JILL KISMET

THE COMPLETE SERIES

EVERY CITY HAS PEOPLE LIKE US,

those who go after things the cops can't catch and keep the streets from boiling over. We handle nonstandard exorcisms, Traders, hellbreed, rogue Weres, scurf, Sorrows, Middle Way adepts...all the fun the nightside can come up with. Normally a hunter's job is just to act as a liaison between the paranormal community and the regular police, make sure everything stays under control.

Sometimes—often enough—it's our job to find people that have been taken by the things that go bump in the night. When I say "find" I mean their bodies, because humans don't live too long on the nightside unless they're hunters. More often than not our mission is vengeance, to restore the unsteady balance between the denizens of the dark and regular oblivious people.

And also more often than not, we lay someone's soul to rest if killing them is just the beginning.

Praise for
Jill Kismet:

"Jill Kismet is, above all else, a survivor, and it is her story that will haunt readers long after the blood, gore and demons have faded into memory." —*RT Book Reviews*

"...Loaded with action and starring a kick butt heroine who from the opening scene until the final climax is donkey kicking seemingly every character in sight." —Harriet Klausner

"Lilith has again created a vibrant, strong, female heroine who keeps you running behind her in a breathless charge against forces you just know you would never be able to walk away from completely unscathed." —Myfavouritebooks.blogspot.com

"Lyrical language and movie-worthy fight scenes are staples in Saintcrow's novels, and this one is no exception." —Midwestbookreview.com

"This mind-blowing series remains a must-read for all urban fantasy lovers." —Bittenbybooks.com

"...ideal for readers who enjoy nonstop rough-and-tumble action combined with compelling characterization and a plot that twists and turns all over the place. Saintcrow...never fails to deliver excitement." —*RT Book Reviews*

Praise for
Dante Valentine:

"She's a brave, charismatic protagonist with a smart mouth and a suicidal streak. What's not to love? Fans of Laurell K. Hamilton should warm to Saintcrow's dark evocative debut."

—Publishers Weekly

"Saintcrow's amazing protagonist is gutsy, stubborn to a fault and vaguely suicidal, meaning there's never a dull moment...This is the ultimate in urban fantasy!" *—RT Book Reviews*

"The characters are rich in detail and the storyline continues on its own unique path of magical death and destruction."

—Darquereviews.blogspot.com

"Hands down, one of the best series I have ever read."

—Blogcritics.org

"This hard hitting urban fantasy will keep you on the edge of your seat and the conclusion delivers a shocker that will both stun and please." —Freshfiction.com

"Without a doubt, Lilith Saintcrow has penned a fabulous, unforgettable story that will have readers lining up to buy her previous releases and waiting with bated breath for her next book in this outstanding new series." —Curledup.com

"...Dark, gritty, urban fantasy at its best."

—Blogcritics.org

Praise for

The Iron Wyrm Affair:

"Saintcrow scores a hit with this terrific Steampunk series that rockets through a Britain-that-wasn't with magic and industrial mayhem with a firm nod to Holmes. Genius and a rocking good time."　　*—New York Times* bestselling author Patricia Briggs

"Saintcrow melds a complex magic system with a subtle but effective steampunk society, adds fully-fleshed and complicated characters, and delivers a clever and highly engaging mystery that kept me turning pages, fascinated to the very end."
　　　　　　　　　　　　　　　　　　—Laura Anne Gilman

"Innovative world building, powerful steam punk, master storyteller at her best. Don't miss this one...She's fabulous."
　　　　　　　　　　　　　　　　　　　—Christine Feehan

"Lilith Saintcrow spins a world of deadly magic, grand adventure, and fast-paced intrigue through the clattering streets of a maze-like mechanized Londonium. *The Iron Wyrm Affair* is a fantastic mix of action, steam, and mystery dredged in dark magic with a hint of romance. Loved it! Do not miss this wonderful addition to the steampunk genre."　　　　　　　　　　—Devon Monk

"Lilith Saintcrow's foray into steampunk plunges the reader into a Victorian England rife with magic and menace, where clockwork horses pace the cobbled streets, dragons rule the ironworks, and it will take a sorceress' discipline and a logician's powers of deduction to unravel a bloody conspiracy."　　　—Jacqueline Carey

JILL KISMET

THE COMPLETE SERIES

LILITH SAINTCROW

www.orbitbooks.net

Compilation copyright © 2013 by Lilith Saintcrow
Night Angel © 2008 by Lilith Saintcrow; *Hunter's Prayer* © 2008 by Lilith Saintcrow; *Redemption Alley* © 2009 by Lilith Saintcrow; *Flesh Circus* © 2009 by Lilith Saintcrow; *Heaven's Spite* © 2010 by Lilith Saintcrow; *Angel Town* © 2011 by Lilith Saintcrow
Excerpt from *The Iron Wyrm Affair* copyright © 2012 by Lilith Saintcrow

Orbit
Hachette Book Group
237 Park Avenue, New York, NY 10017
www.HachetteBookGroup.com

First compilation edition: January 2013

Orbit is an imprint of Hachette Book Group, Inc.
The Orbit name and logo are trademarks of Little, Brown Book Group Limited.

The Hachette Speakers Bureau provides a wide range of authors for speaking events. To find out more, go to www.hachettespeakersbureau.com or call (866) 376-6591.

The publisher is not responsible for websites (or their content) that are not owned by the publisher.

Library of Congress Control Number: 2012947710
ISBN: 978-0-316-20919-9

10 9 8 7 6 5 4 3 2 1

RRD-C

Printed in the United States of America

Contents

Book 1

Night Shift

*For Nicholas Deangelo,
who never asked why.*

The most terrible thing to face is one's own soul.
—Anonymous

Prelude

"Sit. There."

A wooden chair in the middle of a flat expanse of hard-wood floor, lonely under cold fluorescent light.

I lowered myself gingerly, curled my fingers over the ends of the armrests, and commended my soul to God.

Well, maybe not actually commended. Maybe I was just praying really, really hard.

He circled the chair, every step just heavy enough to make a noise against bare floorboards. My weapons and my coat were piled by the door, and even the single knife I'd kept, safe in its sheath strapped to my thigh, was no insurance. I was locked in a room with a hungry tiger who stepped, stepped, turning just a little each time.

I didn't shift my weight.

Instead, I stared across the room, letting my eyes unfocus. Not enough to wall myself up inside my head—that was a death sentence. A hunter is always alert, Mikhail says. Always. Any inattention is an invitation to Death.

And Death loves invitations.

The hellbreed became a shadow each time he passed in front of me, counterclockwise, and I was beginning to wonder if he was going to back out of the bargain or welsh on the deal. Which was, of course, what he wanted me to wonder.

Careful, Jill. Don't let him throw you. I swallowed, wished I hadn't; the briefest pause in his even tread gave me the idea that he'd seen the betraying little movement in my throat.

I do not like the idea of hellbreed staring at my neck.

Silver charms tied in my hair clinked as blessed metal reacted to the sludge of hellbreed filling the ether. This one was bland, not beautiful like the other damned. He was unassuming, slim and weak-looking.

But he scared my teacher. Terrified him, in fact.

Only an idiot isn't scared of hellbreed. There's no shame in it. You've got to get over being ashamed of being scared, because it will slow you down. You can't afford that.

"So."

I almost jumped when his breath caressed my ear. Hot, meaty breath, far too humid to be human. He was breathing on me, *and my flesh crawled in concentric waves of revulsion. Gooseflesh rose up hard and pebbled, scales of fear spreading over my skin.*

"Here's the deal." The words pressed obscenely warm against my naked skin. Something brushed my hair, delicately, and silver crackled with blue sparks. A hiss touched my ear, the skin suddenly far too damp.

I wasn't sweating. It was his breath condensing on me.

Oh, God. I almost choked on bile. Swallowed it and held still, every muscle in my body screaming at me to move, to get away.

"I'm going to mark you, my dear. While you carry that mark, you'll have a gateway embedded in your flesh. Through that conduit, you're going to draw sorcerous energy, and lots of it. It will make you strong, and fast—stronger and faster than any of your fellow hunters. You'll have an edge in raw power when it comes to sorcery, even that weak-kneed trash you monkeys flatter yourself by calling magic."

The hellbreed paused. Cold air hit my wet ear. A single drop of condensation trickled down the outer shell of cartilage, grew fat, and tickled unbearably as it traced a dead flabby finger down to the hollow where ear meets neck, a tender, vulnerable spot.

"I'll also go so far as to help you keep this city free of those who might interfere with the general peace. Peace is good for profit, you know."

A soft, rumbling chuckle brushed against my cheek, with its cargo of sponge-rotten breath.

I kept my fucking mouth shut. "Stay silent until he offers all he's going to offer, *milaya*." *Mikhail's advice, good advice. I was trained, wasn't I? At least, mostly trained. A hunter in my own right, and this was my chance to become . . . what?*

Even better. It was a golden opportunity, and if he thought I should take it, I would. And I wouldn't screw it up.

I would not let my teacher down.

So stay quiet, Jill. Stay calm.

I kept breathing softly through my mouth; the air reeked of hellbreed and corruption. Tasting that scent was bad, as bad as breathing it through my nose.

I just couldn't figure out which was worse.

Something hard, rasping like a cat's tongue, flicked forward and touched the hollow behind my ear, pressing past a few stray strands of hair. If I hadn't been so fucking determined to stay still, muscles locked up tighter than Val's old cashbox, I might have flinched.

Then I probably would have died.

But the touch retreated so quickly I wasn't sure I'd felt it. Except that little drop of condensation was gone, wasn't it?

Shit. I was now sweating too bad to tell.

The hellbreed laughed again. "Very good, little hunter. The bargain goes thus: you bear my mark and use the power it provides as you see fit. Once a month you'll come visit, and you'll spend time with me. That's all—a little bit of time each month. For superlative use of the power I grant you, you might have to spend a little more time. Say, five or six hours?"

Now it was negotiation time. I wet my lips with my tongue, wished I hadn't because I suddenly knew his eyes had fastened on my mouth. "Half an hour. Maximum."

Bargaining on streetcorners taught me that much, at least—you never take the john's first offer, and you never, ever, ever start out with more than half of what you're willing to give.

Sometimes you can pick who buys you, and for how much.

That's what power really is.

"You wound me." The hellbreed didn't sound wounded. He sounded delighted, his bland tenor probing at my ear. "Three hours. See how generous I am, for you?"

This is too easy. Be careful. *"An hour a month, maximum of two, and your help on my cases. Final offer, hellbreed, or I walk. I didn't come here to be jacked around."*

Why had I come here? Because Mikhail said I should.

I wondered if it was another test I'd failed, or passed. I wondered if I'd just overstepped and was looking at a nasty death. Bargaining with hellbreed is tricky; hunters usually just kill them. But this wasn't so simple. This was either a really good idea or a really bad way to die.

A long thunderous moment of quiet, and the room trembled like a soap bubble. Something like masses of gigantic flies on a mound of corpses buzzed, rattling.

Helletöng. The language of the damned. It lay under the skin of the visible like fat under skin, dimpling the surface tension of what we try to call the real world.

"Done, little hunter. We have a bargain. If you agree."

My throat was like the Sahara, dry and scratchy. A cough caught out in the open turned into a painful, ratcheting laugh. "What do you get out of this, Perry?"

That scaly, dry, probing thing flicked along my skin again, rasped for the briefest second against the side of my throat, just a fraction of an inch away from where the pulse beat frantically. I sucked at keeping my heartrate down, Mikhail warned and warned me about it—

"Sometimes we like *being on the side of the angels.*" *The hellbreed's voice dropped to a whisper that would have been intimate if the rumbling of Hell hadn't been scraping along underneath.* "It makes the ending sweeter. Besides, peace is good for profit. Do we have a deal, little hunter?"

Christ. Mikhail, I hope you're right. *I didn't agree to it because of the hellbreed or even because the thought of that much power was tempting.*

I agreed because Mikhail told me I should, even though it was my decision. It wasn't really a Trader's bargain if I was doing it for my teacher, was it?

Was it?

"We have a deal." *Four little words. They came out naturally, smoothly, without a hitch.*

Hot iron-hard fingers clamped over my right wrist. "Oh, good." A slight wet smacking sound, like a hungry toddler at the breakfast table, and he wrenched my hand off the arm of the chair, the pale tender underside of my wrist turned up to face cold fluorescent light. My heart jackhammered away, adrenaline soaking copper into the dry roof of my mouth, and I bit back a cry.

It was too late. Four tiny words, and I'd just signed a contract. Now we'd see if Mikhail was right, and I still had my soul.

CHAPTER 1

Every city has a pulse. It's just a matter of knowing where to rest your finger to find it, throbbing away as the sun bleeds out of the sky and night rises to cloak every sin.

I crouched on the edge of a rooftop, the counterweight of my heavy leather coat hanging behind me. Settled into absolute stillness, waiting. The baking wind off the cooling desert mouthed the edges of my body. The scar on my right wrist was hot and hard under a wide hinged copper bracelet molded to my skin.

The copper was corroding, blooming green and wearing thin.

I was going to have to find a different way to cover the scar up soon. Trouble is, I suck at making jewelry, and Galina was out of blessed copper cuffs until her next shipment from Nepal.

Below me the alley wandered, thick and rank. Here at the edge of the barrio there were plenty of hiding places for the dark things that crawl once dusk falls. The Weres don't patrol out this far, having plenty to keep them occupied inside their own crazy-quilt of streets and alleys around the Plaza Centro and its spreading tenements. Here on the fringes, between a new hunter's territory and the streets the Weres kept from boiling over, a few hellbreed thought they could break the rules.

Not in my town, buckos. If you think Kismet's a pushover because she's only been on her own for six months, you've got another think coming.

My right leg cramped, a sudden vicious swipe of pain. I ignored it. My electrolyte balance was all messed up from going for three days without rest, from one deadly night-battle to the next with the fun of exorcisms in between. I wondered if Mikhail had ever felt this exhaustion, this ache so deep even bones felt tired.

It hurt to think of Mikhail. My hand tightened on the bull-whip's handle, leather creaking under my fingers. The scar tingled again, a knot of corruption on the inside of my wrist.

Easy, milaya. *No use in making noise, eh? It is soft and quiet that catches mouse.* As if he was right next to me, barely mouthing the words, his gray eyes glittering winter-sharp under a shock of white hair. Hunters don't live to get too old, but Mikhail Ilych Tolstoi had been an exception in so many ways. I could almost see his ghost crouching silent next to me, peering at the alley over the bridge of his patrician nose.

Of course he wasn't there. He'd been cremated, just like he wanted. I'd held the torch myself, and the Weres had let me touch it to the wood before singing their own fire into being. A warrior's spirit rose in smoke, and wherever my teacher was, it wasn't here.

Which I found more comforting than you'd think, since if he'd come back I'd have to kill him. Just part of the job.

My fingers eased. I waited.

The smell of hellbreed and the brackish contamination of an *arkeus* lay over this alley. Some nasty things had been sidling out of this section of the city lately, nasty enough to give even a Hell-tainted hunter a run for her money. We have firepower and sorcery, we who police the nightside, but Traders and hellbreed are spooky-quick and capable of taking a hell of a lot of damage.

Get it? A Hell of a lot of damage? Arf arf.

Not to mention the scurf with their contagion, the adepts of the Middle Way with their goddamn Chaos, and the Sorrows worshipping the Elder Gods.

The thought of the Sorrows made rage rise under my breastbone, fresh and wine-dark. I inhaled smoothly, dispelling it. Clear, calm, and cold was the way to go about this.

Movement below. Quick and scuttling, like a rat skittering from one pile of garbage to the next. I didn't move, I didn't blink, I barely even *breathed.*

The *arkeus* took shape, rising like a fume from dry-scorched pavement, trash riffling as the wind of its coalescing touched ragged edges and putrid rotting things. Tall, hooded, translucent where moonlight struck it and smoky-solid elsewhere, one of Hell's roaming corruptors stretched its long clawed arms and slid fully into the world. It drew in a deep satisfied sigh, and I heard something else.

Footsteps.

Someone was coming to keep an appointment.

Isn't that a coincidence. So am I.

My heartbeat didn't quicken; it stayed soft, even, as almost-nonexistent as my breathing. It had taken me a long time to get my pulse mostly under control.

The next few moments were critical. You can't jump too soon on something like this. *Arkeus* aren't your garden-variety hell-breed. You have to wait until they solidify enough to talk to their victims—otherwise you'll be fighting empty air with sorcery, and that's no fun—and you have to know what a Trader is bargaining for before you go barging in to distribute justice or whup-ass. Usually both, liberally.

The carved chunk of ruby on its silver chain warmed, my tiger's-eye rosary warming too, the blessing on both items reacting with contamination rising from the *arkeus* and its lair.

A man edged down the alley, clutching something to his chest. The *arkeus* made a thin greedy sound, and my smart left eye—the blue one, the one that can look *below* the surface of the world—saw a sudden tensing of the strings of contamination following it. It was a hunched, thin figure that would have been taller than me except for the hump on its back; its spectral robes brushing dirt and refuse, taking strength from filth.

Bingo. The *arkeus* was now solid enough to hit.

The man halted. I couldn't see much beyond the fact that he was obviously human, his aura slightly tainted from his traffic with an escaped denizen of Hell.

It was official. The man was a Trader, bargaining with Hell. Whatever he was bargaining *for,* it wasn't going to do him any good.

Not with me around.

The *arkeus* spoke. *"You have brought it?"* A lipless cold voice, eager and thin, like a dying cricket. A razorblade pressed against the wrist, a thin line of red on pale skin, the frozen-blue face of a suicide.

I moved. Boots soundless against the parapet, the carved chunk of ruby resting against the hollow of my throat, even my coat silent. The silver charms braided into my long dark hair didn't tinkle. The first thing a hunter's apprentice learns is to move quietly, to draw silence in tight like a cloak.

That is, if the apprentice wants to survive.

"I b-brought it." The man's speech was the slow slur of a dreamer who senses a cold-current nightmare. He was in deep, having already given the *arkeus* a foothold by making some agreement or another with it. "You'd better not—"

"Peace." The *arkeus*'s hiss froze me in place for a moment as the hump on its back twitched. *"You will have your desire, never fear. Give it to me."*

The man's arms relaxed, and a small sound lifted from the bundle he carried. My heart slammed into overtime against my ribs.

Every human being knows the sound of a baby's cry.

Bile filled my throat. My boots ground against the edge of the parapet as I launched out into space, the *arkeus* flinching and hissing as my aura suddenly flamed, tearing through the ether like a star. The silver in my hair shot sparks, and the ruby at my throat turned hot. The scar on my right wrist turned to lava, burrowing in toward the bone, my whip uncoiled and struck forward, its metal flechettes snapping at the speed of sound, cracking as I pulled on etheric force to add a psychic strike to the physical.

My boots hit slick refuse-grimed concrete and I pitched forward, the whip striking again across the *arkeus*'s face. The hell-thing howled, and my other hand was full of the Glock, the sharp stink of cordite blooming as silver-coated bullets chewed through the thing's physical shell. Hollowpoints do a lot of damage once a hellbreed's initial shell is breached.

It's a pity 'breed heal so quickly.

We don't know why silver works—something to do with the

Moon, and how she controls the tides of sorcery and water. No hunter cares, either. It's enough that it levels the playing field a little.

The *arkeus* moved, scuttling to the side as the man screamed, a high whitenoise-burst of fear. The whip coiled, my hip moving first as usual—the hip leads with whip-work as well as stave fighting. My whip-work had suffered until Mikhail made me take bellydancing classes.

Don't think, Jill. Move. I flung out my arm, etheric force spilling through my fingers, and the whip slashed again, each flechette tearing through already-lacerated flesh. It howled again, and the copper bracelet broke, tinkled sweetly on the concrete as I pivoted, firing down into the hell-thing's face. It twitched, and I heard my own voice chanting in gutter Latin, a version of Saint Anthony's prayer Mikhail had made me learn.

Protect me from the hordes of Hell, O Lord, for I am pure of heart and trust Your mercy—and the bullets don't hurt, either.

The *arkeus* screamed, writhing, and cold air hit the scar. I was too drenched with adrenaline to feel the usual curl of fire low in my belly, but the sudden sensitivity of my skin and hearing slammed into me. I dropped the whip and fired again with the gun in my left, then fell to my knees, driving down with psychic and physical force.

My fist met the hell-thing's lean malformed face, which exploded. It shredded, runnels of foulness bursting through its skin, and the sudden cloying reek would have torn my dinner loose from my stomach moorings if I'd eaten anything.

Christ, I wish it didn't stink so bad. But stink means dead, and if this thing's dead it's one less fucking problem for me to deal with.

No time. I gained my feet, shaking my right fist. Gobbets of preternatural flesh whipped loose, splatting dully against the brick walls. I uncoiled, leaping for the front of the alley.

The Trader was only human, and he hadn't made his big deal yet. He was tainted by the *arkeus*'s will, but he wasn't given super-strength or near-invulnerability yet.

The only enhanced human being left in the alley was me. Thank God.

I dug my fingers into his shoulder and set my feet, yanking him back. The baby howled, emptying its tiny lungs, and I caught it on its way down, my arm tightening maybe a little too much to yank it against my chest. I tried to avoid smacking it with a knife-hilt.

I backhanded the man with my hellbreed-strong right fist. *Goddamn it. What am I going to do now?*

The baby was too small, wrapped in a bulky blue blanket that smelled of cigarette smoke and grease. I held it awkwardly in one arm while I contemplated the sobbing heap of sorry manflesh crumpled against a pile of garbage.

I've cuffed plenty of Traders one-handed, but never while holding a squirming, bellowing bundle of little human that smelled not-too-fresh. Still, it was a cleaner reek than the *arkeus*'s rot. I tested the cuffs, yanked the man over, and checked his eyes. Yep. The flat shine of the dust glittered in his irises. He was a thin, dark-haired man with the ghost of childhood acne still hanging on his cheeks, saliva glittering wetly on his chin.

I found his ID in his wallet, awkwardly holding the tiny yelling thing in the crook of my arm. *Jesus. Mikhail never trained me for this.* "Andy Hughes. You are *under arrest.* You have the right to be exorcised. Anything you say will, of course, be ignored, since you've forfeited your rights to a trial of your peers by trafficking with Hell." I took a deep breath. "And you should thank your lucky stars I'm not in a mood to kill anyone else tonight. Who does the baby belong to?"

He was still gibbering with fear, and the baby howled. I could get nothing coherent out of either of them.

Then, to complete the deal, the pager went off against my hip, vibrating silently in its padded pocket.

Great.

CHAPTER 2

Cities need people like us, those who go after things the cops can't catch and keep the streets from boiling over. We handle nonstandard exorcisms, Traders, hellbreed, rogue Weres, scurf, Sorrows, Middle Way adepts...all the fun the nightside can come up with. Normally a hunter's job is just to act as a liaison between the paranormal community and the regular police, make sure everything stays under control.

Or, if not *under control,* then at least *reasonably orderly.* Which, as a definition, allows for anything between "no bodies in the street" to "just short of actual chaos."

Hey, you've got to be flexible.

Sometimes—often enough—it's our job to find people that have been taken by the things that go bump in the night. When I say "find" I mean their bodies, because humans don't live too long on the nightside unless they're hunters. More often than not our mission is vengeance, to restore the unsteady balance between the denizens of the dark and regular oblivious people. To make a statement and keep the things creeping in the dark just there—creeping, instead of swaggering.

And also more often than not, we lay someone's soul to rest if killing them is just the beginning.

We work pretty closely with the regular police, mostly because freelance hunters don't last long enough to have a career. Even the FBI has its Martindale Squad, hunters and Weres working on nightside fun and games at the national and cross-state level. It's whispered that the CIA and NSA have their own divisions of hunters too, but I don't know about that.

For a hunter like me, the support given by the regular cops and DA's office is critical. It is, after all, law enforcement we're doing. Even if it is a little unconventional.

Okay. A *lot* unconventional.

The baby I unloaded at Sisters of Mercy downtown, the granite

Jesus on the roof still glaring at the financial district. The hospital would find out who it belonged to, if at all possible. Avery came down to take possession of the prisoner, who was sweat-drenched, moaning with fear, and had pissed his already-none-too-clean pants.

I must have been wearing my mad face.

"Jesus Christ. Don't you ever sleep?" Avery's handsome, mournful look under its mop of dark curly hair was sleepy and uninterested until he peered through the porthole in the door. He brightened a little, his breath making a brief circle of mist spring up on the reinforced glass.

"I try not to sleep. It disturbs the circles I'm growing under my eyes. This naughty little boy just brushed with an *arkeus,* didn't get much." I leaned against the wall in the institutional hallway, listening to the sound of the man's hoarse weeping on the other side of the steel observation door. Sisters of Mercy is an old Catholic hospital, and like most old Catholic hospitals it has a room even the most terrifying nun won't enter.

A hunter's room. Or more precisely, a room for the holding of people needing an exorcism until a hunter or a regular exorcist can get to them.

A lot of hunters have trouble with exorcisms. They're perfectly simple; the trouble comes from the psychological cost of ripping things *out* of people. Some hunters who won't blanch at murdering a half-dozen Traders at once quaver at the prospect of a simple tear-the-thing-out-and-dispel-it. Maybe it's the screaming or the bleeding, though God knows there's enough of that in our regular work.

Mikhail hadn't been a quavery one, and I guess neither am I. Exorcisms are straight simple work and usually end up with the victim alive. I call that an easy job.

"A standard half-rip, then. Not even worth getting out of bed for." Avery stuffed his hands in his pockets, rocking up on his toes again to peer in the thick-barred window. I'd kept the Trader cuffed and dumped him in the middle of a consecrated circle scored into the crumbling concrete floor. Etheric energy running through the deep carved lines sparked, responding to the taint of hellbreed on the man's aura.

"He was about to hand a baby over to a hellbreed. Don't be too gentle." I peeled myself upright, the silver charms tinkling in my hair. "I've got to get over to the precinct house, Montaigne just buzzed me. Maybe I'll bring in another one for you tonight."

Avery made a face, still peering in at the Trader. "Jesus. A baby? And shouldn't you be going home? This is the fourth one you've brought in this week."

Who's keeping track? Traders *had* been cropping up with alarming regularity, though. I snorted, my fingers checking each knife-hilt. "Home? What's that? Duty calls."

"You gonna come out for a beer with me on Saturday?"

"You bet." I'd rescheduled twice with him so far, each time because of a Trader. People were making bargains with hellbreed left and right these days. "If I'm not hanging out on a rooftop waiting for a fucking *arkeus* to show up, I'll be there."

He came back down onto his heels, twitching his corduroy jacket a little to get it to hang straight over the bulge of his police-issue sidearm. "You should really slack off a bit, Kiss. You're beginning to look a little..."

Yeah. Slack off. Sure. "Be careful." I turned on my heel. "See you Saturday."

"I mean it, Kismet. You should get some rest."

If I took a piña colada by the pool, God knows what would boil up on the streets. "When the hellbreed slow down, so will I. Happy trails, Ave."

He mumbled a goodbye, bending to dig in the little black bag sitting obediently by his feet. He was the official police exorcist, handling most of the Traders I brought in unless there was something really unusual about them. He only really seemed to come alive during a difficult exorcism, the rest of the time moving sleepily through the world with a slow smile that got him a great deal of female attention. Despite that, not a lot of women stayed.

Probably because he worked the night shift tearing the bargains out of Traders or Possessors out of morbidly religious victims. Women don't like it when their man spends his nights somewhere else, even if it is with screaming Hell-tainted sickos instead of other women.

I hit the door at the end of the hall, allowing myself a single nosewrinkle at the stinging scent of disinfectant and human pain in the air. The scar burned, my ears cringing from the slightest noise and the fluorescent lights hurting my eyes. I needed to find a better way to cover it up, and quick.

It's not every hunter who has a hellbreed mark on her wrist, after all. A hard knotted scar, in the shape of a pair of lips puckered up and pressed against the underside of my right arm, into the softest part above the pulse.

Two days until my next scheduled visit. And there was the iron rack to think about, and the way Perry screamed when I started with the razors.

My mouth suddenly went dry and I put my head down, lengthening my stride. I'm not tall, but I have good long legs and I was used to trotting to keep up with Mikhail, who didn't seem to walk as much as glide between one fight and the next.

Stop thinking about Mikhail. I made it to the exit and plunged into the cold, weary night again, hunching my shoulders, the silver tinkling in my hair.

CHAPTER 3

The precinct house on Alameda wasn't very active tonight. I nodded to the officer on duty, a tall rangy rookie who paled and looked down at his reports instead of nodding back. I placed his face with an absent mental effort—yes, he'd been in the last class I'd conducted. The one where I told each batch of shiny new faces about the nightside, and how and when to contact their local hunter.

Or as Detective Carper calls it, "Puking Your Guts Out While Kiss Talks." Each desk has a wastebasket sitting next to it during that class, and the janitor is busy those days. Still, few of the rookies leave the force after that little graduation ceremony. The nondisclosure clauses they sign are very rarely breached.

Most humans don't *want* to know about the nightside, and they unconsciously collude in making a hunter's secrecy easy.

I don't blame them. Some days even hunters don't want to think about what they do for a living.

Montaigne, his dark hair rumpled, was in a pair of blue-striped pajama pants. He wore a button-up and suit jacket over them, and palmed a handful of Tums as I came into his office, his bleary dark eyes rising to meet mine. He didn't flinch at my mismatched eyes—one blue, one brown—but I noticed he wore slippers instead of his usual polished wingtips. His ankles were bare.

Oh, God. I halted just inside his door, resting my right hand on the whip-handle. *This looks bad.* "Hi, Monty. Sorry I'm late, I had to drop off a Trader. What's up?"

"Jill." His cheeks were actually cheesy-pale. "There's something I need you to take a look at."

As usual, he sounded like he didn't quite believe he was asking a woman half his size for help. I barely come up to Monty's shoulder, but even if I gave him an Uzi and a little help he'd still be no match for me. Still, he'd never doubted my ability, once Mikhail introduced me as his apprentice.

We're back to Mischa again. Dammit, Jill, focus. "Animal, vegetable, mineral?"

"Homicide." Most of the time, that was the case. Monty ran his hand back through his hair again. It vigorously protested this treatment, becoming even more ruffled.

"How many bodies?" I was past uneasy and heading into full-blown disturbed. The charms in my hair tinkled, rubbing against each other. I realized I was slumping and snapped up to stand straight, dispelling the urge to yawn. I would be up to greet the dawn again and probably go all day, too. If I had to.

"Five."

A respectable number. But you're just calling me in now? "How fresh?"

"Two hours. I'm due at the morgue as soon as you show up, Stanton's going to do the dicing." Montaigne's jaw set. I began to get a bad feeling, hearing the way his heart was pounding, ticking off time. He reeked of fear, not just the usual uneasiness of facing me down and being reminded of the nightside. Monty had decided he didn't want to know about anything other than when to call me, which made him wiser than most.

"Come on, Monty. Drop the other shoe." I folded my arms. "Five bodies? *Found* two hours ago, or—"

"Killed two hours ago, Kiss. And they're all cops."

CHAPTER 4

The morgue's chemical reek and fluorescent glare closed around me, and I was glad for the weight of my heavy leather coat. No matter how many autopsies I attend, the cold always seems to linger.

Still, I'll take an autopsy over a scene any day. The dispassionate light and medical terminology helps distance the ordinary horror of death a little bit. Just a little, just enough.

Sometimes.

Stanton was whey-faced too, wheezing asthmatically as he shuffled down the corridor behind us, his white coat flapping from his scarecrow-thin shoulders. His hair stuck up in birdlike tufts as well, and he was fighting a miserable cold. "It looks weird, Kismet." His nose was so stuffed the sentence came out mangled. *Ith lookth weird, Kithmet.*

"How weird?" *Am I going to have to kill them again? Please don't let it be scurf, or an Assyrian demon. I'm too tired for that shit.* "And if it looks this weird, why weren't the bodies left onsite for me? You all know the rules."

"They're *cops.*" Montaigne hurried to keep up, his slippers shuffling. I kept lengthening my stride to keep him slightly behind me, just in case. "We couldn't leave 'em out there in the middle of the freeway."

"Freeway?" *This just keeps getting better and better.* "Take it from the top and give me a vowel, Montaigne."

The corridor was thankfully deserted, stretching through infinity to a pair of swinging doors at the end. Stanton's shoes squeaked against the flooring. He'd put on sneakers from two different pairs, as well as two different colors of socks—acid green and dark blue. Whatever had happened, both Monty and Stan had been dragged out of bed in a hell of a hurry.

Of course, matching his shoes wasn't really something Stan was too concerned about. Geniuses are like that.

"A pair of traffic cops reported something odd and called for backup at about 0200. The backup got there and reported seeing the first squad car sitting on the side of the road. After that, no communication. Dispatch kept trying to raise both of them, got no response. So another black and white goes out. By this time they called me, and I got in about 0300. The third fucking car had a rookie in it; for some reason the vet had the rookie stay in the car and went to go look for the others. Everyone was converging at that point, looked like a real clusterfuck in progress." Montaigne stopped for a breath, his pulse thundering audibly, and dropped behind me. I slowed a little. "Four other cars got there at once and found the rookie bleeding quarts. Something had opened up the car like a soda can and dragged him out. He's at Luz General in trauma and last I heard it wasn't looking good. The other five— the first two teams and the vet—are all in pieces."

Pieces? The scar was hard and throbbing against my skin, burrowing in. It never got any deeper, but the uncomfortable wondering of what it would be like if it ever *did* hit bone often showed up in the middle of long sleepless stakeouts, keeping me company along with Mikhail's ghost.

"Pieces?" I sounded only mildly curious. I couldn't make any sort of guess until I'd seen the evidence, and maybe not even then. A hunter is trained thoroughly not to make any conjectures in the initial stages. You can blind yourself pretty quickly by starting out with the wrong assumption.

A hunter blinded by assumption doesn't live long.

"Yeah, *pieces.* Whatever killed them tossed them out on the Drag like garbage. In pieces. Bleeding pieces." Montaigne's voice dropped.

We reached the swinging door, and I stopped short, forcing the other two to skid to a halt. "Before or after it carved the rookie up?"

An acrid stink of fear wafted out from Montaigne as he and Stan paused, following procedure now. They shouldn't have brought the bodies in until I'd been able to make sure they were truly dead and not just incubating something.

Monty reached across his wide chest, touched his sidearm, clasped in its holster under his armpit. "We don't know."

Jesus Christ. I took a deep breath, motioned them both back.

"All right, boys. Let big bad Kismet go in and see what the monster left us."

Montaigne actually flinched, but he understood. It sounds brutal and callous, but a hunter learns mighty quick to take the gallows humor where she finds it. Just like a cop.

It's the only way to keep from suicide or weeping, and sometimes it doesn't work. That's when you start drinking, or getting some random sex.

See what I mean?

I came through low and sweeping with both guns as the swinging doors banged against the walls on either side. Nothing but the glare and hard tiled floor of a ghastly-lit body bay, each table now full. It had been a busy night in Santa Luz. The five bags on the left-hand side were all shapeless, looking wrong even through heavy vinyl. The bodies on the right were bagged and normal, if there is any such thing as a *normal* dead body.

It used to bother me that each bag was a life, the sum of someone's breathing and walking around carrying a soul. Then the things that bothered me were details. Hair left crusted with blood, a missing earring, a bruise that had half-healed and would never fade now, or—worst of all—the smaller bags.

The ones for children.

I took a deep breath and smelled something I didn't expect—the sweet brackish rotting of hellbreed, added to another smell I hadn't expected. A dry smell, blazing with heat and spoiled musk, like matted fur and unhealthy dandruff-clotted skin. My nose wrinkled. I took another deep whiff, sniffing all the way down to the bottom of my lungs and examining the bags with both eyes. My smart eye, the blue one, saw no stirring or unevenness hovering in the ether over the bodies. My dumb eye, the brown one, ticked over their contours and returned a few impressions I wasn't sure I liked.

"Clear," I called, and holstered my guns. Montaigne's gusty sigh of relief preceded him through the door.

"Are you staying for the slicing, Jill?" Stan sniffed, and his bleary gaze skittered away from my breasts, roved over the five bodies on the right-hand side, and came back up to touch my face, uncertain.

Five autopsies take a lot of time. "I'll take a look, but I'll leave the deli work to you and Monty. I'll need the report. This is one of mine."

Stan's face fell. So did Monty's. They both looked sallow, and it wasn't just the fluorescents.

"Christ." Monty didn't quite reel, but he did take a step to one side, like a bull pawing the grass, uncertain what to charge. "What the fuck is it?"

"Don't know yet." That was the truth. "I'll go by the scene, see if I can pick up a trail. From what you're telling me, it either got what it wanted or was scared off by the black and whites. I'm guessing they didn't come in silently."

He rolled his eyes as Stan rocked back on his heels, stuffing his hands in his lab coat pockets and eyeing both of us. "Suppose you can't tell me anything useful."

Not yet. I haven't even looked at the bodies. "This is hunter's work, Monty. How much do you want me to tell you?"

Monty shook his head fiercely. If he could have clapped his hands over his ears like a five-year-old, he might have tried to do so.

Wise man.

"I'll take a look," I repeated, "and then I'll hit the street and try to find a trail. Nobody gets away with killing our brave blue boys in my city, gentlemen. Stan?"

He shrugged his thin shoulders, the pens in his breast pocket clicking against each other. "Be my guest."

He very pointedly didn't offer to unzip the bags for me, or caution me not to destroy any evidence. I couldn't even feel triumphant. Maybe it was just his cold.

I set my back teeth, the charms in my hair tinkling against each other, and paced cautiously up to the first body bag. Nothing stirred, and none of my senses quivered. I touched the zipper and let out a soft breath, glad the two men were behind me.

I pulled the zipper down. I have never figured out if it's easier to do it in one quick swipe, like tearing off a Band-Aid, or slowly, giving yourself time to adjust.

I usually go with the quick tear. Call it a personality quirk.

The body had been savaged, great chunks torn out. The face

had been taken off, and his short cop-buzz haircut had beads of dried blood sticking to its bristly ends. The only thing left intact was the curve of a jaw, slightly fuzzed with stubble. He hadn't shaved, this man.

"That one's Sanders." Monty shifted his weight, his slippers squeaking a little against the tile. "About forty-five. Retiring next month, early."

A lifer. And before my time. Now he'd never retire. I drew the zipper down more, studying the mass of meat. His feet were stacked neatly between his knees, and his right arm was missing. The ribs were snapped, and the smell boiled up into my nose and down into my stomach, turning into sourness.

That's hellbreed, and something else. Something I should know. A reek like that is distinctive, and I should be up on it, dammit. Are we looking at a hellbreed working in concert with something else? They're not like that, most of them are jealous fucks. Still, it's possible. But nothing a hellbreed can control smells like this. The shudder bolted down my spine. I drew the zipper up, went to the next one.

"Kincaid," Monty supplied. "Twenty-eight. Good solid cop."

I nodded, pulled the zipper down in one swipe.

This one had a face. A round, blond, good-natured, blood-speckled face. I swallowed hard. The rags of his uniform couldn't hide the massive damage done to this body either—the purple of the torn esophagus, white bits of bone, a flicker of cervical vertebra peering up at me. His throat had been torn out and his viscera scattered. The bathroom stink of cut bowel flooded the chilly air. Both his femurs were snapped.

Marlow, the third, had been savaged. He'd been the driver in the first traffic unit, and whatever had attacked him had plenty of time to do its work. There was barely enough left to be recognizable as human.

The fourth—Anderson, Marlow's partner—was the worst. His arm had been torn off, something exerting terrific force to break the humerus just below the shoulder. The force had to have been applied at an angle for the bone to yield before the shoulder dislocated. His other limbs hung by strips of meat. *All* of them. And his head.

There wasn't enough of any of them left for an open-casket service.

As always, the shudder passed and the bodies became a puzzle. Where did this piece go, where did that piece go?

Then I would catch myself, horrified. These were *human beings*. Each one of them had gotten up out of bed this morning expecting to see sundown. Nobody is ever really *prepared* to die, no matter what you see in movies or read in fairytales.

My stomach churned, a hole of heat opening right behind my breastbone. Marty's Tums were starting to look pretty good. He bought them by the case, he wouldn't miss a few hundred.

I zipped Anderson's bag back up. Turned to find both Stan and Marty staring at me. "I'll drop in later for the files." My eyes burned, stinging, from disinfectant married to the smell of death. "What *exactly* did the first on-site traffic unit report?"

"Just 'something weird.' There wasn't a code for it." Monty's paleness had long since passed from cheese to paper. "Jill?"

"I don't know yet, Monty. Give me a little time to work this thing. Have traffic units take precautions; if it's weird and there's not a code, *don't stop.* Tell the beat cops too—they're vulnerable. If they see *anything* weird, they're to report so I can get a pattern of movement, but they are not to pursue. Got it?"

He nodded. "Do you have an idea, at least? I don't want to know," he added hurriedly. "But..."

But you feel better when the hunter at least has an idea. I know, Monty. I know. I could have given a comforting lie. "No." I looked at the bodies, lying slumped under their rubber blankets. All safe and snug, never having to worry about the job or the cold winter again.

Bile rose in my throat. "No. But I'm going to find out."

Because whatever this is smells like hellbreed and rips things up like no hellbreed should. The claw shape is strange. If I didn't know better I'd think it was a Were. But no Were, even a rogue, would go near anything hellbreed.

Great.

CHAPTER 5

False dawn gathered gray in the east, veils of fog from the river reaching up like fat white fingers as I gunned the engine. I winced as my orange Impala's full-throated purr took on a subtle knocking. *Need to get that fixed. Should change the oil soon too.*

The interstate—or the Drag, if you're a local—comes up out of the well of the city in slight curves north through Ridgefield toward the capital, striking for the heart of desert and sagebrush once it's out of the low-lying area watered by the river. Coming down into the city it veers through suburbs, taking advantage of the high ground and flying over deep gullies and concrete washes built to siphon off flash floods. Once it hits the actual city limits it becomes three lanes in either direction, jammed during rush hour and perfect for illegal races once normal people are in bed.

Just south of downtown there's a stretch with hills on either side, thick with trees and trashwood, the green belt going up to chain-link fences facing the blank backs of businesses and warehouses. The scene was still crawling with forensic techs, and when I parked at the periphery a thin, nervous traffic cop came bustling up to tell me to move along—and retreated as I rose out of the Impala, meeting his eyes and keeping my silence. He recognized me, of course.

They all do.

I've heard they have a pool on where I'm going to show up and when, and the betting is fierce; there is a whole arcane system of verifying sightings left over from Mikhail's tenure. Hunter sightings are comforting for them; lets them know I'm still on the job.

It's when I disappear for a while that they get nervous.

Two lanes of southbound traffic were blocked off, and traffic was extremely light. Still, the infrequent cars were slowing down to gawk, and the scene was being trampled.

I couldn't blame them. Cops never like to lose one of their own. Most of them were observing a respectful silence. Quite a few of them looked like they'd been rousted from bed, too. I saw Sullivan, his red hair catching fire on top of his lanky frame as the sun began its work in earnest. His partner, a short motherly woman in a sweater-coat and knit leggings, stood beside him staring at one of the long garish streaks of wetness on the road. The streaks everyone was hypnotized by.

Blood doesn't dry as quickly as everyone thinks, even out here at the edge of the desert. It stays tacky-wet for a long time before it turns into a crust. A flat iron tang rose to my nose, like a banner through the stew of humans milling around and the sharp dual stink of hellbreed and something else, something I'd never smelled before.

Mikhail would have mentioned something like this if he'd ever come across it, wouldn't he? I caught myself. *Concentrate on the job. Jesus, you're getting punchy.*

Too bad I wasn't going to get any rest anytime soon.

I threaded my way through the milling crowd. As fast as people arrived others left, to go back to work or home after paying their respects. It was eerily quiet, and the scar throbbed on my wrist, tension and frustration in the air plucking at it. *Got to cover that goddamn thing up.*

Word of my appearance spread quickly, a murmur through the crowd. Foster, his sleek dark hair pulled back in a ponytail, was the only one brave enough to approach. Of course, he was my Forensics liaison this month since Pepper was out on maternity leave. He ducked carefully under the yellow tape keeping everyone back—in this crowd, there was no shoving. The mannerly silence was almost as eerie as the palpable grief.

"Hey, Jill." Dark circles bloomed under Foster's blue eyes, and the silver stud in his right ear glittered. "How you?"

I don't often use the Forensics liaison; most hunters don't. We work most closely with Homicide detectives and next with Vice; they do the grunt work in getting files ready. Most of the time a hunt goes so quickly we don't have time for that type of legwork, and we don't want the human law enforcement getting close to the nightside anyway. They're our eyes and ears, since a hunter can't be everywhere at once.

Nobody wants their eyes catching flak.

"Hi, Mike. Monty called me in." I pitched my voice low, my

hands thrust deep in my coat pockets. Leather creaked as I shifted. "What do we have?"

He was pale under the even caramel of his skin. "A total goddamn mess, that's what. Five goddamn bodies and that rookie bleeding all over everything. The main scene is up in the woods, there." He pointed to the ordered commotion on the hillside. "They didn't get more than twenty feet before something leapt on 'em. Just like shooting fish in a fucking barrel."

I winced at the mental image. And why would cops get out of their cars and pursue something up a hillside? "Any body parts you can't find?"

He shrugged. "Too soon to tell. Come up the hill. If Monty hadn't called you I would've. This is grade-A weirdness, just your type."

"I hate to be pigeonholed." I followed him, skirting the three traffic units parked in standard pattern on the shoulder, inside the cordon of yellow tape. Their lights still revolved, running off the batteries.

The last car in line had been shredded, its windshield broken and the roof ripped open, jagged metal edges exploding. Bits of broken colored plastic and glass from the lights were smashed to the side.

Christ. My blue eye didn't see any sparking and smoking of etheric energy, though the whole scene reeked of hellbreed. They are stronger and faster than humans, but a 'breed that could do something like this without sorcerous help...

What the hell is this?

The rapidly lightening sky triggered another idea. I glanced overhead. No circling copters yet. "The press?"

"Captain Bolton's putting together a release about a car bomb or something. We've been able to keep the goddamn vultures quiet so far, but it's only a matter of time." Foster snorted, as if he wanted to spit but couldn't bring himself to do so. The two wide lanes of pavement were streaked and spattered with gore.

I was surprised the vultures hadn't scented it yet. *Last thing we need is footage of this getting out.* We crossed the ditch, me in a single leap and Mike over a piece of plywood someone had laid down, and plunged uphill into the bushes. The sharp smell of sage

and pine stung my nose, mixed with the belching tang of death
and that horrible stink of hellbreed and something else.

Dry fur. Dandruff clotted in drifts. Desiccated, exhaled sickness, as if a dog had crept into a hole to die.

What is that? I wished I could find something to cover the scar
up. Preternaturally acute senses are useful, but it *stank*.

There was a clearing ringed with pine trees, their bark tinder-
dry and needles crunching underfoot. Silence broken only by the
shuffling of the techs' feet and occasional muttered directions.
Flashes popped, taking merciless pictures, drenching the scene in
brief shutterclicks of light.

There was so much blood. I've seen plenty of butchery, but this
was... The stench of a battlefield hung over the small clearing, cut
bowel and wet red iron, as well as the heatless fume of violence.
The smell of hellbreed and *something else* was so deep and thunderous my eyes watered.

The spindly tree trunks were shredded, and I stopped to examine the deep furrows carved in them. They were all vertical, and
my eyes caught a thin reddish glint.

"What the hell?" I leaned closer, examining the long strands.
Red-gold, and with a springy curl unlike anything I'd seen. It was
all over, in the scratched furrows and rough bark. "Mike?"

"What, that shit? Hair. We don't know if it's human or animal
yet."

"Where is it? All over?"

"All over. On the... the victims too." His voice didn't break,
but it was close. "There's even some out on the road, in the blood.
Patches of it."

Weird. "What about the scratches?"

"Just on the trees around this clearing."

"Huh." I thought about this, circling the clearing as Mike
peeled off to exchange low words with a woman from the medical
examiner's office, her dark hair pulled back in a sloppy ponytail. I
took care not to disturb the techs at their work, and they took care
not to get in my way. We're all happier that way.

You'd think a hunter wouldn't have to worry about evidentiary
procedure and the like, but it always pays not to piss off the techs.
And you never can tell when something small and insignificant

they find is going to turn a whole case on its head, or spin it so you can see the pattern behind the events.

The stench was deep and dark enough I had trouble finding a trail. My nose stung and my eyes prickled with tears. One slid hot down my cheek and I palmed it away, silver chiming in my hair. The creaking of my boots and coat was very loud in the predawn hush.

I had unusual difficulty making a coherent pattern out of the scuffed and blood-soaked dirt. The chaos must have been intense at night with nothing but handheld flashlights—not even the current illumination of false dawn and the portable floodlights at the periphery of the clearing, mixing a throat-coating wash of diesel into the equation. I finally gave up on trying to reconstruct the fight. There simply wasn't enough on the hard-packed dirt scattered with pine needles.

For a moment I imagined being out here in the dark, something chasing me and nothing but a human's reflexes and one police-issue Glock to fight it off with, and my skin chilled.

I finally zeroed in on a usable trail, but it was a bust. The scent led away from the scene at a sharp angle, back down to the cars; I followed. Then I picked it up again at the edge of yellow tape down on the freeway, and pursued it across the open lane and the meridian before it vanished into thin air. One moment, nose-watering stink, the next, nothing but the smell of damp wiry grass in sandy soil and the scent of morning.

Dammit. If it's hellbreed it might be able to mask. A hellbreed and something working in concert? What would work with one of them? Even their own kind don't trust them.

Still, that's what the evidence points to. Hellbreed plus something else. In other words, a big fucking problem.

I let out a sharp frustrated breath. Traffic was beginning to pick up, and dawn was well under way. I heard the distinctive thrupping of a chopper and looked up. Channel Twelve had arrived.

Dammit.

CHAPTER 6

My warehouse smelled like dust and there was nothing in the fridge except a takeout container of fuzzy green something that had once, I think, been chicken chow mein. I pushed the fridge door shut and leaned my forehead against its cool enamel for a moment, inhaling.

There was nothing I could do just now. When dusk hit I'd start canvassing the city. Anything that smelled that bad was leaving a trail, and that taint of hellbreed would give me a place to start. If any of Hell's citizens were developing a taste for cop, someone would know *something*. I had just the place to start, too.

You know what this means. You're going to have to visit him early.

I pushed the thought away. Hauled myself up and away from the fridge. Eating could wait. I opened up the cabinet over the dishwasher and got out the bottle, poured myself a stiff jigger of Scotch, and downed it. Poured another, tipped it down my throat, and relished the brief sting.

It helped, a little.

Mikhail had left me the warehouse. Its walls creaked, each sound echoing and bouncing. Nothing could sneak up on me here, between the acoustics and the wide-open spaces. My bed was set out in the middle of its own room, well away from the walls. The sparring-space was clean, swept regularly. A long spear-shape under amber silk hummed on one wall, beside the other weapons, all racked neatly.

Mikhail's sword hung in its sheath, its clawed finials and long hilt with the open gap in the pommel reflecting golden light. The sheath glowed—worn, mellow leather—the sword drawing strength from the square of sunlight resting over it, metal vibrating with its subliminal song. The skylight above had turned fierce, an open eye letting down a blade of light.

I shuffled out of the kitchen, swiping halfheartedly at the piled dust on the counter with one hand. Across the living room and down the short hall into the bedroom, my feet making little shushing noises against hardwood. My coat hung over the single chair, and my bed—two mattresses and a pile of messy blankets—beckoned.

Maybe just a short nap, so I'm fresh for tonight. The phone sat next to the bed, the answering machine blinking its deadly red eye.

I touched "Play" as I sank down on the bed, wriggling until knife-hilts didn't poke so badly, burying my face in the pillow.

"Jill? It's Galina. I have some more copper that might work for your wrist. Come by anytime."

Will do. My arms and legs were heavy. So heavy. Sunlight is a hunter's friend, it means rest and relaxation. Bad things generally don't come out during the day. They wait for cover of darkness to sneak around and cause trouble.

"Jill. It's Monty. I've buzzed you, something's up. Come by."

Already did, Monty. I'm on the job. I closed my eyes, breathing into my pillow. The smell of dust and my home gathered close and warm around me. I sighed.

"Kismet." A bland, blank voice. My breath caught. "It would profit you to visit me. Come tomorrow, after dark, and bring your whip." A soft gurgling laugh drew fingers of ice up my spine.

He said more, but I stopped listening, shivering as I burrowed into the bed, stopping my ears with the pillow. The sound of his voice faded.

Goddammit, Perry. Calling me wasn't part of the deal. But I was tired. So bloody tired. I decided to leave it for a few hours. I'd get worked up about it when I woke up.

I tipped over the edge into sleep, the answering machine saying something else to me in a low male tone. I didn't hear it, just slid under the edge of the world without a murmur as day walked the sky above.

Five months' worth of training ended up with me facedown on the floor again, aching all over, battered and bruised, sweat dripping from my split ends. The blond dye had begun to work its way out of my hair, the constant workouts made me scrawnier than ever no matter how much he fed me, and my heart pounded so hard I thought I was going to pass out.

"Get up, milaya.*" Pitiless, the accent weighting his words. "Or I will hit you again."*

He meant it, I already knew him enough to know that. I gasped in deep heaving breaths, my chest afire, staring at his bare hairy feet against the canvas. My arms were bars of leaden pain, my legs wet noodles. Still, when a man told you to do something, you did it.

Didn't you? Obedience wasn't optional, either in the place I'd been raised or during the years hooking for Val. It was a survival mechanism. One I cursed even as it stubbornly forced me to do what Mikhail told me, one more time.

Hate *you, I thought, and buried the words as soon as they drifted across my consciousness. God would surely strike me down if I ever allowed myself to truly think it, wouldn't He?*

He was a man, too.

I pushed myself up. My left arm trembled, shivers spilling through the muscle meat, before it dumped me back facedown on the canvas-covered mat. I tried again. My arm refused to hold me, rebelling, so I pushed myself up with the other one.

"Get up." His cane clove air, a silken swish; I didn't flinch. I'd learned enough not to flinch, no matter what he did.

"How?" I wasn't being fresh—I honestly didn't know. When your body starts giving out on you, what do you do?

I was stupid, then. I didn't know it was the mind that rules the flesh. What you truly will, the body will do. But that's not the kind of truth you learn walking Lucado Street, you know.

CRACK.

Right across the lower back, gauging it perfectly, the thin bamboo cane would sting like hell and leave a bruise but not damage me. Unfortunately, my legs now refused to work, and I let out a dry barking sob. I wanted to do what he wanted. I needed *to do what he told me to—this was my only chance, my only ticket out.*

It was my road away from Lucado and my pimp's empty eyes as he slumped choking over a coffee table, a neat hole in his chest and blood trickling from the corner of his mouth, the clock ticking, ticking, ticking on the wall.

I didn't ever want to visit that room again. I would do anything I had to, to keep walking away, keep locking that door.

Mikhail said he would find me a job and a place, some therapy, something. But anywhere I went that room would be waiting. It was all I knew, and I'd be back on the street again sooner or later.

Probably sooner. I was a damned soul anyway. Who cared what I did?

Nobody. Nobody except the man in the long coat who had plucked me out of the snow as I lay bleeding, the .22 clutched in my scraped, bruised fist.

Mikhail didn't want to train me, he didn't need the trouble. But I wanted to do what he did.

I wanted to make him proud of me.

Mikhail sighed. "Get up, little snake. Don't crawl." Heavy, the words slid between my pounding ears. He sounded sad.

I tried again. Made it up to my knees. Red spots danced in front of my eyes, turned black. My feet hit the mat, I was upright without quite knowing how I'd gotten there. My left arm hung useless, the hand nervelessly clutching a knife, and he moved in on me again.

I threw my arm up just in time. Swallowed a harsh bark of pain as the cane clipped my elbow. The knife skittered away across the mats, and my eyes flew to his face, my right hand coming up instinctively, just the way he'd shown me and made me practice. Exhaustion sang in my ears and blurred my eyes, he shifted his weight and I responded, my knees flexing as I dropped into a crouch, knife lifted along my right forearm and a grimace of effort peeling my lips back.

I was too slow and too late, and I waited for the bamboo cane to descend again, braced myself for the pain. Blinked, gasping again as my lungs informed me they weren't taking any more of this shit. My arms and legs seconded that emotion, with my heart pounding out its own agreement.

It was official. My entire corpse was in rebellion.

"Very good."

For a moment my brain struggled with the words. I thought he'd spoken in Russian, it was so unexpected. Sunlight poured through the room, dusk coming on but the last half-hour of direct light working its way in through skylights, dust dancing in each golden column. Sweat dripped stinging into my eyes. I stared up at his beaky nose, the brackets around his thin-lipped mouth, Mikhail's pale hair turning to layers of ice.

"Very good, milaya. *Come."*

He bent down to take the knife from me, and I was so far gone I almost didn't let him have it, shifting my weight back, bicep and triceps tensing involuntarily, preparing for the slash.

My teacher froze. Wariness crossed his blue eyes, and the world stopped.

"I—" I'm sorry, I began to say. The magic words. Sometimes they would stave off a beating if I said them quickly enough. If I was placatory enough, pliant enough.

"Very good." A broad smile turned up the corners of his thin mouth and made him almost handsome, even if he was too old. "I think, there is more to the little snake than meets the eye, eh? Now hand me knife, milaya, *and we shall find arnica for bruises. I think we go out for dinner tonight."*

I stared blankly at him for a long moment. Did he mean it, or was he going to punish me?

He made a quick movement with his blunt, callused fingers. He never hit me unless we were sparring, and he always tended the cuts and bruises gently. So far he hadn't laid a hand on me except to correct me when I was holding a weapon, or to point out some flaw in my movements.

Or, of course, to beat my ass in sparring. But he was capable of more, wasn't he? He was really able to put the hurt on someone, you could tell by the way he moved.

He was playing nice with me. For now, the hard cold survivor whispered in the back of my head. I tried to ignore her. She wasn't a good girl.

I reversed the knife. Already the movement felt natural instead of awkward. Offered him the hilt, watching, waiting.

He took it, and the blade vanished into a sheath. He stretched, muscle moving under his red T-shirt, and held out his hand.

"Are you deaf? Come, your teacher is hungry. Hard work, training little snakes."

My fingers closed on his, and Mikhail hauled me to my feet, then clapped me on the shoulder. I almost went down again, my legs weak as a newborn colt's.

"Go clean up. We go out for dinner." The kindness in the words was almost as foreign as his accent. *"Good work, little snake. You are worth keeping, I think."*

It was the first time anyone had ever thought so, and my heart swelled four big sizes. I made it about three steps before I passed out from the strain.

I spent two days in bed recovering, and when I got up again, my training started in earnest.

CHAPTER 7

Night rose from the alleys and bars, spreading its cloak from the east and swirling in every corner. No matter how tired I am, dusk always wakes me up like six shots of espresso and a bullet whizzing past. It's a hunter thing, I suppose. If we aren't night owls when we begin, training and hunting make us so before long.

I surfaced from the velvet blankness between dreams, slowly. All was as it should be, the warehouse creaking and sighing as the wind came up from the river like it does every sunset, smelling of chemical-laden water and heat. My eyes drifted open, finding a familiar patch of blank wall. A knife-hilt dug into my ribs, hard. I blinked.

Then I rolled out of bed, catching myself on toes and palms, and did the pushups. Just like every time I woke up. Press against the wooden floor, bare toes cold, shoulders burning. Up. Up. Up.

Like a wooden plank. Nice and straight. Mikhail's voice again, so familiar I barely noticed it.

When I finished the second set, it was time for the sit-ups. Then I padded, yawning and scratching, out into the practice room. Mikhail's sword glittered in one last random reflection, dying sunlight jetting through a skylight to touch the hole in the hilt. The glitter was gone as soon as it happened, I hung the harness that held my knives and guns up on its peg. Yawned one more time, the silver charms in my hair shifting, as I settled, my feet hip-width apart, and found my center.

The fighting art of hunters is a hodgepodge. Name any martial art, and we've kiped a move or two. Savate, kung fu, plenty of judo, we do a lot of wrestling on the floor, actually. Escrima, karate, good old streetfight fisticuffs—which is mostly common sense and retraining the flinches out of you than anything else—t'ai chi...really, the list is endless and a hunter is always picking new things up. There's even a style of fighting Weres train their young with, relying on quickness and evasion, that Mikhail thought was good for me. It's like a dance, and several hunters take ballet for flexibility and balance. Every hunter accumulates a set of favorite moves that work well, but you always have to revisit even the ones you don't like.

You never know what will save your ass.

After a half-hour of katas, I grabbed a pair of knives from the rack on the wall and really went to work. Knife fighting is close and dirty, and it's my forte. I'm smaller than the average hunter, and even before the scar on my wrist I had quicker reflexes than most.

Women usually do.

Mikhail had to train nastiness into me, though, and the ruthless willingness to hurt. Without it, even the quickest reflexes won't save you.

Mikhail.

Get up. My knives clove the air, whistling, spinning around my fingers, elbow-strikes, smashing the face with the knee. *Get up, milaya. Or I will hit you again. Get up!*

My own helpless sobs echoed in my ears, from years and miles away. My body moved easily now, gracefully, forms as strict as a dance become muscle memory, instinctive now. That wasn't always the case. I had been gawky and helpless when he'd found me, a teenage girl more used to streetwalking than lunge-kicks. The first year of my training had been hell in more ways than one.

Step, kick, turn, take out the knee, upward slash, break the neck with a quick twist, stamp and turn. The blades gleamed in the dimness as the last light of day leached out of the skylights. Metal sang as I flung both knives, the solid *tchuk* as they met the scarred block of wood set across the practice room reassuring. "Not so bad," I whispered, then it was time for the heavy bag.

I started out easy, double and triple punches, working myself into a rhythm. I have to be careful; if you've got a hellbreed-strong fist, you have to hold back even when your heavy bag is reinforced. Elbow strike, knee, the rapid tattoo mixing with exhaled breath at the end of each blow.

Sweat dripped stinging into my eyes. Not because of the effort, but because I'd been dreaming again. Memory rose like a riptide, swallowing me whole.

Snow. Shivering, the cold nipping at fingers and toes, exposed knobs of my knees raw and aching. Taste of iron and slick tears at the back of my throat. The place where he'd hit me throbbed, a swallowing brand of fire, and the gun was heavy in my hand.

I'd done it. I had committed murder, and I'd taken Val's gun. Still, the thing I worried about most was the money. The thought that he'd cut me, hurt me, maybe mark my face if he found me now, wasn't eased in the slightest by the fact that I'd shot the motherfucker.

The clock was still ticking inside my head. Tick tock, tick tock.

A white Oldsmobile eased by, its windows down even in the blinding cold, and a beer bottle smashed on the pavement. They yelled, and my dry eyes barely blinked. The gun was on my right side, hidden by my thin cotton dress.

I had already killed. I had already committed the greatest sin possible, to crown all my other sins.

If the car slowed down, if they stopped, it would be the last time. The last *time.*

Split lip. I'd had a split lip and a damn-near dislocated shoulder, and a busted-up spleen—and those were only the lightest injuries. Mikhail told me later it was a wonder I'd been walking, he could smell the blood and hurt on me even across the street.

Punch, bag shudders, follow it up with elbow, lift the knee, move in low, the force on a punch has to come from the hip just like whip-work or it's useless.

Useless. Like I used to be.

The purring of the Oldsmobile's engine returned, growing

louder. I stopped, head hanging, fingers tightening on the cold
metal. Men. All of them, men. The same type of men I'd been so
close to, so many times, swallowing if I had to, spitting when I
could, letting my body do things while the real part of me retreated
into a little box—a box that grew smaller and smaller each time.
When it finally became too small, would I vanish?
I had already sailed off the edge of the world. Now I just had to
take as many of them with me as I could before I was finally put
down. I turned, eyes wide, headlights blinding me, gun lifting—
and warm fingers clamped around my wrist.

No, the tall white-haired man had said, another language
blurring through the words, a song of a foreign accent. Not
tonight, little one.

Kick. Kick. Stamp down, both fists smacking the heavy bag. Fists
blurring, low sound of effort through clenched teeth.

I struggled, but he was too strong, and I squeezed the trigger as
the car eased past. The sound of the .22 was lost under a blare of
the horn and catcalls, and he twisted the gun out of my hand,
ignoring the car. I tried to punch him, he didn't seem to move but
the punch went wide, and I spun aside, falling. My arm stretched,
my injured shoulder screaming. He let go, and I landed in snow,
my skin burning. I coughed, and a bright jet of blood smashed out
through my teeth.

The last thing I felt was gentle fingers in my ragged, strawlike
dyed-blonde hair. I tried to curse at him, hooked my fingers and
tried to take off some of his skin. My broken nails scratched only
air. I tried to scream, choking on blood.

He had watched me for a few moments, weighing me.

My fists thudded into the bag. I stopped. My ribs flickered as I
took in deep heaving breaths. How had he seen anything valuable
in that broken girl in the snow? And the gun had vanished; he
never mentioned it afterward.

Had he guessed how desperate I'd been, and what I'd done with
the goddamn gun before he'd seen me? Did he care? Monty never

mentioned my police record. Then again, my name was different by the time he met me. *I* was different, all the way down to the bone. Sometimes I wondered if my fingerprints had changed.

I gave the heavy bag one last punch, listening as it swayed on its chain. The creaking was familiar, and echoed through the warehouse. My breathing evened out, and my eyes tracked across the wall. A long slim shape under a fall of amber silk, the crossbow and hunting bow, the mace and the wooden spear with its tassels rusty and clumped together, its tip gummed with black residue.

And Mikhail's sword, a faint glow running through the clawed finials, the empty space in the hilt watching me.

The carved ruby in the hollow of my throat warmed, responding. Air brushed my skin, the scar twitching as I noticed it again, the preternatural acuity of my senses almost normal now that I'd spent a while with it uncovered. I would have to visit the Monde Nuit early, both to gather information about whatever hellbreed was killing cops, and also to express my displeasure to Perry. He shouldn't be calling me.

It wasn't part of the deal.

Not tonight, little one. I had not known my teacher's voice then. I hadn't known it was the voice of salvation.

As if I *deserved* salvation, deserved to be plucked from the snow and given a new life.

I don't want to think about this. "Mikhail," I whispered. The whisper bounced back, taunted me. He was dead, choked on his own blood, betrayed by a viper in woman's clothing, and I was still here. I hadn't been able to save him.

All the training, all the striving, all the pain—and I still had not been able to save *him*.

The heavy bag stilled, its chain making a slow sound of metal under tension. I wanted to kick it again, listen to the familiar creaking, but I didn't. Instead, I turned on my heel and stalked for the door, grabbing my harness from its peg.

I needed a shower.

One thing about being a hunter—sometimes your night doesn't work out exactly as planned. All I wanted was a few drinks to brace me before I had to go into the Monde, so I headed toward Micky's on Mayfair Hill, among the gay nightclubs and high-priced fetish boutiques. Micky's is a quiet place, an all-night restaurant where trouble never starts—because not only is it the place where the gay community comes to canoodle over blintzes, beer, and specialty pancakes, it's also staffed with Weres. Pretty much any night you can find a few nightsiders drinking, or stuffing themselves with human food, or just sitting and having a cup of coffee under the pictures of old film stars watching from the walls.

If you're on the nightside and you're legal, you're welcome in Micky's. Even if you're not-so-legal you're welcome, as long as you pay your tab and don't start any trouble.

I was heading up Bolivar Street to the foot of Mayfair when something brushed against my consciousness, and I put the Impala into a bootlegger's turn, headed back and around the corner onto Eighteenth. Tires smoked and screeched; a horn blared behind me, and I zagged the Impala into a halfass parking spot in an alley and was out of the car in a flash, my senses dilating.

The reek of the thing I was hunting smashed through my nose, and I felt more than heard its footsteps like a brush against a drum. Moving fast, and moving *away.*

I bolted out into the street, plunged into an alley on the other side, and scaled the side of the building by tearing my way up the outside of the fire escape. Vaulted over the side of the roof and began to *run,* my coat flapping behind me.

The baked smell of daylight still simmered up from pavement and rooftop, but the stink cut right through it with a harsh serrated edge. I leapt, etheric force pulled through the suddenly blazing scar, and hit a tenement rooftop going full speed, barely rolling to shed a little momentum, glad once again that I wear leather pants. Denim can get shredded when you're going this fast.

I don't wear leather because it makes my ass look cute, you know.

Fuck this thing's quick, watch it Jill, cross street coming up, you can head it off if it keeps going in a straight line—

But of course it couldn't be that easy. I landed *hard* in the middle of Twenty-Ninth Street, the shock slamming up through my hips and shoulders as I ended up on one knee, concrete smoking and puffing up dust under the strain of my sudden application of force. Air screamed away from my body, my coat snapping like a flag in a hard breeze. Two blocks down, an indistinct quadruped shape—the streetlight had burned out—squeezed down into the road itself.

Oh, shit. Please don't tell me it did what I think it just did. But I was already moving, and lo and behold things were about to get interesting.

The son of a bitch had just gone down through a manhole. The manhole cover lay off to one side, dents in its surface I didn't have time to examine. I *also* didn't have time to drag it back so a car wouldn't break an axle in the hole. No, I just breathed an imprecation and leapt, dropping down through the hole with arms and legs pulled close, bracing myself for whatever waited at the bottom.

And hoping I didn't hit anything on the way down.

The resulting thud had a splash attached, liquid splattering up to paint the crumbling concrete walls, and a new and interesting smell of waste threatened to knock me off my feet. Mixed with the gagging stench of the thing I chased, it was a heady bouquet.

Well, at least if it stinks that bad I can track it. No ambush waited for me down below. I finished sliding a knife from its sheath and noticed something strange.

The smell of the thing was *different.* It didn't reek of hellbreed, just purely of sickness and fur. The silver in my hair and against my throat didn't start to burn; Mikhail's apprentice-ring on my third left finger didn't prickle with heat.

No time for questions. The water was knee-high and I splashed through, automatically noting how deep I was—it'd been a hell of a fall. *Christ. It couldn't fall into a nice clean department store, it had to pick a goddamn storm drain. Smells like something's dead down here too. Lovely.*

Running. Breath coming harsh and tearing, the knife held reversed along my forearm, my coat snapping and popping like a guitar riff, the liquid turning even soupier as tunnels began to branch off. I followed the worst smell, my gag reflex triggered—I didn't have *time* to throw up. *Jesus. This is foul. Why doesn't it smell like hellbreed? My coat is never going to be the same.*

Branching tunnels. A left, a right, a soft left in an intersection of four ways—did this thing know where it was going? Was it running blind or luring me into something?

I hate this sort of thing. The sludge started getting deeper, and the tunnel slanted downhill. *I really hate this sort of thing.*

Covered in guck, stinking to high heaven—there *was* something dead in the water—I reached a wide, deep chamber with a cleaner smell. A faint green glow bounced off the water's oily surface and dappled the walls. Above, pipes tangled, and several different round openings led off in different directions.

For the second time, maddeningly, the smell just *quit* between one step and the next. I skidded to a stop in thigh-high water, throwing up a sheet of it, and cast about frantically, trying to catch the thread again. A distant clang, like something sharply striking a pipe, tightened every nerve in my body.

To top it all off, the charms in my hair shifted, tinkling, and the silver chain at my throat began to burn. Mikhail's ring heated up, too. The knife blurred back into its sheath even as my blue eye scanned under the surface of the world and found nothing.

The smell was *gone.*

Goddammit, I REALLY HATE this sort of thing.

I backed up a step or two, and there it was again—but it was fading under the onslaught of fresh water lapping into the chamber, a cold current mouthing my thighs. Breaking a trail with running water, a trick so old even normal humans do it.

But the ability to mask a scent so thoroughly was pure hellbreed. I didn't know of anything else that could do that so cleanly, like a scalpel slicing off a nerve.

And hellbreed meant *possible nasty surprise* lurking somewhere.

This would be a really good time to get out of the water, Jill. Unfortunately, there was nowhere to go but one of the pipe openings, and God alone knew what was in those.

My guns cleared leather in both hands, and I turned in a full circle, my eyes—smart and dumb—traveling over every nook and cranny. No use. Whoever it was, they were gone.

The heat drained from my silver. The scar on my wrist prickled, working in toward the bone, unhealthy heat spilling up my arm, jolting in my shoulder as I pulled force through it, worked into taut humming readiness.

"God*dam*mit." The word couldn't carry the weight of my frustration. I searched for others. "*Shit.* Shit*fuck.* Mother*fucking*cocksucking fuck* on a cheese-coated *stick!*" My voice bounced and rippled off the water.

A slight sound, behind me.

I spun, water tearing up in a sleek wave as etheric force swirled with me, both guns trained on one particular pipe, big enough for something very nasty to fit in. My pulse smoothed out, quit its hammering, and I tasted copper on my tongue through the reek of rot coating the back of my nose.

A glimmer, down low. Green-blue and flat, like an animal's eyes at night. My fingers tightened on the trigger even as I sensed another presence and half turned, one gun locking onto the first target, the other locking onto the second. *Come out and play, shitheels, whoever you are.*

The second one spoke. "Jill?" A female voice, low and husky with a touch of purr behind it. "Don't shoot. I'm coming out with my hands loose. Dominic's with me."

What the hell?

Memory placed the voice. One gun lowered slightly. "Harp?"

Harper Smith slid out of the second pipe. My pulse thundered in my ears as I twitched, amped on adrenaline and oh so close to pulling the trigger.

She's tall—Weres usually are, even females. She moved with the fluidity and precision of a cat Were, all slinking graze and laziness. Long dark hair pulled back in two thick braids, wide liquid dark eyes, and a mouth that always seemed just short of merriment below an aristocratic nose and wide high cheekbones, she was beautiful in the negligent way almost all Weres are. She hung for a moment full-length from a slimmer iron pipe, then curved to land on a larger one, her booted feet placed for maximum effect. Her battered canvas jacket flapped briefly, showing her sidearm, and the feathers braided into her hair fluttered as she cocked her head, examining me.

Her mate, Dominic, peered out of the same pipe she'd been in. "Hey, Kismet." His voice was lower, a bass purr, and his sandy-blond hair was as long as Harp's but pulled back and bound in a club with leather thongs. His eyes glittered briefly too, and I caught a flash of the straight line of his mouth before he withdrew a little, into shadow. "Put the iron away, willya?"

The Terrible Two of the Martindale Squad. What the hell is the FBI doing out here? And two Weres without a hunter...that means a Were problem. I promptly turned my back on them, both guns pointed at the first pipe. "Hey, Dom. What are you guys doing out here?" My fingers tightened on the triggers. "And is that your fucking friend? If it is, you'd better speak up *now* before I ventilate him."

"Easy, hunter." The third voice was male, low with an edge of vibrating bass like Dominic's. "Don't make me take that gun away from you."

Oh, you did not *just say that to me.* "Come and try it, cheese-cake. Weres don't scare me. Who the fuck are *you?*"

"Calm down, both of you!" Harp sounded annoyed. "Jill, he's one of ours. He's a tracker from out on the Brightwater Reservation. Saul, come out and introduce yourself. This is Mikhail's student."

I kept the guns trained as the Were moved cautiously forward. He was a long rangy man, his dark hair shoulder-length and left loose, dark eyes flicking down my body to where the water lapped at my thighs and coming back up again. He had the classic Were face—high cheekbones, red-brown skin, thick eyelashes, chiseled mouth.

He looked Native American, like most American Weres. Native American on the cover of a romance novel, that is, a really bodice-ripping one. Jeans and a hip-length leather jacket, a black T-shirt stretching over his chest. The healthy clean scent of Were mixed with the stink, and I was abruptly conscious of being dipped in fetid goo and wet almost clear through.

"Saul." He gave his name grudgingly. "Saul Dust-circle."

"Jill Kismet." I lowered my guns, holstered them both. Measured

him for a long moment. *I am not going to say it's a pleasure.* Then
I rounded back on Harp. "What the fuck is the Martindale Squad
doing down in the drains in *my* city, Harp? *Without* contacting
me, I might add?"

"Left you a message yesterday." Dominic eased forward a little
more, crouching with easy grace inside the pipe mouth. He reached
up, scratched his cheek with blunt delicate fingertips. "You been
busy?"

"That's the goddamn understatement of the year." *I should
have listened to messages this morning; I knew there was something I'd missed last night.* I let out a long breath. "Five cops
attacked out on the Drag last night. Montaigne called me in.
Something that smells goddamn awful, and has a habit of cloaking itself. I repeat, *why are you in my city?*"

I should have been a bit more polite, but my nerves were a little
thinner than I liked. This disturbed me badly. Something that
smelled that terrible should *not* be able to disappear like a hellbreed could. Plus, I was covered in guck, and they looked cool and
imperturbable like Weres always do.

To top it all off, I'd sensed hellbreed, I *knew* I had. It just kept
getting better.

"Easy, Jill." Harp spoke up, soft and calm. "We just blew into
town a couple days ago, and had to wait for Saul. We've been trying to reach you."

She took a deep breath, and her eyes met mine. The other male
Were—Saul—made a slight scuffing sound as he moved, and I
quelled the urge to twitch. He came goddamn close to getting silverjacket lead in his flesh.

I suddenly had a very bad feeling.

Then Harp went and said just about the worst thing she could
have. "We have a rogue Were."

CHAPTER 8

Some days the worst part of the job is cleaning up. I tossed the damp towel in the hamper, buckled my harness on, and stalked out of the bathroom. My coat was dripping in the utility room, having been hosed off thoroughly, and I suspected I was never going to be able to get my boots clean again. So I was barefoot, in a fresh pair of leather pants and a *Jonathan Strange* T-shirt, the weight of the harness comforting against my shoulders and back.

I heard voices as I padded up the hall.

"This place is a sty."

It seemed Mr. Dustcircle didn't think much of my housekeeping. Weres are inherently domestic, and my empty fridge was probably scandalous to the country boy. If he was fresh off the Rez, he probably hadn't had much contact with hunters, either. Most Rez Weres take a dim view of humans, and hunters are only tolerated because they're good backup when the scurf start infesting again.

I almost shuddered. At least I was fairly sure we weren't dealing with carnivorous bits of contagion. I've never faced a scurf infestation myself. God willing, I never will.

"Don't get snitty." There was the tinkle of glass—Harp was probably getting herself a drink. "She's a good hunter. Mikhail Tolstoi trained her."

My heart twisted with pain, kept on beating.

"She stinks of hellbreed." Dustcircle didn't sound mollified. "And she's not one of us."

It shouldn't have annoyed me, but it did. I stepped out of the hall, my fingers falling away from a knife-hilt. "Will you shut him up, Harp? That country shit is getting on my nerves."

Harp stood at my breakfast bar, and Dustcircle stood in the kitchen, his hands loose at his sides. The female Were kept pouring Jack Daniel's, steadily, into one of four chunky glasses. No Were strategy session is without munchies unless the situation's dire, and JD was as close to food as I possessed unless you wanted to count the science experiment in the fridge.

"Dominic went to get some takeout." Harp's dark eyes rested on the glasses. "I wanted to ask you, Jill, could you put Saul up while he stays in town? I would, but we're at the Carlton on expense account, and the pencil-pushers in Accounting don't look kindly on such things."

I leaned against the living-room wall, folding my arms. I couldn't see Dustcircle's face; the kitchen cabinets hanging over the breakfast bar blocked my view. "Why can't he stay in the barrio?"

It was rude of me, but he'd just called my house a sty. Which it probably was, to a Were. But at least I scrub my own toilets, and there was nothing rotting in the kitchen.

Well, except for the science experiment in the fridge.

"Because," Harp said steadily, finishing her pouring, "he doesn't have kin in the barrio, and because I don't want to worry about you while this is going on. This neatly solves both my problems."

Worry about me? What do you think I've been doing out here, holding hands and having bake sales? "Heaven knows I live to solve your problems, Harp. Quit fucking around. I don't take in boarders, especially ones who can't even insult me to my face. Stash him with Galina, that's what a Sanctuary's for." I restrained the urge to rub at my right wrist, wishing I'd had time to drop by Galina's and take a look at the new copper cuffs. I could *smell* the alcohol in the glasses, and I badly wanted a jolt.

"What, and have a rogue battering at her front door? She won't thank me for that, and even if it doesn't matter to her it'll endanger everyone who pops by. Besides, I want this kept quiet, and everybody and their mother goes to Galina's. Come on, Jill. He'll behave, I promise." Harp scooped up two of the glasses, and stalked over the bare wooden floor to hand me one. Her skin was warm, a Were's higher metabolism bleeding heat into the air. "Let's sit down, shall we?"

"Help yourself." I indicated my ugly-as-sin secondhand orange Naugahyde couch. "Come on, Harp. Spill. Even if it is a rogue Were, what the hell is the FBI doing in on it? Rogue Weres are the responsibility of regional territory holders in conjunction with hunters. The Norte Luz pride should be in on this."

Harp settled herself on the couch. I downed the respectable dollop she'd poured me, felt it burn all the way down, and stamped over to the counter to snag the bottle. Dustcircle eased around the corner of the breakfast bar, eyeing me disdainfully. He smelled faintly of cherry tobacco and cigarette smoke, and he was much larger than me, being a Were. His gaze met mine, flicked down my body again.

I loudly ignored him.

"Well?" I prompted, when the silence stretched a little too far. "Come *on,* Harp."

"The rogue has crossed state lines." She was choosing her words with care. "And his kills are ... disturbing. Very disturbing."

You know, when you say disturbing, *I bet it means something totally different than when* I *say it. And neither definition is very comforting.* I had a bad feeling about all this. "Would it have anything to do with the way the trail keeps vanishing? Or with the hellbreed I keep smelling?"

"You'd know all about that, wouldn't you?" Dustcircle's tone was tight and furious. He didn't like being dismissed.

"You going to muzzle him, Harp?" I settled down cross-legged on the floor near the couch. "I'm not as patient as Mikhail when it comes to dealing with little boys who bark too much."

To give her credit, she didn't roll her eyes. "Jill made a bargain with one of the resident powers in town," Harp said quietly. "With Mikhail's support and approval, I might add. She's a good hunter, Saul. Either be a polite little kitten or shut the fuck up, will you? I would hate to have to call your mother."

"I'm not a kit, Harp." Most of the growl left his voice. He picked up one of the drinks, paced smoothly across the room, and settled down on the floor about six feet from me, facing the couch. There was no other piece of furniture in the living room except the lamps, big antique iron things that had stood in Mikhail's bedroom, once upon a time. "I apologize, hunter. I haven't slept much, and I'm impolite."

By Were codes of etiquette, that was a bare-throat submission. I stared at him for a good thirty seconds. The mellow shine of electric light in his hair was tinted with red. "Forgotten," I said finally. "And forgiven. Nice to meet you."

Which, by Were codes, was a magnanimous refusal to prove my dominance.

That earned me a startled glance, but I turned my gaze back to Harp, who wore a wide white-toothed smile. I touched the back of my right wrist, scrubbed at it with my fingers. Touching the scar wasn't a good time, so when I had it uncovered for a while I rubbed at the back of my wrist, a nervous tic I was helpless to stop. "Fine. But one nasty comment and he's out the door. I haven't been half-drowned in storm-drain shit tonight to take lip from a Were you can't babysit. Now start talking."

The warehouse creaked as the side door opened. I smelled food, and Were. Dominic made no attempt to keep quiet. Wise of him.

Harp knocked back her drink in one smooth motion. I poured myself another.

"It started out in Massachusetts—this rogue is ranging further than any I've ever seen. The kills look strange, very strange. About three-quarters of the kills are a regular rogue's—tracked from a resting-site, muscle meat gone, a high level of violence, souvenirs taken. The other quarter are... well, too savage to be a Were, blood for the hell of it and no muscle meat taken." She took a deep breath as Dominic padded into the room.

"Your plates still in the same place, Jill?" He sounded unwont-edly cheerful. "That Thai place on Seventy-second is still open. Go figure."

I didn't know there was a Thai place on Seventy-second. Trust a Were to know where all the munchies are. "Everything's where it should be," I told him, leaning back braced on my hands. "Drop the other shoe, Harp."

She did. "He's killed two hunters already. Devon Blue in Boston, and Jean-François Roche in Louisiana. Saul's sister was running backup for Jean-François. Our rogue killed her. It was a hell of a fight, from what we can tell."

My stomach turned over hard. "Holy *shit*." My eyes jagged over to Dustcircle, who was staring into his drink. Killing another Were's sister is a big deal. The only thing bigger is killing another

Were's mother. It's one of the few completely taboo things among them.

"I'm sorry." My voice dropped. No wonder he was in a bad mood.

And Boston and Louisiana were too far apart for a regular rogue. They tend to stay in familiar territory, which makes them easier to track. Rogues are normally completely predictable, behavior-wise, at the mercy of instinct run amok. To have a rogue acting *un*predictably was bad, bad news.

Or it wasn't a rogue at all. But if Harp said it was...

Saul glanced up, and I thought I saw surprise in his dark gaze before Dominic came out with plates and chopsticks, carrying two large plastic bags as well. He must have bought one of everything on the menu. "Chowtime, boys and girls. Kiss, you need to eat. You look like you're trying to diet yourself to death."

"Don't call me that." I wrinkled my nose as chili pepper and coconut crawled up into my sinuses and made themselves at home. "You got everything four-stars again, didn't you."

"Live it up, baby." Dominic handed me a plate and a pair of wooden chopsticks. "We've got the files, and you might as well take a look at them. You know the city better than we do, and we'll need to start checking everywhere a rogue might go to ground."

I caught the look he flashed to Harp, and was suddenly sure there was more. "If it's a rogue Were, why is it acting unpredictably, and why does it smell like hellbreed?" *But only sometimes. Still, even "sometimes" is enough to give me nightmares.*

God knows I don't get nightmares easy anymore. I just dream about Mikhail.

It's anyone's guess which was worse.

"We don't know." Harp sounded cautious again. "We were hoping maybe you'd have an idea. Operations suggested bringing you in, and when the trail veered this way we thought we'd pick you up."

Aha. Suddenly more about this makes sense. I tapped my chopsticks against my plate, meditatively.

Silence, broken only by the rustling of plastic. Dominic plopped down on the wooden floor between me and Saul, and Harp slithered off the couch to sit with us, folding her long legs up with inhuman grace. Warm air swirled, touching my cheek—their skins throwing out heat like sidewalks on a summer day.

Shit. Sometimes I wish I couldn't hear what people aren't *saying.* I set my plate down, my skin going briefly cold. Laid the chopsticks across them. *They want to talk to Perry.* "No way, Harp. He'll eat you alive."

"We just want to ask some questions." Her eyes met mine.

"Dinner first," Dominic said. "Eat, then argue. Come on, Kiss."

"Hellbreed *don't like* Weres. And this one's different, he's not your average shiny-eyed weirdo." The chopsticks rattled as I shifted, my knee brushing the plate. "Give me what you want to ask him about, I'll take it in. I've got to go in there anyway, I might as well."

And the more business I have to handle, the more I can put off going in there to make my monthly payment. My skin chilled afresh, gooseflesh prickling up hard all along my back.

"We're curious about this hellbreed, Jill. It's a golden opportunity for the Squad to find out what's going on inside his little domain. We have half a dozen cases he might have his fingers in, and nobody can get close enough to even snap a picture of him."

No doubt. "That should tell you something." I poured another healthy cupful of JD, set the bottle down, and tossed the whole glass back. "Jesus Christ, Harp. Don't push this one. You know better, Mikhail would tell you the same thing. *Did* tell you the same goddamn thing."

Harp decided to push it. But carefully, her voice soft and uncertain. "Not even a meeting in a neutral place?"

Perry doesn't do neutral, sweetcheeks. "*No,* Harper. Not a chance." I shifted restlessly, and Dustcircle twitched. Dominic, a takeout container in his hand, studied me with lambent eyes. Brown feathers in Harp's hair stirred, and the warehouse echoed, little chuckles and sighs as my voice bounced back to me.

"I had to ask. Operations feels it's a priority." She dropped her eyes, looking at her plate.

Two submissions from as many Weres in under ten minutes. It was a record of sorts, but one I didn't feel good about setting. "You can tell that snake to slither back into his hole, I'm not taking you to see Perry. I can barely keep my own skin whole around him, and looking out for you is a distraction I *don't* need. You *know* how hellbreed feel about Weres." I poured myself another healthy dose of amber alcohol, knocked it back, and set the glass down with a small, precise click. Decided it was time for a subject change. "So we have a rogue ranging out of accustomed territories, a quarter of the kills not following a rogue's standard pattern, and the stink of hellbreed. A hellbreed manipulating a rogue Were, maybe?"

Dominic busied himself with dishing up the food. Harp settled into her seated posture, rubbing at her eyes as if tired. She looked so lovely and languid, it was hard to believe she could shift and tear an ordinary human to shreds in less than fifteen seconds.

Dustcircle piped up. "A rogue Were is hard to control."

Bingo. "Easier than a Were with his wits about him." I stared at my empty plate, the white circle with the cheap chopsticks bisecting it. "You said something about files, Harp?"

"Yeah." She accepted a filled plate from Dominic with a nod of thanks, one blonde braid dipping forward over her shoulder. The feathers were brown and stippled, hawk from the look of it; her tribe was allied with the Washington D.C. hawkflight. "But not until after we eat."

Good idea. My stomach rolled uneasily, but I put a bright face on it. "The night's young. I'll peek at the files and then you can start canvassing the barrio while I go through the hellbreed clubs. I want to find out what hellbreed's tangled up in this, or we're just shooting in the dark."

"A rogue should be predictable," Dustcircle muttered, as Dominic glorped some pad Thai onto his plate. "We've missed something. But regardless, we should hunt him first."

My temper all but snapped. "You've done a bang-up job of catching this *predictable* guy so far. And for your information, *Were,* I am the resident expert when it comes to hunting hellbreed."

"Is that why you smell like one?" Dustcircle nodded his thanks to Dominic, not bothering to glance at me.

Harp already gave you my bona fides, country boy. I counted to ten. It didn't work, so I counted again. Harp's hand paused halfway to her mouth, as if she wanted to clap it over her lips but couldn't quite make it there. Dominic, his chopsticks in midair, sighed wearily. Being mated to Harp must mean a whole lot of uncomfortable moments, and he was a smooth-it-over type of guy.

To top the whole damn unsatisfactory conversation, my pager buzzed against my hip, clipped to my belt. The damn thing was waterproof, which I alternately vilified and blessed. I unclipped and glanced at it, barely seeing the number. *Perfect. Just what I need.*

I got to my feet slowly, the floor creaking underneath me. "Duty calls." My voice sounded unnatural even to myself. "Harp?"

She made a small noise, as if the breath had been knocked out of her. "Jill."

"While I'm gone, will you teach the country boy some manners? My job is hard enough without assholes complicating it. I presume you have a copy of whatever file you want me to face Perry down with. Leave it here, lock up when you're done."

I turned on my heel and stalked away, the warehouse echoing and my teeth clenched so tight my jaw ached. They were silent. I was hungry. And my coat was still sopping-wet.

Great.

CHAPTER 9

Avery clasped the bag of ice to his face. "Don't say a word," he groaned, leaning back in his chair. "Not one single fucking word, Kiss. I'm warning you."

I hunched my aching shoulders, bracing my elbows on my knees as I inhaled, exhaled, dangling the bottle of beer in my right hand. "I'm not saying anything, Avery." My wrist burned, I'd pulled a hell of a lot of etheric force through the scar. "I'm not even thinking it."

"Liar." His leg was tightly bandaged, his throat bruised, and the tiled hall echoed as he let out a gusty sigh. Here at the downtown jail, below the five stories that held the normal criminals overnight or during trials, this corridor terminated in three rooms, each with a circle scribed on the floor. Sometimes they were empty for two or three days at a time.

Then there were nights like tonight. Two exorcisms referred in by the two Catholic parishes, one by the local Methodist church, and another three dragged in by Eva and Benito, two-thirds of the regular exorcists in town responsible for doing straight rip-and-stuffs. Wallace was visiting his mother in Idaho, and on a busy night like this I could have strangled him, though he needed the vacation.

Regular exorcists shouldn't do more than two a night. It's draining psychic and physical work, and for anything out of the ordinary they were supposed to call me in. Avery had tried to take on his third exorcism of the night by himself, and I'd arrived just as the possessed—a meek little morbidly religious shut-in on Benton Avenue who was even now unconscious inside one of the holding cells for the night—did her level best to tear his eyes out after chewing his leg open and throttling him. She was lucky to still be alive, as I'd had to tear the Possessor out of her in a hell of a hurry and drag both her and Avery downtown for some medical attention.

Possessors are nasty little things, and once an exorcism gets referred it's almost a given that they've wormed their way into someone with weeks of effort, driving them crazy a little bit at a time. Most of the possessed have no memory of the whole time—big chunks of their life gone—maybe an unconscious reflex, the psyche shutting away the trauma of having a parasitical psychic rider. It's one of the biggest violations imaginable, your mind and soul not your own—and the fact that Possessors, the little worms, tend to prey on the religious and naive, not to mention the middle to upper-middle class, isn't much of a comfort. For once the poor aren't targeted by a species of hellbreed, but that was small reassurance at best.

Plus, Possessors find it easier to slide in while the ambient psychic temperature is fermenting-hot. Like right after one hunter passes away and a new one takes his place. All in all, big fun.

I took a long drag off the beer. It was ice-cold, filched from the small fridge under Avery's desk, the same desk I leaned my knee against as I eyed him. Technically you're not supposed to have alcohol anywhere near you on duty, but exceptions were sometimes made for exorcists.

You don't last long without a drink or two—or six—in this line of work.

Wrestling on the floor with a woman who was no doubt very nice and sweet when she didn't have a Possessor inside her just made a cold beer go down that much better. My shoulders ached, and she'd gotten her teeth in my throat, worrying at the band of the sternocleidomastoid muscle. If she'd been true hellbreed or even Trader, that might have given me a problem. But Possessors are the low end of the hell pool, I could handle five or six of them on a given night without getting tired like a regular exorcist. Still, more than one or two a night wasn't good for anyone involved.

"How you doing?" Avery's good eye blinked furiously, tears running down his scraped cheek from the stinging of ice against swelling tissue. "You look pissed."

No, what I am is tired. Though I just had a snotty-ass Were country boy run his mouth off about hellbreed at me. "New case."

"Heard about that." Avery shifted a little in his chair. The entire jail above us seemed to hold its breath. I cocked my head and took another long draft of cold beer.

"News travels fast."

"Five cops."

"Yeah." I sighed. *I don't even know if that rookie survived the night. No matter, if he wakes up and he's coherent Montaigne will buzz me.* "Christ, Avery. Jesus Christ."

"You'll get whoever it is." He lowered the ice, the plastic chair creaking as he shifted. "If something ever happened to me, you'd kill the bastard that did it."

You're right, Ave. I am the avenger, it's my job. But Jesus. "Let's hope that never happens. I'd hate to have to train your replacement just when I've gotten used to your silly punk ass."

He shrugged, one corner of his mouth lifting painfully. He would be bruised all up that side of his face tomorrow. "Hand me a beer, willya? And tell me what's really bothering you." A flash of his pale chest showed through his torn shirt, and the St. Anthony's medal glittered briefly on its silver chain. I opened the small fridge and passed over a fresh cold bottle, his skin briefly touching mine. The scar on my wrist throbbed. I heard moans and shuffles overhead in the holding cells, and a subliminal thrill ran under my skin.

Dawn. A hunter always feels it, the sun rising and the city settling into daytime geography.

Yet another night spent on the run. I opened my mouth, but my pager buzzed again. "Jesus *Christ*." I sighed, knocked back the rest of the bottle in a few long swallows. Avery let out a sharp little adrenaline-jag laugh, his dark hair sticking sweat-damp to his forehead. He smelled like a good hard workout on a clean human male, no taint of hell. No exotic corrupt smell of hellbreed.

Not like me.

"Why don't you get a cell phone?" He clasped the ice to his eye again, hissing out between his teeth. His other hand was occupied with the beer.

"As many times as I get dumped in water? Or shot? Or hit with levinbolts?" I shook my head. "Can't afford it. Pager works fine, and the buzz won't give me away when I'm playing snake-under-the-rock." I unclipped the pager, setting the empty bottle down. Avery's desk always looked about to disappear under a mound of paper, and he'd stuck slim candles into the bottle mouths, some burned down and others pristine.

Well, an exorcist usually ends up eccentric. It's the nature of the job. Eva paints and gilds hollowed-out chicken eggs. Benito likes hanging upside-down in a gravity rack, says it helps him sleep. And Wallace likes going out into the desert for jaunts with only a loincloth and a canteen for company.

The number on the pager blurred as I blinked at it. Then I let out a soft breath, my ribs squeezing down, and the sound caught in my throat became a low reedy whistle, as if I'd been punched hard and had to suck the air back in.

When I could talk again, I said, "Fuck."

"What's up?" Avery didn't sound very interested. He leaned back, his good eye closed, the ice clasped to his face.

"Got to go. It's past dawn, you should be all right for a while. Call if you need me." *Shut up, Jill. You had to go see him anyway.*

But he shouldn't be calling me, dammit. Christ. Why am I so upset?

It wasn't just the prospect of going into the Monde Nuit. I did that every month.

She stinks of hellbreed.

That was it. I smelled like hellbreed. Like the very things I fought. Usually I ignored the point successfully enough to function.

Thanks to a stinking country-boy Were, I now had to think about it.

I stood up. Avery waved his beer bottle, languidly. "Another parade of heart-stopping excitement, brought to you by the Santa Luz Exorcist Squad." The ice crackled as he shifted it against his face. "I'm going to go see Galina, have her fix this eye. Don't forget about Saturday."

"I'll see if I can squeeze it in," I tossed over my shoulder, settling my coat with a quick shrug. The whip brushed my thigh as I strode away, and the ruby warmed in the hollow of my throat.

I was grateful for that warmth. It crawled down inside me, and as I hit the stairs at the end of the hall—one exit and entry for any exorcist's lair, it works out better that way—I looked down at my left hand. The ring was there, silver still bound tight around my third finger. Mikhail's promise, Mikhail's mark, given to me before I even knew Perry existed.

I blew out between my lips as I swung up the stairs, my shoulders coming up and a welcome heat beginning behind my breastbone. It was anger, and I fed it with every last scrap of energy as I blew down another long hall and out the back door of the administrative section of the jail, into the cold, clear light of dawn.

CHAPTER 10

I knelt in a back pew at Mary of the Immaculate Conception, my forehead against the hard wood of the seat in front of me. Candles flickered dimly, and despite the simmering heat of midmorning outside it was cool and quiet in here. My pager had stopped buzzing.

Get it together, Jill.

There was only one thing to do, and I was putting it off. I swallowed dryly, heard my throat click.

"Thou Who," I began, and heard Mikhail's voice next to mine as he taught me the prayer. "Thou Who hast..."

I couldn't say them, so the words unreeled in my head as I forced my shaking hands together in tight fists.

Thou Who hast given me to fight evil, protect me; keep me from harm. Grant me strength in battle, honor in living, and a swift clean death when my time comes. Cover me with Thy shield, and with my sword may Thy righteousness be brought to earth, to keep Thy children safe.

A tall order, even for God. In a fight between God and hellbreed, I would rather have a good stock of ammunition on my side.

That's blasphemy, Jill, no matter how much it helps. But you're damned anyway, aren't you. What does it matter?

I lifted my face. The crucifix over the altar was a gentle one, not like the twisted screaming monstrosities I've seen in some churches. This Christ looked almost tranquil, as if there had been no pain at all, as if death was a balm and not something to fight tooth and nail against.

Maybe that's what Mikhail saw in me. Fighting tooth and nail. Like a Were, tooth and nail. So I stink of hellbreed, do I? Well, it keeps the innocent safe. Or safer, at least.

That was the trouble with the prayer, Mikhail told me. Even if you only mouthed it, you ended up doing it. *Believing* in it.

Stupid, he would snort after a few shots of vodka. *They call us heroes. Idiots.*

But I didn't want to think about that. If I started brooding about how much I missed Mikhail, I might inadvertently give Perry an opening. And nobody wanted that except Perry himself.

I started again. "Thou Who," I whispered, my lips numb. "Thou Who..."

I could not frame the middle part of the prayer. There was only one part that mattered, anyway. I whispered it into my sweating hands, clasped together in prayer. "O my Lord God, do not forsake me when I face Hell's legions."

I've had enough of being forsaken, God. You think you could cut me a little slack? Run, running, my brain like a rat in a cage.

You're not too tightly bolted right now, Jill. Maybe you should do something to take the edge off. But what?

I dropped my forehead down again and breathed in, smelling incense and wood and candle smoke, the particular mix that means *Catholic*. Get out your guilt and your rulers and your smell of wax and wine, and you had my childhood. Or at least the part of it that gave me the reflex of prayer.

As a hunter, I was barred from both Confession and Communion for the sin of murder repeated every night, not to mention trafficking with Hell's minions. But I could still pray, and I would, by special dispensation, be buried in hallowed ground if there was enough of me left to bury.

Unless I died contaminated. Or unless, like Mikhail, I wanted to go into Valhalla with flame licking my bones.

Mikhail. The anger rose again, tattered and threadbare, and I petted it, coaxed it, mulled over it to give myself strength. Rage was my best friend, for all I kept it a banked fire most of the time. You cannot fight effectively if your head's full of anger. You have to think *past* the rage, let it fill you and see the world in front of you as action and reaction, with your own path laid clear and shining in front of you, whether through a fight or to the door of a hellbreed nightclub.

Oh, fuck. Get going, Jill. You have shit to do and a rogue Were to catch. Get out there and kick some ass. You've done it every month since you made the bargain, sometimes twice, and you're still here. You smell of hellbreed and you're tired and your temper's a little frayed, but you're still here, goddammit. Now get up, and go twist Perry's arm until he gives up what you want.

And teach him to stop fucking with you. Be unpredictable.

I licked dry lips and pushed myself up. The hard wooden back of the pew slipped under my slick palms. My voice was a bare whisper, but it came. "O my Lord God, do not forsake me when I face Hell's legions. In Thy name and with Thy blessing, I go forth to cleanse the night."

Though it's more like midmorning. My bootheels clicked as I reached the end of the pew, genuflected, and turned my back on the altar. I dipped both hands in the holy water, lifted its coolness to my face, hissing out slightly as a thin tendril of it rolled over the scar with a tracer of acid fire. I wiped the holy water in my hair, smeared it over my shoulders, and took a deep breath.

Then I got going.

The Monde Nuit is a long low building, and it sits in a bruised depression of etheric energy. The silver on me warmed, responding to the contamination of hellbreed in the air. The parking lot was mostly paved, but the far edges were gravel, and a spindly, thorny edge of greenbelt looked sucked-dry, clinging to the edge of contagion. I left my Impala parked in the fire zone and headed for the door, eyeing the bouncer. This early in the day, there were only six cars in the lot, not counting mine. One was a low black limousine, its windows blind with privacy tinting, pristine despite the dust and haze of the day.

My coat flared on the edges of a hot afternoon wind. This close to the desert, up on the fringes of the valley the Rio Luz kept watered and kind-of-green, everything smelled of sand and heat. The whip tapped against my thigh and I kept my hands loose and easy. Touching a knife now would show nervousness. Weakness.

You *never* show a hellbreed any weakness. It's a cardinal law, not to be bent or broken like so many other laws.

The bouncer didn't stop me, though his was a face I hadn't seen before. He was a massive slab of muscle with a flat sheen to his eyes, and he didn't quite meet my gaze. His submachine gun, slung on a leather strap, was a flagrant violation.

Goddammit, Perry. You son of a bitch.

My heart stopped pounding by the time I palmed the doors open and saw the Monde's interior, vast and cavernous during the day, no shaft of sunlight piercing its gloom. Nightclubs always look saddest during the day, and even though the Monde pulsed with the glamour of Hell, it was still a broken sight at this particular hour, dappled bits of light sliding over the deserted dance floor, the tables all empty, and the electric lights on overhead. Two janitors—ancient, decrepit, broken things that might once have been Traders—shuffled aimlessly, pushing brooms.

The massive bar was off to the left, and as usual Riverson was

there, his blind filmy eyes widening as he took me in. "Kismet."
His tone was flat, and he reached behind himself for the bottle of
vodka. "You're here."

Score one for you, blind man, stating the goddamn obvious. I
kept the words behind my teeth.

Mikhail had brought me in here to meet Riverson, who for a
human with no taint of Hell was extremely knowledgeable about
Hell's citizens, not to mention still alive to be questioned—both
incredible achievements. The blind man hadn't been blind back
when Mikhail first met him, but by the time I saw him he was a
scarecrow with a shock of white hair and those filmed, useless
orbs that seemed nevertheless to notice a good deal more than
most of the sighted ever would.

And the first time I'd come here, Perry had shown up at the end
of the bar, looking *very* interested. Mikhail had almost drawn on
him, but Perry made an offer... and a few months later, I'd sat in a
chair with Perry circling me, negotiating the bargain that made
me able to do what I do so well.

Murder, chaos, and screaming, that is. Hey, when a girl's got
talents...

I shoved the memories back down into their little black box,
took the shot Riverson poured, tossed it back, and slammed the
shot glass down on the bar. The sound was a rifle crack in the
hush. "I'm early." My voice was flat, uninflected. "I'm here on
business. Put it on the tab."

"You can wait up in his office. They're finishing the meeting—
Kismet! For God's sake, *don't!*"

The old man actually sounded concerned. *A meeting, eh? Wait
in the office? I don't think so. Perry, your meeting's about to be
adjourned.*

And by making a statement here I could probably find out
something useful. I bit back an iron-edged laugh and stalked
through the open maw of the building, skirting the dance floor
and aiming to the left of the stage. The painted-black door opened
smoothly, and I found myself in a back hall lit with red neon tubes
along the ceiling. The light tinted everything bloody, and I strode
down the linoleum, my heels clicking even more sharply and the
charms in my hair chiming sweet and soft.

Perry, you have been a very bad boy.

The scar prickled, a fiery loathsome tendril of pleasure twining up my arm. I'd had it uncovered for so long it almost felt normal.

Almost.

The door I wanted was at the end of the hall, and as I approached it I heard the mutter, like flies magnified by the space inside a stripped-out skull. It was Helletöng, the language of the damned, and my heart gave a smothered leap and settled back into its regular pace.

Do it quick, Jill. Just like ripping a Band-Aid off. Do it hard and quick.

The door—blank steel, no knob on my side—was maybe three yards away. I gathered myself and skipped forward two long strides, kicking it inward and adding a generous portion of etheric force pulled through the scar on my wrist turned hard and hurtful, a bruised swelling. The steel crumpled, smashing inward, and I rode the motion down as the door crashed into the floor.

Two of them, one on either side. I took the first with a quick upward strike, smashing him across the face with a hellbreed-strong fist braced by the handle of my whip. The gun was in my other hand, speaking for me, smashing the shell of the hellbreed on my left. The whip struck, its thundercrack lost under the noise of the gun, and I uncoiled in a flung-wide kick, both boots smashing hellbreed flesh, one on either side. They folded down, both of them stinking now that I'd shattered their shells and dosed them with silver, and the whip coiled itself as I landed, both feet striking the battered curve of the door again.

As entrances go, it wasn't bad.

There was a long table polished to a mirror-shine, and tasteful sconces along the wall with yet more red neon, dyeing the air with crimson. Candles hissed in branched iron candelabra, their warm glow somehow bleached.

At the end of the table, a pair of blue eyes met mine. Perry sat in a high-backed iron chair, the red velvet of its cushions contrasting with the pale linen of his suit. His face under the expensive sandy-blond haircut was bland and interested, but I thought I caught a steely glint far back in his pupils. His fingers were tented together, and he didn't look surprised to see me at all.

Then again, he never did.

Gathered on either side of the table were other hellbreed, none as bland or unsurprised as him. The damned are always beautiful, and these were no exception—black leather, exquisite silk, frayed lace, glittering liquid eyes and sculpted lips, four or five had leapt to their feet on seeing me. The table was full, except for the seat directly to Perry's left.

And there was another surprise, oh friends and neighbors. Most of the damned in the room were instantly recognizable. The movers and shakers of the entire hellbreed population of Santa Luz, the maggots every smaller hellbreed answered to in their network of feudal obligation. There was the tall, sloe-eyed female who owned the Kat Klub downtown; the broker who ran the influence net out in the financial district; the short tense male in the black cloth half-veil that did assassinations for one faction or another, according to who hired him first or paid him most.

A meeting, and the resident hunter wasn't invited. Why am I not surprised?

My boots grated against the door, I took another two steps and leapt, landing catlike at the foot of the table, the whip coiled neatly in my hand. The gun tracked onto the nearest 'breed—a slim dark male with a leather vest over his hard narrow chest. I suspected him behind a large chunk of the cocaine trade that had recently soaked the poorer quarters with a wave of overdoses from whatever the supplier had cut it with. The current bet over in Vice was twelve to eight in favor of simple Drano, but Forensics hadn't come up with a verdict yet.

Jesus, with a submachine gun and some heavy-duty sorcery I could make the world a much better place in about ten minutes.

The trouble was, there were always more. If I erased this batch others would move in, and I'd have to threaten them into behaving all over again. Talk about your futile efforts.

Still. . . . My finger tightened on the trigger. "So many scumbags, and all in one room. Fish in a barrel." My lips peeled back from my teeth. "Feels just like Christmas."

The silence crackled, and leather made a slight sound in my right hand as my fingers bore down on the handle of the whip. The candleflames hissed. *Jesus. I should have thought about this before I kicked the door in. Good one, Kismet. Get out of this alive.*

But still, for what I wanted, this wasn't a bad situation. Odds were they knew about a hellbreed misbehaving in my town, and by getting a little nasty in here I might be able to avoid nastiness later.

The silver chain at my throat burned fiercely, and Mikhail's ring scorched. The charms in my hair shifted and jingled sweetly. I took another few steps down the table, bracing myself, as my eyes came up and met Perry's.

He finally spoke, his words a mere murmur. "So good of you to join us, Kismet."

It was like a slap of cold water across a dreamer's face. The other hellbreed blinked, shuffled, one of the females baring her teeth at me and hissing. I stilled, looking down at her. The Kat Klub figured in one or two cold cases I wanted to get to the bottom of as well, though its owner usually followed the rules.

Do we need another example here? Because I'm just aching to teach you motherfuckers the rules of operating in my goddamn town. The table resounded like a drum under my soles. I locked gazes with the hellbreed female. "You want to repeat yourself a little louder, bitch?"

"There's no need to be rude." Perry hadn't moved. His eyes had turned a little darker, that was all. Indigo spread through his irises, but his whites were still clear. My mouth had gone dry, and the scar on my wrist sent a jolt of heat up the bones of my arm to my shoulder socket. "You were, after all, invited to this meeting."

Invited? Fuck that. "I must have missed the engraved invitation." My lip lifted, in an almost-snarl. Our eyes locked, two magnets pushing against each other with invisible force. Pure repulsion.

Or so I hoped.

"We called this meeting today to address ... extraordinary circumstances." He pressed his fingers together, his mouth making a little *moue* of distaste at my obtuseness.

I beat him to the punch. *Keep it business, Jill. You might just get out of here without having to spend more time with him than necessary.* "Five cops, out on the Drag. Dead. The scene stank of the damned. Hand over the 'breed responsible, and we'll all get along just fine."

The wet, icy silence that fell warned me. One corner of Perry's mouth lifted, and a chill worked its way all the way down to my bones. Except for the scar. The mark of his lips on my skin warmed obscenely, burrowing in toward the bone.

I suddenly wished I'd been able to get out to Galina's and get another copper cuff. Without the bar of blessed copper between the scar and the outside air, I was wide-open to him fiddling with it.

"You are all dismissed." His voice made the candle-flames twist. "Spread out through the city. Find the one we seek."

Wait just a goddamn minute. I thumbed the hammer back, the small click loud in the dim-lit silence. "I didn't give any of you permission to move, Pericles." My soft killing tone couldn't rival his, but it was pretty good anyway. Too bad my lips were numb. My heart began to pound, and that was very bad. They could all hear my pulse, just as I could hear the subliminal rumble of Hell-etöng warping the walls and the strings of energy below the surface of the world.

The other corner of Perry's mouth lifted, a small smile running steel ice along my skin. "We are already apprised of a hell-breed causing trouble with the police. We are seeking her even now."

"Her?" My right eyebrow raised. I noticed with a thin thread of gratification that none of them had moved a muscle. The dusty, exotic, corrupt smell of them filled my nose, coated the back of my dry throat.

Perry's smile was full-fledged now. He wasn't hurtfully beautiful like the other hellbreed, which made him—once you thought about it—even scarier. *Much* scarier. "Her name is Cenci." His tented fingers relaxed a fraction. "I will tell you all we know, my dear Kiss. *After* you have paid me my due." He now looked extraordinarily happy, and my heart sank, turning to heavy steel inside my chest.

Oh, fuck. I suddenly, frantically wished I'd thought to stop by the warehouse and pick up the FBI files. They would make an excellent excuse for keeping this meeting all business.

Like he's going to be fobbed off. You just cost him some face in front of his little lieutenants.

Then, wonder of wonders, my pager buzzed. I swallowed bile

as other hellbreed rose to their feet from the small iron chairs; the ones already standing merely waited. They shuffled out, avoiding the dead bodies at the door, the masked one watching me with eyes blank from lid to lid, black as the devouring darkness between stars. I ignored it.

If one of them moved on me now, it would give me cause to get the hell out of here without spending quality time with Perry.

I wasn't as comforted as I could be by the thought.

As soon as the last one had left the room, I lowered my whip. The gun swung around, fixed on Perry while I dug in the padded pocket. The number displayed on the pager's display couldn't have been more welcome.

Montaigne. Which meant there was another body. Or three.

Which *also* meant Perry would have to wait. Guilt curled hot and acid under a bald edge of relief. What did that say about me, that I was glad about someone's murder because it would get me the hell out of here?

I looked up from the pager, trying not to let the relief show. It was useless, he saw it anyway and his smile broadened, cold sweat bathing my back.

"It's the police." I had to work for an even tone. "I'm on the job, Perry. You're going to tell me what you know now, and I'll come in to pay you when this is over."

He didn't move, but his eyes darkened slightly. "I have waited an entire month for the pleasure of your company, and I don't intend to deny myself that pleasure any longer."

Oh, Christ. God help me now. "Tough." The gun settled, pointed right between his eyes. He wasn't a low-level grunt like the 'breed at the door. If I popped him in the head, it might just make him angry. "Bodies in the street take precedence over our bargain, Pericles. You know that. Start talking."

"I could talk to you for hours, dear one." His tone had turned silky, and the scar throbbed. The heat in my lower belly dipped down, and I had to choke back a sharp inhaled breath. He was doing it again, using the scar to fiddle with my internal thermostat and mimicking the physical aspects of desire.

It had to be a mimicry. *Whore,* the voice in my head snarled. *Just like a goddamn whore.*

God help me, but it felt familiar. Did he guess that was where I was weak? How much did he know about me? About my past?

Stop it. Mikhail made you stronger than this. Don't let Perry get to you.

I set my jaw. He liked playing with the scar while I was near him. Each time I visited it was the same—him messing with my pulse and my nerves, trying to make me respond.

At least I wouldn't have to use the flechettes this time. Or my whip.

Most of the time, he liked to be strapped down, and he liked to be cut while he bled the blackish ichor of hellbreed. Sometimes he would even talk while he made me cut him, and that was the worst. The closest he came to worming inside my head was while I was frantic with loathing at what he told me to do, cursing myself for ever making the goddamn bargain despite anything Mikhail ever said.

Oh, God. Come on. Get me out of here. "Stick to the *point,* Perry, or I'll track it down from the other end. That'll mean I won't come in when it's done, since you've refused to help."

"When have I ever refused you anything, Kiss? I could give you so much more than you've ever dreamed." His voice dropped, and the lights dimmed, candleflames twisting and hissing, sputtering as darkness spilled through the air. Silver shifted and chimed in my hair. The chain holding the ruby was a thin thread of fire, the ruby's setting hot against the hollow of my throat. It had never singed me yet, but each time I wondered.

My legs were shaking. I braced my knees. "Cut the crap. Give me what you have on this hellbreed. That's my final word, Pericles."

"You're no fun." He sounded genuinely regretful, but that smile was like sharp rocks under icy water, just waiting for naked feet. "All we have is her name and her general description. Fair, but with dark eyes, and for some reason, allied with a Were. Surprising, no? She is far from her master and should be returned. Which we have undertaken to do. We cannot, after all, have our vassals going about with animals. It destroys the general sense of order so necessary for a smoothly running society."

"Why is she hanging around with a Were?" *And a rogue one, to boot.* My mouth was parched, the fumes of the Jack Daniel's I'd taken down reaching my head. I hadn't eaten; my body was starting to get that funny shaky feeling it usually did just before Perry ordered me to strap him into the frame and start.

I knew that shaky feeling. It's the same thing as when your body rebels and tries to collapse on you, but your mind won't let it.

Sometimes he wanted the knives. Most of the time it was the flechettes, razor-sharp and silver-plated. On a few very bad nights he made me use my fists until his preternatural skin broke and bled, and the only sounds would be my sharp exhales of effort and his low, bubbling breath right before he gurgled *More.*

Just the single word. Each and every time.

I'd given up wondering why he wanted me to hurt him. Maybe it was just another move in the game he played, trying to get inside my head. Maybe he couldn't get it anywhere else. Still, my mouth tasted sour and my hand felt like it was shaking, though the gun was steady.

"If we knew, Kismet, I would not be allowing this show of defiance from you, however charming I find your homicidal little displays." He finally moved, waving one elegant finger at me. "When I receive more information, I shall bring it to you." A meaningful pause. "Personally."

That's mighty nice of you, Perry. Not like you to be so accommodating. "Who's her master, then?"

"A certain gentleman in New York. One who is most displeased with her disobedience, and intends to teach her a lesson as soon as she is returned to him." Perry's smile broadened. "See what a very *good* boy I am being, my dear? And all for your sake." Two of the candleflames died under the weight of his voice, and his hands came down, curled over the ends of the chair arms. He pushed himself up to his feet, very slowly, his eyes on mine the entire while.

New York? Jesus. The master of the Big Apple's hellbreed was so old and frightening I'd heard even the city's contingent of hunters steered clear of him. I hoped the one looking for this hellbreed was just a smaller fry from that pool. "Fine. Thanks for the information." Slowly, so slowly, my thumb came up and uncocked the gun. It took all my fading courage to holster it. "If this pans out I'll have the mayor give you a medal."

."Stay with me for ten minutes, Kismet." His tone had turned soft as velvet, cajoling, and the stretched-wide smile was gone, replaced by a look of utter seriousness that might have been almost human except for the indigo staining the whites of his eyes. "Only ten minutes. I will forgive your visit this month and wait until the next if you stay with me for that short while."

Shock threatened to nail me in place. This was something new, and my busy little brain started worrying at it, trying to decipher his angle. "You'd give up this month's visit for ten minutes now?"

He stood at the end of the table, looking up at me. Two more candles snuffed, then another two. The light darkened, even more bloody now. I should have felt a little better, having the physical high ground here.

I didn't.

"Ten minutes now, and I will forgive your payment on our bargain this month. My word on it, Kiss."

I wish he'd stop calling me that. I licked my lips, wished I hadn't when his eyes fastened on my mouth. "I don't suppose you'd forgive next month's too."

That earned me a sardonic look. He said nothing, merely stood there, and just that much was enough to make a shallow trickle of sweat trace its way down the channel of my spine.

"Fine. Starting from when I came in the door." I backed up, hopped off the table without looking, and breathed out through my mouth. The two 'breed I'd killed stank.

He didn't even quibble. It was a bad sign. "Come here." He indicated the seat on his left, the one that had been empty. "Sit...there."

I walked slowly down the table, my coat rustling and creaking. Here in the meeting room the floor was mellow hardwood, not linoleum. More candles snuffed, and my breath came short and sharp. I looked at the chair, tested it with one finger, and sank down in it.

The iron was hard, and cold. Velvet and horsehair pillows did nothing to stop the chill from biting immediately through the layers of my coat and leather pants. The ruby at my throat sparked, a single bloody point of light in the charged silence.

"Good," Perry murmured. He lowered himself down in the tall chair. "Put your hands flat on the table."

I swallowed. Did it, the mirrorshine surface cold and slick under my sweating palms. The last of the candles died. I was alone in the neon-lit dark with Perry and two rotting hellbreed corpses by the door.

God, do not forsake me now. Then I quit praying. God was fine, but He was often busy. It was up to a hunter to pick up the slack.

Perry exhaled, a soft sound of satisfaction like a sheet drawn up over a cold dead face.

What is he going to do? Best not to guess. Best just to wait and see.

It was, after all, bound to be unpleasant.

When his hand came down over my right wrist I started nervously. "Shhh." He made a low cold hissing noise, maybe meant to be soothing. "Be still."

His skin was warm, and felt human except for its supple invulnerability, like metal made flesh. The shell of a hellbreed, hard to breach without a lot of luck and firepower.

Silver. Lots of silver, and lots of luck. I swallowed again, pressed my hands into the table. *If I killed him, would his mark fade? Do I chance it? If Mikhail was here...*

But Mikhail, like God, wasn't here. I was on my own.

"Have you visited your teacher's grave?" Perry's voice was so soft I almost didn't catch the words, my every nerve strung tight.

What the hell? Mikhail's grave, where his ashes were buried in consecrated ground, its headstone with curved Cyrillic script scored deep into granite, hoping to last a little longer than other, more perishable things. Like flesh. Or memory.

Bile rose in my throat again. I made no reply. It was all part of Perry's game, trying to worm his way into my head. Less than ten fucking minutes, and I'd be free for another month.

"Answer me, Kiss. Have you?"

My mouth was so dry I had trouble with the word. "Yes."

His thumb moved a little, a slight flexible movement. The mark jolted another wire of unhealthy heat through me, my ears suddenly picking up sounds from the rest of the building. Creaks. The rumble of Helletöng. Running water from the bar. If I looked down with my smart eye I would see the mark flushing with power, swelling with corruption.

"And?"

"And what?" *Don't, Perry. Keep your fucking mouth off Mikhail's name.* But I wouldn't say it. That would be like blood in the water.

"Did his ghost rise to comfort you?"

"No." *I poured out a bottle of vodka, though. Wherever he is, he's sleeping sound.* I drew my breath in, shut my eyes. Exhaled.

"You need some small comfort." His thumb moved again. "You allow me so little. I could help you so much more."

If this is a sample of your help I'll go my own way, thank you. I bit back the words. He hadn't asked me a direct question, I could get away with silence. It was the safest course.

Perry made a small annoyed sound, his fingers suddenly biting down. Small bones in my wrist creaked and crackled. The pain was almost a balm.

"Why do you make this so hard?"

I found my voice. "Make *what* so hard?" *I don't need to make this hard. You do that very well, thank you.*

Besides, the harder Perry found this game, the better I liked it. It gave me an edge.

He tried again. "Think of what it could be like." His tone had dropped to a murmur. "If you sat here, with me at your right hand. Imagine what I could do with you to direct me. There's nothing I wouldn't do for your asking, my dear."

I had to swallow a braying, hysterical laugh. "You're *hell-breed.*" It was all I needed to say. If I bit into the apple of that offer, the snake wouldn't be far behind. It was the same old song. Take a little, then a little more, and before you knew it you were up to your eyeballs in filth—your own, and a good deal more.

What makes you different, Jill?

I knew what. Mikhail had made me different. And as long as I was true to him and what he taught me, I was on the side of the angels.

Figuratively, of course. God needs killers as much as Hell does, I guess.

Maybe more.

"What kind of hellbreed?" Perry sounded only mildly interested.

I had to admit it. "I don't know."

"Ah." Now there was amusement, the lazy grin of a shark evident in his voice. "All I ask is that you turn a very little, Kiss. Just a very, very little."

It was a jolt of cold water. He could fiddle with the scar and try to worm his way in all he wanted, but Perry was just too fucking impatient to crack me. And I wasn't a stupid teenager anymore, ready to believe anything a man told me.

Just a little bit. I've heard that line before. Just do something small for me, and I'll give you everything you ever wanted. How stupid do you think I am, Perry? I set my boots against the floor, tensing in every muscle. "We have our bargain. You won't get anything else from me."

As soon as I said it I knew it was a mistake. My wrist ached as Perry squeezed, a fraction of a hellbreed's strength enough to make sweat break out along the curve of my lower back.

"I have enough time. I've broken stronger Traders than you."

So I've heard. Since I'd already pissed him off, I might as well go with it. "I'm not a Trader." *I'm a hunter, and one day I'm going to kill you too. When I do, Perry, I'm going to throw a party afterward. Hell, I'll have it catered and bring out the barbeque. It'll be a red-letter day.*

His fingers eased up on my wrist, caressed the back of my hand, and finally slid between mine. How could such a small touch feel like such a violation?

I flinched, yanking my hand back, but those gentle fingers turned to steel again and pain tore through the hard knot of the scar as he pulled my hand up, turning the palm toward the ceiling and baring the pale glimmer of my wrist under the pushed-back cuff of my coat.

"Naughty, naughty," he murmured, as if I was a puppy. An edge of delight coiled under the words. He'd made me react.

Good for him.

His mouth met the scar, something cat-rasping against my skin, a brief caress.

I set my jaw, my neck aching with tension. Perry chuckled, a low satisfied sound, his breath oven-hot and swamp-wet against my skin as I went rigid in the chair, an invisible knife twisting in the scar, tangling and ripping at nerve-strings. Great pearly drops of water stood out on my forehead, my neck, the curve of my lower back, the backs of my knees.

At least it was pain this time, and not the sick gasping-sweet heat of the first time his lips pressed into my flesh, his aura injecting a nugget of corruption into mine. Pain can be controlled, even if it's your skin being torn off one millimeter at a time. Even if it's the nerves themselves turning traitor and running with hot acid.

Even if it went on until I made a small betraying sound in the back of my throat, instantly swallowing it. It was a half-broken, hurt little cry, as if I'd been punched.

Immediately, he let go, his head coming up, his fingers sliding free of mine. My hand fell limply to the table and I slumped, the sudden relief almost enough to wring another sound out of me.

Perry let out a long breath, jagged, as if he had just finished spending himself. It was an intimate sound, and I cringed away from it. A filthy feeling circled my skin, as if I'd pressed my naked body against a cold grimy windowpane.

Silence returned, neon buzzing finally intruding on my ears like a bee caught on a dead dry windowsill.

I was shaking. I pressed my hands into the table's slick glassy surface and wished I could kill him. The need to get up, to empty a clip into his body, to flick the whip forward and listen to him scream like an *arkeus*—the temptation shook me. Like a dog shakes a toy in its sharp teeth.

"You may go." Dark amusement burbled under his light even tenor. "Unless you want to stay, my dear. I'd like that."

"Fuck you." It managed to come out steady. I pushed myself up to my feet, managed to stand. Sweat cooled icy on my forehead. The charms in my hair tinkled. "I won't be back until next month."

The urge to kill him shook me even harder. A physical need, like the need to eat or empty my bladder or even the need to *breathe.*

Kill him, one part of me whispered. *You can do it. It might not be easy but you can do it.*

The rest of me dug in heels and resisted. If I killed him now, I'd be violating the bargain. And I knew what that would make me in my own eyes.

Just as bad as the things I hunted, that's what.

The amusement intensified. Perry sounded almost goddamn *gleeful.* "You'll see me before that. Tell your friends from the government I'm hunting their little problem, too. We'll be quite a cozy little bunch, won't we. Like *family.*"

I could have replied, but I didn't. I hit the broken door at a run, his laughter rising behind me, and got the hell out of there.

CHAPTER 11

I ducked under the yellow tape and breathed out through my mouth. Foster hopped down from a Forensics van and hurried over, his dark-blue windbreaker glaring wetly under the afternoon's heat haze.

I still felt cold, and more shaky than I liked to admit. Especially since I'd gotten off easy. *Way* too easy for Perry. He usually liked to mess with me more.

I had the sick unsteady feeling that he probably would before this was over.

Don't think about that. I blinked the thought back and met Foster's eyes. "What do we have?"

The gully at the edge of Percoa Park was stony and full of trash, and I smelled the thunderous odor of the thing I was chasing, but with no exotic taint of hellbreed. My hair was dry from the heat in the Impala, both windows rolled down, but salt still filmed my skin. I hadn't even managed to stop for a burrito. My stomach was unhappy, and the rest of me wasn't too prancing-pony either.

Still, I was free until next month. I'd make it. Piece of cake.

"Three, we think. Maybe more." Foster was pale, his sleek dark hair slightly mussed. "The Feebs are looking at it."

I shook my head. "Is Juan with them?" Juan Rujillo was the local FBI liaison, and a good one. Not like the last asshole.

"No, he's on vacation." Mike gave me an odd look. It wasn't like me to forget that kind of detail. "You look like shit, Jill."

"Thanks." *I just played patty-cake with a nightmare.* "How many feds?" *I hope the country boy stayed at home.*

"Two. Man and woman. She's a looker."

"Hands off if you know what's good for you. I'll just follow my nose." Since I hadn't covered the scar yet, I could smell it all—reek of rotting trash, anemic out here in the dryness, the gassy ripe smell of human death, and the smell of a rogue Were.

Well, at least it was cleaner than the stench of dead hellbreed. And at least now I knew what a rogue smelled like.

Good. Keep thinking about that, Jill. Don't think about Perry. You've put it off until next month. Clever girl, aren't you?

I walked down the gully, the sides rising above me, fringed with succulents and other scrub. This was still part of the river-fed, low-lying cup most of the city rested in, the closest park to my house. Still, the gully at the back showed traces of desert, especially since it wasn't watered until the flash floods came along in fall—an event that wasn't too far away, this being the beginning of September. Percoa was just a slim wedge of a park anyway, a piece of land nobody wanted because it was a buffer between an industrial zone and a patch of suburbs undergoing urban renewal and becoming higher-class every year.

Guess which side my warehouse sat on. Still on the wrong side of the tracks, even after all these years.

Around the bend, a sudden knot of activity swallowed me. More forensic techs, snapping pictures, triangulating. Montaigne, in a gray suit and a brown tie I knew his wife hadn't picked—it was far too ugly—stood sourly to one side, his hands dangling by his sides. He saw me, and I watched as if from behind myself the curious relief, then even more curious flash of dread cross his haggard face. "Jill!" He almost slipped on a loose patch of gravel, his wingtips not meant for grubbing out here in the brush. "You look—" He pulled himself up short, and I felt a click in my head, a door shutting away the feel of Perry's lips on my skin and the shaking temptation to just start killing until there was nothing left that could hurt me.

It was a good thing, that click. I felt cleaner, though I knew I would strip down and scrub myself raw as soon as I could get home. It took a lot of harsh scrubbing and the water turning pink-red as it went down the drain before I *ever* felt clean after a visit to the Monde.

I don't keep a wire brush in the house because I'd be too tempted to use it.

"Hi, Monty." I squinted against the hot oven glare of sunlight, shifted inside my coat. When I lifted my left hand to push a strand of hair weighted by a silver horseshoe back, the charm glittered in my peripheral vision. Like a mirage. "Just tired. What do we have? Foster said three, maybe more."

I spotted Harp up further on one side of the gully, bending down to examine something, her braids fastened back. Dominic stood next to her, his hair bound and his shoulders straight.

"It's over there." He pointed at the beehive of orderly activity. Half-moons of sweat darkened his suit under his arms. "Jesus. Do you have anything yet, Jill? Anything at all?"

I nodded. "Some things." *Not nearly enough. A runaway hellbreed and a rogue Were. If ever there was an unlikely combination, that's one.* "How's your man? The rookie?"

"Still in critical." Monty sighed. It was a weary sound. "Jesus fucking Christ. Sullivan and the Badger are next up, do you want them on this?"

I shook my head. The last thing I wanted was a homicide detective or two dealing with a rogue Were. "The feds over there are my people, I don't want any more of yours getting killed."

He took it better than I thought he would. He only paled more, and shivered despite the heat. Indian summer had struck with a vengeance this year. "It's bad, then."

Worse than you can probably imagine, cheesecake. "I'll go take a look." I wanted to touch him—clap him on the shoulder, maybe. Offer some comfort. But if I did, he'd just flinch away from my essential difference.

My essential taint.

She stinks of hellbreed. It hadn't been so much the words as the tone in which they were delivered. What should I care what a country-boy Were thought of me?

Because of the other voice whispering in my head, bland and

weighted with terrible finality, as if he considered the deal already struck—a newer deal, one Mikhail hadn't approved. *I've broken stronger Traders than you.*

It wasn't so much that he said it. It was that I suspected, deep down, that he might be right. Without the steady compass and experience of my teacher, things were getting more precarious by the day.

I was getting more precarious every day. Out on the edge with nowhere else to go.

I flinched inwardly as I inserted myself into the dance of gathering evidence. A few of the techs looked a little green.

The bodies were tangled together in a messy heap under torn-down branches that had wilted in the heat. I saw a long scarf of brown hair crusted with sand, and thought maybe that one was female. But they were such a mess I couldn't tell for certain. Some of the bigger bones—femur, humerus—had been gnawed, sharp splinters worried up. The faces were marred with deep claw marks.

I looked again at the brush cover. The techs were photographing, picking up, and bagging each torn branch. The ends were ripped, not broken with leverage but torn straight out from the tree or bush that had hosted them. The tougher ones—juniper, sage, pine from the park, probably—were still springy and sap-full.

They were fresh.

So were the bodies. *Really* fresh, even though they stank in the heat.

Had the rogue just blown into town, killed a few cops, and started on an orgy of murder? It was a distinct possibility. The usual rogue Were rules—a kill every few days, mostly for food, a pattern of familiar places—wasn't holding true. What other rules was this case going to break?

A prickle touched the back of my neck, cold even under the sun's assault. Was it just nervousness from dealing with Perry, or was it intuition? As raw as my nerves were, I couldn't tell.

That's bad. You've got to take the edge off or you aren't going to be good for anything. I looked up, shading my eyes, as one of the techs, a slim Asian woman with her hair cut in a sleek bob, approached me.

"Can we move the bodies?" She didn't look me in the eye, rubbing her fingers together against the latex gloves. Latex was miserable in this weather, with the sweat and cornstarch. "Or at least start to? The Feebs said to wait for you."

I should have been looking at the bodies, marking each one and swearing to avenge them. I should have looked to see what had mangled them so badly, what had stripped the face off each one.

A rogue Were kill, dehumanizing the victims? That *was* standard behavior for them, but the shape of the marks on the faces were wrong somehow. Another click sounded at the very bottom of my head.

Why would a rogue Were kill cops? But some of them are *Were kills, I recognized that claw shape on the others. And look at the bodies,* those *are Were claws. Why the different marks on the faces? Dammit. This isn't making sense, and there's a hellbreed in it somewhere.*

The prickling at my nape slid down my back, gooseflesh rising hard. The mark on my wrist was a mass of tiny hair-fine needles, responding to the uneasy swirl of my aura as my senses dilated to take everything in.

Something about to happen, Jill. Look around. Be aware.

I looked up. Harp had come to her feet, immobile, even the feathers braided in her hair motionless despite the soft breeze. Her lovely face was set, color draining away and turning her ash-pale. Dominic unfolded slowly, like a cat will rise quietly from its haunches when it sees prey. My blue eye, hot and dry, saw the deep thrumming swirling through both of them.

"Hey." The tech was still trying to get my attention. "Can we move the bod—"

I was already moving, extending in a leap over the pile of bodies, touching down, and bolting for the end of the gully. A few pebbles drifted down, and the slim shape silhouetted against the sky vanished hastily with a flutter of pale hair. I heard scrabbling behind me, and a scream. Didn't care. My skin came alive, flush with heat, leather coat flapping as I sank one hand into the scree of the slope and made it up the hill, throwing up a chunk of gravel as I catapulted over the edge, recklessly pulling etheric energy through the scar.

I'd just paid Perry, I was going to use it.

The whip uncoiled, each individual flechette burning itself into my retinas as metal flashed, the small sonic booms of the crack like a tattoo against my hellbreed-sharp ears.

Improbable became flat-out impossible, gravel shifted under my boots, and I *missed.*

It was a woman with the full-lipped beauty of the damned, wide liquid dark eyes and a cloud of platinum hair. Her eyes were rimmed in red and her skin flushed from the anathema of the sun, and she wore long sleeves and jeans, the sunglasses she'd been peering through knocked off her face as she scrabbled away.

She skittered back, showing white teeth in a snarl, and spun, her heels digging in as Harp rocketed past me, driving her shoulder into the other woman's midriff. I heard the coughing roar of a panther behind me, and Dominic thundered past me too, engaging with the hellbreed. He had *shifted,* the sunlight gilding his dark hide as he leapt, with all the grace and authority of a Were. They are a little bigger than humans in human form, and a little bigger than normal in their animal forms, and when a Were shifts quickly like that he means business.

"No!" I yelled over the noise, yanking the whip back. *"She's hellbreed goddammit stop it!"*

It was too late. Blood exploded and a high cat-whine screeched across my senses. I was still moving forward, dropping the whip, my fingers closing around knife-hilts, metal singing free of the sheath as I uncoiled in a kick, my boot thudding solidly into Dominic's side. The panther curled away, snarling, and I promptly forgot about him, twisting in midair to collide with the spitting growling mass that was Harp and the hellbreed.

Who was out here in full sunlight, in the middle of the *day,* at the site of a rogue Were kill.

Or something that had been made to look like a rogue Were kill. Something that had been *altered.*

I took a hit low on the side, pain spiking up my ribs like oil against the skin, and heard something snap. Harp was flung away, and I drove the knife in my left hand forward, a flickering slash meant to come under the ribs and open up the hellbreed's abdominal cavity.

She twisted, snarling, and the world turned over, the side of my head ringing with pain. Gravel boiled up and I made it to my knees, panting, scooped up my left-hand knife. No blood or ichor on it. Warm wetness spilled into my eyes, ran down my neck. I blinked it away, irritably.

I'd missed again. The sun beat mercilessly down, and I heard the retreating drumbeat of the hellbreed's footsteps. Filled my lungs with the spoiled, delicious, unique smell of a hellbreed, let the smell sink below the conscious level. Without the other reek of death and Were, it was easier.

I could track her now, if I could get close enough to break through whatever masking-sorcery she was using to cover her scent. My head felt light, strange, stuffed with cotton.

A low whining sound of pain intruded. I gained my feet, shaking gravel out of my hair, heard shouts and scrabbling below. Harp was bleeding badly, and Dominic had shifted back, rumbling the low throbbing distressed note of a cat Were whose mate was injured.

Goddamit. Fucking around with a hellbreed can get a Were killed. I decided now was not the time to tell him so.

They were scrabbling up the slope behind us. Dominic glanced up, the lambent glow in his gaze warning me. I could either pursue the hellbreed, who was too far away and probably had enough breath to cloak herself now, or I could defuse Dominic and keep the humans away from him. He might not hurt anyone, but he'd make them awful uncomfortable, and forensic techs don't deal well with that kind of discomfort. They like more conventional uncertainties, probabilities, percentages.

Not the crazy logic of the nightside when it erupts in daytime. Most human brains stall when presented with something like that.

I blinked away more wetness, heard liquid pattering on dry dusty ground, and ignored it. The copper reek of blood boiled up.

I swore viciously, shook more gravel out of my coat, and edged past him, not turning my back. Harp would be all right, she'd already stopped bleeding but lay pale and gasping-still. Weres don't often come away breathing from tangling with hellbreed.

Especially hellbreed who don't need night's cover to come out and cause havoc. That meant she was high up the chain of Hell's citizens, capable of doing a lot of damage and possibly unfettered by feudal obligation. Was a hellbreed looking to horn in on Perry's territory?

You know, I almost wouldn't mind that. Even if he is the devil I know.

I almost didn't see it. A thin glint caught my eye, and I bent down, picking out a long platinum strand. It twisted around a red-gold curling hair, twined tight, and curled in on itself even as I watched, the hairs tangling together.

More wetness fell in my eyes, and I couldn't seem to take a deep breath.

Curiouser and curiouser. Nothing about this is making sense.

Blood sliding out from the ragged claw gashes along my ribs pattered on dry dusty ground in an almost-painless gout. The world turned over, and I pitched headfirst off the drop and into the converging cops.

CHAPTER 12

Mikhail's hand spread against my belly, calluses scraping. The carved chunk of ruby at his throat glimmered with its own secret life, and sweat dried on his forehead. "What is best way to kill utt'huruk, you think?" He hadn't smoked a cigarette yet, so the day's lessons weren't over.

I lay on my back, looking up at the skylight full of afternoon gold. A hard nugget of silver pressed into the back of my head; I shifted so the charm wasn't digging in. Mikhail had started giving me the charms one by one, mostly when I'd performed well, and I'd taken to tying them in my hair with red thread, just like he did.

Hey, anything helps.

"Holy water? After you've punctured the shell?" I thought about it some more as his fingers tapped my belly idly, obviously unsatisfied with my answer. Of course. I'd been caught assuming again; assuming Assyrian bird-demons had a shell, like hellbreed. You can't ever assume, so I asked the question I *should have asked straight-up. "What's the weakness in their anatomy?"*

He shifted a little under the covers. The air conditioning was on, but even so sweat cooled on my skin and my body sparked pleasantly. Four years ago I'd've called Mikhail an easy dime— street lingo for a john who wants vanilla, straight-up, and doesn't get nasty with you. They're also called milks—as in, you milk them and go home.

He was my teacher, not a john, and falling into bed with him felt more than natural. Here was no sparring and no hurt. Here, in this queen-sized, hip-high monstrosity covered in threadbare red velvet, with the iron lamps standing guard on either side, was the place where I became more and more thoroughly what Mikhail made me.

To hear Mikhail talk, it was normal for two reasonably hetero-sexual people so close in such extreme circumstances to end up in bed. It was even to be encouraged, the sex made the bond between teacher and student stronger and balanced out the harshness of training.

I didn't care. I just liked that... well...

Me. Of all people. He'd chosen me.

"There is seam that runs through their heads." His fingers left off my belly, touched my forehead and ran down my nose. "Like so. Hit them there, and head explodes. Very dramatic."

I laughed, pushed my hair back with my right hand. Mikhail caught my wrist and turned it, looking at the bracelet of pale skin. I'd taken to wearing a copper cuff over the mark.

The lip-print was a bruised purple now, the color slowly leach-ing away, but thankfully not into the surrounding flesh. I held very still, watching the skylight. Golden sunshine filled my eyes, safe warm light.

"Does it hurt?"

"Burns sometimes." I settled my naked hips, my salt-touched shoulders. "But it's okay. It just looks funny." And I had to be careful, having a hellbreed-strong fist was... interesting, to say the least. I was still getting used to it.

"Eh." He let go of my wrist, one finger at a time, and settled down next to me. Then came my favorite part, his arm over me,

and we cuddled together. The feeling of safety returned, palpable enough to set a lump in my throat. "Woman always has edge in bargain like this, little snake. You remember that when old Mischa is gone."

The lump got bigger. "You're not going anywhere, Mik. You're too nasty."

He pinched my arm, but gently, and I giggled. It was a little-girl sound, a laugh I only heard here in the bedroom with the silk-screened Japanese scrolls on the walls. Only in Mikhail's arms.

"Someday, milaya. *It comes for us all. But we have a choice of how to meet it."*

This one I knew. "Head high," I said.

"Guns out," he answered. "Good, little snake. Now rest. Night soon, time to work."

It came sooner than either of us thought, but after that day we never spoke of it again. I fell asleep easily in his arms, but I don't know if Mikhail slept. I rarely saw him relax, and he was always awake when I dropped off, and awake again when I surfaced.

Of all the men I ever knew, all the men whose bodies pressed over or into mine, he was the only one I ever felt safe with. He was also the only one who held me in the middle of the day when I woke crying from nightmares I remembered all too clearly.

More and more, the longer I go without him, the more I wish I could have seen him sleeping.

Of all the things I expected to smell, frying bacon was the very last.

My head boiled with pain. I groaned, turned over, and buried my face in my pillow, which smelled different. Like...fabric softener?

It *was* fabric softener. I didn't use frocking fabric softener. I had a hard enough time running the damn washing machine without frou-frous like that.

What the hell? I lay very still, my awareness suddenly dilating. The last thing I remembered was falling headlong off the high drop into the crush of people struggling to find some way up the almost-vertical slope. I dimly remembered Montaigne yelling, and Harp's voice, thin but determined.

Sleep beckoned, warm and wide and full of welcome oblivion.

It was no use. I couldn't crawl back into unconsciousness. I had too much to do.

I rolled slowly, lethargically, onto my back. Blinked at the angle of sunlight. It was all wrong—low and gray, with the peculiar translucence that meant morning. How long had I been out?

What had happened out there on the streets while I'd been out? How was Harp?

I pushed myself painfully up to my elbows. My belly was tender, as if I'd taken one hell of a sucker punch. My scalp itched and smarted too. But that wasn't what surprised me the most.

I was on my mattress in the middle of my bedroom, but the sheets were on the bed instead of tangled and wrecked, clean and smelling freshly washed. The messy pile of blankets had been washed too and the bed, despite my usual thrashing, had obviously been neatly made. The blinds had been dusted, and the hardwood floor looked suspiciously shiny. On top of that, the maddening smell of bacon in the air was joined by the smell of coffee brewing.

What the flying fuck?

I was in a battered extra-large Santa Luz Warriors T-shirt, again, not usual. There was no knife under my pillow, but one of my guns lay on the milk crate next to my bed, which now sported a red bandanna as covering and a lamp I'd been meaning to fix.

I grabbed the gun, then touched the lamp. It flicked on, warm electric light flooding my suddenly strange bedroom.

It looked like the floor had been *waxed* or something, for God's sake.

Hello, Toto? Are we still in Kansas?

I slid my feet out of my warm nest. They met cold hardwood, I rocked up to my feet—and collapsed back down again, my head pounding and my muscles rebelling. I'd run myself into the ground. I'd need food to get back up, something to digest so I could fuel my body's now-unnatural ability to heal.

I heard footsteps, deliberately loud, and raised the gun. It pays to be cautious. The warehouse echoed, and my heart thudded in my ears. Copper lay against my palate, the taste of fear.

Saul Dustcircle appeared in my bedroom door. He was

barefoot, in jeans and the same black T-shirt. His hair was pulled back from his face with two small braids on either side, the rest of it loose against his shoulders. His dark eyes passed over me once, not pausing at the gun.

He carried, of all things, a plastic tray I used for holding bullets while I refilled clips, so they didn't roll around. Steam rose from it, and I smelled coffee and maple syrup.

If that wasn't enough, the first thing he said was utterly confusing, too.

"Breakfast." His voice was neutral enough. "And an apology."

I'll admit it. I goggled at him, my jaw dropping but the gun remaining steady.

"I was rude to you. I shouldn't have been; my mother raised me better. I was just tired and frustrated. We've been chasing this bastard a long time, and he keeps slipping through my fingers." His mouth turned down at both corners, bitterly, but his eyes still held mine. "You're a hunter, and a good friend to Weres. I apologize."

I still stared, my jaw suspiciously loose. Of all the things I've heard in my life, a Were apology is high on the "real seldom" list. They don't often say the words out loud.

But when they do, they mean them.

He watched me for another few moments before one corner of his mouth quirked. His eyebrow raised. "Truce?" He indicated the tray, lifting it slightly, and I set the gun down on the milk crate with a click, suddenly ashamed of myself.

"Jesus." My voice cracked. "How long have I been out? How's Harp?"

"Thirty-six hours or so. Harp's fine, she and Dominic just left to meet with some of the Norte Luz lionesses. Captain Montaigne called to make sure you were all right, and some guy named Avery called twice and left messages for you. Something about missing a beer date." He approached with the tray. "You need to eat first. You passed out from blood loss and exhaustion, and you look like you've been pushing yourself lately. If you go killcrazy it won't help us."

Only Weres go killcrazy. On us hunters it's called suicidal. I swallowed the words. Harp was okay. Thank God.

The tray held a plate of buckwheat pancakes, buttered and drenched in syrup, toast with strawberry jam, a mound of scrambled eggs, and six strips of bacon. There was a huge glass of orange juice, and a coffee cup that smelled absurdly good. Not to mention the mint sprig to garnish everything, and the decoratively cut strawberry fanned out in thin slices.

"Holy *Christ*." I managed to sound horrified. "Where did you—"

"Harp and I went shopping. You had nothing but ketchup and some green lump I think was achieving sentience in your fridge. I figured the least I could do was clean up a bit around here and make you something to eat—I don't know how you like your eggs, so I scrambled them. Come on, it won't stay hot forever. Scoot back."

He even fluffed the goddamn pillows and settled the tray across my knees. Then he turned around, without so much as another word, and left the room with a long loping stride.

I stared down at the food. *Wow.* Most Weres, especially the males, are pretty domestic. It was a peace offering instead of a violation for him to clean up my house, since he wouldn't understand much about personal property—again, being Were. And the food...if I didn't trust the verbal apology, the food would have convinced me.

It looked ridiculously good, and I started in. It tasted even better than it looked, and I was munching on nice crispy bacon and feeling my blood sugar level rise slowly but surely when he came back, carrying a coffee cup and something that looked suspiciously like a stack of files. "When you're done." He laid them at the end of the bed just past my toes and settled down, crosslegged, on the floor a respectable distance away. His dark eyes half-lidded, and he relaxed abruptly into the peculiar lazy alertness of a Were.

I took a gulp of the coffee and almost closed my eyes. *Goddamn.* Finished swallowing, and examined his face. "I'm sorry." The tray balanced itself on my knees, I cut myself another bite of pancake. "I wasn't very polite either. Guess I'm strung a little tight. It's been a bad year out here."

He nodded. "Harp told me. About your teacher."

The sharp pain in my chest was expected and natural now. I swallowed hard against it and took another bite.

I chewed, and decided he had a nice face. Most Weres are handsome, at least, but he actually looked approachable. Like Theron at Micky's, who's a goddamn headache to have on a hunt but who manages to be good backup anyway. "Yeah? What else did she tell you?"

"Not much." He grinned, acknowledging the uselessness of the words. "Just to keep your skin whole. Can't stand to lose another good hunter."

So you've decided I'm worthy of being called "hunter" instead of "hellbreed trash." My eyebrows rose. "Harp told you that?"

He nodded, took another sip of coffee. His hair had reddish highlights, and his aura—plainly visible to my blue eye—swirled a little, different from a hellbreed's brackish stain. He was most likely a cat Were, he had that grace.

I decided it was time to ask a few questions, or hopefully just get the conversation off the subject of me. "So where are you from?"

"South Dakota way, 'round the Black Hills. I'm 'cougar.'"

I would have guessed it anyway, from the tawny immobility of him. His face was a little broader than a panther Were's, but not as broad as a lion's, and his dark eyes held a gold tint that made me think of dappled shade along a muscular cat's side. He smelled healthy, a little like Dominic but muskier, with the edge of dry maleness boy Weres give off. Human testosterone smells slightly oilier than theirs, especially to my sensitive nose.

"You're a ways from home."

"Promised myself I'd get the rogue that did in my sister." His face changed a little. "She and Jean-François were friends, too."

"I'm sorry." *If it makes you feel any better, we'll get him. Nobody kills cops in my town and gets away with it.*

He shrugged, a fluid movement. "How are the eggs?"

In other words, time for a subject change. "Good. I don't cook much." *At all.* "Don't have time."

"I guessed as much." Silence fell, his eyes hooding and the staticky sound of a not-quite purr rumbling out from him. I finished most of everything, took a long draft of orange juice, and found my hands had stopped shaking.

He got up to take the tray, and when he loped out of the room I scrambled from under the covers to get to the bathroom. I had to pee like nobody's business, and I wanted to get some clothes on. Just wearing a T-shirt was bad for my image, even if he was a Were.

CHAPTER 13

A New York hellbreed, connected to the rogue?" Harp chewed at her lower lip gently for a moment. "How far can you trust the information, Jill?"

Sunlight fell in through the skylights, but the warehouse was cool, air conditioning and a small beneficial sorcery adding up to ward off the heat outside. I stretched, my back crackling as I reached for the sky. Then I leaned forward, my legs out to either side, almost touching the floor. It wasn't a perfect split but close enough, and I needed the stretch. The stack of files stood just beyond my fingertips as I exhaled, letting my neck relax. I spoke into the floor, shutting my eyes. "He doesn't give me information unless it's true. That's the agreement. If he lies to me, we renegotiate and I get the upper hand. He doesn't want that." My toes pointed, I shuddered, relaxing into the stretch again. "I'm beginning to think there's more to this story, though."

"How so?" Dominic lay on the couch, one arm flung over his eyes. He didn't look good, dark circles under his eyes and his face hollowed out. It was probably Harp getting hit that did it.

Weres are serious about their mates. They have no conception of civil or religious marriage; they simply pick their mates and settle down. I've never seen a Were mating that isn't happy. Like so many other things, they do it in a way far more humane and relaxed than humans have ever learned to.

"I looked through your files. There's a pattern. First there's the rogue kill, then there are these other bodies—but the other bodies only show up with someone disturbing the Were. We have a rogue, killing for meat in an irregular cycle, and someone else killing whenever someone disturbs him." I exhaled again, then inhaled, bringing myself up and bending over my right knee, the leather of my pants creaking slightly against the floor. My forehead touched my knee. "The bodies we just found were a regular rogue kill. Four bodies, muscle meat gone, faces missing—but the faces weren't Were work, those were hellbreed claws—and bones chewed. The cops were *mostly* rogue kills—except the rookie. He's an exception, not only because he's still alive. A rogue won't tear off the top of a car to get at prey; it'll take opportune bits of meat."

"Humans," Harp corrected softly. Dishes clinked in the kitchen—Dustcircle was washing up, or cooking something.

Nice of him.

"Humans," I agreed. "The point is, something peeled open that car and slashed at him to kill him quick and messy. It's a hellbreed kill."

Dominic perked up. "The hellbreed's covering a rogue's tracks?"

"Or trying to." I straightened, my eyes still closed, and bent over my left leg. My *Dies Irae* T-shirt rode up, a finger of coolness along my lower back, my breasts pressed against my thigh. A knife-hilt jabbed into my ribs again. "And this hellbreed— Cenci—is desperate enough to come out during the day and tangle with a hunter and two Weres."

"Suicidal," Dominic muttered.

I pushed myself up and brought my bare soles together, then leaned down, feeling the stretch in the insides of my thighs. "Not necessarily. Who expects a hellbreed to attack during the day? If indeed she intended to attack, which I'm not convinced of."

That got Dominic's attention. "You're right. She was hanging out up there like she wanted to stay hidden."

I shrugged. "She almost made chow mein out of Harp, and if I'd been down with the bodies and tangled up trying to keep the humans out of her way she'd have gotten away scot-free, maybe with both of you dead."

Dustcircle came around the breakfast bar, wiping his hands on a towel. "Tell me this one again, where Harp gets bitch-smacked by a hellgirl." He was trying for levity, but it didn't go well with his deadly set face. "Because, you know, that never gets old."

Harper stuck her tongue out at him, a thrumming growl rattling the air. But it was a playful sound, and she went back to looking at the stack of files with a line between her eyebrows. That thoughtful look, when she seemed distracted, was when she was most dangerous.

"Shut up." Dominic sighed, sinking into the couch. "I'd have been mincemeat too, if it wasn't for Jill. Christ."

"Glad to be of service. Besides, I'd hate to break in a new set of Feebs." I sighed, leaned forward again, pressing my knees down. The stretch filled my hamstrings with prickles and I had to remind myself to breathe out and relax my lower back. "So, boys and girl, we have our work cut out for us."

"Well, we've been chasing this asshole across the goddamn country, I'm ready for a change." Harp yawned. "I'm *hungry*." She actually sounded plaintive.

"Working on it," Dustcircle replied, easily. "So what is the plan, then?"

I was hoping you'd ask. The warehouse echoed and rang around us, its midday song of a building ticking and expanding under the sun's weight. "I put in a call to the hunters up in New York and ask them to dig, tell 'em it's urgent. Set them to finding out exactly why this Cenci left and what her story is, and why a high-up hellbreed out there is so all-fired set on getting her back—because something about that smells, there's a piece we're missing. You three go down in the barrio and rouse every Were you can, get them spreading through the city to flush the rogue out."

"Wait a second—" Harp tried to dive in. If I was a Were I might have let her have the floor.

But I'm not, so I rode right over the top of her. "Meanwhile, I start burning hellbreed holes out here until someone comes forward. She can't hide in my city without *someone* knowing about it, and I'm going to find out." I straightened and stretched my legs out, sighing. I was already beginning to feel more like myself. I didn't have to see Perry for another month.

Small favors, but I'd take it.

"Saul goes with you." Harp said it like it meant something. "It's a rogue Were, and you're not going to handle one of those on your own. We leave the hellbreed to you, you leave the rogue to Saul."

"I don't need a babysitter." I rose to my feet in a smooth wave, charms tinkling and shifting in my hair. "And where I'm going tonight, Weres aren't welcome."

"So he'll wait outside in the car like a good little boy." Harp folded her arms and glared at me. "Don't make me sit on you, Jill. This is serious."

"You think I don't know that? You got eviscerated, I got clipped, and we lost thirty-six hours because of it. Someone else could be dead right now, or dying. Or *several* someones." My voice rose a little, I took a deep breath and contained myself. "I might have to move quickly tonight, Harp. He won't be able to—"

The country Were in question decided to pipe up. "I can keep up," Dustcircle said dryly. "Believe me, I don't want to tangle with any hellbreed. I'll leave them strictly to you, and stay out of your way. Now if you'll excuse me, I think the pot roast needs attending."

Pot roast? Just what did they put in my fridge? I folded my arms and glared back at Harp. But she had a point. Hellbreed I could handle—hopefully. A berserker Were gone over the edge and looking for meat I might not be able to take without losing some serious blood. If I ran across them both together a little backup might be nice.

I *really* wanted to leave the country boy at home. But part of being a hunter is being allied with Weres, and the idiot had apologized. I'd be rude and stupid if I kept this up, and while I don't mind being the first, the second can get you killed.

"Fine." I gave in. "You're right. Backup's far from the worst idea when it comes to something like this. But still, it bothers me. Why would a hellbreed be cleaning up after a rogue? It just doesn't make *sense*."

"Unless she's not cleaning up, she's somehow directing him." Harp leaned back on her hands, looking relieved. Dominic let out another gusty sigh and began to purr, the throaty rumble shaking dust out of the couch. He was relaxing.

I restrained the urge to pat his belly like a cat's, touched a knife-hilt instead. "If she was directing him, she'd have picked better targets. Killing cops in a hunter's town is just *asking* for trouble, and none of the victims have any nightside ties at all."

"There is that." Dominic sighed.

The phone shrilled, and I let out a curse, striding into my bedroom to pick it up. "'Lo." I stared at the fall of sunshine through a skylight, my abdominal muscles tightening as if expecting a punch. I was still sore as hell. The scar's channeling of etheric energy meant I healed a lot faster then even the ordinary hunter, but I never felt quite right while my body was knitting itself back together. The food helped, but the sheer animal part of the body doesn't bounce back so easily from a wound that could have been mortal.

Each time you get close to death the body gets a little nervous.

"Jill." It was Monty, again, and my back went cold and prickling with gooseflesh. But he had good news—sort of—for once. "Saddle up. The rookie's awake. You want to talk to him?"

CHAPTER 14

Luz General rose like a brooding anthill. It isn't a Catholic hospital like Sisters of Mercy, but it's still an old building, and the ER doctors there know me. Eva and Benito usually brought their exorcism cases here to be checked out afterward, but they were probably in bed at this hour.

"You scared the shit out of Forensics." Monty didn't mince words, running his hands back through his thinning hair. The bags under his eyes could give mine a run for their money. "You were bleeding pretty bad. What the fuck happened?"

You're better off not knowing, Monty. "Do you really want me to tell you?" I matched his stride as we set off down the corridor. Harp and Dominic would finish dinner and head out into the barrio once dark fell, to gather the Weres and start hunting.

Behind me, Dustcircle's footsteps were almost soundless. Whatever Monty thought of a big man in a brown leather jacket who looked like Crazy Horse in white-man drag shadowing li'l ol' me, he didn't say a word. I was oddly, pointlessly grateful. It's good to work with normal people who might not understand but don't actively fear you.

It reminds you of what you're fighting and bleeding for every night on the streets.

Monty sniffed. "Guess not. The Psych Department is earning its cookies on this one, that's for damn sure. I had to send four of the techs in for trauma counseling."

"Seeing the unexpected does tend to knock the wind out of them. Sorry."

"It wasn't you. It was the goddamn werewolves."

"Cat Weres, Monty. Your pop culture is showing." My trench coat made a slight whooshing sound as we turned a corner. Fluorescent light coated the walls and linoleum floor. It was unforgiving glare, harsh and institutional. Or maybe the smell of Lysol and suffering in the air made it that way.

"Fuck you." He said it a little louder than he'd intended to, as we passed a bustling nurse in the hall. The heavyset woman gave him a glance of disapproval, her graying hair cut short in a cap of curls. I smelled disinfectant, pain, and the smell of filth that always lurks under the bald edge of sanitation in a hospital. "I never get used to that," he muttered. "How do you stand it?"

"A finely developed sense of the bizarre. Plus a good bottle of booze every now and again." *The human mind is amazingly adaptable, Monty. You'd be surprised at what you can live with once you see it often enough.*

"Christ, it's that easy?" Monty pointed, and we went through the glass doors to the ICU.

Immediately the air turned thick with tension, and I felt Dustcircle draw a little closer to me. It was, dare I say it, almost comforting. "It's not that easy. But the booze and random sex help a lot." I heard my own tone, hard and falsely bright. "What's our lucky boy's name?" I should have asked before now, but Monty didn't even shoot me a disapproving glance.

"Cheung. Jimmy Cheung." Montaigne had gone pasty-pale. He pointed again, with a nicotine-stained finger. He'd smoked cigars for years before his wife made him give it up, but old habits and addictions die hard and he still chomped a Cuban or two when the going got really rough. "He knows you're coming. Down there, in room 4."

No shit, Monty. The only room with a couple of uniforms guarding it. "He's coherent?"

Monty's shrug was a marvel of ambiguity. "In spates, I guess. He's pretty well sedated. The doc says not to agitate him, but..."

"But we need whatever I can get out of him. I'll be gentle." *A regular angel of mercy, that's Jill Kismet.* "He's one of mine, Monty. I'll be *very* gentle."

"Good." Monty folded his arms. "I'll be down in the caff if you want me. Gonna get some fucking coffee." His eyes flicked past me, the question implicit.

"He'll come with me. Backup." I watched Monty's eyes widen and the blood drain from his face again. He really did go alarmingly pale sometimes, for such a big tough slouching bear of a man. "I don't expect any trouble. But better to be safe, right?"

"You got it. Just don't shoot up the fucking hospital, I don't need the paperwork." He turned on his heel and left me there, and Dustcircle moved a little closer.

Right into my personal space, as a matter of fact.

I took a deep breath, controlling my twitch. Weres don't have the same concept of space humans do, and most every hunter gets itchy when someone else gets too close. When a Were moves in like that, it means they're offering support. Cat and canine Weres are very touchy-feely, and bird Weres have a whole elaborate protocol for brush and flutter. Snake Weres like to get right up into your aura and breathe in your face, all but rubbing noses like Eskimos.

And let's not even talk about Werespiders. I shivered, the hair on my nape rising briefly. Decided to let him know I didn't feel too chummy, despite his offer of comfort. "Any reason why you're in my personal space, Dustcircle?"

"Just being friendly." He didn't retreat, setting off down the hall with me, matching me step for step. "He's a friend of yours?"

"Monty? Yeah, he's a good guy." We were approaching the uniformed officers, standing to attention at either side of room 4's door, which was slightly ajar. I could almost feel Dustcircle breathing on my hair. *Even for a Were, this is too close. Get him away.*

I didn't have time. I nodded to the uniforms—Tom Scarper, a good cop, and his partner Ramon, both guys I remembered from their rookie class with me—and accepted their quiet murmurs of welcome. Even foulmouthed Fuckitall-Ramon looked serious, his dark eyebrows drawn together.

Then I was through the door, the Were right behind me, and in a hospital room full of tubes, soft sterile light, and the sound of machines beeping softly, monitoring heartbeat and respiration, standing their ceaseless watch.

"Jesus," I whispered. The thing on the bed looked vaguely human, but it was bandaged to within an inch of its life.

Get it? Within an inch of his life? Ha ha, Jill. Very funny. I swallowed with an effort, moved up to the side of the bed. Half of Jimmy Cheung's skull had been shaved, and a wet glaring line of unbandaged stitches showed where his scalp had been opened up. I calculated the angle of the scar and felt my heart thump sickly inside my chest.

Not Were claws. Those are likely hellbreed marks, if I spread my fingers just so and had curved claws the marks would look similar. So it was probably our girl Cenci who opened up the car like a tin can and reached in for this kid.

One liquid brown eye was open. He was awake. His breath hissed in, hissed out without the aid of a ventilator, at least he was breathing on his own. An oxygen tube lay under the bandages that covered his ruined nose.

I found my voice. "Officer Cheung." My tone was soft, respect-ful, and Dustcircle bumped into me from behind. I shoved back, subtly, pushing him away with my hip. "It's Jill. Jill Kismet."

The eye widened. Blinked. His other eye was lost under a sheet-ing of gauze. I wondered if I wanted to see the damage, decided I didn't. The rhythm of his breathing didn't change, and his heart-beat didn't waver. It was uncanny, seeing the EKG spikes match the pulse my preternaturally sensitive hearing was picking up.

The Were moved closer, bumped me again. I suffered it, my eyes on the bandaged face resting against the pillow's whiteness. The blankets were pulled up on his chest, and I smelled the sharp-ness of urine. He had to have a catheter; no way he could make the bathroom in this condition.

God. Tangle with the nightside and this is what you get. Even if you're innocent. Do your job, Jill.

"I'm going to take down whoever did this to you," I promised the slack face on the pillow. "But I need you to tell me anything you can about the attack. If you can't, just shake your head. Or blink, or something." I kept my tone very soft, conciliatory. "But if you can, it would help me. A lot."

When he spoke, I was surprised. His voice was strong but reedy, and his lips weren't bandaged. They were bloodless, and a thin crust hung at their corners, the effluvia of sickness. "It was a woman." He exhaled, took a gasping breath, and I smelled the peculiar sick burning scent of the human body struggling to cope with damage. "They radioed, said they'd seen something by the side of the road—a dog, or something. Coyote. But *wrong*. By the time we got there..." A slight cough, and I eyed his IVs. He was on morphine, which explained the dreamy tone and his lack of affect. "She came right through the windshield. Tore...the top of the car open. So quick. And quiet, nothing but the metal screaming..."

"What did she look like?" I pitched my voice low, respectful.

"Blonde. Pretty. Red eyes." His own eye closed briefly. Opened wide. "She was going to kill me, but it scrambled over the hood. She went after it."

My breath caught. "It?" *Coyote? Dog? A canine Were, stuck between human and animal form? Likely, but don't make assumptions, Jill. This is tenuous enough.*

But there was no more. His eye drifted closed again, and the rhythm of beeping from the machines smoothed out. Gone into the dark depths, just like a submarine sinking.

Blonde. Pretty. Red eyes. The glow of a maddened hellbreed? It meant she wasn't a Trader, their eyes didn't change, just acquired the flat dusty shine.

Besides, no Trader could have fought off both me and Harp. It wasn't possible. Still, I felt a thin thread of unease, and was glad I'd received at least one hard piece of information to hang *that* assumption on.

I reached down. Mikhail's ring glinted on my left hand. My middle two fingers touched the rough gauze over his hand, then the very edge of one knuckle showing through the swathed white and the bumps of the IV. His skin was cold, inert.

"I promise," I whispered. "I'm on the job. Rest easy."

There was no reply. I took my hand back, straightening, and

bumped into Dustcircle again, acutely aware of how much taller he was. *Dammit. What's he doing?* I half-turned, pushing past him and heading for the door; I had to damn near ooze around him, he stood so still. My heart lodged in my throat as he turned to follow me, each move as graceful as a dance.

Outside, the Were left the door ajar again, fluorescent light glowing in his dark hair. I nodded at Ramon, the obstruction in my throat turning dry and massive.

Scarper's cheeks flushed under his stubble. "Hell of a thing," he said, the words falling dead in the corridor.

"Yeah. Hell of a thing." My voice didn't seem to want to work quite properly either.

"Gonna fuckin' get 'em, Jill?" This from Ramon, whose dark eyes were bright with unspecified emotion.

I met his gaze, and for once someone didn't flinch when I looked at them. "Of course I am. Nobody fucks with cops in my town and gets away with it, gentlemen." I turned on my heel and stalked away, almost tripping as Dustcircle moved in close again.

I waited until we reached the end of the hall to bring it up. "What the hell are you *doing?*"

"Just being friendly," he repeated, his steps matching mine. "You take this seriously, don't you."

You have got *to be kidding.* "Is there any other way to take it? I'm a hunter, this is my town. Aren't Were-cougars territorial?" *And what the fuck do you care anyway, country boy?*

"About some things." He was still too close, his warmth brushing my coat.

I rubbed at my right wrist, delicately avoiding the scar's pucker. It throbbed uneasily, reacting to the spill of pain and grief in the air. *Give him something a Were would understand.* "They're my people. Nobody messes with them and gets away with it."

He eased off a bit, giving me a few inches of space that felt damn wide by then. "What's next?"

My lungs filled, a deep breath like a sigh mixing his smell and my own, plus the comforting, ever-present aroma of leather from my coat. "Next I drop by the warehouse and our local Sanctuary to pick some things up, and as soon as dusk hits I go out to torch a few holes."

"Sounds like fun." Was that amusement in his voice? It felt like he was getting really personal, but it just could have been some Rez Were custom I didn't know about.

"Lots of blood and screaming, severed limbs—the usual." I sighed, and moved away as he homed in on my personal space again. It took a half-skipping motion that looked awkward, my coat swirling, but he quit trying to plaster himself to me. "Lucky you. You get to wait in the car. Now quit rubbing on me."

CHAPTER 15

Galina held up a handful of thin silver bracelets, her soft green cat-tilted eyes troubled under dark bangs. She looked like a thirties film star, between her paleness and the marcel waves in her sleek hair. "You want to try these, Jill?"

I swept four hinged copper cuffs off the counter and into my largest pocket, laying down a fifty-dollar bill. Eyed the chiming bracelets speculatively. They were blessed, I could see the clean blue glow running just under the surface of the silver, spilling out into the ether. "You think they might hold up better? The copper's taking a chunk out of both of us."

Westering sunlight fell through the high windows of the small shop. Galina lived up on the second floor, and very rarely left these four walls. Sanctuaries are tied to their particular houses; it's the bargain they make. They finish their training, settle, and drive roots in deep; a Sanctuary's house is well-nigh invulnerable. If they're caught out in the open, several nightside species consider them a tasty snack.

For all that, the local Sanctuary is where hunters, Weres, and other nightsiders go for supplies—silver, icons, bullets, other things—and gossip. Name it, and your local Sanc can get it for you. If your credit's good, that is—and if you haven't been too irritating lately. And lots of Weres or hunters will smack you down hard if you're caught messing with a Sanc.

Sancs have a lot of discretion once the Order finishes training them, and if you start trouble inside one of their houses you'll be on your ass in seconds flat. The sorcery they use is weak out in the world, but inside the confines of their own Houses, a Sanctuary's will is law.

Sancs most often die old in bed after a few hundred years. Hunters don't.

Galina shrugged, her smile flashing for a moment as the sun picked out highlights in her hair. Saul had busied himself in the corner, playing with the Were toys—drums, claw-shaped knives, feathers and other bits for making amulets and fetishes.

"If it'll help you with that thing, I'll import it until the cows come home. But I get these—" The silver chimed in her hand, responding as the walls of her house creaked a little, fluxing in answer to her smile. "—from Mexico; they're cheap and readily available. I can even *make* them, if I have to. They might corrode less easily, too."

The glassed-in counter between us was full of little trinkets: Saint medals—Anthony, Jude, and Andrew, as well as George and Catherine—all specially blessed by Father Guillermo over at Sacred Grace, who had a dispensation from the Vatican to use some of the...ah, *older* blessings. Small stuffed alligators yawned, and a collection of rock-crystal scrying orbs glittered under the golden light.

Galina is slim and even smaller than me, her short stature belied by the shifting cloak of red-gold energy that is a Sanctuary's trademark. She wore the traditional gray, a tunic-top and a pair of bleached jeans, but was as usual barefoot. A silver pendant with the mark of the Order—a quartered circle inside a serpent's curve—winked at her throat.

I took one of the thin hinged bracelets. *If I wear more than one to cover the scar, it'll make a hell of a lot of noise when they tap together. But if it works, I might have her make me a cuff.* "Well, let's see." I snapped it shut over my wrist, held my hand out, and shook it a little to make the bracelet fall against the scar's ridged pucker.

An amazing jolt of pain leveled me to my knees, Galina's short blurt of surprise echoing uneasily against the walls. The defenses on the building sprang into humming alertness, but I couldn't have cared less, my arm was on *fire,* as if I'd just stuck it in an oven and the flesh was crisping all the way down to the bone. I fell over, scrabbling at the bracelet with my other hand, but the hinge had locked, silver ground against the scar and I let out a sharp cry as the pain spilled down my chest, reaching for my heart with clumsy clawed fingers.

Abruptly the pain receded, hot thick tears squirting out of my eyes. I exhaled, blinked, and found myself flat on the floor, Saul Dustcircle crouching next to me. His fingers locked around my wrist, the silver bracelet—curled like paper in a hot fire—was busted open in his other hand.

"Jesus," I whispered.

His eyes were very dark, and they held mine for a moment. He didn't ask a single question, just turned my wrist up and looked at the scar, his eyebrows drawing together.

Shame boiled up inside me, hot and vicious. Galina arrived, having vaulted the counter; she slid her arm under my shoulders and helped me sit up. "Christ, Jill, I'm sorry, I'm so sorry, my God, are you all right?" The defenses settled back into their humming, and I was grateful for that. Triggering Sanctuary defenses would make the pain from my arm seem like a cakewalk.

"F-fine." I tried to yank my wrist out of Saul's hand. His fingers bit down, a Were reflex, but I tore free, dispelling the urge to examine my arm and make sure I wasn't burned. My nerves twitched and screamed. "That was interesting." The words rode a breathy scree of air.

"Are you okay? Do you need to sit down, a glass of water, anything?" Galina was close to tears, her eyes glimmering and pale now. "I didn't think it would do that. Honest, I didn't."

Jesus, Galina, I know. "No worries." I sounded shaky even to myself, took a deep breath. "At least now we know silver won't work to cover it up. What'd you do to that batch?"

"I blessed it using a Greek invocation to Persephone. An old one I dug up out of some of Hutch's books." She was even paler than usual, helping to haul me to my feet and trying ineffectually to dust me off. "Are you really all right?"

Saul rose gracefully, holding the bracelet. It had twisted into a tight little corkscrew and sang a thin little note of stress before it stopped quivering. I didn't blame it, I felt the same way.

Goddamn. Well, let's call that an experiment and chalk it up to experience. All hail Jill Kismet the scientist.

I shook my hands out. The pain had vanished, leaving me weak-kneed and a little sweaty. "Fine. It was just a jolt, that's all." *And I hope nobody finds out about this, because having someone do that to me for torture would be unpleasant at best.* "I'll stick with the copper for now. We'll think of something."

"I'm sorry." She really was contrite. Galina was a gentle soul, when all was said and done. It was why she was a Sanctuary. The Order is concerned with preservation and peace; it's a pity so few pass the entrance tests. Human nature, I guess.

"Don't worry." A sudden idea struck me. "Can you bless all the silver for my bullets like that? It's heap powerful mojo."

Her sleek hair brushed forward over her shoulders as she nodded. "I can do that. How much do you need?" She didn't mention what any fool could see: I was wearing my ammo belt and bandolier, preparing for serious trouble tonight.

If she'd seen the trunk of my Impala, she might have been even more worried. I thought about it for a second. Took a shaky breath in, my heartbeat finally smoothing out. "Enough to refill my ammo belt. I'll stop by tomorrow if I have time." Translation: *if I'm not getting shot at, or dealing with another crisis.* I gauged the fall of sunlight. Near dusk. In another forty-five minutes it would be night.

The thin taste of copper laid itself over my palate again, my body reacting both to the pain and to trouble coming. I was going to throw myself into something dangerous and potentially deadly tonight, and my animal instinct was having a difficult time with the thought. Dumb idiot body, getting all worked up before the fun started.

Going out to torch hellbreed holes is just *asking* for trouble. But sometimes asking for trouble heads off even deeper trouble up the road.

"All right." Her eyes moved past me, to Saul. "Anything you need, sir?" Her tone was polite, and I thought I caught a twinkle in her eyes. Theron and some of the others from the barrio were regular visitors; the Order and the Weres are old friends. Back when the churches both Catholic and Protestant used to hunt the furkind—not to mention the feathered and scaled—the Order was doing its best to protect them. European Weres had caught the worst of it, but those in the New World have suffered enough to remember in different ways.

On other continents Weres had—and have—different problems.

"Leather. A strip this long—" His hands shaped the air. "And these." He laid a handful of stuff on the counter. Probably meant for amulets, and Galina nodded, patting my shoulder.

"I'll ring you up in a moment. Are you sure you're okay, Jill?"

Don't sound so worried, kiddo. I do this for a living, remember? I've been trained. "Peachy keen." I tried not to sound sarcastic, turned away. When she got this soft and worried I felt an acutely uncomfortable need to reassure her, and always ended up sounding like an idiot. Safer just to change the subject. "I'll wait out in the car."

"Be safe," Galina called after me. I made a noise of assent— what *can* you say, to something like that? I couldn't be safe if I tried.

I didn't even know if I wanted to. I was, in my own special way, as much an adrenaline junkie as Avery. Or even more. Hard not to crave the jolt of staring down death or the feeling of skating the edge of terror and coming out on top, once you've tasted it.

The bell on the door's crossbar tinkled as I stepped outside the safety of her shop, taking in the street with a quick glance. My Impala sat at the curb obediently, her orange paint gleaming. My baby.

Dustcircle came out a few minutes later, carrying a small bag. He settled into the passenger's seat as I roused the engine. "Nice lady."

"Just don't start any trouble around her, and she stays that way." I shifted into first and pulled away from the curb. "Find everything you needed?"

"Yup." He paused as I accelerated, heading up Fairville. I'd catch Fifteenth and drop down toward Plaskény Square.

My first stop of the night. My heart thudded once under my ribs, settled back into its regular rhythm.

"Mind if I smoke?" He dug in his pocket and came up with a pack of Charvils. The smell of cherry tobacco reached my nose.

It was oddly pleasant, especially since he'd stopped looming over me.

"Knock yourself out. Just roll down the window." *I redid the upholstery in here, I don't want it reeking.*

"Can I ask you something?"

Depends on what you ask, furboy. "Ask." I hit my turn signal, eased us around a corner.

"What happened to your teacher—Tolstoi, right? He was famous."

"Harp didn't tell you?" My heart leapt up into my throat, my palms suddenly slick. "He fell in love and she killed him." *He fell in love with a Sorrow, she stole his amulet and tore his throat open. If I ever get the chance, I'm going to kill her.* "The Weres gave him a pyre. He deserved it."

The pause was uncomfortable. I shifted, ramming the clutch, and opened my mouth again. "He was the only man who ever thought I was worth a damn."

Shut up, Jill. He doesn't need to hear that. He's just a visiting Were. Stop it. I reached forward, twisted the radio knob angrily, and got lucky. They were playing Jimi Hendrix, and I turned it up, accelerating, the sound of music and wind through the windows sweet enough to drown the lump in my throat.

Mostly.

The Diablo was a hellbreed hole on Plaskény, a long, low vaulted basement at the bottom of a flight of dusty, narrow, filth-drifted stairs. I poured a thin tidal wave of vodka on the bar before smashing the bottle, a nice theatrical touch. The screaming had stopped, but there were still moans and little clicking sounds from the *arkeus* I'd just finished mostly dismembering. The clicks dissolved into a gurgle, and a titanic stink rose.

One more hell-thing dead, more or less.

Most of them were dead, draped over chairs, dissolving on top of tables. The dance floor was chaos, and my shoulders hurt. So did my face, I'd taken a shot right on the cheek that could have broken a human hunter's neck. My shirt was torn, and my long leather trench had ragged claw marks in it. It was just one rip short of the dustheap.

Burning a hellbreed hole is never easy, especially for just one hunter. The only good thing about it was I didn't have to watch where my shots went, eventually they'd hit someone who deserved it. When I used to do backup with Mikhail we'd have to be careful not to clip each other—but working with your teacher is like working with a telepath who *anticipates,* and if you're a good student you get to the point where you can anticipate too.

Or at least stay the hell out of the way.

I held the gun steady on the bartender, a thin ragged hellbreed with a shock of piebald hair and a twisted upper lip. Despite that, he was attractive, in a worn sneering way, with that aura of the exotic 'breed carry. He eyed the gun and opened his mouth to say something—

—and I half-turned, lashing out *behind* me, the whip flicking, striking with a crackle across the face of a slick little female 'breed sneaking up on me through the wreckage. She collapsed, screaming, holding her face. If she lived she'd be scarred by the silver.

Hot nasty satisfaction spilled through my veins like wine-fumes. I was grinning madly, blue sparks crackling over the blessed silver tied in my hair, charms chiming a sweet counterpoint to the violence.

"Spread the word." I turned back to the bartender. The gun didn't waver. I used to use baby Glocks, being cursed with smaller wrists than a man. No more. I like the big ones, my bones can handle recoil a lot better now. "Whoever's hiding this New York chippie 'breed is on a one-way track back to Hell. I want her, and I want her *yesterday*. Got it?"

He made a thin whining sound as the whip returned, wrapping itself neatly in my fist. My fingertips tingled. I ached to pull the trigger—someone had hit me with a chair, crunching my leg and almost cutting my throat with a broken bottle. Most of the hellbreed in here I'd just wounded and put down to bleed out, but that one I'd killed.

The hammer rose back as I squeezed the trigger, delicately, gently. It clicked into the up position. "I am not going to tell you again." My voice was deadly soft. My ribs ached—having a couple 'breed pummel you will do that. It had taken a ridiculous amount of ammo, but I'd wanted the first one messy enough to make a statement. Enough of them had escaped to spread the word that I was on the warpath.

It had certainly *been* messy enough to satisfy. A chaos of blood and screaming, the music pounding through it all until a stray shot had thankfully knocked out a vital connection in the DJ's booth. Then just screams and shouting, and hellbreed cries.

And death.

The bartender scrambled away and fled toward the shattered front door. I hadn't been particularly subtle. Red and purple light flickered, random reflections cast by the blastball hovering over the dance floor. The rest of the place was wreckage.

It had taken me only fourteen and a half minutes. Give or take. There's something about working overtime and double semiautomatics that makes a girl capable of kicking serious ass.

I filled my lungs. My fingers prickled, the heat becoming uncomfortable. The scar pulsed wetly, thrumming with the force I'd pulled through it. Hey, I could afford it; I was paid up through the month.

Don't think about that, Jill. I flicked my fingers.

Vodka on the bar ignited with a *wump!*

A thin pale-blue flame smeared like oil. Banefire. It would spread to thin flammable hellbreed blood and more spilled liquor, and this place was a firetrap anyway. I spent a few moments examining the shell of etheric energy on the concrete walls—the concrete would keep the fire from spreading, but this flame would consume every trace of hellbreed, cleansing the entire interior and leaving a thin coating of inimical-to-hellspawn blessing behind.

Thank you, God. I did *not* want to burn down more than I needed to.

I turned on my heel, the ragged strips of my coat fluttering. Under its protection, I was mostly whole. I hadn't lost much blood tonight.

Yet. This is only your first stop. Don't get cocky.

The place began to smoke and flame in earnest. I strode up out of the fire, up the steps past the subterranean iron door hanging by one hinge, stepping over the pool of ick that used to be a burly hellbreed grunt bouncer, finally out into the night's cool sweetness. The bartender had fled, and I faintly caught the echo of his running feet, heading north and veering to the west.

Probably heading for the Monde. Happy birthday, Perry. I sighed, rolling my shoulders in their sockets, as something detonated behind me and the flames started to lick and sizzle in earnest. Banefire doesn't sound like real flame. It sounds like whispery, papery voices screaming behind you, like a cold sweat in the middle of the night. It is a flame of cleansing, not like the black twisting fire a hunter can call upon to fashion levinbolts.

And definitely not like hellfire.

The scar throbbed aching tension against my wrist. Mikhail's ruby warmed the hollow of my throat. I crossed the street, heels clicking, since I didn't have to be quiet at all tonight.

Dustcircle leaned against the hood, smoking one of his cherry cigarettes. He smelled of tension, musk, and sleek electric fur on end. Seeing the bartender blunder up out of the hole and into the night must have been worrisome.

His eyes flicked past me to the doorway. My back prickled. If any 'breed came out now they'd be angry but wounded, and not much of a threat.

That's pride talking, Jill. Even a half-dead 'breed is dangerous. Do not *get cocky.*

"How many were down there?" He asked it so calmly I almost didn't believe the tense thrumming coming out of him, the Were version of a fidget. Not quite a growl, but certainly more than a purr.

"I stopped counting at twenty." I fished my pager out and checked it. No calls, and it was early still. "I've got lots to do tonight, Dustcircle. You want to get in the car?"

He remained where he was, staring across the street. I restrained the urge to look back over my shoulder.

He took his sweet time examining the twisting blue shadows of banefire. Finally, he spoke. "Were you kind to them?"

I almost went slackjawed in amazement. Kind to them? They were *hellbreed.* Spoilers and corruptors, sorcerous maggots, predators.

After a moment, I understood. When Weres kill, they do it swiftly. They don't play with their prey.

Unless they're rogue, gone berserk and violating the oldest of Were taboos.

Thou shalt not eat people.

It irked me that he'd even asked. What did he think I was? "I've killed more 'breed than you can possibly imagine," I told him, flatly. "Not a single one of them was ever what I'd call happy, and I put them down as quick and clean as I can. You can call that kindness if you want. I like to think I'm being kind to the innocents they prey on. Get in the *car*."

He did.

CHAPTER 16

Two holes and a short streetside gunfight to mop up later, I was tired more than physically. I braked to a stop down the street from the Random, a step above the norm.

Most 'breed like their holes underground, with one entrance. It just shows the burrowing instinct in them. The holes are womblike and thump with music during the night, and any human dumb enough to wander or be lured inside is lucky to escape with only psychic damage.

The Random, however, was a Trader club. If hellbreed came here, they were actively looking to make a deal. Any humans that showed up were the same.

It was a ramshackle building, its windows painted black and its door guarded by two beefy Traders with glittering dusted eyes. I watched through the windshield and let out a soft breath, the scar throbbing. It was time to open up the trunk.

Unfortunately, Dustcircle picked that moment to open his mouth.

"What exactly is this supposed to accomplish?" He sounded uneasy.

You idiot. What do you think I'm doing, having Captain Kangaroo *sing-alongs and eating caramel corn?* I had to work for an even, nonsarcastic tone, and suspected I failed. "The 'breed community functions on profit and loss. If it becomes too expensive for them to hide this Cenci, they'll police themselves and turn in any information they have. Besides, I'm a new hunter, kind of, I've only been knocking around on my own for half a year. If Mikhail was alive we wouldn't have to do this; he'd visit a few of his sources and we'd track her down that way. They'd *know* not to mess with him. Me, I'm still teaching the bitches who's boss."

"Proving you're alpha?" He sounded dubious. "Do we have time for this?"

"It's the quickest way to get what I want, which is no more bodies in the street." I felt the shiver even as I said it. It wasn't the whole reason I was clearing out these places. Every 'breed I killed tonight was a slap directly to Perry's bland blond face.

Fuck around with my head, will you? Just see how easy it would be for me to fuck right back. I pushed the flare of murderous rage down. *Save it for the Random, Jill. Do it just like you were trained to.*

Make Mikhail proud.

"All right." He sniffed, inhaling deeply and tasting the air. "This smells different."

Sure it does. "It's a Trader club. General rule, above ground it's Traders, below it's pure 'breed." *Though there are exceptions. Like Perry's place, which switches back and forth according to some weird rule I haven't figured out yet.* I eased my hands off the wheel. "This one might take me a while."

"I can come with you." He didn't ask, he just *said* it, and tossed the remains of his most recent cigarette out the half-open window. "I'll leave the 'breed to you and stay out of your way. Watch your back."

It wasn't a half-bad idea, except I'd never worked with him before. This wasn't a place for amateurs. "Probably not a good idea," I said, diplomatically enough. "Harp wants—" *Harp wants her deposit back on you,* was what I intended to say.

"Harp wants me to keep your skin whole, hunter. I can handle Traders." He rolled up the window, his profile austere in the wash of orange lights from streetlamps. The twin braids on either side of his face moved with him; he opened the car door and stepped out.

I weighed the situation for a few moments, opened my own door. Cool air touched my skin, and dried sweat crackled as I moved. I'd had to scrub the blood off my face more than once tonight.

He stopped at the rear of the car, much bigger than me and wider in the shoulders. He loomed over me with very little trouble, but I had the scar and enough experience to give him a serious run for it. The thought passed through my head, circled, came back, and was gone again.

You can't shut off that part of your brain when you're a hunter—the part that jots everyone down in columns according to how easy or difficult they'd be to kill. The part that doesn't really care *why,* the part that just wants to survive, by hook or by crook. That cold, calculating, utterly amoral part you have to harness, use—but never let completely free.

I was suddenly very aware that I smelled like death and hellbreed blood, as well as sweat and effort. Dustcircle, of course, looked immaculate and smelled of clean male Were.

He won't be pretty for long if he goes in there. Apparently it was my night for not-very-nice satisfaction. I felt a quick burst of shame, discarded it as useless.

"All right." I popped the trunk and started exchanging spent ammo clips for fresh ones, tucking them into my belt and bandolier. "Pop quiz. A Trader comes at you with his eyes glowing red. What do you do?"

"Get out of the fucking way and let you handle it. Trader eyes don't glow." He folded his arms, his leather jacket creaking a little. One eyebrow raised briefly, and his lip almost curled.

So he's not a complete novice. "What do you do if a hellbreed has me down on the floor with her hands around my windpipe?"

"Stay out of the way and let you handle it. If a 'breed's that close to you it's stupid, doesn't deserve to live." His eyes glowed, a flat green-blue sheen covering them for a moment as the streetlamp overhead reflected against a nonhuman pupil. Just like a cat's eyes, when the light hits them right. "I'm not a complete idiot, Kismet."

So I'm Kismet now, not "hunter" or "hellbreed-smelling bitch." I've been upgraded. "Good to know. Last question." I reached down, picked up the slim length of Mikhail's sword, its clawed finials capped with leather and its blade wrapped in a soft sheath. "We walk in the door and immediately a Trader jumps you. What do you do?"

"Rip its heart out, break its neck." He didn't even blink as I ducked through the strap, settling it diagonally across my body so the sword rode my back. The snaps on the soft sheath clinked a little; if I reached up for the sword a quick sideways jerk would free it, since it was too long to really draw or hang at my side like a rapier. "That's a big chunk of metal, kitten. You know how to use it?"

Kitten? If I didn't know better I'd think you just called me a little kid. The smile that rose to my face wasn't pleasant at all. I made sure all my guns had a full clip and one in the chamber. "That's the advantage of having a hellbreed scar on my wrist, fur-boy. I get to play with all *sorts* of toys that are too big for me." I slammed the trunk and turned. "You can come and play. Stay low, stay away from the 'breed, and try not to get clipped. Harp would kill me if I let something happen to you."

"I'll do my best." He sounded sardonic. When I glanced at him, he wore a slight smile, a feral light shining through his dark eyes. He looked ready to cause trouble, with the edgy good humor of a Were about to explode with frustration. "If I'm a very good little boy will you stop fussing at me?"

Fussing at him? I was so irritated I almost forgot how tired I was, and how I did *not* want to be doing this. "I don't *fuss.* Now shut up—I've got work to do."

"Sure."

I darted another quick glance at him as we stepped out into the street. He stared straight ahead, toward the Random's neon signs and the huddled mass of people lining up at the front door, threads of contamination swirling through the ether around them.

Nobody paid us any mind. We hopped on the sidewalk, and I plunged into an alley slicing off to the side.

"Back door?" Was that grudging admiration in his tone? That rubbed me raw too. What did he think I was, a dolt or a novice? Both? Plus a hellbreed-smelling almost-traitor to the good guys?

"Of course." I tried not to sound too sarcastic. "I wouldn't be much of a hunter if I didn't know where the back doors are."

"Guess not." Grudging, barely giving an inch. I supposed it would kill him if he admitted I knew how to do my goddamn job.

I wondered what he'd say when I told him the back door was on the roof.

We dropped down into a bath of crimson light and a dancing mass of Traders. I landed hard, the dance floor cracking in a radial pattern as the force of my breaking a law of physics crackled out in random spiderweb spokes. My aura flamed, visible suddenly in the inky etheric contamination, a sea urchin made of light. Then I came up all the way from the floor with a punch that sent one Trader flying, blood from his smashed face hanging in the air for a moment before splashing out. The knives left their sheaths, and I started weeding through them in earnest.

Twenty seconds later, I forgot about Dustcircle. It was apparent he could take care of himself—except for when one Trader leapt for his back, and the knife left my hand with a glitter, a short wordless cry like a hunting falcon's escaping my lips. Just afterward I took a shot right in the gut from a squat bearded Trader who gibbered when I snarled at him, the silver in my hair burning and the ruby sparking at my throat, and I brought up the Glock in my free hand. The whip uncoiled, and I was just about to leap down from the dance floor into the club proper through strings of swaying glass beads when something smashed into me from the side.

I went flying and twisted, getting my feet under me and skidding across the bar, bootsoles smoking as I *kicked,* another Trader going flying. Then it came after me again, so fast it almost blurred, and I recognized the veiled 'breed who did assassinations.

Oh, fuck. I dropped to the side, firing with both hands now, trained reflex tracking the 'breed as he leapt above the bar and sank his fingers into the concrete wall, hissing at me with bared teeth I could see through his fluttering veil.

He was unholy quick, but I'd been trained by the best and aimed *before* him, knowing he would twist in midair to get leverage so he could bring his claws to bear on me. Silver-loaded bullets punched through his shell, black ichor flying, then I *rolled,* gaining my feet with a convulsive movement most people don't think a woman is capable of using—knees drawn in before feet flung out, back curving, feet coming under to catch, I spun in a

tight half-circle and caught the next hellbreed—a female with flying black-ink hair—as she was at the apex of an arcing leap down
on me. Silverjacket lead flew, the nightclub suddenly a roil of
screaming chaos, and I heard the deep coughing roar of a Were in
a rage.

Hope he's all right. I was too busy to worry about him, I had
troubles of my own. My eyes found the whip again, but it was too
far away and the veiled 'breed thrummed in Helletöng, the curse
flashing past me and slicing through a pair of Traders who had
been looking to leap on my back.

Thank God I brought it. My right hand flashed up, closed
around the hilt, and I gave the sharp sideways jerk that burst the
snaps on the sheath. Leather parted and the ruby at my throat
flamed into bright bloody light.

Okay, you sonofabitch. Let's tango.

I actually had time to let go of the hilt, flip my hand while the
sword was in midair, and close my fingers on it again before the
veiled 'breed crashed into me yet once more. The shock tore
something in my side, and my scream rose with his growl, an
inhuman sound that caused no few of the Traders to drop to the
floor, clapping their hands over their ears—but my aura flamed
again, blocking the force of his cry, and all I heard was the horrible choking of a gallows-dropped man whose neck has not kindly
snapped. I got my feet underneath me and dug my heels in, the
bright blade coming up as my other hand closed on the hilt.

Orange flame burst along the sword's long straight line. It was
a two-handed broadsword, with its point on the floor the finials
reached my ribs and the blade was as wide as my hand at the base.
The hilt's metal claws sparked, flexing down to feed power into
the blade, and a crimson gleam showed in the empty place in the
hilt, echoed by the bloody gem at my throat.

You can't use a sunsword without a key, after all.

Fighting with a broadsword isn't like knifework. It's a matter
of hack and slash, and the speed that gives me such an edge when
it comes to knifing is handicapped by the sheer weight of the blade
and the pommel, still too absurdly big for my fragile-seeming
hands. Still, the ruthlessness trained into me comes in handy. I
don't hesitate to hack *or* slash.

And once all that mass gets moving, the momentum gets easier to control. My speed kicks back in, becoming an asset once more.

The sword coughed, reacting to the contamination of Hell's citizens in the air. Then it burst into its true flame, golden like the noon sun dawning from hilt to tapered point.

Howls. Screams. The veiled 'breed ran right into the slash as I stamped, driving forward with the long muscles in my legs. Preternatural flesh parted, and the 'breed gave a deathly scream, spiraling up into a falsetto squeal. I half-turned again, continuing the motion and sweeping the sword up, meeting the second wounded 'breed. *What do you say, God, let there just be two of them, please, what do you say, give me a break*—The thought was gone in an instant as ichor sizzled on hot steel, and another squeal tore the space inside the Random. Flame dripped, and the flooring smoked. It was only a matter of time before the place started to burn with sunfire.

My side healed in a brief burst of agonizing pain as I *pulled* on etheric force, sweat dripping down my back. The scar on my wrist screamed with agony, but the ruby pulsed reassuringly. The sword still recognized me, and *didn't* burn me to a crisp. That, at least, was comforting.

Then the world exploded into chaos. I heard Dustcircle's short yell of warning and whirled, only getting halfway before an amazing, terrific weight smashed into me from behind.

I *flew.* Good thing I wore leather, my skin would have been erased as I landed, fetching up against the floor and skidding into a pile of rotting Trader bodies. It was on me again, fingers sinking into my hair and yanking my head up, before I shook the dazed noise out of my head and found myself still holding the burning sword. A pile of decomposing Traders was beginning to smoke, waves of heat spreading out in concentric shimmering-air rings.

My hellbreed-strong right arm came up, and I used the clawed pommel to smash the side of the thing's head in.

It tore away from me, and cloth ignited with a low hissing sound. I staggered to my feet, bracing both hands around the hilt, and got a good look at him.

He was slim and dressed in black, with dusty black eyes. When I say black eyes I mean the iris and pupil were so dark as to be indistinguishable yawning holes in his face, and that blackness spread through the whites, staining them with rage. He wore, of all things, a nice pair of Tony Lamas in plain black, and his hair was scorched on one side but appeared black and curly, his coppery skin and hooked nose giving him a vaguely Italian cast.

The world fell away. Etheric force hummed through the scar, cycling up as his aura tightened, a black hole of swirling force.

Oh, shit.

The sunsword hissed, coming up and dappling the air with heat. It blocked the force of the hellbreed's eyes, and I tilted the blade, deflecting the second curse he rumbled at me in Helletöng. Still, I felt it pass me like a train rumbling past at midnight, and my knees almost buckled.

This wasn't just a hellbreed.

It was a monstrously powerful hellbreed, and I'd just pissed it off big-time.

I dug my feet into the floor, filled my lungs, and got ready for a fight I would almost certainly not win even with the sunsword's help.

CHAPTER 17

Stasis. The world slowing down, stopping, as the hellbreed stared at me, force crackling over him in an egg-shaped shield. Everything hung in the air—drops of blood, shattered bits, a Trader falling from the roof where he had tried to get some height to leap down on Saul Dustcircle, who had finished rolling aside and was ready for him, a Bowie knife somehow appearing in his hand, a random dart of light jetting from the blade.

Goddamn Weres and their damn little camouflage tricks.

The 'breed's eyes met mine. He was old, and I bet he'd produce hellfire in at least the green spectrum. Anything above red is seriously bad news, and anything above yellow means kiss-your-ass-goodbye-hunter-it's-time-to-die.

Unless you have a share of hellbreed strength yourself. I drew in an endless breath, the tatters of my coat brushing out on a breeze coming from nowhere, my own aura extending, spiking with a random pattern of brightness. A hunter's aura: disciplined by the training and each exorcism I've performed, a hard shell of etheric energy that makes sure I stay in me—and *nothing* else gets in.

The sunsword roared with flame, more than I'd ever seen, a tail of orange and yellow like the sun's corona spiking up to touch the ceiling, heat shimmering.

I dared him, silently, and knew that he read it in my eyes, in the slight lift of my chin and the way my fingers grew almost soft on the hilt. You never, ever clutch a sword, it makes the strike inaccurate.

His answer was just as slight—a shifting of weight, an infinitely small smile lifting the corners of his sculpted lips. I realized he was grinning under his thatch of wet-dark hair, and I saw again, *noticed* again, his eyes were almost completely black. Infinitely black, with a pale shimmer like disoriented oil floating on the top of a deep sucking tarn. Those eyes were deadly, threatening to suck me in and drown me.

Riptide. Grabbing, whirling, sinking, arms and legs weighted with lead, even my eyelids suddenly drowsy, heavy as a guilty conscience and just as deadening.

Why are his eyes so deep? The thought glittered like a flung knife, like one of my knives, flying true, its load of silver along the flat of the blade—where it couldn't be sharpened off—hissing with white flame as it streaked under the 'breed's uplifted arm and socked home in his ribs. The sound, a heavy solid thunk like an axe driven into dry wood, smashed through my head as the sunsword swept down, painting a fiery streak after its edge.

The clash—sunsword versus hellbreed—was like Mack trucks colliding. The shockwave threw me back, clutching at the hilt, feet scraping in debris shaken down from the roof. The collision blew every bit of glass in the place, including the lightbulbs and the bottles over the bar. The 'breed screeched, no murmuring rush of Helletöng now but a wounded scream, and there was a rushing confusion.

The sword dimmed. Darkness closed almost-absolute around me, light filtering down through the shattered roof as I gasped, my eardrums rattling and a hot wet trickle of blood sliding down from my nose, matching the hot trickles dripping out of my eyes. I collapsed to my knees, only vaguely aware of Saul Dustcircle's arm under my shoulders as I bowed over backward, fingers still loose around the pommel but other muscles tightening up, convulsing. The scar prickled, wetly, a satisfied little lick that sent revulsion spinning down through my stomach.

Don't throw up, Jill. You're alive, you survived, don't puke. Not in front of the Were.

"What the *fuck* was that?" He sounded a little less than calm. A lot less. It was the first time I've ever heard a Were actually sound *frantic.*

Don't worry, country boy. Everything's under control. I wanted to reassure him, but my mouth for once didn't obey my brain.

"You threw my knife," I whispered.

Then I passed out.

It was only a brief second of unconsciousness. I came to right afterward, the sunsword quenched and weighing down my hand. I heard footsteps crunching through smashed and shattered bits. The reek of dead hellbreed and crisped Trader was incredible.

A slight sound to my left brought me fully back into myself. The scar ran with wet heat, as if hot, inhuman breath was touching the ridged skin.

"Look at this mess." Perry finished lighting a cigarette, flame caressing his face with gold for a moment before he clicked the lighter shut. My eyes stung, then adjusted. We'd caused a hell of a lot of damage. "I am going to be hard-pressed to make amends for this, Kiss. You really do know how to complicate matters."

Oh, Christ. Not now. I coughed and choked on the reek, wetness smearing my cheeks. Blood or tears, I couldn't tell. The sunsword keened a little, metal vibrating as it cooled. The red glimmer in its hilt didn't quite go out, but I could tell it would need several hours of direct sun to recharge it. Time to use Galina's greenhouse again.

Am I still alive? A mental inventory returned the verdict that I was, indeed, still alive. And conscious. Plus possessing all my usual bits and pieces.

Hallelujah.

"Who the fuck is that?" Dustcircle jerked me upright, rising to his feet with one fluid motion and dragging me with him by default.

"Friendly," I managed, between whooping retches. I bent over, and my stomach did its level best to rebel against the rest of me. It was declaring its own country and seceding from my union, so to speak.

"Doesn't smell friendly," the Were muttered. "Are you all right?"

He doesn't smell friendly because he isn't, but if you jump him it's going to get real ugly in here real quick. I got in enough air for a word. "Fine."

"You'd better put a leash on that Were of yours," Perry remarked. He stood in a fall of orange citylight creeping through the shattered ceiling. The fires, all of them, were snuffed. And it was *cold.* My breath made little icy puffs as I gasped. The red eye of Perry's cigarette winked as he inhaled, the smell of burning tobacco and another darker perfume cutting through the death-reek for a moment. "Do you know what you just did?"

Miracle of miracles, the amount of breath I could get in doubled. Enough for two words. "Fuck...you."

"Charming. Do you think we should? It would certainly put a whole new shine on our relationship. I repeat, my dearest, do you know what you just did?"

I just cleared out the Random and almost got hooked like a fish by a 'breed with dark eyes and probably an accent. You know how I am for those tall dark and gruesome boys. I couldn't get in enough oxygen to say it, settled for glaring at him between retches. Silver in my hair chimed, and Saul rubbed at my back over the shredded rags of my trench coat.

I didn't have the heart to tell him to stop.

"Take it easy," he murmured. "You looked dazed."

No shit I looked dazed, it almost had my guts for garters. "C-compulsion." My teeth chattered over the word. *"Christ."*

Never. My brain shuddered, came back to itself. *Never met any-*

thing like that before. Jesus Christ. Mikhail, why didn't you tell me about this? I could handle everything a lot better if you were here.

The heaves stopped, and Saul steadied me until I could stand again. "Made a hell of a mess." His voice was back to calm and even, maybe even a little disdainful. "Nice trick, with the sword."

Nice trick, hell. You saved me by throwing my own knife. Is it the one I tossed at the Trader who almost jumped you? There were more pressing questions. I held the ember-dim sunsword away from both of us, awkwardly, and shook him off. Faced Perry over the heave-cracked floor of what had been, a very short time ago, a thumping, jiving Trader nightclub.

I sure know how to throw a party, don't I. "What the fuck are *you* doing here, Perry?" It came out hoarse, and my throat burned with bile even though I was forcing my stomach to stay with the program.

"Saving your delicate skin from being peeled off in strips. Do you know who that was?" The hellbreed cocked his head. He was pristine in a pale suit, as always, and the lamps of his eyes scored a hole in the darkness. They weren't deepening to indigo yet, which was a good thing. If Perry got seriously pissed off, I was in no condition to handle it right now.

"Some jackshit little hellbreed with a nice pair of eyes." I waved my left hand, dismissive. My apprentice-ring ran with blue threads of light, not breaking the surface of the silver yet but close. "I repeat, Pericles, what the everloving *fuck* are you doing here?"

"I told you, saving you. You just committed violence against Navoshtay Niv Arkady." The faint orange light caressed his pale hair, sliding over its smoothness.

I froze. Passing out again began to sound like a really good idea.

"Who?" Saul didn't sound impressed.

My lips were numb, so Perry answered for me.

"The head hellbreed of New York and the accompanying territories, Were. Our little Kiss just clocked the highest-ranking 'breed on the East Coast—here on diplomatic business, I might add— over the head and gave him a sunburn. And *you* tossed a knife into his ribs." Perry actually, damn his eyes, sounded pleased as punch at the thought. "Oh, Jill, my pretty little Jillian, do you have any *idea* what you are going to owe me when this is all over?"

CHAPTER 18

I held up the coat.

My hands were still shaking.

Blood dripped from its tattered leather edges—my claret, and the thin black fluid that passes for hellbreed blood. My head felt a little too big for my neck, and the ringing in my ears wasn't doing me much good either. Hunger crawled under my ribs along with a sickish feeling. The battered, comfortable knee-length Santa Luz Warriors T-shirt didn't help, nor did the idea that I wasn't alone in the warehouse.

My washing machine finished filling and started agitating. Through the glass door, I saw the suds were deep pink. I'd been bleeding a lot lately, and most of the clothes I was bothering to wash were useless rags now. I was going to have to get another two or three *Dies Irae* T-shirts. A one-woman support for cottage industry, that's me.

You just committed violence against Navoshtay Niv Arkady.

Perry had hied himself off to do whatever it was hellbreed do when they aren't fucking with me. He was also going to go and do his diplomatic best with the head of New York's nightside.

I wished him luck. *Lots* of luck. Of course, Perry thought I was still useful for his purposes, so he didn't want Arkady to kill me. On that count, at least, I was in total agreement, even if Perry was a hellbreed.

My hands lowered, so did my head. Silver in my hair chimed. I'd fastened a copper cuff over my wrist, and the resultant blunting of preternatural acuity was both welcome and frightening. I could smell onions sautéing—Saul was messing around in the kitchen again. Get a Were close to death, and he does something domestic. Like cooking, or trying to do my laundry until I outright snarled at him to *leave me the fuck alone.*

Get a hunter close to death, and she gets the jumping jitters. No place for all that adrenaline to go except sawing along the nerves.

The coat dripped thick red and thin rotting blackness on the floor. I had to hose it off and dispose of it, transfer everything into the pockets of a new black leather trench. But I just stood there, shaking.

I could have died. If it wasn't for the Were I would have died. The 'breed had me hooked neat as a trout. He could have just reeled me in and…

The trembling refused to go away. From scalp to heels, the animal side of my body was taking revenge. It knew how close it had come to death, and wasn't fooled by my continued breathing and heartbeat. Mikhail called this part the "rabbit shaking in a hole" and had some long involved Russian prayer he would use whenever things had gotten dicey and we'd pulled through once more.

Me, I just shivered. And shivered some more.

I put the coat up on its rack, forcing myself to move. My laundry room was painted yellow, a nice sunshiny color. The sunsword was back at Galina's, in her greenhouse for charging all day tomorrow under the near-desert sun. She hadn't said anything, but her eyes had gotten big, and she'd taken the sword without comment.

I hadn't stayed in her shop long. Maybe I was afraid of what might happen *next,* for Chrissake. I was done. Stick a fork in me.

The floor in here was tiled, so I hooked up the hose and sluiced the tiles as well as my coat. By the time the water turned clear and went down the drain at the far end, I was jittering so bad my hands almost blurred.

I made it out into the living room, crossed it in long strides, and swung into the kitchen. The floor was cold under my bare feet. I reached up on tiptoes and got the bottle of Jack Daniels down. I had to grab for it a second time, and catch it when I knocked it off the shelf, actually.

"Steak. And onions. I'm not sure if you like them, but no steak is complete without. You need protein." Saul sounded amazingly calm. "And salad, I think. We don't have fresh bread, so it'll have to be store-bought wheat with butter. Sorry about that."

I twisted the cap off the bottle. Eyed the glasses on the shelf underneath the liquor.

Fuck that.

I took a long pull straight from the bottle itself. Most alcohol just goes straight through me—my metabolism runs so high now. It was a goddamn shame, because getting drunk seemed like a fabulous idea.

The bottle fell away from my lips. I had to breathe. Then I lifted it and poured a little more down. It *burned* all the way, and I could finally admit what was bothering me.

Oh, Jill, my pretty little Jillian, do you have any idea *what you are going to owe me when this is all over?*

The trouble was I *did* have an idea, and a good one. Negotiating with Navoshtay fell under the amorphous heading of "other services" that were covered in the bargain I'd made with Perry—at a price of a few more hours of my time. It wasn't going to be pleasant, especially if he decided to fiddle painfully or otherwise with the scar again.

Or if he decided he wanted my blood to flow instead of his. It was always a possibility.

I'm more worried about Perry than I am about the other hell-breed, and that's not right. He's wormed his way into my head, dammit. "Jesus," I whispered, and took another long pull.

Saul's hand closed around the bottle, pushing it away from my lips. "Easy there, hunter." He said it softly, almost kindly. "Easy."

Words I could never say boiled up in my throat, hit the stone sitting there, and died. *Easy? What's fucking easy about this? It's not going to be easy paying Perry what I owe. It's not going to be easy dealing with Navoshtay in my town. And it isn't going to be easy to get my hands to stay still and my brain to stop running in circles.*

I searched for something to say to get him away from me. To run him out of the house, if possible, or just get him to shut up and leave me alone to deal with this in my own way. My gaze snapped up to his. "There is nothing easy about this," I rasped. "Fuck off."

He overrode me, sliding the bottle's hard glass from my fingers. Something sizzled on the stove, but he paid no attention. He set the bottle down on the counter with a slight click, then did something very odd.

The Were took my face in his hands, his palms warm against my cheeks, and stared down at me. His gaze was dark, not the black pit of a hellbreed's but a human darkness, for all the unblinking patience of a cat lived behind it. I saw something pass through his eyes, a long low shape like a hunting animal, muscularly padding through sun and shade.

He didn't flinch. Most people find my gaze hard to meet because of the mismatch; it disturbs them on a deep nonverbal level.

The first time I'd opened my eyes after coming up out of Hell, I'd seen Mikhail bending over me, the bloody gem used to anchor me clasped in his fist and his mouth drawn tight under his hawk nose.

So, he'd said, quietly. *You come back with gift,* milaya. *Come, let us get you in bath.*

The sob startled me. I caught it behind my teeth, swallowed it. Smelled the musk of a male Were and the smell of food, mixing together. Good smells, both of them, and a heady pairing.

Saul's thumb stroked my right cheekbone. "Let it out." He crooned in the particular way Weres have of soothing an injured one of their own, a deep rumbling that shakes the bones loose and the muscles into jelly. "Just let it out, Jill. Let it go away."

He said it so kindly, and he didn't look away. He stared right into my eyes as if they didn't bother him a bit, as if they were normal and natural. Then he leaned down, his eyes not closing, and his mouth brushed mine.

I leapt guiltily, almost knocking foreheads with him, but his fingers tightened and I stilled, letting him touch my lips with his. As soon as I stopped struggling, one of his hands curled warm around my nape, and my mouth opened to his.

I had not been this close to anyone in so long. Not since Mikhail.

The smell of musk and male filled my nose, heat sliding down to detonate in my belly, my eyes fluttering closed as my fingers came up and wrapped in his hair. He pressed forward, his hands sliding down to flatten on my back, and I found myself with my back to the counters, balancing on one leg because I'd ended up wrapping the other one around him, his mouth open and greedy but curiously polite, as if he didn't want to press the kiss any further than I wanted.

As if he was *asking* me. He tasted like moonlight and the taint of whiskey passed from my tongue to his, came back laden with another, newer taste—the one we made together, a mixture of my own breath and someone else's.

My head tipped back. His mouth traveled down past my jawline, onto the curve of my throat, and hovered over my pulse. The low rumbling growl he gave out chattered the bottle against the counter and made the wood groan. The scar had turned hot and tight on my wrist under cold copper, and I realized I was naked under the T-shirt and his hands had roamed, and that I could feel the harsh material of his jeans against the inside of my thigh.

I turned into a statue. My breath stilled, stopped, and I waited for the violence to explode. I waited for pain, for the sharp strike of a hand against my cheek, for him to shove me to the floor, a kick catching me under the ribs with a sound like red fury. Red and yellow shapes tangled behind my eyelids, squeezed shut tight enough to ache.

Even with Mikhail I had sometimes frozen, despite his gentleness.

Saul froze too, a curious stillness, his warm hands flattened against my back and his face in my throat. I felt the hard prickle of a tooth through his lips, he'd paused right over my jugular.

Of course. That would be the most sensitive, most highly charged spot for a Were. The trust implied in letting his teeth near my throat was tremendous.

My fingers had turned to wood in the silky pelt of his hair.

My breath held itself as long as it could. He didn't move.

When I finally let the air free of my lungs with a small wounded sound, he stirred. Set me gently back on my feet, his arms still around me and my cheek pressed against his chest. The rumbling intensified, shaking through the channels of my veins, loosening my muscles, and calming the frantic racing inside my head. It felt safe to rest there, leaning against him, a safety I could never remember feeling anywhere else.

A safety I found I liked a little too much.

Cancel that. A *whole lot* too much. He was just a country-boy Were full of disdain and thinking he knew everything, looking down his nose at me for making a bargain that allowed me to fight better. If he wasn't an enemy, neither was he a friend.

Then why was he holding me? Why had he spent all day bumping into me, herding me around?

He'd saved me with my own knife.

Coherent thought returned. *What the fuck just happened?* My heart pounded against my ribs like an overcharged motor. *Jesus Christ, what the fuck is this? Weres don't...they never...I...*

I couldn't even finish a sentence inside my own head.

His arms tightened briefly, squeezing my breath out. "You go change," he said finally, as if it was a foregone conclusion that I would. "I'll finish dinner. You need some ballast in you." He let go of me, after taking one last long inhale in the vicinity of my hair.

Smelling me. Taking me deep in his lungs, marking me in his memory. Weres did that while tracking, I knew. It was an oddly intimate thing, and I wondered what it *meant*.

I dredged real deep for something smart to say. I settled for spluttering. "What the *fuck*—"

"Jill." He gave me one dark look, shaking his hair down over his eyes and glaring. "Go get changed. I'm making you dinner."

Stubborn endurance has always been enough for me—too much, sometimes. But this time my courage failed me. I fled the kitchen and headed for my bedroom, and by the time I got there the phone on my nightstand was shrilling.

I scooped it up. *Please don't let it be Perry.* "Yeah?"

"Kismet?" An unfamiliar male voice. "It's Clarke, from New York. You set us to do some digging about a disappeared 'breed named Cenci? Real blonde, lots of trouble?"

Relief curled inside me, hot and deep. It wasn't Perry. Of course, it could be bad news in its own right.

That's the trouble with being a hunter. Some days, it knocks the optimism right out of you.

"Yeah." I cleared my throat, repeated it. "Yeah, I did. Do you have anything, anything at all?"

"You won't believe this." Click of a lighter and a long inhale; Jonathan Clarke was a smoker despite being a hunter. You don't live long in this line of work without *some* kind of stress-reduction vice, I guess. "Her name's Cenci all right, but that's only half of it. Guess who her daddy is."

I just got almost killed and kissed by a Were. I think my threshold of disbelief is a lot lower than I started out tonight with. "I give up. Who?"

"Navoshtay Niv Arkady. Old Ark-and-Bark himself. There's more."

He's her father? The strength ran out of my legs. I sat down hard on the bed, the mattress squeaking faintly. Saul had made the bed, neatly, and I felt a moment's guilt at screwing up the pristine blankets.

This just keeps getting better. "Take it from the top, Jon. I'm listening."

Harp called in as I was scraping the last bit of grilled onions up from my plate. I snagged the phone with one hand, licking the fingers of my other hand clean and reaching down to yank at my boots. "Jill here."

"Jill, it's Harp. Glad you're home. Listen, I—"

"Clarke from New York called. I have an earful for you." *Boy, do I ever.*

"Save it to tell me in person. You and Saul need to hightail it down here. We've found what we think is the main nest."

My pulse quickened, my breathing shallowing out. Saul took the empty plate from my hand with a nod. He'd been quiet all through dinner, neither of us meeting the other's eyes, the only sounds the scrape of forks and knives.

The fact that his cooking was good even for a Were was merely incidental. Just like the fact that I was a lot less shaky once I had some ballast in me.

"Where are you?" I must have sounded different, because the Were's eyebrows shot up, and he cocked his head. I saw this in my peripheral vision, unwilling to look directly at him.

She gave me the address—a house down on the south border of Ridgefield, the edge of my territory. "We're keeping the press off, but that won't last long. When can you be here?"

I did a few rapid mental calculations. It was a thirty-minute drive. "I'll be there in fifteen. Is Monty there? Get the ranking officer to tell the traffic detail I'm going to break a few laws and to get someone to cut traffic for me. How many bodies do we have?"

"Four for sure, but I'm not certain about anything else. There's sorcery here, Jill. I hope like hell you have some good news."

Sorcery meant something they needed a hunter to look at, something possibly deadly. I finished pulling my boots on. "News, yes. Good, no. See you soon." I smacked the phone down so hard I was faintly surprised the plastic didn't crack, and looked up to find Saul's eyes on me.

There was no time for talking about anything other than the current crisis. I am such a coward I was actually *relieved.* "Saddle up, furboy. Let's roll."

CHAPTER 19

The Impala's engine cut off, its full-throated purr ceasing and the ticking of cooling metal taking its place. Saul managed to work his fingers free of the dashboard, and gave me a look qualifying as sardonic. "You're a menace," he said flatly, but I was already unbuckling myself. The windows were down all the way, and the sudden cessation of wind-roar was shocking.

"What, you don't like riding with girls in cars? I thought out on the Rez that was the main form of entertainment." *And having a touch of precognitive ability does help in traffic, you know.* I opened my door and stepped out into a predawn hush full of grayness. Prickling filled the air. We would have an autumn thunderstorm before long, the heat was already becoming close and dense.

"Riding I like. Committing suicide by automobile I don't." He actually did seem a little green, and that cheered me up immensely. He fell into step behind me.

The street was quiet and residential, with a few lush greenbelts taking advantage of the river's proximity. I habitually calculated angles of cover as we walked toward the flashing reds and blues, yellow crime-scene tape fluttering as they roped off the entire yard. Forensics was out in force, and I saw three white coroner's vans.

Christ. The banter wasn't easing my nerves. "You're still alive, aren't you? I hope you didn't leave fingermarks in my dash."

He was again way too close to me, almost bumping me as we walked along, perfectly coordinating his steps with mine. "Next time, *I* drive."

I don't think so. "Dream on. Nobody drives my baby but me."

"Your baby?" Again, that faint tone of grudging admiration.

I ran my tongue along the inside of my teeth, wishing my cheeks weren't flush-hot. What was the matter with me?

What was the matter with *him?*

"I rebuilt her," I said shortly. "I drive her."

"You rebuilt her?"

I stopped and rounded on him, my second spare leather trench coat swirling. He stopped as well, with perfect balance, not running into me or even stumbling. The stormlight was good to his face, and silver winked in one of his braids. I took a closer look— it was the twisted remains of the silver bracelet from Galina's, tied into his hair like the charms tied into mine with red thread.

Nameless fury worked up inside of me. I throttled it, kept my voice steady and even. "Look. I don't know what game you're playing, but it stops *here.* I've got a job to do, and the less I'm distracted the less people will die. I want this goddamn rogue *and* this goddamn hellbreed off my streets, and safely dead if at all possible. Whatever you're doing, *quit.* I don't have time for it."

He studied me for a few seconds, his eyes humanly depthless. Not like a hellbreed's at all. "I'm not playing a game."

Then what the hell just happened? Or is that some arcane Were protocol I don't know about? I don't hunt your kind, I don't know all their ins and outs. "Whatever it is, stop." I figured that covered about everything. "I have enough to deal with."

"I'm here to help." Was that a scowl? He looked away, at the plain two-story frame house being swarmed by Santa Luz's finest. "There's Harp."

Just like a goddamn Were, looking away and changing the subject. "Fine. Just stay off my back."

"Huh." It wasn't affirmative or negative, just a sound.

Goddamn Weres and their goddamn noncommittal noises.

I wished the heat in my cheeks would go away, took a deep breath and looked up to find Harp standing, fists on hips, on the porch. She looked tense and furious, the feathers in her braids fluttering and her jaw set.

Great. I ducked under the yellow tape, nodding at the uniform on duty—it was Willie the Mouse, who flinched when his eyes hit mine, his left hand coming up to touch his right shoulder. A Trader had taken a chunk out of him once, before I could get there and put it down in a welter of blood and screaming, not to mention the stink of roasted flesh because the apartment complex had been burning down around us.

So many of my memories are tinged with smoke.

And blood.

I dropped my eyes as Saul ducked under the yellow tape behind me. "He's with me, Willie." I pitched my voice low and soothing. "How's the shoulder?"

Mikhail had once rescued him from two Traders and an *arkeus.* That was before my time. Poor unlucky Willie.

"Still hurts sometimes, Jill. Thanks." He didn't sound thankful—he sounded like he'd prefer I didn't talk to him at all.

He'd needed a solid two years of therapy before he stopped waking up screaming, I'd heard. The chasm between us yawned wide.

But at least he was still alive. That was worth something, wasn't it?

A knot of forensic techs swarmed around a particular spot in the dry grass of the yard. I saw Foster's sleek ponytailed head; he nodded and pointed up at Harp, a quick sketch of a movement.

In other words, *I'll catch you later, go see the Feeb.*

"Hey, Harp. What's a girl like you doing in a place like this?" It bolted out of my mouth, and her quick smile was iron-tense, a mere flicker.

"The usual. Blood and chaos. Smells like you just had dinner." Her eyebrows lifted a bit. "Sorry to miss it."

The edges of her tan jacket fluttered a bit as I hopped up the steps and got a nose-watering dose of the smell from the open front door. Rogue Were, hellbreed, and death; the mixed reek scraped across my nerves and turned them even more raw. "It was the only nice part of the night, sweets. You won't believe who's in town."

"At this point I'd believe just about anything. Come inside, I want to show you something."

"Harp." I couldn't put it off any longer. "Navoshtay Niv Arkady's here from New York; I came across him while I was cleaning out a Trader hole. Perry's off making amends and smoothing the troubled waters, since Saul knifed Arkady and I clocked him with a sunsword. The hellbreed we're looking for—our pretty blonde girl—is Navoshtay Siv Cenci. Navoshtay's daughter." *And I am going to have hell to pay the next time I visit Perry. Maybe even sooner.*

Harp actually went pale. Her eyes flickered up to Saul, who made some slight movement, having climbed the steps after me. Maybe a shrug, since his coat creaked a little. He moved closer to me, looming behind me and actually bumping into me again, softly.

Harp's eyes got as big as the plates down at Micky's. I moved away, irritably, and peered in the front door. "And there's even more, Harp. Hang onto your hat, because this one is *weird*."

She still stared over my head at Saul. I waited a beat for her to give her next line—something like *well, life around you is never normal, Kismet*. But she didn't give it. Instead, she looked at Saul like she'd caught him eating babies.

The Were behind me responded by moving even closer, crowding me so I felt his chest touch my back. I stepped away, to my left, taking in the front door's white paint and two dead bolts. Whoever lived here had been cautious.

Fat lot of good it had done them.

Saul moved in on me again. "Quit it," I snapped over my shoulder. "What is *wrong* with you? Harp, did you hear me? The head hellbreed on the East Coast is in my city, and he's after his daughter. Who, I'm told, has been a very busy girl."

Harp shook her dark head, the feathers in her braids fluttering. Her mouth opened, shut as if she couldn't find the words.

I could relate. I dropped my other bombshell. "I also know why she's hanging around with Our Boy Carnivore. If another hunter hadn't told me I wouldn't believe it."

That seemed to shake her loose. "Jill—" But she stopped, still staring at Saul.

I've had about enough of this. It isn't like you, Harp. "Come on, Agent Smith. You show me yours, I'll tell you mine—and we might have a chance at stopping this thing."

Dominic greeted me with a nod. He crouched, low and easy, in front of the cellar door. I took in his stance and the alert shine to his eyes, the way he settled into immobility after the quick sharp movement.

He was standing guard in case the rogue came back to his little nest and found a bunch of humans here. I felt a chill trace down my spine at the thought.

The ground floor of the house was oddly pristine. Here in the kitchen, where the door to the cellar stood wide open, stairs going down and that smell belching up in waves, there were clean white countertops and a rack full of washed dishes with a thin layer of dust on them. A blue washrag lay folded over the arch of the faucet, dried stiff. The table was layered with papers. The garage, visible through a wide-open door leading off the kitchen, held two cars—one of them a minivan with car seats.

I didn't want to think about that.

The only sign of violence was one of the chairs pushed over backward and a single smear of dark liquid on the clean floor.

"Family of four," Dominic said when my eyes fastened on the chair. "Near as I can figure, someone opened the front door and got subdued, then was brought back here to where someone else was doing bills. Everything on the table's dated for last month. I think this family was the first to go down, and he's probably been dragging kills back here—there's another entrance to the cellar out back, Theron's out there. He's the one that found a trail in this neighborhood."

I nodded. Theron was the bartender at Micky's, a lean, dangerous Werepanther. Good backup, even if he was an arrogant twit. If he was out in the backyard, I didn't have to worry about the people out there. It was a relief to know.

Harp's voice came from the living room, slightly raised. Dominic's eyebrow twitched, an eloquently inquiring look expressed in a fraction of an inch.

"Don't ask me." I spread my hands, indicating innocence. "I don't know what the hell's going on. Your friend Saul seems to have a gift for pissing Harp off." *And I've got other problems.* "So there's car seats in the garage. What's upstairs?" *Please tell me I'm wrong. Tell me we've found the kids alive.*

"Three bedrooms. Two decorated for cubs, both with beds messed up like the little ones just got up for a drink of water." He tilted his head back slightly, indicating the cellar. His eyes glowed briefly, very sad. "My guess is, down there. I'd love to be wrong."

But it's not fucking likely, is it. I swallowed something suspiciously hot, tasting of bile. "Scene's been held for me?" *What else is down there, Dom? Drop the other shoe.*

The look he gave me qualified as scathing. "Of course. Harp and I took a look at it from the stairs, that's all. Something down there stinks of sorcery, and that's *your* job. There's enough in the yard and around the door to keep the humans busy for a while. Take your time."

My, that's awful sweet of you. But I just eased past him and through the door. Wooden steps went down, concrete walls dry-gleaming with oil under the gassy reek of bodies. The smell of dandruff and hot spoiled musk was eyewatering. I was glad I had stopped for a fresh copper cuff, the air itself was caustic.

Add the sweetish rot of hellbreed, and I suddenly wished very hard that I hadn't eaten dinner.

The memory of Saul's mouth on mine rose. I pushed it away with an almost-physical effort. Distraction was the last thing I needed. Shelves on my right held cans and jars—nonperishables, laid in for a rainy day. I caught sight of a can of Chef Boyardee and my stomach turned hard, thinking of two small rumpled beds upstairs.

My heart pounded thinly. *Of all the things about this job I hate, that's the worst. Kids are the* worst.

I wasn't the only one to feel that way. The hardest cases, and the ones the psych officers worked the hardest on, involved the very young. No matter how hardened or seasoned the cop, kid cases can cut you right down to bone and bleed you for months, if not forever, afterward.

I swallowed, my tongue sticking to the roof of my mouth. I kept an eye out for critters—they weren't likely down here in a concrete cube, but you never know.

The steps turned to the right, a one-eighty that slowly revealed a dusty disused cellar. In the back left corner, as far away from the stairs and the door to the backyard—a trapdoor, just like Auntie Em's—as possible, was a tangled mess of shapes.

Oh, God. White bone peeped through, glimmering in the dark. One electric bulb in the ceiling did nothing to dispel the darkness. A curtain of glaucous night shielded the corner, a shimmer like heat off pavement mixed with night's obscurity only pulling aside to show small glimpses of whatever lay beyond.

Tangled over the bodies was a sorcerous shell of concealment, laid with power and exquisite care. The shield drew tight, humming with alertness as my aura fluoresced in the ether, random points of brilliance swirling around me as the sea-urchin spikes of my personal borders poked through, sparked against the contamination of hellbreed, and retreated.

It nagged at me. Even with what Clarke had told me, something was wrong here. One instrument was out of tune, screwing up the whole symphony.

Deal with what you've got in front of you, Jill. Analyze later when the scene's safe.

The ruby warmed at my throat. Silver chimed in my hair, shifting and heating up.

I shut my dumb eye, my blue eye piercing the strings of sorcery, a shifting pattern of darkness and occasional bloody flashes. She did good work, this Cenci.

The copper cuff snapped free of my wrist of its own accord, tinkling down the stairs. The scar turned into a brand, wet heat tracing obscenely up my arm, following the branching channels of nerves and veins. I lifted my right hand, black fire twisting around my fingertips, crackling as I pulled etheric force through the scar and down my wrist, a low humming cycling through the concrete.

Pitch a levinbolt low enough, and you can actually shatter glass or work a hole in pavement. The drawback is, it takes a *lot* of energy—energy I had to burn now. One reason to be glad that I'd made my bargain with Perry, no matter how much I cursed it while I was in the Monde.

*Oh, very nice work. If I push there, it traps me. If I take it apart
here, the backlash knocks me down. Huh. You're a sneaky bitch,
aren't you? Daddy must have taught you well.*

I set my feet on the last stair. My coat flapped, a hot breeze lifting from nowhere, teasing my cheeks and the silver weighing
down my hair. Sparks crackled, Mikhail's ring burning on my
left hand, the ruby at my throat spitting again and again, warning
me.

Levinbolt flames swirled counterclockwise, coming to a tapered
point like a narwhal's horn. Cupped in my palm, the spire of etheric
energy trembled, cycling up to a moaning cry of torched and distressed air.

More, Jill. Give it more. The whisper burned under my conscious thoughts, my attention centered on the levinbolt straining
to wriggle free. It takes a particular relaxed fierceness to hold this
much energy still, corralling it to one's will; sorcery isn't for those
who can't relax and concentrate.

If Harp and Dominic had come down off the stairs, they would
have triggered the trap. I'd have been looking at a severely
wounded pair of Weres, maybe even critically damaged.

Good thing they've got me. I bent my knees, sinking down,
compressing myself. The levinbolt whined, my fingers scorching
where it pulled on the nerves and yearned to fly free. My coat
pooled behind me, clinks and clanks and sparks trembling in the
air as the silver in my ammo, knives, and jewelry responded to the
contamination of a hellbreed curse in the air, straining toward me
just as the bolt strained to escape my control.

Do it fast, Jill. Go for the quick tear.

I leapt, uncoiling, right hand flung forward, the bolt crackling
through the first few layers of the sorcerous shield and piercing,
stuck fast—then, *explosion,* all that contained force suddenly
finding itself free. Potential became kinetic, like a lightning bolt
lancing air and producing a sonic boom. The psychic thunderbolt
smashed the shield wide open, and I landed, driven to one knee by
the backlash of energy bouncing off concrete walls and buffeting
my aura. A shower of sparks fell from my hair, one huge bloody
point of light from the ruby at my throat, and I shook the deep hid-

eous noise out of my head. It was like the world's biggest gong
vibrating inside my skull.

Easy as cake, Jill. Your usual fine work.

A low thrumming growl slid under the ringing in my ears, my
right hand spread against the cold concrete floor, my leather-clad
knee soaking up a chill too. My coat pooled behind me, and I
raised my head slowly. Very slowly.

Oh, shit.

It hadn't been a shield to keep the bodies from being found. It
had been a protection laid on the rogue Were, sleeping in his nest
of meat and snapped bone.

He wasn't sleeping anymore.

His eyes were flat with beastshine in the dim light, and he
crouched on the slope of mounded bodies. He was halfway
between his animal form and human, neither one nor the other,
and as a result...well, most Weres are beautiful and graceful in
their human forms, and just as beautiful in their animal forms.
The state in-between is never someplace they linger, and it is just
as graceful as the rest of them—but subtly *wrong*. Wrong like a
nonhuman geometry. Wrong like a note no human instrument can
produce.

Wrong like a hellbreed's face, when they drop the mask of
humanity.

Wrong like something spoiled, gone rotten, all a Were's power
and glory thrown away for the lust of the hunt and the consumma-
tion of murder. That's what *going rogue* means.

I stared into the rogue's eyes for a long moment, the bizarre
insanity of its gaze terrible because of the near-humanity of its
suffering.

Then it leapt for me, and I had no time to jump free. A hunter
takes on hellbreed, that's true. But a Were gone rogue, gone berserk, is different. Just like for a Were, taking on a Trader is one
thing, but fighting a full-fledged 'breed is something else.

Rogue Weres move with the speed that pulls muscle free of
bone, a thoughtless scary speed married to weight and momentum
that isn't trackable like a hellbreed's tearing through space. On
most hunts, Weres run backup for hunters.

On a hunt for a rogue, hunters most definitely run backup for other Weres. Because if we don't, we tend to catch flak and die.

He collided with me, his claws out, the impact so immense I didn't even feel my ribs snap as I was flung against the concrete wall and into momentary, star-filled black unconsciousness.

CHAPTER 20

Shouts. Screams. The coughing roar of a Were in a rage. Cold concrete against my spinning, motionless body. A shattering sound, another scream, I was picked up and tossed again, bones snapping as I hit another unforgiving surface.

The pain crested over me in a wave, and I yanked instinctively at the scar, flesh scorching as for one vertiginous moment I *pulled* on every erg of etheric energy available to me. The print of Perry's lips on my flesh turned molten with sick heated delight, and I flung my hand out as the rogue came for me again, a bolt of pure power boiling up into the orange spectrum at its edges as it streaked through the potential-path in the air and smashed the rogue ass-over-teakettle into the knot of Weres suddenly crowding into the cellar's dinginess.

The lightbulb broke, smoking dustmotes of glass peppering the air. Sparks hissed and flew, the ruby at my throat singing a crackling note like a crystal wineglass stroked just right before it shatters. Agony raced down my arm, exploded in my chest, tore itself through my belly and detonated in my left leg, where the femur had snapped.

—*ohgodohgodgetupJillgetUP*—

I *pulled* on the scar again. Did Perry feel it, wherever he was?

Right then I didn't care, and it hurt too much for me to feel the queasiness that thought called up.

Bones melded together, all the pain of weeks compressed into a single moment as the scar hummed to itself, chuckling a bass note that sounded so much like Perry my skin turned to ice, great drops of sweat standing out and soaking what was left of my blood-soaked clothing. I coughed, a jet of bright blood from my lungs mixing with fluid as my rib cage snapped out to its proper dimensions, jagged ends of broken ribs sliding free of delicate tissue.

—*hurts it hurts, ohGod, it hurts*—I tried to get up, to fight, to strike back at the thing hurting me. To *meet* the pain head-on, to smash at it, batter it away.

Yet another personality quirk, and maybe the one that made Mikhail choose me. I keep fighting *long* past the point any sane person would throw up their hands and quit.

Snarling. More screams, shaking the house. Dirt pattered down. An explosion of noise, snapping wood, a high chilling wolf-cry of agony. The noise was incredible.

Get up, milaya. Mikhail's voice boomed and caromed through my head, echoing through a corridor of memory turned into a Möbius strip by agony. *Get on your feet, and fight.*

I made it to hands and knees. Felt for a gun with my left hand. My right was so hot I was afraid it would detonate bullets in the clip. A stupid fear, but I wasn't thinking straight.

A burst of fresh air blasted through the cellar, gray light flooding in. Shapes danced, the close thick reek suddenly returning all the stronger for the brief moment of freshness. Shadows fled out against the square of light.

I coughed, my eyes watering. Tears flew, and blood sprayed from my lips. *Losing a lot of the red stuff, Jill. Just think, the Red Cross could follow you around and make a killing. Get it, make a killing? Arf arf.*

Over that hysterical wash of panic, another thought, tolling in my head like a bell. *Get up. Get up and fight.*

"Jill." A familiar voice. Someone approaching, crouching down over me.

The gun came up, my shoulders hitting the wall. My boots scrabbled in blood. *My* blood, thick and slippery on the cracked concrete floor. Heaving breaths echoed as I shuddered on the knife-edge of murder. *Move. Fight back. Kill.*

The Glock pointed straight between Saul's eyes, less than an inch from his skin. I drew in huge gasping breaths, my fingers aching to clamp down on the trigger. Adrenaline sang in my mouth, pounded in my blood.

He didn't even blink. "You okay?" Looking past the gun like it wasn't even there. Like I wasn't crazed with fear and about to snap, sail right over the edge and fill him with silverjacket lead. A shot at this range would *kill* him, even if Weres aren't allergic to silver.

And oh, I ached to shoot something. Anything. When you live from one violent fight to the next, it becomes a habit. A *need* to pull the trigger, an instinctive, life-saving reflex. The animal in you clamors to strike out with claws, teeth, anything at hand.

He must have seen the murder in me. There was no way he could miss it.

Saul's eyes held mine for what seemed like eternity. Behind him, more swirling shapes coalesced. Other Weres. I heard a gasp, a murmur, and someone swore in a low fierce tone.

"It's okay, kitten." Saul's voice was even, soothing. "Everything's under control. It's all fine. It's all right."

My thumb came up. Clicked the hammer all the way back, eased it gently down. The small sound was very loud. The scar throbbed, full and flushed with wet poison heat. I heard a low sob, recognized too late it was my own voice.

Saul's fingers curled over the gun, pushed it aside. As if it was the most natural thing in the world, he took my shoulders and pulled me away from the wall. His arms folded around me, his purring rumble shaking through my bones again. "Easy," he whispered. "You okay? Say something."

My lips were cracked, my throat desert-dry. I heard another greased-skid muttering rumble of thunder in the distance.

I just got kicked around by a rogue Were. That's twice in twenty-four hours I should be dead. Dead. Even with the bargain, I would be dead. Rotting. Gone.

In Hell, probably. Almost certainly. That's where hunters end up, in Hell.

Or so the Church said. No Confession, no Communion, and no Heaven for those of us who come face to face with the nightside. The murders we commit and the foulness we witness remain with us even after death; it is a point of doctrine from 1427 onward. It hasn't ever changed, despite hunters' petitions.

Sometimes I wonder about that.

A shiver passed through me, muscles locking like a seizure. I pulled myself together with an effort that chilled fresh sweat on my skin. "Fuck," I whispered. "Where did he go? Where is he?"

Saul's weight shifted slightly, his arms tightening as soon as I spoke. "He bolted south. There's a full pack of Weres after him, Dominic went with them." His mouth twisted down for a moment, and my brain slammed into overdrive.

What's he doing here? He should be chasing the rogue. "Go." My lips were numb. "You're a tracker. Go."

An electric current bolted from his eyes to mine, something surfacing in his and shooting straight through my veins like a jolt of recoil. I almost flinched, the feeling was so strong. He should have gone after the rogue that killed his sister, but he'd stayed here to make sure I was all right.

Why?

I didn't know, and I didn't care. For that one moment, someone looked into my eyes and saw past every wall I'd ever built to protect myself. And I could swear I saw past every wall he'd ever built in his head too, and that something in me—something deep and buried, something bruised and battered but still strong—*recognized* him.

Knew him. Somehow.

What the hell?

"I'll be back." He rose in a swift wave, letting go of the gun, and was gone through the shattered door into the backyard, his shadow briefly made of black paper against the grayness of a thunderlit dawn. The air swirled with electricity.

I shut my eyes. *Storm coming. Probably hit this afternoon, I can feel the pressure shifting.*

Why did he do that?

The shrieking, gibbering animal part of me didn't care. Blood soughed in my veins, and my skin crackled with drying sweat and other slick drying fluids. I heard my pulse, clear and strong.

I was alive.

This is getting surreal even for me. And that's saying something.

"What the *fuck* is going on?" Harp's voice was loaded with a growl of its own, somehow all the more chilling because of the soft clear femininity of the tone. "Kismet? Care to clue me in?"

I heard my breath, harsh and jagged, leaned my head back against the freezing concrete of the wall. "Jon Clarke called from New York. He told me Navoshtay had trapped a Were for his own amusement, damaged him. But Navoshtay's daughter set the Were free and fled with him." My throat was raw, I tasted blood with the words. "We've got a major paranormal incident shaping up. God knows what she wants that Were for. And I've got a goddamn 'breed capable of a psychic nuke looking to make this more difficult than it has to be."

That was only half of what Jon had told me, but I knew better than to open my mouth about the rest of it.

That's bullshit, Jon. I'm surprised at you. The sick thump under my breastbone wouldn't stop hatching thin traces of nausea.

I have it on the best authority, Kismet. Somehow, Arkady's daughter bred with a rogue Were. She's pregnant, and her daddy's after her.

What authority do you have it on? I'd persisted. Too many stars were moving into alignment, and the constellation they were making was disturbing, to say the very least.

The best authority, Kiss. Watch your ass out there. There's no telling what will happen if this situation gets out of control.

The trouble was, it was already out of control. Were don't like hellbreed, and hellbreed don't like them. But Jon wouldn't tell me this if it wasn't true. Hunters don't lie about this sort of shit.

Even a little white lie can kill a hunter, and there are too few of us as it is.

I should have been screaming in fear or sobbing with the snap-back reaction of passing too close to death and clawing my way through once more. I *should* have been pushing myself to get up, clean myself off, and *do* something to stop this immense clusterfuck-in-progress.

Instead, I was thinking of Saul Dustcircle's eyes, and feeling the electricity that went through me at the memory of his skin on mine.

He *knew* me. Or for one brief, endless second he had seen right through me. It was the same thing. He had somehow recognized what I was, down at the bottom of my soul.

And he had still held me.

Get up, Jill. Get back on the horse. You don't have time for this.

Not while there were people dying and a rogue on the loose. Everything else could wait.

Cleaning up wasn't as bad as I'd feared. Most of the forensic techs had been in the front yard, poking at a suspicious patch of grass dying under the weight of a viscous, rapidly decaying fluid that might have been oil. I couldn't figure out what the liquid was, even after scanning it with my blue eye. It reeked of hellbreed and death, blackening the grass underneath. The techs took samples, but I didn't think they'd get anything. Hellbreed tissues break down quickly once they're damaged, and this stuff seemed no exception.

The rest of the cops hadn't seen the rogue shatter out of the cellar, or the collection of changed and unchanged Weres streaking after it.

Thank God for small favors.

The bodies in the cellar were being untangled by Forensics, gently and thoroughly. I couldn't see the cavalcade of blue rubberized bags going out the front door, but I heard it each time a coroner's van started up and the picture-flashes started popping. My skin would run with gooseflesh and I would repeat the promise to myself.

I will avenge you, whoever you are. I will grant you vengeance on the thing that did this to you. I left the copper cuff off, paying my penance with each eyewatering puff of stench striking across my sensitive nostrils.

I could even tell myself the hot water slicking my cheeks was just from the smell.

Harp leaned against the wall inside the shattered cellar door. I sat on the steps going up to free air and a day overcast with the promise of thunder, yellow-green stormlight drenching my shoulders from behind. She had settled into immobility, her eyes lambent with the weird light.

Mike Foster detached himself from the organized hive of activity and crossed over to us, peeling off his latex gloves. "You okay?" His sleek ponytail wasn't mussed, but his eyes were haunted, with dark circles to rival my own growing underneath.

"What's the count?" That wasn't what I meant. What I wanted to say was, *did you find the children? Tell me you didn't.*

"Thirteen." His eyes met mine, spoke for a long moment. "Two of them..." He didn't have to finish the sentence.

I made a slight movement, closed my eyes. The worst thought of all returned—that there had been dust on the counter and the dishes, and bills from last month on the table.

I should have known. I should have somehow saved them.

Mike sighed. "I think we've got everyone. We'll ID them if we can, there's no clothes or anything hanging around. That's weird."

Not so weird if a hellbreed is cleaning up afterward. It's like them to minimize the information you can get from a scene. "Not so weird." I hauled myself wearily to my feet. "Buzz me if you need me, 'kay?"

I wanted to howl and beat my head against the concrete. I wanted to take off blindly running south, after the rogue and the hunting pack of Weres trailing him. Hopefully he had already been brought to bay and dispatched.

Hopefully.

I rocked forward, standing up and opening my eyes. Foster, at the bottom of the steps, flinched as he met my gaze. The silver chimed in my hair, tinkling sweetly as leather creaked.

"Jill—" He stopped abruptly, tried again. "Be careful, okay? This is *bad*. The bodies, they've been..." His eyes cut over to Harp, and the sharp stink of human fear cut through the reek of death for a moment.

"Savaged," Harper said flatly. The feathers in her hair fluttered as she made a swift movement of distaste. "Chewed up. You'll find muscle mass gone and organs missing, as well as splintered bones."

Mike winced. His watch glittered as he reached up, raking his fingers through his glossy hair. "I wish your friends wouldn't tell me these things." He directed it at me.

I wish Pepper was back on duty. She had a higher tolerance for this sort of thing. Still, I couldn't blame Mike. This would bother any reasonable human being.

Should I be glad or upset that "reasonable" doesn't describe me? I almost shot Saul, and nothing I've done has turned out right on this job. I should have picked up on this long before now.

I reached out, blindly. Mike's hand met mine, and I squeezed briefly, gently. The scar pulsed on my wrist, sensing human flesh and high emotional distress. I reined myself in with a physical effort, more sweat slicking the waistband of my leather pants. Things would start chafing if I kept this up.

There was something in my throat, a difficulty like talking through mud. "Sorry, Mike. Give a call if you need me, and see the psych boys for some downers if you have to. Okay?"

"It's not me I'm worried about, Jill. It's you. You're looking a little worn out."

I wonder why. I made a face, freeing my fingers from his. "So they tell me. When the nightside slows down, I will too." I turned on my heel and was gone up the steps before he could respond.

Harp matched me step for step, and she waited until we were in the backyard before her fingers closed around my arm. "Jill."

I stopped, staring across the yard at the greenbelt behind the house. There were bushes back there, and a screen of trashwood trees. Dusty greens and grays ran together in front of my eyes, and I was suddenly sure it would be a good place to watch the house from. I caught no breath of *being* watched, but you don't live long as a hunter without checking the terrain.

Harp's fingers didn't loosen. She could break my arm without half trying, with a Were's strength.

Of course, I could heal in moments and repay her with interest.

What am I thinking? She's my friend, and she's a Were. I'm too close to the edge if I'm even thinking *like this.* But the engine in my head didn't stop turning over the probabilities, evaluating every single living thing around me.

When you can't turn that machine off, it's time to get some rest. Unless, of course, you *can't* rest because the bodies are piling up.

Harp didn't shake me, but I got the idea she wanted to. "What's going on?"

I tried not to feel relieved. "I wish I knew. I only have half the pieces of the—"

Her face went through frustration, a flash of anger, and settled on impatience. "No. I mean with you and Saul."

Dammit. I suppressed a guilty start, knew she would feel it anyway. "Don't know there either. You're the one who sicced him on me. Besides, he thinks I'm tainted."

Good one, Jill. Why did he swap spit with you, then? And so nicely, too. I felt the flush creeping up my cheeks again, couldn't stop it. Cursed inwardly.

"He apologized. He didn't understand, and you know what Rez Weres are like." Harp's tone was so dismissive I felt my teeth want to grind together.

"Not so much. I never worked with a Rez Were before." I pulled away from her hand, achieved exactly nothing. Felt the temptation to grab her wrist and lock it, give the quick jerk to dislocate and bring my knee up...

Calm down, Jill. She's not the enemy here. "Let go, Harp. I'm not in the mood."

"He's acting possessive." In her *you-are-being-dumb* tone.

So I played dumb. "Who?"

"Saul."

"Is that what it is." Then, mercifully, my pager went off. I dug with my right hand in my pocket and fished the damn thing out. "Let go. It's Galina." *Thank God it's her. Anyone else calling, it'd be likely to be another body in the streets. The Weres are chasing the rogue, and that just leaves this blonde hellbreed and her loving daddy to deal with.*

She gave up, letting go of my arm and making a short noise of annoyance. "Just be careful, Jill. Don't break his heart."

I cannot believe I am having this conversation with you. Why don't you keep him away from me? "Weres don't date humans, Harp." I swung away from her. "Now I'm going after that goddamn hellbreed. Buzz me if you need me."

"You're not exactly fully human anymore, Kismet." She had to raise her voice a little, and thunder underscored her words. I took a deep breath of the dusty green smell of impending rain and hunched my shoulders.

Yes I am, I wanted to shout back over my shoulder. *I am still human, and humans don't date Weres.*

Yeah, the snide little voice of my more sarcastic side piped up. *But rogue Weres don't work with hellbreed either. And hellbreed don't make bargains with hunters. Pigs are going to start flying any moment now.*

CHAPTER 21

Galina's shop was shut up tighter than an oyster, the sign turned to "closed" and the blinds on the front windows drawn. Her back door was closed and locked too, and the red-orange carapace of Sanctuary shielding wedded to the walls resounded uneasily, crackling with the charge in the air. The storm was coming in fast, breathless expectancy hanging thick under the clouds, pressing on pavement and hurrying people.

I knocked at Galina's red-painted back door for a long time, more uneasy than ever. I couldn't break in and poke around inside her house without dealing with the Sanctuary bindings, and if she wasn't answering she was either out or had retreated to her inner sanctum for some Work. The latter was most likely; Sancs don't often go abroad.

Then who the hell called me from here? And would Galina be out with a rogue Were on the streets? Not to mention the hellbreed action recently.

I thought about it, eyeing the porch roof over her back door.

A few moments later I was on the roof, and I cased it thoroughly, even sweeping behind the glass cube of the greenhouse where Galina grew all sorts of fun stuff. I mean, where else are you going to get your hellebore and mandrake, if not from your local Sanc?

I don't like this. Who called me? Where's Galina?

My boots creaked, dyed dark with dried blood. My coat flapped, lifting on stray breaths of breeze as wind flirted uneasily between earth and storm-laden sky. The scar pulsed, random little soundless chuckles of wet delight spilling up my arm from its puckered tissue.

Even the emergency hatch behind an AC unit was closed and stubborn. I moved to the edge of the roof and peered down the deserted street, not liking the feeling I was getting.

A slight prickling between my shoulder blades, as if I was being watched. Was it nerves? God knew I was having a little trouble with mental balance, lately. Getting almost-killed twice in one day can do that to you.

It's not the getting killed that's worrying you, Jill. It's a Were. Specifically, a Were who's "getting possessive," in Harp's immortal phrase.

It took a physical effort to get my mental train off *that* track. *Stay focused, Jill.*

I eased along the edge of the roof to peer down at the front of the store. Stray bits of paper rustled, skipping down the pavement. I caught a breath of diesel and a powerful hit of green-gray river water, and the ozone smell of approaching lightning. The street was deserted, lamps flickering into life in the gathering artificial twilight.

A glass and iron box a block up caught my eye, and my skin roughened instinctively. I felt cold all over, my breath shortening and my nipples peaking under my T-shirt, hard as chips of rock. *Phone booth. Galina's got her number stenciled on her front window, and my pager's not exactly a secret. I'm a goddamn idiot.*

The cloak of red-orange energy over the building shivered restively, like a horse.

I froze.

The click of a hammer cocking sounded very loud behind me.

"Don't move," Navoshtay Siv Cenci said, in a pleasant, light tone. "Keep facing the street, hunter."

I've been shot before, hellbreed. But I stayed where I was, my back alive with gooseflesh and the knowledge that a 'breed who had nearly eviscerated me and made mincemeat out of Harp was behind me, with a gun. The click sounded like a large-caliber model. Or maybe that was just my nerves again.

Behind me. She had to have come up from the porch roof. Had she been watching from down the street? How had she gotten my pager number? It wasn't a secret, but still—

Galina had better be inside her sanctum. If you've touched her I will kill you. Rage worked its way up inside me. Subsided with an effort that left me shaking, struggling to think clearly through the adrenaline haze. It wasn't logical—even a hellbreed couldn't harm a Sanc inside her own House. Galina was too smart to go outside, wasn't she?

Wasn't she?

I waited. *Patience,* milaya. *It is soft and quiet that catches mouse.*

Only this mouse had the drop on me, and a gun to boot.

"You've killed to find me. To flush me out of safety." Cenci's voice was calm and pleasant, with only the tinkling wrongness of it to tell me *hellbreed.* I could sense it now, the contamination in the air around her. Silver shifted in my hair, heating up, blue light running under its surface. Thunder roiled faroff, coming closer.

"The Were's being chased," I said to the street. "He'll be killed mercifully. You, however, are a whole different ball of wax." *Two children. And Jimmy Cheung, you bitch. Cleaning up? What kind of game are you playing?*

The silence behind me took on a predatory cast, the pause of a shark in the moment just after blood hits the water and right before frenzy. Galina's building thrummed underneath me, quivering with unease. Slowly waking up, catching the current of bloodlust passing between my unprotected back and the hellbreed behind me.

"I should kill you," Navoshtay Siv Cenci whispered. "We don't want trouble. I just wanted to be left alone to do what I have to do. Is that so much to ask?"

Left alone? "When your father's Navoshtay Niv Arkady? *Alone* doesn't happen, sweetcheeks. You're 'breed. You know that."

"So you're going to do his dirty work." Did her voice actually break? Amazing. I gathered myself. My right hand curled loosely around the whip-handle.

Keep talking, bitch. I'm a few seconds away from changing your whole religion for good. "I don't do dirty work. I avenge my people. Like the rookie cop you put in the hospital." *He'll never be right again, even with therapy and the best of care. You ruined a life, and you did it so easily.* I eased my weight forward onto the balls of my feet, a millimeter at a time.

"They shot at him." She dismissed it, I could almost envision her shrugging. "I was quick, I was *merciful* as I could be. But you,

you're doing my *father's* dirty work." Yes, a definite break in her sweet, corrupt voice. Did she use it to hook her prey, like Arkady used his black, black eyes?

I rose, the flesh on my back crawling with the knowledge that a bullet might be coming any moment. If she was aiming for my head, this might all be over very quickly. I would find out if hunters really went to Hell when they finally got unlucky. "I'm doing what I should, to protect the citizens of my city. I'm a *hunter,* hellspawn. It's what I *do.*"

Another thought slid through my head. *She's not shooting me. Why? She's not acting like a hellbreed.*

Fat sizzling drops began to patter down dispiritedly. They made stinging quarter-sized dollops on the dusty, hot rooftop. Sweat pricked under my arms and at the small of my back, dried blood crackling as my clothes moved on the breeze. My fingers shifted slightly, ever so slightly, on the whip handle.

"I told you not to move." Cool, now. She'd made up her mind what she was going to do. Maybe I'd been premature in thinking she wasn't acting like a hellspawn. Maybe she was just playing with me, cat with mouse.

In other words, bad luck for you, Jill. But if you're a mouse, you're a mouse with claws. I polished my very best *fuck you* tone and flung it at her. "What are you going to do? If you shoot me, other hunters will take my place. Your daddy's in town, and he's pissed off because you stole his Were toy. There's a major incident shaping up over him even *having* a Were toy—"

"He isn't my father's!" she screamed. "He's *mine!*"

I spun, diving, the whip flashing free and my left-hand gun clearing leather. The whip's ribbon curled through the air, screaming, and struck across her face as she hung in midair, claws outstretched, her own gun falling unheeded to the rooftop as mine spoke. Time turned to gelatin, closing around me as I *moved.* Black hellbreed ichor flew in a flattening arc before she smashed into me, catching me in midair and throwing us both over the edge.

Wind whistled, and we hung in freefall, the silver in my hair spitting and crackling. She struck me across the cheekbone, a good punch if she'd had all or even some of her weight behind it, a hot gush of pain as her claws buried themselves in my chest, tangling in my ribs before she could jerk her wrist down and spill my guts. Back arching, scream bursting through my blood-slick lips, we fell in a thrashing tangle of tortured air and a sudden booming as the protections on Galina's house woke in a sheet of blinding crimson and orange flame.

She sure doesn't act like a pregnant woman. Maybe it's hormones. The thought was tinged with deep screaming hilarity over a well of panic that training shoved aside.

Cenci thrashed, but I had one hand fisted in her long platinum hair and I brought the gun up, pistol-whipping her across the face.

Falling and Fighting 101: brace someone's head when you're bouncing a gun off them. It hurts more.

More black ichor flew, spattering my skin in stinging drops. I got in another two shots on the way down before we hit pavement, a snapping in the structures of my skeleton—again—and her claws were torn free, a hot gush of blood following them. *No wonder I need steak.* Another flash of a thought, there and gone in a moment that paradoxically seemed to last forever. *I'm losing iron left and right.*

Cenci rolled free, dazed and shaking her head. The smell of scorching rose, and Galina's protections flamed again, dilating like a camera shutter. A scream of toasted air boiled away from the shop, the plate-glass window in front bowing and making a wobbling noise.

The sky opened its floodgates on us both.

I rolled, *get away get away* shaking my right arm out as the scar boiled with acid, desire-laced pain and shot a jolt of power up my arm, sinking into veins and jacking through my system like a needle-load of something deadly. A sharp clarity bolted through me, I made it to my knees with both guns out, the whip slithering along the pavement with its metal bits tinkling as it landed, dropped like a bad habit.

My first two bullets caught her, but she collided with me again. There was no technique, it was sheer blind rage and overwhelming strength—which is a hellbreed's downfall.

They get so used to bullying humans around, they don't use their strength effectively. Hunters are trained to *never* stop thinking about how to most efficiently fuck up the nightsider giving us trouble right *now.*

Reflex had loosened my knees and let go of my right-hand gun. I socked my hip into her midriff, bootsoles squealing on pavement and a long trail of sparks hanging in midair behind her, and I didn't need to do much, just grab a fistful of her and *shove* to deflect a critical millimeter or two, her blind rush providing all the impetus necessary to throw her directly into Galina's plate-glass window.

BOOM.

A wall of concussive force slammed outward, tossing me like a rag doll across the street and into the brick facing opposite. Heat bloomed, and superheated air broke the sound barrier, thunder rolling down the street. I slid down to the pavement, coughing and retching, and heard stumbling footsteps as the hellbreed fled.

Galina's defenses settled, rumbling through the pavement like a subway. Sanctuary rule numero uno: do *not* throw yourself at the Sanctuary's walls. The protections respond without any conscious effort, and the response is ... energetic, to say the least.

Other footsteps, softer ones, approaching me at what seemed a very slow rate next to the rapid pitter-patter of little hellbreed feet. Noise returned through the white buzzing of my dazed ears. Rain pounded my skin.

"—ogodjillareyou—"

I am getting really tired of being flung around. I shook my head. Warm trickles of blood slid down my neck from my ears, dripped from my nose. I blinked more warm wetness out of my eyes. The pain came then, a great rolling breaker of it as my body coped with the damage.

I'm racking up one hell of a bill with Perry. Then, a small, noiseless thought: *I wish Saul was here. I'd like to see him.*

When had I started being happy to see a disdainful country-boy Were? When he'd kissed me? Or when he'd stayed to make sure I was still breathing after tangling with a rogue?

You've got bigger problems, Jill. Get up and start fighting. It's what you know how to do. So do it.

I blinked and looked up. Galina's hot mortal fingers pressed against my clammy forehead. "Get *up!*" she screamed, and thunder rattled. Coruscating energy sparkled in the air around her—

she was actually *dividing her Sanctuary spell,* protecting me as ripples of power boomed and echoed, potential-paths opening as lightning blurred down, the sound like cannonades. Smoke boiled up, and the rain began to slash down in earnest.

I made it to my feet. Leaned on Galina as she half-dragged my heavy self—muscle-dense, hellbreed-strong, weighed down with leather and metal and ammo—across the street under lashing rain slicking down her hair and mine. She smacked the door to her shop open, and the bell tinkled merrily as she dragged me into safety. I collapsed on the floor near her glassed-in counter, next to a bookcase and a rack of candles. My body curled into a ball, and I decided on the spot to spend the next few hours shaking and drinking some of her spiced rum.

Alas, such was not meant to be. Because as soon as I shut my eyes and sagged against the floor, really wanting to shut the world out for a while, the bell tinkled again, and a soundless step filled the shop. The protections thrummed, a high mounting note of energy just aching to be unleashed.

Galina spoke with the sonorousness of church bells chorusing morning in some ancient, smoke-decked city. "Take one more step toward her, Pericles, and you will be thrown back to Hell screaming." She paused, the heavy static-breathlessness of power not abating one iota. "And while you're at it, close the door."

Perry wrapped his long pale fingers around the steaming mug. It was peppermint tea, the vapor rising from it assuming angular screaming shapes before dissipating. Galina swabbed at the blood on my cheek while rain smashed against the skylight overhead. Her marcel waves were tousled and she moved with quick, sharp birdlike movements, her necklace glinting at odd moments as the protections fluctuated.

I took another jolt of rum. The scar on my wrist throbbed. Perry's blue eyes lingered on my throat, and I was suddenly very glad Galina had made him sit at the other end of her long scrubbed-pine kitchen table.

"The Weres lost him, you know." His words were underscored with a booming rattle of thunder, and every once in a while a small mouselike tremor would run under the surface of his skin, flickering and gone in a heartbeat as whatever shape lurked under his semblance of bland, almost-handsome male humanity responded to the raw energy in the air. Still, even Perry didn't dare make trouble in a Sanctuary, and he sat very still where Galina told him to. "He slipped their hunt. Rogues sometimes do, I'm told."

Not often, Perry. As a matter of fact, hardly ever. Just one more thing about this case that isn't what it should be. I set the bottle down on the table with a click. The scar flushed, a knot of poisoned delight. I wished I'd tucked a spare copper cuff in my coat along with everything else, instead of leaving them at home. "I'm getting blood on your floor." I sounded mournful. "I'm sorry, Galina."

"No problem. I'm just glad I came out in time to see what was happening." She grinned, her slanted eyes dancing with merriment for a moment before she sobered, glancing back at Perry.

Who sipped his tea, quietly. And sat still.

Hallelujah and pass the ammunition, there's a single place where Perry won't fuck with me.

The only trouble was, I couldn't stay here. I had too much to do.

Galina's eyes caught mine. Her fingers were gentle as she sponged more blood from my face. Silver buzzed in my hair like a rattlesnake's tail, responding to the humming tension of the storm overhead and the echoes of the Sanctuary protections' lunge into wakefulness, reverberating in the ether.

I took another jolt of rum. "I'm fine, sweets. Thanks." *I had no idea you could divide your Sanc protections. Still, that's not the question I'd like answered most right now. Right now I want to know who called me, and where Cenci was hiding. I should have felt her in the neighborhood, especially after driving her off Harp. I should have fucking smelled her.*

Which meant either she could cloak herself from me more effectively than any other hellbreed, or she hadn't been waiting for me in the neighborhood.

Galina made a small derisive sound. "Your pupils are all over the place, Jill. I think you have a concussion." She wrung out the washcloth, water dyed thin crimson squeezing through her fingers. "What were you doing on my roof?" The question was casual, but her shoulders were a little too tight.

I don't even know what I was doing on your roof. "Someone— I'm betting it was this hellbreed Cenci—buzzed me. Maybe it was to lure me away from Harp and Dom, get me where she could at least put me out of commission for a while. Probably so she could get back and move her Were buddy." *The spell in the cellar was laid to protect and conceal him, neatest trick of the week. This just keeps getting more tangled the deeper I dig.* My eyes flickered across the table to Perry's, interested and bright over the rim of his cup. "Any light you can shed on this, Perry?"

He set the mug down, a slight smile playing over the corners of his lips. His linen suit was, of course, pristine and unwrinkled, though he must have been outside in the downpour. "I've interceded with Arkady for you. As long as we keep you out of his way, I think we can avoid further unpleasantness."

A flickering tremor slid through his face, as if something had shifted just under the skin. His grin widened a trifle as he adjusted his cuffs, his forgettable face turning sharp and predatory for a single moment.

Which doesn't explain what you're doing here. My skin chilled. Galina's mouth drew down sourly. She carried the bowl over to the sink, glanced at the water washing the window outside, and dumped the bloody mess down the drain. Her silence was full of the kind of loathing most people associate with pale wriggling things in spoiled meat.

"Very kind of you." I picked up the bottle, took another swig. Then, because not to do it would be weak, I met his eyes again. The scar turned to an agonized infected burning burrowing into bone, a reminder that he could tweak it into pain or pleasure as his mood called for.

"A pleasure." The smile widened, white teeth exposed. Electric light shone mellow in his sandy-pale hair; a flash of lightning outside bleached everything briefly. "Especially when done for my Kiss."

Do not call me that, Perry. I hate that. Again, I didn't say it. "Why did he come all the way from New York to fetch his daughter instead of sending you a request to have her sent back? You are, after all, the ranking hellbreed in the city."

His eyes hooded. "Especially since you recently thinned our ranks so drastically. You're gaining quite a reputation for impulsiveness." The sibilants slid over the scar, each sending a thread of soft poisoned delight into my flesh. The old carrot-and-stick approach.

I wondered which he thought worked better, the reward or the punishment.

"You're not answering my question." *That gives me wriggle room on our bargain.* Cautious relief warred with fresh unease.

A single shrug, infinitely evocative of nothing, pulled up his shoulders. His eyes flicked away, roving the surfaces of the kitchen, leaving a thin vibration of slime on everything they touched. "Other families and their dirty laundry hold no interest for me. He is here, he wants his earthborn progeny, under our laws she belongs to him." Perry's gaze flicked back to me, and the faint smile he had settled into now seemed a grimace of distaste.

"Earthborn progeny" means Navoshtay impregnated a Trader. A shiver of loathing went up my back, jingling the silver in my hair. It still didn't answer why Navoshtay was here to collect her personally. By what I knew of hellbreed customs, Cenci was born out of a human and therefore not pure 'breed. She had the same "legal" rights as a chair or a coffee mug and theoretically not as much power as a pure 'breed; it should have been a simple case of Perry cooperating with me to send her back trussed up like a pig on a spit, with an apple in her mouth—if it was necessary to send her back *alive,* that is. If he could control the unruly hellbreed of Santa Luz and the surrounding metro areas, he could apply enough pressure to find one troublemaking 'breed female and kick her ass over the river.

Then again, she was powerful. *Disturbingly* powerful. Navoshtay's spawn in a body that might be old enough to burn out some of its mortality...the thought was nightmare-worthy, and that's saying something. Besides, I'd never seen Perry unveil the extent of his power, not even when he marked me.

Sometimes I let myself think he might just be tricky instead of strong.

Perry paused for a moment, then went on, silkily. "She is making quite some trouble with the *human* law—of which you are still a part—and you have made it adequately clear that the trouble will not stop if she remains in my territory. There is no profit to keeping her here and angering Arkady. For all these reasons, I could care less *why* he wants her. My interest is that this matter be concluded quickly, so it doesn't interfere with my own pleasures more than it has already."

It was a nice pat explanation. Too bad I didn't buy it. It was *not* like Perry to merely obey another hellbreed, no matter how powerful. Hellbreed don't do obedience and they don't do charity. Their net of feudal obligation runs on one thing: fear. There's no trust among 'breed. They turn on each other at a moment's notice, whenever they think the benefit outweighs the risk.

Thank God it does, too. Otherwise they *might* rule the world, instead of just hanging in the dark corners and buying power and privilege.

"Well, thanks for telling me. I'll call you if I need you." I lifted the rum bottle again, touched it to my lips.

Perry's eyes fastened hungrily on the bottle's mouth, and by default on mine. "Are you dismissing me, my dearest?" One pale eyebrow raised.

Oh, goddammit, I am so *not in the mood for this.* "Why are you here?"

Perry slid off his seat. He looked about to say something, but Galina turned from the sink and regarded him, level and easy, her mouth a straight line.

"Don't make me, hellspawn." Her tone was just as even as her mouth.

He ignored her, but he didn't move forward. "I came to tell you the Weres lost their rogue. I *also* came to tell you Arkady will not pursue you. As long as you stay out of his sight, he will... forgive... your impoliteness."

"And you just *happened* to be in the neighborhood when I came by?" I tossed it at him as if it didn't matter. *Who did call me down here, Perry? If it was Cenci, why didn't she shoot me? And if it was you... that would mean that you knew she was in this area.* My brain pawed lightly at the problem, turned it over, and dropped it in disgust. I was too tired, blunted both by adrenaline fatigue and the shock of almost-dying so many times in a row. I needed some rest before I could even begin untangling this out.

"I can always find you, my dear." The grin widened again,

white teeth showing their sharp pearly edges. I thought of shark's teeth when I saw him smile like that. "Think on that, for a while. See you soon." A nod to Galina, his sandy hair falling over his forehead in a soft wave—and he was gone, the Sanctuary shields settling back into taut humming alertness as the bell on the shop door downstairs tinkled.

I let out a sigh and put my forehead down on the smooth wood of the table. It felt good, cool against fevered flesh. *Great. Just... great.* Dried blood crackled on my skin, but my hair was still wet from rain.

"Every time I talk to him I feel slimy." She shuddered, a movement I could sense without looking. The shields shivered too, responding. "I don't know how you stand it."

I don't. Not very well, at least. I'm so scared he's going to get in, Galina. The more he plays with my head, the better he gets at taking me apart.

The better he got at that, the more dangerous it was for me and everyone I protected. "I don't stand for much. Thanks for bringing me in." I closed my eyes, tried to relax my shoulders. They wouldn't go down, tight and taut and aching.

The faucet started to gurgle. Was she refilling the bowl? She wouldn't be able to dab much more blood off me with just the one washcloth. "I had to," she said quietly. "We can't afford to lose you."

I took refuge in bleak humor. "I'd hate to be lost." Thunder boomed again, the storm slacking despite the massive disturbance of the roused Sanctuary shields that had contributed to the instability of the weather pattern. You can always tell when a Sanc gets pissed off, it gets rainy over their little castles.

"Seriously, Jill. Perry was just up the street, I sensed him as soon as I hit my doorstep. He was standing around, waiting."

I lifted my head, bracing my chin on both hands and slumping in the chair. She shut the water off, brought the bowl to the table, and dipped the washcloth in again.

"Up the street?" I turned this over in my head and got exactly nowhere with it, again. *He was waiting. If he knew Cenci was waiting here too...*

What the fuck is going on?

"I wonder if he was going to ride in to save you." Her touch was gentle as she sponged at the crusted blood along my hairline. "Or if *he* lured you down here in the first place."

Me too. My face wrinkled up, hard. I tasted blood and the sourness of failure. "Thank you. I was trying not to think that out loud."

"Just one more service I provide. You want something to eat?"

"More rum, if you've got it." I finally succeeded in pushing my shoulders down a little, unstringing the nervous tension in them. "Then I've got to go home. I'm calling it a day."

CHAPTER 22

My pager was battered and busted despite its padded pocket. The lightning hadn't helped; even insulated electronics can have a little problem when you start messing around with potential-paths in thunderstorms. I had a spare at home, courtesy of the Santa Luz Police Department, and I needed more ammo anyway.

And—I'll admit it—I was feeling a little shaky.

Cancel that. A *lot* shaky.

I pulled through silver curtains of rain into the garage, was out of the car in a heartbeat, and walked through the utility room. It felt good to be home, for the first five seconds.

Then I realized the entire place was buzzing and resounding. Unhappy Weres will do that.

I didn't blame them for being upset. If they'd lost the rogue they were likely to be a little *more* than upset. They'd be downright cranky. Which meant more food. It's a wonder they weren't all butterballs. Damn Weres.

Of course, their metabolisms run high and hot, like mine, and the *change* is metabolically expensive. I just had a hellbreed scar working on forcing my body to heal fast enough to stand up to the abuse I was taking.

I was hanging up my coat when I discovered they were arguing, and not quietly either. The acoustics of my home are good for a *reason,* I like to know when even a roach is scuttling in the walls.

Not that I have a roach problem. Sorcery is *occasionally* a practical thing.

"How am I going to tell your mother this?" Harp's voice, raised as it seldom was, edged like an axe and flung at someone.

"You won't have to." Saul Dustcircle's tone was quieter, but no less sharp. I hadn't heard this particular tone from him before, and I was glad of it. "I am not a kit, Harper. I'll tell her my damn self, like I should."

"What are you going to *do?*" Harp hit a pitch usually only reserved for a screaming-meemie fit at Dominic during a bad stakeout or shadowing. I couldn't remember ever hearing her sound this upset, even that time they came out to help Mikhail deal with the hellbreed who *used* to run Santa Luz.

The one who had declared it open season on Weres, and did his best to turn the barrio into a death-hole. I hadn't been allowed out onto the streets during that, since I'd barely started my training. But I'd heard plenty, and seen enough of it to fill in most of the blanks afterward—especially in my nightmares.

Saul's voice, again. "I'm going to do what I *should,* for once. Don't push it, Smith. I've made up my mind."

"You're a stubborn, arrogant, self-centered—"

I came around the corner out of the utility room to find Dominic leaning against the wall in the short hallway. His hair was pulled back into its leather-wrapped club, but a single tendril fell in his face, a sure sign of exhaustion. He nodded and laid one long finger over his lips, then made a pushing-down motion with his hand.

In other words, *stay out of this one, Jill. It's Harp on the rampage again.*

"That's *enough.*" I almost didn't recognize Saul's voice. A touch of growl to it shook the walls and rattled the *ikon* of the Virgin hung in the hall, a gift to Mikhail from Father Gui over at Sacred Grace Seminary. I'd only heard this tone from a Were once or twice, usually an alpha snarling at a pack member who'd stepped out of line in a big way. "I didn't ask for your editorial. I did not ask you what you thought. I told you what I'm going to do, and that's final. I'm of age, I'm legal, and I've made up my god-damn mind. End of story."

Harp changed tactics. "Your sister—"

"Don't you dare." Saul's whisper was more effective than a shout. "Don't bring the dead into the business of the living. You know better."

Dominic saw his moment and took it. "Hey, Jill." He didn't have to say it very loudly, they all probably knew I was here. That's the drawback to good acoustics; everyone knows when I'm at home.

Unless, of course, I don't want them to.

I folded my arms to disguise the way my hands were shaking. Dried blood crackled in my hair and along my hairline as I lifted an eyebrow. "Heard the rogue slipped through."

"Only a matter of time. Weres are patrolling the entire city. When we flush him again, it'll be the last run he'll ever have." His dark eyes traveled down my body, and his nostrils flared a little. "You look awful. What happened?" He jerked a thumb at the end of the hall and lifted both eyebrows, an eloquently silent warning. Good old Dominic.

"Got tangled up with our rogue's girlfriend. Tossed her into a Sanctuary's window." *With Perry waiting down the street, for some nefarious purpose, no doubt.* I didn't mention that part. I also didn't mention that I'd been lured down there by one of them, and I wasn't sure yet which one.

Dominic actually laughed, a mellow, relaxed sound. He had a nice face, attractive in a strong-jawed way. His sidearm was briefly visible as he reached up to tuck the one stray strand of hair behind his ear, an absently graceful motion. "You have all the fun. I just ran my ass off after a rogue who seems to know how to disappear."

"Yeah, well, it's been rough all 'round today." I followed him out into the south end of the living room, wishing the house was empty so I could start shedding clothes. A shower sounded *really* good right about now. Along with a nap, and a case of hard booze— and a flamethrower to take care of some unruly hellbreed.

Harp dropped down on my couch, pale with anger. Even the feathers in her hair seemed bleached, and they were slightly askew—just as shocking, in its way, as Dominic's mussed hair. They were both so contained and precise that the small imperfections blared like a bullhorn.

Saul, his arms crossed over his chest, dropped his hands to his sides. His face was pale and drawn under his coppery coloring, and his eyes were live coals, more like a cat's than I'd seen before. He looked literally spitting mad as he glared at Harp, and I had the sudden mental image of a housecat with every hair on end, eyeing a dog. Since they were both feline Weres, the image was even funnier.

I managed not to laugh. But it was a close call.

Saul's eyes met mine, and the entire world stopped for a moment.

It was still there. That electric sense of *contact,* as if he knew something about me. Saw something about me, something nobody—even Mikhail—had ever bothered to look for.

It wasn't fair. What gave him the right to look at me like that?

"You okay?" Saul's gaze didn't move, but he would have had to be blind not to see that I'd been dipped in blood and air-dried, then dumped in again and run through a downpour once or twice.

Rain beat at the roof, splashing and overflowing the gutters. We would have flash floods out in the desert, and maybe a brief blossoming. Greased ball bearings of thunder fell through the roulette wheels in the sky. Maybe God was gambling with human lives again, hoping for a better turnout.

"Been worse." I seemed to have lost most of my breath. *I wish he'd stop staring at me like that.* "You?"

"Been better." The corner of his mouth quirked up. I could feel it in my own lips.

Oh, yeah. Something strange is going on here. I got a good deep breath in. We looked at each other. I could almost feel a taut line humming between us—me leaning back away from the connection, him shifting slightly forward, pursuing it.

"You hungry?" The fur had gone down, and his tone softened.

I still got the idea that wasn't what he was really asking.

"I could do with a bite." I didn't look away. I got the idea that wasn't what I'd really answered.

"I'm on it." He turned sharply on his heel, his coat flaring briefly open. Stopped. Swung back, as if he'd forgotten something. "I'm glad you're all right," he said, abruptly. Like a challenge.

Not now. Don't pick a fight with me now. "Me too." I could have slapped myself, it was such a stupid answer. I was *trying* to be conciliatory, a new skill for me. "I'm glad you're okay, too. I mean. Yeah."

Who said you couldn't teach an old hunter new tricks?

Dominic made a slight muffled noise. When I swung around to look at him he wore an angel's innocent face, his mouth pressed down tamely and his eyes roaming away, searching for something to fix on.

"You two." Harp leaned back on the couch, the curve of her throat exposed and her arm flung over her eyes. A single feather fluttered out of her hair, came to rest on the orange Naugahyde, and I suffered a deep acute flash of shame for the shabbiness of my house. "Can we please have some answers here? What the *fuck* is going on?"

Just like the forensic techs; she didn't deal well with this kind of uncertainty either.

I took a deep breath. Saul's eyes were very deep, very dark, and quiet.

I dropped the bomb. "I saw Cenci, at Galina's. She didn't initially try to shoot me." That got me everyone's attention and a full ten seconds of silence, which I broke by dropping the other shoe. "I think she might need help. I think she and the rogue are together, and I have it on good authority that the 'breed female's pregnant. She might be carrying a hybrid."

CHAPTER 23

Harp shook her head. "I don't believe it. It's *not possible*."

What's that Sherlock Holmes thing about the impossible? "It's only a theory." I gulped another mouthful of scorching amber alcohol. The smell of chicken frying wafted under the green oily curtain of rain and the ozone of lightning strikes. "You've got to admit, it fits better than anything else we've got. It also explains why Navoshtay's hot to trot out here and drag her home personally. I hear he's big into experimentation."

We were at the breakfast bar. Saul moved around the kitchen, each step graceful as a dance. He'd shed his coat, and I tried not to watch the movement of muscle under his black T-shirt.

Harp knocked back her glass of Jim Beam and frowned into the dregs. "Experimentation." She shuddered, mussed feathers quivering in her glossy hair. "Someone should kill that son of a bitch."

Yeah, someone should. But right now he's further down on my list than you'd think. "It's been tried. Several times. Not very successfully, I might add."

"Why is he experimenting? And for what? A hybrid? Assuming that's even possible, genetically speaking." Dominic set his beer down, stretched his hands out with fingers interlaced, stretching. His ponytail lay tame against his neck, raveling down his back now that it was free of the leather thongs.

"There's legends about Were females raped by 'breed." My mouth felt dry and clumsy, even mentioning it. "It could be Navoshtay's looking to find the truth of those legends."

"There *is* no truth to them." Harp moved, a sudden sharp twitch like an irritated cat. "Besides, we're human. They're not."

"Still…" Dominic drummed his fingers on the counter, thoughtfully. "Navoshtay's a sadist. Who knows what his real reason is for this…experiment? Assuming it is one, and we're not just going down the garden path."

"Who knows why hellbreed do anything?" I muttered, staring into my glass. My eyes weren't focusing properly. Exhaustion weighed down every limb.

"Hunters." Harp didn't sound mollified. If anything, she was sharper than ever.

If we knew that much, we wouldn't have people vanishing into the nightside. "Even the best hunter can only make an educated guess, Harp. Don't ride me." I reined in the flare of irritation. She didn't mean a word of it, she was just frustrated and probably as tired as me.

That got through to her. She sighed, leaning forward and resting her chin on her hand. I could smell the sharp iron-tang of dissatisfaction mixed with her peppery female musk. "I'm sorry. I just...we *had* him, and he slipped through our fingers. More people are going to die, and all I can do is sit around and *wait*."

"A rogue Were runs on instinct. He shouldn't be this hard to predict *or* catch." Saul set a plate in front of me, and another in front of Harp. "Eat, both of you. Don't sharpen your claws on each other, they'll wear down."

I stared at the wheel of food in front of me. Fried chicken, new potatoes with rosemary, a small mountain of greens, and actual biscuits. I could *smell* the iron in the greens, craving waking up behind my palate. I'd lost a lot of blood.

Dominic made a small sound of pleasure as Saul handed him a plate.

Everyone blessedly shut up, which gave me a moment to think. *We've got a rogue who isn't behaving, really, like a rogue should. We have a hellbreed covering his tracks and trying like hell to keep him away from Navoshtay—not that I blame her. I wouldn't want my worst enemy trapped in one of Arkady's games.*

Well, maybe Perry. That would be nice, and I would sleep a whole hell of a lot better. The colors on the plate blurred together as my eyes narrowed, both of them trying to pierce through time and matter to find the pattern, catch the rhythm and anticipate my opponent's next move.

Opponent? No. Prey.

Still, something was bothering me.

You're doing my father's dirty work....He's mine. Odd words for a hellbreed. Clarke swore she was pregnant, and swore he had it on good authority.

Pregnant with *what?* Another one of her father's experiments? Dark stories were whispered about Navoshtay, even darker than usual horror tales hunters like to swap. Most hunters are men, and love to bullshit endlessly over brewskis.

Stories about New York's oldest hellbreed were *always* whispered, though. Even Mikhail had referred to him as "one scary motherfucker, *milaya.*" Nobody wanted to talk much about Navoshtay. I was frankly surprised Clarke had called me back so soon.

If there's something a hunter won't talk directly about, you *know* it's bad news. Something a hunter won't mention unless it's daylight and the doors are bolted is the worst news around.

Pregnant with what?

Do I really want to know?

And who lured me down to Galina's, and why? Why is Navoshtay here to pick up his bastard daughter himself? And last but certainly not least, why is she protecting the Were? That's what she's doing. It's the only way her actions make any shit-for-sense. The kaleidoscope of events shifted this way and that as I tried to figure out what the pattern was—or even where the blank parts in the pattern fell enough to give me a glimpse of the underlying cause of this whole huge mess.

Saul's voice broke my trance. "Jill? You don't like it?"

"Huh?" I surfaced, blinking irritably. My skin crawled with sweat, the residue of rain, and dried blood. I suddenly wanted a hot shower and a long uninterrupted thinking-session.

"I thought you'd probably like the chicken." He leaned on the counter, his dark eyes level with mine because he was bending down, hunching his broad shoulders. The silver bracelet lay tangled in one of his braids, winking wickedly at me, as if it knew a secret. "You look a little pale, kitten."

"Oh. No, I was just thinking."

The silver glittered, sharp darts of light. Why was he wearing it?

"About what?" he persisted.

Well, if you want to hear it out loud I might as well. It might help me think. "About how this doesn't add up, any of it. All I have is one question after another, and the deeper I get the more weirdness crops up. By now I should be getting some *answers,* not more goddamn questions. Which can only mean one thing."

He nodded, took a hit off his beer. A Corona, and he'd even rubbed the mouth of the bottle with a slice of lime. He'd make someone a fine wife someday. "What's that?"

"It means I'm barking up the wrong trees. It *also* means someone's lying to me." I picked up my fork, took a mouthful of butter-drenched potatoes. *My God. Weres can usually cook, but this is* really *good.*

"Do you know who?"

I wish. The pattern still refused to make sense. "No. But I know what about."

"What about, then?" Soft, logical, reasonable, as if he'd done this before, giving me the questions to help me shape everything inside my head out loud.

I began with the central question. "About what exactly is going on between Cenci and this Were. Who doesn't even have a name yet, and that's another thing that bothers me. His kin should be looking for him too. You said the first murder was out in Massachusetts, but I'm willing to bet it wasn't. Harp, I need you to get on the horn with your boss and get them tracking all the kills following a certain profile."

"You really think we've been off-base?" Harp took a gigantic bite of fried chicken. She must have been hungry, and Weres need more protein than the rest of us.

My brain settled into functioning again. It was going to be a short-lived burst of productivity—I needed some rest in the worst way. "I don't think you've been off-base. I think you've been misled. Navoshtay's capable of hushing some things up on the state level but might not have his pretty fingers inside the Martindale Squad. Though I wouldn't put it past him. If there's something he doesn't want us to find out, it's going to be in New York. Have them liaise with Clarke and see what they dig up, and for God's sake give the hunters out there some protection while they do it."

"It's a good idea." Dominic's tone said just the opposite. "How much of this is based on what that hellbreed told you?"

"Practically nothing," I admitted. *It's what Perry didn't tell me that has me curious.* "Which is why I'm probably on the right track." Thunder muttered softly behind my words, echoing in the warehouse's spaces. Windows vibrated a little, bouncing under the sound.

Harp finished chewing. "So what are you going to do next?"

The only thing I can. I braced myself. "Call on Perry to set up a meet for me. I'm going to do my best to drag something useful out of Navoshtay. *Before* then, though, I'm going to do something I haven't done since Mikhail was alive."

The feathers in her hair fluttered as she made a sharp restless movement. She visibly restrained herself from waving a denuded chicken bone at me by sheer force of will. "What, go out for a movie? You're killing me here, Jill."

I winced. *I wish you wouldn't say things like that.* Picking up a chicken wing, I bit into it. Chewed thoughtfully, and swallowed. Licked my fingers, and stared at the white meat under the crust of breading. "I'm going to go *between*."

No sound except rain dripping, splashing through the gutters, swirling on the roof. "You're going to what?" Saul said it very quietly, as if he didn't understand.

He probably didn't. Harp had gone still. I took another huge bite of chicken, stalling for time. Then indicated my blue eye with a quick sketch of a gesture, still dangling the chicken. "I came back from Hell with a sort-of-gift. I've got a dumb eye and a smart eye. One can see the normal world. The other sees *below* and *between*. If I need to, I can see more of the *between*. All it takes is blood." *And since I've spilled so much already, I might as well.* I let out a soft sigh. "I just need someone to hold the other end of the line for me while I go down. Mikhail's not here, and I doubt Perry can be trusted with that. Maybe Galina, or Avery."

"I'll do it." Saul's tone had stayed soft, but there was an edge to it. "If you're really determined to do something so risky."

I don't think I'll let you hold the other end of that line for me, Were. I don't know you enough. "Nobody involved in this is going to tell me the truth, and none of my guesses satisfy me." I laid my fork down. "The rogue's going to kill someone else. Or *she* is. Or Navoshtay. I want the killing to stop."

"But...*between*." Harp, out of all of them, sounded like she understood what I was talking about. "Jill, I don't know if that's such a good idea."

What about me facing down both Perry and Navoshtay? *Between I can handle. Hellbreed who each want to take a bite out of me I might have a little trouble with.* "Screw *good idea*. I want *results*." I stared at my plate some more, wondering how on earth I was going to get the food in me. "And I want 'em yesterday."

"You won't get anywhere on an empty stomach." Apparently Saul had decided to get all Jewish-mother on me. "It won't stay hot forever, either."

I picked up my fork again. *If I go* between *I'll probably lose everything I ever felt like eating in my life. Not to mention dealing with Perry and what he's going to ask in return for setting up this meet. Might as well enjoy something while I can.* "Guess not," I mumbled.

"You're not really intending on..." Dominic took a quick mouthful of potatoes when my eyes met his. He also shut up in a hurry.

The warehouse clattered with the sound of rain and the static of tense, unhappy Weres. *I'm not exactly happy about this idea either, guys.* "If I don't do it, who will? I'm the resident hunter."

"You should take better care of yourself." But Saul dropped his eyes, and the words didn't have the usual sting.

"Hard to do when I'm running from one goddamn thing to the next." I settled down and applied myself to my plate. "But I'll keep it in mind. Maybe I'll even learn how to cook."

For some reason, both Harper and Dominic laughed their fool furry Were asses off at that. Dom laughed so hard he almost choked on a potato. It's a damn good thing he didn't spit it across the kitchen.

Harp and Dom headed back to their hotel room, needing a change of clothes and some sleep. Even Weres get tired.

I had other plans.

I started dialing Perry's number three times, hanging up in the middle each time. I dialed *four* times before I could let it ring through without hanging up.

Getting braver all the time, eh, Jill?

I told that voice inside my head to go away. I didn't think it would, and I was right.

One ring. Two. Three. The shadows of rain reflected all through the room, ghostly dapples against the wall and my skin, a mottling like hellbreed contagion in an aura.

My aura. The scar turned hot and hurtful, straining in anticipation. My pulse thundered so loud I almost couldn't hear the ringtone, kept my breathing even only by sheer stubbornness.

No, that's not true. My throat had closed to a pinhole, that's why my breathing was shallow. I shouldn't have been doing this, I was too tired. I was going to make a mistake.

Mistakes are not allowed, Jill.

He picked up. "Hello." A silky, smooth, bland voice that raised both my hackles and gooseflesh the size of eggs on my arms.

My mouth was bone-dry. Dry as a chickenbone in the desert. Dry as my palms were slick and wet. Still, I sounded good. Steady, even. "Perry."

"Oh, my dear. I've waited ages for you to call me." His voice crackled through phone wires, diving underground to come up and bleed into my ear like snakes aiming for my brain. He chuckled, a warm pleased sound, and I felt condensation collecting on my skin again, the touch of a scaled, rough tongue too flexible to be human *or* animal.

"Can the sentiment, Pericles. I want you to set up a meet for me." The words came out hard and fast, just as if I wasn't scared out of my mind. "With Navoshtay Niv Arkady."

Silence, crackling like lightning. I got the idea he didn't think too much of the request.

Tough luck, hellbreed. "I've got questions that need answering. This is *my* town, after all. You'll set up the meet and keep my skin whole through it. It'll count toward the time I owe you. And you'll keep your nasty little maggot fingers off me the whole time, too."

More silence. When he spoke, it was the rasping of sharkskin against the palms of a drowning diver. "If I am to perform this miracle, it will *not* count toward what you owe me. That's ridiculous, my dear."

A hot jet of nasty satisfaction curled through me. *He didn't say no outright. Thank you, God.* I tossed the dice. "Ridiculous or not, it's what's going to happen. You're not coming clean about something, Pericles. That violates our agreement. You can either be in violation, or you can set up the meet and have it count toward my balance."

More silence. I prayed I just hadn't opened up a can of worms, and I further prayed he wasn't thinking up a lovely way to get back at me for outwitting him this once.

I don't care. I'll put up with it. The important thing is to stop the killing. My palms ran with fear-stink sweat, a trickle of ice sliding down my back. I couldn't tell if it was sweat or merely dread. I did not close my eyes—I didn't want to imagine him on the other end of the phone.

The shadows dappling my bare arms had all turned angular, though the water falling on the skylight hadn't changed its shape.

"Very well." Sharp and curt, the words were knives. "I shall arrange it, and go to some trouble to ensure your safety. I will further allow you some leeway on your repayment. Don't think you've avoided me, my dearest. I do this because it pleases me."

You do this because you think you can worm your way into my head a little more, and because you are *in violation—you* haven't *come clean with me. I've won this round.* "Go borrow a quarter and call someone who cares. Call me when you've got the meet set up. And Perry?"

A long exhalation of hot diseased air I could almost smell vibrated over the phone line. My skin flushed with heat, then chilled, pearly drops of sweat re-wetting my torn, dirty, blood-stained clothes.

"Yes?" Quiet, but with an edge.

I suppressed the urge to scream-laugh like a maniac. A terrified maniac with one hand on the trigger and the gun under her chin.

The laughter receded, and when I spoke I was steady. "The next time you lure me into a setup with a mad hellbreed I'll send you back home, and it won't be a pretty trip."

"I was watching over you, Jillian. Protecting my very *dear* investment." Each word frosted with black ice. Thunder boomed overhead, more lightning crackling. It was turning out to be a hell of a night.

Sure you were. "Yeah. Fine fucking job you did too, since a Sanctuary had to rescue me."

"You are still alive. Don't press your fine luck, hunter. I like this conversation less and less." His tone had dropped from a tenor to a baritone, the throbbing of Helletöng rubbing hurtfully underneath. The warning was clear.

He's already mad, you might as well. I couldn't help myself. "Poor little hellbreed. I could almost pity you." Then I slammed the phone down, before he could respond.

My legs trembled. I sat down hard on my bed, my knees spilling out to either side and my arms turning to wet noodles, every muscle shuddering and rubbery. My pulse beat high and thin in my throat. A sharp bloody noise trembled on my lips, burst free, and echoed like the voice of a bird battering at the side of a cage.

An iron cage, with horsehair cushions and old rusty stains crusting the elaborate scrollwork, while sick remembered pain roiled through my nerves and the scar puckered and prickled, tingling.

You did it. Good job. Very fine work, Jill. Now stop shaking. Stop it.

My room was dark except for the reflections of rippling water covering the walls, stippling my forearms. The shadows had relaxed, no longer full of sharp edges. Gooseflesh remained, hard and cold, swelling up through my flesh like a disease.

Are you listening, God? I was actually wringing my hands like some bargain-basement Lady Macbeth. *It's me, Jill Kismet. I just pulled the tail of a huge sleeping dog. I'll be lucky to get out of this without losing a few more gallons of blood. Not to mention a few pounds of flesh.*

There was a small sound, like an indrawn breath or a restless movement. My nerves were scraped so raw I almost flinched.

"How much did you hear?" At least my voice was still steady. I had to hold myself very still, denying the urge to reach for a gun.

A patch of wall near the door rippled. He laid aside the camouflage trick, the one Weres use to keep from being seen by ordinary humans. But I could see the blurring of the real world, with its strings of energy, underneath the mere refraction of light.

If I'd just kept to that little skill and told Perry to go fuck himself when he offered that bargain, would I still be alive? I'd certainly be a lot more cautious—and there were a lot of people who might be dead instead of just traumatized.

Was it worth it?

"I smelled fear." Saul's voice was quiet. "That was the hellbreed? The one you made a bargain with?"

My fingers knotted together. *If he makes one snotty comment, I swear to God I'll ... what? What will I do? Something I'll regret. Make him go away.*

That was the goddamn trouble. I was unpredictable even to myself when Perry started playing with me. And just because I'd come away the winner in this round didn't mean anything. Next time would be just as uncertain.

I brushed my lips with a dry tongue, wished the spit in my mouth would come back. "Just leave it alone." *Just leave me alone. All I want is to lie down and shiver for a bit. I'm getting a little sick of the merry-go-round.*

He paced into the room, one slow step at a time. "You're shaking."

No shit, Sherlock. "Really? I hadn't noticed. Leave me alone. Go bake some cookies or something."

"Did he scare you like this before the bargain?" Saul sounded curious. The marred light slid over him, his eyes glinting a little as he sank down into an easy crouch, halfway between the door and the bed, not getting too close. For once, observing my personal space.

I shut my eyes. The darkness was not comforting. *Go the fuck away.* "Of course he did. But Mikhail ..."

"Your teacher." Soft and easy, the same tone I suspected he'd use on a frightened animal.

Well, I was certainly one half that description, wasn't I. The other half ... well, who knew? You had to be a little bit of an animal to work this job. "I loved him." My voice broke. My fingers ached, I tried to yank them apart and couldn't. "I still do. But he's gone. I wasn't strong enough or fast enough when it counted, even after the goddamn bargain. And now—" My voice rose. "Now I've got this mess on my hands and nothing's going right and I can't even keep my people from being killed in the streets and my God, there were two *kids* and the scene was a month old, they've been here for at least three weeks if not the whole goddamn month and I didn't know, I've been so busy but there were *kids,* for Christ's sake, just *children,* fucking *children*—" The words spiraled up into a gasp that wasn't a scream because I bit it back, swallowing it. Pushing it down, pushing it away.

It didn't want to go. It had been waiting a long time, this cheated howl. For six months at least, ever since I'd stood beside my teacher's pyre and felt the chill wind against my tear-slick cheeks, as the sobs I couldn't let go bolted down into my stomach and turned into a steady red flame of rage. Against hellbreed, against Sorrows, against Mikhail—yes, I committed that sin. I raged against my teacher for leaving me alone.

But most of all, I turned that blowtorch of agonized grief on myself. Because I had failed to save him.

And now, here I was.

"Shhhh." Saul was on the bed next to me. I flinched, throwing up an elbow—but he caught the strike with one broad hand, shoved it down without missing a beat. His arms circled me, a cage I wanted even as I leaned away from it. "Let it out. Let it go."

"I *can't.*" Heat and water slicked my cheeks. A sob broke the second word halfway, and I went rigid, leaning away from him. "I've got w-work to d-do tonight—"

More hellbreed holes to torch. Because tonight's as good a night as any to do a little murder in the name of getting Perry's voice out of my head. I don't c-care if I'm too t-tired—

The thought trailed off into a hoarse gasp as he pulled me off-center, into the shelter of warmth and the sound of someone else's pulse. Were filled my nose, a musky boy scent mixed in with something that was one of a kind, his, unique. When had I started recognizing that smell?

An even bigger question—when had I started liking it? When had it become *safe,* as safe as Mikhail's long-gone odor of pepper, leather, vodka, cordite, and foreign skin?

That was what broke me, finally. The remembered smell of my teacher, a powerful sensory memory of the only man who had ever protected me. Gone forever now, buried with him, nothing of that ephemeral imprint of a soul remaining except in my faltering human recollection.

My cold, comfortless, pitiless memory of everything I would rather forget.

I clamped my jaw down over the sobs. Swallowed them one by one as they rose, juddering me like an earthquake. My own personal set of seizures, rocking me off the face of the earth. I made no sound. He was silent too, not even thrumming the deep hum Weres use for wounded animals. He stroked my hair, silver chiming and tinkling; slid his hand under the heavy weight and cupped my nape, his thumb moving soothingly just under my ear. He simply breathed, and held me.

The shakes quieted bit by bit. Thunder in the distance. There would be flash floods out in the desert, the gullies and channels cut through Santa Luz would be full for once, liquid pumping through the city's dry veins. The simple fact was, there was nothing I could do tonight, even if I wanted to. If I went *between* in this state I'd get lost, my focus gone. If I went down into a hellbreed hole I'd end up getting myself scorched. I was too tired, too nerve-strung, and too goddamn edgy.

I'd just hit the wall, big-time.

Finally I rested against Saul, awkward, my upper body twisted and my cheek pressed against his shoulder. His hand had moved down from my nape, stroking my back evenly. Stopped, his fingers playing with the arch of a rib. Came back to my spine, tracing muscle definition through my T-shirt.

"I don't even like you," I whispered mournfully into his shoulder. Could have kicked myself, taking a deep breath of him. Then one more. Maybe just one more. *You do much more of this, Jill, and you're not going to want to stop.*

He didn't take offense. Maybe he even understood. "Give it time. I'm told I grow on people."

"Why are you doing this?" I squeezed my eyes shut until starbursts of red and gold burst, my blue eye still seeing the complicated strings of energy in his aura that shouted, *Were.*

A shrug, careful not to dislodge me. "Because you need it. Because I want to." A careful tone, giving nothing away. "Good enough for now?"

Not nearly good enough. I don't even know what it is you're doing. You're fucking up my head and I need to be clear for this. "You need to stop." I couldn't make the words louder than a whisper. "I can't afford this." *I can't afford any of this.*

"No strings, no payment, no bargains. I'm not hellbreed." Was that a new coolness in his tone?

I hoped so, and I didn't hope so. "I didn't—"

"Shut up." No anger, just flat finality. His pulse beat steady under my cheek.

I did. He held me, and for a while it was enough. Long enough for me to promise myself a hundred times that this next breath I took of him would be the last—and to break that promise, each and every time.

CHAPTER 24

Y*ou spend a lot of time on rooftops as a hunter. The high ground is always best, it's another cardinal law.*

Of course, when you're tracking someone else who hangs out on the roof as a matter of habit, it can get a bit tricky. But my quarry didn't even look up. He glided through shadow and streetlamp light, flickering through belts of orange glow, pausing only to catch the rhythm of a street before sliding along on the tangent least likely to draw notice.

When you have the preternatural sensitivity of a hellbreed, you can afford to stay far back. But the scar burned and prickled so much, the welter of sensation so deep and terrible each time, Mikhail had suggested covering it up. Galina had copper cuffs, and they seemed to work just fine ... but I could still hear the slight scrape of Mikhail's boots against concrete, his pulse hammering. I could almost taste his pheromones on the air, a lingering trail of phosphorescence.

I hung back, just at the very edge of his sensing range. But he wasn't watching for a tail—who would follow him?

Nobody except a stupid girl, that's who. Just finished with her training, and curious about where her teacher had taken to disappearing so frequently. Curiosity might have killed the cat, but satisfaction brought it back—that was one of Val's sayings.

I tried not to think about Val.

The new coat made a slight flapping noise and I cursed silently, stopping still. But my teacher didn't even break stride. He had a bounce in his step, and plunged into a network of alleys at the fringe of the barrio.

What was out here for him? I fell further back, following him only as a faint faraway song, more a pressure against sensitive ear membranes than music.

It was wonderful, and I couldn't wait to surprise my teacher with this new dimension to the mark we'd bargained so hard for. Although how I could do that without him knowing I'd tracked him ... that was the question.

I was so busy thinking about it I almost stepped over the silent edge of Mikhail's field of awareness. He had stopped in a deep well of shadow in the lee of an alley, and the air itself listened when he told it to.

Silence folded itself around me, my heartbeat smoothing out. I dropped into a crouch and drew that silence like a blanket around my shoulders. It was a trick he himself taught me, and the small burst of pride inside my chest from performing it so successfully warred with caution and growing unease. What was he doing?

Did it matter? He had a right to privacy, didn't he? That was why he wasn't sleeping in the same bed with me anymore. I had my own room and my own blankets now.

A slim shadow unmelded itself from the end of the alley. I would have held my breath, but training had me in its grip—you do not rob yourself of the advantage of oxygen while you're on a rooftop watching a shadow in an alley. You just don't.

She swayed toward him, blue silk whispering, and my mouth gaped open, both to provide me with soft shallow breaths and also so the shock could escape my throat in a soundless puff. Long dark hair and pale, pale skin, she was willow-graceful and must have smelled of incense and honey.

Under that smell of female attractiveness was an edge. It was rusty, blotted with old iron blood, and somehow wrong. My left eye twitched and watered, seeing the strings under the surface of the world resonate in response to sorcerous pulsing.

Whoever she was, she wasn't wholly human. But Mikhail stood still, light gleaming in his pallid hair, as she swayed toward him, moving so supple and soft I could imagine anything but legs under her skirts. A faint murmur reached me, satin-soft; she was talking to him.

My hackles rose.

Mikhail reached for her like a drowning man grabbing at buoyant wreckage, and they drew back into the alley's shadow. The clink of his belt buckle unloosing under those pale fingers was as loud as a shot to my tender ears, and I looked away, my face and ears burning with a shame that poured down my throat in a river of bitterness.

The soft sounds—her murmurs, his gasping for breath, the wet sound of lips and tongues meeting—tore across my eardrums like copper spines. Heat and shame alternated with burning cold, laid on my skin like a heavy fur coat. The scar prickled, running with gleeful vicious pain.

Was it my anger? Or was it that I was even now, nailed to the edge of this rooftop in an easy crouch, obeying my training and staying quiet and still as an adder under a rock?

Mikhail's little snake under the rock. The trouble was, there were more things under this rock than just snakes.

I eased back, one step at a time, but not quickly enough to escape hearing the climax. I knew that full-throated hitch in Mikhail's breathing, the body brought to bay, the way he would stiffen and sometimes drive his teeth into my shoulder to muffle any sound.

Training doesn't stop in the bedroom, either.

I thought it was because of the mark. *The thought came from nowhere, rising to fill my head like bad gas in a mineshaft.* I thought he didn't want me because of the scar.

A hard, cold truth surfaced underneath it. Is he Trading? That doesn't look like a hellbreed. First you've got to find out what it is, Jill. How would you do that?

I knew how. First a visit to Hutch, the man with the library of rare texts. Then dropping by Galina's and casually, oh so casually, asking a few questions.

Then what? What the hell was I thinking? He was my teacher.

I eased away. Soundless, even my coat didn't flap. Alternating hot and cold waves started at my crown and ran through to my soles. I was burning and freezing to death at once, but my body kept moving, training becoming instinct.

I did not run blindly. I just kept moving through the city, leaping from roof to roof with my coat flaring behind me, no sound except a huff of effort when I landed, etheric force pulled tingling through the flushed hard knot of the scar until I ended up under the granite Jesus atop Sisters of Mercy, hunched over, arms crossed tight and squeezing down to hold my heaving ribs in. Hot salt water slicked my cheeks, and now that I was out of the danger zone I heard soft weak sounds spilling from my throat.

I was sobbing.

The terrible thing was, I swallowed each sob, and they sounded like a woman in the ultimate crisis of sex, helpless shudders racking me. Each sound was a weakness, and reminded me of my teacher's body clasped against something in a dark alley, the stabbing motions of any cheap john taking a hooker against the wall.

The shame was worse than the anger, because both were marks of how I'd failed once more to be what a man needed. If Mikhail was Trading, how could I trust him? How could he trust me, with a hellbreed scar turned into a hard knot of corruption on the inside of my wrist?

I never told anyone, but that was the moment I truly became a hunter. Because I suddenly knew I could not even rely on my teacher—if he was Trading with something inhuman, he was a question mark until I figured out what was going on. He had taught me well, and the logic was inescapable. He was hiding something, and I wouldn't be able to rest until I knew what it was.

Until the rock was lifted and I saw the pale squirming things underneath.

I had not been an innocent when he found me, but the last dregs of whatever innocence I had left me under the granite Jesus. Because even while I cried, I was planning.

The tears would not last nearly long enough.

CHAPTER 25

I flipped on the radio next morning to hear the bad news, and only relaxed a little when no messages or news of murders came in. Autumn floods had arrived with a vengeance, and the rain lasted long enough to spring a leak in my ceiling. I stuck a large plastic tub I used for soaking blood out of leather under the silvery drops and promptly forgot about it. I had other things to worry about.

Galina was regretful. "I can't, Jill. I've got serious Work to do in my sanctum for the next three days, I'm closed down and tapped out. I would, but this is for the shields, and—"

I said I understood. And I did.

Avery was a bust too. "The exorcisms are kicking my ass. I'd slip, Jill. I'm not strong enough and you know it. Eva and Benito are out too, we had to sweep the whole city last night. It's turning into a madhouse out here."

Guilt, a hot rank bubble, rose in my throat. "I'm working on it, Ave."

He made a short sound of annoyance. Behind him, phones rang and someone shouted something. It sounded like he was up in Vice, probably bullshitting with his buddy Lefty Perez. "Since when do you stop working on it? Can the martyr trip, Jill. Clear your head out and get this bastard sewn up so we can have that beer together."

I made my goodbyes and hung up, chewing at my bottom lip. Saul handed me a cup of coffee. "No breakfast?" he asked for the third time.

My stomach clenched into an iron fist. "Not before something like this."

"I told you I'd anchor you. I wouldn't be much of a tracker if I couldn't." He'd showered, and his hair lay glistening-dark against his shoulders except for the twin braids on either side. It was a good look for him, framing the classic purity of his cheekbones, balancing out the line of his jaw. He wore the same T-shirt, and I wondered how light he traveled. I hadn't seen a suitcase yet.

"I don't know you that well. No offense."

An easy shrug, as if I couldn't offend him. "None taken, but it looks like I'm all you've got. Harp's not a tracker, and Dom's her mate."

In other words, she wouldn't like it if Dom got close enough to anchor me. I could call Theron, I supposed. I could even scare up a few more people if I had to, including Father Guillermo down at Sacred Grace.

But Gui wasn't strong enough for something like this. Anyone else I could call in would be a risk—and *at* risk, not only because I'd be vulnerable, but because the process itself was so dangerous.

I studied Saul in the fall of sunlight through the skylights. It was pale, washed-clean light, fresh and bled white by the storm last night. The weather report said the storms were moving in, coming from a ridge out in the desert meeting another ridge coming up the Rio Luz's broad slow muscular bends. We'd have heat lightning tonight and more rain tomorrow when the weather finished rolling up like a parade of barrio low-riders.

Saul's jaw was set, his eyes sleepless and fierce. The silver twisted tighter against one of his damp braids pulling the hair out of his face. I didn't ask him where he'd slept last night, because my bed had smelled like both of us this morning. I smelled a little like him too, the tang of Were mixing with cordite and silver and leather, and the faint trace of hellbreed and death that clung to my skin. It was a heady mix.

The bracelet was unrecognizable now, twining through his hair like a morning-glory vine through a fence. I stared at the gleaming metal for a moment, memory boiling up under my skin.

He paused in the act of taking a sip from his own coffee cup. Steam drifted up, touching his face. "What?"

The blonde hair, and the red hair, twisting around each other. I set my coffee cup down and bounced to my feet from the rumpled bed. I moved in on him so fast I half expected him to flinch, but he kept still, watching me. His eyes were very dark, and very deep.

The silver was warm from his heat. I touched the metal, running my fingers over the tight curves married to the silky texture of wet hair. "Did you do this? Make it bend like this?"

"It happened." He didn't move, but I sensed a shrug. "It happens. So what?" The faintest hint of a challenge, his chin lifting just a fraction. Mulishly defiant, and a startlingly young look for a Were so contained. How old *was* he?

I ran my tongue along the inside of my teeth, shelving the question. Something else bothered me, the shape of an idea just under the blanket of my consciousness.

He isn't my father's ... he's mine. "So what does it *mean,* Saul?"

His fingers flicked. He caught one of the charms tied into my hair with red thread and gave it a slight tug, his eyebrow quirking meaningfully and his mouth firming into a straight line.

Knowing Weres, that was the only answer I was going to get from him. I'd have to talk to Harp about it. Something about the two hairs twining together bothered me. Or not precisely bothered me, but gave me the tail end of an idea I didn't much like, one I had to tease out with an hour or so of hard thinking. An hour or so I didn't have right now. The unsteady feeling behind my pulse told me this thing was wending its way to a conclusion, and not a pleasant one.

You don't live with adrenaline and intuition, not to mention sorcery, for very long without getting a feeling about when a situation's going to blow sky-high. I let out a soft breath, frustration blooming sharp under my breastbone. My palms were damp again. "All right. You'll anchor me. I hope to hell you know what you're doing."

"I usually do." He let go of the charm, patted my hair back into place. The look of defiance was gone, replaced with calm steadiness. "Don't worry. I won't let you fall."

It was oddly comforting to hear him say it.

"It's not the falling I'm worried about. It's the climbing back up out of *between*." I eyed the coffee cup longingly, heat from the mug burrowing into my fingers. Handed it back to him. "Let's do it before I lose my nerve."

"I can't imagine *that* happening," he muttered as he turned away.

Ridiculously, I was hard-pressed not to smile.

I rarely used this narrow room, as the padlock and the chain on the door proved. It was little more than a closet set to the side of my practice-room, the empty wall opposite that had held Mikhail's sword lying under a rectangle of thin sunlight. I made a mental note to pick up the sunsword from Galina's and led the Were through the door. Darkness swallowed us, broken only by a faint silver glow.

The altar was at the other end of the room, and the walls were covered with an intaglio of spray paint, blue and black, protection-symbols from almost every religion since the dawn of time. Fat lines of paint shifted like tentacles, responding to my presence, and the air hummed as my eyes adapted, pupils flaring wide.

Cut into the hardwood floor was a double circle, spiky symbols carved between the inner and outer rings. The pentacle, inscribed just as deeply, glowed with silver hammered into its sharp lines. Hardwood inside the circle was stained darker than the surrounding floor, the silver pale and drained but glittering faintly, like a half-busted neon sign.

"Huh." Saul peered over my shoulder, his heat burning through his T-shirt and mine. "Nice."

If you think so. My fingers tightened on the knife I carried, the only weapon I had on me. I felt damn near naked. "Mikhail did it. As a present." *And also so I don't have to use a church to go* between, *since most churches are tactical nightmares when it comes to defense and I'm vulnerable while I do this.*

It was the last present he'd ever given me. The warehouse, and this little room, hours of work and love I hadn't thanked him properly for. Three days later, he'd been dead, bleeding out through slashed jugulars in a cheap hotel room as the Sorrows bitch he'd fallen in love with fled with his amulet and I kicked in the door just a quarter-minute too late, unable to save him.

Oh, Mikhail. The familiar bite of shame turned bitter in my throat.

"He must have spent some time on it." Saul pushed past me, lingering for a little longer than absolutely necessary as he touched me, and stepped away to examine the circle, giving it his full attention. There was barely enough room for it, but it was complete, the carved lines deep and still fresh.

A swift pain lanced through my heart. I could remember Mikhail with his arm over my shoulders. *Is for you,* milaya. *Use wisely. Some day old Mischa might not be here to protect his little snake under rock, eh?*

I missed him. I missed him so much, even the slaps and the kicks as he trained me. Even the fear in the middle of the night. You must love your teacher as deeply as you hate him; the love will bring you back from Hell while your teacher holds the line. That love will also save you if you lose your way in the shifting forests of suicide and screaming that are the border between Hell and our world of flesh and light. The love is necessary.

The hate is to make you *strong.* Out in the wilds of the nightside, there is no second chance, and your teacher has to make sure you can survive on your own. It's bad to lose a fellow hunter, there are few enough of us as it is. Losing an apprentice is much, much worse.

So it's love, and hate, and need. All twisted together and made into a rope, a bond, a chain. A fetter each hunter wears with pride, and the reason why we don't lie to each other. You can't lie to someone else who's been loved like that.

No matter what secret your teacher keeps from you. No matter how deep the betrayal.

"He did," I whispered. *He spent weeks on this. Did he know he wouldn't be here forever? Sure he did. He was already old, and he had to know . . .*

Had he known the Sorrows bitch would turn on him? He *had* to have known, Mikhail taught me everything I knew about the Sorrows and their worship of the Elder Gods, their Houses where incense hung heavy in the air and women became hive-queens, their collective energies focused on bringing back the Elders through the veils that kept them from the "real" world. I had to go to Hutch only because I hadn't smelled one before.

Mikhail *had* to have known. So why had he trusted her? Why hadn't he *told* me?

Deal with what you have in front of you now, Jill. Quit stalling.
Saul stepped into the bare space in the middle of the pentacle. I
inhaled, deeply. Then I reached up and unclasped the ruby from
my throat. Its sharp edges dug into my sweating palm as I slid past
the Were. I stepped delicately over the double circle and turned to
face him, my back to the altar. His face was shadowed, only the
glitter of eyes and the glint of silver in his hair reflecting the spent
light from the pentacle below.

I held up the chain. The ruby dangled, bloody sparks drifting
in its depths as it sensed the event looming toward me. "This is
my line back." My voice sounded normal, except for the pain riding each word. "It'll get slippery, and it'll fight you. *Don't* let go. If
you let go, I'm lost."

He nodded, solemn. Silver winked in one of his braids, his fingers brushed mine as he took the gem, its chain dipping and swaying. "I won't."

Jill. Time's wasting. I turned my back on him, walked the four
steps to the altar. It was bluestone, quarried in Britain somewhere
and shipped here on the hush-hush by one of Mikhail's friends in
"exports." A simple thigh-high rectangle of stone, it resonated as I
laid my hand on it, cold burning my fingertips. "O my Lord God,"
I whispered. "Do not forsake me when I face Hell's legions. In
your name..."

*That's the trouble. I'm not doing this in God's name. I'm doing
this for me.*

I hopped up on the altar and spent a few moments arranging
myself. The chill of stone reached even through the leather pants,
and my T-shirt was no barrier to it at all. I didn't wear my weapons, except the one small knife with a leather-wrapped handle. I
lay on my back, arranged my booted feet carefully, and wriggled
my head a little until the silver charms didn't dig so hard into my
skull.

My left hand was pale, my apprentice-ring glittering as I lifted
it. The knife-hilt was in my right hand. I swallowed dryly.

*Don't do it, Jill. Don't. You know what this is like. Don't do it.
Find some other way.*

There was no other way. If there was, I wouldn't be here.

Determination took shape under my skin. A spark crackled

from the ring, a point of lightning-white in the gloom. The spray-painted sigils ran wetly on the walls, whispering like bruised fingers rubbing each other. By now the door of the room would be invisible from the outside, sealed shut. Inside, womblike dark was broken only by the eerie glow of the silver pounded into the pentacle's lines.

Go for the quick tear, Jill.

My breath whooshed out past my teeth. I set the knife-edge against my palm and *cut.*

The smell of blood exploded in my nose. Bile scorched the back of my throat. I dropped the knife to the side, heard it clatter behind the altar, and whipped my left hand out as the scar tightened on my wrist, rumbling a low dissatisfied note.

An arrow of etheric force from my palm smashed into the ruby, an attraction older than time. Blood calling to a bloody, blood-sensitized gem. My back arched, and the rope of force tautened.

Saul had caught the other end. It strained, and I sensed him going down to one knee inside the pentacle, his fist tight around the ruby and blood—*my* blood, transferred through space—welling slick and hot between his fingers. He leaned back against the pull, and I *dropped*—

—into howling wind, buffeting increasing as I fell, a scream like the slipstream past a jet's windows filling the world. Falling, naked flesh stung by air turned hard with velocity. It was dark, the utter dark of blind closed eyes at the bottom of the sea at night.

In this space there is no up or down, despite the sensation of falling. We call it between *because it is; between life and death, earth and Hell, physical and spiritual.*

Between present and past.

The greatest danger is forgetting who and what I am, falling into chaos and dispersing, the psyche unable to contain itself without an outside border. But the bracelet of agony closed around my wrist, crimson light spilling between my fingers as the etheric copy of the jewel closed in Saul Dustcircle's fist almost snapped free of my grasp. A long huuuuuuuuuuungh! *of mental effort burst out of me, the taste of copper filling my mouth to the brim, and I swallowed. With the jerk of arrested motion came the consciousness of who I was, what I was doing here, what informa- tion I sought.*

Time means less than nothing in this space, and so does dis- tance. I became an arrow, translated between one spot and the next without the benefit of moving, the reflex of a physical body turning my stomach inside-out. Gagging, choking, trying desper- ately to remember that I was not in a real body but between *and therefore without a goddamn stomach to reject food, I slammed through the barriers and found myself in a howling ash-choked wasteland with pale copies of skyscrapers glittering through a fog that tore into agonized screaming faces at my approach. Flying, through walls and jets of bright psychic moments crystallized by emotion, until the location that pulled me came into view.*

It was a mansion, its physical shape common enough for the super-rich and paranoid. Its etheric shape, though, was a howl of suffering and pleasure in that suffering, the psychic fume of death and corruption like the belch of an old cancerous dragon, tinted with dark flame having its origin in hell. Into this maw I flashed, the not-me holding a bloody jewel that twisted like a live snake in my grip, trying to break free of this place of horror and flee back to its real physical home.

The mansion swallowed me.

There they were. The hellbreed was a pale sword of diseased brightness, and the rogue Were a twisted mass of fur and flesh, crouched at her feet. The images overlapped with Cenci's face, hair whipping in pale strands as she fought to contain a mas- sive force spilling through her, lips pulled back in a grimace of agony.

It is its own kind of agony to see between. *There is no differ- ence, once you are sideways in that not-space, between the face and the mind behind it, the vessel and the wine. People become smears of reaction, hellbreed spreading vortexes of contagion, hunters straight disciplined arrows of brilliance each with a screaming child on the inside. It is a vision of inner truth that can drive you mad, if you have not been trained—and even then, san- ity is not certain.*

Cenci knelt, the Were bleeding at her feet. The floor was tessel- lated patterns of darkness, black and white linoleum squares stretching to infinity. **Don't** worry, *she whispered to the hulk of shattered fur and animal growl.* I'll take care of you.

The Were screamed with fury, but her slim strong arms came around him—and then, Navoshtay Niv Arkady came.

A tidal wave of etheric force slammed into me, a bat hitting a baseball with the cracking of a sweet swinging-for-the-fences bonebreaking home run. The slippery line between my fingers slid a few inches, my hand loosening, opening, my self *flung through nonspace, skidding for the edges of reality.*

If I went over that edge...

I heard, from very far away, Arkady's voice. I knew it was his because of the black weight of ice it carried, and the unmistakable stamp of black oily eyes and coppery skin, a hook nose and the smell of heatless acid fire. This is unacceptable. *Each sibilant carried a dagger of ice, plunging for the beating heart of whatever living thing it could find.* You are my vessel, and I will break you if I wish.

Comprehension blazed through me as I lunged away from the sound of that voice. A hellbreed that old can sometimes see between, *and if he caught me spying inside his secrets even Perry might not be able to call him off.*

The jaws of the mansion slammed shut as I streaked through, shoulder screaming in pain as the ruby pulled, *and my fingers slipped again, hot blood torn loose from my hand in a painless gout as the gem squirted out of my slippery palm.*

Falling. I had gone too far, the cord sliding between nerveless fingers, stunned and dazed by the impact. Comprehension flashed through me too late, a map of cause and effect stretching back to one image—slim white arms, bleeding from a hellbreed's claws, clasping with more than human strength as a red-haired man struggled and screamed in agony, his flesh cracking and madness bleeding through.

I fell. And fell. Heart stopping, brain bleeding, breath turned to a death-rattle, I fell.

And was caught, deceleration slapping hard against every atom of me.

—come back—

I hung pinned for excruciating eternal moments like a butter-

fly, the world wheeling underneath with a sound like rushing hungry waves. Then another jolt, as someone wrapped both fists around a bloody gem and hauled with every muscle and erg of strength, pulled until lungs and heart both strained, eyes bulging and a cougar's coughing roar smashing against spray-painted walls, a pentacle shifting silver and the line snapping, ripping, tearing me back into a body that glowed with a spiky clear aura, a blot of shining darkness on its right wrist like a live coal.

The part of me that went between *slammed back into this body, convulsing, choking, flung sideways like a rag doll, falling—*

—until my head smashed into the wooden floor. I lay crumpled in front of the altar, hearing my own hoarse screams as my legs jittered and flopped.

The retching eased, every muscle in my body seizing up and relaxing in waves. I could finally *breathe* again. I lay against the altar, my eyes closed, vibrating with pain. The scar pulsed, a wave of sick delight spilling up my arm and curling down my back, as if a warm, manicured hand had just stroked along my spine, a linen cuff touching my skin gently.

Or as if a scaled tongue too wet and warm to be human had touched the vulnerable hollow behind my ear.

I flinched, without the energy to cower away. Got myself up on hands and knees, my left hand singing a thin note of pain before the cut, sucked bloodless, closed. I realized, through the ringing noise in my head, that Saul was calling my name, his voice hoarse as if he'd been shouting a while.

"Goddammit, answer me!" He sounded frantic, and the silver light pulsed as if he'd tried to step over the pentacle's borders. It held fast, singing a warning note of crystalline power.

"Hold...on..." I managed through a fresh set of retches and the howling in my head. It was a good thing I hadn't had breakfast.

He subsided, but the rumbling growl coming from him shook the walls. He was one unhappy Were.

Well, I'm not too happy myself. I struggled for a laugh and couldn't find one.

My arms and legs trembled, as if I'd just pulled through a fever.

I managed to sit up, propping myself against the altar, and made the gesture that released the double-circle and the pentacle. Silver light folded away, its hum diminishing as it bled into the ground.

Saul's feet slid and slipped in the spreading pool of my blood as he launched himself, the silver glow turning bloody as he broke the weakening barriers and landed next to me, almost crashing into the altar. He fetched up hard and went to his knees, grabbed my shoulders, and shook me, my head bobbing back and forth. Sounds came out of him that I only vaguely recognized as words. I was too busy shaking, choking back more retches, and hearing the roaring noise of *between* fade too slowly out of my ears.

I'd made it. The knowledge I'd brought out of the space *between* thrummed in my veins, spilled through my head, and the whole monstrous pattern became clear.

I began to cry as Saul cupped my face in his bloody hands, the ruby a hard hot edge against my cheek. I sobbed until my ribs ached, howling, and when he kissed me I couldn't stop weeping but I also started to scream, and he swallowed my cries as I found out I was once again alive.

CHAPTER 26

I splashed cold water on my face again, flung my head back. A charm chimed against the mirror, whipping at the end of a long strand of hair. The phone shrilled, and I reached it just as Saul appeared in my bedroom door. My guns lay on the nightstand, each with a full clip and one in the chamber.

It was Harp. "We've got him, Jill. His name's Billy Ironwater, and he hails from Connecticut. He went to visit kin in upstate New York—the Alleghany pack—and disappeared about half a year before murders started popping up, murders that until now have been 'lost' in a stack of paperwork. The Alleghany canines have been looking for him and running up against blank walls. Most of those walls lead back to hellbreed, and in *that* state it only means one thing."

I felt the click of a pattern slide under my skin, resounding in my bones. "Arkady," I breathed. I couldn't call him anything else, now. Not when I had brushed him *between* and seen his true face.

"Yeah. We're in the barrio, at the Criz in the Plaza. Can you bring Saul? We've found a trail, and we need him. The entire Were population except for cubs is on this." She was straining and eager, now that she had her prey in sight. Now it was time for the hunt, and all uncertainty was over.

It was a relief. My brain slid into overdrive, the plan crystallizing in a moment. It was a good plan, and might even get me out of this alive. "I'll give him my car keys." Shocked silence rang on the line. I slid one gun into its holster, then the other. "What? I can't go into the barrio, I'm a *gringa*. Besides, I've got shit of my own to do."

"You're giving him your car keys?" She sounded, for once, taken aback. The hard note of glee was gone.

I felt sorry for raining on her parade. "How else is he going to get down there in time? This is worse than you think, Harp. Get moving; he'll catch up." I slammed the phone down and turned to Saul. "Harp needs you, down in the barrio. They've found a trail, and just found out who our mystery boy is. Name's Billy Ironwater and he's a canine Were from Connecticut." My hand shot out, and I tossed the jingling clatter of my spare set of car keys at him. I picked up my next spare leather trench coat from the bed, shook it experimentally, and shrugged into it. I'd put in my tiger's eye earrings, and they tapped my cheeks as I shook my head, freeing my silver-laden hair from the collar of the coat. The blessing in the stones flashed blue for a moment, subsided.

"I thought nobody drove your baby but you." He said it mildly, slipping the keys in the pocket of his jeans.

"If I can trust you to hold the line while I go *between* I can trust you not to scratch my goddamn paint job," I snapped. *Get him out of here, Jill. Hurry up.*

Do it quick.

"What are you planning?" His dark eyes had narrowed, and I allowed myself a few moments of looking at his cheekbones, the shape of his mouth, the loose grace of his hands. He was beautiful in the way only a Were can be, each line arranged for maximum effect.

Like something human, only better, stripped of imperfections. All the flaws burned out, instead of scored in with a hellbreed's kiss. The distance between us yawned wide as the chasm between ordinary waking life and the screaming winds of *between*.

"I'm going to finish my end of this, and you and the Weres will finish yours." *After that maybe it's time for a vacation. I wonder what Tahiti looks like this time of year. Ugh, maybe not. I've had all I can stand of heat and rain.*

He took two steps into the room. "I wonder..." The sentence stopped itself, and his eyes met mine. The stinging communication returned, deeper than ever, the line between us wide open now and humming with force. It felt too good, too familiar.

"Don't wonder. Get going. You can find the barrio from here, and once you get there you can follow your nose." My hands had turned into fists. The scar pulsed, my agitation plucking at it.

Another two steps toward me. *God in Heaven, can't you just go?* I wanted to scream it, folded my mouth against the cry. Clenched my hands even tighter. Silver clinked and jangled in my hair.

He approached me cautiously. When he was within arm's length I made a restless movement and he stopped, his feet poised. "What's wrong?"

What the fuck do you think *is wrong?* "This isn't going to work," I told him flatly. "You have to go. You *have* to. Right now."

His mouth compressed into a thin line. He reached up, and I thought he meant to touch my cheek. I flinched away, but his hand flicked, and one of my charms dropped into his palm, neatest trick of the week.

"Hey—"

Saul retreated swiftly, paused in the door. He held up the charm—a silver wagon wheel, tied to a long lock of my dark hair. His claws had sliced through as effectively as a razor.

I stared at him. That close, and that quick, it could have been my jugular opened instead of a lock of hair sliced. The worst part was that I didn't care. If he was close enough to kill me, he was close enough that I could breathe in that smell of safety, of something too good for someone like me.

"You're not hellbreed," he said softly. "And I'm not rogue. It might work."

There. It was out in the open, it was said. I opened my mouth, let my half of the flawed equation slip out. "I'm contaminated. I'm not willing to take the chance." *Now will you please get the hell out of here?*

"You've been wrong before." He stepped back, his fist closing over the silver charm. His boots made no sound, and it hurt to see his fluid grace, and the way his eyes moved over my face, as if he saw something precious there.

"So have you. Get going, Were." *Go and find yourself a nice pretty Were girl on the Rez and raise nice cublets. Forget about all of this.*

"I've only been wrong once, hunter." Then he was gone, the space in the air where he'd stood crying out to me.

I stood wooden next to my bed, my eyes shut, listening. When the garage door opened and my car's engine roused my shoulders sagged. When I heard the purr of the Impala receding along the street, I finally opened my eyes.

My cheeks were wet. I swiped at them angrily and slid the replacement pager into its padded pocket a moment before the phone shrilled again. I was starting to hate that goddamn noise, and had a brief satisfying vision of emptying a clip into the fucking thing.

I couldn't waste the ammo. I hooked the headset up out of the cradle. "Talk." I sounded a little less than welcoming, even to myself.

"So glad to find you at home, my dear." Perry's voice had turned from bland to venomously gleeful. "I am calling to inform you the meeting you requested is scheduled for dusk, here at the Monde. It is the only place I can be assured of your safety."

You sound so happy I'm going to bet my safety isn't on the agenda tonight. My mouth had gone desert-dry and sandy inside. Cool sweat rose up on my forehead and prickled at the small of my back. I was about to use my own body as the lure in a trap, for the five hundredth time in my life.

As usual, I took refuge in sarcasm. "Gee, Pericles. That's awful swell of you. Do I get a pony for Christmas too?"

"Do not bait me today." The words rattled around my ears, each spilling their load of cool poison. "There is a limit to what I allow you, Kismet."

My temper broke with a brittle snap. "Get one thing straight, hellbreed. Your end of this stinks, and if you want to keep your nice cushy little existence in my city you *will* keep in line. You fuck with me, and there won't be any profit in this for you. It'll be all loss, and I'll personally take pleasure in filling you with silver-jacket lead right before I burn your web to the goddamn ground with you in it. Is that clear enough for even your thick little head?"

Amazingly, he chuckled. The sound was so warm and rich my hands began to shake. "You're coming along quite nicely. See you at dusk, my dear." A sound that might have been a kiss breathed into the telephone, and the line went dead.

I checked the clock, picking up my knives and sliding them into their sheaths. Dusk gave me roughly six hours to nerve myself up for what I had to do.

Get going, Jill. Come on.

I got going.

CHAPTER 27

The next wave of stormy weather had begun to move across the city by the time I reached Galina's. I didn't go through the shop. Instead, I leapt across a narrow gap between the Italian restaurant next door and the rooftop of her building.

Galina's greenhouse glowed with failing light as I cast my glance over the roof again. Concrete was gritty and oily underneath my boots, their leather still dark with my own blood. The stain in the closet next to my practice room had gotten deeper, wine-dark inside the double circle.

How long are you going to keep bleeding, Jill?

Another useless question.

I lifted up the latch and ducked into the greenhouse. The cloak of Sanctuary shields had no reason to stop me, which told me Galina was out of her sanctum and in the house somewhere.

Probably sensing me overhead.

Most certainly waiting. The entire world was breathless with waiting. The pattern, seen with striking clarity in the buffeting nonspace of *between,* had its own momentum now. All that remained was for me to do what came next.

And not get my stupid self killed. *That* was going to be the hard part.

The sunsword lay on a slim table scattered with gardening tools under a shelf of blue frilly orchids. Dozing, drowsy heat encircled me, the scar on my wrist pulsing under its carapace of copper, clipped on just this morning. I smelled decaying organic matter in the potting soil, the healthy powerful scent of green things growing, the sharp pungency of just-watered earth. I closed my hand around the hilt.

The Sanctuary shields shivered, tensing. My skin chilled.

"I'm not going to do anything," I said without turning around. "I just want to talk to her."

"I don't know if that's a good idea." Galina spoke from the trapdoor leading down to her bedroom. She never did like to be far from her plants. "I'm sorry I couldn't tell you, Jill. It's the nature of the Sanctuary vow."

You keep my secrets just as thoroughly, I suppose I can't blame you. I nodded, deciding to piece it together. "Understood. She came here with him, didn't she? They were desperate, looking only for a way out by now, since they couldn't run anywhere else; Arkady was too close. Ironwater suggested a Sanctuary, probably as his last hope."

"I'm always a last resort, Jill. Just like you. I couldn't help him. He had some periods of lucidity, but..." Heaviness tinted her voice. "She's here now, asking for a weapon to kill you with—one I won't give her, by the way. He's gone, broke all her protections and fled. The Weres are hunting him now?"

So he ran away even from her, at last. He must want to die. There would be no torture more thorough for a hellbreed-broken Were with intermittent periods of sanity than to know that he had broken a whole clutch of their oldest taboos and tasted human flesh. "You know they are. This time they'll catch him, because she won't be there to mask his trail and slip him free." I slid the sunsword into the soft leather sheath through the side snaps. The clicking of the snaps was very loud in the stillness. The walls hummed their song of Sanctuary. "I wouldn't have put the pieces together, except I went *between* this morning. I saw what she's hiding from, and I know she wouldn't shelter with any hellbreed. That's why I couldn't flush her out by burning hellbreed holes. She moved him around as much as she dared, and she hid the last place anyone would suspect—with a Sanctuary. A *human.*"

It's official. Perry called me here to flush her out of hiding, but didn't pursue her. Why? What's his game?

Even with all I now knew, that part was still murky. It was enough of a wild card to give anyone cold sweats.

"I took my vows." Her voice didn't tremble. "And I'll keep her here to give you a head start. I don't want any more fights on my roof, and you're my friend as well as our hunter, Jill. This city can't stand to lose you."

Mighty nice of you, Galina. "I just want to talk. That's all."

I sensed the sad slow shake of her head. "I said that's not a good idea. You'd better get out of here. Once the Weres catch him there will be hell to pay."

A chill touched the base of my spine. "There's going to be hell to pay all right." I picked up the sword, buckled the diagonal strap so it rode my back, a heavy comforting weight. "But she's not going to be dealing it out. I am." The glass walls rattled a little, responding both to my voice and the cycling-up of the Sanctuary shields.

Did Galina think I was going to turn on her?

A hunter is supposed to be unpredictable. Still, a Sanctuary should have no doubts about my trustworthiness. But Galina knew I'd been too late to save Mikhail—and maybe she suspected *why.*

You can't lie to yourself as a hunter. But I still couldn't decide if I had been too late because of some lingering traces of trust and respect for Mikhail keeping me too far back when I followed him that night, or if I had hung back because some part of me knew something was going to happen—and wanted to punish him for betraying me, not as a teacher or as a father, but as a lover.

Did it matter? I had been too late, in any case, and Mikhail had bled out, choking on his own blood. Melisande Belisa, the Sorrows bitch, had stolen his most precious amulet, the one that should have gone to me, and fled into the night.

And now here I was.

"You should go," Galina repeated softly. Conciliatory, but with a core of steel.

For fuck's sake. Can't you see I'm trying to finish this and stop all the killing? "Tell her this, Galina. I've got a meet with Perry and Arkady tonight at the Monde. Arkady started this whole mess. He's liable, but I can't take him on without help and Perry's about as useful as tits on a boar hog in this situation. He'll be too busy trying to figure angles for himself. Billy Ironwater's death will be clean and merciful. If she goes with me up against Arkady, I promise her revenge on her father—and a clean death, as painless as I can make it." My voice caught. I turned, and saw Galina standing at the edge of the trapdoor, her green tilted eyes alight with sorrow and raw power. An ageless look, and one I almost felt sure my own face was wearing.

Galina was in full Sanctuary robes, gray silk with the wide hood thrown back, the undersleeves of crimson glowing eerily. Her necklace—quartered circle, serpent shifting—glittered with hard darts of light. "I'll pass it along. Now get out." She held a gun, her slim fingers loose as it dangled by her side. Was it for me, or for the hellbreed brooding below? I almost imagined I could *feel* Cenci's breathing in the hot stillness.

Waiting, like a pale blind adder under a rock. Were we both snakes hiding under the same stone?

No. I'm not hellbreed. I backed toward the door, feeling my way with each footstep. "No hard feelings, Galina." She was, after all, a Sanctuary. She had no choice.

Just like I had no choice.

"None on my end either, Jill. I'll hold her until you're gone. Be safe out there."

I finally said it. "You know I can't. It's not in my goddamn job description." I eased out of the door, closing it behind me with a click. The sunsword vibrated on my back. My boots ground the rooftop as I took a running leap and launched myself out into space, landing on the street below and pulling etheric energy through the scar, streaking away.

Clouds covered the city under a yellow-green dome, heat held close and breathless under glass. Out in the desert there would be heat lightning, and animals scuttling to shelter. Here in the valley, in my city, there was scurrying to get under cover too. Even the humans could feel something lurking in the heat and the boiling sky.

Something with teeth, just looking to close on the unwary. No wonder they sought cover.

My pager went off four times. Harp, trying to track me down. I didn't respond. The game was set and the pieces were moving, and there was nothing to do now but see how it finished out. I had my own moves to make.

I sat for a long time in my usual back pew at Mary of the Immaculate Conception, watching candleflames shudder as uneven currents of storm-charged air brushed them. If Perry was watching me, I'd drawn him away from Galina's house to here, where I usually came before I braved the Monde to make my monthly payments. My eyes drifted across the crucifix, Christ hanging with his attenuated limbs and peaceful face. A quiet, aesthetic representation of a death gruesomely paraded in front of the faithful for centuries—I wondered why they hadn't chosen the Last Supper instead. Religion might be a little more civilized if a picture of a feast instead of a Roman torture was pasted up in the churches.

Still, I know better. Humanity doesn't go in for gentle gods. I wished Mikhail was alive; I would have wanted to hear what he would say about my forays into philosophy. Probably something practical, like how all the philosophy in the world wouldn't stop a bullet.

Oh, Mikhail. I loved you. I love you so much.

Did I kill you? Even now I didn't know.

It all boiled down to simple starkness. There was light and there was darkness; and there were those in the light who fought the dark. It made us worse, sometimes, than the darkness itself.

We were so close to that edge. It was impossible not to step over sometimes, whether from momentum or choice.

Did that mean we should stop fighting? What decent person *could,* even if the job itself wasn't decent at all?

You know better than to think that, milaya. It was Mikhail's voice, a baritone purr. *I do not force you. You force yourself.*

"Bullshit," I whispered. But he was right. He had lifted me out of the snow, a battered and broken girl still clawing and fighting back with her last vestiges of strength. He'd fed me, and sheltered me, and would have turned me over to social services for therapy and reclamation; indeed, had tried to several times. I'd *chosen* to stay with him, stubbornly sleeping on his floor and following behind him as he did his daily practice until he took me on. There was no obligation laid on me. There never is, on hunters. We can give it up and walk away at any moment. Nobody, not even the Church, blamed us if we did.

Sure you can walk away. Now that you know what's out there in the night preying on the weak, you can turn tail and head for the hills. You can move to another city and take up tatting lace for fun and dealing blackjack for profit.

Sure you can.

He had saved me because I'd let him. Because I didn't want to die in the snow. I wanted to *live.*

Had I killed him for it? Had I been deliberately late?

I sat very still, my hands white-knuckled on the back of the pew in front of me. Raised my eyes once again to the crucifix, silver tinkling in my hair from the slight movement. The scar gave out a throbbing murmur of dissatisfaction edging on pain.

My eyes traveled up the long nerveless legs, past the loincloth and the tortured chest, paused at the throat, and watched the slice of dreaming face I could see under the heavy tangle of thorns and curly wooden hair. No glitter under his slackened eyelids answered mine. He was asleep. "I don't do this for you," I whispered. "I never have. Is that my sin?"

Or is my sin greed? I want something for myself. I always have.

I felt Saul's mouth on mine again. I still smelled, a little, like him. When he went back to his life, I was going to keep the sheets unwashed for as long as I could stand it. I would take deep lungfuls of that scent every time I needed to, until it faded like everything did, especially everything good.

There was so little unmitigated good in the world. The corruption crept in everywhere. How long would it be before I could no longer lay claim to my own soul?

Had I just made the same mistake Mikhail had, trusting a woman who wasn't truly human, tainted with hellbreed? Did that mean that everyone who trusted me had made the same mistake?

Did I kill you, Mikhail? I wish you could tell me. I need to know.

I leaned forward, my clammy forehead on my tense and clutching hands. Dusk was coming, I could feel it like a compass must feel north. Thunder rattled; the storm would probably wait until nightfall and the great gush of cool nightly wind from the river to unleash its fury. Somewhere in the city the Weres were hunting a rogue, and they would be kind when they caught him. He wouldn't feel a thing.

But for me, it was going to be vengeance. Whether Cenci took my bargain or not, it was going to be fury and hatred and messiness, spilled blood and screaming.

After all, that was what I lived for, right?

Just stop it. Mikhail's dead no matter what you intended, and you have a job to do. Just be happy Saul is out there somewhere in the world, that he even exists. Quit moaning and get on with it. This is your big night, you don't want to be late.

I could have been happy with being a *little* later. But I stood up, and I did something I hadn't done since my teenage years.

I approached the altar with slow steps, climbed the steps, and stood right next to the bank of candles and flowers, in the midst of their heady fragrance. They adorned what in pagan times would be a site of bloody sacrifice, whether done kindly or cruelly.

Times have changed a lot less than we think.

I looked up into the wooden face of the man on the cross, under the shelf of carved hair and runnels of painted decorative blood from jagged thorns. A great howling cheated scream rose up inside me, was savagely repressed, and died away.

What could I say to a God who had never spoken to me and a Son who slept?

"You give out redemption, don't you?" My whisper sounded

very loud in the silence, broken only by the hissing of candle-flames. "If you're not too busy right now, I could use a handful. Maybe even just a pinch."

I was still begging. Just like the girl I had been, before. The weakling.

I'd been taught a better prayer, hadn't I?

O my Lord God, do not forsake me when I face Hell's legions. In Thy name and with Thy blessing, I go forth to cleanse the night. My lips shaped the words, and the candleflames flattened. The scar on my wrist grumbled uneasily, a hot hard knot under the skin, infected.

I shut the thought of Mikhail away, along with the thought of Saul. It took a physical effort, a tensing of every muscle. When it was done, I inhaled, let out a long huff of air.

The click sounded inside my head. I'd never told Mikhail about this switch in the very bottom of me, the one I could now flip. I could lift off, shutting away everything but the job that had to be done, the shining path of vengeance laid out before my feet. That road might eventually end at Hell's bony clutching gates, but at least I'd take plenty of the predators who preyed on the weak with me. Maybe a few innocents would survive a little longer because I was out getting dirty.

Enough whining. The night could use some cleansing. I was just the girl to get it done. *If* the Weres kept the rogue out of my way, and *if* Cenci's need for revenge on her hellspawn father was greater than her need for revenge on me, and *if* Perry's interest in me would keep him from interfering, and *if*...

I was counting on a lot of *if*s, and on a lot of hellbreed jealousy. I was also counting on Navoshtay Niv Arkady being killable, which was by no means certain.

"Only one way to find out." My voice echoed in the church's cloistered quiet, the sunsword ringing softly underneath it. The ruby at my throat was warm and comforting. I had never seen a priest in here, but the doors were always open. I was glad on both counts; if I did see a priest now, I wasn't quite sure I could control my sarcasm. It would hurt too much to be respectful, and in any case I've never done submission well.

Did the man on the cross mind? Did he forgive me for it, knowing

I was as I'd been made? By the same hand that had made him, the same hand that abandoned him to be nailed up for sins he didn't commit? Sins he had no choice but to pay for, over and over again?

Was memory a curse for the man on the cross too?

Quit fucking around, Kismet. Get your ass moving.

I did. But as I left the church I felt comforted, for once. I pushed open the doors and stepped out into an early evening eerily dark with storm clouds covering the sky's bright eye. In the west was a crimson streak. Dusk was coming, the sun sinking under the rim of the earth and night rising to start its games.

CHAPTER 28

I didn't have to walk out to the Monde *or* take a cab. I wasn't more than four blocks away from the church when a pristine black limousine detached itself from parking up the street and crept toward me.

It was absurdly anticlimactic.

I got in, taking one last drowning breath of heavy muggy air crackling with approaching thunder before air-conditioned calm and the smell of hellbreed closed around me. I had to unbuckle the diagonal strap and lay the sunsword across my knees, a bar between me and the blue-eyed 'breed who lounged, patently unconcerned, across from me on the white leather seat. The blondness of the interior matched his sandy hair, and the scar on my wrist leapt with sick hot delight under the copper cuff.

"Alone at last," Perry greeted me. His suit jacket was unbuttoned, and the stickpin in his pale blue tie was a diamond. I suspected it would have a flaw like a screaming face in its depths. "That is an exceedingly undainty tool for such a pretty thing as yourself, my dear."

You're not the first man to tell me that. I stared out the window as the quiet residential streets around Immaculate Conception flowed by.

The driver was behind a pane of smoked glass, and Perry sat with his back to the driver and regarded me. "No word for your faithful slave, dear Kiss? You're even surlier than usual. I've decided to forgive your insubordination this time as well. Comforted?"

There's nothing you can do that would comfort me, Perry. Except stop breathing, and maybe not even then. I wouldn't put it past you to rise from a grave or two. I caught myself, focused my eyes out the window. Mikhail had always told me a woman had an edge in this kind of bargain.

I was about to use that edge for everything it was worth. Besides, my head was full of colorless gasoline fumes, and all I needed was a spark. I hoped I was as dangerous as I felt right now.

He fell silent for a short while. I could feel his eyes crawling avidly over me, leaving behind a sparkling, oozing trail like the wetness coating a hot scaled tongue.

The driver was taking the direct route to the Monde.

Like that's a blessing, Jill.

The scar turned warm. Heat oozed up my arm, a pleasant bath of sensation. I set my jaw as the limo turned left, bracing my foot against the floor.

"You make this so difficult." He managed to sound mocking and contrite at once. I didn't dignify it with a response. "I've done what you wanted. Arkady is waiting at the Monde, enjoying such blandishments as might make him a little more amenable. I've spent a great deal of time and effort soothing his ruffled feathers and persuading him to overlook—"

Now, Jill. Go on the attack. "Bullshit." My voice slashed through his. "You've convinced him I can be used as bait for his daughter, since you've deduced—or maybe you even *know*—that the Weres are hot on the rogue's trail. Can the act, Perry. I'm tired of this game."

"There are other games to play." His eyes half-lidded, a movement I could sense, though I kept my gaze out the window, by the sudden heat brushing my cheek. Every nerve was agonizingly aware, waiting for the violence. "You should take that abominable thing off. I like to hear your pulse."

"The cuff stays on, Perry." *At least until I start getting my ass beat by Arkady.* The limo's engine opened up, accelerating up the slight hill of Mendez Road.

"You're harsh." Delicate, dainty as a cat. "What have I done to deserve your ire, avenging one?"

You're here instead of in Hell, Perry. And you're fucking with my head. Watch me fuck right back. "Just don't start with me. I'm not in the mood."

"Changeful woman," he murmured. I sensed his eyes lighting up with predatory glee. The scar prickled, burrowing wetly into my skin. "It's your prerogative, I suppose."

Keep going, you scumsucking hellspawn. I was an idiot to think I could manipulate a hellbreed, especially one like him.

Still, even idiots get lucky sometimes. I felt lucky tonight. Or maybe just reckless.

He kept his voice low, thoughtful. "You've grown quiet. And very thoughtful."

I glanced at Perry. His profile was presented to me, he glanced out the opposite window, one leg crossed over the other, his hands folded on his knee. He looked like a mild-mannered businessman.

I let him have it with both barrels, a mismatched stare and my seeming-full attention fixed on him. "I'm wondering how far you can be trusted when Arkady decides he wants to rip my throat open." *Or just use those eyes on me until I do it myself.*

Perry's head slowly turned. His blue eyes met mine, a shadow of indigo clouding the whites. "That is one thing you *don't* have to worry about, Kiss. You're signed, sealed, and *mine*. Navoshtay Niv Arkady isn't what you should fret over." His colorless tongue stole out, touched his bottom lip in a flicker of motion. "You should worry more about satisfying me once this meeting is over. You've put yourself right into my hands."

Oh, have I? Amazingly, I felt the corners of my mouth tilt up. It was a crazy, suicidal smile, and I heard Mikhail's voice from a long time ago—it seemed like centuries. *When you stop fearing them,* milaya, *you have made first mistake.*

"That's what you think, you hellspawn fuckhead," I informed him sweetly as we bumped across railroad tracks, the limo braking. The Monde was less than ten minutes away, along an extended stretch of road packed with slaughterhouses and warehouses, as well as rumbling bits of railroad track freighted with commerce. I'd never approached the Monde from the meatpacking district before.

It put a whole new shine on things.

Perry paused, his head tilted to the side. The indigo swelled through his eyes, and his hair stirred slightly, lifting on a breeze that came from nowhere because the interior of the limo was still as a drowned mineshaft. "I am going to enjoy breaking you," he whispered.

Then the night turned red, and chaos descended from above. I was ready for something to happen, but it still took me by surprise.

CHAPTER 29

The limo was a burning mass of fragments, and the fingers in my throat were pure iron. I thrashed, the sunsword clattering to the ground just out of my reach—I'd been holding it when the limo swerved and the bolt from the heavens descended, tearing through metal like it was paper and igniting like a Molotov cocktail.

Navoshtay Niv Arkady crouched over me, his shoulders hunched and hellfire in the yellow spectrum dripping from his oily, curly hair. His eyes were black from lid to lid, and the sheen of oil on their tops was scorch-hot, sucking at me as I went down, black water closing over my head. His teeth were serrated edges of pure ivory bone, and they champed as he sizzled at me in Helletöng, the rumble making the silver in my hair crackle and scorch. A bloody spark spat from the ruby at my throat, and he hissed back. The silver chain against my neck began to *burn*.

He'd gotten tired of waiting for me, despite whatever promises he'd made to Perry. I'd thought that might happen. Powerful hellbreed are touchy about hunters who make them look bad in front of their peers. Sometimes they can't contain their little tempers.

What a joy, I've finally figured a hellbreed out.

The copper cuff clanged on pavement as I surged up, fighting with almost-hellbreed strength. He bore down, grinding me into the pavement. *"You."* His voice was the death of stars, was the cold bleakness of space, his sterile breath scouring my face as I gagged and fought for air, the fingers of my left hand scorching too as I tried to pry his grip loose. He had his foot on my right wrist and he ground down, my scream lost and bottled in my throat. *"You stink of the beast!"*

A secondary explosion rocked the burning limousine. *"Animal."* A load of disgust and hatred made his voice stagger even under its awfulness. His weight, like the pressure at the bottom of the ocean, crushed down on me, my bare skin crawling with acid and loathing. His eyes dug at me, slicing, burning, nerves dying, the rope at my throat and the knife drawing up my arm, riptides of black oil sucking me down.

His breath roared hot and rancid over my face as he *sniffed* me. *"You reek of it!"* he screamed, and I remembered the tang of Were that overlaid my scent.

I realized too late that Navoshtay Niv Arkady was utterly and completely fucking insane, and that he had a big problem with anything smelling like Were. Like I did, now, after hanging out with them—and sleeping in the same bed with one.

If he hadn't intended to kill me before, he certainly did now.

The limo exploded once more, shrapnel flying. Lightning sizzled, thunder sounding very small when compared to the noise in my head. My eyes rolled up, and I dug for every erg of strength I possessed. I convulsed, pitching to the side, trying to throw him off, and got exactly nowhere.

I'm going to die oh shit I didn't plan for this think of something oh my God I'm not ready yet I didn't even tell Saul—

Arkady paused, his wetly gleaming head coming up like a lizard's, his tongue sliding out and poking the air. His cheek was scarred under its copper tones by the sunsword's finials.

FOCUS! Mikhail's voice roared inside my head.

My left hand stopped its fruitless digging and flashed down, closed on a gun.

I had almost cleared leather, my fingers suddenly clumsy and black spots crowding in on my vision, when Cenci simply resolved out of the air with the unholy screech of a basilisk and knocked dear old daddy on his ass.

I rolled onto my side, coughing and choking. The noise was terrific. I was glad the street was deserted, because Arkady slid across pavement, bumped up the curb, and flew right into the side of a warehouse with a snapping sound like a really good bowling strike. Cenci vanished, flung back by the strike her father dealt even as he flew, a long coiled serpent of pure force.

Crap. Now she was out of the picture.

Get up, milaya. Mikhail's voice, tender and pitiless. *Get stupid ass moving, woman!*

I did, dropping flat again from my half-crouch and rolling as the side of the warehouse exploded and Arkady stepped out, siding and drywall—not to mention glass—whickering through the air. Little bits peppered the street; my coat made a snapping sound as the blowback pushed at its long flow.

My fingers curled around the hilt of the sunsword, and Arkady moved. He didn't so much seem to walk as to sidestep through space, as if he folded the street like a cloth and stepped from one wrinkle to another. He kicked me, and the massive impact against my side flung me back across the street, pain exploding and no more breath in the world, lungs starving, almost into the shattered burning heap of the limousine.

He could have snuffed me out. Arkady was playing with me before he killed me.

Now would be a really good time to have Perry on my side. Hell, I'd settle for anyone. The cough drove splintered bits of bone through my lungs, and the scar on my wrist turned almost as hot as the roasting from the burning limo. I smelled cooking hair and my entire body seized up, bones crackling as a long strangled sound of effort burst out of my blood-slick lips.

I was vaguely surprised I had the breath left to still try screaming.

I'm getting really tired of bleeding. Someone stop the world, I want to get off.

But the sunsword was still in my hand. I managed a walloping painful breath in, sucking at it like wine. Even tainted with hellbreed and burning metal, that breath was the sweetest I'd tasted for a long time. My ribs snapped out, and I screamed again as Arkady stepped mincingly nearer, the pavement groaning under his weight of insanity.

More thunder arrived, shatteringly close. I had my legs under me and a complete lungful of air as Arkady reached down, his fingers curling in my hair and hauling me up, probably to throw me around again.

The silver in my hair woke in a coruscating whirl of blue-white etheric flame.

He inhaled a scream like a black hole sucking in a star, dropping me. I landed on my feet, and pumped four shots into him at point-blank range, my shriek lost in the massive noise of his. Blood gushed from my ears and slicked my upper lip under my nose.

Then I brought the sunsword around, and slashed at him as the blade sputtered and burst into flame. I would have hit him too, if Cenci hadn't collided with him from the side again, her face twisted up in a mask of hatred and her claws making a snapping sound as they dug for his black eyes.

Her momentum slammed them both back into the wreck of the burning car, great gouts of oily smoke gushing up. I didn't hesitate, unhealthy strength flooding me from the burrowing burning of the scar, a tidal wave of heat and etheric force jolting up my arm and through the rest of me. My hunting cry mixed with the guttural scream the hellbreed female made, a chorus of female destruction.

I threw myself into the burning wreck of the car, my boots smacking down on something that crunched wetly as I swung the sunsword, flame suddenly belching in a white-hot blowtorch arc. This wasn't just sunfire—this was nuclear fission, the very soul of flame itself, responding to evil and to my throat-cut yell as I drove the length of bright whiteness into Arkady's chest.

He backhanded me, a fist narrow and hard as a crowbar landing on my cheekbone, snapping my head aside and flinging me out of the inferno. I landed hard, teeth clicking together with a snap that would have taken a piece of tongue out if I hadn't almost swallowed it while sucking in breath to scream again. The gun clattered and spun out of my left hand, and I scrabbled back, erasing the skin on my palms in my haste, as the flames made a sound like the world ending.

I saw her, in the middle of the conflagration.

Navoshtay Siv Cenci crouched on her father's chest, her face a mask of keening inhuman rage as she tore at his face. His eyes were already deep gaping holes welling blackish ichor. Lightning smashed down, a gunpowder flash etching every detail into my retinas.

Slim female hellbreed with long pale hair and a nose that echoed his, her eyes mad and alight with crimson as she hunkered down in the middle of fire crippling for an ordinary 'breed, ignoring the weak jerks and twitches as Arkady's old, immensely strong body fought to live, not knowing the battle was over. She held up the eyes with one hand, each with its long string of raveled nerve root, and her mouth opened once, twice. Dribbles of darkness spilled from the corners of her mobile mouth, and I saw the flames flinch away from her. Her other arm reached up, fingers clasped around the hilt—slim fingers, blackening and curling at the touch of holy sun-fired metal.

I sat in the middle of the street with eyes that felt as wide as plates, staring like a child listening to a fairytale too horrible to be unreal.

The sunsword sang a high keening note of agony before the fire—even the burning gasoline—flattened and died with a *wump,* as if starved of oxygen.

I felt around blindly with my stinging hands, the reek of burning gas and scorched paint in my nose. Found my lost gun. My legs didn't want to work, but I pushed myself up, shaking, as the first spatters of rain began again. More thunder caromed through the sky's unhealthy orange cityglow. Lightning spattered between clouds.

The sounds Cenci made as she ripped even further at decaying hellbreed flesh brought everything I'd ever thought of eating up to the back of my throat. I doubled over, heaving so hard black spots danced in front of my eyes again.

There's even a limit to what a hunter can stand, I thought, amazed. Shotglass-sized drops of rain dotted the cracked asphalt. Crazy loops of scorching and cracking marred the entire surface of the street. Had I done that, or had the dueling hellbreed done it? The road was a mess. I spotted two lampposts and a telephone pole down, and a couple more buildings smashed. Down the street there were lights, and I caught the distant sound of sirens.

I'm alive. I didn't believe it even as I thought it.

Hands were at my shoulders. "It's over." Perry sounded very pleased with himself. "There now, my dearest. That wasn't so bad, was it? One little thing left to do, and we will go home."

My forehead left a bloody, soot-grimed streak on his immaculate, linen-clad shoulder. Not a hair out of place. He wasn't even bruised, or scorched.

The sounds behind me ceased. Tension tightened between the raindrops. I jerked away from Perry, whose hands dropped back to his sides.

Cenci stood amid the wreckage of the limousine. Ice now marred the edges of shattered steel and broken glass. I thought I caught sight of the driver's body in there, but my gaze locked on Arkady, who was swiftly collapsing into runnels of foulness.

They rot quick, when they're older. It was a comfort to imagine Perry like that. More of a comfort than I liked.

Navoshtay Siv Cenci's eyes met mine. They were crimson, glowing, and entirely crazed, but I saw...

No. I thought I saw...

No. I *saw.* I saw comprehension in them, and devouring grief, and shattering pain. I saw agony in those eyes, and my guns dropped to my side.

The anguish burning in her eyes was almost human.

"Kill her," Perry whispered, sweetly. His breath touched my cheek, hot and laden with moisture. "Kill her now, hunter. She murdered your people."

Blackness smeared Cenci's chin. Her clothes were smoking rags, and I wanted to look down, see if her belly was curved. I suspected not. I remembered the pool of oily viscosity in the front yard of the death house, and I thought of her crouching in the dark of night, her arms crossed over her midriff and her eyes gone crimson just as they were right now while she bit her lip so as not to make a sound, as one of her father's filthy experiments slid out of her body and onto the mortal grass.

She's not human! She killed them! Kill her! Kill! My brain shrilled it at me, but my hands were limp and cold. The guns dangled.

No. Not human. The body bags loaded with bits of her ravaged victims I'd seen screamed for vengeance. That was my function, that was my job. To put her down like a rabid animal, no matter what I'd promised.

But I didn't shoot. I held her eyes, and I thought of Saul. I thought of a rogue laid under spells of concealment and protection, and I thought of the trail vanishing each time.

Because *she* had protected a Were whose name I now knew. Billy Ironwater.

My muscles strained between the two urges—the urge to kill, to do my job and be the vengeance of her victims, and the small still voice of my conscience, trying to speak through the soup of rage and destruction. Trying to show me the way.

I hesitated, on the knife-edge. Why was I not killing her? Which was the right path to take?

Did I even care?

Then Perry made his mistake. The mistake that put the last piece of the puzzle in place.

"Do as I *tell* you!" he hissed, vibrating with rage and impatience. *"Kill her, you stupid bitch!"*

I came back to myself with a jolt. Uncertainty vanished, and my conscience spoke with the voice of brass trumpets. I knew the right thing to do, and what Perry wanted me to do, and found with relief that I could still make that choice.

No. My lips shaped the word, without breath to make a sound. It was wrong. Just how I couldn't say, but I *knew* it was wrong.

If I killed her, I would no longer be a hunter.

I would be as bad as Perry if I cut her down now. Worse, even. Had that been his game all along?

Certainly, something deep whispered inside me. *He's been watching and waiting to trap you, and Arkady gave him a perfect opportunity. It's just another game for him, maneuvering you into taking a life you shouldn't. Damning you just like a Trader, and taking his payment. Then it won't be him in the rack, screaming.*

It will be you. And he will not let you go.

Cenci nodded. It was a slight movement, her chin dipping faintly. Then she turned, the rags of her clothing fluttering on the sudden sharp rain-laden wind, and was gone, into the black mouth of an alley. Masked as thoroughly as ever a hellbreed was.

Perry twitched.

I threw myself back and to the side, avoiding his clawed hand. The guns spoke as I squeezed both triggers, staggering them. Each shot hit him full in the chest. Once, twice, three times. Four. Black ichor burst out, his diamond stickpin vanishing in a mess of gore.

He snarled, lightning etching sharp shadows into his face. They were the lines of an ancient inhuman hunger, and for a moment I saw beneath the screen of blond bland humanity and glimpsed the truth, as if I was *between* again.

I *saw* him, and my heart stopped, sanity struggling with the flash of revealed evil before my brain mercifully shut it away, unable to remember the full horror. My breath stoppered itself in my chest, heart struggling to function.

A clotting, cloying reek of spoiled honey and rotting sweetness boiled over me before the rain flashed through where he had been standing, and I heard retreating footsteps. Perry ran in the direction of the Monde Nuit, and I lay on the cold street as the slashing fat needles of water soaked through leather, cloth, and my scorched hair.

My breath came back, spilling into flaccid lungs. My heartbeat kept going, the stubborn muscle not knowing when to quit.

Thank God. Thank you, God.

If I lay there with my face upturned to the rain, the shaking juddering sobs wouldn't matter. I had very little time to cry, because the sirens were getting closer, and I had to find a phone.

CHAPTER 30

It took an hour for me to clear the scene, mostly waiting for Montaigne to get there so I could tell him to start the paperwork for a major paranormal incident. The shattered hulk of the limousine, full of the water falling from the sky, was hauled away, and I used Monty's cell phone to reach Harp as I stood in a doorway, looking at the yellow tape and flashing red and blue lights. Monty palmed a handful of Tums while Harp's cell phone number rang.

"What?" she snarled, and I cleared my throat. I felt like I'd tried to swallow tacks instead of Monty's antacids.

"Harp. It's me." I coughed, each breath a broken husk. I was soaked to the bone, and would have been shivering if I'd had the energy.

"Jesus *fucking* Christ! Where the fuck have you *been?*" She was coming unglued.

That meant the job was done. Billy Ironwater was dead, the hunt had been successful. "Arkady's dead," I husked. "Where's the pyre?"

"The barrio. Barazada Park. Jill—"

"I'm on my way. Don't start until I get there."

"It's *raining,* Jill. Where the *fuck* have you been?"

"I will explain. Later." It hurt to talk. I tasted blood. "Hold the fucking pyre for me, Harp. It's necessary."

Silence, crackling. Thunder spilled through the clouds again, reminding us little mortals below of angels bowling and lightning striking.

I'd been so close to falling into Perry's trap. The idea that he'd used this to set up a snare just to catch me made me feel weak and sick.

The idea that I'd been so *close* made me feel even sicker.

What had stopped me?

"All right. Get here soon." Then she hung up, and I thought privately that her cell phone had probably been flung at a tree. Harp always got a little nervy after a successful hunt. She was coldly lethal during, but all the tension snapped like a rubber band afterward.

We know someone else who functions like that, don't we, Jill? Someone else who needs just a little push to go over the edge. Someone who almost fell right into a hellbreed's trap.

I ignored that voice in my head. The sunsword was a cold weight against my back, spent and icy. Working it free of the shattered metal and the pavement underneath had been hard for even my hellbreed-strong right arm.

Monty's bald spot glowed under the glaring lights. "Is it over?" He hunched his shoulders miserably under the assault of the rain.

"It's over." I would have sounded relieved, if it hadn't been for the broken glass scraping in my throat. "No more bodies, unless there's a site we haven't found yet. It's done."

"I don't even wanta know." He was pale. Fishbelly pale, and the water on his skin wasn't all from the rain. "You okay, Jill?"

The question was so absurd I almost laughed. I didn't only because it would have hurt too goddamn much. My ribs were tender, and I was so tired of being flung around and breaking them. The blood was washing off my face, and I was tired of losing it.

My throat was on fire, and I was tired of talking. I was just plain *tired*.

"Right as the fucking rain," I croaked. "I need a ride to Barazada Park, on the double. Can you?"

His tired, mournful eyes met mine. Lightning flashed, another tattoo of brightness. The bright yellow slickers of the emergency personnel wavered like fish at the bottom of a pond.

"I can do that," he said. Someone yelled his name and he waved fretfully over his shoulder. "Anything else you need?"

Another laughable question. There was so much I needed, so much I would never have.

But look at what you've got, Jill. A big fat pile of nothing. Isn't that grand?

At least I still had my soul. That, I now knew beyond a doubt. I had not fallen into a hellbreed's trap. I might be tainted, but I wasn't gone.

I was not damned. And if I wasn't now, had I ever been?

It was enough. For now.

"Not a thing, Monty. Thanks." Then I shut up and let him make the arrangements for a black-and-white to break a few traffic laws getting me down into the barrio.

There's a corner of Barazada Park that butts up against a graveyard, the Church of Santa Esperanza sitting gloomily off to one side. Weres don't have much use for Catholicism—and they have their reasons, the Inquisition in the New World being a big one— but they understand the symbol of the sacred as well as anyone.

Bile and slick copper lay foul in my mouth. My throat still throbbed. My hellbreed-enhanced healing capability had other things to worry about, like replacing the few gallons of blood I'd lost lately. Little things like a sore, bruised throat were last on the list.

I sent the black-and-white with its nervous rookie driver away, hunched my shoulders against the driving curtain of cold downpour, and plunged into the park's pines, aiming for the back corner. I crashed through the brush without trying to move quietly—after all, they were Were. They'd hear me coming.

I tumbled out finally on the top of a low rise, looking down into the shallow depression where a stack of brushwood lay slick and dark, a long male shape arranged atop it. Lightning flashed somewhere else, spilling light and silver shadows onto the wet grass.

I felt them watching, from the trees. Lambent eyes and glitters of teeth. But none of them came out. Had they guessed, or was it just a courtesy they paid me? Where was Saul?

Just as I thought it, another shape resolved out of the trees beside me, avoiding each wet clinging branch easily. Tall and broad-shouldered, two bits of silver glittering in his hair, Saul Dustcircle stopped short, staring at me.

I heard more branches crackle and whirled, held up my hands. *"Leave her alone!"* My harsh crackle of a voice was a crow's unlovely scarring on the sweet silver sound of rain and the clean roll of thunder. *"Leave her alone! She's not here for you!"*

Thank God, they retreated. A pale glimmer showed between the trees. The bone-splintering growl of threatened Weres rose under the collage of storm sounds.

Saul moved restlessly. "Jill?"

The growls died down. It took a while.

"Let her be," I managed through my swollen throat, struggling to pitch it loud enough to be heard. "I promised her."

He stepped away, twice. Both quick graceful movements. According to Were custom, it was his right to light the fire, since his kin had died at the hands of the rogue.

Water dripped icy down the back of my neck. I stared at the pale glimmer in the trees, willing it closer. Finally, Cenci stepped out.

She looked different, without the insanity of crimson glowing in her eyes. She had been washed clean, all the black ichor and scorching sluiced off. Her rags fluttered as she walked past, head held high with a hellbreed's pride, and stopped, staring down at the pyre.

Her face crumpled, once. That was all. She darted me a glance, and her eyes were dark without the shine of 'breed. Her throat swelled as she swallowed. She was taller than me by a good head, and so thin I saw the shadows of her bones.

Finally, she spoke. "Was it quick?"

I nodded, but it was Saul who answered for me. "Quick and painless." His voice was tight, almost as throat-locked as mine. Another restless movement on his part, and I stepped forward, steeling myself as I came within range of her claws. I kept my hands loose and free with an effort.

I hope I'm not being stupid.

She shot me a look that might have qualified as amused, if not for the sheer veneer of mute madness. Her profile was classic and serene, despite her father's nose. The damned are beautiful, all of them. Except maybe Perry, and he wasn't ugly.

The thought made my breath catch and my stomach go tight with stark terror. I'd shot him, and outwitted him by the barest of margins. If I'd fired on Cenci like he'd wanted me to, I probably could have killed her with a headshot. But what would have happened? *Really* happened?

I could guess, but I never wanted to know. I *never* wanted to find out. I never wanted to be that close to the abyss again.

Too bad, Jill. This is your life.

"I suppose you want an explanation." Her jaw set, her eyes flicking past me. Down to the pyre, as if she couldn't wait to get started.

"Don't need one." The rasp in my voice was better. I longed for a cold beer, for a hot bath, for a decent meal and a week's worth of sleep. "Arkady had a toy, and he had you. You did something hellbreed don't do."

"I'm one of his *experiments,* too. He impregnated a human. A *Trader.*" Loathing burned through her heatless voice. The sound of thunder retreated, the storm sweeping through and relaxing. The rain would be over soon, and fall would begin treading through the desert. Which meant colder nights, and the occasional seventy-degree day, and not much else here in Santa Luz.

The nightside doesn't take vacations. Neither do I.

"It doesn't matter." I didn't say that I knew, that I had seen it, in the way of things I saw *between*. A sudden flash of comprehension, and I'd understood so much more about her. Another toy, kept for some of Arkady's games, and a Were driven to madness after being trapped and subjected to God alone knew what.

They had done the impossible, both these broken creatures, and relied on each other. I didn't know if I could call it love. I would swear on a stack of Bibles that hellbreed can't love.

Yet she had put herself in danger, for a Were. Protected him as best she could, moving him across the country one step ahead of Arkady's search for them—because hellbreed do not like their toys to escape.

She had protected the Were the only way she knew how—with her sorcerous ability, and with spilled blood. His periods of lucidity grew less and less until he no longer recognized her—had that been a particular type of torture? And when he broke from her and ran, brought to bay at last by others of his kind, what was left for her?

Nothing but this.

"Are you ready?" I tried to sound kind, probably failed miserably.

"I'm ready." But she paused. "You know of Hell, hunter." It wasn't a question.

I shivered, not from the cold. Nodded. Rain peppered her skin and mine. She stared at the pyre still, her entire body leaning tensely forward, down the slope of the hill.

"Do you think he'll be there?" Abruptly, she sounded very young. I don't know how I knew who she meant, unless it was the human softness in her voice.

The rock in my throat wasn't just the swelling from being half-strangled. "Wherever you're going, Billy's waiting for you, Cenci."

She nodded. Stepped forward, and I noticed her feet were bare and battered, bleeding sluggish black that didn't look like hellbreed ichor. It was too thin, and though it looked black... well, blood often does, at night.

Human blood, at least.

Dear God, let this be the right thing to do. Let this be enough.

Her right hand was curled into a blackened claw—and I saw it again, her holding the sunsword's hilt, keeping her father pinned amid the gasping flames.

I stumbled. Saul's hand closed around my upper arm, kept me upright. The hillside was slick and treacherous as we picked our way down.

A Were pyre is lit with the peculiar practical sorcery they use. The flames aren't crimson, or black, or any of the spectrum of hellfire, banefire, or levinbolt flame. A Were pyre burns clean and hot, and it is white, with a dancing leaping thread of joyous yellow in its heart.

Saul Dustcircle stood beside me after lighting the wet wood. The tapering rain hissed and splatted, underlit white smoke billowing as the Weres lifted their voices in an ancient chant wishing peace to the departed. If you have ever heard it, you don't need it translated. It is the very color of grief.

Navoshtay Siv Cenci, her white arms closed around the slumped body of a Were, made no sound as the flames crawled through her flesh.

And I don't want to talk about that anymore.

CHAPTER 31

Harp's jaw jutted tensely, and the feathers rebraided in her hair fluttered. She wasn't speaking to me.

The platform was a chaos of noise and activity. Bright sunlight glittered on the ranked cars—Weres very rarely fly. They don't like it, so it was the train for all three of them. Harp and Dominic would drop Saul off near the Rez and use the rest of the trip to eat up a few days of recuperation time. They deserved it.

Harp and Dom had finished the small mountain of paperwork to report an interstate major paranormal event, and I would get a lump sum from the FBI's backstairs funding. With a little bit of fudging, the official story held up; a rogue Were was put down and a meddling hellbreed toasted. Cenci wasn't mentioned except in passing. All in all, it was a neatly tied package.

Perry still hadn't called me.

Dominic glanced at Harp, who had drawn away down the platform. "She'll get over it," he murmured to me. "Thank you, Jill. I mean it."

Same old Dominic, still smoothing things over for her. I nodded, silver shifting in my hair and my dagger earrings swinging. The bright sun was an excuse to wear wraparound shades, and I'd left the sunsword, blackened and still icy, at Galina's. If it ever recharged enough I might use it.

Or I might not. I shuddered at the thought. My replacement black leather trench creaked slightly with the movement, and I had my next pair of boots on. I hoped I could get through a week without bleeding on them.

Then again, the town had quieted down enormously. Maybe my reputation was finally scary enough to keep it that way. "Don't mention it, Dom. Why don't you come out some time when there's *not* an impending apocalypse? It'd be nice to just have a barbecue or something." My tone was far too falsely bright. I coughed into my hand, as if my throat was still troubling me.

"Sometime." Dom grinned. "I'd better go get Harp on the train. She'll call you in a few weeks."

I doubted it. She wasn't the forgiving type, and my putting a hellbreed on a Were pyre must have rubbed her hard the wrong way. Probably some other Weres, too.

I don't care. It was the right thing to do.

At least Dom agreed with me, in his own quiet way. Saul . . . he didn't say much one way or the other. It could have been that I was avoiding him.

If *could have been* meant *definitely,* that is. "See you, Dom."

He gave me a salute, sketching the motion with two fingers, and turned away. Harp had moved further down the platform, and I saw him slide an arm over her shoulders as he hustled her onto the train. They were a beautiful couple, I saw a few admiring glances tossed their way.

Saul stood with his hands in the pockets of his leather jacket. His eyes were on my face.

I studied him behind the sunglasses. My heart hurt. My head hurt. The pain ran through me.

"I guess this is goodbye," I said brightly. Blinked furiously behind the shades.

He shook his head a little, glancing across the platform behind me. The silver wheel and the twisted unrecognizable bracelet threw back sharp darts of reflected light. I tried to memorize everything about his face, storing it up like a thief.

"Take care of yourself," I added. I babbled. Like a complete idiot.

His jaw set, his mouth thinning. He nodded, privately, as if wrapping up a long internal conversation.

Saul's right hand came out of his pocket, and he held up something I had to squint at to make sense of. The shades didn't help, and neither did the water in my eyes.

It was a leather cuff, with buckles. Just wide enough for a wrist; for my wrist. He held it out, and I took it. I was helpless not to, my hand just flew up and grabbed it.

"That should last you longer than the copper." He stuffed his hand back in his pocket and cocked his head, regarding me. The departure announcement began blaring in the background, as last goodbyes were said all around us and people hurried to file onto the train. "When it gets worn or the buckles snap, I'll make you a new one." His voice dropped, as if he had something in his throat too. "I have to go home. My mother deserves to hear from me about...everything."

"I know," I jumped in. "Don't make it worse. Just go. Get the hell out of here." *Don't go. Stay. Please, stay.*

But I couldn't say it. I closed my teeth against the words. There were so many reasons why he shouldn't stay. He was Were, and I was human—tainted with hellbreed.

Corrupted, even if I retained my soul. No matter how hard I fought it, I was going to Hell eventually. And I'd just had an object lesson on what could happen to Weres once they tangled with anything hellbreed.

It wasn't fair. It was monstrously, hideously, absolutely unfair.

It doesn't matter, I told myself. *God, just make him go. Keep him safe.*

His eyebrows drew together, stubbornly. It just made him

handsomer, the richness of his skin almost too real under the sunlight. "I have to say something."

Oh, Christ. Don't draw this out. "Just *go,* will you?"

"I'm going." His shoulders hunched. "But I'm coming back. You can't cook worth a damn."

With that he was gone, flowing away with the peculiar Were economy of motion. I stayed nailed in place, buffeted by a stream of people who were heading for the exits now that everyone was safely stashed on the train. When his feet left the platform and he hopped up into the carriage Dom and Harp were already in, the snap of his feet leaving the ground of my city echoed in my chest like a broken guitar string.

I turned blindly away. It was a miracle I was able to make it to the parking lot and my Impala with the cuff clenched in my sweating fist. The tears blurring my eyes and sliding down my cheeks didn't stop even when I dropped into the driver's seat. I put my head down on the steering wheel and heard the lonely sound of a train whistle blaring as the five o'clock special pulled out of the station and chugged out of town.

Epilogue

Life went on. I cleaned out a nest of Assyrian shapeshifters, busted a ring of child-pornographer Traders, and wasn't thrown out of Micky's the next time I ventured in for beers with Avery. Theron simply nodded to me from the smoky dark lounge in back. I actually got to have beers with Ave every week, and we even went to see a horrible movie about zombie-slayers once. It was that calm. Unfortunately, I caught myself playing with a knife-hilt halfway through the film, and one of the supporting actors had shoulder-length dark hair and broad shoulders, not to mention a supple grace that was human enough to bring tears to my eyes. Avery didn't notice.

The weeks rolled by, and it came time for the payment. I finally nerved myself into a visit to the Monde on a gray Saturday night when fall had settled a blanket of sere monochrome over Santa Luz. Perry didn't act surprised to see me—but then again, he never did. In fact, he didn't talk much at all, beyond ordering me to strap him into the frame and use the long flat silver flechettes. The sounds he made were almost worth it, and I was so close, so close to cutting his throat. It would have been easy.

I could have killed him while he was strapped down. I *could have.*

I didn't. I don't know what stopped me, but I suspect it was the memory of silver in a man's dark hair, and his hand holding mine as yellow-white flames burned and the Weres sang their ancient, sad melody.

Cenci wasn't the only one a Were had saved. I could finally admit as much to myself.

By the time the hour was over, I was sweating while I cut, thinning black hellbreed ichor spattered over the frame and the white, white enamel floor of the room Perry reserved for his little games with me. I left him hanging in the frame, bleeding, and headed for the door, the flechette falling from my hand and chiming as it hit.

The edge was there, the temptation to kill him overwhelming. But he was strapped down, and if I murdered him now, or even tried to...

He spoke again. Just five little words. "Come back," he whispered, the sound sliding through the air and kissing the scar with a finger of soft delight. "Finish the job."

I did not pause. I ran, and his silky laughter followed me, falling from his bloody mouth. I knew his mouth was running with blackness because I'd punched him hard enough to make his lips a mess of meat.

When I finally got home that night I stood in a hot shower, sobbing and scrubbing at myself with coal-tar soap until I was raw all over, the water sliding down the drain turning ice-cold and running pink and red. I collapsed on my bed afterward, hugging sheets that still smelled faintly of a man's smoky musk.

Nothing had changed.

Everything had changed.

No rest for the wicked. I cried myself to sleep, got up the next night, and went back to work. But not before I visited Mikhail's grave with another bottle of vodka.

It was a relief to finally know I had not killed him. If I'd hung back, purposely waiting, on that night, it was only because I loved him. Had it been otherwise, I would have pulled the trigger on Cenci. You are either damned or you're not, and if you're not, you can stop worrying about your teacher's death in a shitty little hotel room.

Whatever responsibility I carried for Mikhail's death, it was not because I had deliberately robbed him of backup that night. I could swear that much with a clear conscience now, and if the keening infection of grief under my heart didn't stop, at least it got easier to bear.

Things picked up after that. There was a scare about a scurf infestation moving up from Viejarosas to the south—Leon's territory. We found a few *arkeus* who had a nice little Trader stable specializing in rape and extortion, busted it up. I took almost half a clip of heavy ammo before Leon knocked out one of the Traders. He told me later he'd thought I was a goner.

Not yet, I told him. *I'm too mean.*

He laughed, thinking I was joking.

There was the regular rash of exorcisms around Halloween, and I finally nabbed the hellbreed flooding the city with adulterated cocaine. Right after I beat him to a brackish pulp another one moved in to sell adulterated heroin, and I lost a few pints of blood teaching *that* hellspawn that if you were going to import drugs into Santa Luz, cutting them with shit wasn't good business sense.

Then came damn near a month of almost-quiet, and I roamed the streets at night looking for trouble and not finding any.

It was a good feeling, but also a faintly unsteady one.

I came home on a chill winter night. The mountains in the distance were wearing their hoods of snow again, and as soon as I pulled into the garage I knew something was different. I slipped out under my closing garage door and padded around to the side entrance, silent as death.

The door closed quietly behind me. I had the whip loose and easy in my right hand, the Glock in my left, and I eased down the short hall, the warehouse creaking and booming with wind coming from across the desert, laden with cold and the smell of sage.

There was another smell. I sniffed cautiously, then deeper. My chest hurt with a swift deadly pain before ice closed the feeling away.

What the hell?

The lights were on in the long living room. I edged out into the open, caught a flicker of movement in the kitchen, and leveled the gun.

He didn't even turn around. He wore a long-sleeved black thermal shirt and jeans, and he was barefoot. The sheaf of hair that used to touch his shoulders was shorter now, shorn, glowing red-black under the kitchen lights. He hummed a little as he added something to the saucepan.

My heart pounded so hard I thought I would faint. I actually considered it.

"It's late," Saul said over his shoulder. Silver glittered, threaded into his hair with red thread. He'd picked up a few more charms, and the glints looked good against the silky darkness. It would look even better once some of it grew out. "Or early, with you working the night shift and all. So I thought, omelets. Hope you like pepperjack cheese; it's hard to find decent pepperjack back on the Rez. I was craving it. And hash browns. Baked, this time. You don't have the right oil for frying them. Did you throw out *every-thing* in the fridge?"

My jaw was suspiciously loose. My ribs ran and boiled with pain that burrowed under and into every vital organ, but most of all my heart. I was having a heart attack. Jill Kismet, kickass hunter, dropping dead of cardiac arrest over an omelet.

He looked back down at the stove, the back of his neck oddly naked without a Were's long hair. "It took a little longer to finish up out in the Dakotas than I thought it would. I was going to call, but then I thought you don't answer your phone much."

I dropped the whip. Closed my mouth with a snap, and kept staring at him as the leather slid onto the floor, metal flechettes tinkling.

He was in my kitchen. Again.

Oh, God, I am not strong enough for this.

He shut off the stove, picked up the pan. Flipped one omelet off onto a plate arranged just so on the counter, repeated the process with a slightly bigger saucepan. Fragrant steam rose. "I'll leave salt and pepper to your discretion," he said, and I realized he sounded a little nervous, for the very first time.

I cleared my throat. That was the sum total of my conversational ability.

He turned, holding my battered plastic thrift-store spatula. "We're going to have to talk about your taste in kitchen utensils, too." His eyes met mine, dark and level, and he dropped his hand. The spatula dangled easily, loosely.

I summoned up every scrap of courage I had. "I'm no good at this sort of thing," I managed, in a squeak that sounded more little-girl Minnie Mouse than confident hellspawn-murdering hunter.

"I got that," he answered gravely. He didn't look away.

My heart cracked open inside my chest. *Please, God.* The

prayer was no more than that, an incoherent mass of longing right behind my breastbone like Monty's indigestion. "I'm not a nice person." *I kill, Saul. I kill hellbreed and Traders and other nasty things. I'm corrupted. I'm tainted. You have no idea what I was, or what Mikhail made me, or what I am now. What I almost did, how close I came to handing over my soul to Perry. It's not just in the stories that people get taken by hellbreed.*

He sighed. Laid the spatula down on the counter. I remembered I was holding a gun, and holstered it. The creak of leather sounded very loud.

"Mikhail wasn't the only man who gives a damn about you." Saul said it very quietly. "No bargains, no deals. We'll see what happens."

One choked word struggled to get out. "Why?" *Why me? Why this? Why couldn't you have come here before Perry? Before I was a teenage streetwalker with a serious rage problem? Before I was broken?*

He shook his head slightly, as if I'd just asked a stupid question. "Because you need me. Because I want to," he said softly, and because he was a Were and he said it so quietly, it made *sense.*

God help me, but it did make sense. He was here *now,* he was saying. He was right here. In my kitchen.

With omelets.

The bubble of tears broke in my throat. One slid down my cheek, hot and accusatory. "I don't know how to do this." That finished up all my ability to speak, because if I said anything else I was going to start screaming.

He shrugged. Picked up a plate, and I saw with a kind of mad hilarity that he even had a sprig of parsley stuck in each neat mound of hash browns.

"It's not that hard, Jill. You just sit down and eat something. Then we talk."

"Urgh," I managed, with a slight inquisitive sound at the end. What I meant was, *talk about what?*

And God have mercy on me, but he understood. He smiled, a sweet slow smile as he stood under the lights, and I lost every bit of good sense I had left.

"We can talk about anything, kitten. Come on, it won't stay hot forever."

Book 2

Hunter's Prayer

For Miriam Kriss,
whose honor is impeccable.

From ghoulies and ghosties
And long-legged beasties
And things that go bump in the night,
Good Lord, deliver us . . .
—Traditional prayer

Thou Who hast given me to fight evil, protect me;
keep me from harm. Grant me strength in
battle, honor in living, and a swift clean death
when my time comes. Cover me with Thy shield,
and with my sword may Thy righteousness
be brought to earth, to keep Thy children safe.
Let me be the defender of the weak and
the protector of the innocent, the righter of
wrongs and the giver of charity.
O my Lord God, do not forsake me when
I face Hell's legions.
In Thy name and with Thy blessing,
I go forth to cleanse the night.
—The Hunter's Prayer

CHAPTER 1

It's not the type of work you can put on a business card.

I sometimes play the game with myself, though. What *would* I put on a business card?

Jill Kismet, Exorcist. Maybe on nice heavy cream-colored card stock, with a good font. Not pretentious, just something tasteful. Garamond, maybe, or Book Antiqua. In bold. Or one of those old-fashioned fonts, but no frilly Edwardian script.

Of course, there's slogans to be taken into account. *Jill Kismet, Dealer in Dark Things. Spiritual Exterminator. Slayer of Hell's Minions.*

Maybe the one Father MacKenzie labeled all females with back in grade school: *Whore of Babylon.* He did have a way with words, did Brimstone MacKenzie. Must have been the auld sod in him.

Then there's *my* personal favorite: *Jill Kismet, Kickass Bitch.* If I *was* to get a business card, that would probably be it. Not very high-class, is it?

In my line of work, high-class can cripple you.

I walked into the Monde Nuit like I owned the place. No spike heels, the combat boots were steel-toed and silver-buckled. The black leather trenchcoat flapped around my ankles.

Yeah, in my line of work, sometimes you have to look the part—like, *all* the time. Nobody takes you seriously if you show up in sweats.

So it was a skin-tight black T-shirt and leather pants, the chunk of carved ruby at my throat glimmering with its own brand of power, Mikhail's silver ring on my left third finger and the scar on my right wrist prickle-throbbing with heat in time with the music spilling through concrete and slamming me in the ribs. With my hair loose and my eyes wide open, maybe I even looked like I belonged, here where the black-leather crowd gathered. Bright eyes, hips like seashells, fishscale chains around slim supple waists—all glittering jewelry, silken hair, and cherry lips.

The damned are beautiful, really. Or here in the Monde they always are. Ugly 'breed don't come in here, or even ugly Traders. The bouncers at the door take care of that.

If it wasn't for my bargain, I probably would never have seen the inside of the place shaking and throbbing with hellbreed. Even the hunter who trained me had only come here as a last resort, and never at night.

I might have come here only to burn the place down.

Nobody paid any attention to me. I stalked right up to the bar. Riverson was on duty, slinging drinks, his blind eyes filmed with gray. His head rose as I approached, and his nostrils flared. He could sense me, of course. Riverson didn't miss much; it was why he was still alive. And I burn in the ether like a star, especially with the scar on my wrist prickling, the sensation tearing up my arm, reacting to all the dark hellbreed energy throttling the air.

Plus, a practicing exorcist looks *different* to those with the Sight. We have sea-urchin spikes all over us, a hard disciplined wall keeping us in our bodies and everything else *out*.

Riverson's blind, filmy gaze slid up and down me like cold jelly. "Kismet." He didn't sound happy, even over the pounding swell of music. "Thought I told you not to come back until he called."

I used my best, sunniest smile, stretching my lips wide. Showing my teeth, though it was probably lost on him. "Sorry, baby." My right hand rested on the butt of the gun. It was maybe a nod to my reputation that the bouncers hadn't tried to stop me. Either that, or Perry expected I'd show up early. "I just had to drop by. Pour me a vodka, will you? This won't take long."

After all, this was a hangout for the damned, higher-class Traders and hellbreed alike. I'd tracked my prey almost to the door, and with the presence of 'breed tainting the air it must have seemed like a tempting place to hide, a place a hunter might not follow.

It's enough to make any hunter snort with disgust. Really, they should know that there are precious few places on earth a hunter won't go when she has a serious hard-on for someone.

I turned around, put my back to the bar. Scanned the dance floor. One hand caressed the butt of the gun, sliding over the smooth metal, tapping fingers against the crosshatch of the grip— blunt-ended fingers, because I bite my nails. Pale flesh writhed, the four-armed Trader deejay up on the altar suddenly backlit with blue flame, spreading his lower arms as the music kicked up another notch and the blastballs began to smash colored bits of light all over the floor.

Soon. He's going to show up soon.

I leaned back, the little patch of instinctive skin between my shoulder blades suddenly cold and goosebumped. Silver charms braided into my hair with red thread moved uneasily, a tinkling audible through the assault of the music. I had my back to River-son, and I was standing in the middle of a collage of the damned.

Life just don't get no better than this, do it, babydoll?

"You shouldn't be here," he yelled over the music as he slammed the double shot of vodka down. "Perry's still furious."

I shrugged. One shrug is worth a thousand words. If Perry was still upset over the holy water incident or any *other* time I'd disrupted his plans, the rest of my life might be spent here leaning against the bar.

Well, might as well enjoy it. I grabbed the shot without looking, downed it. "Another one," I yelled back. "And put it on my tab."

Riverson kept them coming. I took down five—it's a pity my metabolism just burns up the alcohol within seconds—before the air pressure changed and I *moved,* gun coming up, left hand curling around the leather braided hilt at my waist and the whip uncoiling.

People have got it all wrong about the bullwhip. In order to use one, you've got to lead with the hip; you have to think a few seconds ahead of where you want to be. Like in a fast game of chess.

You get a lot of assholes who think they can sling a whip around ending up with their faces scarred or just plain injured, forgetting to account for that one simple fact. A whip's end cracks because it's moving past the speed of sound; little sonic booms mean the small metal diamonds attached to the laces at the end can flay skin from bone if applied properly—or improperly, for that matter.

Despite his ethnic-sounding name, Elizondo was a dirty-blond in blue T-shirt and jeans, dust-caked boots, his hair sticking up in a bird's nest over the face of a celluloid angel. His eyes had the flat hopeless look of the dusted, and I was willing to bet there was still dried blood under his fingernails. What he was doing here was anyone's guess. Was Perry involved in the smuggling? It wouldn't surprise me, but good luck proving it.

The whip curled, striking and wrapping around Elizondo's wrist; blood flew. I pushed off, my legs aching and the alcohol fumes igniting in my head, the butt of the gun striking across his cheekbone. *Not so pretty now, are we? When I get finished, you won't be.* I collided with his wiry-thin, muscular body, knocking him down. Heat blurred up through my belly, the familiar adrenaline kick of combat igniting somewhere too low to be my heart and too high to be my liver.

He went sprawling, landing hard on the dance floor, the thin graceful figures of Traders and hellbreed suddenly exploding away. They were used to sudden outbreaks of violence here, but not like this. It wasn't the usual dominance game played out for flesh or sex, or even darker hungers.

No, I was playing for keeps. As usual.

I landed hard, the barrel of the gun pressed against his temple, my knee in his ribs. "Milton Elizondo," I said, clearly and distinctly, "you are *under arrest*."

I should have expected he'd fight.

Stunning impact against the side of my head. Judo stands me in good stead in this line of work; I spend a distressing amount of time wrestling on the floor. I got him a good one in the eye, my elbow being one of my best points. He had a few pounds on me, and the advantage of being a Trader; he'd made a good bargain.

Still, I put up a good fight. I was winning until he was torn off me, his fingers ripping free of my throat, and flung away.

A pair of blue eyes met mine. "Kiss." Perry's voice was even, almost excessively so. "Always causing trouble."

I made it up to my feet the hard way; pulling my knees up and *kicking,* back curving, gaining my balance and standing up. It was one of those little things you see in movies that's harder to do in real life but worth it if you want a nice theatrical touch. Nobody ever thinks a *girl* can do it.

The whip twitched as my arm tensed, flechettes chiming against the floor.

Perry is a few bare inches taller than me, and slim in a casual gray suit. Blue eyes, long nose, a thin mouth, and a shock of pale hair completes the picture. If he wasn't so damn *bland* he might be more frightening—but the fact that he's unassuming, that he blends in, that the eye just kind of slides past him, makes him scarier when you think about it.

Much scarier.

Especially with the kind of beautiful damned hanging around him.

I pointed the gun at him. He held Elizondo up with one hand, the other hand in his pocket, casual as if he wasn't doing something no normal man would be able to do.

The music bled away in throbbing fits and starts. The scar on my right wrist turned molten-hot, the ruby at my throat began to vibrate, the silver charms tied with red thread in my hair tinkled. Mikhail's ring thrummed against my left ring finger; the finger that according to legend held a vein going directly to the heart. "He's under arrest, Perry. Put him down."

One blond eyebrow lifted slightly. He examined me the way a cat examines a nice, sleek bird, one the cat isn't quite sure if it's hungry enough to chase. A flicker of his tongue showed at the corner of his mouth, almost too fast for human vision to track.

The tip was scaled, and too wet cherry-red to be human. "Unwise to come in here, hunting."

Elizondo struggled, but Perry didn't even have the grace to pretend it mattered. Instead, his blue eyes held mine. I kept the Glock absolutely steady. Last time I'd shot Perry he'd bled buckets; I'd sent him a cashier's check to cover the damage to his suit. Which he promptly sent back with a dozen red roses and a little silver figurine of a scorpion that I'd picked up in a bit of newspaper and had Saul melt down. The silver had gone to coat more bullets, I burned the newspaper and the roses—and scattered salt all through the warehouse.

It pays to be cautious when dealing with the damned; especially hellbreed. The trouble is, nobody knows what *type* of damned Perry is, not even me, and he was a legitimate businessman. Deeply involved with all sorts of quasi-legal shit, but still legitimate, and able to afford a good lawyer. Or ten. Or twenty good lawyers, if it came down to it.

I cashed the check, though. I'm not a fool.

Then there was the holy water incident about a month ago. Which I was hoping he'd forgiven me for, or at least wasn't going to kill me over now.

Not when he could make me pay later, in private. I was banking on that, as I did so often. "I follow the prey, Perry. You know that. Hand him over, I'll cuff him, and the rest of you can get on with your revels. End of discussion." *And I'll even assume you have nothing to do with his business, but since he ran here like a rat once I blew his other hidey-holes I'm thinking it ain't a fair assumption. If I find out you're into slaving, Perry, our business relationship is going to undergo a drastic renegotiation.*

Perry's smile widened. "And what do I earn for my cooperation, Kiss? What is *this*," he shook Elizondo, negligently, "worth to you?"

Elizondo made a whimpering, whisper-screaming sound like an exhausted rabbit caught in a trap. I thumbed the hammer back with a solid click. Most women use baby Glocks because of their smaller wrists; I'm one of the stupid bitches who likes a big one. What can I say, I find it comforting. *Very* comforting. Plus I can handle the recoil, since I'm much stronger than your average girl.

Or even your average human. "Put him down, Perry. I'll cuff him." *I am not going to negotiate with you on this one.*

"A few moments of your time, Kiss? Since we are in such a very *special* place right now."

He's still mad about the holy water thing. Maybe it wasn't so easy for him to fix the scars. My throat went dry. I was acutely aware of the Traders and hellbreed, solemnly watching with their bright eyes and pale faces. I was outnumbered, and if Perry made it open season on me I was going to have a hell of a time.

Get it, Jill? A Hell of a time? Arf arf.

"Suck eggs, Pericles." I had four and three-quarter pounds of pressure on the five and change–pound trigger, and this time I lifted the gun. I would hit him right between the eyes, my pulse suddenly slowed and the sweat turned to ice on my skin. "Put him the fuck down before I blow your motherfucking head clean off your scrawny little body."

"Such ladylike language." But Perry dropped him. Elizondo hit with a thump and scrabbled briefly against the floor. "What is the nature of this one's sin, avenging angel?"

Sometimes hellbreed ask me that. *Do you really want to know? Are you sure?* "Child molester." I moved forward, carefully keeping the gun on Perry. Dropped the whip and gave the body on the floor a kick, he moaned and coughed. All the fight had gone out of him. I knelt, and managed to get the left bracelet on him. It took a bit of doing one-handed, but I also got his right hand wrapped, tested the silver-coated and bespelled cuffs, and decided it was good. "He had a thing for cutting out little kids' eyes. Once he finished raping them, that is. Then there's his habit of passing older kids along for a slave ring, that's what he's facing charges on now. Trouble is, this boy's a clairvoy. Always knows where the cops are going to be, jumps ship like a rat." My fingers curled in Elizondo's greasy hair, I wrenched his head up, examined his face. Yep, under his fluttering eyelids there was a sheen to his eyes. *Trader.* He'd bargained with one of Hell's denizens for an advantage over humans. It would be useless at this point to try to find out which one in town had given him what he'd asked for.

When Elizondo got to the jail Avery would exorcise him, and he'd go back to being a petty little meat-sack; he wouldn't have any clairvoyance left either. Psychic ability gets ripped out by the roots during a Trader exorcism, partly to deny hellspawn a further foothold inside a human being and partly because of the weird internal logic of exorcism ritual.

It would be excruciatingly painful.

Well, that was the price of being a Trader criminal in my town.

I dropped him, looked up at Perry, the gun still held steady. "Back up."

He shrugged, his hands in his pockets. "Your lack of faith wounds me, Kiss. It truly does."

Will you quit calling me that? I didn't say it. Giving Perry that opening would mean no end of trouble. "Back the fuck *up*."

He took one single step back. "You owe me. I expect you here for two hours tomorrow. Midnight."

"I'm busy."

"With an attitude like that, you'll never pay your debt." His voice had turned silken.

Like I owe you for more than a month at this point. "I'm serious, Perry. This isn't my only job. I'll come on Sunday." I decided it was probably safe, holstered my gun. His eyelids dropped a little, but that was all. I tried not to feel relieved. "Midnight." *You don't own me. We just struck a deal, that's all. And it was a good deal, we both get something we want.*

You just don't get all *you want. You won't, either. Not while I'm breathing.*

He shrugged. "Two full hours, Kiss."

"You already said that." The bullwhip coiled back up as I flicked my wrist, I stowed it at my hip, and just for the hell of it I gave Elizondo another kick. My eyes never left Perry's. The pretty blond man on the floor vomited, a sudden sharp stink. I bent down, snagged the cuffs, and hauled him to his feet. "Sorry about that." My tone said clearly I wasn't sorry at all. "Thanks for the assist. I'll see you get some credit with the Chamber of Commerce."

A ripple ran through the ranks of the damned. Their eyes bored into me, bright little points of light; I heard Riverson mutter something under his breath. Something like *bitch*.

Perry's mouth twitched. If the smell bothered him, he made no sign. His eyes ran down my body, but his hands didn't leave his pockets. "A round for everyone, on the house," he said quietly. "Let's celebrate the end of a successful hunt, for our Kismet."

They shuffled, a polite and sarcastic cheer edging up from the crowd. I hauled Elizondo for the door as the movement to the bar started and the music began at low volume, ramping up slowly. They gave me a wide berth, and I heard the usual whispers.

I didn't mind. After all, next week I might be hunting any one of them; Trader, hellbreed, or whatever else hung out in the shadows. Once damned, *always* damned, it was a piece of hunter's wisdom.

What does that make me? The scar on my wrist ran with cold prickling, Perry's attention on me the whole time.

Elizondo was an almost-dead weight by the time I shoved him out through the front door, past the glowering twin mountains of bouncer. My orange Impala was parked at the curb, in total violation of the fire lane, and Saul Dustcircle leaned against the hood, smoking a Charvil. He was tall and rangy, his skin a sweet burnished caramel; straight shoulder-length red-black hair glittering with sacred charms and small silver amulets tied with red thread. The tiny bottle of holy water on the chain around his neck, next to the small leather bag, glittered a sharp blue like a star. This close to so many Traders and hellbreed, the blessing in the water was reacting to the charge of power in the ether. To OtherSight, the Monde Nuit was a depression full of murky fluid, clearly a place where those allied with Hell came to party down.

Saul's dark eyes brightened as he saw me pushing Elizondo along. He shifted inside his hip-length leather coat, and his white teeth showed in a smile I was very glad to see.

I finally began to feel like I might have survived my latest trip into the Monde.

CHAPTER 2

Every city has people like me. *Every* city. Usually the police and the local DA's office have us on payroll as consultants; when all's said and done it's law enforcement we're doing. Freelancers are rare, mostly because without the support system the regular cops provide we have a tougher time. Besides, even though most of us don't play well by rules or with others, we *are* on the side of the good guys. Our methods are a little different, but that's just because the criminals we catch are a little different.

Okay, a *lot* different. We do, after all, go after the things the cops can't. What ordinary cop can face down a Were or even an ordinary shapechanger, or an Assyrian demon? Not to mention the contagion of scurf or Black Mist bloodsuckers, the adepts of a Sorrows House trying to bring back the Elder Gods, or the Middle Way and their worship of Chaos? What ordinary cop stands a chance against a Trader, even? The very idea will send the more flighty of us into hysterical fits of not-very-nice laughter. We are what we are because we *know* what's out there in the darkness. People disappear all the time. It's a fucking epidemic; some of the disappearances are murder, some are fugitives, some are kidnapped by other human beings. Some of them are even found again.

But a good proportion of them are taken by the things that go bump in the night. And then it becomes a hunter's job to bump back.

Hard.

Morning isn't my best time, so I cradled a double vanilla mocha breve, extra whip, while I waited for the room to fill up. Bright, shiny new rookies; each one with a pretty badge and that look every rookie has, eager but trying to contain it, like a dog straining at the leash. Buzzcuts were in for both genders this year, and they came in laughing and joking, sobering when they saw me leaning against the dry-erase board. My back was to the defensible wall; it was why I taught in this room with its gallery of windows looking out onto the Vice squad's forest of cubicles. Each desk had an empty garbage can sitting next to it, and there were a couple of jokes about that, too.

I blinked sleepily and sipped at my coffee while they chose their seats, jostling and good-naturedly bantering back and forth.

On the other end of the dry-erase board, Captain Montaigne shifted his bulk. This was one of his less-favorite parts of the job. I heartily agreed.

I'd dressed normally, for me. Most hunters are sartorially odd, to say the least. So today it was leather pants, low on the hips; a tight *Mark Hunt* T-shirt, my long leather coat heavy on my shoulders. A gun rode my right hip, but I'd left the bullwhip at home. Instead, I wore extra knives. My hair was pulled back from my

face with two thin braids, the rest of the long mass hanging down
my back, silver amulets tied in with red thread. The braids were
also woven with red thread and tiny silver charms; I wore the silver ankh earring in my left ear and the long fanged dagger earring
on the right. A brown leather bracelet sat on my right wrist over
my scar; my short-bitten nails were painted dried-blood red. The
combat boots were steel-toed and scuffed; the tiger's-eye rosary
dangled down and touched my belly while the black velvet choker
with the medal of St. Christopher moved as I swallowed. Just
below the choker, the chunk of carved ruby on its short supple silver chain was warm.

I also wore enough eyeliner to make me look like a hooker. My
eyes stand out even more when I outline them with kohl. One blue,
one brown, the mismatched gaze a lot of people find hard to meet.

I didn't paint them to accentuate it before. Not until I met Saul.

The rookies finished dribbling in, and Montaigne cleared his
throat. I looked at the slide projector again, allowed a small smile
to touch my lips.

Monty looked at the sheet in his hand, called roll. I let the names
slip past me. They were like every other class of rookies, eyeing
me nervously, wondering what I was, fiddling with the folders on
their desks. Nobody had been brave enough to open one yet.

"Everyone's here." Monty shifted his weight again, a board
creaking under his mirror-polished wingtips. He had a nice tie on,
probably a gift from his wife. She had far more taste than he ever
would. "Now listen up, boys and girls. This is Ms. Kismet. She's
going to give you the class you've heard whispers about. Listen to
her, and don't give her any shit. If you play nicely with her, she
might even show you her tattoo, and believe me, it's worth it. You
will be tested on this material, and it could save your life. So *no
shit*." He glared at them with his watery gray eyes, and my smile
widened. I could have repeated the speech word-for-word. Every
class, though, some jerkass decided to get cute with me.

We'd see who it was this time.

"They're all yours. Don't kill anyone." Monty ran his eye over
them one more time, then stalked away. The door closed behind
him with a click.

I let the silence stretch out, taking a sip of my mocha. Then I set it down on the small teacher's desk set to one side, and folded my arms. "Good morning, class." I took perverse pleasure in speaking as if to a bunch of nine-year-olds. "I'm Jill Kismet. Technically, I'm an occult consultant for the Santa Luz metro area; my territory actually runs from Ridgefield to the southern edges of Santa Luz; Leon Budge in Viejarojas and I split some of the southern suburbs. If you *really* want to get precise and technical, I'm the resident head exorcist and spiritual exterminator, not to mention liaison between the paranormal community and the police. But the most popular term for what I am is a *hunter*. I hunt the things the cops can't catch."

A ripple went through the room. I waited. Phenomenal self-control, not one of them had made a smartass comment yet.

"I'm sure you all come from many diverse religious backgrounds, and you will probably think I'm doomed to go to some version of eternal torment after my inevitable demise. It is, I will tell you, too late. Strictly speaking, I've been to Hell and come back, and that's what gives me some of the abilities I possess. Most of you are probably wondering what the fuck I'm talking about, or wondering if this is a practical joke. Lights."

The lights flickered and died. Not a one of them glanced at the switch by the door. I snapped my fingers, and the slide projector hummed into life. "I assure you," I said into the thick silence, "I am not joking. These are crime-scene photos from a case you may recognize if you read the papers a year and a half ago."

"Jesus Christ," someone whispered.

"No. This is a rogue Were attack. Can anyone tell me what differentiates this from a regular homicide scene?"

Someone coughed. Choked.

"I didn't think so. By the end of this day, you'll be able to. If you'll open your file folders—"

"What the shit is this?" This from a tall, jarheaded rookie who smelled of Butch Wax.

Here it comes. I wasn't far wrong. He made the same little movement a lot of civilians do when confronted with the nightside—a jerk of the head as if shaking off oily water, like a dog or a horse. "This some kinda joke? What the fuck?"

"This isn't a joke, rookie. It's deadly serious. Your employment with the police force is contingent upon you passing this day-long course to my satisfaction. Because believe me, I do *not* want to visit any homicide scene starring any of you yahoos in the victim role. The simple rules I give you will keep you safe. Lights."

The lights flicked back on, and my smile wasn't nice at all. They stared at me, dumbfounded.

"I will be blunt, rookies. You'll all be required to memorize the number for my answering service, which will page me. Pray you never have to use that number. Three or four of you will have to. A few of you won't have time to, but you can rest assured that when you come up against the nightside and get slaughtered, I'll find your killer and serve justice on him, her, or it. And I will also lay your soul to rest if killing you is just the beginning."

Thick silence. Vacant stares. They were too stunned to speak.

"Saul?"

He resolved out of the shadows in the far end of the room, stalking between their desks. Several of them jumped. It was a nice bit of theater, even if I do say so myself. He reached the front of the room, a tall mahogany-skinned man with his hair starred and hung with silver, two streaks of bright red paint on his high, beautiful cheekbones and lean muscle rippling under his T-shirt. He was armed, too, and when he turned on his heel and raked the rookies with his dark gaze, not a few of them leaned back in their chairs.

"Saul here is a Were. You didn't know he was in the room even when he flipped the light switch, and believe me when I say he could have killed every motherfucking one of you in here and walked out the front door of this precinct without so much as breaking a sweat." I took two steps away. "Do it."

Saul blinked, and complied.

No matter how often I see it, I always get a little shiver down my spine when he *shifts*. The mind is trained by the eyes to make a whole hell of a lot of assumptions about things, and seeing a tall man who looks like the romance novel ideal of a Native American melt and re-form, fur crackling out through his skin, eyes becoming amber lamps with slit pupils, can wallop those assumptions out from under you pretty damn quick. It doesn't help that my blue eye can *see* what he does, how he pulls on the ambient energy around him to break a few laws of thermodynamics and turn into a big-ass cougar.

Where Saul had stood, the cougar now sat back on its haunches. It blinked again, deliberately, and muscle rippled under its pelt.

Someone let out a thin breathy scream. The first vomiting spell began, in the back of the classroom. The blond jarhead's mouth worked like a fish's.

Saul *shifted* back, spreading his arms and shaking himself. Looked at me again. I nodded, he drifted over to the door, his step completely silent... and he proceeded to disappear from their sight again, the little camouflage trick Weres are so fond of.

The vomiting began in earnest, and I picked up my coffee, took a long drink and wrinkled my nose. When they were finished and the janitor had taken away all the pukebuckets, we'd get down to work.

CHAPTER 3

Lunch was pizza, but none of them were in the mood to eat much. I had three pieces, Saul stopped at five; we didn't bother with dinner. I finally let them go at about six, mostly shell-shocked and bone-tired. The psych staff was on hand to give them each tranquilizers and a good talking-to. I was packing up the slide projector while Saul picked up all the leftover folders, when Montaigne breezed in the door again, this time accompanied by Carper from Homicide.

"Hey, Kiss." Carp could barely contain himself. "Another long day of bile?"

I wasn't in the mood. "How hard did *you* throw up when I trained you, Carp? I seem to remember you passing out and moaning near the end of the slide show."

Saul straightened. He didn't like Carp, and the feeling was

mutual. His dark eyes fastened, unblinkingly, on the tall, broad-shouldered detective. My scar itched, under the leather cuff, prickling in the presence of antagonism.

Montaigne sighed. "Mellow out, both of you. How's it going, Saul?"

Saul shrugged. He went back to picking up the folders, each movement economical. "Good enough. Dragged one in last night."

"I heard; Avery was delighted." Monty finally dropped it. "There's something I need you to take a look at, Jill."

The script never varies. *Something I need you to take a look at, Jill.* Each time delivered wearily, as if Montaigne himself doesn't believe he's asking a woman just a little over half his age and half his size for help.

I gave my line. "Sure." I put the slide wheel back in its box. "Animal, vegetable, mineral?"

"Homicide. Carp examined the scene."

"Male or female?"

"Hooker."

Oh, for God's sake. "Male or female?"

"Female. The autopsy says so, at least."

"How fresh is the body?"

"Last seen last night. Out on Lucado."

Lucado, the flesh gallery. A cold finger touched my back. "Where was she found?"

"82nd and Varkell. On the side of the road, just on the margin of Idle Park." Carp finally spoke up. He might enjoy baiting Saul and giving me a hard time, but he was a good homicide deet and knew what to look for in a scene. If it had triggered his fine-tuned sense of the weird, I should definitely take a look.

I stretched, my lower back protesting as it often did after one of these things. "All right. Lead the way; send someone to box this up and put it back in the vault. Saul?"

"I'm with you." He fell into step behind me, and we left the file folders and the slide projector behind. "From Lucado to 82nd is a fair way."

"'Tis." I followed Monty's broad back and Carp's thinner, younger one. *And a body in what kind of shape that they can't tell*

male or female without an autopsy? That doesn't sound good.
Saul bumped into me, crowding me just like a Were. He liked
physical contact, and herding me around was his way of showing
it; it was also meant to make the point that I spent my off-duty
time with him.

Weres get a little territorial like that.

I pushed him away, the leather cuff on my wrist brushing his
arm. He jostled back as we strode down the hall. He was getting a
little antsy; it would probably degenerate into a shoving match
once we got home. We'd spar for a while, and it would end up very
satisfactorily for all concerned.

He was always a little on edge whenever I had to go into the
Monde. So was I.

We made it to the Homicide department, and a perceptible
quiet entered the room when I did. I didn't pay attention, not anymore. Instead, we made it all the way through to Monty's office.
Saul shut the door, not bothering to do his camouflage trick; he
knew how Monty hated it. Instead he loomed behind me. One
hand brushed the small of my back, a private caress.

I tried not to smile as I crossed the room to Monty's desk. He
handed me the file. "Take a look. Want a drink?"

"Sounds good. Saul?"

"None for me." His voice was a pleasant rumble, he looked
over my shoulder. I didn't flinch. I'd long since gotten used to
hearing his voice in my ear, his heat brushing my back.

Monty handed me the bottle; I took a slug as I opened the file.
The liquor burned all the way down, and I choked, slamming the
bottle down on the desk. I nearly followed it with a fine mist of
Jack Daniels, the picture snapping into coherent shapes behind
my eyes. "Fuck." I backed away from both Monty's desk and
Saul's heat, stalking over to the window. "Holy *fuck*."

"All the internal organs are gone," Monty said quietly. "Took
her eyes too. *Everything's* gone, there are chunks taken out of the
upper arms and legs that look like...bites. The only reason the
ME could make determination of sex was because of a lucky fin-
gerprint. Her legs were still mostly there, but everything between
them and her neck is *gone*."

The picture was brutal, taken under the glaring high-intensity lights of autopsy. No wonder they'd had to get her on the table to find out *he* or *she*. The body was almost unrecognizable as human. *No hair. No clothes. Was she dumped naked? Are those claw marks? Teeth? What is this?* "She was seen on Lucado, and then found near Idle Park? How iron-clad is the sighting?"

"She was seen by Vice cops at ten-thirty. At two in the morning the body was found. Her right middle finger was left intact, they printed and ran it just on the off chance, got lucky. Sylvie Mondale, teen hooker and heroin addict." Monty's tone wasn't dismissive or harsh. Just blunt, to cover the aching sadness of it. I checked the vitals sheet.

She was fifteen. I'd been fifteen on Lucado once.

Jesus. They get younger all the time. Or is it that I'm getting older? The picture glared at me, something about it still subtly wrong. *No breasts. And the viscera's gone. Where did it go?* "Parents?"

"Father's in Hunger Central, doing life for murder. Real winner. Domestic violence, petty theft, assault, grand theft auto, rape, breaking and entering. That's not counting the attempteds. Mom was a heroin addict, dead two years ago. Kid ran away from Blackman Hall and hit the streets, been in on prostitution charges every once in a while. Part of Diamond Ricky's gang."

"Grew up fast, this kid." Saul said it so I didn't have to. I turned the photo over, laid the file down on the desk, and began to look in earnest.

The pictures taken at the scene were also merciless. Someone had dumped her just at the edge of the park, right on a fringe of gravel bordering the road. Varkell Street slid away from 82nd at an angle, and she was left just at the dividing edge. Each photo was a different angle, with marks for triangulation. The body lay on its side, arms and legs flayed and crumpled together, blood soaking into the gravel. I looked, but didn't see any sign of entrails.

If they killed her somewhere else it's bound to be messy. Lots of trace evidence. But Carp's right. This is...this is something strange.

A chill finger caressed the back of my neck just as my pager jolted into life against my hip with a blurring buzz. The small sound made the sudden quiet in the room more noticeable.

I unclipped the pager, held it up, glanced at the number.

Christ. Never rains but it pours.

"This is one of mine." I gathered up the file with quick swipes. "Is this my copy?"

"Take it. I thought you'd want it." Carp had gone pale. "What's it look like, Kiss?"

I don't know, and that's a little disturbing. "We'll see. I'll be in touch. If another one like this shows up, call *and* page me. All right?"

"You got it."

I handed Saul the file and nodded to Montaigne, who was looking decidedly green. Of course, Monty hated it when I clammed up. Almost as much as he hated it when I opened my mouth and told him about the nightside. He'd run up against a Trader once, a guy who had bargained for near-invisibility and superstrength; Monty'd had the crap beat out of him and some good sense scared in by the time I showed up and dusted the Trader with four clips of ammo and a trick I picked up working the Santeria beat in Viejarojas under Leon's teacher Amadeus one summer.

It took Monty three months in the hospital to recover. He hasn't wanted to know shit about the nightside since.

Wise man.

"See ya round, Monty."

"See ya, Jill. Good luck."

It was the closest he ever came to thanking me. Or telling me goodbye.

CHAPTER 4

Father Guillermo kept in shape by playing basketball, and his curly mop of black hair framed a face as pale, serene, and weary as a Byzantine angel's. "Daughter Jillian. Thank the gracious Lord."

I grimaced, but if anyone could get away with calling me that, he could. "Morning, Father. You rang?" Darkness pressed close behind me as I stepped over the threshold, from night chill into seminary quiet. Saul followed, his step silent, baring his teeth in a greeting to the priest, who was used to it by now and didn't flinch. Weres don't like the Church, and I can't say I blame them. There's only so much of being hunted an innocent species can take.

Of course, the fact that some Weres weren't so innocent didn't help. But still, they didn't deserve the Inquisition.

Nobody deserved the Inquisition, at least in my humble opinion. And the other half of Saul's heritage had suffered at the hands of Christianity too.

They remember, out on the Rez.

"I'm glad you've come." Guillermo, at least, was always happy to see me. Of all the priests I'd worked with, he was by far my favorite. "We have...another one."

Of course you do, otherwise you wouldn't call. I took a firm grip on my temper. Teaching a class of rookies always puts me in a bad mood. "Age, sex, details, Father. You know the drill."

He closed the high narrow door, locked it with shaking hands. I smelled incense, candles, the smell of men living together, and the peculiar fustiness that screams *Catholic.* My heartbeat kicked up a notch, and Saul bumped into me again, his hand this time smoothing down my hip through the tough leather of my coat. The brief touch was soothing, but I still moved away, following the priest's long black cassock. Sour fear roiled in the air behind Guillermo, despite the placidity of his face and the habitually clasped rosary. As a matter of fact, as soon as he was finished locking the door he clutched his rosary again, twisting it through his capable brown fingers.

"Twenty-four, male. The...it's odd."

Male? That *was* a little odd; women are statistically higher at risk for possession; it works out to about seventy-thirty. The Catholics blame it on Original Sin. I blame it on being taught to be a victim from birth, plus a higher incidence of psychic gifts—and less training for those very gifts, in our rational culture. We would just have to agree to disagree, the Catholics and me. "Odd how?" *You've had every conceivable type of person in here suffering from possession, Father. What makes this one different?*

Although I would have to admit there were patterns in

possession, just like in everything else. Most victims are morbidly religious innocents, since Traders have the benefit of an agreement, no matter how shoddily phrased, to protect them from being taken over; also, the *arkeus* who comes through to sign the agreement usually loses out when the Trader's hauled in and exorcised. It's in their interest to make a good deal. Also, most victims are middle-to-upper-class; the poor seem to be ignored by the Possessors. For once, there was a predator who *didn't* feed on the lowest end of the economic pool.

The priest's footsteps echoed, mine brushed quietly along behind him, and Saul's were silent. "It's *different,*" Guillermo insisted. "This time it's . . . different."

I'm really starting to hate that phrase. I took a firmer grip on my temper. But then we reached the end of the hall, and instead of making the sharp right that would lead to the basement, the priest turned to the left and led us toward a smaller private chapel. I could see that the chapel door was barred, a four-by-four with a rosary hanging on it, swaying gently as whatever electric current was behind the door strained and swirled.

Uh-oh. Bad news. Why don't they have the victim downstairs in the exorcism chamber? "Gui? You want to give me a vowel or something here? Why aren't we heading to the chamber?"

"The victim is . . . a student, Jillian. It's Oscar."

My heartrate kicked up another notch. I didn't know Oscar, and the dreamy shocked tone in Father Guillermo's voice was beginning to worry me. "A seminary student? Victim to possession?"

"He was missing from evening prayers; Father Rosas found him in here."

Big fat Rosas, the jolly one. I eyed the chapel's high pointed doors. The four-by-four rested in iron brackets that hadn't been used since the great demonic outbreak of 1929. Now *that* had been a bad year for hunters all over. "Where's Father Rosas?"

"Father Ignacio took him to the hospital. He's suffered a heart attack. I entered the chapel and saw Oscar. He . . . he was *floating.* And gabbling in a strange tongue. I pronounced the name of Our Lord and he screamed in pain. Then I came out, barred the door, and called you. The rest of the students are in their dormitory; Father Rourke is standing watch there with the crossbow."

I heard the hiss-flare of a match, light briefly dappling the high
narrow hall with its black-and-white tiles. Saul had lit a Charvil.

Oh, for Christ's sake. But I let it go. He had more than one
reason to hate the Church. Guillermo didn't mention it, just pointed
at the chapel doors. "He's in there. Please, be merciful. If...if
he..."

I nodded, reached out. Touched the back of the good Father's
hand. His fingers curled so tightly in the rosary it was a wonder
his knuckles weren't creaking. "There." I pointed with my other
hand, to a spot in the hall on the opposite wall, where a bench
would provide him with a place to sit that was out of the way
should the door get busted down, and out of the sight-line should it
be busted down by whatever was in the chapel instead of by me.
"Sit over there. Keep your rosary out, and repeat your Hail Mary.
Okay?" That would keep him occupied and provide him with
some protection—calling on a goddess is one of the oldest reme-
dies against evil. Gui had once admitted to me that he loved God,
certainly—but Mary was intercession, and a Jesuit is predisposed
to Marianism anyway.

It was part of why I liked Gui. That, and his taste in microbrew
beers.

I would have reassured him, but what priest would want reassurance from *me?* I'm a hunter, and condemned to Hell—or Pur-
gatory at least—even as the Church quietly funds training for not
a few of us.

Guillermo nodded. "Be...be merciful, Jillian."

"You know me, Father. I'm a regular angel of mercy." I regretted it as soon as it left my mouth. His face crumpled slightly, took
back its serene mask. I saw just how badly shaken he was and
regretted it even more. "Go sit down, Gui. I promise I'll take care
of him."

A few moments later, with the priest out of the way and mumbling his prayer, Saul glanced at me. "Ready?" The cigarette
fumed in his hand, resting casually on the four-by-four. His fingers
brushed the dangling rosary. The wooden beads were charred.

Holy shit. What the hell's going on here?

I didn't reach for the whip. Instead, my left-hand fingers crept
to my right wrist.

Saul's eyes widened a little. He dropped the cigarette to the tiles, stepped on it, ground it out. He said nothing.

The scar burned and buzzed under the cuff. I could feel my left eye—the blue one, the smart one—starting to get dry. I eyed the rosary as it swayed, the cross tapping the door with tiny little sounds. The closer I got to it, the more violently the cross swung.

Tap. Tap. Tap.

I took a deep breath. Saul's hand came up, the bone-hilted Bowie knife lying flat against his forearm. *Be careful,* his eyes said, though his mouth wouldn't shape the words. It would be an insult, implying I couldn't take care of myself. Weres are touchy about that sort of thing.

It briefly warmed me, that he would consider my pride. High praise, from a Were.

I unbuckled the cuff, and the shock of chill air meeting the scar made me inhale.

Did Perry, across town in the Monde—maybe sitting in his office, maybe in his apartment up over the dancefloor, staring at the walls or an empty chair—feel it when I did this? I'd never asked.

I didn't want to know.

Colors became sharper, the sting of cold air hitting the back of my throat, my skin suddenly sensitive to the faintest brush of air. My vision deepened, darkness taking on color and weight, new strength flooding my limbs.

As usual, the thing that scared me most was how *good* it felt. My hair lifted on a slight warm breeze that came from nowhere, and I lifted my eyes to find Saul smiling, a private little smile that reminded me of all *sorts* of delicious things.

The scar twinged. Open for business, working overtime.

"Ready," I whispered, and focused *through* the door.

Saul flipped the four-by-four out of its bracket as the charms tied in my hair made a low, sweet tinkling. The wood clattered on the floor, the rosary splitting, its beads kissing the tiles gently before shattering into fine ash. He kicked the door open, force splintering the wood in long vertical strokes as they flew wide. My boots brushed the floor lightly as I leapt through, right hand

up and fingers spread, heatless black flame twisting at my fingertips. Skidded as it darted for me, my hand twisting through a
motion that sketched flame on the air.

I collided with a levinbolt, hit hard, the voice like brass bells
stroked with a wire brush. It was muttering in Chaldean, and it
had just thrown a concentrated bolt of energy at me.

Oh, for fuck's sake. Just what I need. The scar on my wrist
flushed with heat, shunting the levinbolt aside and leaving me
only breathless instead of knocked senseless on the floor.

Saul was suddenly *there,* appearing out of thin air, spinning
into a crouch with the fingers of his free hand tented on the floor.
The young boy in the long black seminary-student almost-frock
(because they believed in old-fashioned clothing here at Grace)
tumbled over him, the twisting ripping sound of Old Chaldean
spoiling the air. I spun, the flame on my fingertips arcing, and
caught him, boots skidding across the floor as kinetic energy
transferred, mass times velocity equaling an elbow to my mouth.

That's why I don't get my nose pierced like I want to. I get
clocked in the face too goddamn much.

Tasted blood; locked the kid's wrist and wrestled him to the
ground. A few moments of heavy breathing and twisting, my coat
rucking up, and I finally had him down on the floor. "Saul!" *For
fuck's sake, where are you?*

He appeared, locking the boy's arms over his head. Pressed
down with a Were's strength, his dark eyes meeting mine for just
a moment and the paint streaked on his cheeks suddenly glaring
in the darkness.

The chapel was narrow, pews on either side; the altar would
have been beautiful if the *utt'huruk* hadn't leached all the life
from the flowers, torn the cloth and the dead plant matter to
shreds. It hadn't been able to breach the shell of belief and sanctity
over the windows and walls, though; that was something to be
grateful for.

Oscar was a tall blond corn-fed boy. I got my knee into his gut
and held him down, his legs scrabbling uselessly against the tiled
floor. *Don't crack his skull, Gui wants his deposit back on this
mother.*

"Show thyself," I hissed in ceremonial Chaldean, the syllables harsh and curdled against my tongue. "Show thyself, unclean one, carrion one. *Show thyself! In the name of Vul I command thee!*"

It howled, and the smell of spoiled milk and dry dusty grave-wrappings coated the back of my throat. More important than the words of any exorcism is the psychic force put behind them, the undeniability of command. You have to be a little bossy with the bitches, or they start laughing at you.

Then you really have to kick some ass.

So I bore down, not physically but *mentally,* a long harsh breath of effort hissing out between my teeth. Struggling, my will locked against the *utt'huruk,* pressing, *pressing.*

A subliminal *pop!* and the world exploded. I passed out for a fraction of a second, the outward pressure I was expending slamming me out of my body and back in as the elastic defenses built around my mind snapped the thing away from me and deflected most of its blow. I came to with scaly, horny hands around my throat, digging in, and Saul's chilling cough-roar. The pews we'd landed on had shattered, wood-dust swirling crazily as the *utt'huruk*'s bulbous red compound eyes stared into mine, its beak click-snapping shut twice.

I'd pulled it out of the kid.

Good fucking deal.

I balled up my right fist, my left fingers scrabbling uselessly at its claws around my throat. The scar on my wrist ran with flame, burrowing in toward the bone, *burning.* The thing was wiry but tremendously strong, it hissed a curse in Old Chaldean that would have turned a civilian's hair white.

My right hand throbbed, the scar turning white hot as if Perry had pressed his lips on the underside of my arm again. A bolt of agonized desire lanced through me, I punched the bird-headed demon right square between its ugly eyes, where the seam of almost-flesh made an imperceptible weakness. *Utt'huruk* Anatomy 101: if you've got a hellbreed-strong fist, use it on the thing's skull.

Its head exploded in gobbets of stinking meat, its predator's beak curling like plastic in an oven. The smell was incredible. Choking, I scrabbled at the horn-tipped hands digging into my throat, worked them free. My breath came harshly. Little charms knotted into my hair dug into the back of my head, my shoulders.

"Fuck." I coughed, rackingly. The *utt'huruk*'s body slid bonelessly to the side, hitting the floor with a thump. "Man, I hate it when they do that."

"You okay?" Saul, his voice low. But he didn't move from his position, holding down the kid.

God, it was good working with him. "Peachy keen." I rolled aside, made it up to my feet. My coat rustled as I strode back to him. One boot on either side of the boy's hips; I squatted down and ran my right hand down the front of his cassock. Buttons parted, I pushed material aside, looked at his narrow pale chest.

No mark. The chest was the most traditional place, but...

I checked the inside of his wrists, his ankles, his knees. I even checked the inside of his thighs; Saul helped me turn him over and I checked his buttocks, the base of his spine, the *backs* of his knees.

His nape was covered by the high black collar. I tore the rest of the material aside, my heart beating thinly.

Nothing. I even smelled his *hair*. And checked his testicles.

"He doesn't appear to be a Sorrow," I said finally, and Saul let out a relieved sigh. I, however, was not relieved, not in the slightest. How could an *utt'huruk* get into a kid in a seminary? "Pick him up; let's go. Guillermo's probably having a fit by now."

Behind me, the *utt'huruk*'s body was caving in, noisome liquid running from its breaking skin in runnels of filth. Being a hunter was exhausting, but at least I wasn't a janitor.

Saul hefted the boy's weight, pale naked skin looking exotic against his more familiar mahogany darkness. "You hungry?"

My pulse was starting to come back to normal, the copper of adrenaline leaching out of my dry mouth. And despite the smell, my stomach rumbled. "Yeah. Want to go to Micky's?"

"Sounds good." His white teeth flashed in a smile that was like his hand on my back. "Bacon cheeseburger? Pancakes? Omelet?"

As if anything could match your omelets. "Tease."

CHAPTER 5

Father Guillermo knew better than to be unhappy about the state of the chapel. He took the news calmly, all things considered, only almost-fainting; I held him up and made an appointment to come back and interview the kid's friends. I did search the kid's room and look over the visitors log, but none of the names seemed familiar or suspect; Oscar himself hadn't had any visitors and he would probably be in a coma for a good week before he woke up and could give any answers. There was nothing in his room. Nothing abnormal, that is.

It didn't matter. I'd find out. Chaldean meant the Sorrows, and if they were looking for fresh meat they would have to look somewhere else. I didn't allow a Sorrows House in my city.

That didn't mean they wouldn't try to sneak one in. Still, they should know better. Some hunters just keep an eye on the Sorrows and bitch-slap them every now and again to keep them in line.

I kill them on sight. And each time I do, I earn a little piece of myself back.

Saul and I hit Micky's at about midnight. Micky's is on Mayfair Hill, in the gay section of town; the nightclubs were just hitting their most frantic pace. But Micky's is a little more quiet, being an all-night restaurant of the quality the locals guard jealously and tourists only hear whispers of. Inside, the walls are covered with posters of film stars from the forties and fifties, and the bar is tucked in the back, smoky and murmuring but always well-mannered. Start trouble in Micky's, and your ass will be on the street in seconds flat.

Because along with being a safe place for the gay community to canoodle in the booths and kiss openly at the tables, Micky's is run by a Were and has Were kitchen staff. Some other nonhumans work there, too. Though a few of the waitstaff are civilian humans, Micky's is where nightsiders come to eat late at night.

Nightsiders on the right side of the law, that is.

I shrugged off my coat and slid into the red vinyl booth, giving Saul the side with his back to the wall. Chas was on duty, and he brought a martini and a Heineken, setting the beer down in front of Saul with a grin. "Heya, dude."

"Dude." Saul's answering grin lit up his eyes. "How you, Chas?"

"Can't complain. Hey, Jill." Chas looked like Puck on steroids, flirting his eyes at Saul while he put my martini down. Tonight his T-shirt was pink, with *Fancy Boy* in curlicue script across his broad chest. Jeans just short of indecent wrapped around his lower half. It was a safe bet that he was commando under them.

"Hey, Chas. What's the word?"

"All quiet around here. My sister says hello."

I stifled a smile. Marilyn thought she owed me for saving her baby brother's life. Chas had gotten tangled up with some trouble once, having to do with a circle of Traders running a dope-smuggling outfit from a house on Mayfair itself. Two SWAT teams had already been wasted by the time they called me in; I cleared the house and found Chas naked and shaking like a rabbit, chained in a small filthy room with only a mattress. I could still see the marks on his wrist from the chains if I looked closely. But after rehab and five-odd years of therapy, he was much better.

And Marilyn was everlastingly grateful.

I never told her that I'd almost killed Chas, I'd been trigger-happy after taking out five Traders and a little doglike demon that looked disconcertingly like a Lhasa Apso. That had been before Saul, but only by a few months.

"Tell her I say hello back." I settled for empty cliché politeness. "How are you, Chas?"

"Better all the time. The usual?" The frightened-rabbit look had gone out of his eyes, and he'd stopped flinching when I moved too quickly.

After five years, that was a blessing. "The usual, hot stuff. Don't forget the strawberry jelly." I made a face, and was rewarded with Saul's slow smile. Chas bopped away, switching his cute little weightlifter ass, and Saul handed the file over the table.

"Dammit, I hate it when you anticipate me," I lied.

"You're just so transparent." Saul's smile widened, turned wolfish. "Rookies put you in a bad mood."

"I'm always in a bad mood. It's part of my girlish charm." I flipped the file open, turning over most of the grisly photos in the same motion. Instead, I studied other shots of the scene. "What do you think, Saul?"

His eyes met mine. Deep, dark eyes, as veiled as a cat's gaze, he rubbed his chin. No stubble yet; he doesn't have the usual Were problem of being hairier than an Armenian wrestler. The red paint was crackling, drying on his cheeks. It meant the day was over.

Thank God. I could do without days like today.

"Has it occurred to you," he said slowly, "that we've been really busy lately? You haven't had a week off since the spring equinox and that serial-rapist guy."

I thought about it, staring at the photo of the wet stain left under the body, gravel showing up sharp and slick under the glare of lights, evidence markers bright yellow.

He was right. It had been one thing after another. I hadn't even had a pedicure in months. Of course, being a hunter means being outnumbered. Most psychics are women, but most hunters are men; they can quite frankly take more damage.

We female hunters are a tough bunch, though.

Still, we have large territories, and even with Were and other alliances it's still hard work. Plenty hard, plenty dangerous, and unremitting.

But there should have been a lull or two since spring. We were just past New Year's, that made it almost a year since my last real break.

The trouble was, there wasn't anyone I'd even felt had a *chance* of surviving training, even if I had time to take on an apprentice or two. Saul was fast and tough, but he was a Were. There were some things a hunter dealt with that would kill him, if only because he didn't have the breadth of knowledge I did when it came to Possessors or *arkeus*. Or, say, a Sorrows adept.

Or, God forbid, a Black Mist infestation. No, Saul was great backup, the most marvelous backup in the world, but I couldn't train him to be a hunter. Even if he'd wanted to, which wasn't at all likely. He went with me because we were involved, not because he had any pressing need to even the scales. No *mission,* unless it was keeping his lover's skin whole.

Don't think I'm not grateful.

"Doesn't look like things are calming down much lately either." *I'd call for reinforcements, but who am I going to call? Leon? He can barely keep Viejarojas under control. Anderson up north? His territory's twice the size of mine. Anja, over the mountains? She's got all she can handle with the Weres fighting the scurf over there.* I tapped my fingers on the glassed-over tabletop.

"I miss you." The smile had fled. He picked up his beer, took a long draft, his throat working as he swallowed. Set it down, licked his lips. "I mean, I miss hanging out with you. We haven't been to a movie in months."

We spend every ever-loving day together. But you're right, our R&R has been sadly lacking of late. "I miss you too. What's playing?"

"Probably nothing much. The point is, you need to take a break, Kiss."

I made a face. "Don't I always. But you're right, we should spend some quality—"

"I want you to stop."

I actually dropped the file on the table, closing it. I stared at him. "What?"

It was his turn to make a face, a swift grimace. "Not stop hunting, kitten. I know you too well. I want you to take a vacation with me. A real vacation, to someone else's territory. Where you're not always looking over your shoulder."

Do you think this is like a nine-to-five job, where if I leave I'll come back to paperwork and phone calls? I'll come back to dead bodies and mountains of work to catch up on. Christ, Saul, what are you thinking? "If I could get someone to cover—"

"Leon and Andy could both help; they've both got apprentices, for Christ's sake. Anja would be more than happy to ask a few Weres to come out on patrol—it'll be fun for them. Not to mention the Were population here in your own town. I want to get away."

He nodded, sharply, as if he was finished speaking. Then he continued. "I want all your attention, for a change."

Were jealousy? Or something more? I glanced down at my right wrist, the scar covered and feeling flushed, full, ripe since I'd drawn on it. "Is this about—"

"It's not about that goddamn bastard and his goddamn Monde. I just want you to take a vacation. With me." He looked down at the tabletop, his long expressive fingers playing with the beer bottle. A ring of condensation marked the table, he moved the bottle slowly, blurring it, drawing it out. "Want to take you to meet my people."

Holy shit. My heart gave a leap that felt like zero-gravity had suddenly kicked into effect. "You want me to...meet your people." *Christ, I sound stunned. I feel stunned.*

He shot me a dark look from under his eyebrows, the charms in his hair stirring as he tilted his head. "That's what I said."

Oh, Lord. That was news. *Big* news, coming from a Were. I picked up my martini, downed half of it. It burned all the way down. "Sure." I tried to sound casual. "I want to dig a little deeper in this murder. But I'll call Andy and Leon tomorrow. Okay?"

His slow smile was a reward in itself. "You sure?"

As if I didn't know anything about Weres. I took a deep breath. "I'd be honored to meet your people, baby. Nobody better try to bite me, though."

"Aww, come on. I thought you liked that." The smile widened as he settled back in the seat, vinyl creaking and rubbing against his coat. I slid my boot over, touched his under the table, and had to catch my breath when his eyes half-lidded. Just like a big sleepy cat.

"Only from you, catkin. Only from you." I opened the folder again, looked down, and took the rest of my martini in one gulp, hoping Chas would come back soon with the food.

All of a sudden I couldn't wait to get home.

CHAPTER 6

I woke up with Saul's heavy muscular arm around me so tight I could barely breathe, his face in my hair, and an ungodly racket right next to my ear. Late-afternoon sunlight came thick and golden through the blinds, and the sound echoed. One of the things about sleeping in a warehouse: the acoustics are screwed-up. Which means I can hear every sliding footstep, every insect in the walls...but it also means the phone's ring turns into something like an air-raid siren. Especially when I'm tired.

Saul stirred slightly. I pushed his arm away and stretched, yawning, fumbled for the phone. His fingers slid over my ribs, warm and delicate for all their strength. I finally managed to grab the phone and hit the talk button. "Talk." *This had better be good.*

The warehouse on Sarvedo Street was mine, a last gift from Mikhail. I'd been trained as a hunter by one of the best ever to take the field, and he'd left me this space; enough room for a fully equipped gym, a meditation space, a double kitchen for entertaining and cooking up supplies, and a nice big bedroom with plenty of space around the bed so I could be sure of nothing sneaking up on me. And since Saul had moved in, the place looked much better; he had a genius for finding thrift-store gems and bargain luxuries.

What can I say? Weres are domestic. He even does dishes.

The phone crackled in my ear. "Jill? It's Monty. Wake up."

Adrenaline slammed through me, cold and total. I curled up to a sitting position, Saul's hand sliding free and the green cotton sheets rustling. "I'm up. What do you have?"

"We have another body."

"Another..." *So far, Monty, this discussion is frighteningly familiar. How many times have we had this little talk?*

"Another dead hooker with all her guts and her eyes gone."

My mind clicked into overdrive. "Where? And where's the body?"

"Scene's at Holmer and Fifteenth. Recero Park. They're hold-ing it for you, but it won't be long before the press jackals—"

"Recero? I'll be there in twenty. *Hold the scene.* Don't move even if the press finds it, put a tent over the body, and *leave it alone.* Okay?"

"Okay." But Monty didn't hang up. "Jill, if you know anything—"

"Who found it?" *Monty, I don't have anything yet, and even if I did I wouldn't tell you, dammit. You don't want to know.*

"Jogger. Being held at the scene. Medics are treating him for shock."

"I'm on my way." I hit the off button and bounced out of bed, heading for the bathroom at a dead run. My feet slapped the hard-wood floor.

"Jill?" Saul's voice, all sleepiness gone.

"Another murder," I tossed back over my shoulder. "Get your coat."

I took one look at the body and my gorge rose. It takes a lot to upset my stomach, but this managed to do it. I stood at the edge of the crumbling sidewalk and contemplated the gentle rolling grassy strip, about six feet wide, that was the very edge of Recero Park. The trees started with a vengeance, erupting with scrub brush and thick trunks as if the forest couldn't wait to spill out; if it hadn't been the beginning of winter there would have been more shade. My breath hung in foggy ribbons in front of my face.

This one lay on her back, sprawled in the shade below a large oak tree right off a jogging path. Her ribcage was cracked open, her face savaged and the empty sockets of her almost-denuded skull were already hosting flies even in this chilly weather. There wasn't even enough hair left to mark her as female. I stood for a few moments, letting it sink in.

There was nothing left between the broken petals of her ribcage, and nothing left in her belly either. I could see the glaring gouges where something had ripped and gouged through the periosteum covering the lumbar vertebrae. Little shreds of what had to be her diaphragm hung from the broken arches of her ribs; her arms, like the other one's, were terribly flayed. Her legs weren't touched much, but they were oddly flattened, as if the bones had been crushed.

The femur's an amazing bone; it takes a hell of a lot of stress per square inch with every walking step and even more while running. To crush and splinter a femur so slim slivers of bone poke out through the quads is . . . well, it takes a lot of strength.

Saul had gone pale. I didn't blame him. He hung back at the very periphery of the makeshift tent that had been erected to shield the body from the press, who had just started to show up in droves.

I shut away the sound of people, slowly closing my awareness until I could hear the wind moving in the trees of Recero Park. Naked branches, most of them; there were evergreens further in the center of the park, but out here along the fringes it was scrub brush and sycamores, a pale beech standing like a sentinel at the corner of Fifteenth up to my left. Again, the body had been dumped less than ten feet from the street, just at the margin of the park. The sidewalk here was cracked and beaten; this was a forlorn little stretch of road. Across the street a dilapidated baseball diamond for Little League stretched behind its rattling chain link fence, its dugout set off to the side, first base right across the street. The parking lot was a field of gravel and weeds behind the dugout and the stands, which looked rickety enough to collapse the first time someone sat on them.

Not a lot of witnesses, despite it being broad daylight. And nobody to hear her if she screamed. Assuming she was killed here. No, there's not enough blood.

The trees rustled.

Dumped here. Why? Anything that causes this much damage usually eats what it takes; why take the eyes? What is this?

I closed my dumb eye, the one that only saw the surface of the world. My blue eye stared, focusing *through* the scene, and I saw the faint fading marks of violence. She hadn't wanted to stick around, even as a disembodied soul; I didn't blame her. It was strange; she must have left in a hell of a hurry for the etheric strings tying her to her body to be torn like that. That wasn't too terribly out-of-the-ordinary for a violent death, but the scale of the damage was a little . . . odd.

"Paula Lee," Carp said, right next to me. I returned to myself, the sound of people swirling around me. "Those boots."

She did still have her boots on, distinctive pink leatherette numbers with stiletto heels. The pink was splashed with still-sticky crimson. "The boots are familiar?"

"I called Pico over in Vice, figured since the last one was a hooker and this one's wearing fuck-me hooves I might save myself some time. Peek knew the boots. She was also seen last night, early, on Lucado. Another one of Diamond Ricky's girls."

Crap. My stomach flipped, settled. "How old is this one?"

"Don't know. Caruso says she's young, though. Street name is Baby Jewel." Carp looked a little green, this morning he wore a thick gray sweater and jeans, a pair of battered Nikes. *Must have called him out of bed early. Was he sleeping in? It's almost 4 P.M.* His sharp blue eyes rested on the corpse; mine returned unwillingly to the ravaged face.

Baby Jewel. Christ. "I'd better have a talk with Diamond Ricky."

"He'll enjoy that." Carp's mouth pulled habitually down at the sides, making him look like the fish he was nicknamed for. He had run his hands back through his hair more than once today, I guessed. It stood up in messy spikes. His partner Rosenfeld was talking to one of the forensic techs; Rosie's short auburn hair caught fire in the afternoon light.

"You did the prelim, Carp. What's up?"

"Jogger came along, his usual route. Found the body, called it in from the pay phone at the corner of Fifteenth and Bride, two blocks up. Vomited right there before he did so, though. No tracks, even though the ground's fairly soft; there's some leaf scuff. It's the damnedest thing..."

I waited.

"Rosie looked at it and thought maybe the body had been *thrown* to land that way. Look at where her arms are, and where her head ended up. I think I agree."

You guys are amazing. "I'd carry that motion." I let out a heavy sigh. "Christ. Do you want to be there when I question Diamond Ricky?"

"Shit, yeah. Love to be a fly on the wall during that discussion. You gonna beat him up?"

I'd love to. "Only if he gets fresh with me. Try to keep your excitement under control." I motioned to Saul, who detached himself from the shadows he had begun to sink into and approached, his step light on the cracked pavement.

"I hate to ask." Carp's tone warned me. "But...Jill, do you have anything? Anything at all?"

"It's not a Were." That much, at least, I was sure of. "Mind if Saul does his thing?"

"Go ahead." Carp sounded relieved. I wondered when he'd figure out that I had no idea yet. Just like him.

And that bothered me. A kill like this was anything but subtle. When things shout this loud, they usually want a hunter to hear them.

Saul lifted his head and sniffed, rolling the air around in his mouth like champagne, tasting it. He stepped off the pavement, delicately, knowing the forensic techs were watching where he moved. His boots were soundless as he approached the body.

He paused four feet from the sticky pool of blood under the broken corpse. My gorge rose again; I pushed it down.

He bent his head, spreading his left hand, tendons standing out on the back, his fingers testing the air. Shuddered, his shoulders coming up.

He backed up without looking, retracing his steps. Reached the sidewalk, turned on his heel to face me. His dark eyes glittered, and under his dark coloring his face was cheesy-pale. His mouth turned down at both corners. He reached out blindly, his hand closing over my shoulder, fingers digging in.

I reached up, covering his hand with mine. Stared into his dark, dark eyes. He didn't speak—he would wait until he had everything clear inside his head before he gave me anything. But for the moment, we stood there, and copper filled my mouth.

In all the time I'd known him, I had never seen Saul Dustcircle look frightened before.

CHAPTER 7

Failing sunlight dipped the flesh gallery in gold. The tenements slumped, tired as the women who walked below, go-go boots and hot pants, fake rabbitfur jackets, each on her prescribed piece of sidewalk. The overall impression of this section of Lucado Street has always been motion, hips swinging back and forth, eyes blinking and glittering under screens of makeup, teased hair, candy-glossed lips most often marred by cold sores. The older girls worked the north end, the bargain basement; Diamond Ricky's turf was further south, prime real estate I could remember pacing years ago when it was Val's territory.

I never like thinking about that, though. It was a whole lifetime and a trip to Hell away from me. Thank God.

Ricky had some of the best merchandise, the youngest and prettiest; teenage girls who each would have sworn that Ricky *loved* her and was *protecting* her. And of course, we suspected him of running an escort service that provided underage action for rich businessmen. No proof.

Yet.

His number one was a girl a little older than his usual crew; she tossed back her long brown hair, sniffed, and wiped at her nose with the back of her hand as I tilted my head, taking in the apartment: huge entertainment system, white leather couch, trendy-in-the-eighties Nagel print hanging on the wall. Ricky's tastes ran to chrome, glass, and leather, and every piece in here was bought with the money he took from the young girls outside, peddling their asses scraping together enough to feed his appetite for luxury. Normally he'd be sitting out on the street in his Cadillac with some muscle, overseeing the action, but we'd managed to catch him at home with nobody but his girl.

Lucky us.

I took a deep breath. Pulled the chair out from the dining-room table, dragged it across the spotless white carpet. You wouldn't think to look at this place that it was merely a modest brownstone sandwiched between sloping ramshackle apartment buildings filled with the desperate.

Slim greasy Ricky lounged on the white leather couch. He wore a black cowboy hat with silver scallops on the band, black silk button-down shirt, and leather pants. Cowboy boots with silver tips were propped on the low glass table in front of him. He gestured at the small square mirror tile laying on the table. Two lines of white powder were prominently on display.

Christ. Do pimps ever change? I shook my head, set the chair on the carpet at precisely the right angle. Saul leaned against the door next to Carp; Rosie was still at the scene. Carp's blue eyes were avid, flicking over every surface.

I settled down on the chair, folding my arms and resting them on the back, knees on either side. Turned my unblinking gaze on Ricky while the number one wiped at her nose again, snuffling, and padded into the kitchen.

Ricky grinned, his fingers dangling loosely in his lap, an advertisement. He indicated the powder on the spotless mirror again, with a nod of his hat. "Feel free, *puta*." His grin widened; we wouldn't bust him unless it got difficult. "Or you here to make some money? I turn you out after I test the merchandise, see."

You son of a bitch. The scar on my wrist throbbed. The smile began down deep, I let it rise to my lips. Waited for the right time to speak, as Ricky shifted. It was that tiny movement, a flinch, that told me I had already unsettled him. He was a man who lived off mindfucking women, and I was just aching to do a little in return. Even it out for the female species, so to speak.

I waited. Let the smile bloom. He was Puerto Rican, so I let the tiger's-eye rosary dangle, hunching my shoulders and resting my chin on my crossed forearms. My eyes would do half the work for me. It's funny how many cultures have weird legends about people born with different-colored eyes.

Only I was born with brown eyes. The blue one is a gift—or a curse. Whichever, as long as it worked.

I looked at Ricky's nose. If you stare right at the bridge of a man's nose, he thinks you're looking him in the eyes. The gaze grows piercing, intense, and the man starts to sweat. Especially if he's done something wrong.

"What you want, huh?" His eyes flicked past me to the door. Carp was probably grinning. Saul, of course, would be staring unblinkingly at Ricky, daring him to make a move. "What you want, *puta?*"

I slid the gun free of its holster, rested my elbow on the chair back and pointed the barrel at the ceiling. The pimp stiffened. "Call me a whore again, Ricky, and I'm going to shoot your balls off." My smile widened, became sunny. The charms tinkled in my hair as I moved slightly. "Baby Jewel."

His eyes widened. "What about her? Hey, man, she swears she's eighteen, you can't pick no—"

I leveled the gun, cutting him off midstride. "Did she get uppity with you, *cabron?* Stopped handing over her cash? What was it?"

I've never seen a man turn white as curdled milk so fast. There was a gasp from the kitchen, and his number-one girl came around the corner, her eyes as big as dinner plates. I didn't move—if she needed taking care of, Saul would handle it.

"Jewel? She..." His eyes flicked over to Carp, widened, came back to me. "Oh, shit. Listen, I did no—"

"Shut up, Ricky." I pulled the hammer back.

He shut up.

"Now. Jewel was working for you last night. When did you last see her? When did she drop off her last load of cash?"

He flinched. "Nine," he finally squeaked. "She work the early shift, man."

Vice had seen her at just past ten or thereabouts; she must have hit the street again, maybe trying to make her rent now that she'd paid Ricky off. Or had she? "How much did she give you, Rick? And keep in mind that I can smell a lie, you greasy little piece of shit."

The girl behind me was quivering with terror, exhaling a high hard musky smell dipped in copper. She knew something. Good luck getting her to spill; if she told us anything Ricky would probably demote her, a fate worse than death.

Still, I might be able to try, if I could catch her alone. A lot would depend on the next few minutes.

And a lot would depend on if I could keep my temper.

Ricky reached up, took his hat off. "Four, five hundred," he said cautiously. "Sent her back out, her pink ass can make four *times* that if she works. Lazy bitch. They all lazy."

And you're such a self-made man. "She didn't show up all day today, and you didn't check on her?"

"Check on her?" He laughed, snuggling back into the couch, his hips jerking up. It was macho, and I let it pass. *Let him get comfy. I'm going to make him pretty damn uncomfy soon enough.* "The bitch comes back. She begs for a little Ricky love, *bruja.* They all do."

So we've gone from calling me slut to witch. It's an improvement. I raised an eyebrow. "Just like Sylvie? Did she come back begging too?"

Despite being lazy, Ricky wasn't a fool. His eyes returned to Carp. "Oh, *shit.*" He could barely get the breath to whisper.

I moved. The chair squealed, glass shattered as I brought it down squarely on the table; the sound was incredible. The girl screamed; Ricky let out a yell, and I was on him.

My knees sank into the leather of the couch. My left-hand fingers sank into his throat. I smelled *quesadilla* and cologne, not to mention the thin acrid funk of a coke fiend. I pressed the gun to his temple and smiled into his eyes.

This was pure terrorization for its own sake. I am not a very nice person, and if there's one thing I hate with a vengeance that surpasseth all understanding, it's *pimps.* I never pass up a chance to make a pimp feel my displeasure.

"I would as soon blow your head off as look at you, you greasy little cocksucker." My breath touched his lips. He shook like a rabbit in the snare. "I am going to ask you a few simple questions. Sylvie. Jewel. What did you do to them?"

I didn't think for a second that he had much to do with it. Mostly because the girls were worth more to him alive and peddling their wares. And also because Ricky was, like all pimps, a fucking coward.

He spilled a lot of babbling in Spanglish, enough for me to determine a few things: he hadn't even known Jewel was dead before we came calling. He also was more than willing to spill about the escort service, and I let him talk about that for a little while. Then he dropped one more piece of news.

I let go of him, reholstered the gun, and was off the couch in one motion. "You're sure?" The number-one girl stood by the entrance to the kitchen, her fingers pressed to her mouth and her eyes huge, dark, and full of tears.

"Course I'm sure, the stupid bitch!" Ricky moaned, turning his face into the couch. There was a ratty little gleam to his eyes I didn't like. "There's a doctor on Quincoa—Polish fucker, name's Kricekwesz, he takes care of that shit, but it ain't cheap. Stupid bitch. Stupid *fucking* bitch."

"You're a real prince, Ricky." I looked over at Carp, who was almost purple with restrained glee. It did him good to see me do something like this, something a regular cop wouldn't be able to do without worrying about a brutality lawsuit. "You want to take him in?"

Carp shook his head. He sounded excessively casual. "Not worth our time right now."

I silently agreed. Looked at the girl. Tears slicked her cheeks, and the way her eyes jittered away from mine told me there wasn't much hope of questioning her. There was a fading bruise just visible under the scoop collar of her pink shirt. She couldn't have been more than eighteen, but was already looking old.

"Do yourself a favor, honey." My voice was harsh. "Get out of the biz." *Before you end up just as dead as those other two girls.*

Then I stalked for the door. *Pregnant. Sylvie was pregnant.*

This puts a little different shine on things, doesn't it. Two counts of murder for her and her baby; and all her internal organs gone. Why? What is this?

Outside in the hall, Carp eyed me while Saul curled his hand around my nape and reeled me in. I spent a few moments leaning against Saul's chest, hearing his heartbeat, the shakes going down slowly. Very slowly.

I'd never told him about Val, but it wouldn't surprise me if he guessed. I'd never told Mikhail either, even in the long, sun-filled afternoons we spent in the same bed. But I wouldn't be surprised if Mikhail had known, too—he had treated me so gently in that one space, the space where we became more than just teacher and student.

Saul didn't want to let me go, but after a few moments I slid away, and his hand fell back down to his side. But a little of his warmth remained against my skin, as much as I could hold on my own without his hands on me.

"Well?" Carp couldn't restrain himself.

I checked the hall, set off for the end of it, where stairs would take us down to the door and the street below. "My initial reaction? He's got nothing to do with it. Could be chance, you know how it is. The escort service, though..."

"Yeah?" Carp was almost begging for me to give him something, anything.

"It gives me an idea." More than an idea, in fact.

Shit. I'm going to have to go see him early.

CHAPTER 8

Rosenfeld had short auburn hair, a strong-jawed, too-striking-to-be-pretty face, and wrists that put mine to shame even though mine are hellbreed-strong. She settled into the booth next to Carp and examined me suspiciously. "Don't suppose you've got anything useful."

"Not yet." I blew across my coffee to cool it.

Carp I could lie to, Monty encouraged me to keep it close to the vest—but Rosie liked it out where she could see it and tried to act like working with me didn't bother her.

Rosenfeld had only questioned my judgment once. That was during the Browder case; the next day she'd seen an *arkeus* up close and personal. I had almost been too late to save her—and she had seen me take my wristcuff off and battle the thing hand-to-hand. After a week in the hospital, she'd actually come down to the warehouse and *apologized,* something I had no idea a cop could do.

She was probably still dyeing her hair to cover up the white streak. I had no idea if she was still undergoing therapy, and I didn't ask.

Carp snorted. "You shoulda seen it. Diamond Ricky pissed his pants."

Rosie's eyes didn't sparkle, but it was damn close. "I heard the Vice guys giggling about it. Are you really gonna eat that? My arteries are hardening just looking at it."

"I need protein." I smothered the pancakes in butter and strawberry jam; picked up two slices of bacon at once. "Got to keep my girlish figure."

"We should all be so lucky." She studied my face. "So what do you think?"

"Sylvie was pregnant. Ricky was going to send her to a doctor on Quincoa. I'll check him, leave you two to talk to the other hookers. See if they can describe the last trick of the night for either of our girls."

"I don't have to tell you we gotta work fast." Carp dumped more creamer in his coffee. "There are only so many man-hours they'll spend on this."

I knew. If the dead had been nice middle-class churchgoing girls, the public outcry would be tremendous and we'd have a whole task force paid for by John Taxpayer. As it was, the only thing drawing attention to this was the shock value of the killings. Who cared what happened to hookers? Certainly not the same John Taxpayer who handed over a twenty for a blowjob or a bendover in one of Lucado's dark corners.

Same old story, different day.

Saul stirred restlessly next to me, tucking into his hash browns. His eyes flicked over the inside of the restaurant, a hole-in-the-wall diner on Holmer. I passed him the salt and the green Tabasco, shuddering at the thought of kissing him afterward.

I will never understand men and Tabasco sauce. "Two dead women in two days. If this accelerates we're going to have problems." I looked down at my cheese and ham omelet. The pancakes were substandard, but the bacon was crisp, at least.

"Thanks for that lovely thought." Rosie grimaced into her yogurt and granola, produced from her purse. "Anything you want us to do other than talk to hookers and try to keep the press off our backs?"

"I've got someone to visit who might be able to shed a little light, after I talk to the doctor. At least, he'll be able to tell me if someone's moved into town without permission." *And I've got to go back to the seminary and question a few kids, not to mention call Andy and... Christ, my dance card's full. As per usual.* "Just be careful, okay? This isn't looking good."

"Be more than careful," Saul piped up. "Be *cautious.*"

I glanced at him. He'd been extremely quiet since this morning, and while I appreciated his restraint—he more than other people understood how I felt about the sex trade—I still felt a little alarmed at how pale he'd been.

But he probably didn't want to talk in front of the cops, and I couldn't say I blamed him.

"Great." Rosie waved her spoon. "Be *cautious,* Tonto says. Care to give any specific pointers, or will you just settle for being cryptic?"

"Shooting our mouths off before we know precisely what's going on will get us exactly nowhere," I pointed out. "Don't give Saul a hard time. He works for me, not for you."

"We all work for the taxpayers, baby," Carp weighed in.

Yeah. So do the hookers. I rolled my eyes, flicked a long, charm-weighted strand of hair back over my shoulder with a slight chime. "Eat up, boys and girls. There's work to do today."

The abortion clinic on Quincoa was closed by the time we got there. I used the payphone on the corner to leave a message on Carp's cell that we would try the doc tomorrow. Next we could either stop by the seminary or go to the Monde Nuit. I wanted to get the Monde out of the way first, and Saul just got that look again, so I drove. I left him in the Impala smoking a Charvil and staring at the building with narrowed eyes.

I walked up to the door, fitting the silver over my right hand. It was technically a set of brass knuckles, but made out of alloyed silver with just enough true content to hurt anything damned but enough other metal to be twice as hard.

The usual daylight bouncer was on duty, a massive guy with a tribal-tattooed neck; I nodded to him and strode past. My blue eye widened, taking in the flux of bruised hellbreed-tainted atmosphere.

It was still daylight, never mind that the sun was fading fast; the Monde was almost deserted. One or two Traders were in there drinking whatever it is the damned drink, and Riverson was at the bar again; a couple janitors were cleaning everything up and wait-staff were getting ready for dusk.

Perry was at a velvet-covered table in the back, three other hellbreed with him. They were playing what looked like a card game, and cigarette smoke fumed in the air. He didn't even glance up at me, but the scar on my wrist ran with throbbing prickles, a hurtful bloom on the underside of my arm.

I was glad it was covered.

"Hey! *Hey!*" Riverson yelled. I ignored him. There were a few musclebound idiots in the shadows, too far from the hellbreed to be any help; my pace had quickened. By the time I reached the table they were converging on me. Perry's profile was supremely unconcerned, bent over his cards. A low murmur like flies above a corpse filled the air.

Helletöng, the speech of the damned. The ruby warmed against my throat on its silver chain.

I kicked the chair out from under Perry and *punched,* catching him across the cheek and flinging him down and away. The next kick shattered the table; oversized cards, cigarettes, and a half-bottle of Glenlivet went flying.

I reached down, grabbed Perry's shirt, hauled him up left-handed, and punched him again. Blood flew, the silver armoring my fist would hurt him more than the force of the blow. I drew back, silver suddenly hot on my fingers, and did it *again,* dropped him, and kicked him twice. The gun left its holster left-handed, a feat I practiced long and hard to achieve in the dim first days of my training, and I set my feet on the floor, turning in a complete circle to see what I was up against.

Seven of 'em, not counting the goddamn breeds I just inter-rupted. Splendid.

Perry coughed, and the sound of his laughter cut the air into a thousand wet, shivering pieces. "Sweet nothings," he managed through a mouthful of blood. "Kiss. So nice to see you again."

The muscles stopped, each leather-clad mountainous one of them. I drew in a deep soft breath, the gun held level. "Back off," I told them. "Or I'll fucking kill you all."

Silver in my hair rattled just like a diamondback's tail.

They backed off. I reholstered the gun, bent down, and hauled Perry upright again. "I put up with a lot of shit from you, Pericles. You and the rest of your hellspawn scum. But *no underage cooch.* The rule's simple: no dabbling in the under-eighteen pool in my territory. Right?"

As usual, he got cute with me. "Would we dare disagree?"

I'd damaged one whole half of his bland pale face, his blood-masked eyes glared at me but he remained still, perfectly still.

Inhumanly still.

I let go of the front of his shirt. Blood dripped from his chin, the skin over his cheekbone mashed into hamburger, his lacerated eye puffing up. *Never pretty in the first place, and a whole lot worse now.* I discarded the thought, lifted my fist again.

"Spare me your kisses, Kismet." He raised his hands, loosely. But there was no shimmer of etheric force around them, he wasn't getting ready to throw anything nasty at me. "We know this decree of yours. We *obey.*"

Like shit you do, if you think you can get away with it. "Oh yeah? Someone's breaking it. Using Diamond Ricky's teenage whores to feed a few bad appetites. And right now my suspicion is squarely on the hellbreed population. I know how little self-control you bastards have."

His unwounded eye narrowed a little, that was all. I could tell nothing from his face, and he probably had the idea that I was just fishing.

Still, it was therapeutic to bash his face in every once in a while. It was also good for my image. "Whatever escort service supplying underage cooch you've got your fingers in, get out. Now. Or next time I come back I'll *shoot* you in the fucking face. *And* I'll see this place loses its incognito appeal with the police."

His lip curled—at least, the half of it that wasn't split and bleeding. "Human police?"

And whatever nightside help I can beg, borrow, and threaten to erase you from the face of the earth. "I'm sure they can be given a little help." I held his eyes, unblinking. The scar on my wrist sent waves of heat up my arm, each wave deep, soft, and deliciously warm. My heart rate rose a little, but I was trained too well to have a little sex magic distract me. "Don't fuck with me, Perry."

"Someday you might want me to." He reached up, touched his bleeding lip with delicate fingertips, and the smile in his blue eyes chilled my blood. "I'll live to hear you beg, hunter."

Not if I have anything to say about it. "Dream on, hellspawn. Do we understand each other, or do I have to kick your ass around this cheapshit little shack?" The back of my neck prickled. I could *feel* them moving in on me. *Got to think of something quick here.*

Perry waved them away. Thin black ichor spattered on the floor, the wounds closing slowly. Very slowly. Silver's deadly to them, something about the Moon and how she rules the tides of both sorcery and water. We don't fully understand *why* silver works, but no hunter I've ever run across cares. It's enough *that* it works.

Perry's eyes burned laser-blue. The tip of his cherry-red scaled tongue flicked over the black ichor oozing over his lips like a tiny crimson fish. "I understand you perfectly, dear Kiss. Do you even understand yourself?"

"Spare me the psychobabble." I turned on my heel, my hand throbbing inside the silver weight. My back ran with electricity— a damned I'd just punched in the face was right behind me. *Right* behind me. In front of me, two mountains of muscle, both wearing sunglasses, both armed with assault rifles. "See you Sunday, Perry. Maybe I'll ruin another one of your suits."

"I look forward to it. Try not to break anything next time."

"Don't piss me off, and maybe I won't. Keep your ears open." I strode straight for the muscle, and they moved aside to let me pass.

I let out a soft breath of relief, though I shouldn't have. Perry's voice floated through the air behind me, wet and chill with glee.

"You could've just asked, Kiss."

You fucker. "You wouldn't have told me jackshit," I tossed over my shoulder. *And I'm not so sure you don't know anything. This was an exercise in futility, but at least I got to hit you.* "Besides, maybe I like smashing your face in, *hellspawn.*"

With that, I hit the door. Mercifully, he didn't say anything else. Maybe he was getting smarter.

My orange Impala gleamed at the curb, once again in the fire zone, Saul's cigarette sending lazy whorls of smoke into the air out the passenger's-side window. I got in, dropping down in the driver's seat, and looked at the red fuzzy dice hanging from the mirror. Let out a sigh.

Saul said nothing.

"I think we're fucked." I stared through the windshield as the last of the daylight poured out of the sky's cup. "He knows something, maybe, but he won't give it up. Yet."

Saul exhaled a long sheaf of smoke. I worked the silver knuckles off my fingers; they were grimed with Perry's thin black blood.

They don't bleed red, Hell's scions. No, they bleed silt-black, in thin runnels like grapeseed oil, and it stinks as it decays.

"It isn't Were," Saul answered softly. "It isn't hellbreed, at least not any hellbreed or damned Perry has control over. It isn't a type of damned you've seen before. Whatever it is, it stinks of violence, and fur. I haven't ever smelled anything like this, Jill. It's definitely not human, but I don't know *what* it is."

I turned my head, meaning to look at him, but instead staring at the front door of the Monde guarded by its huge bouncer. Why the muscle kept letting me in I don't know, except for the scar on my arm and my bargain with Perry. Still, they should have roughed me up once or twice, just to keep things standard. "Something neither of us knows about. Something that attacks teenage hookers and divests them of their internal organs."

"It stinks of ice and rotting flesh. And magic. Bad, old, nasty magic."

I stared at the door as if I could will a part of the puzzle to come clear. "You think he's involved?"

"This isn't his style. But I wouldn't rule him out." Saul flicked the Charvil out the window. "What next?"

"The seminary. We need to figure out how an *utt'huruk* got into a nice corn-fed missionary boy. Then home to pick up a few things, and call Andy." I gave him a tight smile. "No, I haven't forgotten. And I want to pick his brains as well as ask him to send his apprentice down here to cover for me."

Saul looked troubled. I twisted the key and the Impala purred into life. Good old American heavy metal. "Jill."

"What?"

"Do you like visiting *him?*"

What? Saul had never directly referred to my bargain with Perry since coming back from the Rez after the rogue Were case two years ago. "What the hell are you talking about? One of these days, when I've figured out a lesser evil, I am going to kill him. He's useful, Saul. Don't start."

"I don't like the way he looks at you."

You're not the only one. I put the car in gear, released the parking brake, and pulled out. "Neither do I, baby. Neither do I."

CHAPTER 9

I was on a hell of a run of bad luck, and more came in the form of information, as usual. The still-unconscious Oscar hadn't had any visitors, but he *had* been in the room when another seminary student's aunt had visited. The aunt had been tall, dark-haired, and nobody could describe her face; not even the priest who had signed her in and watched the visit—who just happened to be the heart-attack victim, Father Rosas. The kid who'd been visited was a transfer student from out of state, a thin ratlike teenage boy whose narrow eyes widened when I shoved the gun in his face and told him to strip.

Red-nosed Father Rourke choked, but Saul had him by the collar. Father Guillermo stood up so fast his chair scraped against the linoleum floor. "Jillian?" He sounded like the air had been punched out of him.

"Sorry, Father." And I was. "But this kid might be dangerous. It's insurance."

"You...*you*—" Father Rourke was having a little trouble with this. "You *witch!* Gui, you won't let her—"

"Paul." Gui's voice was firm. He backed up two steps from the teenager I had at gunpoint. "Remember your oath."

"The Church—"

"The archbishop *and* the cardinal have given me provisional powers once there is proved to be supernatural cause," I quoted, chapter and verse. "Keep yourself under control, Father, or Saul will drag you outside. Don't make him cranky, I don't recommend it." I nodded at the kid. "Strip. Slowly. The cassock first."

The boy trembled. The whites of his eyes were yellow, acne pocked his cheeks, and I was nine-tenths sure there would be a mark on him. Maybe not on his back, but somewhere on his body.

A Sorrow doesn't leave the House, living or dead, without a mark. One way or another, they claim their own, from a Queen Mother down to the lowliest male drone.

The question of just what a young Sorrow would be doing here in a seminary was the bigger concern, though.

And just as I was sure the kid wasn't going to strip, he slowly lifted his hands, palms out.

Uh-oh. This doesn't look go—

The spell hit me, *hard,* in the solar plexus, I choked and heard Saul yell. The cry shaded into a Were's roar, wood shattering, and I shook my head, blood flying from my lip. Found myself on my feet, instinctively crouching as the ratfaced Sorrow leapt for me; I caught his wrist, locked it, whirled, and had him on the ground. He was muttering in Chaldean.

Saul growled. I spared a look at him; his tail lashed and his teeth were bared. In full cougar form, but his eyes were incandescent—and he was larger than the usual mountain cat. Weres tend to run slightly big even in their animal forms. He made a deep hissing coughing sound, the tawny fur on the back of his neck standing straight up and his tail puffing up just like a housecat's. "Shift back," I snarled. "I need this bastard held down."

"What is she—what is she—" Father Rourke was having a little more trouble with the program. Gui had his arm, holding him back; Rourke's face was even more florid than usual. He was actually spluttering, and I felt a well of not-very-nice satisfaction.

I leaned down, the boy's wiry body struggling under me. "I can help you," I whispered in his ear. "I can help you, free you of the Sorrows, and give you your soul back. You know I can. Cooperate."

His struggles didn't cease; if anything, they grew more intense. He heaved back and forth, rattling in Old Chaldean like a snake.

It was always a fool's chance, to try to free a Sorrow. Hunters always offer, but they almost never take us up on it. The Mothers and sorceress-bitches have things just the way they want them, all the power and none of the accountability—and the boys are drones, born into Houses and trained to be nothing but mindless meat.

The Sorrows worship the Elder Gods, after all. And those gods—like all gods—demand blood. The difference is, the Elder Gods like their claret literally, with ceremony, and in bucketfuls.

Saul's hands came down; tensed, driving in. Immediately, it became *much* easier to keep the kid down. Working together, we got him flipped over; I held down the boy's hips while Saul took care of his upper torso. The Were's eyes were aflame with orange light, he was *furious.* He slid a long cord of braided leather into the kid's mouth, holding down one skinny wrist with his knee. "No poison tooth for you," he muttered. "Jill?"

"I'm fine." I spat blood, he'd socked me a good one in the mouth. Thank God my teeth don't come out easily. Sorcery is *occasionally* useful. "Hold him." *Where's the mark, got to find the mark, got to find it; what's a Sorrow doing in here?*

The boy's spine crackled as his eyes rolled into his head. He mumbled, and I wondered what he was cooking up next. *God-dammit, and he's gagged. Christ.* I tore the front of his shirt, ran my hand over his narrow hairless chest. No tingle. Where was the mark?

"Jillian?" Father Guillermo, by the door. He sounded choked.

"You *witch,* that's one of our *kids!*" Rourke was still having trouble with this one.

I snapped a glance back over my shoulder, checking. "Transferred from out of state? Your kid's in a ditch somewhere, Father. This is a *Sorrow.* Probably just a little baby viper instead of a full-grown one, though." *Or he'd have tried to crush my larynx instead of socking me in the gut.* I got his pants off with one swift jerk, breaking the button and jamming the zipper. "I suggest you wait outside in case he chews through the gag." Blood dripped into my right eye, I blinked it away, irritably. "The question is why the Sorrows are so interested in this seminary. And when I find the mark we'll find out."

I got lucky. It was on his right thigh, the three interlocked circles in blue with the sigil of the Black Flame where they overlapped. He was a young soldier, not a man-drone only fit for sacrifice or a pleasure-slave. Of all the ranks a male could hold in a House, the soldiers had maybe the shortest life—but at least they weren't tied down and slaughtered to feed the Eldest Ones. "Bingo," I muttered, and held out my hand. The bone handle of Saul's Bowie landed solidly in my palm.

The Sorrow hissed and gurgled behind the gag. Saul reached down, cupped his chin, and yanked back, exposing the boy's throat and making sure he couldn't thrash his shoulders around.

I laid the flat of the knife against the mark and the kid screamed, audible even behind the gag. Steel against Chaldean sorcery, one of the oldest enmities known to magic.

The Elder Gods would have us all back in the Bronze Age if they could. They would have us killing each other to feed their hungry mouths as well. Still, there are some Elders the Sorrows don't invoke, because their very natures are inimical to the worship of darkness. Belief is a double-edged blade, and a hunter can use it as well as any other weapon.

"Thou shalt be released," I murmured in Old Chaldean. "Thou unclean, thou whom the gods have turned their face from, thou *shalt* be released, in the name of Vul the Magnificent, the lighter of fires—"

He screamed again. I paused. Next came sliding the knife up and flaying the skin to get the mark off. I could add it to my collection. Each little bit of skin, drying and stretching and marked with their hellish brand, was another brick in the wall between me and the guilt of my teacher's death. Each time I killed a Sorrow, I felt *good*.

Cleansed.

I am not a very nice person.

"Last chance," I said. "Before you go to your Hell." *And believe me when I say that's one place you don't want to visit even for a moment.*

The kid went limp.

There, that's more like it. I looked up at Saul, whose eyes still glowed. No, he was not in the least bit happy. But he nodded, a quick dip of his chin, and released the pressure on the gag just a little.

The rat-faced kid's eyes met mine. A spark flared in their tainted depths, swirling now he had revealed himself. His skin began to look gray too, the Chaldean twisting his tongue and staining his body.

Wait a second. He isn't even an Acolyte. What's he doing out of a House? "Ungag him."

Saul hesitated.

"Christ, Saul, ungag him."

The boy jerked. Leather slipped free. But Saul was tense, and I saw his right hand relax from a fist into a loose claw, nails sliding free and lengthening, turning razor-sharp. If the Sorrow made a move, my Were would open his throat.

"What are you out here for, Neophym? Who's holding your leash?"

He had apparently decided to talk. "Sister," he choked, gurgling. "My...sister...*please*..."

I bit my lip, weighing it. On the one hand, the Sorrows were trained to lie to outsiders.

And on the other, no Sorrow would ever use the word *sister*. The only word permitted for female within the House was *mistress*. Or occasionally, *bitch*.

Just like the only word for man was *slave*.

I considered this, staring into the Sorrow's eyes. "What's a Sorrow doing in my town, huh? You've been warned."

"Fleeing...*chutsharak*." His breath rattled in his throat.

Chutsharak? I've never heard of that. "The what?"

It was too late. He crunched down hard with his teeth, bone cracking in his jaw; I whipped my head back and Saul did the same, scrambling away from the body in a flurry of Were-fast motion. I found myself between the body and the priests, watching as bones creaked, the neurotoxin forcing muscles to contract until only the crown of the head and the back of the heels touched the floor. A fine mist of blood burst out of the capillaries of his right eye.

Poison tooth. He'd committed suicide, cracking the false tooth embedded in his jaw.

Just as his heels slammed back, smashing into the back of his head, his sphincters released. Then the body slumped over on its side.

"Dammit." I rubbed at the cuff over my right wrist, reflectively. "*Damn* it."

"What's a *chutsharak?*" Saul's voice was hushed. Behind us, Father Rourke took in a deep endless breath.

I shook my head, the charms in my hair shifting and tinkling uneasily. "I don't know." My throat was full. "Gods above. Why are they sending children? I *hate* the Sorrows."

"It's probably mutual." Saul approached the body carefully, then began to mutter under his breath, the Were's prayer in the face of needless death. I left it alone. The poison was virulent, but it lost its potency on contact with a roomful of oxygen. He was in no danger.

"Jillian?" Father Guillermo sounded pale. He *was* pale, when I checked him. Two bright spots of color stood out on his cheeks. "What do we do next?"

"Any other transfers in the last year? Priest, worker, student, anyone?"

"N-no." He shook his head. "J-just K-Kit. Him." His eyes flickered past me to the body on the floor. The stink was incredible.

Father Rourke kept crossing himself. He was praying too. His rubbery lips moved slightly, wet with saliva. Probably an Our Father.

Sometimes I wished I was still wholly Catholic. The guilt sucks, but the comfort of rote prayer is nothing to sneeze at. There's nothing like prepackaged answers to make a human psyche feel nice and secure. "I'll need to go over the transfer records. Why would a Sorrow want to infiltrate a seminary? Are you holding anything?"

His face drained of color like wine spilling out of a cup.

"Gui? You're not holding anything I should know about, are you?" I watched him, he said nothing. "Guillermo?" My tone sharpened.

He flinched, almost guiltily. "It is...Jillian, I..."

"Oh, for *God's* sake. I can't *protect* you if you don't tell me what I need to know!"

"Sister Jillian—"

"What are you holding?"

"Jillian—"

I snapped. I grabbed the priest by the front of his cassock, lifted him up, and shook him before his shoulders hit the wall. "Guillermo." My mouth was dry, fine tremors of rage sliding through my hands. The scar on my wrist turned to molten lead. Behind me there was a whisper of cloth, and Rourke let out a blasphemy I never thought to hear from a priest.

"Take one more step and I hit you," Saul said, quietly, but with an edge.

"I could have died." I said each word clearly, enunciating each consonant. "*Saul* could have died. If I'd known you were holding something I could have questioned him far more effectively. You *cannot* keep information from me and *expect me to protect you!*"

"He's a Jesuit. He can't tell you anything." Rourke spat the words as if they'd personally offended him. "He took a vow."

I dropped Guillermo. *Fuck. I'm about to beat up a priest. Man, this is getting ridiculous.* "If you don't start talking in fifteen seconds, Gui, I'm going to start searching. I'm going to tear this place apart from altar to graveyard until I find whatever you're holding. You might as well tell me now. What is it? What are the Sorrows looking for?"

"It's nothing of any use to them." Gui rubbed at his throat. He was still pale, and the smell swirling in the air was beginning to be thick and choking. I was used to smelling death, but he wasn't. "Merely an artifact—"

"What. Are. You. Holding?" The scar pulsed in time to each word, and I was close to doing something unforgivable, like hauling off and slugging a *priest*. Dammit. This disturbed me more than I wanted to admit.

"The Spear of—" Rourke almost yelled.

"*No!*" Gui all but screamed.

"—*Saint Anthony!*" Rourke bellowed, his face turning crimson. Gui sagged.

I turned on my heel, eyed Rourke. *Come on, I used to be Catholic. Don't pull this shit on me.* "Saint Anthony didn't *have* a spear. He gave his staff to Saint Macarius."

"It is the spear he blessed with his blood when the citizens of a small town were overwhelmed with the hordes of Hell. He didn't use it; Marcus Silvacus used it." Father Rourke's flabby cheeks quivered, and he was pale too. I couldn't tell if I was smelling the stink of a lie on him, or the reek of fear.

I am going to have to check that out. As far as I knew, Marcus Silvacus never met Saint Anthony, and Saint Anthony didn't have a fucking spear. I could feel my teeth grind together. I tipped my head back, my jaw working.

"I'm sorry, Guillermo. But you took a vow." For once, Rourke's tone wasn't blustering.

"An artifact here, and it somehow slipped your mind to tell me? This isn't looking good, Gui. Years and years I've trusted you, and I've done the Church's dirty work peeling demons out of people before I was even fully trained. *This* is how you repay me?"

"The Sorrow said he was fleeing," Saul's voice cut across mine. "It might be unrelated."

I wasn't mollified, but he did have a point. "Still, that's something I needed to know."

"Agreed." His hand curled around my shoulder. "It stinks of death in here. And we have work to do."

Damn the man. He was right again.

I shook out my right hand, my fingers popping as tendons loosened. "All right." I sounded strange even to myself. "Fine. But I won't forget this, Guillermo." *I will not ever forget this.*

"I would have told you everything, Jillian. When I was released from my vow." Gui slumped against the wall, rubbing his throat, though I hadn't held him by anything than his cassock. "I swear it, I would have. I didn't think the two were connected, and I can't speak of it."

I waved it away. The charms tinkled in my hair, uneasily. "Get that cleaned up. And give him a decent burial; he was only a kid."

"Not in consecra—" Rourke stopped when my eyes rested on him. I felt my face harden. My blue eye began to burn, and I knew it was glowing, a single pinprick of red in the center of my pupil.

"Give him his last rites," I said, very softly and distinctly. "If indulgence is required, *Father,* I'll pay. But for God's sake bury him kindly."

I left it at that. And for once, so did he.

Saul drove. I wasn't in the mood. We didn't speak on the way home. As soon as I swept the warehouse and determined it was safe I headed for the phone. Which began to ring as soon as I got within three feet of it.

I hooked it up. "This better be good news."

"Hello to you too." Avery sounded serious, as usual. "Jill, there's a problem."

Oh, Christ. Not another one. "The Trader I just brought in?"

A short, unamused laugh drifted through the phone line. Avery was a professional exorcist, not a hunter like me. It was his job to exorcise the Traders I brought in, just like it was Eva, Benito, and Wallace's job to handle other straight exorcisms in my city and refer the extraordinary ones to me. "No, he was an easy rip-and-stuff. Screamed like a damned soul, though. He's on meds. No, the problem's different. I wanted to talk to you about it."

I considered this. "Micky's? At—" I glanced at the clock, juggled his probable freedom from work. "Eleven?"

He agreed immediately. "Sounds good, I'll buy you a beer. Um..."

"Um, what?" I glanced over my shoulder as Saul began rummaging in the kitchen. He was probably hungry; I was too. The light shone mellow off his long red-black hair, silver glinting against the strands; his cheeks looked a little pale without the paint. He glanced up, probably feeling my eyes, and gave me a half-smile that made my legs feel decidedly mushy.

"Will Saul be there?"

What? "Of course he will. He's my partner." *And a damn fine one, too.*

"I just...well, yeah. Bring him. Sorry. Look, eleven o'clock. See you then."

I hung up feeling even more unsettled, and that was rare. Avery didn't have anything against Weres.

Not that I knew of, anyway. Nothing out of the ordinary.

I dialed Andy's number from memory and got his answering machine, left a message. The heavenly odor of sautéed onions tiptoed to my nose, and that meant steak. *Bless Weres and their domesticity.*

I stared at the phone after laying it back in the charger, my eyebrows drawing together. Then I picked it up again, and dialed another number from memory.

"Hutchinson's Books, Used and Rare." This was a slightly nasal, wheezing voice; I had to bite back a laugh.

"Hutch, it's Jill."

He actually spluttered. "Oh good Christ, what *now?*"

"Relax, baby. I just need to use the back room. Want to do some research for me?"

"I'd rather gouge my own eyes out." He was serious. Wise man.

"That makes you much more intelligent than a number of people I know. Listen, scour for everything you can find about the Sorrows. Brush up your ceremonial Chaldean and find me every mention of something called a *chutsharak.*"

"Zuphtarak?" He mangled the word. I could almost hear his teeth chattering. Cute, nervous Hutch was not cut out for hunter's work, but he was hell on wheels when it came to digging through dusty old tomes; which Hutchinson's Books held as a hunter's library in return for a number of very nice tax breaks that kept it afloat.

Hey, hunters believe in supporting local indie bookstores.

"Chutsharak." I spelled it for him. "But the *ch* is sometimes *j,* and sometimes—"

"—those goddamn seventeenth-century translations, I know. All right. Fine. You still have your key?"

"Of course I still have my key." *I am exceedingly unlikely to lose it, Hutch. And anyway, I built those fucking locks. They'll open for me anytime I want.* "I won't come by while you're in. Leave your notes in the usual place."

"Thank fucking God."

I snorted. "I thought you liked me, Hutch."

He gave an unsteady little laugh. I could almost see his hazel eyes behind his glasses and his thin biceps. "You're hot, yeah. But you're scary. I'll work on it. *Chutsharak.* Chaldean. Got it."

"One more thing."

"Oh, Christ."

"Can you look up Saint Anthony's spear?"

"Saint Anthony didn't have a—"

"I didn't think so either. But check it. And check to see if there's *any* connection between Anthony and Marcus Silvacus. Just to be sure." I rubbed at the bridge of my nose, feeling a headache beginning. Just my luck. But why would Rourke lie to me? Of course, I wasn't Catholic anymore, I wasn't a priest, and I was female; he would probably just confess and be forgiven and not lose any damn sleep over lying to *me*. And if Gui really was under orders not to say anything about an artifact hidden at the seminary, an artifact the Sorrows wanted for some unholy reason, things were getting stickier by the moment.

"Fine." Hutch said it like I had him by the balls—and not in a good way.

"Thanks, Hutch. I'll bring you a present."

"Keep me out of this."

I laughed, and he hung up. I laid the phone back in its cradle and stared at it, daring it to ring again.

It remained obstinately mute.

"Red-sauce penne with steak, and fresh asparagus." Saul made his happy sound, a low hum like a purr. "Want some wine?"

"Please." I rubbed at the back of my neck under my heavy hair. "You're a good partner, Saul."

His eyes met mine, he peered under the hanging cabinets. The copper-bottom pans glowed behind him. "Yeah?"

I folded my arms. "Yeah. Avery wants to meet us at Micky's. And then I've got some research to do."

"Research?"

I know, I know. I don't like it either. "Then we'll come back, and I'm all yours."

"I like the sound of that. Make yourself useful and open the wine, kitten."

CHAPTER 10

A very slumped in the booth, tapping his long fingers on the glass-topped table. Directly over him, Humphrey Bogart stared somberly out of a framed print. Curly brown hair fell in Ave's face, over sad brown eyes; he looked like a handsome little mournful beagle. Despite that, he was quick and ruthless during exorcisms, seeming to come alive only when a particular Possessor or *arkeus* was giving him trouble, or the victim started to thrash. Of all the exorcists I knew, he was the one who came closest to being a hunter, if only because of the sheer nail-biting joy he took in skating the edge of danger.

We are all adrenaline junkies, really. You have to be. Hunting is 95 percent boredom-laced waiting punctuated with the occasional bursts of sheer and total terror. No middle ground.

Ave's badge hung on a chain around his neck; he had shrugged out of his motorcycle jacket and was staring at his fingertips like he had bad news.

I was really getting a rotten feeling about this.

I slid into the booth, Saul right next to me. "Hey, baby." I gave a smile, but Ave didn't grin back. Not even a glimmer of his usual sleepy good humor. "Wow, looks grim."

Vixen swished her hips up to the table, her sleek brown hair clinging to her head like an otter's. "Hey." She plunked down three Fat Tires, her lip lifting as she glared at me, then smiled at Saul. He, as usual, looked supremely unconcerned.

She sighed, turned on her heel, and her tartan skirt ticked back and forth as she switched away with a Were's grace.

"In heat again, I see," Saul murmured, and I choked on my first sip of beer, the laugh bubbling up.

Avery didn't even crack a slight smile. I sighed. "So what's up, Ave?"

He finally shifted, picking up his beer and tipping a sarcastic salute to Saul. "Hey, furboy."

"Hey, skinman." Saul's tone was even, chill.

"I heard something." Avery addressed this to me.

"Yeah?" I waited, rolling my next sip of beer around in my mouth. Stifled a small pleasant burp; it tasted of grilled onions. At least I had the memory of dinner to get me through this. Whatever *this* was.

"One of my stoolies; he's a drunk. But he picks stuff up—it's amazing. He manages to get around. Anyway, he knows someone who saw something." Avery produced a white square of paper, held between his fingers like a card trick. "And the worst thing is, I believe him."

"What did he see?" *And what the fuck does this have to do with anything?* I shifted uneasily, the leather of my pants rubbing uncomfortably against the vinyl seat.

"Guy's called Robbie the Juicer. He saw them dumping Baby Jewel last night. Black van, no license plate. Said there were four of them, one looked to be a woman, and two men. The last one was . . . he said it was big, and it stank, and it threw the body like it weighed nothing."

Huh. I absorbed this. "Big. And stinky."

"Yeah. He said it looked like an ape. Like it was *furry*." He darted a look at Saul. "Could it be a rogue Were? No offense, understand, I just thought I should ask."

It was a good question, considering what he'd been told. "A rogue Were would hide the bodies," I said, slowly. The memory of the last rogue to hit Santa Luz was far enough away that I could consider the notion without a gut-clenching burst of slick-palmed fear. "Wouldn't work with anyone else, that's why they're rogue. And wouldn't eat the organs unless it was starving; they like muscle-meat first. Who is this witness, and where was he?"

"My stoolie said something about a baseball diamond; the witness is homeless and sometimes sleeps in the dugout. He heard the van's engine and looked out; the van sat there for a while and he decided to go take a look." He offered the square of white paper. "Here's his name and vitals, and a list of the places he usually hangs out. He's scared to death."

"He should be. This is nothing to mess with." I took the paper; it was thin and innocent against my fingers. "Thanks, Avery."

Christ, I bet I'm not going to sleep for a while. Behind my eyes, the vision of the edge of the park and the baseball diamond flashed, and I cautiously decided it was possible. The dugout was at an angle and it was *extremely* possible someone hidden in there could have seen something. It was just *slightly* possible someone hidden in there could have been unremarked, which was the truly incredible part. Whoever this Robbie Juicer was, he'd probably used up his entire life's worth of luck.

Avery was decent, after all. He looked up, at my Were. "I'm sorry, Saul. I just—Christ. This thing's *awful.* There's talk going around."

My ears perked. "What kind of talk?"

"Talk of a bounty on Weres. Someone's saying that this is a rogue Were, and why shouldn't the rest of them suffer for it? And there's talk about you too, Jill, that you're marked and it's only a matter of time before the damned drag you back to Hell."

"Marked. By who?" *I've been marked all my life, Avery.* But if he was hearing whispers on the nightside, little bits of rumor from the occult shops and not-so-human stoolies that kept on the exorcists' good side, it could only mean bad trouble.

"I dunno. But you hear shit, you know. Something big is going down, and I can't get more than whispers." He hunched his shoulders, looking miserable. "You just be careful. We can't afford to lose you. *Or* your furry friend there."

Well, at least that was something. "Guess not." I bumped Saul with my elbow, but gently. Just to let him know I was there. He was still crowding me, a little closer than usual. Taking comfort in closeness. "We've got Sorrows adepts in town, Ave. At least one. I pulled an *utt'huruk* out of a kid the other day and there was a Neophym who gurgled something about *chutsharak* before biting his poison tooth. You know that term?"

"I never was good at that prehistoric shit." He shook his brown head, curls falling in his eyes. "I thought you didn't let the Sorrows in."

"I don't. When I find their bolthole I'm going to burn them. Just watch yourself. You hear anything that sounds like Chaldean, you *run.*"

"You bet. Hey, be easy on this witness. He's not bolted too

tight, I guess. And he doesn't want any police static, or I woulda met him and brought him to you."

Go easy? I'm an easygoing gal. "That goes without saying." I lifted my beer bottle and he lifted his, we clinked the glass together. He suddenly looked a lot easier about the whole thing. "I'll be gentle, I promise."

"Yeah, right." His color began to come back. "Sure you will."

I could almost feel my eyebrow raise. "You're a cynic, Avery. One day that's going to catch up to you." I lifted my beer again, and took a long hard swallow.

It tasted a little more sour than I liked. Or that could have been the taste of bad luck in my mouth.

Instead of research, we hit the street looking for Robbie the Juicer, the nervous witness. It was a cold night, clouds moving in from the river but not fast enough to give us rain before five or six in the morning; the hard points of braver stars pierced the veil of night and orange citylight. Outside the city limits, out in the near-desert, the waning moon would shine on yucca and sandstone. It was a night for sharp teeth and quick death. The air itself was knotted tight with expectation.

We canvassed the easier places on Avery's list first: the missions, Prosper Alley, the shooting gallery on Trask Street, the fountain in Plaskény Square. Nada. Not a whisper of our target.

Plenty of the people we saw that night had no idea we were there. I stayed close to Saul, and Were camouflage took care of hiding us both. Weres are traditionally hunters' allies, and plenty of times a hunter has been grateful for the furkind's ability to conceal. I was odd among hunters in that I actually slept with my backup, but by no means unique. Most Weres don't like bedplay with humans; we're too fragile.

But with the scar on my wrist, I was no longer so fragile. It made things interesting.

Just the way Saul's initial distrust and distaste for me and my helltainted self had made things interesting. Sometimes I wondered why he had come back.

You can find bums in any city. Looking for a *particular* homeless man in Santa Luz is needle-in-a-haystack frustrating. You just roll around a lot and hope to get stuck in the right place.

We were casing the second large mecca of the dispossessed in Santa Luz, Broadway. I walked beside Saul carefully, occasionally glancing down at the cracked sidewalk, threading between groups of street kids gathering in doorways and sharing cigarettes of both legal and nonlegal origin. Quite a few had bottles in brown paper bags, and a good number of them were younger than Baby Jewel. Dreadlocks, dyed hair, piercings, layers of clothing as they struggled to stay warm in the desert night, gangs and streetfamilies drawing together for comfort and protection—it was enough, really, to make a cynic out of anyone.

I caught sight of a thin, nervous-looking man with a scruff of brown hair, sharing hits off a bottle with a taller scarecrow of a black man in army fatigues. The brown-haired scruff wore a dun coat and a red backpack, black boots, and a shocking-blue T-shirt.

Saul marked him a full fifteen seconds after I did. "That him?"

"Coat, backpack, boots, and a serious case of nerves. Looks like it." I started forward, but Saul's hand closed around my arm. "What?"

He tilted his head. "Someone else is looking."

I looked. There, tucked into a slice of shadow like a professional, a skinny man in a long dirty duster finished un-smoking a cigarette. The red eye glowed as he dropped it, and he was too clean-shaven to be a homeless man. And it's not just strange to see a homeless man drop a smoke halfway to the filter, especially when he doesn't take a drag before he does it.

It rings every wrong bell in a hunter's head to see something like that.

"Got enough metal on him for me to smell, and he's hunting," Saul murmured in my ear. I barely nodded, letting him know I'd heard him.

Mercenary? Or something else?

I thought this over, examining our new player. Was he looking for Robbie or just for trouble? He didn't seem to have the nervous witness in his sights, but he was certainly up to no good. And if Saul could smell gunplay and violence on him, he was probably someone I should have a nice little chat with.

You can call me paranoid, but I rarely believe in pure coincidence. Usually coincidence gets a little help in a situation like this.

"Get our witness. Question him if you feel like it." I slid a slim,
black-finished blade out of its sheath and reversed it along my
arm. "I'll see what's up with our little friend over there."

"You got it. Where should I take the jitterboy?"

I did a rapid mental calculation of location and distance. "Take
him to Woo Song's and buy him dinner, but don't let him drink
any more. I'll meet you as soon as I can. Get *every* scrap of information you can from him. And play nice."

"I will." He looked, again, like he wanted to say *be careful*. But
he didn't. He merely bent down, kissed my temple, and slid away,
leaving me without a Were's camouflage.

I set off across the street at an angle calculated to bring me into
our mysterious visitor's blind spot.

Unfortunately, I realized as I was halfway across Broadway,
our friend wasn't alone. His backup was on the roof, and as bullets
chewed into the pavement behind me and the screaming started, I
realized that this wasn't normal at all. Nothing about this was
usual. And that usually added up to one very *fucked* Jill Kismet.

I rolled, taking cover behind a parked car. Glass shattered;
whoever it was had a fucking assault rifle and was spraying the
car. The knife vanished, and I spared a brief prayer for the civilians on the street. *Let's have no casualties, Jill.*

That is, except for the ones you *want to inflict.*

CHAPTER 11

A running gunfight is not like you see in the movies. Most gun
battles are over in just under seven seconds, and most end
with nobody getting hurt. Or at least, among the normal dayside
population, that's what it's like.

A nightside gunfight is a different beast. We don't engage in
them often, mostly because a lot of hellbreed and other things
hunters deal with are tough enough not to need guns most of the

time. A hunter is armed with heavy firepower merely to even the score.

These boys, however, were not nightsiders. They were human, and professional troublemakers unless I missed my guess. The one on the ground vanished as the one on the roof peppered the car I'd taken cover behind; I tore the cuff off my right wrist and stuffed it in my pocket, gasping as air hit the scar and a flush of chill heat slammed through my nervous system. I could have dealt with these jokers with the cuff on, but I was feeling a little unsettled. Besides, why not use near-invulnerability if you have it?

It used to be I wouldn't use it unless I *had* to. *God, Jill, you've changed.*

My own guns spun out, and I gathered my legs underneath me. Sighed, blew out between my teeth, and whirled, skipping back two or three steps before pitching forward, legs burning as I *pulled* on all the etheric force the scar could provide. My boots smashed into the car's hood, using the mass of the engine underneath to *push* against.

Wind screamed as I *flew,* gravity loosing its constraints for one brief glorious second.

The only trouble with doing this is a simple law of physics: the landing, once you're going that fast, is a lot harder than you think.

Impact.

I smashed into the man on the roof, heard human ribs snap like green wood, the rifle went flying. Skidded, my boots dragging and heating up with friction, hitting the roof *hard* as I lost my balance, teeth clicking together. The man let out a choked burble, I bounced up to my feet.

This is why I wear leather pants. Less goddamn road-rash when you hit a rooftop going faster than you should. Jeans would be shredded. It's not just a fashion statement—though they do make my ass look cute, as Saul so often reminds me.

I grabbed the man. He was in night-camo and streaky face-paint, and there was a whistling sound that told me one of his broken ribs had punctured a lung.

Shit.

"Who sent you?" *I'm going to take you to a hospital and have them patch you up so I can break every bone in your body for shooting down at one of my streets like that. You could have killed a bunch of innocents, you asshole. My innocents.* "Who? Tell me and you'll live." I held him up one-handed, my fingers tangled in straps that were some kind of harness to keep his weapons on, he was armed to the teeth. He even had a couple of grenades. Just the thing for urban combat. "*Who,* goddammit?"

He would have screamed if he could have gotten enough air in.

Then it smashed through his chest, spraying me with blood and chips of bone, I yelled and hit the ground for cover, hearing the clack of pulleys as well as the meaty thud of the body hitting the ground. *What the bloody blue fuck?*

Silence. Sirens in the distance, screams and shrieks from the street below. *Goddammit. What the fuck was that?* I *extended* my senses, felt nothing.

The man in camo lay slumped on the rooftop, something protruding from his chest. I took a closer look.

It was an arrow. The head was heavy-duty, a nasty piece of work; the sound of pulleys suddenly made sense. Probably a compound hunting bow.

It took some doing to yank the arrow free of the meat. I traced its path, both from sound and from instinct; came up with a rooftop due east, higher up—a perfect place to lie in wait and shoot. The bowman was gone now.

Who used *arrows* anymore? This was getting weirder by the second.

The scar on my wrist pulsed, ripe and obscenely warm. Silken warmth slid against my skin, under the dampness of fear-sweat and sudden chilled adrenaline gooseflesh. My breath came harsh, torturous, echoing in my ear.

What the fuck was going on?

The scar twinged. I let out a long frustrated breath. Laid the cuff back against my wrist. It was hard to cover the puckered, seamed mark back up. What if there was someone else out there with a bow trained on me? It might not kill me, but it would be a mite uncomfortable.

Well, there are Sorrows in town. A bow is just their speed, the filthy little Luddites. But why? Don't assume this is connected—but neither can you assume it's not. Great.

I stuffed the cuff back into my pocket. Hefted the arrow. Thought about it for a moment.

A sudden bite of bloodlust swam across the current of darkness. More of them, moving in. *Ah. More fun and games. I should have known an arrow wouldn't be the end of it.*

I stepped to the edge of the building and leapt out into space. Just as I did, the secondary team moved in, and bullets smashed into my chest. Blood tore across the night sky as I landed, and if I'd been human it would have killed me.

The knives slid into my hands. It was knives instead of guns this time because I wanted some of them left alive.

I hit *hard,* rolling, wet splotch of blood on the pavement as my bleeding back pressed down briefly, made it to my feet. A hunting cat's scream tore from my throat as I saw them, moving down the street in standard mercenary formation, with high-powered rifles and body armor.

I took the first one with a knee to the midriff, snapping a few ribs. The street behind me roiled with screams. *Get down and stay down, everyone, I'm on the job. Jill Kismet's going to work.*

Knocked the gun out of his hand; another kick sent him careening away, crashing into the left flank guard. Punched the secondary through the faceshield of his helmet, a short kick dislocating his patella at the same time. The pounding of bullets didn't stop, one flicked past my cheek. *You boys are really starting to piss me off.*

"SURRENDER NOW!" I yelled, and threw my left-hand knife. It buried itself in one of the rear-guards. That left four of them on the left wing, they were moving in to surround me, bringing in the flanks. *Well-trained, they're well-trained, boys like this don't come cheap, who's paying for this?*

Oh, no. That isn't a combat pattern. That's a holding patte—

And then, it happened. The thing streaked down the street, tearing through dappled streetlamp light and shade, and it hit me squarely before I could even begin to move.

The massive impact smashed *through* me. Whatever it was, it was *big,* it was *fast,* and its claws tore through my right arm. The knife went clattering. *"Move move move!"* someone yelled. The mercenaries. They were retreating. The scar on my wrist gave out an agonized burst of heat.

It stank. It *stank,* a titanic massive smell that tore through my sinuses and made me gag, bile rising hot and whipping through my throat.

I hit the plate-glass window of a pawnshop, which wouldn't have been so bad if this part of town hadn't needed iron bars so badly. Agony as my ribs snapped, I fell to the concrete as it streaked for me, a low hulking shape that was *wrong,* my eyes refused to focus, even my blue eye refused to *see* what it was, blood hot and slick on my face, splashing against the pavement.

Cold. It was *cold,* frost starring the pavement. Little curls of steam slid up from my skin, my breath pluming in the air as I gasped. It was so cold.

I lay there as it roared, coming for me again, I had to get up, couldn't, *there's a limit to the damage I can take even with the scar oh God oh God it hurts—*

The night turned peacock-iridescent with flame. The bolt hit it low on the side, hellfire crackling and fluorescing into blue, scarring my eyes. *Holy shit, that's hellfire in the blue spectrum! Who is it, a hellbreed come to dispatch me personally?*

The thing went flying, snarling. The sound was like adamant nails on the biggest fucking chalkboard ever. There was a crashing—metal and glass crumpled like paper. I choked on blood and tried to make my body obey me, struggling to turn over onto my side and push myself up. The frozen pavement burned my skin.

"Keep still, Kiss." The voice was familiar. *Too* familiar. "Let your body mend. This will only take a moment."

What the fuck is he *doing here?*

The thing snarled again. I pushed myself up on my feet, ribs snapping out and crackling as they melded back together but too *slow.* Far too slow. I coughed, bending over, a great gout of blood and lung-fluid fountaining out of my mouth and nose, splatting and steaming on the ice-starred sidewalk.

"Be *still,* Kismet." Now he sounded irritated.

I lifted my head.

Perry, in a loose, elegant gray suit, stood with his hands in his pants pockets, the streetlamps shining on his blond hair like a halo tilted just-so. He cocked his head as if listening, looking at the creature, which hunched in the middle of a shattered car. Hell-flame dripped from its smoking hide, melting glass and metal, and I opened my mouth to scream.

The gas tank ignited. Flame belched, and the thing's squealing roar choked off midway. Glass whickered, metal shrapnel flew. I flinched, throwing up my unwounded left arm to shield my eyes. Grating pain tore all the way down my ribs.

Soft padding feet with claws snicking, retreating so quickly the sound blurred. The sound was distinctive, and habit noted it; if I hadn't had the cuff off I wouldn't have been able to track it as the sound faded a couple of miles away to the south. I coughed again, spat blood. Pain ran up my right arm from the scar, throbbing and delicious, sinking into torn muscle and broken bone.

His fingers sank into my left arm, a bolt of agonized heat going through me. Glass and metal groaned as the awful numbing cold retreated. "Idiot. Little *idiot*. Look at this mess."

I coughed again, choked on blood, bent over and vomited more blood. *I didn't know I had this much claret to lose. How many pints is that?*

I hate wondering things like that. But I usually only have time to wonder when the danger's past and I'm still breathing, so I guess it balances out.

Perry's fingers tightened. He propped me against the shattered glass and twisted iron. I'd made quite a dent, must have been going at a fair clip when I hit. The sirens were closer now, and everything was creaking as the terrible devouring cold fled the air.

Montaigne is going to have a fit. Pain ground through me again and I made a weak moaning noise.

My right arm hung in strips of meat, the humerus snapped. "Look at this," Perry repeated, warming to his theme. "You idiot. You fool. You *stupid* little *id*iotic *feather*brained *ninny*."

The scar pulsed hotly, pleasure rising with the pain, a horrible writhing python smashing through my nervous system. His other hand closed around my bloodslick wrist. I tried to fend him off. He slammed me back against the jagged metal, grinding the edges of my broken arm together with exquisite care, at just the angle to produce maximum agony.

I screamed, my ribs creaking. Choked on more blood. The ferocious cold was gone as if it had never existed.

He lifted my right hand, giving it an extra savage twist. Bone ground and I screamed again, weakly.

"Damage my fine work, will you? How is *this,* Kiss? Do you like the pain? *Do you?*"

I collapsed, panting, hanging onto consciousness by a thread. My lips were hot and slick with blood. "F-f-f-fuck...y-y-you..." I could barely shape the words.

"Promises, promises." His breath touched the scar, and the jolt of maggot pleasure that slid through me dipped me in fiery slime. It even drowned the pain for a moment, and I moaned. "Someday, Kismet. Some fine day, when I'm getting a little bored. We'll play a few games."

His lips met the scar, and mercifully it was pain again. Great roaring waves of pain as hellfire tore through my body, each wound rubbed with acid and ash, sadistic waves of agony as he took his time melding my shattered body back together. The scaled, hot, slick-wet touch of his tongue against the puckered tissue coated the roaring agony with slime, burrowed into my hindbrain, and ripped at the roots of my sanity.

When it was done, he dropped me. I hit the pavement hard, weak as a newborn but whole. Blood soaked into what clothes I had left. My coat was a mess. The charms in my hair tinkled, and my carved-ruby necklace sent waves of warmth spilling down my chest.

Perry turned on his heel, surveying the street. Smoke billowed up from the burning car, and condensation rose into the air as merely-chill met freezing and mixed. "This is highly unpleasant." His tone was too mild to be called *anger.* Distaste was as far as it went.

What, you think I'm having a ball? I lay against chill hard concrete, gasping like a landed fish.

"*Highly* unpleasant," he continued, meditatively. "I might almost suspect..." He seemed to remember I was at his feet. "You make this so fucking difficult, Kiss. I've broken stronger Traders with ease."

As usual, he picked exactly the right thing to say to piss me off and break the spell of lethargy. "I'm...not...Trader." Strength returned, the mark sending a wave of fiery pleasure up my arm. Flush, again. Full. Ripe. I could feel the warming trickle between my legs. My hips jerked forward. I gasped. "I'm *hunter*," I managed to say it all in one breath. "And some...day...it's going to be...you."

"Pray it never reaches that point, Kiss. You won't like being hunted."

I'm going to be the one hunting you, you bastard. "What was...that thing?" Blessed air whooped into my lungs. I was going to live. *Thank you, God.* I was going to *live*.

I can't explain the feeling. If you've ever been close to the edge of leaving the world entirely, you know what I'm talking about. If you haven't, I'm glad for you. But don't expect to understand. It's like every Christmas and every disappointment in your life wrapped up in cold air and set on fire with a napalm strike while your bones tremble inside the meat.

Something like that.

"How should I know?" Perry said, thoughtfully. Fog gemmed his blond hair with tiny jewels. "You're lucky it didn't kill you. Is this about your latest visit to the Monde?"

As if you can't guess. But Perry just liked to pretend he had his fingers in every pie; he really might have no idea. Strength returned, slowly. I pushed myself up to sitting, broken glass grinding against shredded leather. Levered myself up, balancing on unsteady feet. The sirens were getting closer. "Kind of." I had my breath back now. "What are you doing here?"

"Watching out for my investment, Kiss. I've put a lot of effort into you, and you're coming along quite nicely." The faint obscene happiness tinting his bland blond voice reminded me of maggots squirming in bloated meat.

Fuck you, Perry. God, I wish I could shoot you now. "Leave the mindfucks at home, Pericles."

"No mindfuck, Kiss. Strictly fact. Now, are you waiting around for the cops? I have other business to conduct tonight. You know, places to go, people to kill."

"Go bother someone else." I coughed, rackingly, my ribs

reminding me they weren't designed for this kind of thing. The mark pulsed, wetly. Pleasure slid up my back like fevered sweating fingers, married to skincrawling loathing, like having a scaled tail run across your skin while you're dreaming safe in your bed.

He showed no sign of leaving. "Where's your pussycat? Have you finally sworn off bestiality?"

Lord, I wish Saul was here right now and there was a bullet or two in your head. That would make me very happy. "Lay off, Perry. I'm warning you."

"I only ask out of curiosity. See how patient I'm being? A good little hellspawn." He was smiling. I have only seen that smile on him once or twice, and each time it chills my blood. He looks so damn happy and interested, as if he's examining a fine piece of art—or ass. Something he knows he can pick up and is just stretching out the anticipation of. It makes his bland, nondescript face into the picture of "terrifying."

Especially when his eyes sparkle.

I finally felt as if I had enough air. "That was a trap for me." I didn't sound choked, but I was beginning to feel it.

"Gee, you think?" He didn't bother to weight the words with much sarcasm. But there was a ratty little gleam in his eyes I didn't like, though I was too tired and sore to think much about it.

Besides, there's *always* a gleam in Perry's eyes I don't like. I rolled my eyes. Dragged more sweet air in. "What are you really doing here?"

"I told you, looking after my investment. You think you can go for a few hours without getting shot or torn up? I really do have important things to do."

I waved my right hand experimentally. It worked just like it always had. The fog was retreating, evaporating up from the street in long white trails. "Thanks, Perry. Now get the fuck away from me."

"Sweet talk will get you nowhere." He grinned, his chin tilting up slightly. "I'll see you tomorrow night."

My heart thudded, my body too drained to even produce adrenaline. Still, the bite of fear just under my skin was sharp as a new blade, and hard to hide. "Midnight." I kept dragging in deep healing breaths. "I haven't forgotten."

The first cop cars arrived on-scene. I braced myself. When my eyes flicked back to where he had been standing, Perry was gone.

I hate it when he does that. I swallowed, tasting blood and bile, and peeled myself away from the twisted iron bars. *Monty is just going to die,* I thought, as flashing blue lights converged. The burning car smelled awful, and the stink of the creature still hung in the air. *Gah, that's foul.*

The shakes had me. Beating under every thought was the same sentence, repeated in frightened panicked-rabbit jumps across my brain.

I could have died. I could have died. Oh God, my God, I could have died.

CHAPTER 12

Woo Song's is a little hole in the wall, a neon dragon buzzing over a single door, no windows, and the smell of foreign cooking belching out each time someone entered or left. Since I was battered, bloody, and generally not in a good mood, I stood outside across the street until Saul appeared, shepherding our nervous witness. Once more I was grateful to have a good partner.

Robbie's eyes widened as he took me in; Saul himself barely raised an eyebrow. His gaze did flick to the leather cuff on my right wrist, which was conspicuously *not* blood-soaked. His hand was over Robbie's shoulder, and he moved with an awareness and grace that, as usual, comforted me and unsettled me a little at the same time.

Sometimes I wondered what would have happened if I'd still been just a human hunter when I met Saul. The scar was Perry's claim on me, true...but it also meant I wasn't so easily damaged during bedplay. And there were several times I could have died if not for the fact that I was tougher and quicker now, which would have put a distinct crimp in our relationship.

Go figure, I meet the perfect man after I'm in hock to a

hellbreed, and if I wasn't tainted I couldn't have had a relationship with a Were.

Sometimes I don't just *think* God has a sadistic sense of humor.

I kept to the shadows, beckoning them into the alley across from Woo Song's. I suspected Robbie the Juicer would be a lot more comfortable where he couldn't see the bloody rags I wore. Half my left breast was peering out, my shirt was never going to be the same, and the tough leather of my pants was shredded. My long leather coat wasn't ever going to be the same either.

Clothes get expensive when you're a hunter. I was going to have a hell of a time getting the blood out of my sodden boots, if it was possible at all.

Dammit.

Monty hadn't been happy, but at least the Feeb on duty—sleek, dark Juan Rujillo—was actually a decent sort who wouldn't make any problems. Both of them were a little pale when I presented them with the scenario that scares everyone the most: something out there a hunter doesn't know about, and hasn't had any luck stopping.

Rujillo had promised to get me a list of all the professional operators in town, even if he had to twist a few interagency arms. That is one thing about being a hunter, you're usually assured of getting cooperation from even the stingiest intelligence agencies. Turf wars end up with a lot of dead civilians and uncomfortable media attention, and that's two things no intelligence or law enforcement agency wants. *Especially* the latter. There are very few spooks, Feebs, ghosts, or rubber pencils who want to interfere. The FBI has its own hunter division, the Martindale Squad, and it's whispered that the CIA has a few operatives that are a little more than strictly human.

I wouldn't know about that, though.

Though strictly speaking, a list of mercs in town wouldn't do much good. This had been a one-time shot; now I was wary and whatever mercenaries they'd set on me had suffered horrific casualties. It would be inefficient to send another mercenary cadre after me and expect it to delay me or hold me for the creature, whatever it was. And whoever was pulling the strings here wasn't stupid or inefficient.

That, at least, I was sure of.

Ruji had once again accused me of being a menace to property, but he'd done it with a twinkle in his eye. Monty was chewing Tums by the bucketload; he was the one who had to deal with the media showing up in droves and demanding an explanation.

And I was ready to explode from frustration.

"Start at the beginning," I said, and Robbie shot a nervous glance at Saul.

"You wanna come in and eat something?" Saul looked down at the alley floor, his shoulders hunching. It was a show of submission, almost shocking in a Were much taller and bulkier than me.

I must have been wearing my mad face.

"I don't think Wu-ma would like it if I showed up all bloody." I was trying for a light tone. *She'd probably feed me MSG just to express her displeasure, too.*

His nostrils flared. "You stink."

"Thanks. I just had a run-in with something big and hairy that looks like a Were on steroids and reeks to high heaven." I eyed Robbie the Juicer, who was beginning to tremble. "Relax, Robbie. I'm not going to hurt you. As a matter of fact, I'm your new best friend. I'm going to keep you alive."

"Very goddamn kind of you." Robbie's voice was thin and reedy. His shock of dark hair was greasy, and he smelled like dumplings. "What the fuck happened?"

You do not want to know, civilian. Trust me. "Who did you tell? About the other night?"

His shoulders trembled. He stared at me like I was Banquo's ghost. "Couple people. Shit, man, after that I was happy to be alive. Got a cigarette?"

"I suggest we take him somewhere safe." Saul straightened, his eyes reflecting green-gold for a moment in the dimness. "I don't like this."

"I heard that." Even this alley wasn't likely safe. "Micky's? The bar, not the front?"

He nodded, the silver shifting in his hair; the little bottle of holy water at his neck sparkled summer-blue once, maybe reacting to the scar still pulsing hard and heavy under the cuff. Or maybe it was because I smelled of hellbreed, Perry's etheric fingerprints all over me from the work he'd done patching me up. "Good idea," he said. "I'll drive."

I didn't argue.

Robbie stared into his coffee cup while I scrubbed at my hands with baby wipes. I'd changed in the bathroom, into fresh pants and a T-shirt kept in the Impala's trunk, but my coat was still tacky-wet with blood and my boots were squishy. It had dried under my short bitten nails and crusted in my hair.

Thank God it was only *my* blood. One thing to be happy about: no civilian casualties. I'd managed to keep anyone innocent from being hurt.

It wasn't as comforting as it should have been, but it was enough for me.

The bartender, Theron, brought me a stack of damp washcloths and a beer. Ther was tall, lean, dark, and intense. He also happened to be a Werepanther. I'd only seen him *shift* once, during a fight with a nest of Middle Way Chaos-worshipping wannabes out on Chartres Street. I didn't want to see it again. Panther jaws can crack bones, and Theron was *big;* Weres tend to run bulkier than both humans and beasts but some of them just look too huge to be real. He was good backup but extremely unpredictable; not someone to call unless you wanted to play it his way. Still, he was a good sort, and part of the reason why nobody stepped out of line in Micky's.

"Stinks," he said, giving a nod to Saul.

Who visibly bristled. "I know, Theron. Thanks."

"Want a shot, Saul?"

"No. Thanks." Saul was extraordinarily still, his shoulders spread wide and his eyes luminous. Theron gave him a toothy smile, and retreated. In the dominance game between Weres, Saul and Ther were roughly equal; sometimes Ther pushed it a little, moving in on me, getting a little too close. It was a Were's version of social game-playing, and I didn't like being a chit in the middle. Another night I might have been amused.

Not tonight, though. Getting almost-canceled will cut your sense of humor dead short.

"Why don't you start at the beginning, Robbie?" My temper was fraying badly. Saul's arm pressed against mine; I stopped wiping at the blood on my hands and leaned my head against his shoulder. He leaned back, subtly, then turned his head, his chin rubbing across my still-damp hair.

My chest eased a little bit. The shaking in my hands began to go down.

Robbie glanced up, looked hurriedly back down at his coffee. "I got ta the field at about ten-thirty. I wasn't drunk, but I was tired. So's I wanted a place where I could think, right? I pissed about back and got my sleeping bag all set up, got my stuff situated. Then I settled down and I was almost asleep, man. I thought of lighting a J to get myself all nice and mellow, but I was finally warmin' up. It was a cold fuckin' day, I tell you, out on the streets."

Well, yeah, we're past New Year's and in the chilliest part of the year. I sighed. Saul slid his arm around me, pulled me into his side. I wiped at my face with the first wet washcloth, scrubbing the wet terry across my cheeks, digging at my closed eyes. I can be covered in filth, but I like my face clean.

Call it a quirk.

The silver charms in my hair shifted, chiming softly. Saul's braid bumped my cheek as he turned his head, taking in the bar.

"So I dunno what time it was, but I heard an engine. And not a cop car or anything, just a very soft, nice purring engine." Robbie's dark eyes were wide, his spotted cheeks pasty. He was sweating, and he smelled like too few showers and too much drinking, with a healthy dash of fear-sweat on top. His fingernails were brutally short but still grimy.

The scar on my wrist tingled. *Perry.* What had he been doing out there? He didn't usually leave the Monde, preferring to sit in the middle of his web like a big fat waxy-pale spider.

That mental image made me shudder, and Saul kissed my temple.

"I got this weird feeling. Just a weird feeling. You live on the street long enough, you start to get a kind of feel for the nutzoid things. Like when the crazy shit is gonna start going down. Sometimes you don't get no warning, but most of the time there's this feeling before crazy shit starts up. Y'unnerstand?"

I certainly understood that. One of the things a hunter looks for in an apprentice is a certain amount of psychic ability; I wouldn't have survived to become an apprentice if I hadn't had more than my fair share to begin with. "Like instinct," I supplied.

His face brightened a little. He grinned into his coffee, with yellow teeth. "Yeah, instink. Thatza word. I just got that feeling. So I got up, and I went to the end of the dugout, real low-like. Creeping. And I looked out."

His fingers tightened on the cup; dirt grimed into his knuckles and under his short-split nails. "I saw this black van sitting there. Just sittin'. And then I notice it ain't got no license plate, and I think maybe the cops are doing a sting, and I'm getting ready to get my ass out of there nice and quiet-like. Then the door opens up, and out jumps this thing. And damned if it don't look like a goddamn ape, but it hunches down—like them things you see in movies. You seen that movie, where there's these things, they look human, but they don't move no human way?"

Honey, I don't need movies. I see them in living color. "I guess so." I didn't want to lead the witness, so to speak, so I didn't give him more.

"Like this movie where guys change into werewolves, and they run on their hands and feet, but their shoulders are all funny. And they've got weird-shaped heads. Lots of teeth. Anyway, the goddamn thing hopped out, and started snuffling. And I started thinking maybe it could smell me, 'cause I could smell it. Smelled like a wet dog puking its guts out in a whorehouse."

That was a revolting but extremely apt way of describing it. I leaned into Saul's side, for once not caring that my hair was crackling with drying blood and my toes were damp inside my boots. "Okay."

He continued. "Someone's gotten out, and they're moving around. A woman. Light hair, but not blonde. I can see her haircut, she's got it cut like that bitch on Channel Twelve—"

"Susan Zamora? The anchorwoman?" Zamora had a sleek, leonine bob dyed a fashionable chocolate-cherry color. She was a barracuda in human form.

There's no love lost between me and the press. I like to keep things quiet, because let's face it, normal people don't *want* to know about the nightside. Reporters have just enough orneriness to *think* they want to know, that's all. Which equals a huge pain in the ass for a hunter *and* the cops.

Don't get me wrong, I love the Fourth Estate like any red-blooded American. But Jesus *wept,* they make my job harder. Fortunately, they get stonewalled by everyone except UFO nutjobs and fake psychics.

Anyone who knows about the nightside knows not to talk about it.

"Yeah, her. That way. She's moving around, there's nobody else out there. And I've got a bad, bad feeling about this, because the furry smelly thing is snuffling, and I got this feeling like I'm going to throw up. Anyway, the woman barks something, and the furry thing leaps up into the back of the van and I can see the entire thing rock a little bit. Then it brings out something real pale, and I can see it's not right. The only thing that big is a body, but it handles it like it's nothing. The furry thing kind of shuffles to the edge of the sidewalk, and it *throws* the thing, and I see it is a body but something's wrong with it. It hits with a kind of thud and the furry thing is back in the van, and the woman gets in. Then the engine gets to purring again, and they're gone." He shivered, despite the close muggy warmth of Micky's. His eyes came up to meet mine, and they were dark enough that I reached up and pushed my beer across the table.

"Take it. It'll do you good."

He did, setting down his coffee, and took down about half the cold bottle in one long throat-working swallow. He wiped his mouth with the back of his dirty hand. "I bet it did smell me," he said miserably. "I bet it did."

"Don't worry about that right now. Was there anything else? Did she talk, laugh, move around the van at all?"

"Moved around looking up. That's all." He finished the rest of the beer. "What the fuck was that thing? It *warn't human.* I warn't drunk, ma'am. It warn't human 'tall."

The more worked-up he got, the more hillbilly he sounded. "Maybe, maybe not," I soothed. *I'll take him to Galina's and leave him there; that's the safest place for him right now. And she won't stand for any street bullshit.* "But what's important for right now is to keep you out of sight. I've got someone you can stay with, if you don't mind a bit of work. It's either that or hit the streets where these people—whoever they are—are looking for you. Think back, and tell me everyone you told about this. *Everyone.*"

He did, and the list was depressingly long and imprecise, finishing with: "That kid who hangs around Plaskény Square, with the blue hair and the rings in his nose. Tall kid. I mentioned it to him. That's all."

That's all? Oh, man, this just keeps getting better and better.

"Tell her what you told me," Saul said suddenly. "About what the woman said."

"Oh, yeah. Almost forgot." His mournful face brightened. "It sounded like French."

Huh? "French?"

"I took four years of French in high school. I think that's what she was speakin'. Somethin' about ... well, shit, I'm rusty. But I'd swear it was French."

"French." I nodded, my head resting on Saul's shoulder. Suddenly I was incredibly, bone-crunchingly weary. It's the reaction of coming very, very close to certain death: after the adrenaline and the urge for sex wear off, the only thing left was terrible exhaustion, as if every appendage is dipped in lead. "Okay."

Wonderful. A French-speaking broad with fancy hair, multiple murders and more on the way, and something so tough even Perry's frightened of it. Not to mention the fact that I think Perry knows more than he's telling. For a moment I closed my eyes, listening to the clink of glass from the bar, the clatter of silverware and murmur of voices from out in the restaurant, the sound of water and frying from the kitchen, a waitress's voice lifted in a snatch of song along with Bonnie Raitt on the restaurant's speaker system, giving "them" *something to talk about, a little mystery to figure out.*

Coincidence. Getting a little help again.

Saul was warm and solid beside me, his arm tightening, and he didn't let go until I opened my eyes and leaned away.

This just kept getting better. But for right now, all I wanted to do was go home and sleep.

CHAPTER 13

Saul collapsed, his lax weight resting on me for a brief moment, his hipbones digging into the soft insides of my thighs. The tattoo high up on my right thigh writhed, its winged tingle running under my skin. I kissed along the edge of his jaw, found his mouth again. He tasted of night, of cold wind and wildness and the Scotch I'd taken down four mouthfuls of before he'd slid his arm around my waist and half-dragged me to the bed.

My hair was still wet, the charms tinkling slightly as the spillfire of orgasm tore through me again, my hips slamming up. The third was always the nicest; I gasped into his mouth and heard the low rumble of his contentment begin, a purr that shook through every cell, every bone, and chased away all remaining fear. Sweat mixed with the water from the shower, his smell of Ivory soap and animal musk making a pleasant heady brew.

"Shhh," he whispered against my mouth. "Kitten, shhh. It's all right."

I quieted, more air gasped in, flavored with his breath. He kissed my cheek, my temple, my mouth again, bracing himself on his elbows.

As usual, he didn't want to let go, nuzzling along the line of my jaw and down to the hollow of my throat, teeth scraping delicately as aftershocks rippled through me. It had taken months of patient trying before I could let him touch me anywhere covered by a bikini, and even longer before I could rest there under his weight, utterly vulnerable. We were branching out, experimenting, and I finally felt like I'd trampled some of the demons of my adolescence.

But coming so close to death raised demons of its own. I went limp, closed my eyes, let him nibble at my throat. It was a highly erogenous zone for Weres, especially Weres of the cat persuasion. A sign of trust, and a sign of territorial marking. A hickey on the neck of a Were's mate means seriousness, means *don't touch this, it's mine.*

He was Were. He wasn't a human man, and sometimes I wondered if that was why I *could* let him touch me. With Mikhail it had been different—he had been my teacher, trusted absolutely even in the confines of the bed, always in control.

Until Mikhail had no longer wanted me.

My hands relaxed, slid down Saul's arms. The leather of the cuff touched his shoulder. He nuzzled deeper in my throat, the sharp edges of his teeth brushing the skin just over my pulse. A strand of his hair, freighted with a silver charm, lay across my chin.

"Saul," I whispered. He sucked at my throat, a spot of almost-pain, gauging it perfectly. I could feel the blood rising to the surface, blossoming on the skin, the bruise would be flawless. A dark mark, almost like a brand.

One last gentle kiss against my carotid artery and he moved, sliding out of me with exquisite slowness. Off to the side, the bed creaking as it accepted his weight, and the usual slow movement ended up with my head on his shoulder and his arm around me, my body slumped against his side. He was warm, flush with heat, and purring contentedly.

I thought he would fall asleep, as usual. But instead he pulled the covers up with his free hand, tucking us both in. "Better?" The rumble didn't fade when he spoke. Nobody could ever figure out where a cat Were's purr came from. If they know, they're not telling.

"Much." I kissed his shoulder. My neck pulsed with a sweet pain. "Good therapy."

"Happy to provide." He paused. "You looked pretty bloody."

It was the closest he would get to an accusation.

"It beat the shit out of me," I admitted. "I didn't hit it."

He was still. The rumble kept going. "A trap."

"Yep." I dropped the bombshell, even though he would have smelled it on me. "Perry showed up."

His purr stopped.

"Hellfire didn't even damage the thing, but he blew up a car and it ran off. Then he patched me up."

"Patched you up?"

"Says I'm an investment." I kissed his shoulder again. *Come on, Saul. Please.*

His silence was eloquent.

"Saul?"

He moved, a little, restlessly. A movement like a cat settling itself for the night, curling into a warm bed.

"Please, Saul. *Please.*" There was nobody else I would use this tone on. Pleading, cajoling, trying to convince. Almost—dare I say it—*begging.*

"I don't like it," he said, finally. He had gone tense, muscle standing out under his skin, the utter stillness of a hunting beast crouched low in the grass.

Oh, for God's sake. "You think *I* do? You think I *like* it?"

"Why keep going back?" As soon as he said it he made a restless movement, then stilled again.

"He's fucking useful. And if it hadn't been for the goddamn bargain I would have *died.*"

"I can take care of you." Stubborn. "If it wasn't for the goddamn bargain I wouldn't have left you there."

"And they might have killed us both and our witness as well. I'm a *hunter,* Saul. Perry's a tool. That's all. One day I'll kill him."

"Not soon enough."

Not soon enough for me either. "Amen to that." I rubbed my chin against his shoulder. My voice dropped to a whisper, I swallowed and felt the hickey on my throat pulse again. It was better than the scar on my wrist, a cleaner pain. "I love you, dammit."

"I know, kitten. I love you." But anger boiled under the words.

"It's just a tool," I repeated. The thought made me shudder with frantic loathing, remembering bargaining for the mark, remembering the press of that scaled tongue against my flesh. A hundred other unpleasant and downright horrific memories crowded behind that one, threatening like piled black clouds announcing a cataclysmic storm.

"I know." Saul brushed my wet hair back from my face, I tilted my head against his fingers, savoring the touch that pushed bad dreams away. "I know. I just...I'm gonna breathe a sigh of relief when I see that hellspawn motherfucker draw his last breath. I wish I could tear out his throat myself."

You're not the only one. "I love you," I repeated, desperately.

Under that desperation the deeper plea—*don't leave me. Please don't leave me.*

Not like he would. Weres settle down with their mates, and that's that. They do it much more easily and cleanly than humans manage to.

But I wasn't Were. I was an aberration.

The tension left him, bit by bit, and the rumbling purr returned. "Loved you the first minute I saw you, kitten. Covered in muck and swearing at the top of your lungs. God, you were a sight."

The memory made me smile, drowning the press of other memories not even half as pleasant. I could smile, now that I was almost two years away from that hunt. "Why do they always hide in storm drains? I hate that."

"Hm." He was sleepy now, going as boneless and languid as a cat in a patch of sunlight. The danger was past, thank God. "Go to sleep."

"I will," I whispered. "Stay with me."

Because if you leave me, I don't know what I'll do. As usual, the thought sent panic through me, plucking at my hard-won control over my pulse, tightening every muscle against postcoital lassitude.

"Not going anywhere, kitten." He held me tighter, even as he slid over the edge into sleep, the purr growing fitful but still comforting.

Thank God for you, Saul.

I listened to him breathing. It was the sound of safety, of good things, of comfort and pleasure and trust. After imagining what it might be like sometimes in the deep watches of the night, I now knew—and I had no desire to ever go back to being lonely.

My wrist prickled. The scar always felt like it was burrowing deeper, trying to reach bone. I'd given up wondering if it was phantom pain; it wasn't any more deeply scarred than it had ever been. It was just part of the deal.

If it came down to a choice, I was going to have to welsh on a deal with a hellbreed and take my chances. Damned if I did, possibly damned if I didn't...there was no winning here. The best I could hope for was as long with Saul as I could get.

Is that enough?

It didn't matter. It was all I was going to get. The bruise on my neck settled into a dimple of pleasant heat as I slid over the border into sleep's country. For once, I had no dreams.

The next day brought bad news, another body—and the first break. My pager was destroyed from last night's fun, and it would take me a day or so to get a new one; but they called me at home and I made the scene in less than half an hour.

"We don't know her name yet," Carp said. His hair was back to standing up in messy sandy-blond spikes. "Christ."

The abandoned parking lot was deserted under thin winter-afternoon sunshine, weeds forcing up through cracked old concrete. The body—if there was enough left of it to qualify as a body—lay slumped in the middle, blood lying sticky-wet on sharp thistle leaves and dead dandelion plants. The ribs were twisted aside, viscera and other organs gone, the eyes had been plucked from the skull and long strands of blood-matted hair stirred gently under the wind's stroking fingers.

Off in the ambulance, the kid who had found the body as he cut through the parking lot on his way to school made a low hurt sound. He was crying messily, and his mother was on her way to pick him up. No more shortcuts for him.

"God." I folded my arms. I'd gotten the blood off my coat, but it hung in tatters, clearly showing where the thing had clawed me. The right sleeve had needed patching before I could even put it on, and I wore my second-best pair of boots. "All I have is more questions."

"A black van with no license plate. A redhead who speaks French, and something that smells like—what was it?" Carp sounded grimly amused.

"A wet dog puking its guts out in a whorehouse," I quoted. I thought he'd enjoy that. Carp's laugh was sharp and jagged as a broken window.

Saul picked his way around the body, watching where he stepped. The sun touched the red-black of his hair and the silver of the charms tied in it, ran lovingly down his coat and brought out the glow in his dark skin. *A fine-looking man. A very fine-looking man.*

Saul stopped. He lowered himself slowly, staring intently at the ground. Then he reached down, his fingers delicate, and picked something up.

I held my breath.

He continued on his circuit, examining the cracked concrete and frost-dead weeds.

"Looks like Tonto's found something." Rosie arrived at my side. "How you feeling, Jill? Heard you caused some damage last night."

"Wasn't my fault. The Feebs treating you right?"

She shrugged, her eyes hidden behind mirrored sunglasses. Today she wore a hooded Santa Luz Wheelwrights sweatshirt jacket and a black leather coat, jeans and black Nikes. She looked like a fresh-scrubbed college kid, especially with the shades. "Rujillo. He's okay. Not like that bastard Astin."

I winced. Astin had been a good agent, but a rigid one; he believed the local cops were all incompetent or mismanaged. Having him reassigned had been a distinct relief. "Yeah, he's different. Little more flexible."

"You all right?" Her tone was excessively casual.

So you heard I was covered in blood. Rosie, I didn't know you cared. The thought was snide, unworthy of me. She *did* care. A cop who didn't care wouldn't have limped down to the warehouse in her bandages and apologized to me. "I got beat up a bit, but I'm okay."

"You know what's going on yet?" This from Carp.

"Not yet, Carp. Can't rush these things." *I'm beginning to feel distinctly out of temper.* Thin winter sunlight caressed my shoulders, the wind had veered and was coming from the faroff mountains; we would have deep frost. Living in semi-desert meant that winters were miserable cold times, especially with the war between the river wind and the mountains breathing on us.

"Wish you could. Press is crawling on our backs. All sorts of wackos coming out of the woodwork."

I knew. I'd seen the papers. *Serial Murderer Haunts Ladies of the Night!* was the kindest headline. Even the respectable rags were trotting out the Jack the Ripper comparisons. And the nightly TV news was in a frenzy. "Any incredibly weird, or just the usual weird?"

"Just the usual. Crystal-crawlin' psychics. Copycats. Nutcases." Carp sighed. "This is starting to piss me off."

"Me too." My tone was a little sharper than usual. I didn't like being in the dark, and I was failing them. "I'm working as hard as I can."

"We know," Rosie soothed. "We know, Jill." And they did. I'd worked with them for long enough that they *did* know, and I was grateful for that.

Saul approached. He held up his hand, and something dangled: three thin leather thongs, braided, interwoven with feathers and bits of fur. There were complex knots in a pattern that looked vaguely familiar. A single dart of darkness was braided into the end of it.

An obsidian arrowhead, carefully flaked and probably genuine. Saul's fingers flicked, and the arrowhead dangled. "Found something." His face was grim. "Smells awful. Probably related."

I plunged a hand in my pocket, already hunting for a drawstring bag. Found one, fished it out, and opened it. "Finally," I breathed. "Come to Mama."

He dropped it in, and wiped his fingers against his leather pants. The thing was oddly heavy, and coldly malignant. And he was right, it did smell. I caught a faint whiff of a familiar reek.

"I don't like this." Saul drew himself up, still scrubbing his fingers against his pants. "That thing is evil, Jill."

"They usually are." I was too relieved to finally have a piece of usable evidence to mind much. "Do you recognize it?"

He shook his head, his jaw setting grimly. I stuffed the bag in another pocket, and studied the body. Now that Saul had circled it I approached, cautiously; he had point-blank refused to let me get near it until he had a chance to look. He stayed back as I edged closer, but I felt his eyes on me.

No, Saul wasn't happy either. But whether it was the case or Perry, I wasn't going to guess.

Now that I'd seen the creature, I could see marks that matched its claws. There were ragged slices in the flesh, chunks taken out of the thighs and the breasts gone, just divots with glaring-white splinters of rib poking through sodden meat.

I peered into the cavity left by the taking of the viscera, and my eyes narrowed. *Wait a second. Wait just a goddamn second.*

I looked through the rest of the scene, too, found exactly zilch. But my heart was beating quickly as I nodded at the forensic team and went back to Saul. "There's something else," I said.

Rosie and Carp both went still, attentive. Like bloodhounds straining at the leash. I took a deep breath, a chill finger sliding up my spine; it was the feeling of the first piece of a pattern falling into place. "There's claw marks and *other* marks. The thing I saw last night had claws shaped like *this*." My hands sketched briefly in the air. "The other marks, inside the abdominal cavity and around her eyes—those are too clean, and they're almost covered by the claw marks. The ones covered up are made by something *sharp*. Like a scalpel."

"A scalp—" Rosie trailed off. Her mouth pulled down, meditatively.

"Scalpel." Carp scratched at his chin. "Well. Okay. So?"

"I assumed the creature was eating what it took. It may be. But it might also be getting a little help. Or eating leftovers." I folded my arms against the chill in the air, the butt of a gun digging into my left hip.

Carp kept scratching at his chin. "Or it's covering something up."

"Either way." The smile pulled up my lips, baring my teeth in a feral grimace. "Cheer up, boys and girls. This constitutes our first bit of good luck."

"How so?" Rosie didn't sound convinced.

"Well, it's more than we had before. And if that little thing Saul found is from it, we can track it. Tracking it's the first step to finding it, which is the first step to taking its sorry ass apart. And that will make me very, very happy."

Saul stirred next to me, and I didn't have to read his mind. He was thinking that I'd run up against this thing once before and nearly died, so why should tracking it make me happy?

But I did. I felt irrationally happy. If it would make a mistake like dropping something, it could make other mistakes. Unless this was a challenge, a *fuck you, Kismet. We nearly got you last night; we'll get you eventually.*

"Do we know the time of death?"

"Hard to tell with the body so torn up. But it ain't frozen. And if it ain't frozen with this kind of cold, and on pavement, it's still pretty fresh." Carp sounded as unhappy as it was possible to sound without sarcasm.

"The blood's still a little tacky-wet too." I cast around. Good luck getting tire tracks on this concrete, and how did they get the van here? If they *did* get the van here. "The question is..." I sorted through all of the questions in my head, still far too many for my taste. I picked the most useful one. "The question is, why get rid of the bodies like this? What purpose does it serve?"

"Make our lives miserable," Carp muttered.

"Not as miserable as hers." Rosie jerked her chin toward the body, now being swarmed with forensic techs.

"I'm going to go do some research." I rocked back on my heels as Saul bumped into me, crowding me again. His heat was a comfort in the early morning chill. They were right, the body hadn't frozen yet. Whoever she was, she was freshly killed. "Buzz me if anyone else dies."

Black humor, maybe. Bleak gallows humor. But you spend enough time looking at dead bodies and hanging out with cops, and that kind of humor becomes necessary. It's a shield held up against the dark things we see, against the horrific things that can happen to anyone.

I'm lucky. I see inhuman things and how they prey on humanity. I see the aberrations, those who bargain away their souls for power, those who trade everything for the sweet seduction, the canker in the rose, the dominion of the earth. The cops have it so much worse.

They have to see the things human beings do to each other without any help from Hell.

Saul's chest brushed my back. He had stepped behind me, looming just like a Were. The fresh hickey on my neck throbbed.

"Yeah, we'll call you. Why don't you get a goddamn cell phone?" It was an old complaint. Carp hunched his shoulders, fishing a pair of latex gloves out of his jacket pocket.

"Can't afford to replace 'em, as many times as I get beat up and dumped in water. Not to mention electrocuted, stabbed, shot—"

"Okay, okay. I got it." Carp rolled his eyes. "Get this one corralled quick, Kiss. Rosie's getting pissy with the long hours."

Rosie wasn't amused. "Fuck you. Glad you're okay, Kiss."

I leaned back into Saul before moving away, feeling his hand brush mine. "Me too, Rosie. Thanks."

Saul followed me to the Impala, sitting tucked out of sight on Edgerton Street. He was sticking so close he might have been glued to me, and after dropping into the driver's seat I waited for him to come around and get in. He did, and I looked at the red fuzzy dice. They swung gently when I reached up and touched them, a gift from Galina.

I should go see her and have a cup of tea, it always helps me think clearer. But we had a witness stashed at her house, and it wouldn't do to go visiting her again and perhaps bring trouble to her door.

Saul didn't buckle his seat belt. Waited, staring out through the windshield. His profile was beautiful. I looked at his mouth—he had such a lovely mouth, his upper lip chiseled and his lower slightly full, a little bruised from kissing. *One of these days, I'm going to leave a hickey on him. He'll like that.*

"This is a break," I told him. "A good one."

He shrugged. "I don't like it. Broadway's only four blocks away."

Meaning they're playing with me. They dumped the body less than four blocks away from where they tried to kill me. Or did it come straight from dumping the body to mangle me? Either way, it's not good. "I know. But this is still a break."

"You're visiting Perry tonight."

Thanks for reminding me. The skin on my back roughened. I buckled myself in. He reached for his own seatbelt.

I twisted the key. The Impala's engine purred into life. *Sixty-seven was the best year in American car history.* My hands gripped the wheel. I decided silence was my best option.

What he said next destroyed *that* theory. "I want you to stay there."

"What the *fuck?*" I twisted my head to look at him so quickly a silver charm flew and smacked the window on my side, my hair ruffling out. It almost hit me in the eye, but thankfully the red thread held and it was snatched back as my head turned.

"I want to go do some research. I want you to stay at the Monde until I get back. It might take me a little while."

"Why? Where are *you* going?" I heard my voice hit the pitch just under "shriek."

"Just out to the barrio. I got a few things on my mind." He stared out the windshield.

"Like *what?*"

"Just a few things."

Fuck that. "I'll go with you."

"No, kitten. There are some places down there you shouldn't go."

It didn't help that he was right. The barrio was a good place for someone of my racial persuasion to end up dead; the Weres ran herd out there and only called me in if something boiled over. "People are dying, Saul. I'll go anywhere I need to." I settled back into the seat, listening to the engine's steady comforting purr.

"Please, kitten. If you're at the Monde, I know you're at least alive. I don't want to take you into the barrio." His eyes dropped, he looked at the dash.

"You'd rather leave me with Perry." Was that accusation in my voice? Wonders never cease.

"He's got a vested interest in keeping you alive, *you* keep reminding me of that. And he chased that thing off last night."

"I don't think he chased it off."

"It left when he showed up. Good enough for me. Come on, Kiss. Please."

This is something I never thought I'd hear from you, Saul. I looked at my knuckles, white against the steering wheel. Then I reached down, shifted into first to pull out onto Edgerton. "Jesus Christ, Saul. What the hell's going on?"

"I wish I knew, kitten. I really do." He did, too. I could hear it. Whatever he suspected, it had to be *really* bad if he was going into the barrio; doubly bad if he wanted me to spend any more time with Perry than was absolutely necessary. "I just want to ask some questions."

"Like what questions?"

"Like some Were questions. Watch your driving."

"Shut up about my driving." I took a right on Seventh, turning up toward downtown. "Talk to me, Saul. Come on."

"I just want to ask about that braid and knot pattern, that's all. It looks familiar, but I can't quite place it."

"Is the arrowhead genuine?"

"You're a sharp girl. I think it is." He shifted in his bucket seat, leather moving against the red fur of the seat covers; he fished a Charvil out of the box in his breast pocket. Rolled the window down a little, lit it with his wolf's-head Zippo. I reached down and yanked out the ashtray.

"The hair?"

"Human." His voice was shaded with distaste.

"Christ." I shifted into fourth, the tires chirped a little when I stamped on the gas. "Give me a vowel here, Saul."

"Wish I had one to give. It just *looks* familiar but I can't place it. Makes my hackles go up."

Yours too? "Instinct."

"Trust it."

"I do." *I have a healthy respect for a Were's instinct.* "All right."

He obviously hadn't expected me to give in so easily. "You'll stay there?"

"I will, Saul. If you want me to, I'll put up with Pericles. Just do what you have to and don't leave me there long, for God's sake. I suppose you want my car."

"I'll clean out the ashtray." He inhaled, blew out a long stream of cherry-scented smoke. His unhappiness mixed with mine, a steady tension between us. "And I won't grind the gears. We going to the hospital?"

"I want to check in on Father Rosas. Something about a Chaldean in a seminary after a Catholic artifact doesn't sit right with me. And an artifact I've never heard of—and that Hutch hasn't, either?" I paused, hit the left-hand blinker and turned left on Pelizada Avenue. *Then we're going to visit that doctor on Quincoa.*

He inhaled a deep lungful of cherry-scented smoke, blew it out the window. "Catholic rites do offer protection against Chaldean sorcery and possession. That bird-thing couldn't get out of the chapel."

You've been studying, you naughty boy. My wrists weren't steady enough, a tremor running all the way up to my elbows I ignored. "Catholic immunity only started in the sixteenth century with the creation of the Jesuits and their Shadow Order. Loyola created the Society in 1534 and the Shadow Order in 1536 by secret charter; the Sorrows started to feel the pinch in 1588 when their House in Seville was cleared and torched. That was Juan de Alatriste." I knew I was babbling, couldn't help myself. "And then Alatriste went against the scurf in Granada and—"

"Breathe, Jill."

I took a deep breath. My knuckles almost creaked, my fingers were clenched so tightly. "The only thing worse than going there is anticipating it."

"He counts on that."

"And you want me to stay there after he's finished with me." *You hate him. The very first thing you learned about me was that I smelled like hellbreed. You hated me, as much as a Were can hate, I guess.*

His silence answered me. He inhaled again. Dry cold air bloomed through his slightly open window.

My heart twisted. I still didn't know why Saul had changed his mind about me. I didn't know what he got out of staying with me. All my life I've stayed alive by knowing the motivations of every-one around me, especially everyone who could hurt me. Anyone who made me vulnerable.

I could understand, I guess, why Saul wanted me somewhere he knew I'd be protected if that thing—whatever it was—came after me again. What I didn't understand was why he was with me at all. He was Were, and human rules didn't apply. I mostly thought that was a good thing.

Now I wondered.

I'd trusted him this far, with my body and whatever was left of my heart. I'd trusted him with everything Mikhail had left me. And I'd trusted him to watch my back more times than I could count.

It would have to be good enough.

"Okay." I downshifted as the light on Pelizada and Twelfth changed. "Okay. You got it. Okay."

CHAPTER 14

Sisters of Mercy rose above downtown like a giant brooding concrete bird. The old hospital was lost in a welter of pavement, but the great granite Jesus tacked on the roof still glowered in the direction of the financial district. We went in through the side entrance and suffered the immediate attack of linoleum, disinfectant, floor wax, and the smell of suffering.

Saul reached down and took my hand as soon as we walked in. I've grown to hate hospitals. Don't get me wrong—they're mostly wonderful places, staffed by some of the best and most dedicated around. But like schools, they just raise my hackles. So much suffering and free energy floating around, whether from illness and dying or from kids squeezed into little boxes and told to behave; so much *pain*. It's a charged atmosphere, which is good for a hunter—we kind of amp up to meet that charge—and bad for a hunter as well. There's only so long you can stay with your hackles up before going a little wack.

Of course, the case could be made that we're all permanently wack anyway.

We took the stairs up to the fifth floor, post-cardiac. My footsteps echoed in the hall, and I began to feel a little uneasy. My fingers tightened, and Saul gave me a single inquiring look.

I spotted Father Guillermo down the hall, and felt my face harden. It still rankled. The Church funded training for quite a few hunters, but it was an article of faith and doctrine that we were going to Hell for our traffic with and contamination by the nightside. Still, I'd thought I could *trust* Gui, that he wouldn't... well, hold out on me.

Treat me like just another layman.

God knew I'd handled enough exorcisms for him. I deserved a

little bit of warning if his seminary was holding a relic or arti-fact—even if it was very likely that the Sorrows had no interest in the fucking thing.

Why were they there, then? What the hell's going on with that?

The scar tightened, sending a flush of heat up my arm. I stopped dead. My nostrils flared. Saul went still and dangerous beside me.

"You smell that?" I asked, as he let go of my hand and reached for the hilt of his Bowie.

"Incense," he replied. "And blood. A blue smell."

Not just a blue smell, but a smell I remembered. A smell that made my hackles not just rise, but stiffen into steel spikes and pulse with bloodlust.

God, how I hate them. Hate them.

"A Sorrows adept." I shook my hair back. The hallway was cluttered along the sides with little stations for doing paperwork, bits of medical paraphernalia, doctors in doors talking quietly or striding away purposefully—and Father Gui, his stare blank as he leaned against the wall three feet away from a door that was slightly ajar.

Probably Father Rosas's room.

I went for my guns, they cleared leather in a heartbeat. Kept them low, glanced up at Saul. His cheeks were pale under his darker coloring.

"Keep track of Gui," I whispered. "If he starts to act possessed, just back off and keep him in sight. Okay?"

"'Kay." He knew the drill. "Gonna kill a Sorrow, baby?"

As many of them as I can in this lifetime. "You better believe it." I started down the hall.

They don't tell you in training how the world slows down with each footstep as you approach a fight. Each breath takes forever. The palms get sweaty, the heart beats thick and fast, the hair on the back of the neck tries to stand straight up.

All in all, great fun.

Father Gui stared straight ahead. He made no move, and I didn't sense anything demonic in him. His tumbled black curls rested sleekly against his head, and his eyes were glazed, half-closed. The smoky oddness of a hypno-spell wove in the air around him, and I cursed inwardly. Finding out if the Sorrow had planted any triggers in him would be uncomfortable at best.

I pushed the hospital door in with my foot, every nerve aware of Gui leaning against the wall. If he moved with the eerie speed of the possessed, this could get really ugly really quick.

I saw a slice of the hospital room, a pale blue curtain drawn around the bed, the door to a small bathroom standing ajar. *Christ. Take your pick. Do you think a Sorrow's going to be hiding in the can, or behind the curtain? Standing next to Father Rosas with a knife to his carotid, maybe? It'd be just like a Sorrow to take a hostage and kill 'em anyway.*

I paused. The beeps of a heart monitor sounded, brightly ticking off cardiac squeezes. The sound came from behind the blue curtain, and the room was full of the blue, incense-laden smell of a Chaldean whore.

"You can come in," a familiar voice said. "I'm at the window. And I'm alone."

A woman's voice. My entire body went cold, then flushed with the heat of rage. I knew that voice. Of all the adepts of any Sorrows House, it was the last one I would think stupid enough to put herself in a room with me.

It was the bitch herself, Melisande Belisa.

The woman who had killed my teacher.

She *was* in the window, but I checked the bathroom and ripped aside the curtain. Jolly fat Father Rosas, his cheeks ashen, slumbered the sleep of a tranquilized and tired old man. The red blossoms on his nose and upper cheeks were testament to his love for the bottle, and his graying black hair was lank and greasy, beginning to go bald on top. But he was whole, and still alive—and he had a visitor.

She had long black hair, blue-black, and a hint of tilted-catlike to her eyes. Her skin was a little darker than the Sorrows usually preferred, but well within canons, and her eyes were the limitless black of the adept who has practiced for more than four cycles of their calendar; black from lid to lid, no iris or white to break the sheer gelid orbs. She wore delicate golden eardrops, and the bruising of Chaldean my blue eye could see in her aura was disciplined, a parasitical symbiote. A sickness that helped, like an *arkeus* helped a Trader.

The Elder Gods give to those who serve them well, almost as often as they consume them.

She wore blue silk, in utter defiance of passing for normal. A Chinese-collared shirt, loose pants, slipperlike shoes. As if she was still in a House's quiet, incense-laden darkness, shafts of sunlight piercing the dim smoke.

If it was the end of a cycle by their calendar, the air would be full of crackling expectation; and as night fell there would be a black flashing knife and the gurgle as a drugged prisoner—or more likely, one of their own, a male raised in the House's gloom for just this purpose—would wind up throat-slit, sacrificial death fueling ceremonies from a time when the Elder Gods walked the earth.

The Elder Gods were gone now, locked behind a wall so old even hunter legends only whisper of its making. But sometimes the smaller Chaldean demons come through and wreak havoc. The Sorrows accumulate what they can and spread their Houses like a sickness, praying for the return of their hungry masters.

I lifted both guns. My fingers tightened. Sunlight fell over her, bringing out the highlights in her hair, the mellow burnish of her skin.

"I need your help," she said.

Oh, for Christ's sake. I've had all I can stand of people saying utterly incomprehensible things. "For Mikhail," I whispered. Father Rosas's heart monitor beeped, incongruous in the charged, suddenly buzzing quiet.

She lifted both hands, palm-out but loose, with no tingle of sorcery surrounding them. "I loved him too. I just had to kill him."

I felt it again, Mikhail's body in my arms as he choked on blood and her mocking freezing laughter as she disappeared. As I screamed Mikhail's name until the Weres—small consolation that they were watching him just as I was—came to bear him away from the shitty little hotel room where he'd breathed his last and give him a clean-burning pyre.

And not so incidentally, to restrain me as I tried to throw myself after the Sorrows adept. She would have killed me then.

I was stronger now.

Shoot her now, goddammit! Shoot her! "I told you. No Sorrows in my city." My voice cracked, I could barely force out a whisper through my rage-tightened throat.

"You killed my brother." A swift grimace pulled down the corners of her pretty mouth. "We thought he could stay here unnoticed. In a seminary."

"Was an *utt'huruk* in one of his classmates part of the plan?" My voice was ragged. *Kill her. Kill her now.*

But she had used that word. *Brother.* It wasn't like a Sorrow. And he'd said, *sister.*

They lied, though. It was SOP when dealing with Sorrows: *don't believe a fucking word.* Masters of the mindfuck, sometimes they even make Perry look simple.

And this one had taken in my teacher, probably the smartest fucking hunter on the face of the earth. She had done it so easily.

"The Chaser was sent to bring him back. It took you to kill him, hunter."

Like hell. How did it get in Oscar? By mistake? "He bit his poison tooth." The words tasted like ash in my mouth. The situation began to resolve behind my eyes—maybe the Sorrows boy *had* been hiding out in the seminary. It was almost likely, and almost logical.

"I don't blame him. We know how...unkindly you view us." The sunlight faded, a cloud drifting across the sky. She looked out the window, presenting me with a profile I had only seen before in shadows, through a haze of bloodlust, rage, fear, grief. And a slice of her throat, visible above the Chinese collar. "I am in violation, hunter, and I've come here for your help. One of our adepts has escaped us, and is engaging in forbidden acts."

I felt one eyebrow raise. "I didn't think there were any acts forbidden to a Sorrows House adept. Except, of course, being a decent fucking human being." I eased back on the triggers a little, kept the guns pointed at her. Saw Mikhail's face again, the light dimming in his eyes, the last gurgle as blood pumped free of the gaping razor-made wound in his throat.

And oh, how he had loved her, meeting her in furtive alleys and motels, keeping his relationship with her a secret even from me. Even though I'd been his apprentice, closer to him than anyone else, Mikhail had kept his secrets. A hunter, snared in a Sorrow's net, Belisa's plaything in a game still murky to me. After his death the Weres and I had cleared the Sorrows House on Damietta Street.

I had not left a single one of them alive. But Belisa had already stolen Mikhail's amulet, the Eye of Sekhmet. It was probably in a Sorrows treasure-room right now, a pretty prize that had probably bought her the right to move up a few more ranks in the stifling cloister of priestesses.

True to form, she didn't even offer an apology. "Both New Blasphemy priests are alive." She kept looking out the window. "And so is your pet cat. Be grateful."

Let me take off my cuff and thank you, bitch. "You have twenty seconds before I blast you out that window and into Hell," I informed her. *Calm and steady, Jill. See what she knows, if anything.* "You might want to start talking."

"Her name is Inez Germaine." She smiled as she dropped this piece of news. "Blood-colored hair, very sleek. From the North House in Alsace-Lorraine."

I stared at her. Could Robbie have mistaken Chaldean for French?

No way. They don't even sound similar. "I'm still not convinced." I thumbed the hammers back slowly, hearing two small clicks. *Ten. Nine. Eight. Seven. Six.*

"She is attempting an evocation, hunter. She is fueling it with death and acquiring funding from the sale of bodily—"

Four. Three. I'll admit it. I lost my temper and fired early.

I pulled both triggers at the same time, the sound was deafening. I kept firing, glass shattering, she was gone in a flurry of blue silk. I leapt to the window ledge, clearing the bed in one swift movement, and almost plunged out, just in time to see her land on the pavement below, roll gracefully, and bolt down Sarcado Avenue. Glass ground under my feet as I crouched on the windowsill, both guns leveled.

Five stories is nothing to a Sorrow, going after her now will just make everything messy. She had an escape route planned. This was the first step in the game. Just like she played with Mikhail.

No getting away this time, bitch. Not on my watch.

I took careful aim with my right-hand gun, closing out everything around me, including Saul bursting through the door and
the sudden scramble of sound from the hall. Sighted at her fleeing
back, inhaling smoothly; *squeezed* the trigger.

Roaring sound, smell of cordite. I swear I could almost *see* the
bullet as it leapt from the gun's barrel, a brief burst of muzzle flash
lost in the weak cloudy winter light.

She stumbled, red blossoming as her right shoulderblade shattered. *That's going to hurt as it heals, isn't it. No matter. I'll hunt
you slowly. And before I'm done, bitch, you're going to beg. Just
like Mikhail did.*

Six months I'd spent eating myself alive, wondering if I'd been
too late to save my teacher because of jealousy, like any jilted
lover. Until Saul and a hunt for a rogue Were had crossed into my
city, and Perry's game to eat up whatever was left of my soul had
shown me with stark clarity that I had not been to blame.

I had not killed my teacher. *She* had.

"Jill? *Jill?*" Saul. He grabbed my shoulders, dragged me back
from the window. "What the *fuck?*"

"It's her," I was saying, in a monotone. "It's her. The bitch. It's
her." The beeps of the heart monitor were steady in the background; Father Rosas hadn't even twitched. He must have been
tranked out of his mind.

"Christ, was that really a Sorrow?" He shook me as I heard
yells out in the corridor, running feet. "Jill? It reeks in here.
Jillian!"

"It's okay." I shook my head. I was shaking, and my voice hit
the level just a hair under "blood-chilling": soft, chanting in a
singsong, tasting each word. "I'm okay. It's her. The bitch herself.
I'm going to take her apart joint by fucking joint—"

"Come on." He pulled me under his arm and dragged me
toward the door, the peculiar blurring of his Were camouflage
beginning just at the corner of my vision. "Jesus Christ, you were
only in here for a minute. Can't I leave you alone for ten seconds
without gunfire? This is a *hospital.*"

Do you really want me to answer that, Saul? I let him pull me
along, numbly. *It's her. The bitch. It's her.*

"To hell with dead whores," I heard myself say. "I'm going to hunt myself a Sorrow."

Then my left hand came up, I would have clapped it over my mouth if it hadn't still been full of heavy metal gun. "Christ," I choked. "I think I'm going to be fucking sick."

"Hold it for a few seconds," he replied, practically, palming the door open and dragging me out into the hall. He got me down the hall, neatly avoiding the chaos of security guards and running nurses, and out through a fire door, adding to the general fun. I felt sorry for the poor cardiac patients, fleetingly. And sorry for Father Rosas, though he probably hadn't heard a damn thing. She'd probably drugged him; poison and chemicals are a Sorrow's stock-in-trade. And Guillermo would mean less than nothing to her. Belisa's game right now was with me.

In an alley below I lost breakfast and everything I'd ever thought of eating for lunch. Saul held my hair back as I retched and swore, alternately, hearing the little gurgle of Mikhail's life bubbling out through his throat and her laughter like tinkling glass.

All in all, for facing down Belisa again, I handled it pretty well.

CHAPTER 15

This is beginning to piss me off." I stared at the small brick building. The office on Quincoa—Kricekwesz's—was closed again, this time at three in the afternoon. "Doesn't this doctor ever open up?"

Saul lit a Charvil. "You want to go in and take a look around?"

My stomach flipped. I studied the front of the place: windowless because of the chance of projectiles, *Family Planning Clinic* in gold on the door that had a peephole and an intercom box with the *Closed* sign hanging from it as well as a *UPS NO!* stenciled underneath on white-painted bricks. There weren't any protestors out here, and I supposed that was a good thing. A doctor who did abortions needed to be circumspect and safety-conscious; if he didn't have a crowd of Jesus freaks out front it meant that he hadn't pissed off the religious fanatics.

Yet.

I took my time, looking at the roof, the security cameras, the steel door. "Ricky didn't say anything about needing an appointment."

"Kind of odd for the doc not to be here."

"He doesn't keep night hours either." I sighed. My mouth tasted sour even through the cinnamon Altoid Saul had given me. My hands were no longer shaking, but I still felt a little... unsteady.

I couldn't believe something so callous had come out of my mouth. *To hell with dead whores. I'm going to hunt myself a Sorrow.*

It was exactly the sort of thing a hellbreed would say. Or a Middle Way adept, one of those selfish bastards. I couldn't *believe* myself.

"Christ." I let out a sharp breath. "If I'm going to do any breaking and entering, I want it to be for a good cause. We'll come back tomorrow. All the doc will be able to do anyway is confirm Baby Jewel wanted to get rid of a career impediment." Shame twisted under the words as soon as I heard my own voice. "Christ, Saul. I can't believe what I'm saying."

His hand closed over my nape, warm and hard. Saul reeled me in as he leaned back against the wall of the alley we'd chosen for surveillance. "Relax, kitten." He exhaled smoke over my head. "Just take a breath."

I closed my eyes and leaned against him, my head cradled below his collarbone and shoulder. My cheek rested against his T-shirt, and I pushed his coat aside and breathed him in.

His thumb worked along the tense muscles at the back of my neck. He took another sharp breath in, inhaling the smoke, and blew it out. "She really got to you."

"Mindfuck central." I jagged in another breath. *God, Saul, what did I ever do without you?* But I knew. I worked myself into the ground and killed myself by inches, that's what I did. Just like every other hunter. "They probably have a dossier on me a mile thick." *And it doesn't fucking help that I have to visit Lucado again. I hate pimps. Jesus Christ, but I hate pimps.* I shoved the thought away. It went without protest, used to being pushed under the rug. I was no longer vulnerable, I was a grown-up, kickass hunter, and I wasn't going to forget it.

"What do you think the game is?"

"There's a vanishing possibility she actually knows something." My voice was muffled in his shirt. He was warm, warm as a Were, a higher metabolism radiating energy. "The trouble is, there's nothing Chaldean that does this. The demons like to possess, not eat. And the Sorrows don't *use* body parts. They like the whole person, bleeding and screaming. After they've mindfucked the hell out of them and torn them into little bits and slit their fucking throats and—"

"Jill."

"What?"

"Shut up."

I did.

"I need you calm, baby. Nice and calm. You start going off the deep end and your pheromones get all wacked-out, and that makes me *real* unhappy. 'Kay?"

I nodded, my cheek moving against his shirt. He smelled of spice, woodsmoke, Charvil cherry tobacco, and familiar musk. *I don't want to make Saul unhappy. That's the last thing I want.*

"'Cause I like you nice and sweet, kitten." His voice rumbled in his chest, not just the words but the sound soothing me. "I like you sleek and I like you purring. I don't like no fucking Sorrow playing with your head, and we'll fix it just as soon as we can. But for right now, baby, honey, kitten, Jilly-kiss, you need to calm the fuck down before I give you a *dose* of calm. Okay?"

"Okay." I heard his heartbeat, even and unhurried. This was rapidly getting out of hand. "I'm calm."

"No you're not." Amusement in his voice. "But close enough."

"I could still use a dose." *At least when you're in bed with me I'm sure you're not going to vanish.*

That thought vanished too, like bad gas in a mineshaft. I couldn't afford to start on that particular mental path right now.

"Bet you could. Me too." He moved a little, bumping me, I leaned into him. "Business before pleasure, baby." His voice rumbled against my ear.

"Who made up that rule?" *I am handling this very, very well. All things considered.*

"You did. Want to break it?"

Shit. "We'd better get to Hutch's. I've got books to hit before I have to face a few hours with a hellbreed."

"You want dinner?" Christ, did Saul sound *tentative?* Why? I wasn't going to break. I'd handled worse than this. The enemies I didn't like were the ones that surprised me, that's all. Once I knew they were in town, it became a clear-cut problem: seek and destroy.

Knowledge is the hunter's best friend, Mikhail always used to say.

Oh but it hurt to think of Mikhail. Hurt down deep, in a place I shut off from the rest of my life, the place that only bloomed when I was up alone at night with the wind mouthing the corners of the warehouse, low-moaning its song of streetcorners and loneliness. A place that hadn't shown up too often since Saul had waltzed into my life and first irritated the hell out of me, then worked his way inside my defenses and ended up twined around my heart. Worked in so deep I wasn't sure where he ended and I began.

The trouble with love is that it leaves you so fucking vulnerable. It's a weak spot. But without that weak spot, what the ever-living fuck is a hunter fighting for?

"No." I stepped reluctantly away from the shelter of his warmth. "I'd better not. Hanging around him tends to upset my stomach." I sighed, rolling my tense shoulders, and blew out a long breath. "Feel free, though. You can hit the stands for a burrito or something while I'm in Hutch's."

"You think I'm going to leave you alone in the bookstore with Hutch?" His eyebrow rose, and the world suddenly jolted back into its familiar configurations. "I know how hot he thinks you are."

Hutch's was a bust. Hutch hadn't had time to do more than pull the sources he thought were most likely and skim for translatable passages. The term *chutsharak* didn't appear to mean anything at all. Hutch himself turned white when he saw me, showed us into the back room, then closed down and hightailed it. Which meant we spent the better part of the day into the night poking through moldering books and not finding much that I didn't already know about the Sorrows.

He *also* hadn't managed to find anything on Saint Anthony's spear. Which meant that either Hutch was slipping—or Rourke had lied to me.

Guess which one my money was laid on.

When the time came, Saul drove—my hands were a little shaky. Our first stop was Mary of the Immaculate Conception, and I spent twenty minutes in a back pew with my eyes closed, smelling the peculiar odor of a church. Incense, vestments, ritual wine, the dash of hope, belief, terror, pleading. A familiar mix, comforting and spurring in equal measure.

The beads of the tiger-eye rosary slipped through my fingers as I sat, swaying slightly, the prayer repeating itself inside my head.

Thou Who hast given me to fight evil, protect me. Keep me from harm. Grant me strength in battle, honor in living, and a quick clean death when my time comes. Cover me with Thy shield, and with my sword may Thy righteousness be brought to earth, to keep Thy children safe. Let me be the defense of the weak and the protector of the innocent, the righter of wrongs and the giver of charity. In Thy name and with Thy blessing, I go forth to cleanse the night.

It is the Hunter's Prayer. Several different versions are extant: Mikhail used to pray in gutter Russian, singing the words with alien grace; I've heard it intoned in flamenco-accented Spanish and spoken severely in Latin, I've heard the greased wheels of German clicking and sliding, I've even heard it chanted in Swed-ish and crooned in Greek, spoken sonorously in Korean and sworn languidly in French, and once, memorably, spat in Nahuatl from a Mexican *vaduienne* while cordite filled the air and the snarls of hellbreed echoed around us on every side. Me, I say it in English, giving each word its own particular weight. It comforts me.

Faint comfort, maybe, that hunters all over the world had just said or were about to say this prayer at any particular time. Faint comfort that I was part of a chain stretching back to the very first hunters of recorded history, the sacred whores of Inanna who used the most ancient of magics—that of the body itself, with the magic of steel—to drive the nightside out beyond the city walls. The priestesses were themselves heirs to the naked female shamans of Paleolithic times; those who used menstrual blood, herbs, bronze, and the power of their belief to set the boundaries of their camps and settlements, codifying and solidifying the theories of attraction and repulsion forming the basis of all great hunter sorceries. They had been the first, those women who traced ley lines in dew-soaked grasses, drawing on the power of the earth itself to push back Hell's borders and make the world safe for regular people.

Faint goddamn comfort, yes. But I'd take it. Each woman in that chain had added something, each man who had sacrificed his life to keep the innocent safe had added something, and all uttered some form of this prayer. *God help me, for I go forth into darkness to fight. Be my strength, for I am doing what I can.*

When I was finished I genuflected, candles shimmering on the altar; an old woman eyed me curiously as I dipped both hands in the holy water. She looked faintly shocked when I smoothed the water on my hair and the shoulders of my ragged coat, wiping two slashes of the cool blessed water on my cheekbones like Saul's war-paint. I genuflected to the altar one last time, winked at the old woman, and met Saul in the foyer, where he was absorbed in staring at the stained-glass treatment of the Magdalene welcoming repentant sinners with open arms over the door. He dangled the obsidian arrowhead on its braided leather absently in his sensitive fingers, turning it over and over, smoothing the bits of hair and feathers.

He said nothing, and drove the speed limit all the way out to the familiar broken pavement of the industrial district, where the Monde Nuit crouched in its bruised pool of etheric stagnation.

He pulled up into the fire-zone, reached over, took my hand. Squeezed my fingers, *hard*. Let go, a centimeter at a time. Another ritual.

He would come into the Monde with me if he could. But a Were in a hellbreed bar like this would only spell trouble, and something told me Perry would love to have Saul on his territory.

That's exactly the wrong thing to think at a time like this, Jill. I stared out through the windshield. The long low front of the Monde beckoned, its arched doorway glowing with golden light. One hell of a false beacon.

"Stay here until I come get you, kitten. Okay?" If the words stuck in his throat, he didn't show it.

I nodded. The scar on my wrist was hard, hot, and hurtful, a reminder that Perry expected me. A reminder I did most emphatically *not* need. The silver charms in my hair tinkled uneasily.

"He doesn't own you." Now Saul's voice was thick. "He *doesn't.*"

"I know." I barely recognized my own whisper. "He doesn't own me. You do." *You're the only man other than Mikhail who has ever* owned *me, Saul. You mean you don't know that?*

"Christ, Jill—"

But I had the door open and was out, the chill of a winter night folding around me. I walked to the door, my bootheels clicking on the concrete; there was a line as usual. Hellbreed and others stared at me, whispering, I reached the door. The bouncers eyed me, the same twin mountains of muscle, their eyes normal except for red sparks glittering in their pupils.

Please, I prayed. *Let it be one of the nights he's bored with me. Let him have other business.*

Fat fucking chance. Last night he'd actually left the Monde Nuit and expended serious effort on me. Tonight I was probably going to pay for that.

Probably? Yeah. Like I was probably breathing right now.

I stalked between the bouncers, daring them to say anything; if they turned me away I could go back to the car and blame it on his own fucking security. But no, they didn't make a single move. In fact, one of them grinned at me, and the thumping cacophony of the music inside reached out, dragged me into the womblike dark pierced with scattered lights, the smell of hellbreed, and the jostling crowd of the nightside come out to have a little fun. The ruby at my throat warmed, and Saul's hickey pulsed.

Was it shameful of me to hope Perry wouldn't notice it?

I kept my chin up and a confident swing to my hips as I stalked for the bar. Riverson was on duty again, and his blind eyes widened. He immediately reached for the bottle of vodka.

Not a good sign.

I reached the bar, and he poured a shot for me, slammed it down. "You're supposed to go straight up," he shouted over the noise. "He's waiting for you."

I winced inwardly. Outwardly, I gave Riverson a smile, picked up the shot, and poured it down. It burned. "Not like you to give free drinks, blind man. But I guess my tab's still good."

His mouth pulled down, sourly. His filmy eyes flicked past me, evaluated the dance floor. There was very little he didn't notice. It used to be that a visit to the Monde would be during daylight, to visit Riverson and hear what he had to say, coming in as a hunter's apprentice and watching Mikhail's back. He'd never liked coming in here, even during the day. It was a very last resort, and one he hadn't had to use too often.

Perry had taken an interest the first time I'd covered Mikhail in this hole. Mikhail had nearly fired on him when he made that first appearance, leaning against the end of the bar and eyeing me.

Stop thinking about Mikhail, Jill. You have other things on your mind.

Of course, that was a losing battle. There wasn't a day passing by that I didn't think of him. After all, he'd rescued me, hadn't he? Better than any other father figure I'd ever had.

He had taken a shivering, skinny little girl in out of the cold, and he had trained me to be strong. Mikhail had pushed me, shaped me, molded me—and held the other end of my soul's silver cord as I descended into Hell to finish my apprenticeship.

Sometimes I wondered what he'd felt, watching my lifeless body on the altar, holding the silver cord steady with the ruby I now wore pulsing and bleeding in his palm, wondering if I was going to come back. Wondering if I would survive the trip down into the place hellbreed call home.

Or did he not wonder? Did he know he'd trained me as best he could, and given me every weapon possible to use against the nightside? Had it been any comfort to him?

"You should stay away from here, goddammit." Riverson

shook his head, his filmed eyes focusing past me. "You stink of Were."

"And you stink of Hell, Riverson. Keep your fucking advice to yourself." I slammed the shotglass back down on the bar, turned again, and walked toward the back as if I owned the place. My tattered coat swung like the fringe on a biker's jacket.

Feets don't fail me now.

In the back, the tables were full of hellbreed—playing cards, drinking quietly, murmuring in Helletöng that threaded under the blasting assault of the music thudding through shuddering stale air. Their glittering eyes followed me as I strode through, heading for the slender black iron door at the very back, behind its purple velvet rope.

A chair scraped, audible even under the noise. When one of them half-rose, reaching under his bottle-green velvet coat, I barely blinked. The gun was in my hand, pointed at him; his sharply handsome fine-boned face was a pale dish under the warm bath of electric yellow light. Cigarette smoke wreathed and fumed in the air. Yellow eyes glittered with the preternatural fury of a hellbreed, and a powerful one too.

Well, hello, whoever you are. What's your goddamn problem, you suddenly got tired of living? I kept the gun trained on him. The scar pulsed, hard and hot, on my wrist.

Give me a reason. Come on, just one little reason. Oh, please. Come on.

My finger tightened on the trigger. I could see the ether gathering, the black bruise of hellbreed swirling around him. I couldn't believe my luck. If he moved on me, I was well within my rights to shoot him and leave.

Then, out of nowhere, Perry's hand closed around my right wrist. The scar turned so hot under the leather I almost expected to smell scorching.

He said nothing, his fingers gentle, his bland interested face turned to the hellbreed who stood awkwardly, caught in the middle of pushing himself up to his feet and reaching under his jacket.

Without warning, Perry's fingers on my wrist turned to iron. He *squeezed,* I heard bones creaking, and he subtracted the gun from my grip with a negligent twist of his free hand. He leveled the gun, drew the hammer back, and pulled the trigger.

The shot sliced through thumping music, black blood flew. The hellbreed's head evaporated. The head is one of the surer places to kill a hellbreed—that is, if they're not actively leaping on you, being spooky-quick fuckers. And my ammo is coated with silver. True silver bullets are a bitch when it comes to ballistics. Luckily you only need enough of the moon-metal to pierce the hellbreed's shell and render them vulnerable. It poisons them as well; two for the price of one.

Perry replaced the gun in my hand. Then he guided my hand down to holster it, his fingers still on the leather cuff over the scar, swelling up prickling and infected-painful to meet him.

The music swallowed echoes of the gunshot. Nobody moved. The hellbreed's body slumped to the floor, meat deprived of life, the mess of the head thocking wetly onto the laminate flooring back here in the inner court of the Monde Nuit.

Oh, fuck.

I didn't know who the 'breed was, or what his problem with me had been—hell, I was obviously a hunter, and he was probably wanted for something. But still, if Perry had wanted to make the point of just what I was here for, he could hardly have written it larger and underlined with neon. I was here because I had business with him, and I was under his protection.

In other words, Perry had done the hellbreed equivalent of a Were leaving a big ol' hickey on my neck. As if anyone in the room didn't already know my face.

Except the dead hellbreed in bottle-green velvet, that is.

Perry indicated the door, and let go of my wrist. I swallowed, set my jaw, and stalked forward. My back ran with tingling cold awareness. *He's behind me. Behind me. Oh God he's behind me.*

The door opened, a slice of blue light widening. I stepped behind the purple velvet rope, saw the stairs going up. My skin chilled all over.

Christ. I wish Saul was here.

No, no I don't. I'm glad he's nowhere near here. That means he's safe.

Behind me, Perry's soundless step filled the air as the iron door swung shut. "A little touchy, aren't we, my Kismet?" His tone was even, interested, calm. "I wonder why."

Let the mindgames begin. I swallowed. "Lots of people trying to kill me lately."

"Not in my house." He didn't sound amused, for once.

"You can never tell when a hellspawn's going to get funny ideas." I kept my pace slow. This counted toward the two hours. Every moment I spent in the Monde counted toward the two hours.

God, get me through this.

"No. You never can." The soft, meditative tone was new, and gooseflesh began to swell on my back. I was glad I had my coat on. "Are you wondering what I'll ask of you tonight?"

"Safer not to wonder. Bound to be unpleasant." I reached the top of the stairs, pushed the wooden door wide. It squeaked a little on hinges I suspected he left unoiled on purpose.

"If you relaxed a little, you might like it." There was a chilling little laugh. "But tonight, you're going to sit down and have a drink with me."

Oh, Christ. "What are we drinking?"

"Whatever you like. And I am going to have your full attention, Kiss. It's been too long."

Not for me. I stepped into the room, my boots sinking into plush white carpet.

The room was large, and music from below thudded faintly through the floor. At the far end in front of a sheet of tinted bulletproof glass the bed stood—pristine, swathed in white, and loaded with pillows. The wet bar at the other end, to my left, gleamed with chrome and mirrors; artful track lighting showed the Brueghel on the far wall next to the bank of television monitors, some showing interior views of the Monde, others showing satellite feeds of news channels. The walls were painted white. The smell of hellbreed floated thick and curdled on still air.

On the expanse of white carpet, two chairs: recliners in white leather. Which brought up the inevitable choice. Did I sit with my back to the door so I could pretend to watch the television images of death, destruction, and hellbreed dancing, or did I sit with my back to the bulletproof glass and have Perry be the only focus for my eyes?

Choices, choices.

"Sit down, take it off. What do you want to drink?" He moved to the bar, and I swallowed dryly again. He was being far too polite.

Wonder if I should put a new strategy into play? Make him dictate every damn move. It was worth a try. "Where should I sit?"

"Wherever you like, my dear Kiss. Just take that idiot cuff off. I like to hear your pulse."

I reached down, unbuckled the leather, and slowly drew it off. Tucked it in my pocket. Air hit my skin again; the scar tightened deliciously, and I choked back rising panic. What was he going to make me do to him this time? The whip again, or would it be the flechettes?

And would I enjoy it? He *liked* the pain. And sometimes, dear God, I liked making him bleed.

If there was a valley of darkness for hunters, that was it. You can't live with the violence, blood, and screaming for long without getting a taste for vengeance. Every time I made Perry bleed it felt suspiciously close to justice.

It felt good.

"Sit down," he said in my ear, hot too-moist breath brushing heavily and condensing on my skin. I gave a violent start, whirled away, my hand closing around the butt of my right-hand gun. I had to work to make my fingers unloose as Perry cocked his head, the light shining off his blond hair. He held two brandy snifters, an inch of glowing liquid in each. "Oh, come on, Kiss. Tonight's not a night for those games. If you would only relax a little, we could be *such* good friends."

"You are *not* a friend." My hands curled into fists. "You're a hellbreed. Hellspawn. Just one step up from a goddamn *arkeus,* that's all. One more type of vermin."

He shrugged, then held out the glass in his left hand. "And yet you keep coming back."

"I made a bargain. One that allows me to hunt more effectively." My fingers avoided his, I took the glass like it was a snake. The silver ring on my left hand spat a single white spark, reacting to his closeness, the carved ruby at the hollow of my throat gave a single reassuring pulse of clean heat.

The spark didn't seem to upset him, as usual. "Mikhail warned you about me." He pointed at the chairs. "Sit." Incredibly, he chose the seat with its back to the bulletproof glass, settling down and bringing the bowl of the glass to just under his nose. He inhaled, his eyes half-closing.

Almost purring with pleasure, as a matter of fact. He looked tremendously pleased with himself.

Why the fuck is everyone talking about Mikhail now? The ring warmed on my left hand. My chest tightened. "He did."

"What did he say?"

I swallowed memory, set my back teeth against it, and got ready to lie. *He told me you wanted me for reasons of your own, and I'd best remember that. And that a woman always has the edge in this situation. I believed him. I always believed him.* "That nothing you could give me was worth what I'd end up paying for it." I settled gingerly into the other chair. My heart beat thinly. *I still believe him.*

"You didn't listen to him."

"I evaluated the benefits and risk of the bargain." *I'm still alive, aren't I? And still playing patty-cake with you. Still coming out ahead by a slim margin, I'd say.*

Just don't mention how slim.

"Just like a Trader." He looked, of course, amused. And generous, so early in the night's games. He could afford to be.

"I'm not a Trader. I'm a *hunter.* And one day, Pericles—"

"Spare me." His blue eyes turned dark and thoughtful. I began to feel *very* uneasy. This wasn't like the usual visit; he would normally be asking me to slip the cuffs on him by now, strapping him into the iron frame. "I find I like you threatening me less and less, Kiss."

"Get used to it." Silver burned against my neck; it was the chain the ruby hung on. And my left ring finger, the burning spreading up my wrist. My earrings were beginning to get warm too, the silver and steel of my jewelry turning against me as I sat in the hellbreed's office with the scar uncovered.

His smile was gone. Instead, he studied me with an interested, somber expression for the first time since our initial meeting. It was a good thing I was already sitting down, my knees were weak.

I was also starting to sweat.

He swirled the liquid in the glass once, precisely, and eyed me. "Oh, I am *used* to it. I console myself with the thought that eventually, you'll beg me. It's only a matter of time."

I decided to go on the offensive. Strobe lights flickered against the huge window behind the bed, red and green drenching the white coverlet. The television monitors buzzed, throwing out blue light. On one, grainy footage of a prison riot played. On another, bombs dropped from a plane's sleek silver belly into a verdant green jungle, giving birth to bursts of liquid orange flame. "What are you, Perry?"

"Just a humble hellspawn. Your most respectful servant, Kiss." He smiled, a thin curve of thinner lips. His tongue flicked once, briefly visible, shocking-wet red. With the cuff off, I could almost see the overlapping scales.

I am beginning to think you aren't so humble. You did, after all, produce hellfire in the blue spectrum. Maybe you're not a hellbreed. Maybe you're a full-fledged talyn instead of an arkeus? *But no. You're physical. You're* real. *I know that.* "I know better. You don't serve, Perry. You like to think you're the one pulling all the strings. Even mine."

"There now." The smile widened. He took a small sip of his brandy, exhaling with a small, satisfied smile. His eyes hooded, glowed bright blue like gas flames. "I told you, you're coming along quite nicely."

All right, you son of a bitch. "I saw Melisande Belisa today." I drew in a deep, smooth breath. "She sends her regards."

That wasn't *quite* true, but if I could distract Perry with the news that the Sorrows were in town I might buy a few minutes without him poking at the inside of my head.

His eyes flickered, but he didn't take the bait. "I find it extremely unlikely that she mentioned me. It was only a matter of time before her path would cross yours again."

My mouth was dry. I badly wanted to bolt the brandy, restrained myself with an effort of will. Sweat slid down the channel of my spine, a cool tickling finger. "You knew she was in town. That's why you were following me. Keeping an eye on your *investment*."

An eloquent shrug, giving me nothing. "You're playing blind."

Aren't I always, when it comes to you. "What do you know about this? Dead teenage hookers and something bullets don't even dent, something hellfire doesn't even touch?" *Though the hellfire may have touched it; I couldn't see. I was hardly a disinterested observer at that point.*

"Tonight is not for business." His tone had cooled. Point one for me.

He knows something. My pulse abruptly slowed. "That's part of the bargain, Perry. Your help on the cases I'm working."

"And your part of the bargain is time spent with me, in the manner I choose. Which you are violating, by the way." The silken reminder closed around my throat.

My temper broke with a brittle snap. "What is it this time, Perry? Am I supposed to whip you until you bleed? Or cut you until you feel like you're real? Or—oh, here's a thought. Maybe I should just beat you up. Give you a black eye and mar that unpretty face of yours. We could probably sell tickets. I'm sure all your fucking hellspawn friends downstairs would love to see you taken down a peg or two again."

He lifted the snifter. "I could simply send a pair of mercenaries to remove your little pussycat from the land of the living. That would, in fact, please me a great deal."

My fingers tightened on the glass. It was suddenly difficult to talk around the lump of dirty ice in my throat. "You leave Saul out of this."

He barely raised an eyebrow. "I allow you your regrettable taste for bestiality. You will do me the honor of living up to your part of our bargain."

You son of a bitch. "Bestiality would be if I was fucking a hellspawn. You're *not human*."

"Can you call yourself human, after the things you've done? Not to mention the punishment you've meted out to one uncomplaining, passive hellspawn who has done nothing but aid you? Or the countless souls you've sent screaming back to Hell?"

I took refuge in sarcasm. "I do love my work."

"But you don't, Kiss. You don't like causing pain. You don't like it when you have to kill. You don't like it when you have to—"

"I like it just fine," I interrupted. *This is the only part of the goddamn job I hate. This, and looking at dead innocents.*

"They were *all* pregnant, Kismet."

The breath left me in a walloping rush. "What?" I sounded about ten years younger, and breathy as Marilyn Monroe to boot.

He blinked, both blue eyes suddenly much darker than usual. Almost black, indigo spreading and swelling through the whites. And in the back of each was a glimmer of light, a pinprick of infinity. "There is much more to this than you think. And I am warning you, my dearest little whore of darkness, tread carefully. My protection may only extend so far in this matter."

Holy fucking shit. I rocked up to my feet, the glass dropping from my hand and spilling its cargo of liquor onto the pristine carpet. "Are you telling me what I think you're telling me?"

"I am telling you it is possible that I can only protect you *so far.*" He lifted his own glass, carefully. He looked far more immaculate than usual, his cheekbones seemed a little higher, his eyes still indigo, swelling through and staining the whites. Almost...well, if he hadn't had Exorcist eyes, he might have looked almost handsome. "Though I have made it adequately clear that you are mine, there are...extenuating circumstances."

Yours? If you think so, you've got another think coming, Pericles. But there was a more important point to be addressed. "Extenuating circumstances? Like *what*—like you know what's going on? Like you're *involved?*" I was repeating myself. Goddammit. I'd dealt with so many hellbreed. Why did this one give me so much trouble?

He took another sip, totally unmoved. And yes, friends and neighbors, he was changing shape right before my eyes. Still recognizably Perry, but much handsomer, higher cheekbones and his mouth ripening, his eyebrows subtly remodeling. Was the blandness a front, or was this the lie? "You have an hour and forty minutes left to give me, Kismet. I suggest you rein in your impatience."

An hour and forty minutes. My hand curled around—not a butt of a gun. No, it was a knife I went for. Was he trying to make me so angry I attacked him? *I can make him bleed, but I can't make him tell me.*

Not when I'd just gone and given away how interested I was in the whole deal.

The reek of spilled brandy filled the air, fuming. I eased my hand away from the knife, felt the scar on my wrist go hard and hot, infection pressing against the skin, stretching before the bursting of pus. Perry's lips thinned even more, turning up into a facsimile of a smile. His eyes turned depthless, with the sparks of infinite darkness dancing far, far back.

His face finished transforming from bland to sharply handsome, bladed cheekbones and perfect proportions, subtly wrong but still...attractive. In a graceful, hellbreed sort of way; the type of beauty that wormed into the apple and ate it from the inside out. Giving a blush of tubercular crimson to the fruit before the blood started to cough up.

I dropped down into the chair and stared at him. *One hour, forty minutes. God help me.* "If you want anything out of me at all, you had better start talking, Pericles." Even as it left my mouth I knew it was the wrong thing to say.

"I could speak to you all night. For example, I could begin to extol the virtues of your mouth and move to your eyes, which are charming in their mismatched splendor. Perhaps I could quote from the Bible. I'm told there is some wonderful poetry in there when one overlooks the rape, pillage, plunder, and murder." The smile touching his lips didn't resemble anything human at all. "Then again, that might appeal to you, *hunter.*"

I crossed my legs and closed my eyes. Deepened my breathing. He waited, but when I didn't respond I heard cloth shifting, as if he'd moved.

I breathed deeper, deeper. Relaxed, one muscle at a time. One of the wonderful things about being a hunter: you take your sleep where you can get it, and unless you learn to relax in a dangerous situation you don't last long.

Perry didn't see it as a gift, apparently. "You can't escape me that easily. I have your time."

Fine. But it's time I'm going to be spending feigning sleep. I settled myself more comfortably, loosened every muscle. *Saul.* The hickey on my throat burned, a different fire than the scar on my wrist. A cleaner fire.

Not going anywhere, kitten. Saul's voice scratched at the inside of my head, the roughness of his hair under my fingers. Was he right now driving into the barrio, parking my car in some hideous little spot and going into a bar or some little dive to dig for information on the little bit of knotted leather and arrowhead?

I relaxed. Perry wouldn't kill me, and even if I couldn't fall asleep completely I could give a go at faking it. It was a new strategy, I could give it a try.

Then he touched me.

The contact slid against my cheek, warm skin; he traced the arc of my cheekbone. Then his fingertips slid over my lips, trailed against my jaw, and brushed down my throat.

Christ, stop it. Make him stop. Please make him stop. I clamped down on control, heartbeat, respiration, everything. Tension invaded my body. The scar turned liquid, a traitorous outpost on my own flesh.

He'd never done this before.

Another, softer touch brushed my lips. There was no stink of rot, but the breath was too hot and humid to be human, and condensation prickled at the corners of my mouth.

He sipped my breath, and the scar exploded on my wrist, spilling fire through my veins. I heard my own voice, crying out weakly as I spilled off the chair and onto the floor. The riptide of sensation drifted away.

My hips tilted up. My heels dug into the ground, the scar burned again. *No, not again, please not again, please—*

"This does not have to be so difficult," he whispered against my damp cheek. Was he crouching over me? A brushing, feathery sound filled the air.

Tears slid down my face. The scar pulsed. *Oh, Christ. Christ help me. Still a whore. Once damned, always damned.*

The whisper continued, as the scar pounded another hot acid-burning tide of pleasure through my nerves. "All you must do is give in. I can be forgiving. I can wrap you in silk, I can make your life a series of delights, little one. I can be so kind, if you would simply *let* me. If you would only bend just the smallest bit and let me turn you, just a fraction. Just a hairsbreadth. Not so much at all. You are already so very, very close."

I've already turned all I can. I gasped, heard an agonized moan. Like a woman in the throes of love. Or death. *As a new strategy, Perry, this one sucks. I was being fucked better than this when I was fifteen years old.*

The moan sent a hot curdled wave of shame through me. My voice. It was my own voice. I braced myself against the welter of sensation spilling from the scar's puckered little mouth. "Fuck...you," I gasped. "*Hate* you." My voice caught, I gasped again.

"Oh, Kiss. My poor, poor Kismet." His breath was against my cheek now, loathsome oily moisture dewing my skin. The scar began to throb harder, the darkness behind my eyelids bursting with fireworks as the ragged leather of my coat rasped against the carpet. "Why do you force me to be so cruel to you?" His hands tensed against the front of my coat. My head fell back, the ruby at my throat hissing a blood-red spark. Perry hissed back in the shapeless grumble of Helletöng. "Shall I show you what you've been missing?"

My hand curled around the knifehilt as he lifted me, the silver ring turning hot against my skin. Hard to think past the spill of desire, the flare of heat as the scar was brushed with a random curl of air, it smashed through me again and my hips tilted, body convulsing with poisoned delight. Fingers clamping down, oiled metal leaving the sheath, I slashed with all the strength I could find and felt flesh part like water.

Fell. My head hit something—a bedpost. He'd *thrown* me, weightlessness and a jarring crash. The impact rang in my head for a moment until I shook it free and hauled myself to my feet. The crotch of my leather pants was warm, too warm, the sodden material of my panties rasped against delicate tissues and I bit back a curse. Turned on just like the whore I was.

No. The whore I *had* been. Now if I fucked someone, I *meant* it. I wasn't a working girl anymore.

Not anymore. Not now.

Not since I'd killed the man who'd turned me out. Not since I'd descended into Hell and been pulled back by the first man to ever rescue me, the man who had knelt in front of my death-altar with his hand knotted around the ruby, our mixed blood dyeing the gem and dragging me back into the light. The first man and only man who had seen not just tits and ass but my anger, my talent, my strength, my reflexes.

My ability to become a hunter.

I gasped, gathering myself. Hoped like hell Mikhail was right and that I had the advantage here.

It sure as shit didn't feel like it.

Perry lifted his bloody fingers to his mouth and delicately licked, his tongue flickering coal-red along thick black fluid. The cut was low on his belly, I'd scored a good hit. "Another sweet nothing, from you."

I lifted the knife. Got my balance back. My head rang. "You do that again, you son of a bitch, and I'll kill you."

"Kill me, and your strength is effectively reduced by a few orders of magnitude." He touched the wound on his stomach again. Thinning black ichor slid down his trouser leg. I'd cut through his suit, ruined another fine shirt. "I'm the devil you know. You should treat me better."

"I don't care if I go back to being a human hunter," I flung at him, getting my balance and my bearings. "You do that to me again, Pericles, and *I will kill you.*"

"I'm only trying to be nice." His smile widened as he licked his fingers clean of blood. "Wouldn't you like me to be nice? I can be very, very *nice* to you."

If you only knew how many times I've heard a man say something similar. "Sit the fuck down." I pointed the knife at the chair. "Now."

He did, very slowly. I decided it was safer if I got away from the bed. My hands shook, but the knife was steady. Or at least, I hoped it was steady. I took an experimental step. Another. Kept going until I could see his profile, and the glass of brandy spilled on the carpet.

It was time to get back to business. He wouldn't be satisfied with just that exchange, but I might get something out of him nonetheless. "They were all three pregnant? How the fuck do you know?"

He closed both eyes, settled back in the chair. "Ah, now I have your attention. The sum of your regard. The sunshine of your—"

"Stop fucking with me, Perry. What do you know about this?" I licked my lips, wished I hadn't. The scar gave a small twinge, another jolt of pleasure sinking through my bones.

"I know they were all pregnant." He said it like it meant nothing. He did hear all sorts of things, and I would have to check, but it was a damn good clue.

If I could follow it. And if he wasn't lying.

"And?" *How do you know anything about this case at all, Perry? How deep are you in? And what the fuck is that thing that nearly killed me?*

"And nothing more, my dearest whore, unless you pay me."

Oh, God. "In what coin?"

"You know what I want."

Rage rose. The knife *did* shake, perceptibly, as my grip tightened on it. "If you are involved with these murders, Perry, I will—"

"What? Kill me? You've made that threat already. Don't be boring. If I were involved, would I tell you anything? Besides, there are some things even I will not stoop to profit from. But you should beware. My protection, as I've said, may only extend so far." His voice dropped intimately, like a hand between my legs. "But you could have *all* my protection, and so much more besides."

Some things you won't stoop to profit from? There's a short list. I took a deep breath. *Christ, Saul. Come back soon. Please come back soon.*

"Sit down," Pericles said softly. Almost kindly. "No more of this, tonight. Though I do love to hear you whimper."

"Go to hell." It wasn't very creative, but I was kind of at the end of my leash. This was far worse than any other encounter I'd had with him. He'd been watching me for a while, and hellbreed were masters at finding out what made people tick and taking them apart, piece by piece.

Seducing them.

"Oh, no. I like it here ever so much better. Sit down, my dear. In a little while I'll fetch another drink."

My breath turned harsh in my throat. But he kept his eyes closed, the black blood stopped soaking through his clothes, and the scar didn't erupt on my wrist. He tilted his head back against the white leather of the recliner. Resting. As if he was satisfied.

Christ, Perry. What happened to you? You kept trying to make me react by making me hurt you, and now you pull this? The thought that he might have figured out a way to make me react the way he wanted was chilling, to say the least. It meant I would have to find a whole new way to relate to the bargain I'd made, a whole new way to deal with him.

Like I don't have enough problems.

Or maybe he was just moving in on me because I was vulnerable, because this case was bothering me more than I wanted to admit. I lowered myself down in the chair opposite him, the knife's blade throwing back colored light. Blue from the TV screens, red from the glare in the bulletproof window, gold from the track lighting.

"One day." His voice was very quiet, very soft, and almost human. "One day, Kiss, you will have to face just how much like me you can become before you give in."

"You can't turn me, Pericles." But my throat was dry as sand. I knew better. If he kept getting better at pushing me, things might get sticky.

I'd have to kill him.

"I don't have to. You'll turn yourself, given enough time. Now be quiet. I want to listen to you breathe." All semblance of life left him, draining away until he was only an icon painted on the white leather of the chair, a black-splashed icon with his arm clamped against his side. The silver content in my knife must have hurt like a mad bastard even as it healed.

For the first time we sat there, Perry and I, and he didn't speak. Neither did I. And when the two hours were up I left. I made it to the iron door at the bottom of the stairs, buckling the leather cuff on, before I started to run. I had promised Saul, yes.

But I couldn't stay there a single moment longer.

CHAPTER 16

I hit the door still running as the cab pulled away. Tossed my torn and battered coat over the habitual chair at the end of the hall and pounded into the practice space, barely hearing the creaks and echoes as the warehouse registered my presence.

The reinforced heavy bag hung, its scuffed red sides repaired with tape several times. Before I reached it, both my fists were balled up so tight I felt my bones creak.

I began.

Leather and vinyl popped. The charms in my hair jingled. Left hook, uppercut, right hook, combinations Mikhail had taught me, my second-best boots scuffing the mats on the floor, the heavy bag shuddering as sweat began to drip down my spine, my arms, my legs.

My teacher's voice, with its harsh song of gutter Russian under the language we shared. *Use it, use it use it! Zat is best friend right there. Should be able to do this in sleep, milaya, use it! Hurt it! Kill it! Do it!*

How had he seen the potential in me, the scared, skinny, beaten girl in the snow? He'd never told me.

Of course, I'd never asked, too grateful for his care. For the attention he paid me, attention I was starved for. We are supposed to love our teachers, otherwise it's unbearable. You have to trust your teacher with your heart and soul, with the other end of the thin silver-elastic cord that is your only way of escaping Hell once you descend. And Mikhail and I had been lovers, of course—it was inevitable, so much adrenaline and prolonged contact, two people closer than siblings or spouses or even twins.

But we are also supposed to hate our teachers, because they must teach us how to *fight*. A teacher cannot afford to be an apprentice hunter's friend. Soft in the training room means unprepared out in the dark depths of the nightside, and that's something no teacher wants. Losing a fellow hunter is bad.

Losing an apprentice is a thousand times worse.

So to hear Mikhail's ghostly voice was a double-edged comfort. I was making a sound, too. A low, hurt sound, as if I'd been stabbed. The skin on my knuckles broke and bled, leaving wet prints on the thick red vinyl. The blood would grime the ring he'd given me when he accepted me as an apprentice, the ring that was singing a thin distressed tone as my furious pain communicated itself to the metal. The carved ruby spat spark after spark, each a guncrack of frustration.

Sweat fell in my eyes, stinging, and I pounded on the heavy bag. The doorbell rang, but I ignored it. Anyone knocking at my door would either come in and get shot or go away.

Throw elbow, solid, tighten up, hit so zey know zey been hit! Not like that, want to lose fucking hand? Tighten up! Vurk it, vurk it, vurk it—Mikhail's voice, barking through the painful hole in my memory, the years of training peeling away until I was the girl standing on the streetcorner again, cold wind against the backs of my bare legs as the cars crept by, each with its cargo of hungry-eyed men.

The mousy little brown-eyed, skinny-legged smartass girl. Not *me*. Not Jill Kismet, kickass bitch.

Not me. Not anymore.

The horrible moaning sound stopped. My hands throbbed. Punches slowed, stuttered, I gave one last blow—solid contact, a right cross, the scar on my wrist running with heat—and stood, head down, shuddering, sweat soaking through my clothes as the broken skin on my knuckles melded together, painfully, twitching as it healed.

"God." My voice cracked, fell to the floor. "God. Jesus. God."

I heard a sound. The east door opening; the front door, the only door that gave onto the street, unlocked because I'd been going so fast. Stealthy movement in the hall, probably human.

I whirled, gun coming up, the sound of it clearing the leather holster loud in the deafening cavernous draft of the warehouse. The heavy bag creaked as it swayed.

Standing at the end of the hall, the front door open behind her, was a thin brown-haired girl with a terrific bruise spreading up the side of her face. I had to look under the split lip, the bruise, and the painful, hitching little sounds she made when she breathed before I recognized her.

It was Diamond Ricky's number one girl.

"Jesus fuck," I yelled, my voice slamming through unprotected space, "what are *you* doing here?"

She jumped. She had her hands up, a battered backpack hanging off her thin shoulder. Her legs were bruised and battered too. A short pink skirt and a green sweater with holes in it completed the picture of a woman at the end of her goddamn rope.

And I knew what that felt like, didn't I? I'd once looked like that, standing in the burning snow with my life in flames, a stray cat with no place left to go.

It was official. Perry had gotten to me, and the past was about to swallow me whole. I jerked myself back into the present with an effort that made fresh sweat spring up in the hollows of my armpits and the curve of my lower back.

She would never know how close she came to eating a bullet, this girl.

Holy Christ. Echoes faded, bouncing off walls and ceilings. I took a deep breath. Sweat dripped in my eyes, stinging. "Jesus." I finally managed to get some control of my voice. "What the *fuck* are *you* doing here?"

Her face crumpled a little. Her big brown eyes were the size of dinner plates, and they welled with silent brimming tears.

I put the gun away, sliding it back into the holster with a creak of leather.

"My n-name is C-Cecilia," she whispered. Then she said the magic words. "I...uh, I...can you h-help m-me?"

I checked her for needle marks, for the nasal deterioration that would mean coke, for the smell of burnt metal that means meth. She looked pretty clean other than the familiar tang of weed and beer. She was also so painfully thin I wasn't surprised as she stuffed herself with leftover penne and steak. "Go easy on that." I poured myself a double jigger of Scotch. *Drinking too goddamn much.* "Don't get all bulimic."

She gave me a pitiful, owlish look, and I immediately felt like the biggest bitch in the universe. I poured her a glass of orange juice, and looked at the clock.

Three-thirty in the morning. How long had she been sitting outside waiting for me? One shoddy human, and I hadn't noticed. Was I slipping? Then again, I was tuned to notice things like *arkeus* and Traders trying to ambush me. Not one skanked-out little girl.

"You're Ricky's number one, aren't you? His head girl?" *The one that keeps all the others in line?*

She nodded, stuffing another mouthful of penne in. I didn't blame her, Saul makes a kickass red sauce. She wiped her mouth with a paper napkin and sniffed loudly. "I ... I met him when I was in high school. I—"

Jesus. Don't. I shook my head. "Honey, it's all the same story, getting into that life. Don't need to hear it. Now, what's going on?"

She stared down at her plate, seeming to lose her appetite. I tried again, pitching my voice low. It cost me to be gentle.

"Did Ricky bust you up?"

She nodded. Tears welled up, brimmed out of her sad brown eyes. My frustration mounted another notch. It was like pulling teeth. I settled myself down on the stool at the kitchen counter next to her. "Because?"

"I ... I know some things."

No shit. But what are you doing at my door, woman? "Like what? What do you know?"

She gulped in air. "I knew Baby Jewel. And Sweet Sylvie. There's ... you know, an awful lot of the girls have gone missing lately. It's hard to keep track of people, they move in and out, some of them go north on the circuit, some go back east—it's just really hard."

I nodded. Sweat had dried on my forehead, my shirt stuck to me. I smelled like a hard workout and spilled brandy.

And hellbreed. Let's not forget the hellbreed. Goddamn you, Perry. He had wormed his way into my head with startling ease, and with a suddenness that left me breathless. Had he just been waiting for the right moment and pretending to misunderstand me all along? "I know what that's like."

She shoveled another spoonful of penne in. Chewed and gulped it down. "They've been going missing for a while. There were whispers, before. But it's been really bad since...oh, since spring. When the rain moved in that one week and we had flash floods."

I remembered, there had been people caught in the floods. Idiots, mostly, but that rain had made the hunt for a Trader serial rapist miserable. *You haven't had a week off since spring,* Saul's voice whispered in my head. He'd be going back to the Monde to look for me. Dammit.

"How bad?"

"Bad enough that girls are starting to get desperate. They..." She gave me an uncertain look, as if gauging my comfort level with details about the night trade. It made me want to laugh. Did she think I was a john or a nine-to-fiver?

To hell with dead whores, my own voice rose up to haunt me. "It's okay," I said, as gently as I could. "Believe me, kid, nothing you could say could shock me." *I've probably done it all twice if it's human, or killed it at least once if it's nightside.*

She probably didn't believe me, but she continued anyway. "They won't get into cars with a trick they don't know. Everyone's trying to buddy up, to get a good look at the last trick anyone else goes with. But it's hard. And there's been...well, Bethie Stride disappeared, and Mercy. And Lucy Long, and Star and Hope and Alexis—and these are all girls who wouldn't leave the city. But the worst is, if a girl gets pregnant she *vanishes.*"

Pregnant. Even with condoms and spermicide it happened. Not a lot of working girls could afford the pill, or could remember to take it every morning. And then there were pimps, and tricks who paid more for skin jobs. An occupational hazard, in the sex trade. "How many pregnant girls are there on the strip now?"

"Not a lot. They all keep disappearing." She tore off a bite of wheat bread; I'd buttered two slices for her.

Pregnant hookers. Pregnant women, with all their organs gone. And their eyes. I frowned at my glass, seeing the amber liquid inside swirl gently as my attention touched it. And those marks, too clean and sharp to be claw-marks. Scalpel cuts.

The scar on my wrist throbbed under the leather cuff. My back ran with gooseflesh.

Profit incentive. "There are some things even I will not stoop *to profit from." What if one of those things is the sale of bodily organs and stem cells?* "Holy fuck," I breathed. "Holy mother of fuck."

"She is attempting an evocation, hunter. She is fueling it with death and acquiring funding from the sale of bodily—"

And I'd fired on Belisa, who may have been trying to mind-fuck me with the truth.

Oh yeah. This just keeps getting better.

"Yeah." She pushed her stool back and dug in her backpack as I watched. "Look." And she came up with a thick wad of crumpled, dirty bills. "I've got two grand in cash." She laid it on the counter between us. "Most of it's mine, but five hundred's from Ricky's stash. If I go back he won't just beat me up, he'll mark my face. Maybe kill me. He's done it before." Her eyes met mine. "Can I...I mean, they said you could help people. Can you help...me?"

Those little words. Those little magic words. *Can you help me? You're my only hope. Help me. Please, for the love of God, help me.* Of all the words a hunter hears, those are the most common. And those were the words that drag us in, again and again.

Well, we sure as hell weren't in it for the money, were we.

"You want out of the life?" I said it as flatly as I could. "You get one fucking chance, doll. *One.* You fuck up with any help I give you and you're on your own. I don't care how you got on the street; if you're determined you'll get the help you need to stay off. But *don't fuck with me.*"

"You think I don't know that?" She yanked her stool back up to the bar and hunched over her plate, beginning to eat again in great starving bites. I saw the deep ugly freshness of the bruise on her face and winced inwardly. "There's stories about you," she said between mouthfuls. "All sorts of stories. Ricky calls you a witch."

"Not a witch. Exorcist, sorceress, and tainted with hellbreed, but not witch." I didn't have to work for a dry tone. "Don't let that concern you, though. You're better off not knowing." *Believe me, you are better off not knowing.*

She shivered. I didn't try to console her. I was having enough trouble consoling myself.

Fuck Perry. You've got a job that needs doing here, Kismet. You just forget about him for a little while, you're paid up until next month when it comes to His Royal Hellbreedness. One problem at a goddamn time.

I decided. "Okay. I'm going to clean up a little and then we're going to have a nice long chat. Then I'll call a friend of mine who might be able to give you a safe place to stay until this is all over. But I warn you, you'd better not fuck with anyone I call for you. No drugs, no tricks, no nothing. Strictly legit. You got it?"

Her eyes couldn't get any bigger. I squashed the little voice inside my head telling me I was being a bitch for no good reason.

She nodded. "I got it." She sounded about five years old.

"Cecilia. You got a last name?"

She started as if pinched. "Markham."

"Well, Miss Markham, you're officially under my protection as a witness. I'm gonna go get cleaned up. There's more juice in the fridge." I paused, looking down at the grubby pile of bills. "And put that cash away. You'll need it to start a new life."

The way her pinched, bruised, split little face lit up was enough to make me feel like an even bigger bitch than before.

I am not hellbreed, I told myself as I headed for the bathroom. *I'm a hunter, goddammit. And whoever's harvesting hookers in my city is going to get a little taste of Judgment Day real soon now.*

I couldn't help feeling better.

CHAPTER 17

I didn't call Galina; I had already dumped one witness on her. Instead, I called Avery and wished Saul had a cell phone. Then again, if he was down in the barrio, he didn't need any distraction. He'd catch up with me soon enough.

Ave promised to drop by and pick up the girl as soon as he could, which meant three hours since he was on his Sunday overnight shift. One of those hours I spent questioning her. She was bright and relatively observant, and living on the street had fine-tuned her instinct for what was bullshit and what was truth left unsaid.

What Cecilia could tell me was almost as interesting as what she couldn't. The doctor on Quincoa—Kricekwesz—had been taking care of street girls as a profitable side gig for a long time now. Recently, though, whispers had started. The flesh gallery was alive with rumors, because girls that told their running mates or coworkers (if such a word could be used for girls that worked for the same pimp or walked the same bit of street) that they had a little "trouble" started disappearing. And the girls that visited the doctor came back with appointments to see him again—but never got there.

"It's not just girls," Cecilia told me. "Some of the street kids, the young ones, get taken too. And some of the older rummies on the street have started to talk about weird things. Seeing weird things." When pressed, she shook her head. "I dunno. I've heard everything from UFOs to Sasquatch. Real crazy shit."

If other people had seen what Robbie the Juicer had seen, no wonder the street scene was boiling with rumor.

The most interesting piece of news was the pimps all getting together after I'd put the squeeze on Ricky. A meet was something that only happened in dire circumstances, thanks to the egos of the petty thugs involved. There was always fresh meat, but one or two of the flash boys had been grumbling about something cutting into their profit by picking off the girls. Ricky had thrown a fit, but he was small fry even though his girls had some prime real estate.

Another pimp, a heavyset black man with gold-capped front teeth who went by the name of Jonte, had told everyone to shut up, because they would be getting paid plenty. He'd told Ricky in no uncertain terms that the little shit hadn't been let in on the action because he couldn't keep his mouth shut. Ricky had gotten fresh and got bitch-smacked for his pains. Which explained why the smacking had devolved onto Cecilia, incidentally.

And then there was the bombshell. The meeting had also been attended by a representative from the local Mob, Jimmy Rocadero, with two bodyguards. Beyond supporting Jonte's claim that the pimps would be paid plenty for going along with the program,

Rocadero hadn't said much, but his mere presence had scared some of the smaller fish in the pond. Every pimp in Santa Luz paid a percentage to the Mob. It was just how business is done.

"Do you know if the strip clubs are having similar turnover?" I asked.

Cecilia, the worst of her scrapes Bactined and a few Band-Aids applied, as well as arnica to take down some of the worst swelling, no longer even looked eighteen. Instead, she looked twelve. A very frightened twelve. She curled up on my couch with a battered teddy bear she'd fished out of her backpack and jumped at the slightest noise. I hoped her ribs weren't busted up; she sounded horrible when she breathed. She had nothing but short skirts and hot pants in her backpack, so I'd rustled up a pair of paint-splattered sweats for her. She shook her head. "I dunno. I never did the strips. By the time I was old enough I was already turned out for Ricky."

I sat on the floor, cross-legged in leather pants and a *Prospero's Housewives* T-shirt, thinking about this. The need for *action* boiled away under my breastbone, but there was nothing I could do right at the moment except get every scrap of information I could from this girl.

I had brought out a package of Oreos, and she was putting them away at a steady rate. *I hope she doesn't make herself sick.* I had a sudden vision of holding her long brown hair back while she retched.

It wasn't pleasant.

I took a closer look at her. She'd been pretty, and bright enough to escape getting hooked on something deadly. I pegged her as smart but terribly needy, probably a cheerleader in high school with a bad home life that she thought running away would save her from.

Like looking into a fucking mirror, eh, Jill?

I pushed that voice away. It was time for the most inconsequential but revealing question.

"So why did you bail out on Ricky?" I tented my fingers and leaned forward, bracing my elbows on the coffee table. Saul's slippers lay neatly underneath, and my knee touched one of them. I found it absurdly comforting.

She actually blushed. Her cheeks turned red, and she looked down at the package of Oreos.

I caught the message. I should have smelled it on her, but under the fume of hellbreed and fury from my own skin and yeast-alcohol beer from hers, it would have been a miracle to catch it.

Christ. "Okay. Please tell me you haven't been out to Quincoa."

"I haven't," she whispered. "But Ricky called the doctor to make the appointment for me. I said I wouldn't go. He..."

"That's when he got all nasty on you." I nodded. *Great.* It must have been the last straw.

"I told him I'd go after he hit me. But I...there are people who know stuff. I went to this head shop on Salvador Avenue, I told them I was looking for you. That I needed help. The woman there said to come here. I walked the whole way."

And if I'd checked my messages, I'd probably have heard one from Jordan letting me know someone in need was heading my way. Dammit. "All right." I stared at the tabletop, my finger tracing an invisible sign on the wood. "The best thing to do—"

I stopped. Tilted my head a little. *What was that?*

The sound came again. A scrambling, and a stroking of claws on cold concrete. Far away, but growing closer, coming from the east.

Oh shit. The sensation of danger was immediate, palpable, and hair-raising. My head snapped up, my right hand automatically blurred for a gun, and Cecilia gasped.

"Get up," I snapped, leaping to my feet, barking my knee a good one on the coffee table. Wood cracked, but I hardly noticed the brief burst of pain. "Get the fuck up. Come on."

"What's happened? What's going on?" She flinched, her eyes getting even rounder as she saw the gun. I stalked for the recliner by the small table where I did tarot card readings, scooped up my battered leather coat, and shrugged into it, passing the gun from hand to hand.

"Something's coming. I just heard it. It'll trip the first line of defenses and alarms around my house in, oh, ninety seconds." I couldn't restrain a hard, delighted grin. "You don't think I'd sit in here *helpless,* do you? Move, girl. You're going to play mousie and hide in the hole."

*   *   *

It was probably a good thing she was trained to immediate obedience, even if I could have cheerfully ripped Diamond Ricky's nuts off for the beating he'd given an underweight girl. She scrambled up the rickety wooden ladder, her breathing coming short and hard. Her bruised ankles were terribly thin. When she reached the top, her battered face peered down at me.

"Pull this up." I helped her get the ladder up. "Now close that fucking trapdoor and lock it. Stay up there until I come get you, or until dawn. If it takes me out, go to the precinct house on Alameda and ask for Montaigne. He'll take care of you. I know you don't like cops, but he's all right."

She nodded, biting her lip. Tears rolled down her pale, bruise-mottled cheeks. "Why are you doing this?"

What the fuck do you mean, why am I doing this? I'm a hunter. I protect the innocent. "This is what I do. Now close that door *and lock it, bitch!*"

She scrambled to obey. The heavy lead-sheeted trapdoor closed; the little hidey-hole was in the bedroom, where the mixed scent of Were and hellbreed hunter would help mask her fear and human smell.

I'd also wanted the bedroom for the extra ammo stash, and it took a few seconds I didn't have to load up on silverjacketed lead, each full magazine slid into the loops sewn in my coat. Better to have the ammo and not need it, especially if what I had in mind didn't work. I wished I could use the bullwhip, but that was for Traders. The little distance a thin bit of leather would give me, critical for facing down a full hellbreed, wasn't going to be any frocking help against something this fast.

So I ran for the practice room, my breath coming hard and harsh in my chest. Skidded against the hardwood and reached it just as the front door shuddered under a massive impact. It had taken the thing two and a half minutes to reach my home; maybe they'd let it out in Percoa Park or down on Lucado somewhere?

I shelved the question as the door shuddered again. *Wonderful. Didn't your mother ever teach you to knock?* I ran along the side of the room, each step seeming to take forever, toward the long shape lying under its fall of amber silk on the far back wall, its shape reflecting in the eight-foot mirrored panels.

The silk slipped in my fingers as it crashed onto the front door for the third time. *I hear you knockin',* a lunatic Little Richard screamed inside my head, *but you cain't come in!*

"Shut up," I gasped to myself, and tore the silk free.

There, humming with malignant force, was the long, fluidly carved iron staff. A slim dragon head snarled at either end. The leather cuff I tore from my right wrist, gasping as air hit suddenly sensitive skin. I felt the humming of etheric force begin to cascade around me as my right hand closed around the staff's slim length.

The iron burned, pain jolting up my arm. "Thou shalt serve me," I whispered. "By the grace of the Destroyer, thou shalt *serve* me!"

The staff subsided as I lifted it down, my knuckles white against its oiled metal gleam. It had tested my will only once, in a massive struggle inside a consecrated circle, the final test before my Hell-descent, before I was a full-fledged hunter in my own right. It rumbled in my hands, restive—too much blood and violence swirling in my aura and way too long since the last time I'd used it, even to drain off its excess charge. I would have to drain it to about half-strength soon, and deal with a couple of days of nosebleeds.

That is, if what I was about to do now didn't drain it, and if I survived.

I really wish I could use the whip. My hands tightened. I whirled, testing the heft, the dragon heads clove the air with a sweet low whistling sound. Then I gathered myself and ran for the front door.

The etheric protections in the walls screamed and tore as the physical structure gave way too. I dug my bootheels in, skidding to a stop in the living room, the staff held slightly tilted in front of me, both hands aching where they gripped its coldness. Then it began to warm, vibrating with eagerness, and the scar on my wrist turned hot and hard again.

"Come to Mama, you hunk of shit," I whispered, and the creature slammed through the crumbling wall. Rebar snapped, chunks of concrete and wooden paneling flying, and the staff jerked up in my hands, coming alive. There was a soft *snick,* deadly curved blades springing from the dragons' mouths. Warm electric light drifted down as the thing came for me, a faint silver glimmer showing at its low unhealthy neck.

As usual when I was holding the staff, things seemed oddly slow. Shift the weight, throwing the hip forward—in both whip and staff work, the hip leads. A sweet low sound as the blades cut the air, the complicated double-eight pattern becoming a blur of motion.

Then, *impact*.

It smashed into me again, the low, fluid somehow-*wrong* shape that my eyes hurt straining to see. The staff jerked in my hands, supple and alive, singing its low tone of bloodlust as it clove both air and preternatural skin. Fur flew, and the gagging stench of it enveloped me, *can't breathe can't fight* but I was going to give it an old college try, something black and foul exploded and the cold smacked through me, a cold like a razor burn with the bile in my throat, good thing I hadn't eaten anything because the Scotch boiled in my stomach looking to escape the hard way.

And as always, when the staff was in my hands and time blurred around me, the dragons beginning their long bloodthirsty moaning and the blades slicing the air as I retreated, shuffling, I felt it. The cold clear chill of the world falling into place, everything stark and simple.

Kill or be killed.

Another gagging, retching breath, pluming in the frozen air as the staff executed a complex maneuver, going so fast it almost seemed to turn on itself, Mikhail's voice screaming in my head and the entire world narrowing to *don't get dead move move move,* no time for thinking, only time for pure trained reflex that is nonetheless informed with a great deal of thought. The fastest fucker in the world can still do something thoughtless and end up dead. Moving is not enough; one must move *correctly.*

The creature howled and came at me again. It was vaguely humanoid despite the claws. Which clanged off one blade—but the staff was working hard, humming to itself contentedly as if it had finally found something to wake it up and exercise it a little. My arms ached, especially the scar that was a knot of fire against my wrist, etheric energy humming through it; but the fierce high excitement beating behind my breastbone didn't let up, and I knew who was making that terrible sound under the snarling and foul nails-on-chalkboard howling of the creature.

It was a high chilling giggle, clear as crystal and cold as midnight in a moon-drenched room. It was my own voice, laughing, crazed with bloodlust. The scar turned blood-warm, strength like wine flooding my limbs, and the charms in my hair rattled and struck together with cracks like lightning.

The creature backed up and snarled. I snarled back, almost twitching in my eagerness to kill, ice painting the air as my breath froze. It was human-shaped, and I was so far gone by then that I peered underneath its scrim of hair and blinding blur. Only for a moment, trying to decipher the silver glimmer at its throat—a chain? A leash? Who knew?

Then it backed up, holding its front left limb up as if I'd wounded it. Black sludge dripped on the floor, smoking in the cold.

I laughed again, that chilling tinkling sound that broke glass and shivered the wooden flooring into splinters. *Kill it. Kill. Kill.*

A crackling bolt of blue hellfire lanced through the shattered air, splashing against the thing's side. It howled again and streaked away, its footfalls heavy and off-kilter now. I heard it drumming the surface of the earth as I whirled on the balls of my feet to meet this new threat.

The scar turned hot and hard. I felt Perry like a storm front moving through, a change of pressure that meant lightning. But that wasn't what made me freeze. Standing amid the shattered wreckage, his eyes dark and infinite, Saul shoved his hands deep in his coat pockets and regarded me. Steam drifted up from his skin. The couch was a shambled mess, the kitchen was torn all to hell, every mirror and window in the place was shattered and crusted with ice.

And still, my hands tightened on the staff. The blades hummed, alert, vibrating with bloodlust. *Kill?* the slim length of iron, old when Atlantis was young, hummed in its subsonic language. *Kill? Kill? Destroy?*

What civilization the staff was an artifact of, I didn't know. Mikhail hadn't known either. But ever since that highly advanced people had shaped this length of steel into a long wand with stylized dragon heads at either end—and don't ask me how we know they're dragon heads, we just *do*—it has been used for one thing.

Bloodshed. Destruction. The secret to handling it has been passed down from hunter to hunter in an unbroken line since its creation—or so Mikhail told me.

I had no reason to disbelieve him. Once, and only once, I think I saw what the world had looked like when the staff was created. The fact that I wasn't howlingly insane meant I had passed the test and was ready to descend into Hell—and come *back,* a full hunter.

My muscles spasmed. The terrible battle began, me trying to wrench my fingers free of the iron, the staff screaming to be set free, to whistle through the air again, to cleave flesh and anything harder, anything at all, to maim and rip and tear. Blood trickled hot down my side, down my leg, down my arm from my left shoulder, turned into hamburger by the thing's claws.

But Saul's eyes were dark, and he didn't look away. He didn't move. The electric current between us—the thing in him that saw past every wall I've ever built to defend myself, the thing in me that *recognized* him—went deeper than all the bloody raw places in my head, deeper than my breath and bones and blood, and deeper still.

He *knew* me, even now.

It seemed to take forever but was in reality only a few seconds before I could *make* my fingers unloose. The staff slid toward the floor, I spun it, turning with a scream of agonized muscles and a cry that shattered each iota of broken glass into smaller shards and tore the scrim of ice into steaming fragments. The staff tore free, taking the skin on my palms with it, and smashed into the wall. Stuck there, sunk six inches into the concrete, quivering.

I let out a low harsh sound. Swayed, the small spattering sound of blood hitting the floor very loud in the stillness. I suddenly became aware that I had been moving in ways a human body hadn't been designed to move, even one with the help of a chunk of meteoric, pre-Atlantean steel and a hellbreed scar on one wrist. Everything *hurt,* a scalding fiery pain.

But my heart still beat, so fast the pounding in my wrists and throat was a hummingbird's wings. I was still taking in great ragged breaths, panting, my ribs flickering as they heaved, fiery oil spreading up my left side. My shoulders felt dipped in molten lead and my legs felt like wet noodles and my *head,* my God, my head felt like it was going to crack down the middle, like some demented dwarf was driving glass pins through my brain.

I swayed again, sour taste of adrenaline in my mouth. Heard someone else moving and knew it wasn't Saul approaching me, *knew* it wasn't him, and moved without thought.

My fingers had turned into claws, and I screamed as my nails tore through Perry's face, the scar on my wrist giving an agonized flare of pleasure. Then Saul had me in his arms, was talking to me as I struggled, he had me caught in a bear hug and took my legs out from under me, we hit the ground among debris and melting ice and I struggled, getting wood dust, glass, plaster, water, all sorts of crap in my hair before Saul snarled at me, burying his face in my throat, and I went utterly still. The sharp edges of his teeth could open my carotid in a moment.

I made a low sobbing noise, gongs clanging inside my head. "Si-si-si-si—"

I was trying to tell him there was a civilian in the house, someone I had been protecting, when I passed out.

CHAPTER 18

I woke up with one hell of a hangover.

Using the staff does that. It's not something to be done lightly, as Mikhail had reminded me until he was blue in the face. But really, I was just happy it had *worked*.

I opened my eyes, saw something hazy that qualified (maybe) as light, and let out a low moan. Immediately, someone slid an arm under my head and held the foulest concoction in the whole wide goddamn world to my lips.

The best cure for a bad case of overstrain goes like this: nuke room-temperature Coke until you get the fizzies out, about ten seconds in the microwave on defrost will do it. Then mix it half and half with Gatorade. You dump about a quarter of it and fill up the huge old mug with *very* strong valerian tea. Mikhail always used to spike it with a little vodka, but he was crazy.

It tastes unspeakably foul, especially when your stomach is trying to crawl out through your throat without so much as pausing to say goodbye. But it works. The Gatorade settles your electrolytes; the caffeine and sugar in the Coke bring your blood levels back up and the nixed carbonation settles the stomach, and the valerian if strong enough is almost as good as Valium to calm down a hunter who's just gone through the wringer.

The vodka, of course, was because nothing medicinal could be without a touch of that finest of elixirs. I heard Anja's brews involved imported absinthe, but I've never had the dubious pleasure of having her mix up a concoction. God willing, I never will.

I took down four mugs of it before swearing at Saul and thrashing, trying to get up out of bed. "Calm down," he told me, in a tone that brooked no argument. "Or I'll strap you down, goddammit. You stupid bitch."

"Fuck you," I flung back. My head was splitting. My stomach sloshed. I felt like I'd been put together sideways.

"I told you to fucking stay with Perry."

He was right. And he was furious.

"Si-si-si-*civilian!*" I managed to get the word out.

"She's okay. She's with Avery. Just settle down, Jill. Come on."

I went limp. Lay with my breath whistling in my throat. *Thank you, God. Thank you.*

He stroked my hair back from my damp forehead. "I told you to stay with Perry." But this time, less anger. He sounded worried.

I squeezed my eyes shut. Found I could speak. "I couldn't." My voice cracked.

"Guess not. What'd he do to you?"

How could I answer that? *He suddenly found his way in, Saul. He got to me.* "The usual m-mindfucks." I dragged in a deep breath, let it out. "Saul." It was so hard to *think* through the dragging pain in my head.

"Right here." His fingers threaded through mine. "You want more backlash brew?"

Oh, God, no. "Shit no. What'd you find out?"

"Interesting stuff. Just rest, okay?" His hand was warm, and he leaned in, his lips meeting my cheek. "I'll kick your ass later."

"Promises, p-promises..." But I passed out again.

When I surfaced, I felt better, the brew had done its work and my head no longer felt like something monstrous was trying to birth itself from the center of my brain. Late afternoon sunlight fell in through the window; I was in my bed. Plenty of space all around, so nothing could sneak up on me.

Saul was a warm weight on the other side of the bed. His dark head rested on his arm, because as usual he'd thrown off the covers and ditched his pillow. Unlike usual, however, he was clothed, boxers and a T-shirt. He smelled of Were and sweat and musk, and the charms in his red-black hair gleamed under the light.

I sat up slowly. My head felt tender and my body was a little sore, but other than that, I felt surprisingly good. It was the first time I'd used the staff since striking my bargain with Perry, and I didn't feel like I'd been run over by a truck.

I stretched, yawning. *First order of business is to get that goddamn doctor and throttle him until he squeals. And then a quick visit to Jimmy Rocadero, and—*

Saul's hand closed over my wrist. One of his eyes had slid open a bit, and he yawned. "And where do you think you're going?"

"Hey, baby." I didn't have to work to sound relieved to see him. "How are you?"

"Pissed as hell," was his languid reply. "How you feelin', kitten?"

The tension in my chest eased at his calm tone. "Okay. Not going to be running a marathon anytime soon, but I can work. Saul—"

"Goddammit, Kiss. I told you to stay with Perry." He opened his eyes and curled up to a sitting position, shoving blankets aside.

How a man in boxers and a Santa Luz Wheelwrights T-shirt could look so delicious was one of the wonders of the world. I swallowed hard and wrenched my mind away from that. *It's just the survival thing. You know that. Chemical cascades and psychological necessity to prove you're still fucking alive after a dicey situation. No time for that now.* "I couldn't." The words stuck in my throat. *Christ, Saul. I couldn't stay there. Not around that mindfucking bastard.*

"What did he do to you? Huh? *What did he do to you?*" The charms in his hair tinkled, moving against each other; his fingers sank into my arm. I took another deep, lung-stretching breath. A shiver of pleasure went through me. Even though he was holding me hard enough to bruise, I liked it. The thought that he was touching me was enough to make me catch my breath, threatened to make me melt.

What didn't he do? "Nothing. Just...*nothing.* Mindfuck. Like usual. There's a reason why I don't want to *stay* there when he's finished with me. Last night it was bad."

"Two nights ago. Perry's been putting the house back together. Avery has the girl. There are three more bodies. I've got files."

Lovely. Great. Wonderful. I'll read 'em in the car. "I got things to do. We have to get that doctor. And Jimmy Rocadero—"

"Rocadero?" Saul snorted. "He's one of the bodies, kitten. And I want to make it *abundantly* clear to you how fucking unhappy I am with the chain of events that ended up with you, here, facing that thing alone with *no fucking backup*. Very, *very* fucking clear." His eyes glowed with a Were's peculiar lambent orange tint.

"Rocadero's dead?" *Holy shit, that's news.*

"Straight-up dead. But he's still got his internal organs— they're just spread all over his goddamn house. I also found out a few things in the barrio."

I stretched. My entire body ached. *God, I hate using that thing. But I'm alive. Alive. And Cecilia is too.* "What did you find out?"

His fingers flicked, and the length of cluttered leather braid and obsidian arrowhead dangled. A venomous dart of blue light splintered from the arrowhead. "I found out what this is."

"Well?" I stretched, loosely. My skin twitched and rippled with soreness. The headache was returning, circling like a shark, though with less of its former virulence. "You're killing me here, baby."

"Don't fucking say that." His fingers flicked again, the

arrowhead vanished. Neatest trick of the week. "Want to wash up, then we'll talk?"

"Okay." But I reached out to grab his arm as he turned away, his skin warm and hard under my fingers, under the T-shirt's sleeve. "Saul?"

"Don't ever do that again." He stared at the window, his profile suddenly clean and classic. His mouth turned down bitterly at the corners. "I dropped by here to pick up fresh clothes and ammo for you so we could track down the leads I found straight from the barrio. Imagine my surprise at finding Perry and that goddamn thing here before me."

"Perry was here?" *What the hell was he doing here so late? Protecting his investment?*

"He'd just arrived, I saw him coming down the street. That thing was tearing up the inside of the house. We came in and saw you beating the shit out of it. You looked..."

I winced. With the staff in my hands, I probably looked feral, my hair standing on end as I moved in ways a human body shouldn't. And the laugh, the chilling crystal laugh, bruising the vocal cords as it ripped free. "Horrible," I said flatly.

"Deadly. Beautiful." His eyes dropped. "Jesus Christ, Jillian. You could have died."

I know that. "I had to."

"For one of Diamond Ricky's girls?"

Just a whore, right? Just another teenage hooker on the cold street. I swallowed the words. Saul wasn't like that; I was just...edgy. Too willing to think the worst, no matter what anyone said. "A civilian. She asked for my help."

He made a short, vicious growling sound. "And those are the magic words, aren't they? Well, I need your goddamn help too."

Please, baby. Don't do this now. "Saul."

He turned his head, his eyes trapping mine. "You listen to me. You end up dead and you know what happens to me? *Do you?*"

A Were dies when his mate does, but I'm not Were. I'm human. Fucked-up with hellbreed, but still human. "Saul—"

"I put up with Perry. I put up with you throwing yourself into every goddamn mess in this city. But god-*dam*mit, Jillian, I do *not* want to lose you!"

"Saul."

"I want you to meet my people," he said softly. "I want you under the Moon with me."

Holy Christ. My mouth dried up. "That's serious." Then I kicked myself. Couldn't I come up with something less stupid to say?

"Very serious." He removed my fingers from his arm gently. His hand was warm. "As serious as it can get. Need a shower?"

For a moment, I thought the stone in my throat would stop me from speaking. "You offering to seduce me?"

His teeth flashed in a white grin before he levered himself off the bed. "I'd love to, but duty calls. Hurry up."

"Where in the barrio did you go?"

"Couple of places," he said over his shoulder on his way to the closet. "But I found what I needed in a little bar off Santa Croce. A real dive. You'd love it."

I peeled the sheet away. I'd bled on it, nosebleed and from the wounds that were now pink scars, rapidly fading. It had marked me a couple of times. Left side up my ribs, shoulder, leg. I was lucky to be alive. "I suppose it was a smelly place full of nasty characters."

"Just like usual, baby. You've broadened my social horizons, that's for sure." He opened the closet door, and I spent a few moments in artistic appreciation of his boxer-clad ass before hauling myself up out of the bed.

There was work to be done.

I called Hutch from the cordless in the bedroom, but he had still not had any luck digging up whatever *chutsharak* meant. I was beginning to think it was a dead end.

Just like Saint Anthony's spear. Gui and I were going to have a little talk about lying to hunters, just as soon as I had some time.

Hutch did have other news, though. "Hey, it's the end of the Sorrows' three-year cycle this year." His voice whistled slightly with excitement.

"Three-point-seven," I corrected, shoving my feet into my second-best boots. My coat was still torn up, but better than nothing. I wriggled my toes, rocked up to my feet, and accepted a cup of coffee from Saul. It was thick black mud, and I could drink about half a cup before I needed food in me to balance out the caffeine. I nodded my thanks to Saul, bracing the phone against my shoulder. "So they're in the Dark Time now."

"Looks like it. Though if you ask me, those motherfuckers are *always* at thirteen o'clock. So, the Dark Time. Cleansing within Houses, hunting down apostates—and evocations of the Elder Gods."

That rang a teensy bell. "Wait a second. Evocations?"

Saul's eyebrows rose.

"Miguel de Ferrar says it's SOP for a House to evoke their patron Elder at this time. Lots of demonic activity, that sort of thing. It's when they believe the veil between this world and the world of the demons gets real thin, like Samhain for witches."

I leaned back in the chair, taking a sip of coffee. "So. What's necessary for an evocation of this magnitude? Say, if a Sorrow was doing it alone?"

"They *can't* do it alone. That's why houses are collective, it takes a full House to hold a door in the world open for an Elder to reach through even briefly. We're talking granite floors carved with the Nine Seals, perfect-tallow candles, velvet robes, ambergris and amber incense, the whole nine. The *whole* nine, including gold laid in the circle for the Elder, the sacrifice, and the psychic energy needed to rip a hole in the ether." Hutch was sounding more cheerful by the moment. He did indeed love his research.

She is attempting an evocation, hunter. She is fueling it with death and acquiring funding from the sale of bodily—

"So it's a massive financial as well as sorcerous effort," I said slowly. "Hutch, what's the market like in Santa Luz for black-market organs?"

"Organs? What kind of—"

"Human organs. Kidneys, livers, that sort of thing. Stem cells, too."

"Hell, I don't know. But I can find out. Five minutes on the Internet and—"

"Never mind. Listen. Which patron Elder rules the end of this cycle? I know each House has their special dedication, but which one of the Ninety-Nine rules this *particular* cycle in general?"

Saul's eyes met mine. I took a scalding mouthful of coffee.

I heard paper rustling and his breath whistling as he dug around for it. "I just had it, I just had a copy of Luvrienne's *Chaldeans* open...ah-ha. Here we are." More paper rustling. "Let's see...if we calculate from the Chaldean calendar...carry the one...leap years...the Gregorian...okay. This year's winner is...oh, *shit*."

"What?" *Hutch, I hate it when you say oh shit.*

"It's the Nameless." His voice dropped to a whisper. "And the cycle ends in four days."

It felt like all the hair on my body was trying to stand straight up. It probably was. The charms tied in my hair tinkled. I set the coffee cup down on the nightstand. "Jesus, Mary, and Joseph," I whispered. "The Nameless?"

"Destroyer of babies. Eater of worlds. He-Who-Rewards—"

"Shut up, Hutch." *I know the titles.* I swallowed dryly. "Listen to me. Leave the bookstore right now. Go over to Galina's. Stay there until I come get you. Take the Luvrienne and de Ferrar with you, I might call there. Okay?"

"Oh, God," he moaned. "What have you gotten me into now?"

"I haven't gotten you into anything, stupid. I just want you safe. Better safe than eviscerated. Get my drift?"

"Oh, shit, Jill. I hate you."

"Galina will be glad to see you."

"You bitch." But I heard more paper rustle, and knew he was getting ready to do as I asked. "Okay. I'm on my way. I'll leave everything locked. If you come in, try not to burn the place down, okay?"

"Hutch!" For once, I sounded scandalized. "I wouldn't ever burn down a *bookstore*. Jeez, what kind of hunter do you think I am?"

"One who's made it her personal mission to get me into trouble. Bye, Jilly."

"Don't call me that." I hung up and stared at my bedroom phone, feeling my forehead pucker. *Holy fuck. The Nameless. Why would a Sorrow break away from her House and do an evocation? It makes no sense.*

Well, there was one person who could explain it. The catch, of course, was if I could trust her explanation.

Saul was silent. He stood by the window, sunlight touching his hair, making the silver sparkle and bringing out the richness of his skin. He had his hands in his jeans pockets, the black *Cazotte Lives* T-shirt strained at his shoulders. The tiny bottle of holy water on its silver chain at his chest glittered, throwing darts of hard light from the glass.

All right, Jill. I looked at the fall of sunlight against his hair. *Think. What pattern do we have here? Having a pattern is the first step.*

If what I was suspecting was really going down, why hadn't there been bodies showing up earlier? Or if there *were* bodies, where were they now?

That isn't a very comfortable line of thought.

I didn't have enough pieces of the puzzle to make a pattern I was happy with logic-wise. Once Saul told me what the arrowhead was, I would have a little more. Hopefully.

And the thing, the clawed and furred thing that I couldn't quite get a mental picture of no matter how hard I concentrated . . . what did that have to do with it? Was it a piece of Chaldean sorcery I hadn't seen before? It wasn't exactly likely, given the study of the Sorrows I'd done. But was the furry thing the *chutsharak?* If it was, and Belisa and the younger Sorrow were fleeing it—

No, that didn't make any sense. Was the furry stinky thing unrelated to the murders? But no, its smell was gagging-strong over the scenes. *That doesn't necessarily mean they're related. Does it?*

I coiled the bullwhip at my side, checked my guns, my knives, and shrugged into my coat. I caught a fading whiff of iron, pre-Atlantean bloodlust, and furry stink on the tattered leather. "Saul?"

"Yeah?" He looked away from the window.

"It's time. You can tell me what that thing is."

"Come on out into the kitchen first."

"Why?"

"You need breakfast, and Perry's here."

Jesus Christ. "*What?* He's still here?"

His dark eyes were fathomless. "Of course he's still here. He's patched up the windows and everything, he thinks he should shadow you until this is over. I happen to agree."

"What?" My jaw threatened to drop completely. The charms tinkled in my hair, and my palms itched with the memory of a slender piece of steel, reverberating with bloodlust. "He left the Monde Nuit and he's in our *kitchen* and you want him to *stay there?*"

He shrugged. "I want him to stick around. You're safer with both of us looking after you."

"Saul—"

He held up the arrowhead. "I found out what this means, kitten. And believe me, you don't want *any* of it."

"Well, spill it."

"Come on into the kitchen and I will. I'll make you breakfast, and we'll strategize." He was utterly serious.

I held up both hands, Mikhail's ring glittering in the thin hard sunlight. "Wait just a goddamn minute. You don't like it when I visit him, whether to track down a hellbreed or pay my dues for the bargain I made. What the hell are you doing playing pattycake with him now?"

"If he's going to help get your stubborn ass through this in one piece I don't care." Saul folded his arms, muscle sliding under the T-shirt's thin cotton. "This is *bad,* Kiss. As bad as you think it is, it's worse."

My heart was doing something strange, pounding so hard I felt faint. I didn't like the thought of Perry in my *house.* The thought of something so bad Saul didn't care if Perry was running around unchaperoned inside the warehouse was even worse. "Why? What *is* that thing?"

"Come out, have some breakfast, and I'll tell you. Then you can decide what you're going to do."

In the end I gave up. Saul had a good reason for anything he asked me to do, and I trusted him. But for Chrissake, something so bad he wanted Perry around as backup....

It was enough to give even a seasoned hunter the willies.

CHAPTER 19

Saul set the plate down in front of me. "Eat."

I eyed it. Eggs, pancakes, bacon, more coffee, an English muffin. Another plate of eggs with hollandaise, and a peach, cut up carefully and decoratively. Nothing experimental, and nothing fancy. For Saul, this was the culinary equivalent of a polite non-answer to a question that hadn't even been asked.

Perry hunched on the stool at the end of the kitchen counter, his gray suit sharply and immaculately creased. He seemed not to like the sunlight falling through the windows, and I was secretly glad. For all that, his hair glowed and his eyes burned blue, and the warehouse—while smelling of hellbreed—was neat and repaired, the ice gone, every inch of glass swept up and new panes put in, the wood fused back together, shattered furniture either patched up or replaced. It was a massive expenditure of cash and sorcerous power, and one I wasn't quite sure I liked the thought of incurring.

I finished examining my plate and glanced at Perry, who snickered into his coffee cup. "Don't worry, Kiss. Saul and I negotiated terms. This doesn't enter into our bargain."

"Is that so." I tried not to look relieved; tried also not to feel a little wriggle of panic that he had guessed what I was thinking. Picked up a piece of bacon, crunched it between my teeth. "Well? Care to clue me in, Saul?"

He leaned against the counter on the other side, and I realized he was keeping Perry in the corner of his eye. "I found out what our hairy little friend is." Saul poured himself a glass of orange juice. "You want the bad news or the bad news first?"

"Just tell me *something*. I'm getting impatient." I tucked in with a will, finding I was indeed hungry and my stomach would, indeed, accept nourishment. Hallelujah.

Perry snickered again.

Saul didn't even glance at him. "It's a wendigo."

I choked on a bite of pancake. "Urf? Mrph murfr *mrph!*"

"They're not myths. I wish to Christ they were." Saul had actually paled. "I had to take the arrowhead to a Moonspeaker in the barrio, an old one. She'd seen a wendigo before and remembered the smell. She said it was a *hund'ai,* part of a fetish meant to control or create a wendigo. The sight of it turned her into a sobbing heap and her mate nearly had my liver and lights for upsetting her. I ended up at a little bar with a werespider; she'd actually hunted a wendigo up Canada way. She started to shake while she talked about it." Saul's tone was dead level. His eyes were as dark and serious as I'd ever seen them.

I glanced at Perry. He stared into the coffee cup, his face arranged in a mask of bland interest. All the same, he looked miserable. My blue eye twinged a little, I could see the edges of his aura fringing a little bit, wearing down.

Maybe our favorite hellbreed didn't like being out during the day. I was suddenly immensely cheered by the thought. Inside his jacket, pants, and open-collared crisp white shirt he looked almost normal, and profoundly uncomfortable.

Don't fall for that, sweetheart. It's just another dirty little façade. If Saul wasn't here we'd see a different Perry indeed.

"Wendigo." I crunched on another bit of bacon. "A flesh-eating spirit, with its lips and nose frozen off. Come on, Saul."

"Jillian, if you don't cut the crap, I'm going to take your breakfast back and drag you into the sparring room. And make you wash the goddamn blood off the goddamn sheets, too. Look at your *coat.* This is no fucking laughing matter." Even, chill, cold. Saul had never spoken to me like this before. "A wendigo is something else. It's a spirit made mad by neglect and violence, a spirit that has done what is *taboo*—tasted human flesh, developed a craving for it."

A craving for human flesh and black-market organs. Why is this fitting together far too neatly for my comfort? And the unearthly, deadly icy chill of the thing rose briefly in memory. I shivered again. "A Were spirit? That thing wasn't a Were. I know Weres."

"It's not Were, it's a *spirit* we know about. Totally different kettle of fish." Saul folded his arms. "Some of the legends say they're maybe Weres dying without burial rites, or a Were who was *taboo* in life. I don't know. The legends are confused. It's not like hunting scurf. Weres *know* scurf. These things...humans might get confused about them, but whatever they are, they're not Were."

"Jesus." I was having a little trouble with this. The *last* thing we needed was it getting out that the Were had anything to do with something like this. This thing was as unlike Weres as....My brain failed, trying to come up with the simile. But a non-hunter, even one with some nightside experience, wouldn't understand that. Hell, plenty of nightsiders with grudges against the furkind wouldn't understand it either.

Perry finally weighed in, as if he couldn't help himself. "Really, dear Kiss, you should listen to furball here. He knows more than you think. After all, he didn't go into the barrio to seek facts. He went to confirm."

My fork paused halfway to my mouth, and I looked up at Saul. His mouth had drawn down bitterly, and he pushed his hair back with one hand. But his other hand was on the counter, and his knuckles were white.

What, did Saul think a transparent little ploy like that would work on me? How far inside my head did he think Pericles had wormed his little hellbreed way?

However far Saul thinks he has, he's probably gotten in further. Last night proved that, didn't it? "You suspected it?" I felt like an idiot with my fork in the air, I set it down gently, carefully, on the cobalt-blue counter. "Saul?"

"I didn't know." He picked up his juice again, took a sip, his eyes not leaving mine. But I got the idea that if he could have, he would have darted a venomous look at Perry. "Until I knew for sure, I didn't want to open my mouth and muddy the trail."

I nodded. Looked down at my plate. "Well, that's why you're my partner." *Nice try, Perry. But no dice.* "So you're absolutely satisfied that this thing is a wendigo?"

He nodded. The silver in his hair tinkled, and his dark eyes lost their hardness and for a moment were lambent orange, a Were's hunting glow. "I'd bet my life on it."

"It's not your life we'll be betting, it's mine." I stared down at my plate, forced my fingers to curl around the fork again. "Whatever it is, I'm taking it down. What kills a wendigo?"

Saul sighed, heavily. "I don't know yet. The legends are...confused. The werespider was part of a team that tracked one of those things for fifteen weeks, through a few snowstorms, and finally killed it by driving off the edge of a crevasse and dynamiting a mountainside down on it. The creature and the dynamiting combined to knock out most of her team."

"How many?" Werespiders aren't known for being pack animals; like werecats they tend to be independent, loosely affiliated in tribes rather than in pack-groups. Except werelions, of course. Always excepting werelions. Some bird Weres were highly social, and most of the canine Weres except the occasional albino shaman. Then there were the *khprum* and the scorpiani, who some sources said weren't Weres at all, not to mention the kentauri and the wererats, who are highly social and stratified to a fault. The wererats, incidentally, are the closest in physiology and outlook to humans.

Nobody but me usually sees the humor in that.

"Fourteen in the team. The spider and a wereleopard made it back. The wereleopard died of matesickness two months after; his mate was lost in the dynamiting. If they hadn't been out in the middle of nowhere the casualties might've been higher. Humans and such."

Crap. I mulled this over, tapping my fingertips on the countertop. In an urban setting, this didn't bode well. "An evocation in four days. Bodies being dumped, clean of organs.... Saul, where are the autopsy files? I wonder how much other body mass was lost. Muscle, specifically."

"Belly muscle was gone on the ones we saw. Some bites on the thighs and the arms, too." He edged down the counter to a stack of file folders. "But Rocadero wasn't found with his organs gone."

I snorted. "Given his proclivities, I'm not sure his own side didn't murder him." I was chewing on more egg when a terrible idea hit me. "One of the traditional evocations of the Nameless is done with perfect-tallow candles. Victims' omentums would be perfect for that. All you'd need is a place to render it down." My gorge rose; I swallowed it and took a gulp of coffee. "Ugh. This is going to be a messy one. How about Rocadero gets sliced because he's no longer useful?"

"How so?" He slid the folders down to me. Perry had subsided, but I get the feeling he was only biding his time. Some essential quality of scariness had drained away from him in my sunny kitchen, Saul's territory in the middle of my house, and I was grateful for that.

But not grateful enough to relax. Or to think he was finished yet. "Let me pass this theory by you. A Sorrow escapes, she decides for whatever reason that she's feeling a little apocalyptic. She starts laying her plans and moves into Santa Luz, finds a Mob man, and starts supplying him with black-market organs, taking a healthy cut to fund her dreams of world domination. She gets the organs out with the help of a trained doctor—our friend Kricekwesz. Then she throws whatever bits she doesn't need to the wendigo, who sits in the van and snacks until she needs to get rid of an inconvenient hunter." I buttered my English muffin, very pleased with myself. "Only why does she start dumping pregnant hookers?"

"Once-pregnant hookers," Perry corrected, pedantically.

"They were still pregnant when they were killed." I looked at him, hunching on the stool, and had a moment of dangerous pity. He looked miserable.

But even a miserable rattlesnake can kill.

"We don't know that. They were visiting an abortionist." He pronounced the word with no audible weight, just a slight emphasis on the last syllable that made it sound vaguely French.

Where do you come from, Perry? "Thanks for putting my house back together," I said suddenly. "Why did you follow me?"

"The cat wasn't at the Monde to pick you up. I thought you might be in a state to harm yourself."

Well, isn't that decent of you.

Saul pushed the folders closer, hitting my elbow. Subtle of him, but I was glad of it anyway. "Fetal tissue?" he hazarded. "Valuable stuff, to the right buyer."

I swallowed another wave of nausea. *Goddammit.* I needed the nutrition if I was going to stay on my feet and bounce back after using the staff. "Oh, yuck. That's a wonderful thought to have with breakfast." *Not to mention one I've been kicking around for a bit.*

"Troubled by a delicate stomach, my Kismet?" Perry was suddenly all solicitude. The oil in his voice reminded me of the terrible devouring spill of pleasure through my nerves, the mark on my wrist suddenly swollen-hot with his attention.

I closed my eyes, chewing the English muffin. Swallowed. "Our first stop is this Kricekwesz. If he's not in his office I want to tear the goddamn place apart until we find something, anything. I want to get Carp and Rosie to start leaning on the organ trade in town. And I want to find Melisande Belisa. She knows something, and once we get our hands on her I want to make her squeal." My eyes opened, met Perry's. "You ever menaced a Sorrow before?"

Did I imagine it, or did a flicker of a snarl cross his face? "They don't like hellbreed. With good reason." He set his coffee cup on the counter. "If you will agree to stay in my sight until this matter is finished, I will agree to find this Sorrow and make her fit her name."

"I thought your protection only extended so far."

"That was before you were attacked in your own home, Kiss." He slid off the stool, and I tensed. What was it about daylight that made him seem so bloody human? "All bets, as they say, are now off. I want to repair some of the holes in the walls. Call me if anything *interesting* happens."

He glided away, and I sighed. *I don't like this. I don't like this at all.*

Saul muttered something unprintable. I silently agreed. "I don't like this," I said quietly. "So he shows up just in time, both times. I dragged Elizondo in on a slave-ring charge and he was in the Monde after we scorched that hole on North Lucado. And now this organ thing, and a wendigo. Saul, you're *sure?* Absolutely sure?"

"Hundred percent." He hunched his shoulders, his eyes on me. "The truly bad news is I don't know if we can kill it. It's a *spirit,* kitten. Hunger incarnate, hunger distilled. It's taboo. Not a real physicality at all, now. Just...appetite. And ice."

I took a long gulp of coffee that had cooled just enough to be reasonable. "It cut me." The finality in my voice surprised me. "If it can cut, it can *be* cut. There's nothing out there so bad it can't be killed. Except for maybe a god, and we're not facing one of those. Not for four days, at least. What can you tell me about wendigo? How they're created, what can kill 'em, that sort of thing?"

"Not much." Saul straightened, looking relieved. "But I can get in touch with someone who knows more."

"Good." I turned my attention back to my plate. "This is good, Saul. You do a mean pancake."

I didn't look up, but I could feel his smile. "Glad you like it, kitten."

Monty was going batshit.

"What the fuck are you telling me, Jill? Black-fucking-market organs? What the hell?" He stalked through his office as if expecting the perp to be hiding behind a stack of paper. "Why didn't you *tell* me?"

If I'd known, Montaigne, I would have. Don't get pissy. "I had no idea organ heisting was part of it. I was looking for a supernatural explanation. It was the scalpel marks that clued me in."

"Sullivan and the Badger have been tracking a string of black-market organ harvestings that end up leaving the donors dead with a .22 hole in their skull." Monty's tie was loose and his collar crumpled, he was working round the clock. It wasn't good for him.

Then again, police work isn't, strictly speaking, *good* for anyone. Eating your Glock, ulcers, cynicism, depression—the list goes on and on. I took a deep breath. Hunting wasn't good either, but at least a hunter could take the edge off with sex or some hard sparring. "Huh. Maybe they're related?"

Monty's office seemed too small to contain his rage. Not at me, thank God. He stalked behind his desk and dropped into his chair, almost disappearing behind the flood of paper files and assorted other crap. "Go talk to them, look over their files. We'll pick up this doctor, Kricky—"

"Kricekwesz. Polish, I think." *Like it matters.*

Monty rubbed at his eyes. "Whatever the fuck his name is. We'll pick him up. Though if whoever this is decides to take out some more scumbags like Rocadero I might throw a fucking parade."

"For cleaning the streets of pregnant hookers too?" My tone was harder than it needed to be. But goddammit, everyone was forgetting the victims here, the girls that walked the streets, the girls who had been abandoned too many times already.

Don't get up on your high horse, Kismet. You did it too. They're less than human because they're still in the life. On the street. Swallowing God-knows-what and doing what nobody wants to talk about, and turning over a cut of their pay to the professional pimp or the dealer or the man who "loves" them. Christ. Even I look down on them.

And I should know better.

Monty's silence warned me. I dropped my eyes to the tough short russet carpet of his office. Outside the door, Saul waited. Perry was in a limousine circling the block. I was alone in here with Montaigne, who was a good cop—and even more important, a friend. He'd never let me down.

"I'm sorry, Jill," he said finally. "You know it ain't that way."

Carp and Rosie cared about everybody they came across; even the pimps and the hookers and the drug lords. There is something so unutterably final about death, some robbing of human dignity from every corpse, even the ones that die naturally. And Montaigne cared too. Even the impossible cases, where the perp was never found, he and his detectives circled like a tongue circles a sore tooth, unable to forget.

"I know it isn't. I'm just fucking frustrated." *This is getting to me far more than it should.* I blew out a long breath between my teeth. "I'm sorry, Monty. Really."

"You're gettin' punchy." *Bitchy* was the word he wanted to use, I guessed, and I was grateful he hadn't. "When this is over, you wanna take some time off? I guess we can keep everything under control for a little while. Mebbe."

Oh, Monty. The fact that he had brushed the nightside once and knew a little bit about it made the offer that much braver. "I'm planning on it." I stretched, my bones still aching and tender from the demands the staff had made on my body, demands engineered to keep me alive. "I'm sorry, Monty. I'm sorry as shit. I should have thought of the organ thing sooner."

He waved one limp, sweating hand. Rubbed at his eyes. "Don't worry about it. Just go out there and stop this shit, will you? I got to go home to Margie one of these days. Okay?"

"Okay." I squared my shoulders. "I'll get this done ASAP, Monty." *Because if I don't and a rogue Sorrow brings the Nameless through with an evocation, all hell's going to break loose. And that's not even half of it.* "Do you want to know any more?"

"Christ, no. What you just told me is going to give me fuckin' nightmares. Get out of my office; get to work. Give Carp and Rosie something new to do, and Sullivan and Badger too. I'll keep the press distracted as long as I can. Just make this shit *stop*."

"Okay, Monty." I paused. "You're good to work for, you know that?"

Another languid wave of the hand. He reached down into a half-open drawer and set a bottle of Jack Daniels and a bottle of Tums on his desk. "Get the fuck out of here, Jill."

"See ya."

I left, closing the door softly. Saul, leaning against a cubicle wall directly across from the door, examined me. I met his dark eyes for a long moment.

"This is getting too big," he finally said, quietly, under the clamor of ringing phones and the shuffling sounds of the homicide division. "We need help. Not just human cops."

What he didn't say, we both thought. *And a hellbreed neither of us trusts.* My tattered coat rustled as I stepped away from Monty's door. "What are we supposed to do? Call in a bunch of Weres to waste themselves on a suicide attack? No. We figure out how to take the wendigo out on our own. There's got to be a way."

"What about this Sorrow?" It was a good question. He fell into step beside me, shortening his stride to mine, and I was so abruptly grateful for his presence that my eyes prickled, both my dumb eye and the smart one.

"If Belisa's telling the truth, she probably knows how to short-circuit whatever evocation this bitch is trying to perform—and if the wendigo's involved. I just have to get a message to her that I'm willing to talk."

"How are you going to do that?"

"Simple. Just drop a word in the right ear, and it'll get to her."

"Which ear?"

"Relax, Saul. It's taken care of, Perry put the word out this morning." I slid my arm through his. "We're going to set Rosie and Carp to digging with the Badger and Sullivan, and then we're going to go have a little chat with this doctor. And after that, we're going to visit Hutch's bookstore and see what we can dig up on wendigos."

The Badger was a short round motherly woman with a streak of white over her left temple, and Sullivan a thin, tall red-haired Irish with a penchant for cowboy hats. They were sometimes called Jack Sprat & Wife by the braver practitioners of cop humor, and put up with it estimably. They had reams of information on the organ trade in Santa Luz, too much for me to absorb. The Badger, bless her forward-thinking little heart, had photocopies of the more interesting cases as well as a few fact sheets.

I read in the car while Saul drove and Perry's limo cut a narrow black swath behind us. I wasn't sure I liked that albatross following us around, especially during the day, but the tightness of Saul's jaw warned me not to say anything about it. I wondered what deal he'd made with Perry. Swallowed the question.

We made it to Quincoa against light traffic, and Saul parked in the same alley as before. Perry's limo, in magnificent defiance of its own incongruity, idled, gleaming and black, across the street. I checked the sky—sunlight, still. He didn't seem as scary in sunlight, but the limo had smoky tinted windows. He made no appearance, and I wondered once again what he was.

Vulnerable to sunlight? Or just not showing himself? Playing a game?

This time we didn't lie in wait and examine the building.

No, this time Saul kicked the hermetically sealed door in on the second try, the deadbolt tearing free of softer metal. I had my gun out, swept the inside of the hall, and recoiled as the stench boiled out.

"Jesus *God!*" The reek drove me back a full three paces, to the edge of the steps. Death, and a loud zoolike odor. Saul wrinkled his nose, glanced at me. He had drawn his Sig Sauer, he covered the door. I swallowed bile. "What the *fuck?*"

"Stinks. And a sealed door." He didn't sound strained, but I caught the edge of disgust in his voice. "I smell more than one."

"How many?"

"I can't tell."

"The wendigo—"

"I smell it too. But old. It hasn't been here for a day or two."

"Jesus." I coughed, my eyes watering. "All right. Call Montaigne; tell him we've got a scene. I'm going in."

"Jill—"

"Come on, Saul. I'm the hunter. There's a pay phone on the corner. Or there's a cell phone in Perry's limo, if it comes to that. Hurry up so you can come back and cover me." *Though I don't think the thing's here. I don't think anything's left alive in here.*

His jaw set, hard as concrete. Then he was gone, his coat flapping as he took the stairs with a single bound, brushing past me. Silver chimed angrily in his hair. I waited until he was half a block away before I peeled the leather cuff off my right wrist one-handed.

Cool air hitting the scar sent a shiver down my spine. I stuffed the cuff in my pocket and closed my left hand around my secondary gun. Then I stepped forward, into the miasma of death.

Breathe. Dammit, Jill, breathe. The smell will fade.

But I knew it wouldn't. It *wouldn't.* The receptors in my nose might shut off, but the smell would work its way into my skin. And even deeper, into memory. How many bodies?

Let it be only one or two. What do you say, God? Even as I crossed the threshold and stepped into the flickering fluorescent light of a perfectly normal waiting room, I knew it wouldn't be only one or two. No wonder the clinic hadn't been open.

The air was stuffy, dead still. I peered behind the nurse's counter—no, nobody there. A neat stack of files sat next to a keyboard, under a dead dark monitor. I wanted to take a look, but rule one of sweeping a scene is *give assistance to the living.* Of course, I doubted there was anyone in here alive. Not with that smell.

I pushed open the swinging door that should lead to patient

rooms and the back hallway, and the odor of death belched out, enfolding me.

I peered into the hall, and my fingers loosened on the gun. "Dear God," I whispered, then wished I hadn't because the smell rushed into my mouth and the vision of...

Sweet Jesus, dear God, it burned its way into my skull.

How many of them are there? Arms, legs... this is a lair. Or it was. The smell of the creature was fading, but enough remained to make the intaglio of twisted rotting limbs seem to move. Open mouths, eyes torn from skulls, torsos cracked like nuts—

I backed up, the gun bumping against my leg as my grip slipped still more. *Oh, God. God in Heaven.*

The sight scored itself deeper behind my eyes, and the scar on my wrist pulsed, gruesomely warm and wet as if a rough-scaled tongue had licked it. I backed up again, ran into something soft, and leapt, raising the gun.

Perry's fingers locked around my wrist. "Just me, Kiss." His blue eyes glanced past me as the swinging door closed, a soft sheaf of pale hair falling in his face. He looked just the same, and the fringing of his aura had stopped. Of course, there was no sunlight in here. "There is nothing living in this place."

"It's—" Words failed me, and the reek closed thick and cloying. Pressed against my skin like rancid oil. "God—"

"God is not here. Of all people *you* should know that." His fingers tightened on my wrist, the scar gone hot and swollen. "Catholic, weren't you? A schoolgirl."

I pulled against his grasp. His fingers tightened, but I tore my hand away. My grasp firmed around the butt of the gun.

My shoulder hit his as I pushed past him. He didn't even bother to pretend I could move him, I bounced off and stumbled. I aimed for the door, a rushing sound in my ears and the back of my throat suddenly whipped with hot bile.

"Jillian." Perry's voice echoed with soft chilling glee in the still, muffled air. "You do know that, right? God is a fiction. There is nothing godly about this."

Shut up, Perry.

I made it outside before I threw up. The air was cold and full of knives; I hung over the spindly iron railing and lost everything I'd ever thought of eating.

Perry held my hair back, ignoring the silver charms. His fingers rubbed soothingly between my shoulderblades until the sirens started in the distance and Saul came back.

Maybe I should have been grateful. But I wasn't.

CHAPTER 20

They were stuffed everywhere. Bodies and *bits* of bodies, in varying stages of decomposition; there was not an inch of carpet that wasn't soaked with blood and fouler things. Maggots exploded from torn flesh, noisome liquids ran, and the techs brought the remains out in bags much too small for a human corpse. There was only so much piecing together of individual corpses that could be done at the scene. The rest had to wait for the lab.

The only thing worse than the stench inside was the smell of vomit outside. Even the hardened forensic techs who had seen the worst stumbled out to void their stomachs and staggered back in, grimly determined to do their work. Voices were hushed, even the most cynical and jolly of the homicide deets taking hats off and speaking as if we were in a church.

The whole building was cordoned off, thank God we didn't have to worry about a crowd. This was a quiet part of town. Quincoa was a limbo that only happens in cities—a long seedy street zoned for both industrial and residential and holding precious little but vacant buildings and the occasional professional office lingering from better days, when it had been a thriving highway. Perry's limo sat sleek and black across the street in a parking lot, not idling but simply...sitting. Perry himself stood off to one side, watching the human hubbub while the sun went down. Most of the paramedics, cops, and forensic techs instinctively avoided him, as if he was a cold draft or a nasty smell. His hair glowed, and his suit was still immaculate.

The almost-worst had been finding the operating theater, scrubbed and glistening; there was a close narrow back hall that gave onto a haphazard bay where they had most likely pulled the van in. A stack of Styrofoam coolers; a supply of dry ice, scalpels and clamps laid out with gleaming precision. Everything you needed to harvest organs.

Especially if you weren't too concerned about the owners of those organs surviving the experience.

The medical examiner's office was not going to be happy with this.

What was even worse than the operating room were the fading marks of violence, the etheric strings of souls torn and violated as surely as the bodies had been. My blue eye could see those marks, where a Sorrows adept had performed that most foul and tricky of feats: eating a soul. Taking the psychic energy of death, harvesting it to fuel something unspeakable.

An evocation of the Nameless, powered by this kind of terrible agony and brutality, would tear a hole sky-deep in the fabric of reality. We were looking at a psychic wound the people of this place would probably never recover from—and God help us all if the Nameless was set loose. It would mean three and seven-tenths years of indescribable corruption, agony, and degradation, a cancer eating its way into the heart of the world.

Not here, goddammit. Not in my city.

I sat on the curb, my head on my knees. The last failing vestiges of sunlight fell across my shoulders, edging with gold the weeds forcing up through cracked and failing sidewalk. I heard the faint roar of traffic and the mutter of official activity, pencils scribbling and the faint sounds of flashes going off. Footsteps. The dry heaves of someone who had seen all they could take for the moment. The paramedics, talking in hushed tones.

They were treating some of the officers for shock.

I pulled further into myself, forehead pressing into my knees, my arms wrapped tight around my shins.

Since spring. God knows how many there are in there. Right under my nose, a Chaldean whore and a wendigo.

Right under my goddamn nose. Some hunter I am.

Saul sat next to me, close enough I could feel the heat of him.

He didn't touch me, though. He knew enough to leave me alone, silently offering his presence while I suffered the worst wound any hunter could ever suffer.

Guilt.

God. Under my very nose. How could I overlook something like this? And the not-so-comfortable thought, *in my city. My city. Why?*

The images were burned into the darkness behind my eyelids. A cavalcade of horrors, Hell reproduced in miniature, and Perry's soft corrupting voice, smooth as velvet and so, so amused.

God is not here. Of all people you *should know that.*

Dark exhaled up from the cold pavement, the sun sliding below the rim of the earth. "How is she?" Rosie's voice, soft and respectful.

"Quiet." Saul's deadpan reply held no trace of levity. "Taking it a little hard."

"I brought some coffee." Wonder of wonders, Rosie sounded shy. "Jill? Want some coffee?"

Get up, Jill. Mikhail's voice, the harshly weighted syllables, as if he was tired and wounded. *Get up, and do your duty. You are hunter. This is what you do.*

I raised my head. Slowly. The sun was on her tired way back down under the rim of the earth, and night was rising.

Rosie's freckles stood out garishly against the paleness of almost-shock. Her hair was pulled sleekly back, but she still looked tired and frazzled. Carp was talking to a forensic tech, leaning against a squad car, a defeated slump to his shoulders. He looked a little green, and his hair stood up as if he'd run his fingers back through it more than once.

"Thanks." The word cracked, my voice as dirty and disused as an empty room. I took the Styrofoam cup of coffee sludge Rosie offered. The laces of her white canvas sneakers were dirty, and that one small detail suddenly filled my eyes with tears. "I'm sorry, Rosie."

"For what?" She shrugged. "Better we find these people now. We have a chance of identifying them. Hopefully, that is." One side of her mouth pulled down. "You look like hell."

Not yet I don't. But soon I probably will. I took a sip of the burned coffee. "Thanks."

"You gonna be okay?"

No. Not even close. No way. "Fine."

Saul leaned over, bumped me with his shoulder. The coffee splashed inside the cup, its surface oils swirling.

"What do you want us to work on, Carp and me? We've been getting up to speed on this organ stuff with Badger and Sullivan."

I returned to myself like a heavy sigh, sinking back down into my body. Leather creaked as I sat up straight, I heard a car door shut quietly. Someone else started to heave. I took another swallow of the liquid masquerading as coffee. "You and Carp can process the scene and keep on the lookout for another one. Other than that, nothing. It's too goddamn dangerous to have you guys poking around, I don't want to lose either of you."

I suppose I should have taken it as a compliment that she didn't argue. "What are you going to do?" She sounded less like a seasoned detective and more like a teenager frightened to death by ghost stories told around a campfire. It just showed how sane she was.

"Find the Sorrows bitch responsible for this," I answered quietly. "Take her out. And her entire happy crew of helpers. Kill them and leave them in stinking gobbets somewhere, and curse their bones so that their souls find no rest in this world or the next. *Nobody* fucks with my city."

A short pregnant pause was broken only by the sound of someone still heaving. Quiet murmurs.

"Well," Rosie said finally. "Nice to know you have a plan. Anything we can do?"

"Keep your heads down." I rocked up to my feet, my knees protesting. I felt bruised and tender all over. "One way or another this is all going to be over soon. Either I'm going to kill them all...." I glanced at Perry, who had finally moved and came silkily through the organized chaos of processing one of the worst murder scenes in Santa Luz history.

"Or?" Rosie prompted. "Do I really want to know?"

"Or you'll need a new hunter, and quick. Not to mention you'll want to get as far away from this fucking city as possible." I handed the coffee cup back.

"Lovely, Jill. That's really reassuring."

"Not my job to be reassuring. You're a good cop, you know that?"

"Coming from you, that means something." A tired, sour smile lit her face. "I'll go tell Carp the good news. You might want to slide away before he decides to corner you and tell you not to do anything stupid."

"You're not going to tell me that?"

"He thinks you'll listen; I know better. Be careful." She looked up at Saul. "You too, Tonto."

He nodded, silver chiming in his hair. Perry reached us as Rosie stepped away, heading back to Carp.

"Jill—" Saul began, rising like a dark wave.

"Hang on. Perry?"

"Kiss." A tilt to his chin, a raising of one blond eyebrow, and his eyes began to glitter. He looked far more like the hellbreed I was used to seeing inside the walls of the Monde Nuit.

"Find Melisande Belisa. Bring her to me."

He was about to protest, I suppose. At any rate, he opened his mouth as if he was going to say something, then stopped, studying me intently. I was safe enough right now, if the wendigo was going to attack me it would have to find me first. Which wasn't a comforting thought, but we needed someone on our side who knew what this other Sorrows bitch was up to.

And Belisa, damn her eyes, was the only one I could think of. Besides, if she gave me any trouble I'd have Saul and Perry hold her down while I took her spleen out the hard way.

And I would enjoy every goddamn moment of it.

I am not a nice person.

I held Perry's gaze for a long, restless eternity. Then I folded my arms, the ruby at my throat beginning to vibrate. The scar, slumbering since I'd found the bodies, tingled. His aura tightened, the bruised sludge that marked him as hellbreed. Funny, but nothing with an aura like his should be able to produce hellfire in the blue spectrum.

Just what was Perry, anyway?

He dropped his eyes. "Certainly, my dear. Anything for my Kiss. It shouldn't take too long."

"Good." I watched him turn with an oddly uncoordinated grace, and begin walking away. "I want her alive, Perry. But I want her frightened."

He waved one hand above his shoulder, as if I was bothering him with trifles. Saul bumped into me, crowding; I bumped back. The taste of ashes, burned coffee, and sourness still hung in my mouth. The scar on my wrist pulsed, but quietly, a soft mouthing caress, scales rasping seamed and puckered skin.

"Saul." My voice sounded strange, as if I was several miles away and hearing myself talk. Pushing everything else away, boiling everything down to the simplest possible essence.

Distilling it.

"Right here." And he was. I could feel his attention like sunshine on my face—but from far away.

From very far away. I focused on the gleaming paint of Perry's limo as dusk spread over the sky, turning the blue to purple and tinting the clouds with pink in one last gasp of brightness. "I need you to go down into the barrio and find out what kills a wendigo. Keep digging until you find something, then come back to me. Take the car, I won't need it."

"Jill—"

"No. I need you to do this for me."

"What are you going to do?"

"Some things." *Things I don't want you to see me do, Saul. I love you.*

"What kind of things?"

Bloody, screaming things. I watched as the headlights turned on and Perry's limo smoothly banked out of the parking lot, heading north on Quincoa. "Please, Saul." *Don't make me say any more.*

"Try not to get into trouble," he said, heavily. "Give me your keys."

I dug in a pocket and handed them over, still staring at the spot where Perry's limo had sat. My eyes blurred, and I felt the final *click* that meant I was lifting off, sliding away from the earth, into the space where there was no room for what I was feeling. The space that would hold me until it was safe to feel something again.

I have had enough. My city. They are trying to do this to my city.

"Jill?" Saul bumped into me again. Just like a Were, crowding me so I knew he cared. "I'll come find you as soon as I know how to kill it. I promise."

That made me smile, a gentle abstracted smile I could feel against the foreign material of my face. I turned my head and looked up at him. "You don't need to promise."

"I like to. So you know I'm serious." His dark eyes scorched mine for a moment, and feeling threatened to come back. I shoved it away. "Jill?"

"Go. Find out what kills the thing." I pushed him, gently. "Then come get me. Okay?"

"Okay." A short nod, his hair falling forward over his shoulders. Silver glittered, and his high cheekbones caught the last of the dusky light. He always looked good in dimness, and even better in strong light. "You got it." He turned and headed for the Impala. I don't know if he looked back, because I took the opportunity to fade into a pool of shadow between the unnecessary SWAT van and an ambulance, then ran soft and light for the alley that cut between an old abandoned grocery store and a newer but equally abandoned building that had been an auto parts supply store. I could cut over to 142nd and get a cab there. I had enough cash for anywhere I would need to go tonight.

I did not look back. I kept going.

CHAPTER 21

The flesh gallery was just starting to pulse with nightlife. Long legs in ragged fishnets under short skirts, the motion of hips back and forth, the glitter of eyes under mascara and thick eyeliner, cheap jewelry and the ubiquitous jackets now that the wind had risen. Coming down off the mountains, the winter wind was cold, full of the smell of sage and stone. It whistled in the canyons between skyscrapers, and here on Lucado it filled the night with knives.

The girls were nervous, and I didn't blame them. I examined the street from a good vantage point on the roof of a tenement, pulling my tattered coat around me. I waited, taking deep lungfuls of the cold wind.

The street danced; they were like shoals of fish glittering and turning in sync. Clicking of platform heels against concrete, the sound of car wheels, catcalls as the girls stamped their feet and tried to keep warm. Cars pulling in, cars pulling out, doors slamming, windows creaking as they slid down.

I had stripped the cuff from my wrist, and the scar burned under the cold kiss of wind. The night came alive, colors and sounds curdling under the lash of preternatural attention, my mind open, still, receptive.

I saw it. The Cadillac.

It slid like a stiletto through the shoals of tired girls, and some of them cast frightened glances at it afterward. I *moved,* brief wind in my ears as the world turned over and gravity caught me, plummeting, hitting the ground and rolling to bleed momentum. Cold concrete, pebbles digging into my back, then I was sliding through the shadows, just a flicker of motion in the darkness.

The scar, the scar, I'm moving like a hellbreed. Like a Trader. A five-story drop off a roof and here I was, running.

By the time I reached the quiet little brownstone he was already inside, and one of his muscle troop was on the front steps. The muscle, thick and heavy in a long coat with a bulge under his left arm where the gun was, never even saw me. I simply came straight out of the shadows and hit him, the crack of bone breaking in his face a sharp sweet sound.

Then I was inside, and the other thug was at the end of the hall. I took him too, a short tubby man powerfully built for all his lard, smelling of *frijoles* and grease; with the heatless scent of a killer on him too. *Well, Ricky certainly doesn't skimp on the help, does he?*

The short one went down easily and quietly, I pulled the strike at the last moment so as not to break his neck.

I slid up the stairs on cat-soft, cat-quick feet, and burst into the bedroom.

Diamond Ricky had a girl in there with him, a half-naked child with high brown breasts who was rolling the top of a stocking down her thigh. I saw her from very far away and spared her less than half a thought. There was a low table with a mirrored tile fouled with cocaine holding down a fan of twenties, a white leather couch; the ceiling held mirrors too as well as the closet on the far wall. Electric light was soft and dim from three green and blue lava lamps on a glass shelf; the nightstand held a paper bag (full of something illegal, judging by the smell) and a 9 mm that would do him no good.

The thick musky-green smell of pot filled the room, both old and new; Ricky had just lit a joint and was reclining on the bed, his hand inside the open fly of his trousers. He saw me and his mouth fell open, the joint falling from his fingers over the side of the bed. I was on the bed in one leap, my left-hand fingers sinking into his throat and the gun in my right hand rising up to lock onto the girl, who hitched in breath to scream. Her face hadn't lost its babyfat yet, she was barely old enough to be walking to school by herself, let alone be in a room with a pimp.

"Shut up," I snarled, cutting through her gasping inhale. "Shut the *fuck* up."

She did, clutching an incongruous bit of feathers to her chest. Some kind of lingerie, probably Ricky's contribution to the fun and games. Her long dark hair quivered, and the lipstick smeared on her lips made her mouth into a wet dark hole.

"Pick up the money." I pointed the gun toward the table, she edged over and looked at Ricky, then jerked the money out from under the tile. The cocaine scattered on the tabletop. Snow on glass plains.

I made a tiny motion with the gun toward the door. "Go out the back door, or you'll be shot." The softness in my voice made it a promise. "Go home, if you have a home. If you don't, check into a hotel. But if I see you on the street tonight, or if you tell *anyone,* I will find you."

It was an empty threat. I wouldn't have cared. But she believed it, and her eyes darted toward Ricky. I tightened my fingers in the pimp's throat, and he moaned, a shapeless sound of terror.

She scrambled for the door, and I heard her bumbling along as she tried to get dressed on the stairs while running. I listened— yes, she went out the back door.

Good girl. I turned my attention to Ricky, who was choking as my fingers tensed. "Ricky." I sounded meditative. The gun swung around, settled against his forehead. "Now you and I are going to have a little chat, *cabrón.* A very cozy little talk. You're going to tell me about your playmates, and we are going to have a lovely special moment right here on your bed. Bet you like that, don't you?"

Ricky was wet with sweat; it rolled in great beads from his brown skin. He had a hard-on, and he smelled of oil and smoke, as well as fried cheese. A thin curl of smoke lifted from the joint on the floor.

The smile pulled my lips back into a snarl of effort as the scar on my wrist pulsed, every fiber of my body straining to pull the trigger. But instead, I loosened up a little on his throat.

"Now," I whispered. "Your meeting. With Jonte and the boys. Who else was there, and what was said? Take it from the top."

He did.

Pimps are predictable creatures. They have their routines and their habits, and the fact that most of them are into petty drug dealing doesn't change that. If a pimp gets picked up, his girls bail him out, usually with the help of his lieutenant.

But if a pimp ends up dead, with his second and his muscle crippled, the girls freefall for a while. The drugs come from other dealers, some of whom are weak and move into the power vacuum to become pimps. Or they come from new pimps that rise like maggots from a corpse to take the place of the old one.

I wish it was harder for them. God, do I wish it was harder.

Wish in one hand, Kismet. Spit in the other. See which fills up first.

I followed the chain up, each pimp telling me a little more, and saved Jonte for last. He was a big, broad, soft-in-the-middle black man with a wide genial smile and two front teeth cased in gold that rang sweetly against the floor the second time I backhanded him. Eleven pimps, each of whom had been at the meeting with Rocadero, who was dead probably because the redheaded Sorrow didn't need him any more. The pimps being alive either meant that they weren't important or that she still needed them to supply something, whether it be flesh or cash.

It was from Jonte that I got the most important piece of news.

It would take a stronger man than a pimp not to give up everything he knows when a hellbreed-strong fist flexes and a testicle pops like a grape. At heart, the men who make their living like that are cowards. It's why they engage in the mindfucks instead of getting real jobs. What they don't realize is that the mindfucks eat them alive too.

Now's not a time for philosophy, I told myself as the boneless body of the big man slumped to the tiled floor. Jonte had a nice place, for all that I'd busted up a good deal of it. He'd also had some half-decent help. I was bleeding down one side of my face, and there was a fresh bloody hole in the left thigh of my pants, closing rapidly.

Now is the time for showing these fucks what happens when you mess with my *city. Had enough, I have* so *had enough of this. The* scar on my wrist pricked wetly, a thick welter of heat spilling up my arm. Fresh cold wind poured in through the busted French door, glass broken in sharp slivers in the tide of sticky blood that washed across the tiles.

I let out a long soft breath as Jonte gurgled his last, pieces falling into place. Taken separately, the pimps hadn't known much. But putting all the pieces together gave me a picture. Just like a jigsaw, even if you don't have all the pieces you can make a guess if you have enough of them.

And now I knew, too, where the redheaded Sorrow had her little bolthole. It was a stroke of genius, one I admired coldly while I considered how to break in and kill her.

The pseudo-adobe house groaned under the lash of wind. I'd taken four men with assault rifles, three with handguns, and another two that apparently had little use other than as hangers-on. They were only human, all of them, and I'd found Jonte gibbering with fear in his kitchen, crouched under the counter and trying to load a .38 revolver—whether for himself or me I wouldn't want to guess. And now that the shooting and moaning was over I heard something else.

I tilted my head. Scratching sounds.

Mice in the walls, Kiss? The voice, strangely enough, was Perry's; his jolly happy tone when he'd just discovered something to make me flinch. *Little mice fingers scratching at the plaster. Mmmh.*

Glass crunched under my feet. The sound was coming from downstairs, in the basement. Jonte was quite a successful pimp, probably because of his connection to a few of the larger drug dealers in town. He actually had a suburban house, in depressed real estate less than five minutes on the old highway from the strip downtown where his girls paraded. All the comforts of home but close enough to keep a tight leash on his moneymakers. Yes, ol' Jonte was quite the operator.

"Was" is the operative word. Now he's pimping in Hell. The thought brought another one of those frozen smiles to the surface of my face.

The house was utterly silent except for the scratching and the faint whimpers. If I'd been wearing my cuff, I probably wouldn't have heard it.

I had both guns out. Jonte's taste in furnishings was Mission-style, with a few tribal touches; it was nice for a fatass pimp, I supposed. The kitchen gave onto the living room, I stepped past the body of one of Jonte's thugs, the one dressed all in night camo. *Where do they find these people? Then again, reputable mercs don't like to work for pimps; they prefer a little higher on the food chain where the money's better.*

I turned into the entry hall, lifting both guns. There was a door at the end, probably going down to the basement and locked with a shiny brand-new padlock. Behind it was whatever was making those stealthy sounds.

Hamelin Town's in Brunswick, by famous Hanover City; the poem rang inside my head with dark glee. *Vermin, 'twas a pity.*

The hammers on both guns clicked back. *Focus, Jill. What the fuck is that?*

I caught a muffled sob, and the sound of movement again. More than one.

What lovely little surprise do we have waiting for Kismet in here?

I approached the door, cautiously, quietly. More muffled sobs. *What the fuck?*

I holstered my right-hand gun, closed my fingers around the padlock. Drew on the scar for a quick hard yank, and metal squealed, snapping. I twisted, tossed the padlock, and drew my gun again.

It pays to be careful.

I backed up. "Come out," I called, ready for submachine gun fire, zombies, scurf, or anything else that might pop out to surprise a hunter who had just had a very bad day.

Anything except what confronted me. More sobs from behind the door, which was thick heavy old wood. Women's sobs. But I kept the guns level. There was simply no telling, and I was here without backup. *I hope Saul's having some luck in the barrio.*

The door creaked. They were fiddling with it from the inside.

"Goddammit!" I yelled. *"Come out right fucking now or I will come in there shooting!"*

More soft sounds of distress, and the heavy iron doorknob twisted violently. A slice of darkness widened as the door slid open, and my fingers tightened on the triggers.

A naked human woman emerged, blinking. She carried a long splinter of wood that looked utterly useless as a weapon, and for one of the longest and most exotic moments of my life (and that's saying something) we faced each other over the expanse of tiled floor, under the gently tinkling chandelier Jonte must have paid a fortune for.

She had wide dark eyes and close-cropped dark hair, and she couldn't have been more than eighteen. She also recovered first, as another girl—this one just as naked, and quite obviously just as young or younger—stepped blinking out into the light.

"Are you one of them?" the first one demanded. "If you are, goddammit, I'll kill you."

Brave of her, considering how I must have looked. And considering that I was armed, I was smoking with violence, I was spattered with blood, and I was ready to kill whoever I had to.

What the fuck is this? I stared. "What the fuck?" I couldn't come up with anything better. Then I recovered, slightly. "I just killed Jonte. What the hell were you doing in the basement?"

Her shoulders went back and her chin lifted a little. I heard more soft sounds behind her. More women? Naked women? "What, you think we *wanted* to be locked up down there in the dark?" She lifted the splinter of wood, and I remembered I was holding both guns on her.

I lowered them, slowly. A horrible idea began forming under the surface of my conscious mind. "Are any of you pregnant?"

"What?" She stared at me. It was another exotic moment. "Are you fucking *high?* We've been down there for *weeks!*"

I decided this would be a good time to holster my guns, did so. "I just killed the pimp who owns this house," I said. "Let's call 911 and find you ladies some clothes."

The suspicion she eyed me with would have been insulting if I hadn't suspected that I'd stumbled across the reason why Jonte had been left alive by the redheaded Sorrow. Three days to the invocation of the Nameless, and a clutch of young girls held here in a pimp's house, fed and trammeled like prized rabbits.

Oh, God. And what she said next convinced me I was maybe right. She stared at me like I was her own personal nightmare.

"You're *her,*" she whispered. "You're the one who bought us."

"I don't buy people. Nor do I sell them." My voice was a little sharper than usual, and the chandelier overhead tinkled restlessly. I must have been wearing my mad face, because the girl gasped and dropped the splinter; it clattered on the tiled floor.

It was a good thing I had the cuff off, because otherwise I might not have heard it. But I had been functioning with preternatural senses most of the night. Sensitivity is a wonderful thing, once you get used to it.

Clawed feet brushing the earth like fingers on a drumhead, incredibly fast. Far away, but getting closer.

Much closer. Someone was coming to dinner. The hair on the back of my neck stood straight up, and the charms in my hair tinkled together sweetly. The sound was suddenly loud in my hell-breed-sensitive ears, moving to the forefront. Impossible to ignore.

I whirled, the tattered edges of my coat flaring out. Stared at the half-open front door, the one I'd busted through. "Holy fuck," I whispered, forgetting the naked women for a moment. I heard individual heartbeats; there had to be a good twenty of them in there. Defenseless, and from the smell, sanitation hadn't been as good as one could wish. But they were in good health, so they had probably been fed.

Just the thing to fuel your evocation of a hungry Elder God with.

Shit. Goddammit. I turned back to the women. The girl behind the leader had folded her arms over her bare breasts defensively. I saw more spilling out, none of them a day over twenty if I guessed correctly. They clustered behind the dark-haired girl, who was obviously the leader, and I saw a glint in her eyes I recognized from a lifetime ago and miles away.

She wasn't ready to die yet, and she was one tough cookie.

What am I going to do here? "Listen to me. Jonte's got cars, the keys are hanging in the kitchen. Be careful, there's broken glass. Get the fuck out of here, all hell's going to break loose."

She took it better than I thought she would. "Where should we go? Shut *up!*" She yelled the last, over her shoulder, and I heard the sniffles and soft moans behind her quiet down. Wide wet eyes were wiped, the girls holding on to each other, more pushing up from what looked like dark stairs. "Goddammit, I'm going to get us out of this, but you have got to stop *whining!*"

I like this girl, I decided. "Get downtown. I think he's got a fucking Humvee in there, get downtown and get to a police station. Tell them Kismet sent you. Got it? K-I-S-M-E-T. Kismet."

"Kismet. Okay. Show me the car, I've got my learner's permit." Yes, she was definitely the leader. "Amy, Conchita, you two get the girls organized. Let's go. Come on. Quit crying, Vicky; hold her up." She sounded like a battlefield general, but I heard the quick thunder of her pulse. She was scared half to death. And so young.

Holy fucking shit. I can't just leave them here. "Come on." The chandelier overhead tinkled again as I spoke. I sounded two short steps away from murder. The scar abruptly cooled on my wrist, turning chill as an ice cube pressed into the flesh. "What's your name?"

"Hope," she replied, moving forward, seemingly utterly unselfconscious of the fact that she was completely unclothed. But I saw the bruises on her thighs and the way she held herself, as if she couldn't stand to even have the air touch her. "Hope Melendez." Goosebumps rose on her skin, and I heard the footsteps in the distance stutter, pause . . . and redouble their effort.

Shit. Fucking shit.

"*Move* it!" I yelled, and several of the girls flinched. "This fucking way, and hurry up. Hurry *up!*" I had a good guess where the garage was, and Jonte was known for his car collection.

I've got to get them to a car or two. Christ, I hope more of them know how to drive.

Then I've got to hold the wendigo until they can get away.

CHAPTER 22

Two of the longest minutes of my life later, we were in the garage with the huge door creaking open. "They kept us down there in chickenwire cages. I've been working on tearing a hole through the wire in one." Hope held up her left hand; her fingertips were mashed and bleeding. "We heard the gunshots, figured either we were next or we were going to be left down there in the dark. So I broke open my cage. They told us we'd been bought by a woman, and that she was coming to take us away." She shivered. "*Jesus.*"

Closer. It was getting closer. I didn't have time to offer any comfort. They were barefoot and naked, and miserable. But I got them all loaded into two cars—a black Humvee and a silver Escalade; Jonte had certainly liked pimp rides. Finding the keys was no problem, there was a neat pegboard with all the keys we could ever want. Seatbelts *were* a problem, but if it was a choice between seatbelts and getting them out of here I'd pick getting them *out*. They were packed like sardines, some of them openly sobbing now.

Hope clambered into the driver's seat in the Humvee. Her second-in-command, a plump blonde girl with wide blue eyes and bruised, blood-crusted thighs, was already strapped into the driver's seat of the Escalade.

"Jesus, this is big." Hope's breathing was short and rapid, and I thought some of the girls were going into shock.

"Go easy on the brake. If you get pulled over, it's okay. Tell them my name and they'll take care of you." The garage door finished opening, I flinched as the sound of the creature's footsteps—distinct from a thousand other sounds—pounded my ears, communicating itself up through my bootsoles. *I'm sensitive to it now. Of course I am, it almost fucking killed me.* "And for God's sake be careful. It might help if everyone in there prays. Turn the heater up as soon as you can, you don't want anyone going into shock. Okay?"

"Who the fuck are you?" Her eyes were wide and haunted. "Jesus."

"Kismet," I repeated. "Tell the cops I sent you." I spelled it out for her again. "Now go. For fuck's sake, go. *There is no time.*"

The footsteps were very close now, drumming against the earth. The cars roused themselves, and the Humvee pulled out, slowly. The Escalade followed, torturously slow, and slid down the circular driveway. *Oh, please, oh please...*

I saw them make the turn out onto the street, so goddamn slowly, the footsteps almost on top of us by now and coming from the north. Which made not much sense, if she was hiding out where I thought she was, where Jonte had told me he had "taken a few bitches."

It didn't matter. I wondered if it had slipped its leash and come hunting or if the redheaded Sorrow had let it loose in another part of town.

Then it howled, a long chilling spun-glass growl of blood-thirsty hunger rising from the north. My skin crawled like it wanted to run away from both me and the creature; I turned around, hitting the button to close the garage door. *Fucking Christ. I could have been out of here already.*

I wanted to examine where they'd held the women, but it was enough to know that they were supposed to be kept alive and relatively unharmed except for rape. Opening up a door in the ether and bringing a Chaldean demon through requires a massive effort, and that effort could be fueled by harvested death. But something simpler was fresh death, done ritualistically; Traders sacrificed snakes, rabbits, dogs, horses, goats—anything they could catch and get rid of the husk afterward. But to bring through the Nameless, not even the death harvested from organ theft would do.

And to bring him through and bribe him into doing something nice for a renegade Sorrow would take even more. It made sense. Appalling, wasteful, *mad* sense, but still, it was a pattern. It was a workable theory.

Now I just had to stay alive long enough to figure out the rest of it and *stop* it. Brooding wouldn't help—and the slight nasty thought that the renegade Sorrow might have killed Jonte herself for allowing his boys to play with her sacrifices was amusing and gratifying, but wouldn't help me now.

I ducked under the garage door and set off across the driveway, my legs aching with the need to run. *Decide which way to go, Kiss. Move with a plan, for Christ's sake don't do anything stupid, taking off like a rabbit. This thing is fast, it's deadly, and you've got the scar, your whip, your guns, your knives—all of which are fucking useless if it gets too close—and you've got your teeny little noggin. Which has to save you now.*

This was a bad part of town to be trapped in. But if I cut across the old highway and ran for a bit, I would be at the edge of the barrio's dark, night-pulsing adobe warren. I knew that warren, knew some good hiding spots and shortcuts.

Going into the barrio was a good way to end up dead. But still, given the choice between killing me and killing what was chasing me, I was comfortably sure self-interest might strike the deciding blow in my favor.

It was getting close. Very close. Night wind brought the first threads of its scent, a noxious stink that raised the hairs on the back of my neck. Gooseflesh prickled up under my skin.

That thing almost fucking killed you. You have no staff now, goddammit, and it's fast. It's too goddamn fast. Oh, God. Oh, God.

I told the rabbit-panicking part of myself to shut up, reached the street, and picked up the pace, my coat flapping and the sour taste of fear on my tongue.

CHAPTER 23

I don't mind being shot at. I don't *like* it, mind you, and I don't seek out flying lead. But I don't mind it. I don't mind knives, I don't mind a bit of fisticuffs. I don't even mind it when someone springs a trap on me and does their best to kill me.

I am a hunter; it comes with the job.

But Lord God on high, I hate to be *chased*. I hate to run with no other thought but the rabbit's thought of finding a way to escape certain death.

It was too fast. I paced myself, and drew on the cold, pulsing scar on my wrist as hard as I could. But even though I had the benefit of hellbreed-bargained strength, I was seriously flagging by the time I reached Merced Street and the Plaza Centro.

The PC isn't really a plaza. It's a gutted five-story building full of tiny shops, botanicas, and bodegas, with a vast central well thronged with people at any time of the day or night. It takes up a whole city block and was once a train station before the barrio reached in from the slum edge of town and took it captive.

It also has the biggest concentration of Weres in the city. Something that smelled this bad and was obviously intent on mayhem was likely to attract some notice. And while I didn't like the thought of luring the wendigo right through a heavily populated area and risking some casualties, I also didn't like the thought of meeting my death on a lonely street where there was no bloody *cover*. Weres mean smell, and smell was likely how this thing was tracking me. If I could confuse it, maybe I could escape.

These considerations flashed through my mind as I turned down Merced and saw the lights of the Plaza Centro in the distance, glimmering like fool's gold. My boots pounded the pavement, the scar no longer cold on my wrist but *hot,* so hot I expected it to steam in the chill night air. It poured pure etheric force into me, and I spent it recklessly—speed was imperative, since I could *hear* the thing behind me, and whenever the wind shifted I could smell it too. How it was tracking me through windshift I didn't want to know.

I didn't even want to guess.

At this point, I would settle for just keeping my miserable life. My breath rattled in my chest, my ribs heaving, it had almost caught me once on the top of a tenement on Colvert and Tenth. I knew my city, knew every dip in the streets, knew every shortcut and back alley, and it was only knowledge that kept me one scant sliver ahead of it, this thing—wendigo, whatever it was—that roared its glassine screech behind me doing its own personal imitation of a Wild Hunt.

Christ I'm glad it's not smart, if it was smart I couldn't have fooled it and it would have me by now. I pounded up the slight slope, flagging badly now, headlights blurring past. If the normal humans sensed me at all it was only as a cold draft, a flash out of the corner of the eye, something not-quite-right but gone before they could take a second look.

A ghost.

Grant me strength in battle, honor in living, and a quick clean death when my time comes— The prayer trembled just at the edge of my exhausted mind. *But don't let it come yet. Please, God. I have served well; help me out a little here. God? Anyone?*

Then, the impossible, the smell of the thing gaggingly close, I had slowed too much, no alley in sight, no way to jag left or right, I was running for the PC and maybe an escape in the tunnels underneath but oh *God,* I was tired. So tired. And I was hit from behind, a massive impact that smashed *through* me as the thing collided with its prey and sent me flying.

I heard the scrabble of claws and the screams as I flew, trying vainly to twist in midair, get my feet under me, something, anything, and heard the snarling crash into a wall behind me.

Hit. Hard. Snapping and shattering glass, I'd gone through a window and fetched up against shelving that fell over, bottles breaking, glass whickering through the air and the sudden smell of smashed vegetables all around me.

Lay for a moment, lungs burning and heaving, legs and arms too drained to move, scar a burning cicatrice on my wrist. *Oh God oh God, let it be quick, if it has to take me let it be quick, Saul, oh God Saul. Saul—*

Then, as if a gift from heaven, something familiar. "Get up. Jesus Christ, Jill, *get up!*"

A familiar voice, a prayer answered. I levered myself up just as the thing smashed through the glass searching for me, a massive ball of hunger and gagging stench suddenly freezing the air. It moved too *fast* and I was tired, so tired, arms and legs weighted with lead.

Crash. He hit the thing from the side, screaming his warcry, a roar halfway between man and cougar. Flame suddenly belched out, garish in the darkness and the fluorescent light of the grocery store, I heard screams and popping sounds as the fire, bright crimson-orange, speared through the night. More vital, more impossibly real than regular fire or hellfire, heat scorched the air so badly it stripped the hair back from my face, a holocaust of flame.

More screaming, and the barking, coughing growl of more Weres. I heard chanting—a shaman's voice lifted in the high keening screech of Were magicks, those bloody, animalistic, and strangely pure works of sorcery that are their peculiar heritage.

Saul yelled his warcry again, moving with fluid grace as the shining thing he held glittered with heat. More glass smashed, the smell of mashed vegetables and fruit suddenly turning caramel-brown shot through with the disgusting stink of the cancerous thing that screeched and tried to bat Saul away.

Seeing a Were fight in midform, dancing between human and animal, is...We never really think of how they shift to animal forms, forms that are precise and graceful. In most cases, far more graceful than human beings ever manage to be. And in their human forms they're graceful too, blessed with quick reflexes, regular features, an uncanny ability to move economically and efficiently through space.

Midform, they have the best of both worlds, a beauty that is so weird and alien it catches at the throat and dries the mouth. The movies don't do them justice at all. And midform is not somewhere they linger, unless they are rogue—or unless there is no other way to fight.

Saul was somehow not there as the creature swiped with its bloody claws, and seeing its speed and power up close I slumped to my knees, jaw hanging open in wonder and my breath rasping in my throat. It wasn't fair, it just wasn't *fair,* that I had to bargain with a hellbreed to get even a fraction of his grace and *still* I was so much less.

So acutely aware of being so much less.

Steam billowed. The thing Saul held, its flame liquid and hissing, broke the soul-devouring cold of the creature. Another scream from the shaman, and a massed snarling tide of power rode through the air. Were magic, tasting of nights out under open skies, black air against the back of the throat like champagne, hard crusted snow under feet no longer human, and the joy of *running* on four legs, the air alive with scent and the hard cold points of the stars overhead singing their ancient songs of lust and slow fire to those of us on the ground who had ears to hear.

The glowing thing, a long slim wand, struck. Saul yelled, ducking aside as the wendigo clawed for him, slowed by the weight of furred heavy power smashing through the interior of the store. More glass shattered, cardboard exploded, and the smell of cooking food shaded through goodness and into burning.

Saul *kicked,* a perfectly placed *savate* blow, then somehow twisted, using the kick to propel his body back and up, uncoiling to avoid the creature's claws as it fumbled for him again. The slim shape, burning white-hot, scored through my eyes, I flung up a hand to shield them and heard a death-scream unlike any other. Clapped my hands to my ears and screamed as well, a little sound lost inside the massive wrecked howl like frozen mountains colliding.

If glaciers feel pain when they rub against each other and split off whole mountainsides, they would scream like that. It...no, there is no way to describe the enormity of that cry. It broke whatever had not broken and flung me back; I hit the wall with my boots dangling six feet off the floor and slid down, landing in a medley of shattered glass and exploded packets of meat sizzling in the heat. Smelled my own hair burning as the silver charms heated up.

The scream stopped just before my eardrums burst. I rolled

free of the bubbling, steaming mess, gained my knees again, had to try twice before I could make it up to my feet. The air abruptly chilled, became the normal cold of a Santa Luz winter night.

Steam and vapor drifted in the air. There was murmuring, the ancient words Weres mutter when they come across death from bad luck or humanity. A forgiving of the spirit, in the midst of clear red rage. They have never had to translate that prayer.

You don't need to, if you've ever heard it. No translation is necessary.

My breath sounded harsh in the sudden silence. I was suddenly aware of my legs, strained and unhappy, making their displeasure known. My ribs, heaving, almost pulled loose by the demands placed on them. The scar, pulsing obscenely against the inside of my wrist, as if Perry was kissing my arm again and again. Pressing his hellbreed lips to human flesh, his scaled tongue flickering and his hot humid breath condensing on cooler human skin.

Veils of mist in the air parted. Saul stood over the shattered body of the wendigo; he tossed the arrowhead with its cargo of leather, feather, and hair onto the mess. Now that it was dead, it was a twisted humanoid figure running wetly with icy gray fur and long bits of different colors where its victims' scalps had been plastered to its mottled hide. Its face was tipped up, the eyes collapsing into runnels of foulness, its lipless mouth open in a silent blasphemous scream. And its claws, obsidian-tipped and deadly, lay twitching against the prosaic bubbling linoleum of a devastated grocery store.

It looked strangely small now, its face like a wizened ugly child's despite its frozen, rotted nose and nonexistent lips. Its genitals were pendulous, and black with frostbite.

And around its neck was a thin silver chain, winking in the light, squirming with unhealthy black Chaldean sorcery. The chain was broken about a foot below its jaw. Had it escaped and come looking for me?

Shoved through its heart was a spike of glossy black obsidian-like material, popping and zinging as it shrank. It had been white-hot just moments before. The steam whooshed away, evaporating into the night.

I sounded like I was dying of pneumonia, my breathing was so hard and labored. I half-choked at the titanic stink in the air. Bile caught in my throat.

Oh please don't let me throw up again. Oh please.

The hair of cougarform had melted from Saul; he stood straight and in profile, staring down at the defeated creature, his lips moving with the prayer of the massed Weres, their eyes bright and their mouths cherry-beautiful, crowded in through the window. I saw several different types: a kentauri tossing his long silvery mane, a were-spider whose face was gray and haunted under her mop of silken hair, another werecat who folded her hands and had closed her eyes, mouthing the ancient sounds. There were others, but I was too tired to see them. And then, in the back of the crowd, I saw a pair of familiar blue eyes, a sheen of pale hair. Perry. Had he found Belisa?

At the moment I didn't care. I closed my eyes. The breath that knifed into my lungs was not less sweet because of the stench it carried. No, it was *air,* and I was still alive to breathe it, no matter how foul it smelled. *Oh, Saul. Saul. Thank God for you. Thank God.*

Then I stumbled away, looking for a place to throw up. There was nothing left in my stomach, but I felt the need to purge anyway.

CHAPTER 24

I had never been so glad to see my own four walls again. The warehouse clicked and rang as I collapsed on the couch, keeping a wary eye on Belisa as she moved to perch on a chair opposite, glaring at me through her good eye while she clasped the pack of ice to the other side of her face. When she wasn't avidly peering at the interior and the furnishings, that was.

Storing up little bits of deduction to mindfuck me with later, no doubt.

Perry stood slightly behind her. He was immaculate, gray suit, the first two buttons of his crisp white dress shirt undone, his shoes shined to perfection. He looked very satisfied with himself, in his bland blond sort of way.

Belisa was moving gingerly, and her blue silk shirt was crumpled, her slippers were battered. It had probably been a hell of a fight, but for tangling with Perry she was strangely unharmed. I wondered if it was because I'd threatened him.

Not likely.

Saul went straight for the kitchen. I heard the cupboard opening, glass clinking. "Anyone who wants whiskey better speak up now," he said, calmly enough.

"God, yes." *Oh, Saul. Thank God for you.* I rested my head against the couch's back, almost beginning to feel like I could breathe again. Leather creaked, I hadn't bothered taking my coat off.

"If you have anything decent, I'll take it." Perry's eyes rested on me. Under the leather cuff, the scar ran with rancid flame, trailers of heat sliding up my arm. Smoky desire, sliding through the map of my veins as if he was touching me, running his fingers up the inside of my elbow.

I didn't look away, but I did clamp down on my self-control. I was vulnerable now, exhausted after expending so much power. And any time human animals get close to death, sex is the easiest thing to tempt them with afterward. "Belisa?" I kept my tone neutral.

She almost flinched, recovered. "That would be nice."

Perry leaned on the back of the chair. "What?" It was a soft inquiry, and I saw the blood drain from her face.

She looked terrified, and I couldn't blame her.

"That would be nice, mistress." All the color had leached out of her tone too. She shivered, hunching her shoulders.

Mistress. The term for a bitch-queen, a Sorrow higher in status than herself. What had Perry done to her? Abruptly, I felt sick all the way down into my stomach. He'd found her and brought her, and from the looks of it she'd resisted; and now he was rubbing it in. For her benefit, and also for mine; just to drive home that I owed him for bringing her in.

Christ. Well, you knew what he was when you struck the bar-

gain, Jill. Don't pretend otherwise. "Drinks all round, then." I sank into the couch.

The two cars full of naked women had made it to the police station; Montaigne had left a message on my answering machine, alternately swearing at me and thanking me, then swearing at me again. I'd sort it out later.

Right now I had other things to worry about. A few clipped sentences in the Impala, with Perry's limo right behind, had laid out the chain of events for me: Saul had gone into the barrio and poked around, not finding much of anything until Perry showed up with Melisande Belisa in tow and a long thin iron-bound case—the firestrike spear Father Guillermo knew was hidden under the altar in the seminary's main chapel, a secret kept by Sacred Grace since its inception. Perry swore whatever was inside should kill the wendigo.

The catch? He hadn't actually opened the case yet. Both of them felt my wild plunge into the barrio, Saul had left Perry to corral the bruised and beaten Sorrow and set off as fast as he could to find me and either kill the thing chasing me or buy me enough time to escape.

He didn't want to talk about killing it, and he didn't want to talk about how the spear had burned his palms. *It doesn't matter,* was all he would say. *It's fine.*

Saul brought the bottle and four glasses. He poured, slamming the bottle down when he was done, and left two glasses on the table. He handed me a glass half-full of amber liquid. He took his own and settled on the couch, and I wished I could cuddle up next to him, feel his heat.

But he was still angry, the musky fume of fury hanging on him. He was wound tighter than a clockspring, I knew enough to leave him to himself right now. Werecats are dangerous and unpredictable; if he snapped now I would have to calm him down the old-fashioned way. The thought sent a spike of heat through me, cleaner heat than the spoiled spillage of the scar, and I tossed down half my drink in one motion. I didn't think Perry and Belisa were to be trusted poking around the warehouse while Saul and I attended to some demons of our own.

Besides, there was this redhead bitch of a Sorrow to catch.

But first things first. "So Rourke lied. It wasn't Saint Anthony's spear. I *knew* there wasn't such an artifact."

Saul shrugged. Belisa leaned forward, took a glass, and handed it up to Perry, flinching. Then she took the last one for herself.

I don't think I like the looks of that. I eyed her over the rim of my own glass. Whiskey exploded in my stomach, another clean brief heat as my metabolism burned through it. *I'm alive. Alive. Thank you, God. I'm alive.*

Saul's tone was carefully neutral. "Gui didn't want to lie to you, but he'd taken an oath to keep the secret. I wonder what else they're hiding in there."

I don't care right now. Sort it out later, too. I shivered. The thing had glowed, white-hot, and part of the smell of burning had been Saul's hands charred down to the bone. "How are your fingers?"

He wriggled them, almost fully healed. I caught a flash of pink scarring rapidly shrinking. "Hurts a little. But fine." He spared me a tight smile, the corners of his mouth and eyes crinkling. Even though smoky musk rage pounded in the air around him, he still wanted to put me at ease.

I love you. The words choked me for a moment. I looked back into my glass. Another piece of the puzzle fell into place. "So *you* were looking for the spear, too. And your brother."

Belisa hunched her shoulders, staring into her glass. The warehouse creaked and muttered around us. The ice crackled against her face; her other eye, black from lid to lid, seemed oddly unfocused. "The plan was simple. We were to find the spear, kill the creature, and bring back Inez Germaine. Use her to buy our way back into the good graces of our House. It was my inattention that allowed my brother to escape, and we were both due for punishment and liquidation once we were returned unless we achieved something...extraordinary, something that could be legitimately seen as needing an escape as part of the plan. I visited him, explained the plan; he was to bring me the firestrike once he found where it was hidden. The New Blasphemy priests hid it well, and we were running out of time. When I visited him he had *still* not located the spear. And our House sent the Chaser for my brother, and—"

"And I got involved. So you decided a little mindfucking was in order?" I couldn't help it. *I should kill her right now. Goddammit, she killed Mikhail and she's sitting on my goddamn couch. In his house, the house he gave to me. Goddammit.*

"I know you have reason to hate me," she said evenly. "You've killed my brother. Tit for tat, we're even. Are you happy? We have less than a day before the evocation of the Nameless will alter the balance of power in every Sorrows House in the *world*. Inez isn't just playing in your little city, hunter. She will be a new Queen Mother above even the Grand Mothers, and we will—"

I choked on my whiskey, my protest that he had cracked his own poison tooth with no help from me dying in my throat. "Wait just one goddamn second. Less than a day? But the end of the cycle isn't until—"

"It's tomorrow. Your calculations are off. They usually are, when you add the Gregorian calendar to the mix." Belisa's shoulders hunched even further. "We are doomed. All of us, doomed."

Oh, for Christ's sake. "I'm not going to give up yet. When *exactly* does the cycle end? Tomorrow, *when?*"

"At 1:15 P.M. And thirteen seconds." She eased the ice away from her face and took a gulp of the whiskey. She looked as dejected as it was possible for a Sorrow to look, but her black eyes were oddly empty. As if they were painted on.

Perry took a small mannerly sip, raised his eyebrows, and took another. But he was crackling with awareness; he looked ready to leap on Belisa if she so much as twitched. I found that comforting—but still, seeing her flinch away from him rubbed me the wrong way.

Hard.

I finished mine and reached for the bottle. The bottle neck chattered against the mouth of my glass. I poured myself a tall one.

"Jill?" Saul. Carefully, quietly, his *you want me to kill someone or what?* tone.

"One in the afternoon." I settled back on the couch, leather creaking. The charms in my hair chimed, shifting, the scar on my wrist pulsed as Perry's eyes rose to meet mine. Why was I looking at him? Because he was right in front of me, and I didn't want to look at Belisa. "Will freeing the human sacrifices help stop it?"

Belisa shrugged. "For an evocation of this nature, she would keep them close at hand. The ones you freed were probably decoys, or only to reward her human tools. You said they had been used?"

Used. What a pretty little euphemism. "They were raped." My voice was flat, and loaded with terrible anger. "Probably repeatedly." *They're probably going to need therapy for the rest of their lives.*

Belisa nodded. "And several of the victims were pregnant?"

I nodded. The ruby nestled in the hollow of my throat was comfortingly warm.

"Then it's simple." She took another gulp of whiskey. "The harvested fetal tissue is probably to provide a base matrix for the Unnamed's entrance and physicality. She's going to create a *Vatcharak*—an Avatar." Admiration, probably unconscious, shaded her voice. "The other organs went for cash to build her new House, and still others went to feed the creature. Which was insurance, I would guess. The chain around its neck carried a powerful control spell. I wonder if she created it herself?"

I don't know and I don't care. "Why dump the bodies?" Of all questions, that was probably the most useless, but the one I most wanted to have answered.

"Probably because she had run out of places to hide them. And also, every place where a victim of this evocation lay slain would become a node-point when she succeeds in bringing the Unnamed through."

"A node-point." *I sound shocked.* "Of course. So the Avatar could have ready-made taplines into the ambient energy of the city, draining it like an orange. Which would widen the psychic scar in the ether and give it a *hell* of a lot of power."

She nodded, like a teacher pleased with a good student. "Very good. I begin to see why your file is red-flagged."

"Red-flagged? Forget it, I don't want to know. Why did this bitch pick my city, huh?"

"You allow no House here. No House, no scrutiny by other Sorrows who might discover her plans."

What, so it's my fault? I swallowed the flare of temper and closed my eyes, tilted my head back against the couch, and swore inwardly. Blew out between pursed lips, not quite a whistle. "Jesus *fucking* Christ."

"I can get almost every Were in this city ready in a few hours," Saul said tentatively.

"And there are hellbreed who can be coerced——" Perry began, his voice a dark thread, for once not supercilious.

Well, would you look at that. Even Perry's scared. "Not enough time. And once this is dealt with, there'd be a free-for-all I'd have to sort out." I sagged into the couch. *Tired. So fucking tired. I need a vacation. God. How many other graves are there out there, do you think? And other bodies. God. Dear God.* "Why a wendigo?"

"I suspect she came across it in her travels and thought it could be useful. She was in the Alps, and there have been ... stories." Belisa shuddered. *"Chutsharak."*

Curse my curiosity, I had to know. "What is a *chutsharak,* anyway?"

"It's House slang, not the ceremonial shorthand-garbage you know. It means—well, the best translation is, *oh fuck.*" Belisa managed to sound amused. "Or something of that nature. It depends on inflection."

Well, one mystery solved. For a moment I was tempted to just curl up on the couch and go to sleep. Just let whatever was going to happen, happen. The animal inside me just wanted to bury itself in a hole and sleep off the shakes and unsteadiness that came from almost-dying.

Silence crackled, tense and deadly. Unbidden, padding soft and clean into my head, came the sound of Mikhail's voice. Not singing the prayer in Russian, but growling it out in his accented English, every word a slap against the gray cotton of shock and apathy threatening to close over me. My own voice following along, uncertain and tired, but strong enough.

Cover me with Thy shield, and with my sword may Thy righteousness be brought to earth, to keep Thy children safe. Let me be the defense of the weak and the protector of the innocent, the righter of wrongs and the giver of charity. In Thy name and with Thy blessing, I go forth to cleanse the night.

That is what you swore, Mikhail's voice continued. *That is what you prayed. And that is what you will do, milaya.*

I gathered myself. When I opened my eyes I found Perry and Belisa staring at me. Black eyes and blue, waiting avidly. For what? It was in Perry's interest to keep me alive—at least, until he got tired of my resistance. And Belisa? If she could get me to distract this Inez bitch for long enough, she might have a shot at stepping into her shoes.

I rolled my head along the back of the couch, looked at Saul. He was staring into his glass, the musky smell of anger draining away. *Look at me, Saul. Please. Let me know what you're thinking.*

He might even have heard the thought, because he glanced at me, his mouth pulled tight in resignation. No, he wasn't happy at all. But he said nothing, merely giving the slight headshake that meant he would wait until we were alone.

Uh-oh. I made up my mind. "All right. Perry, you can take the Sorrow back to the Monde and wait for me. If all hell breaks lo—"

"No." Perry leaned against the back of the chair. Belisa cringed away from him, and bile rose in my throat. *Stop it. Don't feel sorry for her. That's like feeling sorry for the rattlesnake a bobcat's playing with.*

But still, she cringed just like a hooker waiting for a pimp's slap. And I knew what that felt like, didn't I.

Every blessed thing about this case seemed engineered to remind me what that fucking felt like.

"Excuse me?" The temperature might have dropped a few degrees, or it might have been my tone. "Last time I looked, Perry, you weren't the one in charge here."

"I brought you the Sorrow. You promised to stay in my sight for the duration." The scar on my arm prickled wetly, as if he had just licked it, and I steeled myself.

"I didn't—" I began.

Perry gestured languidly with the glass, his tone laden with flat finality. "The creature's dead. Very well, very good. But you are my investment, dear Kiss, and I am not about to let another little viper such as this one interfere with my very *interesting* plans for your education. That wouldn't be very wise of me, would it."

"You're not known for wisdom, Perry. A certain type of cunning, maybe, but not wisdom." It was out before I could stop myself. "Cut the crap. You want to go along? Why should I let *you* wander into a fire zone where I'll have to split my focus between worrying about what's in front of me *and* worry about you slipping a knife into my back?"

Even I couldn't quite believe I'd said it. Saul didn't move, but I felt his attention sharpen, and reminded myself that he was Were. If Perry moved on me, Saul might try to stop him, and however fast and dangerous a Were was, a hellbreed who could produce flame in the blue spectrum was not my idea of a good time.

And I needed Saul alive.

Amazingly, Perry laughed. But Belisa was suddenly examining me, her mouth slightly open, as if a new thought had occurred to her.

"There are more enjoyable things to do than slip a knife between your ribs, my dear Kiss." He saluted me with his glass, then downed the rest of the whiskey, rolling it around in his mouth and swallowing. "Now, just tell us where the icky little Sorrows hidey-hole is, and we'll finish this matter and turn our attention to other things." He reached down and gently, delicately smoothed Melisande Belisa's sleek dark hair. "Like what I should do to teach this viper some manners. We have a room at the Monde specifically reserved for—"

White-hot rage boiled up. I snapped.

I had the gun out, barely aware of drawing it. I was on my feet, my shins hitting the coffee table with a short sharp sound. Then I'd leapt on the coffee table, still forward, and ended up with my feet between Belisa's, the gun pressed to Perry's forehead.

Oh, Jesus Christ, Jill, you stupid little prat.

I didn't look down. "Your services are no longer necessary, Pericles," I informed him. Even, level, and with my unprotected belly less than three feet away from a Sorrow who probably wouldn't cry too much in her coffee if I ended up with a serious case of dead.

But she needs someone to take on Inez for her. That's why she bothered meeting me at the hospital, that's why she let Perry catch her, that's why she's still sitting here instead of trying to escape. Isn't it?

His eyes were so deeply, infinitely blue, indigo clouding the whites along traceries just like veins. His pale fingers tensed on the glass. "Put the gun down, Kismet."

You will not take a woman into that room at the Monde Nuit if I can prevent it. I have had enough of seeing women raped tonight.

That room at the Monde...I knew what it was used for.

I'd seen it used. I'd seen what happened afterward.

My thumb reached up, pulled the hammer back. The sound of the 9 mm cocking was very loud in the sudden hush that seemed to have descended on the warehouse. "Get. Out." I had to work to get the words out through the obstruction in my throat. "Of my house. Get. *Out.*"

"I am losing patience with you, Jillian. Or should I call you Judith? Didn't you prefer tha—"

Shock slammed through me. How did he know that? How *could* he know that?

I *squeezed.*

Saul yelled, a short sharp cat-coughing bark of surprise. Perry fell, dropped like a stone. Blood gouted, so much thick black blood, shooting a hellbreed in the head is messy.

No more. My hands shook and my breath came hard and harsh. *No more.*

No more of it. No more women raped, no more mindfucking, no more of it, *no goddamn more.* I could take no fucking more. And if it took killing Perry and slaughtering a houseful of Sorrows and an Elder God too, I would do it.

It was that motherfucking simple.

My hand dropped. The scar on my wrist began to burn, tearing in through my skin toward my bones. I looked down at Belisa, whose head was bowed. Her shoulders were shaking under the blue silk.

Don't worry, I wanted to say. *I fixed it. I stopped him. He won't hurt you now.*

The faint voice of rationality piped up. This was a *Sorrow,* the one who had killed my teacher. What the hell was I doing protecting her?

She's still a woman. And no woman deserves Perry, dammit. Or gang-rape by hellbreed. "Saul." My voice cracked, my throat denying itself a killing scream. "Go get the car warmed up."

"Jill—"

Goddammit, Saul, I'm not safe right now. I think I just did something stupid. "Do it."

He got up, I heard the couch squeak. Then he was gone. I heard the front door slam as I stepped back from the Sorrow who hunched in the chair, her hair falling forward over her face. The smell of rotting blood cooking in a gun barrel painted the air. My hands were shaking. *Point blank, you shot him point blank, hope that's enough. Pray that's enough.*

And under that, the other thought, repeating like a bad record. *No more. Not to another woman. No fucking more.*

"Belisa?" *I still sound like a stranger. What have I done?* "Melisande?"

Her shoulders were still shaking. And God help me, but my fingers tightened on the gun again, and it was all I could do not to shoot her too.

"Goddammit, get up. Let's go. We've got a world to save, you Chaldean bitch."

Then her face tipped up, her black eyes meeting mine, and I saw she was laughing. Tears rolled down her cheeks, and she smiled, a death's-head grin that told me she was having a hell of a good time. Her hand stabbed forward, the broken glass ampoule spewing something that smelled oddly sweet; my body sagged, not hitting the floor because of her slim iron arms around my waist. Her fingers were at my throat, I heard a snap as she tore the ruby away and tossed it, its sweet chime as it hit the floor. I choked on the poison and heard her laughter ring in the rafters. She laughed as if she had just heard the world's funniest joke.

Laughed, in fact, fit to die.

Blackness. I floated.

I'm dead. Any minute now I'll see Hell again. I'll sink into it, and they'll start on me, every hellbreed I've killed, everyone I've laid to rest. I'll start screaming, and it will never end, and I'll be back on the streetcorner with the wind on the back of my legs and that car coming toward me. I will. In a moment. When I finish being dead.

Something hard against my back. Cold hardness seeping into

my skin. My nerves were on fire with pain, creeping up my arms and legs. Any minute now I would wake up to find myself in Hell. There was no reason to fight it. I was dead.

Dead. Floating in a blackness that started to sting in all my fingers and toes, as if I was wrestling with a jellyfish.

Belisa. The traitorous bitch.

Did she kill me? Why? She wanted me for a diversion so she could take out this Inez bitch.

Didn't she?

A nagging little idea began growing in the back of my mind. I tried to push it away, to concentrate on being dead, but it wouldn't go away.

The file on you is red-flagged for a reason. She had given a picture-perfect imitation of being scared to death of Perry, and she probably had been. One false move, one note out of tune, and he might have killed her before he could bring her to me. I certainly wouldn't put it past him. But she'd had an ampoule of something. Poison, the Sorrows trademark. Poison in word, deed, and fact.

Belisa knew too much. This was, again, Mikhail's voice. *Far too much. How she know what the redhead bitch is planning? And here is thought, milaya, is there reason why you haven't seen zis redhead Sorrow yet? There's such a thing as wigs.*

But that made no sense, did it? Nothing about this made much sense.

Wake up, kitten. The tone of my conscience changed, mutated into a voice I knew as well as my own, deep and soft. Saul's voice, whispered in my ear. At least he'd been outside when Belisa made her move. *Time to wake up. Come on.*

But I was dead, and I was so *tired.* So goddamn tired of it all. Being a hunter is just one disgusting fight after another, and there were endlessly inventive ways people could be shot, stabbed, tortured, burned, hurt. Every hunter got tired of seeing it, even if we were luckier than the cops who only dealt with humans. A hunter had to remind himself—or herself—about *why* we did this. Why we put ourselves through this.

Well, why, cream puff? This time the voice wasn't Saul's or Mikhail's. It was another voice, one I knew very well, the voice of a man who had picked up a lonely shivering girl and made her feel worthwhile, made her feel *loved,* before he'd turned her out on the street and set her to earning her keep. *Why d'ya do it at all, then?*

I didn't want to hear Val; I'd *killed* him. I pushed that voice away with an effort so hard it felt physical, heard a shapeless sound. It sounded like someone was moaning, coming to, swimming up out of dark water. Metal clashed, and the fierce cold against my back and my heels ratcheted up another notch. It burned across my buttocks, my shoulders, digging into the back of my head and my neck. And the inside of my right wrist hurt, a sharp stabbing pain.

Oh, *shit.* Maybe I wasn't dead.

Val's voice wouldn't go away. *Why d'ya do it, babydoll? Huh? You don't do it to save the world or any fucking shit like that. You want to know why you put yourself through this?*

I pushed that voice away again. I knew why I did it. I didn't need to be reminded.

Why are you a hunter, kitten? Saul's voice, on the edge of breaking. We did fight, sometimes volcanically, and he had asked me once or twice *why* I seemed so determined to fling myself into the worst trouble I could find. There's no retirement plan for hunters—none of us live that long. There's also no Higher Authority, even though the Church trains a lot of us. If a hunter wants to quit he just *quits,* just disappears. You aren't a hunter because you're forced into it, or because you fill out an application and have to find a replacement.

No, a hunter *chooses* to put his body on the line. And each hunt is another conscious choice. Nobody would blame you if you stopped, backed out, laid down the sword, and walked away. As a matter of fact, that was the sanest option—part of finding an apprentice is doing everything possible to dissuade the candidate from even thinking about taking the training.

We all do zis for one reason, milaya. It is for to quiet ze screaming in our dreams. It is for to kill our own demons. And they call us heroes. Idiots. Mikhail, again. Why was I hearing voices? I could even smell him. Vodka metabolizing out through the skin, the smell of someone raised in a different climate, foreign darkness and the smell of his hair as he leaned over me to correct my form, the copper charms tied in his hair tinkling sweetly.

His voice dropped to a whisper in the very center of my head. *Now is time for ze waking up, milaya. Wake up.*

I didn't want to. I wanted only to drift. But the stinging in my fingers and toes sharpened, as if they were coming back to life.

As if I was coming back to life.

If you do not wake up, milaya, I will hit you.

I lunged into consciousness, fully aware and awake, because when Mikhail said that he never lied. Metal clashed as I tried to leap to my feet, springing up—and was grabbed mercilessly at wrists and ankles, my head hitting cold stone as I was yanked back. Stars slammed through my head, actual bright points of light.

Shit. Oh shit.

I was on my back on cold, hard stone that felt glassy, like obsidian. And I was chained, the cold cuffs closed around ankles and wrists. Stretched out like a virgin sacrifice.

Well, if that's what they wanted they certainly have the wrong girl. My forlorn little laugh half-choked its way out of my throat, I blinked, breathed in a long lungful of air so cold it burned, and looked around.

I pulled against the chains first. No give, and they were orichalc-tainted titanium, just the thing to hold down a hellbreed-strong hunter. Stronger than they had any right to be, and probably with staples driven deep into the granite of the floor and concrete underneath. I pulled all four chains until I was sure I couldn't just wriggle out. It wasn't likely, but sometimes even Sorrows made mistakes.

Not this Sorrow. A respectable foe, smart, accurate, canny, and unwilling to take chances. Just my luck. The chains were too tight for me to pop a shoulder out of its socket and wriggle around, too.

Dammit.

Vaulted ceiling, made of poured concrete, ribbed and beautiful, in perfect proportion. Hammered into the concrete were the Forms, the squiggles and sharp curves carved and filled with thick gold wire, glinting as they channeled etheric force. The place was humming, alive with sorcerous power.

By craning my head I could see the floor was granite blocks fitted precisely together, and was also full of wrist-thick gold lines twisting; the altar was inside a square, set inside a pentacle, set inside a triple circle that held the Nine Seals, each in its prescribed place. Between the pentacle's outer orbit and the beginning of the triple circle was another smaller altar, this one curved like a dolphin's back without the fin. Channels were carved into this concrete curve, deep fresh channels that were already dark and crusted.

The first sacrifices had already been performed.

Candles burned, their flames hissing in the dimness. Candles that smelled sickish-sweet. In the trade they are called perfect-tallow.

The layman would call them, with respectable horror, *made of human fat.*

"Christ," I whispered, and the sound bounced off the high vaulted roof. There were braziers, and heat simmered up from each of them. This little hole hadn't come cheap, especially with all the gold. She must have funneled an amazing amount of cash into it.

Perhaps the final indignity was that I was naked except for the leather cuff buckled securely over the scar—*under* the chain-cuff. My ruby was gone, and I could tell the silver ring Mikhail had given me was gone too. The silver charms in my hair, each one painstakingly braided in with red thread, were gone as well. There was no comforting weight of silver in my ears either.

Which made me feel even more naked.

Crap. Well, I'm still alive, aren't I? That's one. But the sinking sensation under my breastbone just wouldn't go away. Because if Belisa had drugged me, stripped me of my jewelry, and dragged me here, there was only one reason why.

The deep sharp blood-channels cut into the smooth glassy surface of the altar underneath me told me just what they had planned for me.

Saul. Did she hurt Saul? How did she get me here? I shut my eyes. *Don't panic, Jill. Don't you fucking dare panic.*

How could I not panic? Had she hurt Saul? *Had* she? Or had she just dragged me out of there, content to elude him?

The prayer rose under the surface of my mind. *Thou Who hast*

given me strength to fight evil, protect me. Keep me from harm.
Grant me strength in battle, honor in living, and a quick clean
death when my time comes—

"Fuck that," I whispered. I didn't want to die at all.

There had to be something I could do. Even if the preliminary
sacrifices had already been performed, I still had at least an hour.
Or at least, I hoped I did.

Time to think fast.

CHAPTER 25

The stone was cold and my head hurt. I kept my eyes closed and
my breathing steady, and the scar had turned hot. *Very* hot. As if
a blowtorch was held against it, the skin crisping and turning black,
burning down to bone but never quite getting there, *burning.*

Was Perry dead? Probably. I'd shot him in the head with silver-
coated ammo. If he wasn't dead he was very unhappy—and
unlikely to forgive me. He would probably peel the scar off me
himself, and overload my nervous system with sick wriggling
pleasure while he did it.

If he does that, Jillian, you'll be alive to feel it. Which will
mean you'll have escaped this. So don't worry about it right now.

The scar was *hot.* And when the first acrid scent of burning
found its way to my nostrils I was elated—but not so happy my
concentration slipped.

Fire, from a hellbreed mark. Part of the bargain, even if Perry
was mad at me.

He shouldn't have called me that. Shouldn't have threatened to
have a woman raped, even if it was a Sorrow.

The thought disturbed my concentration, but the heat didn't
slip. I heard a rustling, and swallowed hard, opening my eyes just
as the last shred of the tough battered leather charred. I couldn't
see it under the metal cuff that held my arm stretched at an awkward angle, just in the precise place that robbed me of any leverage. It was the same with my legs.

The Sorrows are good at trussing people up.

The soft sounds were velvet capes, brushing the floor. I heard another soft, chilling sound.

A long drugged moan, impossible to tell if the voice was male or female. The cold air brushed my skin, and I shivered.

The sudden wash of sensation from the scar was enough to make gooseflesh rise all over my body. I could, if I wanted to, look down and see if my nipples were hard.

A fine time to be naked and chained to an altar, Jill. With you the fun times never end. I drew in a long soft breath, watching as they came in two by two.

Two. Four. Six. Eight.

I was beginning to get a very bad feeling about this. I had assumed that Inez was a rogue Sorrow, but that was because Belisa had told me so. For there to be more than one Sorrow here was bad, bad news. Which one of the robed bitches was the one who had killed my teacher and maneuvered me so neatly?

Ten. Twelve; these two carrying between them a long pale shape that was a woman's body. The shapeless moan came again, it was from *her*. Drugged.

Oh, thank God, she won't feel a thing if I can't save her in time. Christ, how am I going to get out of this?

They were hooded and draped in black-blue velvet, but the thirteenth entered with her hood thrown back. A sleek shock of darkish hair glowed with bloody highlights in the candlelight, and she walked to one of the brass braziers—the one nearest the curved sacrificial altar—and tossed something in. Sizzling filled the air for a moment, then sweet smoke billowed out.

Ambergris. Amber. And clove.

The incense of evocation. My skin chilled again. I was going to go into shock.

Stop it, Jillian. Listen. Look. Plan.

What plan? I was trussed up tighter than a Christmas turkey. But the stink of charred leather told me I wasn't completely helpless.

Think, Jill. And open your goddamn eyes.

"It won't help, you know." Her voice was soft, accented with fluid French and wrapping its velvety ends around me; digging in, squeezing, looking for a way inside. She glided up to the altar on cat-soft feet, this blood-haired Sorrow.

I found myself looking at a strong-jawed, not unpleasant face; her eyes were black from lid to lid and the bruising of her aura was deep and severe. I caught a whiff of something else, too, a fume that shimmered out from her robe in waves of olfactory scarlet and gold.

She was far more than a Sorrows adept. That fume could only mean one thing.

I was looking at a Grand Mother of a House of Sorrows, one of the most efficient praying mantises the world has ever seen. Just one step below a Queen Mother, a brooding termite capable of hiving off Houses and *calling* potential suicides to her as Sorrows Neophyms.

In other words, I was in deep fucking shit.

My brain jittered like a rabbit; I inhaled sharply, and she smiled. Set just under her hairline, above and between her eyes, was her mark: the three circles, the black flame, and a colorless glitter that was the seal of a Grand Mother.

I cleared my throat. "Inez Germaine, I presume." My voice was harsh, cracked, and only human after the softness of hers. Like the cawing of a raven after a dulcet song.

Quit it, Jill. She's a fucking Sorrows mantis, she'll chew you up if you're not careful. I gave her my most winning smile. She was going to have to work harder than that to squeeze her way in through my mental defenses. I was toughened by so many exorcisms that I wasn't even sure I could let something in if I wanted to.

I didn't want to test that theory, though. Not at all.

She put one hand down, and a velvet sleeve brushed my belly as her fingers closed around my left breast. I made my face a mask, but she smiled, a very gentle smile that sat incongruously on her strong face. Her thumb moved a little. "Inez Germaine Ayasha, if you wish to be specific." She paused, examining me thoroughly; scalp to toenails. If I'd been embarrassed by nakedness, now would have been the time to show it. But dating a Were will give you a whole new definition of naked, and having a hell-breed kiss on your wrist will too.

But her hand let go of my breast, trailed down my ribs. I sucked in a shallow breath. *No.*

Her fingertips brushed my belly, passing over old ridged scars and the furrows of abdominal muscle from hard training. I was too stringy, really, not much room for big curves when you're fighting like hell all the time and having a hard time taking in enough protein to fuel that sort of muscle burn.

Sometimes I wondered if Saul would have liked me a little softer. A little more feminine.

The touch lightened as she brushed my pubic hair. *"Tranquille, enfante,"* she murmured. Calmly, lovingly. "I would not crack so fine a vessel."

Her fingers dipped, and my entire body closed. My eyes rolled up into my head, and I curled up into the quiet space inside my own head. That space was small, and dark, and smelled like a kid's closet stuffed with shoes and plush animals. Bad things could batter at the door, men could howl outside, but inside I was safe.

It was the space that I used to go to whenever Saul touched me. With Mikhail it had been heat and combat, but with Saul...it had been gentleness.

He had coaxed me out with infinite patience, one night at a time, holding me when I sobbed. Stroking my hair, reassuring me, easing me along. Until I could have my body belong to me again, and like anything that belonged to me it could be shared.

But not now. Now I didn't want to share. I went rigid, sweating, my jaw so tight my teeth ground and sang a thin song of agony, red and black explosions playing out behind my eyelids as she probed with first one finger, then another.

I made a low harsh sound. Metal clashed as I struggled, hit my head against the stone altar, and suddenly knew that if she kept going I would beat my skull against the stone until one of us broke.

And I didn't think it would be the altar.

She finally returned her black eyes to my face, sliding her fingers free and stroking my belly again with the flat of her palm. "You should have been born into a House, *cherie.*" Her tone was gentle, kind. "We would have known how to bring out the best in such a...delicate temperament as yours, without causing such regrettable side effects."

High praise, from a Sorrow. "Horseshit." *If you think I'm going to beg, bitch, think again.* "Nice trick, sending Belisa to play the Sorrow in distress. That brother bit almost got me."

"Melisande's brother was genuine. I picked both of them, *ma cherie.*" The smile widened. "So brave." Her fingers stroked, came back up to cup my breast, and I could feel that my nipple was indeed hard. Hard as a chunk of rock.

Goddammit. But six years of Perry's scar burning on my wrist and his fiddling with my internal thermostat was now paying off in prime. My heartrate stayed the same, though my breathing was a little harsher than I liked. I felt soul-bruised, savagely stretched, and just one thin hair away from raped.

If I belong to me, then I can share or not share, and I don't want to share with you, you bitch.

Besides, if she wanted to mindfuck me with just a paper file to work from, she was going to have to work for it. Perry was harder to deal with.

No he isn't, goddammit. Perry's interested in seeing you remain breathing so he can break you. This bitch is going to kill you anyway; she's calling you "dear" as if you're her Neophym. You're dead. Get something for your pains, Jill.

"The bodies were to draw me out and create taplines." I sounded steady. Steady enough for being chained naked to a rock. "Belisa was just to spice the mix, draw me in, keep me around. But why the wendigo?"

She laughed, a marvelously soft sound. I sucked in a deadly breath as her warm fingers continued to stroke my breast. "You think I'm going to make the mistake cartoon villains make and tell you my plans while you work on burning away that ridiculous leather bracelet?" She tweaked my nipple with her fingertips, I kept a straight face. Heard more soft moans.

Oh, God. They're starting the second sequence.

"I see the lamb's voice disturbs you more than mine does, hunter. The wendigo was a useful tool, and its habits kept you looking in the wrong place. But your first encounter with it was carefully scripted."

"You were on the roof with a bow." I sounded bored. But I wanted to look past her to the curving altar. Controlled myself. "Killing your own employees."

"They were men, my darling. Useful, expendable, but over-whelmingly useless—"

"I'm female, and just as expendable." Interrupting a Grand Mother is a good way to piss her off; they were the rulers of their Houses. Big egos and big brains, not to mention enough sorcerous ability to power a blimp. Her eyes were so *black,* from lid to lid, infinite holes in her pleasant face. Deep. So deep.

The scar on my arm was growing hotter by the moment, as if Perry had breathed on it, turning it to lava. I could almost feel acidic saliva trickling down my wrist, too. The pain scored up my arm, jolted me out of the sticky web of her eyes.

"You, *ma belle,* are not expendable. You are my greatest achievement. The pregnant victims were selected for fetal tissue, yes, but that tissue has already been harvested and sold to the highest bidder. They paid for the vault over your head."

Well, that's a fucking relief. Thanks for giving me that wonderful piece of news. I was beginning to get a very bad feeling about this. "You're doing an evocation," I said flatly. "And you want me to be the host for your psychotic little fucknut of a—"

The blow came out of nowhere, smashing across my cheek, my head rang and I saw stars again. Then her fingers were back on my breast, caressing, kneading my flesh. I felt a warm trickle of blood trace down my chin and rolled my head back to look at her. "Damaging the merchandise, bitch." My voice was husky.

"You are merely required to be whole, not undamaged. Think of it. One of the Old Ones, the *summa* of negation, inside a body—a female body, a body capable of creation and destruction, a body strengthened with a hellbreed mark and possessing a soul gifted with murder and mayhem in the finest degree? You are a fit vessel, and once you are filled there will be enough blood, enough *destruction,* to remake this world as it once was. The Elder Gods will live through you, hunter." Her smile was calm, beautiful, and so sane it was crazed, and I began to *really* get a bad feeling about this.

I heard the last breathless sigh of the drugged woman near the door. *Oh, God. Please, God. No.* Then a terribly final *cessation,* the act of slitting the throat down to the vertebrae. And the gurgle of life and blood leaving the body.

The golden marks on the ceiling writhed, a fresh humming charge flooding them. "Try again, you bitch," I whispered. "I'm a hunter. Your Chaldean filth won't stick to me."

"A hunter who has just killed a dozen men." Inez Germaine's smile broadened. She stroked my breast once more, lovingly, and I jagged in a sharp breath. The gentle touch reminded me of Saul, something I couldn't afford. "You slaughtered them like pigs, *bebe.* You heard the screams for mercy and you disregarded them. You were judge, jury, and executioner, you took your God's place."

It wasn't like that. "I did not."

"You killed them, didn't you?"

"They were your accessories. Willing, in Jonte's case. Unwitting in others. But they were—"

"We're all aware of your feelings about pimps, Judith."

That *name* again, the name of a dead girl. The air left me as if I'd been punched. Oh, Belisa had gotten her money's worth when she'd rifled Mikhail's private papers.

Stop it, the voice of reason said, desperately. *Stop it. Of course she's dug that up. You aren't her anymore. That girl died and you came back from Hell. That's not you.*

But my voice was ragged. "Cogs in a wheel, bitch. One steps out, the next steps in. Try another sticky-finger attempt to get inside my head. You've failed."

"Pas necessaire." The smile that broke over her face now was a marvel of sincere serenity. I heard more velvet shushing and another slow, disoriented moan. Another victim. The second sequence.

The touch on my breast gentled. "The ritual will proceed, *cherie belle.* And when you look in the face of the Old One who will inhabit you, we will see how much your protests avail you." A final gentle tweaking of my nipple and she was gone, shushing back in her long velvet robe. The sound of the candles hissed, and there was another soft gurgle as blood spilled, steaming, into the air. The copper reek thickened.

I looked up at the ceiling. Golden marks revolved in their stately dance, thick gold wire scoring new channels through the concrete, twisting and healing their former runnels without a sigh. And as soon as Inez Germaine cleared the square around the altar, the golden border of the square flushed with etheric force and began to move too.

By the end of the second sequence of sacrifices the pentacle would be revolving as well. Then the third sequence, but that one would be the harvested death Inez was carrying behind her black eyes, ready to release with a Word. A Word in Chaldean, which would charge the Nine Seals and the triple circle, containing the psychic force and enforcing the collective will of the Sorrows hive on the space inside.

After that, the final sequence, which would rip open a hole in the fabric of reality. And I was right at ground zero. A tasty little snack.

Her voice was soft and utterly merciless, dropping into my head like a bean into a furrow. Ready to germinate, the seed of doubt. *You slaughtered them like pigs, bebe. You heard screams for mercy and you disregarded them. You were judge, jury, and executioner, you took your God's place.*

And what had I told Saul? Told him to go to the barrio, because I didn't want him to see what I was capable of. What I could do, once I decided it was *necessary.*

My breath hissed in my throat. Hopeless. It was fucking hopeless. Nothing left to do but pray.

Cover me with Thy shield, and with my sword may Thy righteousness be brought to earth, to keep Thy children safe. Let me be the defense of the weak and the protector of the innocent—

I balked, sheer stubbornness rising up under the words, shunting the prayer aside. It would work when I was gearing up to face Perry, but not now. Not now. Oh God, not now, I didn't want to die like this, stretched out like bad fantasy-novel art on a moldy old twenty-five-cent paperback.

I was going to die.

Fury rose in me. *Shit on that, Jillian Kismet. Shit all* over *that.*

You're a hunter, there's work to do and your city to save. Think up a way to get out of this one, you stupid whore. You didn't even tell Saul where her little bolthole is. How could you be so stupid? Assuming, of course, that Belisa left Saul alive.

Another breath, this one deeper and smoother.

You're chained naked to an altar and they're killing people over there, and there's a Sorrows Grand Mother who is crazy as a bed-bug with a thumb in your door. And all hell's about to break loose.

It wasn't working. Panic set in. I thrashed, once, twice, the chains jangled.

I heard it again, the gurgle of another life wasted. Women, probably, the reserve Inez had kept here in this place, a Sorrows House hidden so wonderfully well in my own city. Hidden so well I hadn't had a clue—but I'd been busy since spring, hadn't I? Dreadfully busy. A spike in violence and crime that was a clear sign of Sorrows moving in, with twenty-twenty hindsight I could solve *every* fucking problem, couldn't I?

They were killing people. People from my city. *My* people.

But why should you care? You killed eleven of them last night. Not twelve, like that bitch said—unless you count Perry and he's not a pimp, he's a hellbreed. Just one step up from a pimp in my personal pantheon of evil, but still.

The voice was soft, seductive, stroking me. *Why should you care, Jill? Why should you care how many they kill?*

"Mine," I whispered, and closed out the sound of the candles burning and the sudden hiss as someone threw a gout of incense into another brazier. "My city. *My* city."

Santa Luz was *my* city; and whoever was in it—especially anyone a Sorrow would want to sacrifice—was under my protection. *I* kept the law in my city, goddammit, and if this jumped-up praying mantis thought she was going to kill pregnant hookers and Mob bosses in my town and without my say-so, she had another think coming.

But doesn't that make you just like them, Jill? Doesn't it? You decide who lives, who dies? Judge, jury, executioner?

The scar on my wrist turned excruciatingly hot. Pain rolled up my arm, a great golden glassy spike of pain. The scream burst from me, raw, wrecked, and agonized, like the dying scream of the wendigo. I'd killed it too, hadn't I? No matter that Saul had held the spear, I had caused its death.

Who was I to decide that?

I am the law, goddammit! I protect them, the innocents. I am the sword of righteousness.

But I'd murdered, hadn't I? Eleven pimps. Eleven *men,* never mind that they'd given me the information I needed. Never mind that the world was probably better off without them.

Cogs in a wheel, bitch. The world is not better off without them. More will rise to take their place.

And with every pimp I killed I bought some hooker on a corner a little breathing room. Not much, not ever enough—but some.

It was worth it.

I sagged against the altar's cold unforgiving glass at my back. The chains clashed. The golden marks on the ceiling were twisting madly now, running with the black crackling lightning of Chaldean sorcery.

Another gurgle. Guilt slammed through me, a hot steamy nauseous guilt. I had fallen right into the trap, and people were dying for it. Innocent people.

I tilted my head over, tucking my chin, and *looked.*

Black lightning ate the body whole once the blood had been spilled. Where there had been a pale human form, veined in black fire, now there was nothing; the etheric discharge of death, visible through my blue eye, was trapped and funneled, the soul tearing itself free and disappearing, the etheric strings holding it to the body snapped. Cleanly severed. The wendigo's violence and reek had covered up the signs of theft on the other bodies. How many of them? How much death was the blood-haired bitch carrying?

No wonder she's fucking mad, I thought, and it was like a slap of freezing water.

They dragged another drugged naked form in, and ice slammed through me. Pure, clean, marvelous ice, the little *click* as I disconnected again, taking off, rising. Becoming that other person, the Jill Kismet who could go from house to house like the Angel of Death, sparing and striking according to her will.

The girl had long sandy hair, and was drugged out of her mind. She didn't struggle, but suddenly it wasn't her I was seeing. It was another girl, with long brown hair and a severely bruised face, whose ankles were thin and bruised too, who flinched when I yelled.

Oh, dear God. I knew it wasn't Cecilia; she was with Avery. Or at least, so I hoped.

But goddammit, the light wasn't good, and when I looked at the pale body they bent back over the curved altar all I could see was Cecilia's face. The face of a tired young hooker who had once been a bright needy little girl, who had escaped from Hell between four walls of a home and found a different hell out in the cold world, in backseats and hotel rooms and up against walls and wherever a dark corner could be found and sometimes, not even then.

And under Cecilia's face, I saw another face. A face of a girl with dark hair and brown eyes, a very intelligent but terribly crippled child who had grown up too fast.

She's dead, Jill. The only one left alive is you. She went into Hell and you came back.

I struggled, but silently. Pulled. *Pulled.*

I pulled against the chains, my breath coming out in a long *huuuuuungh!* of effort, veins popping out and muscles protesting. The scar turned white-hot, agony bolting up my arm, and I heard a slight groan of overstressed metal.

I was still looking when they tipped her head back, the vulnerable curve of her throat glaring-white in the smoky dimness. More incense had been thrown on the braziers. The air crackled with humming etheric force, the thick golden wires whispering now as they remade themselves, livid lurid golden fire writhing and undulating through granite floor and concrete vault.

They use curved knives, the Sorrows. Curved black obsidian blades, with hammered gold in the blood groove.

I screamed as the knife descended, my cry taking on physical shape and smashing through the incense smoke, my back arching as if in the throes of orgasm. I convulsed with every iota of strength, mental, physical, *everything,* straining, tearing at the prison of metal around my wrists. My left shoulder popped, tendons savagely stretched, almost dislocating itself, and I heard a scream of metal stretching and stone bubbling hot. Heat blasted up, reflecting from the altar's surface and careering across the cold vault in a gunpowder flash.

Inez Germaine Ayasha laughed, and she pronounced the Word in Chaldean that set loose the third sequence and tore the three circles into screaming life.

Then everything broke loose.

I think I passed out. At least momentarily. But that moment contained a lifetime.

Darkness enfolded me, smothered me, pressed down deep upon me. A bulging pressed obscenely against the fabric of the physical world. Spacetime curving, the black curved mirror *slanting,* a pregnant hollow of cancerous pus as something, sensing its time was near, strained to be let out. Strained to rip through etheric and physical reality, strained to unzip the barrier of the world and step through. There had been much work to prepare for this, much toil and suffering, and there was a body ripe for the taking. A matrix of probabilities meshed, caught, turned... and *tipped.*

It dropped like a baby's head into the waiting hollow of the pelvis, descending preparatory to labor. The mother draws a deep breath, relieved for the moment, unconscious that around the corner lies the straining of birth.

And then, it *pushed.*

Screaming, torn past rationality, an animal shriek as if my guts were ripping out on glassy sharp claws. Screaming as if the veil had been torn away and I'd seen the naked face of existence leering down at me.

Maybe I had.

The howl was an animal's, yet it shaped *words,* a language that had not been spoken since the War between the Chaldean gods and the Imdárak, the Lords of the Trees. The Imdárak were gone, their victory in banishing the Chaldeans from this plane Pyrrhic in the extreme, something only whispered faintly of between hunters, passed down in the dead of night as part of a hunter's inheritance. Yet I screamed aloud in that language, tearing my vocal cords until the screaming trailed off in a long rasping gurgle as if my throat was cut.

It bore down on me. An immense weight, seeking to get *in,* to crush me and fill me, boiling wine trying to shatter the cup it was poured into. Or lava, forcing its way through a brittle stony crust. Forcing its way into me, to possess me.

Something in me resisted. A hard piece of tinfoil between the teeth, a small germ of irritation, a pinprick to a creature this mighty. Every exorcism I'd ever done—had it felt like this to the victims? Locks smashed, drawers pulled out, mental furniture reduced to matchsticks, personality shredded, *breaking,* the essence that was me stretching in a thin film over something too horrible to be described, like the shape of a monster under a blanket that is so instantly *wrong* you know it cannot be human.

Is nothing even close to human.

Then, pain. Fresh pain, a slice straight through the middle of me. A fist curled in my hair and *yanked,* metal snapping at my wrists and ankles, and I spilled off the altar in a boneless heap, my head hitting granite with skullcracking force. The gurgle died in my throat, giving way to a whimper.

Like a beaten dog, whining in the back of its throat.

"No," Perry's almost-familiar voice said, and the scar on my wrist suddenly turned blowtorch-hot again under the metal of the broken cuffs. And every pain in the world was suddenly a thin imitation of this agony, excruciating because it was physical and yet a relief because it wasn't the soul-destroying violation of my innermost self.

"She is *mine,*" the voice continued, calmly but with a terrible weight of anger. "Signed, sealed, and witnessed, Elder. She is not for you."

The world stopped on its axis, though I could now hear other sounds. Crimson sparks danced behind my eyes, and I heard clashing, screams, and the coughing roar of a Were in battle-fury. *Saul?* My dazed brain staggered.

The *thing* spoke again, a long string of those horrible, horrible alien sounds. I cowered, chains clashing as I clapped my numb hands over my bleeding ears and huddled against something solid. Something absurdly comforting, twin hardnesses poking into my ribs, as if I was at the foot of a statue. I choked on blood and bile, drew in a shuddering breath, and the scar turned to liquid on my arm. Pleasant oiled honey, sliding under my skin. Soothing.

OhGodplease let it be over, please let it be over. I sobbed without restraint, huddling down and making myself as small as I could.

"Let's ask her, shall we?" Perry's voice turned cheerful, razor-edged with sheer goodwill, and I flinched. I knew that tone. I knew that voice, though I had never heard it unveiled in its full aching power before. "I think she likes me better. But then, I'm handsomer."

More screams, more sounds of bloodshed, the steady roar of an enraged Were doubling, trebling. How many were there? *Saul? Is that you? Oh, God. God help me.*

It was my first coherent thought, and I welcomed it, even as I clung to someone's feet. My eyes cleared, bit by bit. The air was full of ambergris, clove, copal, and a horrid, foul, rotting stench; a smell so alien the brain shuddered each time it drifted across the nasal receptors. *Oh, God. God, thank you. Thank you.*

It spoke again, that sound tearing at the world. With it, quiet seemed to envelop us, the choking quiet of a nuclear winter.

A laugh like a flaming steel sword to the heart. "How very crass, Elder. Wherever you have been, you have not learned manners. No wonder they banished you. Did you not hear me the first time? I said *no.* This one is *mine.* See?"

The scar bloomed hotly again, and I moaned against his feet. Spilled over onto my back, my body not obeying me but I had to look, had to see. He was hellbreed, and he was *dangerous,* but he was better than that . . . that *thing.*

Perry stood, his hands in his gray trouser pockets, immaculate as always. There was an angry red healing mark on his forehead, perfectly placed, and his blue eyes blazed with holocaust flame over the indigo spreading through the whites like a cobra's hood. I was looking from beneath, from the floor, so he seemed taller than he should have, and thinner, and his face was full of a wasted light like the dying of the sun on a knife-cold winter day. His pale hair had become a halo, and a breeze touched my face, choking with the smell of dusty feathers and spoiled, rotten honey. I heard buzzing—wasps? angry hornets? flies?—and couldn't tell where it came from. He stood straight and slim as a sword, and his face was no longer bland but terribly, sharply beautiful.

Beautiful in the same way a mushroom cloud or the sterile white light of reaction is beautiful. A devouring beauty.

Above the altar, darkness pulsed. Only it wasn't darkness. It was like the wendigo, shapes running like ink on wet paper. Shapes that were so completely divorced from the geometry of our normal space that I tried to throw up again, seeing them twist and try to leap free.

If that carnivorous thing broke through...

It spoke very softly, the words still dimpling and scoring the fabric of reality. But it was fading, drawing away like the cry of a distant train. It was no less menacing and alien.

Perry shrugged. It was a marvel of Gallic fluidity, that shrug, expressing resignation and uncaring disinterest. "Perhaps. But you are *there,* and I am *here,* and I own *this.*" His foot moved slightly, nudging my hip now since I had turned onto my back. The scar boiled with spiked honey, pleasure creeping up my arm and spilling down my chest. Soothing, calming. I heard my own shapeless, helpless moan again.

Just like one of the drugged victims they had slit open.

Oh, God. God help me.

The thing replied with a thick burping chuckle, like poisonous mud boiling. I twitched against the sound, the raw places inside my head stinging under another salted lash.

"Empty threats bore me, Elder. Go contemplate cold eternity elsewhere. It is *our* time now."

Reality closed together like a camera lens shutter, and I convulsed as it tried to drag me, but Perry's foot came down on the skein of my hair, nailing me in place with a jolt. A soon as the telescoping hole closed I shuddered again, strength spilling back into my bones.

But not enough. Nowhere near enough.

Perry glanced over his shoulder, gauging the situation. Then he squatted, his left hand dangling, his right reaching down to thread through my hair. There was no silver for him to avoid. He made a fist, pulling my head up. My throat curved helpless, and the cold floor scorched my hip, my back, my buttocks, my heels. "Look at this," he said softly. "My poor darling."

His blue eyes burned into my brain, even as the scar writhed with curdled pleasure. "Here." A jolt smashed through me, as if I was in cardiac arrest and had defib applied. I cried out, weakly, the cuffs on my ankles and wrists chiming and clattering against the floor.

Just like a newborn screaming.

"My poor, poor Kiss," he whispered. "Look at this mess."

I was getting very tired of him saying that. I couldn't help myself. "Saul," I whispered in reply.

Perry's face didn't change, but I flinched nonetheless. "Oh, stop it." He sounded annoyed. "You'll tire of him soon enough. Can you stand?"

I'll sure as hell give it a try. "No . . . dancing," I managed, in a thick choked voice sounding not at all like myself. "For a . . . while."

He actually laughed, a chilling, happy little chuckle. "Brave to the last. Stand, I'll help."

The growling of Weres had subsided. Now I heard only moans and the soft low thunder of still-angry shapeshifters; the battle was evidently won. He slid his arm behind my shoulders and picked me up as if I weighed less than nothing. I'm tall for a girl, and muscular, but he handled me as if I was made of straw.

Or spun glass.

"One moment." His fingers curled around the metal of the cuff over my right wrist, sank in and twisted. He tore the metal as if it was cardboard, freeing my hand. Then he closed his warm fingers over my wrist, the scar pulsing in his palm. My head lolled, resting against his shoulder. "There. Isn't that better?" The fabric of his suit was expensive, rich, soothing against my cheek, and I felt muscle flicker underneath as he stroked my hair. Warmth spilled through me, strength like wine flooding through my abused flesh. Unhealthy strength, like the jitter of a drug smashing through my system—but I'd take it.

Perry sighed. "Just relax."

Delicious, wonderful safety spilled down my skin. "Saul," I whispered against Perry's suit.

"The cat is in fine form, little one. No worries. We have averted a little unpleasantness. I think we shall renegotiate your visits to me, no? Come. Walk. You can walk."

"Ch-chains—" I was trying to tell him to take the other cuffs off.

"Let them be a reminder," he replied, inexorably. "You should have listened to me, Kiss. You've racked up a heavy debt."

"Fucking...romantic." Humor would help, I decided. My brain shivered, jagging between the unreality of the Chaldean obscenity straining to break through into our world and the sanity of a normal day.

Normal for a hunter, maybe.

"I've never been accused of romanticism before." Perry's fingers dug into my upper arm as he steadied me. Just short of bruising.

Broken bleeding husks in velvet robes lay scattered, the fluid golden wires of the Nine Seals and the three circles pale and still, useless. There was a blackened path—Perry's passage through the circles and the pentagram, breaking into the center, slashing through the careful work Inez had done.

All that work, all that life, wasted. I slumped against Perry, metal anklets clinking and the broken bits of chain chiming sweetly against the floor.

There were Weres in the shadows, a whole contingent of them. Among them I saw four lionesses from the Norte Luz pride, and two 'pards, both shamans, from the Anferi confederation, and then there was Saul and two more werecougars—and, oddly enough, Theron from Micky's, his dark eyes luminous orange in the candlelit dimness. Some of the candles had been knocked over, and someone was snuffing the braziers. Of course, the smell would make the Weres nervous. I also saw a werefalcon, his feathery hair ruffling as he checked the borders of the room, passing his hands over the walls, checking for hidden doors.

Where did they come from? I didn't want them in on this, Sorrows are dangerous for Weres.

Saul approached, rage crackling in the air around him. He didn't pause, shucking his hiplength leather coat as he walked. He had recently *shifted,* I could see the glow swirling through his aura. The deepest thrumming snarl was coming from him. Muscle slid under his T-shirt; he was armed to the teeth and had a dark streak of warpaint on each high, beautiful cheekbone.

He took me from Perry with a single scowl, his lip lifting. But he didn't fully bare his teeth, Perry didn't protest, and in short order Saul had the metal cuff off my left wrist and the coat closed around me. The clean musky smell of him rose, and warmth flooded me. I felt like I could stand up, but I leaned into him. The coat swallowed me whole, sleeves hanging far below my finger-tips and the hem coming down to my knees. "Christ," he whispered into my hair. Then he swore, vilely, in deep guttural 'cougar. "Are you all right? *Are* you?"

No, Saul. I'm very far from all right. But there was work to be done. "How many bodies? Theron? How many?"

"Ten dead, hunter." Theron sounded grim. "The other two are unhappy, about to be worse."

"Show. *Show* me." I coughed, rackingly, my throat afire. I wanted to sink into Saul's arms, shut my eyes, and scream. I wanted to black out, flinched away from the screaming well of darkness threatening to swallow me whole. "There's another one. *Find* her. There are probably prisoners, too. Search this hole, but for God's sake don't do it alone. Go in pairs. How many do we have on our side?"

"Twenty or thirty, Boss. There's already a group scouring for survivors. Let us work." Theron waved one long-clawed hand in an elegant brushoff.

Saul lifted a silver hipflask to my lips. Brandy burned my throat and exploded in my empty stomach, I retched, managed to swipe at my lips with the back of one hand while he picked me up and hugged me with ribcracking force. "Jillian," he whispered into my hair, his breath a warm spot against my skull. The butt of a gun poked into my ribs, a blessed sensation. I felt a little better now.

A little. Not much. The scream boiled under my skin, I pushed it down. Trembling weakness settled into my bones. *Alive. I'm alive.* "Show me." *I have to see. I have to.*

Perry laughed again, a bitter little sound. "Have no fear, little one. These vipers are most dangerous in darkness. *Fiat lux,* and they are vulnerable as maggots." He stood a little distance away, his hands back in his pockets and his shoulders slumped. "Belisa is not here. But the head viper is."

Saul half-carried me to the crumpled bodies; two of the Weres were methodically checking them. Wet crunches came as the necks were snapped, Weres believe in being thorough. They were searching for marks once the necks were snapped; all of them were Sorrows, probably Adepts.

Dear God. It had been close. Very close.

I could have died. Or worse, definitely worse. That was definitely worse.

"Casualties?" My voice was husky, a ruin, I'd broken it screaming on the altar. The inside of my head echoed with the filthy squealing of Chaldean; I pushed it away with an effort that left me shaking again. *Please God, be kind. Tell me nobody died rescuing my stupid ass from this.*

One of the 'pard shamans looked over her shoulder. "Not on our side. They were all looking the other way, didn't even have a guard." She was a lean, rangy female, gold earplugs dangling as her head moved; her sleek short spotted hair was chopped and feathery. Like most Were shamans, she kept her arms bare, cuffs closed around her smoothly muscled biceps. The tattoo on her left shoulder slid under the skin, its inked lines running almost like the gold wire had in the ceiling and floor.

Nausea rose sour under my breastbone. I wasn't sure I was still alive, after all. Saul was warm and solid and real, but everything else wavered, dreamlike. The world was retreating into the fuzziness of shock, dangerous if I passed out now. Holding on to consciousness with teeth and toenails; I had to make *sure*.

Two Sorrows left alive. One of them was Inez Germaine, her red-dark mane draggled and slicked with blood, chewing at the leather gag as Theron finished tying her legs together. He snarled at her, lifting his lip, and I saw the other 'pard shaman—this one a male, his spotted hair pulled back in two high crests—reach down to cup the other Sorrow's face in his hands, tenderly.

"Go in peace," he said, huskily, and made a sharp movement. The crack echoed through the room.

My gorge rose hotly again. More killing. Christ.

Theron reached for Inez's head.

"Stop." This was from Perry. "Give her a gun, Saul."

"You're out of your fucking—"

"He's not talking about Inez." The weary huskiness in my voice cut through Saul's automatic protest. My head lolled, I gathered my shattered strength. Heard movement, stealthy cat feet padding; they were searching this place, however big it was. *Be careful. There could be little traps set in here, it is a Sorrows House. Right under the Santa Luz garbage dump. Perfect, absolutely perfect. No wonder everything reeked so bad. How did they find me?* "He means give *me* a gun, and I agree." I stopped to cough, a deep racking sound I wasn't sure I liked.

I am really going to feel this in a little while. But for right now, I was in shock, standing just outside myself, watching as a hollow-cheeked, almost-naked woman with bruised wrists and long tangled dark hair missing its usual silver stood next to Saul, swaying. He steadied me before reaching down and unholstering a Sig Sauer.

"This do okay?" he asked, and tears rose in my throat.

I denied them. *Oh, Saul. Thank God for you.* If I started to cry I was going to laugh, and if I started to laugh I was going to scream, and if I started screaming now I wouldn't stop until I passed out or battered myself senseless. I nodded, reached up with my right hand. Closed my fingers around the heavy gun.

The scar throbbed, and cold air kissed my exposed skin. My legs shook, Perry's borrowed strength not covering up the deep well of exhaustion underneath. With the gun weighing down my hand, I eased Saul's arm aside and made my way, unsteady as a newborn colt, to the spill of black velvet and draggled slicked-maroon hair.

Her black eyes stared up into mine. Her wrists were working against each other, trying to loosen the Were-tied bonds. Good fucking luck—when a Were tied something up it *stayed* tied.

At least, most of the time.

I shook. Tremors spilled through me, each wave followed by another feverish-warm tide of false strength from the puckered, prickling mark on my wrist. I looked down at her, the broken bits of chain from the anklets making sweet low sounds against the floor.

Lifted the gun. Sighted. Right between those fucking black eyes, just below where the colorless gem glittered at her hairline.

You slaughtered them like pigs, bebe. You heard the screams for mercy and you disregarded them. You were judge, jury, and executioner, you took your God's place.

Her soft, merciless voice chattered inside my head. So close to being outplayed. I wondered who had tracked me here, Saul or Perry, and I wondered just how deep into debt with Perry I'd gotten.

The thought of paying off that debt made me shiver.

Maybe she mistook it for weakness, or indecision. Her eyes lit up, sparks dancing in their infinite black depths, and her mouth curved up despite the distortion of the cruel gag. The Weres learned a long time ago not to take chances with a Sorrow.

So did I. I should have killed Belisa on sight. But I hadn't.

"Judge, jury, executioner," I said, harshly. The rest of the world fell away, leaving us enclosed in a bubble of silence. "Just like you, you fucking Sorrows bitch."

Her eyes widened.

"There's just one difference, Inez." My mouth was dry, I wanted another swallow of that brandy. I wanted to start screaming.

Most of all, though, I wanted to stay in that clear cold place where nothing mattered but the job at hand, the killing that had to be done. Everything there was so fucking simple. It was mercy that fucked things up; it was kindness and compassion that tangled everything together.

The smile spread razor-cold over my face, and watched as her struggles to free her hands intensified. She began to move on the floor, velvet whispering and a thin choked sound bubbling up from behind the gag.

I took a deep breath, air so cold it burned going down. "I'm a hunter. I *am* the fucking law in this town, bitch. Sentence pronounced."

I squeezed.

The muzzle flashed and her body jerked. Her head exploded— Saul had loaded with the hollowpoints, and as tough as Sorrows become, they are still human at the bottom. Not like Perry.

Did that make them bigger monsters, or smaller?

I lowered the gun slightly. Squeezed the trigger again. Again.

He must have had a full clip. I kept squeezing, firing into her body again and again and again as it twisted and jerked. Then there were only dry clicks, two, three, four, five of them before Saul twisted the gun out of my weakening hand, took me in his arms, and dragged me out of there. I wanted to stay, to find Melisande and kill her with my bare hands, I raged in my cracked and unlovely voice that I was going to do just that. I did, until the shakes got so bad my teeth chattered and cut the words into bits.

Then I screamed, again and again, in Saul's arms until he carried me outside, where the reek of the garbage piled around was overwhelming but at least there was sunlight, thin and sad through high clouds. But it was Perry who clapped a hand over my mouth, finally, and hissed a word in my ear. It was Helletöng, a long sliding subvocal whisper, and it sent me into a sleep that was, again, like death.

And I went gratefully.

CHAPTER 26

'd been wrong. It had been Perry who had tracked me, through the scar, disregarding the wound in his head. It had been Perry who suggested spreading the word among the Weres about the trouble I was in. They had stopped by Micky's and made Theron their first contact.

The Weres had come because I was a hunter, and because I was Saul's lover—but, more important, because they respected me. It was nice, I supposed, to know I was regarded so highly among them. They're notoriously hard to impress.

I spent the first two days in a deathly daze, dealing with one thing after another in between passing out and having Saul threaten to tie me down in bed if I didn't stop and take some time to heal. Belisa had escaped, her trail led out of the House underground in the very heart of the Santa Luz garbage dump and then...vanished.

There were no surviving sacrificial victims. They recovered eight bodies, Belisa had stopped long enough on her way out to slit a few throats herself. They were all vanished prostitutes, not a one over twenty, and they were folded into the murder statistics for the year. Five of them had family, but I wasn't able to attend any of the funerals. I wanted to, but I just...I had my hands full with other fallout.

Demolition boys from the Santa Luz bomb squad brought out some type of explosive, wired the underground complex while the Weres guarded them, and blew it. There was a rumbling sound, a crater, and the slight depression in the ground was buried under tons of refuse.

Montaigne finished another economy-sized tub of Tums. Juan Rujillo filled in the requisite forms to report a Major Paranormal Incident as well as requisition hazard pay for me from the FBI's backstairs funding since the mercenaries had come from out of state, sent it off in its courier pouch, and told me to get some fucking rest. Montaigne seconded that emotion, and thanked me with profanity-laced gruffness for sending him two carloads of naked sobbing women who understood very well they were not supposed to talk to the press about their ordeal. The women had been turned over to counselors and social services; in a few years they might be okay. Maybe.

Two of them had already committed suicide. But not Hope; I asked specifically after her. "Tough cookie," Montaigne had sighed. "Keeps asking difficult questions about you."

"She'll get over it," I said, rubbing the new leather cuff Saul had made to go over the scar.

Montaigne paused, leaning back in his chair. Saul was just outside the door, and the sound of phones ringing and people moving was so comforting I almost closed my eyes right there. Swayed on my feet.

Monty cleared his throat. "About those pimps."

I braced myself. *I won't apologize, Monty. What are you going to do? Fire me? Bring me up on murder charges?*

His mouth twisted up on one side. It was a facsimile of a smile, more like a grimace of pain. "Turf wars. Wish they'd kill each other more often." Monty dropped his eyes to his paper-strewn desk.

Bile rose in my throat. *Judge, jury, executioner. You took God's place.*

It was true. But like most truths, it had an edge that would cut—and an edge that didn't cut me. I found out, with relief, which one was pointed at me. "Monty—"

"Shut the fuck up, Jill."

"I was only going to say thank you."

Monty told me to get the hell out of his office, and I complied meekly.

I missed Carp and Rosie's visit, being sound asleep for once. They came, Rosie left a bouquet of flowers, Carp left a bottle of Jack Daniels. Nice of them.

Father Gui called, offered to come by and pray with me. Saul told him in no uncertain terms where to stick it and hung up. I guess he was still upset. At least it saved me the trouble of hanging up on the priest. I wasn't ready to forgive him yet.

And I was still weighing whether or not it would be worth it to go down and tear apart that fucking church to find what else he had hidden from me.

The Weres, of course, said nothing. Except Theron, who came by the warehouse and squatted down by the couch, which was the only place I could stand to sleep. I kept staring at the chair Belisa had sat in. My eyes would close as I heard Saul moving around the warehouse, cleaning up, cooking exquisite little meals I tried to force myself to eat.

I usually woke up screaming. Nightmares are usual after something like this; better a nightmare than waking up to the real fucking thing. You go long enough with post-traumatic stress from nightside fun and games and you learn that very quickly.

Theron examined me for a long time, his dark eyes moving over my face. He was here on business, not socially, so he didn't try any of his usual little games with Saul. Instead, he simply *looked* at me. Saul had tucked a wool blanket around me, pulled it up to my chin, and spent some time braiding more charms into my hair. My throat felt naked without the ruby, and Mikhail's ring was probably gone.

The Sorrows don't like holy objects. Anything consecrated with love is anathema to them. The ruby, a soul-link between me and my teacher, would be doubly so.

"You weren't planning on calling in Were backup," Theron finally said, his hands dangling loosely as he crouched with peculiar ease. "Right?"

I blinked. Shrugged under the blanket. "Sorrows." My voice was husky. "Dangerous."

He waved that away with one sharp, economical movement. "You need to take some time off and clear your fucking head out. That was a stupid fucking decision, hunter. We're allied with your kind for a *reason*."

"I didn't know what it was." I sounded exhausted even to myself. And pained.

"When Saul came 'round asking questions about wendigo, that was the time we started taking notice. We could have trapped it more effectively if you'd coordinated with us." He sighed. Eyed me speculatively before getting to the point. "Mikhail would have kicked your ass for this Lone Ranger shit."

Mikhail. I'd failed him; his killer had outplayed me and gotten away. Again.

Theron shifted a little, as if preparing to stand upright. "We put the word on the wind, Jill. Wherever that bitch goes, sooner or later she's going to run across a Were. She's under the Hunt."

"But—" I started to protest. Sorrows were *dangerous,* and Weres coming across them often died.

"But fucking nothing. We'll deliver her head one of these days, or she'll come back to fuck with you again and we'll joint her like a pig. Quit the Lone Ranger shit, Jill. It's detrimental to the safety of the citizens of Santa Luz." His smile broadened. "Besides, your ass is a lot cuter than Mikhail's. I'd hate to have to chat up a whole new hunter."

"I heard that," came Saul's voice from the kitchen. "Get out of here, Theron. Go chase some chickens."

"You're a fine one to talk, Dustcircle. I'm going." Theron rose to his feet with the fluid grace of a Were. He leaned down and touched my forehead, smoothing my hair back. His voice dropped. "Peace in your dreaming, hunter. We'll bring you a head one of these days."

Then he was gone, and I shut my eyes, curling into the couch, and cried. Saul left the kitchen and half picked me up, held me, we ended up on the floor under the blanket while I sobbed and he murmured soothing nonsense in my ear, until I fell asleep again and woke up in my own bed with him beside me, trying to calm me down as I screamed from the dream of being chained to the cold glassy stone and feeling the thing from *outside* try to force its way into me.

But Saul was there. And his warmth was enough to keep that thing at bay.

I shrugged into my new leather trenchcoat, my fingers running over the handle of the new bullwhip. Replacing gear gets expensive, but the FBI's hazard pay was a nice chunk.

"You sure you want to do this?" Saul's mouth pulled down bitterly. Afternoon sun slanted through the windows, bars of thick gold. Spring was right around the corner, or at least I hoped so.

I held up a hand, watched it shake just a little. Concentrated, and it kept steady, my fingers easing. The scar was warm under the new leather cuff. "I've got to tell him I'm going on vacation. Five minutes."

"You shot him in the *head*." Saul folded his arms. His dark eyes rested on me, then slid down to the floor. "He wasn't happy, kitten. He said some pretty nasty things."

"He broke through a Sorrows circle and faced down a Chaldean god to—"

"Because he thinks he owns you, kitten. Because he's hellbreed. He'd rather kill you himself than have another demon touch you. Why don't we just go?" He'd already loaded the suitcases in the Impala, and I wasn't due to get a new pager for another three weeks.

Because I have to finish this. I checked the action of each gun before I holstered it; the knives were new too. "I wish we could have found my gear," I muttered. "Goddammit."

Then another fit of trembling hit, and Saul was suddenly there, his arms around me. He hunched down a little so I could bury my face in the hollow of his throat and breathe him in, deep. All the way down to the bottom of my lungs.

But still, I smelled ambergris. And a breath of foul reek that seemed to stay on my skin no matter how raw I scrubbed myself.

Andy's apprentice was staying up above Micky's, in the apartment kept for visiting hunters. Anja's apprentice, nearly a hunter himself, was due in on the evening train; Galina would meet him and get him settled. The Weres would come out of the barrio and run regular patrols. But it had been quiet since the demolition of the Sorrows House.

Thank God.

Saul stroked my back, slid his hands under the coat, and pulled my T-shirt up. His palms met my skin, he flattened his hands and pulled me closer, closer. I could barely breathe, but that's the way I wanted it.

The waves of trembling went down, silver charms shifting and chiming against each other in my hair. Each wave was a little less intense than the last. He murmured soothingly, little nonsense-words, purring in 'cougar until they stopped. Even then he held me.

I swallowed the lump in my throat. Breathed him in. Musk, male, leather, the best smell in the world. Safe. I whispered his name, over and over again.

The fit passed. He rubbed his chin against the top of my head, his heartbeat thundering against mine. "Sorry," I finally mumbled into his chest. "Sorry, Christ I'm sorry—"

"Mmmh. What the hell for?" He kissed my hair. "I like holding you."

My eyes were squeezed shut, dampness slicking my cheeks. "Saul?"

"Jill."

"I did something wrong. I...I'm not a nice person." That wasn't what I wanted to say.

I didn't want you to see what I was capable of. I didn't want you to know. What am I going to do? I can't stand to lose you. Oh, God, I can't stand to lose you.

I wanted to tell him. I wanted to tell him about the little click inside my head, how I could move outside myself and calmly, coldly, commit murder. How I had slaughtered eleven men who hadn't had a chance, because they were human and I'm a hunter.

And not only that, I'd ruthlessly used the advantage of my bargain with Perry not only to get information but also to...to what? I could have gotten the information and left them alive. Crippled, maybe, but alive.

I could have. But I didn't. I evened the score, *my* score.

I played God.

"No," he agreed. "You're not."

Silence. His hands tightened, pulling me even closer.

"But." He nuzzled my hair. "You're a *good* person, Jillian. Not nice, but good."

"I killed them." The words were dust in my mouth.

"Yeah." Neutral agreement.

"I killed them because of someone else, what someone else did to me." Another shudder slammed through my abused body. He steadied me. "Don't leave me," I whispered, so softly I wasn't sure he could hear, even with a Were's acuity.

He sighed, a heavy movement that pushed against my own ribs. "Not going anywhere, kitten. Count on it."

Relief smashed into my heart, a pain so sharp and sudden I might have been having a cardiac arrest. "Saul—"

"I want you to meet my people," he said, slowly and clearly, as if talking to an idiot. "The sooner we get this over with, the sooner we can go and get formal. Hitched. Under the Moon. Full ceremony, with a feast afterward. You thinking of backing out?"

"No. *No.*" I shook my head, rubbing my chin against his shirt. "Good God, no. I just...I'm not a nice person, Saul. I'm *not.*"

"Hell, kitten, I knew that when I met you. It's part of your charm. You're a *hunter.* Being nice would be a weakness. Right?"

He sounded so sure.

Is mercy a weakness, Saul? Doesn't killing like that make me worse than what I hunt?

"Right?" he prodded, moving slightly to bump my hips with his.

I wish I was as sure as you sound, catkin. I swallowed the stone in my throat. "Right. You bet."

"So let's get this visit to that goddamn hole out of the way so we can get out of town. Okay?"

I firmed my jaw, set my shoulders, and gently slid away from him. He let me. I touched the handle of the bullwhip. "Okay."

But I sounded more like a scared teenager than a hunter. He didn't mention it, just picked up the duffel with spare weapons and ammo in it and motioned me toward the door. "Let's go, then."

Oh, Saul. Thank God for you.

CHAPTER 27

The Monde was just getting ready for the night. Outside, winter sunlight was slanting thinly toward the end of the day, cold breath of wind coming not from the mountains but off the river, filled with a chemical tang.

There was a new bouncer at the door, daytime muscle, but he just nodded and let me by. Food for thought—or maybe, even as drawn and haggard as I was, I looked like nobody to mess with.

Riverson, his gray-filmed eyes widening, was at the bar. The charms in my hair shifted and rang as he reached behind him for the vodka bottle. The air turned hot and tense, the few hellbreed having crawled out of their holes before dusk suddenly stilling, several Traders clustered around a table near the dance floor looking up, disturbed by this new feral current.

I passed the bar for once and headed for the back, for the iron door behind its purple cord. I heard Riverson call my name.

"Kismet! *Kismet!*"

Sounded like he was trying to warn me. Nice of him, really, considering we hated each other.

I stepped behind the purple velvet and reached for the doorknob. It was unlocked, as usual. I twisted it, pushed it open, and went up the stairs, stopping halfway to lean against the banister and try to calm my racing heart.

What are you doing, Jill?

Only what I have to, I replied. *Only what I must.*

And Mikhail's voice, barely a whisper. *Head high, guns out, milaya. Meet what chases you.*

I pushed the creaking wooden door at the top open and the

room hove into sight: white carpet, pristine, no sign of spilled brandy or blood. The glimmer of glass and chrome that was the bar. The other two doors, neither of which I ever wanted to see what lay behind. The bed, perfectly made, as always.

The two chairs, facing each other.

Perry stood straight and slim in front of the bank of television monitors, his hands clasped loosely in front of him. His back was to me, and I could see he'd gotten a haircut. A nice, short, textured cut, the latest thing for boys this season. Nothing but the best.

He wore, for once, jeans and a pale ash-gray sweater instead of a suit. A pair of dark leather engineer boots. Blue light from the monitors touched his hair, picked out paler highlights in the blond.

I closed the door behind me. Waited.

"It is not safe for you to be here," he said finally, very softly. Static blurred across the monitors, they cleared up. On one satellite feed, Court TV was just getting underway with a serial killer's trial. On another, explosions ripped through a Jerusalem restaurant in slow motion. There were more explosions on the third, some Eastern European country purging again, riots in the streets.

I took a deep breath. "Three things."

He waited. The trembling started, I leaned against the door. *Stop it, Jill. Just stop it. You planned what you were going to say. Do it quick.* The scar pulsed under the new cuff, sweating.

Push him off balance, Jill. "First of all, thank you. For saving my life."

He didn't move. His shoulders were absolutely straight. More static fuzzed across the monitors, moving in an oddly coherent pattern; a cold breeze touched my cheek. Spoiled honey and dusty feathers. The air behind him shimmered like pavement on a hot day; the shimmer swept back and forth, combing the air.

Double or nothing, Jill. Do a mindfuck of your own. Make your teachers proud. "Second of all...I owe you an apology, Pericles. I should have listened to you about Belisa. I should have let you kill her. It...what I did to you wasn't right. I'm sorry. For shooting you in the head and for not listening to you. You didn't deserve that."

The static drained away. The silence in the room was now shocked, as if I had walked into a high-class party and started

yelling obscenities. A murmur slid through the air, circling; the
shimmer behind him died down.

His shoulders were still straight, but some essential quality of
murderous rigidity had drained away. I waited.

"Surprising." His tone was flat. "But not entirely unexpected."

Holy fucking shit. It worked. I peeled myself away from the
door, cautioning myself not to get too cocky. Next came the trick
of the week, if I was good enough to perform it. "What do I owe
you?"

His laugh made the glasses rattle uneasily at the bar, the hanging material over the bed billowed as if caught in a breeze. Glass
bottles of liquor groaned, chattering against their shelves. "More
than you can comfortably repay, Kiss. More than you can *ever*
repay. I have angered an Elder for your sake, though I was well
within my rights. You are *mine*."

I don't think so, Perry. "The deal was that you would help me
in my cases in return for a slice of my time. That hasn't changed."

Another fluid, almost Gallic shrug. "If it pleases you to think
so, by all means, continue."

Now for the sting. I braced myself and tossed my dice. "There's
just one thing." My right hand rested on the butt of a gun, a new
Glock 9 mm. I wouldn't need to draw it. At least, I hoped not. I
was in no condition to deal with him if he got nasty.

But I'd certainly give it a go if this went south.

"What?" This was a snarl, more glass rattling. The windows
looking down over the empty dance floor flexed in their frames.

"How much did she take *you* for? Belisa, I mean. How deep in
their venture did you have your tentacles?"

Silence.

A warm bath of satisfaction started at my toes and worked its
way up. *I guessed right. You fucking hellbreed bastard. God damn
you.*

It had become clear to me in a blinding flash while I stood
shaking in the shower trying to scrub the smell of the Nameless
off my skin yet again. Just before I'd shot him in the head, Perry
had spoken that name, the name of my dead self. A name he could
have had no fucking way of knowing unless he'd chatted cozily
with someone who had taken a peek at Mikhail's private papers.

Someone like Melisande Belisa, who had put the information in the Sorrows file for Inez to read too and taunt me with.

I'd suspected, of course. A Trader known for slaving showing up in the Monde when I'd blown all his other boltholes, Perry trailing me before he should have known I was in serious danger, his warning that his protection might only extend so far—which by itself would have meant nothing, since he liked to pretend he knew everything going on in the city. But with everything else, it added up to a pretty picture.

A *damning* picture. Not to mention him finding her with a minimum of fuss, and her only showing up with a black eye and tender ribs.

Just to make it look good.

I continued, surer of myself now. My arms and legs stopped shaking. "She crossed you, didn't she. They moved into town and I was kept busy chasing my tail on other cases, but you didn't know Inez's big plan was to have *me* in the starring role when her lord and master came calling. That's also why you intervened when it came to Elizondo, he was a bit player but you couldn't have him talking to me." I swallowed dryly. "How much, Perry? How much did you lose on the deal?"

Another shrug. "Money. Only money." His tone told me he was lying. He'd lost something else too.

And I had a pretty good idea of what that *something else* was. "Belisa played me like a fiddle. And she played you, too."

"The cat was supposed to be with you," he informed me, flatly. "When the wendigo was allowed out. You were not the beast's target."

That's why they were in a holding pattern. Only I sent Saul away; they couldn't have known I would do that. My skin went cold, flushed hot. "But nobody expected us to be searching for a witness down on Broadway." We were supposed to be out there canvassing the street scene for clues about missing hookers, not meeting with a witness.

Oh, Christ. And once Saul was gone, was I supposed to turn to Perry for solace? Fat fucking chance.

Belisa had probably told him to wait, to bide his time and she'd take care of Saul. She had maybe even set the wendigo free the second and third time—not guessing that the creature, balked and hurt when it came for Saul the first time and Cecilia the second, would fixate on me. Hard to get much coherence out of a thing built only for appetite and destruction.

Though the silver chain around its neck had been broken. Maybe the wendigo had broken free on its own. I didn't know. I would probably *never* know.

So Perry had been waiting, not just watching over me but waiting for the assassination of my lover to step in and take his cut of the whole rotten deal. And once I had bloodied my hands cleaning up the expendable bits of their operation, Belisa had to have guessed I wouldn't take kindly to Perry moving on me. That I would, to some extent, *identify* Perry with the men I'd just killed.

And with the man I'd killed before I ever became a hunter.

She had only to wait until the ticking bomb inside my head went off. Belisa had applied the pressure neatly, and if Perry hadn't been so all-fired eager to use his newfound psychological leverage on me himself I might have been a little less likely to shoot him in the head.

It was so neat, so perfect, that I began to laugh. I leaned against the door to his little chamber of horrors and chuckled. I damn near *guffawed*.

No hellbreed likes to be laughed at. But Perry suffered it, static crawling over the TV screens, while I fought for breath, tears running down my cheeks.

"You poor bastard," I finally wheezed, hanging onto the door, wiping at my cheeks with the back of my left hand. "You poor silly bastard."

He twitched, and I jerked the gun up out of the holster. His hand clapped around mine, shoving it back in; he leaned into me. The door creaked, Perry pressed his body against mine, and I could feel he was shaking.

And he had a hard-on. A quite respectable one, as such things went. Shoved right up against me.

Well, at least now we know he's generally built like a human. Hellbreed usually are, but reserve judgment, Jill, he could have something else in there entirely. Like his tongue.

The scar went white-hot. Desire spilled hot through me, my

legs turning weak; his breath was hot on my lips. It smelled of dry
hot desert winds and spoiled boiling honey. At least it wasn't the
clotted reek of the Nameless.

*The devil I know, at least. Be careful, Jill. Oh, God, be
careful—Saul's right outside.*

"Do not," he breathed against my skin, "make the mistake of
thinking you can treat me like I'm *human*. You made a bargain
with me."

He was strong, wiry-strong. I went limp, not even trying to
fight, staring unblinking into his blue eyes. They were human,
maybe a little *too* human, except for the hellbreed sheen to them
and the spreading indigo stain. And the far points of distant light
in the very center of his pupils. A remote, shimmering spark, of
no color I could have identified.

The static twisting behind him came up to twin high points,
combing the air.

My throat wouldn't let me speak, so I whispered. "You broke
the bargain when you sold me out."

"Then I will make you a new one. I will leave the cat alive, and
you may play with him all you wish. But you will give me your
time as always, Kiss."

The pinpricks in his pupils revolved, swelled. I stared through
them, the scar thundering on my wrist, pulsing in time to my
heartbeat. Heat curled through me, down low.

Whore, I heard in the furthest-back reaches of my memory,
from the dead time before I'd been a hunter. *You whore. Spread
your legs for anyone, won't you.*

Not anymore, the hunter's voice of steel replied. I found my
physical voice, a raw, cranky whisper. "No deal, Perry."

Then I brought my knee up, swift and sharp. He avoided the
blow, but I shoved him while he shifted his weight and he let himself be toppled over. He sprawled on the plush carpet, and the gun
left the holster in one smooth oiled movement. Slender, silver-
coated bullets, and his head would explode just like Inez's. And I
wouldn't just count on one shot to do it, either. Not now. I would
fill him full of silverjacket lead and when he was down I'd hack
off his head with one of the knives I carried. Then, just to be sure,

I'd smash a few bottles of liquor and set his carcass ablaze; and with enough etheric force spilling through the scar I could burn this whole place down.

That is, if the scar was still a conduit for a hellbreed's power after he was dead.

He leaned back against the carpet on his elbows, looking up at me, one eyebrow slightly raised. "Fun and games, Kiss? Go ahead. Pull the trigger. Show me how far you've come."

The gun trembled. *Judge, jury, executioner. Playing God.*

Downstairs there was a clatter, and a loud swearing. Riverson. The sound brushed my ears, not as acute as they would be if I'd stripped the cuff off. Still, I heard it, and the red haze over my vision cleared. My heart pounded in my ears.

I reached over with my left hand, unsnapped the cuff. Slid it off, and fresh strength flowed through my veins. My skin turned exquisitely sensitive, brushed with the chill air and my clothes, hot and confining. The leather crumpled in my hot sweating palm, creaking slightly.

Perry took in a small avid sip of air, tensing.

My right hand tightened. The hammer rose, clicked into the up position. I stared into those blue, scorching, mad, inhuman hellbreed eyes and temptation dried my mouth, made my hand shake. My pulse roared in my ears. The low grumbling sound of Helletöng rattled through the building, the hellbreed on the first floor conversing.

Mikhail's voice rose again in my memory, swirling and trembling. It was a good memory, of his gruff voice in English and my own lighter tone repeating each line of the prayer.

Cover me with Thy shield, and with my sword may Thy righteousness be brought to earth, to keep Thy children safe. Let me be the defense of the weak and the protector of the innocent, the righter of wrongs and the giver of charity. In Thy name and with Thy blessing, I go forth to cleanse the night.

I stuffed the scrap of leather in my pocket. "I'm going on vacation, Perry. When I come back, I'm not visiting. When I need you, I'll call. And if you 'arrange' for anything to happen to Saul, I'll put a bullet through my own fucking head and spoil all your pretty plans for me. So you'd better take *real* good care where you drop your quiet words."

His face froze. I could almost feel the air pressure shift. "Sooner or later you will come to me." He said it quietly, as I groped behind me for the doorknob with my sweating, suddenly clumsy left hand.

I felt the smile sink into my face, my lips pulling back from my teeth. "Hold your breath until I call, hellbreed." My fingers closed around its slick roundness. My right hand quivered, but I managed to ease the hammer down with my thumb. The big muscles on the front of my thighs were shaking too.

"You can't escape it." His voice rose as I backed out, my foot seeking behind me for the first step, finding it. Lowering me down. I backed up another two steps, swung the door closed. "Come back and kill me or walk away now, it's all the same." His shout rattled the door as I pushed it closed. The click of the latch catching seemed very loud. "*I will have you, hunter! I will have you!*"

"Not today," I muttered, and made it down the stairs without having to stop. It helped to be going down.

I pushed the iron door open, stepped out. Slammed it behind me. Leaned against it for a moment, studying the room.

Riverson stared at me. The hellbreed, all frozen, stared at me. One of the night bouncers, leaning against the bar for a quick drink before going on duty, stared at me.

All eyes on you, Jilly.

I walked across the Monde Nuit with my head high, the heels of my third-best steel-toed boots clicking against the floor. The boots would need hard use before they were as soft and comfy as my favorite pair. I was going to have to figure out a better way to get blood out of boot leather.

"Kiss. *Kismet.*" It was Riverson, out from behind the bar. Nobody made a move to help him as he stumbled for me, his hands out. As if he was truly blind, and not more capable of finding his way around—at least in here—than anyone else.

I didn't stop, didn't slow down. But he reached me anyway, and grabbed my coat sleeve. "Kismet."

"Fuck off." I didn't have breath or energy to waste on him. I had to get out of here.

He grabbed my hand, shoved something into it. A box, a small cardboard box like they have for jewelry. "Goddamn you." His fingers bit into my sleeve. "Take it and go, you fucking bitch. Take it and go if you know what's good for you. Don't ever fucking come back here."

Oh, God, I can kill you now if you push me. Don't push me. "Fuck *off*, Riverson."

"These are yours," he insisted. "Fucking take them, or he'll destroy them. And for the love of God, *don't come back.*"

He let go of my sleeve, and I made myself keep walking. My fingers crumpled the edges of the box, I felt the harshness of some kind of ribbon. What kind of present would Riverson give *me*?

These are yours. Take them or he'll destroy them.

That was a laugh. How much more could Perry take or destroy? *Nothing but what you let him, Jill. It's that goddamn simple.*

I was past the bar and four steps away from the door when I heard shattering glass and a screech of inhuman rage from above. The air turned hot and tight, but I didn't pause, and nobody moved on me.

Outside, I stepped past the day bouncer. The parking lot was filling up, and the sun was sinking. The sky was fantastic, crimson and gold, indigo moving in from the east. Night's dawning, ready to spread over the vault of heaven.

I stopped, looked down at the box. It was wrapped with a piece of silvery ribbon that slid off because I had crushed it. But I felt a familiar tingle in my fingers, and tore the top of the box off.

There, sitting on a cushion of white padding, was a silver glimmer. Mikhail's ring. And tangled around it, the supple silver necklace and the chunk of carved ruby, glowing and pulsing with its own inner light.

The gem that Mikhail had held as he pulled me out of Hell, and the ring he had given me when he accepted me as an apprentice. Both shining with their own inner light here, at the edge of the brackish pond of hellbreed energy.

My eyes filled with tears. I fitted the ring on my left third finger, clutched the necklace, and dropped the box. Looked up.

My orange Impala was parked in the fire lane, like the good girl she was. The engine was running, and Saul had lit a Charvil. I made it to the passenger's side on unsteady legs and dropped into my seat with a sigh. Slammed the door. Locked it.

Saul said nothing.

I rubbed at the top of my right wrist. There was a paler patch of flesh where the cuff had protected and softened the skin, a brace-let of weakness. The marks from the Sorrows' chains had healed over.

The ruby glowed up at me. My fingers fumbled with the clasp of the necklace, the ruby settled right in the hollow of my throat. Home again, home again, Jill Kismet.

Pulled out of Hell.

Who was holding the line this time?

Jesus. Jesus Christ.

If Perry had planned to give them to me, why did Riverson have them? Had he filched them from his master? I always stopped at the bar first; did Perry think it would soften my mood to have the blind man present me with my own jewelry?

Take them or he'll destroy them.

Saul's profile was even, serene. He watched the door of the Monde, the Charvil dangling from his left-hand fingers, his other hand on the wheel.

I found my voice. The ruby warmed against my skin, settling into its familiar tingling readiness. "Ready to go, baby?"

He tossed the cigarette, touched the wheel with both hands, his fingertips gentle as if he was stroking my back. "Born ready, kit-ten. You?"

"Get us the fuck out of town, catkin." I swallowed roughly, closed my eyes. Felt Saul shift into first. "Let's not stop for a few hundred miles."

"You got it." The Impala slid forward, he cut the wheel, and as we pulled out of the Monde's wide broad lot, he slammed on the gas and left a respectable streak of smoking rubber. I slumped in the passenger seat, and didn't open my eyes until we hit the freeway.

Book 3

Redemption Alley

To L.I., Because I promised.

Si vis pacem, para bellum.
—Unknown

Bonis quod bene fit haud perit.
—Plautus

CHAPTER 1

Right before dawn a hush falls over Santa Luz. The things that live and prey in the night are either searching for a burrow to spend the day in, or looking for one last little snack. *The closer to dawn, the harder the fight,* hunters say. Predators get desperate as the sun, that great enemy of all darkness, walks closer to the rim of dawn.

Which explains why I was flat on my back, again, with hell-breed-strong fingers cutting off my air and my head ringing like someone had set off dynamite inside it. Sparks spat from silver charms tied in my hair, blessed moon-metal reacting to something inimical. The Trader hissed as he squeezed, fingers sinking into my throat and the flat shine of the dusted lying over his eyes as they narrowed, a forked tongue flickering past the broken yel-lowed stubs of his teeth.

Apparently dental work wasn't part of the contract he'd made with whatever hellbreed had given him supernatural strength and the ability to set shit on fire at a thousand paces.

I brought my knee up, hard.

The hellbreed this particular Trader had bargained with hadn't given him an athletic cup, either. The bony part of my knee sank into his crotch, meeting precious little resistance, so hard some-thing popped.

It didn't sound like much fun.

The Trader's eyes rolled up and he immediately let go of my trachea. I promptly added injury to insult by clocking him on the side of the head with a knifehilt. I didn't slip the knife between his ribs because I wanted to bring him in for questioning.

What can I say? Maybe I was in a good mood.

Besides, I had other worries. For one, the burning warehouse.

Smoke roiled thick in the choking air, and the rushing crackle of flames almost drowned out the screams coming from the girl handcuffed to a support post. She was wasting both good energy and usable air by screaming, probably almost out of her mind with fear. Bits of burning building plummeted to the concrete floor. I gained my feet with a convulsive lurch, eyes streaming, and clapped the silver-plated cuffs on the Trader's skinny wrists. He was on the scrawny end of junkie-thin, moaning and writhing as I wrenched his hands away from his genitals and behind his back.

I would have told him he was under arrest, but I didn't have the breath. I scooped up the handle of my bullwhip and vaulted a stack of wooden boxes, their sides beginning to steam and smoke under the lash of heat. My steel-reinforced bootheels clattered and I skidded to a stop, giving her a once-over while my fingers stowed the whip.

Mousy brown hair, check. Big blue eyes, check. Mole high up on her right cheek, check.

We have a confirmed sighting. Thank God. Now get her out of here.

"Regan Smith." I coughed, getting a good lungful of smoke. My back burned with pain and something flaming hit the floor less than a yard away. "Your mom sent me to find you."

She didn't hear me. She was too busy screaming.

I grabbed at the handcuffs as she tried to scramble away, fetching up hard against the post. She even tried to kick me. *Good girl. Bet you gave that asshole a run for his money.* I curled my fingers around the cuffs on either side and gave a quick short yank.

The scar on my right wrist ran with prickling heat, pumping strength into my hand. The cuffs burst, and the girl immediately tried to bolt. She was hysterical and wiry-strong, choking, screaming whenever she could get enough air in. The roar of the fire drowned out any reassurance I might have given her, and my long leather trenchcoat was beginning to smoke. I was carrying plenty of ammo to make things interesting in here if it got hot enough.

Not to mention the fact that the girl was only human. She would roast alive before I got *really* uncomfortable.

Move it, Jill. I'd promised her mother I'd bring her back, if it was at all possible.

Promises like that are hell on hunters.

I snapped a glance over my shoulder at the Trader lying cuffed on the floor. He appeared to be passed out, but they're tricky fuckers. You don't negotiate a successful bargain with a hellbreed without being slippery. Of course, since I'd caught him, you could argue that his bargain hadn't been *that* successful.

More burning crap fell down, splashing on the concrete and scattering. A lick of flame ran along an oily runnel in the floor, and the girl made things interesting by almost twisting free.

Dammit. I'm trying to help you! But she was almost insane with fear, fighting as if I was the enemy.

It probably messes your world up when you see a woman in a long black leather coat beat the shit out of a Trader, using a bullwhip, three clips of ammo, and the inhuman speed of the damned. Silver charms tied in my long dark hair spat and crackled with blue sparks, hot blood slicked several parts of me, and I'm sure I was wearing my mad face.

I hefted the girl over my shoulder like a sack of potatoes and spent a few precious seconds glancing again at the motionless Trader. Burning bits of wood landed on him, his clothes smoking, but I thought I saw a glimmer of eyes.

She beat at my back with her fists. I sprinted down the long central aisle of the warehouse, hell-lit with garish flame. Fire twisted and roared, stealing air and replacing it with toxic smoke. Something exploded, a hurricane edge of heat mouthing my back as I got a good head of speed going, aiming for a gap in the burning wall.

This might get a little tricky.

Rush of flame, a crackling liquid sound, covering up her breathless barking—she had nothing left in her to scream with, poor girl, especially not with my shoulder in her stomach—and my own rising cry, a sound of female effort that flattened the streaming flames away with its force. The scar—my souvenir from Santa Luz's biggest hellbreed—ran with sick wet delight as I pulled force through it, my aura flaming into the visible, a star of spiky plasma light.

Feet slapping the floor, bootheels striking sparks, back burning—I'd wrenched something when I'd brought my knee up. *Probably still feel better than he does. Hurry up, she can't take much more of—*

I hit the hole in the wall going almost full speed, my cry ratcheting up into a breathless squeal because I'd run out of air too, darkness flowering over my vision and starved muscles crying out for oxygen. Smoke billowed and I hoped I'd applied enough kinetic energy to throw us both clear of the fire.

Physics is a bitch.

The application of force made the landing much harder. I don't wear leather pants because they make my ass look cute. It's because when I land hard, something snapping in my right leg and the rest of my right side taking the brunt of the blow, trying to shield the girl from impact, most of *my* skin would get erased if I wasn't wearing thick dead cow.

As it was, I only broke a few bones as we slid, muscles straining against the instinct to roll over on her to shed momentum. I managed just to skid on my right side. Spikes of rusty pain drove through each break, right leg cramping, ribs howling.

Concrete. Cold. The hissing roar of the fire as it devoured all the oxygen it could reach. The girl was still feebly trying to struggle free.

It was a clear, cold night, the kind you only get out in the desert. The stars would be bonfires of brilliant ice if not for the glare of Santa Luz's streetlamps and the other, lesser light of the burning warehouse. I lay for a few moments, coughing, eyes streaming, while my leg crunched with pain and the scar hummed with sick delight, a chill touching my spine as the bone set itself with swift jerks. My eyes rolled up in my head and I dimly heard the girl sobbing as she stopped trying to get *away.* She'd be lucky to get out of this needing a few years of therapy and some smoke-inhalation treatment.

Sirens pierced the night, far away but drawing closer. *Here comes the cavalry. Thank God.*

Unfortunately, thanking God wouldn't do much good. *I* was the responsible one here. If that Trader was still alive and the scene started swarming with vulnerable, only-human emergency personnel...

Get up, Jill. Get up now.

My weary body obeyed. I made it to my feet, wincing as my right tibia and my humerus both crackled, the bones swiftly restructuring themselves and all the pain of healing compressed into a few seconds rather than weeks. My hand flicked, I had both guns unholstered and ready before the warehouse belched a torrent of red-hot air and the Trader barreled through the hole in the wall, flesh cracking-black and his eyes shining flatly, the sick-sweet smell of seared human pork adding to the perfume of hellbreed contamination.

Traders are scary-quick, not as fast as hellbreed but fast enough. I tracked him, bullets spattering the sidewalk as my right arm jolted under the strain of recoil going all the way up to my shoulders, broken bone pulling my aim off.

My teacher Mikhail insisted I be able to shoot left-handed, too. I caught the Trader with four rounds in the chest and dropped the guns as he reached the top arc of his leap, his scream fueled with the rage of the damned.

I'm sure the fact that half his meat was cooked didn't help his mood.

My hands closed around knifehilts. Knife fighting is my forte, it's close and dirty, which isn't fun when it comes to hellbreed or Traders. You don't want to get too close. But I've always had an edge in pure speed, being female and little. And *nasty,* once Mikhail trained the flinching out of me.

The scar helps too. The hard knot of corruption on the soft inside of my wrist ran with heavy prickling iron as I moved faster than a human being had any right to, meeting the Trader with a bonesnapping crunch.

The idiot wasn't thinking. If he had been, he might have done something other than a stupid kamikaze stunt, throwing himself at a hunter who was armed and ready. As smart and slippery as Traders are, they never think they're going to be held to account.

The knife went in with little resistance, silver laid along the flat part of the blade hissing as it parted flesh tainted by a hellbreed's touch.

The Trader screamed, a high gurgling note of panic. My wrist turned, twisting the blade as the force of his hit threw us both, my right leg threatening to buckle under the momentum. I stamped my left heel, the transfer of force striking sparks between metal-reinforced bootheel and aggregate stones in the concrete.

My other hand came up full of knife, blurred forward like a striking snake as the blade buried itself in his chest, and I pushed him *down,* pinning him as the shine flared in his eyes and roasted stink-sweet filled my mouth and nose.

I wrenched the first knife free and cut his throat. Blood steamed, arterial spray bubbling and frothing as the flat light drained from his eyes. I didn't want to kill him. I wanted to question him and find out what hellbreed he'd made a bargain with.

But you can't have everything. Besides, I could still hear the girl sobbing, the supsucking sound of a child in a nightmare that doesn't go away when she opens her eyes. The thought of what he must have done to her—and what he'd probably *planned* on doing, based on his other victims—drove my hand just as surely as the instinct of combat.

The body began to stink, sphincters loosened by death. I'd almost decapitated him. *Better safe than sorry.* I let out a long shuddering breath, my smoke-roughened lungs protesting with a series of deep hacking coughs. Helltaint drifted up from the corpse, the body contorting in odd ways as contagion spilled through its dying tissues, sucking the life from it. It was an eerie St. Vitus's dance, limbs twisting and jerking as they withered.

If Traders could see what happens after one of them bites it, maybe they'd think twice about making deals with hellbreed.

Or maybe not. *Details, details, Jill. Get moving.*

I turned on my steelshod heel. The knives slipped into their sheaths, and I found my guns, reloaded and holstered them, barely noticing the habitual movements. The warehouse was burning merrily and the girl lay crumpled on the pavement, barely getting in enough breath to sob. She looked pretty bad, and would be terrifically bruised.

But she was alive. The broken bracelets of handcuffs jingled as she tried to scrabble away from my approach. I squatted, ignoring the flare of pain in my right calf, the bone finishing up its healing now that I'd stopped putting so much load on it. My coat, torn,

ragged, and now scorched, whispered along the concrete, dragging behind me like a dinosaur's tail.

"Regan." I pitched my voice nice and low, soothing. "Your
mom sent me to get you. It's okay."

She cowered, gibbering. I didn't blame her, if I was a civilian
I'd probably do the same. So I just stayed where I was, in an easy
crouch, listening to the burning as the sirens drew closer.

Goddamn. I think I can count this one a win.

The precinct house on Alameda was still hopping. The graveyard
shift hadn't gone home yet and the late drunks were being wheeled
in for processing. Montaigne was waiting for me in his office,
looking a lot better than usual—no bags under his eyes and a few
inches slimmer. Vacation did him some good.

His tie was even still on straight. That meant a relaxing day, for
him. Of course, it was still early, and he'd been yanked out of bed
to come in and tie off the Regan Smith disappearance/reappear-
ance, and sign the forms for what little remained of the Trader to
be cremated. You don't bury them—you never know when a hellbreed will have a need for a nice fresh-rotting zombie skeleton.
Why give them one?

"Harvey Steiner," Monty said, leaning back in his chair. A
fresh bottle of Tums sat unopened on his desktop, next to his overflowing inbox. "Mild-mannered accountant by day, wacked-out
serial killer by night."

"All he needed was a cape and Spandex." I reeked of smoke
and foulness, my back ached, and under the buckled leather cuff
on my right wrist the scar tingled and prickled like a wire whisk
vibrating against the skin. "And all it cost us was one lousy
warehouse."

"Plus four insurance claims that need to be filed for the cars
you jumped on while chasing him. You're a menace to property,
Kismet." Streaks of thinning, graying hair combed across his
shining head, Monty raised tired gray eyes to meet mine. "How's
the kid?"

I shrugged, leather creaking. Monty's one of the few who don't
have much trouble meeting my mismatched gaze. One brown eye,

one blue, somehow it just seems to disturb people on a very deep level when I stare them down.

My fingers were at my throat, touching the carved chunk of ruby on its silver chain. I dropped my hand with an effort. "She'll need therapy. But she's alive. Her mom's on the way down to pick her up." *After they finish with the rape kit and the sedation. Poor kid. At least she's still breathing. Quit second-guessing yourself and count it a win, Kismet.*

I *did*. But I didn't think Regan or her mom would appreciate the news that she'd gotten off lightly, all things considered.

The half-open door to Monty's office creaked a little as someone went past. A burst of laughter sounded through the shuffling paperwork, ringing phones, and general murmur of cops doing their work. Homicide was up early, as usual.

Murder doesn't sleep.

Most of the time a hunter interacts with the Homicide division, closely followed by Vice. Murder, sex, and drugs, that's the list of symptoms of hellbreed in your town. Not like humanity ever needs much help to start killing, getting high, and looting.

No, indeedy. But hellbreed do like to help out.

Monty let it rest for a few beats. "How's Saul?"

I don't know, I'm not home enough to answer the phone. It was a pinch in a numb place. "I talked to him a couple days ago. His mom's doing better."

It was half a lie. Once Weres get a particular lymphoma they tend to go downhill quick, bodies burning up from the inside. They call it "the Wasting."

"Good." Monty nodded. His chair squeaked as he shifted, uneasily.

My back still hurt, a lead bar of pain buried in my lumbar muscles. I wanted to go home and scrub the smoke and fear off my skin. I wanted to check the messages and see if Saul had called again. I wanted to hear his voice.

Too bad, Jill. There were other things to do before dawn.

Like whatever Monty was sitting on. "Spit it out, Montaigne." I folded my arms, leaning against the file cabinet. My bullwhip tapped the metal, a soft thumping sound. I had to pick up more ammo soon, drop by Galina's and get a whole run of supplies.

He gave me a look that could have peeled paint and his eyes flicked toward the open door.

Subtle, Monty. I hauled myself upright, padded across thin cheap industrial carpet, and swept the door closed, without even a sarcastic flourish. "That better?"

"I need your help. On a case." He looked down at the drift of paper covering his desk, and I began to feel uneasy.

Normally, he says *There's something I need you to take a look at, Jill.* Like he can't believe he's asking a woman half his size for help.

What the hell. I had nothing else I was doing tonight, other than visiting Galina and patrolling the streets for stray *arkeus* and other hellbreed. There weren't any leads to chase for tonight's Trader—the 'breed who had given him the ability to fling fire was still out there, free as a bird.

It didn't matter. I'd catch up with him, her, or it soon enough. You don't get away with things like that. Not when Jill Kismet's on the job.

I dragged the only unburied chair over to his desk, pushing a stack of files out of the way with my boot. I settled down, resting against the straight wooden back, and fixed my eyes on the piles of paper. "Talk to me."

He opened up a drawer and set a bottle of Jack Daniels down. Amber alcohol glowed under the fluorescents.

Uh-oh. I leaned forward, closed my fingers around the bottle, and twisted the cap off. "A case? One of mine?" *If it is, why haven't you said something before now? It's the rules, Monty. You've done this before.*

"I don't know." He reached down, digging in another drawer as I took a swig. The alcohol burned, and I was reminded that I hadn't eaten yet today.

Come to think of it, I couldn't remember eating yesterday either. Once you get going it's hard to slow down.

And Saul was gone.

"Will you just tell me, Monty? The cloak-and-dagger routine gets old."

"You'd think you'd enjoy that." He didn't quite raise an eyebrow, but it was close.

I sighed, exaggeratedly rolling my eyes. A very teenage movement, which he acknowledged with a sour smile. Neither of us had
seen our teens for a decade or two, or three. I doubt Monty even
remembered his teen years, and I had no urge to recall mine ever
again. "Just get on with it. I have other shit to do tonight." *Or this
morning, as the case may be.*

"You're always in such a fucking hurry." He had a file in his
hands, a thin dog-eared manila number held shut with a rubber
band.

"Hellbreed don't take vacations." *When they do, I'll be the first
to celebrate.* I sniffed smoke, still rising from my clothes and skin.
Maybe not with a barbeque, though. "What's this all about?"

"Marvin Kutchner." He held up the file. "Cop. Ate his Glock
about two months ago."

"Has he come back?" In my line of work, that's always a possibility. If you run up against the nightside in Santa Luz—or
really, anywhere in my territory, which runs from Ridgefield to
the southern edges of Santa Luz; Leon Budge in Viejarosas and I
split some of the southern suburbs—you'll see me sooner or later.
I will avenge you, if you fall prey to the things that go bump in the
night.

And if you come back, I'll lay you to rest. Permanently.

Monty shook his head. "Buried out at Estrada. No sign of him
since."

Well, that's a relief. I eyed the folder. "So what's the deal?"

"I want you to look into it."

"A cop suicide? No offense, Monty, but—"

"He was my partner, back in the day." His weak, smoke-
colored gaze fixed itself over my shoulder, and his mouth turned
down at the corners.

The bottle of Tums on his desk wasn't open, and the whiskey
bottle was mostly full. He was laying in for a siege.

I studied him for a long few moments. *What aren't you telling
me?* "Is there a suspicion of homicide?"

"Something just don't smell right, Kismet. I don't know. I didn't
think Marv was the type, though God knows any cop can be driven
to it." He spread his hands, helplessly, like people do when they try
to express the inexpressible. "It just don't *smell* right."

Scratch any cop hard enough and you'll find intuition. Most of the time it's an educated guess so reflexive it seems like a hunch, courtesy of working the edges of human behavior for a long time.

A hunter, on the other hand, is normally a full-blown psychic. Messing around with sorcery will do that to you. Po-tay-toe, po-tah-toe. Doesn't matter.

Still... *why me, Monty?* "Why not just set IA on it?"

"Them?" He made a dismissive gesture. "Look, Marv was a good cop. Maybe it got to be too much for him, maybe not. He had a wife, she's getting his pension, and if something..."

I waited.

"He was my *partner,*" Monty finally said, heavily. As if it explained everything.

Maybe it did. If he was just uneasy, or wanted to know *why,* he was no different from the people who come to me looking for their loved ones. Everyone who disappears is someone's kid, someone's friend, someone's lover. Even if they're not, they deserve someone to care about finding them.

Even if that someone is only me.

Kutchner had pulled the very last disappearing trick anybody ever does. If it didn't look kosher to Monty and he wanted to do right by the widow by having someone *quietly* look at it so the pension wasn't interrupted, it was reasonable. More reasonable than a burning warehouse and a throat-cut Trader.

I leaned forward, holding out my right hand. The leather cuff on my wrist slid a little bit under my coatsleeve, over the scar. "I won't promise anything. It's not my type of case."

Monty's shoulders sagged as he let me take the file. It could have been relief or a fresh burden. Vacations never last long enough. "Thanks, Kiss. I mean it."

I almost winced. Leather creaked as I made it up to my feet, sighing as my back twinged and settled into aching. The scar burned, a reminder I didn't need, just like the reek of smoke clinging to me. "Don't call me that, okay?" *A few days looking into this, it's the least I owe him.*

Monty wasn't just a liaison. He was also a friend.

Even if he sometimes couldn't look me in the face.

I left with the file tucked under my arm, heading out into the rest of my night. The gray of false dawn was coming up, sky bleaching out along its edges, and I kept my windows down as I drove. The cold air was a penance, but at least it didn't smell like fire.

CHAPTER 2

The phone shrilled. I rolled over, blinking hazily. My bed was rucked out of all recognition, blankets tossed everywhere and my clothes in a stinking pile on the floor next to the mattresses. I'd been too tired to shower when I got home midmorning—just shucking off, putting a knife under the pillow, and passing out in the square of sunlight that travels through the skylight every day.

If you're not nocturnal when you start out, being a hunter will make you that way before long. Afternoon is the best, a long slow sleepy time of safe daylight. Dusk will wake you up like gunfire, because darkness is when the nightside comes out to play. Sunlight means safety.

At least most of the time.

I was just going to let the machine take it. But the thought that Saul might be calling when he knew I was probably home brought me up out of deep dreamlessness and set me fumbling for the phone. I hit the talk button and managed to get it in the vicinity of my face. "'Lo?" *Saul? Is that you?*

There was a moment's worth of silence, and I knew just from the sound of breathing that it wasn't my very favorite werecougar. Cold water ran down my spine and I lunged up into full wakefulness a bare second before a low, throaty chuckle echoed in my ear and made the scar on my wrist run with wet heat.

"My darling Kiss," he said. "It has been too long."

I knew he hadn't forgotten me.

It'd be nice if he would, wouldn't it, Jill? My mouth turned dry and slick as desert glass, and the scar thundered under its leather hood. The buckles on the cuffs Saul made for me regularly snapped off or corroded, and I didn't help matters by tearing off the cuff when I needed the full extent of helltainted strength.

I didn't move to sit up in bed. Perry would hear material moving and know he'd gotten to me. Instead, I froze, lying on my belly, one hand under the pillow around the knifehilt and the other clutching the phone to my numb ear.

I'd wondered just how much chain he was going to give me before yanking. I'd left town six months ago in the aftermath of the Sorrows incident, and on my way out I'd paid Perry a little visit. I *knew* he'd been in it up to his eyeballs, thinking he could play both sides of the fence and use the Sorrows to get his wormy little fingers inside my head.

It hadn't worked. I'd spent a lot of time between then and now wondering when he was going to make his next move. The scar didn't twinge much, and it still functioned the same as before, feeding me enough etheric force to make me exponentially more dangerous.

It's not every hunter who has a tainted hellbreed mark. It's saved my life more than once.

And driven me right to the edge of the abyss.

"Perry." I sounded normal. Or about as normal as you can sound, awakened from a deep sleep with a hellbreed on the line. My palms were wet and my nipples, pressed against the mattress since I'd shucked every stitch of smoke-fouled clothing, were hard as chips of rock. I'd tossed most of the pillows off the bed. "Didn't I tell you not to bother me?"

I didn't even have to put any *fuck you* into my voice. Just weariness, as if I was dealing with a spoiled child.

Oh be careful. Be very goddamn careful, Jill. My pulse kicked up as if it was dusk. High, hard, and fast, right in my throat, too.

"Would you like my mark to start spreading, Kiss?" Bland, smooth, and even, as if he was discussing the weather. I could almost see his blue eyes narrowing.

Most of the damned are beautiful. Perry is just blandly mediocre-looking. It's why he's so goddamn scary, and why my left hand started to quiver a little bit.

The woman always has advantage in situation like this, my teacher Mikhail's voice whispered from the vaults of memory.

I hoped he was right. It sure as hell didn't feel like it, sometimes.

"Or perhaps," Perry continued, "you would like it to start rotting and turning black. I believe the proper term is necrosis."

I know what necrosis is, hellspawn. "That would put a little wrinkle in our bargain." I didn't swallow audibly only out of sheer force of will. "And since you're already in dutch by cavorting with the Sorrows not so long ago—"

"Oh, let's not fight. Come see me, Kiss." Silky-smooth, his voice could have been an attractive businessman's baritone except for the rumble behind it. It sounded like freight trains in a deserted switchyard at midnight, rubbing against each other and groaning in pain.

Helletöng. The language of the damned.

The mother tongue of Hell.

"Hold your breath until I show up, Pericles." I peeled the phone away from my ear and hit the talk button again. It disconnected— but not nearly quickly enough to suit me.

I rolled over and stared at the skylight. Late-afternoon sunlight filled the Plexiglas rectangle with gold. I was under the messy blankets, except for my bare foot, with the sheet wrapped around my ankle like a manacle. My toes flexed as sunlight scoured my vision, comfortable safety filling the inside of my skull with white noise. I tuned my mind to a blank, meaningless hum, but my hands were shaking, one of them braced with a knifehilt.

My warehouse resounded with tiny noises. I like to hear every little thing moving in my place, right down to the mice in the walls. Though sorcery is sometimes practically useful—I don't *have* mice in my walls. Creaks as sun-heat made the building expand, the low moan of the wind from the desert, a faraway rumble as a train slid along the tracks, since I live in an industrial district. Nowadays I was liking the solitude more and more.

You knew he wouldn't forget about you. I was cold even under the blankets. The scar, under its shield of leather, ran with moist warmth. It wasn't much to look at, a puckered lip-print as if someone had painted lye on the skin and kissed with a wet mouth. It still functioned the way it always had, feeding me etheric force, hiking my physical strength and just generally making me a lot harder to kill.

I hadn't been in to the Monde Nuit to give Perry payment for that power since Saul and I returned from the Dakotas.

I was all right with that. And technically, he had betrayed the bargain we'd made. I was within my rights never to darken the Monde's doorstep again, never to make another payment no matter how much power I pulled through it.

It's too easy. And it was. Perry wasn't the sort to let a hunter slip through his immaculate fingers. He'd miscalculated badly last time, and I'd outwitted him.

Hellbreed don't like that.

Add to that the fact that he'd done a few things I hadn't suspected he could—like producing hellfire in the blue spectrum— and you had a very unsettling situation developing.

Worry about it later, Jill. For right now you need to get up and start poking around after Monty's dead partner. The sooner you get that looked into, the sooner you can get back to those disappearances on the east side of town. Four women gone, and the whole thing stinks.

The trouble was, I might have to wait until someone else disappeared before I was sure last night's player didn't have anything to do with the situation. But the fire-slinging sonofabitch hadn't bothered going out to the east, he'd concentrated slightly south of downtown, in the warehouses and freight yards near the river. Lots of places to hide where nobody could hear a woman scream.

Regan Smith had been the lucky one. Her mother hadn't been able to look me in the face when she asked me to find her daughter, *or* when I left her outside the curtain to the ER bay her child was behind. Maybe it was my eyes. Maybe it was my long leather coat or the skintight black T-shirt, or the silver tied in my hair.

Maybe it was even the guns. Or the bullwhip.

Or maybe it was her raped, traumatized daughter whimpering even through the sedation. Sometimes people aren't prepared for their loved ones to be brought back hurt or marred. The disappearance itself throws everything off, screws everything up, and life is never normal again even if their loved one comes back.

That was Perry on the phone. A galvanic shudder spilled

through me, from top to toes. *He's about to start messing with you again, Jill. It figures he would wait until Saul is out of town.*

I wanted to call Saul, but he would immediately be able to tell something was wrong. He didn't need another burden right now. He already sounded too worried. When he could get me on the phone, that is.

I repressed another shiver. I could still smell smoke, my clothes on the floor sending out invisible waves of stink like Pig-Pen in the old *Peanuts* cartoons.

I should get up, work out, and hit the street.

For a few minutes I lay there, breathing, my eyes full of light. Trying not to follow the inevitable chain of logic.

You know what this means. Perry's thinking about you.

I wished it didn't make me feel so unsteady. He'd almost gotten into my head more than once. Almost pushed me over that edge every hunter lives on.

We commit murder on an almost daily basis. It doesn't matter if it's hellbreed, Trader, scurf, Middle Way adepts, what-have-you. It's still killing sentient beings. The fact that most of these sentient beings are kill-crazy predators doesn't absolve a hunter of responsibility.

The Church, after all, does not admit us into Heaven, even if we're buried in hallowed ground.

Sometimes I wonder about that. I wonder more and more, the longer I do this sort of work.

Getting that close to the edge is necessary. You can't kill a hell-breed if you hesitate or flinch. But no matter how close you get to that edge, no matter how you put your little toesies on it and peer over into the howling abyss that lies beyond, you cannot go over. It's a razor-thin line, but you cannot, ever, go over it.

I had been so close.

Get up, Jill. Work out, and go out and do your job. Let Perry suck eggs in his little hellbreed hole. When he pops back up you'll deal with him.

It sounded good.

I just wished I believed it.

I rolled up out of bed, taking the knife with me, and got ready to face another night.

CHAPTER 3

'd just given the Impala a tune-up, so my baby purred as I took her up into the suburbs, the red fuzzy dice Galina had given me dangling from the mirror. Kutchner's widow lived in the Cruzada district, nice little houses from the seventies, fenced yards, and neighbors as old as Methuselah—on the right streets. On the wrong streets, the neighbors have bad crack problems that make them *look* like Methuselah.

Only in the 'burbs do you find this combination. No wonder they need sitcoms to dull the pain.

The wrong streets tend to cluster on higher ground, further away from the artery of the river. Closer to the desert. Mrs. Kutchner lived on the edge, high enough up that security bars on the windows were not just a fashion statement. Still, it was an okay neighborhood, and as the sun slid bloody below the rim of the mountains, I slammed the Impala's door and eyed the house, a neat little adobe with a trim, if weedy, yard and a chain-link fence. Out here the grass was yellow; people had better things to spend their money on than astronomical water bills.

I leaned against the car door and examined the place. The right-hand neighbors had kids—someone had to play with the toys scattered around their yard. On the other side, a scraggly greenbelt cut through the neighborhood, edging a ditch that would take runoff in flash-flood season. The fence was higher on that side, and so were the weeds.

The blinds were all pulled behind blank windows and vertical iron security bars. The red-painted door looked like a tight-pursed mouth, and the high arched windows gave the street a perpetually surprised glance. The brick-colored roof tiles were still fresh, not bleached by a few high-grade summer scorches.

Now why does this not look right? I pulled my sunglasses off as the sky turned indigo, pink and orange lingering in the west. The mountains glowed, furnace teeth spearing up to catch high thin cumulus clouds. The original seven-veil dance, performed nightly, hold the applause, just throw cash.

Wind came off the desert, smelling of sand and shimmering heat. Oven-warm, drying the sweat along my forehead and tinkling the charms knotted into my hair with red thread. My silver apprentice-ring rested against my left ring finger. I played with it as I watched the house, hairs rising on my nape.

My smart eye—the blue one, the one that can see below the surface of the world—watered a bit as I focused. A pall lay over Kutchner's house, etheric energy turned thick and bruise-clotted.

There could be a number of reasons for this—grief, or any strong negative emotion over time. A murder or suicide in the recent past—this was listed as Kutchner's last known address before he ventilated his own skull.

Hellbreed contamination, or even just plain sorcery of the darker variety, will also congest the ether around a place, just like a bruise is congested blood.

Kutchner had been found in a flophouse hotel on the edge of the barrio. Still, brooding about suicide for a while, especially if you're serious enough to actually do it, can cause your house to get a bit stale, etherically speaking.

I dunno. That's an awful lot of static.

Well, no time like the present to stick my nose in and find out.

I crossed the street and opened the squeaking chain-link gate. A narrow strip of concrete unreeled to the steps leading to the entryway, and dried husks of yucca flowers rattled in the breeze. The sound was like clicking small bones together in a wooden cup, and my right hand crept for a gun.

Great, Jill. Show up at the widow's door and scare the crap out of her with a Glock shoved in her face. Monty said he wanted this quiet, you know.

Quiet's one thing, and disregarding your instincts is another. A hunter who ignores instinct is half dead already. The other half comes when you do something stupid, like not drawing when every nerve in your body screams *something's behind Door Number One, sweetheart!*

I drew, keeping the gun low along my side. Leather rustled as I walked up the path, and the dead blossoms rattled, rattled. Like handcuffs. My coat brushed my ankles as I stepped cautiously, the transition to nighttime taking a breath all along the edges of my city. Sometimes I *feel* that deep breath just after dusk, right under my sternum. It's like every instrument in an orchestra tuned to the same key and suddenly giving out the deepest tone it's capable of.

The entryway held pots of cacti, different spiny little things that might have been flowering if they weren't desiccated enough to be used for tinder. The charms in my hair tinkled as they rubbed against each other. Deep shadows at the end of the roofed entryway moved as I stepped forward, cautiously, and my sensitive nose picked out something it was all too familiar with. A ripe, overwhelming smell.

Under my leather cuff, the scar pulsed hotly. It didn't seem to be getting any bigger.

Stop thinking like that, Jill. My entire body flushed hot, then cold.

The wind was coming from behind me, or I would have noticed the smell earlier. The door creaked a little bit as the breeze pushed it.

It was open.

Monty swiped at his forehead. Sweat sheened his face. "Jesus," he said, for the third time.

Usually we only get one *Jesus* out of him per crime scene.

Jacinta Kutchner's corpse hung from a white and blue striped nylon rope looped over an exposed ceiling beam creaking slightly as the house settled for the night. She wore a pale blue housedress and one slipper, and had been dead for a while, if the state of the body was any indication. The air conditioning had been turned off sometime in the recent past, and the house was breathlessly hot and stale.

Not to mention reeking of decay.

I folded my arms, doing my best not to lean against the wall. The forensic techs were hard at work, gathering evidence, photographing, trying to ignore the smell. A few of them had Vicks smeared on their upper lips, it was that bad. A few days in desert heat will dry a body out, but hot moisture in an enclosed house is bad for dead human tissue.

"I don't like this." I kept my voice low. The techs were giving me little sideways looks, except for plump brunette Piper. She was off maternity leave and slimming down again, my very favorite forensic tech and my particular liaison with that department. Not much disturbs her serenity.

Maybe it's having kids that does it. I've never seen Piper even blanch. She's even been known to whistle Disney tunes at scenes.

The mind boggles.

"I don't either." Monty looked miserable. I didn't blame him. One suicide is chance, two coincidence.

I didn't want a third.

"This isn't my type of case," I said again. "There's no smell of anything hinky on this one. Not extra-human hinky, that is."

"What about human hinky?"

You don't want me to tell you anything you don't already know, Montaigne. You just want someone else to say it out loud. I glanced around the living room. "What the hell did she stand on? She's only five-three, recent stretching notwithstanding." It felt horrible, but you don't last long around violent death without evolving some black humor. I ticked them off on my fingers. "Where's her other slipper? Not to mention most women want to look pretty right before they take the plunge. They usually hang themselves in more private places, too."

A fresh wave of stench rolled toward me. There was a large stain on the carpet below the body, and the insect life was having a ball. Not as much as there would be outside, but you'd be surprised how little time it takes for six-legged critters to find a recently deceased piece of meat.

"I thought about that too." His gaze came up, touched my face, skittered away. He palmed a couple of Tums up to his mouth and started chewing. "Goddammit."

Full night had folded around the house, darkness swirling in corners where it wasn't driven away by electric fixtures and portable lights brought in by the crime-scene team. The shadows in the corners had weight, only seen through my blue eye.

Seen from *between,* violent death has its own eddies and currents. She had suffered before passing out of this place and into whatever awaited her.

This isn't one of yours, Jill. Get going, there's other things out there tonight you should be taking care of.

But I made no move to leave beyond shifting my weight from one foot to the other.

"What the hell are you doing here?" Carper said irritably from the entryway, hunching his shoulders. His sharp blue eyes flicked once over the scene, taking everything in.

In his sneakers and tweed jackets, Carp looks more like a college professor than a homicide deet. Behind him, his partner Rosenfeld was conferring with the blue holding down the site log. Rosenfeld's spiky auburn halo threw back what little light made it past the long mirror on the wall.

"Relax, Carp." I let my shoulders drop. "It's not one of mine."

He looked only barely relieved. "Great. What're you *doing,* then?"

"Conferring with Montaigne. If that's all right with you." *Don't get snitty with me, Carp. I'm not in the mood.*

"Hi, Jill." Rosie ambled past her partner, bumping him with her shoulder. Her jaw would have done a prizefighter proud, and her leather jacket creaked a little bit. The Terrible Two of the Homicide department, appearing nightly on the scene. "What's going on?"

It was an excessively casual question. Santa Luz's finest get a little bit nervous around me, though they take bets on where I'll show up next. There's a whole system of verifying hunter sightings left over from Mikhail's time.

It's when they lose track of me for a few weeks that everyone gets jumpy.

Still, very few cops *like* being around me. The mandatory class I put all rookies through takes care of that. My tiger's eye rosary bumped my stomach as I shifted again. "Not much for me here. See you later, Monty."

He couldn't quite bring himself to ask me, but he spread his hands as I passed, brushing close to Carp and almost enjoying when the man stepped away. He used to be able to get a rise out of me. Now Carper and I just go through the motions. It's a comforting routine on both sides.

He rolled his eyes, and I grinned at him. The corner of his

mouth twitched, and he looked away, the twinkle going out of his baby blues as he studied the shape of Jacinta Kutchner hanging, the edge of her robe fluttering a bit. "Goddamn," he said, softly.

I paused at the entryway, next to the blue. He didn't offer me the site log, but he gripped it until paper crackled. If I looked closely I would probably remember his name. "Monty."

"Yeah?" He palmed another couple of Tums. The vacation was wearing off.

What else could I say? He wanted me to look into it, and someone else was dead. *Worst case of suicide I ever saw,* the tagline to an old joke floated through my head. "I'll be in touch."

Then I was out the door, plunging into the night, crossing the street to the Impala. She stuck out like a sore thumb, having no flashing lights, and I noticed something else about the neighborhood.

Jacinta Kutchner's neighbors didn't come out to see what the fuss was. At all.

So much for suburbia.

CHAPTER 4

Gray predawn was breaking, again, when the phone rang and my pager went off simultaneously. I left my trench dripping on the rack in the utility room and hobbled through the hall, through the cavern of the sparring space and living room, every muscle I'd pulled singing its own separate note in the orchestra of pain. I'd broken my *left* arm this time, the *arkeus* I'd run across on the east side of town had put up a hell of a fight.

Get it, Jill? A Hell of a fight? Arf arf.

But I'd found out, to my lasting satisfaction, which pile of hell-soaked waste had given the mad accountant his power. It was unmistakable, especially when an *arkeus* pulls a flame-jet six feet long out of its mouth and tries to feed it to you.

The scar provides me with faster healing and damage regeneration, but when it's busy splinting bones and replacing a few quarts of blood, pulled muscles heal more slowly. I didn't want to think about what would happen if it started spreading, or if Perry decided it wasn't such a hot idea to have me drawing on a hellbreed's tainted power if he wasn't getting anything in return—even if it was his own damn fault.

Don't think like that. The phone brayed, the pager buzzed against my hip, and I stopped short of picking up as the answering machine clicked. There were a few moments of silence, then a beep.

"Hey, kitten." A voice I knew as well as my own slid from the speaker, only slightly distorted. "Guess you're out—"

My pager quit buzzing. I was already scrambling for the phone. I scooped it up and pressed the talk button, and the machine clicked over with a feedback squeal. "Sorry about that." Breathless, now, I folded down on the bed. "God, it's good to hear you."

"Hey." Saul sounded tired. "Glad I caught you too, kitten. What's happening in the big bad city?"

A sharp ache welled up in my chest. *I miss you, and Perry called.* "Not much. A couple things Monty wants me to look into. A Trader."

"Bad?" He had a nice voice, to go with all the rest of him.

I shut my eyes, imagining him right next to me. Tall darkhaired Were, looking like a romance-novel Native American except for the gold-green sheen off his eyes in certain light, the rods and cones reflecting differently. "Nothing out of the ordinary. I even got a civilian out alive."

"That's my girl." A warm rumble of approval, carried through a phone line and suddenly threatening to ease every muscle.

"How's your mom?" I swallowed sudden dryness in my throat. Saul's mother hadn't been too happy to meet the hellbreed-tainted hunter he'd given up his place in the tribe for, but with faultless Were courtesy she'd accepted me into her home as a guest and cooked for me. She'd even introduced me to the extended family and officiated at the firelit ceremony that formalized everything. As far as Saul was concerned, we were formally mated.

As far as his tribe was concerned, we were as good as married, even if I was... well, disappointing. But they hadn't said a word, just welcomed me with Were politeness.

I wondered if they regretted it now.

"There's morphine." Saul's tone changed now. Deeper, and just a bit rougher. "It's not bad. My aunts are here. They're singing to her."

Oh, Christ. She must be close to passing. No more needed to be said.

I listened to him breathing for a few moments, knowing he was doing the same thing. "I love you," I whispered. *I can't make it better. If I could I would. I'd hunt down the cancer and put a gun to its head. Slit its throat. Kill it for you.*

"I know that, kitten." A thin vibration came through the phone—he was rumbling, deep down in his chest, a werecougar's response to a mate's distress. "You sure you're okay?"

His mother was dying and he was out there alone, because I couldn't leave the city—nobody was around to take some of the load; the apprentices who had come out last time to handle the overflow while we were honeymooning had gone home and were needed desperately there.

And he was asking if *I* was okay.

I don't deserve you, Saul. The charms in my hair jingled as I played with my pager, unclipping it from my belt. It was habit to take the damn thing with me everywhere, in a padded pocket except when I was hosing blood and stink out of my coat. "Right as rain. Wish I could be there."

"I wish so too. You be careful for me, you hear?" He was already worrying about the next thing, or he wouldn't have told me to be careful. He almost never did that, because it implied I couldn't take care of myself.

Weres are touchy about things like that. "Always am. Do you need me?" *Say the word, Saul. I can't leave now, but I will if you ask me to.*

Should I feel grateful, or more guilty, that he understood and hadn't asked? That he had insisted I stay in Santa Luz, because he knew my responsibility weighed as heavily as his?

"I do, but I'm okay. They need you more." A long pause, neither of us willing to hang up just yet. He broke it first, this time. "I'd better go back in."

"Okay." *Don't hang up. Perry called me, and I'm scared. Come home.* I swallowed the words. "You take care of yourself, furboy."

"You too. Tell everyone hello for me."

"I will." I waited another few moments, then straightened my arm to put the phone down. He hated saying goodbye.

So did I.

I laid the phone in its cradle and watched as the light winked off. Let out a long breath, muscles twitching and sore under my torn, blood-stiff T-shirt. My pants were shredded—the *arkeus* had just missed my femoral artery in its dying desperation, brought to bay and made physical enough to fight at last.

I lifted my pager. The number on it was familiar, and I scooped up the phone and dialed again without giving myself time to think. It rang twice.

"Montaigne," he barked.

"You bellowed?" I even sounded normal, sharp and Johnny-on-the-spot. All hail Jill Kismet, the great pretender.

"We got another disappearance on the east side. And there's something else. Can you come in?"

My entire body ached. I hauled myself up from the bed, looked longingly at the rumpled pillow and tossed blankets. Saul was the domestic half of our partnership, I've never been good at that sort of shit.

The hurt in my heart hadn't gone away. It was still a sharp piercing, like a broken bone in my chest. I made it over to the dresser, wincing as my leg healed fully and the scar flushed under the damp leather cuff. The urge to tear the cuff off and make sure it wasn't spreading suddenly ignited, I pushed it away.

"Jill?" Monty sounded halfway to frantic.

I snapped back into myself and jerked a dresser drawer open, scooping up a black *Frodo Lives!* T-shirt. "I'm on my way."

The message light on the machine was blinking. I ignored it and bolted for the bathroom, another pair of leather pants, and quite possibly a sleepless day.

CHAPTER 5

"Michael Spilham." Monty laid the file down on his cluttered desk. "Vanished from a bus stop out near Percoa Park last night. We have a verified sighting at ten-fifteen, when a coworker drove by and saw him waiting for the bus due at ten-twenty-six. The driver on that route doesn't remember him, says she wondered about that because he's a regular. His mother filed a missing-persons when he didn't come home on time; says it's not like him. It might be nothing, but it's in the same area as the other disappearances."

I nodded. Percoa Park. A brief cold wave slid down my spine—we'd found bodies there before. "That's a small window."

"The bus might have been off by five minutes or so. Still, you're right."

If Monty hadn't had something else up his sleeve he would have given me the location over the phone, and I'd already be there searching for clues. The other disappearances on the east side were all the same—people vanishing without a trace, outside, often in very short spaces of time. Small windows in disappearances are common enough, but this one smelled fishy to me.

It stank of hell, actually. Or *something* unnatural. Still.... "I dunno. Everything about this fits except the gender of the victim."

But that meant very little too. Women are just bigger targets of opportunity most of the time.

"Can you look at it?" He stared down at his desk. The bottle of whiskey was down by a quarter.

"That's the plan. Want to tell me what's bothering you?" I hooked my thumbs in my belt, my dangling fingers brushing the bullwhip's oiled curve. The precinct building quivered, phones ringing and thin predawn wind boiling against the windows. Monty's office didn't have any outside portholes. It was more of a luxury than you'd think—on a summer's day, the air conditioning didn't have to fight for primacy.

"I got autopsy reports on the widow." His shoulders dropped, and he cast a longing look at the Jack Daniels.

I picked up the bottle, uncapped it, took a swallow. It burned on the way down. I used to drink a lot of this stuff, before Saul happened along. "And?"

"Hyoid crushed and damage to the strap muscles, but no cervical vertebrae snapped and no rope burns." Monty dropped down in his chair. "We're waiting for toxicology, but there was...she was...there was vaginal bruising. And semen. We might get DNA."

Oh, Christ. "So we're looking at a murder here, not a suicide." I said it so he didn't have to.

"Whoever set it up didn't work that hard. There was nothing for her to stand on to get up there. The rope was tied to the—"

"I saw the scene, Monty." I didn't want to revisit it. As gruesome as hellbreed get—and they get pretty *damn* gruesome—I'm still more upset by things human beings do to each other without needing any extra help. It's in a hellbreed's nature to be vicious, just like a cancer cell or a rabid animal.

I'm still not sure why people do it.

Monty stared at his desk. "Her bedroom was torn apart. Looks like someone was looking for something, or maybe the attack started there. Carp and Rosie are betting on both. The screen in the master bathroom window was torn loose, but it's too small for anyone but a five-year-old to shimmy through."

That was odd, too. I replayed the scene in my head. Something about that bathroom nagged at me. "Who sleeps with their window open in *that* neighborhood? Even with bars on the window." *And why not tear up the rest of the house if they were looking for something?*

"The neighbors aren't worth jackshit." Monty smoothed the fresh manila folder on his desk, the one with Jacinta Kutchner's name on the tab. "Nobody can remember anything out of the usual."

I exhaled sharply. "Monty. This isn't my type of case. There's no inhuman agency at work here. I've got those disappearances to look into and—"

"Jill." He dropped down into his chair and glared at me. "I

never asked you for anything like this before. Marv was my partner."

I looked down at the file. Lots of people don't understand that about cops. The partner isn't quite a spouse, but they're the person whose head you think inside of, whose judgment and reactions you trust your life to, the person you spend so much time with you might as well be twins.

It may not be love, but it's close.

It wasn't Monty's tender feelings that made me reach across the desk and tug the file out from under his hand. It was the vision of Jacinta Kutchner's body, gently swinging just the tiniest bit as her empty house breathed around her.

Hyoid crushed. Vaginal bruising. Bedroom ripped to shreds.

"I'll look into it. Can't promise anything." Even though I already had.

Monty almost visibly sagged. His chair creaked, and he dropped his gaze to the top of his desk, drifted with paper. Silence bloomed between us, a new and uncomfortable quiet.

Finally, he shifted and his chair creaked sharply. "Thanks."

"No problem." *What are friends for, Monty? And if you've got one, you might as well use her.* "I'll check in."

"Yeah. Try not to destroy any property, will you?"

For Christ's sake. I was already at the door. "I can't *promise* anything, Monty. See you."

His curse was like a goodbye.

The plastic of the bus shelter's window-walls was scarred and starred with breakage. I examined it minutely. Cigarette butts, an overflowing trashcan, the smell of despair.

Just like waiting for the bus anywhere, really. Dawn was coming up fast, the sky full of scarves dyed indigo, rose, streaks of gold and soft threads of orange over the furnace in the east. There was a blank brick wall behind the bus shelter, and a drift of paper trash in an alley to the side. Across the street, Percoa Park simmered under a pall of early morning half-vapor, trees breathing in relief as the sun rose.

Michael Spilham. Thirty-four, college dropout, living with his mother and working in a shipping warehouse four blocks away from here. He'd be tired at the end of his shift, overtime wearing down his feet and shoulders. So, he'd probably stand here, leaning against the shelter's support post. A nonsmoker, the file said, so he didn't light up while waiting. He probably just stared down the street, thinking a normal man's thoughts.

I closed my eyes. Took a deep breath. Smelled exhaust, the odor of poverty and footsore wandering, trash and concrete.

A sudden cessation of subaudible buzzing made my eyes fly open. The streetlamp to my left had switched off. I glanced down the street to my right. Edges of broken glass glittered like diamonds as the star we all roll around lifted itself higher over the horizon.

I left the shelter, cautiously. Intuition tingled and prickled down my spine, raised the fine hairs on my nape under the weight of silver-laden hair. My trenchcoat, still damp from hosing, whispered and fluttered. Time for a new coat; hellbreed claws are death on leather.

This lamp was busted, broken glass on the pavement. A star-shape of expended force glittered, bits and pieces arranged along rays of reaction. Intuition turned chilly, raising prickles along the backs of my arms. A faint distinct perfume evaporated as soon as I got a whiff. Corruption, and sweetness like burned candy.

Huh.

I crouched easily, my bootheels digging into the pavement and my leather pants making just the faintest noise as dead cowskin rubbed against itself. My smart eye saw the strings under the surface of the world resonating to a powerful burst of bloodlust and fear.

My dumb eye wasn't so dumb. Streaks and smears along the base of the streetlamp gleamed. Blood dries fairly quick out in the desert, but this close to the misty park it wasn't completely flaking off yet.

Huh again. These were transfer prints. Someone with bloody hands had clasped the bottom of the streetlamp. Now that I was crouched down I could see smears on the filthy sidewalk too, oddly pale—pink instead of red.

Blood shouldn't look like that. Another chill touched my nape, tickling little fingers. "Shit," I breathed, reaching down to touch the smears on the post's concrete base. *"Shit."*

My fingers came away with powdery pink clinging to them. As I lifted my hand, I turned a little so the sunlight hit my skin.

The powder vanished, little puffs of steam rising from my fingertips. "Goddamn shitsucking son of a *bitch*," I whispered. "Motherfucking *hell*."

There's only one thing that dries blood to powder evaporating in the sun. And as much as hunters hate, hunt, and loathe hellbreed, there's only one thing that a hunter fears enough to cross herself and shiver, one thing that sends us looking for backup and polishing whatever weapons make us feel a little safer.

I settled on my haunches, my right hand dropping to the butt of a gun. "Shit," I breathed one final time, before rising slowly to my feet and looking down at the long jagged wet-looking marks on the sidewalk. They pointed toward the mouth of an alley, yawning and shadowed even with the clear light of dawn coming up.

No time like the present, eh Jill?

I headed for the alley as traffic ran like water in the distance. The next bus wasn't due for about ten minutes and the street was deserted. A ruffle of paper twisted in the intersection two blocks away, and I eased a gun out with my right hand and a knife in my left. *Wish I had a flamethrower. Dammit.*

The alley swallowed me with shadows you only get in the morning—knife-edged and clear, like stiff black paper cut into animal shapes. A Dumpster loomed in the alley's throat, and I sniffed cautiously, seeking that perfume of burnt sugar and weirdness. *Should have recognized that first-off. Goddammit.* My heart kicked up, high and wild in my throat, a bitter taste in the back of my mouth. Training clamped down on my hindbrain, regulating the cascade of adrenaline through my system. Too much and I'd be a jittery mess, and if this turned ugly . . .

I eased into the dark maw, clicking the hammer back. *They're not going to be in the alley, not with day coming on. But they dragged him back here, you might find something. Pray you don't find something.*

One step. Two. Easing down the side that held a little more light, though the entire alley was shaded. The Dumpster was full of garbage, and as a stray breath of breeze touched my cold cheeks, the smell strengthened.

Oh God. Please. I quelled the tremor in my hands by the simple expedient of putting it out of my mind. Whatever was going to happen was going to happen. Nothing to be done about it now.

I stepped toward the Dumpster. It was a big green number, half its heavy plastic lid closed and the other half open, resting against the wall of the alley. At the end of the alley's confined space was a huge rolling door, probably for whoever took out the trash. I scanned the alley again—no, it was a blind hole. No place else to hide.

Don't let me find anything, God. Please. Cut me a break on this one.

Unfortunately, God wasn't in a giving mood today. I saw telltale frosting along the metal edge of the Dumpster, a fine powdery substance drifting in complicated whorls. And I heard, straining the preternatural acuity of my senses, a faint rustling.

Yup. God's not in a good mood today, Jillybean. You've got a scurf infestation on your hands.

CHAPTER 6

Scurf aren't like Traders or hellbreed. There's no pattern to their movements, no training, no instinctive predator's grace. They're just engines of messy hunger, ravenous and unpredictable.

And contagious.

I emptied two clips into the motherfucker and ended up burying my knife in its side. Brick puffed into dust and the Dumpster's side was stove in, garbage spilling out into the alley, body-sized dents in the walls, and blood everywhere. My blood, which just served to drive the thing into a feeding frenzy.

They can smell it. And even though they like it fresh from the vein, so to speak, they'll lick it up from concrete if they have to.

In the end, I drove the skinny naked thing out of the alley, my fingers clamped in its throat and its claws tangling in my ribs. He wasn't fully changed yet, the virus hadn't turned his bones all the way to flexible cartilage or given him the thick slimy coating that makes scurf so slippery. But his eyes were blank pale orbs without iris or pupil—they don't need to *see*—and even though he was newly infected and didn't have the developed instincts for carnage, he was strong and desperate.

When they're newly changed, they're even *more* unpredictable than usual. It snarled and champed, teeth snapping with a sound like heavy billiard balls smacking together; foam splattered rank and foul, burning the skin of my hand and smoking on my leather sleeve. I cried out, miserable loathing beating frantically under my heart, as we tumbled out into the street and a flood of early morning sunlight.

The scurf screeched, damage runnelling its face and its blind pupilless eyes popping, smears of buttery eyefat glistening down its gaunt cheeks. Thin acrid smoke gushed, pale powdery drifts rising as the thing that used to be Michael Spilham squealed and imploded. The smell was gagging-strong, the reason most hunters don't like cotton candy or caramel. Burnt candy, sweetness, and *bad,* all rolled up in one pretty package.

It screamed again, foam splattering in harsh droplets that sizzled where they landed. It took every ounce of hellbreed strength I had to hold the thing *down,* even as its flesh began to run like plastic clay, stinking and smoking. I held it, *held it,* and heard far-off traffic under its screams, the sound of the wind in the park trees.

Lord, take this soul into Thy embrace. I couldn't help adding my own little touch to the prayer—*and will You do it quickly, please?*

Its throat collapsed into stinking sludge, powder lifting on the wind and sparkling in the sunlight. I coughed, deep and racking, struggling for purchase on the still-moving mass of almost-liquid ooze. *Keep it in the sun, ohGod Jill keep it in the sun, for the love of Christ don't let it go now....*

It squirmed and heaved, almost squirting free. If I lost my grip now it would scurry off into the alley and I'd have another fight on my hands. The longer I fought, the bigger the chance of a bite.

The scurf that had been Michael Spilham collapsed into final true death, and I let out a whispered prayer that was half a sob. *Got off lucky.* It was only then I realized I was bleeding from its claws, the gouges whittling deeper as acid in the powdery slime exhausted itself. The charms in my hair ran with blue sparks and the scar on my wrist throbbed. The dead body subsided, bubbling into powder, and I scraped both palms on the pavement as I backed away hurriedly, staring at the smear. *Lucky, lucky, lucky.*

"OhGod," I whispered, as my left hand grabbed a gun and I cleared leather, pointing it at the stain on the pavement.

That's the trouble with the damn things. Sometimes scurf just don't stay dead.

My heart leapt and shivered inside me. I coughed, tasting blood and adrenaline, stripes of fire along my ribs as acid hissed and bubbled in my flesh. There was another clawstrike on my thigh, and one down my back. Hot blood dripped down my cheek. It had damn near taken out my eye.

Lucky. Jesus Christ I'm lucky. The scar pulsed, pulsed under the cuff. The burning bubbling went away, preternatural healing replacing tissue faster than the acid could burn. Most hunters are walking factories of scar tissue, healing sorcery notwithstanding, I should have been glad I don't need healing spells.

I wasn't. I almost never am.

After a little while I decided the flood of sunlight was enough to take care of the scurf. Besides, I couldn't sit here with a gun out all day, could I? I cautiously hefted myself to my feet, and forced myself nearer the bubbling grease spot.

My tiger's eye rosary bumped against my midriff. The chunk of carved ruby at my throat was warm, humming with power. The scar throbbed. Silver clinked and chimed in my hair. Everything was present and accounted for.

No bites. I'm up to date on my garlic shots anyway, thank God. I stared at the smear for a long time before holstering my left-hand gun. *Scurf. What next?*

Get going, Jill. You've got work to do, and not a lot of time to do it.

Jacinta's killer was going to have to wait. I headed for the alley to collect my other gun and the dropped knives. My knees only trembled a little, but when my pager went off, buzzing silently in its padded pocket, I almost leapt out of my skin.

*   *   *

Micky's on Mayfair Hill is the type of restaurant locals like to keep to themselves. Good food, quiet atmosphere, and pictures of silent and classic film stars on the walls. I'm not used to being in Micky's during daylight, unless it's just before dawn and I'm tired and bloody. Normally I wouldn't go around civilians like that— but Micky's isn't just the best restaurant on the Hill, where the gay nightclubs rollick and roll all night long.

It's also the only restaurant on the Hill run by Weres.

I didn't stop to be seated, just stalked through the tables—very few of them occupied at this hour—and headed for the bar. Two steps down into the dark cavern where it was always dusk glinting off bottles and the jukebox in the corner, and I caught Theron's eye.

The tall lanky dark-haired Were raised an eyebrow and cocked his head. I went behind the bar for once, without breaking stride, and a bleary-eyed businessman with the perfume of something unnatural hanging on him blinked, shifting uneasily on his stool. Micky's is where the nightside comes to drink, and if you don't make trouble you're welcome here.

If you *do* make trouble, well...the staff will have you out the door on your ass in seconds flat. Probably minus a few body parts, too. And if I'm around I'll help.

I snagged a bottle of vodka off the rack and headed for the back door. Theron followed, setting his towel down. He waited until I swept the door open and stepped out into the alley, where Amalia, one of the lionesses of the Norte Luz pride, leaned against the wall and made a slight moue of surprise to see me. I'm sure I wasn't in my finest form.

"You going to pay for that?" Theron stopped short when I rounded on him. "Jesus, Jill. What's wrong?"

I twisted the cap free and took down a jolt of colorless liquid courage. "Disappearances on the east side of town. Four women and a man, probably more." I took another slug, wiped my mouth with the back of my hand. The habit of drinking steadied me more than the alcohol would, since I burn it off so quick anyway. "I need every Were in the city running sweeps." I took a deep breath. "We've got scurf."

Amalia paled and straightened. She was golden-blonde, with a cat Were's characteristic dark eyes and wide cheekbones. Feathers knotted into her long honey hair fluttered as she pitched her cigarette into the buttcan with a clean economy of motion. Muscle rippled in her bare arm, the sleeves torn off her Cruxshadows T-shirt. She shot Theron one eloquent look.

"You're sure?" The lean dark Were reached for the vodka. I surrendered it without demur. It was formulaic—I wouldn't be here unless I *was* sure.

I pointed to my leg, where the leather was shredded. Underneath, the angry red of clawswipes was visible, with the trademark jagged curl at the end. "I'm pretty goddamn sure, Theron. I need patrols run in every inch of the city. I'm going home to call Leon right now."

"How many did you tangle with?" Theron passed the vodka over to Amalia, who barely touched it to her mouth to be polite. Most lionesses are teetotalers—when they drink they like to hunt, and not many men can keep up, Were *or* human.

But what a way to go, eh?

"Just one. New one, vanished last night. I found him this morning. Hadn't gotten all chewy and bendy yet, and was probably just a random infection. There was no sign of a nest." *But there has to be one, and he would have found it tomorrow night. Ugh.* My pulse trembled, came back to regular. "Have everyone be on the lookout, and I'll drop by Galina's on my way home. She'll break out the emergency garlic."

Amalia made a mournful face. "I hate that."

"Better than waking up slimy." Theron actually shivered. It was utterly unlike him—but the Weres have been fighting scurf for longer than anyone. There's not a single one of them, even a pup, who doesn't have a scurf scar or two. Of course, they heal faster and better than humans, but still. "The east side of town, you say?"

"Yup. There were disappearances, but nothing out of the ordinary—if you can call anything on the nightside ordinary." My pager buzzed again, but I ignored it. It didn't make me jump this time, thank God. "I'll be digging for the entry point soon. There's *got* to be more disappearances I haven't heard about."

"Okay." Theron's face thinned out, his dark eyes taking on an orange cast in the alley's shadow. One end was blocked off by another Dumpster, and there was a row of castoff plastic deck-chairs for smoke breaks near the door to the kitchen. That door was ajar, and I smelled the grill, hot oil and bacon frying.

My stomach gurgled. I turned sharply on my heel, heading for the mouth of the alley. "Put the vodka on my tab, furboy. See you soon."

"Get your garlic up to date, Jill. And eat something!" He yelled the last, but I was already gone, gathering myself to leap, one hand thudding onto the Dumpster's lid to push me up and over. My boots touched home and I hit the street, up the slope of Mayfair to where I'd parked the Impala. Along the way I stopped right out-side the Episcopalian Church—*ALL Welcome,* its sign said, with a rainbow arching over the words to drive the point home—to use a payphone. I dropped spare change in and dialed.

"Montaigne," he snarled.

"It's Jill. Listen, Monty—"

"Where the hell are you?" He sounded about halfway to fran-tic. "There's another disappearance on the east side. This time it's a cop."

My skin went cold. "Who?"

"A blue named Winchell. Just walked away from his cruiser. We found it locked on Rosales and Fifteenth. He missed his four A.M. call-in."

I did a few swift mental calculations. That was pretty far away from Percoa, but again in a shabby clutch of industrial buildings and railyards.

Plenty of dark little holes for scurf to live in. If they had a range that big we were looking at serious trouble. "Keep everyone away from the scene. If you have people there pull them *back.* Stay away and set up a cordon."

"How big?" A good lieutenant will never question a hunter. In Monty's case, he'd known Mikhail. And he'd once screamed his lungs out while watching me take down a Trader whose bargain had included a deep, nasty hunger for human flesh—mostly sau-téed, with garlic and onions. Monty had a chunk missing from his right buttock, probably the only tender part on him.

After that, there was never a quibble. Most cops are smart

enough, after the obligatory orientation, to just do what I tell them. Very few dig their heels in after a brush with the nightside. And word gets passed around, by hook or by crook.

I don't know, Monty. "Forget the cordon. I can't answer for anyone's safety down there. Pull everyone out. If he's still alive, I'll bring him to Mercy General." *If he's still human, that is.*

"Jesus Christ, Jill." He sounded a little pale. "How bad is it?"

You don't want to know, kid. "Nothing I can't handle," I lied. "See you around."

"Jill—"

"*What,* Monty?" The high sharp edge of fear in my voice could be mistaken for irritation. I wasn't known for having the best temper.

Still, he persisted. "The widow. Do you have anything, anything at all?"

What do you expect, miracles? It would do me no good to say it—I was in the business of providing miracles. "Not yet, Monty. Just hang in there."

"Jill—"

"Got to go, Monty. Keep everyone out of the way, will you?" I hung up, dropped in another handful of change. Payphones are expensive these days, but nowhere near as expensive as replacing a cell phone, with as many times as I get shot, dumped in water, knifed, electrocuted, thrown off buildings. Pagers are slightly less expensive, and they're harder to break most of the time.

It rang six times and the answering machine picked up, a passionless recital of the number I'd just dialed. I waited for the beep.

"Leon, it's Jill. We've got scurf. Anyone you can send will be welcome. Call me, I'm dropping by my house tonight to pick up ammo. Yes, I'm up to date on my garlic. Hurry." A terse message, but it got the job done.

I hung up, and the desire to call Saul shook me with its intensity. I pushed it away and headed for my car.

CHAPTER 7

I parked behind Winchell's black-and-white on Rosales Avenue. The patrol car was parked neatly at the curb, tires turned out toward the street and doors locked. Its shadow cut knife-sharp toward the sidewalk. It was a little after noon.

Not enough time. Still, that was no reason to be sloppy. I sat for a few moments in the Impala, listening to the engine tick as it cooled, heat shimmering up from the pavement down the road. Dry desert air keeps me from sweating much, and my internal thermostat takes care of the rest. Hunter training is good for that, conserving energy and keeping you from drowning in sweat when you're wearing leather in the desert. With the windows rolled down I could smell sand and the river, baking stone and the effluvia of concrete canyons and human scrabble.

I could also smell the mineral tang of hosewater and a sharp whiff of cordite.

Cordite? What? I inhaled deeply, passing air through my preternaturally sharp nose. If I took off the leather cuff I could track it better.

Gooseflesh crawled up my back. *Would you like the scar to start spreading, Kiss?*

"He can't do anything." My own voice startled me. Go figure, I was talking to myself again.

But he can, Jill. If he figures out how to up the ante on this, you have no recourse except the bargain. Hellbreed aren't known for sticking to their word.

Then I could kill him. But then I'd go back to being strictly human again, wouldn't I.

Would I? Was it a chance worth taking?

Not yet. So shut up and get to work. I got out of the car, slammed the door, and cast an eye over the street. Deserted in the middle of the day, all it needed was a lone tumbleweed mincing down the pavement to make it a cliché. One block over I heard heavy machinery rumbling and the sound of voices, traffic in the distance, and a low moan from the trainyards stitched under every other noise, something normally only heard at night.

The scar twinged sharply, maybe because I was thinking about it. Maybe because I could still feel the scurf's acid-drenched claws dragging through my flesh. Maybe because somewhere, Perry was thinking about me.

Worry about what you've got in front of you, hunter.

I approached the car, sniffed delicately. No sweet taint of corruption. Nothing except baking automobile paint and the faint fading odor of a man's cheap cologne.

I cast around. There was another shadowed alley not fifteen steps away. I skirted the car and headed for it, my right hand easing a gun out, pulse pounding hard against the back of my throat. Adrenaline boiled copper on my palate. My coat fluttered, tattered by claws and crackling with dried blood.

The alley held nothing. Scraps of meaningless garbage, all the way back. No place for even a scurf to hide, and a locked door leading into a warehouse that didn't move even when I applied a little pressure to it. The whiff of cordite had gone away, too.

Huh.

I slid out of the shade and into the hammerblow of southern sun again. Tested the wind direction and got another fading noseful of gunfire and something else. It was more a pheromone wash than a smell, brittle copper fear and something invisible I'd smelled before.

Death.

I tracked the flaring and fading of the scent as the wind veered, a block down and two over, turning back, zeroing in. I had to backtrack even farther to skirt the side of a falling-down building that might have held offices once.

What's wrong with this picture, Jill?

The structure wasn't up to code, and there was crime-scene tape over the doors. The tape was bleached and fluttering, no longer a bar to passage. The door itself had been broken in and repaired with plywood, also bleached out.

But the padlock through the hasp screwed into the plywood, holding the door shut, was so new it glittered like a diamond under the fierce light.

Huh. I touched the lock tentatively, sensitive fingertips scraping rough new-bought metal. The smell was stronger here.

I thought about it for a little bit. Then I set my heels, wrapped my hellbreed-strong right-hand fingers around the clasp, and wrenched it free of the thin plywood. I could have broken the padlock itself, but why do it the hard way?

I toed the door open and peered into darkness. Spiderwebs fluttered, and I thought of scorpions, the tattoo high up on my right thigh prickling briefly. A concrete-floored hallway vanished into gloom, and I kept my back to the wall as I stepped in and started working my way down.

There was no hint of scurf, but that reek of gunpowder and death called me. A hunter is trained pretty thoroughly not to make assumptions at the scene, it clouds your thinking and can bite you in the ass pretty hard.

Still, this was a disappearance on the same side of town that other people had been going missing in. A chill that had nothing to do with external temperature drifted down my back. I kept the gun low and ready, and my left hand curled around a knifehilt.

Locked doors frowned at me. None of them smelled very interesting, and they all had dust on the doorknobs that gritted under my fingers. The corner took a sharp bend—I covered it and swung around, found the walls and roof soaring away from me as the hall turned into the interior of the building proper. The lower floors had been converted to open space for something, once upon a time.

Seventeen steps in, on a concrete floor littered with slow-rotting cardboard junk, was Officer Winchell, a curly-headed tall young man in blues with a mask of bruising. Nylon rope knotted around his wrists, his arms pulled grotesquely far behind his back as he lay sprawled in the final indignity of death. A lake of congealed blood spread out from him, and the wooden chair he'd probably been tied to was overturned another four steps away, one of its legs sitting right in the still-wet-looking stain.

He'd been shot four times in the chest, close-range. His back was soaked through—hollowpoints can puncture and bleed you dry, sometimes even if you're wearing a vest. Extremely close range, and he'd bled out under the Kevlar intended to keep him alive.

What the hell is going on here? I looked away from the body.

Glanced at the hall. Someone had to have locked the door on the outside. Had Winchell let himself in over there, or had he been overpowered and dragged in? His gun was gone.

Four shots to the chest was serious business. The mask of horror that was his face was premortem, but only just. Tied to a chair, untied and shot.

Why do you assume he was tied to the chair, Jill? I examined the chair, then. There was some bloodspatter, and a hank of blood-stained nylon rope still clinging to it.

Blue and white striped nylon rope. I chewed at my lower lip, thinking it over.

Jacinta Kutchner had hung with blue and white striped nylon. Just this kind. The same kind Winchell's hands were bound with.

A cop commits suicide, the widow gets killed and there's this rope at the scene, and now this. This type of rope's as common as a sneeze; they sell it in hardware stores—but to have it here in two out of three murders related to police officers? Something smells here indeed, Jill.

I was wasting daylight even looking at this. A scurf infestation would spread until burned out or contained; this was a stack of human murders with no inhuman agency I could see behind them. Not my problem, I was already stretched thin enough as it was.

But Jacinta's body swung gently, her house creaking to itself in my memory, and Officer Winchell—I didn't even know his first name—didn't stare at me because his eyes had puffed closed. Someone had beat the hell out of him and shot him.

So we were looking at revenge or money, most probably. You don't get beaten like that just because someone hates your haircut.

Sudden certainty bloomed under my breastbone like a poisonous flower. *It just don't smell right,* Monty had said.

I agreed, one hundred percent.

I straightened, looked down at Winchell's grotesquely puffed face. Noticed all at once how hot it was, and wondered why I'd smelled the cordite first and not the death. Maybe because I've gotten used to the smell of decay.

As used to it as you *can* get, that is.

Daylight's wasting, Jill. Call this in to Homicide and have a word with Piper when you can. Get your ass in gear.

But first, I stood gazing down at Winchell. The lump curdled in my throat. Nobody should have to die like this. Or like Kutchner's widow.

My voice startled me, breaking the eerie quiet over the sound of freight trains and traffic in the distance. "Monty's called me in, Winchell. You tell Jacinta I'm on the job." I paused. "You can let Marv Kutchner know too."

Then I headed out into the daylight to look for a phone.

CHAPTER 8

Galina looks like a film star from the thirties. Her sleek dark hair is marcel-waved, and her cat-tilted green eyes, set in a pale face, would have been worth a lot of hope in Garbo's Hollywood. Each All Hallows Eve I want to buy her a flapper's dress and an ostrich feather, but I never get around to it.

Besides, she'd probably take offense. You never can tell, with a Sanctuary. They've got some funny ideas.

She pushed the plunger down and pulled the needle free, tamping a cotton ball down and taping it with deft motions. "You're already up on your garlic, but a little more won't kill you." Her rain-gray skirt whispered as she turned away, laying the tape down.

I leapt to my feet and swung my chickenwing-bent arm. Garlic serum burns like *hell*. "Jesus. Christ. *Hurts*."

Her snort was unsympathetic. The Sanctuary snapped the point off the needle deftly in a pint-sized biohazard container and scooped up the tray. Sunlight veered through the skylights and burnished her kitchen table. She lived upstairs over her shop, just a regular garden-variety occult store unless you know what you're about. Then you realize you could find just about everything a serious practitioner of sorcery needs—and practically everything a Were or witch might need, as well—in her little store. "Well, if you'd prefer getting all slimy and bloodhungry…"

"It might be an improvement." I sighed as the burn settled down, spreading up my arm. "I should stock up on ammo." *I want all the goddamn ammo I can carry if we've got scurf. And a few more hours in the day would be nice.* Monty was probably climbing the walls by now, I'd phoned in the location of the body and not much else.

"Again?" But she didn't demur. "Hang on, I'll fetch it. Will it be on account? I can spot you a few hundred."

"No, I've got it. Business has been good lately." Hunters get backstairs funding, both from the city and county; it's a small price to pay for most municipal or county administrations. We also get federal funding if a paranormal incident is big enough to qualify, or if it crosses state lines.

"Defense spending" isn't only for mundane threats.

Plus, the Church subsidizes training no few apprentices. Even if they do bar us from Heaven, they try to make sure we're funded enough to hold back the tide of Hell. We're usually overworked and just-barely-paid-enough, but that's better than nothing. Resident hunters don't need to worry about rent or their next meal, thank God.

We just have to worry about damnation.

And being psychic has its perks when it comes to investing. Mikhail had done very well for himself. Screw that "not using your powers for personal gain" bit. When you're getting shot, knifed, electrocuted, strangled, dumped in rivers, thrown off buildings, or almost eviscerated protecting the common citizenry, the *least* the world can do is give you a break or two on the stock market.

Of course, living long enough to claim a retirement fund is the problem.

"Are you going to keep the Glocks or switch to something else?" She paused, the sun shining off her lacquered hair.

I have regular Glocks, not the smaller ones most female cops use. My wrists look small, but hellbreed strength means I can handle the recoil better than most men. One of the best days of my life was switching to bigger guns. "I'll stick with the Glocks. But fill me up on hollowpoints and the silver-grain armor-piercing rounds. I want to be nastier than usual."

She nodded, tilted her head as the bell jingled downstairs. "Were," she said shortly, and vanished.

Coming to take me to the dance. I picked up my shredded coat and shrugged into it. The walls quivered slightly, the Sanctuary binding responding to my nervousness and Galina's as well. Inside their little houses Sancs *are* the law; the price they pay is being more vulnerable outside than even a weak untrained psychic. But they usually fix it so they don't have to go outside much—and hunters and Weres, not to mention most hellbreed, will beat the tar out of anyone hassling a Sanctuary. Neutral supply of necessities is the least of the services they provide.

I gauged the fall of sunlight and glanced at the kitchen clock—Elvis in a red jacket, his hips swaying regularly. The days were long, but still, every hour of sunlight gone heightened the possibility of a nightfight with scurf.

Enough to give any hunter shivers. If I wasn't *already* halfway to twitched-out between tripping over dead cops and getting shot full of garlic.

The scar throbbed. I reached over, fingers trembling, and stripped the leather cuff off my right wrist. Stared down at the band of paler-even-than-my-usual-milk skin.

On our too-short honeymoon I'd left the cuff off, and I'd even gotten a bit of a tan. For all a hunter's sun-worship, I stay out too much at night to be anything but fishbelly. I was back to putting the cuff on when I didn't want to be distracted by the wash of sensory acuity.

Air hit my skin with a thousand sharp needles, suddenly alive again. My nose tingled, picking up the reek of garlic, silver, the dry smell of herbs hung in the large pantry, wet earth from the greenhouse on the roof. Fur and cologne that was a Were downstairs, Galina's perfume, the incense and Power of her shop.

I examined the lip-print. It wasn't any bigger. It was just the same as it had always been, and when I tipped it up into the sunlight uncomfortable, allergic warmth spilled up my arm.

Goddamn you, Perry. Getting into my head again. *Worming* his way in.

My exhaled breath stirred the leaves of small potted herbs growing in the windowsill, under a double drench of light. Air conditioning sent a cool draft across my shoulders. I'd have to change into my first spare and place another order with Jingo out on Cortada Street for another two or three custom jobs.

They don't sew ammo-loops into regular leather trenches, you know. And I don't have time anymore for sewing, if I ever did.

I was shaking. My fingers almost blurred. It had been so *close* last time, and the time before that. Perry had brought me right to the line, made me look over, and I still didn't know how I had stepped away from the edge.

Yes you do. Get moving, Jill. I slapped the cuff on and buckled it as footsteps sounded on the stairs. *"Jill!"* Someone shouting, and I knew the voice.

I met Theron halfway. "What's up?"

"Barrio's emptying out." He wasn't even out of breath, though his dark hair was disarranged and his eyes were lambent, sheened with orange. An excited Were is like an excited hellbreed, the eyes get all glowy. "One of the 'cougars ran across spoor on the east side, right near where you said. They're tracking now."

My heart settled into a high fast thumping and I pushed a strand of dark hair, weighted down with a silver wheel-charm double-knotted with red thread, out of my face. It clinked against more charms. "Great. Let's roll. Galina, that ammo, please?"

"Be careful." She was at the bottom of the stairs, the pendant at her throat winking with its own light as the air conditioning kicked off again. Her hands were full of cartridges stacked on a red cloisonné tray.

She's pretty much the only person who tells me that. Anyone else knows it's useless. Then there's Saul, who would never tell me that because it implies I couldn't take care of myself. Except he had last time . . . because he was worried, and tired, and watching his mother die by inches.

More unpleasant thoughts, arriving right on schedule. "I can't be careful, Galina. It's not in the job description. Is the sunsword still black?" It was a good weapon in a dark hole, but it had been drained past recovery a while ago.

When it had been shoved through Navoshtay Niv Arkady's chest by a half-crazed hellbreed female crouched on a burning car. Just another day in the life of a hunter.

I wish shit like that wasn't so routine.

"No, it's silver now, but nowhere near fully charged. You want it?" She looked almost pathetically hopeful, but her eyes didn't stop at me. Instead, her gaze touched my face, flinched away, and found Theron, who leaned against the wall between us, running his long fingers through his hair.

I stowed the ammo and made sure the guns were easy in their holsters, ran my fingers over the knifehilts. "Not unless I'm sure it won't snuff out and leave me in the dark. Come on, Theron. I'll drive." *If you can peel yourself away.*

"Give me a second, Jill." Quiet and courteous, not like the unpredictable smartass I knew. Still, everyone minds their manners at Galina's.

Even Perry.

Stop thinking about that. "Fine." I headed for the front of the shop, brushing past the Sanctuary. The scar throbbed wetly. I couldn't resist one bad-tempered little goose. "Stay inside, Galina. We'd hate to lose you."

I didn't miss her muttered reply, which contained at least one term highly unsuitable for a lady's use. We all mind our manners at Galina's—but sometimes it's fun hearing her cuss like the rest of us.

Outside, it was a solid ninety in the shade. I stamped across the street toward my Impala and stopped, suddenly, right in the middle of the ribbon of concrete, heat waves shimmering up on either end of the block.

The sensation of being *watched* spilled gooseflesh down my back. You don't live long as a hunter by ignoring that feeling. I turned a full three-sixty in the middle of the road, scanning the buildings, roofs, the sidewalks, contemplating all the angles.

Who would be watching me? And in the middle of the day, no less, when the sun's power is at its highest.

I concentrated, still as a cat watching a mousehole. *Come on. Stick your nose out, whoever you are. Come and get me.*

The wind quieted, ripples dying in the cauldron of the day. Inside the scurfhole, wherever it was, it would be hot too. They would be piled in on top of each other in a lump of contagious slime, dozing through the danger of daylight. Shedding heat while they breathed sickness on each other.

I need more flash grenades. Three just isn't going to do it. It was one of those random thoughts that floats across your mind right before all hell breaks loose.

Something punched me hard in the chest. I staggered, the wind knocked out of me, and folded down as the hammerblows continued. It didn't hurt until I tried to roll over and pain crested in a fierce wave, driving iron spikes into muscle and bone. Little twisting jitters of sparkling agony slammed through me, each one so individual I could name it.

The world went dark, heaved, turned over, and rammed me back into myself with a shock like lightning striking. Only it wasn't lightning. It was the scar on my wrist exploding with furious power as my punctured heart struggled to beat, bullets tearing through my body, shattering, spilling, blood steaming on the road and chips of concrete flicking up.

Someone was *shooting* me. Doing a handy job of it, too.

More pain, a river of it, a new brand of pain. By *brand* I mean shape and type, and burning hurting *godpleasemakeitstop*—

Half-choked screaming. The walls of Galina's shop tolling deep notes of distress. The coughing roar of a Were having a fit, and it sounded like Saul—but he was somewhere else, wasn't he?

Saul? My lips tried to shape the word, a bubble of something hot broke on them, ran down my chin. Alone and unprotected in the middle of acres of burning road, except I was being dragged by one arm, shoulder popping out of joint with a short *thop!* that would have been funny if it wasn't mine. The scar burned, working inward toward the bone, burrowing in with sick delight. My heart exploded again, body convulsing as weightlessness swallowed me whole.

The scar had actually shocked me, just like a defibrillator. Sparks crackled from the charms lacing my hair.

"Don't you *dare,* Jill!" Galina screamed. The sound was a bright ribbon through dark water closing over my head as I thrashed, moaning sounds spilling from my lips along with the bright red. *"Don't you dare die on me!"*

Scratching, scrabbling sounds. I opened my eyes and gasped as another lightning-shock, this one different from the first, slammed through me. The flayed, exploded meat of my heart was a live coal buried in my chest, systems struggling to deal with the sudden trauma and loss of blood pressure.

WHAM! This time it was Galina, the power had her distinctive flavor of incense and growing green things. Slamming into my heart, *making* it beat through the damage as cells regrew, each one a scream of pain.

I coughed, choked, and yelled, striking out, dislocated arm flopping uselessly. The blow was deflected, and my chest was an egg of red-hot pain. Tearing, horrible, agonizing heat coalesced, snapped into a lump in the upper left quadrant of my ribs; the scar chortled to itself as electricity popped, and I arched, mouth full of blood and eyes bulging, a scream locked behind the clotted stone in my throat.

Heartbeat. I had a heartbeat again.

"—*fucking* dare die on me, Jill Kismet, I've seen two hunters go in my time and I won't lose you, now *breathe!*" Galina's voice was deep and irresistible, she leaned on my chest, thumping me a good one, then clamping my nose shut and blowing into my mouth, trying to inflate my lungs but doing a good job of drowning me in my own claret.

I spat blood, a good chunk of it geysering out through nose and lips both. Galina let out a yelp, choked midway by the volume, and I stopped myself from instinctively striking out again. The walls thundered, wavering like seaweed. If I hit a Sanc in her own house, it would get pretty damn uncomfortable pretty goddamn quickly, and I was uncomfy enough already.

The trouble with almost dying is that it makes you weak as shock sets in and the body struggles to function. I curled over on my side, spitting to clear my mouth of blood and lungfluid, the deep drilling ache in my chest intensifying with each labored pulse. My dislocated shoulder throbbed, a bass note drowned out by a whole orchestra of nasty sweating pain. I twitched, several times, nerves firing without any real reason except *holy shit, we're still here? Still working?*

"Good girl," Galina whispered. "That's my good girl." Patting my back as I retched, coughing and choking to clear passageways violated by lead and fluid.

The ridiculous little bell she had on the shop door tinkled. "Gone." It was Theron's voice. "Tell me she's okay."

"Just fine." The Sanctuary, wonder of wonders, sounded *nervous.* "Or as fine as you can get when you've lost all your blood."

I haven't lost all of it, dammit. It still hurts, there must be some left. But I felt weaker and more unsteady than I liked. Agony receded, becoming just garden-variety pain.

That I could deal with.

Get up, milaya. Mikhail's voice, memory sloshing inside my skull. *Or I will hit you again.*

He never said anything he didn't mean. I struggled to get *up,* to fight.

"Relax, killer. Take it easy." Hands on my aching shoulders, so familiar. A deep rumbling sound—a Were, purring to ease another's distress.

Saul? No, he's miles away. What?

Lassitude poured over me, a sucking swamp of lethargy so huge it threatened to close my eyes and drag me down. "Wha-fuck?" I slurred, my tongue too thick, not working properly.

"Someone just tried to kill you, Kismet." Theron, uncharacteristically serious. No wonder he sounded like Saul. "An assault rifle from a rooftop halfway down the street. You know anyone who drives a blue Buick?"

It was so ludicrous I could only repeat myself. "Wha*fuck?*"

"Just lie still for a moment." Galina's skirt swished. The walls calmed down, settling into regular lath, plaster, and paint instead of shimmering curtains of energy ready to enforce a Sanctuary's will on physical and psychic space. "I'm going to get the first-aid kit."

Best of luck to you. I don't think I need a Band-Aid. "Arm," I whispered, through another mouthful of blood. *Stop bleeding, Jill. Goddammit.* "My arm."

"Sorry about that." The Were crouched over me, a bulk radiating safety. He didn't smell exactly like Saul, but it was comforting nonetheless. "Had to get you out of the middle of the street, dragged you too hard."

It's not the first time that's popped out of the socket. At least

I'm still alive. "Thanks." My voice was a thin thread. I passed out briefly, a stripe of warmth across my face reminding me that daylight was slipping away, and someone had just tried to kill me.

In the middle of the day, with an assault rifle, no sorcery or claws or teeth. Just like a human would kill.

Why?

CHAPTER 9

I shifted, let the clutch off, and the Impala responded, leaping forward. Theron grabbed for the dash. Dried blood crackled in my hair, and I rammed the car into third gear like it was going out of style, goosed it, shifted up to fourth and put the pedal to the floor.

"Jesus!" Theron yelled over the rush of wind.

Men. They never like my driving. Of course, nobody likes my driving. I've never been in a single accident—basic precognition takes care of that—and the cops all know my car well enough to leave me alone when I'm bending the laws of physics and traffic to get somewhere.

They don't like to think about why I hurry. Or what I might be hurrying to get to.

Rubber screamed as we took a corner like it was on rails, and I thought about who would want to kill me. A blue Buick and regular ammo—not even silver.

Not even silver. Anyone coming after a hellbreed-tainted hunter is going to have silver ammo. It wouldn't kill me but it would at least mean someone knew what they were doing, knew it would take me longer to heal and hurt like a motherfuck. Or is that a red herring? I stood on the brake as the intersection ahead of me ran with traffic, the red light looming, juggled probability and precognition, felt the little tingle along my nerves that meant *okay GO NOW* and stamped on the accelerator again.

The Impala zoomed through the light just as it turned green, skidding around a red Caprice as I jerked the wheel and shot us through traffic like a greased pinball.

Who would try to kill me right on Galina's doorstep, too? Someone who had a bone to pick with both the Sanc and me? Someone who wanted to make a statement, or who knew I'd still be alive afterward?

Or just someone who knew I could be found at her place every few days? Which was just about anyone on the nightside and quite a few regular folks.

We roared onto the east side a few minutes earlier than I'd thought. My traffic karma was still holding. Theron worked his fingers free of the dash while I unclipped my seatbelt. More blood crackled, drying on my skin, and I felt a little pale.

"You okay?" Theron's knuckles cracked as he stretched.

"Never better," I lied. "Getting shot just pisses me off, furboy. Now I'm aching to take it out on a whole nest of scurf."

"You'd better calm down." He confined himself to that mild statement, and the glance I shot at him splashed right off the concern on his lean dark face.

I didn't dignify the obvious with a reply. Angry is the last thing you want to be in a nest. Anger is good fuel, yes—but it clouds judgment, and a hunter can't afford that. *Not thinking straight* is one step away from *getting your ass blown off.*

And I'd already had that today, thank you very much.

Another thought occurred to me, terrible enough to make my hackles go up again.

I got shot in the heart. I felt it. Worst piece of lead I've ever caught—and the scar just sewed me up and zapped me, Galina zaps me, and I'm fine.

Well, maybe not fine. But still alive. That's what counts.

But if I'd still been meeting Perry every month at the Monde to pay for using the scar, what would he have made me do? How could I have paid for that much power thundering through my still all-too-human flesh?

It doesn't matter, Jill. It's a non-issue. Worry about who's trying to kill you now, for Christ's sake.

Put that way, the question of Perry began to take on different dimensions. But he would have sent someone with silver, wouldn't he?

Wouldn't he? If hurting me more was the point, yeah. But not if just half-killing me is the point. Perry wouldn't send a human, either—he'd send a Trader. Stop thinking about him, Jill.

Percoa Park lay under a motionless flood of hard bright light, the trees looking dusty and grass scuffed to yellow wherever the sprinklers didn't reach. A baseball diamond simmered kitty-corner, and the streetlamps over the bus shelter Michael Spilham had spent his last human moments on earth standing in were just visible.

The park thrummed. I caught flickers of motion between the trees, and Theron's face eased a bit. The Were's stride lengthened, and I glimpsed the predator in him. It's easy to forget, sometimes, that they're built for hunting. They do it, just like they do most things, far better than humans. He raised his head, his dark hair suddenly more alive, curling a bit longer, and sniffed the air.

My nose was sensitive even with the cuff on. Fur. Musk. The smell of healthy animals, sandy dust, and tinder-dry bark. An outside smell. A good smell, one that means safety. Weres have been allied with hunters ever since the beginning, working back-to-back. Even through the Middle Ages, and that was a right fuck of a time to be a Were *or* a hunter, between the Inquisition, the open mouths to Hell, and the general state of chaos.

Weres provide muscle and speed when it comes to hunting rogue Weres, backup when facing down Traders, and general support, since human hunters are spread so thin. Hunters keep things smoothed over with the police, function as leaders who don't have to work by consensus during crisis times, and take on hellbreed—one of the few things Weres can't do as well as a human.

It takes a hunter to kill a hellbreed. Or a Sorrow.

The thought of the Sorrows tasted like bitter ash before I turned it aside.

"Good turnout," was all Theron said, before loping down a slight hill toward a stand of cottonwoods. I followed, my coat flapping, suddenly aware I was covered in dried blood again, my shirt shredded and my leather pants two steps away from the rag bag.

At least my weapons were still okay, and my rosary. Shoot me all you want, but if you shoot one of my knives, my blessed charms, or God forbid my guns, I'm going to get *pissed*.

The scar brought me back, or I'd've bought it. Not even Galina could get me back after that much lead poisoning. The sudden certainty was chilling.

Had Perry felt it, etheric force thundering through the scar to keep my body alive? Was he up during the day, sitting in the quiet of the Monde Nuit, staring at the television screens in his office? Maybe fondling the flechettes, stained with black hellbreed ichor, though they were always pristine each time he told me to open up the flat rosewood case.

I shivered. My coat flapped and I touched my guns, the knife-hilts, the other little surprises strapped to leather and taped down to cut the clanking. Silver chimed in my hair since I didn't have to be quiet, and the rosary bumped against my belly.

Quit thinking about it, Jill. You almost-die every week. Just get over it.

Maddeningly, it didn't seem quite *right.* I was too busy to tease out why just yet.

The small clearing was full of Weres, and lambent eyes turned to me as soon as I brushed past an anonymous trashwood bush and into full view. They were too polite to ask what the hell had happened, and sadly it's more common than not to see me when I've just been through the wringer.

Hunting is a messy business.

"Trackers are on it," a lean tall woman said. Lioness from the look of her, she had the characteristic broad face and sleek arms, muscle moving supple under honey skin. "Not too far from here, zeroing in on a couple blocks."

"We're burning daylight." A slim young male, barely past puberty if you could believe his skinny build, with the prominent nose of a bird Were. Brown feathers were tied into his shag of a haircut, and he made a graceful, contained movement expressing impatience and controlled enthusiasm all in one.

"Patience, Rubio." Theron's entire face wrinkled into a snarl of a grin, smoothed out.

"It's not a virtue," the lioness added. "It's a survival tactic."

That caused a ripple of laughter, and the kid laughed too. It wasn't the type of nervous laughter you get in an autopsy room, but its intent was the same. To bleed off a little steam, make the waiting palatable.

I set my back against the bole of a cottonwood and closed my eyes. My heart was thumping a little harder than I liked. A rebuilt heart, shattered by a bullet less than half an hour ago. Good thing I was a domestic model, maybe they had a hard time getting import parts for a ticker.

Get it, Jill? Arf arf. You're a regular comic. Should go on the circuit.

Now think about something useful. What the hell is going on here? A blue Buick, Theron had said, speeding away down Macano Street. Nothing but shell casings left on the roof, some of them jingling in my coat pocket. And a smell. Male, Theron had said, human, and sweating. But a professional, to pump me full of lead and get the hell out of there.

Or very lucky.

Why? If I knew the why I'd know the who, wouldn't I.

Pure lead bullets and a professional hit. My life was certainly never boring.

The air pressure changed and my eyes snapped open. Every Were in the clearing was standing poised and looking in the same direction, the same way a flock of birds will wheel with tremendous in-flight precision. As if by prearranged signal they broke, some running, others merely loping, Theron glancing over his shoulder at me.

No muss, no fuss. The trackers had found something, and communicated in that way Weres sometimes have, through instinct, pheromones, or just sheer air.

No more time for thinking. The hunt was underway.

CHAPTER 10

Running with Weres is like hunting on full-moon nights, when everything goes just slightly sideways and it can either be dead quiet...or a sliptilting screamfest from beginning to end, not even stopping at dawn. There's the same breathless expectation, the same pulse in the air, hitting the back of the throat like copper-tinged wine.

I know almost every hollow and corner of my city, and it's that knowledge that lets me keep up. Even hellbreed speed has a hard time when it comes to Weres in full asshaul mode. They run like quicksilver, not like the hellbreed's habit of blinking through space too fast for mortal eyes.

Pounding feet, exhilaration, the heat of the day shimmering off pavement, alleys and fire escapes flashing past, we swept through the industrial district in a tide of half-seen shapes. Most hunts are run at night, when there's less chance of normals out on the street.

When there's a scurf infestation, the Weres run by day. They use that little *don't look here* trick they're so fond of, the same trick animals use for camouflage. It's more of a blending-in, really, but it makes the eye slide right over them.

Me? I rely on sheer outrageousness. People don't *want* to see violations of the laws of physics. They don't want to see anything un-ordinary. Their brains will convince them their eyes aren't telling the truth. It's part of what makes eyewitness testimony so tricksy. Given enough time, people will talk themselves out of seeing just about anything—if they're lucky enough to survive seeing it, that is.

And if they're lucky enough not to crack under the strain.

So we ran, me skipping and skidding, not as graceful as the Weres but just as fast, until they coalesced around me and there was a pause, my ribs heaving, silver shifting and chiming in my hair as I took a deep breath and peered off the roof of a dilapidated trucker's depot right on the river's edge.

"Goddammit," I breathed. I'd've suspected someone's nose was off, but hunting scurf is a Were specialty. "Near the *water?*"

"Funny." Theron crouched in the shade of an old HVAC unit. "They usually hate water. And the place is up on stilts, for Chrissake. Hard to keep warm."

"Not in summer." My coat flapped as I shrugged. "It'll be a regular tinderbox in there."

"I hate getting sweaty." He actually delivered the line with a straight face, too, damn him. "Whenever you're ready, Jill."

I don't think you can ever be ready for this, Theron. "Let's not burn any more sunshine." My fingers tingled, aching for a gun, and my mouth turned dry and slick again.

CHAPTER 11

It wasn't just a nest. It was a full-blown nightmare.

Coughing howls, barks, growls and the exploding sweetsick smell everywhere, sinking into hair and clothes and even the boards of the decrepit building. No time for thought, only motion, because I'd popped the hatch on the roof and dropped straight down into a pile of scurf, Weres suddenly swarming through the boarded-up windows and kicked-in doors, more tearing off the HVAC vents on the roof and boards from the windows, letting in sword-shafts of sunlight as the scurf began screaming their keening glassine cries.

Theron landed lightly, half-changed, the cat in him overcoming the man as he dropped. They are creatures of power and grace, and no matter where on the continuum between human and animal they are they still express the best of either. His claws sprang free, the cat rising to the fore like smoke, and he unzipped the scurf leaping for me in one graceful motion. I spattered bullets through it, missing him by a miracle of reflex, and clocked a scurf on the head with the butt of my pistol. Another Were leapt with a spitting snarl, colliding with the scurf and knocking it away.

Most fights, a hunter takes point and the Weres watch her back. Facing down a rogue Were or scurf reverses that—a hunter is there to coordinate, to provide a leader who doesn't have to function by consensus, and to clean up any problems with the authorities afterward.

In the middle of a fight with scurf—especially full-blown scurf with cartilaginous bones, powdery-slime acid coating, and active viral agents in their saliva and coating, even in their exhalation and pheromone wash—you want Weres. Because they do not hesitate, and they are largely immune to the viral agents, their systems peculiarly antithetical to scurf infection.

It mostly falls to a hunter to give the *coup de grâce,* and keep out of the way otherwise. It's only a little harder than it sounds.

The smell coated everything. Cloying burnt sugar and illness, like the breath of a dying child given a lollipop. And there were so many of them—fifty at least, drifts of them jammed into corners, wedged between boxes, waking to find Death moving among them with fangs and fur, claws and lambent eyes.

That was the first wrongness. There should not have been so many. People go missing all the time, it's true, it's a fucking epidemic, but a nest this big should have made a *huge* pattern of disturbance.

The second wrongness was how old they were. Scurf get more bendy and vicious the longer they survive, and these were full-blown, two weeks to a month old, the scurf equivalent of Methuselahs. Their skin glowed with pallid moonsickness, and their bodies had become humanoid instead of human—potbellied, loose flaps and wattles under hyperdistending jaws, skinny arms far too long and attenuated to be as strong as they are, spindly legs that bend in ways no human's would, and new tadpole legs beginning from the muscle mass of what had been the glutes and also to a lesser degree from the groin, sexual difference only showing itself in the savagery and thrust of a scurf's attack.

Those that used to be male go for your throat. The used-to-be-female go for the chest or the gut, impatient to get at the entrails.

Battle of the sexes, right there. If it wasn't so deadly, it might even be funny.

I jammed the muzzle against a hairless skull as the scurf screeched, its cry like a rabbitscream, and pulled the trigger. No time to think—Weres were pouring into the building's wide-open inner space, reinforcing their brothers and sisters.

The sense of wrongness grew as I killed another wounded scurf, poisonous fluid spattering, acid hissing on my sleeves and against my pants. My boots slipped and slid in powdery slime, and I choked on hot candied fumes as the warning crested, running down my back in rivers of sharp metal insect feet.

I jerked around to see a slice of floor opening, darkness at its mouth as more scurf boiled out from the trapdoor and leapt for me, and I fell back, firing, as the Weres wheeled and poured past me, a tide of glowing eyes, feathers, and fur. The noise was incredible, and I was just beginning to think that maybe we had a handle on this one when the world turned over, the scar clotting with iron prickles on my wrist and burrowing into the bone.

Another hole stove itself into the wall, sunlight streaming as a body hurtled through. A male hellbreed with a glaring white stripe in his black hair hit me so hard my teeth snapped together, I twisted in midair and the knife was in my hand, a natural movement, I rammed it forward and it hissed as it touched Hell-tainted flesh. Wood snapped as we shot sideways, the 'breed's teeth champing scant millimeters from my cheek and the *smell,* the sweet corruption of its breath and the sick candy of scurf mixing to bring up everything my stomach had ever thought of digesting in a painless mess, but I couldn't throw up—I was too goddamn busy.

Wood splintered and crackled as I was rammed through it, splinters popping up. Hellbreed hate Weres, and the feathered and furred return the favor. But while a Were is built to handle scurf, it takes something different to deal with a hellbreed's stuttering, awesome speed, not to mention the corruption that fills them.

Yeah, for scurf you need Weres. But for hellbreed, nothing but a hunter will do.

The problem was, I had just been tossed into a natural enclosure, wooden boxes stacked up on three sides, the hellbreed coming in fast—and scurf on every side, hissing as they bared their teeth and scented me.

Thin blades of fire ran up my leg and I made it upright, reflex moving my entire body with jerky, fantastic speed. The knife was still buried in the skunk-haired hellbreed's chest, and my free hand came up with another one, the gun still in my left hand speaking as the 'breed jerked and twisted in midair, coming down on me, claws out, and the oddly narcotized flood of hot blood as scurf teeth clamped in my calf and the hellbreed collided with me, flinging me back even as it bled runnels of dying foulness. The corner of something clipped my head hard enough to break a human neck, and consciousness left me all in a rush. I didn't even have time to worry about what would happen when the scurf swarmed my unconscious body.

"…jill…"

Drifting. Patches of glaring white. The smell of blood and roasting sugar.

Whafuck?

"...hold her head..." A deep thrumming, like a Were in distress. Sounds came in shutterflashes—cries, moans, the high yip of hurt animal. No nails-on-slate squealing of scurf, though. That was good.

...bit me. It bit me. I've got a bite. I tasted blood and foulness, then something heaved off me and I could breathe again.

Pain broke over me. It was red and smoking, the flesh of my calf boiling as the viral agents worked their way up. The scar ran with sick hot delight, burrowing into skin bubbling with heat, and the agony became immense, compressed, a point of hurtfulness in the gloom of twilight consciousness.

I hate this part. Coherent thought snagged, turned into a soup of confused reaction as etheric force slammed through me again, spiraling out through broken bones, fusing them together, rebuilding tissue. The low deep hum of the Weres gathered around me helped, taking the edge off the pain, smoothing sonic jelly over my flesh as the scar fought with heaving infection running up my leg. The garlic should have been helping too, but I couldn't feel it.

I was *bitten.*

I moved. Silver chimed, hitting the pavement—my hair, flung around as I tried to leap up and failed. I blinked, finding I had eyelids after all. Consciousness returned along with sound and color, rushing into the cup of my brain. I wasn't ready for it— who is?

But the pain receded a little bit, and that meant I could function. And if I *could* function, I *had* to.

My lips refused to obey me, but I made a garbled sound anyway.

"Jill." Theron, as close to frantic as I'd ever heard him. "Stop it. Calm down. We're trying to help."

I'm not moving. It was a lie as soon as I thought it, and I pulled the punch even before strong fingers twisted on my wrist, pushing the momentum of the blow aside. The rumbling didn't die down.

How bad was I hurt? It was hot, heat like oil against the skin, a nova of pain exploding as my entire leg cramped. *This is ridiculous. Can I go home now?*

The cramping eased slightly. I went limp.

"Something is not right," Theron said grimly.

No shit, you think? I couldn't say it, my mouth refused to work. Even for a hunter, dying twice in one day is a little too much. *I'm tired. So tired.*

"Where's Dustcircle?" A female Were, the voice hushed under a thrumming purr.

"He's on the Rez. His mother has the Wasting." Theron braced me, his hands on my shoulders oddly familiar for a stranger's touch. It felt like Saul holding me, the purr he used when I was really hurt but the danger was past resonating in my bones.

"We should call him."

No. I opened my eyes. "N-n-n—" My mouth *still* refused to work.

Even if the body is patched up after something like that, the psyche shivers and jolts like a junkie doing cold turkey. The human animal isn't built to take this type of damage and live, and it can shake certain floor-deep bits of your mental furniture around and around until you're no longer sure who you *are.*

"Easy there, hunter. Relax." A sharp edge under Theron's tone, he was worried. "Just give yourself a second, Jill. Lay back, or I'll sit on you."

I didn't think he *would,* but my muscles were limp as wet noodles, the skin over them throbbing as if I had the mother of all sunburns. I could have gotten up to fight, but it would have taken gunfire and some screaming. The entire conscious surface of my brain retreated from the glare of sunlight, seeking a deep dark hole to hide itself in, to wrap itself in velvet unconsciousness until it got over dying *twice* in less than two hours.

The bite on my calf lost its pulsing heat, the feeling of infection retreating along a map of veins.

"Someone's trying to kill her," Theron was saying. "Maybe more than one someone."

This is news? I wanted to say, but darkness closed over me, my brain finally having enough and shutting off. The party was over.

CHAPTER 12

I came to on my couch, a huge orange naugahyde monster that was actually pretty respectable once Saul got around to slipcovering it with some cream linen he'd found on sale. The warehouse creaked and settled, singing its usual greet-the-dawn production number.

Darkness was kind, but I had to open my eyes. As soon as I did, Theron's face loomed over me, and I smelled bacon, Were, and a hot griddle.

"Just stay where you are." His eyes glowed orange in dimness. Gray dawn edged up through the skylights and the lights in the kitchen were on, sharp yellow blocks throwing shadows into the living room. A single lamp burned at the far end of the couch. "I thought I heard you. It's five A.M., nobody else has died, we're running sweeps. Your ass stays on that couch, Jill. Clear?"

I blinked. My lips were cracked and dry, I licked them before I could speak. "How many—" *How many did we lose?*

"Two down. The scurf swarmed your body; we had a hell of a time with it." He nodded shortly, turned on his heel, and stalked toward the kitchen. "Saul called," he said over his shoulder.

Oh, Christ. "What did you tell him?" It was hard work to pitch the words loud enough, my throat was dry as desert glass. I felt feverish, my body fighting off the viral infection. But I was conscious and talking, and if Theron hadn't killed me I wasn't in any danger of getting chewy and bendy.

Or at least, so I hoped.

"What did you want me to do, lie? He'd skin me." Dishes clattered, steam hissed. "We're supposed to look after you, hunter."

Blankets slid aside as I gingerly levered myself up. I felt like I'd been drawn and quartered, then sewn back together all wrong. *Jesus. What the hell is going on?* "He doesn't need to be worrying about me, Theron. I can take care of myself—"

"You got bit, Jill. You're fighting off the infection, but it was

close. How many times have you almost-died recently?" It wasn't
like him to interrupt me. An egg cracked, and the sizzling was
bacon, I was sure of it. "What the hell's going on?"

*Scurf. And people trying to murder me as if I was a normal
human being instead of a hunter.* "I wish I knew." Guilt pricked
under my skin—two Weres, probably with families, dead because
I hadn't been fast enough to kill a hellbreed popping up in the
middle of a scurf hole. I would have asked Theron who, but it
would be rude—they don't speak much of the dead, and they
especially don't often name them.

I could have asked Saul. If he'd been there, what might have
happened?

Theron made a short sound of almost-annoyance. "Well, start
at the beginning. What's been going on?"

Where do I begin? "There was a Trader that burned down a
warehouse. An *arkeus* I killed the other night—last night? Or
something. The scurf, those disappearances have only been going
on for a week or so." *And Perry called. And Monty.* My brain
refused to work just right. *What was a hellbreed doing there?*

"Anything else?"

"A friend asked me to look into something." Dried blood
crackled on my clothes. I held up my hands, tendons standing out
under pale skin, the cuff dyed with blood and noisome fluid on my
right wrist.

"Like what?"

"Some murders without a nightside connection. So far all I
have are three bodies and nothing else." There was a small pile of
silver charms on the coffee table, tangled in red thread. They'd
probably fallen out when the hellbreed hit me, or gotten torn off in
the heat of battle. I *did* feel like handfuls of my hair had been
ripped out. I almost never get my hair cut. Saul sometimes trims it
for me, but I was probably rocking the punk look right about now.
The back left of my skull was tender, and I could feel the scab
there when my face moved. My neck ached, a vicious dull pain.

*Goddamn. Sonofabitch hit me hard enough to knock me out of
my hair. That's a first.* I almost wished I hadn't killed him, though
you can't second-guess things like that in the heat of battle.

What the hell was a 'breed doing there during the day? And in a scurf hole?

"I didn't know you did murders without a nightside connection."

"*All* the murders I personally commit have nightside connections, Theron. Don't burn my bacon, Saul bought those pans." I tried to lunge up to my feet, sank down on the couch with an internal curse, holding my head. Dehydration pounded in my brain like a padded hammer rolled in glue and ground glass.

"Why he cooks on copper bottoms I will *never* understand, not when there's perfectly good stainless steel around. There's orange juice on the table, Jill. Drink the whole thing, it'll help with the headache."

"How do you know I have a headache?"

"You're usually much nastier than this. Not up to your usual speed right now."

I half-groaned, spotted the glass pitcher Saul usually made ice tea in. There was a clean glass set right next to it, which told me Theron had washed dishes. "Fuck you, Were."

"Nice try, but doesn't have your usual snap. Drink something, will you?"

I poured myself a huge dollop of orange juice, couldn't resist. "Where's the bourbon?"

He was having none of it. "Do the non-nightside murders have anything to do with someone using plain lead to kill you?"

"I don't know, Theron. The bigger mystery is a fucking hellbreed in the middle of a scurf nest." *Not to mention the nest was in a place where no scurf would build it, and...Jesus.* It made my head hurt to think about it.

No assumptions, milaya. *Never assume.* Mikhail's voice, the injunction repeated so many times it was worn into memory like a groove on a record. *Shortest way to get ass blown off sideways.*

"So more than one person is trying to kill you."

"Christ, I'd hope so. If this is only *one* enemy I'm going to turn in my hunter's union card." The banter came naturally, punctuated by the sounds of cooking; it was so much like home I could have cried.

"You guys have a union?" The sizzling ended, and he came out of the kitchen with two plates. Fragrant steam rose. I'd never had any of *his* cooking before, but Weres—especially Were males—are very domestic. It was likely to be good.

Missing Saul rose like a hand clamped around my throat. I took a long draft of orange juice, acid stinging my chapped lips and dry tongue. It took a physical effort to stop before I drank myself sick on it, but I put the glass down only three-quarters empty. "Of course not. Did you make any coffee? How long have I been out?"

He set a plate down in front of me. "I'll go turn the coffeepot on, and you've been out about fourteen hours. Missed a whole night of fun and games, cleaning up scurf stragglers and all."

Shit. "Anyone call? Other than Saul, that is?"

"Your pager buzzed once or twice. Otherwise, quiet as a mouse."

I spotted said pager on the table, scooped it up, and blinked through the layer of blurring closing over my eyes. The plate held scrambled eggs, crispy bacon, and a mountain of grits holding up a pat of butter. It looked *good.* "Thanks."

"I'm running backup on you until this is over." His lean dark face didn't change, but his eyes flashed orange before settling back into their ordinary darkness. "Saul's request. So don't argue."

"What exactly did you tell him?" Monty had paged me twice, Carp once, and the last number sent a cold finger tracing down my spine.

Goddammit.

The Were shrugged. "I told him you were fine, and sleeping, and that we have scurf. Told him you were playing everything by the book and there was no need to worry, but I'd keep an eye on you. He asked me to not just keep one eye but both on you, since you have—and I quote—a habit of getting yourself beaten to a pulp. He calls it your particular brand of charm."

"I do love my work," I muttered, and set the pager down, exchanging it for the plate. Everything else could wait. I was *hungry.* "Did you mention coffee, or not?"

"I did. I *didn't* tell Saul someone tried to assassinate you." One shoulder lifted, dropped, Theron's particularly ambiguous shrug added to a raised eyebrow. "If he finds out, we'll both be in dutch. So you'd better get cracking."

I couldn't answer, I had a mouth full of grits. But I glared at him, and Theron snorted, set his plate down, and went to turn the coffeepot on.

Damn Weres.

My eyes snagged on the pager again. But first things first.

I peeled up the remains of my trouser leg and looked at my calf. There was an angry red chunk taken out of the muscle, already scabbed-over. It *looked* nasty, but the flesh around it wasn't inflamed. There was no telltale blue network of viral spreading around its edges. It was just a bit of missing meat, about the size of a mouth, and I couldn't tell which shape the final scar would take. It was healing far slower than anything else, and the scab on my head was still throbbing as I chewed.

I pushed the shredded leather down, smoothed it over my leg. Let out a heavy, only half-relieved sigh. Took another bite, ignoring the way it turned to ashes in my mouth. The orange juice started going down easier once I had some food in me.

Why would Perry be calling me now? *Especially* now, with someone trying to kill me and scurf in town? It was too neat a coincidence not to be suspicious, coming from him.

And with a hellbreed bursting in on a bunch of scurf. A skunk-haired 'breed who didn't look familiar. Well, I didn't know *every* hellbreed in town. That would be impossible.

But still.

I weighed the idea of going into the Monde Nuit to ask Perry a few questions—preferably up close, personally, with a few silver-loaded bullets—and shivered. Took a huge bite of bacon, chewed mechanically, and sighed as the coffeemaker started to gurgle and Theron came out. He didn't make his bacon like Saul did, but it was still crispy and good, and he'd added cheese to the eggs.

"There's more when you're finished with that plate," he said, settling himself on the couch and picking up his own plate. "Want to tell me what's really going on?"

"If I knew, I would. Whoever's bringing in scurf probably wants to kill Weres as well as me."

"Things have been awful quiet lately. I should have known that would change." He stretched out his long legs and got down to the serious business of eating. "Eat up, Kismet. When are you gonna slow down and start eating properly?"

"Why waste time on that when I could be killing hellbreed?" I shoveled in another mouthful of grits. I *also* waited for him to get the last word in, as usual, but he didn't.

Jesus. Miracles do *happen.*

CHAPTER 13

Monty was out of his office. I left a message on his voicemail and dialed Carp's cell, popping the last bit of buttered toast in my mouth as I dropped down to sit on my bed, taking a deep inhale of the mixed smell of hunter, leather, and Were that reminded me again of Saul. My hair dripped. I'd taken a few minutes to reattach all the loose charms, braiding some in with red thread, tying others close to the scalp, and shaking my head to hear the reassuring jingle.

It rang twice. "Carper," he snarled, the sound of open car windows roaring behind him.

"It's Jill. You bellowed?"

A full five seconds of silence, and the wind-noise cut down. He must have rolled up his window. "I need to see you. Somewhere private."

Well, miracles never cease. "I'm a married woman, Carp. What's up?"

"No shit, Kismet. It's serious, and I *need* to see you. Now." Did he actually sound *nervous?* It wasn't like him at all.

I juggled everything in my head, sighed. "Is it a case?"

"It's the Kutchner case."

My heart gave a bounce, my innards quivered, and I let out a short sound that might have been a curse if I hadn't swallowed the last half of it with my mostly chewed toast. *Now this is really too much, Carp. Goddammit.* "Where?"

"You know Picaro's, on Fourth?"

It was downtown, a little hole-in-the-wall bar. I was going to have to wear my replacement trenchcoat. "I can be there in half an hour. Care to drop me a clue?"

"Not without seeing you. Try to be inconspicuous."

I'm a hunter, Carp. I could be standing right next to you and you wouldn't know, if I wanted it that way. "I'm bringing a friend."

"Come alone."

You know, I would if people weren't trying cut me in half with machine-gun fire or sic scurf on me. A shiver of reaction cooled along my skin, the scar a hard quiescent knot. "Can't. Don't worry, it's one of my people."

"Fine." Bad-tempered as usual, he hung up, but not before I heard the click of a lighter and a sharp inhale.

I hope he's not driving, smoking, and *juggling a cell phone.* I laid the phone back in its charger. "What the *hell* is going on?"

The empty air of my bedroom gave no answers. I heard Theron humming as he did dishes, rattling and clinking and sounding so much like Saul tears rose in my throat again.

Jesus. How was it possible to miss someone this much?

I touched the soiled leather of the cuff. He'd left me three, each custom-made with snapping buckles, fitting close to the wrist. This was the last one. I wondered if he'd thought he was going to be home sooner.

Two Weres were dead. Someone had tried to kill me, or kill them. A whole mess of old, contagious scurf—*and* a hellbreed. Which was like seeing a snake in a beehive—something you don't expect at all.

What did it *mean?*

I don't know. But I'm damn well going to find out.

To get into Picaro's, you have to go down two flights of stairs from a plain door on the blank side of a skyscraper set in a hill. The main part of the bar doubles as a restaurant, a dim little hole with frayed carpet, sticky-tabled red vinyl booths, and stained-glass lamps hanging everywhere.

Picaro's main claim to fame is their two-dollar drink specials, and large cheap breakfasts you can nurse a hangover on. Of course, they're nothing compared to a Were's cooking, but you take what you can get.

I was actually even contemplating a second breakfast as I slid into the booth opposite Carper, my replacement trench creaking as it folded. There were deep shadows under the deet's blue eyes, and he'd taken off his tweed jacket. An actual *tweed* jacket, for Christ's sake. He looked like an English professor in mufti, except for the shoulder holster and the flat oily stare of a cop who's seen too much. He was also scruffy, sandy stubble standing out on his chin and the flat planes of his cheeks. Carp's face is built like a skewed skyscraper, all angles that should work together but don't. He's handsome in the untraditional way of a character actor.

Theron dropped into the booth right next to me, and Carp opened his big mouth.

"Jesus. Are you dating *another* one of those fur rugs?"

I know you like ruffling Saul's fur, but this is different. I winced, and opened my mouth to reply. The Were beat me to it.

Theron gave him a wide, toothy, sunny smile. "Maybe she just likes a little more than skinboys can give, Officer."

For Christ's sake. Save me from males and their pissing contests. "It's *Detective,* Theron. And you're looking at my temporary backup, Carp. Which means he's deputized, and technically fellow law enforcement. So quit yanking his chain and tell me what's on your tiny little mind. Sunlight's wasting." *And I have other business to handle. Like finding out who's trying to kill me, and why. If I knew one, I'd know the other.*

Carp cupped his coffee in both palms, studying Theron. His gaze flicked to me, and he let out a loose, gusty sigh. The waitress came back, stepping into our armed truce with a bored "whaddalya have?"

I asked for orange juice and two orders of bacon, extra-crispy. Theron politely declined.

The place was deserted except for the bar, where a blue haze of cigarette smoke whirled slowly. A few anonymous male shapes sat in the cloudbank, and the waitress became a ghost among them as she headed for the kitchen. I touched the fork laid at my place—cheap metal, poorly stamped. "So why don't you want anyone

seeing you with me? Afraid people might start to talk?" I meant it
as light banter, but Carp's face immediately set itself hard like
he'd sucked on a lemon.

He reached under the table. Theron stiffened, an infinitely
small movement, and I wanted to roll my eyes. Carp's hand came
up holding nothing but his badge, which he flipped open and set
on the table between us.

"I'm Internal Affairs." He said it baldly, like it was a bad taste
in his mouth. Maybe it was. "I had a hell of a time getting away
this morning, but I had to talk to you. What were you doing at the
Kutchner widow's place, Jill?"

I studied him for a few moments. *Internal Affairs? No wonder
you're paranoid.* Still, Carp was a good cop with a finely-tuned
sense of the weird; he knew when to call me in and get out of
my way.

He *also* taunted Saul mercilessly and came off as a cracker asshole sometimes. Nobody's perfect.

"Marv was Monty's partner back in the day, and the suicide
didn't look right. So Monty asked me to poke." I rubbed the fork's
surface, wishing it was a knifehilt. But Carp was already jumpy.
"I have to say, it's looking less and less like suicide and more like
someone's hiding something."

"Only a few million dollars and thirty dead people at last
count." Carp leaned back against creaking vinyl. "Kutchner was
dirty, Kismet. As dirty as they come."

Huh? I replayed the three sentences inside my head. Yes,
Carper had just said what I thought he'd said. "But Monty—"

He dropped another bomb. "Montaigne's under review. I don't
like it any more than you do. Do you think he's involved?"

Monty? Hell, no. "Why would he ask me to take a look at it?" I
picked up the fork, tapped it on the tabletop. "Would there be any
reason for someone to try to kill me because I'm poking around in
this?"

Theron shifted uneasily, staring off into the distance. He
looked bored.

Carp shrugged. "Let me put it this way, I wish I was wearing
some fucking Kevlar assplugs. This is *big,* Kiss."

The waitress returned with a stack of pancakes and eggs for

Carp, filled his coffee cup, and plunked down my orange juice. "Be a sec on the bacon," she announced to the air over my head, before shuffling off.

Yeah, thanks. I got that. "Are you going to take it from the top, or are you going to be all cryptic? This isn't the only iron I have in the fire."

"Actually, I was going to ask you to help me." He stared at his plate like it contained a pile of snot. I got the idea maybe Carp had lost his appetite. "Since you're already involved, might as well."

I so do not have time for this. But I heard the creak of a nylon rope rubbing against a ceiling beam, and saw a mask of bruising on a dead man's terrified face. "What are we dealing with? Use small words, and speed it up."

He stuck his fork into the pile of eggs, worked it back and forth. "You remember a barrio case, about three years ago? Two illegal immigrants found in a cheap-ass room, kidneys gone, blood on the walls?"

A quick fishing trip through Memory Lane produced zilch. "Nope. Unless something my-style hinky was involved, I don't."

"I remember," Theron said quietly. "The *Herald* did a long series on organ thievery. An all-time high nationwide, they said. Whole underground economy."

Cold fingers walked up my spine again. The last huge paranormal incident in the city had touched on black-market organ trade, but only briefly. By the time I'd unraveled it, everyone was already dead, the organs were sold—and I'd almost become a host for a Chaldean Elder God.

I still have nightmares from that. Just like the hundreds of other cases I have nightmares about. At least if I'm dreaming about it I know it's over and done with. "Sullivan and the Badger were on that, weren't they?"

"They got yanked. Sullivan thinks someone high-up is involved, since there were more deaths than could be accounted for even with whatever happened with those hooker murders you were chasing." Carp had turned milk-pale. Those homicide sites had probably figured in a few of his nightmares too. "But still, they were pulled off it and the files were put in a deep freeze. We think whoever's profiting mostly strips wetbacks of their kidneys, because they're a transient population."

I nodded. Illegal immigrants are victims in more ways than one. Coming to look for the American dream, they usually end up raped one way or another. If they're lucky, they get more of a wage than they would back home while it happens.

If they're *un*lucky, they become just another statistic. Or not even that.

I blew out a long frustrated breath. "Okay. So what does this have to do with—"

"I think there's cops finding illegals for stripping, and cleaning up after it happens, a real body farm. It's a safe bet the cash is laundered, but I don't know how. I don't think Marv Kutchner ate his Glock. He was in too deep and making too much money. That shitty little suburban house was small potatoes. He had plans to retire to a nice tropical paradise."

"Who doesn't?" I was only half sarcastic. And another question arrived, flirting at the corner of my consciousness. *I never found out who they were selling the organs to. I assumed it was out of town, since I didn't find anything here afterward and—*

There I was, caught *assuming*. There was always a market for organs. I hadn't thought the Sorrows would foul their own nest, but I'd been kept running around after other cases, chasing my tail. By the time I'd caught wind of their operation they were winding down. They could very well have been supplying brokers inside the city; the distribution network for organs was probably even better-funded than the one for drugs. Where there's a will— and a profit—there's always a way to get a product to someone who needs it.

If they can pay.

The waitress came and plunked down my bacon, or some charred sticks that resembled something that might have been bacon in the distant past. "Anything else?"

"No thanks," Theron said promptly, and we waited until she disappeared into the smoke-filled bar.

I wondered if she smoked—I didn't think she'd need to, breathing that fug all day. *So this could have been going on for longer.*

Or it could be the tail-end of the Sorrows' operation. Too many variables. "So if it wasn't suicide, why did Kutchner die?"

"Jacinta Kutchner was an accountant. Her office was tossed as well as her bedroom. We think she had a set of cooked and uncooked books, either in the office or in the safe in her closet. Yesterday a blue bit it—"

"Officer Winchell," I supplied helpfully. "Was he implicated too?"

A vintage Carper shrug, his shoulder holster peeping out. He didn't look surprised at my supplying the name. "Only up to his eyeballs. Would it surprise you to know Winchell and Kutchner's grieving widow were having an affair?"

Huh. That puts a new shine on things. I picked up a slice of charcoaled bacon. "You do such fine police work, Carp. What do you need me for?"

"The trail dead-ends with Marv's retirement fund disappearing. All half-a-million of it. I think the widow was about to blow the whistle on the whole dirty deal, or she double-crossed someone and hid the money. Maybe she even loved her husband, I don't know. But without her and without the books—and without Marv and Winchell—we have exactly what we started out with. Dead wetbacks and a whole lot of nothing."

And here I was getting all bent out of shape over victims. The thought was too bitter to let out of my mouth. "That doesn't tell me what you want."

"I want to know how far up this goes." He blinked at his food as if he couldn't believe he'd ordered it, took a long draft of coffee. "I have to tell you, Kiss, I'm willing to break a few laws to do it. And you're one of us, but you don't have a lot of the same...limits...that I do."

"Someone tried to kill me the other day." *Jesus. Was that only yesterday?* "They didn't use silver-coated ammo. Which leads me to believe someone knows Monty's called me in and feels just a wee bit threatened."

"You think?" Carp went pale. He was sweating. If it was concern for me it was awful cute. "Marv and Winchell weren't the only ones to end up dead over this. Six months ago Pedro Ayala over in Vice stumbled across something, gave me a call, and turned up dead less than four hours later before I could meet him. It's filed as a random gang-related shooting, since Ay did the gang beat. He was tight with a few of the old-school 51s, their territory's a chunk in the barrio near the Plaza. He used to run with the oldsters before he turned all law-abiding. I can't get any of them to talk to me about him."

I vaguely remembered Ayala from rookie orientation—slim, dark, and intense. They blur together inside my head sometimes. All those cops, each and every one of them passing through my hands before they're allowed out on the streets.

You'd think I'd feel better about that. "Jesus."

"Yeah. They won't talk to me or to Bernie—his partner—but it doesn't seem possible that one of them pulled the trigger on him. He was out of *la vida* since he was sixteen, but he once or twice brought in some of the 51s as material witnesses during a turf war."

I let out a low whistle. That was a not-inconsiderable achievement. "Did they walk afterward?"

"When the killing stopped. Ay was a good cop. He didn't deserve lungs full of lead. The coroner said it probably took him ten minutes to suffocate on his own blood."

I could relate. *Jesus.* I poked at the bacon some more, nibbled at a bit of it, set it down. "You want me to go into the barrio and poke around the 51s."

Theron made another restless movement. But he held his peace, which was more than I would have expected.

Carp held my gaze, did not look away. "I'm asking for a hot chunk of lead if I go down there. Monty's already called you in, Jill."

He was serious. The trouble was, *I* was asking for more than one hot chunk of lead if I went into the barrio. The Weres run herd out there and keep everything under control. I *know* the streets and alleys—there's not a slice of my city I don't know by now—but going into the depths of Santa Luz's *other* dark half isn't something to be done lightly if your skin is my color.

I can't spend more time on this. There's scurf, goddammit. And the widow and Winchell weren't victims in the usual sense.

But still. The rope made a small sound inside my head, a

human being reduced to a clock pendulum, and I knew I couldn't let this rest. Something else was bothering me about the whole goddamn deal, but damned if I could lay a finger on it.

I hate that feeling. It usually means something is about to take a big bite out of my ass in a very unpleasant way. "All right. Hand over the paper."

His hand slid under the table and came up with a manila file, rubber-banded closed. It was dauntingly thick. "This is what I've got so far. A collection of fucking dead ends. If you can make something of it . . ."

"Dead ends don't mean the same thing to me that they do to you." I pushed the bacon across the table, took the file, and laid a ten down to cover a bit of breakfast. "Keep your head down, Carp. I would hate to lose you just when I've gotten you toilet trained."

His reply was unrepeatable. I slid out of the booth, following Theron's graceful motion. I tipped Carp a salute, he shot me the finger, and we parted, friends as usual.

As soon as we got up the stairs and stepped outside, the Were took in a deep breath, rolling it around his mouth like champagne. "No news," he announced, needlessly. "Maybe that was the main nest, maybe we got them all."

I'm not so sure. They were too old. "I'd feel better if we *knew* instead of guessing." I slid my shades on; the sun was a hammer-blow even this early in the morning. "And I'd feel a lot better if we could have ID'd some of the scurf as our missing people." *Good fucking luck doing that, scurf all look the same.* "Or if I could have asked that skunk-haired 'breed some questions."

"*I'd* feel a lot better if you hadn't just volunteered to go down in the barrio." He fixed me with a sidelong stare. "I suppose this is something else I'm not supposed to tell Saul about?"

"I never told you not to tell him anything." I set off for my Impala, parked in a convenient alley some two blocks away. It was going to be another desert scorcher of a day. "I go where I have to, Theron."

"This sounds like a human affair." His tone was carefully neutral.

"So are scurf, if you look at it the right way." Sarcasm dripped from each word. "Don't ride me, Were. I know what I'm doing."

"Easy, hunter. I'm just pointing it out." He didn't crowd me like Saul would have. He didn't smell like Saul, not really. He was just similar enough, his bulk just familiar enough, to remind me of what I was missing.

"Thanks." *You don't have to come along.* But that would be a direct insult, since Theron had appointed himself my backup. It would imply I didn't have any faith in his capacity to defend himself.

Weres are funny about things like that.

He apparently decided he'd pushed me far enough. "When are you going in?"

Well, if I wait for nightfall it will only get more dangerous. But sunlight's best for hunting scurf. "If they find anything while doing sweeps you'll know, right?"

"Of course." He didn't sound offended that I'd asked. "Do you think they're connected?"

A hot breeze came off the river, ruffled my hair. Carp hadn't said anything about me looking torn-up and exhausted. Dim light and some breakfast must have done me some good, though I'd never win any prizes in the looks department. "What?"

"The scurf, and this."

Jesus in a sidecar, I hope not. "I don't know. I'm not assuming they are. There's no visible connection." But he knew as well as I did that I wasn't ruling it out, either.

He digested this. "Something's off. They were too old, and too many of them."

Just what I'd been thinking. "I know. But a hellbreed, busting in on a scurf nest..." *There's one small note off here, and it's throwing the entire orchestra out of whack.* "If this gets much deeper I'm going to have to do something drastic."

"Huh." He visibly restrained himself from making a smartass comment. "Like what?"

"Like something unsafe."

"More unsafe than the barrio?"

Visiting Perry makes the barrio look like a cakewalk, Were. "Much, Theron. Now shut up, I need to think."

"*I'll* say you do."

I let it go. A Were sometimes needs the last word. It makes them feel better.

CHAPTER 14

Santa Luz's barrio isn't a shantytown, though it has a forest of shacks on the edge between "suburb" and "desert" where even the Weres go in pairs when they have to run through. There is the Plaza Centro, which used to be a railroad station but is now a *mercado* with a giant mezzanine, the center of the barrio's seethe. There are bodegas on every corner, and Catholic or Pentecostal churches sprinkled throughout, sometimes even in abandoned storefronts.

The rest of the barrio is quiet, watchful streets. Violence occurs pretty rarely in most of its sprawl, but it's always a breath away. The feeling is like a storm hanging overhead, ready to toss thunderbolts at the slightest provocation. A crackling edge of expectation blurs the air, and your entire skin turns into a sensitive canvas, ready to catch any breath, any faint tingle that might warn you a half-second before a bullet punches through your meat.

The 51s run in the south part of the barrio, in a wedge-shaped territory with its thin end pointing at the Plaza Centro and the wider, trailing hind end spreading almost halfway through the closest slice of shackville—what bigots in my fair city mostly call Cholo Central or, in slightly more politically correct terms, "that goddamn sinkhole."

I surveyed the pockmarked sloping street. Ranchero music blared from the bodega on the corner, *cholos* lounged on every front porch. Two driveways down, a vintage orange Nova was up on blocks with someone's head under the hood, two men in flannel shirts with only the top button buttoned offering advice while clutching cold bottles of Corona. *Frijoles* and sweat, beer and cumin, chili sauce and hot burning wax from novenas all mixed together, with the tang of poverty underneath—a bald edge of desperation, marijuana fumes, and old food.

Theron slammed his door. Down here he looked normal—the

darker tone of his skin and the strangeness of his bone structure became *mestizo* instead of just-plain-brown-person. "You sure you want to do this?"

I shrugged. "I go where I have to. Why don't you put that nose of yours to good use and find me a 51?"

"This whole street is theirs, hunter. But we're going to see Ramon."

"Head honcho?" I didn't ask how he knew all this—he was a Were; this was his part of town. Most Weres in Santa Luz live either on the fringe of the barrio or in a narrow corridor between it and Mayfair Hill where the houses have been in the same families, packs, and prides for generations.

"Lieutenant. He'll give you a safe-conduct if you act nice and polite. Let me do the talking."

"I wouldn't have it any other way." I slid my shades on, silver chiming in my hair. The sensation of eyes on me was palpable, my hackles rising and the scar prickling with dense wet heat. Almost-living heat, like a flower opening under sunlight.

It's not growing. Don't even think about that.

Instead, I thought about the black-market trade in organs. I would have to meet up with Sullivan and the Badger if I had time, and if I could do it without endangering them. I thought about why a hellbreed would burst in on a scurf nest in the middle of a fight, and the thing that occurred to me was so plain and simple I stopped in my tracks for a good five seconds.

"Jill?" Theron looked over his shoulder. Morning sunlight touched off a furnace of highlights in his dark hair. "Everything copacetic?"

"Scurf don't attack hellbreed. Their ichor doesn't carry any hemoglobin or the right proteins for the viral agents."

He didn't think my revelation was worth the name. "No shit."

I suddenly wished for Saul. He would have understood the way my thoughts were wending. "Which means someone might have laid the scurf like bait in a trap. A nightsider who's not only able to handle them, but who knows I'd go after them with Weres."

"Yeah?" Theron folded his arms. *Time's a-wasting,* his body language said.

"So someone is probably *profiting* from the scurf. Nobody

would want to kill me in the middle of a scurf hole just because I'm annoying. Someone is making some money, and there *could* be a connection to this other case. Profit's a strong incentive. And what makes scurf so dangerous?"

"They're contagious," he said, flatly. But his head tilted a little, listening instead of dismissing.

"*And* cannibalistic. What better way to get rid of bodies?" I hated to assume these two cases were linked, but it wasn't out of the ballpark. And part of not assuming, as every hunter is trained to realize, is also not ruling out the possible. "Murder attempts from nightsiders and normals when I'm working a nightside *and* a normal case means they could very well be connected."

"It's a lot of assuming." Theron scratched at his temple, thinking. His dark eyes had gone distant.

"If a better idea comes along, I'll latch onto it." I fell into step beside him as he set off again, heading for a ratty adobe house sandwiched between a gas station and a ramshackle tenement taking up most of a block. Its sliver of lawn was weedy but neat, and the sidewalk in front of the chain-link gate had been freshly swept and sprinkled with Florida water, if the ghost of orange perfume in the air was any indication.

Interesting. But of course, down in the barrio you find all sorts of... interesting... things.

Theron opened the gate for me, and the feeling of being watched intensified. My hands itched to touch a gun butt, but I carefully kept them loose and easy. I know I look odd—wandering around in a black ankle-length leather trenchcoat in the middle of a Southwestern summery simmer isn't the best way to appear harmless. Plus there was the silver in my long dark curling hair, throwing back darts of light. And the pale cast to my skin wasn't guaranteed to blend me in either.

The porch creaked under my boots and Theron's weight. He opened the screen door and knocked, and I heard stealthy little sounds inside the house, my ears pricking. All human.

The thought that I had my back to the street touched my nape with gooseflesh. It was *too* quiet, eerie-quiet, under the ranchero blast from up the street. The kind of deep silence right before a gunshot and screaming.

The door opened, and a young *cholo* with a fedora, a white dress shirt, red suspenders, and a pair of natty sharp-creased chinos eyed us. He had a face that could have come off a codex, it wouldn't have looked out-of-place under a quetzal-feather headdress. Dark eyes met mine, flicked down my body, and dismissed me, moving over to Theron. "Eh, *gato, que ondo?*"

"*Que ondo,* homes." Theron actually grinned, showing a lot of teeth. "Ramon in?"

"Who's *la puta?*"

"This is *la señora bruja grande de Santa Luz, cabron.* Watch your mouth. Is Ramon in, or do I get to go to the cantina?"

"*Bruja grande?*" The boy snorted. He peered at my face again, I slid my shades a touch down my nose and gave him the double-barrel impact of my mismatched stare.

The reaction was gratifying. Sudden chemical fear glazed his smell of healthy young man, and he forked the evil eye at me. "*Madre de Dios,*" he muttered, and looked hurriedly away, at Theron.

"Ramon," the Were said, quietly, irresistibly. "It's business."

The *cholo* backed away from the door. "*Mi casa, su casa, gato.*" But the sweat breaking out on his forehead said different.

Don't worry, kid, I'm harmless. At least, to you. I didn't say it, just followed Theron over the threshold and into the quiet cool of a real adobe. The floor was tile, and my steelshod heels clicked on it.

"Iron," the kid said, in the entryway's gloom. My eyes adjusted to see his swift gesture, index fingers out, thumbs up, a short stabbing motion.

"Come *on.*" Theron gave short shrift to the notion, probably guessing there was no way in hell I'd hand my weapons over to this kid. "You know the iron mean less than nothing. Who the hell are you, anyway?"

"Paco. Ramon's *mi tio.*"

"Then go fetch him, Paquito. I don't like waiting." Theron still hadn't put his teeth away. He also seemed to get a few inches taller, his shoulders broadening, and a slight crackle told me he was puffing up for my benefit.

Gangs are all about face, really. Paco was in that dangerous stage where he was still a young *wannabe* and not a full-fledged *is*. Which meant if Theron made this a pissing match, the boy might feel compelled to throw him some sauce.

The prospect was amusing, but I didn't have time to fuck around. Sunlight was wasting and someone was planning on trying to kill me again, I could just *feel* it.

Theron stepped forward, looming over Paco, still showing his teeth. The boy flinched, covered it up well, and retreated up two swift steps before turning on his heel and hurrying into the adobe's gloom.

"I take it these are friends of yours." My fingers relaxed, and I controlled a sharp flare of irritation. My heart rate had picked up, walloping along harder than it should. Theron shut the door with a click and leaned against the wall, all hipshot Were grace.

"We like to know who's doing what out here. You okay?"

"Peachy." Adrenaline coated my tongue with copper. I was all twitched-up. Dying a couple of times a day will do that to you, redline your responses even to garden-variety aggressiveness. As hard as hunters are trained to deliver maximum violence in minimum time, we're also trained to clamp down on the chemical soup of the body's dumb meat responding inappropriately.

The scab on the back of my head had come away in two graceless chunks in the shower, blood clots large enough to give even me pause. I still felt them peeling free of my scalp, bits of dead tissue clinging to my fingernails under the hot water.

Focus, Jill. Now's not the time to go postal. Save it for later. Save it for hellbreed or scurf. Relax. I took in a deep cool breath, aware of the prickle of reaction-sweat along the curve of my lower back, calming my heartbeat with an effort.

Mercifully, Theron let it go. I slid my shades back up my nose. The dimness gave me no trouble, even through dark lenses my vision was acute enough to pick out the clean tiles, the pattern in the plaster on the wall, and the way Theron tilted his head slightly, testing the air.

I smelled Ramon before I saw him. The cologne was musky, mixing with the smell of healthy male and dominance every charismatic man exhales. I also smelled metal and cordite, and my palms itched for a gun.

*Settle down, Jill. He's only human, after all. He couldn't even
break you out in a sweat.*

The voice of reason didn't help. I calmed myself with an effort.
The scar prickled, sensitive to the tightening of my aura.

Cholos run to two types: beanpole and brick shithouse. Ramon
was the latter, wide and chunky, the 51 colors showing on his
do-rag and knotted around his left biceps. He had a broad cheerful
face and eyes as cold as leftover coffee. He also had a cannon of a
.45 stuck in his waistband and looked about ready to blow his own
balls off with pure *machismo*. "Eh." He greeted Theron with a
lazy salute. His gaze barely flicked over me, lingered on my
breasts under my T-shirt, completely dismissed the guns and
knives, and returned to the Were. "Paquito's a fuckin' idiot. You
wanna beer, *ese?*"

"Love one. This is Kismet. *Bruja grande.*" Theron was making it, in essence, impossible for Ramon to dismiss me.

The gangbanger eyed me. I eyed him right back through the
shades. My heart rate settled down. The body sometimes likes to
pitch a fit, thinking it can stave off death or injury by working
itself up into the redline *after* the fact.

Still, you can't blame the body. It's wiser than the idiot pushing
it through the valley of danger.

Ramon said nothing. He was still deciding. I tilted the shades
down a bit and gave him my second-best level glare.

He took it well, only paling and stepping back once. The scar
prickled under its cuff, responding to the sudden fog of blood-
colored fear tainting the air.

It's not getting bigger, Jill. Goddamn it.

Theron laid an easy hand on my shoulder. "She'd probably like
a beer too."

Ramon said something under his breath, probably a prayer.
When I didn't disappear or scream in pain, he shrugged. "C'mon
back, then. Whatchu here for?"

That was my cue to open my mouth. "Pedro Ayala." I left it
open-ended.

Ramon took another half-step back, his gaze sharpening and
his hand making an abortive movement for the .45, stopping in
midair and dropping to his side. "What for? He dead."

I didn't relax, but I was glad he hadn't put his hand near the gun. "Whoever killed him is fucking with me and mine." I didn't mean it to come out quite so baldly. "You're not the only people who take care of your own."

Gangbangers, if they're smart, understand loyalty. This one didn't look like an idiot, and he was capable of thinking twice. Both good signs, but you never can tell.

Ramon studied me for another few moments, no sign of warming in his cold-coffee stare. "Pedro was one of yours?"

He was a cop. That makes him one of mine. "He was. I'm after whoever unloaded on him, *señor.*" I let it hang for five long seconds. "I would *also* like a beer."

The gangbanger's eyes didn't get any warmer, but his shoulders dropped. He eyed me from top to bottom again, then shifted his inspection to Theron, who spread his hands and shrugged in the particular way Weres have—not volunteering an opinion, but giving polite consent to listen to whatever the questioner wants to say next.

My fingers stopped itching for a gun, and the scar quit prickling as his fear stopped drenching the close air of the foyer.

Ramon visibly decided it might not hurt to be sociable. "C'mon into the kitchen, *bruja*. I tell you about Ay."

CHAPTER 15

It was a productive half-hour.

I ended up with a bandana in the 51 colors, a short lesson in how to wear it and where in the barrio *not* to go when I had it on, and a full rundown on Pedro Ayala—the scene of his death, and who rumor said saw him gunned down and where to find *them*. Ramon promised to make a few calls so I was greeted with courtesy and not a hail of bullets if I went from door to door in 51 territory asking about a murdered cop.

It was more than I'd hoped for. The beer didn't hurt, either.

Even my Impala wasn't stripped at the curb, which showed

someone was watching when we trooped into Ramon's house. It was a good thing, too.

There were three *cholos* in flannel despite the heat, watching the car. They looked amused when I went around to the driver's side instead of Theron. Women's lib hasn't penetrated much into the *barrio*. Still, none of the *vatos* hanging around would dare dishonor or disregard their *abuelita*. If they had one.

I almost thought we would get out of there without a fight.

"Eh *gato*," one of them called. "Who's *mamacita puta*?" A long stream of gutter Spanish followed, asking in effect how much I cost for a few acts that might have been funny if the *cholo* in question could have gotten it up at all.

Yes, I hate men catcalling at me. It doesn't precisely *bother* me—I quit walking the flesh gallery of Lucado Street a long time ago—but I dislike it so intensely my hands itch for a gun each time.

"Does everyone in the barrio know you're a Were?" I said over the car's roof, controlling both the urge to drop down into the driver's seat and the persistent itching for a weapon in my hands. A thin scrim of sweat filmed my forehead, prickled along my lower back.

Control, Jill. It's just a mouthy little boy. Don't go off the deep end.

"Not everyone." Theron showed his teeth again. He was just as · on edge as I was. "But they know how to see us down here. *Gringos* are stupid."

Gee, thanks. Sour humor took the edge off my temper. "Yeah." I heard the footsteps behind me and didn't tense, but my hand did move a bare half-inch, ready to draw and fire if necessary.

They're civilians, Jill. You can give them a few free shots and you'll still come out ahead.

But even civilians can get a lucky headshot in. And I had no desire to die again today. I turned on my heel and heard Theron take in a long sharp breath, as if bracing himself.

For a moment I was almost angry. But then, I couldn't blame him if he was nervous. I was pretty goddamn nervous myself, and hunters are meant to be unpredictable.

The kid standing on the sidewalk couldn't have been more

than fourteen, but his dark eyes were empty as a vacant lot, an emptiness I haven't seen on many non-nightsiders. Acne pocked his lean face, and I couldn't tell how long his hair was, since it was slicked down and trapped in a hairnet knotted on his dewy brown forehead. He wore a shining-white wifebeater over a torso all scrawny muscle, and I knew he was carrying just from the way he moved.

He stopped, considering me, and a chill rippled along the edge of my skin. The scar prickled.

Even among normal humans with no scent of the nightside, there are killers.

This one stood easy and hipshot, his dead eyes flicking down my body once, not with a regular man's ticking-off of breasts, ass, and desirability. No, this young man looked like he was evaluating my ability to interfere with him, and coming to an answer that had nothing to do with my gender.

Score one for a surprise in the barrio, Jill. I eyed him, and my hand eased a little closer to a gun.

He didn't move. Didn't even shift his weight, but a line of tension unreeled between us.

His voice had broken, thank God. Because if he'd had a reedy little whine with a Spanglish accent, I'm not sure I wouldn't have smiled from the sheer lunacy of the juxtaposition. And *that* might have gone badly.

"You lookin' for Ay, *señora?*" A light tenor, not piping. He hooked his thumbs in the pockets of his well-pressed chinos and his mouth turned into a thin line.

Say what? Word travels fast down here. "Pedro Ayala's dead, *señor.*" I kept my tone respectful enough and throttled the uneasy smile once again. It died hard, my lips wanting to twitch. "I'm looking to serve whoever did him in."

A spark of interest died a quick smothered death under his ruler-straight eyebrows. "Why you wanna do that?"

I took a firmer hold on my temper. *Easy, Jill. He's just a kid.* "Why do you want to know?"

His thin shoulders went back and his chin lifted. The sun gilded his thin arms and a chest that stood a good chance of being sunken, and the sullen fury passing over his face was shocking in its intensity—and just as shocking when the emotion fled and he was back to flatline.

Of all things, he unhooked his right hand and offered it to me. "Gilberto Rosario Gonzalez-Ayala." The words were a monotone. "Ay was *mi hermano.*"

Brother, huh? My nose itched and the heat, while not enough to make me sweat, was still oppressive. My entire back prickled with vulnerability. "They tell me he was shot in the lungs and drowned, *señor.*" I kept the words just as flat as his. "Whoever did him is doing others just as bad. Worse, even. I'm going to stop it." I slowly clasped his hand, careful not to squeeze too hard. Hellbreed-strong fingers can make for a goddamn uncomfortable handshake.

He was under no such compunction, bearing down with surprising strength. His entire arm tensed. "Then you better watch your back, *chiquita.*"

That's enough. I doubled the pressure and watched his eyes widen as something creaked in his hand. It sounded like a bone. I tilted my head down, looking over the rim of the shades, and let my lips curl up in a wide, bright, sunny, and utterly false smile. "Thanks for the warning." A deliberate pause. *"Señor."*

It might have been a misstep, but I don't like threats *or* veiled warnings. You get them every day in this line of work, and pretty soon the gloss gets worn off. Yawn.

Now those dead dark eyes had lit up, and the change made him boyish. Under the acne and the hairnet, that is. "Ain't no warning. It's fact."

I let him take his hand back. *Get into a pissing contest with a hunter, gangboy? Not the best way to stay breathing.* "I'm sure of that, Gilberto." One thing about living in Santa Luz for a long time, my accent was dead-on. *"Gracias."*

His thin face wrinkled up into a smile that might have actually been handsome if not for the boils of acne. He would scar badly, this boy, and with those dead eyes . . .

"Call me Gil, *chiquita.*" Thin brown fingers flicked, he lit himself a cigarette. "You do who did for Ay, you come down to *nuestra casa* here. I give you beer."

Thanks, kid. Like you're old enough to drink. "I'll keep it in mind." Making friends and influencing people among all walks of life, that's your friendly neighborhood hunter.

"Jill?" Theron, his tone halfway between *what the hell are you doing* and *can we go now please.*

"Let's roll." I dropped down into the driver's seat and slammed the door. A faint breath of cherry tobacco lingered in the car—Saul smoked Charvils. Right now I was half wishing for one myself. "Where next, *gato?*"

"Christ, don't you start too." He closed his door with fussy precision. "Go west, we'll cut across on Antilles. Isn't that where he got shot?"

"Antilles and Tabasco, the 3100 block. Good idea to check it out, at least. Put your seat belt on." I buckled myself in and twisted the key in the ignition, the engine roused with a sweet purr that turned a few heads. Sunlight skipped heat off the road, the buildings all leaning tired and sweaty under the assault. I seconded that emotion—one beer was not *nearly* enough, the way things were going. *Go ahead, Theron. Say something. I dare you.*

He responded with all the valor of discretion. "Well, that's not 51-friendly, over there. Put that bandana away."

We crossed out of 51 territory in ten minutes, and I had a mounting sense of unease, precognition not specific enough to really mean anything. About twelve blocks later I realized the popping, pinging sounds were someone shooting at my *car.* By then a lucky shot had taken out a tire and the entire contraption—tons of metal—was jigging and jiving like a hellbreed jacked full of silver.

Oh no. No. Skidding, skipping, a flapping noise as the tire gave up the ghost and I struggled against the sudden drag on the steering wheel, time slowing down as if dipped in cold molasses. The engine leapt, straining against inertia, and things got *very interesting.*

I steered into the skid, mashing the accelerator to the floor to get us out of the firezone if possible, and heard Theron's coughing roar as the car bucked once more and lifted, physics taking her revenge in a big way. The silvery crinkle of glass shattering married to the crunch of metal folding in ways it didn't want to. The world blanked out, down was up and up was down, for a long moment. I was picked up, shaken, tossed a few different ways at once, and thrown into that blank spot between normal life and disaster for an endless moment of disorienting darkness— and roared out on the other side in an explosion of too-bright color and sharp pain.

The edged reek of spilled gasoline burst in my sensitive nose. I blinked something wet and warm out of my eyes.

At least I'm right-side-up. Or am I?

It took me a second to figure out which way gravity was dragging, the blood in my eyes streaking in fat globules down my cheeks. *Must be a head wound, they're messy. Bleed a lot.*

More pinging and popping sounds, my body moving instinctively, seeking what cover it could, *that's gas I smell, move, Jill, get the fuck out of here, Theron, where's Theron?*

Broken glass littered the seats. The Were was gone. I tore myself free of the seat belt and squirmed around the gearshift, its head ripped free of the shaft. The red fuzzy dice Galina had given me had disappeared and the car had rolled, coming to rest right-side-up. *Goddamn. I'm still alive. Again. Go figure.*

I braced my shoulders against the seat and kicked. The jolt slammed my shoulders deeper into glass-strewn upholstery. No dice—the entire car was crumpled, I couldn't bust the door open.

The passenger-side window had been rolled down and was now an irregular hole. Stink of flammable fluid rose gagging-thick. *Get out of here, Jill. All it takes is a spark.*

I wormed my way toward the window. The pings and whines of bullets still smacked the side of the car. More glass broke. It was a regular fusillade. *Jesus wept. What NOW?*

The choice was to stay where I was and possibly roast if the car went up, or get shot as I wriggled out the window. I froze, half a precious second trickling away through molasses as the body, idiot meat that it is, expressed in the strongest possible terms that it didn't want to get shot again, thank you.

MOVE!

My arms shot out, fingers closing around the edges of the hole, jagged metal slicing deep. I didn't care, hauling myself free, a high keening sound I realized was my own voice, yelling filthy obscenities I probably would have blushed at a few years ago— before I was a hunter.

Now I know how toothpaste feels when it's pushed free of the tube. It's a good thing I'm skinny. I worked my way free while the crackling sounds receded from the forefront of my consciousness. Black smoke belched and the unholy reek of vinyl burning scoured hot water from my eyes. My coat got stuck, was sliced, I wriggled free and fell on concrete, fetching my head a stunning blow. Rolling, trained reflex bringing me up to my feet just as my baby, my beautiful Impala I'd bought from a junkyard and nursed to apple-pie order, exploded.

The shockwave flung me flat, leather scraping the pitted surface of the road and my head snapping back, bouncing as I hit again. I scrambled away from the car, already going in the direction the blast had pushed me.

I picked myself up. My ears were bleeding, thin trickles of evaporating coolness down my neck.

Goddamn. My car.

The rest of the world returned in a rush of diluted noise. A woman was screaming in Spanish, high-pitched babble. Kids were yelling. *Oh God did I hit someone? Hope not. Cover, find cover*—I rolled, heading for the far side of the street, my back wrenching in a quick burst of red pain.

They were still shooting at me, but the bulk of the burning car shielded me from view. It was a small mercy, and as soon as the smoke thinned a little they would have a clear field of fire.

There were acres of cracked sunstruck pavement and no cover. Then Theron landed gracefully, his fingers tented on the concrete as bullets spattered. He grabbed me, shifting his weight, and I *pushed* with the long muscles in my legs, uncoiling in a leap as awkward as it was effective. My back wrenched again, and the scar woke, prickling and roiling as I *pulled* blindly on etheric force, a completely nonphysical movement that nevertheless echoed in the physical world, adding lift.

The alley opened up like a gift, swallowed us whole, shadows sharp in the flood of sunshine. *"Car!"* I gasped, and Theron's hand closed on the collar of my coat. He hauled me back as I tried to reverse direction and take off.

"Goddammit *they're still shooting!*" he yelled as I lunged again for the mouth of the alley. More bullets pinged against adobe and brick, puffs of dust turning gold. Black smoke belched up— my car was absolutely totaled, a twisted wreck at the end of three loops of black rubber smeared on patched, cracked pavement.

My baby. Gone in a heartbeat.

Theron yanked at me again, so hard my head bobbled. "Jesus *Christ!*"

I seconded that emotion. "They blew up my *car!*"

"Woman, you're lucky they didn't fill you full of lead again. This is getting ridiculous." His hair was wildly mussed, two spots of high color standing out on his cheeks.

"They blew up my *car!*" I sounded like they'd pissed in my Cheerios. Blood dripped salt-warm and stinging in my eyes. "Goddammit, you fucking Were, *do something useful!*"

"What am I supposed to do?" He dragged me further into the alley, swearing under his breath. "Jesus Christ. Who wants you dead this bad, Jill?"

"How the hell should I know? It's someone different every fucking week." I had to suck in breath, burning muscles starved for oxygen and complaining.

Shadows moved at the mouth of the alley. Theron pulled me behind a Dumpster and shoved me down. We both crouched there, my ribs flickering with deep hard breaths and the hot explosive reek of garbage climbing down my throat. "Where are we?"

"Shush." He waved a hand and cocked his head, a cat's inquiring movement. His eyes glowed orange, swords of sunlight piercing the high blank wall of a ratty old tenement across the alley. There were still screams and spatters of gunfire and a low harsh tearing sound—my car, burning.

Oh, my God, I swear I am going to kill *whoever is responsible for this.* I softened my breathing, drawing silence over myself. More movement at the mouth of the alley. A fire-escape jagged up on our side further back, but it looked rickety and rusted; both of us were probably too heavy for it. It's the price you pay for heavier muscle and bone—less vulnerability, but more mass in the ass.

Still, if they come through we'll either have to kill or flee. There's no third option, we can't vanish here. And it's the middle of the goddamn day.

Quick liquid streams of Spanish, tossed back and forth. I listened hard. *"Acqui?"* someone asked.

"Nada, ese. Caray."

More voices. Men's voices, and the piping of boys. Their heartbeats were so high and fast I heard them even though the cuff half-blinded the scar. I *smelled* them—sweat, cordite, beer, and grease, along with the deep brunet scent of dark-haired men.

Theron's hand tightened on my shoulder. My hand had curled around a gun butt.

My car. Goddammit.

Then it came, at the tail end of a string of expletives. "You better tell *el pendejo gordo.* He said you had to see the body."

My skin chilled. *Think, Jill. Think.*

Someone asking for kill verification was someone serious about murdering me. And *el pendejo* has two meanings.

One is *fool,* or *stupid idiot.* A looser translation is *sonofabitch.*

Not very PC, you know. Because the other meaning, in Santa Luz, is *cop.*

CHAPTER 16

The blue Chevy Caprice smelled of sourness. It was clean enough, despite the bottle of bourbon shoved under the passenger's seat and the funk of burned and mashed cigars. It was hot, but the heat was bleeding away as the sun retreated and shade fell over the parking lot.

He parks out here because it's the only time he gets alone. The insight was unwelcome. I lay in the back seat, still and quiet as a stone. Of course I was pretty much in plain sight, except for the thin thread of sorcery running through my aura. Complete invisibility is expensive, energetically speaking. It's much easier, and cheaper, to simply avert the gaze. To hook onto that quality of the repeatable in the physical world that lulls most people into sleepwalking.

It makes them good prey. Even cops, who notice more than most.

Dappled shade from a tall anemic pine tree clinging to life at the edge of the lot fell over the car, yet another reason for him to park here.

I waited.

Shift change swirled through the lot, snatches of conversation, car doors slamming, engines rousing. My quarry opened the driver's door and dropped in, pushing his battered briefcase carefully over into the passenger's side. I waited until he buckled his seatbelt and sighed, reaching over for the bottle tucked under the folded newspaper in the passenger-side footwell.

I curled up into a sitting position, glad for the liquid shadows. I clapped a hand over Montaigne's mouth and poked the gun into his ribs. "Drive. Take your usual route home."

I was sorry about the gun. But I had to make sure. *Completely* sure.

His eyes got really, really wide. But he didn't question me— just twisted the key to grind the starter, got the Caprice running, and pulled forward through an empty spot, taking a right and sliding through pools of orange as the lamps in the lot tried ineffectually to light the gathering dusk. Once I was sure he wasn't going to yell, I eased my hand away from his stubble.

Monty kept quiet, but sweat dewed the back of his neck. His tie was loosened and his jacket rumpled. He was still chewing a mouthful of Tums, a chalky undernote to his tang of heavy maleness, not at all clean and musky like a Were's smell.

We hit Balanciaga Avenue from the lot, and he began to work his way toward the residential section. He still didn't ask any questions.

I decided it was time. "Someone's been trying to kill me, Monty. Someone not on the nightside, someone who doesn't know you need special bullets and a lot of luck to take me down. A real execution-style hit uptown, and then just today a whole bunch of gangbangers took exception to me and started talking about cops wanting kill verification on my sweet little behind." I kept the gun steady. "You want to tell me why you wanted me to look into Marv's death so much?"

"Jesus." He was still sweating, and it smelled sour. "Put that thing away, Jill."

I wish I could, Monty. "Not a chance, not yet." I paused as his eyes flicked up to the rearview mirror, then cut longingly over at the passenger side. "Bourbon in the *car,* Montaigne? What the hell is going on with you?" Leather creaked now as I shifted my weight, he was keeping nicely to the speed limit.

Drinking in the front seat on the way home from work is a Very Bad Sign.

Score one for him, he sounded dry and academic. "It's the stress of putting up with you, goddammit. Your car was reported firebombed in the fucking barrio. They're whispering you're dead. Everyone's nervous."

"Well, as far as the Santa Luz PD is concerned, I'm going to *stay* dead. You're not going to tell anyone you saw me. But before I go deep and silent to flush this one out, Monty, you're going to level with me." I took a deep breath. "You knew Kutchner was dirty."

More sweat beaded up on Monty's neck. He leaned forward— slowly, slowly—and flipped a switch. Hot wind blasted into the interior—the engine hadn't been on long enough for the air conditioning to do much. "It didn't feel right. I just suspected *something,* I didn't know what. Goddammit, he was my *partner.*"

You must have done a lot more than suspected, Montaigne. What, you think I'm stupid? "His widow's dead and so is Winchell. And so is Pedro Ayala. How many other cops are dead, Monty? Was I supposed to end up one of them?"

"Ayala? What the fuck?" Monty sounded baffled. But he was sweating.

But it was hot as hell in the car. What precisely did *I* suspect?

Not much. Except who else would know where I was likely to be, if not my primary contact on the force?

And the whole betting pool, who would be tracking hunter sightings. I didn't bother hiding from the police; they were my allies.

Or at least, most of them were. It looked like not all of them felt
the same way. "Ayala over in Vice. Got himself taken down a bit
ago, shot on gang territory—but it wasn't a gang hit, it was
because he uncovered something." I slid the gun into its holster,
he wasn't going to do anything silly now. "Listen to me, Monty.
You need to keep your head down and stay away from all of this. I
don't want you catching any flak. Who did you tell?"

"Tell?"

"That you'd called me in on the Kutchner case. Who did you
tell? Anyone?"

He took a hard right on Seventeenth, still driving like a prissy
old maid. "Not a fucking soul, Kismet. Jesus, you think I'm stupid?" His eyes flicked up to mine in the rearview, returned to the
road. Traffic was light. "How big is this?"

"You've got some suspicions, don't you. You did from the start.
God*dam*mit, Monty, you should have told me. I don't like to go
into something like this with my ass hanging out."

He looked just the same—an aging fat man, with haunted eyes
and a stained tie. "So Marv was dirty? How dirty?"

When I didn't answer, he stared at the road. After a few tense
seconds he slammed his palm on the steering wheel and let out a
string of curses, finishing with, "And I didn't have a fucking clue,
Jill. I woulda told you, for fuck's sweet fucking sake!"

Christ. Monty had never held back on me before, I didn't think
he had it in him. Still, I had to be sure. If there's one thing I hate,
it's someone supposedly on my side sitting on the information I
need to pursue a case. I still hadn't forgiven Father Gui over at
Sacred Grace for that episode with the wendigo and the firestrike
spear, and I wasn't sure I ever would.

I wasn't sure I *should,* either.

"I know. But something here stinks." *Who would guess you'd
ask me to look into the Kutchner suicide? Or was it showing up at
the widow's house that did it, I wonder? Jesus, twenty people must
have seen me there.* I stared thoughtfully through the windshield
as cold air spilled through the vents. The car rapidly became more
comfortable, but didn't smell any better. "You can go ahead and
smoke if you want to."

"Gee, thanks." But he pulled a Swisher Sweet from his breast pocket and champed, lighting it while he steered with one hand. I glanced away from the flash of the lighter, a star in the darkness. Orange streetlight bounced off the road's hard paleness. He rolled his window down a little and exhaled oddly scented smoke.

I suddenly, completely, missed Saul like there was a hole in my chest. Again. It was like missing a hand, or a leg. I'd grown so used to working with him, having his quiet presence clear up any mess in my head.

"So you think I should leave this alone?" Monty sounded uncharacteristically uncertain.

No shit, Batman. "Let me put it this way. I don't want to avenge you too. I like you breathing."

"That bad?"

I let the silence answer him.

"How dirty was he?" He braked, we were fast approaching a stop sign at Tewberry and Twenty-Eighth. I coiled myself for action.

"Don't worry about that, Monty. Worry about keeping out of this. Don't go anywhere alone. Be careful. And for God's sake don't tell anyone I'm still alive."

"That's going to be rough. What if someone else shows up missing on the east side?"

That's more likely than you can possibly know. I wish we knew we'd gotten all the scurf. "Don't worry about me doing my job. You just keep yourself out of trouble." The car rolled to a stop, I hit the door, and was gone before he could even curse at me. I watched his taillights vanish from the roof of a convenient apartment building and hoped like hell he wouldn't do anything silly.

Theron was waiting in the darkened doorway of a bakery, doing the little Were camouflage trick. If my blue eye hadn't been able to look under the surface of the world, I would have had to depend on the thin thread of *wrong* touching my nerves, and really *looked* to see him. I also would have had a gun out while I did it.

Theron's eyes fired orange in the gloom, like and unlike the streetlamps. "Is he clean?"

"Squeaky." *Or if he isn't, I haven't given him anything to go on other than I'm alive—and if word gets out I'm still breathing, I'll know where it came from.* "He suspected something was wrong, that's all. Intuition still happens."

The Were shrugged. My back prickled—other Weres were still out running sweeps, but they hadn't found any trace of scurf. Yet.

And I'd lost a full day.

It was enough to turn anyone into a pessimist.

"What next?" He moved restlessly.

"You stop by Galina's and pick up some ammo for me, drop by the barrio and squeeze your gang friends for the word on why a cop would want me dead, and I'm going home to change clothes."

Predictably, he decided to argue. "Like I'm going to let you out of my sight."

This isn't negotiable. I need a few minutes to myself and some hard thinking. "Everyone thinks I'm dead, Theron. There aren't many cops who know the amount of damage I can really take, or what it would take to kill me. Nobody is going to be looking for me just yet. Besides, the longer you wait to go talk to your friends in the barrio, the more chance they'll 'forget' something." *If you were Saul we wouldn't be having this conversation; you'd be doing what I told you. Goddammit.* I rolled my shoulders in their sockets, a habitual movement easing muscle strain.

"I don't like it. I promised Saul I'd look out for you."

"I'm just going *home,* Theron. I promise not to talk to strangers and to look both ways before crossing the street." I stepped out of the doorway, smoke taunting my nose. It drifted up from my coat, the smell of burning vinyl, cooked leather, and gasoline.

What a reek. I'm never going to be able to wash it out.

The Were shrugged. "You'd better," he muttered darkly, before easing out of the shadows himself and taking a few steps in the opposite direction. Then he gathered himself and blurred, running with fluid finicky feline grace.

I strangled the urge to get the last word in. It would take me about a half-hour to get home, longer if I had to wait for a cab. I might as well use my own share of preternatural speed.

What I hadn't said hung in the air. Hunters depend on the police, they are our eyes and ears. What we do is law enforcement, in its strictest sense. And as Carp had pointed out, we didn't have some of the restrictions ordinary cops had. No hunter was ever hauled into court.

When you couldn't depend on your backup, where did that leave you? *Fucked* was the only term that applied. And until I knew more about who was trying to do me in, I couldn't even answer my pager. If someone else went missing or a new case popped up...

Then you'd better finish this quickly, Jill. Start thinking about how you're going to do just that.

CHAPTER 17

I hate having guests. Especially uninvited guests.

And most definitely, especially, uninvited guests who barely wait until I'm through the door before they try to kill me.

Word of advice: If you are looking to catch a hunter by surprise, *don't* do it in her house, for Chrissake. Any place a hunter sleeps is likely to be well-defended, and if it's easy to break in you should be wondering how hard it's going to be to escape. A hunter does not sleep somewhere without knowing every crack and creak in the walls—which includes knowing when some sloppy-ass hellbreed has slithered through a window and is breathing heavily behind your door.

So I was ready when I stepped through and dropped down into a crouch. The dirty-blond 'breed hesitated, flew over my head and smacked himself a good one on the jamb. Wood splintered and I drove upward with the knife, the silver laid along the blade hissing with bluespark flame as it met Hell-tainted flesh.

The 'breed twisted on himself in midair with that gut-loosening spooky agility they all have. The hardest thing to get used to is how they *move,* in ways human joints can't and human muscles never would. I spun a full one-eighty, bootsole scraping the linoleum just inside the door, and went down flat on my back in the entry hall.

Come to Mama, you stupid fuck. The bleeding 'breed didn't disappoint, dropping down with claws outstretched, face twisted into a grinning mask of hate. Maybe he thought I was vulnerable, since I was on the floor.

I spend half my fighting life on the floor. Judo's not just fun, it's a lifesaver. Once you ground a 'breed or, say, a Possessor, their advantage in speed is gone and their edge in strength is halved if you know anything about leverage. But I had no intention of wriggling around with this jerkwad.

No, I shot him four times, punching through the shell of hellbreed skin, and flicked a boot up to catch his wounded belly, deflecting his leap by a few critical degrees so he sailed over me and splatted, screaming like a banshee, onto the hardwood floor.

I was on my feet again in a trice, knife dropped chiming to the floor, kicked away so the 'breed couldn't reach it, and my fingers closing around the bullwhip's handle. A quick jerk, a flick of my wrist, and braided leather snapped through the air, the tiny sharp bits of silvery metal tied on the end of the whip breaking the sound barrier and scoring hellbreed flesh.

This is why hunters use whips. It gives us reach we otherwise wouldn't have. I was already pulling the trigger, firing twice more, the reports booming and echoing through my silent house. I was only a half-inch off on the right shoulder, but my first shot took him right through the ball-joint of the left. That took some of the pep out of my unwanted visitor—but not all of it.

The whip flickered again, like a snake's tongue weighted with razorblades. It tore across the 'breed's face, and by now I'm sure both of us had figured out I wanted him taken alive.

I wanted answers.

He still put up a fight, but when I broke his left arm in three places and got him down on the floor, the silver-loaded blade of another knife to his throat, the squealing from him took on an animal sound I was more than familiar with.

I didn't recognize this chalk-skinned scarecrow of a 'breed. He was definitely male, catslit blue eyes glowing even in the wash of electric light. *Fucker left my lights on. How stupid can you be?* "Do I have to cut your throat?" I whispered in his ear, knowing he would feel the brush of my breath through the matted fringe of blond hair. He was bleeding thin black ichor, a wash of the stinking stuff all over my dusty wooden floor.

Once the hard shell is broken, the bad in a hellbreed leaks out. Once that shell is breached with silver, an allergic reaction sets in too. The blade ran with blue sparks, reacting to the brackish foulness of Hell the scarecrow exhaled. He wore a black silk buttondown and designer jeans, but his battered, horn-callused feet were bare, the toes too flexible to be human and graced with curling yellow nails.

He went still. I bore down with all my hellbreed-given strength. The scar pulsed, sensing something akin to its corruption. He whined, right at the back of the throat, and went limp, the subvocal groaning of Helletöng rattling in my ears.

"I don't speak anything but human, asshole." I kept the whisper down, my breath heaving. My head hurt, a pounding stuffed between my temples. *Hell of a day. Stay focused, Jill.* "You going to settle down?"

He writhed a little, testing, but subsided. I was braced and exerting leverage on the broken arm, grinding both shattered shoulders into the floor. He was losing a lot of ichor. *Don't you dare fucking die before I find out who sent you.*

A long string of obscenities, made all the more ugly by the tenor sweetness of his voice. The damned are always beautiful, or the seeming they wear to fool the world is. I've never seen an ugly 'breed—except for Perry, and he wasn't truly ugly.

Did Perry send you? "Who sent you?" I ground down again, was rewarded by a hiss of pain. My arm tightened, and the silver-loaded knife pressed lacerated skin.

The hissing yowl of his pain was matched only by the sound of sizzling. It ended on a high almost-canine yip when I let up a bit.

"I've got all night to make you talk." My throat was full of something too hot and acid to be anger or hatred. The smell was eyewatering, terrific, colossal, burning into my brain. I ignored it, braced my knee, and tensed. "And I enjoy my work, hellspawn."

"Shen," he whispered. *"Shenan—"*

Oh holy shit. But there was no time, he heaved up and my grasp slipped in a scrim of foul oil. I set my teeth and my knees and yanked, twisting; an easy, fluid motion and a jet of sour black arterial spray. His cry ended on a gurgle, and his rebellion died almost before it had begun.

Cold night air poured through the open door, cleaner than any-thing inside. I coughed, rackingly, my eyes burning as I struggled free of the rapidly rotting thing on the floor. A young, hungry blond 'breed, maybe thinking to prove something.

But. *Shen. Shenan.*

There was only one thing that could mean.

Shenandoah. Or, if you had your accent on right, *Shen An Dua.*

In other words, seriously fucking bad news. If Perry was the unquestioned leader of the hellbreed in Santa Luz, keeping that position through murder and subterfuge, Shen was the queen, or an *éminence grise.* She was the biggest contender for replacing Perry if he ever got unlucky or soft—and *that* thought, friends and neighbors, was enough to break out any hunter in a cold sweat.

Gender means less than nothing when it comes to 'breed, but all in all I'd rather deal with a male. Female hellbreed just *seem* deadlier.

I coughed so hard I retched. The stink was amazing. It had been a day of varied and wonderful stenches, that was for god-damn sure. Theron was due to come back and find this mess lying around. If there's anything I hate more than cooking, it's cleaning up hellbreed mess from my own goddamn floor.

I toed the door closed, wishing I wasn't silhouetted in the rect-angle of golden electric light. Locked it, and stood for a moment. Fine tremors began in the center of my bones, the body coming down from a sudden adrenaline ramp-up and successive shocks. I shook so hard my coat creaked, responding to my weight shifts. An internal earthquake, and me without any seismic bracing.

Jill, you're not thinking straight. You could have handled him, gotten more information. You're beginning to blur under the pres-sure, who wouldn't? You have got *to get some rest.*

Yeah. Great idea. Unfortunately, like all great ideas, this one had a fatal flaw. There was no rest to be had.

Not if one of the most powerful hellbreed in the city—and one that had a reason to bear me a grudge—was sending 'breed to kill me in my own house. But why would she send a callow idiot like this, one who didn't know the first thing about hunters?

One who hesitated before attacking me?

It didn't make any *sense.*

I gathered my dropped weapons with shaking hands, tacked out across the broad expanse of floor for the kitchen. A sudden shrill sound yanked me halfway out of my skin, guns clearing leather with both hands and fastened on the disturbance—that is, in the direction of my bedroom.

The phone was ringing. I tried not to feel like an idiot as I reholstered my guns.

It never rains but it pours. Black humor tilted under the surface of the words. I made it to the kitchen, letting the phone ring, the noise sawing across my nerves. A cupboard squeaked when I opened it, and I lifted down the bottle of Jim Beam as carefully as if it was a Fabergé egg. *Jesus. Jesus Christ.*

The habit of drinking helps more than you'd think with something like this.

The ringing stopped. The answering machine clicked on. The same few seconds of silence as always, then a hiss of inhaled breath, static blurring over the line as he started to speak.

"Kiss." Carp sounded ragged. "Goddammit, Kismet, answer your fuckin' phone. Pick up if you're there."

Sorry, honey. No can do. I uncapped the bottle, took a healthy draft. It burned all the way down, but the heat helped to steady me. My metabolism burns off alcohol like nobody's business, but it's still . . . comforting.

"Things are gettin fuckin' ridiculous," he continued, the words spilling over each other. "Jesus. There's a lead. If you're there, if you get this message, there's this place downtown on First and Alohambra. It's a club, the Kat Klub. I got a line on someone who knows something, she works there. A waitress named Irene. I'm goin' in."

My heart did its best to strangle me by climbing up into my throat. I slammed the bottle on the counter, sloshing the amber liquid inside, and bolted for the bedroom.

"Carp!" I yelled, pointlessly. *"Goddamit!"* As if he could hear me. But he hung up before I could scoop the handset out of its cradle.

"Shit!" I yelled, and almost hurled the damn thing across the room. "Oh, fuck. Fuckitall, no."

I barely paused to grab a dose of ammunition, wriggle into a fresh T-shirt and leather pants—the ones I wore smelled of hell-breed, gas, and burning vinyl, as did my coat—and to take another long jolt off the bottle before hitting the door at a run.

Please, God, don't let me be too late.

CHAPTER 18

First and Alohambra is a ritzy northern part of downtown. Despite spending most of my time in alleys and on rooftops, I also know where to find gentrification if I need it—upscale eateries, boutiques, art galleries, and the smell of money. A fair amount of the nightside has its fingers in high-cash trades; the rich can pay for pleasures that might not be strictly earthly.

I like to think it doesn't matter, that I pursue every criminal equally. God knows I try to care a bit more for the poor, since they get shafted most often. What's that old song? *It's the rich what gets the pleasure, and the poor what gets the blame.*

Truer words never spoken. No matter how hard I try to even the score, basic inequality looms over human life from cradle to grave.

Getting more pessimistic all the time, Jill. Why is that?

I crouched on the rooftop, watching the front of the Kat Klub, a long-time fixture of downtown Santa Luz.

Its current incarnation dates back to the Jazz Age. The normals think it's just a restaurant with a cabaret dinner show that turns into a nightclub at about midnight, shutting down just before dawn in merry defiance of the liquor laws. It's a venerable institution, housed in the bottom of the granite bulk of the Piers Tower, one of the oldest skyscrapers in Santa Luz. Mikhail told me once that the property had been a mission long ago—before the town got big enough to attract hellbreed.

One thing is for sure, there is no sacredness left in those walls.

The heat of the day had run out like the heat of the Beam in my belly. I crouched, and considered.

If I went in my usual way, guns blazing, there would go my advantage in being thought dead. On the other hand, if Carp was in there he needed all the help he could get. And hellbreed would know better than to think a burning car would do *me* in.

The thought that any hellbreed would know that one punk scarecrow wouldn't be enough to do me in, either, was not particularly comforting. Something about this was stinking even worse than the mess left on my floor. *That* was going to be a pain in the ass to remove.

Why are you dilly-dallying, Jill? If Carp steps inside that place, you'll have to do more than bleed to get him out.

I weighed every possible alternative. Cold hard logic said to just keep watch, see what happened, and return once I'd developed some other leads—with the benefit of whatever cops involved in this thinking I was dead, so I didn't have to worry about more bullets flying my way from *that* quarter, at least. It was the way I was trained to think, a straightforward totting up of averages and percentages, the greater good balanced against personal cost.

Screw that. Carper's in there.

You don't get to be a hunter without knowing when to buck the odds.

I rose to my feet slowly, breathing. *Just like burning a hell-breed hole, Jill. Go fast and deadly, you don't have Saul with you this time. You did it on your own before he showed up.* My fingers crept to the leather cuff over the scar; I undid the buckles and peeled it away.

Cold air mouthed my skin with hundreds of vicious little wet lips. I let out a soft breath, every muscle tightening as the welter of sensation spilled through nerve endings already pulled taut with worry and stress.

It's gotten stronger. Hasn't it? Oh, God.

The cold machine inside my head jotting down percentages replied that if it had, that was good; it would give me an edge I sorely needed. I would worry about the cost later. Story of my life. I was mortgaging myself by inches—the most dangerous way to do it.

Well, I never did like doing things by halves. Go for the quick tear, Jill.

The rooftop quivered slightly, the world flexing around me. I was pulling on etheric force, the scar moaning and thundering against my wrist. Too much power for me to really control, it wasn't obeying my will. A piece of my own flesh, turning traitor. My aura sparkled in the ether, a sea-urchin of light.

I leapt out into free air, physics *bending* and the pavement smoking under a sudden application of strain. I hit the street like a ton of bricks, bleeding off some of the etheric force boiling through me and leaving behind a star-shaped pattern of cracks; streaked through a gap in late-night traffic toward the door—a massive, iron-bound oaken monstrosity, guarded by two bouncers just this side of gorilla with flat-shining Trader eyes behind smoked sunglasses and the taint of Hell swirling in their once-human auras.

A waitress named Irene. But first, we get Carper, and we make a statement.

The only question was whether or not to shoot the bouncers. I was already going too fast; I hit the door with megaton force, sharp-spiked edges of my aura fluorescing into the visible as blue sparks crackled off every piece of silver jewelry I carried. Oak splintered, iron buckled, and my boots thudded home, I rode the door down like a surfboard, my knees bent when it hit the parquet inside; I was already leaping, a compact ball of bloodlust and action, my coat snapping like a flag in a high breeze.

The restaurant was down a short hall behind swinging sound-proofed doors. A skinny hat-check girl with the brackish aura of a Trader bared her teeth, cowering back into the plush darkness of her booth. Three more bouncers converged on me, I shot two, pistol-whipped the third, and plunged down the hall. I hit the swinging doors so hard they both broke against the walls and was suddenly in an oasis of silk palms, hanging fake greenery, and the quiet tinkling sound of a fountain made of whipped glass and creamy spun metal.

Glass eyes regarded me, shining in the soft light. There were at least a hundred stuffed cats, maybe more, draped in the greenery, their fur brushed and glossy and their fangs exposed. From little calico housecats to sleek stuffed panthers, even four or five (I shivered to see them) cougars arranged artistically on branches with bark too rough and shiny to be real.

The place was stuffed with hellbreed and Traders. Linen-draped tables in nooks shrouded by false plants clustered around a wide glassy dance floor, currently hosting a set of contortionists in spangled costumes—three unbreasted girls and two stick-thin boys, tall and stretched-out, all with blank dusted eyes and empty loose mouths—writhing around each other. They didn't even pause when I shot the maître d'.

Murmured conversation stopped. The maître d' collapsed, half his head blown away and the sudden sharp stink of hellbreed death exploding with the oatmeal of his brain.

I eyed them all, they watched me. The scar thundered and prickled, running with sharp diamond insect feet against my skin. "Huh." My voice was unnaturally loud in the stillness. "Must have forgotten my reservation."

Forks hung, paused in midair. The fountain plashed, sequins on the contortionists' costumes scratched, and the sounds of clinking and cooking came from the open kitchen, set along the back wall. Later on in the night it would convert to a bar, and ranked bottles of liquor glowed mellow behind a counter where hellbreed bellied up, the old-fashioned equipment of a soda fountain gleaming as it dispensed booze—and other liquids and powders.

I scanned the whole room once. Everything was frozen in place except the contortionists, twisted into pretzels. One of them distended her jaw with a crack, and made a low groaning sound as her spine extended into a hoop.

Great. "A waitress." I kept my tone conversational. "Named Irene." One thumb clicked back the hammer on a gun, the *snick* very loud. *"Now."*

A clattering crash, my eyes flicked toward the sound. A black-haired Trader, as thin and beautiful as the rest of them, had dropped her tray. The short black skirt on her French-maid uniform made a starched sound as she backed up under my gaze, blundering into a knot of hellbreed and Traders who scattered in a flash of uniforms—harlequins, maids, one female in a super-retro Batgirl costume—*what the hell,* I thought, and promptly dismissed it.

I took two steps forward before a table full of Traders erupted

into motion and things got *seriously interesting*—but not before I
got a flash of hellbreed and Traders parting to show a slumped
body on a table, blood bright red and human decorating the linen,
and Carp's blue eyes wide open with terror and glazed with either
death or unconsciousness.

Four shots, whip cracking across a Trader's face and snapping
back, I *kicked;* my steel-toed boot caught the snarling hellbreed
just under the chin with a sound like thin glass wrapped in bread
dough when you drop a hammer on it. Clearing a hellbreed hole is
messy, even with heavy-duty sorcery and silverjacket lead. Thin
black ichor coated the floor, not yet ankle-deep but we were going
to get there.

I landed on the table, heels slamming down bare inches from
Carp's head on either side. Stood over him, gun in one hand, whip
in the other. Spared a quick glance down—his eyes had half-
closed, and his mouth wet-flickered, closing, opened again.

He's alive. Thank God. Now to get him out of here.

The world froze between one moment and the next, every hellbreed and Trader in the place dropping to the ground like they'd
all been caught with cyanide Kool-Aid. The doors from the
kitchen swung open, a wave of coldness pouring through the
room, and the tinkling of the fountain began to seriously get on
my fucking nerves.

Dainty, delicate, and dolled up in a red kimono, Shen An Dua
stepped between the doors. They swung shut behind her and
framed her with blank industrial steel; it was a good look for her.
Catslit yolk-yellow eyes cradled in slight epicanthic folds swept
the room, waist-length blue-black hair with the body of well-oiled
straw was pulled into some sort of elaborate confection atop her
well-modeled head. *Probably matches the fountain,* I thought
with an internal snigger, and the scar on my wrist gave such a
burst of burning pain my fingers almost clenched.

Great. Just great. Her aura was the deep sonorous bruising of
a full hellbreed, the taint of Hell warping the strings of the physical world. Plucking, like little flabby fingers, the harpstrings of
this place of flesh.

I pointed the gun, let it settle naturally so the bullet would follow its own path of consequence right between her eyes. Decided that the best defense, so to speak, would be a good offense.

Hey, it's my usual method. Along with ripping Band-Aids off in one quick jerk and throwing myself off buildings after hell-breed, you could even call it my job.

"All right, bitch." I bit off the end of the sentence. "Irene. The waitress. Bring her out, and maybe I won't burn this whole pile of bad taste to the ground."

Shen placed her small hands together and bowed from the waist, a slight inclination of her upper body. "Kismet. You honor our humble business with your presence."

"Can the so-solly routine, Shen. Bring out the fucking wait-ress, or I start wasting paying customers *and* staff. Your call."

The tip of a tongue, far too pink and far too glistening-wet to be human, crept out and touched her candy-apple lips. "What is the nature of her sin, avenging one?"

Perry asks me that occasionally. It's some kind of formula in their weird twisted society, I suppose. Not that I cared enough to ask. "You just let me worry about that, hellspawn." My pulse eased, settling into a hard rhythm, slower than the energy demand of combat but a helluva lot higher than just lounging on my couch. "Hand her over for questioning. And while you're at it, sit yourself down and prepare to answer a few questions yourself."

Her smile broadened. Her teeth were white bone behind bleed-ing lips, and her cheeks plumped up adorably. The kimono swished slightly as she settled—maybe on her heels, maybe not. I didn't know what was under the long skirts she habitually wore, and experience has taught me not to even guess. "I do not think you understand the situation, hunter."

Oh, you did not *just start this game with me.* I didn't lose my temper. Instead, I squeezed the trigger. The report smashed all the air in the room, silver in my hair alive with blue sparks, their crackling suddenly a counterpoint to the dishes crashing in the kitchen.

"Huh. Will you look at that." I sounded damn near gleeful, a laugh riding the razor edge my voice had become. "A thousand apologies, most honorable Shen An Dua. I must have become irri-tated. Do you want to see what'll happen if you make me *angry?*"

Black strings of hair fell in her face. I'd shot whatever architecture underpinned her elaborate coiffure—a trick no less amazing because it was only half-intentional. It had occurred to me at the very last moment that maybe just killing her would be a tactical error in here.

But oh, it would be so satisfying.

That was a bad thought to have, because it was treading right on the edge.

I didn't care as much as I should right now. Getting killed a few times will do that to you.

Carper made a thin moaning sound. I didn't want to think about what had probably happened to him before I quit dithering and busted down the door. Instead, I shook the whip a little, its flechettes jingling. The circle of hellbreed and Traders around the table, like darkness pressing against a sphere of candlelight, shivered at the tinkling sweet sound.

The situation quivered on the edge of violence. If I was going to really get into it here, I would have Carp to protect. It would handicap me.

Deal with it, Jill.

Shen's fingers flicked. I tensed, but a blood-haired female— the mop was really amazing, crimson hair to her nipped-in waist, a sequined maroon sheath just like Mae West's hugging dead-white curves—was pushed forward out of the crowd. She had a pale, hard little face with the rotten bloom of hellish beauty on it like scurf powder on blood, and her eyes were dark and liquid under the flat shine of a Trader.

"This is the one you seek." Shen hissed.

Great. Now I had to figure out how to get us all out of here.

"Now we're all going to be civilized, aren't we?" The whip moved, tick-tock, just like a clock pendulum, before it coiled almost of its own accord and was stowed in its proper place. My free hand now touched a gun butt, but I didn't draw just yet. "I'm taking the waitress and this—" My heel gently prodded Carp's temple, he made a thin moaning sound of a man caught in a nightmare, "with me." My gun eased away from Shen, the assembled hellbreed flinched under its one-eyed stare. Then it came back to the mistress of the Kat Klub, settled on her forehead. *If I kill her, the rest of them will swarm me. She knows it. Think fast, wabbit.* "Anybody have any *problems* with that?"

Dead silence. The kitchen had quieted too, maybe finally noticing something was amiss out here in the dining room.

Shen made another quick movement, her dainty hands fluttering. I almost pulled the trigger—but no, the assembled damned pulled away, crawling or skipping, pressing back as if I had the plague.

Leaving a nice clear corridor between the mistress of the Kat Klub and yours truly.

Great. Wonderful. Jill, this is going to hurt.

"You and your master will pay for this." Fat, oily strings of black hair writhed over Shen An Dua's face, tangling together like live things. She didn't look half so pretty now, her eyes alive with running egg-soft flame and her upper lip lifting like a cat smelling something awful.

My master? Mikhail's dead. "My teacher's in Valhalla." Nothing in the words but flat finality. If Shen thought mentioning Misha would yank my chain enough to get me to make a mistake, she was either stupid—or holding something in reserve. And whatever else Shen An Dua is, she's not stupid. "You can't touch him, bitch."

"His is not the hand that holds your leash, hunter." Her razor-pearl teeth showed in a snarl, all the more chilling because of the full-cheeked sweetness of her face. The kimono's skirt rustled, shapes bulging underneath it. "Tell the master of the Monde *he will pay for this.*"

It was so out of left field I almost couldn't connect the words together. *Perry? Oh good God. Please.* "If you think I'm here for him, you're wrong. Perry has no hold on me." *Other than the fact that I'd rather deal with him than you any day of the week, since he has a vested interest in keeping me alive so he can fuck with me.* I hopped down from the table, the gun tracking smoothly. The waitress flinched, cowering, I eyed her. "Pick him up, Trader."

"You will not—" Shen began, and my heartrate eased, smoothing out, as I lifted my head and regarded her again. They could all hear my pulse, and the sudden calm washing over me was as ominous as a thunderstorm.

Talk your way out of this one, Kismet. "This is one of mine, hellspawn. You don't get to eat him tonight."

There are six pounds of center-trigger pull on a Glock and I was at about four and a half. The world had turned into a collection of edges too sharp to be real, all my senses working overtime and amped up into the red.

Shen's face contorted once, smoothed out, crumpled again. The bruise of her aura tightened like a fist. I watched, waiting. If Shen was more than normally upset at Perry or needed to regain some face in front of her minions and clients, this would get ugly really quickly.

"You are only one, hunter. And we are legion." The black strings of her hair rubbed against each other, squealing as she subvocalized. Helletöng rumbled through the floor, vibrating against my bootsoles.

"That does not particularly bother me." I sounded like it didn't, too. "I've killed more in a night than you have in this dining room, Shen." I paused. "You, Trader. I told you to pick him up."

The Trader squeaked as if she'd been pinched and moved to obey. I kept both guns on Shen. *I might get out of this alive. All hail the poker-faced hunter and her ability to talk smack.*

Shen took two long strides forward, the fabric of her kimono's lower half moving in odd ways, silk groaning and stretching. "You will not leave this place alive," she promised, and the hell-tainted on every side moved closer. A rising growl slid through them, Helletöng rubbing at the walls.

Oh, so that's the way we're going to do this? My free hand was suddenly full of Glock. "Outside, Irene. And *gently.* If he dies, you're fucking next." I waited until I heard her start moving, Carp's shapeless groan as he lay cradled in her stick-thin, dead-white arms, her purple satin gloves now stained with blood. This I took in through my peripheral vision, my heartrate cool and steady, both guns still locked on the mistress of the Kat Klub. "Is that the way you want to play it, Shen?"

Nothing human lived under the skirt of that antique kimono. The scar prickled, a mass of hot needles burrowing into my wrist, and the world got very still again, clarity settling over each edge and curve. The contortionists were still writhing on the stage, joints crackling and sequins scraping.

"Take her," she whispered. But none of the assembled 'breed or Traders moved.

Apparently, right at this moment, even fear of Shen An Dua couldn't make them swarm me. It was an indirect compliment.

I showed my teeth. My entire body relaxed into the flow of the moment, the absolute chilling certainty of violence taking all indecision out of the equation. "Bring it," I whispered. My forearms tensed, cords of muscle standing out as I edged toward that last pound and a half of pressure on the triggers.

A new voice cut across the warp and weft of the interior, slicing cleanly even if it was loaded with Texas so thick the drawl dripped over the sides. "Jesus fuckin' Christ. What the hell's this?"

I almost twitched. Relief threatened to unloose my knees, and the situation tipped from *ohmyGod I am not going to survive this* to *Thank God someone else is going to die with me.*

Shen's head turned, a slow movement like a servomotor with oiled bearings. I kept both guns trained on her. I'd once seen her unzip a Trader's guts and lift a double handful of wet intestine to her plump little candy-apple-red mouth.

Things like that will make a hunter cautious. Add to that the fact that I'd wanted to question the Trader about a certain stable of high-priced underage sex slaves, and Shen's calm inscrutable smile as strings of human gut hung from her mouth, and you had bad blood between us. I knew she'd been in it up to her eyeballs, but I hadn't been able to make any of it stick. I couldn't *prove* it to my own satisfaction.

I could prove little of what I suspected when it came to her. Which meant I couldn't kill her with a clear conscience. Or even just a reasonably clear conscience, which, some days, is all you're going to get in this line of work.

"Hi, Leon," I said. "Nice to see you."

"You've got crappy taste in restaurants, darlin'," Leon Budge drawled. "Why don't we go somewheres civilized where I can get me a got-damn drink?"

Shen surged forward again, and there was a familiar, ratcheting sound. Leon had worked the bolt action on his rifle. "Oh, now, sweetie-pie, don't do that. Me and Rosita here, we gets nervous when a slope-eyed gal like you gets twitchy."

Jesus, Leon, how much of a racist cliché can you be? I took two steps, sidling away from the table. Helletöng crested, the sound of skin slipping as drowned fingers rubbed together, chrome flies buzzing in chlorine-laced bottles—the scar sent a wet thrill up my arm, hearing its language spoken.

Two more steps. I took a quick glance, made certain I was out of Leon's field of fire.

He stood in a battered leather trenchcoat, plain dun instead of black, his hair a crow's nest of untidy brown waves, copper charms threaded on black heavy-duty waxed thread and clinking slightly as a breeze ruffled his hair. The wreck of the swinging doors smoked around him, and he held the rifle like it wasn't capable of blowing a 'breed in half with the modifications he'd put on it.

Chubby cherub's face, wide shoulders, a body kept in shape by a hunter's constant training but still managing to give the impression of pudginess. Leon looked like a newscaster trapped in goth-boy drag, an impression helped along by the eyeliner scoring rings around each hazel eye and the clinking mass of amulets around his neck on cords, thongs, and thin copper chains. Four plain silver rings on his left hand ran with blue sparks, echoing the silver in my hair. One of them was the apprentice-ring his teacher had given him.

Leon was smiling under a scruff of dark stubble, white teeth peeping out. "Should I put 'er down, Kiss?"

Don't call me that, dammit. "If she moves." I turned my back on Shen An Dua and her assembled footlickers and customers, guns sliding into their holsters. "Or hell, even if you don't like her hairstyle."

"It's somethin'." The cheerful, thoughtful tone never wavered, and he didn't blink. The bandoliers crossing his chest held small silver-coated throwing knives, each one sharp enough to take a finger off.

Or pop right into a 'breed's eye and pierce the brain with blessed metal.

"Well, the barber was an amateur." I shrugged, my knees threatening to buckle with each straight, strutting step.

Rule of dealing with murderous hellspawn: try not to look weak. It gets them all excited.

"You have earned my hatred," Shen was back to whispering. "Hell and Earth both witness my vow, hunter. *You will pay for this.*"

Yeah, one way or another. Sure. "You already said that, most honorable Shen An Dua. Don't be boring." I would have pantomimed a yawn if my hands weren't quivering with the urge to take the guns out again, turn around, and put this murderous hellspawn down like the parasite she was.

Leon's gaze flicked to mine for a fraction of a second. It was a purely professional look, gauging what I was likely to do next. I sounded cool and calm, but something in my cheek twitched like a needle was plucking at the flesh. The glance was also a communication, one I heard as clearly as verbal speech—*are you gonna throw down, darlin'?*

If I did, he was willing to back me. But Leon knew just as surely as I did it would be a terrible mistake. These hellbreed and Traders weren't surprised anymore, and they'd had plenty of time to think about how to take the two of us apart. Shen could threaten all she wanted now and still retain some semblance of face, but if we killed her it wouldn't be a free-for-all that would allow us to divvy them up and pick them off. No, if we insulted her, *then* killed her, whoever wanted to step into her shoes would have to kill us to prove they were worthy of taking Shen's place.

Well, Jill, you fucked this up six ways to Sunday. Cool night air poured down the hall, touching Leon's hair. He backed up, covering me with the rifle as I retreated from what had certainly been a bad idea in the first place.

We made it through the hall, past the crumpled bodies of the bouncers. The hat-check girl was nowhere in sight. Sirens wailed in the distance, and I was suddenly struck by an entirely new feeling.

I was used to the sound being a relief, as in *the cavalry's on its way.* Now I felt the way any criminal feels—like the sirens were baying hounds and I was the fox.

The crowd out front had vanished. Most of them were likely to be Traders and hellbreed, probably thanking their lucky stars they hadn't been inside.

"Fucking *hell*." I restrained the urge to kick something.

The blood-haired Trader was gone.

So was Carp.

CHAPTER 19

Leon drove, of all things, a big blue Chevy half-ton. The interior smelled of grease and jostled as the engine labored.

"This thing needs a tune-up," I told him. "What the hell are you doing here? Not that I'm not happy to see you."

"Where the fuck's your car, darlin'? And I'm here because you called, and because someone's been trappin' scurf in my neck of the woods. I wouldn't mind, since we got enough and to spare, but trappin' 'em means they have somethin' planned, and that I don't like. I tracked 'em over the city limits. We got ourselves a genuine grade-A problem goin' on here."

"My car blew up. What do you mean, *trapping* scurf?" I clung to the oh-shit strap while he took a corner, working the gears like they were going out of style. Beer cans rolled around my ankles and a metal footlocker containing ammo and various other odds and ends rattled, sliding forward to smack my boots.

Then Leon did something I hated. He closed his eyes.

Oh shit.

I came back from Hell with a gift or a curse, depending on which way you look at it. My blue eye can see *between* and *below* the surface of the world. It is that ability to go *between* that sets me apart from other hunters—that and my bargain with Perry. Most of us just come back from Hell with some interesting instincts, a grasp of sorcery, and the ability to see through the masks hellbreed like to wear.

But some of us return with more.

Leon came back a tracker. You name it, he can follow it. All it requires, he says, is the right mindset.

And a healthy amount of Pabst Blue Ribbon to dull his sensitivity the rest of the time. If Budge wasn't half-drunk, things were very bad indeed. The only good thing about it was he needed a bathroom about as often as a female hunter does.

Beer does that to you when you've got a human metabolism. Me, I can't drink enough of the damn stuff to even get a buzz.

I didn't ask who we were following. Leon had seen Carp, unmistakably human and bleeding in the middle of a hellbreed haunt, and had further seen me unwilling to leave without him. Some things are just understood.

Leon floored it, and the pickup began to shimmy in interesting ways. "Movin' fast, and agin the wind."

Not like wind matters to Traders or hellbreed, Leon. I hung on for dear life as he slammed us through traffic, missing a semi by bare inches and almost dinging the paint job on a showroom-bright black SUV that blared its horn and dropped back. Leon's eyelids flickered like he was dreaming.

"What do you mean, *trapping scurf?*" I repeated. That was bad, bad news on all fronts.

"I mean catching the little bastards and shipping them out of town, both by rail and by water. I didn't think it was possible—who the hell would *want* 'em, huh? Hang on."

Hang on?

Leon twisted the wheel, hard. We cut across two lanes of traffic, he floored it, and I started to feel a little green. It wasn't the speed, it was the fact that he had his eyes shut tight.

Even when you're used to Leon, it's creepy.

"You might want to slow down. I'm having some problems up here."

"What kinda problems?"

Where do I start? "There's a case. Some dirty cops. They've already tried to kill me."

"Holy *shit*." That snapped his eyes open for almost fifteen seconds, but it wasn't comforting at all. His dark gaze was filmed as if by cataracts, shapes like windblown clouds rolling over the eyeballs. Wind roared through the half-open window; I didn't have a hand to spare to roll it up. I was busy hanging on.

For some reason, nobody ever says a goddamn thing about the way Leon drives.

He closed his eyes again, stamping on the accelerator, and I was seriously considering commending my soul to God yet again that night when he jagged over, zipped into an alley neat as you please, stood on the brakes, and bailed out like his pants were on fire.

I followed, sliding across the seat and hopping out his side. He'd taken the keys with him, so I swept the door closed and pounded after him. He was only capable of human speed, but human speed is pretty damn fast when you're a hunter.

He plunged through an alley, up a fire escape, zigzagged across a low rooftop and came to an abrupt halt, staring across the street. I skidded to a stop right next to him, gave the street a once-over, and looked up at the granite Jesus glowering at downtown.

"Holy shit. She brought him to the hospital?" I didn't mean for it to come out as a question. *Well, I told her that if he died she was next. I suppose it's logical.*

"That's one almighty-big statue there," was all Leon said. He blinked a couple times, his shoulders coming down and the colorless fume of urgency swirling away from him.

"That's Sisters of Mercy. Used to be Catholic. I thought you were in there once, when Mikhail and you—" I bit off the end of the sentence, swallowed it, and looked for a way down. "Well, let's go on in, then. I need that Trader and I need that cop, too."

"He's a cop?" Meaning, *I thought you said they was tryin' to kill you.*

"He's one of mine, Leon. Move your ass." I paused. "It's good to see you."

And it was, too. Some things only another hunter will understand, and moreover, sometimes you don't want to be questioned. It didn't matter to Leon what the hell was going on, if I was in it, he was going to be in it too. Up to the eyeballs, if necessary, and without counting the cost or thinking twice about it.

And while we were at it we would find out who was shipping scurf around, for God's sake.

I hopped up to the ledge, but Leon's fingers curled around my arm. Only another hunter—or Saul—would be able to do that without me instinctively twitching away. "Jill."

The street below looked quiet. I took a second look, to make sure. "What?"

"You doin' all right, darlin'?" Quiet, with absolutely no Texas bluster.

The street swam with light as if underwater, wavering, and snapped into focus when I made an almost-physical effort to clean up my mental floor. "No. I'm not." The truth burned my tongue, but you can't lie to another hunter.

You just *can't.*

His hand fell away. "Well sheeee-*yit.*"

"I heartily concur. Now come on." I leapt out into space, pulling etheric force through the scar at the last moment, and slammed down on the pavement, smoke flashing in the air as the sudden violation of a law of physics rippled around me.

Jesus, Jill, what would have happened if the scar failed? You'd be lying on the pavement bleeding, now.

I told myself not to borrow trouble and stalked for the entrance to the ER. Leon would find his own way down.

Of all the wonders the world has to offer, a Trader hovering by the bedside of a foul-mouthed homicide detective is surely one of the most uncommon. Carp was beaten up, bruised, and had bled all over Kingdom Come from a couple shallow head wounds and a more serious one on his right thigh that looked like a huge dogbite.

I kept one eye on the Trader while I examined Carp. A phlegmatic Filipina nurse swabbed the hole in his leg. He was shocky but not too bad, and I was worried about being seen here.

Leon crowded into the curtained cubicle, eyeing the Trader in her evening gown and blood-colored hair just exactly as he would eye a critter crawling on his boot before he crushed it.

"You stupid son of a bitch." I kept my tone calm, low, quiet. "Carp, I should peel your skin off in strips. You *idiot.*"

"Mom . . ." He shivered, mumbling. The nurse—*Concepcion,* I remembered her name with another one of those wrenching mental efforts—merely glanced at me. They see a lot of me at Mercy, and they've long since stopped caring what I do or look like as long as I don't shoot anyone.

Sometimes they get disappointed, but they're used to that in the ER.

"Kismet?" His tone was too dreamy, and I glanced at Connie.

She shrugged, brushing me aside with one soft shoulder as she handed his wallet and badge over. Her shoes squeaked on the linoleum. "Shock. Head wounds are messy. And this thing. Looks clean, but the edges are ragged. *Madre,* you bring in some interesting things, no?"

"No other wounds?" Raw disbelief married to unwilling hope inside my chest. I hate those pairings. They usually end up badly. The edges of the leg wound weren't discolored, and held no trademark candy-sweet corruption. He wasn't poisoned, thank God.

"They only wanted to play with him before Shen came down." Irene tilted her head, a tendril of that fantastical hair brushing her flour-pale cheek. "I tried to—"

Leon made a restless movement, as if he couldn't believe she was stupid enough to open her mouth. "Speak when you're spoken to, Trader."

"How soon can I get him out of here?" I gave Connie the full benefit of my mismatched stare.

She paled, but gamely rolled her eyes. "*Señora,* this needs stitching. And he's in shock—"

"We can fix that. Get some sutures."

"I am no doctor—"

"*Now,* Connie." I said it very softly. *I am not going to wait around here for someone to come to finish him off.* "Get some fucking sutures and get him ready to travel."

"Galina's?" Leon made another restless twitch, and I glanced at him.

"Of course." *There's no place else in the city I can be sure he's safe, not after tangling with Shen like that. Jesus. I shot her* hair. *She'll really be after me now, and I have to question this Trader. Hard.*

The nagging sense of something not-quite-right returned, but I didn't have the leisure to ferret it out.

The Trader chose that moment to pipe up again. "I brought him here, I was worried—"

I barely saw Leon clear leather, his Smith & Wesson suddenly pointed at her forehead. The knife in his other hand pressed its flat, silver-loaded blade against one milky shoulder, and the Trader shuddered. A slight sizzle; the silver ran with blue sparks. Under the smell of Lysol and human pain endemic in emergency rooms, the sweet-pork foulness of burning Hell-tainted flesh cut sharp, a serrated edge.

Concepcion gasped.

"Shut the fuck up," Leon said, conversationally. "You one small step from being sent to face Judgment, Trader. Got that?"

No flush crept up through Irene's sick pallor, but a greenish tinge bloomed along her cheeks. Her jaw worked, her gaze shivering back and forth between Leon and me, but otherwise not a muscle flickered. She nodded, and my fingers eased off the gun butt. My gun remained in its holster.

Why would a Trader help Carp? There must be an advantage in it for her. Of course, not having me kill her is an advantage. Am I really that scary?

When he peeled the knife away, an angry line of blisters boiled through her skin. They weren't reddened either, but tainted with green like the pale underside of a poison-bearing frog.

I wondered if she would bleed green, and didn't want to find out. What had she bargained for, to end up like this?

Not your problem, Jill.

I could sense no sorcery hanging on her, and she didn't appear to have much in the way of invulnerability or superstrength. Of course, I hadn't tried to kill her yet, so that didn't mean much. "Sutures, Connie. And move it along, I'm on a schedule here."

"Sí, señora." Concepcion didn't waste further time arguing, just brushed past me and pushed the curtain aside.

"Jill?" Carp sounded even more dreamy and disconnected. It was a bad sign.

"Right here." I did something that surprised me—I picked up his hand where it lay discarded against the remains of his slacks. Whatever had made the hole in his leg had chewed right through his clothes; thank God it hadn't hit the femoral artery.

His fingers were limp, cold and clammy. I squeezed them. "What were you doing there, Carper?"

"Waitress. The waitress." His eyes rolled up into his head and he shivered. "Teeth. They all had teeth."

No shit, Carp. They all do. My pager went off, the slight soundless buzz against my hip a reminder of how vulnerable I was. I fished it out of its padded pocket with my free hand and glanced at the number.

It was familiar. Someone paging me from my own house, most probably Theron. He was likely to be climbing the walls by now.

Concepcion reappeared with handfuls of medical supplies. "I should not do this, *señora*. He needs to be admitted."

"He'll be admitted all right, Connie. Suture him up and give us a few cc's of adrenaline in case he goes under, and something for the pain."

"There are more *policía* here," she whispered, shoving the crackling plastic into my hands. Sterile packaging, each tool in its own little pouch. "They are asking if any of their kind has been admitted. Go."

"Oh, *Christ.*" Would this ever end? "All right. We'll go out the back. Don't worry, I'm not going to let your patient die."

She shrugged. "Tonight I have many patients, not just one."

"And you can't remember this particular one, right?" I handed over a fifty-dollar bill—hey, she had kids to feed, I knew that much—and nodded to Leon, shoving the packets in assorted pockets of my trenchcoat. "Help him. I'll watch the Trader." A few moments' work had a tourniquet above the hole in Carp's leg. He wasn't bleeding badly but moving wasn't going to be a fun experience for him. Leon got him up off the bed, and I heard raised voices toward the Admissions section of the ER.

The Trader stared at me, her lips parted. All of her had a matte finish except her lips and the dark holes of her eyes. In dim light, or nightclub shine and flicker, she was probably a sight to behold. Here under the fluorescent wash, she just looked tubercular, but with a green undertone instead of consumptive flush.

"Get moving." I pointed. "You're still alive because you brought him here. Don't make me reconsider."

CHAPTER 20

"Where have you *been?*" Galina got that much out before she saw Carp, who was pale as death and hanging onto Leon like a shipwrecked man clinging to drifting wood. His injured leg wouldn't work quite right. She moved forward to help him without missing a beat. "Goddammit, Jill, you just missed Theron."

Dammit. I made another one of those gut-wrenching physical efforts, trying to prioritize. There were too many things to do. "Is he okay?"

"He said something about your house infected with hell-breed—oh, my goodness. Hello, Leon. Get him in here, lay him on the table. Open up that cupboard on the left—"

I started unpacking medical supplies from my pockets. "Infected with hellbreed?"

"He barely got out in time. Says there's at least six there. And they've found more scurf—" Galina's eyes widened as she took in the Trader, but she didn't mention it, just helped Leon get Carp onto a table in the small room off the main showroom of her store. The table, an old butcher-block number matching the one upstairs in her kitchen, had legs carved with the winged serpent of the Sancs and a system of straps that could hold down a pain-maddened hunter or a dangerous, untreated victim of a Possessor. The old thick leather straps also sheathed thin flexible silver wires, blessed and knotted specifically to constrain harm and evil. Coupled with a Sanc's traditional protections in the house walls, this was an excellent place for stopgap exorcisms, interrogating reticent Traders, or engaging in a little trauma surgery when a hunter's life gets interesting.

Though not as interesting as it is right this second. "Scurf? Where?"

"Near the river. The 3700 block of Cherry, he says you'll know when and if you get there. Good God, what happened to this guy? Who is he?"

"Homicide detective. Name's Carper. Keep him here, and keep him alive for me. This Trader stays here too, I need her in one piece and available. You." I pointed at Irene, who jumped as if pinched. "You come with me into the other room, I've got a few questions. Leon, we're going scurf hunting in a few minutes. Stock up on ammo and whatever else we need."

Some days it's nice being the resident hunter. It means some decisions are just not consensus. Leon nodded and sidled against the wall. Galina hunched over Carp and kept working to patch him up.

"The ammo is in that cabinet there. Take what you need," Galina said as I left the room.

The Trader followed me out into the darkened front room, the walls humming and alive with Sanctuary shielding. Crystal balls in the glassed-in case under the counter sparked, swirling softly with golden light. The stock rustled, books and materials all alive in their own specific ways in a store that has the advantage of being completely useful—unlike a few other occult shops I've had the bad luck to try to supply myself from.

Sometimes I wonder what hunters do without Sancs in their territories. Santa Luz is lucky to have Galina.

"All right. Start talking." I rested one hand on my bullwhip, the other on a gun butt. If it made her nervous, she didn't show it.

Much. Her eyes were wide. The dim light was kind to her, making her bloody hair a river of softness and her shell-like hips curves of delight. The stain on her lips made her look just-kissed. She must have been pretty in her own way, while human. "I'm allowed to talk now?"

"Don't get cute. Carper had a lead in the organ-theft case, and it was you. You have exactly thirty seconds to tell me what you know, everything you know, leaving nothing out, or we learn if you bleed green too." I didn't even have to snarl, the flat matter-of-factness in my tone was more chilling than ranting and raving would be.

I was too tired to rant and rave. The successive shocks were beginning to wear on me.

Get over it, Jill. Focus.

"Organ theft." Did she sound relieved? She nodded, and a curl fell forward, sweetly and fetchingly, into her face. A shadow of hardness in her eyes told me the attractiveness was only skin-deep. There was something else under that thin crust.

"And dirty cops. Start talking." I kept one eye on the clock.

"Oh, that. It wasn't even work, just something I learned on a house call." When I gave her a blank look, she smiled, a thin tight curve of lips that brought the hardness out and made her look a lot less sex-kitten. "I'm one of Shen's dogs, hunter. We're available for reasonable rates if you have . . . desires, and the money to pay for them."

That was nothing new. And neither was the way her face changed. Even paranormal hookers learn how to calculate, and they learn how to try and hide that calculation. She wasn't very good at it. Maybe she hadn't had a lot of practice yet.

"About two weeks ago I had a client, a police officer. Normally run-of-the-mill detectives can't afford us, you know. It's mostly the brass we service, and the politicos. But this one was flush, I guess, and paid up front." A gleam touched her eyes at the mention of money—a ratty little gleam I wasn't sure I liked.

"How much?"

"Seven thousand to secure the appointment, another five for the standard consultation, and four for . . . extras." Faint dislike tinted her voice, swirled away. She shifted her weight, licked her lips again.

Those heels must be murder. I waited for the rest of it.

"He wanted the usual, and my specialty. Most of all, though, he wanted to talk. His conscience was bothering him. That's what I do, I provide . . . discipline."

I got the feeling she wanted to call it something else. That gleam in her eye turned into a hard little diamond, assessing how much of her story I was buying. I still waited. Silence is the best weapon in conversations like this.

"Anyway," she continued, "he was really upset. Kept repeating that he hadn't signed on for murder. He'd just wanted to make some money, some of the money he was spending on me. It was getting too big. He wanted out, but couldn't see any *way* out. I just gave him the usual and left. I didn't tell Shen about it—it didn't seem important, the man wasn't Trade material. Too guilt-

ridden." Her shrug was soft poetry, like a Venus flytrap just waiting to close. "Anyway, tonight *this* detective shows up and asks for
me. He stinks of human and doesn't seem to notice the place isn't
safe for him. Turns out he had access to my client's credit card
statements and traced me from there. We're independent contractors, you see, and—"

"Names. Your client, anyone else he mentioned."

Her eyes flickered from side to side, and a pale tongue-tip crept
out, touched her glossy lower lip. "I don't know, the confidentiality—"

For fuck's sake, what are you, a psychiatrist? "I don't give a
shit about confidentiality, I want names. That table in there can
hold a Trader down, you know. You've been cooperative so far, I'd
hate to have to *convince* you to give me what I need."

She shrugged again, satiny flesh moving against the velvet of
her gown, and I had one of those irrelevant flashes of memory that
happen when you've been going for too long on not enough rest.
I'd been idly trying to figure out who she was dressed to resemble,
and I had it now. She looked *just* like Jessica Rabbit in real life,
right down to the high wide forehead.

I hadn't seen that movie in forever.

"It doesn't make much difference. Shen will kill me anyway."
Her gloved hand flicked nervously and produced a long thin
brown cigarette with a gold band. The pulse ran high and hard in
her throat, despite her show of indifference. "The name on his
credit card was Alfred Bernardino. Italian, greasy, built wide and
hairy. Do you want to know what he wanted me to do?"

Bernardino? Why does that sound familiar? Most cops' names
do sound familiar, since I put every rookie through the obligatory
orientation class. But this sounded *more* than familiar—it sounded
like I'd heard it in the past couple days.

My memory's normally like a steel trap; I only have to concentrate for a second or two to make a connection. The tip-of-
my-brain feeling around the name hovered and, maddeningly,
retreated. *Shit. Goddammit.* "I don't much care. What did he tell
you about the organ trade? Is Shen involved?"

"All I know is that they're getting them somehow. There's a
buyer from out of state, they pack them up and send them in

shipments from a private airfield out of town. There are lists, you know, people too rich to stand in line like the rest of us." Another shrug. Her voice quivered, but I didn't blame her. Facing down a hunter in a bad mood should give anyone the shakes. Especially a Trader with something to hide.

And she was most definitely hiding *something*.

Jesus. "What do the cops do?" *I should have dug harder to find the clients that Sorrows bitch was shipping organs to. I should have kept an eye on Sullivan and the Badger and their case, too. God*damm*it.*

Hindsight is twenty-twenty, but no hunter likes that sort of vision.

"They find the donors and cover everything up. It's just under the table, he said. Like hiring illegals for yard work."

What a lovely way to look at it. "He told you all this?"

"He had a lot on his mind." She waved the cigarette. "Can I get a light?"

"No. Galina doesn't like people smoking in here, and you're not going outside. At least, not until I know you're telling me the whole truth." *This is a nice neat little story, but something's off. It just doesn't make enough sense.*

"Come on. Shen's going to kill me, this is the only chance I've got. I'm trading this for some kind of protection. They say you're fair."

Goddamn Traders. "Who says?"

"They. You know, *them.* Everyone."

"They say I'm fair?" *Now that's news. Traders saying I'm fair?*

"Mostly. I'll tell you something else if you protect me."

I eyed her in the gloom. The taint of Hell on her aura and that ratlike gleam in her pretty eyes told me not to trust her as far as I could throw her over my shoulder with a broken arm, but I was holding most of the cards here. She was right. Shen An Dua wouldn't take this Trader back unless it was to make an example of her, both for consorting with me and for being party to Shen's humiliation.

Which made Irene officially my problem. Except she was a *Trader.* And there was still a very significant unanswered question.

"Does it have anything to do with one of Shen's people trying to kill me in my own house?"

For a moment, something hunted flashed in her dark, liquid eyes. She lowered the unlit cigarette. "To kill you?"

Bingo. She knew something about it. This was looking up. "Yeah, a blond scarecrow. I'd be insulted, except it's easier when they send stupid-ass kids to kill me instead of people I'd have to work up a sweat over." My fingertips tapped the whip's handle, a solid comfort. "So, any light you can shed on this?"

"A blond...Fairfax? Why would she..." Now her hands were limp as boned fish at her sides. Her mouth loosened a little, and the shock made her seem more human. "He's...dead?"

Fairfax? What a name. "I don't play pattycake when murder comes calling, sweetheart." It answered a question—Shen had wanted me dead, but not enough to send a 'breed with the balls to do it. Or maybe she just wanted me looking somewhere, and the blond 'breed was supposed to send me in another direction. I hadn't given him enough time to lie to me.

Irene actually staggered, as if the heels had been too much for her. "He was..." It was a bare whisper. "He wasn't there to kill you. If he managed to get out he was there to warn you. One of the higher-ups wants you dead for interfering with an experiment."

Huh? Then why did he jump me? "What kind of experiment, and why would Shen warn *me?*"

"Maybe he escaped. But Shen might send him, if she didn't need him anymore. And she's got a grudge against the owner of the Monde."

"Perry?" *Well, who else?* "He's involved? What kind of experiment?"

The air swirled with darkness and the scar on my wrist tingled. Irene actually flinched when I said his name.

I didn't blame her one bit.

"I don't know. Fairfax is dead?" The green tone was back under her paleness, pronounced even in the dark. And the hard, calculating gleam had fled her face. "My God."

Well, at least that solves one mystery. Why are there other hellbreed at my house, though? "Sorry." I didn't *feel* sorry, but she looked so lost for a moment I almost couldn't help myself. "Look…" *What are you about to do, Jill? This is madness. She's a* Trader, *goddammit!*

But still, she'd made the right choice, taking Carp to the hospital. Sure, she'd done it because I told her she was next if he died— but still. It had to count for something, didn't it?

"Do you have what you want?" Her shoulders sagged, she dropped into her heels. "If you do, I'll be going back to the club."

What? "What the hell for? You just said Shen's going to kill you."

Her shoulders hunched. "If Fax is dead, I don't care."

Say what? "Oh, please. We're talking about a hellbreed, right?" I watched her flinch, dropping her gaze to the floor as her lips twitched. *Can it, Jill. Stick to the matter at hand.* "What kind of experiment, and who was running it?"

"Fax might have known. I don't." She glanced at me sidelong. A bleeding, shifting light had lit far behind her eyes. Did she actually look relieved? "Are you done?"

All my chimes rang at once. *Not even close. Not until I'm sure you're not hiding anything. And not until I'm sure you're telling the truth.* "You're staying here for the time being. How far is Perry involved in this? Is he the one who wants me dead?"

"No, it's one of the *other* higher-ups." Irene shivered. Now tears glimmered in the corners of her wide eyes. One had even tracked down her cheek, and I couldn't tell if it was grief or relief, her face was changing so fast. "But if you, say, owed Shen a favor, she could use it to her advantage against the owner of the Monde. She'd like that."

I eyed her. The idea that she might know a few things about how Perry interacted with the other hellbreed in Santa Luz was…intriguing, to say the least. Not to mention the "higher-ups." That was worth a good hour or two of hard questioning.

An hour or two I didn't have. But Galina would keep her here for me, all safe and warm.

"Jill." Leon stepped out into the shop's main room. "Everythin' even, darlin'?"

I don't know if you could call it that. "Even-steven. Want to go kill some scurf and find out why someone's shipping them?"

"Can't wait." His eyes narrowed as he took in the Trader, who slumped, splay-footed, on her high heels. "What are you gonna do with that?"

"She may be useful." I hated the words. It was the sort of thing a hellbreed would say. "How's Carper?"

"If he can pull through, Galina will pull him through. He seems okay." My fellow hunter shrugged. "We going?"

"Certainly." I weighed every priority I had, found each one jostling with the others, and wished wringing my hands was an option. "Let's roll."

CHAPTER 21

The aftermath of a scurf fight isn't pretty. There's slime all over everything; most of it breaks down into powder but it will steam on any night under seventy degrees. The footing is treacherous, and everything that can be broken probably is. Weres are very rarely messy, but scurf are not the neatest kills in the world.

They just won't stop wiggling.

We arrived too late for any of the fun, and the Weres were gone. Instead, the warehouses were a shambles, the rail doors dented as if stroked a good one from inside by a huge hammer. There was a smell of fur and clean fury lying over the choking terrible candied sweetness of scurf, and Leon was pale as we started checking, covering each other.

Nothing living remained. The Weres had done a good job, and I could see where the battle had been particularly fierce. I hoped nobody *else* had died.

"Huh." Leon lowered Rosita. "Would you look at that."

The slime was merely a thin scattering near the rail doors—a spur here joined a yard about a hundred feet away. One of the doors was half-open; we ducked out into the cold and examined the tracks.

They weren't brand spanking new, but they weren't disused either. Our eyes met, and Leon's mouth firmed. We slid into the warehouses and he held Rosita pointing straight to the ceiling, gapping his mouth a little bit as he breathed to try and relieve some of the stink. "You thinkin' what I'm thinkin', darlin'?"

I pointed. "Pens, to hold them? You could herd them out through here....If you were stupid enough to do so, I guess. But *why?* And where the fuck are the Weres? There should have been one or two here hanging around, waiting for stragglers—or for me."

He nodded, curling dark hair flopping into his face. "Yeah. And look here."

Part of the wreckage was metal gates, chain link knocked down in sheets—and a row of pegs holding slim black cattle prods. Some of them had been knocked down.

"Oh Jesus," I whispered, nausea biting under my ribs.

"Yeah. This definitely qualifies as big fuckin' problem." Leon shuddered like a horse scenting a snake. "What the *fuck?*"

I touched one of the cattle prods, lifted it down. The end crackled slightly when I depressed the trigger. One hell of a magic wand. "This is getting weird. Where are the Weres? One or two should *be* here."

He shrugged. "Suppose we look around after we give the rest of this the eye. Maybe..." But there was no way to make the situation any less odd. Neither of us said what we were thinking.

This has got to be a trap.

Nothing happened as we checked the rest of the building. Three interconnected warehouses, an L-shaped nightmare; we'd check the bottom of the L next. Even the roof was spattered with powder-slime.

Why weren't there more disappearances? This much scurf, there had *to have been something, someone else missing! Unless they were shipping them in quantity—but how were they feeding them? Scurf* need *the hemoglobin or they go into brainrot.*

There was a foreman's office up a rickety, smashed staircase neither of us could trust our weight to. Leon scabbarded Rosita and gave me ten fingers, lifting with a grunt, and I caught the edge of a window that might have sliced my fingers down to bone if glass had ever been put in it. For once, cheap shoddy work was to someone's advantage.

It was a moment's work to muscle myself through into the

office. The light was uncertain, the few unbroken fluorescent fixtures buzzing like Helletöng through broken teeth.

The office was torn to shreds too, claw marks dragged into the cheap rotting drywall. Were claws—and *others*. Once you've seen them a few times, it's easier to differentiate claw marks than normal people would ever believe.

"Shit," I breathed, and started casting around. The candy-reek of scurf covered up the rotten smell of hellbreed, but once I scented it the aroma of Hell moved front and center.

And I hadn't been here to protect my Weres, goddammit.

Drifts of slime-spattered paper covered the floor. A metal desk sat in one corner under a refrigerated cabinet; I looked it over and gingerly swung the powdered door open. Bottles of a rusty-dark liquid stood neatly on the shelves.

My gorge rose, pointlessly. Blood. But not nearly enough for the number of scurf formerly housed here.

Not to mention the obvious question—who were the donors, and were they willing? "Leon? Any refrigerators down there?"

"I'll look. What's up there?"

"Blood canisters stacked like Bud Lights. And a desk. There was at least one hellbreed here."

"Sheeeeee-yit." Maybe it was the Texas in him, but he could put an incredible amount of disgust in two stretched-out syllables.

The desk drawer was locked, but a simple yank took care of that. It was almost frightening, how casually I tore the reinforced metal apart.

The scar skittered with unhealthy heat, flushed and full. It was getting disturbingly easy to rip things up. I yanked a handful of folders up out of the drawer and flipped one open.

Nothing but shipping manifests. I eyed them, a sick feeling beginning under my breastbone. The information in them started to click over into the coldly rational part of my brain, and intuition kicked in. I scattered more papers, found pictures—eight-by-tens of an airfield. The picture started revolving inside my head, and I began to feel sick.

Oh, God. I spent at least ten minutes moving around, digging through paper. Bureaucracy is a bitch. You can't run an operation without it, but it leaves slimy little pawprints all over everything.

"Jill?" Leon, moving downstairs. "You should come take a look at this." Sound of movement. "Jill?"

My throat was dry and my hand actually trembled. "Jesus," I whispered. "Jesus Christ."

"Jill, get the fuck down here, darlin'." Leon's voice didn't tremble, but it was firm. "Come on."

"One second," I said around the rust in my throat. The pattern was clear. Infrequent shipments from down south and slightly to the west, Viejarosas way. Mostly regular shipments from due south, with notations attached to the irregularities that I could well imagine. Smaller, more frequent notations in another column for shipments to ARA, wherever that was. I had a sinking, chilling feeling that I knew.

Oh, Jesus. Jesus God. No wonder there haven't been disappearances I could track.

"Goddammit, Jill! What the fuck's going on?" Leon looked relieved when I appeared at the window. He looked a little less relieved when I landed right next to him, boots thudding and the force of the landing almost driving me to my knees. The jolt was a bitch—three-quarters of a story isn't enough for me to brace myself, there just isn't time.

"I've got an idea. What are you bellowing about?"

He pointed. "This way."

As we worked our way down into the bottom of the L-shape, the pens got more and more reinforced—and more terribly shattered. How many scurf had been here, rattling against the chain link, tearing at the metal that held them?

Jesus. I had a good idea what we'd find around the corner.

Leon had already checked it, but we still covered each other as we slid around into the bottom of the L-shape. The light was a little better here, not so many fixtures damaged, but it wasn't the sterile white glare it would have been before the fight tore through.

More pens on one side, not torn apart, but with each cage door open. These weren't reinforced like the other ones. At the end was another rail door, with a line of tasers hanging along the side.

On the side opposite the cages were huge industrial refrigerators, their slick chrome sides dewed with scurf slime . . . and blood.

The scurf powder was running in thin crackling trails across the tacky-wet handprints and whorls of human claret. I knew what fridges this size were used for, but I was still miserably compelled to open one cautiously, with Leon and Rosita covering me.

Racks and racks of bottled blood. Hanging corpses, just like sides of beef, swaying gently when I touched them. Each fridge could hold about twenty bodies on neat rows of hooks, each cased in crackling plastic—and each with brown skin, an undertone of gray death to them. When I approached I could see the neat excisions—organs taken out, the cavities of the belly and chest opened with surgical precision, the rest of the body just plain muscle mass to be disposed of. The thighs were flayed, probably for bone marrow harvest.

"What the fuck?" Leon was having a little trouble with this.

So was I. "These are probably all illegal immigrants. The manifests up in the office have them shipped over the border by *coyotes,* by the truckful. They're transferred to a rail line and shipped in. Held in the pens with the doors there. We'll find surgical facilities here—"

"For what?"

"Organ donation, *definitely* unwilling. The scurf take care of the remains. They were in the other pens. There's hellbreed involved, and cops. The organs are taken to an airfield about twenty miles out in the desert if the gasoline receipts are any indication. With the initials ARA. Shouldn't be too hard to find."

"Huh." He didn't ask the next question, knowing I'd answer it anyway.

"Selling to rich people who don't like waiting in line for transplants." My stomach twisted again. Each crackling plastic bag was a *life,* goddammit, someone who had wanted the American dream badly enough to risk being shipped over the border one way or another. If they hadn't ended up here, they probably would have ended up working dead-end jobs, trying like hell to keep their heads above water. Maids, construction workers, fruit pickers, yardworkers, carwash hands—all those jobs people with my skin color couldn't be bothered to do for themselves or pay someone decently for.

And this is where it ended up. Used and discarded one way or another, human beings reduced to empty soda cans.

"Why the scurf, though?" Leon shuddered. "There has to be more. *Has* to be."

"Getting rid of evidence? And it's a good way to keep me occupied and off their back. Not to mention if someone has a grudge against me."

"And the cops trying to kill you?"

"Probably without the hellbreed's knowledge, whoever it is. If the 'breed knew they'd have 'em use silver bullets and I'd've been in much worse shape." My own shudder ran below the surface of my skin. "Let's finish checking and get the hell out of here."

"You got it, darlin'."

Checking the other fridges was a matter of minutes and nausea. Leon was definitely green by the time we finished, and I wasn't far behind.

I stepped out of the last fridge, my eyes on the pen opposite, its gaping door. The padlock was busted—probably Weres. If anyone survived this mess, the Weres would test them for scurf, and probably try to get them home.

Not that it mattered much. Whoever was locked in these cages would have nightmares the rest of their lives, survivor's guilt, and probably be back over the border within a month working at a low-paying dead-end job because their family had to eat.

Jesus.

"I've heard of some goddamn stupid things in my life, but *this* takes the cake and the whole fuckin' picnic too. What sort of short-sighted idiot would ship scurf into a clean territory? Even hellbreed ain't that stupid." Leon touched a busted padlock, watched as the whole chain-link cage shivered.

I closed the fridge door. The sound of it clicking shut was loud in the stillness. *Something still isn't right here. Something—*

I'd opened my mouth, but Leon and I both froze, our eyes meeting. I didn't have to ask if he'd heard it.

A footstep, sliding and soft, and definitely not human. Instinct placed it—around the corner of the L, someone had come in the main door and was picking their way, quietly, over the rubble.

I slid a gun easily from its holster. Drew silence over myself like a veil, and started considering my options just as other sliding sounds told me our guest, whoever and whatever it was, had brought company.

CHAPTER 22

own!" I yelled, and Leon dropped as I opened fire, silver-laden bullets punching through the shell of the third hell-breed. Two down, six to go, and things weren't looking good even before the whip crackled; Leon rolled and I already knew he was going to be too slow, *too slow* as the 'breed snarled, thin black ichor splattering in a high arc as I brought the whip around, the strike uncoiling from my hip as chain-link rattled under my boots. Not the best footing in the world, but the chance bounce propelled Leon on his way as I leapt, my focus narrowing to keeping them *off* him.

It was a mistake, one I realized even as I was in the air, committed to the movement and turning to present as small a target as possible, my boot solidly cracking against the 'breed's already-lacerated face. Kinetic force transferred, I stopped dead and dropped down to land splay-footed. The brunet 'breed went flying back, crashing into two of his fellows with a sound like sides of beef flung together hard enough to crack steel-reinforced bones.

I caught my balance and heard Leon scrambling to his feet behind me. My lips peeled away from my teeth, a silent snarl that shook the whole building, light fixtures swaying and making the shadows do a knife-edged dance.

No. It wasn't my snarl. It was someone else's, thrumming sub-sonic like tectonic plates grinding together.

"Hold!" The command spilled darkness like wine through the air, and the 'breed all dropped, cringing, flattened under a wave of Hell-tainted power. "Stay your hand, avenging one. We are not your enemies."

Of all the things you could say, that's probably the biggest, fattest lie. I froze. I knew that voice.

"Shit," Leon whispered, and I wholeheartedly agreed.

The whip coiled, stowed safely in a half-second. I had both guns out and trained on the corner when he stepped into view, his cream-pale hair catching the light. It wasn't the hip super-short cut he'd sported last time I saw him but slightly longer, just as expensively trimmed, and it still did nothing for his expressively bland face.

Most of the damned are beautiful. The owner of the Monde Nuit is merely average, and that dries up the spit in your mouth like desert sun dries up a single lone drop of water.

Especially when his eyes are eaten alive by an indigo stain swallowing the whites, leaving the irises burning gasflame-blue. Eyes should not look like that.

He held his hands up, a classic *hey man I'm harmless* stance that didn't fool me for a second. His suit was pristine, gray wool instead of his usual white linen, sharply creased in all the right places. His shoulders were a touch broader than I remembered, and something new glimmered at his throat—a metal chain, with a small gem set in iron filigree flashing under the swinging, dancing light. It was a red-tinted diamond, and I would have bet everything I owned that it held a flaw like a screaming face in its blood-gleaming depths.

I swallowed dryness, settled my guns—one covering him, the other one covering the group of hellbreed, spilled or standing, he'd brought with him. "What the fuck are you doing here, Pericles?"

His hands dropped a fraction, the indigo swirling through his eyes like ink through water. "Why, my darling Kiss, helping *you.* What else would I be doing?"

"There's hellbreed stain upstairs, and this is right up your alley. Give me one good reason I shouldn't ventilate you now. Didn't you learn *anything* from last time?" *Calm down, Jill. You're sounding like a fishwife instead of a goddamn hunter. Chill out.*

He didn't shift his weight, but all the bloodless shark's attention was on me. "Oh, I learned, my sweet. It was a truly regrettable series of events, but so far in the past. I think we have other problems now, don't you?" A slight, expressive movement, indicating the shambles all around us, and the indigo stain retreated from the whites of his eyes, like the tide along a wreckage-filled beach. "You have not been keeping a clean house."

"You have ten seconds to tell me what the fuck you're doing here, Perry. And even less than that to convince me you don't have anything to do with this." My guns clicked, a nice piece of theater. Leon's breathing evened out, and I knew without looking that he was covering the other 'breed. The one I'd shot lay moaning on the floor, and Perry didn't spare him a single glance.

"This place is *mine;* it belongs to me. Why would I invite such filth in?" A shadow of distaste crossed his blandness. "They foul the carpet and stain the very air. Give me some credit for business sense, as well. There is no profit in having such things contaminating my territory—as I would have told you, had you bothered to speak to me."

Don't, Jill. He's just trying to get inside your head. The scar chuckled wetly, my pulse hammering as a wave of heat jolted up my arm. He liked doing that, fiddling with my internal thermostat when he was in the same room.

Another of those physical efforts to regain control and get my priorities straight made stress-sweat prickle along the curve of my lower back. The guns, however, did not waver. "You're just as much an infection as scurf, hellbreed. Start talking."

He opened his mouth—probably to taunt me—and visibly reconsidered, calculations crossing his face like the shadows of airplanes over baking sand. "I have been engaged in finding the source of this...corruption...for some time. No hellbreed claims to know about it, and each small marker I sent to be my eyes vanished. Three promising young ones gone without a trace, and I have decided to take personal interest in the matter. I have traced the corruption this far, and arrive to find you here and the work of Weres all over the walls—and the smell of my last protégé's untimely death upstairs." He folded his arms, still not sparing the hapless, bleeding 'breed on the floor a single glance.

One of the higher-ups wants you dead. I eyed Perry. "You wouldn't be the only one sending hellbreed after me, would you? What about skunk-haired idiots busting in on a nest-cleaning and trying to kill me?"

"Skunk-haired? His eyebrow lifted. "None of my protégés deserve that appellation."

"What about a 'breed sent to kill me in my own home and whisper someone else's name?" I pressed. I got a half-second of some other emotion flickering across his face. Did Perry look, of all things, *surprised?* "So you ride in to my rescue, huh? You're *helping* me. How very congenial of you." *Like shit you are. You're probably neck-deep in this too, God knows you always are.*

My tone must have warned him. His eyes narrowed a fraction, and instead of looking at me like a prize entrée, he eyed me like a cobra eyes a mongoose.

It was a welcome change. Still, it bothered me. What had calmed him down enough that the staining on his whites retreated?

I holstered both guns, though my entire body fought it. They were my protection, and these were *hellbreed,* for Christ's sake. "You can start by telling me which of your little hellbreed friends wants me dead."

"And what will you pay for that information?" He cocked his pale head, still regarding me with that cautious, unblinking reptile stare. His coterie cringed even further.

Jesus Christ, Jill, what are you going to do now? There was only one thing I *could* do. "I don't need to pay you, Pericles. You were in violation and we renegotiated. And you can threaten all you want, but if the scar goes sour, I'll be well within my rights to erase your sorry little ass from the face of the earth and send you screaming to Hell. Your choice."

There it was, as plain as I could make it. If he made trouble, better it was here with Leon backing me up and the scar still mostly workable.

"And that would reduce your power by an order of magnitude or two." Perry was very still, a statue carved of gray ice and platinum hair. His eyes had half-lidded, their gasflames burning down.

Why isn't he angrier? "Maybe I'm willing to risk it. What other hellbreed wants me dead, Perry?"

"There are many who wish your death, hunter. Aren't you happy we have such a marvelous little agreement?"

Oh no you don't. "The only *agreement* we have, Pericles, is that you trade information for your continued survival. You're in this city on my sufferance. This is the last time I'm asking, hellspawn."

Leon didn't move, but I could almost *feel* him tensing. Had I been backing up a mouthy hunter, I would have been getting a little itchy too. This was wrong. *All* wrong.

Perry didn't move, but there was a general scurrying and his hellbreed scrambled away like roaches once the light's on. The moaning hellbreed on the floor tried to scrabble away from Perry's slow, even footsteps.

Perry stopped, looking down at the mess of thin black-welling ichor and torn flesh. *"Haasai,"* he rumbled in Helletöng, and the injured 'breed drew in a huge hissing breath, as if preparing to scream.

The owner of the Monde didn't even seem to move. One moment he stood, hands in pockets, looking down at a wounded member of his species.

The next, his foot came down, and the injured 'breed's skull shattered like a watermelon dropped on concrete. I skipped away, guns clearing leather again, and braced myself. Preternatural flesh steamed, scurf slime cringing away from the deeper contagion of hellbreed ichor, and Perry made a short satisfied sound. A low chuckle, to be exact, as if he had just been surprised by something enjoyable.

My stomach turned over hard, rebelled against its moorings, and then I was too busy to care, because Leon let out a short sharp garbled word and Perry had taken three steps in a rush, with that same eerie darting quickness.

My left-hand gun spoke, a brief muzzle-flash and a roar. The bullet whined and pinged, and Perry stopped short. The sleeve of his suit coat smoked; a crease not intended by the tailor along his shoulder.

It was my night for trick shots, I guess.

"The next one goes in your head." My heart thundered, the scar snapping and twanging with pain like a rope in a high wind, puckering the flesh of my arm. *It's not doing anything, Jill, you know it's not, goddammit focus!* "Settle *down,* hellspawn."

Perry's head cocked like a lizard's, a flicker of tongue too red and wet to be human showing between his white, white teeth.

Once before I'd seen what lurked under the pretence of bland humanity he wore, and my brain had shunted that memory aside, refusing to hold it. I was goddamn grateful at the time, and even more so now.

We stood like that, Perry's head not six inches from my right-hand Glock's muzzle, my left gun settling slightly lower, zeroed in on his mouth.

"Argoth," Perry whispered. The rumble of Hell's mother tongue under the word made the shadows turn angular, the lights buzzing and crackling. "Argoth is coming. You should be thankful, my dear one, that I've kept this little ant farm safe. You should get on your knees and pray to your bloodless Savior. I can only hold the tide so long."

"What tide?" *Argoth? Nobody I've heard of before. I'll bet I don't have time to run by Hutch's and set him to working on it, either.* The 'breed behind Perry drew back, with scary nimble quickness, making little inhuman sounds wherever they stepped.

"Silly, stupid little hunter." Perry leaned forward on his toes, for all the world as if wanting to tango and waiting for a dancer unwary enough to join him. "You truly think you owe me nothing? You think we *renegotiated?*"

Don't fall for it, Jill. But I did. My fingers tightened on the triggers, and the little clicks sounded very loud, especially when echoed by another, sharper, more definite click from Rosita. "Take one step closer, Perry, and *fucking find out.*"

We stood like that for five ticking seconds, the scar working a red-hot coathanger up the channels of my nerves and veins, but my arm never wavered. It was only pain, and if it got too bad, I would shoot him now and keep shooting until I was sure the fucker was dead.

If I ever *was* sure, that is. And it wouldn't stop me from parting out the body and burning each steak and hamhock down to ash.

And scattering the ash.

Miles apart, *continents* apart if I could.

The owner of the Monde stepped mincingly...away. He retreated, his eyes still bright blue, and it unnerved me more than if they *had* been turning indigo with fury.

Six feet away he halted, came back down on his heels, and

pointed to the 'breed on the floor, a quick sketch of a movement. "He was becoming troublesome, you know. You killed him just in time."

"I only wounded him, Perry. You murdered him all on your own. What's Argoth?" *Have I heard that name before? Don't think so. Shit. Never rains but it pours.* My pulse was struggling to thunder again, but control clamped down. The switch inside my head trembled—the one that could flip and make the world into a chessboard, every move clear and clean, with nothing even resembling hesitation to keep me from what had to be done.

The uncomfortable thought arrived right on schedule. *Like bashing a hellbreed's head in? Did that just have to be done? Does Perry think of it that way?*

"Not *what,* but *who.* He is Death come calling, and you will see him soon enough." Perry smiled broadly, his teeth gleaming. "You think you can manage without my help? Go and see, my dearest."

"Don't even think of welshing, hellbreed." The switch trembled again, I forced it to stay still. I had never even told Mikhail about that part of me, the way I could lift out of my own body and just do what was needed.

What was necessary.

"Oh, you may have rope to hang yourself and to spare. Have no fear of that." Perry took a gliding step away, and another, as if it was a dance. Chain-link rattled under his feet like metal bones. "Enough rope, and a noose as well. Goodnight, sweetheart."

He all but vanished into the sudden darkness, the lights at the bend of the warehouses failing utterly, and there was a sound like pipe organs chuckling in some deep subterranean cavern while a madman pounded on the keys. I let out a long shaking breath, forcing my arms to come down and rest stiff at my sides, weighed down by the guns and their cargo of deadly silver.

"What. The fuck. Was that?" Leon spoke for both of us.

"I don't know." I sounded tired even to myself. "This does not look good."

"Every time I see that motherfucker he looks like he just won the lottery."

Just like any other hellbreed. "He can't cash the check as long as I'm around, Leon." My eyes dropped down to the quick-rotting 'breed on the floor. The stink had just officially gotten worse. Runnels of decay poured from the smashed head, down the neck and through the chest cavity, fouling the clothes—a pale blue shirt that was Brooks Brothers, unless I missed my guess, and a pair of high-end designer khakis. Alligator wingtips, too.

I felt a momentary flash of guilt. It hadn't been necessary to kill them, if Perry was telling the truth and he'd come here to help.

Get real, Jill. What kind of "help" do you think Perry's going to offer you? Nothing you'd want to accept. You made the deal with him because Mikhail said it was a good idea, and now you're sitting pretty.

As pretty as you can sit with a hellbreed mark on your wrist and Perry laughing at you. Cold fingers touched my spine as I stared at the collapsing face.

It was a relief it didn't look human. Well, much.

You're not thinking straight. Focus.

Just as I prepared to make another of those gut-clenching physical efforts to tear my mind out of a psychological dead end, I froze and tipped my head back, staring up at the fixtures slowly losing their dangling momentum.

"Jill?" Leon was getting to the edge of not-quite-frantic-but-definitely-uncomfortable. "I'd like to buy a fuckin' vowel, please."

Me too. But I think I just got one. "Shhh." The thought circled, returned, and I leapt on it.

Irene's voice floated through the cavern of my skull. *The name on his credit card was Alfred Bernardino. Italian, greasy, built wide and hairy.*

Echoing against it came Carp's voice, from a few days and a wide shoal of darkness away. *They won't talk to me or to Bernie— his partner—but it doesn't seem possible that one of them pulled the trigger on him.*

Bernie, in Vice. Italian, built like a dockworker, with a foul mouth—always an asset in the Vice department—and stubby fingers always holding a filterless cigarette. Pedro Ayala's partner.

The insight hit me in a flash of blinding white, the fluorescents overhead beginning to buzz again, the warehouse brightening as hellbreed contamination ebbed.

"Holy shit," I breathed. "Leon, I'm an idiot."

He magnanimously refused to comment on that. "Can we get the fuck outta here now?"

"Sure thing. Let's go back to Galina's, I need to talk to Carp."

CHAPTER 23

Dawn leached gray through the sky. Galina's eyes were smudged with sleeplessness. "Thank God you're here," she greeted me. "Your detective's all right, but that Trader—"

Oh, Jesus. What now? "Do I have to kill her?" I only sounded weary, which was a bad sign. Leon sighed, leaning against the door, and Galina handed him a cold can of Pabst.

That's your local Sanc. On tap with whatever you need. Galina made a slight moue of distaste. "She's up in the greenhouse, crying. Tried to get out, but you said you wanted her here. Something about Fairfax, and—"

"I can kill her," Leon volunteered hopefully, popping the top and taking a slurp. The eyeliner turned his eyes into dark holes, and made the smudges of exhaustion under them deeper. "Put a real capper on my night."

It's not like a Trader to cry, unless there's an advantage in it. Still, she saved Carp. Under threat of death, but still. I let out a sigh that was mostly weariness, with a soupçon of irritation thrown in. "Not yet." *Not tonight, at least. Or today, since it's dawn.* "Where's Carp?"

"In bed. He's sedated. I think he'll be fine, if he can get over the nightmares." Galina sighed, too. She really was a gentle soul.

It made me wonder sometimes. If I'd ever been a gentle soul, would my life have knocked it out of me? Would I have survived hunter training and the nights afterward if I'd had any gentleness left in me?

Stay with the here and now, Jill. "Can he talk?"

Galina shrugged, slipping her hands in the pockets of her gray knit hoodie. She looked like she could use a night or two of rest as well. "Depends on what you want to talk to him about. He's not going to be doing quadratic equations, but he's coherent."

Upstairs, in the spare room over the shop, Carp lay still as death under a vintage yellow counterpane. He was cottage-cheese pale, his sandy hair a bird's nest, and even though the blood had been washed off the wound on his head was glaring. He stared at me through the gray light spilling through windows humming with a Sanctuary's powerful defenses, and I knew that look in his eyes.

Carper was now haunted. He'd seen the nightside up close. Not just the fragrance of difference that hung on a Were, not just the bodies left after a nightside eruption into the civilian world. He'd been in the nightclub for forty-five minutes or so—more than enough time for him to see up close what lurked under the fabric of reality.

They just wanted to play with him before Shen came down, Irene had said. God alone knew what game they had played. One that involved taking a bite out of him, apparently.

I dragged a straight-backed chair over to the side of the bed. "Hey." Even though I needed words out of him, needed them quickly, I spoke slowly, softly. "How are you?"

He managed a harsh little thread of a laugh. "Kismet." It wasn't an answer. "Jesus."

"Just the former, Detective." A little humor, to set him at ease.

Who was I kidding? No way was Carp going to be set at ease. He'd seen under the mask.

I decided to get down to it. I couldn't make the shock any less, but I could at least get usable information out of him if he was coherent. "Bernardino, Alfie Bernardino. Ayala's partner. What do you know about him, Carp?"

Still, even as I said it, I hated myself. He needed sedation and a therapist, not me digging around and reminding him of things he was probably goddamn eager to start forgetting.

He blinked. Made an internal effort, things shifting behind his eyes. "Ayala. His partner. Slippery fucker."

Man, this just keeps getting better. "He's in it up to his neck, and probably deeper. But then you know that, right?"

"Credit card statements about this waitress—Irene. She—" He

coughed, weakly, his eyelids falling down. "Kiss, their eyes. Their eyes were glowing."

They always do, Carp. I laid a hand against his forehead—my left hand, since the right was humming with fever-hot hellbreed-tainted force. "Just rest. It'll fade."

I was lying. Things like this don't fade. They come back in nightmares and in waking dreams, flashbacks and stress disorders you need antidepressants for—or something stronger.

Something like a steel-cold barrel in the mouth, or the bottle in the hand, or pills you can't get in the States. Something, anything, to make it go away so you can face the normal world.

Except sometimes you can't.

"Do you have anything else on Bernardino?" I didn't want to push him...but I had to know. I *had* to.

"File. Maybe in the file...their eyes. And the teeth..." His eyelids drifted down, and Carp took refuge in the sedation.

I didn't blame him.

I sat there for a long few moments, gray gathering strength through the windows, dawn coming up. My left hand lay human-cold and limp on Carp's sweating forehead, under the gash that ran along his hairline and jagged into his temple, sutured up and quiescent under a dabble of green herbal paste running with the clear gold of Sanctuary sorcery. Galina's work, fine and gentle, stitching together damage.

I wished she had something that would stitch up the damage inside him. I'd have to get him to a trauma counselor; there were a few on call that took care of things like this and billed the police department.

What comes next, Jill? Come up with a plan. Your brain works just fine, now for God's sweet sake, use it.

I took my fingers gently away from Carp's feverish, damp, *human* skin.

It took longer than I liked, breathing deeply and staring at the gray filling up the cup of the window, for my mental floor to clear. I needed sleep, and food, and a good few hours of hard thinking.

So many things I needed. What I was going to *get* was a long mess before this was all through.

When I finally pushed myself up, leather creaking, I stood

looking down at Carp's slack face. He was still shocky-pale, but breathing all right. He might wake up not remembering much, the brain outright refusing, to keep the psyche from being further traumatized. Or he might wake up reliving every single second of it, replaying it like a CD on repeat until he had a psychotic break.

It was too soon to tell.

"Jill?" Leon stood in the door, the copper tied in his hair clinking and shifting as soon as he spoke.

"Where's the Trader?" I kept staring at the planes and valleys of Carp's unhandsome face, as if they would turn into a map that would lead me out of this.

The amulets around Leon's throat jingled a bit as he touched them, his version of a nervous tic. "Up in the greenhouse, Galina says. Are we sitting tight or moving out?"

I swallowed hard, juggling priorities. *Rest easy, Carper. I'm on the job.* "Moving in fifteen, Leon. Get what you need."

"Where we going?"

The next step is to find Bernardino—after we visit Hutch. "Hutch's, to find out what we're up against. Then we're going cop-hunting. Leave your truck here."

CHAPTER 24

Hutch pushed his glasses up on his beaky nose. "Oh, Christ." At least he didn't try to slam the door in my face. I pushed past him and into his bookshop, the familiar smell of dust, paper, and tea enveloping me. "I hate it when you do this."

"Hey, Hutch." Leon grinned. "How you doing?"

"Not you too." Hutch backed up to give both of us plenty of room. *Chatham's Books, Used and Rare,* was painted on a weathered board out front as well as in peeling gilt on the front window, and he did a good trade in repairing old texts. Most of his business is done over the Internet, which is the way he likes it.

Still, the place would've probably gone under if it wasn't for the back room. That room gets Hutch a subsidy from the resident hunter *and* resident law enforcement—a room with triple-locked doors, long wooden tables, and high narrow bookcases stuffed with leather-jacketed tomes on the occult, the theory and history of sorcery, accounts of the nightside, and just about every useful book a hunter needs.

Hey, we're not savages. Sometimes research is the only thing that keeps a hunter's ass from being knocked sideways by the unexpected. Ninety percent of solving any nightside problem is figuring out exactly what you're up against.

And if it wasn't in books, Hutch could *still* probably find it for you. He'd discovered computers in the dark ages when they still used floppy disks; they were still talking about his raids on government databases in law-enforcement classes.

He hadn't wanted to use the information, Hutch always pointed out. He'd just wanted to prove it *could* be hacked.

Nowadays he collects information the resident hunter might need—enough of an exercise for Hutch's skills to keep him out of trouble. If he did anything more, at least he didn't get caught. Which is all I *or* Mikhail ever really asked for. In return, we kept him out of trouble with the law when he went a-fishing and a-hacking on our behalf.

Today Hutch wore a Santa Luz Wheelwrights sweatshirt and a pair of khaki shorts, his thin hairy calves exposed. His beaky, mournful face twisted as he locked the front door and flipped the sign to "closed." "I *really* hate it when you do this. What is it now?"

He isn't one for excitement in the flesh, our local nightside historian. Wise man.

"Internet trace, Hutch. Find me the vitals on one Alfred Bernardino. He's in the Precinct 13 Vice squad. Hack if you have to, but don't leave any fingerprints." I barely broke stride. "And make yourself some tea, we're going to be here a while."

"Why aren't you asking Monty to do this? Or someone else?" Hutch pulled all his angles in, from his thin elbows to his knobby knees, and I considered telling him we had a scurf infestation and all sorts of trouble boiling into town.

I erred on the side of mercy, for once. "Because this time it's the police that are the *problem,* Hutchinson. Find the cop for me, and we're spending some time in the back room. I need to know about something."

"About what?" He didn't quite perk up, but any chance of poking through dusty old books brightens him considerably, even if he's allergic to the idea of seeing *anything* abnormal up close.

I'm not the only one with personality quirks.

"Something called Argoth. And something about an airfield just outside of town."

The milky pallor under his freckles deepened. *"Argoth?"* He actually squeaked.

I halted next to the counter with the antique cash register. A brand-spanking-new credit-card reader sat next to the old brass machine. I turned, on the balls of my feet, my coat swaying with me, and met Hutch's eyes, swimming behind their thick lenses. "You know something about Argoth?"

"Only that he's a hellbreed, operated mostly in Eastern Europe. The last time he surfaced was 1929, he went back down in 1946." Hutch's thin shoulders came up, dropped. The bookstore breathed all around me. "You can guess where he was stationed."

And indeed I could. Both World Wars created enough chaos, pain, and horror to blast the doors between here and *other places* wide open; the battlefields and camps were playgrounds for all sorts of nastiness. Some places on earth still haven't recovered— like Eastern Europe, the hunter population out there is *still* scrambling to get a lid on some of what was let loose decades ago.

"Christ." Leon sneezed twice. It *was* dusty in here.

I'd heard rumors about the war before, but this was unexpected. "Pull me the basic references on Argoth, then get me that cop's vitals. And I need you to find me everything you can on an airfield out of town, possibly called ARA."

Hutch had produced a small steno pad, a mechanical pencil, and was scribbling furiously. "And after that I change water into wine, right?"

If you could, I'd ask for a bottle or two of a nice pinot noir. "Don't get cute. After that you're going to Galina's while I poke around in here some more."

His eyebrows shot up and his pencil paused. "Again?"

Yes, again. Because if they know I'm alive and they know I go to Galina's, they probably know I come here too. "Yes, again. Unless you want to get a severe case of lead poisoning."

"What have you gotten me into now?" But he went back to scribbling. "Okay, come on into the back room. Christ on a crutch, why did I ever take this job?"

"Because you thought it would be interesting, Hutch, and Mikhail saved you from being locked in a six-by-nine." I really must have been feeling savage, because for once even mild-mannered Hutch shot me a dirty look and I realized that was a really, really bitchy thing to say to someone who had risked his ass over and over again to help me. "I'm sor—"

"Oh, shut up. Get into the back room. I just got a new machine, best way to break it in." He made little shooing motions with his hands, for all the world like a farmer's wife herding chickens. "Come on, kids. Let's go see what Uncle Hutch can dig up."

It's certainly something to see an underweight, glorified librarian poke and prod two fully trained and armed hunters around like a chicken herder. If I was less tired, I might even have been amused.

Hutch left about an hour later. I should have taken him to Galina's, but there was precious little time. The next half-hour passed slowly, both Leon and I up to our eyeballs in reading material. He'd taken the Argoth references; I took Carp's file and Bernardino's stats as well as whatever Hutch could dig up on the airfield.

"We are looking at some serious shit," Leon said quietly.

I glanced up from Carp's file. "How bad?"

He tapped the thick, dust-choked leather-bound tome sitting open in front of him. "Bad enough that I've got the heebie-jeebies, darlin'." Copper clinked in his hair, and he took a pull off the only beer Hutch had stocked—a brown-bottled microbrew Leon wrinkled his nose at but took down three of. "Says here that Argoth surfaced earlier than Hutch thought. First recorded instance of him is in 1918, something involving a batch of three hundred shell-shocked soldiers in a hospital ending up with a serious case of dead and half-eaten."

"Charming." I didn't quite shudder, but it was close. "Any verification?"

"Some British hunter thinks it was him, anyway. Then he shows up in Germany in 1924. A couple of Alsatian hunters living in Munich ID'd him hanging around with an Austrian wannabe rabble-rouser who came to power a little later."

I let out a slow whistle, air bleeding between my lips. *Ugh. Nasty.* "A *talyn?*" I hazarded. It certainly seemed likely. When they come out of Hell, they come hungry. And shell-shocked, vulnerable humans would be a nice snack.

"Could be. Sources ain't specific enough. Went through the hunters in Germany like a hot knife through butter all the way through the war; the Allies had to bring in their own hunters attached to the armies just to stay afloat of all the nasty." Leon's mouth pulled down like he tasted something sour. He probably did.

I dimly remembered hearing about that time from my own training, one of the long sessions with my head on Mikhail's chest and his fingers in my hair, his voice tracing through the history of what we know—and even more important, what we suspect. "Mikhail mentioned that."

It was a bad time all around. Here in Santa Luz there had been the great demonic outbreak in '29, and the few hunters remaining stateside during the war years had been overworked almost to death. The Weres suffered high casualties too, and pretty much the only thing that kept any kind of lid on the situation was the Sanctuaries letting hunters move into their houses and training halls, quietly taking sides even though they were supposed to be neutral.

Patriotism isn't just for normals, you know.

Leon looked down at the page, tapped it with one blunt fingertip. "Says here Jack Karma—the second one, that crazy fucker—takes credit for killin' him, in February of forty-five. In Dresden. That must've been a goddamn sight."

"Jack Karma, huh?" I eyed the book speculatively. "He moved to Chicago after the war, didn't he."

"Think so."·Leon didn't need to say any more.

I had Jack Karma's apprentice ring, blackened and vibrating still from the incident that had killed him, tucked safely away in the warehouse on a leather thong with five other silver rings. Each one was a story, passed along the way family history is.

Mikhail hadn't spoken much of his teacher, and I supposed it was normal—as normal as a hunter ever gets. Losing your teacher is much worse than losing a mother or a father. It's almost as bad as losing an apprentice.

And I still could not think of Mikhail's death without an ache in the middle of my chest. "Huh. So we don't know exactly how high-up in the hierarchy this Argoth is. But Jack killed him or sent him back, right?"

"Probably just sent him back, if that blond 'breed is talkin' him up now. Which means he's worse news than a fuckin' *talyn*. But there ain't been anything in the news lately big enough to break anything big out of Hell. Not on this continent, anyway." Leon sighed. "There ain't nothin' else of any use here. What you got?"

In other words, Perry could be leading us down the garden path. Even though I didn't think it was very likely. Still, first things first. "A whole pile of not very much," I admitted. "Carp's right. The file's a bunch of dead ends. There's only initials in witness statements, and witnesses have a habit of disappearing. Want to bet they all ended up as scurf chow?"

"Now why do you want to take an old man's money, darlin'?" Leon rolled his shoulders in their sockets, easing tension, and pushed the book away, leaning back in his chair and eyeing me.

"There's one common note in here—someone high up in the police structure, identified only as *H*. Pedro Ayala told Carp that he knew who H was, that it was bigger than Carp thought, and suspected wiretapping so bad he wouldn't even talk on a pay phone. Then he ended up dead." *And I still have to find time to find out who took him down. Christ.* "Sullivan and the Badger had four different leads who referred to a big-time cop as ringleader, but all four of them petered out, mostly with the people giving the leads disappearing."

"There's an almighty big mass grave out somewheres, then."

And a cop so dirty he makes Perry look almost clean. I swallowed hard. "Not if it's scurf-related. Listen to this. Twelve murders of illegal immigrants, organs stripped. Then everything stops—just when that Sorrows bitch moved in last year. Want to bet this little organ ring came to the attention of someone on the nightside once the Sorrows started putting their fingers in?"

I cocked an ear, listening. Traffic on the streets outside. The shop was dead quiet. All was as it should be, hot sunlight trickling away with every moment we spent in here. Prickles of sweat touched the curve of my lower back even through the air-conditioning. Last year had been bad in more ways than one.

And somewhere out there in the world was Melisande Belisa, the Sorrow who had killed my teacher. Free as a bird, again.

Get it together, Jill. Belisa's not your problem right now. Scurf are your problem, and whoever is killing your people is your problem. Even Argoth isn't a problem—yet. Prioritize.

I took a deep breath laden with the smell of paper and dusty knowledge. Forced myself to pull it together.

"Huh." Leon thought it over. He sneezed twice, lightly. Took another swallow of beer.

It felt good to say it out loud, to string the events together. It's always handy to have someone else to bounce things off. "The scurf we've found have all been too old. If they're escapees from that warehouse on Cherry, they're communally sharing kills. Which means the disappearances we've had fit a pattern. If you dropped a mature nest in the middle of a populated area you'd have exactly the sort of disappearances I've been seeing lately."

"So it's a pattern." He nodded. "Good fuckin' deal."

"Amen to that." If it was a pattern, it could be anticipated—and interrupted.

"So we're gonna go find this cop? Bernardino?"

I gained my feet, pushing the chair back. "Yup. Let's just hope he hasn't gotten twitchy. Or a case of the vanishings."

Leon hauled himself up. "Never knew you was an optimist. What you gonna do about this Argoth character?"

Pray? Hope he's not hungry? "I don't know yet. But it might be time to visit the a few hellbreed dives and twist some arms—*after* I find out who's shipping scurf into my town."

"Sounds like a plan. I'm gonna piss."

"Thanks for sharing." I didn't say what we were both thinking. If hellbreed were connected to the scurf, and a major hellbreed's name was being bandied around, and one of Shen's Traders said a "higher-up" wanted me dead...

Well, it wasn't looking good. But at least we had something to look *at* now, instead of a maddening half-baked mass of weird occurrences with no rhyme or reason.

I sat staring at Carp's file while Leon vanished. Shut my eyes, breathed deep, and tried not to think of Carper lying in bed, his mind at the mercy of suffocating terror. Or of Jacinta Kutchner's body hanging like a rotten fruit from a blue and white nylon rope. Or of Saul and how much I wished it was him I was bouncing ideas off.

It was looking like the Kutchner case was my sort of case after all.

CHAPTER 25

Bernardino lived on a quiet little street, not quite suburban but close enough. He had a nice ranch-style, freshly painted, and his yard was greener than many of his neighbors'. I wondered if he had a landscaping service staffed with illegals out to take care of it, and spent a good few moments wrestling with nausea at the thought as we slid through a neighbor's yard and up to his front door, seeking maximum cover. It wasn't easy, with a high-noon summer sun beating down.

He had no alarm system on his house, and he was probably at work in the Vice department.

Dear God, the irony.

I held my right palm in front of the doorknob and concentrated, a thin thread of etheric force snaking out and bifurcating. One thin thread slid into the doorknob, the other quested blindly and found the keyhole for the deadbolt. A moment's worth of the fierce, relaxed concentration peculiar to sorcery, and the deadbolt eased back, the doorknob lock clicking as it cleared.

"You'd make a great housebreaker," Leon mouthed.

Yeah, that's just one of the many career options open to a hunter. "You think?" I whispered. I eased aside, toed the door open while Leon covered me, and slid into Alfred Bernardino's home—only to recoil and straighten, the reek so intense it scorched the back of my throat.

Dead, decomposing human tissue. "Goddammit," I whispered, my eyes watering, and plunged into the house. Leon swept the door shut behind us, and we cleared and checked every room, working through a place that had obviously been searched. Drawers were pulled out, cushions slit, paper scattered everywhere— and that horrible, nose-eating stench.

And the smell of hellbreed or Trader, a subtle, sweetsick corruption. "There's been 'breed here," I whispered. The kitchen was torn to shreds, a drift of takeout containers and cheap dishes. The living room was a shambles, the dining room smashed too. Bernie's taste had run to cheap mismatched bachelor furniture, but the huge state-of-the-art plasma flatscreen on one wall was new, and the stereo system still smelled of its packaging. That is, through the fume of smoky violence—even these toys bought with blood money had been broken.

I don't know if it was a fight or a hell of a search. Leon covered me down a hallway, we checked a bathroom and a room that had been left empty and bare except for a stain on the carpet and a silver tangle of handcuffs. The reek of sex fought briefly with other varied stenches; Leon's eyebrows went up and I shrugged, moving on. I pushed a door open softly with my foot and saw the source of the worst smell.

Alfred Bernardino lay spread-eagled on his bed, his body bloated by several days' worth of decomposition. His ribs had been torn free and wrenched back, the lungs carefully pulled free and shriveled by exposure to dry outside air. His legs were flayed and his belly opened; a feast of insect life swarmed in the cave of his entrails.

If I'd had any gag reflex left on this case, the sight would have done it.

"Jesus," Leon breathed.

Another fucking dead end. "This is *ridiculous.*"

Leon moved past me, checked the closet. Neither of us put our guns away. Bernardino's clothes were tumbled off the hangers, his cheap white-painted dresser drawers pulled out and disemboweled, and I leaned against the wall, silver tinkling sweetly in my hair.

"You think…" Leon glanced at me. "How long would you say he's been dead?"

I glanced at the window. It was suffocatingly hot in here, and the bedroom window was open a crack, the screen slit. Easy enough for insects to find their way in. The air conditioning wasn't on, and a cool bath of dread touched my spine, working downward from my nape. "With that window open and the critter buffet sign out? Couple days to a week. But we have his credit card run by Irene…" *A Trader, the last known contact we have with this man. Huh.*

"Four days ago," Leon supplied.

Looks like there's more here than meets the eye. My brain gears turned, meshed, caught. "It could fit with the widow's death. We have someone killing the cops to cover this up. Jacinta's account books are missing. Bernie's having second thoughts…" I sighed, then winked, shutting my dumb eye. The smart one, the blue one, showed me a room swirled with the etheric contamination of violent death and desperation. But nothing for me to latch onto, no thread that I could pull to unravel the mess.

Leon let out a gusty sigh, one he probably immediately regretted because he had to take a breath. "Someone tore this fuckin' place apart. And I don't like it—why hasn't anyone come by to check on him? He's a cop."

"A cop with a dead partner. If there weren't cops trying to kill me I could call in and find out if he was on administrative leave or something. Though if this is *el pendejo gordo* they were talking about, he can't have called in the gang hit on me." I lowered my guns, thinking, and my attention snagged on something.

On the bed, actually. It was stripped down to bare mattress and boxspring, but both of them were new, blue with pink flowers, a matched set of Sealys. Intuition tickled under the surface of my brain, and I stared at the mess of Bernardino's body, unseeing, for a long half-minute before Leon moved, checking the master bathroom again. Copper chimed in his hair, a deeper sound than the silver in mine. "Screen's slit in here, too. Window's open."

"The screen was cut in the widow's place. But the window

wasn't open." I replayed the Kutchner scene in my head, walking through mental rooms taken in by a hunter's ground-in, thorough training in observation.

Yes, there above the bathroom window, two patches in the paint.

Curtain rod, ripped down. The screen hurriedly cut. The space between the screen and the window, just the right size to hold...

I let out half a soft breath, opened my eyes. "Come on."

The garage held two cars—a puke-green 1971 Dodge Charger that had seen much, much better days and was drifted with fast-food wrappers inside, and a brand new red Mustang with none of the grace or fluidity of the old models. A fiberglass piece of shit and a horribly mistreated piece of heavy American metal. There was detritus stuffed everywhere; Bernie had been a terrible slob.

But leaning against the wall next to the Mustang was an old mattress, dingy yellow and broken-in.

"Pop the hood on that and check the engine." I indicated the Charger with my chin and slid between the Mustang and the wall, reached the mattress, and started looking.

Twenty seconds later I found what I was looking for—a long slit in the fabric sheathing. I held my breath and reached in as Leon rummaged under the hood.

My fingers closed on something. Hard plastic, book-shaped, and thick. "My God," I whispered.

"What? What is it?"

I yanked the ledger free, tearing the tough material. It must have taken some doing to get the goddamn thing into the mattress, but the hiding place had done its job. "Leon, my dear, we have a break." I ripped it the rest of the way free and flipped it open, riffled through the pages, then fished around again inside the mattress and yanked another one free. "We've just found Jacinta Kutchner's account books. Cooked and *un*cooked, I'm betting."

"Is that so. Looks like this car will run, too. I ain't no mechanic, but nothing seems wrong with it." He dropped the hood.

"Let's find the keys, then. And get the hell out of here." Something stopped me, looking at the Mustang. For some reason I wasn't even considering taking it—for one thing, it was too red.

We'd left Leon's truck behind for the same reason—it was too conspicuous a vehicle.

And for another, the Mustang reeked of hellbreed. Or Trader.

My instincts tingled again, and I looked for license plates. Nada. Not even a dealer tag. The Charger was registered to Bernardino, all its papers in order. "Someone's lying to me."

"You think?" Leon sighed. "The shit's just getting deeper. I'll look for car keys."

I wasn't looking forward to it, but we had to go to Micky's. I expected to see the regular Were waitstaff and I expected Theron at the bar. What I did *not* expect was to be almost-mobbed by Weres as soon as I set foot in the door. It looked like a regular lunchtime crowd, but it was full of cat Were and bird Were, and I was hugged, slapped on the shoulder, fingers brushing over my face and touching my hair. A very big, very angry Theron came pushing his way through the humming, thrumming crowd.

Even the framed pictures of film stars on the walls vibrated, glass and wood chattering. Theron grabbed me by the shoulders, gave me a once-over, and shook me twice, sharply, so my head bobbled and my ears rang a little.

I let him. A tide of sound rose through them, swirled, and Leon was clapped on the shoulder a few times. A bird Were breathed in his face, greeting him, and he nodded and grinned, giving a thumbs-up, especially when someone passed him a cold, foaming can of Pabst.

"God*dam*mit, Jill!" Theron shook me again. "What am I going to tell Saul about this, goddammit? Where have you *been?* There's hellbreed all over your house—"

"Settle down." My tone sliced through the hubbub. I shifted Carp's file and the ledgers under my left arm. "There's not much time."

The rumbling swirled down, and I caught sight of an anomaly—a human face among the Weres.

Gilberto Rosario Gonzalez-Ayala leaned over the counter, watching the Were cooks as they moved around the kitchen. Amalia passed him, handing off a bottle of microbrew the kid looked far too young to drink, and the kid turned around, his eyes sweeping Micky's interior and stopping on me. "What the hell is he doing here?"

"Showed up. The 51s sent him to check with us, since you got firebombed on your way out of their territory. Then the guys that blew up your car moved into the 51 slice of the barrio. Things have been hopping down there."

Shit. How was I going to sort that out too?

Priorities, Jill. As much as I hated it, gang warfare wasn't my problem. I had bigger fish to gut *and* fry.

Someone flipped the "closed" sign and Weres crowded close as I commandeered a table near the back of the dining room, away from the windows. "Pipe down, everyone." I took a deep breath as they settled, eyes shining expectantly. "What we have here, ladies and gentlemen, is a situation. We have a hellbreed operating inside Santa Luz, shipping in scurf with the help of several members of the police force, and using them as the cleanup crew after a nasty little organ-stripping campaign. Illegal immigrants are being shipped in by *coyotes,* parted out like junked cars, and the remains disposed of. The organs are sold—and the scurf are *not* just here for cleaning up what's left. There's experiments." The quiet had become dead heavy silence, pressing against my skin. "Experiments on scurf, with scurf tissue, and funded by this organ operation."

"What kind of experiments?" Amalia balanced her tray on spread fingers, tense and alert, not even the feathers in her hair stirring.

"I don't know." I set down the ledgers and Carp's messy, stuffed-to-the-gills file. Taken together, they were a pretty damning picture of corruption, at least from the organ-theft side of it. Looking below the surface, there was another shape, something looming over my city like a hand about to crush a struggling ant. "Corruption in the police department goes high up. I'm not sure how high just yet. The cop we thought put out the hit on me down in the barrio's been dead for a few days." I let my eyes travel past the Weres to the fringe of the group, to where Gilberto stood, leaning hipshot against the long lunch counter where truckers sometimes sat—or anyone who didn't mind their breakfast slid to them along the counter like a hockey puck. His dead eyes narrowed.

I held his gaze for a long moment. "Señor Gilberto?" *What*

does this kid know about the nightside? He knows about Weres, that much is certain.

Gil stepped away from the lunch counter, and the Weres parted to let him through. Leon took in the kid with a swift glance and sucked another long gulp off his beer.

"He's representing the 51s," Theron didn't twitch, but he was tense at my shoulder. "They . . . feel bad, that you were attacked."

And they don't want to piss off a witch allied to the Weres. "It wasn't their fault. I wasn't on 51 territory. I'm worried about them catching flak from associating with me."

"They had you marked the minute you crossed off our turf, *chiquita*." Gilberto paused, took a sip. He was sorely out of place, a human kid with bad skin and the smell of neglect hanging on him like mildew amid the crackling hum of perfection from the Weres. "Now how you suppose they did that?"

I shrugged, my tattered coat flapping. "I'm a *gringa?*"

It was the right thing to say, because he laughed, a reedy little sound. *"Sí, bruja.* But nobody knew you come down to see us but *el gato* here. Right?"

And Carper. "There was one other person—the cop that gave me the lead on Ay. Gil, your brother's partner killed him."

Gil's utter stillness might have fooled a human, but not a roomful of Weres. Theron sighed. I held the boy's dark soulless gaze, watching the color bleed out from under his cheeks until he was sallow instead of Hispanic.

"His partner's dead too," I continued. "His house was torn apart, but I've got a rough timeline. He had the widow's ledgers, and—"

"Hold up, *bruja*. Ay. His partner, you say? Bernie kill him?"

Silver clinked and shifted in my hair as I nodded. "It appears that way. I'm going to keep digging, though. Until I find out everything about this, I'm still on the job."

"Then the 51s stay on the job too." He darted a glance to Theron, sweat sheening his forehead and upper lip. He'd lost the hairnet, and his hair was surprisingly soft-looking, with a hint of childhood curl. "I go to Ramon. *Es un traidor en nuestra casa, bruja,* because there was no way they should know you visit us." Another silence rose, uncomfortably, between us.

I had to say it.

"The traitor may not be among the 51s, Gil. Because if Ay's partner was dead, my contact sent me into the barrio. But he's not fat. The name *el pendejo gordo* mean anything to you?"

The kid thought it over. "Lot of *pendejos gordos* in *el barrio, bruja*. Lot of them."

"Don't declare war on the cops." It came out harder and faster than I intended, and Gil stiffened slightly, his wiry shoulders coming up. "The last thing we need is a bloodbath in the barrio." He shrugged, the kind of evocative shrug street kids learn early. I pressed a little harder. "Do *not* fire on the cops." *Why do I feel like a den mother?*

The kid seemed to feel comfortable enough in a room full of Weres, and had only given Leon the same passing glance he gave me—measuring, calculating, and not frightened at all. Curiouser and curiouser. "I take it to Ramon. He decide."

Good enough. Ramon's smart enough to keep things quiet down there—I hope. "Can someone go with him?"

Two of the Weres—a lean cub whose face looked very familiar and a bird Were with sleek black feathers knotted in her straight dark hair—volunteered for the job. Gilberto left without a backward glance.

"Nice kid," Leon said, sarcasm tinting his tone.

He'd just as soon kill someone as look at them. Nice kid my ass. Still, Gilberto was smart enough to see my point about firing on cops. And if the 51s had sent him here, he couldn't be entirely lacking in brains *or* discretion. Still. . . . "How much *does* he know about the nightside?"

"Enough, Jill. They all know enough, down in the barrio." Theron folded his arms, leaning against a table. "You want to tell me why there's hellbreed swarming your house?"

I suppose I should be grateful he held off grilling me for this long. "If I knew enough to fill you in, I'd be gunning for the 'breed behind all this. So far all I know is . . ." I ran up against the wall of incomprehensibility, glanced outside to gauge the fall of sunlight. There was a pattern, sure, but it wasn't clear enough. "Any more scurf? Anything?"

"Not a whisper. We cleaned them out."

Thank you, God. "Did we lose..."

"Two more." Theron's jaw firmed, and a rumble swirled through the assembled Weres, drained away.

Goddammit. Futility clawed acid at the back of my throat. Two more of my Weres dead, and I didn't even know their names. "Were there hellbreed there? At the warehouse site?"

He shook his dark sleek head. "Not a one. We would have held back and waited for you awhile if there had been."

So the smell of 'breed up in the office had been *after* the fight? I chewed at my lower lip, considering. The cold dread had turned into a hard rubber ball in my stomach, and the smell of food taunted me. No Were strategy session is without munchies, but if they were closing down Micky's and feeding people for free the situation was dire indeed.

Weres can eat a *lot.*

I stared at the stack of paper on the table as if it might tell me something I didn't know instead of just taunting me with half-seen connections. "I want two or three Weres on Montaigne. Watch him, don't let anything get to him. He's a target now too. I also want some of you watching Galina's house. They tried to kill me onsite before and I've got a wounded human and a Trader in there. Hutch will be there too, for the duration."

Which meant only one thing. I expected serious trouble and didn't want anyone else to get burned. In other words, war. A fresh tension spilled through the Weres, a tautening of attention.

Good allies to have, Weres. But if something bigger than a *talyn* was coming down the turnpike, it might be time to evacuate them.

Deal with that when the time comes, Jill. For right now, get going on what you know *you have to deal with.* I glanced up to gauge Theron's reaction. He nodded. Then I dropped the bomb. "Tell the 51s we want a meet with the gang that opened fire on me. If we can find out who *el pendejo gordo* is I'll feel a lot better about this."

Of course he didn't think much of the idea. "Oh, for Chrissake, Jill, the barrio—"

Shut up, Theron. "You'll be standing in for me, I'm not going into the barrio again. Leon and I are going to make a run on this airfield where they transport the organs out. There's bound to be something out there."

"We'll go—" the Were began, but I shook my head, silver chiming. Rested my fingers on the butt of a gun.

"No, you won't. No Were will get within ten miles of that place. It's hunter business, Theron, the kind that doesn't mix with Weres. There's rumor of a hellbreed involved with this." *More than a rumor. This has sticky little hell-fingers all over it.*

Theron digested this, looked up at the other Weres. "Maybe that bastard that runs the Monde?"

They were quiet, watching us. Apparently Theron had been elected to talk to me about that. "Not him." Of that much, at least, I was reasonably certain. "Another hellbreed. Seriously bad news, if the sources are right."

Which was the understatement of the year. My brain returned to the problem, probing at it like a sore tooth. There is a strict hierarchy in Hell, and we usually only saw the lower orders, it being too goddamn hard for the biggies to come through into the physical plane. The biggest we usually see is a *talyn,* and they're mostly insubstantial anyway.

Except Perry, who might or might not be one. Which I didn't want to think about right now. He couldn't be a *talyn,* he was all-too-substantial on a daily basis.

I didn't want to think about that either.

If half, or even a quarter, of what Hutch had in moldy books about this Argoth was true...

"Leon and I will take care of it." I even said it with a straight face. "But I need every Were watching the city. Keep the barrio from boiling over, and see what you can do about finding out exactly *which* cop gave the kill order on me. Got it?"

"I don't like this," Theron said. "You should have backup."

Shut up. "I *have* backup, Theron. He's standing right here. What I don't need is you second-guessing me."

Another rumble rippled through the Weres. Theron tried again. "This is Lone Ranger shit, Jill. You know how—"

I interrupted him, rude by any standard but especially by Were etiquette. "Shut *up,* Theron!" I rounded on him, both hands loose, and felt the tension in the room tip and shift. "Leon and I will *handle* it. You have no idea what's about to go down, goddammit, and I need my city kept safe while we avert a goddamn apocalypse or two!"

The Were studied me for a long moment, orange light shifting in his eyes. Dressing down a cat Were in public isn't a safe thing to do.

But goddammit, this wasn't a democracy. Weres function by cooperation and consensus—they *have* to. But when the city's under fire, with scurf and 'breed and God knows what going on, it's the hunter's call.

Still, Theron was my friend. And good backup. I shouldn't be taking out my frustrations on him.

The Were slumped, his shoulders going down. "All right." It was a submission, a virtual baring of the throat. "You got it, Jill. We'll keep the city together."

Leon was downing his third beer. I considered telling him to take it easy, decided not to. If the quick, strung-out jerkiness of his movements was any indication, he felt exactly how I did about this whole thing.

"Good deal." I pointed at the ledgers and the file. "Keep that for me, will you? I don't know where else to put it."

"Anything else?" He was suddenly all business. I didn't blame him.

"Just keep Santa Luz on the map and spinning like a top, Leon and I will take care of the rest." I nodded sharply, turned on my heel, and headed for the front door. Leon grabbed another Pabst from Amalia and fell into step behind me, the sound of him popping the ringtab loud in the stillness.

We got almost to the door before Theron spoke again. "Jill."

I didn't turn, but I did stop. *Don't hassle me now, furboy. Just don't do it.*

"We can't afford to lose a hunter." Which is as close as he would ever come to telling me to take care of myself. *And* Leon, for good measure.

Goddamn touchy Weres. You can't even get mad at them when they're so concerned about you. The thought of Saul rose like choking smoke in my chest, I shut it away.

"We won't," I tossed over my shoulder, and made it out the door. Leon followed, guzzling for all he was worth.

The green Charger sat across the street, in a rare bit of shade and free parking in front of a whole-foods store and a video rental place. I got behind the wheel, Leon slammed his door, and I looked at my fingers on the steering wheel. Bernie's keychain, a heavy brass Playboy bunny head, swung through the hot stillness of the interior.

"You just lied to a roomful of Weres." Leon took another hit off the can. "Jesus, Jill."

"The shipments should stop now that we've hit their distribution center." My fingers moved restlessly, Mikhail's apprentice-ring glinting on my third left finger. *In other words, Leon, you can go home. You don't have to see this through.*

Yeah. Right. Like he was going to go for that. I shouldn't even have thought it.

"I been curious all my life." He shrugged, finished off the can with a long slurp and a massive belch that threatened to fog the windows. "Ain't gonna stop now."

The unspoken lingered just under the day's heat. *And if this Argoth is closer than we think, I'll need all the help I can get. Since neither of us is Jack Karma. Not even close.*

I twisted the key. The Charger roused, nowhere near my Impala's sweet purr. Bernie hadn't taken care of this car. *I could fix that, if I hang onto this hunk of metal after the case ends. Have to clean it out, too.* "We need ammo, but I don't want to draw any more attention to Galina's. I've got a cache in the suburbs. We should get to the airfield in about two hours."

The sun would be past its highest mark, the day hot and still in its long afternoon; blessed, safe sunlight everywhere. With a bit of luck, we could disrupt anything going on at the airfield and be home in time for dinner.

I was hoping I'd finally be feeling hungry by then, too.

"More ammo." Leon nodded sagely. "And I'll be praying my ass off, Jill. This is suicide."

You don't think I know that? "It beats sitting in front of the TV." I checked traffic and pulled out, sedately for once. I didn't know how far I could abuse this engine, and I didn't want cops marking this car. Not for a while, anyway. With Bernie's partner dead and me driving like Granny Weatherall, there shouldn't be a reason for anyone to run the plate number either.

If we were lucky.

"Amen." Leon belched again, dropping the can on the floorboard, and I rolled my window down.

CHAPTER 26

The Anabela Rosenkrantz Memorial Airfield sits about twenty miles outside the city limits. It's a dusty, claptrap place, hangars set on one side of a long strip of pounded-down desert, leveled by a wheezing bulldozer after every gullywasher. Hutch had done his digging well, and now I knew all about it.

ARA was where prop-plane enthusiasts stored their machines and the Santa Luz Police Department trained their two or three helicopter pilots. The county fire department trained out here too, sometimes, rather than at the bigger airport situated halfway between Santa Luz and the state capital.

All in all, the dusty little place saw a lot of activity. That is, until last year.

Hutch had discovered ARA had been "closed for repair" last winter, and never reopened. The amateur enthusiasts had moved closer to the county seat, and the cops hadn't been out here at all this year.

At least, not the honest ones.

Which is why I wasn't surprised, when we crested the rise on a Forestry Service road cutting off the highway at an angle and heading into the canyons, to see more tin roofs throwing blinding spears of sunlight at the sky. It was the eight-by-ten I'd found in the Cherry Street warehouse. That picture had been taken recently, for some reason—probably to familiarize a pilot with the layout so the cargoes could be flown out.

The drug runners move through further east, trucking things up through the border, carrying them through with illegal immigrants, and paying flyboys top dollar to play tag with Border Patrol. The last time I tangled with serious drugrunning into

Santa Luz had been that hellbreed motherfucker selling tainted E, but most of that had been cleaning up the pipeline for ingredients, since the actual drug had been made in the basement of an apartment building at the edge of the barrio.

"What?" Leon glanced up through the windshield as we rolled to a stop below the top of the rise.

I gestured briefly, switched the radio—AC/DC moaning about the highway to hell, since we're both classic rock fans—off. Heatwaves blurred the distance and poured in through the open windows. "They've built more onto the airfield."

We exchanged a long meaningful look. Rosita was in the back seat, out of sight but close at hand should he need her. "Shit." He leaned over the seat to grab her.

I agreed. Coming in this way we had some cover, but the airfield was...well, an airfield, and out in the middle of nowhere where you could see somebody coming. We would raise a roostertail of dust into the stratosphere, and if they had assault rifles—

We'll deal with that when we get there. I tipped my shades down my nose, looking over them and memorizing the layout. Light stung, water wrung out of both my smart and dumb eyes. And yes, friends and neighbors, wasn't there a plucking in the fabric of reality around the airfield? Little dimples of swirling corruption lifting like pollen on the air, rising with the heat, and a brackish well of contamination centered right over the airfield, welling up like crude from a deep, dark secret place.

Leon eyed it too. "Gives me the willies," he said finally, a world of hunter's intuition boiling down to four little words.

"Contamination. Can't tell what it's from, yet." Baking, sand-smelling wind scoured the inside of the car. Junkfood wrappers rustled and blew. *Thank God we're downwind.*

"Yay." His blunt fingers touched Rosita the way they would touch a lover's hand. "This ain't gonna be pretty, darlin'."

"I know. If half of what Hutch has archived is true we're stuck hoping he hasn't found a door yet." *That's a hell of a run of luck we're expecting.* "This bothers me, Leon. It bothers me a *lot.*"

As usual, he took refuge in understatement. "You get the feelin' we're bein' led by the nose?"

"All through this goddamn thing. I just don't see how anyone would think Monty would call me in to look at his ex-partner's 'suicide.' And I don't see how anyone could expect me to find scurf and take them out, even if I was looking into disappearances on the east side. Those were probably escaped stragglers, unless the 'breed was outside to watch over them. It was probably luck pure and simple, and..."

"And anytime we get that lucky, someone has to be planning something." He shifted uneasily in his seat. "So what we gonna do?"

"We find out what's going on at this airfield, and what those new buildings are. And with any luck, they won't be expecting us to hit them *here*." *Luck. Again. Never a substitute for proper planning, ammunition, or intelligence, as Mikhail would point out to me.* The nagging feeling of something missing, of a trap about to spring, hovered over me again, retreated. "Fuck."

"My sentimentals 'zactly. So what's the plan?"

"What would you do?" *Since you'd do exactly what I'd do.*

He sniffed, tasting the air. Made a face. "Drive this piece of shit straight in and keep my eyes open. Then I'd send you out to draw their fire, darlin', while I bulwark myself in and Rosita covers you. That's assumin' they have guards."

"I don't see anyone moving, but that's no assurance." Headache pounded behind my eyes, and I slipped my shades back up my nose. The world took on a better contrast, but I'd have to take them off for the last few miles of approach. "This baby's heavy metal, like my Impala. Should be good as long as nobody hits a gas tank. After blowing up one car already on this case, I don't think I want to blow up another."

"Amen, darlin'." He sighed, copper clinking as he settled himself in his seat. The look on his face told me he was wishing for another beer.

I waited for him to add more, but he didn't. So I dropped the car into "drive" and hit the gas, glad to have him with me.

Dust rose in a choking swath as I worked the steering, swinging the rear end out and standing on the brake. I bailed out as Leon did, and we both scrambled for the defensible angle between the back of the car and the farthest hangar. From here we had a straight shot down the runway or a good chance of cover while bobbing and weaving to the new buildings.

When no shots rang out and nothing happened, it was absurdly anticlimactic.

I crouched, my coat hanging behind me. The copper in Leon's hair chimed. "Go," he whispered, Rosita socked to his shoulder, his keen eyes alert down the alley for any muzzle flash.

I *moved,* etheric force pulled through the humming scar on my wrist, almost faster than I could control. *It's acting up. Dammit, Perry.* The thought was gone in a flash. I reached cover, pointed my guns down the way, and found no breath of anything stirring. It was as quiet as a grave.

Get it, Jill? Quiet as the grave? Arf arf.

I whistled, and Leon tore down the same path I'd taken. We covered each other, leapfrogging, because it was goddamn evident there was nobody here. I couldn't even hear a heartbeat. Just the rasp of sand sliding over the desert, carried on the back of an oven-hot wind.

Just like scales moving in a dark hole.

"This is creepy," I muttered. Then I shut up, brain working overtime. It had to be a trap. *Had* to be.

The largest of the new buildings crouched under a shiny tin roof, and Leon and I both stopped, considering it for a moment. There was a door, a nice double-reinforced number, on the side of the prefabricated trailer. A brand-spanking-new set of wooden steps and a ramp large enough to wheel a forklift up led to the door, its latch and padlock glimmering like fool's gold.

"Are you—" he began.

I noticed it too. "No windows." I answered. "And locked on the *outside.*" Just like the Winchell murder site. Gooseflesh rose cold and hard under my skin, and I made another one of those wrenching mental efforts to stay clear. Leon was depending on me, dammit. So were my Weres and my city.

But what's behind that door, Jill? Hm? You're so smart, what's behind that door?

"Yeah," he breathed. "You go first."

"Sure you don't want to take this one?" Black humor at its finest, I glanced at him and Rosita. The spark was back in Leon's eyes, and high hard color stood out on his cheeks. Otherwise he was dead white. A sheen of sweat not from the incidental heat of the day—because as a hunter you learn to regulate your body temperature pretty thoroughly—touched his forehead.

"Aw hell, darlin', ladies first." His attention never wavered from the padlocked door.

I grinned, a fey baring of teeth Saul would recognize as my *get ready* face. "Age before beauty."

"Pearls before swi—"

But I was already moving, bolting out of cover. The sun lay in a white glare like a hot sterile blanket over a corpse, and I hit the door like it had personally offended me. It gave, buckling, built to withstand more than ordinary pressure, but the extra force I pulled through the scar blazed through my arm and it crumpled like paper. I landed hard, weight on the balls of my feet, and swept with my guns.

The Trader hit me just as hard, knocking me ass over teakettle down the three wooden stairs I'd just bolted up. I landed on my back, already firing, and heard Rosita roar.

At the apex of his leap, the dirty-blond Trader, wearing an eerily gleaming long white coat, was tumbled sideways by a load of silver ammo punching into his side, curling up like a spider dropped into a candleflame. His screech tore the simmering air, and I was on my feet again in a moment—pull the knees in, *kick,* use the momentum to jackknife and get your feet under you, then leap sideways as well, *get on him Jill, take him down are there more Leon cover me goddammit—*

"Mercy!" the Trader yelled, and I landed with one gun trained on him and the other on the door of the trailer. *"Mercy don't kill me Kismet don't kill me please!"*

Whafuck? I replayed it in my head and decided that yes, he *had* really said it. "How many more?" I shouted. "Who else is in there?" I felt naked, horribly exposed, no cover, if they wanted to open fire on me like they did at Galina's I was right in the crosshairs.

No heartbeats. There's nobody here but this Trader. But you didn't hear him, you might have missed someone else, dear God—

The Trader moaned. Bright blood welled between his fingers, clamped to his side. The white was a lab coat, now grinding into the dirt and fouled with blood. Lots of blood, only faintly tinged with black corruption. "Mercy..." The sibilant at the end of the word trailed between a ridge of triangular teeth sharp as a shark's. "Irene...Irene—"

What the hell? I eyed him. Nothing happened for a long taffy-stretching moment. Hellbreed crawling all over my house and now this Trader moaning a Trader waitress's name.

Hang on a second. Hold the phone for just one goddamn minute here.

"Fairfax?" I hazarded, not lowering my guns. Every hair on my body stood on end, quivering, scouring the air currents for the next weird happenstance. *Wait a minute. I thought I killed you. But I just said blond, and Irene...*

Caught assuming. Again. Goddammit. And Irene had looked relieved when I insisted the blond was *hellbreed*—I hadn't said *Trader.*

The Trader froze. His eyes, blue under the flat shine of the dusted, half-opened. "Nobody...here," he gasped, and took in a huge sucking breath. "Just the...the subjects. And me."

"Jill?" Leon was getting nervous.

That made two of us.

"Subjects?" The hammer on the gun pointing at the Trader clicked up. "And how the *fuck* do you know Irene?"

"The *subjects!*" He whisper-screamed it, losing air. "She's my *wife*, goddammit!"

I holstered a gun and hauled him up from the crumbling dirt by his lapels, dragged him toward the blown-out door, his body in front of mine like a shield. "Move." I prodded him, both guns back out. "Inside. And if there's someone in there, *you die first.*"

"They say you help—" He stumbled. He was losing a lot of claret through that hole in his side. When Rosita talks, she's not to be taken lightly. "Help...people."

They certainly say that. What they don't say is that I'm a right bitch. "Sometimes." I stepped in front of the open door, prodded him again. He stumbled, took two steps inside, and dropped down in a heap, his eyes rolling up inside his head.

The smell boiled out and hit me. Candied, foul, rotting sweetness. My hackles rose, adrenaline dumping into my bloodstream like pollution into a river.

"Jill?" Leon, getting even more nervous.

I scanned the inside of the building. "Jesus," I whispered. "Jesus Christ." Then, over my shoulder, "Come on, Leon!"

And I plunged into the smell, stepping over the unconscious Trader. I didn't even cuff him. He was losing blood too fast to need it.

CHAPTER 27

The tanks were huge glassy cylinders of greenish liquid. In each clear tube, a scurf floated, in varying stages of maturity. The smell was enough to make my eyes run even with the door blasted open and sunlight scouring a rectangle of yellow linoleum.

There were two rows of the green tubes, each lit with ghostly non-UV light. There were dissection tables, and a long bookcase along one wall, stacked with reference works and binders.

Leon helped me drag the Trader to a table and bandage him. Leon also snapped silver cuffs on him, just in case. Meanwhile, I stared at the closest tube full of green viscous stuff, and the scurf floating, eyes closed. "They're preserved." My gorge rose, hot and hard at the back of my tongue. "Jesus."

Leon gave them barely half a glance and turned an interesting shade of pale. His amulets clinked. "What the fuck is going on?"

"Check the books." I tipped my head at the bookcases and holstered a gun, then set about trying to wake the Trader up. It was hard—he'd lost a lot of blood, but he was tougher than the average human. Then again, it didn't look like he'd Traded for anything good, like superstrength or invulnerability.

But then, there were those teeth. And his hands looked funny, bonelessly flopping and too delicate. Strangler's hands.

"Virology. Chemical composition of antidepressants. *The Anarchist's Cookbook,* even." Leon snagged that one, it vanished into his coat pocket. "Looks like a first edition too."

"Kleptomaniac." One whole wall of the trailer/hangar was taken up with chem-lab equipment. They'd been cooking something up, out here in the desert. The Trader started to come around, his eyes rolling back down in his head. He shifted uneasily, the silver cuffs clanking, and cringed when he caught sight of me. "He's waking up. Check that stuff over there, will you? Didn't you take chemistry?"

"Once in m'benighted youth, darlin'. Left as soon as I figured out how to make beer and fertilizer explosives."

"Now *there's* a combination." Both of us took care not to turn our backs to the door. The scurf floated eerily in their green tubes. They didn't look dead, just...sleeping, caught in a moment of rare immobility, like during daylight when they pack themselves together like sardines.

I shuddered. Leon was all white now, pale even under the fishbelly of "night-walking hunter." His eyeliner had turned garish against the new pallor. From the cold feeling in my cheeks, I probably wasn't far behind.

The smell was incredible. Fresh tears trickled down my cheeks—and the scar puckered itself up into a tiny mouth, a thrill of painful heat running up the branching channels of my nerves.

"Irene..." the Trader moaned. He woke up all the way and blinked at me, like a six-year-old coming out of a nightmare.

This is goddamn ridiculous. "Hey, Sleeping Beauty. Start talking."

"You're her." He gasped in breath again. He really did sound awful, but then he'd taken a load of silver in the side from Rosita. I wouldn't be too peppy myself under those circumstances. "Kismet. You're actually *her.*"

"No shit." *Who else would be doing this?* "The question is, who the fuck are you? But that can wait. Is there anyone else here? Anyone at *all?*"

"J-just the subjects." He winced and the cuffs clanked, blue sparks running just under their surface, responding to the contamination of hellbreed on him. As Traders went he was a lightweight. "They're in the east building, two down. It's not due in the s-south building for another week—"

Another week? "What's in another week?"

Blond stubble covered his cheeks. He looked like a watered-down version of Hutch, weak-eyed as a mole. The lab coat covered a frame that wasn't even wiry-strong, just wiry.

Still, he knocked me over. Must be something in there. Looks can be deceiving, especially when it comes to Traders. And what's the story with him and Irene?

"The Summoning," he whispered. "They're not due for another week. When the moon's dark. Then they...they—"

Oh shit. A summoning? "They what?" I had a sneaking suspicion I knew.

Argoth. Or other seriously bad news.

"They won't tell me." He cringed against the surgical table we'd laid him on, instruments rattling. It took me a moment to figure out why he looked familiar—there was the same ratty little gleam in his eyes as in Irene's, a gleam I wasn't sure I liked. "Only that *he* is coming, and *he* wants this place. I keep my ears open, so does Irene. When *he* comes...they have the formula, they'll make as much of it as they want—"

"Formula for what?" *And why do I have this sinking feeling like I know who "he" is?*

"For the sickness." He cringed again as I loomed over him, even though I hadn't moved. "For Dream."

I frowned. "What sickness?"

He made a short sketching motion, arrested when I twitched, a hair away from breaking his arm. "Bioweapon. They came to me with samples. I thought they were from the government. They said, what can you do with this? It was a good job, I took it—and then they took Irene. Said I had to start working, and working quick, or Irene would be dead before—"

Bioweapon? Oh Christ Jesus. "Samples?" *Keep him on track, Jill.*

"From—" His eyes flicked nervously to one of the green tubes. But his face had lit up, just like a mad scientist talking about his monster. "From them. They got live ones from somewhere, a lot of them. Finally figured out to put 'em in the xarocaine and the cellular burn stops, they die but don't rot. It's a preservative. Used the same process for—"

"There's some Day-Glo purple powder over here, Jill." Leon's tone cut through the Trader's babble. "All in little Ziplocs. Looks ready for shipment."

The Trader nodded jerkily, his hair flopping. "It *is* ready. It starts changing on the first hit, you can deliver it through the water supply; it could possibly go airborne if I had enough time. But I can't figure out how to stop the replication yet. The side effects—"

Dear God. The smell was worse now, because drafts of fresh air were spilling in the open door. A fresh gout of stench hit each time the wind shifted, and the breaths of not-so-bad air only served to underscore the reek. "Side effects?" It was like questioning a waterfall, hard to keep him on one topic, words spilling out past those sharklike teeth.

Oh yeah. Definitely Dr. Frankenstein material.

"These things, whatever they are . . . the viral replication is just endless, it remodels the genetic code and eats up hemoglobin like nobody's business. So the Dream—that's what I call it—hits hard and fast like a Mack truck, but the side effects, they can't go out in the sun, their pupils get all dilated, and they get thirsty. They tear each other up, and when one of them starts to bleed—" His shudder echoed mine. "It's in the blood. I could engineer the effect for just a quick death and stop the mutation if they would give me more *time.* But they said—I thought they were from the *government.* Who else would want something like this?"

"Holy shit." I eyed him. *Is this for real?* "You're kidding."

"Once it's perfected—"

"Shut up." *Men like you made the atom bomb, you waste.* I didn't need any help putting together the consequences. No wonder hellbreed were crawling all over this, it had all the things they like in a weapon. But what was the connection, where was the other half of the puzzle? The sense of a missing puzzle piece returned, nagging.

Was it just because it would cause enough death to feed a hungry high-class hellbreed just out of Hell? Something even worse than a *talyn?*

I hate those sorts of questions.

"I say we put a fuckin' bullet in his head and burn this place to the ground." Leon racked Rosita, but his eyes were steady.

The Trader squealed like a rabbit in a trap. *"Nooo! Please, no don't kill me, please—"*

"For Christ's sake." I'd heard enough. "Shut the fuck up. I'm not going to kill you yet. You said something about subjects. What subjects?"

"The test subjects. Some of them just get addicted to the

Dream, they don't die. They exhibit side effects. They're in the east building." He flinched again, cowering, even though I hadn't moved. "They had Irene, I had to do what they said, I *had to!*"

Fax might know, I don't, I heard Irene say, in her flat little voice. *Definitely* more to this than what Mr. Skinny was telling me. On the other hand, Irene wasn't the most dependable source either. So, two lies to choose from?

That's not the issue, Jill. The issue is what we're going to do now. Leon and I locked eyes for a long moment, weighing the situation. When he nodded, fractionally, I knew his mental calculus was the same as mine.

I stepped back from the surgical table. "Cover him. I'm going to check the other buildings."

"Have fun." Leon drew a Glock from a hip holster. "If I hear any ruckus, Doc-Boy here gets one in the *cabeza.*"

"I'm sure there won't be anything." I looked down at the Trader. "Am I right?"

As good-cop-bad-cop routines go, it was a good one. If Fax could have lost any more color without turning transparent, he would have. "Just the subjects," he whispered. "They...you won't believe it until you see it."

Leon snorted. It was unintentionally funny, and I found myself wanting to smile too. Dispelled the urge. *You have no idea what I might believe, kid.* I turned on my heel, sharply, and headed for sunlight. The water on my cheeks dried as soon as I checked the angles and stepped out into the harsh glare of daylight. The fresh air was a balm after the reek of scurf, hellbreed, and lies.

CHAPTER 28

Ten minutes later I stumbled back out into the glare and made it, then grabbed at the side of the building and retched, my eyes spouting water. Again, a tearing heave that came all the way from my toes. One last time before control clamped down, stomach cramping, aware I was making a low hurt sound and hating it.

Focus, goddammit! It wasn't Mikhail's voice in my head this time, it was my own, harsh as if I had a throatful of smoke. *Get a handle, Jill. Any handle will do.*

I made it to the laboratory. Leon barely glanced at me, did a double take. "Jill?" For once, all Texas bluster and drawl was erased from his voice.

I had to try twice to speak. "Get him in the car. Take him to Galina's and *chain him the fuck up.*" I wiped at my cheeks. "I'm going to stay here and rip this fucking place apart."

"We been havin' a little chat in here." Leon's eyes were watering from the stink too, and he looked none-too-happy. "It's worse than you think. Some guy named Harvill—"

My brain shuddered with what I had seen inside the south building. *Dear God, their eyes... their arms, and the smell—*

I lunged into the present. *Harvill. The District Attorney. Big fat redhaired good ol' boy. Ran last year on a tough-love, three-strikes ticket. You voted for the guy, remember?* "The DA is in on this?" *The H. in the file. A big-time cop, one of the witnesses said. But I didn't think of the DA's office. Jesus. It makes sense. It makes too much goddamn sense.*

That's the trouble with hellbreed. Sooner or later they find someone high-up to seduce. It never fails.

"I don't know who he is," the Trader whined. "Just that he was a bigshot, he came in with—"

I found myself at the side of the table, the Glock out of its holster and pressed to his forehead. "Shut. Up." *He did this. Willing or not,* he *did this. He made those... things. Dear God.* "I should kill you now, for what you did to those people."

The weak blue eyes shimmered with tears. But under the gleam there was that hardness, the animal calculating how to survive. I've seen it too many times in Trader eyes—the little gleam that says everything is disposable to them, as long as they get what they want.

I've seen that gleam in ordinary people too. I grew up with that avid little light shining at me from the faces of people who should have loved and protected me. I hit the street to get away from it and found out it only got deeper. I *hate* that queer ratlike little shine in people's eyes.

And sometimes I wonder if my own eyes hold that little gleam. When I'm considering murdering someone, Trader or criminal or hellbreed. When I've got my toes on the cliff edge and am staring down into the abyss.

Get a hold on yourself, Jill.

Tremors ran through my arms and legs. *Don't kill him.* The voice of reason in my head was Saul's, and I was grateful for it.

If it had been any other voice, I'd've spread his brain and bone all over that fucking table.

"Hellbreed," I rasped. "Who came with Harvill? Which one of the motherfuckers is behind it? Who did you Trade with?" *I think I already know. And if you lie to me, so help me God, I will send you to Hell right now.*

Cringing and sobbing, he told me, and quite a few things fell into place. *Don't kill him, kitten,* Saul's voice repeated. *You know what you have to do.*

"Jill?" Leon asked again.

Daylight's wasting. I had too much to do, not enough time to do it in. Story of my life.

"Those things in the east building. Are they vulnerable to UV light like—" I tipped my head back a little, indicating the scurf floating peacefully in their green tubes.

Oh Jesus. Jesus and Mother Mary. The urge to vomit rose hard and sharp under my breastbone again. I shoved it down.

"Y-yes—" He looked ready to plead for his life again, but something in the geography of my face changed. I felt it, skin moving on bones, from somewhere outside myself.

The Trader shut up. Wise of him.

"And this stuff, Dream, fire destroys it? It doesn't become toxic in midair?" *It better not. If it does, I don't know what I'm going to do.*

He nodded, a quick little jerk of his head. The movement ended with a flinch, because the gun's blind mouth was still pressed against his forehead so hard I felt the trembling running through him.

"One more question." Every muscle in my body protested when I took the gun away from his head. *They know it's possible now. Some hellbreed somewhere is going to do something like this, unless I can cut it off at the root.* "Is this *all* of it? All the weapon, the drug, whatever it is? Everything you've got onsite here? Is there a backup to your research?"

"Everything's here—my work, all the computers. No backup, nothing. The first shipment is in planes in the hangars—"

That was all I needed to know. I dismissed him, looked up at Leon, who stood cradling Rosita. The bright spots of color still stood out on his cheeks, and his aura sparkled through my smart eye, the same sea-urchin shape as mine. A flicker of disgust crossed his face, and I was terribly, sadly grateful that it wasn't me he was disgusted with.

My voice didn't want to work properly. "Get him the fuck out of here. Now."

He didn't think much of the idea. "Jill—"

I was not in the mood. "If you don't get him out of here, Leon, I am going to lose my temper." Flat, quiet, just as if I was telling him what was for dinner. "Stay in touch with the Weres and keep my city together. If I'm not in town by dawn tomorrow—"

"What the fuck are you thinking of doing?" But Leon was already moving, racking Rosita, sweeping the Trader off the table and onto his feet with a gun pressed to his side. "Give me a vowel here, darlin'."

"First, I'm burning down this building." *I have to erase every trace of this, or it'll be used somewhere else.* I holstered my gun with another one of those physical efforts that left me shaking, shook out my right hand, and drew on the scar. A hissing whisper filled my palm, and pale-orange, misshapen flame burst into being between my fingers.

I barely felt the burn against my skin, I was so cold under my leather and weight of weapons. It was the absolute chilling freeze beyond rage, beyond pain, and beyond fear.

I could wish it didn't feel so familiar. "Then I'm burning down *every* fucking stick of this place, and consigning every soul in that east building to God." I paused. "If He will take them."

Leon had the Trader, was dragging him toward the door. Their shadows moved in the ragged rectangle of clean sunshine, and the flames dripped from my fingers, scorching the floor. The sorcerous flame hunters are trained to call on—banefire—devours all trace of hellbreed and leaves a blessing in its wake, but for this, I needed something more.

I needed pure destruction.

The hellfire made a sound like strangled children whispering. Like dead souls filling up a room with angry cricket-voices. Like the click of a bullet loaded into a magazine, over and over again, with a feedback squeal as my fury escaped my control for a single moment, a breath between thoughts.

The bookshelves burst into oddly pale orange flame. The hellfire laughed, wreathing my fingers, and I flung it in a wide arc, smashing against the beakers and shelves on the back wall like napalm. Glass screeched and exploded, and I backed toward the door, fire scouring wetly in a trail from my right hand.

The frightening thing wasn't how easy it was to pull that sort of power through the scar, or even the agonizing plucking against every nerve running up my right arm and into my shoulder, branching channels full of magma played like dissonant violin strings.

The frightening thing was that the hellfire turned yellow, a clear pure yellow like sunlight, and I jerked my hand away from me, toward the green columns of floating dead scurf. Glass shattered and slime flooded the floor, bodies falling with wet thumps as the backdraft pushed me out the door, just in time too. I landed sprawled on the wooden ramp, hearing the Charger's engine rouse itself just as the first explosion—of course, there were stocks of chemicals in the building, I was basically torching an ammo dump of viral weaponry—rocked the desert air and the fire took a deep, vast, hot breath. A belch of greasy black smoke rounded itself like bread dough rising and flared for the sky.

Burn, someone whispered inside my head. *Burn it all.* And this last voice sent me scurrying, trying to shake the yellow hellfire away from my hand like hot grease, because it was Perry's voice, and I knew that for once I was going to do exactly what it said.

Smoke rose in a huge black smudge, a beacon underlit with bright yellow leaping flame. I shot the last mewling, crawling, burned-black thing skittering in the ashes in its approximation of a head.

My gorge rose again, pointlessly, receded with a sound like a choking-dead laugh. The hangars were burning, sharp guncracks of explosions sending flaming debris arcing across the runway.

The entire place looked like a bomb had hit it, except the last building. The sun hung low in the west, a gigantic bloody eye. *Someone has to have noticed this by now.* A tired sound escaped my lips, sounding suspiciously like a giggle.

The only building I'd left almost untouched was the southerly new one. The Trader said the evocation was due in a week, and a glance inside the kicked-in door had shown me a fresh concrete floor with a pentagram carved deep—and it was definitely a penta*gram,* not a penta*cle*—inside a circle and square, candles ranked on fluted iron holders, and the reek of hellbreed so strong and thick it almost knocked me over despite all the varied and wonderful stenches that are a hunter's life.

The hellfire, burning steadily on my fingertips now, running from the scar like greasepaint, had turned green at its tips. Most sorcerous flame works on a spectrum, and I shouldn't have been able to produce more than red flame tinged at the edges with a little orange.

Instead, I was cycling up through the spectrum. I'd seen Perry produce blue hellfire once or twice, and it made me wonder. How much of this could he feel, sitting in his office in the Monde? Was he curious about what I was doing? Was I using up all my stock of preternatural power in this one futile gesture?

If I was, I'd cross that bridge when I came to it. There were more immediate problems to solve. *They have a backup somewhere. They would be stupid not to. Or this* is *a backup.*

Still, the statement I was making might make any hellbreed think twice before visiting my town. Even the ones still burning in Hell's embrace.

Even one who had killed my teacher's teacher? Wasn't that the sixty-four-thousand-dollar question? If they released Dream— drug, bioweapon, whatever it was—on my city as this Argoth climbed free of Hell, the massive suffering would be a huge banquet. It would *feed* him, and with that sort of energetic jolt he'd become a very serious proposition indeed.

And I wasn't a Jack Karma, capable of containing that sort of thing. Not even close. Not even with Perry's scar on my arm—a scar that might turn into a liability if Perry was ordered by a much stronger hellbreed to Do Something About Me.

Get cracking, Jill. There's work to do.

In the center of the pentagram the altar stood, a chunk of wood probably from a hangman's tree under draped black satin stiff with noisome fluids. Various implements, hissing with malice, scattered over the altar's surface. I took them all in with a glance, shaking my hand. The hellfire didn't want to go away. It kept popping and hissing, chortling at me, drawing strength from the contagion in the air.

Each piece of silver I wore spat blue sparks. I shut my eyes, my smart eye piercing the meat of my eyelid to show me the shape of things under the surface of the world. The evocation was indeed very close to being finished. Had this continued, on some night under a dark moon the walls between the physical plane and Hell's screaming, shifting flames would have gapped for just the tiniest moment, and something could have slipped through, not just as a bad dream or a walking shade like an *arkeus,* only able to coalesce into physical form when someone bargained with it and gave it a toehold.

No, something real would step through. It only took a moment, a knife's-edge worth of time. And what would a creature like Argoth want with my town? Revenge on a hunter of Karma's lineage? Something coincidental? A darker purpose?

Always assuming Perry was telling the truth and it *was* Argoth waiting to come through.

If it wasn't that hellbreed in specific, it was probably one just as bad. And its corruption would spread until burned out, fueled by the suffering of my people. My civilians. *My* city.

Not in my *city.*

The sharp clarity of my rage was comforting, but I couldn't stay there. It took a long while, me wrestling with the scar, a battle of wills that ended with sweat breaking out all over my body and my eyes snapping open to see that darkness had gathered in the corners. A dry lion's cough of an explosion sounded. *Did I really do all that?*

I held up my right hand.

In the uncertain light, the puckered lip-print on my inner wrist

was just the same. There was no mark on my skin of the power I'd
pulled through it. It felt flushed, obscenely full, pulsing in time
with my heartbeat.

"God," I whispered. Blue sparks hissed.

The banefire came slowly, whispering around my fingers in
wisps, almost drowned by the pressure of hellbreed contamination in the ether. It tingled, like a numb limb right before the pain
of waking up starts.

The prayer rose inside my head. *Thou who hast*... It circled
the rage, came back. *Thou Who hast given me to fight evil, protect me; keep me from harm.* The prayer, skipped, skidded, and
returned to the most important part. "O my Lord God," I whispered, "do not forsake me when I face Hell's legions." My voice
cracked; I licked my dry lips. From some deep place inside me the
idea of calm rose, and I grabbed for it with both mental hands.
The last sentence fell into a well of silence. "In Thy name and
with Thy blessing, I go forth to cleanse the night."

I opened my eyes.

Oily, pale-blue banefire wreathed my hand in living flame,
whispering to itself, a cleaner sound than hellfire's greasy chuckling. It boiled up, sheathing my skin, and I threw it at the altar
with every ounce of hellbreed strength my right arm possessed.

It hit, dimmed, and roared up, a sheet of avid blue flame crawling
over cursed implements and scouring the black satin. The curved
knife, the twisted claw of no animal that crawled under the sun, the
chalice full of noisome, clotted scum, other things that had no other
purpose but to hurt and wreak havoc—all wrinkling like paper in a
flame, the banefire gathering strength as I stumbled back on legs as
weak and rubbery as noodles, hit my shoulder on the wrecked door,
and almost went down in a heap out in the dust beyond.

Jill, you're in bad shape.

I let out a hard jagged sound. Better shape than those...
things...in the east building. If hunters were allowed to go to
Confession and Communion I might have turned a priest's hair
white, sharing the horror.

It was worse because they'd been human once, and worse even
than scurf because of the—

My mind reeled violently away from the thought. There are

only two or three things in my life as a hunter that have that effect—memories so terrible the fabric of the brain itself refuses to hold them, human comprehension shying away.

Good, you can't remember. Which means it's over. Which means you need to get on your fucking feet and finish the rest of this job. Monty. Theron. Carp. They're all in danger, and it's up to you. So quit your bitchmoaning and figure out how you're going to get the hell back to your city.

I came back to myself on my knees in the dust with my head down, hair hanging in dark strings starred with blue-sparking silver, and the hissing of banefire behind me underlying the crackle of other flame. If anybody was giving out prizes for laying waste, I'd have won one. The entire airfield looked like a picture of an artillery attack I'd seen in an old magazine. Every hangar was a roaring shell, and the new buildings were burning merrily, mostly with orange and yellow flame.

I struggled up to my feet, taking harsh deep barking breaths. The crimson stain in the west was the sun finally dying. And the plume of black smoke stretching up into the gathering dusk was a huge fucking neon sign.

Priorities, Jill. Your city's in danger. They could have another evocation site, and you're stuck here without a car. What are you going to do?

Why weren't there news helicopters circling? Someone had to have seen this from the highway. Out here in the desert, you could see forever, couldn't you? A pillar of smoke during the day, miles from the city—

Instinct, and instinct alone, made me raise my head. I wouldn't have heard the car's tires over the snap and crackle of flame. Behind me, banefire exploded, and the heat of it against my back was comforting enough to make my knees sag again.

Or maybe it was the green Charger, slid into a bootlegger's turn and sending up a great spume of dust that did it. Because the passenger door opened, and I ran for the car as if my soul depended on it. I assumed it was Leon, come back to pick me up.

That assumption was my next mistake. A muzzle flashed, and something hit me in the chest like a padded hammer, and all of a sudden it was burning, my heart was a lake of fire inside my chest.

This time, they used silver. They shot me four times, and the last thing I heard was the crunch of feet on gravelly dirt as blackness closed over me, shot through with lead and redness. And a voice that was familiar, a woman's voice.

"We've got them by the balls now. Give me that rope."

CHAPTER 29

Tradeoff for being a helltainted hunter: silver fucking *hurts* to get shot with. The wound closes slowly, not poisoning me the way it poisons a hellbreed, but at about three-quarters the usual speed. I lose blood I can't afford, too, thick trickles of trying-to-clot claret.

I came back to consciousness slowly, in patches. Something hard was against my back, my head lolling, eyelids fluttering. My hair hung down in greasy wet strings, silver charms hanging like odd, blue-glowing fruit.

"They'll be here. They can't afford not to." The woman's voice was familiar. Slight smacking sounds—a wet, openmouthed kiss. "Relax, sweetheart."

"You didn't see what she did." Male. Sounded familiar, too, and scared of his own shadow, with a whining edge that set my teeth to clenching together. "She almost shot me. And the *entire* place, just like a bomb hit it. Jesus."

What the hell? Grogginess receded, and the scar prickled, a pucker of skin, still feeling full and obscenely flushed.

"I saw enough. Even Shen's scared of her. Don't *worry* so much. We have the only samples left, I saw to that. You have the formula, and we have the hunter to trade in. Everything's going to be okay." Another soft, wet kiss and a small moan. *Someone* was having a good time. "Just as long as you do what I tell you."

The world resolved around me, my consciousness sharpening.

I was in a chair. The air pressure was still, swallowing sound, echoing, telling me I was underground. Rope crisscrossed my chest, holding me in the chair. My hands were tied behind my back, fingers swollen, my elbows tied together, my ankles lost in coils of blue and white nylon rope.

I shifted my weight a little, looking for slack in the ropes. Found some.

Whoever had tied me up had done a goddamn messy job of it. I stilled, watching the silver in my hair run with blue sparks under the smooth metal surfaces. Hellbreed contamination in the air, but not a lot of it.

I saw concrete, a crumbling wall threaded with thin trickles of dried nameless fluid. I was in the dark, but electric light played over a vertical edge, a corner with teeth where the concrete had been worn away.

My eyes fell shut again. I was so tired. Even my toes hurt. Even my *hair* hurt. And I was starving. I would have given about anything for a chicken-fried steak right about then. And a nice cold beer.

Jill, wake up. My own voice, soft and urgent. *Wake the fuck up. Something's happening right in front of you.*

The scar ran with wet heat. My wrists rubbed against each other, and the hunger shifted under my breastbone, turned steely and sickening. I heard nylon rubbing against a cross-beam as a body shifted below, dead fruit. *You're tied up with the same type of rope. Wake up, Jill.*

It was like a bucket of cold water. I snapped into full consciousness silently, my wrists rubbing, the scar turning hot. It burrowed in toward the bone, and I wondered if it would slip my control and fill with yellow flame again.

The idea of burning expanded my chest with unsteady glee. I clamped down on it, reflexively.

Can't afford to do that, no matter how good it feels. I blinked crusted something out of my eyes, felt the tingle along my skin as the last bullet hole in my chest closed over, the silver-coated slug pushed free and no longer hurting me. The scar hummed, the strings of the physical world thrumming like a violin touched by a master's fingertips. Just the slightest plucking, making subtle vibrational music.

Something was about to happen.

Too late. It's too late.

Hopelessness threatened to scour the inside of my head. *Bullshit it's too late,* I answered that whining little voice. *Get out of these ropes, Jill. That's the first step. Everything else comes from that.*

I rubbed my wrists together like Lady Macbeth. The skin on my entire body tautened. They hadn't even taken my trench off, the dumb bunnies. And the rope had plenty of give in it—enough for my purposes, anyway. Etheric force tingled in my swollen fingertips, my concentration falling into itself like a rock down a bottomless well, and tough nylon frayed, parting.

It took all my waning energy to keep the state of fierce relaxation so necessary for sorcery. Strand by strand, the rope parted. Nervous silence ticked on the other side of the wall, broken only by the sound of breathing and the occasional wet kiss or moan.

"What if they don't show?" the male said, fretfully.

"They have to show," Irene said, with utter mad certainty. "We're holding all the cards, Fax. Just relax."

I wondered, for a few seconds, how she'd gotten free of Galina. Either she'd tricked the Sanctuary—hard to do, but Galina had that core of blind decency that made her able to do what she did— or there had been violence. It was vanishingly possible that she might have overwhelmed Galina physically for long enough to escape, but treachery was more likely.

Inside a Sanctuary's house, the owner's will is law. It *had* to have been a trick. But if she'd hurt Galina, the Trader bitch was going to pay in blood.

That's not the only thing she's going to pay for, Jill. Get out of the rope.

My concentration slipped. Sweat trickled cold down the valley of my spine, a flabby fingertip tracing. I regained myself, felt more strands slip, fraying loose under the knife of my will.

"They're late," Fairfax whined.

If it hadn't been so critical to keep quiet, I might have laughed. *They're expecting hellbreed they've double-crossed to be on time. Silly them.*

"They usually are. Will you just *relax?*" Irene's tone held less fondness and more command now. Movement in the light told me someone was pacing, sound of high heels clicking. No more kisses, and no more soft words.

The air pressure changed like a storm front moving over the city, pushing thunder in front of it. These two Trader idiots were about to get a huge surprise, either from their visitors—or from me. Copper coated my palate, adrenaline dumping into my bloodstream to sharpen me and deaden the edge of exhaustion. *This is about to get real ugly real quick. Hurry, Jill.*

A general rule of sorcery is that more haste equals less speed— but the rope fell loose, and I eased my shoulders out of its coils. My hands were numb and tingling, but they worked. I just couldn't pull a trigger for a little while. Pins and needles raced up my legs, and I almost blacked out when I bent over to take care of the rope messily looped and pulled tight around my ankles.

Rule one of tying up a hunter: you'd better be *damn* sure she can't wriggle out. Nylon's useless. Hemp's better, but it stretches too. Orichalc-tainted chains are the best, but even those are workable if the hunter's left alone and conscious long enough.

I've only been chained up so bad I couldn't get out *once*. That was enough for me.

They'd taken my guns. But my knives were still all present and accounted for, along with my whip and everything else, even all the ammo in my pockets.

Jesus. People this stupid shouldn't be playing with hellbreed. The air sharpened, the swelling in my fingers going down too slowly, *way* too fucking slowly, and I heard them arrive.

The air was suddenly full of hissing like laughter, the subliminal reverberation of Helletöng rubbing painfully against my ears. I eased myself off the chair, quiet, quiet, stopping when my right thigh cramped viciously. I kept my breathing soft and even. Raised my hands over my head to help my fingers drain. I would need them soon.

My hands turned into fists. Rivers of sparkling pain ran down my arms. I eased them open, and made a fist again. It would help the edema drain. *Come on. No time, Jill.*

On the other side of the wall, there was a wet crunching sound. A sudden impact, like a side of beef dropped three stories onto simmering pavement.

Funtime's over, kids. Everyone out of the pool.

Irene let out a shapeless, garbled yell.

In the ringing silence afterward, Shen An Dua spoke. "Oh, I am sorry. I was supposed to negotiate, wasn't I."

There was a slobbering wet noise, and another crunch. "Dear me." Shen giggled, a little-girl sound. "So sorry. I just keep making mistakes."

"You *idiot*." Irene's voice trembled. "Now you've killed the only person who has the formula!"

Another chill giggle, edged with broken, freezing glass. "Oh, I haven't killed him. He'll heal, with the proper care—care I can provide, as your liege. Besides, now I know what is *possible,* and it is easy enough to find more scientists." The hellbreed's tone darkened. "Where is the hunter?"

I dropped my hands. *So glad I'm not tied up right now.* My fingers curled around knifehilts, clumsy and aching. More copper adrenaline dumped into my blood, enough to sharpen me, not enough to blur. I'd pay for it later, when my body's reserves finally gave out.

I let out the soft breath, took another, my lungs crying for oxygen I couldn't take in. No use in gasping and advertising my position and status as awake and reasonably ready to kick ass.

"Fax?" Sounds of material moving, probably her long sequined dress. The hardness had left Irene's voice. "Fax, hold on—*Fax! Fairfax don't you leave me!*"

She sounded like a victim. Maybe like one of her *own* victims. I doubted she'd see the irony if someone else pointed it out, though.

"Oh, shut *up.*" Another impact, and the wall in front of me quivered imperceptibly as something human-sized was thrown up against it hard enough to crack bones. Shen let out a little satisfied sound. "Whining. Always *whining.*"

I tensed all over. The scar thrummed against my wrist, a high-voltage wire.

Shen suddenly turned all business. "Spread out. Search for the hunter. She's close, I can smell the bitch's shampoo."

Lunatic laughter bubbled up in my throat. I swallowed it. *What's wrong with my goddamn shampoo?*

"That's the last order you'll ever give," Irene snarled, and I crouched reflexively as gunfire rang through the small space, echoes tearing and re-tearing at my sensitive eardrums.

Maybe I could stay right here and let them sort it out. But something hit the other side of the wall again, bone-crunchingly hard, and I was out of my little hole and in the light of a swinging, naked electric bulb before I even noticed moving. The flap of my abused coat followed me like the smell of burning, clinging to me in tatters.

Four of them, and all you've got is knives.

Well, that wasn't quite true. My left hand had been smarter than me, curling around the whip handle and jerking it free. I guess Irene and Fax had thought I was tied up too tight to use a whip.

Fucking morons. They shouldn't have been playing with hellbreed.

Confined space, a concrete cube, the smell of blood cooking on an incandescent bulb as it swayed crazily, making the shadows dance. A slight hiss of steam echoed the longer hiss of hellbreed.

Shen An Dua stood, incongruous in a pale-pink kimono patterned with plum blossoms, her narrow golden hands folded and her eyes running with yolk-yellow flame. Her hair was piled atop her head in a complex patterned knot, held in place by lacquered shine and chopsticks with dangling things reflecting hard darts of light. And here was my first piece of good luck. In her monumental arrogance, Shen hadn't brought full 'breed to the party.

No, she'd brought four Traders, all male, and the whip smacked across flesh and dropped one, screaming, to the floor, clutching at his face and howling loud enough to shake the entire concrete cube.

Shen screeched, but the knife left my hand, flickering through the dance of shadow and blood-dappled light, and I had a second piece of good luck. It buried itself up to the hilt in her right eye as the whip crackled again, catching the next Trader at the top of his leap. I moved aside, spinning on feet gone numb and scraping-slow, and my hand flicked again, coming up full of steel.

Move move move! The screaming inside my head was no match for the noise bouncing off the walls until I tuned it out, focusing instead on the Trader closest to me, a cute little number who might have been Puerto Rican while he was human. Now he was small, brown, and unholy quick; the mirrored surfaces coming up from his cheekbones and inserting into his eyebrows gave him permanent sunglasses. He was right next to me before I realized it, but instinct saved me again—my fist, full of knifehilt, blurred forward and his trachea collapsed with a crunch.

Guys always expect you to go for the nut-shot. They never expect a rabbit-punch to the throat. And no matter how good you are, if you can't breathe, your fighting effectiveness is numbered in bare seconds.

Just to be safe, I slid the knife between his ribs, high in the left side of his chest, punching with a generous share of hellbreed strength to get through the pericardium—if I was that lucky.

Shen hit the floor, wailing, and I got a glance up her kimono skirt. If I'd eaten anything recently I would have thrown it all up, again, but the animal in me was concerned with survival first, snapping me aside with a half-skip and a clatter of steelshod bootheels to free my footing from the Trader's spasming legs.

Gunfire echoed again, and the third Trader—a stocky motherfucker in motorcycle leathers, his ears coming to high bristling points—collapsed, a neat hole appearing in his forehead and the back of his head vaporizing. Irene was picking her shots.

Let's just hope I'm not her next target, eh?

I hit the ground, rolled, and kicked the knees of the last Trader, he went down in a heap and I fed him a few knives to keep him quiet.

I lay there for just a second and a half too long, my sides heaving and my body suddenly failing to obey me. *Wait just a minute, bitch,* my muscles informed me. *We're declaring mutiny. You've fucked with us for too long.*

The body will do what the will dictates, yes. I learned that in my first year of training. But sometimes, even the will isn't enough to get the body up off the floor, when you've forced flesh past the point of no return. Even a berserker will eventually get tired.

Shen landed on me, tentacles swarming, thick black gore slicking her right cheek. Probing, flexible hairy pseudo-fingers bit hard, helped along by tiny vicious suckers, each rimmed with sharp cartilaginous protrusions resembling teeth. *Peeked up the skirt of destiny, did we?* the merry voice of impending doom snarled inside my head. *About to pay for it, Jill. And pay for it big.*

Slim strong human-shaped fingers tightened around my throat, and if my cervical spine hadn't been hellbreed-reinforced, my neck would have snapped. I kicked, my knee sinking into fleshy pulsing warmth nesting under her kimono and finding precious little bone to bounce off. My abraded wrists swarmed with tentacles, and she exhaled sicksweet foulness in my face, squeezing harder now, black ichor dripping from her pointed chin and splashing my face.

I spat, defiant to the last, and heaved up. No dice. She had too much leverage. Judo doesn't teach you how to fight off *tentacles,* goddammit.

The gun roared again.

The unwounded half of Shen's head disintegrated. Silver grain loaded in hollowpoints will do that. Black ichor spattered my face, stinking as it rotted.

The tentacles spasmed. Her hands bit in once more, terribly, but I wriggled free. My own fingers tore hers away, and I took in a gasping, whooping breath.

Irene was sobbing. The Trader whose larynx I'd crushed was suffocating to death, thrashing on the floor, a knifehilt protruding from his chest. Someone else was dying in leaps and spasms. I scrabbled through the crowded space, noticing for the first time that I was bleeding. Someone had clawed me in the side, my wrists were wet and dripping, my legs ached savagely, and I was blinking away both crusted and fresh blood. Not to mention the hellbreed-stinking gore dumped all over me.

There was the click of a half-depressed trigger, and I looked up. *Ohshit.*

But Irene stood, straddle-legged, over the Puerto Rican Trader. "Bobby," she whispered, and pulled the trigger. I tried not to flinch. "You should have listened to me." She let out a sound like a choked sob, and again the gun spoke.

Silence descended. There was a smear of thick crimson beginning near the ceiling, on the wall I'd been tied up behind. It looked about the size of an adult male, as if a man-sized canvas bag of blood had been flung at the wall and slid down, sopping-wet.

I gained my feet in a convulsive movement. The entire goddamn place was only about ten by ten, too small a space for the carnage it held. Pipes clustered at the far end. The naked, blood-spattered bulb swung in ever-decreasing arcs.

Irene hunched over something near the wall. The gun dangled limply in her hand. "Fax," she whispered.

I coughed, deep and racking. Fax wasn't going to mix any more bioweapons for anyone. Pretty much every bone in his body was broken, and the odd shape of his head meant his skull was crushed. Thin red blood, only a little tainted with hellbreed black, slicked his face and spattered his now-grimy lab coat.

I tried to feel something other than hot nasty satisfaction. *Got what you deserved.* Bile whipped the back of my throat as the thought of his "subjects" crawled under the surface of my consciousness, refusing to surface fully.

Thank God for small mercies. It wasn't much, but I'd take it.

I found my other guns near the ruins of what looked like a wooden chair. It had been smashed to splinters, and it looked like the chair Winchell had been beaten in.

Shen must have thought I'd be easy to take out. My, isn't this tying up nicely. Three guns, Irene had the fourth, and I had a bead on her even while my left hand picked up the two leftover Glocks and holstered them independently of me.

I coughed again, tasted blood and the bitterness of exhaustion. My neck was going to be bruised.

"Fax," Irene whispered again. "Oh, God."

I checked all the other bodies. They were twitch-rotting, fast, contagion spreading through tissues and loosing a powerful stench into the air. I kept the gun trained on Irene.

Dead and rotting meant they were no threat. But God, it *smelled.* If there's anything I hate about my job, it's the varied odors of rot and corruption.

Not to mention almost getting killed on a regular basis. Or getting lied to so frequently I barely even trust *myself* anymore.

Or how even a job that ties itself up can feel almost like a failure. I'd been caught assuming too often on this one, and how many people could have died if I hadn't been lucky? Or if I'd been just, simply, too late and a high-class hellbreed had stepped through to sit down and have himself a feast?

I took two steps forward, over the tangled ruin of a body. Fury worked its way up inside me, I blinked more blood out of my eyes.

Irene didn't move, crouched on her high heels, her knees

splayed. The green tint to her skin was pronounced under the bloodspattered light.

"What did you do to Galina?" I husked.

"I threatened to shoot the detective unless she let me go." Her slim fingers opened. The gun clattered, came to rest right next to Fairfax's dead, crushed hand. "Goddammit."

"You're playing out of your league." The gun barrel met the back of her head, through that blood-colored hair. She didn't move. "Who else is in on this? Harvill, Shen, who else?"

"They're mostly dead." The words were colored with a sob, but I didn't miss her shifting her weight slightly, very slightly. She froze when I shoved the gun against her skull again, harder. "Fax and I, we were trying to fix it, once we realized what they were planning. Bernardino killed the widow and I took care of Winchell, but we didn't find the ledgers. We couldn't pressure Harvill without them. Shen sold me to Bernardino to keep him quiet, he was a pile of filth. I *enjoyed* killing him, but he didn't have the ledgers and it all went...Fax. He was..."

Yeah, you were trying to fix it, and blackmail a few people in the process. A nice little nest egg, there for the taking, but Bernie had plans of his own. Enough double-crosses to make everyone dizzy, all of you little fucking rats scurrying once the lights turned on.

It might have been funny if it hadn't been so pathetic. Or if so many people hadn't died, used like Kleenex and discarded without a thought. And now she was sniveling over her dead bio-weapon-making boyfriend. *I'll bet it never even occurred to you to look in the garage, either. Even with the car you arrived in sitting in there.* "What other higher-ups were involved? *Who*, goddammit?"

She kept talking. Maybe she thought that if she kept going, she'd find a way out of the hole. Or maybe it didn't matter to her now. "Just Shen. She wanted to ingratiate herself with the *big* guy, he wanted a way through, into this city. She thought the owner of the Monde knew and sent you to blackmail her so he could get in first."

Perry? Evoking Argoth? I don't know, he likes being the biggest fish in town too much. I cleared my aching throat. "Was there a backup for the evocation?"

"I don't think so. Shen was always going out to the airfield, every dark moon for six months. It was the only time I was allowed to see Fax." Her voice broke again. But the calculation was back in it, the slightest hesitation masquerading as sorrow.

When you've spent a lifetime listening for that hesitation, it blares like a bullhorn.

"You realize I have to kill you." It didn't hurt to say it. Cold clarity had settled over me again, the part of me that didn't count the cost or hesitate when something had to be done.

It wasn't the same as the cold calculation or the ratty little gleam. It *wasn't*.

At least, I hoped it wasn't. What else was I doing this for, if it was?

"Just do it," she whispered. "Do it fast."

My hand tensed. I struggled to think clearly. This wasn't like taking a life in combat. This was something else.

"Did you hurt Galina? Or Carp?" I pushed against her skull with the gun, just a little. Her head bowed, pliant. "Tell me the truth, Irene."

"What the fuck does it matter?" Cold weariness, now.

"Oh, it matters." *It's the difference between me killing you mercifully . . . or otherwise.* The scar plucked at my arm, humming to itself. It wanted me to kick the Glock near her hand away and beat the living shit out of her personally. It's a small step from knowing how to fight to knowing how to stretch out hurting someone.

It's an even smaller step between knowing how to do it and finding a *reason* to do it.

She sighed. "I dumped the detective at the end of the block and ran. He was okay enough to squeeze off a few shots at me."

Thank you, God. I don't have to hurt her. "You're going to Hell." I couldn't sound comforting.

"Fine." She shrugged, pale greenish shoulders smeared with blood and other matter. An exhausted rat in a cage. "Like it's so different from here. Just get it over with, Kismet."

I wanted to tell her Hell *was* different. That's why they call it *Hell,* for Christ's sake.

But in the end, I didn't.

Let her find out for herself.

CHAPTER 30

When I surfaced on the street, I knew exactly where I was. Irene and Fairfax's little hidey-hole turned out to be the half-basement of a shabby little deserted office building on Rosales, less than two blocks from Winchell's murder site. Everything tying together into a neat little package. *Bumbling incompetents getting themselves killed. Avarice, arrogance, and envy are the hunter's friends; if it wasn't for that I wouldn't have found so many loose ends to tie up. And if not for monumental fucking arrogance, Shen would have brought hellbreed.*

And that would have been a goddamn clusterfuck.

I stood in the shadows in the lee of the building, night wind rising off the desert brushing the street and curling down the alcove. Did it smell like burning, or did I? I swayed, my fingers catching at the wall and leaving smeared prints behind. Blood and stinking hellbreed ichor, and more blood. Forensics would have a field day with that little room, if anything was left after a night's worth of decay. I hadn't been able to muster up the strength to force banefire off my fingers.

Think, Jill. Think.

What was my next move?

The Charger was easy enough to find, tucked into an alley across the street. One of them had topped off the tank with gas and done a passable hotwire job on it. Irene's work, I was betting—Fax hadn't seemed like he could tie his shoelaces, much less hotwire a car.

But he'd been enough of a genius to engineer a weapon likely to completely bash my city out of recognition, loosing a tide of darkness and corruption that would feed a huge hellbreed. *And* turn people into blood-hungry fiends or...those *things*. And he'd done it all without asking where his "subjects" came from. Probably talked himself into thinking it was real bang-up science he was doing, too.

I shouldn't have felt sorry for either of them. But a few more minutes of questioning Irene before I sent her on her way meant I'd found the link between Shen and Fairfax. An intent-to-distribute conviction for mixing up designer drugs to make some cash, and the concurrent threat to a promising career, had brought Fax into Harvill's—and Shen's—reach. And with him, Irene, who had taken to being a Trader like a duck to water. But then, when you're dating a mad chemist, I suppose you can get used to bargaining with Hell one slice of flesh at a time.

Just like I was mortgaging myself an inch at a time. I didn't have the energy to argue with myself over whether or not I was different.

The only loose end was the district attorney, the nodepoint of corruption. How had he gotten involved with Shen? Had she gone looking for someone amenable or had he committed some indiscretion that brought him to her attention? Did it matter?

It was probably the latter. The happy little organ-theft ring that had intersected with Melisande Belisa's plans last time had intersected with Shen's *this* time, and I had a chance to pull it up by the roots.

I rested my head on the steering wheel and breathed in, breathed out. The crusted blood in my eyes irritated me, I blinked it away.

It wasn't just the crusties. It was hot water filling up my eyes and trickling down my cheeks.

Jesus. I'm in bad shape.

The wind rattled and rolled down the street, deserted because it was after dark. So much of a hunter's life is played out on an empty street, or in places where no light shines. Places nobody can share with you, or wants to share. Not if they're right in the head at all.

Saul. He would be worried. I wondered if his mother was sliding over the dark edge into finality.

Theron would be climbing the walls too. Leon, if he knew Irene had slipped the leash, would have gotten the situation at Galina's under control and would be coordinating the Weres in my absence. Faithfully keeping the city under wraps. I wondered how long I'd been unconscious. My bet was on not very long, since Shen would have been anxious to get the formula and her pet chemist back.

And kill me, of course, both for interfering and for making her look bad while I did it. And probably to make points with this Argoth guy.

I lifted my head, peered blearily out the windshield. The old moon hung, a nail-paring, low in the sky. It was approaching midnight.

I knew Harvill lived in Riverhurst, the tony part of town, north and a few minutes out of the downtown sector. Keeping tabs on high-level law-enforcement personnel in your town saves a lot of trouble when you're a hunter, whether you need heavier bureaucratic guns to take care of a case—or the case itself involves them.

What are you going to do, Jill? You're in no shape to take anyone on.

It didn't matter. This was mine to finish off, and by God, I was going to.

I stroked the Charger into starting. It was an automatic, so I didn't need to worry about shifting the way I would have in my Impala. Which was good—my legs were still weak and my fingers painfully swollen. The headlights came on without any demur, cutting a swath through the night.

You're not even in any shape to drive. Find somewhere to rest, get to Harvill tomorrow.

Fat fucking chance. I slid the car into drive. Eased my foot off the brake and the car slid forward, the engine sounding overworked and underpaid.

Just like the rest of us, honey. Never mind about that. We'll fix that right up. I always wanted a Dodge.

A roaring sheet of darkness beat at the edges of my vision. I blinked. The tears slicking my cheeks came faster, dripping off my jaw and wetting the ruins of my shirt.

It's about a twenty-minute drive, Jill. Do it in ten.

The Charger nosed at the street, I turned, and reached for the little tingle of precognition along my nerves. It didn't happen for a long thirty seconds, so I cruised along the dark street, my fingers still swollen and aching. The wheel slid smoothly under my hands, and I turned left on Twelfth. I could zig crosstown and avoid the major cop activity, which at this hour would be around the bars and nightclubs as they hit their stride. Drunks would be getting rowdy just about now, and domestic disturbances reaching their peak for the night too.

The Kat Klub won't be reopening anytime soon, folks. I done put that bitch out of business, as Leon would say.

And I would be lying if I'd told myself it didn't feel good to know Shen An Dua was dead. The only trouble was, her replacement was likely to be an even bigger bitch. Cogs in a wheel—one corruptor rolls out, another clicks in. Way of the world.

When the tingle came, I shook myself. I was weaving, and one tire kissed the curb before I snapped into my own skin, each new ache in my overstressed muscles not just a weight against the nerves but a balm, keeping me awake.

Come on, Jill. Just one more thing. Then you can rest.

I was lying to myself and I knew it. But I tightened my dirty hands on the wheel, shook my hair back, and jammed the pedal to the floor. The Charger had some life left in him yet, and he lurched forward like someone had just stuck a pin in him. Speckles of streetlight ran up the hood, and the buildings on Twelfth all yawned at me, sliding past as if greased. I let out a painful, half-hitched laugh; it sounded rusty under the wind from the rolled-down window rustling all the fast-food wrappers. First thing I had to do, when I had time, was clean this goddamn car out. It was a dirty crying shame for a good piece of American metal to be so filthy inside.

Complain about my driving now, goddammit. I dare you.

He had the wrong house for a DA. It was a nice ranch-style pseudo-adobe, all done up with red tile roof and everything. The garden, what little there was of it, was immaculate, and he had a lawn that probably guzzled a winter's worth of water every week.

The Charger looked sorely out of place in Riverhurst. It's the rich section of town, well insulated both from pesky downtowners and from the stink of the industrial section. The rule here is wide sidewalks, lovely expanses of thirsty grass, and more often than not a wall and an iron gate. And trees. This is the only place in the city, other than the parks, where you find honest-to-God trees, mostly left over from the quiet neighborhoods of the twenties and early forties.

Harvill's house was easily the shabbiest, but still worth a nice chunk of change in property tax alone. The windows were all dark and deserted, only the porch light burning.

What are you going to do? Go up and ring the doorbell? Is he married, does he have kids?

I couldn't remember right now.

What are you going to get into if you walk up the path and knock on that door?

I was still considering this when another car approached, nosing down the street. It was a little red import number, and the engine sounded like an overworked sewing machine. Even more out-of-place than the Charger. I slouched down, keeping it in view. *What's this?*

The little red car—I could identify it now, it was a Honda— chugged to a stop in front of Harvill's house under a big old elm tree in full leaf. The engine shut off, and the door opened, squeaking. A slim male shape rose from the tiny front seat, and I smelled someone familiar. I had trouble matching it to a face for a few seconds.

Gilberto Rosario Gonzalez-Ayala went up the front walk. He checked the house number, then rang the bell.

Jesus. What the hell?

Two full minutes ticked by. He pressed the bell again.

A light came on.

Twenty seconds later the door opened, a rectangle of golden light. Harvill stood in the door, a man-mountain in pajamas. He looked ruffled and sleepless, and my blue eye saw a faint stain of Hell's corruption on him. He wasn't a Trader, but he'd been fucking around with a hellbreed.

Gilberto said something I didn't catch.

"Who the hell are you?" Harvill's voice carried across the street, the stentorian tones of a man used to the courtroom and television appearances.

The gun spoke, a faint pop. He had a silencer.

Harvill went down hard. I reached for the door handle.

Gilberto stepped forward, fired twice more. Stood watching. I heard a slight sound, like an exhale. Like someone sinking down into a bed. The breath of corruption intensified, taking hold as the soul fled the body and quit fighting to reclaim the flesh.

Do I have to kill him too?

"That was for my brother, you piece of shit." Gilberto's young voice broke on the last syllable. I slouched further in the seat. So Gil had been conducting his own little war, and found the hand behind his brother's killer in his own way.

It all made sense—Harvill putting whatever cops he was sure of on me, and using his position to start a little gang war on me too. I wouldn't be able to question him and find out *exactly* who opened fire on me, though.

Life's not perfect, Jillybean. Take what you have.

The 51 retraced his steps. He stopped by his driver's side door, eyeing the Charger. I touched a gun butt, ran my fingers over it, and was glad I was in deep darkness.

I didn't want to kill this kid, no matter how scary his flat dark eyes were.

"Eh, *bruja*," the young man whispered. "Still on the job, me."

I can see that, Gilberto. I turned into a stone, drawing silence over me like a cloak. Could he sense the change in the night, an absence where before there had been listening?

How much did he know about the nightside?

Just who was this kid, anyway?

He dropped down into the Honda. The sewing-machine engine started up again. He backed into Harvill's sloping driveway and pulled out, heading away down the street. Somewhere in the deep water of darkness a dog barked.

Before he turned the corner I saw a brief flare of orange light. Gilberto had just lit a cigarette.

Jesus. A shudder worked its way down my body. I stroked the Charger into starting again, watching the street. Not a hair out of place, except for that faraway hound. Everyone sleeping the sleep of the rich and untroubled.

Jacinta Kutchner's neighbors hadn't heard anything either.

I put the car in drive and pulled out. Took a right on Fairview. The city stayed quiet. Darkness beat at the edges of my vision again, my body reminding me that it had put up with a lot of shit from me in the last forty-eight hours.

I made it to Galina's, parked drunkenly crosswise in front of her store because I couldn't see well enough to do more than bump the car up against the curb. I fell sideways across the cushioned center console and darkness finally took me. I struggled on the way down—there was more I had to do, wasn't there? There was *always* more to do, and something I'd forgotten.

I dreamed of yellow hellfire chuckling and groaning to itself. I dreamed of scuttling, crawling things that forced themselves through cracks in the walls and licked up the corruption running from the corpses left stacked in a ten-by-ten basement room, runnels of foulness seeping through the walls. I even dreamed of the time before I'd become a hunter, curling up in a small space while adults fought outside and someone cried softly into a teddy bear's wet fur.

I struggled a quarter of the way into consciousness while someone carried me, the heat and a deep rumbling purr reminding me of Saul. But my body mutinied again and dragged me down, and in this fresh darkness there were no dreams.

CHAPTER 31

Sunlight poured through the window. I lay and stared at it for a long time before moving, wincing a little bit as my head and body both protested. Even hellbreed strength has to be paid for, and I'd cycled enough etheric force through my body to give myself a *hell* of a hangover.

Get it, Jill? "Hell" of a hangover? Arf arf. I groaned, stirred slightly, and pushed weakly at the covers. I was tucked into Galina's own bed, the huge mission-style monstrosity she'd hung with white netting to make a sort of cloud to sleep in.

I heard footsteps. Voices. Nobody was yelling, and one of the voices was Galina, calm as always. So she was okay.

Good.

I lay in the bed a few moments longer, staring at the fall of sunlight through the window. My trench, battered and still smelling of smoke, was draped over a high-backed wooden chair. It was cool in here, air conditioning soughing through a vent near the door. Mellow hardwood shone through layers of polish and care.

My fingers were back to their regular size. I was still filthy with crusted blood and smelling of smoke, and my head ached, ached, a pumpkin on the stem of my neck. I felt the bruises from Shen's narrow delicate hands still digging into my throat.

How long was I out? Is it darkmoon yet? I killed that evocation site, but maybe Shen had another one. Irene didn't think so, but she could have been lying.

Coherent thought halted. I didn't have enough energy for it.

I blinked. My cheeks were hot and chapped. There was grime ground into my face and under my nails. I almost never fall asleep without washing my face, even if I'm covered in guck I like scrubbing my shiny little flower smile, as Sister Mary Ignatius called it in kindergarten.

I tried moving again. Rolled over on my back.

Get up, Jill. Get moving. You're not done yet.

Footsteps on the stairs. I listened—Galina's softly distinctive tread, and someone else's. Probably Leon, the way he pushed lightly off of each step was familiar. I pressed myself up on my hands, ignoring the shaking in my arms, and found out I was wearing a T-shirt reduced to bloodsoaked, bullet-holed rags, and my leather pants stank of hellbreed guck.

And here I was in Galina's nice clean bed. Why hadn't she put me in the spare room? Was Carp still in there?

Rest easy, Carper. It's all tied off. Well, mostly. I hoped he was sleeping. I hoped he'd pulled through.

"You're awake." The Sanctuary's sweet face was solemn. "I'll have to let Theron know. He threatened to kill you as soon as you woke up."

I cleared my dry throat. Leon came into sight behind her, expressionless, with a beer can in one hand and a bottle in the other. The copper in his hair gleamed, and Rosita was snugged safely against his back.

"Charming." My voice was a dried husk of itself. I coughed, and Leon slid past Galina, offered me the chilly bottle of micro-brew. Why he drank canned piss when there were better things around was beyond me. "How long was I out?"

"Don't worry." My fellow hunter settled himself on the end of the bed with a sigh, easing down as if he hurt all over too. "We found a primary evocation site at that nasty-ass nightclub. I took care of it."

I sagged in relief. So the one at the airfield had been Shen's backup. One worry down.

"Jill—" Galina began, but Leon interrupted her.

"Why don't you go get her somethin' to eat, darlin'? I'll make sure she doesn't hurt herself. You go call Theron too, so he can stop worryin'." Leon's dark eyes were steady, and his mouth was drawn in a tight line.

Oh, shit. What's gone wrong now? "More scurf?" I hazarded, but Leon shook his head. Copper chimed in his hair. There were dark circles under his eyes.

"Naw. Town's clean as a whistle. Go on now, Lina." He toasted her absently with the Pabst can, and she made a face as if he'd told her to drink it.

"I'll bring up coffee." She cast one short, troubled glance my way, but I was too aching and muzzy-headed to decipher it. Instead I took a pull off the bottle and winced at the havoc it was going to play with my headache.

We listened to her go down the stairs. Leon shifted a little bit inside his clothes. Copper clinked, and he touched one of the amulets hung around his neck, then put his hand down with an effort. "Talked to that lieutenant. Your contact."

"Monty," I supplied. *Thank God he's okay.*

"Big fucking mess for him to clean up. I guess this Harvill ass-hole came down with a serious case of the dead." Leon's tone was a careful nonquestion, and my silence a careful nonanswer. "Dangerous, being in bed with hellbreed."

I shrugged. Took another pull off the bottle. Waited for him to get to the point.

"Your town should be clean, but you know how scurf are."

I knew. I nodded. One of my earrings was lighter than the

other; it had probably broken sometime or another. My skin crawled. I couldn't wait to get cleaned up.

"That cop you brought in from that nightclub." Leon sank a little heavier into the bed, took another long swallow from his can. Condensation beaded on the aluminum, I could hear the liquid going down his throat. Downstairs a refrigerator door opened, and Galina began to hum.

My heart turned to a stone inside my ribs. *Oh, shit.* "Carper? Is he okay?"

Leon sighed. "He talked Galina into letting him go home yesterday. Waltzed out, went home, and ate his Glock."

No. Oh, no. "What?" I sat bolt upright, then wished I hadn't because my head immediately started pounding. "What the *fuck?*"

"Galina blames herself. Said she never should have let him go. I was with the Weres, cleaning out that nightclub." His shoulders hunched. "She said she figured the cop was up and walking around, and everything was tied off..."

"Carp?" I couldn't wrap my brain around it. *"Andrew?* It can't...he wouldn't..."

Leon's face set itself. "He wasn't too tight-bolted, Jill. Sometimes when civilians see the nightside, they go nuts. He was in that hole run by that Asian bitch for a while and they played with him, Lina said."

While I sat outside and worried over who would report me as not dead. "Jesus," I whispered. "You're sure it was suicide?" *Because Kutchner's death looked like a suicide too, but maybe someone pulled the trigger on Carp too. Because...oh, God. Carper. Why?*

But I knew why. Sometimes, when you pull a civilian out of a tangle with the nightside, they don't stay out. They go into the black hole. A peek under the surface of the normal world throws them off the back of reality, and they never return.

Leon spread one hand, made a helpless gesture. "I'm sure, Jill. That's where I talked to that lieutenant—Montaigne. Good ol' boy, that one. Worried about you."

"I'm sure he was." The words tasted bitter. I drained the bottle in a few long, long swallows. It was ashes going down. The carbs would give me a quick flush of strength, but I needed protein if I was really going to bounce back. "Jesus Christ. Carper."

"Funeral's this Saturday. I got it all written down if you want it." His shoulders slumped for a moment, and so did mine. Silence rose between us, under the safety of sunlight.

He knew what it feels like to lose one of your own. Only another hunter understands. We are here to protect, and when our protection fails sometimes we don't pay the cost. Others, less trained, less equipped to bear the strain, pay what *we* should.

And oh, God, it hurts.

There was nothing he could really say.

So he was quiet.

I rested the chill of the bottle against my forehead. The thick brown glass came away spotted with flecks of dirt and dried blood. A sharp bloody stone lodged in my throat, with beer carbonation trapped behind it. My eyes were hot and dry.

"He was a good cop," I finally whispered.

Leon eased himself up to his feet. The sun brought out highlights in his hair, made his copper charms shine. The amulets around his neck clicked as he shifted his weight, and Rosita's blued-steel barrel shone with a fresh application of oil. "I gotta get home. Some things to clean up back there. You gonna be okay?"

No. I guess so. What choice do I have? I made another one of those physical efforts to focus. It came a little easier now that I'd had some rest. "I'm not sure I'm done yet. Harvill might not have been the only bigshot involved. But I'll keep digging." *Andrew. You shouldn't have. Why couldn't you have waited?*

He balanced on the balls of his feet. "Good fuckin' deal." A nervous glance toward the door. Galina was still humming downstairs. "Thought you were a goner, darlin'."

"I could have been." *Two steps behind an arrogant hellbreed and a stupid-ass set of Traders the whole time, and Carp paid the price. I should turn in my badge. If I had a badge.* "Leon?"

He grunted, a truly male sound, and took another shot of his piss-masquerading-as-honest-beer.

I had to settle for two of the most inadequate words in the English language, words too pale to express what I needed to say. "Thank you."

"Aw, shit, girl. We all do what we can." His shrug was a marvel of indifference. "Be cool." *I'm sorry,* his eyes said.

"You too, Leon. Get your truck looked at, will you?" *Me too,* I thought. *I'm sorry too. I can't call this a win. Can't even call it a tie.*

"All right. Goddamn nagging." He waved his beer can, slopping the liquid inside, and stumped for the door. Stopped halfway there.

I waited, but he didn't say anything else. Just squared his shoulders and walked away without a backward glance. Classic Leon.

Then again, most hunters aren't much for goodbyes. You never know which time will be the last. Better to just walk away and carry on the conversation the next time.

If there is a next time. It's superstition, but you take what you can get.

I pushed the covers away. Someone had taken my boots off; they were in a puddle of stink right next to the bed. But I padded in sock feet across the room, stopping when my head started to spin or my legs threatened rebellion.

The bedroom window overlooked the street. Galina's humming stopped, and I heard low voices again. Leon's question, her soft reply. Then his footsteps, speeding up. The door to her shop jingled a few moments later, and Leon headed across the street to his truck.

My entire chest hurt, a pain that wasn't physical. The copper in his hair caught fire. He got behind the wheel and the engine turned over.

I lifted my hand to wave, found it full of the empty beer bottle. He wasn't looking anyway.

The air in the room changed imperceptibly. I lowered my hand.

"Just like that," Galina said. "Jill—"

"He told me. It's not your fault." *It's mine. I was too far behind the game. Should have done something more, seen something more.* The heavy weight of responsibility and disappointment settled on my shoulders.

Galina sighed, the sound hitching in the middle. "I shouldn't have let him go. I thought the danger was past."

It was and it wasn't. "It was." The carbonation crept past the blockage in my throat, I exhaled beer and the taste of failure onto the glass. Faint condensation swirled. "Sorry about your bed."

She was quiet for a long few seconds. Nerving herself up to it, probably. "It's what it's there for. Jill—"

Christ, Galina, if you apologize one more time . . . "Did you say something about food? I'm starving."

"Coming right up." Mercifully, she left it at that. "Theron brought you some clothes. He says your house is clean, no more hellbreed. I've got to call him and let him know you're awake."

"That'd be good." I kept my stiff back to her. Exhaled again on the window and watched the condensation fade, like a ghost. My head ached. "You got any coffee?"

"I'll bring some up to you. You know where the bathroom is." Again, she hesitated.

"Food, Galina." I said it as gently as I could. "I'm not done yet."

"You got it." She turned quick and light as a leaf, and was gone down the stairs.

I tipped my head back, looking at the slant of the roof. Across the room, the mirror atop her antique cherrywood vanity held my reflection like a black stain. The plaster on her ceiling was in whorls, spiraling in and out.

The tears trickled from my eyes and vanished into my filthy hair. *Jesus. Carp, you asshole. Why didn't you wait for me?*

When the pressure behind my eyes faded a bit and the smell of something good frying began to waft up the stairs, I tipped my head back down. The street was full of hot liquid sunshine, and there was light traffic. The Charger sat across the street, behind the empty spot that had held Leon's truck.

It was a fine-looking piece of heavy American metal. It needed a bit of work to get it into shape, sure, and Monty would roll his eyes when I asked to requisition the car. But there was no reason to let it go into impound.

No reason at all. Except I didn't want to drive it, now.

I turned away from the window and hobbled on my stiff legs toward the other door. Galina had a shower in there, and I needed one. Then as much food as I could stuff into the bowling ball my stomach had become. After that, on to the next thing.

And if the tears came when I was standing under the hot water, if I made a low hurt sound like a wounded animal, if I scrubbed at my flesh like it was an enemy with her pretty pink floral-scented soap, it was nobody's business but mine. It was between me and the water, and the water wouldn't talk. It would carry my tears along with the dried blood, the dirt, and the beer I vomited back up down below the city into the dark.

CHAPTER 32

I t felt strange to walk into the precinct house again. Nobody said a word, but conversation failed when I appeared and turned into a tide of whispers in my wake. I stalked up to Montaigne's office, ignoring the nervous looks and whispers both.

Who among them was happy I was alive?

Who wasn't? Which one of them had a secret and an assault rifle? And access to a blue Buick? And a connection to Harvill?

I might never know now, if he kept his head down and his mouth shut.

Monty was out, so I stepped into his office and waited. When he stamped into view, armed with a load of paper and a scowl, I had to fold my arms and school my face. A relieved grin wouldn't help him in this mood.

He grunted. "Jesus fucking Christ. *There* you are."

"You don't look happy to see me." I stepped aside, let him lug his papers past me. "Are you okay?"

He gave me a look that could have peeled paint. "I got to buy more Tums. I got a dead DA and two more dead cops—"

I winced internally. "Leon explained it all?"

He swept the door closed with his foot and dropped the pile of paper on his desk. "You see this? These are the forms I have to fill out. You burned down an entire goddamn airfield, Kismet. You're a menace to property."

"It's better than the alternative." I didn't mean to sound harsh, but each word was edged. *Better than some sort of poison engineered from scurf taking over my city and a high-up hellbreed waltzing through.*

"Jesus, don't you think I know?" He dropped down behind his desk and regarded me. "He saw something, didn't he. Carper."

You could say that. "He got tangled up in nightside business. There was a connection after all." I swallowed. Galina's steak and eggs still weren't convinced they wanted to stay down. "How much do you want me to tell you, Monty?"

He considered it for a long thirty seconds, then reached down in his desk drawer. "You want a drink?" He brought out the Jack Daniels, amber liquid shaking inside the bottle. There was half of it left. Bully for him.

Oh, Monty. I nodded, not trusting my voice.

He actually rustled up two almost-clean coffee mugs, one with a badge in worn gold foil and the other with a picture of a disgusted-looking hippo on it. Both were probably from his house. He poured me a generous measure, himself a little less generous one, and we both knocked back without waiting.

That way, I could pretend the slow leaking from my eyes was a result of the booze scorching my throat and uneasy stomach.

The short silence between us no longer had sharp edges. "Ballistics on the DA didn't come up with a goddamn thing. It's a clean gun. Goddamn .22s are like fuckin' cell phones, everyone's got one." He set his cup down. "No more disappearances on the east side. The papers are calling Harvill a fucking saint and the airfield's blamed on a propane tank explosion." Monty rubbed at his tired eyes.

Nice and neat. Everything smoothed over. "Bernardino's car is parked out front. Stick it in impound." I set my own mug down, balanced carefully on the messy stack of paper.

"You sure? I mean, what with your car and all . . ."

"I'm sure. I don't want to clean the fucker out." I licked the last traces of whiskey away. "Carp was clean, Monty."

"And Marv wasn't?" He set his jaw.

I opened my mouth to tell him the truth, shut it. He already knew. There was no point in putting salt on that wound. Instead, I looked past him, to the picture of his wife propped right next to a dormant computer monitor. "How's Rosenfeld taking it?"

A single shrug, his shoulder holster peeping out from under his jacket. "Dealing, I guess. The funeral's Saturday."

Tomorrow. I nodded. Silver shifted in my hair. "I'll be there. Anything else?" My cheeks stung, but I didn't wipe at them.

"Not much. There was a warehouse fire down near the rail-yards. The 3700 block of Cherry. Whole place was burned down. Some interesting wreckage in there, but not anything to go on."

"Hm." I contented myself with a noncommittal noise. Cold air blew against my wet cheeks, drying them.

"Other than that, quiet as the western front out there. No weird-ness. Just garden-variety rapes, murders, and larceny."

"Glad to see everything's back to normal." I straightened. "Thanks for the drink. I'll be in touch—I need another pager, too." *Since my last two have died inglorious deaths.*

"Jesus H. A menace to property." He waved me away. "Go burn down something else, will you? I'd hate to get bored."

"Have a nice evening, Monty." I turned on my heel and headed for the door.

"Jill?"

I stopped, one hand on the doorknob. The noise from out-side—phones ringing, people talking, breathing, working—faded. "What?"

I don't know what I expected him to say. Why would he thank me? But at least he knew, now. There wasn't the nagging doubt.

It's cold comfort. Sometimes knowing doesn't help. Some-times *understanding* doesn't even help. It just drives the knife in deeper.

He cleared his throat. "Glad you're around. Now get the fuck out of my office."

A police funeral has its own etiquette. In some places, bagpipers play. Here in Santa Luz there's the official ceremony, and then the wake, usually in the back room at Costanza's Pub downtown.

Hunters don't go to those.

Saturday dawned bright and fresh. I hadn't slept yet, but I'd made sure I was wearing my tiger's eye rosary and my dagger ear-rings. I'd hosed off my trench coat, so it was at least clean, if torn and a bit shabby.

He had a full escort of blues, and they laid him to rest in Beacon Hill's lush greenness, under the trees. I stood in the shadow of a century-old oak in the south corner of the cemetery, watching, my hand against the treetrunk.

Monty was there, and Rosenfeld. Rosie's hair was on fire under the fierce desert sun; she wouldn't stand under the portable awning. The glitters of her dress uniform were sharp enough to cut diamonds.

The scar puckered hungrily, tasting the tang of misery and grief riding the air. Mikhail's headstone is in the northern half of Hill, where there was a good view of the rest of the valley, a light scum of smog lingering against the rising towers of downtown.

I know that view like the back of my hand.

There was Lefty Perez from Vice, and "Fuckitall" Ramon. Other familiar faces—Anderson, McGill, "Shooter" Kirby and Rice, all from the Vice Squad. Sullivan and the Badger from Homicide, the Badger's gray hair pulled severely back, shoulders square. Carson and Mathers from Homicide too, and Frank Capretta. Some rookies, and some blues, all dressed their best. Piper and Foster, from Forensics. Other faces I put names to, matching them up slowly.

I knew them all, and drew deeper into the shadows under the tree. The chaplain's voice reached me in fits and starts, carried by the faint wind from the river, smelling of greenness and mineral water.

There was no blue Buick parked on the single strip of asphalt cutting through the rolling green. I hadn't expected it, but it was a relief.

Soft footsteps behind me. I didn't turn around.

"I should kick your ass," Theron murmured.

Just try it, Were. My hand tightened, loosened on the treetrunk, Mikhail's apprentice-ring closed around the third finger. "Show some respect."

"Sorry." And he was. "You gave me a scare, Jill."

It was my turn to apologize. "Sorry."

Silence. The chaplain stopped, then the recital began as the coffin lowered slowly into the waiting darkness.

I duly swear myself to the service of the citizens of Santa Luz, to protect and to succor. I swear to act without fear or favor, to protect the innocent and to safeguard the living. I swear to be honest and true, to be a servant of the law, and to do my best each and every day, so that the citizens who place their trust in me are well and truly served by the power of Justice.

I mouthed it along with them. Hunters have their prayer, I suppose cops are no different.

A few of them said *Amen* afterward. Very quietly.

My chest hurt, a sharp tearing pain. Something too sharp and smoking-hot to be grief loaded the back of my throat. My fingers tightened on rough treebark, I dropped my hand to my side, shook out the fingers so they were nice and loose.

"Gilberto sends his regards," Theron said softly. He stood so close I could feel the heat of his metabolism, but he carefully didn't touch me. "He says he owes you a beer."

I nodded. "Tell him…" *What, that he's safe? That I watched him commit a murder and didn't interfere?* "Tell him I understand." *And that he'd better not get in the habit of killing people in my city.*

Rosie stepped forward. Neither of Carp's ex-wives were here, and even if they had been Rosie probably still would have been the one to take the small shovel and scatter the first handful of dirt into the hole.

I heard it clearly, small pebbles striking the roof of the coffin. A hollow sound of finality.

"The warehouse on Cherry is cleaned out," Theron continued, in a monotone. "No sign of scurf. We found an evocation altar downstairs in the Kat Klub. Looked pretty nasty."

"Leon told me." I swallowed sourness. This morning's breakfast had been a few mouthfuls of vodka, the sting relished before I hit the door running. "You're good backup, Theron. Thanks."

He let out a sound that might have been a dissatisfied sigh, smothered in respect for the dead sleeping all around. "Saul's been calling. He's pretty upset. I haven't been home much."

Shit. But it was a Were's tactfulness, asking me what I wanted him to say. If he and Leon had thought I was in serious trouble, or dead, Theron would have been the one to bring Saul the bad news.

It would not have been pretty.

I braced myself. "Neither have I. But I'll get hold of him soon. Let me talk to him." *In other words, Theron, this stays between you and me.*

He absorbed it. "How close was it, Jill?"

What do you want me to tell you? "Close enough. I can't count this one a win." I stared unseeing at the tableau around the open, yawning grave, a mound of dirt covered with Astroturf sitting neglected to one side. Rosie's chin was up. Monty had his arms folded, his shoulders slumped. Sullivan looked down at the ground, Piper's cheeks were wet.

"City's still standing. And that 'breed who ran the Kat Klub—"

"She's dead." I said it too quickly, on a breathy scree of air. *Carp, I avenged you without knowing. I wish I could do it again.*

Sometimes avenging isn't enough. They don't tell you that when you're training. You have to learn it on your own. It is one of the lessons that makes you a hunter, not an apprentice.

The service began to break up. The honor guard marched away to their flashing vehicles; the knot of uniforms and suits at the graveside fraying. Theron watched with me, in silence. Monty stayed while car doors slammed and engines started.

So did Rosie.

The chaplain, an unassuming, balding little man in a black suit, exchanged a few words with Monty, who neatly cut him away from Rosie. She stood in the sun, her hair throwing back its light with a vengeance, her hands knotted into bloodless fists at her sides. She stared at the hole in the ground, then lifted her head, scanning the cemetery's rolling greenness.

I made a restless movement. Theron was still, the peculiar immobility of a cat Were.

The chaplain headed off toward his own car, a sunny yellow Volkswagen Beetle. I stepped forward as he drove away. Picked my way with care around headstones and plates set in the ground, passing wilted flowers and the occasional shrub. The last twenty feet or so were the hardest, because I could feel Rosie's eyes on me and the grave opened like a mouth. Strata of sprinkler-wet earth striped its sides.

I came to a halt outside the awning's shelter. The sun beat down.

Monty clapped me awkwardly on the shoulder and handed me a new pager. "We're going to Costanza's." The words hung in still air, the breeze had died.

I nodded. Silver clanked as my hair moved.

Rosenfeld sounded steady enough. "Give me a minute, Monty?"

"Sure." He shifted his weight, awkwardly.

I could feel his gaze on me, maybe he was trying to tell me something. I didn't look up. There were a few handfuls of dirt scattered across the coffin's lacquered top, and someone had dropped in a rose. Probably Piper.

Monty retreated. I steeled myself, raised my gaze, and met Rosie's head-on.

Rosenfeld was crying.

Oh, hell.

"He was Internal Affairs." She lifted her prizefighter's jaw a little bit, as if daring me to make something of it. "Jill..."

So she knew.

She was his partner, and probably knew him better than he knew himself. Of course she would at least suspect he was IA.

"He was clean, Rosie." The words came out in a rush. "I did my best. He saw something, something awful. I didn't get there in time."

"Oh, Jesus." Her mouth gapped a little, her nose inflamed— redheads can't cry gracefully, at least not any redhead I've known. Then again, the whole point of crying is that nobody does it gracefully. "I thought... his ex-wives, and the case he was working. I thought..."

"I got the people responsible." My voice didn't seem to work quite right. "I tied up the case."

"They're dead? The motherfuckers that did for him?" She searched my face.

Do you even need to ask me that? "They're dead." *Except the other dirty cops Harvill had on a string. But sooner or later, I'll get to them. I swear it, Rosie.*

It would be vengeance, and it wouldn't help. But it was the least I owed her.

She glanced at the grave, her mouth firming and twisting down, bitterly. "I've been thinking, I should have seen it. It was all there. He's been withdrawing all year. Just sinking deeper and deeper into the pit. I should have nagged him into something. Counseling. *Something.*"

Oh, Rosie. "It was the nightside, Rosie. Not him." *Give her that much, at least. Don't let her blame herself for this.* "I should have kept him under tighter wraps, made sure he was okay. It was on my watch. I'm . . . sorry."

"It isn't your fault. He was already cracking."

I smelled the sweat and the misery on her. The heat was immense, Biblical, no shred of air moving to break the bubble of silence laid over us. We stood in the sun and watched each other.

Once, Rosenfeld had checked herself out of the hospital and marched into my warehouse, all in order to apologize to me. Seeing the nightside up close had put a streak of white in her hair she had to dye and given her nightmares she'd needed two years of therapy to face. The guilt would eat at her, because she had seen the naked face of darkness and survived.

And Carp hadn't.

I broke the silence. "He was a good cop. A damn good cop."

The air started moving again, flirting and swirling as the breeze came up the hill, laden with heavy green rainsmell. We'd have thunderstorms as soon as the season started changing. Fall would ride in with afternoon rains, and winter. And here, sleeping under the earth, would the dead take any notice of weather?

There was never any rain in Hell. I knew that for a fact.

"He was," Rosie agreed. "Don't . . ."

Don't blame myself? "If you won't, I won't."

"Deal." She held out her hand. I took it gingerly, and we shook the way women accustomed to men shake—a brief squeeze, eye contact, and a half-embarrassed smile.

The scar throbbed, sensing the misery saturating afternoon scorch. I let go of her hot fingers. A thin trickle of salt sweat oozed down my spine. "You'd better go on. Monty probably needs a drink."

She let out an uneasy half-cackle of a laugh, choked off midway as she glanced toward the scar cut in the green earth. "I feel like I should stay with him."

"They'll be along in a few minutes to fill in the . . . to fill it in. I'll stay." *It's my job. It's the least I can do.*

She nodded once, sharply, her spiky hair drooping, plastered to her skull. We stood there for a few more moments, nothing left to say hanging between us.

Her shoulders finally dropped. "I guess I'll see you around?"

Why did she make it a question? "I'm not going anywhere." *This is my city. And when I find the other dirty fucking cops, I'll serve vengeance on them too. I promise.* "Rosie? Take care of yourself." *Please.*

"Yeah. You too, Kismet." Military-precise, she turned and headed for Monty's car, running now. I thought of the air-conditioned comfort inside and breathed out softly through my mouth, since my nose was full.

Monty pulled slowly away. Theron approached, and I heard a golf cart buzzing along. The diggers, two broad Hispanic men in chinos and blue button-downs—*of course,* I thought, *white would show the sweat and the dirt, and we can't have that*—arrived, and gave me a nervous glance.

I headed for the strip of asphalt and paused there, watching. One of the diggers had shucked his button-down and was in a black wifebeater. The other was still eyeing me. They began filling in the grave. Heat bounced, shimmering, up from the black asphalt, clawed at me in colorless waves. Still, I didn't sweat much, even under the leather.

I did wonder, standing there and watching them work with their shovels, if they had come over the border. I wondered if they'd been born in my city. I wondered if either of them had any idea who they were burying, or if it was just another job to them. I wondered if they resented the fact that they were cheaper than a machine, or if they were grateful for the work.

And I wondered if they would ever want to know how hard I tried to keep them safe too. I couldn't fix economic inequality, but I could stop hellbreed from preying on the poor and marginalized. One at a time and piecemeal, but it was better than nothing.

They call us heroes, Mikhail sneered inside my head. *Idiots. There is only one reason we do it, milaya, and it is for to quiet the screaming in our own heads.*

One of them said something in an undertone. The other

laughed, replied with a snatch of softly-delivered song. It sounded oddly reverent. Even if it was just another job, they spoke quietly around the dead.

"Jill?" Theron, at my shoulder again. "Come on. I'll buy you a drink."

"Hunters don't go to police wakes, Theron." *It hurts too much. Far too much.*

"At Micky's. I'll spot you some lunch too. If I know you, you haven't eaten."

I waited in the sun for another ten minutes. It didn't take them long to fill in the grave and tamp it down. The taller one elbowed his partner, and they glanced at me again before loading their shovels and the Astroturf into the golf cart. They buzzed away. Maybe they had other holes to fill.

Sleep well, Carp. My chest ached with all the things I could never say.

I wiped at my face again. *Jesus, Jill. Quit it.* "I didn't have much breakfast," I admitted.

Theron manfully restrained himself from commenting. "I'll drive."

CHAPTER 33

The sun went down in a glory of red and orange. Wind shifted, veering in off the baking desert, but it carried a breath of something other than sand and summer on its back. A faint tang that meant autumn was coming. Not for a while, but still coming.

I'd considered calling Perry. I'd even considered waltzing into the Monde Nuit and questioning him about Argoth. And about just what he'd known about Shen's little bid for a bigger slice of domination in the city.

Questioning him *hard.*

In the end I dragged the cut-down discarded end of a metal barrel from the railyards behind my warehouse and fed it a mound of barbeque charcoal. I doused the briquettes with lighter fluid and wadded up bits of waste paper, lit a match.

When the coals were glowing red to match the sun's nightly death I dug in my pocket and pulled out the little Ziploc baggie.

The purple crystals inside were slightly oily, giving under my fingers with a faint crunching through the plastic. I'd searched both Irene and Fax pretty thoroughly, but only Fax was carrying a sample and several folded sheets of paper covered with arcane notations.

I never took any chemistry in high school, so they might as well have been Greek. They burned just like any ordinary paper.

When they were ash I tossed the Ziploc in. There was a brief stench of burning plastic, and flame flared like the yolk-yellow light in Shen's eyes.

It still bothered me. Why hadn't she brought other hellbreed to finish me off? Then again, if she was trying to make points with one of Hell's higher-ups, she would have been greedy for the credit and unwilling to share. A big drawback to being hellbreed—they can't trust each other, and barely even trust Traders mortgaged to their eyebrows.

Which meant that maybe, just maybe, nobody else knew about this little foray into experimental chemistry.

Dream, he'd called it. More like a nightmare. A nightmare nobody would wake up from. Cold sweat prickled along my arms, along the curve of my lower back. With this shit to provide a banquet, Argoth could have stuffed himself to the gills on death and destruction. He could have made an entire continent a living hell.

Hey, he'd done it last time.

The only thing about averting a goddamn apocalypse is that it happens so routinely. None of the civilians have any idea how close the world is, *all the time,* to going up in smoke.

Sometimes I wonder if that ignorance is really a blessing.

The purple crystals sizzled, I poked at the fire with Saul's barbeque tongs to make sure every little scrap was consumed. Sparks rose, and I kept my face well out of the hot draft. Who knew what this shit could do to you?

I did. I'd seen it.

Argoth is coming... I can only hold the tide so long.

How much had Perry known? Only as much as he'd told me? Or was he hoping I'd disrupt Shen's plans?

I didn't want to know badly enough to let him fiddle with my head again.

Getting cowardly in your old age, Jill?

It didn't matter. If another hellbreed was crazy enough to try following in Shen's footsteps, they'd get the same treatment. I knew what to look for, now. And even if Perry hadn't been involved... well, we'd just have to see.

I hate just waiting to see.

The scar pulsed under a copper cuff, one of the old ones Galina had dug up for me. With Saul gone I was back to the copper, since I can't work leather to save my life.

The sun finished sinking below the horizon. My city trembled, waking up to nightlife.

The phone shrilled. I made sure every scrap of chemical and paper was gone, then stamped inside and scooped it up right before the answering machine would click on. "Talk," I half-snarled. *What now? Goddammit.*

"Hey, kitten." A familiar voice. He sounded sad, and bone-deep exhausted. "Glad to hear you."

Oh, God. "Saul." I sounded like all the air had been punched out of me. "Jesus. Good to hear you too. What's going on?"

"I was about to ask you that. Can't get hold of Theron. Everything okay out there?"

I closed my eyes, throttling the sigh of relief in my chest. "Just fine. Been a little busy, is all. How are you? What's going on out there?"

"You sure you're okay, kitten?" The rumble hid behind his voice. Distress.

"Just fine. Fine as frog's fur." *I just fucked this thing up six ways from Sunday and almost lost my whole city. But it's cool.* "We had a scurf scare and some Traders getting uppity. The usual. It's all packed away now." I stopped myself from babbling with sheer relief. "How are *you*? What's happened?"

"She's gone." A world of sadness in two words. "I'm coming home. Due in Tuesday at eleven P.M., I'm at the train station now."

Oh, thank God. "I'm so sorry." My breath caught. *He's coming home.* "You sound awful."

"Thanks." A dollop of wry humor lightening grief for just a moment. "She went peacefully. My aunts were there."

I listened to him breathe for a few endless moments. "I love you." Soft, high-pitched, as if I'd just been caught in the wrong bathroom in junior high.

It must have been the right thing to say. The rumble behind his breathing lessened. "I love you too, kitten. Pick me up?"

"With bells on." *Where am I going to find a car? Shit, I don't care. He's coming home.*

"You sure you're okay?" Now he sounded concerned. "You seem a little—"

"It's just been a long couple of days. And I miss you, and I feel bad for you." *And I almost lost my city. I almost didn't catch what was happening. I got lucky.*

Except hunters don't really believe in *luck.* Another reason to feel uneasy.

Like I needed one.

He didn't question it further, thank God. "All right. I've got to go, the train's boarding."

I squeezed my eyes shut even tighter. Yellow and faintly-blue stars danced under my eyelids. "Go on. I'll pick you up at the station. I love you."

"Love you too, kitten." A disembodied voice echoing behind him. Last call for boarding, probably. "See you soon."

It can't be soon enough for me. "See you."

He hung up. I listened to the dial tone for a little bit, then reluctantly put the phone in the charger and hauled myself up, paced back out to the barrel. The coals were back to glowing red. The formula and the sample were history. Apocalypse averted, again.

Saul's coming home. Thank God.

I made sure the barrel wasn't close to anything flammable and watched the last few dregs of light swirl out of the sky. When it was full dark, I shrugged into my trenchcoat and checked my ammo. I locked my home up safe and sound and headed out into the newborn night despite the stiffness in my legs and the aching in my heart.

He's coming home. He's on his way.

A thin fingernail-paring of waxing moon hung low in the sky. My city lay below, drowning out the night's lamps with streetlight shine. A field of electric-burning stars covering up holes of darkness, some Hell-made, some human.

And one more grave.

I went back to work.

Book 4

Flesh Circus

To L.I.

Bonitas non est pessimis esse meliorem.
—Seneca

CHAPTER 1

Just outside the Santa Luz city limits, the caravan halted. I rolled my shoulders back under heavy leather, my fingers resting on a gun butt. They tapped, once, four times, bitten nails drumming.

Out here in the desert, the two-lane highway was a ribbon reaching to nowhere. The stars glimmered, hard cold points of light. A new moon, already tired, was a nail-paring in the sky, weak compared to the shine of cityglow from the valley. I'd parked on the shoulder, and dust was still settling with little whispering sounds.

They were pulled aside, on a gravel access road, as custom dictated. Or fear demanded.

Their headlights were separate stars, the limousine pointed directly at my city, a long raggletaggle spreading out behind it. Minivans, trucks, trailers, and one old Chevy flatbed still wheezing from the '60s with bright spatters of glittering tie-dye paint all over its cab. One black limousine, crouched low to the dusty ground. The animals were sprawling or pacing in semi trailers. I could smell them all, dung and sweat and glitter and fried food with the bright sweet corruption of hellbreed laid over the top.

Another pair of headlights pierced the distance. I waited, leaning against a wine-red 1968 Pontiac Bonneville. She wasn't as sweet as my Impala, or as forgiving on tight corners, but she was a good car.

Cirque de Charnu was painted on everything except the glossy limo, in baroque lettering highlighted with gold. Under the fierce desert sun it would look washed-out and tawdry. At night it glittered, taunted. Seduced.

They're good at that. I sometimes wonder if they hold classes for it in Hell. It wouldn't surprise me. Nothing much would surprise me about that place, or about hellbreed.

Saul lit a Charvil, a brief flare of orange light. He studied each and every car, and the taut silence around him was almost as tense as the way he tilted his chin up, slightly, sniffing the air. Testing the wind.

"I don't like this," he murmured, and turned his sleek, new-shorn head slightly to watch the headlights arrowing toward us. A few silver charms were knotted into his hair with red thread. He had a small copper bowl of them in the bathroom, all the ones he'd worn before his mother died, tied back in as his hair got longer.

I contented myself with a shrug. The scar on my right wrist pulsed, the bloom of corruption on the caravan plucking at it. I'd stuffed the leather wristcuff in my pocket, wanting my full measure of helltainted strength tonight.

Just in case.

Baked, sage-touched wind off the cooling desert ruffled my hair, made the silver charms tied into long dark curls tinkle sweetly. I had no reason to draw silence over me like a cloak right now. We'd arrived at the meeting spot first, slightly after dusk. They'd shown up as soon as true dark folded over the desert, a long chain of bright, hungry headlights. The caravan still popped and pinged with cooling metal, its engines shut off one by one. Nobody moved, though I could see a few faint flickers when someone lit a cigarette, and a restive stamping sounded from one of the semis. Their lights were a glare, but not directed at me. Instead, the flood of white speared the desert toward my city, etching sharp, hurtful shadows behind every pebble and scrubby bush.

The other headlights, coming up from the city's well, came closer. My pulse tried to ratchet up, was strictly controlled.

Anticipation. Fear. Which one was I feeling at the prospect of seeing him?

Faint dips in the road made the sword of light from the approaching car waver. Still it came, smooth and silent like a shark. Mostly, you can see a long way in the flat high desert. But he was speeding, smoothly taking the dips and curves. It took less time than you'd think for the other car's engine—another limo, sleek and freshly waxed—to become audible, purring away.

"I don't like it either," I murmured. A hunter spends so much time holding back the tide of Hell, it feels just-damn-*wrong* to be inviting hellbreed in. *Come into my parlor*—only it was the fly saying it this time, while the spider just lolled and grinned.

And I would much rather put off seeing Perry again. No visits to the Monde to pay for a share of a hellbreed's power, thundering through the scar on my wrist. And I'd used the mark more or less freely for months now.

I was in the right, of course, and he'd welshed on the deal first, but...it made me more nervous than I liked to admit. Especially since it seemed stronger now than it ever had while I was visiting the Monde every month. Strong enough that I had trouble controlling it every once in a while.

Strong enough that it worried me.

His limousine coasted over the near rises. The wind dropped off, the desert finishing its long slow exhale that starts just after dusk. I marked the position of every vehicle in the caravan again.

There were a lot of them.

I heard it was always a shock to see how big the Cirque was when set up. How many souls they pulled in for their nightly games. How during daylight it always seemed exponentially smaller but still the shadows held secrets and dangers. And *eyes*.

It wasn't comforting information. And some of the pictures and old woodcuts Hutch had dug up for me before he went on vacation were thought-provoking and stomach-churning at once.

The black limo coasted to a stop. Sat in its lane, purring away, the gloss of its paint job powder-bloomed with fine crackling threads of bruised etheric energy.

The engine roused again, and for a mad moment I thought it was going to peel some rubber and speed off into the dark. Of course, if it did, I would be able to refuse entry. The Cirque would go on its way, and I'd breathe a huge sigh of relief.

But no, the shark-gleaming car just executed a perfect three-point turnaround, brought to a controlled stop on the other side of the road.

"Show-off," Saul muttered, and I was hard-pressed not to grin.

The urge died on my face as the door opened and Perry rose from the back of the limo, immaculate as always. Only this time he didn't wear his usual pale linen suit. It was almost a shock to see him in a tuxedo, his pale hair slicked back and the blandness of his face turned by a trick of light into a sword-sharp handsomeness before settling into its accustomed contours. His eyes lit gasflame-blue, and he didn't glance at the dingy collection of cars huddling on the access road.

No, first he looked at me for a long, tense-ticking ninety seconds, while the limo idled and he rested his bent arm on the door. There was no bodyguard to open it for him, no gorilla-built Trader or slim beautiful hellbreed to stand attentively beside him.

Another oddity, seeing him without a posse.

Why, Perry, what a nice penguin suit you're wearing. A nasty snigger rose over a deep well of something too hot and acid to be fear, killed just as surely and swiftly as the smile. The contact of cooler night air on my skin turned unbearably sharp, little prickling needles of sensory acuity.

The scar turned hard, drawing across the nerves of my right arm like a violin bow.

I kept thinking the memory of him pressing his lips there would fade. Silly me.

He finally stepped away from the limo. The door swung closed, and I tensed, muscle by muscle. Perry strode loosely across the road, gliding as if on his own personal dancefloor, and the caravan took a deep breath. Another door swung open, I heard feet hitting the dusty ground. Two pairs, both with the sound of hellbreed or Trader—too light on the toes, or too heavy, a distribution of weight no human musculature would be capable of—and if my ears were right, from the limo.

Hellbreed like limousines. I've heard politicians do too. Oh, and rock stars. Thought-provoking, isn't it?

I peeled myself away from the Bonneville's hood. Saul stayed where he was, but I felt his attention. It was like sunlight against my back as I strode forward, steelshod bootheels cracking down with authority.

If it was a dance, it was one that brought us all together just where the road met the shoulder. I ended up with one foot on the tarmac and the other on dirt. Perry, to my left, stopped a respectable six feet away on the road, and as he came to a halt I saw he was wearing mirror-polished wingtips. The crease in his pants was sharp enough to cut.

To my left, the Ringmaster halted. Thin membranous curls of dust rose from his footprints, settling reluctantly with little flinching sounds.

The Ringmaster. A tall thin hellbreed with a thatch of crow-dark hair over a sweet, innocent face with bladed cheekbones. They're all beautiful, the damned. It's the blush of a tubercular apple, that beauty, and it rots in the gaze if you keep looking steadily enough. Little things that don't add up—bones a millimeter too high, a skin-sheen just a degree or two off, a chin angled in a simulacrum of humanity but with *something else* under the skin—grab the attention, then the attractiveness reasserts itself. It's the mask they wear to fool their prey, but a hunter back from Hell can see under it.

We can see the *twisting*.

This one wore a thin-lipped smile that was far, far too wide. I looked for his cane and didn't see it. His black suit was a shabby, fraying copy of Perry's, a worn top hat dangling from loose, expressive strangler's fingers. When his lips parted, a long ridge of sharp bone with faint shadows that could be tooth demarcations showed. The ridge came down to points where the canines would be, then swept back into the cavern of his mouth.

In very dim light, human eyes might mistake him for one of their own. A hunter never would. Diamond insect feet walked up my back, leaving gooseflesh in their wake. A muscle in the Ringmaster's elegant cheek twitched, but it was Perry who spoke first.

"Kiss. A delight, as usual."

Don't call me that, Perry. I eyed the second one from the Cirque, a small, soft boyish Trader with huge blue eyes and a fine down on his round apple cheeks. My stomach turned over, hard. "Let's just get this over with." I sounded bored even to myself. "I have work to do tonight." *Got a childkilling Trader to catch, and you assholes are wasting my time.*

"As do we all." The Ringmaster's voice was a surprise—as hearty and jolly as he was thin and waspish. And under that, a buzz like chrome flies in chlorinated bottles.

The rumble of a different language. Helletöng.

The speech of the damned.

"Always business." Perry shrugged, a loose easy movement, and I passed my gaze down the small, doe-innocent Trader. He was thin and birdlike, in a white T-shirt and jeans, and he made me uneasy. Most of the time the bad is right out there where you can see it. If it's not, you have to keep watching until it shows itself. "Welcome to Santa Luz, Henri."

The Trader leaned into the Ringmaster's side, and the 'breed put one stick-thin arm over him. A flick of the loose fingers against the T-shirt's sleeve, probably meant to be soothing, and the parody of parental posture almost made acid crawl up the back of my throat.

"Thank you, Hyperion. This is Ikaros," the Ringmaster said. He focused on me. "Do you have the collar?"

I reached into a left-hand pocket, my trench coat rustling slightly. Cool metal resounded under my fingertips, and I had another serious run of thoughts about stepping back, turning on my heel, and heading for the Pontiac.

But you can't do that when the Cirque comes to town. The compact they live under is unbreakable, a treaty between dark and light. They serve a purpose, and any hunter on their worldwide circuit knows as much.

It just goes against every instinct a decent hunter possesses to let the fuckers keep breathing.

Perry rumbled something in Helletöng, the sound of freight trains painfully rubbing against each other at midnight, in some deserted hopeless trainyard.

I paused. My right hand ached for a gun. "English, Perry." *None of your goddamn rumblespeak here.*

"So rude of me. I was merely remarking on your beauty tonight, my dear."

Oh, for fuck's sake. I shouldn't have dignified it with a response. "The next time one of you hellspawn rumbles in töng, I'm going back to work, the Cirque can go on down the line, and you, Perry, can go suck a few eggs."

"Charming." The Ringmaster's smile had dropped like a bad habit. "Is she always this way?"

"Oh, yes. Always a winsome delight, our Kiss." Perry's slight smile hadn't changed, and the faint blue shine from his irises didn't waver either. He looked far too amused, and the scar was quiescent against my skin.

Usually he played with it, waves of pain or sick pleasure pouring up my arm. Fiddling with my internal thermostat, trying to make me respond. Tonight, he didn't.

And that was thought-provoking as well. Only I wasn't sure what thoughts it was supposed to provoke, which was probably the point.

My fingers curled around the metal and brought it out.

The collar was a serious piece of business, a spiked circle of silver, supple and deadly-looking. Each spike was as long as my thumb from middle knuckle to fingertip, and wicked sharp. Blue light flowed under the surface of the metal, not quite breaking free in response to the contamination of two hellbreed and a Trader so close. My silver apprentice-ring, snug against my left third finger, *did* crack a single spark, and it was gratifying to see the little Trader shiver slightly.

I shook the collar a little, the hinges moving freely. It trembled like a live thing, hypnotic blue swirling. "Rules." I had their attention. My right hand wanted to twitch for a knife so bad I almost did it, keeping myself loose with an effort. The charms in my hair rattled against each other, blessed silver reacting. "Actually, just one rule. Don't fuck with my town. You're here on sufferance."

"Next she'll start in about blood atonement," Perry offered helpfully.

I held the Ringmaster's gaze. My smart eye—the left one, the blue one—was dry, but I didn't blink. He did—first one eye, then the other, slight lizardlike movements.

The Trader slid away from under his hand. Still, their auras swirled together, and I could almost-see the thick spiraled rope of a blood bond between them. Ikaros took two steps toward me and paused, looking up with those big blue eyes.

The flat shine of the dust lying over his irises was the same as every other Trader's. It was a reminder that this kid, however old he really was, had bargained with Hell. Traded away something essential in return for something else.

His lashes quivered. That was his first mistake.

The next was his hands, twisting together as if he was nervous. If the Ringmaster's hands were flaccid and delicate, the Trader's were broad farmboy's paws, at odds with the rest of his delicate beauty.

I wondered what he'd Traded for to end up here.

"We'll be good." His voice was a sweet piping, without the candy-sick corruption of a hellbreed's. He gave me a tremulous smile. There was a shadow of something ancient over his face, a wrongness in the expression.

He was no child.

"Save it." I jingled the collar again and watched him flinch just a little. The hellbreed had gone still. "And get down on your knees."

"That isn't necessary." The Ringmaster's tone was a warning.

So was mine. "I'm the hunter here, hellspawn. *I* decide what's necessary. Get. Down on. Your knees."

The Trader sank down gracefully, but not before his fingers clenched for the barest second. Big, broad hands, and if they closed around my neck it might be a job and a half to pry them away.

He might have looked like the sort of tchotchke doll old ladies like to put on their shelves, but he was *Trader*. If he looked innocent and harmless, it was only the lure used to get someone close enough for those strong fingers. And that tremulous smile would be the last thing a victim ever saw.

I clipped the collar on, tested it. He smelled like sawdust and healthy young male, but the tang of sugared corruption riding it only made the sweetness of false youth less appetizing. Like a hooker turning her face, and the light picking out damage under a screen of makeup. The stubble on his neck rasped and my knuckles brushed a different texture—the band of scar tissue resting just above his collarbone. It was all but invisible in the dimness, and I wondered what he'd look like in daylight.

I don't want to find out. I've had enough of this already, and we're only ten minutes in.

I stepped back. The collar glinted. My apprentice-ring thrummed with force, and I twitched my hand, experimentally.

The Trader let out a small sound, tipping forward as he was

pulled off-center. His knees ground into the dust. Every bit of silver I wore—apprentice-ring, silver chain holding the blessed carved ruby at my throat, the charms in my hair—made a faint chiming sound. My stomach turned. It was just like having a dog on a leash.

I nodded. Let my hand drop. "You can get up now."

"Not just yet." Perry stepped forward, and little bits of cooling breeze lifted my hair. I didn't move, but every nerve in my body pulled itself tight as a drumhead and my pulse gave a nasty leap. They could hear it, of course, and if they took it for a show of weakness things might get nasty.

Ikaros hunched, thin shoulders coming up.

My left hand touched a gun butt, cool metal under my fingertips. "That's close enough, Perry."

"Oh, not nearly." He shifted his weight, and the breeze freshened again. His aura deepened, like a bruise, and the scar woke to prickling, stinging life.

A whisper of sound, and I had the gun level, barrel glinting. "That's close *enough.*" *Give me a reason. Dear God, just give me a reason.*

He shrugged and remained where he was. The Ringmaster was smiling faintly, his thin lips closed over the tooth-ridges.

I backed up two steps. Did not holster the gun. Faint starlight silvered its metal. "The chain, Perry. Hurry up."

He smiled, a good-tempered grin with razor blades underneath. It was the type of smile that said he was contemplating a good piece of art or ass, something he could pick up with very little trouble. His eyes all but *danced.* A quick flicking motion with his fingers, the scar plucking, and a loop of darkness coiled in his hands, dipping down with a wrongly musical clashing. His left hand snapped forward, the darkness solidified, and the Trader jerked again, a small cry wrung out of him.

Ikaros's eyes rolled up into his head and he collapsed. Spidery lines of darkness crawled up every inch of pale exposed flesh, spiked writing marching in even rows as if a tattoo had come to life and started colonizing his skin.

Perry's hands dropped. The Trader lay in the dust, gasping.

"Done, and done." The Ringmaster sighed, a short sound

under the moan of freshening breeze. "He is your hostage." Now his cane had appeared, a slim black length with a round faceted crystal the size of a pool ball set atop it. He tapped the ground twice, paused, tapped a third time with the coppershod bottom. The crystal—it looked like an almighty big glass doorknob except for the sick greenish light in its depths—made a sound like billiard balls clicking together, underlining his words. "Should we break the Law he will suffer, and through him, I will suffer; through me, all shall suffer. He is our pledge to the hunter and to the Power in this city."

The Trader struggled up to his hands and knees. The collar sparked, once, a single point of blue light etching sharp shadows behind the pebbles and dirt underneath him. He coughed, dryly. Retched.

"So it is." Perry grinned. The greenish light from the Ringmaster's cane etched shadows on his face, exposing a breath of what lived under the mask of banal humanity. "May your efforts be fruitful, brother."

"No less than your own." The Ringmaster glanced at me. "Are you satisfied, hunter? May we pass?"

"Go on in." The words were bitter ash in my mouth. "Just behave yourselves."

Ikaros struggled to his feet. He moved slowly, as if it hurt. I finally lowered the gun, watching Perry. Who was grinning like he'd just discovered gold in his underpants. His face wavered between sharply handsome and bland as usual, and the tip of his tongue flickered out briefly to touch the corner of his thin lips. Even in the darkness the color—a wet cherry-red, seen in an instant and then gone—was wrong. I had to clamp down on myself to stop the sweat rising along the curve of my lower back.

The Ringmaster took the Trader's elbow and steered him away, back toward the convoy. Their engines roused one by one, and they pulled out, a creaking train of etheric bruising, tires shushing as they bounced up onto the hardtop from the access road and gained speed, heading for the well of light that was my city below.

Last of all went the limo. The Trader slumped against a back passenger-side window, and the inside of the vehicle crawled with green phosphorescence, shining out past the tinting. Its engine made a sound like chattering teeth and laughter, and its taillights flashed once as it hopped up onto the road and passed the city limits.

As they wound down the highway, they started to glitter. Each car, even the ancient Chevy, dewed with hard candy of false sparkling. They wasted no time in starting the seduction.

Jesus.

Perry stood, watching. I swallowed. Took another two steps back. The scar was still hard and hot against my wrist, like almost-burning metal clapped against cool skin.

I waited for him to do something. A conversational gambit, or a physical one, to make me react.

"Good night, sweetheart." He finally moved, turning on his heel and striding for the limousine.

It was amazing. It was probably the first time in years he hadn't fucked with me.

It rattled me more than it should. But then again, when the Cirque de Charnu comes to town, a hunter is right to feel a little rattled.

CHAPTER 2

Mine is definitely not a day job. The day is for sleeping. A long golden time of sunny safety hits about noon and peters out at about five in the winter, somewhere around eight in the summer. I like to be home, curled up in bed with Saul's arms around me.

I do *not* like wrestling with a Trader in a filthy storm sewer reeking of the death of small animals. I don't like being thrown and hitting concrete so hard bones break, and I hate it when they try to drown me.

So many people have tried to drown me. And I live in the *desert,* for Chrissake.

This close to the river there's always seepage in the bottom of the tunnels, and the Trader—a long thin grasshopper who had once been a man, filed teeth champing and yellow-green saliva spewing as he screamed—shoved me down further, sludge squirting up and fouling my coat even more.

I clocked him on the side of the head with a knifehilt-braced fist, got a mouthful of usable air, and almost wished I hadn't breathed. The smell was *that* bad.

Candlelight splashed the crusted, weeping walls. The Trader had set up an altar down here, bits of rotting flesh and blood-stiffened fur festooning the low concrete shelf. Cats and dogs had gone missing in this area for a while, but the Trader hadn't bumped above the radar until small children started disappearing.

I had more than a sneaking suspicion where some of those children could be found. Or *parts* of them, anyway.

The Trader yelped, losing his grip on me in the slime and scudge. The knife spun around my fingers, silver loaded along the flat of the blade hissing blue sparks like the charms in my hair, and I slashed with every ounce of strength my bent-back left arm could come up with.

The blade bit deep across one bulbous compound eye. I've long since stopped wondering why a lot of Traders go in for the pairing of hellish beauty and bizarre body modifications. It's almost as if they want to be Weres, but without the responsibility and decency Weres hold themselves to.

Green stuff splattered, too thick to be slime but too thin to be pudding. The Trader howled. I exploded up from the bottom of shin-deep water, the carved ruby at my throat crackling with a single bloody spark, and shot him twice. The recoil kicked almost too hard for even my helltainted strength—I'd finally gotten around to getting a custom set of guns, like most hunters do after a while, and I'd wondered since why it had taken me so long. Nine-millimeters are nice, but there's nothing like something bigger to pop a hole in a Trader.

Some male hunters go for guns on the maxim that "bigger is better." Female hunters generally go for accuracy of fire. I decided to go for both, since I've got the strength and have no complex about the size of my dick.

My pager went off in its padded pocket. I hoped it hadn't gotten wet, ignored the buzzing, shot the Trader a third time, and flung my left hand forward. The knife flew, blue light streaking like oil along its blade, and hit with a solid *tchuk!* in his ribs. Even that didn't take the pep out of him.

Kill kids in my town, will you? I blew out a short huff of rancid foulness, clearing my nose and mouth at the same time, wet warmth dribbling down from my forehead, more wet sliminess sliding down from my nostrils. My chin was slick with the stuff. Right hand blurred to holster the gun, other hand already full of knife, my feet moved independently of me and I hurled myself at him.

We collided with ribsnapping force. I feinted with my left hand and he took the bait, grabbing at my arm since the knife was heading for his face again. Stupid fucker.

It was my right hand he should have worried about. No gun meant I was moving in for the kill, since knifework is my forte. I'm on the tall side for a woman, but comparatively small and fast compared to 'breed and Traders.

Even without the hellbreed scar jacking me up past human and closer to the things I kill.

My right hand flicked, sudden drag of resistance against the blade, and we were almost cheek to cheek for a moment. I exhaled, inhaled, almost wished I hadn't because the smell of a ripped gut exploded out, a foul carrion stench.

Who knew what he'd been eating down here in the drains?

I did. I had an idea, at least.

The scar pulsed wetly against my wrist, feeding hellish strength through my arm. I twisted my wrist, hard, breaking the suction of muscle against the blade. My knee came up, I shoved, and he went down in a tangle of too-thin arms and legs, twisting and jerking as death claimed him and the corruption of Hell raced through his tissues. It devours everything in its path, the bargain they make claiming the flesh and quite possibly the soul, and the body dances like a half-smashed spider.

Some hunters swear they can see the soul streaking out of the body. Even with my blue eye I can't see it. Sometimes I've sensed a person leaving, but I don't talk about it. It seems so...personal. And once you've gone down and seen the shifting forest of suicides bordering Hell, a lot of New Age white-light fluff palls pretty quickly.

The Trader collapsed, his compound eyes falling in, runnels of foulness greasing his cheeks. The stench took on a whole new depth. I watched until I was sure he was dead, noticing for the first time that my ribs were twitching as they healed, the bone painfully fusing itself back together. I was bleeding, and my right leg felt a little unsteady. Liquid sloshed around my shins. I took in sipping breaths, my lungs starved for oxygen but the reek, dear God, it was amazing.

The candles kept burning. Lumpy, misshapen tapers, their thin flames struggling in the noxious air, stuck to any surfaces above the water's edge. I waded toward the altar, my blue eye smarting and filling with hot water as it untangled the web of etheric bruising hanging over every surface. Little crawling strands, pools of sickness a normal person would feel like a chill draft on the nape or an uncomfortable feeling it seems best to ignore.

The drift of small bones on the altar, some tangled with fur, others with bits of cloth that might have once been clothes, made small clicking sounds as I approached. Random bits of meat quivered, and if I hadn't already been on the verge of retching from the stench I'd probably have lost my breakfast right there. As it was, it had been a while since I'd eaten, and my stomach was near empty.

My fingers tingled. It took a short while before the thin blue whispering flames of banefire would stay lit along my fingers, a sorcery of cleansing almost drowned by the tenebrous air.

I'm sorry. My lips twitched. I almost said it. *It's my job to protect you. I'm sorry.*

Four kids we knew about. Three we suspected, another two I was reasonably sure of. Nine little vulnerable lives, sucked dry by a monster who had bargained with Hell.

Who knew what those kids would have grown up to do? Save lives, find a cure for cancer, bring some joy to the world. But not now. Now there was only this vengeance in a filthy, stinking sewer.

I cast the banefire, my fingers flicking forward and long thin jets of blue flame splitting the dimness. The candles hissed, banefire chuckled, and I stumbled back, blinking the blood out of my watering eyes. The bane would burn clean and leave a blessing in its wake, a thin layer inimical to hellbreed and other contagion.

I'm so, so sorry.

It was getting harder and harder to keep the words to myself.

The banefire had taken hold and was whispering to itself, a sound like children crying. I tried not to think about it as I went through the sodden pockets of whatever was left of the corpse on the floor. Luck was with me, and I found a wallet. It went in my pocket, and I half-dragged, half-floated the squishing, still sluggishly contorting body over to the burning altar. When I dumped him on it, a shower of snapping sparks went up, and I suddenly felt queasy at the thought that he was lying on top of his victims. Nothing to be done about that—I had to burn them all, or the hellbreed he'd Traded with might be able to reach out and get himself or herself a nice fresh-rotten zombie corpse or two.

Now that I had his ID I had a fighting chance of finding whatever 'breed he'd Traded with and serving justice on him, her, or it. I headed back, sliding and slipping, for the tunnels that would take me to the surface. It hadn't been a long or particularly grueling hunt, physically. No, this one had just hurt inside.

God, I hate the kid cases. The cops agree with me. There's no case that will drain you drier or turn you cynical faster.

It took me a good twenty minutes to retrace the route I'd tracked him along. When I finally found my entry point—a set of metal rungs leading up to an open manhole, welcome sunlight pouring down and picking out bits of rust on each step—I looked up, and a familiar shadow moved at the top.

"Hello, kitten," Saul called down. I started climbing, testing each rung—that's the price of greater strength and endurance, a muscle-heavy ass. And I hadn't precisely climbed through, just dropped into the manhole after my quarry, hoping I didn't hit anything on the way down.

I wish that wasn't so much business as usual.

"Hey," I called. "How's everything up in the daylight, catkin?"

"Quiet as a mouse." He laughed, and it sounded so good I almost hurried up. Exhaustion dragged against my shoulders. "Smells like you had a good time."

"The fun just never ends." Crumbling concrete held a spider-map of veins right in front of my nose. I kept climbing. "He's bagged."

"Good deal." Tension under the light bantering tone—he hadn't wanted to stay topside, but I'd needed him up there watching the manhole in case the Trader doubled back.

Or at least, that's what I'd told him. He didn't make any fuss over it, but his tone warned me that he was an unhappy Were, and we were probably going to have a talk about it soon.

There were other things to talk about, too. Big fun.

I reached the top, skipping a rung or two that didn't look sanguine about holding me, and Saul put a hand out. I grabbed and hung on, and he pulled me easily out of the darkness. He magnanimously didn't mention how bad I must have smelled. "You okay?"

My boots found solid ground. It was a dead-end street down near Barazada Park, the spire of Santa Esperanza lifting into the heat haze. Blessed sunlight poured hot and heavy over me, just like syrup. In the distance the barrio weltered.

"Fine." I paused for a moment. "Not really."

He reeled me in. Closed his arms around my shoulders and we stood for a moment, me staring at his chest where the small vial of blessed water hung on a silver chain. No blue swirled in the vial's depths.

He pulled me even closer, slid an arm around my waist, and I could finally lay my head down on his chest. We stood like that, his heartbeat a comforting thunder in my ear, for a long time. The rumble of his purr—a cat Were's response to a mate's distress— went straight through me, turning my bones into jelly. It didn't stop the way I was quivering, though, body amped up into redline and adrenaline dumping through the bloodstream.

When the shakes finally went down I let out a long breath, and immediately felt bad about smearing gunk on him. He didn't seem to mind much—he never did—but I felt bad all the same.

"Want to tell me about it?" He didn't try to keep me when I eased away from him. He just let go a fraction of a second later than he *had* to.

I sighed, shook my head. "It's over. That's all." A flood of sunlight poured over the dusty pavement, the drop-off at the end ending in a gully that meandered behind businesses and the chain-link fence of a car dealership.

"Good enough." His hands dropped down to his sides, and he studied me for a long moment before turning away. The manhole was flung to the side—I hadn't been particularly careful at that point, I just wanted to get *at* the motherfucker. It was bulky, but he got his fingers under it and hauled it around, and I fished my pager out of its padded pocket, the silver in my hair chiming in a hot draft. "Who's calling?"

The number was familiar. "Galina. Probably got another load of silver in." *Christ, I hope it's not more trouble.*

"Least it's not Monty." The manhole cover made a hollow, heavy metallic sound as he flipped it, gauging the force perfectly so it seated itself in its hole like it had never intended to come loose.

"You're such an optimist." The smile tugging at my lips felt unnatural, especially with the stink simmering off my clothes and the sick rage turning in small circles under my heart. The scar twinged, the bloom of corruption on my aura drawing itself smaller and tighter, a live coal.

He smiled back, crouching easily next to the manhole cover. The light was kind to him, bringing out the red-black burnish in his cropped, charm-sprinkled hair, and the perfect texture of his skin. He tanned well, and a fine crinkle of laugh lines fanned out from his eyes when he grinned. They smoothed away as he sobered, looking up at me.

We regarded each other. He of all people never had any trouble meeting my mismatched gaze. And each time he looked at me like this, dark eyes wide open and depthless velvet, I got the same little electric zing of contact. Like he was seeing past every wall I'd ever built to protect myself, seeing *me.*

It never got old. Or less scary. Being looked at like that will give you a whole new definition of naked. It's just one of the things about dating a Were that'll do it.

We stood there, oven heat reflecting off the concrete, each yellowed weed laid flat under the assault of sunlight. Finally my shoulders dropped, and I slipped the pager back in its pocket. "I'm sorry." The words came out easily enough. "I just..."

"No need, Jillybean." He rose fluidly, soft boots whispering as he took two steps away from the manhole. I was dripping on the concrete, but drying rapidly.

"I don't mean to—"

"I said there was no need." He glanced at the street over my shoulder. The Pontiac crouched, parked cockeyed to block anyone from coming down here, a looping trail of rubber smeared on the road behind it. I'd been going at least seventy before I stood on the brakes. "You really wanted this guy."

I really want them all, sweetheart. The words died on my lips. *And each time I kill one, the itch is scratched. But it always comes back.* "Kids." Just one word made it out.

"Yeah." He scratched at his ear, his mouth pulling down in a grimace. Weres don't understand a lot of things about regular humans, but their baffled incomprehension when faced with kid cases is in a league all its own. "You must be hungry. We can stop for a burrito on the way to Galina's."

In other words, *you haven't eaten in a while, shame on you. Come on, Jill. Buck up.*

I took a deep breath, squared my shoulders. "Sounds like a good idea. That shack on Sullivan Street is probably still open."

The pager went off again. I fished it out again, my hair stiffening as it dried. Ugh.

This time it was Avery. It never rains but it pours. "Shit. On second thought, maybe we'd better just go. Avery probably needs an exorcism, and I can call Galina from his office afterward." I stuffed the pager away and turned on one steelshod heel, headed for the Pontiac.

"Dinner after that?"

"Sure. Unless the world's going to end." Adrenaline receded, leaving only unsteadiness in its wake. I made sure my stride was long and authoritative, shook out my fingers, wrinkled my nose again at the simmering reek drifting up from my clothes.

He fell into step beside me. "You know, that sort of thing is depressingly routine. How about calzones, at home? I've got that dough left over."

It *was* routine. People have no idea how close the world skates to the edge of apocalypse every week. If they did know, would it make them stop killing each other?

I used to think maybe there was a vanishing chance it would. But I'm getting to be a cynic. "Calzones sound good." I was already wondering what Avery needed, and the pager finished its buzzing as I walked. "Let's get a move on."

CHAPTER 3

The apartment was on Silverado, in a slumping, tired-looking concrete building—the old kind with incinerators in the basement and metal chickenwire in front of the elevator doors. The wallpaper had once been expensive, but was now faded, torn, and a haven for creeping mold. If the elevator worked the place could probably have gotten on a historical register.

As it was, the whole building smelled of fried food, beer, and desperation. We took the stairs, found the right hall, and the door was cracked open.

I don't usually show up for exorcisms covered in gunk and stinking to high heaven. The victim doesn't give a rat's ass by the time I'm called in, but my fellow exorcists probably do.

This time, however, Avery didn't even seem to notice. His brown eyes sparked with feverish intensity, his mournful-handsome face animated and sharp despite the bruising spreading up his left cheek. A gurgling noise scraped across my nerves, and we came to a halt at the foot of the bed.

I studied the body thrashing against restraints for a few moments. Don't ever, ever rush an exorcism in the beginning stages, no matter how pressed for time you think you are. That was the first thing Mikhail said when he began training me to rip Possessors out of people.

"Guy's name is Emilio Ricardo. Thirty. Dishwasher. Not the usual victim." Avery spoke softly, but his entire body quivered with leashed energy. I folded my arms. The carved ruby on its short silver chain at my throat sparked once, a bloody flash in the dimness. Silver moved uneasily in my hair. Saul stood near the door, leaning against the wall with his eyes half-closed.

The apartment was small, with none of the usual signs of possession. No hint that the victim was a shut-in, nothing covering
the windows, no scribbles of demented writing in whatever substance was on hand on the walls or mirrors. No smell of rotting
food. No foul slick of etheric bruising over every surface.

And Possessors aren't that fond of poverty. They like to get
their flabby little mental fingers in the middle and upper class. It's
almost enough to make you feel charitable, finding at least *one*
thing that doesn't prey on the poor.

There was a metal bed the victim was tied to, a chair and a
table in the greasy kitchen, and an old heavy television balanced
on a TV cart. The floor was linoleum, and the whole place was the
size of a crackerbox.

No, definitely not the usual victim. But they are creatures of
opportunity too, the Possessors.

The victim was male, another almost-oddity. Women get possessed more often, between the higher incidence of psychic talent
and the constant cultural training to be a victim. But a man wasn't
unheard of. It's about sixty-forty.

Still.... Male, dark-haired, babbling while he strained against
the restraints, leather creaking. "How did you get him tied down?"

"Cold-cocked him. He'll have a headache for a while." Avery
didn't sound sorry in the slightest. He rubbed at his jaw, gingerly.
"Assuming he ever wakes up."

I kept my arms folded. Ave had done a good job strapping the
man down. He looked thin but wiry-strong, fighting against the
restraints, his skin rippling. The candy-sick scent of corruption
was missing.

That was what bothered me. "He doesn't smell right."

"Smells like BO and fish." Ave's nose wrinkled. "But it just
seems off. That's why I called you. Didn't feel right, and you're
always bitching about trusting those instincts."

"Because when you don't, you end up getting your ass handed
to you." I paused. "And then you get all embarrassed when I do
show up to bail you out."

"Humility's a virtue, Kismet."

"So's discretion. I suck at both. Didn't you notice?"

The banter wasn't easing our nerves, but he gave me a tight, game smile. The bruise was coloring up quite nicely. "I was too bowled over by your witty repartee. Not to mention your leather pants. What do you think?"

"I think he's possessed, but I don't know by what yet. Grab a mirror."

He backed up two steps and bent to dig in his little black exorcist's bag on the greasy linoleum floor, metal and glass clinking. I approached the end of the bed and considered the thin man, who was still ranting and raving in glottal stops and harsh sibilants. It didn't sound Chaldean. It had a lilt to it unlike Helletöng, and it was vaguely familiar.

"Here." Avery had a small round hand mirror, the type exorcists buy by the case. I took it and hopped over the end of the bed, which squeaked and shuddered as my feet landed on either side of the victim's hips. I crouched easily and kept the mirror out of sight, tucked against my leg.

My trench coat settled over the victim's legs, and I could see his eyes were blind—filmed with gray. A fine tracery of overloaded veins crawled away from the corners of his eyes, right where laugh lines should be. They were gray as well, pulsing as if thin threads of mercury were running under his skin.

Now *that* was interesting.

Let's see what we're dealing with here, shall we? I leaned down, examining him closely, my gaze avoiding his blindness. My aura quivered, sea-urchin spikes almost visible, my blue eye turning hot and dry.

The victim kept twisting against the restraints. I shifted my weight, the cot groaning. Waited. The blind eyes wandered, back and forth in random arcs. He didn't respond to my nearness, which could have meant anything.

Seconds ticked by. Avery was breathing high and hard, tension spreading out from him in waves. Saul was a quietness by the door, watching. I settled, my heartbeat picking up just a little. I forgot what I smelled like, crouching there, my attention narrowing to stillness.

The mirror jabbed forward just as his gray-filmed eyes wandered across the precise, unavoidable point in space that would force him to look at himself. The reflection caught and held, my

blue eye straining to pierce layers of etheric interference—like
fine-tuning a radio dial to catch the familiar bars of an old song—
and I caught a glimpse of it before the mirror's surface disintegrated with a sharp horrified sound and the bed itself heaved and
bucked three different ways at once.

The mirror went flying, jerked from my grip; restraints creaked
and the bed jolted. I moved quick as a striking snake, my hellbreed-strong right hand flashing to close around the victim's
throat as leather groaned, restraining a force it was never meant to
bear. The chanting rose, the victim's mouth loose and sloppy, and
I knew what I had hold of.

Oh, goddammit.

I bore down hard, a nonphysical movement accompanied by a
hardening of physical muscles. The sea-urchin shape of my aura
trembled on the surface of the visible, spikes starring out hard
against the air, light popping on the points. My aura, like any
exorcist's, has grown hard and thick over the course of hundreds
of exorcisms, each of them unique—the only commonality is the
undeniable will needed to press something inimical out of its
unwilling host.

But this case needed something a little different. Silver rattled
in my hair, and I heard my own voice.

*"Begone, in nomine Patrii, Filii, et Spiritus Sancti! I command
you, I abjure you, I demand you release this—"*

That was as far as I got before what was in the man exploded, my
fingers slipping free, and threw me ass-over-teakettle. The cot shredded itself, screeching as it tore. The restraints held, just barely—
once-living tissue more resilient than brittle metal, for once. Avery
yelled, diving, and Saul gave a short sharp bark of surprise.

I landed hard, skidding on my hip, hit the wall. Drywall crumbled, puffing out chalk dust. I was on my feet again without knowing quite how, moving faster than I had any right to, adrenaline
pouring copper through my blood. Two skipping steps across the
room, a leap, and I realized just as soon as I was committed to the
motion that I was going to miss.

Crap.

Avery was still yelling as I twisted in midair. The victim rose
from the ruins of the bed, leather restraints squealing as his body

strained against them, a sound like the wind rushing from the mouth of a subway tunnel thundering through the apartment and blowing out the windows in a tinkle of glass.

He was shouting, still in that lyrical tongue, and the curse flew past me as I twisted even further, my coat snapping taut like a flag in a stiff breeze. I touched down, pulling etheric energy recklessly through the scar, a pucker of hurtful acid wetness inside my right wrist humming with power. My foot flashed out, weight shifting back, and I caught him full in the face right before full extension, the precise point where a kick has the most juice. The jolt went all the way up my leg.

He went flying, Avery yelled something else shapeless, and I coiled myself, getting my feet under me. Now I was prepared.

The wall disintegrated as the victim hit it, and I had no time to think about the damage that might be done to the host body. I centered myself, drew myself up to my full height, and the charms in my hair rattled and buzzed.

"Papa Legba!" I had to shout to hear myself through the volume of noise the victim was producing, gabbling and screaming. *"Papa Legba! Papa Legba close the door! Papa Legba close the door! PAPA LEGBA CLOSE THE DOOR!"*

Silence fell, sharp as a knife. My blue eye—the left one, the smart one—watered. The ether swirled, the sensitized fabric of the room resounding like a plucked thread. Everything halted, droplets of crystallized water hanging in the air—Avery, chucking a bottle of holy water at the victim, whose mouth was open in a trapped, contorted scream.

Well, at least Ave was thinking. Holy water's far from the worst ally in a situation like this.

The room filled with a colorless cigar-smoke fume. I tasted rum, thrown back hard against the palate, and spat, spraying the air. A silver nail ran through me from crown to soles, and I remembered Mikhail's pale face after my first introduction to this type of magic.

Be careful it does not eat you alive, milaya, he'd said. *These sorts of things do.*

The victim toppled, a long slow fall to the greasy linoleum floor. Before he hit I was on him, my aura sparking in sudden swirling darkness despite the flood of sunlight rushing through the windows. The shape of the things inhabiting him rose like smoke—three small humanoid forms, weaving in and out of each other. There was a high chilling childish laugh, and a gabble of weirdly accented Spanish.

"Usted va a pesar de que, bruja." For a moment I saw them— little boy and little girl, both with crystalline eyes and bowl-cut black hair, the girl in a shift and the boy in a brown loincloth. The shape between them was androgynous, melting first into the girl's body, she mutated into the boy, and the third shape whisked them both back out of sight, receding down a long tunnel. The sound of a door closing, sharp and firm, echoed through shocked air.

I sagged. The victim was unconscious, his face slack and empty. "Ogoun," I whispered. "Legba, Ogoun, thank you. *Muchas gracias.* Thank you very much."

"What. The. Hell?" Avery didn't finish the thought. He didn't have to.

"It's bad news." I glanced at Saul, who hadn't moved from the door. He leaned forward, though, tense and expectant, his dark eyes not leaving me. He was pale under his coloring, and I found out I was still smelling like rotting goop.

I couldn't *wait* to get home and take a shower.

"I got that much." Avery crouched gingerly. I let go of the victim, who slumped to the floor, breathing heavily. "That smelled like cigars. And...rum?"

"Put him in a holding tank downtown. Get me a file on him, too. I need two headshots." I straightened. Every muscle in my body cried out in pain, then subsided into a dull howling. "Keep the door bolted. Watch him. If you have to, buzz me again."

"Great. Okay." Ave visibly restrained himself from asking me why, and I checked. I get so used to dealing with one thing after another that sometimes letting someone else in on the situation doesn't occur to me. But Ave would do his job better if he knew what he was dealing with.

"You've never seen a *loa* before? An *orisha?*"

"Holy crap." His eyes got really wide, and he eased back a few steps, as if it was catching. "That was a—"

"Not a normal one, no." I cast a critical eye over the apartment. "Get going. He won't stay knocked out forever, but you should be able to get him downtown. If he wakes up in the back of the car and gives you trouble, smack him in the face with holy water and keep repeating a Hail Mary or something."

"I'm *Protestant.*"

For Christ's sake, like that matters. "Then recite the Nicene. Or the goddamn Wheelwrights lineup, whatever works." I straightened. "Go on. I'm going to look around."

"What for?"

"For signs of what he's mixed up in. You don't just trip and fall and get a spirit in you, you know." Even Possessors had to spend weeks of effort to worm their way into a human host.

"Ha ha. I suppose you're not going to help me carry him?"

"Saul will." I glanced over at my Were again. He nodded slightly, and his jaw was set. I couldn't think why, until something warm and stinging dropped into my eyes. "Shit." I touched my forehead, discovered a shallow slice. "I'm bleeding." I actually sounded surprised.

Avery rolled his eyes. "Hanging around you is a never-ending adventure."

It's that way for me too. "Shut up and get this guy locked up before he does anything else."

Bare fridge, bare cupboards—only a can of refried beans and a paper bag of Maseca, as well as a bottle of vinegar, for some reason. Threadbare clothes, two uniform shirts with the victim's name embroidered on them. A pair of busted sneakers in the closet. It was like a monk's cell.

I poked at the remnants of the cot. Was standing, staring at the twisted curlicues of metal and sharp sheared-off ends, when Saul reappeared, closing the door with a slight click. "Anything?"

"Nothing. If he's a follower, he's got it well hidden."

"That wasn't a Possessor."

"Nope, it wasn't. It was an *orisha.* Or a *loa.* Six of one, half a dozen of the other. Whatever branch of magic this guy's into—"

"He didn't smell like magic." Saul paced forward, stopped at my shoulder, and looked down at the mess of the broken bed. "Why didn't it cut the leather?"

"Leather was once living. And it has a greater elasticity when it comes to that kind of load. No, he didn't smell like magic. And the Twins don't usually take people without—"

"The Twins?"

"Yeah. You've heard of voodoo, right?" I glanced up. He looked blank. I tried again. "Santeria? Candomblé?"

"Santeria? A little. Popular down in the barrio." A shadow of a grin eased the tension in his face. He hadn't even had time to smear warpaint along his beautiful cheekbones, we'd been running so hard and fast. "I suppose now isn't the time to admit I'm behind on my reading."

This is why Weres run backup—they don't have the breadth of knowledge a hunter does. They're busy with their own spirits, their own particular sorceries. They rarely mess around with human magics.

Or human predators.

"Well, forget what you've seen in the movies. Voodoo is different. People don't just make bargains with hellbreed—there's a bunch of other inhuman intelligences out there. They make contact for all sorts of reasons. We have things spirits want, they have things we want, and everybody trades."

"Got that. So, voodoo in particular? Santeria? Candomblé?" His pronunciation wasn't off by much.

"Basically they interact with the same *species* of intelligence, but not the same *groups*. There's some crossover, but they're like different families. Spirits halfway between us and God, they say." I had to choose what to tell him, boiling a complex subject down to a few sentences. "They're not from Hell, and generally a practitioner is safe from being contaminated by a Possessor." I frowned down at the shattered bed. "Though they're not immune to physical harm from a hellbreed. Hell generally doesn't mix with voodoo." Now I was thinking out loud, good to do with him in the room.

"That's not what's bothering you, though." His fingers touched my hip. He crowded a little closer, his heat wrapping around me. It felt nice.

I let out a long breath. "What's bothering me is that the *loa* don't step in where they're not invited. At least, not without a good reason. And that was the Twins. At least, I'm reasonably sure it was one of their aspects."

"Bad news?"

Well, not particularly good news. I shrugged. "We'll see. If he was mixed up in something, we'll find out. I'll pick up the file from Avery and—"

"Dinner first?" It wasn't like him to interrupt me.

I was tired, my head hurt, and I smelled like death warmed over. "Dinner first," I agreed, scrubbing at the quick-drying blood on my face with my free hand. "This doesn't look right. It makes my weird-o-meter tingle like mad."

"That's saying something. Come on. Let's close this up and go home."

"In a second." I gave him a squeeze, freed myself, and checked the small bathroom. A bar of coal-tar soap in the ringed bathtub; toothbrush, box of baking soda, and a straight razor in a ceramic mug next to the sink.

The razor was a nice one, antique. Had to be 1920s, if my guess was good. A black scale with mother-of-pearl inlay, and a well-preserved steel, sharp as a suicide's whisper. I flicked it open, saw the shadow of blue swirling under the surface of the metal. I blinked, and it was gone.

Now that's interesting. I closed it carefully, dug in my pocket for a Ziploc baggie, and found one. Slid the straight razor in and sealed it. *I wonder...*

"What have you got there?" Saul said from the door.

"Clue." I slipped the razor in my pocket, turned. My coat brushed the sink, and the mug clattered down into its rusted bowl, spilling the toothbrush as well. "Shit."

"Which one? Clue or shit?" It was a pale attempt at humor, but one I appreciated.

"The former, catkin. Come on, I'm hungry." *And I need to work some of these nerves off. Maybe you'll help me with that.*

"Mh." He let me out of the tiny, tiny bathroom. Hot air soughed through the broken windows. "Sure made a mess."

"Can't have an exorcism without breaking a few beds. If he's clean we'll figure something out."

"And if he's not?"

I didn't have to work to sound tired. "Then a smashed-up apartment is the least of his worries."

CHAPTER 4

Dust swirled like oil, covering my city in waves. Autumn was moving across the mountains, the nights getting chillier and the days only slightly less hot. Soon the thunderstorms would start rolling in. But for now the far hills were tawny, and the clouds only stayed, threateningly, in the distance.

I hit the ground hard. Drew my knees up and shot my bare feet out, using the momentum to fuel a leap, propelling myself up. Whirled, my hand shooting out; he avoided it with a liquid jump to the side. My hand turned into a blade, chopped down.

He caught my wrist, brown fingers locking, and twisted, pulling back as he dropped into a crouch, swinging his center of gravity down and back. My arm almost yanked out of its socket, his foot smacked into my midriff as he hit the mats on his back, and I flew. Twisted in midair, doubling on myself like a gymnast, and landed a bare half-second before he was on me, a fast hard flurry of strikes and parries. Each one pushed aside, combat like a dance, no more than the barest touch needed to redirect, to score a hit, pulled at the last fraction of a second.

A hunter relies on firepower and sorcery to even the playing field. Still, we never fight Weres, even rogues. They're just too quick, too powerful, too graceful. They have no corruption, like in a hellbreed, that a human can latch onto and track.

I've wondered about that. I wonder about a lot of things, the more I work this job.

I'm harder to hit now, and a hell of a lot harder to hurt. And it was times like this that the bargain seemed a better thing than just a stopgap measure until I could figure out how to send Perry screaming back to Hell.

Hard.

Saul drove me across the length of the sparring room, dying sunlight falling liquid through the windows, sweat on both of us and the sounds of deadly serious mock-combat echoing. I stamped my back foot down hard, dipped, and spun as he advanced on me, taking his legs out from under him. He hit hard. I leapt and had my fist drawn back, my other hand tangled in his silver-scarred shorn hair.

"Give up?" I asked, sweetly.

A fine sheen of sweat highlighted each plane of his face. He blinked, a cat's quick flicker of eyelids. "You haven't won yet."

I grinned, lips pulling back from teeth. "Wanna keep going? Best two out of three, or should we take this somewhere else?"

"Don't know if you're ready." An answering grin, but his teeth kept well hidden.

Oh, I'm ready. I was ready for more than just sparring.

He heaved up, I pushed him back down. A few more seconds of wrestling ended with me still on top for once, the scar burning against my wrist and hot strength spilling through my bones. "It's looking like you're the one not ready, catkin."

"Just biding my time." He surged again, I pushed him down and realized my mistake a split second too late as his knees came up, my balance off by a critical fraction. A confused welter of movement, his forehead hit me in the mouth, and we rolled. Judo took over, and I began fighting in earnest. Reflex turned me into a dangerous snake writhing in his arms, but Saul knew how to handle this.

He always did. Or at least, he always *had.*

Stinging salt, my body suddenly just a welter of reaction. Saul held me down, silver chiming as his head dipped. Smell of leather, of cherry Charvil smoke, the good scent of a healthy male and the dry sleekness of catfur. We became one body with twisting limbs, rolling and seeking advantage, the floor a hard sea we only touched the surface of.

His mouth found mine, and it was no longer tossing on an

ocean. It was a softness blooming, nailing me in place. My body loosened, tingles flooding me. It was a far cleaner feeling than the scar's sick heat. I kissed him with my heart flooding out through the play of tongue and lips. He was purring, a rumble spreading out in waves. Each concentric circle of that purr stroked along my skin.

I broke away to take a breath. He nuzzled down my jawline, his mouth settling lower, just over my pulse. I quieted, the instinct of struggle sliding away.

"Saul," I whispered.

"Hm?" He nipped, playfully, and I arched.

"I think we should take this somewhere else." *Like a bed. Like our bed.*

"Here's nice." He nuzzled again. I squirmed in a new way.

"Saul—"

"Shhh."

I stilled. He inhaled deeply. Let out the breath in a chuff, a warm spot on my vulnerable throat. My pulse strained toward him. I held still as long as I possibly could. Finally wriggled a little bit, and he didn't immediately move. "What's wrong?" My wrists, braceleted by his fingers, both throbbed. He was holding me a little too tightly.

"Nothing," he whispered back. "I just want to hold you."

Goddammit. I want something else entirely. But I breathed in, the urge retreating low in my pelvis, a dull ache spiking for a moment as bloodflow reversed itself. *I'm going to be cranky if this keeps up.* "Okay." I swallowed, my throat moving against his lips. Another slight touch; it became very difficult to throttle my hormones back.

Mikhail had always been on me to control my pulse. I was much better at it than I ever had been, but one whiff of my cat-boy and the hormones started jacking me up again.

As problems went, it was a nice one.

Deep breathing. My eyes closed. The dark behind my lids was safe for once. Pushing the feeling down and away, reasserting control.

It used to be damn near every sparring session ended with us rolling around in an entirely different way to take the edge off.

Since Saul had come back from the Rez with his hair cropped, it hadn't happened. He wanted to be close, and wanted to be held.

I was okay with that. But the no-sex thing was beginning to take its toll.

God, Jill, how selfish can you be? His mom's dead. For a Were, that's like the end of the world. I kept my breathing slow and even. He didn't let go. We stayed that way, knotted together. Frozen.

"I love you," he finally said against my skin. "Jill?"

"I know that." And I did. "I love you too, catkin. Just rest for a minute. It's okay." I told the persistent tension in the bottom of my belly to go away. *I refuse to be dragged around by my clitoris, for God's sake. Come on, Jill. Rule the body, the body doesn't rule you.*

"I..." Maddeningly, he stopped. We lay like that for another thirty seconds or so, hardwood floor holding me up but not in the most comfortable way.

He levered himself up all in a rush, easing over to the side and ending up cross-legged, sitting and watching me. Something flared in his dark eyes. I watched his face, alert for any sign.

"I'm sorry." The little bottle of holy water on its silver chain around his neck shifted as he moved again, twitching, and stilled. "I thought..."

"Don't worry about it." I pushed myself up on my elbows. My T-shirt was rucked up, muscle moving under my abdominal skin, scars crisscrossing me. I'd put on a little more weight, but not a lot, and most of it more muscle. "Really."

"Jill..." A helpless shrug. You wouldn't think he was so much bigger than me, he looked so small and lost right now.

"Hey." I scrambled, got my knees under me, threw my arms around him. "Hey, don't. Please don't. Don't *worry* about it."

"I just...I want to..." I'd never known him to be incoherent before. Quiet, yes. Unable to find the words?

No. That was my job, wasn't it? To be the one who couldn't express a single goddamn important thing. I searched for the right thing to say. "I know, baby. Don't worry so much. It's only temporary."

His face fell. "You think so?" It wasn't like him to sound so questioning. Or so tentative.

"Of *course*." I said it far more firmly than I felt. Maybe it wasn't temporary. Maybe he was just having second thoughts about marrying a hellbreed-tainted hunter. Weres don't divorce— they just pick their mates and settle down—but Weres didn't date hunters all that often either, and almost never got hitched to them.

So if this distance between us wasn't temporary, would he go back to his tribe? As far as they were concerned the fireside cere- mony with his mother officiating made me his mate. But...I was an anomaly, and a big one. If he went back to his tribe, I couldn't see anyone protesting.

Least of all me. I'd commence and finish quiet internal bleed- ing before I said a peep. He deserved that much from me. If he really wanted to go back, I couldn't blame him one bit.

God knows you're not the easiest person in the world to live with, Jill. Buck up. Comfort him.

I held him, stroking his hair, touching the silver charms knot- ted in with red thread. Rubbed his nape just the way he liked it, scraping with my bitten-down nails. He eased a little and purred again, in fits and starts. "It's okay," I repeated. "Really and truly. It's all okay."

I don't know what else I would have said if the doorbell hadn't sounded loud enough to cut my ears in half. The thing goes off so seldom, I always forget between times that I have it deliberately loud. I like to hear everything scuttling in the warehouse's walls, down to the smallest insect.

Not that I ever have many insects around, what with sorcery burning all through the paneling and studs, but you get the idea.

I straightened. There wasn't a quiver or a peep from my hack- les. My intuition was quiet, for once. "Huh."

Which didn't mean there wasn't something bad at the door. It could be just a very *quiet* something bad. Then again, why would anything that valued its life and had mayhem on its mind ring my doorbell instead of just busting in to lay some hurt on me?

"Jill—" Saul made a small movement, like he wanted to catch my wrist.

"Hang on, catkin." I bounced to my feet and stalked for the door. A convenient table on the way gave me a gun; I checked the maga- zine as I slipped cat-footed down the hall and toward the front door.

Nothing. Not even a tingle. A series of raps—*human,* I decided, since they didn't have the odd too-light or too-heavy edge that meant something else. I slid up to the door.

Breathing. Slightly asthmatic. A human pulse, just a little elevated. I jerked the door open, the locks parting like water.

A skinny Hispanic teenager smelling of Corona and refried beans stood on my front step. He wore 51 colors, a red bandanna knotted around one thin bicep. Beneath the edge of a hairnet keeping his dark, limp hair back, he had a face that belonged on an Aztec codex.

Or at least, his proud, bird-beak nose did. Sallow, pitted skin and a pair of dead, empty eyes showed why he'd never be handsome. I recognized him a split second after I realized what he was standing there for.

He had the look.

Oh, no. Not now. "What the hell do you want?"

Gilberto Rosario Gonzalez-Ayala blinked once. *"Hola, bruja."*

"Hello, *Señor* Gonzalez-Ayala. I repeat, what the bloody blue blazes do you want?"

"Took me a while to find your house." A ghost of good humor slid through the bottom of his dark, shark-flat eyes.

You're not packing a .22, are you? I eyed him, taking in the flannel shirt, the torn jeans—and there it was under the stark flatness of his expression.

I knew that look. It was hunger.

Crap. I knew I hadn't seen the last of this kid. "There's a reason for that," I said finally. Behind him, the street was empty. The warehouse is on the wrong side of the tracks, of course. I spent the first half of my life trying to get away from the wrong side, and now it's where I spend most of my time. I barely have any idea what it's like over on the decent side of town, unless I'm working a case with its tentacles up among the rich and powerful.

I think that's referred to as *irony*.

He kept quiet, watching me. The sun was going down, dusk dyeing the west in bright pink and orange scarves. It was almost time to get ready for the night. Which would mean racking in more ammo and dropping by Galina's, since she had another load of blessed silver for me. Before that, I had to do some quiet digging, starting with the file on Avery's victim from the last night—

"You know why I'm here, *bruja*." His eyes were fixed on my face. "I owe you a beer. And we got business."

Yes, I do know why you're here. You still have to say it. "What kind of business? I'm not involved with petty gang warfare." *No matter how useful you guys were last time I had big trouble in town.* My heart squeezed down on itself, thinking of a grave and a coffin, and a good cop laid to rest.

My fault. If I had known...

But you never do. I brought myself back to the present with a conscious effort.

The boy on my front step shrugged. "I ain't here for Ramon. We got other business."

"Like what, Gilberto?" *Go away while you still can.*

"*Bruja* business. With what you do."

I held his gaze for a long fifteen seconds, feeling Saul appear behind me, a silent presence. My nostrils flared. It was there, too, the flat odorless reek of desperation with the burnt-sugar edge of wanting.

He didn't quite break, but he did pale the slightest bit and step back, as if my mismatched eyes had somehow changed. I knew they hadn't—there was none of the dry burning that would tell me my blue eye was doing funny things. But even the bravest tend to get a little weirded out when I stare at the bridge of the nose. The gaze grows piercing when you do that, especially if you just soft-focus, and you begin to look like you're staring through someone's head, riffling through their most intimate memories.

It's a tough look to pull off while covered in dry sweat, rucked-up in a T-shirt and leather pants, and frustrated enough to chew nails. I still managed.

"I know what you do." Gilberto dropped his hands. They dangled loosely, reminding me of the strangler-fingered Trader. "I want to do it, too."

I didn't have to put any more bitterness into my laugh. It was already bitter enough. "Go home, *poquito*. Leave the night alone and don't darken my door again." I swept said door to and closed it in his face.

No sound from the other side. None that you could hear with

human ears, that is. I could still hear his heartbeat, pounding a little harder and faster now. Accelerated breathing, too.

I'll bet that didn't go the way you thought it would. I half-turned, and Saul stood close behind me, his hair mussed and high color blooming in his cheeks, one dark eyebrow elegantly lifted.

I shrugged. "Hopefully he'll go away. I'm going to hit the shower."

"What if he rings the bell again?"

"Ignore him." I swung past him, already planning out the rest of the night. "Want a snack before we head out again?"

His broad shoulders dropped. "I'll make you eggs." He even managed to make that sound tentative. His hand twitched again, like he wanted to touch me, but he refrained.

Why?

You've got other problems, Jill. Just let him be. Be supportive, for once. "Good deal. Thanks, sweetie." I paced away, a little faster than I should have, trying not to feel like I was retreating.

Now *that* was a losing battle.

CHAPTER 5

Avery's desk always looked about to disappear under a mound of paper and ranks of liquor bottles. He'd stuck slim candles into bottle mouths, some burned down and others pristine, though I never saw a burning one. If he ever lit them up, it was probably when he was alone.

Cops aren't supposed to drink on duty, but exorcists get a little bit of leeway. However, Ave didn't immediately reach for the mini-fridge under his desk to get me a beer, and that was odd.

The tiled passageway behind me resounded with faint echoes from the downtown jail above. Here, at the very bottom, the long corridor terminated in Ave's office and three rooms, each barred with cold iron. Each with a circle carved into the concrete floor to hold victims hosting a Possessor—or those who had been cleaned out but had to be protected from the demon coming *back* to crawl right in and set up housekeeping.

He handed over the file. "This is seriously weird."

When isn't it? I rolled my shoulders back in their sockets, my coat creaking a little. "What's weird? Where's our boy?"

"He's the winner in Room One. Didn't flinch at the circle or anything. Didn't even know he was awake until I peeked in the porthole about an hour ago, when I finally got the file all together. There's some headshots in there too. He has a record."

I flipped it open and took a look. A couple of drug arrests, one breaking and entering dismissed with time served, and nothing for the last three years. Emilio Ricardo, thirty-six, brown and brown, employed halfway across town at a Mexican restaurant. Avery had even, bless his thoroughgoing little heart, pulled his recent renewal of a food-handler's card. "Huh."

"Yeah. The address on his food permit isn't the place on Silverado where I found him." Avery scratched at his forehead under a flop of brown hair. "It just tingled too funny. I got called in by a patrol car—they'd gone in for a domestic disturbance in the same apartment building and ended up hearing this guy screaming. Couldn't break the door down, and one of them—Jughead Vanner, you know, blond kid, looks like an advertisement for Clairol—radioed me in. He said it made him feel hinky."

That's odd. "Poor Jughead. You know he came across a Trader a couple months ago?"

Ave's sleepy smile bloomed. "He told me. Not in so many words, but...he wanted nothing to do with anything weird. I had to jiggle the door to get it open, and the vic tried to cold-cock me when I stepped in. I returned the favor, we tussled, I knocked him out."

"Where was he when you came in? Right next to the door?"

"Guess so. Why?"

"No reason." The straight razor was still in my pocket. For some reason, it bothered me. "So he's been quiet?"

"As a mouse." Avery's eyebrows were struggling not to rise. "Something wrong, Jill?"

"Not yet." *But this is strange.* "I'll peek in on him, then I've got a couple other things to do. Can you hold him for a bit?"

He made an expansive motion, rolling his eyes. "All things should be so easy. It's been quiet on the exorcism front."

I didn't tell him that with the Cirque in town, exorcisms would probably bottom out for a while. He didn't need that kind of uneasiness weighing him down. "Yeah. I haven't pulled something out of someone for at least two weeks, before this."

"No rest for the wicked." He indicated the first door. "Wanna take a look? Eva and I are going out for beers after I get off-shift. In about twenty minutes."

"You've been spending a lot of time with her. Speaking of Eva, how's Benito? And Wallace? Is Benny's leg okay?"

"Oh, yeah, it itches like hell under that cast but he's all right. Says he feels more stupid than anything else." Avery pointedly didn't mention Eva again, and—was he *blushing?*

I stared at him, my jaw threatening to drop. Ave's got a sleepy smile and big brown eyes, both of which draw women like honey. They don't stay—girls don't like it when their man spends his nights somewhere else, even if it's with possessed people. And Avery never makes much of an effort to keep them, either.

But he and Eva had been hanging out an awful lot lately. She's smart, tough, and a capable exorcist, even if she'd never make a hunter. Both Benito and Wallace have a little-sister thing going for her, and she handles it as gracefully as any woman in a predominantly male field does.

That is, with a smart mouth and twice the moxie of any mere man.

I swallowed the smile struggling to rise to my face. "Mmmh. Serves him right, taking on an exorcism-plus like that without calling me." I put the file under my arm and stepped up to the first door, my back itching a little because it was to the hallway. Only one entrance and one exit to any exorcist's lair.

Getting trapped is a risk we'll take. Letting a Possessor or a victim escape without being cleaned out isn't.

"Eh, well. None of us want to call you without reason." He shrugged when I glanced at him. "I know, I know. Better to call you without need than to need you and not call you. Believe me, I'm down with that."

I eased the bolt on the porthole free, slid the small reinforced square aside. Even this aperture was barred with cold iron, blue light running under its pitted, rusting surface. Reinforcing the protections on a space like this was an every-day, every-other-day job at most. Some exorcists do it twice a day, even.

Considering the alternative, I don't blame them.

Emilio Ricardo crouched in the center of the circle scored in the concrete floor. He rocked back and forth, subvocalizing, and now that the peephole was open I could hear it, a tuneless buzzing plucking at the air. He was hugging himself, and the rags of his shirt fluttered. The restraints lay in a corner, a jumble of leather straps.

Interesting. "Did you untie him?"

"Yeah. Figured he was going to be in there awhile. I'll trank him through the door if we need to take him out for a walk." Avery shivered. "I got a bad feeling about this, Kiss."

Don't call me that. "Me too." I shut my dumb right eye and peered through, concentrating.

There was only a slight, fading quiver of the unnatural around Ricardo. He was just keening, probably in psychological shock. Either that, or . . .

"Huh." I looked closer, my smart eye dry and buzzing.

"I hate it when you say that," Avery muttered.

Lingering cheesecloth veils hung around him, pulsing every time he took a breath. It looked like he was fighting free of the contamination—though contamination isn't the right word when it comes to voodoo or any of her cousins. He was definitely struggling with the mental and emotional damage done by having something inhuman use your body as a hotel room—or getting that something violently evicted.

It didn't look like the regular event of a *loa* or *orisha* "riding a horse." The bargains that priests and priestesses make with those spirits are well-defined on both sides, and initiation into the secrets of any voodoo-esque branch carries a protection against unwanted possession as well as methods of doing it safely.

That is, if any possession can be called "safe."

They are jealous of their followers, those spirits. I learned as much doing a residency, working the voodoo beat in New Orleans. Now *that* had been an education. Just goes to show there's always something more you can learn, even as a hunter.

I slid the porthole closed, locked it. "Has he eaten anything?"

Avery shook his sleek dark head. "Nothing yet. I slide the food in, he doesn't touch it."

I don't like this. I restrained the urge to flip through the file again. "Okay. I'm going to ask some questions. Hopefully I—" My pager buzzed, I broke off and dug for it. "Jesus. Never rains but it pours."

"You say that a lot. I'll just keep feeding him, then."

"Be careful. I'm not exactly sure what's going on here, and until I am I don't want him going anywhere. Okay?" I checked the pager. Galina, again. Which meant I had to get over there—it wasn't like her to buzz right after I'd visited her unless something was going on. Usually she'll just wait for me to drop by every couple of weeks, figuring I have other irons in the fire.

"Okay. Say hi to Saul for me, will you?"

"I will." I pocketed my pager, took another long look at the closed door holding a mystery behind it, shook my head, and turned on my heel. "Say hi to Eva for us."

He *was* blushing. He should've known I wouldn't leave without twitting him. "Go fuck yourself, Kismet."

I laughed and was on my way, pushing up the stairs lightly with each foot. Outside the jail, the Pontiac was parked in a fire lane, Saul leaning against the front left quarter-panel and smoking. The streetlamp shine of just-past-dark was kind, and I stopped on the steps for a moment, just taking a good look at him.

Tall, dark man, silver in his short black hair, jeans and combat boots and a black T-shirt. Broad-shouldered and lean-hipped, and almost too delicious to be real. Weres are generally striking if not beautiful. They just look more *finished* than regular humans.

He was studying the street, presenting me with a three-quarter profile hard-edged as a statue. There were dark circles under his eyes, I noticed, and his mouth was drawn tight. And his shoulders were hunched in a way I'd never seen before.

He looked tired. *Well, his mom just died. Leave it alone, Jill. Be supportive.*

My pager buzzed again, and I fished it out.

Galina, again. A chill touched my nape. "Fuckity."

That got Saul's attention. He ditched his cigarette, a long, thin stream of smoke following its arc into the gutter. "What's up?"

"Galina's buzzing. Twice. I should get over there. Avery says hi, by the way. I think he and Eva are dating." I waited for him to give me a quick smile, waited for his eyebrow to quirk.

Instead, his mouth turned even thinner. "Huh."

He really did look tired. My fingers tightened on the manila folder, making it creak and crackle slightly. "I can drop you off at home."

That earned me a look sharp enough to break a window. "You don't want me along?"

What? "Of course I do. You just look a little under the weather, that's all." *You look tired, and I don't blame you.*

He didn't scowl, but it was close. "I'm *fine.*" He slid along the side of the car, opened his door, and dropped in as my pager sounded again.

Goddammit. I stalked around the front, popped the driver's door, and got in, tossing the file in the backseat. I'd go over it after we found out what was going down at Galina's. "Saul—"

"I'm fine." He lit another Charvil. "If that's Galina we'd better hurry."

"You're actually telling me to drive fast?"

He grabbed for the seat belt as I twisted the key. The Pontiac purred into life. "Christ, when do you not drive fast, kitten?"

When indeed. I dropped the Pontiac into gear. My pager buzzed again, and I floored it while Saul was still trying to get his seat belt on.

CHAPTER 6

Galina's shop windows shone with featureless yellow light behind paper-thin blinds. The telephone poles marching alongside the road in this part of town were festooned with paper. As I cut the engine, looking at the one right next to the car, I saw a huge painted poster stapled over the weathered drift of concert announcements and nudie-bar placards.

Come To The Circus! Art Deco flowers festooned the edges, and in the middle was a grinning clown's face, deep lines in its paint, leering at the street. A suggestion of fangs touched the greased lower lip, and the clown's eyebrows came up to high peaks. A dusting of corruption lay over the paper, visible only to my blue eye.

There was no address. Of course, the people who wanted to would find it. That's the way it works.

My mouth went dry. "Jeez."

Saul barely gave it a glance. "Trashy." He opened his door, flicking his Charvil into the gutter.

A shadow moved in the plate-glass front of the shop across the street. I eyed it for a few moments, took my time opening my door. Blue fuzzy dice hanging from the rearview mirror rocked slowly to a halt—Galina's gift, a replacement for the red ones that had gone up in flames with my Impala.

The thought *still* pissed me off. I'd nursed that car back into shape from a rusted hulk in a wrecking yard. All that work and effort gone in a few heartbeats, dying in the barrio.

Saul hadn't asked any questions when I picked him up from the train station in the Pontiac. I was glad about that.

The shadow in Galina's window moved again. I slid out of the car, slammed my door, and eased a gun free of the holster. Saul had paused at the rear of the car, his head up, hot wind touching his hip-length leather jacket and making the fringe move a little. His dark eyes flicked to the gun in my hand, and he straightened infinitesimally before stepping out into the road.

He followed two steps behind and to my left, carefully out of the way but close enough if I should need him. The skin between my shoulder blades twitched a little when I crossed the center-line—it hadn't been so long ago that I'd been right in the middle of the street and got chewed up by an assault rifle. They'd used copper-jacketed lead, the dumb bunnies, instead of silver to hurt a helltainted hunter.

Everyone skipping and scrambling to kill me, when if they'd just left me alone they could have quietly had their bioweapon and their higher-up from Hell stepping through to make my entire city—hell, probably the entire *country*—a wasteland before I could stop them. There wouldn't have been a damn thing I could do about it. I'd only been poking around the suicide of Monty's old partner, not looking for a serious dose of lead poisoning or a fire-bombed car.

I wasn't far enough away from that case yet for my body to forget. A prickle of chill touched the curve of my lower back.

The body remembers, and the body knows. You can override that knowing with enough training, but it's still never pleasant.

The blinds twitched and one moved aside slightly. The shape in the window was Galina, her marcel-waved hair an immaculate cap as always. Her green eyes sparked as the sheet of etheric energy folding over her shop changed slightly, like light refracting through a waterfall. Even my dumb eye could sense the reverberations, watering and tingling. The scar prickled.

"She looks worried," Saul murmured.

"No shit," I muttered back. Inside her shop, Galina's will is law—she is, after all, a Sanctuary. But anything could happen on the way up to her doorstep.

And who knew what was waiting for us around here? It wasn't like her to call more than once. They all know the drill, everyone who dials me—I'll get around to you sooner or later, unless I'm being shot, strangled, knifed, electrocuted, thrown off a building, or doing anything else fun and interesting.

I opened the door cautiously. The bell jingled. I stepped carefully through the curtain of Sanc warding.

"Thank God." She was in her robes, the pigeon-throat gray shifting and the mark of the Order—a silver medallion, the quartered circle inside a serpent's hoop, snake eating its own tail—at her throat. I gave the shop a quick glance—nothing visible. I relaxed fractionally, didn't reholster the gun. Something was off here. "You won't need that, Jill, I've got everything—"

"Is it her?" A rumble of Helletöng slid under the words, and the windows chattered, both with Galina's wordless shout and the lash of a hellbreed's voice.

Coming from *inside*.

Usually, my instinct would be to dive *away* from something like that. This time, though, I pitched forward, my shoulder smacking hard against the bottom of a display case running along the right side of the store. Glass shivered and whickered loose. Saul let out a short sharp yell, I finished rolling, gaining my feet in a single convulsive movement and ending up with both guns pointed straight at a very familiar-looking 'breed.

The Ringmaster held his cane like a staff, the crystal at its head spitting with venomous green as he stood next to the cash register. His eyes ran with wet orange hellfire. His hair was lifting on a slight screaming breeze from nowhere, standing up in wet black spikes. This time he was in a battered red velvet coat and actual *jodhpurs,* but it didn't make him look ridiculous.

No, he looked like he belonged on a carton of animal crackers. A really twisted, ugly carton sopping with blood and other nasty liquids.

"We came to this town in good faith, hunter." The faint lines on the ridge of bone masquerading as teeth were grimed with something dark. "We came to cleanse and to—"

"Stand down." My voice sliced through his. Behind me, Saul's warning growl rose, rattling the entire place no less than Galina's anger or the wave of hellbreed agitation. "This is a Sanctuary. Calm the fuck *down.*"

"*Both* of you." The air hardened under Galina's words. "You. Stand over there, or I will send you back to Hell. I'm *not* joking."

"She isn't, you know." This was Perry, who stood with his back to the rest of us, bending down to peer inside a glass display case that held several crystal balls, mummified alligators, and a stacked display of Etteila tarot cards. Something rippled on his back, under the white linen suit jacket. "I suggest you calm yourself."

"What the hell's going on?" I didn't lower the gun, and Galina's walls ran with rivulets of etheric force, cascading in sheets. The lightshow was amazing, but it could just as easily turn on me as on the hellbreed. "Galina?"

"Stand *over there.*" Her voice rang like a gong, and the Ringmaster grudgingly paced to the exact spot she pointed to on the hardwood floor, his thin body twitching with mutiny. His hair actually writhed, the spikes touching each other with little balloon-squealing sounds. The fraying nap of his red velvet coat crawled with corruption-dust, and his fingers twisted and twitched.

Galina gave me a meaningful look, and I slowly, slowly lowered my guns. The glass shards on the floor stirred, quivering.
"Someone give me a vowel."

"We are in a very special place right now, Kismet." Perry still
didn't turn to face any of us. "Let us absorb the full implications."

"Where have you been, hunter?" The Ringmaster jabbed his
cane at me, the crystal popping off one diseased-green spark. "We
came here in *good faith!*"

"I've been chasing a child-killer and doing exorcisms." Every
nerve in my body cried out in protest when I holstered the guns.
"More than enough fun and games to keep me busy. Whatever's
happened to you, I'm not involved with it." I licked my dry lips.
Saul straightened from his crouch behind me. It was good to feel
him there, even while I was worrying about two hellbreed in front
of me and the look on Galina's face. "Yet."

"There has been an attack." Perry finally turned, slowly, and it
was almost a relief to see him still wearing his blond, bland face.
He was also grinning, lips pulled back in a rictus and his eyes
burning gasflame-blue. There was no indigo spreading and scarring the whites, though.

That was good news. How good remained to be seen. "Attack?"
That was the bad news. "What kind of attack?"

"A Cirque performer, my dear." Perry stuffed his hands in his
pockets and tilted his blond head. It ruined the lines of his suit, but
I suppose he thought it made him look less dangerous. Or something. "A certain fortune-teller appears to have gone to collect her
eternal reward. With some help, I might add."

For a few seconds the words refused to make sense. Then they
slammed home, and I took a deep breath. My face felt very cold,
and I suspected I'd gone even paler than my usual night-working
fishbelly. "You're kidding." It was the only thing I could think of
to say.

"You see?" Perry's grin didn't alter in the slightest. "I vouch
for her shock, brother. My Kismet is altogether too intelligent for
such a blatant act."

"Shut up, Hyperion." The Ringmaster's cane dipped. He
watched me, his orange gaze swirling with dust and crawling all
down my body. "You will swear you had no part in this, hunter?"

"For Christ's sake." I resisted the urge to draw a knife, or better yet, limber my gun up and make the world a better place with a few well-placed headshots. "The hostage is your good behavior. Why the hell would I want to attack any of your people?" *Other than their being hellbreed, which is enough reason to seriously tempt me.*

"To erase the rest of—" The Ringmaster's eyes flicked toward Perry, who pursed his lips. A number of things occurred to me just then, and I actually had to stuff my tongue into my cheek and bite down to keep from making a snarky comment.

They were actually thinking I'd go after the entire Cirque, given enough reason. But the Ringmaster wouldn't be so upset unless he seriously thought I had a chance at actually pulling it off.

It was an unintentional compliment. Being feared by hellbreed isn't a nice thing, but it's damn useful, and pleasant when it can smooth your way a little bit.

My heart rate eased a little bit. Saul crowded closer behind me. The bell on the door jangled slightly, thrumming under the murderous tension. Galina relaxed, fractionally.

"All right." I tried not to sound relieved. "This is the first I've heard about an attack on the Cirque—which I consider just as bad news for me as it is for you. I give you my word I have nothing to do with it. But I'm about to." I took a deep breath. My pulse smoothed out a little bit more, and my eyes skipped between the two 'breed, each of them vibrating with barely controlled rage. Perry hid it better, but I've been around him too much, for too long, to trust his outward appearance. "I've got some business to transact with my Sanctuary, here. Then I'll be out at the Cirque to take a look at what's going on. I'll find out who's behind this and take appropriate action. In the meantime, you'll keep your noses clean." *Put the sting in the tail, Jill.* "Perry, you'll meet me at the Cirque."

"I do not—" The Ringmaster began.

"I think it's best, don't you?" Perry interjected smoothly, taking a single step closer. "So nobody is tempted to run amok while my dear Kiss is on the scene. It would be so embarrassing to have a hunter become justified in killing a few *more* of your performers." He didn't look at the other 'breed, though. Instead, he was staring at me like he was hungry and I was a bowl of lunch.

I wish I could say I didn't know that look. But men have been giving it to me all my life.

The other 'breed stared at me, the pumpkin hellfire smearing from his irises not abating one iota. I was suddenly glad we were inside Galina's shop. If he moved on me she'd drop him—or more precisely, the Sanctuary warding on the walls would. If all else failed, it would give me enough time to put a few silverjacket slugs in him. And maybe sink a knife right into one of those orange-glowing eyes.

"If I find that you are, indeed, involved in this...unfortunate...event—" The cane twirled smartly, the crystal hissing as it clove unresisting air.

That's the trouble with this job. It's full of threats, both veiled and naked. After a while it gets ho-hum. Except when you're dealing with Hell's scions. The slippery, twisting, twitchy bastards threaten all the time—and they'll get away with what they can.

"I sure hope that wasn't a threat," I remarked to the empty air over his black-spiked head. "Because for a member of the Cirque de Charnu to threaten a resident hunter is exceeding bad taste. Not to mention stupid. And dangerous. And—"

"That's it." Galina stepped forward just as the Ringmaster did, a synchronized movement that would have been funny if the hellbreed hadn't been hissing like a steam kettle. "Both Perry and I vouch for our hunter's innocence. Go back to your home and wait. You've said and done enough here."

Our hunter. A pucker of hot liquid prickling filled the scar. The bottom dropped out of my stomach. Perry grinned like he had just gotten a Christmas present full of snackable entrails. Galina, however, didn't notice anything.

Great.

Crackling tension rose another notch. The Ringmaster paced toward me, and I realized he would have to pass very close to get out the front door. I stepped aside, so did Saul, and I did my best to keep myself between him and the 'breed. The smooth incense quiet of Galina's shop trembled like the skin atop fresh milk. My hands literally itched for a weapon.

The Ringmaster halted for a bare second. Adrenaline spiked through my bloodstream. I caught a whiff of sawdust and glitter, spice and fried food, with the faint thunderous note of rotting underneath. The edges of his red frock coat twitched, as if tiny insect feet were stabbing the threadbare crimson velvet from underneath.

Amazingly, he didn't stop to threaten me again. He just passed by with a sound like fresh-tanned leather crumpling and banged out the door, leaving a scrim of evil little laughter in his wake. I let out the breath I hadn't been holding—I'd inhaled deeply, ready for the explosion.

"Now you, Perry." Thunder smoked and roiled under Galina's voice. "I've business to transact with Jill."

"What if I do, too?" He grinned and leaned forward, his toes digging into the floor. "Business with *my* hunter."

"Perry." Just the one word. Galina's eyes turned incandescent. The silver at her throat sparked, a clean springtime green swirling at the surface of the metal. "It would be *undignified* to be tossed out of here on your ass."

"True." He rocked back on his heels, grinned at both of us. "I bid you a civil adieu, then, ladies." A wink and a flash of pearly teeth between his bloodless lips, and he slid past me like a burning wind. Halfway out the door he vanished, leaving behind strangled little whispers before the door banged closed and I heard footsteps pattering away down the street, far too fast and light to be human.

My shoulders dropped. I let out another, far gustier sigh, and Galina swayed before she pulled herself upright. The glass on the floor quivered again. I watched as the broken pieces of the display case twitched slightly, arranged along spiraling rays of reaction.

Huh. That's interesting.

Saul's hands caught my shoulders. "You okay?" He sounded worried.

I realized the scar was twitching against the underside of my arm as if an enthusiastic seamstress was pleating the skin. At least Perry hadn't really tried to play with it. "Just ducky. Jesus, Mary, and Joseph. Someone's looking to kill Cirque performers?"

Galina said it, so I didn't have to. "Or they have a deeper plan, and they're going to try to pin anything that happens on you. I don't like this."

"Sorry about your display case." I stared, willing the pattern to come clear, and finally blinked it away when it refused. Hunters always become full-blown psychics before the end of their apprenticeships; damn useful when dealing with the nightside. But sometimes intuition won't tell you anything. It will just muddy the waters.

I looked up to find the Sanctuary studying me, a line between her dark eyebrows. "Don't worry about that." Galina was pale, and shaking just the slightest bit.

"Oh, Christ," I said. "Drop the other shoe. And get me some more ammo. I've got a bad feeling about this."

CHAPTER 7

You could find just about anything a serious practitioner needed at Galina's, and if your credit was good you could get a whole lot more. A neutral supply of necessities for all concerned is the least of the services a Sanctuary provides to a city's nightside inhabitants.

She poured us tea up in her kitchen. The night pressed against the bay window over the sink, the green bank of herbs in a cast-iron shelving unit stirring slightly.

Sancs like growing things. They are gentle souls, really. It's a shame so few people pass their entrance exams.

Galina set the tray of silverjacket ammo down on the butcher-block table. "What do you know about the last time the Cirque was here?"

Saul blew across his tea to cool it. He was looking everywhere except at me.

I stared at her for a few seconds, the chill down my back growing more pronounced. "It was the hunter before Mikhail. I know he told them not to come back until he wasn't the hunter here either. Bad blood between him and the last Ringmaster. Or is that the same one?"

"It's the same one. He's been controlling the Cirque for a few generations, which means he's nasty and smart." Her fingers were steady on the teapot; she poured and pushed the ammo tray toward me. It was really strange to see her so pale. Not much disturbs Galina's serenity. "With that goddamn cane of his. The last time..."

I waited while she set the teapot down, the walls echoing slightly with her distress. Sancs don't go outside much; it's the price they pay for being almost godlike inside their nice thick defenses. Being inside a Sanctuary's space when they lose their cool is an uncomfortable experience at best.

Saul slurped loudly. The scar ran with prickles, like icy water on burning skin. I began checking the ammo automatically, sliding yet more extra cartridges into the loops sewn inside my coat. I could probably do this in my sleep, I've done it so many times.

And hell, while I was here for the second time today I might as well load up.

"There was some trouble," Galina finally said, lowering herself down to sit on a stool opposite me. "The hunter before Mikhail was Emerson Sloane; he had a sort-of apprentice. Everything went sideways."

Sort-of apprentice? That doesn't happen. But there are wannabes in this business, just the same as any other. Fucking amateurs trying to get themselves killed, since they're unfit for the job one way or another, or they'd be trained.

Silence stretched between us. I finally broke it. "Mikhail never told me about that."

"He wasn't an *actual* apprentice." The kitchen, with its mellow shining counters and wood-faced cabinets, wavered slightly and solidified around her. "He just kept following Sloane around until Sloane gave up and began training him."

That's how it usually starts. My own apprenticeship hadn't begun that way, but...Mikhail had been an exception all over.

And so, I suppose, was I. And if I was lucky, Gilberto would have vanished off my front step by the time I got home.

Galina sighed. "He got into trouble. There were some problems."

"What type of problems?"

Her brow furrowed. "I...didn't hear much. Sloane never opened up about it. I do know the kid ended up dead, after something terrible."

There's certainly no shortage of terrible things on the night-side. "And no word on what 'something terrible' entailed? Did it have to do with the Cirque, or—"

"I just don't know, Jill." She picked up her own cup, took a small sip. Her shoulders were sharp points under the robes. Some of the shaking had eased out of her. The walls had stopped quivering with etheric distress. "The Ringmaster seemed to think you had a hand in this attack, and he was...excited when he showed up. Perry was right behind him."

Goddammit. I'll just bet he was, with his little fingers in the pie as usual. I couldn't help myself—a sigh to match hers came out hard on the end of the sentence. The smell of incense, dust, and sleepy power in her shop mixed uneasily with the aroma of spaghetti sauce and the fading tang of 'breed—she'd probably been at dinner when they dropped by. "What can you tell me about this trouble?"

The line between her eyebrows got deeper. "Not much that I can recall. It had to do with the apprentice and a woman over near Greenlea, I think, back when that part of town wasn't very nice. Had to be, oh, around 1926 or so. Before the barrio moved, before the big outbreak, and before all that new money moved in and turned it into a shopping district. The kid..." She frowned. "There was something about him. I can't remember. I'll dig through my diaries, see if I can suss it out."

Hm. "It's not like you to have a bad memory."

She gave me an exquisitely sarcastic look. "When you've put in almost a century of tending a Sanctuary, Jill, then we'll talk. Mikhail and Sloane both liked things close to the vest, too. Most of the time I didn't have a clue what either of them were up to."

And I was no different when a case was heating up. It was my turn to shrug as I finished stowing the ammo. "Mischa was a private person, all right. I didn't hear much about the former hunter either. Except that Sloane wasn't of our lineage, he was part of Ben Cross's crowd."

"Yes. Sloane died after the outbreak in 1929." She stared into her tea mug like it held the secrets of the universe. "We were in freefall for years. That was a bad time for any hunter."

"Yeah." The second-biggest demonic outbreak of the past century, 1929 was a bad year for hunters all over the United States, and it got exponentially worse in Europe ten years later. So much of what was unleashed during the two decades after '29 is still out running around—it's like the Middle Ages all over again, only this time we have more firepower to put things down.

Still, the firepower's no good without people trained to use it. And quality apprentices are few and far between.

I thought again of Gilberto and hoped he was gone by the time I got home. Which might not be soon. This had all the makings of a complex situation, which meant a lot of blood and screaming. Not to mention gunfire and ugliness.

"Oh." A sudden, abrupt movement. Galina finished trolling through her memory and blinked. "Gregory. That was the kid's name. Something Gregory. I'll look through my diaries."

"I'd appreciate it." *Great. And I really have to get over to Greenlea, now that you mention it. I've got business there too.* "Hey, has anyone been in to buy voodoo stuff lately? Anyone making a big serious purchase?"

"No. I don't do much voodoo or Santeria here. That's more Mama Zamba on the edge of the barrio, or Melendez. I sometimes send people to either of them." A curious look crossed her round, pretty face. "I wonder..."

I hate going to either of them. Jesus. "Well, give ol' Zamba a call as soon as I leave. Let her know I've got a few questions. It's about time I went and scared her again." I fished out a fifty-dollar bill. "Here's all I've got on me for this load of ammo; I'll take care of the rest when I get my municipal check. Okay?"

"You can put it on account, you know." But instead of saying it with a grin, Galina looked troubled. "Jill, are you sure you want to go out to the Cirque?"

"I'll go where I have to." *You should know that.* "It's just a bunch of hellbreed playing games. Nothing I haven't seen before."

"I really hope you don't mean that," she muttered, but she let it go.

It wasn't like her not to get the last word in, so I left it at that.

Saul finished his tea, I got a few more odds and ends, and we left her up in her kitchen, tracing the ring of spilled tea from the bottom of her cup, drawing it on the table like it might give her an answer.

Of course they would settle near the trainyards, far north of my warehouse and on the fringes of the industrial section. A cold night wind came off the river, laden with flat iron-chemical scent. It was usually a space of empty, weed-strewn lots, a few squares of concrete left over from trailers or something, and a festooning of hypodermics and debris from when it used to be a shackville. The homeless were rousted out during a huge urban renewal drive five years ago, but the drive petered out and the fencing around the lots turned that bleached color everything gets after a winter or two in the desert.

Now it was cleaned up, the fencing was taken down in some parts, replaced in others, and it was starred with lights.

Everyone who told me about the Cirque was right. It *does* look bigger than its sorry little caravan would ever lead you to dream of. It sprawled like a blowsy drunk on a tattered divan, cheap paste jewels glittering.

Cirque de Charnu, the painted boards on the fence barked. The bigtop was up, canvas daubed with leering clown faces and swirls of watery glitter. Faint music rode the flat, whispering wind. The smell of fried food mixed uneasily with the blood-tang of the river, and I caught the undertone of sweat and animal manure too. Shouts and laughter, and a Ferris wheel I would have sworn wasn't part of the caravan spun like a confection of whipped cream and glass. Its winking lights were sterile eyes, and it shuddered as the wind changed. One pair of lights winked out, and I heard the faint ghost of a scream before it righted itself and went whirling merrily on.

We sat in the car overlooking the spectacle; there was a footpath down the embankment leading to the temporary parking lot, already full of vehicles. Little dust devils danced between the neat rows. The fringes of contamination and corruption were thin flabby fingers poking at each tire and dashboard.

Saul was smoking again, cherry tobacco smoke drifting out

his window. The tiny bottle of holy water on a chain around his neck swirled with faint blue. "Smells like a trap," he finally said.

"It is." *A trap for the weak or unwary. Or just for those who don't care anymore.* "You sure you want to come with me?"

A shadow crossed his face. He tapped the ash from the cigarette with a quick, angry motion.

I glanced quickly away, over the carnival. The Ferris wheel halted, its cars swinging and trembling slightly, like leaves in a soft breeze. Its gaunt gantry looked hungry, and a couple lights flickered on the verge of going out.

"I haven't changed my mind yet." He took another drag. His face settled against itself.

I'm not so sure about that. But I didn't say it. "You realize we can't interfere down there. Once we step through the gate—"

"I know the rules. You repeated 'em twice. I'm not stupid, Jill."

"You're right, you're not stupid. But maybe I am." I eyed the layout again. The alleys between the tents looked regular and even, but they also ran like ink on wet paper in the corner of my vision. I had the idea that if I looked away they would move, and snap back together in a different configuration once my gaze returned.

The music halted as the wind veered, then started again. Calliope music, faint and cheery, with screaming underneath. It sounded like a cartoon. The Ferris wheel shuddered again, and another light blinked out. It restarted, creaking, and the music swallowed any sound that might have made its way out.

I blew out between my teeth. Measured off a space on the steering wheel between two index fingers, tapped them both rapidly, a tattoo of dissatisfaction. *Time's wasting, Jill. Get moving.*

When I reached for the door-handle he did too. The Pontiac sat in shadows, her paint job glistening dully. It was a cleaner gleam than the cars in the lot below, or the bright winking lures beyond.

The music struggled up to us as we made our way down the hill, my bootheels occasionally ringing against a stone, Saul silent and graceful. Between the rows of cars, windshields already filmed with dust, gravel shifting under our feet. There was no need to be quiet.

There wasn't much of a crowd milling around the ticket booth.

The scattered people were mostly normal, and they looked dazed. I kept my mouth shut, watching for a few moments as a round brunette in her mid-thirties tilted her head, listening. The calliope music sharpened, predatory glee running under its surface, and she finally stepped up to the booth and handed over a fistful of something. It looked like wet pennies, and the Trader manning the booth—female, heart-shaped face and short black Bettie Page bangs, big dark eyes, and a pair of needle-sharp fangs dimpling her candy-red lower lip—made a complex gesture, then stamped the woman's hand and waved her past.

Saul let out a short sigh. We strode through the confused, each of them averting their eyes like we were some sort of plague. A couple Traders milled with the normals, uncertainly. Most of them flinched and drew into the shadows when they saw me.

The Trader in the booth studied us. She opened her mouth, and I saw all her teeth were sharp and pointed, not just the fangs.

I beat her to the punch. "I'm here on business, Trader. Where's the Ringmaster?"

She shrugged slim, bare flour-white shoulders, her rhinestone-studded Lycra top moving supple over high, perky breasts. Visibly reconsidered when I didn't respond. "Around and about. Probably in the bigtop. Want your hand stamped?"

I snorted. "Of course not. Come on, Saul." I took two steps to the side, heading for the turnstile.

Her sloe eyes narrowed. "Just what are you—" The words died as I stared at her. The corruption blooming over her was strong, and I'd bet diamonds she had weapons under the sightline of the flimsy booth. She tried again. "You can come in. But I'm not so sure *he* can." She actually pointed at Saul with one lacquered-yellow fingernail. It was amazing—I wondered how she wiped herself with claws that long.

Oh, yeah? Quit pointing at my Were, bitch. "He's with me. Go back to seducing suicides," I snapped. We strode past, through the clicking turnstile. Each separate bar of the stile ended in a cheap chrome ram's head, lips drawn back and blunt teeth blackened with grime. The Trader didn't say anything else, but the swirl of corruption lying over the entire complex of canvas and wood tightened.

The spider knows the fly's home.

I didn't like that thought. I also didn't like how the air was suddenly close and warm, almost balmy with a slight edge of humidity. It even smelled wrong—no clean tang of dry desert, no metallic ring from the river or any of the hundred other little components that make up a subconscious map of my city. You spend enough time breathing a place and it'll get into your bones—and when it isn't what it should be, that's when the uneasiness starts right below the hackles.

It was also—surprise, surprise—more crowded inside than out. There wasn't a crush, but it was work threading my way through. The flat shine of the dusted on Trader irises, dazed incomprehension on the shuffling normals, rubbing shoulders and shuffling feet. I saw men in pajamas, a woman in filmy lingerie with her hair in pink curlers, a fiftyish man in work clothes carrying a dripping-wet hammer and wandering walleyed and fish-mouthed like he was six again.

The midway bloomed around us. Pasteboard and flashing lights, buzzing strings of electric bulbs.

"Throw the ball, win a prize!" This was an actual 'breed, female in a red cotton peasant dress. A sleepy-eyed teenager stopped in front of her; she licked her pale lips and smiled at him. Her white, white hands touched his shoulders in a butterfly's caress, but she saw me watching and pushed him aside. He stumbled and rejoined the flow of the crowd.

"Catch a fish!" A Trader in suspenders, a white wifebeater, and a newsboy hat, his ears coming to high hairy points, motioned at a crystal bowl. The fish inside glittered too sharply to be anything but metallic, globules of clear oil bubbling from their mouths. "Win a dream! Lovely dream, freshly colored! Catch a fish!"

A woman hesitated before putting her hand in the bowl. I silently urged her not to, and turned away before she could make her decision. There was a wet, deep crunch. The fish-catcher's savage cry of triumph rose behind me, and I let out a sharp breath, my stomach turning over.

This was what the Cirque did. It separated the weak and suicidal from the just vaguely disaffected. I caught sight of a young woman, mascara dribbling down her cheeks on a flood of tears, mouthing words that seemed to fit the dim seaweed sound of the calliope. Something like "Camptown Races," married to a more savage beat.

Doo-dah, dooo dah.... She shivered, and walked slowly toward an open tent exhaling a flood of beeps and boops like a video arcade. God alone knew what waited for her in there.

Funny, the music should be louder. I shivered, kept pacing. They parted in front of me like heavy molasses, drawing slowly away.

The normals didn't look at me, lost in whatever the calliope was whispering. But the Traders flinched aside, and the 'breed sometimes bared their teeth, or fangs. One, dolled up like a fortune-teller and outside a tent swathed with fluttering nylon scarves, a chipped crystal ball on the round satin-draped table in front of her, actually snarled.

I stopped and stared at her for a good twenty seconds, unblinking, before she dropped her yellow gaze. Her eyes matched her tongue, a jaundiced, scaled thing that flickered past thin lips and dabbed the point of her chin before reeling back into her mouth.

"There's a lot of them," Saul murmured. He kept close, the comforting heat of him touching my back. The silver in my hair was shifting, and the carved ruby at my throat spat a single, bloody spark just as he spoke.

"There always are." *And when the sun rises, maybe a third of them will make it home safe. Those who decide they do want to live after all—or those smart enough to run like hell and make no agreements. Even implicit ones.*

And here I thought I was such a cynic. Probably a lot less than a third would get home.

Lean four-legged shapes slunk in the shadows. Their colorless eyes flashed, and they followed us through the midway. The Ferris wheel rocked at one end, another light winked out, and I heard a shapeless scream, like a man waking from a nightmare in a cold bath of sweat. The calliope music surged, swallowing it. Paper ruffled at our feet—wrappers still hot from popcorn or sticky with cotton candy, gnawed sticks still holding traces of corn-dog mustard or clinging caramel. A man's gold Patek Philippe glittered, flung carelessly on the packed, scuffed dirt. Thick electric cables creaked back and forth under the slow warm breeze.

The entrance to the bigtop was huge, easily as big as a triple garage door. Oiled canvas rubbed against the ropes; tattered pennants fluttered and snapped on seven high-peaked poles. Crowd-noise swelled, and for the first time I heard the rumble of Helletöng bruising the air.

A gangling scarecrow of a male hellbreed lolled in a chair next to a post holding one end of the tattered red velvet rope barring the way. His top hat was pulled down over his eyes, and his spider-like fingers—six on each hand, and a thumb too, bones and tendons flickering under the mottled skin—twitched as I halted.

I eyed him. Threadbare, skintight burlap pants straining every time a skinny leg moved. Biceps so thin I could probably have spanned them with thumb and forefinger. For all that, it was a hellbreed, and usually they aren't so flagrantly unhuman.

Usually they're beautiful, and they like to show it. Except Perry. This one could be a surprise too.

I stepped forward, my heels clicking on gravel, and eyed him. The hat lifted a little, and mad silvery eyes gleamed under a hank of silky dirt-dark hair. The fingers twitched again.

I held the 'breed's gaze for maybe fifteen long seconds, the calliope music drifting up around me in skeins of etheric foulness. The hounds, slinking in the shadows, drew nearer. Saul didn't make a restless movement, but I could guess maybe he wanted to.

"Cut the act." Silver jangled, underscoring my words. "Get me the Ringmaster."

The 'breed tipped his head back further. A pointed chin, hollow cheeks—he was a walking skeleton with mottled skin stretched drum-tight over bones, and I suddenly knew what he was. The knowledge made my hands ache for a weapon again; I controlled the urge.

"Are you sure you want to see him? He's not in a good mood." The 'breed smirked, pointed yellow teeth flashing for just a moment. Strings of thick saliva bubbled behind his lips. I was almost sorry I'd eaten.

"Snap inspection, plague-bearer. And the mood you should be worrying about right now is *mine*. I'm giving you less than two seconds to haul that skinny ass of yours up, and less than ten to bring me the Ringmaster. Or I start shooting 'breed and Traders. Your choice."

It was a nice bluff. Technically, a hunter can snap-inspect any part of the Cirque at any time, and serve summary judgment on any 'breed or Trader caught breaking the rules—for example, pressuring a victim into making a bargain, or in my city, playing with anyone under eighteen. That's pretty much why the Cirque obeys the strictures—first there's the hostage, and then there's *us*, swallowing bile and watching, waiting for them to step out of line.

Of course, people vanish all the time. It's a goddamn epidemic, and whenever the Cirque finally leaves town there's a lull in exorcisms, disappearances, and other nastiness. They eat all they can hold in each town, I guess. And with the pickings so easy once the calliope starts singing, they would be foolish to take any unwilling meat.

Hellbreed aren't fools.

He jolted to his feet, elbows and knees moving in ways human joints weren't designed to, and I almost twitched toward a gun. But he just capered over the red velvet rope and into the bigtop, leaving his chair rocking back and forth, a bloom of powdery yellow dust left behind, eating little holes in the painted wood.

"Plague-bearer?" Saul murmured.

"You don't want to touch that stuff." My nerves were scraped raw, my back crawling with the thought of so many of Hell's citizens in one place, a cancer in the middle of my vulnerable city.

My apprentice-ring cooled, turning to ice on my finger. It twitched, sharply, twice. It was the first time since I'd met the Cirque outside town that it had made any sort of motion at all.

I tilted my head, listening. The calliope music surged, screaming puffs through chrome-throated pipes. I shut it away, despite the plucking underneath the music—*come in, come in, lay your troubles down, play a game, become one of us, one of us, just give in, stop struggling.*

My attention turned, coasting through the flood of sensory information. Dust, hot frying fat, screams, chewing noises, stamping feet, a horse's screaming whinny.

And a long, drawn-out rattling gasp.

I came back to myself with a jolt, spun on my heel, and leapt into a run. Saul's footsteps were soundless behind me.

The bigtop blurred past on one side, yards and yards of canvas. It drew away like a wave threatening to crest, and I plunged into a network of tents and alleys, half-lit. Here was one of the older parts of the carnival—the air was thick with a reek of spilled sex, and the tent flaps were always half-open. Moans and ghastly shrieks ribboned past, the calliope suddenly crooning. Traders with gem-bright eyes, hellbreed with seashell hips and candied mouths, lounging in the entrances to their tents, seducing and beckoning—

I veered off to the left, my apprentice-ring pulling like a fish on a thin line. The tents gave way to trailers, and I passed the limousine sitting still and polished under a rigged-up canvas canopy. The headlights flickered once, green, as I flashed past.

A huge silver Airstream rocked as I left the ground in a flying kick, etheric force booming through the scar and filling my veins with sick heat. My boot hit the door, which crumpled and exploded in. A terrible, sour-sewer smell puffed past me, and I heard Saul's surprised half-yell.

The trailer was small, and every surface inside was crawling. Little bits of darkness moved, fluttering chitinous legs and wings twitched as the roaches spilled over every surface. A pinprick of laser-red light glowed on the back of every goddamn insect, and they startled into flight as I let out a half-swallowed, childlike cry of revulsion.

Hey, they were bugs, and they surprised me.

The tide of insect life streamed past me, little hairy legs touching and brushing. Saul's coughing growl warned me.

I couldn't worry about the inside of the trailer just at the moment. There was something behind me, and Saul barely managed to get the warning out in time.

I threw myself back and down, landing hard on the two portable wooden steps leading up to the crumpled door. I'd blown a hole in the side of the trailer, and I shot the Ringmaster four times as he hung in the air over me, the crystal knob atop his cane ringing a high piercing note as a silverjacket bullet bounced off or past it, whining until it smashed into the side of his leering, screaming face. It even knocked his hat off.

He dropped straight down. My knees jerked up, I rolled backward down the steps. My shoulder grated hard and popped against straining wood, the edge of a step biting the back of my neck before I made a lunging, fishlike twist and was suddenly, irrationally on my feet but facing the wrong way, whirling and dropping to one knee as the whip flicked out. The silver flechettes tied to the end of its length jingled sweetly before they flayed flesh from the Ringmaster's wrist, and his cane clattered away, the crystal bouncing down first as if it was too heavy for the laws of physics.

The 'breed was bleeding, gushes of thin black ichor flooding out from every hole I'd blown in his tough shell. The roaches swarmed him, the pinpricks of red on their back dividing as they multiplied, and he screamed in Helletöng, a sound like the rusted sinews of the world groaning. The fabric of reality bowed around him in concentric circles, and the little insects burst, clattering shells puffing into sick green smoke as they hit the dust. The Ringmaster shouldered his way up out of the curls of vapor, his eyes dripping pumpkin hellfire, and snarled. The stairs splintered and groaned.

When you get to see under the carapace of beauty, the brain shudders aside from their alienness. A hunter who's been to Hell has seen this before, and it gives you a slight edge. You don't run screaming-insane every time they shed their human seeming and show the twisted thing underneath.

But it's awful close.

I remained on one knee, instinct fighting with cold logic. If he leapt for me, my chances were better here, where I was centered and had some clear space, than if I tried to get to my feet now. Training won out, and I stayed where I was, gun in my right hand and whip in the other, shaken free with a jingling sound. Saul was to one side, still growling but staying out of the way—just where he should have been.

A choked rattle echoed inside the gaunt silver trailer. My apprentice-ring cooled, a band of ice on my third left finger. The Ringmaster snarled and doubled over, falling to the ground with a wet writhing thump. Black ichor splashed, and the entire Cirque stilled, the faint ever-present calliope music skipping a beat. It limped and wheezed, gaps opening between the notes.

What the hell?

The Ringmaster screamed, and his cane quivered. The thin cry was echoed from inside the trailer, and I was suddenly sure that something else was happening I'd better take a look at.

I uncoiled, force pulled through the scar, and cleared the busted stairs and the Ringmaster in one leap. Landed on my toes, my center of gravity pulled up high and tight, and plunged into the trailer.

A pale shape lay, seizure bowing it up into a hoop, on the frowsty shelf-bed. It was the hostage, and just as I reached the side of the bed, wading through a drift of empty clicking shells and candy bar wrappers, the Trader began to rattle deep down in his chest.

Oh, fuck.

The hostage was dying. And if he shuffled off the mortal coil now, we were looking at a seriously fucked-up situation.

I dropped the whip, shoved the gun back in its holster, and leapt for the bed.

CHAPTER 8

My hellbreed-strong right hand closed around Ikaros's throat, and I braced myself, knees on either side of his narrow rib cage. "Oh, no you *don't,*" I snarled, and ripped the leather wristcuff free, one of the buckles breaking and hitting the side of the trailer with a sweet tinkle.

A razor-barbed mass of etheric energy pooled in my palm, slammed through the Trader's body. The ratcheting sound from his narrow chest peaked, and I heard the Ringmaster howl like a damned soul outside.

Get it, Jill? Like a damned soul? Arf, arf.

The air turned hard and dark, something alien pressing through the fabric of reality, hovering over the twisting body on the bed. I took in a harsh breath and *pushed,* the sea-urchin spikes of my aura dappling the inside of the trailer with aqueous light. The sudden welter of sensory overload from the scar's unveiling crested

over me, my skin suddenly alive and my nose full of a complicated tangle of scents. Tears welled up hot and hard, my eyes coping with a sudden onslaught, every crack and wrinkle in the world
visible.

The Trader hostage twitched and convulsed again, his teeth
actually grinding. The collar's spikes bit my skin, blessed metal
burning. I let out a short hawk's cry, the force of whatever was
torturing the Trader giving me a short, hard punch in the solar
plexus. It tasted like lit-up liquor fumes and hit the back of my
throat, roared past me like a barreling freight train.

My free left hand jabbed up, two fingers snapping out, lined
with twisting sorcerous flame. Banefire burned blue, hissing, but
there was no helltaint for it to catch hold of.

The thing struggling to come through hit me hard in the face,
my head snapping aside, and blood exploded from my mouth and
nose in a bright gush, droplets hanging in a perfect arc for a long
timeless second before splashing against the trailer wall.

So banefire wasn't going to work. Ikaros surged underneath
me again, his body moving in weird angled jumps, like his bones
were trying to turn themselves into rubbery corkscrews.

Goddammit, what the hell is going on here?

Fortunately, banefire wasn't the only trick up my sleeve. Intuition meshed with recent memory, and as he screamed so did I,
our twinned voices rising in harmony again as my fingers tightened, the collar's spikes dragged at the meat of my wrist and forearm again, and I *pushed* with every ounce of sorcerous strength I
could dredge up in an entirely different direction.

As if I was exorcising him.

The pressure built, excruciating heat behind my bulging eyeballs and under my stomach, the last bit of air escaping me in a
huuuungh! of effort. Ikaros rattled again, but this time it wasn't
the hideous *I'm-dying* type of rattle. No, this time it was the inhale
of blessed sweet air, and my apprentice-ring gave another twinging pull. He began to thrash with inhuman strength, but without
the corkscrewing weirdness.

The thing hovering over him snapped with a sound like thick
elastic breaking, a high, hard *pop!* that might have been funny if
there hadn't been a sudden gush of green smoke and chittering

legs. The roaches swarmed, falling out of a point in thin air directly above us, and both of us yelled in miserable surprise. The roaches vanished as they peppered us, more sickly pea-soup smoke eddied and billowed, and the Trader surged up.

He had a lot of pep for someone who was just being sorcerously strangled a few seconds ago. But I had the upper hand and my booted foot on one of his wrists in a trice, and I ground down with the steelshod heel, a simple flexing movement. The collar slashed even more cruelly at my wrist, but I ignored the pain rolling up my arm, hot blood slicking my grip on the hostage's throat. "Settle the fuck *down!*" I yelled. "Settle *down,* I'm trying to *help!*"

The irony of the situation—I was yelling that I was trying to help a Trader—didn't escape me. He subsided just a little, blue eyes rolling like a terrified horse's. I waited until I was sure he wasn't going to thrash again and eased up just slightly on his throat. He kept breathing in high harsh whistles.

I kept watching, loosening my fingers by increments. They actually creaked, I moved so slowly. Harsh voices babbled outside, a whirlpool of surprise, and I heard a werecougar's low thrumming growl.

That managed to get me off the bed, shaking out my right hand. Blood flew, dripping down from my scored wrist, and I was suddenly glad none of the blessed silver spikes had touched the scar. I'd had silver against the hellbreed kiss once before, and had no desire to repeat the experience.

Ikaros lay, his ribs flickering with deep heaving breaths, on the tangled bed. His eyes closed, heavily, and he curled into a ball as I backed away. I realized he was naked, light dancing and dappling his haunches. Old burn scars traveled up both legs, clasping his buttocks with angry rope fingers. I scooped up my whip without pausing, two strides kicking up a tide of candy bar wrappers. The green smoke began to thin, and the empty cockroach shells were vanishing with little crackling popcorn sounds.

The stairs were indeed shattered, and Saul crouched in front of them, one hand braced on the dusty earth. The trembling in his aura told me he was just on the edge of shifting, and his snarl rose steadily.

I didn't blame him. Because gathered in a loose semicircle, pressing close in an arc of sharp teeth and hellfire-glowing eyes, were hellbreed and Traders. The Ringmaster hooked his cane up with one clawed hand, the crystal spitting spark after agonized green spark and his entire tattered costume swimming and dripping black ichor.

It was going to hurt as he healed, the silver residue poisoning him. *Let's hope it doesn't make him crazier than he already is. Control the situation, Jill.* I cleared leather, pointed the gun up, and squeezed off a shot. The sound crackled through both Saul's growl and the rising noise coming from the hellbreed, a deep thrum of Helletöng like iron balloons rubbing together.

"Good evening, everyone." I paused for a breath. All eyes turned to me except Saul's, and the crowd of 'breed and Traders took in a collective breath. Silver hissed in my hair, the charms moving angrily. "Seems someone has a bit of a grudge against your hostage. I just saved his life." Another pause, this one taking a different tenor as the gun came down and swept slowly, leisurely, along the front of the crowd. "Anyone have a problem with that?"

There's a definite proportion of this job that is just plain theater. The little bitches don't take you seriously unless you act the part. I used to think Mikhail enjoyed the acting, but then I figured out he was really a fan of getting the job done in the shortest amount of time so he could move on to the next. It just goes more efficiently with the right proportion of fuck-you posturing.

The gun swept the front of their ranks again. Saul had stopped growling, but he still quivered with readiness. The Ringmaster straightened slowly, shook himself like a cat shedding water. Half his face was peppered with threads of damage. The black spikes of hair covering his head were plastered down, and thin foul-smelling ichor splashed free of his quick little movements. Little threads of white smoke curled up when the droplets hit the dust.

Silence stretched. Even the calliope was silent, the entire glass bowl of the Cirque holding its breath. If this went on much longer I'd probably have to actually kill someone to keep the peace.

My only trouble was figuring out where to start.

The Ringmaster hobbled forward. "Our hostage still lives," he rasped, and I tried not to feel relieved.

Watch him, Jill. He's a tricky little bastard. I hopped down, avoiding the broken steps. "Of course he does. He ends up dead and I have to kill every motherfucking last one of you. What the fuck are you up to out here?" *And where's Perry?*

"I do not," the Ringmaster husked, slowly, "answer to *you.*"

I made a small beeping noise. The gun settled on him, my pulse cooling immediately. "Wrong answer, hellspawn. This is my town, you *do* answer to me. I am not having my city fucked up because you guys brought bad business with you."

"You blame this on *us?*" He actually bristled.

Yes, *bristled,* his hair standing up in ichor-stiffened spikes, his skin turning mottled and pinpricks of the shape underneath poking out through the skin. Each hole I'd blown in his shell ran with diseased orange foxfire.

An elegantly manicured hand closed around his shoulder and squeezed, grinding. Perry pushed the Ringmaster down, the thin 'breed's knees folding until they hit the dirt.

"Of course she blames you," he said conversationally, his eyes glowing gasflame-blue, a deep indigo inkstain threading through the whites. "I must confess I am halfway to blaming you myself, *brother.*"

The assembled 'breed and Traders drew away in a single coordinated movement. Perry twisted his wrist slightly, and ground his fingers in. It was a slight movement, and didn't look like much unless you know how horribly, hurtfully strong hellbreed are. A meaty popping sound—like bones crunching in a side of beef—cut through the breezy silence, and I heard another short cry from somewhere in the Cirque's depths. It was either a peacock's scream, someone dying, or a woman in full-throated orgasm.

Take your pick. The show must go on, I guess.

"Let me be exquisitely clear," Perry continued. Another one of those meaty sounds, and the Ringmaster turned the cheesy-pale shade of a mushroom in a wet cellar. I'd shot him in that shoulder, and I was suddenly sure Perry was grinding the silverjacket bullet—or whatever was left of it after it mushroomed in hellbreed flesh—in deeper. "Our hunter will follow this attack to its source. If that source connects with you in any way, if this is a bid for domination or spoliation of *my* territory, I will be exceedingly displeased. Do you understand me, carrion?" His tongue flickered out as he grinned, the cherry-wet redness of it gleaming. A low buzzing, like chrome flies in chlorinated bottles, filled the space behind and between each word. The popping of vanishing cockroach shells finally petered out.

The scar had turned to a hot pucker of acid. I swallowed, kept the gun steady. Saul's shoulders were rigidly straight, and I suddenly wished I was in front of him. He was between me and a whole fuckload of 'breed and Traders, and some of them were eyeing him instead of watching Perry and their boss.

Just be cool, Jill. No need to sweat anything. I eased forward two steps, my coat whispering as warm redolent air caressed it.

"Understood." Great pearls of watery ichor beaded up on the Ringmaster's narrow face. He wasn't nearly as pretty now. The prickling hadn't gone away either. The thing that lived under his mask of humanity snarled and cringed.

"That's very good." Perry's gaze flicked across me. The urge to freeze warred with iron training; training, as always, won out. I took another single step, the scar twisting and burrowing, my pulse ratcheting up before I could force it back down. "Kiss?"

Don't call me that, goddammit. God, I wanted to say that to him just once and wipe that smirk off his face. But if I did, it would be blood in the water. Who could guess what he would come up with if he knew something so simple bugged the shit out of me?

It took an effort of will to lower the gun. "Something was definitely attacking the hostage."

"So I gathered." He simply stood there, as if he wasn't holding a cringing hellbreed like a mama cat will hold an offending, writhing kitten. "Who is the offender, avenging one?"

"Don't know yet." I paused, weighing the next sentence. "I'm fairly sure it wasn't 'breed, though."

It had the intended effect. Everyone, including Saul—and he had to twist halfway around in his lean easy crouch—stared at me.

All eyes on you, Jill.

"You are certain of this?" Perry didn't drop the Ringmaster, but his eyes narrowed slightly. His fingers still held the other 'breed immobilized, but some of the hurtful tension drained out of him.

"Fairly certain. Last time I checked, hellspawn don't use voo-doo. Any reason why someone on the side of the *loa* would have a hard-on for a Cirque de Charnu hostage?"

If the silence before was glassy, the silence that followed was molasses-thick. It was broken only by the soundless buzz of my pager in its padded pocket. Bright eyes sparked in the gloom, the hellbreeds' with varying red and orange tones, an occasional yellow speckle; and the Traders' with their flat dusty shine.

Nobody said a fucking word. The trailer behind me rocked a little on its springs, and a faint groan slid from its depths. Ikaros was probably feeling a little better.

Saving a Trader's life was a novelty, and not one I liked.

"Someone had better start explaining things to me." I took perverse joy in using the same tone a teacher would with a class of young imbeciles.

Perry's fingers tightened again. The Ringmaster's pale face contorted, but he didn't make a sound. If this kept up we were going to have yet another Bad Situation.

"Ease up on him, Pericles." I dug for my pager, every nerve alert. It would take very little to turn this entire mob into a melee, especially with the way most of them were now shifting their attention, ever so slowly, toward Perry. And while I didn't particularly mind the thought of them tearing him apart in little quivering pieces, I minded the thought of dealing with the Cirque *and* a scramble for power among the hellbreed who jostled in Perry's long deep shadow. "He's got the most to lose if the hostage bites it."

The number on the pager was familiar, and my intuition tingled. *Huh.*

"Voodoo?" Perry pronounced the word like he didn't know what it meant. Saul rose as soon as I took another step forward, gravel shifting under his booted feet. His was the only warmth in this place that didn't make me feel like slime was trickling over my skin.

"Yeah, voodoo. As in, the *loa* taking an interest in this, or someone who has enough credit with them to make a Trader uncomfortable. Nobody wants to tell me why anyone would have a grudge against the Cirque?" I don't think I could have sounded any more sarcastic. "Or why there were roaches crawling all over your sorcerously-being-strangled hostage not five minutes ago? Or something about this murder I'm supposed to be looking into?"

The bitter, rancid grumbling of Helletöng rose. It cut short when I swept my gaze over them and tapped at a gun butt with one bitten-down fingernail. "English," I said softly. "Good old-fashioned American English. None of this töng shit."

I couldn't even feel good about glaring a bunch of 'breed into silence.

Perry finally bestirred himself to speak. "One of the performers has been murdered." He let go of the Ringmaster, who crumpled and caught himself on hands and knees, ichor splashing and his cane making a soft chiming sound that sliced the stillness. "We shall examine the evidence."

Well, la-di-da. Of course we shall, Pericles. But I didn't want to give him control of the situation just now. "Wait a second. First things first. Who died, who found the body, and who had the last contact with the victim?"

It was amazing to watch them move like quicksilver, exploding away from one tall male Trader who hunched, his eyes grown round and desperate. He wore a straw hat and suspenders, and looked vaguely familiar in the way all blond, dark-eyed men with ferret faces do. You know the type—the narrow-eyed, unreliably handsome, and just waiting to slip a thin knife between your ribs and *twist*.

Yeah. That kind. Especially in a frayed, worn linen button-down and a pair of gray pinstripe trousers that wouldn't have looked out of place on an Edwardian dandy. The flat shine of Trader on his irises looked weird for a moment, like two silver pennies.

Perry beat me to the punch. He sounded kind and avuncular, and the only thing more terrifying was the way everyone in the crowd shivered and pulled back further. "And just who are you?"

The Trader snatched at his hat, his silken thatch of hair damp with sweat. I suspected he'd look vaguely pretty in daylight, but here in the dim shifting light the pointed jaw became strong and his wide cheekbones merely masculine instead of pugnacious.

Then he opened his mouth. "T-T-T-Tr—"

He stammered.

I frankly stared. What kind of joke was this? Hellbreed don't usually Trade with someone so flawed, and Traders usually bargain for beauty as well as weird body mods. This guy must have something else to recommend him—smarts, or viciousness.

"Dear heavens." Perry made a mocking little moue, his lips twisting. "Were you a joke?"

"N-n-nosir. J-j-just a k-k-carny. I'm T-T-Tr-Troy. I w-was H-Helene's t-t-t-t—"

He kept going with the t's, his face contorting. Perry tapped one elegant wingtip, his shark's grin widening.

"*Talker,*" the unfortunate Trader finally spit out. "H-Helene's t-talker."

This is going to take a while. I glanced at the number on my pager again, suppressed a sigh. Stuffed it back in my pocket. "Helene? 'Breed or Trader?"

"'Breed," Perry answered. "You would have enjoyed it, Kiss."

Enjoyed what? I didn't ask. "I do not have all night. You were the last person to see the victim?"

He simply nodded. Thank God.

"All right." I dropped the hand resting on my gun butt with an effort. Saul was still and quiet behind me. "Show me."

"What do you want done with him?" Perry gestured at the Ringmaster, who shivered again, more foul-smelling ichor splattering. "He will survive this night, if you let him. Unless the hostage is attacked again."

What a lovely thought, Perry. Thanks. "Leave him alone." I weighed the words, felt the need to add more. "I've just gotten used to his ugly face. I'd hate to have someone new to deal with."

CHAPTER 9

The 'breed named Helene had died in a gaudy tent painted with screaming-red broken-open pomegranates and big stalks of green vegetable. After a few moments I identified the green stuff as leeks, and weird creeping laughter crawled up my throat, was strangled, and died away. "So what was this Helene's act?"

"Fruit seller?" Saul piped up, and a great scalding wave of relief went through me. He sounded okay.

Perry, a respectful distance away, actually sniggered. It was the sound of a popular kid in high school tittering in the back of the room. "Hermaphrodite."

Suddenly the leeks and pomegranates made sense. "A hermaphrodite hellbreed?"

His bland blond face split in a wide grin. "Hell has its freaks too. Here is where they prove their worth."

Which was another lovely thought.

Troy pushed aside the spangled curtain over the door-opening. "In h-here."

"A stuttering barker?" I had to know. "How did you—"

He half-turned, his dusted eyes glittering sharply. "*Step right up!*" His face contorted, and a thin thread of cold slid down my back. Instead of a piping stammer, what came out was a rich, seductive baritone. "*See the half-man, half-woman, all loveliness! Step right up, ladies and gentlemen!*"

I folded my arms. "That's what you Traded for?"

He shrugged. "H-Helene t-taught me. L-l-like s-s-s-singing. Sh-sh-she was n-n-n-n—"

Oh, my God, is he about to say "nice"? Now I've heard everything.

"Spare me your love song," Perry cut in. "What happened?"

For once I agreed with him, but I might've liked to hear more.

"It was a s-slow n-night." The Trader spoke very slowly, trying to enunciate each word clearly. "I w-was b-barking, b-but there were n-n-no t-t-takers. I w-was d-d-doing my b-best. F-first n-night's always s-s-slow—"

"Get. To the. Point." Perry tapped his foot again.

"Shut up and let him talk, Pericles." *This is going to take even longer if you keep making him nervous.*

"But of course, my dear. Anything for you." The indigo still hadn't left his whites, veining through like cracks in glazed porcelain. His suit fluttered slightly at the edges, white linen mouthed by the warm damp breeze redolent with the smell of fried grease.

"She s-s-sc-screamed." The Trader was pale as milk, his unreliable face twisting as he tried to get the words out. "I th-thought a r-r-r-rube was g-g-getting n-nasty. B-but they d-d-don't usually. S-s-s-so I w-w-went in." He shuddered, the movement rippling through his skinny frame. Beads of sweat stood out on his fore-head. "Th-th-there were b-b-bugs."

Bugs? "Flies? Or mosquitoes?"

Hey, you can't ever trust them to tell the truth.

"R-r-roaches." Another shudder. His red suspenders actually creaked. "All over. W-with r-red spots." He ducked into the tent and I followed, Saul behind me as close as my shadow. I had a moment's worth of worry—Perry was right behind my Were.

Jesus. This is getting ridiculous.

It certainly was.

The smell hit me between one step and the next. They rot fast when they go, just like Traders. There was a wide greasy stain on the small strip of planking serving as a stage. The rest of the place was scattered with pillows and rugs, a bargain-basement impres-sion of a harem helped along by the rusted glass-and-iron hookahs scattered around. Each pipe was at least four feet high, scalloped and decorated to within an inch of its life. Frayed tassels hung everywhere, and behind the stage hung a tapestry of trees and riv-ers that shifted, its stitches running over each other with a faint sound of needles against fabric.

"It looks like a whorehouse," Saul muttered, and I heartily agreed.

"Have you been in one lately, cat?" Perry inquired sweetly.

"Perry?" I checked the circuit of the tent, examined the stage's raw lumber. Three red satin cushions were covered in thin black gunk dried to a crust.

"Yes, my dear?" Silky-smooth, but he didn't look at me.

"Shut the fuck up." I inhaled deeply, wished I hadn't. Under the reek of sex, tobacco, and marijuana lay the rusted-copper tang of blood and a breath of . . . what was that?

Cigar smoke. Candy. And rum. It was very faint, fading even as I inhaled deeply again, trying to catch another whiff. *Now that's interesting.*

"I was only asking." Perry eased into the tent, his lip curling. "Such petty games played here."

"As opposed to the ones played out at the Monde?" It was my turn to inquire sweetly. "If you're not going to be helpful, you can wait outside."

His tongue flickered over white teeth, a flash of wet cherry-red. "I can be singularly helpful, for your sake."

Oh, I'll just bet. "Good. You're going to stay here and keep an eye on the hostage. I've got other business tonight."

"I might have business too."

The scar turned hot, and a spill of poisonous delight threaded up my arm. "Too bad. Now that you've seen the crime scene, you can run along."

"Dismissed by my lady." He sighed, but the scar tweaked.

So he was getting to the point of pulling my chain, was he? Hellbreed hate being outfoxed, and they hate being outfoxed by their own cleverness even more. If Perry hadn't been so eager to use a measure of what he thought was his newfound psychological leverage on me, he wouldn't have lost every bit of his hold— including the ironclad agreement to have me in every month. My time for his power; that had been the deal—and when he welshed, it was his power for nothing.

Except I had to step carefully, or I would get trapped again. And he would make me pay for every insult I offered him.

Still, that wasn't a reason not to twit him while I could. And I wanted him out of the way for the next ten minutes. The stuttering Trader looked ready to die from fright, and couldn't get out a coherent sentence.

I understood. I didn't sympathize, but I completely understood.

"I'm not your lady *or* your hunter, Pericles. I'm the hunter of Santa Luz and I'm telling you to keep a close watch on the Ringmaster and that hostage. You're responsible for their good behavior. And not so incidentally, for the hostage's continued survival." I was apparently staring at the stain on the stage. My attention was all on him, though. The Trader crouched with his face level to the planking, peeping up at the red satin pillows like a kid looking through the banister for Santa Claus. "Now be a good little hellspawn and run along."

The air tightened, and I wondered if this was going to be the

time that Perry pushed it. It was getting more and more likely the
longer this went on.

But apparently, he was just as invested in keeping the Cirque
under wraps as I was. I was banking on that. So often, I was banking on the flimsiest things to keep him from seriously fucking
around with me.

It is the woman, has the advantage in situations like this,
milaya. *You just remember that.* Mikhail's voice, a memory equal
parts pleasure and pain.

I was hoping, like always, that it was true.

"Very well," Perry finally said. "Happy hunting, my dear. I
expect this...situation...to be resolved shortly."

"The longer you stand here jawing, the less likely that is."
*Unless you've got some elegant little finger in this pie, which is
very possible. I'm not ruling* anything *out.*

But still...voodoo. The one thing pretty much no hellbreed
would be involved in.

Perry's presence leached out of the room slowly, like an invisible heavy gas. The Trader still crouched, peering up at the stage,
and I sighed.

"So, this Helene. Did she have any enemies?" I was fully aware
of the irony of the question.

"O-only th-the u-usual." The stammer *did* get better with
Perry out of the room. The ferret-faced blond shot me a glance
that could have meant anything. "You're n-not going to l-look for
whoever d-d-did this."

"Are you kidding? Of course I am." I studied the stage again,
and suddenly saw how Helene probably lay down—in a way guaranteed to show off the goods to the maximum number of people
in the room. "Was she between showings? In here alone?"

"N-no. Th-there were r-rubes. Not very m-many." He was
damn near peppy with Perry out of the picture, and I suddenly
thought I liked him better when he was scared. The self-serving
little weasel glint in Trader eyes always makes me want to reach
for a weapon.

It's that same weasel glint I used to see in my mother's eyes when
one of her boyfriends was on the rampage. A cold calculation—*how*

much can I get? How can I use something else to get out of this? What's in it for me?

"Sh-she was just a 'b-b-breed. I know what y-you h-hunters are l-like."

You do, huh? Well. That's nice. "Is that so." There were tiny pinpricks dotting out from the stain in random twin loops—cockroach tracks. They stopped cold about two feet from the body.

Little skittering roach-tracks. Did they vanish in a puff of green smoke too?

"So what did the...the *rubes* see? Any of them still around?" *Did any of them get home safe, either?*

"D-d-don't kn-know. Was b-busy trying to g-get the b-b-b-bugs—" His face flushed. "Bugs. Away."

"Did the bugs do that?" I pointed at the stain. "Was she making any sound? Choking?"

"S-screaming. And th-they r-ripped h-her ap-p-part. N-n-not m-much l-left."

I questioned him a little more, but he either knew nothing or covered it really well. The way he crouched right next to the stage was unnerving, and the story was even more so. Bugs descending out of nowhere, and an invisible force ripping a hellbreed to pieces? Or strangling a Trader?

There may have been a time when I might've decided to let that pass. But if the hostage ended up biting it...it just didn't bear thinking about. The Cirque would explode out of its boundaries, and I'd have a hell of a time getting things back under control again.

Get it, Jill? A Hell of a time? Arf arf.

Whoever was doing this probably had a beef with hellbreed or the right idea. But they were going about it in exactly the wrong way.

CHAPTER 10

Thank God," Eva said as I muscled up through the attic trapdoor, her dark eyes widening with relief.

She says that every time I show up. It's kind of nice to hear.

She nodded at Saul, her tiny gold ball earrings flashing. She used to wear hoops until they almost got torn off her head five times in a row during exorcisms.

She's stubborn like that.

Eva's black bangs were disarranged, and her suit jacket was torn. It hadn't been any trick finding her here—the victim was still making enough noise to be heard on the street outside. Fortunately (or not), here at the edge of the barrio nobody paid much attention. It wasn't like her to look so mussed, though. She's usually neat as a pin. While Avery, Wallace, and Benito often go in guns blazing, Eva depends more on outsmarting and leverage.

When you're short even compared to me, I guess that's the better way to go. Of course, Mikhail probably trained me because I tend to go in guns blazin' too. Call it a character quirk.

Hey, when you've got a hellbreed mark, firepower, and a serious rage problem, leverage and tact lose a lot of their charm.

"What the hell do you have here?" I looked past her and saw something familiar—a human shape on a pair of stacked mattresses, writhing around under a sausage-casing of leather restraints. And babbling in something that sounded very familiar, too—not the grumbling of töng, but a lyrical rolling song.

"Guy's wife called 911, said he was going weird. The black-and-whites called me in, since he was holed up in the attic and chanting."

"It wasn't Jughead Vanner, was it?"

She gave me a look that could qualify both as *amused* and *what the hell?* "No, it was Connor and the Pole. I sent them both on and the wife's at her mother's. She asked if we could help him, I said I wasn't sure."

Safe answer. "Huh. Did he go to church?"

"Nope. She does. Sacred Grace. Rourke's her confessor. There are a couple of indicators, but not enough to red-flag our boy. I'm stumped."

Saul's lip lifted at the mention of Rourke. He was on the ladder leading up into the attic, his shoulders barely clearing the small entrance. He hadn't said a word since we left the Cirque. It was quiet even for him, and I suspected trouble.

First things first, though.

Huh. I still hadn't really spoken to any of the priests at Sacred Grace since the last incident with the Sorrows. I had decided, after much reflection, not to tear the whole fucking place apart to find anything else Father Gui and his happy band of priests was hiding from me. I hadn't *forgiven* Gui yet, but I hadn't stopped doing exorcisms for them either.

There was being justifiably angry over them hiding necessary information from me, and then there was being stupid.

"Does she bring home novenas?" I stepped past Eva, clearing the way for Saul to come up.

"Yup. There's a whole clutch of them on the mantel downstairs. The husband's supposed to be irreligious, which is a surprise. Part of why I called you. And Avery said—"

"Yeah, Avery. How are you two?"

"He's good." She didn't blush, but she did smile slightly, an ironclad grimace. On her pretty, wide-cheeked face, it was amazing. She has delicate fingers and a strong nose, and is built like a gymnast. It probably helps when she's wrestling Possessors. Of all of my standard exorcists, Avery comes closest to having the qualities necessary for a hunter, but Eva is the one who thinks fastest—and most thoroughly—on her feet. And she's also the calmest. She paints eggshells *a la Fabergé* to relax, I'm told. It's exactly the sort of finicky, delicate thing I'd expect her to do. "This doesn't feel like a Possessor."

It probably isn't. "Good call. Got a mirror?"

"Of course." She wasn't male, so she didn't bother with useless questions. She just dug in her black bag—exorcists favor the old medical bags, since they're just the right size and can be dropped in a hurry—and fished out a hand mirror. "The victim's Trevor

Watson. Male, African American. Forty-three, works as an orderly out at Henderson Hill. Likes beer, soft pretzels, and his wife. The marriage seems happy, the financial side stable but not luxurious by any stretch. *Scratchin'* is what the wife called it. She's Hispanic, thirty-eight, registered nurse."

"He works at Henderson?" That was interesting. Mental institutions can sometimes lead to cross-contamination in possession cases. Not as often as you think, though—plenty of people in institutions are indigent, and Possessors don't go for *that*.

"Yeah. The *new* one." It went without saying, but she said it anyway.

Our eyes met. I suppressed a shiver at the thought of the old asylum. It wasn't a nice place for anyone with a degree of psychic talent, and I'd chased an *arkeus* or two up into its cold, haunted halls. Nobody worked up at the old Henderson Hill but an old, half-blind, mute caretaker who didn't care what happened as long as he could sit in the boiler room with his quart of rye. He seemed more a fixture of the place than the old furnace itself, and I'd given up wondering exactly what he was, since he didn't interfere with any case that took me up there.

The man on the mattresses writhed and gurgled. "He chewed through a gag," Eva said helpfully. "I was worried until nothing happened."

Since Possessors—and *loa*—can snap curses at an exorcist with a victim's mouth, I didn't blame her. "Reasonable of you. How did the mattresses get up here?"

"I don't know. The wife said they never used the attic."

Curiouser and curiouser.

Saul lifted himself up from the steps. "Smells like the other one, Jill."

I stopped, gave him a quizzical look. "Really?"

"Cigars. And candy." He sniffed, inhaling deeply, tasting the air. "An orange-y perfume."

"Florida water?" I hazarded. It was a reasonable guess.

"Could be. But there's a lot of sugar. Like cookies."

Huh. Even with my senses amped up and the scar naked to the open air, I smelled nothing but dust, fiberglass insulation, and the remains of a recent fried chicken. "Well."

"*Bruuuuuja,*" the victim crooned. "*Ay, bruuuuja!* Come heee-eeere."

Eva actually jumped. "What the—"

I shushed her. *Jesus. This can't be what I think it is.*

"*Bruuuuuuja!*" A long, drawn-out sigh. The voice was eerie, neither male nor female, a sweet high piping. "We want to *talk* to you!"

"*Madre de Dios.*" Eva crossed herself.

Amen to that, I thought. "Leave your bag. Go downstairs and start saying Hail Marys. Saul—"

"Not going anywhere." Saul folded his arms as Eva brushed past him. She didn't even argue—another thing I could be thankful for. Sometimes a civilian will try to protest or object or something.

My mouth was dry. "If he gets loose, keep him from getting downstairs. Got it?"

He nodded, his eyes lighting up. I liked seeing that, and wished I had time to ask him what was going on with him. A good hour or so to worm out what was bothering him and maybe get somewhere would have been nice.

But duty always calls. I dug in Eva's bag until I came up with a taper candle and a mini-bottle of blessed wine. Father Gui blesses these tiny bottles in job lots, having a dispensation from high-up in the Vatican to perform some of the, ahem, *older* blessings.

It wasn't rum or tequila, but it would do. The victim started moaning again, and I uncapped the bottle. It was a moment's work to stare at the candle wick, the scar prickling with etheric energy bleeding down a vein-map into my fingertips, until the waxed linen sparked and bloomed with orange flame.

The attic *shifted* around me, turning darker. The shadows took on a sharper edge, hanging insulation moving slightly, though the air was dead still.

One of the oldest truths in sympathetic magic: *to light a candle is to cast a shadow.* If I didn't believe Hell predated humanity—having it on good authority—I'd think that human beings had created it. As it is, we do our bargain-basement best up here on Earth, don't we?

I wonder about that sometimes. Not enough to give myself the blue funks Mikhail used to withdraw into, but enough to make me question this entire line of work.

It's a good thing. Without the questioning I'm just another vigilante with a gun.

The taper's flame held steady. The liquid in the bottle trembled slightly, but that could have been the tension blooming in my midsection. This wasn't your ordinary exorcism, and things were beginning to take on a pattern. *Find the pattern, find your prey;* that's an old hunter maxim too.

"You want to talk to me?" I pitched my voice loud enough to carry. "Here I am."

The victim flopped against the restraints like a fish. I wondered how Eva had gotten him tied down. He looked to be twice her size.

But when a girl's motivated, miracles are possible.

I chose my footing carefully, my dumb eye on the candleflame and my smart eye soft-focused, scanning the etheric congestion over the mattresses. It still bugged me—the floor was dusty, no drag marks—so what were mattresses doing up here?

The flooring creaked. Veils of insulation shifted. It was still warm up here after the day's heat, and a prickle of sweat touched my forehead. It wasn't because of the temperature, though.

The candleflame wavered, but I was quick, shifting my weight just a half-step to the side. The strike slid past me, boards groaning, and I heard Saul skip nimbly aside. *Son of a bitch. You hit him with a curse and I will tear your face off, goddammit.*

The flame guttered; I let out a soft breath and it straightened. My smart eye watered. The mass over the bed was seething, trying to find a purchase. The safe path I was following twisted to the right just as the victim gave another chilling, childlike chuckle.

"Come a little closer, said the spider to the fly," it crooned, out through the man's mouth. "Come closer, *bruja,* and look into our eyes. We want you to see us, yes we do—"

You're about to get your wish, asshole. I reached the side of the mattress, kept my eyes on the flame, and tipped the wine-bottle up to my mouth. Blue light sparked in the fluid, whether it was the blessing reacting against the mark on my wrist or my intent flooding the alcohol I couldn't tell.

The thing inside the man's body chuckled wetly, smacking its lips, and I heard the groaning of leather as his body erupted into wild motion. But I was just a half-second quicker, and the wine I sprayed across the candleflame blossomed into blue flame just a fraction of a second before he would have smacked into me. I flung the taper too, shaking the flame out, and the sudden curtain of darkness gave me another critical half-second before I grabbed him by the throat and *shoved,* still dribbling blue-flaming wine from my lips.

It wasn't pure theatrics. There's not really enough alcohol content in cheap blessed wine to ignite, but sorcery helps—and the contact, mouth meeting flame or spit booze, is a symbol understood by the creatures in this man's body. It's what their followers do as an offering or a protection.

And it's hard for the body's natural protective reflexes not to trigger when there's a ball of blue flame coming straight at the vulnerable eyes. That reaction gave me a thin wedge and a chance to drive it home.

I was on the mattresses over him, my knees on his shoulders, one hand on his forehead, *pushing.* My aura sparkled and flamed, and the thing inside him exploded out with a shotgun's cough.

His screaming took on a harsher tone. I fell, hitting the floor with a thud, various implements in my coat digging into my flesh, and it tried to strangle me before my aura sparked again, sea-urchin spikes driving it away. It tried again, howling obscenities in a sweet, asexual child's voice, and I shoved at it with a completely nonphysical effort, screaming my own imprecations. The scar was a live coal, pumping sorcerous force up my arm.

There was a *crack,* the physical world bowing out in concentric ripples of reaction, and a weird ringing noise. The man on the mattress was still screaming, and Saul's growl spiraled up. Mixed into the noise, there was splintering wood and a sudden weightlessness.

I hit hard, narrowly missing clipping my head on a countertop, and little peppering noises resounded all around me. I blinked, chalk dust and splinters hanging weightlessly before descending in lazy swirls. The peppering noises were little bits of wrapped candy, falling out of thin air and smacking down around me with sounds like a hard rain.

Eva's face came into view. She was chalk-white, dark bruised rings under her eyes, and she frankly stared for a few moments.

Saul peered through the huge hole torn in the ceiling, his eyes shining green-gold. The sound of the victim's rubbery sobbing gradually overwhelmed the rain of candy. There's nothing like hearing a grown man cry like a three-year-old.

Especially when that cry is blessedly, completely human. But we weren't done yet, and I struggled against sudden inertia, my body disobeying the imperatives I was giving it.

"Well," Eva said. "*That* was impressive."

I blinked. Twice. It had knocked me right through the ceiling. "Shit," I muttered, and the world grayed for a moment before I came back to myself with Eva gasping and Saul suddenly *there,* his face looming over mine. *No,* I wanted to say, but I couldn't make my mouth work for a half-second, gapping soundlessly like a fish. *NO, go back up and watch him—*

It was too late. The flexing of the world completed, a hard snap with a thick rubber band. Or maybe it was leather peeling and popping free. The high-pitched, childish laughter came back, ringing, and more candy pelted down like stinging rain. Another rending, splintering noise, and the laughter was receding, along with a wet thudding sound, then light pattering footsteps.

Our victim, Trevor Watson, was on the lam.

CHAPTER 11

This is getting seriously weird." I crouched on the cellar stairs, easily, running my smart eye over the candle-lit walls. "The wife had no idea?"

"She was adamant." Eva, behind me, was round-eyed. "I didn't think to look in the basement."

"Don't worry about it. You did exactly what you should have. There was no indicator the guy was into voodoo." The candles were arranged on an altar draped with green and gold, novenas flickering, a crudely done painting of the Trinity fastened to the concrete wall. A brass dish of sticky candy, a bottle of rum, and a few other implements, including wilted bunches of chrysanthemums. It was thick down here; the padlock on the outside door leading down to the cellar was new, and this whole thing was beginning to take on a shape I didn't like at all.

"Well, there was the chanting. But I didn't twig to it." She folded her arms.

I decided there were no traps lying under the surface of the visible and rose, stepped down another stair, and crouched again, watching. "I said you shouldn't worry about it. This guy wasn't anything more than a low-level novice. Any serious practitioner would have some defenses down here." *Though I'm not sure yet. Slow and easy and by the book, Jill.*

Saul was outside smoking a Charvil. If Eva felt bad about not checking the cellar, Saul probably felt just as bad for letting the victim—or whatever was riding him, to be precise—get away.

To be even more precise, I knew *what* was riding our victim, but I didn't know *why*. I had a sneaking suspicion I'd find a connection to whatever was happening out at the Cirque, though.

I hate those kinds of suspicions. I moved down another stair, scanning thoroughly, but I found nothing that would tell me our victim was anything more than a secret follower. A complete and utter novice who shouldn't have been able to fling curses while under a *loa*'s influence—who shouldn't have even been able to be ridden.

It's called "being ridden." Like a horse. The *loa* descends on one of the followers during a ritual, and gains certain things from inhabiting flesh. Having it happen to a solitary practitioner isn't quite unheard-of, but it only happens where the practitioner has sorcerous or psychic talent to burn.

This guy had no markers of initiation, intuition, or sorcery. At *all*.

I stepped off the last stair, boots clicking and my coat weighing on my tired shoulders. *I really wish I wasn't getting the feeling these things are connected.* The cellar was narrow, meant for nothing more than storing a lawnmower or two, and the candles made it hot and close. The guy was lucky his house hadn't burned down. But if the *loa* were taking such a particular interest in him, his house was probably safe.

They do take care of their followers, mostly. If you can get their attention. But the trouble is, once you have their attention, it's the scrutiny of creatures without a human moral code. Capriciousness might not be cruelty, but when wedded to power it gets awful close sometimes.

The altar looked pretty standard. Twists of paper and ash half-filled a wide ceramic bowl, used for burning incense for communications, or the names of enemies. The only thing that didn't fit was a cup.

It was an enamel camping-cup, a blue speckled metal number that looked easily older than I was. The blue sparkled for a moment, something running under the metal's surface, and my hand arrived to scoop it up with no real consideration on my part. It was a reflex, and one I was glad of, because one of the candles tipped over and spilled flame onto the altar.

"Oh god*dammit,*" I yelled, and yanked the cup back, tossed it into my left hand, and jabbed the right one forward. Eva let out a short blurting cry as the fire ate into dry wood—he had his altar sitting on fruit crates, for God's sake.

Smoke billowed. Etheric force pooled in my palm, and the sudden blast of heat against my face stung both smart and dumb eyes. "*Fuck!*" I yelled, and snapped my right hand back *hard,* the scar singing a piercing agonized note into the meat of my arm as I yanked.

The flames died with a whoosh, all available oxygen sucked away. I backed off in a hurry.

"Jill?" Eva sounded about ten years old, and scared. Of course, producing flame is one of those things that tells a regular exorcist to call me in a hurry, but we weren't dealing with Hell here.

Or at least, we weren't dealing solely with Hell.

Huh. "Everything's cool, Eva." The cup was a big chunk, and my pockets were on the full side already. But I now had a good idea where I could go to find out more about all this. "We're going to clean up here, then I want you to go check on something for me, and I'm going to do more digging."

"More digging? Do I even want to know?"

Smart girl. "Probably not. I have to go out and visit the bitch of Greenlea."

"Great. I'll just let you do that, then. What am I checking on?"

"You're going to call Avery and check on another victim." *One that we've got in the bag, thank God.*

Greenlea is just north of downtown, in the shopping district. If you're really looking, you can sometimes catch a glimpse of the granite Jesus on top of Sisters of Mercy, glowering at the financial district. But Greenlea's organic froufrou boutiques and pretty little restaurants don't like seeing it. Sometimes I think it's an act of will that keeps that particular landmark obscured from certain places in the city, especially around downtown.

Saul waited until I set the parking brake. "I'm sorry."

"For what?" I peered out the window, scanned the avenue.

This district is just one street, with two high-end bookstores, vegan eateries, a coffee shop, and a couple of kitchy-klatch places selling overpriced junk. A few antique stores cluster down at one end, and a fancy bakery and two pricey bars at the other. It's the kind of well-fed, quiet little upwardly mobile granola enclave you can find in pretty much any American city. Sometimes you can find two or three of them in the same metropolis.

Two blocks off the main avenue—Greenlea itself—the cracker-box houses are pushed together behind their neat little gardens. They're old houses, on prime property, and people who have an address out here are jealously proud of it.

On the corner of Eighth and Vine, two and a half blocks away, is Sunshine Samedi. I'm sure some of the trendoid yuppies think it's a Buddhist term, too.

"He got away." Saul's face was shadowed in the half-light. "I thought—"

I didn't want him to keep going with that particular mental train. "Don't worry about it. He didn't come downstairs, right? We didn't have to peel him off Eva, and we'll find him soon enough."

"Still." He even sounded upset. I glanced at him. He looked haggard in the half-light, and I wished I had time to sit him down for a good talking-to. Only what would I say?

"Don't, Saul. You're my partner, and a good one. You did fine." Did he really think I was going to yell at him for being concerned because I'd been knocked right through the ceiling?

But it wasn't like him. He was my partner, and he knew better. Whatever knocked me sideways wouldn't put me out of commission; I was just too tough and nasty. He should have stayed where I put him.

But maybe he wasn't able to. Like he's not able to touch you anymore without flinching.

I looked away and unlocked my door, hoping he couldn't read my expression. "Come on, let's go see if she's in."

Of course she'd be in. She never left the house.

A little coffee-shop and bakery with carefully watered nasturtiums in the window boxes sat in a brackish well of etheric depression, congested like a bruise. It wasn't the congestion of Hell, but it was thick and smelled rancid—not truly *smelled,* but more sensed with that place in the very back of the sinuses where instinct lives. The closest I can figure is that the brain has no other way of decoding the information it's being handed, so it dredges up smells out of memory and serves them up.

In any case, it was more than strongly fermented here, just on the edge of turning bad. Etherically speaking.

The coffee here was horrible and the baked goods substandard, but that wasn't why people came. It most definitely was not why the place was still open, especially in a neighborhood where people were picky about their shade-grown espresso and organic-flour croissants.

Chalked signs writhed over cracked concrete, a ribbon of walkway and a naked patio holding only a terra-cotta fire-dish and chimney on three squat legs. To get back here, you had to lift the iron latch on a high board gate and wriggle past some thorny sweet acacia that hadn't been cut back. The smell cloyed in the nose, curdled and slipped down the throat, and I gapped my mouth a little bit to breathe through it. I'm sure Lorelei left the acacia there deliberately, and coaxed it into growing large enough to pick people's pockets—or rend their flesh.

The backyard was cool, holding only a ghost of the day's heat. There was no moon, and the porch light buzzed a little, illuminating nothing. The garden pressed close, far too humid for the desert.

Her water bill must be sky-high, I thought, just like I did every time I came here. Which wasn't often. Once every three years or

so is often enough for me to keep tabs on the bitch of Greenlea, as
Mikhail often called her. Lorelei kept her nose clean and wasn't
directly responsible for any murders, so all things considered she
was a minor irritant in a city filled with major ones.

I wish prioritizations like that weren't daily occurrences.

"Smells bad." The words were just a breath of sound. Saul
wrinkled his nose.

I nodded. *This spider has the bad business in this whole neighborhood and a few others coming to her door. And I'm sure she
helps it out quite a bit.* "Lot of people around here like to double-
deal their neighbors. They come here for help."

"Hanging around with you always an—" He stopped short, his
sleek silver-starred head coming up in a quick, inquiring movement. He looked more catlike than ever when he did that.

I heard it too. A skittering, like tiny insect feet.

Oh, shit. My left hand closed around the whip handle, my right
touched a gun butt. Saul dropped back, melding into the shadows,
and I *listened* intently. The scar turned hot and hard, and I wished
I had a spare leather cuff. Still, superhuman hearing is far from
the worst ally in a situation like this.

Skittering paused. The scar turned hot and flushed, a hard knot
of corruption snugged into my flesh.

A small creak sounded from the hinges as a random breeze
wandered through the garden.

The back door was slightly open.

Motherfuck. I eased forward, the gun slipping out of its holster
and into my hand like a lover's fingers. The garden behind me
exhaled, and I caught a thread of another scent, fresh and coppery
under the reek of the acacia. *What the—*

I toed the door open, the hinges giving out a loose moan. Shadows fled aside, dim light spilling across yellow linoleum. Runnels
of smeared blackness dragged their way down the back hall
toward a shape in a blue housedress, pink fuzzy slippers decked
with gore at the end of indecently splayed legs.

"Oh, fuck."

"What is it?" Saul, behind me.

"Lorelei's dead," I informed him grimly. "And I think—"

Whatever I thought was cut off as a living carpet of shining, multilegged things scuttled and swarmed from the gloom, their backs marked with pinpricks of red laser light, and raced toward me. It was a wave of black cockroaches, and the skittering of their tiny feet stabbed my ears as my smart eye pierced the etheric veil over them, catching a glimpse of a swirling, ugly intent.

Oh, holy fuck. The gun would be useless on a swarm like this. I skipped back twice, almost running into Saul, who let out a short unamused sound and faded away. The gun went back, the scar running with heat under the wristcuff, and I jabbed my hand forward, two fingers out. Etheric energy ran crackling over my fist, sorcery rising to my lips, and the living tide of darkness scrabbled against my will.

It felt like tiny hairy feet running over my body, bristly little things poking at my mouth and eyes, scrabbling for entrance. My skin literally *crawled* before my aura flamed, bright spikes jabbing through the darkness in points of brilliance. A wet salt smell—ashes doused with rum and stale cigar smoke—thudded down over us, and the garden whispered uneasily to itself. Branches rubbed against each other and the flood of acacia scent didn't pierce the other reek.

The bugs imploded, darkness shrinking into tiny red pinpricks that glowed like cigarette cherries before green smoke puffed out of the place in the world they had occupied. The vapor thinned unnaturally fast, leaving only acridity.

"Jill?" Saul's tone was neutral, leashed impatience.

"Goddammit." I let out a short, sharp sigh. "I think we can cross normal homicide off the list for this one."

"You think?" Sarcasm turned to curiosity. "What *was* that?" His eyes sheened with gold-blue briefly, rods and cones reflecting differently from a human's.

"Don't know yet. Could have been one of Lorelei's defenses." *Although it didn't do her much good, if that's her.* "Could have been the same thing that tried to strangle the hostage." *Much more likely, but anything's possible.* I eased forward, my left hand still playing with the whip handle. It was the equivalent of a nervous flinch. "I'm gonna check the scene, then you can call Monty and have him get Forensics out here. I'll meet you at home—"

"No dice. I'm staying with you." He sounded like he meant it, too.

"I can't wait for Montaigne here. I've got other shit to do." I took another step forward, doing my best to avoid the claret spread on the floor. Blood looks black at night, even human blood. Hellbreed ichor is always black, but it's thin and doesn't splatter the same way human fluid does.

You have to see a lot of both before you can tell the difference with a glance, though.

"Goddammit, Jill." He sounded upset. It was so unlike him I paused and glanced over my shoulder. His eyes were orange-tinged; they get all glowy when he's excited, like a 'breed's. But Weres are as different from hellbreed as it's possible to be. "I'm not a cub."

You just look tired. I'm trying not to burden you more. "You're right, you're not. You're my partner, I need you here."

"Jill—"

I edged forward another step, every sense alert. "You can wait in the car if you're not going to help." *Might even be the best thing, the way this is going.*

It *was* Lorelei. Her black dreadlocks lay in fat limp ropes, soaked with clotted blood and daubed with bone beads and bits of glittering onyx. She hadn't been dead long, I was guessing. There wasn't much insect life.

Except for the cockroaches. Each with a pinprick of red light on its back, coming out of the gloom and vanishing into smoke. *This is not good.*

She lay between the back hall and the kitchen. There was something bubbling on the stove. It didn't smell like spaghetti. In fact, it was a thin brew with nameless chunks of something stringy floating in it, and the remnants of sorcery popping and fizzing on the water's surface. I flicked the heat off, examining the brew.

Bubble, bubble, toil and trouble. I should have left it on, but who knew what would happen when it finished cooking, especially in a house full of forensic techs? And contaminating the scene was a small thing compared to the fire risk, especially when I was sure this was one of my cases.

How about that for ironic? If this was a regular garden-variety murder I wouldn't be touching anything.

I passed my right hand through the steam, greasy moisture

scumming my palm. Sniffed deeply. It smelled like greedy obsession and musk, sex-drenched sheets left to rot in a dark hole.

Ugh. Nasty, nasty. What were you doing, Lorelei?

Three good Cuban cigars lay on the clean counter, next to a bottle of Barbancourt rum. The charms in my hair shifted uneasily. Right next to the unopened rum was a fresh bottle of Florida water and a jar of cornmeal.

She'd been preparing to do something, and the longer I waited the harder the traces would be to decipher. My right palm skipped through the steam once more, and yet more grease-laden steam touched my skin. My blue eye was hot and dry, the right watering from the smell. Cool air touched the rest of me, air-conditioning working overtime—Lorelei liked it cold as a tomb in here.

Get it, Jill? Cold as a tomb? It wasn't funny, and I'd given up wondering why people who liked it freezing had moved to the *desert,* for Chrissake.

Probably no shortage of people who wanted her dead, for one reason or another. But she hadn't survived this long as a black sorcerer by being careless or weak, and there was nobody I could think of with usable psychic talent and a vendetta against her.

And there was the slight matter of *loa* in a young man who shouldn't have them, the very same *loa* in an older man who shouldn't have had them so strongly, and a series of attacks on a hellbreed and a Trader hostage.

The commonality was voodoo, but I couldn't assume they were all directly linked—or could I?

Hunters are trained pretty thoroughly not to make assumptions. But we're also trained not to discount the thing that's staring us in the face. It's a fine line to walk.

My concentration narrowed. *One thing at a time.*

Poking, probing, my hand motionless in the steam, the rest of the world shut itself away. Saul had gone quiet and quiescent, watching my back. Intuition flared and faded, trying to track the traces of sorcery through a shifting mass of intention and weird, sideways-skipping dead ends.

It faded and flared maddeningly, and I came back to myself, exhaling a short dissatisfied huff of air. "God*dam*mit."

"Nothing?" Saul asked cautiously.

"Nothing I can see from here. I'd have to go *between* to track this one." Goose bumps crawled over my arms as I said it, and I hurried to give him the last half of what I was thinking. "Don't worry, I'm not planning on doing it unless it becomes necessary."

"It's not necessary?" He sounded dubious, but the relief of knowing I wasn't going *between* probably made him sound that way.

"Not at this point. I still have a couple other things to track down, like our other victim's other address. And I'm going to go see Mama Zamba. If it's a voodoo feud, she'll know about it. If it's not, she'll want to know someone's messing around on her turf, and she's far from the worst ally in a situation like this." I backed cautiously away from the stove. The surface of the water still roiled greasily, but the sorcery was fading. It hadn't been completed, so all the work and effort Lorelei had put in it was bleeding away, blood from a wound. "If nothing pans out with her, I'm going to have to go see Melendez. Jesus."

"You're not going to *either* of them without me." Flat and quiet.

I turned on my heel and opened my mouth to tell him I'd go wherever I had to, but the look on his face stopped me. Saul looked *worried,* dark circles under his eyes and his mouth a tight line. His hands had curled into fists—shocking, first because he was a Were, and second because he was always so even and steady. He was too calm to be believed most of the time, and I didn't realize how much I depended on that calm until he was gone.

Or until we hit a snag like this.

"What the hell's wrong with you?" I didn't mean it to come out so harsh. *Christ, Jill, his mom just died. Give him a break.* But the words spilled out. "We've got a couple of really serious problems here, and I need you firing on all cylinders. I *count* on you, Saul."

Great. Well, I suck at giving breaks. But Jesus...

"I know." His dark gaze slid past me, as if he couldn't bear to look. "I just..."

"You just what? I know—look, I really know you're suffering. Your mom...I mean, you're grieving, I understand. I'm trying to give you space, you know. It's just hard when I'm running to solve a case. I don't have a lot of time. I'm sorry." The tangle of everything I should have said instead—beautiful things that would help him feel better—rose to choke me, and I swung away from him, looking for a phone. "I'm going to call Montaigne. Take the car and go home, I'll wait for them to come secure the scene; I've got a couple things I need them to take samples of for me. Then I'm going to check out our first victim's address, and visit Zamba. I'll be home when I can and we'll hash this out."

He wasn't having any of it. "You think this is about my *mother?*" He sounded shocked. "So you've been—"

"Trying to give you some space. Which I'm going to keep doing. I've got shit happening here, Saul. If the hostage ends up dead or we're looking at a voodoo war, all fucking hell is going to break loose." *And I'll be on the front lines trying to deal out enough ammo to keep it from killing more innocent people.*

"Jill—"

I cut him off. I had to. "Saul. Go home. I'm sorry, I'm a hunter. That comes first. I love you and I'm going to give you the space you need to get your head clear. Go the fuck home." I took two steps toward the phone. They were hard—every inch of me wanted to turn back, grab him, and hug him and tell him it was all going to be okay.

But I had more than a sneaking suspicion that something was about to break over my city. If the hostage ended up dead, there went the Cirque's promise of good behavior, and I'd have a hell of a time getting another hostage out of them *and* making sure they didn't step outside their boundaries and go hunting instead of just luring the suicidal, desperate, insane, and psychopathic in to play their games. And if a voodoo war broke out at the same time . . . it didn't bear thinking about. There was only one of me, and a lot of uppity assholes to kill to keep the peace once chaos was on the loose instead of still mostly contained.

If the two things were connected, someone was making a lot of trouble for me, and I needed to get a handle on it *yesterday.*

"Jill—" Saul tried again.

"Go on." I didn't want to sound harsh. I really didn't. I tried to take a gentle tone. "Go home. Really. I'll be along when I can. I love you."

Lorelei's phone was at the end of the kitchen counter. I picked it up and dialed a number I knew by heart. Saul's footsteps were heavy. He headed for the back door.

Don't go. Come here and I'll hug you. Everything's going to be okay. I love you, I can love you enough to make the hurt go away. Come back.

"Montaigne," the phone barked in my ear.

Saul pulled the back door to but didn't close it. I *felt* him, each step taking a lifetime, sliding away around the corner of the house.

"Hello?" Monty bit the word like it personally offended him.

I came back to myself with a jolt. "Monty, it's Jill."

"Oh, Christ. What?"

"I've got a body I need taken care of, and I need a scene gone over. I also need Avery to meet me here." I gave Lorelei's address. "Get them here now—I'm on a schedule."

"When are you not?" He didn't ask any stupid questions, at least. "Are things going to get ugly?"

God, I hope not. The pressure behind my eyes wouldn't go away. Neither would the stone in my throat, but I sounded sharp and Johnny-on-the-spot. All hail Jill Kismet, the great pretender. "Time will tell. Get them out here, Monty. I'll be in touch."

"You got it." He hung up, and I did too. Thank God police liaisons don't question a hunter's judgment, even if they don't know what we're dealing with most of the time. Those that do know—and Monty had brushed the nightside once or twice—have a better idea than most, and leap to do what we ask.

The alternative really doesn't bear thinking about, but I'm sure they do.

I turned in a complete circle. I heard the Pontiac's engine purr into life outside. *Oh, Saul. Jesus. I wish I was better for you.*

I had work to do, not the least of which was sweeping the scene so I was sure it was safe for the forensic techs who were about to descend. Time to get cracking.

But oh, my heart hurt.

CHAPTER 12

A very arrived just as I was giving my forensics liaison the run-down. Piper is my very favorite tech. She didn't even blink when I told her what samples I needed. Lorelei's house was clear, her basement altar quiet, and the only problem was three live chickens brooding in wire cages downstairs. It's the kind of problem Piper's used to solving, and not much disturbs her serenity. She's got four kids and a husband who does house duty while she's out at crime scenes, and her sleek brown ponytail is almost never disarranged.

"Chickens?" She barely even raised an eyebrow. Behind me, they were photographing Lorelei's body.

"I don't care what you do with them, sell them or something."

She gave me a look that could only qualify as long-suffering. I'm sure she practiced it on her kids. "Okay. You want a file on the body, of course. Can Stan release it after the autopsy? Anyone likely to want it?"

"I have no clue. Don't release it until I give the okay."

"Is it likely to . . ." Both eyebrows *did* raise this time, slightly.

"If it was likely to sit up and start causing trouble I wouldn't let you keep it." I'd already taken care of piercing the palms and feet with long iron nails. "Have Stan do a full workup, but warn him not to take the nails out."

She didn't even blink. "Your wish is our command. Anything we need to be worried about?"

"Of course not. Take pictures of the altar downstairs, catalog the scene—the usual."

"Got it. Anything I should beep you if we find?"

Someone called her name, she raised a hand to let them know she'd be with them in a second. I mulled the question, shuffling priorities and evidence inside my head. "Nope. Just let me know when the file's done. See if you can find out if anyone visited her—check the phone and have the black-and-whites ask her neighbors."

She nodded. "Got it."

Technically I suppose I should have had a couple of homicide deets there to take care of the legwork, but I'd told Monty not to bother. This was so clearly one of my cases, and there was no reason for anyone to be brought in on call. It wasn't like I didn't know what had happened. "Great. Thanks, Piper."

She shrugged. "Yeah, well. You're *sure* this one won't...."

"It won't come back to life, Piper. I promise. Just tell Stan not to take the nails out."

"Okay." A shadow crossed through her dark eyes, but she shrugged again and went to work. Which officially finished up my job here.

Avery leaned against the hood of his Jeep, and I got a pleasant surprise. Eva was there too, perched on the hood like a Chrysler-approved pixie. The breeze stirred her dark hair, and I could tell just from the tension in her shoulders that she was still upset over losing Watson. Either that or something else, since Ave looked troubled too.

"How's our first victim?" I didn't bother with a preamble. Our second victim was still missing, or I would know about it.

"Funny you should ask." Ave's mouth twisted. "Had to sedate him and tie him down again. He was throwing himself all over the cell. I'm surprised he doesn't have a concussion. He was chanting again, too. It was hinky as hell."

Eva shivered. "It took three darts before he even slowed down. I don't know what we're going to do when he wakes up again."

Interesting. "Anyone there with him?"

"Benito and his bum leg. Wallace is out on a job. It sounded like a regular one," Eva added hurriedly, seeing my expression. "We've traded notes. Nobody's seen anything like this."

I nodded. "Care to come check out our first victim's other address? I want to eyeball it, and if there's anything there I'm going to have you two secure the scene while I go traipsing around following clues."

"Sounds like a good time." Avery grinned. "We were going to go to a movie but this is ever so much better."

Oh, I'll bet. "Bite your tongue. And give me your car keys."

That wiped the grin off his face, and Eva sighed.

"You're driving?" Avery dug in his jacket pocket, but slowly.

"We need to get there this century. Come on, Avery. I've never been in an accident in my life."

"It's not for lack of trying, I bet." But Eva looked angelically innocent when I glanced at her. "Seriously, Jill. You're not quite a menace, but you're close."

"Why does everyone feel the need to comment on my driving?" I held out my hand, Avery dropped his key ring in, and I motioned at them like a mother hen. "Come on, chickadees. Let's get going—Mama's in a hurry."

CHAPTER 13

The address on Ricardo's food-handler's permit was a trim little one-story bungalow on Vespers. The place looked nice enough, despite the dying lawn. Still, we live in the desert, and not many people have the patience or the funds to drench sun-dried dirt regularly enough to make it bloom.

But that kind of bothered me. The lawn was dying, not dead. I sat in the Jeep, eyeing the house, and Avery groaned.

"I think I'm going to be sick."

"Don't be dramatic. You should take this beast in for a tune-up." I unclipped my seat belt, still staring at the house. *What's wrong with this picture?*

Sometimes looking at a scene is like that. Something doesn't jell, and it takes a few moments to make everything snap together behind your eyes in a coherent picture. I've given up wondering if the way hunters turn psychic is the sorcery or the science of informed guessing, or both. It doesn't matter. What matters is listening to that little tingling shock of wrongness as it hits right under the surface of conscious thought, and not ignoring it.

The hunter who ignores instinct is dead in the water.

"That was *fun*." Eva burbled from the backseat. "Damn, Jill, you should rent out as a cabdriver."

"People would drop dead of heart attacks." Avery *was* looking a little green. And he was sweating a bit. "Jesus."

"Come on, buck up." Eva ruffled his hair, and Avery grinned, blushing. The slow grin got him a lot of female attention, but it seemed a bit softer now. An internal happiness, rather than an external show.

He looked like a man in love.

Now I'd officially seen everything. And a sharp pin lodged itself in my heart. I ignored it.

I studied the house some more. *This really, really doesn't feel right. Lawn dying, but it was a nice one until recently. Ricardo worked as a dishwasher; why would he list this as his address if he was on the edge of poverty? And why does it give me the heebies so bad?*

The porch light wasn't on, though that probably meant nothing. It doesn't take a lawn a long time to yellow out here, especially in the autumn before the storms sweep up the river. But there was something else. The swirl of etheric energy over the whole place was congested, bruised. Strong negative emotion will do that, especially over time. But it's only one of the things that will.

"Jill?" Eva, again. Avery knew better than to talk when I went quiet like this. So did Saul.

Saul. Christ. I wish I could go home.

But there's never an excuse for leaving a job half-done. "Stay here."

"You got it," Avery said immediately. "Should we call anyone if anything, you know, happens?"

What, and have this place crawling with vulnerable people to protect? Still, he meant well. "No. If anything happens you should first drive away. Wait for me back at the precinct."

"What exactly do you think is going to happen?" Eva shifted uneasily in her seat. Both of them smelled healthy, with the darker edge of clean brunettes and her light feminine spice. Now the edge of adrenaline and fear touched both distinct scents.

"Can't tell yet." *I'm not even going to guess.* "Just stay here." I dropped Avery's keys in his lap and slid out of the Jeep, slamming the door with a little more care than I used with my own cars.

Quit thinking about Saul. Focus on the work at hand.

I went up the cracked driveway. That was another thing—no

car parked outside. They had a garage, but the recent oil stain on the concrete led to the conclusion that a car was missing. I wondered if it was our victim's, discarded the question. It didn't matter right now, wouldn't until I figured out who belonged here—and who didn't.

The windows were dead dark. It wasn't early enough in the night for that, even though people in this neighborhood probably retired early. You had to work a full day to afford a house in today's economy, and this was the sort of half-depressed area that would slide right over into outright welfare warzone in a heartbeat. All it would take is one little crack house.

The front door was tucked back a little, the walkway running up along a quarter of the garage's length. My blue eye twitched and smarted a little; the concrete walk was littered with yellowing newspapers, rolled up and tossed higgledy-piggledy. Their delivery boy must've had a hell of a good arm.

Now I could see other rolled-up papers hiding in the straggled grass, hidden by the slight downward slope of the lawn. Whoever had been caring for the lawn had watered right over the top of them.

The place felt as deserted as a cheap haunted house the morning after Halloween.

I tapped on the front door with no real hope. Tapped again, toyed with the idea of ringing the doorbell.

The metal doorknob was cold under my fingers. A jolt of something went up my arm, the scar humming to itself greedily, a wet little pucker embedded in my flesh. I jiggled the knob, then twisted, and the wrong notes drowned out the whole fucking symphony.

The door was unlocked.

This is not going to end well. I ghosted the door open, listening hard. The scar listened too. I wished again for a fresh wristcuff to cover it up, drew a gun instead. Eased forward.

The house was soundless.

Well, not quite. There was a stealthy not-sound, a listening silence. I didn't think it was just my imagination.

The smell hit me a breath after I stepped into the front hall. The place was bare, empty white walls and a dead blank television in the living room, set on a wooden crate. The venetian blinds were half-drawn, and the kitchen was empty too. A plate in the sink had congealed, a thick rubbery mass on its surface.

The reek was thick and rotten. If you've even *once* smelled death, you know what it's like and how it clings in the nose, climbing down to pull the strings in your stomach.

The only question was, where were the bodies? There was no cellar, which is usually the first bet in a case like this. I turned down the hall, passed a bathroom, and headed for what was almost certainly two bedrooms, doors firmly closed.

Door number one, or door number two? Which should it be, Jillybean? Come on down, don't be shy. My boots whispered along thin, cheap carpet. It was warm in here, but not overly so. The windows weren't open, which meant there was air-conditioning—but it was set at an uncomfortably high temperature. Probably meant to save money.

Number one or number two, Jill? The one ahead or the one on the right? It makes sense to check the one dead ahead first.

It bothered me. The smell should be worse, if it was so nice and warm in here.

The stealthy non-sounds grew more and more intense, but I couldn't get a fix on them. There's a certain frequency where you can't tell if the sound is truly audible or just a mental echo of something else going on; it burrows under the skin and strokes at your eardrums with little hairy legs. A shiver of loathing went down my skin. My blue eye only caught the stirring of ambient energy, a slow lethargic swirl that told me nothing.

I debated reaching for the doorknob with my left hand or just plain kicking it. The first rule of any scene is to offer assistance to the living, but I was pretty sure nothing was left living in here. Still, if I went around kicking doors in . . .

Take it easy, there, Jill. Think for a second.

The smell was wrong. The silence was wrong. The newspapers, front lawn, blank walls, empty kitchen, and most of all the unlocked door were *wrong.*

My left hand flicked toward another gun just as all hell broke loose. The door crumpled and shattered outward, little splinters peppering me and the wall as a zombie lurched through, dry tendons screaming and half-eaten face working soundlessly. It was dripping with little bits of plated light—it took me a split second to determine the thing was crawling with roaches, each with the familiar little red dot on its back. But worst of all was the smell that belched out of the small close bedroom, and the zombie lifted its shattered arms and blurred forward with the eerie speed of the recently reanimated, roaches plopping off and scuttling for my boots over the cheap carpet.

I'd found Trevor Watson. And he wasn't alone.

The trouble with zombies is that the motherfuckers just won't stay *dead.* I stamped down hard, a short sound of disgust escaping tight-pursed lips, and the skull gave way under my steel-toed and -heeled boot with a sound like a ripe melon splitting. Zombie bones get porous after a little while, something about the body cannibalizing itself to provide enough chemical energy for their restless motion.

The roaches scuttled, but my aura flared, pushing them away from my feet. They ran with greasy green smoke, popping out of existence like Orville Redenbacher's ugliest nightmare. My fist blurred out, hellbreed strength pumping through my bones, and caught the fourth one in the face as well. It exploded, bits of rotting brainmatter splattering me and the walls liberally.

Guns won't do much good against zombies in close quarters. The ones whose heads I'd shattered were still scrabbling weakly on the carpet, sorcerous force bleeding away. Green smoke rose from the sludge their noncirculating blood had become. Identification of these bodies was going to be tricky—they were juicy as all get-out. But it explained why the smell was just awful and not truly, blindingly massive.

And I'd ID'd the first one before he'd tried to chew me into bits. He shouldn't have ended up here and dead, for God's sake. But I had other problems to worry about right now.

The roaches made little whispering sounds, puffing out of existence. Both bedrooms were awash with green smoke hanging at knee level, and a roving hand splatted dully against my ankle. I stamped again, felt flesh and sponge-bones give.

Two left, where did they go, spooky fuckers, they move so

fast—I skipped to the side. When you don't have a high-powered rifle or particular ammo for headshots that will make the entire skull explode, you're down to fisticuffs and whip-work. Unfortunately, the area was too confined for the whip. Knife-work wouldn't do me any good.

I was wishing for my sunsword when one of the remaining zombies made a scuttling run, humping up out of the smoke and heading straight for the wall. I grabbed it, fingers popping skin and sinking into worm-eaten muscle tissue before, and broke the neck with a quick twist. That didn't do much—they're sorcerously impelled, not relying on nerve endings much—but it did slow it down long enough for me to take its legs out, get it on the floor, and stamp its head in.

Everything I'd eaten in the last twenty-four hours tried to declare mutiny, but I was too busy hunting around for the last zombie. It dodged out the door and I gave chase, wading through waves of roaches and spluttering, still-moving corpses awash in bloodsludge and green smoke.

Well, that answers that—the cases are connected. Hallelujah, but I hate to be right. I bolted down the hall, my left hand heading down for the whip.

It zigged around the corner and so did I, clipping the wall with my shoulder and taking away a good-sized chunk of it. Out into the clean, cold night air, where I saw two things—first, Avery was outside the Jeep, standing near the hood and staring at me.

Second, the zombie was scuttling straight for him.

If it reached him, it would probably tear his throat out. Just because I'm tough to kill doesn't mean regular humans are, especially if you're a spooky-quick, sorcerously engineered corpse bent on mayhem. A corpse just aching to do its master's bidding.

Then I'd have to deal with Avery's body too, and right in front of Eva.

I screamed and leapt, the whip coming free and flicking forward, silver flechettes jingling as it wrapped around one of the zombie's legs and almost tore itself out of my hand. The leather popped hard, once, like a good open-hand shot to the face or a piece of wet laundry shaken in just the right way, and the zombie went down in a splattering heap.

"Get in the fucking car!" I yelled. Then I was on the thing, its foul sponginess running away as I broke its neck with a louder crack than the other ones. *This guy must be pretty fresh, too.* I balled up my right fist, my knees popping foul, slipping skin and sinking through muscle turned to ropy porridge.

I *punched,* pulling it at the last second so my fist didn't go through the head and straight on into the dying lawn. Newspapers ruffled in a sudden burst of cold air and the smell of natron. The wet splorching sound was louder than it had any right to be, and brain oatmeal splattered. The body twitched feebly.

No, they don't rely on nerve pathways much. But the head as the "seat" of consciousness carries a magical meaning all its own, and the symbol of breaking the head breaks the force the zombie is operating under.

I just wished it wasn't so messy. You'd think I'd be used to it by now, though.

I considered retching, but Avery was already doing enough for both of us. He was still gamely trying to make it around the car to the driver's side. Eva stared out through the windshield, her mouth ajar and her eyes wide enough to turn into plates.

Bits of dead zombie plopped off my coat as I rose, heavily. Shook myself like a dog heaved free of an icy lake. More bits splattered.

"J-J-J—" Avery was trying to get my name out through retches.

"Get in the car!" I yelled at him again. The scene wasn't safe, for Chrissake.

"Behind you!" Eva screamed, but I was already turning, hip swinging first, skipping aside as the whip sliced air. The silver jangled, bits of rotting flesh torn free, and it hit the zombie I hadn't counted before full in the face.

The thing did an amazing leap, dead nerves trying like hell to respond, the same kind of unholy quick reflex motion a small, partially crushed animal makes as the body dies. It jittered and jived there on the lawn, and I was on it in a heartbeat. When it was finally twitching out its last, I cast a quick glance back at Avery, who finally managed to make his legs work and scurried around the front end of the Jeep. I turned back to the house, waited until he was in the car and had the engine going before taking another step toward it, senses quivering. The whip had transferred itself to my right hand, and my left fingers found my largest knife. It would brace my fist and I could probably lop a hand off if the zombie was old enough.

The sudden wash of sensory acuity turned me into a mass of raw nerve endings. I exhaled, made sure of clear play on the whip by shaking it a little, listening to the flechettes jangle. *Christ. Wish I had my sword. Or that Saul was here.*

But wishes didn't get the job done. I had a whole house to check, and who knew how many zombies to deal with.

I eyed it. One-story, no cellar unless it was hiding around the back, and I'd already cleared out two rooms with two zombies each. Where had the last one come from?

Lord God above, I thought, *I hate attics. Almost as much as I hate basements.*

I got to work.

CHAPTER 14

Piper wasn't happy about bodies spread out in fast-decaying bits, but she took my word that they wouldn't rise again. I'd cleared the whole house and found three more wet ones—not up in the attic or in a surprise cellar, but in the small crawl space underneath. It made sense—they like dark spaces. It was hard to believe so many people had lived here, but the kitchen held dry goods and the bedrooms had mattresses as well as two altars. It was clear the altars were where all the money had gone. They were elaborate three-story affairs, candles burned down, dishes of flyblown sticky candy and bottles of Barbancourt, cigars that cost as much as the television. Whoever lived here was serious, though the wide bloodstain in the weedy backyard under a canopy was probably chicken or goat instead of human. They even had a firepit to grill things, and I wondered how many "barbecues" they'd thrown a month.

Still, the rest of the house was too empty. "It looks like a front," was Piper's only comment, and I didn't have to tell her how right she was.

It was the empty fridge that convinced me, actually.

Piper loaned me her cell phone, too, and I called Avery's desk number. It was a relief when he picked up.

"You okay?" I tried not to sound sarcastic, or too relieved.

He let out a gusty sigh. "Kind of. Jill—"

"The next time I tell you to get in the car, Ave, you *do* it."

"Christ, Jill, I *know.* Don't rub it in. Listen, I—"

"You shouldn't have been outside. If that thing had caught you, Eva would be very unhappy."

"Will you quit? Ricardo's gone. Tore a hole right through the door—the cell is a mess. The circle in there is broken. Something ground the concrete up and broke it, made a gap."

My knees didn't falter, but it was damn close. Bright lights were on inside the house, starring the night. The neighbors didn't come out to check, and I wondered how many of them had an idea about the backyard at this place, and the drumming that would go on all night sometimes. I could have had a homicide pair out here at this scene too, but really, what was the point? I knew where I had to go next.

"He's gone?"

"Completely AWOL."

Goddammit. What do you want to bet he won't end up a zombie too? "All right. See what you can do about getting the room repaired."

"I *hate* contractors," he muttered. "Jill, I'm sorry. I was trying to get around into the driver's side to get us away if we had to. I was just about to go."

That's what I thought. I took a deep breath, watching the shadows of forensic techs in the living room, played against the bright golden windows. "Everything's copacetic. First encounter with a zombie?"

"Yeah. You know, no matter how many times you see weird shit, it always knocks the wind out of you."

Don't I know it. But I didn't really agree. It's amazing what the human mind will accommodate, given a strong enough framework. And the training helps.

Training made me think of Gilberto on my front step again. What would Saul do if the kid was still there? Ignore him, hopefully. And more hopefully, maybe the little gangbanger would have gone on his merry way.

Still, he had the look. Which meant he was a problem I would have to solve soon.

After, of course, I figured out who was attacking Cirque performers and strewing zombies all over. And after I figured out what Saul was—

"Jill?" Avery sounded uncertain.

"It certainly does," I agreed. "See what you can do about that room, and if anything looks hinky during *any* exorcism, buzz me. Don't even go on a call if it feels weird. Make sure Eva and the rest know that, too."

"Okay. Any idea what's going on?"

"Do you really want to know?" I took his silence for a negative answer and smothered a laugh. "I'll be in touch."

I flipped Piper's phone closed. It was time for God's honest truth.

I might not have looked very hard for the perpetrator if it had just been a couple Cirque performers dead, or just Lorelei. If black sorcerers and hellbreed were looking to off each other, it made my life a little easier. It was the chance they took when they signed up for their kinds of fun and games.

But the hostage? If he ended up biting it, the Cirque would be stunned for a little while—and then the guarantee of their good behavior would be gone. And that was bad news for everyone. Even Perry, but while I could *probably* bank on his territorial jealousy, I couldn't bank on him not deciding a certain level of chaos was a good thing for his plans.

Whatever those plans were.

And *zombies,* for Christ's sake. Nobody needed to be unleashing carnivorous corpses on my city. I just hate that.

Especially when it looked like the corpses were people being fed to *loa* in return for something big.

I returned Piper's phone, assured her again the bodies wouldn't reassemble or otherwise even twitch, and realized I was there without a car. *Oh, dammit.*

Fortunately, one of the black-and-whites could give me a ride to the barrio. I ignored the paling of the rookie's face. It was the unfortunately-named Judy Garland, a smug trim blonde with a wide smile and a *summa cum laude* from the police academy. She would probably shape up to be a good administrator one of these days.

After I finish their orientation, very few of them actually want to interact with me in any way. The slide show takes care of most of it, and the demonstrations—I used to do other things before Saul was around to change and show them something their brains couldn't wrap around—did the rest. Most people's interest in the paranormal only stretches far enough to cover a thrill or two, or some white-light bullshit.

"Chesko, right off the freeway," I told her. "Turn your lights on and get me there yesterday."

"Yes ma'am." She sat bolt upright in the driver's seat. It was her bad luck, partnerless for the night and showing up to help secure this scene. I tapped my fingers on my leather-clad knee, suddenly remembering how bad I must reek.

Nothing like a zombie to clear the sinuses.

"You can open a window if you need to." I tried to sound a little gentler. "I must smell bad."

"It's okay," she lied, but cranked down her window halfway anyway. The night rushed in, full of city, concrete, and river. Red and blue strobes dappled the silent streets as we raced through over them, the shocks groaning. She was a good driver, but too slow. "Does this...this sort of thing happen a lot to you?"

What, you mean zombies, or smelling like death and goop? "Often enough."

"You were bleeding."

I'll bet I was. But it had stopped by now, or I would have used some healing sorcery on it. Another benefit to a hellbreed mark on my wrist. "Yeah, that happens too."

"Can I ask you something?"

"Fire away." *Only, how much do you want me to tell you?*

"We—I mean, some of us at the station, whenever your name comes up—" She was still pale, took a deep breath, and rushed on. "Why do you do this?"

Well now, isn't that an unanswerable question. "There's nobody else to do it," I said, and left it at that. I didn't tell her what Mikhail said, and I didn't tell her what I really thought.

Idiots, Mikhail had often sneered. *They think we do this for them. Is only one reason to do,* milaya, *and that is for to quiet the screaming in our own heads.*

He was right as far as it went—he always was. But sometimes, in the long dark reaches of the night when nothing much is happening and I patrol looking for trouble, I follow the logic out a bit further. I think becoming a hunter was preordained for me, but not in any Calvinist way.

There was no grace to save me from these works.

I slouched in the seat, weapons digging into my flesh as I shifted, and watched the city go by. She was doing at least thirty over the limit, and it was too goddamn slow.

When I say it was preordained, I mean that there was nothing else for me to do but die in a snowbank, and I wasn't ready for that. I'd reached the end of my normal life, and I was taken over the edge and into the nightside by Mikhail, for no reason I ever heard him explain. I never even considered doing something else, or taking the other bargain he offered me—therapy and a fresh start. The bargain offered to every apprentice.

No, as soon as I figured out what he was doing, I wanted in. Or maybe not precisely. I just wanted to do what would make him proudest of me. I wanted to please him.

I wanted to be worth whatever had made him pull me out of that snowdrift.

I had probably been moving toward him—and this—all my short unhappy life. I could have taken a detour anywhere, I suppose. Free will means as much.

But there's free will, and then there's being made in such a way that you can only do what you must. There's no law against choosing a different path, and I suppose you could if you wanted to— but that isn't how you're made. It isn't how you *are*.

If the clay cuts the potter's hand, who is to blame—the clay, or the Great Potter who created it? It was an old riddle, and one I was no closer to solving. I was as I'd been made, and I was doing what I was made for.

It was as simple as that. And she wasn't anyone who needed more of an answer from me.

Maybe Saul does. We haven't fought over this in a while. Maybe he's just waiting for me to bring it up. He's probably waiting for me to bring something *up.*

We hit the freeway. It would take less than five minutes to get me to the Chesko exit, and then poor Judy could go back to her rounds. It would take me a short while to work around one edge of the barrio and get to Zamba's, and the night was getting old.

"Can I ask *you* something?" I stared out the windshield, watching traffic slide easily aside, pulling over. It was so much easier with a set of red and blue lights, instead of the usual intuition-tingling run through the streets.

"Shoot," Garland said, and probably wished she hadn't.

"Why do you do what you do?"

I caught her momentary half-shrug. Was she wishing she hadn't opened her mouth, or was she shrugging because she hadn't thought about it?

The road zoomed under the car. We were only a few feet above the concrete. Such a small distance.

"I guess it's what I was supposed to do," she said finally. "There's all sorts of reasons why people work this job. Too many for each person. Otherwise we'd be doing something else." The exit loomed, she braked, and we began the long slow bleedoff up the hill. The barrio pulsed, and her radio crackled, squawking at us.

The light at the head of the exit was green. She rolled to a stop, the reds and blues dappling the run-down gas station and the arching soar of the overpass. This far down Chesko she wouldn't have to worry about her car getting shot at, and she could get right back on the freeway. It all worked out.

"Exactly," I said, and bailed out of the car, slamming the door behind me. I was already two blocks away, the scar tingling as I pulled etheric force through it, by the time her engine roused again. I didn't look back.

Exactly.

The queen of the voodoo scene in Santa Luz lived in a ramshackle split-level on the edge of the barrio. The houses on either side were abandoned—nobody would stay in them long enough to pay rent *or* a mortgage. I often wonder if real estate agents have a clue why certain places don't sell.

The house had a three-car garage, an overgrown jungle garden full of spiny, smelly plants, and a zigzagging, cracked concrete walk up to the spindly porch, concrete stair-slabs laid in an iron framework that looked far too frail to hold them.

I stood across the street, in the shadow of a closed-down convenience store with blind, boarded windows. The area hadn't been so depressed and run-down last time I'd been through, but the edge of the barrio is a no-man's-land. It was a wonder everything hadn't been closed down before, but Zamba's presence had given the place a facsimile of liveliness.

Which brought up, again, the question of just what the hell was going on here now.

The shadows drew close. The night was getting too old, and the streets had no cover. Even the barrio was winding down, its pulse taking on the tired thump of the long dark shoal of three to five A.M., when the old or the critically injured often slip over the edge into deeper darkness. When the parties are winding down, the bars are closing up, and people just want to get home.

Of course, there's also the people who just want to fuck someone up this time of night, too. But they're easy to avoid, and if they haven't caught anyone by this point, they're probably not going to. This is the time when nightly fun and games switches over to alcohol and fatigue-related traffic fatalities and code blues, instead of domestic free-for-alls or substance-fueled fights.

This is the time of night when the scar always turns hot and full, and I wonder if Perry's thinking of me.

It's anyone's guess.

High wispy clouds scudded over my city, and the swelling moon played peek-a-boo. I watched Zamba's house and thought about all this, breathing slowly, my pulse smooth and deep, silence drawn over me like a quilt. It smothered the little sounds that could give away my position—jingles of silver charms, the creak of leather, the subliminal sough of oxygen being taken in.

That silence is the first thing an apprentice learns, and the most thoroughly applied lesson imaginable. Sometimes you'll be deep in thought, and look up when you realize you've been making someone else uncomfortable. The quality of stillness in a hunter can verge on the uncanny.

It never bothers Saul, though. And really, cats can be just as still.

That was a distraction, and I didn't need a distraction inside Zamba's walls. That was officially a Very Bad Idea. The only Worse Idea was being distracted when dealing with Perry.

It's just a night for thoughts we'd rather not have, isn't it, Jillybean. I breathed soft and easy, considering Zamba's house. The peeling white split-level was completely dark. Blind windows watched the empty street.

I checked the moonphase again. No festivals in this particular part of this particular month, at least none that I could pin down off the top of my head. There was no reason for Zamba's house to be lit up, but there wasn't any reason for it to be dead dark either. And she wouldn't be a very good voodoo queen if she didn't have an idea that something was going on and I was likely to show up.

Then again, the sorcerous ability of a hunter usually means that you don't see us before we show up to knock you on your lawbreaking ass.

But I'd asked Galina to give her a ring.

It was the umpteenth time tonight I was feeling hinky as hell. Either the successive shocks were making me jumpy, or it was thirteen o'clock around here.

Although it's *always* thirteen o'clock around Zamba. She's been around as long as Mikhail has, and she's always been the big power on the voodoo scene. If someone had taken her out and was messing with the Cirque as well...

I eased out of cover. Crossed the street, trying not to feel like the house was watching me approach.

Trying not to feel *lured*.

The last time I'd been out to visit her, Saul had been with me. We were digging to the bottom of a case involving two particular black sorcerers who just happened to be her devotees. Zamba hadn't been too happy about how that turned out—I got the feeling she'd been invested in their little rape and extortion stable, not to mention a profitable side-trade in the body parts for some of the, shall we say, less wholesome brand of sorcery you can tap as a *bocor,* the voodoo version of a black magician.

I used to get all twitchy about the less-positive side of voodoo until Mikhail pointed out it wasn't any different from people double-dealing each other in offices. The ambition of a *bocor* who sacrifices his friends and family is the same ambition that makes a workaholic cubicle-farmer double-deal his officemates and ignore or abuse his family. They're the same thing; the only question is one of *degree.* I just deal with the people who leave broken bodies and souls instead of broken careers in their wake. Lives are ruined just as surely by either brand of troublemaker.

And a good, fast, smart black sorcerer of any type can rise in the hierarchy of such things just like a conscienceless asshole can become a CEO. All it takes is the drive and the luck.

Zamba hadn't ever *overtly* gotten her hands dirty, and I hadn't been able to press the point. But this was an entirely different piece of pie. If someone was operating without her knowledge, it was a threat to her primacy. I was hoping it was that—if she had a vested interest in keeping her position, this would go a lot easier. She was a scumbucket, but she was a useful one, and less dirty than Perry by an order of magnitude.

If, on the other hand, the trouble started with her or one of her followers, we were looking at some serious unpleasantness. Best to get started on making it more unpleasant for her than for me.

The concrete walk unreeled under my gliding feet. The rickety stairs didn't move when I tested them, remembering the slip-sliding motion necessary to get up them without the rusted metal groaning and rubbing against the concrete slabs.

I did tell Galina to give Zamba a call, tell her I'd be by to see her. So why is the house dark?

I was too uneasy to ignore the way my nerves were twitching, pulled tight against each other. The sudden double sense—of being watched, and of ugliness about to happen—scraped me down to rawness in less than a second. I eased my right-hand gun out of its holster and breathed in, a long shallow inhale, poised on the steps.

Wait a second. The sense of being watched was coming from behind me, not from the dark windows.

I weighed the cost of looking over my shoulder. Was this a fakeout, or was something going on inside Zamba's house? Since Lorelei had just bit it, Zamba could be next. Or Melendez, or any of the larger fish in the Santa Luz voodoo-or-Santeria pool.

This makes no fucking sense. I think that so often before a case jells, it's a constant refrain. It just meant I wasn't seeing the pattern yet.

Between one blink and the next, I leapt forward, body stretching out. The stairs gave one howling groan as I pushed off, concrete squealing against iron framework, and my boots hit the door. Blue sparks crackled, an etheric strike as surely as a physical one, and the steel-reinforced door busted off its weakened hinges. I rode it all the way down, hitting with a hollow boom on the landing.

Up or down? But the decision had already been made, because something was moving. I leapt up and to the side, catching a banister and propelling myself over, one boot-toe pushing and my left arm doing most of the work. This swung me neatly around, and I hit the ground in the living room, rolling. It was *dark;* she had blackout shades on the windows or something, for fuck's sake.

I hit furniture—felt like the edge of a couch—and something that ground under my coat, sharp edges slicing. One whole wall of Zamba's living room was, if I recalled correctly, a multitiered altar to Ifa and several lesser *orisha,* built around a rock-walled fireplace. Drums should have been stacked against one wall, and the rest of the room should have been lined with furniture—two couches against the window, a long line of cushions for the lower-ranked devotees, and Zamba's thronelike recliner with its back to the altar, wheeled in by a couple of strong young men at the beginning of every court-holding session.

It was there, rolled to a stop on the floor with my eyes straining to pierce absolute blackness, that I remembered Zamba had a close personal relationship with the Twins. They had a whole quadrant on her main altar, and a private altar in her bedroom.

Don't ask how I know what's in her bedroom. Like I said, last time I was here, things got iffy.

My blue eye could get only confused images through a heavy, oppressive screen of etheric bruising. It was thick in here in more ways than one, a stench I was beginning to find all too familiar painting the back of my throat as I waited, full-length on the floor, hearing something shamble around in the living room.

And hearing the tapping skritches of thousands of little insect feet flooding up the stairs. The darkness came alive with tiny red dots blanketing the soaked carpet, and I was suddenly very sure that whether or not Zamba was involved, I'd find nothing living in this happy little split-level.

I was pretty sure I'd find plenty dead and moving around, though.

CHAPTER 15

Fighting in the dark, especially when every footstep crunches with little moving bodies underneath, is no picnic. I couldn't tell how many there were—*a lot* was about all I could think, hearing them shuffle and close in on me. The roaches made little creaking sounds, a dry insect thrumming. My fist crunched through slippery flesh, I hooked my fingers and pulled, a gelatinous eyeball popping and running. Wet splorching hands fumbled at my waist—I kicked back, heard the splutter of contact and the crash as it flew back, hitting whatever was left of Zamba's altar.

And still they crowded me. What a welcoming committee. Either they had orders to kill whoever entered the house, or Zamba had fallen prey to something, or—

My aura flamed, sea-urchin spikes boiling with blue sparks. That was better and worse. Better because the shifting illumination gave me visuals to work on, instead of straining my other senses to place the opposition. Which meant I could afford to unlimber the whip.

But it was worse because it meant the atmosphere in here was boiling, and not about to calm down anytime soon. And the gloom only got more intense, clotting and thickening. A spiritual hematoma.

Bug guts slimed underneath, ground into the carpet. The roaches clattered and chattered, and the sound of dry tendons stropping each other as the zombies lurched around me.

The fighting art of hunters is a hodgepodge. Almost any martial art you can name, from *savate* to esoteric *t'ai chi,* is in there somewhere. You can never tell what move will save your ass, and every once in a while you have to run through everything you know just to keep it fresh. Of course we all have our *favorite* moves, but pulling something out of your ass in a fight is a good way to put your enemy down.

But for this—close combat in a dark space, with things pressing in on every side, more than I could comfortably count because I was too goddamn busy—I fell back on the fighting style Weres teach their young, relying on evasion, quickness, and grace. Whether or not I'm graceful is an open question, but evasion and quickness?

Yeah. Especially with the scar on my wrist whining a subvocal grumble as it spiked etheric energy through me, granting me a measure of inhuman speed.

Hellbreed speed.

These were new, juicy zombies dripping with roaches. Their reek clogged the throat, and if I hadn't had it drilled into me to *breathe, goddammit, breathe* by Mikhail endlessly I might have held my breath and passed out.

That wouldn't have been good. I splat zombies when I'm going fast enough, but a helpless body on the floor wouldn't be so lucky. It would be pulled to pieces.

Step back, swing, fist blurring out to crunch through a rotted leering face, roaches dripping, a high tinkling childish laugh bouncing off the walls as the air thickened to paste, darkness *pressing* down as if I were the thing to be exorcised from this house, boots slipping and skidding in muck—

One leapt on my back and I got free, my legs tangling together. *Goddammit, too many of them, Jesus*—The scar chuckled wetly, pinging the nerves in my arm, sawing them like dry violin strings. The thing on my back exploded away with a wet popping sound, and right before I went down under a crushing weight of bodies I heard a coughing roar and the mechanical popping of a handgun. Sounded like a .22.

What the fuck—

Teeth crunched against my elbow, worrying at the tough

leather. I struck out with fists and feet, something hit me behind the knees, and I starfished again, trying to get them *off* me, roaches skittering, little insect feet probing at my eyes and mouth—

Crunch! The weight suddenly lessened, and the roar became a steady snarl. I *knew* that voice, even though it held no relation to humanity. The world whirled into chaos, ripping and wet splorching noises, foulness gushing out. I was spattered with hot fluids, and the density in the air fled before the clean sound of my Were's battlecry.

I thought I told him to go home! I surged up, fighting for air and life, and they exploded off me.

It *was* Saul. He blurred between man and cougar, the roar changing as his chest shifted dimensions. He didn't pause, either, sliding into cougarform and stretching as his claws took out an abdomen; he blurred up into humanshape, collided into another zombie with ribsnapping force and dropped gracefully back into catform again to avoid a strike. Seeing a Were fight is like seeing a tree bend itself to the wind, leaves fluttering. Every motion is thoughtlessly deliberate, beautifully precise. They never pause between humanshape and animal form, but the glimpses of unhuman geometry between the two are heartstopping in their beauty.

The popping of a handgun sounded again, and a high boy's voice, breaking as he cursed.

I launched myself, my hand sliding greasily against the balustrade, and hit the landing. Broke one zombie's neck, put it down, and ripped the other one off a supine human form. *Goddammit! Civilian.* The priorities of the situation shifted—I reached down with my hellbreed-strong right hand, grabbed a handful of flannel shirt, and tossed him unceremoniously out the door, not hard enough to bruise.

Or so I hoped.

Who the hell is that? I had no time to figure it out, because I heard Saul roar again and bolted up the stairs. A living carpet of roaches was trickling down the first two steep drops, the dots on their backs glaring at me.

Saul feinted, then reversed with sweet and natural speed. Another zombie exploded, foulness spattering both of us, and I leapt, meeting the next one with a crunch that rattled my teeth.

From there it was sheer instinct, fighting, with Saul at my side. We've done this so often—and I knew better than to ask him what the hell he was doing *here* until after things were under control.

There was a popping sound and the smell of wet salt and natron again. The roaches began to puff up into green smoke, and the zombies milled, losing their mass mind for a few crucial seconds. We waded into them, porous bones snapping like greenwood sticks and noisome fluids spraying and spattering.

Forensics was going to have a hell of a time with this place.

The roaches were popping out of existence, green fog knee-deep, and I hoped like hell there weren't more zombies downstairs. Whoever I'd dumped on the porch would be a prime target.

Saul's claws reached out, his fingers blurring between paw and hand, and sheared the last zombie's face clean off at the same moment that I hit it, double-fisted, and snapped ribs like matches. A few more moments' worth of work, and we were done here.

"Hey, sweetheart," he said as I stood panting and collecting myself.

Wouldn't you know it, even spattered with zombie goo he looked too good to be real. And now that the air was no longer paste-thick, ambient light was creeping around. It was no longer darker than midnight in a mine shaft.

I got my breath, ribs flickering. "Hey yourself." I turned on my heel and headed back down the stairs. My glutes were sure getting a workout from this case. "Civilian?"

"Kid," Saul said behind me, understanding immediately. "Gilberto. Says he heard you were coming out Chesko way on the police scanner, figured you were heading for this place."

Oh, great. "For Christ's sake." But it showed promise, and intuition. Neither of which were going to help him once I got my hands on him.

After I secured the scene.

"Seems like an okay kid." That was as far as he would go. "You okay?"

"Fine. Just ducky." *I thought you were at home.* I glanced out onto the front porch.

Gilberto crouched, his eyes huge in his thin, sallow face. His hair was mussed, free of a hairnet for the first time and falling lank across his pimpled forehead. He held the .22 like it was his personal holy grail.

"Happy now?" I didn't have time to say much else. There was half a house that could be crawling with more zombies. "Watch him," I tossed over my shoulder, and plunged down the stairs.

The basement smelled bad but not overwhelmingly so. This used to be where Zamba kept a couple pit bulls all year, and a few goats inside during the autumn rains. The chickens had their own coop in the back yard, but as soon as my eyes adjusted I saw ragged bundles of feathers scattered over the concrete floor.

I hit the light switch. There was nothing living down here.

The dogs were shapeless lumps of fur. The feathers were chicken corpses, strewn around as if there had been some sort of explosion. In the middle of the basement, a chalk-and-cornmeal circle writhed. The lines were moving sluggishly as the sorcery in the air bled out, whispering with a sound like a kid drawing on pavement, a dry hollow whisper. The meal was scattering, bleeding away from the thin lines.

Inside the circle, the three goats were twisted together, their legs stiff with rigor mortis and their bellies bloated. The floor was awash with sticky, almost-dry blood.

This isn't real voodoo. Nobody even made an attempt to cook these, or to kill them kindly. My gorge rose, I pushed it down. Why was it that zombie-smell didn't make me puke, but the dead helpless bodies could?

No, the animals had been killed with sorcery. They lay twisted in agony, their throats ripped open. No self-respecting practitioner would do this. Not even a *bocor* would waste lives this flagrantly.

I examined every part of the scene I could see, gun in one hand, whip in the other. There were no teensy-tiny track marks in the blood here. My blue eye caught the fading marks of etheric violence, souls ripped from bodies.

The explosion of energy when something is killed is one form of food for the *loa;* it is the offering the practitioners use to make bargains or payments. Cooking and eating the animal afterward is a sacrament. Even a *bocor* won't waste good meat that often. But this kind of wanton death bore no relation to voodoo. It was destruction for its own sake—the destruction of souls, which carries its own price and its own charge of dark energy, like jet fuel. This was more like the work of the Sorrows, those soul-eating carrion.

The Church holds it as a point of doctrine that animals don't have souls. I know better. I've *seen* better. It's only one place where we differ, the Holy Mother Church and I.

There are plenty of others.

Oh, God. The basement was clear. I headed back up the stairs. Saul met me on the landing. "No more of them. Some bodies in the bedrooms, though."

In a minute. I nodded. Half-turned. Gilberto was still crouching on the porch, the wreck of the shattered door creaking as I stepped on it. He looked up at me, and before the walls behind his eyes could go up I caught a glimpse of what he must have looked like before whatever had made him into what he was.

The first time I'd met this kid, I'd known he was a killer. Strength, size, and speed are all useless without the willingness to do serious harm; someone smaller with the ruthlessness to hurt can take on a giant and come away a limping winner. The dead-eyed gangbanger had that willingness in spades. We recognize each other, those of us who have come out the other side of decency and settled for survival.

And sometimes, something just gets left out of people, and they don't see anything wrong with killing. That's one of the tests of taking on an apprentice—finding out if they're willing to hurt someone if they have to, or if they're just sociopaths.

You have to be sure. A hunter is a deadly thing, and that deadliness *has* to be disciplined. Otherwise you're no better than the things you put down. You're worse than a Trader, even.

"I told you to go home." I didn't have to work to sound unwelcoming. "Did you not hear me? I said go home, and leave the night alone."

"What was those?" He rose slowly, the gun dangling in his right hand. "Right out of a fucking horror movie, eh, *bruja?* And him, he's *el gato. Lobo hombre, gato hombre.*" He was breathing so fast his narrow ribs flickered. That smell was on him—desperation, wanting so hard the teeth ache as if under a bad load of sugar.

"You're not listening." I glanced at Saul. "He was already here?"

"Yup." Saul's eyes glowed orange for a moment. He stood easily on the stairs, his back to the entire upper portion of the house, and I suddenly wanted to check every single room and cupboard.

It was ridiculous. He said he'd checked, and I trusted him to tell me when part of a scene was cleared. That was the whole idea behind having a partner, wasn't it?

I trusted his judgment, didn't I?

Of course I did. I swallowed hard, prioritized. "And you came out here because..."

"Galina called. She got no answer when she dialed Zamba. Figured you might run into some trouble." One corner of his mouth curled up. "Besides, I like seeing you."

My own lips stretched into a grudging smile. How did he do that, make me feel good with five little words? "Flatterer."

"Hey, whatever works." In this light he didn't look nearly as tired. And no doubt about it, he'd pretty much saved my bacon. I would've survived, but still. "Where's Zamba?"

"Don't know. Any blondes in the wreckage?"

"Not that I saw, but the bodies are a little...well, you'll see."

I looked back out onto the porch. Gilberto was following our exchange. He wasn't pale or in shock. He was just as he'd always been—sallow and dirty-looking. His eyes were a bit wide, but that was all. He seemed to be handling this well.

It could've been an act. Gangs are big on face, and he probably had a lot of practice in not looking scared. But usually, when someone encounters the nightside for the first time, there's more trouble. Screaming, fainting, puking, rage—I've seen it all. The initial reaction doesn't mean much. It's how people deal with having the rationality of the world whopped away from under them over the long term that matters. After a brush with the nightside some retreat into rigid logic, a bulwark against something their upbringing tells them shouldn't exist. Others get increasingly loud and nervous, ending up wearing tinfoil hats and screeching about conspiracy aliens.

Some of them get really, really quiet, go home, and eat a bullet or some pills. It all depends.

On the other hand, in the barrio they know about Weres. Enough not to mess with them, at least.

Gilberto just looked at me, his chin coming up a little. Stubbornness made him look mulish, especially when he hunched his thin shoulders and peered out under strings of hair. *What's it gonna be,* that look asked. *What you gonna do with me? Because I ain't going home.*

I stared at him, trying to make a decision. It's not like snap decisions aren't a part of the job—some days, it's nothing *but,* and you have to make the right one in under a hundredth of a second. But this wasn't a decision that would or could be made without a lot of thought.

Then again, the students come along whether a teacher is ready or not. The world was just full of on-the-other-hand answers today. "You got a car, Gil?"

He shrugged. Even the shrug was right—equal parts stray-cat insouciance and hesitation.

"All right. Here's the first thing: *don't* steal any fucking cars. From now on you don't break or even bend the law. Go back to my house. There's a key under one of the empty flowerpots stacked on the east side. Go inside and don't touch anything, unless you're getting yourself a snack. We'll talk when I get home, and I don't know when that will be. You got me?"

He nodded. The hunted look didn't go away, but at least he straightened a little.

"I mean it," I persisted. "Don't steal a car. Don't break the speed limit. If you have a gun, clean or not, ditch it before you step in my door. You come in clean, or I won't have anything to do with you."

"I'm not stupid." The sullenness returned.

"Prove it by being clean when you step in my door. Stay inside, don't leave until I talk to you. Go on, now."

He shrugged. His slim brown fingers loosened, and he dropped the .22. It made a heavy sound when it hit the porch, and I winced internally. *He's going to be a live one.*

I watched him go down the sobbing, squeaking steps. He headed across the street and vanished into the darkness. I hoped he made it, and I hoped he listened to me.

Then I shelved that hope, scooped up his .22, and got back to the problem at hand.

This was not looking good at all.

"What just happened?" Saul still stood on the stairs, watching. Bits of zombie glop still clung to him, dripping off the fringe of his jacket. It was going to be a job and a half cleaning the suede up. Thank God he believes in Scotchgarding everything. It doesn't do much good with the rags my clothes end up as, but it works wonders for his.

"I don't know yet." *I might have an apprentice, that's all. We'll see.* "Best to keep him out of the way until I do." I checked the pistol, made sure the safety was on, and wondered if it was one I'd seen him use before.

The thought of that case was uncomfortable, to say the least. And Saul still hadn't asked any questions about it. And there was a grave up on Mount Hope, with a good cop sleeping under a green blanket. The people responsible had been mostly cleaned up—but not all of them.

Prioritize, Jill. Get back up on the horse. "When did Galina call?"

"Just as I got in the door. I came out here. Was wondering what the hell the kid was doing here when I heard the fight." He shrugged, stuck his hands in his pockets. "Any idea what's going on yet?"

"Not much. Other than these cases are connected somehow. And if Zamba's not a body here, she might be involved."

"Great." He sounded as thrilled as I felt about that. "What does she look like again?" As if he wouldn't remember her, but he was being sure. Checking. It was a partner's responsibility to check.

"Blond dreadlocks. Tall. Bad legs, but a good smile." I tried a smile on my own face, but it felt like plastic. This was going south fast. "Show me the bodies. Let's get this wrapped."

"Sure thing." But he just stood there, looking at me, for a long moment. "I'm glad I came out."

What do you want, a tickertape parade? But that was uncharitable of me. I could just chalk it up to nerves, couldn't I? "Me too, catkin. Let's see those bodies."

"Are you really?" It wasn't like him to persist. "You sure?"

I exaggerated rolling my eyes, just like a teenager. I'll never see the sunny side of thirty again, but sometimes eyerolling is so satisfying I don't care. "Of *course* I'm glad. Jesus, Saul, what's up with you?" *And can it wait? I've got a city about to blow sky-high here, and a pattern I don't like the looks of underneath.*

"Nothing." He turned gracefully and led me up the stairs. "There are bodies in the bedrooms, nothing in the kitchen but a pot on the stove. Smells like the other place, a little."

"But no blondes? Blond dreadlocks, waist-length?" Wide face, big nose, bad skin, rotting teeth rimmed with gold making a bright-starred smile, and those dreadlocks. Zamba was tall and almost breastless, and I'd sometimes thought she was in drag. Nowadays you can't tell, and dealing with 'breed on a regular basis will wallop some of your assumptions about gender pretty hard.

"Come and see."

Goddammit. But he was right not to tell me, I suppose. I might not have believed it, if he had.

It was nine bodies, all told. I recognized an ebony-skinned trio, male and female, who had been Zamba's longtime acolytes. There was a small, compact Hispanic male—Zamba was truly catholic in her choice of trainees—and a taller, Grecian redhead. A double-gemini of husky dark-haired males completed the sets. They were three to a room, her inner circle all naked and twisted together like the goats in the basement. The beds had been scattered with chrysanthemum petals, and their throats had been ripped out.

They probably wouldn't rise as zombies, though I would nail the palms and feet before Forensics got here. There wasn't enough etheric residue in them to power that kind of motion, though. Zamba's devotees had been *eaten.* And either someone had brushed aside Zamba's protections and killed her followers and her, or...

Jesus.

In the kitchen, a pot on the stove was long cool. A stringy brew of something that smelled vaguely similar to Lorelei's still-bubbling concoction rested under a thick scrim of clotted grease. The kitchen was otherwise spic-and-span, the attached dining room where Zamba fed her acolytes holding a long table, chairs ranked neatly, and an altar on the wall under the window that looked out on the side-yard and the wall of the abandoned house next door.

"What do you make of this?" Saul asked quietly. He stood by

the sink, arms folded, looking at the bottle of dishwashing liquid and scrubbies, neatly placed in a chrome rack.

"I don't like that we can't find her body." *That's just one of the things I don't like about this.*

"Any chance she could be the one behind all this?"

Trust him to say what I was thinking. "More than a chance, catkin. Still, I suppose there's always room to hope she's not. I'd like it better if the bitch was dead."

"Now there's something I don't hear you say often." He peered out the window. "It's almost dawn."

No shit. This has been a long night. I spotted the phone, hanging at the end of the counter. "If Zamba's behind this, it's bad news. If she's just disappeared it's bad news too; it means we might have another body site." I let out a sigh. The smell was bad, the situation was worse, and I had the idea I wasn't going to spend today sleeping, either. "I've got to call in and see who they can spare to come out and process this site too. No rest for the wicked."

"Amen to that." His shoulders went down a little. Had he been bracing himself? For what? "What's our next step?"

I thought about it. "Calling someone to come out and take care of this site. Seeing if I overlooked Zamba's body downstairs or in the back yard. Going over this place with a fine-tooth comb, then going through the files—" I tapped the counter with bitten-down nails, my fingers drumming. "This has all the earmarks of a serious fucking tangle."

As usual, Saul put the question in reasonable terms. "If Zamba *is* behind this, what does she have against the Cirque?"

"I don't—" I straightened, suddenly, and stared at the pot on the stove. "Huh."

Saul kept quiet, looking at the sink, and let me wander around inside my head. It was good to have him there—he served up the right questions, and knew when to keep his mouth shut so I could *think*. I found myself studying the lines of his fringed jacket, his jeans splattered with zombie, the edge of the stove, his boots, my own boot-toes. Eyes roving, snagging on the linoleum as I pursued the line of thought to its logical end, found it wanting—but not wanting enough.

"If a better theory comes along, I'll snag it," I decided out loud.

"Call this scene in, I'm going to check the back yard and the houses on either side."

"I'm coming with you." His jaw jutted, stubbornly.

Oh, for Chrissake. "Of course you are. *After* you call."

CHAPTER 16

Piper was still processing the last scene. This time Foster showed up, his own brown ponytail slick as ever. He surveyed the stinking goop starred with porous bones that had been zombies and sighed. "Busy night. Anything else?"

I almost hated to tell him. Foster always reminds me of an otter—brown, sleek, with a cute little nose and quick clever fingers. "The bedrooms. Don't take the iron nails out of the corpses. And there's animals downstairs."

"Well, shit." But he motioned his team past, Carolyn holding the door log in front of her like a holy grail, Max with his camera, Stephanie and Browder with their matching smiles and bags of gear. "*Beaucoup* overtime."

Behind them, Sullivan and the Badger showed up. The Badger negotiated the stairs with her mouth set tight and turned down, her gray hair pulled back into its usual bun, the white streak down one side glinting, since I'd flicked the porch lights on. Sullivan, scratching at his coppery stubble, gave me a weak grin. He looks like dishwater even on a good day, but that pale, nervous exterior hides a sharp, inductive mind.

The Badger looks like a cookie-baking, kitten-sweatshirt-and-mom-jean-wearing soccer mom—a particularly cuddly and harmless one. She'd added a pair of steel-framed glasses to her round florid face, and moved carefully. I wasn't fooled—for such a rotund woman, she was light on her feet when it counted. And they don't call her the Badger for her hair.

No, she gets that name by being tenacious as hell. She does it in such a nice, unassuming way that people forget her namesake has teeth *and* claws.

Rumor has it she went a couple of rounds with a sex offender once, and busted him up bad by the time backup arrived. The perp thought one plump lady cop would be easy to bowl over. He spent three weeks in the hospital and another couple months in physical therapy, I was told.

I'd lay odds it's true.

"How many fucking scenes you going to give us tonight?" Sullivan said, blinking. He patted his breast pocket, where a pack of Marlboro Lights peeped up at me. For someone who looks so washed-out, he certainly has a big strident voice.

"As many as I've got. Hi, Badge."

She grunted, heaved herself up onto the porch, and eyed me. "Thought you didn't want a team tonight."

I shrugged. Silver tinkled in my hair, falling over my shoulders. "With bodies mounting up like this, I need backup." *I'm glad it's you two.*

"Huh. Should we check the other scenes?" It's amazing, the way her soft, modulated voice can slice through a hubbub. One of the forensic techs was laughing—shrill laughter with that edge of disgust you hear so often at homicide scenes.

It's not disrespectful. It's because sometimes you have to laugh to keep from screaming, crying, or throwing up. "Might as well. This turned out bigger than I thought it'd be. I thought I could save you guys some work."

Sullivan wheezed and the Badger chuckled. "You kidding?" she got out, between snickers. "If we wanted less work we wouldn't have chosen *this* job."

"Very funny. Make sure the techs don't take the nails out of the hands and feet. See if you can get any IDs on the messy bodies; the less-messy ones will be easier but I already know who they are. Find out where they were last seen, see if you can trace the animals—"

"Animals?" Sullivan's pale face twisted up. The short buzz of his coppery, receding hair glittered again as he hunched his shoulders. "Shit."

"Sorry." And I was.

"Well, you didn't kill 'em." He stuffed his hands in his pockets. "Should we go over Piper's scenes too?"

I nodded. Saul moved briefly behind me, a restless movement utterly unlike him. "Please do. Oh, and see if you can dig up who this house actually belongs to. I'd like a legal name, DOB, everything." *I don't know nearly enough about Zamba. That's going to change.*

"That means you have a hunch." The Badger nodded. "Don't worry, I won't ask—I know I don't want to know. I'll page you as soon as we have something."

And bless her thoroughgoing little heart, she would have the full report from chowder to cashews—or as close to it as it was humanly possible to get. "Good deal. Thanks." I eased past both of them—the Badger stood stolidly and Sullivan flinched back. He covered it well, though, turning to look down at the garden.

"Huh," he said. "Go figure."

"What?" I glanced down at the belt of jungle greenery, uncomfortably reminded of Lorelei's backyard.

"Plants are dying. Looks like someone did a lot of work on the yard, though. You'd think, a place like this, they wouldn't have stopped watering before they died. Or are the bodies old?"

"Not *too* old." *Especially the ones that were trying to kill me about half an hour ago.* But they didn't need me to lay that little thought in their heads. "See you."

Sullivan sighed. "See you, Jill. Try not to trip over any more dead 'uns tonight."

"Shut up, Sully. It's our *job*." The Badger sounded long-suffering, as usual, and she herded him inside the house.

What a pair.

Saul drifted beside me as I made my way down the cracked, zigzagging walk. "Car's this way."

I nodded, let him take the lead. Sullivan was right, the garden was just in the first stages of dying. Plants were drooping, but not browned and crispy yet.

I stopped, turned, and looked back at the house, its windows blazing with golden light now. A hose was coiled up next to the porch's listing sneer.

Hellebore. Feverfew. Foxglove. Wormwood. Mugwort. Bindweed. American ginseng under a rigged-up canvas canopy. Some succulents, but not many, and the rest of the plants were useful, in one way or another, to a rogue herbalist or kitchen witch.

Or a voodoo queen.

The zombies were relatively fresh. So were the bodies. Rigor mortis doesn't last *that* long. Bellies were distended on the goats downstairs, but that happens...I'd need an autopsy to be reasonably sure of time of death.

But the garden, though. Things wilt fast out here in the desert, but if things were normal out here at Mama Zamba's—if normal could be the word applied to the biggest wheel in the voodoo community in my town—the garden should be in tiptop shape for a little while after she was dead.

So what had kept her so busy her garden didn't get watered? She had people to do it *for* her.

But those people were dead.

The zombies were too juicy and the human bodies were too fresh. It just *didn't add up*. Unless the reigning queen of the voodoo scene had had something more than gardens on her mind lately—and on the minds of her followers.

Her newly dead followers.

"What are you thinking?" Saul finally asked as I stood staring at Zamba's garden like I was hypnotized.

"I don't quite know yet," I admitted. "It's more and more likely Zamba's involved instead of a victim. I think we should get some breakfast, since dawn's coming up."

"And then?"

I tested the hypothesis in my head. I just didn't know enough to see if it explained everything. "And then we're going to visit Galina again. If she hasn't gone through her diaries yet, I'll wait while she does. I've got a theory, but I can't figure one thing out."

"That one thing would be?"

"Why a voodoo queen has it in for the Cirque. You'd think if she hated hellbreed she'd find some closer to home to murder."

CHAPTER 17

Micky's on Mayfair was just the same as it always is around dawn—almost deserted, clean as a whistle, and staffed with Weres. Some of the waitstaff are humans, true, but the greater percentage including the owner are from the Santa Luz prides, packs, and flights.

Amalia, a lioness of the Norte Luz pride, greeted us at the door. "Jill, nice to see you. Dustcircle." She nodded, and Saul nodded back. "A table? Or is it business?"

I must have looked grim, and realized I was dirty and disheveled. They do usually see me in this state, but I'd been thinking so hard even my nose had shut off.

"A table," Saul said as I cast around vainly for something to wipe off with. "Does Theron have any towels lying around?"

"I'll check." She grinned, her broad, high-cheekboned face lighting up. I suddenly felt even more dirty and mucky, snuck a peek at Saul. He was just the same as ever, his essential difference shining out from under weariness and zombie muck, and I felt myself deflate like a punctured balloon. It wasn't fair. They're so much better than we could ever be, the Weres.

No wonder humans hunted them, during the bad old days of the Inquisition. The only thing humans hate more than ugliness is actual beauty.

Theron, a lean dark Werepanther, actually came out from the bar to greet us, wiping his hands on a white cloth that had seen much, much better days in the bleach bucket. His long fingers danced with it, refolding it so the holes didn't show. "Hey, Saul. Glad to see you back."

"Theron." Saul gave him an answering grin. "How's bartending?"

"Good work if you can get it." Theron's dark gaze flicked past to me, and his forehead furrowed. "Jill."

"Hey. Sorry, I smell. Got a spare towel?" As usual, I sounded more truculent than I really was. They were just so pretty. Amalia's face was flawless, not a pore in sight, and neither of the two males would ever lack for female attention.

It made me wonder what the hell Saul was doing with me. Not for the first time, and a question I was mulling over more and more lately.

"You bet." But Theron stayed where he was, looking first at Saul, then curiously at me, the line deepening. "Um..."

"She's hungry." Saul folded his arms, and a hint of gravel poured through the bottom of the words.

It was so unlike him my jaw threatened to drop. But Theron just shrugged, Amalia tipped me a wink and a salute, and both of them disappeared, leaving us to seat ourselves.

"What was that?" I poked him on the shoulder when he didn't respond. "Saul?"

He gave me a single dark glance, hitched one shoulder up, and dropped it. I sighed and considered folding my arms, but Saul set off for our regular booth along the back wall and Theron showed up again, carrying a stack of damp washcloths.

"Here you go." The Werepanther gave me a meaningful look. I raised my eyebrows, my hands full of warm, sopping wet cloth. "You guys want a beer?"

"Might as well." I wiggled my eyebrows and pointed my chin at Saul's retreating back. *What's up with him? Help me out here.*

Theron just looked confused, a blush sliding along his high-arched cheekbones. His dark hair fell across his forehead, curls and waves damp with sweat. It looked like Micky's had seen a heavy night; he was just cleaning up before dawn.

The liquor laws in Santa Luz kind of don't apply to the nonhumans. Hellbreed and Trader bars go the same way, only they rollick far harder than any place the Weres run.

In *both* senses of the word. Harder, dirtier, and far, far fouler.

"What's wrong?" I mouthed, wishing my eyebrows would go up higher and that my face could communicate the complexity of the question I wanted to ask.

Theron spread his hands helplessly, spun on the balls of his feet, and set off for the hall running alongside the kitchen. It actually looked like he was *retreating.*

What the hell is going on here? The washcloths—they were

bar towels, soaked and smelling of bleach and fresh laundry—
dripped in my hands, rapidly cooling. Nobody was likely to give
an answer. I heard one of the cooks in the depths of the kitchen off
to my right swear, and the hiss of something hitting the grill.

Yeah, sometimes when you go into Micky's around dawn, you
get what the cooks think you should eat instead of anything on the
menu. It's always good, and you should never look a Were's gift in
the mouth, so to speak.

I shook my head, silver clicking in my hair, and headed for the
girls' room. I'd probably feel better about all this once I was a little
cleaner.

Then again, I thought, clutching the washrags, *maybe I won't.*

Saul slid the file across the table at me and tucked into his fried-
eggs-and-ham. I took a long pull off a bottle of microbrew Theron
had slung on the table and eyed the steak-and-eggs combo, hash
browns cremated the way I like them, extra bacon, and toast slath-
ered with butter. It probably had enough calories in it to keep me
fueled through a long night of chasing evil. I wondered if it would
fuel my brain enough for me to figure out the pattern behind the
murders.

Once I started eating, I realized how hungry I was. This led to
a good quarter-hour spent in silence, just the clinking of forks on
plates and an occasional slurp. I finished my beer and another
arrived. So did more toast. Amalia simply plunked down a fresh
plate of it and raised an eyebrow—about the closest she'd get to
telling me I'd better eat it all.

Weres. It's only one of the ways they show they care.

I cut a strip of steak, sliced it up, and was grateful it wasn't
rare. Now that the first edge of hunger was past I could slow down
and enjoy the taste. There had to have been at least five eggs on
the plate.

Fighting off the undead and Hell's citizens all night does work
up a girl's appetite. Sorcery can only do so much, and I wasn't as
young as I used to be. I used to be able to go for days without eating, running from one thing to the next, writing checks my body
cashed without complaining too much.

Not anymore.

Go figure.

I finally looked up from my plate to find Saul chewing slowly, watching me. His eyes were dark and fathomless.

I swallowed a mouthful of steak, glad Micky's was empty. My skin twitched under the sensory overload from the unveiled scar, every noise and photon amped up exponentially. "Hi," I said finally. "Good to see you."

A small smile lifted the corner of his chiseled mouth. "Hi, kitten. Nice to see you, too."

Is it? Or are you just saying that? "This is looking like a huge problem."

"Isn't it always." But his tone was reflective and amused, faintly sarcastic. "You think it's connected?" One lifted eyebrow could have meant that he agreed, or that he wanted to give me a chance to get my thoughts in order.

I ticked them off on my fingers. "Those bugs. Each with a red spot. The green smoke. Voodoo practitioners dead, zombies everywhere, possessed people that shouldn't be, one of them ending up as a zombie, and Zamba missing. The Cirque's hostage attacked, and another Cirque performer dead. Both Zamba and Lorelei had something cooking on their stoves..."

"If it looks like a duck, swims like a duck, quacks like a duck—"

"—it's certainly not a zebra," I finished. "So, they're more than likely connected, all these things. I just don't know *how* yet." I forked up another load of eggs. "What possible connection could the Cirque have with any voodoo practitioner?"

"I don't know."

I took another long swallow of beer. It went down nice and easy. Wrestling zombies gives you a powerful thirst. "Voodoo and hellbreed don't tangle. It's just one of those things."

"They must mix sometimes," he pointed out practically.

I shook my head. Silver shifted and chimed, and some of my curls were stiff with gunk. "The *loa* are jealous, and hellspawn don't like anything interfering with their games either."

"What about..."

I watched him, fork paused in midair, but he merely shrugged. "No," he finally amended. "I got nothing."

"And then there's this." I yanked the plastic-shrouded straight razor out of my pocket, laid it on the table. Next out was the enamel cup.

Put together, they looked shoddy. The straight razor crouched in its swaddling, and the cup's chipped sides reflected fluorescent light.

"A razor? And a cup." He set his fork down. "Huh."

"Yeah. My instincts are all tingling, but I don't know what they're saying."

"Tingling instincts?" He might have looked bland and interested, except for the wicked twinkle in his eyes. "I hear they have creams for that."

A chuckle caught me off-guard. "They're not *burning*. Just tingling. Anyway, and then there's zombies. It takes work and effort to create one with voodoo. Now all of a sudden they're crawling around everywhere—and the Twins are taking an active interest in everything."

It was a huge pileup of events. The more I sat back and considered, the more it seemed like one thing.

"What?" Saul speared a piece of fried ham. "You look like you just thought of something."

"I did." I applied myself to clearing my plate, but I also hooked the file a little closer and flipped it open. There might not be anything in it, but it was best to check.

"Well?" He didn't quite fidget, but he did shift on his side of the table, his long legs stretched out until his boot-toe touched my calf.

"Nothing solid yet, catkin. Let me think." I scanned the file, flipping past Xeroxed pages and paperwork filled in with Avery's neat scrawl. Lucky boy, our first victim, Mr. Ricardo. A green card and everything. Avery, bless his little heart, had even pulled the application for me. I'd bet anything Juan Rujillo, our local FBI contact, had facilitated that little search as a favor. Dear old Juan, a joy to work with. Not like the last Feeb we had.

Hmm. That's interesting.

Ricardo even had a sponsor. The little click of a puzzle piece sliding home sounded in the middle of my head, and I took a long draft of beer. "Hey, Saul. Guess what? Ricardo had a green card."

"Mmmh." He had a full mouth. He was busy slathering even more green Tabasco on the remainder of his ham. "Mmmmh?"

"Guess who his sponsor was."

"Mrph?" He jabbed at his plate and shrugged.

"Lorelei." I slapped the file closed as his chewing stopped and his eyebrows went back up in surprise. "As soon as we finish here, we're heading for Galina's. I'll bet your ham and my entire plate she knows something about this, and she's had a chance to go through her diaries by now."

CHAPTER 18

Dawn came up in gray streaks, followed by rose and gold. Once the sun heaved itself up over the rim of the world, I let out a half-conscious sigh of relief. My pager stayed quiet, and—true to my guess—Galina had spent all night with not only her own diaries but the records of the Sanctuary before her. Huge leather-bound books, each cover stamped with the seal of the Order, stood in stacks on her butcher-block table.

She was covered in dust, her hair held back with a red kerchief, and as ill-tempered as I'd ever seen her. Which was still pretty damn polite.

"Lorelei's dead?" A line etched itself between her winged eyebrows. She swiped at a smudge on her cheek. "And zombies at Zamba's? Christ. Try saying that ten times in a row."

"Tell me about it. No, wait. Never mind. Tell me about the problem Sloane had with the Cirque." I folded my arms and leaned against the wall. Saul was fiddling with the kettle and her stove. Gray dawn filtered through the skylight and the big box window, touching his shorn hair and wide shoulders.

"I've been going back through the records." She spread her hands. "I was wrong. It wasn't Arthur Gregory. The trouble started with Sam."

"Rosehip tea?" The kettle started to chirp, and Saul looked over his shoulder.

"Oh, yes. Yes indeed." Galina dropped into a straight-backed wooden chair, swept the kerchief off. Her marcel waves were disarranged.

"Coming right up." Saul didn't ask if I wanted tea.

I stifled a burp. Now that I'd eaten, I was beginning to realize how tired I was.

No rest for the wicked, though. "Sam?" I prompted.

"Samuel Gregory. Arthur's younger brother. Arthur came to Sloane needing help—his brother had disappeared. The Cirque was in town, and Sloane suspected them, but he couldn't find the boy. Arthur kept following Sloane around, pestering him. He didn't get what he wanted, so he went elsewhere."

"Elsewhere?" It could mean just about anything.

"He apparently decided that since Sloane couldn't help him, he'd make a deal with someone who would."

Not too bright of him. But sometimes civilians make that sort of mistake. "Hellbreed?"

She shook her head. Her earrings—little peridots in marcasite—swung. "Voodoo. Or so I heard. Sloane suspected Lorelei. She wasn't Lorelei then, she was Abigail Figueroa. It was in the seventies that she switched over to—"

"Hold on." *This may be connected, but* how*?* I dropped down into a chair myself, my brain buzzing. "This Arthur. He had a hard-on for the Cirque?"

"I don't know. I do know Sloane suspected that was where Samuel disappeared to, and dug pretty hard to find him. Arthur disappeared, and Sloane went looking for him too. He came across some of the Cirque folk running a game on the side—something to do with child-slaves, I think, though he never said—and put them out of commission. He tried to find either of the Gregory boys, but neither of them ever showed up. He was still working that case, off and on, when the outbreak happened."

Yeah, that would put a dent in working a case or two. "So it never got wrapped up. And it's only vanishingly likely it's connected to what we have going on now. Was there any proof at all that this Arthur kid went to voodoo? Or did Sloane just suspect?"

Of course, a hunter's suspicion is sometimes good as gold. But you can't move without proof, or you turn into what you're hunting. It's just one of those things.

"The last place Arthur was seen was going into Lorelei's old shop. She used to be down near Plaskény Square instead of on Greenlea; I can't believe I'd forgotten that. Anyway, Sloane had a witness who placed him there before he disappeared. There was something else. People who knew the boys turned up dead."

"Like who?"

"Their father, for one. A real winner—the kind who likes to use the strap. He ended up torn in pieces and scattered around his rooming house cot, blood all over the walls. Another man—he'd apparently been their mother's other pimp." She glanced at me, then swiftly back at the table. "It was a different world then, Jill."

I wondered what my face was saying. "Not so different. So the 'father' was a husband, and she had another pimp?" I knew that game, I'd seen it played before, up close. A woman desperate for any kind of attention, selling herself to and for the man who promised to protect her while she nursed bruises from the other man— and when the first one beat her again, she'd go back to the second. It was a vicious cycle.

"Bounced back and forth between them. Poor kids." Galina's eyes were dark and troubled. "There were others. A few police detectives—ones on the take, Sloane said—and a schoolkid who hung out with the Gregory boys, was apparently a bit of a bully."

"That's a high body count. They can't have been unrelated."

"Life was cheap back then, Jill. This was a mining town and a riverport. I remember when you didn't dare go outside at night if you were a respectable female. At least, not without a man and a gun." For a moment she looked much older, her mouth pulled down and her cheeks sucked in. "Anyway, the deaths were all the same. Torn into tiny pieces, lots of blood."

Life is still cheap around here, Galina. At least, if you're brown-skinned or poor. Gold leached in through the skylight, taking on the tenor of daylight.

I rolled my shoulders back in their sockets, trying to ease a persistent ache. "Huh. I wonder...I should still have some of Sloane's records. Can you write down the dates for me?"

"I can do that." She looked, in fact, relieved to be given a concrete task. I didn't blame her. Digging through old records can be deadly boring, and for a Sanctuary it was probably even more so.

They drive their roots in deep and live a long time, but the things they trade for it...you don't make a bargain like that without wondering if it's worth it.

Or at least, that's what I think about every bargain. The world keeps asking you to peel bits of yourself away, just to keep breathing.

The kettle whistled, Saul flicked the stove off and poured. And as usual, he asked the right question. "So is someone settling scores?"

I stared at the leather-bound books. She must have been excavating all night. "Possible. But why try to kill the hostage? That won't damage the Cirque. It will remove the constraints that make them behave. And Helene..."

I hate that feeling—when you think you have a lead, and all you get is more questions.

"It was a long time ago," Galina said softly. "Long and long."

"Do we have any pictures of either of the Gregorys?" There wasn't much hope.

She sighed, a flicker of irritation crossing her round face. It wasn't with me—although heaven knows Galina usually has enough reason. "No, unfortunately. This is so *frustrating*. I feel like there's something I should be remembering." She stared at the books as Saul handed her a mug.

I blew out a long breath. "Well, it was almost a century ago, Galina. It's not like forgetting what you had for lunch yesterday."

"It kind of is, though. This is important. It's just on the tip of my brain. But I should have noted it, and I've been all through my official diary and the private one. It feels unfinished."

"Life is full of unfinished things." I glanced at Saul, who stretched his long legs out. *This is all very historical and interesting, but it sounds like a dead end. There's nothing to tie an old case to what's going on now, unless it's Lorelei. And she had her fingers in so many nasty pies, it's not very likely she was just now killed for something that happened almost a hundred years ago. No, the connection's probably elsewhere. Which means I'm right back where I started—except I have a missing voodoo queen, zombies, dead hellbreed, and a situation that could get Very Messy Indeed.* The exhaustion came back, circling like a shark.

Prioritize, Jill.

I took it out loud, so I could think it through better. "The attack on the hostage was voodoo. Perry's supposed to stay and make sure the hostage doesn't bite it. In any case, it'll be nightfall before someone can try again." *One problem that doesn't have to be solved immediately.* I stared at the leather-bound books heaped on the table, breathed in deeply. Galina blew across the top of her tea. "I've got voodoo practitioners dropping like flies, spirits in people who shouldn't have them—though if they're believers, it changes the equation a little—and one of them came down with a bad case of zombie. *And* Zamba's missing in action. She could quite possibly be needing protection, or she's part of this. Either of which is equally unprepossessing. I've got Forensics collecting evidence, and Sullivan and the Badger doing some digging."

It took me a couple more seconds to piece everything together.

"What's up next?" Saul, as usual, gave the right question.

"Going home and getting cleaned up," I decided. "Figuring out what to do about that kid. Then the next step."

"Which is? And what kid?" Galina took a gulp of her tea. Maybe she needed it to wash the taste of history and dust out of her mouth.

"The kid who's been following me around. And the next step is visiting some *botanicas*. Zamba wasn't the only game in town, just the biggest one." I pushed myself up to my feet and almost regretted it. Aches and pains twinged all over my body.

"An apprentice?" The Sanc looked at me like I'd just expressed a desire to take off my clothes and howl naked in the street. "When did this happen?"

"It hasn't happened yet." I pushed my chair in. The sunlight strengthened. It looked like another beautiful day. "Right now I just want him kept out of trouble."

"That's funny." Galina's tone suggested it wasn't funny at all. "That's just what Sloane said about Arthur Gregory. I remember *that* much, at least."

For once, I observed the speed limit. Saul turned the radio's volume knob and lit a Charvil, and dawn traffic was light. Santa Luz sometimes looks washed out, the sun bleaching buildings and dirt, the dust haze putting everything in soft focus. The greens are pale sage, the whites turn taupe and buff, and any dab of brightness gets covered with a thin film before long.

It's different in the barrio. Bright blocks of primary color are a little more cheerful in the daylight—but a little more carnivorous at night. Even well-tended lawns look anemic under the first assault of morning light. It isn't until the richness of twilight that things take on that mellow gold tinge, like waking up from a siesta with the world scrubbed clean and a little brighter.

It could just be me. But things seem tired in the morning. The day has risen, wearily, from the bowl of night. It's when I get to go home, because the nasty things mostly stick to darkness to do their dirtiness.

They don't call it the nightside for nothing.

And this morning seemed a little darker than usual. The windows were down and the radio was off, early coolness rising from the river and a promise of scorching later, but I thought I heard something else under the purring engine and the rushing air. The scar had been uncovered almost all night, and the sensory acuity was beginning to seem normal. The noise resolved itself into notes from a steam-driven calliope in the distance.

A bright, cheery tune. That "Camptown Races" thing again, but with a darker edge. And the shadows were wrong this morning. Just by a millimeter or two, but they were at strange angles, and darker than the usual knife-sharp morning shadows. Gleams flickered through them—pairs of colorless gleams, low and slinking.

It wasn't precisely against the rules for the Cirque's dogs to be out running—but it was strange.

Stranger than someone with a grudge against both voodoo practitioners and hellbreed? Or stranger than Zamba disappearing and her entire household laid waste?

Stranger than Perry doing exactly what I tell him to?

The more I thought about it, the more my brain just went in circles. Even intuition wasn't any help; it just flailed and threw up its hands. I was too tired, and getting dull-witted. Fatigue is a risk during cases like this.

"Goddammit," I sighed, and Saul exhaled a long tobacco-scented sigh as well.

"Jill." He sounded serious.

"Huh?" *The thing that troubles me most,* I decided, *is not find-ing Zamba's body. That slippery little bitch wouldn't have let any-one kill her closest followers. That was her power base, the ones that ran herd on all the others.*

Always assuming someone *else* had killed them.

"We need to talk."

Oh, Christ. Not now. "What's up?"

Seconds ticked by. I braked to a stop on Chesko. We'd turn and go up Lluvia Avenue. The engine hummed to itself, a familiar song.

The light turned green. Saul still said nothing. "What is it?" I prompted again, touching the accelerator. We moved smoothly forward, and no, it wasn't my imagination. The colorless eyes in the shadows were following us.

Great.

"I love you." He tossed the half-smoked Charvil away. It som-ersaulted in the slipstream and was gone. I checked the rearview. *Just wonderful. Jesus.* "You know that, right?"

"I do." *That's not the problem. The problem is that you can't stand to touch me now. And there's a bigger problem right now, too. It has to do with those eyes in the shadows. The ones watch-ing us right now.*

Why now? Nighttime was their time.

There was another long pause, like he was waiting for me to say something. I kept checking the mirrors. *Is this trouble? Why would they wait for daylight?*

"Are you—" He tapped another Charvil up out of the pack. Held it in his long expressive fingers. I checked to make sure his seat belt was on. Of course it was. I pressed the accelerator a little harder. "Are you listening to me?"

"Of course I am." The needle climbed, slowly but surely. The shadows were thickening, and I got a very bad feeling. "You said you love me. I said I know. You asked—"

"Jill. There's something..." He twitched, looked out the win-dow. "Is something following us?"

"Hang on." My fingers caressed the gearshift. "Half a second."

"Goddammit. There's never a minute alone with you."

"You're alone with me right now." The shadows were growing

blacker, their crystalline eyes reflecting daylight stripped of all its warmth.

I mashed the accelerator. Tires chirped, and the Pontiac leapt forward obediently.

We roared down Lluvia, the shadows keeping pace. They circled as we bounced over the railroad tracks and down a long sun-drenched stretch of road. Here the sun hit a wall of warehouses dead-on to my left, and there wasn't a shadow to be found—except the shadow of the Pontiac, running next to us with its own loping stride. The tires made low sounds of disapproval, I skidded into a turn and jagged right on Sarvedo Street, working the turn like threading a needle in one motion. Saul grabbed at the dash, breaking his Charvil and giving me a single reproachful look.

My warehouse was about ten blocks down, and even from here my smart eye could see the layers of protection on my walls waking in bursts of blue etheric flame.

Oh, holy shit. There's a civilian in there. I sent him in myself.

I jammed the accelerator to the floor and prayed I wasn't too late.

CHAPTER 19

I bailed out in a blur, Saul right behind me, and I didn't have to break my own door down. The entire warehouse was tolling like a bell in a windstorm, and there was a gaping hole where the front door used to be. Green smoke billowed out, thinning in the morning breeze, and there wasn't a shadow to be found.

The fume was acrid, tasting of rotten pumpkins and stale cigar smoke. Down the short hall, bursting into the living room—couch overturned, floors awash with greasy knee-deep smoke—I flashed through, boots pounding, into the long, wood-floored sparring room.

The mirrors along one wall were all cracked, the ballet barre splintered, the weapons hanging on the walls scattered except for one long quivering shape under a fall of amber silk. Gilberto Rosario Gonzalez-Ayala was in a crouch, a Bowie knife flat against one forearm, feinting at a shape made of smoke and nightmare. He was bleeding—a scalp wound, I thought, since his face was covered with blood. His left arm hung, flopping queerly, at his side, but his face was alive.

His eyes damn near *shone.*

I'd never seen Gilberto light up before, and now wasn't the time to pay attention. Still, the computer in my head took note. I hurled myself forward, heard Saul's coughing roar right behind me as he changed, and hit the shape of green smoke with both physical and etheric force. The scar blazed under my skin, vibrating wetly, and my right fist pistoned forward, smashing into the lattice of evil intent.

A ringing sound hit the pitch just under "puncture-an-eardrum," then broke in a cascade of splinters. Just like the smoke, which solidified into breaking crystal shards, raining for the floor. I hit the ground and whirled, boots grinding in the wreckage, and saw Saul, dodging the shambling fingers of a zombie. Four more crowded behind it, all with their jaws working, and just as his claws sheared the face off the one he was dancing with I lurched forward again, fingers unlimbering the whip.

"Six!" Gilberto yelled. *"Seis!* Six!"

What the hell? But then I realized he was telling me how many enemies we had loose inside the warehouse, or at least how many he'd seen.

Well, at least he's got his wits about him. How long has he been in here with them? The whip cracked, silver flechettes thudding home in rotting flesh, and the smell exploded. *Goddammit, and I was looking forward to getting clean, too.*

It was short work putting the zombies down. These ones were old and fragile, porous bones and worm-eaten flesh. Five of them, and I was looking for the sixth when it blundered around the corner, arms outstretched like a bad B-movie villain, and snarled.

The whip hit, my fist arrived a few moments later, and I was struck by just how *satisfying* making a zombie's head explode can be. If only all problems are as simple as setting your feet, uncoiling from your hip, and smashing a hellbreed-strong fist right through something's head, then shaking the gobbets of flesh from your fingers.

But, of course, I have to spoil all that enjoyment by thinking about who the hell would send zombies *into my fucking house*. Just when I was looking forward to a shower and a little bit of rest.

I stood still for a moment, panting, head down. Saul's growl petered out. He cocked his head, still in cougarform, tail lashing. Then the blurring enveloped him, his form running like clay under water, and when it receded he was there again. It's an amazing thing to see, and the fact that I can *see* the strings under the surface of the real world responding with my smart eye, see the quivers of energy as thermodynamic laws are violated, doesn't make it any less amazing.

The human mind can compass an awful lot, but it isn't comfortable even when you're used to it.

"Dios mio." Gilberto coughed behind me. It was the first time I heard him sound anything other than bored. *"Madre de Dios."*

Yeah, kid, calling on God is a good thing to do in a situation like this. I let out a long slow breath. "Jesus Christ. What the hell?"

Saul glanced at me, then turned on his heel and strode back to Gilberto. "What happened?"

"Doorbell rang." The kid winced as Saul touched his left arm, but he didn't let go of the knife. I recognized it—an antique Bowie, with a plain hilt and a blessing running under the metal's surface.

It had belonged to the first Jack Karma, one of the hunters in my lineage. *Why am I even surprised?*

"His arm's broken," Saul said over his shoulder. "Jill?"

"Get it set and find out what happened. I'm going to sweep the house."

"I don't hear any more." But he nodded, and crouched easily next to the kid. "This is going to hurt a bit."

"Chingada, man, just get it over with." Gilberto sounded very young. "There was a blond bitch at the door, but I think she left."

Wait a second. "Blond?"

"Dreadlocks, *bruja.*" He was sweating as Saul probed his arm more. "Right down to her ass. Tall, too. Dressed like *mi abuela,* for fucksake. Flower muumuu and everything."

"Greenstick. Humerus." Saul looked up at him. "Brace yourself."

"Ay de mi, just fucking—"

Saul made a swift motion, Gilberto spluttered and sucked in a breath. He turned the color of cottage cheese under his brown skin. It was amazing—he actually looked yellow. The acne scars stood out, like the cratered surface of the moon.

Tall. Blond dreadlocks. And I wonder if he's talking about a blue caftan embroidered with orchids. "Hold that thought," I said, and swept the rest of the warehouse.

Someone definitely had an agenda. They went straight to my bedroom, where the bed stood away from all four walls and three filing cabinets against one wall were busted open and ransacked. Paper fluttered, and I stood for a few moments staring.

What the hell?

There was nothing in those cabinets except bills and invoices for things like custom leather work, ammunition, artifacts bought—necessary for tax purposes.

Hey, even a hunter has to file. Death and taxes are immutable laws for us, too. I generally end up getting a refund, though. It's the least Uncle Sam can do for me.

All the really revealing personal papers, like Mikhail's birth certificate and mine, files on cases closed or unclosed, immunization records, school records, anything that might give an enemy a foothold or a piece of insight, were locked up in a concrete vault under Hutch's bookstore. After Mikhail's death and Melisande Belisa's rifling of his personal papers, it seemed like a good idea, and I was never so glad as right now.

Sloane's papers are there too—whatever survived the fire in '38, that is. Huh.

I holstered the gun, coiled my whip. The warehouse was fracked-up but clean of zombies, and the shadows were only shadows. Someone had quickly but thoroughly torn through the filing cabinets. I strode out to the kitchen. Someone had opened all the cabinets and torn open the filing cabinet at the end of the breakfast bar. Police and federal contacts, files on protocols for requesting funding from different municipal, county, and state (not to mention federal) contacts—all pulled out and scattered. This was potentially more damaging, so I crouched and searched quickly through the papers, checked the drawers. Each file was labeled in either my spidery handwriting or Saul's firmer copperplate script.

Nothing immediately appeared to be missing. A few files had been yanked out and scattered. That was it.

What the hell?

"Jill?" Saul appeared in the doorway to the living room.

"Someone went through my papers." I rose, surveyed the kitchen. They hadn't pulled the dishes out, but the fridge door was ajar. *Jesus. Wonder what she was looking for?* "How's his arm?"

"I'm going to cast it. Need anything?"

I spread my hands. Silver shifted in my hair. "Just one thing, and it's nothing anyone here can help me with."

"Huh." His shoulder slumped as if he thought I was talking about him personally. "Really?"

Shit, Jill. Sarcasm is *a deadly weapon.* "Not really. You're going to help me find something out."

"Like what?"

"Like what Mama Zamba was looking for in my fucking filing cabinets. And why she's alive if most of her inner circle is dead." Frustration threatened to knot my hands into fists. "And what the fuck is really going on here."

"Oh." He didn't look happy, but who would, faced with that news? "Sure it was Zamba?"

"Tall? Long blond dreadlocks? A bunch of zombies and green smoke? Sounds like Zamba to me. The only things missing are the cockroaches."

"You know, that doesn't comfort me as much as it should. You okay?"

I nodded. Silver shifted and tinkled. "Frustrated as all hell. But okay."

He opened his mouth, shut it, then plowed on. "All right. I'm going to get the kid put back together. Is anything missing?"

"Not that I can figure out." I looked down at the papers, and this time my hands curled into fists despite my deep breathing. I'm just like anyone else—I *hate* having my house broken into. "Get the kid something to eat, too. He's thin as a rail."

"He fought off six zombies." Was that actually *grudging admiration* in Saul's tone?

Wonders never cease.

"Or he was smart enough to stay away from them. Six of one, half a dozen of the other. Get him fixed up."

He shifted his weight back, paused. "And then?"

I struggled with my frustration, kept the words even and calm. "Then we're going to get cleaned up, board up the front door, and get going. We're dropping the kid off at Galina's, where I know he'll be safe. After that we're paying a visit to Hutch's."

"I thought Hutch was out of town."

He's vacationing in the Galapagos. Just when I need him too. "He is. But Zamba was after something. It's a safe bet that whatever-it-is is in the vault. Go on, Saul. Time's a-wasting."

He vanished down the hall, and I heard Gilberto swearing in a high unsteady voice. The kid had some potential. He was also goddamn lucky Zamba hadn't unseamed him from guts to garters. She must have been in an awful hurry.

My pager went off as I stood there, thinking. Zombie-stink rose from my clothes, and we were going to have a hell of a time getting the house back together. I dug in my pocket and brought the thing out, still staring at the scattered papers.

The number was unfamiliar. I snagged the phone, dialed, and was rewarded with a click and two rings.

The connection went through, and my breath froze in my throat. I could tell who it was just by the slight static behind his breathing and the rumble under the words.

Perry's voice crawled into my ear. "My dearest Kiss. I presume you're well?"

Don't FUCKING CALL ME THAT, you goddamn hellspawn. I swallowed, reached all the way down to my toes for patience.

It was a long reach. I settled for my best fuck-you tone. "Why is the Cirque sending its dogs after me, Pericles?"

"That isn't the Cirque, my dearest. It was me, and they are to watch over you." He paused for maximum effect. "Another performer is dead. Your presence is requested."

Oh, for Chrissake.... I took a deep breath, forced myself once again to prioritize. My weary brain rebelled. "Who's dead? Trader or hellbreed? And when?"

"Before dawn. One of my kind. A fortune-teller, I believe you would call it. Moragh."

Moragh. The name meant nothing to me, especially with all my other irons in the fire. *Before dawn* meant that Zamba'd had a busy night. "And the hostage?"

"Safe and snug, and under my *especial* protection and supervision." A low, silky laugh. "Fear not for him, my dear. Come see the latest death and destruction. It has a certain symmetry."

"I'll be there when I get there. And Perry?"

"Yes?"

What was I going to tell him? *Fuck off* was what I wanted to say, but it would just give him an opening. He also hadn't done anything to deserve it—at least not lately. "Take care of that hostage." *If he bites it, this entire city's going to have a very bad night. You don't want that either; it'll interfere with your own games. Don't think I don't know it—and don't think I'm not betting on it.*

"I told you he's safe." Now he sounded irritated. Score one for me. "Why do you make me repeat myself?"

"I just like to make sure you *understand,*" I informed him sweetly, and slammed the phone down.

CHAPTER 20

Hutchinson's Books, Used and Rare, was painted on the window in fading gold—but Saul and I parked four blocks away and slid up to the back door under a punishing wave of sun and heat. Midmorning, and it was already a scorcher. The shadows teemed with shapes, far darker than morning shadows had a right to be. I kept seeing the little glimmers of colorless crystal eyes and twitched for a weapon.

Saul didn't mention it. Whether he was magnanimously refusing to comment or he didn't sense them was an open question. I was willing to bet on the former.

I blinked the exhaustion out of my eyes and touched the doorknob. A thin thread of sorcerous energy slid off my fingertips, stroked the locks I'd built. They eased open, tumblers clicking with thin little sounds.

Saul crowded behind me. Gilberto was dropped off at Galina's, wide-eyed and with a fresh cast on his arm. Galina, bless her, didn't ask a goddamn question, just took one look at my face and clucked and cooed over the gangbanger, promising to get him into fresh clothes and get some healing sorcery on that arm. Technically I suppose I should have charmed the bone before we left the warehouse, but I had other things on my mind.

The whole time, Gilberto clutched Jack Karma's knife. I didn't ask him to let go of it. I guess that answered *that* question. I had a new apprentice. To add to all my other problems.

The door ghosted open. Paper, dust, and air-conditioning closed around us as I swept it to and relocked it. "Zombies," I said for the third time. "In our *living room.* What next?"

"Well, at least we didn't have to kill them in the kitchen." Saul sighed heavily. "That kid . . ."

"He's got the look."

"Great." Saul didn't sound in the least excited. "Another person to get a slice of your time."

"Is that what this is about?" I checked the shop. Books sat quietly on their shelves, leather-bound tomes stacked on chairs and on Hutch's massive mahogany desk, shipwrecked in a sea of papers. A PC that hadn't been there last time crouched on one corner of the desk, a shipshape new Mac on the other corner. The two laptops were in their traveling cases, tucked out of sight under the desk.

Pity he hadn't taken his phone. The whole point of his vacation was to get him out and away from temptation, the little monster. The deal was, he hacked only when the local hunter needed him to, and the local hunter kept his ass out of jail.

Unfortunately, sometimes Hutch just couldn't help himself. He's small and beaky and a Cowardly Lion, but a challenge in cyberspace? Suddenly he's Superman, six feet tall *and* bulletproof. And completely without any goddamn self-control at all. I had to wait until things calmed down and the local FBI liaison, Juan Rujillo, finished smoothing the ruffled feathers before Hutch could come back.

Saul sounded angelically innocent. "What *what* is about?"

"You." I turned past the small kitchen where Hutch heated his lunches, opened an EMPLOYEES ONLY door. "And whatever it is you're sitting on."

"I'm not sitting on anything."

Yeah, that's why you can't touch me anymore. That's why you flinch whenever I get a little frisky. "Okay. When you want to talk about it, fine." The small room was lined with bookshelves, and even the dust in here vibrated with secrecy. Ordinary people wouldn't even *see* the door we'd just ducked through. Though precious few people came in here; this place was kept afloat because of the hunter's library. Hutch got a stipend and dispensation for when he occasionally went breaking a few electronic-surveillance laws in service to whatever case I was working at the time; I got a research library and an extra pair of eyes to go digging through dusty tomes whenever the end of the world drew *too* nigh.

"We never have time." Did he actually sound *sulky?*

Jesus. "You're kidding, right?"

"Do I sound like I'm kidding?" He let out a sharp sigh. "Work comes first. I know. I just have to talk to you sometime."

"So talk to me." I pushed aside the conference table, a big wooden thing suspiciously clean and neat now that Hutch was out of town and I hadn't been bothering him to look things up for me. Saul bent down and lent his strength, even though I was already handling it. The legs scraped across cheap industrial carpet, and it fetched up against one of the overloaded bookcases. A copy of Luvrienne's *Les Chateaux de Chagrin* teetered on a shelf; I prayed it wouldn't fall. There's only six of the copies he produced in existence, and it's one of the best all-around books about the Sorrows to have been written in the last four hundred years.

Nobody knows you like your own. Luvrienne had barely escaped the fate that stalks every male in a Sorrows house, lived to write about it—and they track down and destroy every copy of the book they can find. Just like they tracked him down and took him back.

Fortunately, Hutch scanned it into a digital archive and emailed it to every hunter's library we had addresses for. He gets orders from other libraries for printed copies. The digital age is a wondrous thing.

However, I don't want to touch the damn book if I don't have to. I know too fucking much about the Sorrows to want that.

I snagged the loop of denim sewn into the carpet and yanked up the cutout square. The concrete underneath was smooth and featureless, its expanse broken only by a recessed iron ring. I grabbed the ring, set my legs, and let out a breath while *heaving* up.

A hellbreed-strong right fist helps when you have to lift a concrete slab. But you still have to lift with your legs, not your back. Ergonomics for hunters—a bad back is a liability. Saul kept out of the way—there wasn't enough room for him to help.

I keyed the code into the climate-control pad and slid the glass panel aside. A few items Galina keeps for me; I learned my lesson when that Sorrows bitch stole Mikhail's talisman and rifled all his personal stuff. But the papers are here. All the salvageable vitals on the hunters of my lineage, down from the first and second Jack Karmas. Before the first Jack, we don't know anything.

This isn't the kind of career that lends itself to leaving evidence in the historical record. The day world, the real world, doesn't want to know. Hunters sometimes rely on sheer outrageousness to slide by unnoticed. A regular civilian's reaction to a genuine paranormal event is usually screaming and running in the other direction.

Emerson Sloane's files were very thin. The big Santa Luz fire of 1938 had eaten most of the records he'd left, one way or another. A bare triple-handful of manila folders labeled in a round Palmer script, some with notations in Mikhail's broad firm hand with its Cyrillic notations followed by English translations.

I flipped through them. About twenty had no connection to anything remotely resembling the current clusterfuck we were looking at. My pager went off; I dug in my pocket and pulled out the other thirteen files that looked promising.

I gave my pager a cursory glance. It was the Badger. Maybe she had something for me.

"Do you still want me?" The words just burst out of Saul and hung in midair.

It was like being punched in the gut. I sucked in dust and paper-laden air. The dead quiet of the bookstore closed around the sound, and my hands went nerveless for about half a second. I almost dropped the files.

"Of course I do," I told the hole in the floor. "I always have. What the fuck?"

"My family's gone." It was a simple statement of fact. "My mother's dead. Billy Ironside killed my sister. My mother's sisters are...well, I'm not theirs. They have their own cubs. If I didn't have a mate, it'd be different. But..."

"But there's me. And I'm not a Were." There it was, half the dysfunction in our relationship laid out in plain words. The other half didn't need to be spoken. *I'm tainted. I've got a hellbreed mark on my wrist and a serious rage problem. I'm not a nice person, Saul. I'm not even a* good *person, despite your thinking so. I'm a hunter. End of story.*

"I don't care what you are," he answered quietly. "You need me, Jill. You'd kill yourself over this if someone wasn't reminding you..."

"Reminding me of what?" I flipped through the first file, scanned it. No connection. The second, too. My eyes were hot and grainy, and I was hoping I wouldn't miss anything. My heart was a lump in my throat, the words had to squeeze around it.

Five little words. "That you're worth a damn."

Mikhail was the only man who ever thought I was worth a damn, I'd told him once.

Not the only one, he'd told me later. Tit for tat, we were even, except we weren't.

We would never be even. Not while I was still breathing. Only it wasn't the kind of debt you could repay, or even anything that could be called a debt at all.

I didn't know what it was, except maybe love. Or something so huge it could swallow me, something that terrified me when I thought he might not want *me* anymore. Mischa thought I was worth plucking out of a snowdrift and training, but he left me behind. I wasn't worth enough for him to stay. And that little voice inside my head, buried under a hunter's iron.

You're not worth anything. You're ugly. Too ugly for anyone to love. Even my mother, the bitch, had said so.

And, I mean, come on. Just look at the man. Even gaunt and grieving, he was Native American calendar beefcake, broad-shouldered and dark-eyed.

Who wouldn't want him? Who wouldn't feel their breath catch every time he looked their way?

The third file fell open under my numb fingers. I blinked back hot water and what felt like rocks in my eyes. The little tingle of intuition ran up my arms and exploded under my breastbone. A puzzle piece fell into place with a click so loud I was surprised it didn't knock over a few books.

"Holy shit," I breathed.

There, clipped to the inside of a folder probably older than I was, a singed, faded black-and-white photo glared at me. Saul approached, but I kept staring.

The jaw was the same. So was the blond hair, the sculpted lips, and the straight thick eyebrows. And the glint of gold around the teeth. And the bad skin, but underneath that . . .

All this time I'd thought she was just an ugly woman. Funny how beauty mutates according to expectation.

My Were bent down, and his warmth touched my back. "Huh." The faint ghost of zombie clinging to us both faded under the good smell of him, male and fur. "Is it Zamba's brother?"

"I think it's Zamba." I moved my hand so he could see what Sloane had written on the mat, the fountain pen marks digging hurriedly into the yellowing fibers.

Arthur Gregory, missing, presumed dead. I flipped the file closed. "Jesus."

"Huh. She didn't *smell* male."

"It can't just be a coincidence." I handed him the file and leaned forward, jammed the others back in vaguely where they went. "Right under my goddamn nose all the goddamn time. I *hate* that."

It took under a minute to get the vault closed up. I tugged the carpet square back over the cover and smoothed it down, turned sharply to find Saul just standing there, a line between his dark eyebrows, staring at me.

The urgency of a case heating up bit me sharply, right in the conscience. *Goddammit, can't this wait?*

But no, it couldn't. I braced myself and met the problem head-on. "Don't worry about me." There it was again—that sharp tone, the grating whine underneath it. "I did this job before you came along, Saul. If you're aching to get back to the Rez, you can go. I wouldn't hold it against you. God knows nobody else has ever been able to fucking put up with me."

Jesus. I meant to say something gentler. Like *I love you, don't leave me.* Or even just, *I need you too much. I don't care.*

I *did,* though. I cared that the dark circles under his eyes were getting bigger, that his ribs were standing out sharply, and that his shoulders were hunched. Those were only the first few things in the long list of things I cared about when it came to him. It all boiled down to him maybe not wanting to keep banging his head on the steel wall I couldn't figure out how to drop. The place in me where I'd been broken and remade, beaten until I turned strong. I'd figured he knew the way through the wall without my having to tell him. It was there every time I woke up next to him and my heart hurt because he was next to me, warm and breathing.

Because he *knew* me.

"Do you want me to?" His mouth pulled down at the corners, bitterly. "What did I do?"

Huh? I searched for a handle on my temper, didn't find one. The rock in my throat turned into sharp ice edges. "You? You didn't do anything, goddammit. If you're trying to figure out how to gracefully get rid of me, Saul, don't worry about it. It's okay."

I was lying. It wasn't anywhere near okay. But I would say it was. For him.

"Jill . . ." He made a helpless motion just as my pager buzzed again. "I'm sorry."

I had a sudden, violent urge to grab my pager, throw it across the room, and shoot the motherfucker for good measure. "Don't be sorry. Look, I know something's wrong. It's been wrong since you came back. *I'm* sorry. I should have known it was too good to be true."

"What the fuck are you talking about?" There it was, a spark of anger. It was a relief—when he was angry, the twenty-pounds-underweight-and-unhappy-too wasn't so visible.

I grabbed the file. He didn't resist. "You don't have to make any excuses to me," I informed him. "No promises, no deals, no bargains. You said that the very first night. If you can't stand me anymore, it's okay. I expected it. Just go ahead and go. Find a nice tabby and raise a litter or three. God knows you're domestic enough."

"Are you *insane?*"

Holy hell and hallelujah. He'd actually *shouted* at me. No more moping; he was now officially pissed off.

I closed my eyes, the massive mental effort needed to think clearly dragging at every inch of my body. The shaking had me in its jaws and wouldn't let go.

Zamba, Arthur Gregory. Some kind of beef with the Cirque, and his brother? Who knows? He found a bargain somewhere— probably voodoo. And the Twins, they specialize in androgyny. It would make sense, it would make a whole lot of sense.

He went to Lorelei, Lorelei brokered a deal. Now that the Cirque is back, Lorelei was a liability, and her death would serve as fuel, and payment for the loa *too. As well as the deaths of Zamba's inner circle. The possessions could be aftershocks or for some other part of Zamba's plan.*

And once the possessed had died inside their violated bodies, they were easy meat for reanimation, *and* payment for the *loa.* Zamba was mortgaging herself to the hilt for this, whatever it was. Revenge?

Probably.

There were things I had to do. I opened my eyes, found I was staring at the ceiling. The acoustic tiles all but vibrated until I realized my goddamn eyes had fucking flooded. I couldn't blame it on the dust in the air. Everything shimmered as I blinked, trying to get them to reabsorb the water. "I'm not crazy. I'm just saying that if you can't bring yourself to touch me anymore, something's obviously very wrong. You're torn up over your mother, I know. I *understand.* But don't kill yourself staying with me because you think you have to. If you have to cut me loose and go back to the Rez, if this isn't what you need or want, you're free as a fucking bird. I can't keep you, Saul. I *won't* keep you."

My pager quit buzzing. I tipped my chin back down and got a good look at him.

Saul stared at me as if I had indeed lost my mind. His mouth opened, then closed. I clutched the file to my chest like a school-girl with her books.

"I've got to go," I finally said. It sounded very small in the stillness. "I've got to figure the rest of this out. Any moment now it could blow sky-high." Knowing pretty much who I was dealing with gave me more to work with. The other big question—*why*— could be attacked now, and wrestled to the ground. Not to mention pistol-whipped and shot, if the occasion called for it.

I was so tired it didn't even sound like a relief.

"Jill—" Saul had finally found his voice.

If he was going to tell me that he wanted to go back to the Rez, I was going to start screaming. I couldn't afford to lose it now.

People were counting on me. A whole city full of them. My people, in my city.

"Save it." The words were a harsh croak. "Do what you're gonna do, Saul. If you're going to leave me in the dust, make it quick and clean. If you ever loved me, do it that way. Don't drag it out."

I stamped past him, every string in my body aching to stop and touch him, throw my arms around him, and maybe engage in some undignified begging. Screw the entire city, screw *everything*. I didn't care as long as he stayed with me. As long as there was a *chance*.

But. One teensy-tiny little *but*.

I'm a hunter. It's that simple.

If Zamba-Arthur or whoever it was kept killing Cirque performers, things were going to get sticky. There's very little a really motivated voodoo queen can't do to you, and she'd already hit the hostage, too. Perry was there, but if she found some way past him— or if he decided it was too much trouble and some chaos served his ends—well, it would be party time for the entire Cirque *and* I'd have Perry and a renegade fucking voodoo queen to deal with.

Big fun.

It meant a lot of innocent people dead or maimed. It meant hellbreed thinking they could slip the leash and make trouble in my town. It meant years of steady work keeping things under control wasted.

It meant more victims.

And there was just no fucking way I was going to stand for that.

No matter *what* I stood to lose.

CHAPTER 21

When the Badger gets her teeth in something, she doesn't let go. "It was a job and a half to find out who holds title to that goddamn house." Behind her, another phone rang, and I heard Sullivan's big voice raised. He was probably cussing at his coffee. The way Homicide bitches about the coffee, you'd think someone would have brought in some decent beans by now.

Other than that, it sounded like a cubicle farm on speed. Which is to say, a usual morning in Homicide.

"Huh." I closed my eyes. It was easier that way, with the outside world shut out. "In what way?"

"I had to go rousting." She sounded almost indignant. "It wasn't in the usual databases. I had to go down to the tax assessor's office, they sent me to some goddamn basement. Had to pull records from 1930, can you believe that? They haven't got around to putting that slice of the city in the databases, he said. Weird, since every other district is."

Well, isn't that interesting. "And the winner is?"

"Someone named Ruth Gregory. Utilities, phone, garbage pickup, all under the same name—there were bills in the house. But here's some other weirdness: Ruth Gregory doesn't exist."

"If she gets bills, she must exist."

"That's the thing. None of her information's anywhere we can find it, no DOB, no nothing. But she got bills and paid them. Has a bank account, but if it wasn't for paper statements we wouldn't know, her bank doesn't have her on electronic file. There's not even a listing in the phone book. This woman just came out of nowhere, and she doesn't show up in the databases."

That's voodoo for you. The electronic stuff is easier for the loa *to affect than paper. Dammit.* Ruth Gregory. "What's her middle initial?" It was a small question, but I needed something I could feel good about anticipating.

"Ruth R. Gregory. Why?"

Ruth R. Arthur. A little fuck-you from Mama Zamba. Just like a supervillain. "I don't suppose you've found any hints of other houses?"

"I ran a check. Guess how many Ruth Gregorys there are in the good old United States."

How the hell should I know? But it was just like her to run it into the ground. "Thousands?"

"Less than four hundred. Four in our state. None with the middle initial R. And no hint of a separate identity, though it's a good bet that if she had one we wouldn't be able to find it electronically either. It could take us weeks of sifting paper—"

We don't have weeks. "That's not necessary. If any scrap of another identity comes up from processing the house, let me know. Otherwise, just keep identifying those stiffs. Okay?"

"All right." She sounded almost disappointed. She would run Zamba into the ground over weeks if she had to. Months. Or years.

"Good work." And I meant it. "Did you get everything you needed out of the house?"

"Boxes of paper. She was a real pack rat, our Miz Gregory. We left everything not needed for Forensics there and closed it up. Should we go back?"

No way. "No. God, no." I didn't mean to sound horrified. "Stay away from there. Just keep processing that paper and buzz me if anything else tingles your weird-o-meter, okay?"

"You got it."

"Any ID on the other bodies yet? Other than Trevor Watson?" *At least, the zombies that weren't Zamba's followers?*

"Not yet. They're pretty spludgy."

Well, that's one word for it. "Okay. Thanks." I dropped the phone in the cradle, considered screaming and shooting something.

Prioritize, Jill. Get your head straight.

It was a good plan. I just wasn't sure I could do it.

What next? Come on, what are you going to do next?

There was only one thing to do. And it wasn't going by the Cirque, thank God, or standing around yelling at Saul. I looked up, but the bookshop was deserted. Nothing but empty aisles faced with stuffed-full bookshelves, boxes on the floor, the antique cash register sitting stolidly, gathering dust. "Saul?" The word quivered. Was he gone?

Oh, fuck. I stood there with my hand on the phone, my hip against Hutch's desk, and my heart twisting itself like a contortionist inside my chest. "Saul?"

I checked the kitchen and the EMPLOYEES ONLY room. I even checked the goddamn bathroom.

He was gone. I hadn't even heard him leave.

God. I swallowed something hot and nasty, paced through the entire shop one more time. Blinked several times. My cheeks were wet.

This is one less thing for you to worry about. Get back up on the horse, Jill. Do your job.

It was time for me to visit Melendez.

CHAPTER 22

If Zamba was the reigning voodoo queen, Melendez was the court jester. Don't get me wrong—anyone who bargains with an inhuman intelligence is suspect, and just because I hadn't heard of Melendez doing anything even faintly homicidal or icky didn't mean he didn't dabble.

But it didn't mean the little butterball was harmless, either. Any more than the mark on my wrist meant I was a Trader.

Only I was, if you thought about it a certain way. And while Melendez didn't go in for the theatrical horror and power games Zamba did, he also didn't go out of his way to make things easier on people. *Live and let die,* that was probably the closest thing to a motto he would ever have.

Saul had left me the car. Awful nice of him. I told the sharp spearing ache in my heart to go away and made time through mid-morning traffic, brakes squealing and tires chirping. The shadows leapt and cavorted in my peripheral vision until I began ignoring them, even the colorless crystal eyes and the glass-twinkle teeth. I caught the flow of traffic like a pinball down a greased slide, all the way across town to the northern fringe of the Riverhurst section.

A nice address, all things considered, clinging to rich respectability like cactus clings to any breath of moisture. The houses are old, full of creaks, fake adobes and some improbable Cape Cods. They had bigger yards than anything other than the rest of Riverhurst, and most of them were drenched green. I even saw some sprinklers running, spouting rainbows under the heaving, cringe-inducing glare of dusty sunlight.

Melendez didn't hold his gatherings in his home. He owned a storefront on the edge of the barrio, with a trim white sign out front announcing the Holy Church of St. Barbara, nonprofit and legitimate under a 501(c)(3). His own private little joke, I guess. Seven nights a week you can find drumming, dancing, and weird shit happening on the little strip of concrete that had pretensions of being Pararrayos Avenue.

Mornings, though, he could be found here. It's a good thing the streets are wide even on the edge of Riverhurst, because his followers usually come out for consultations, filling up his driveway and the street for a block or two. Quarter-hour increments, donations optional—nobody leaves without paying *something*—and results guaranteed.

You don't last long in that business unless you have the cash to back the flash.

Today, though, the street was clear and I parked right near the front door. Melendez's faux-adobe hacienda sat behind its round concrete driveway with the brick bank in the middle, holding still-blooming rosebushes, a monkey puzzle tree, and a bank of silvery-green rue. Lemon balm tried its best to choke everything else in the bed, but aggressive pruning had turned it into a bank of sweetness.

I was relieved to see his tiny garden was tiptop. The fountain— a cute little chubby-cheeked cherub shooting water from his tiny wang—was going full-bore. I wondered if there was a homeowners' association in this part of town, and what they thought of his choice in lawn decorations. Not that there was much lawn to speak of. The largest part of his lot was out back with the pool.

The heat was oppressive, a bowl of haze lying over the city. A brown smudge of smog touched downtown's skyscrapers, and high white horsetail clouds lingered over the mountains. I couldn't wait for the autumn rains to move up the river and flash-flood us, just for a change of pace. Hunters are largely immune to temperature differentials, it's right up there with the silence, one of the first things an apprentice learns.

I winced at the thought of apprentices, opened the car door and stood for a few seconds, looking across the Pontiac's roof, sizing up the place. My smart eye caught nothing but the usual stirrings and flickers, an active febrile etheric petri dish.

I wonder if I'm not his first visitor today. Well, no time like the present to find out.

The wrought-iron gate was open, as usual. The courtyard was just as lush as it ever was, smelling of mineral hosewater and the sweet orange tang of Florida water. The splashes across the threshold, where the concrete stopped and the red-brick paving began, were still wet.

Well, Melendez. You've been keeping your house neat and clean, haven't you. I stepped over the barrier, a brief tingle passing over my body. The silver in my hair sparked and chimed, oddly muted. I wanted to touch a gun butt, kept my fingers away with an effort.

He had a fountain in the middle of the courtyard too, a big seashell with a spire rising from the middle of it. It was bone-dry. Masses of feverfew, more rue, a bank of bindweed...and the red-painted front door, open just a crack.

Gooseflesh rose hard and cold on my arms and legs. I wished Saul was behind me. Right now he was probably back at the warehouse, packing. Or maybe he'd already blown town. He traveled light, sometimes just a duffel, most times not even that.

Focus, Jill.

I wanted to kick the door open and sweep the house. Instead, I stood on the front step and rang the bell. The sweet tinkling chimes of—I shit you not—the chorus to Fleetwood Mac's "Dreams" sounded, leaking out through the open door.

The air changed, suddenly full of listening. No matter how many times you get to this point as a hunter, it never gets any easier.

I toed the door open. "Melendez!" I tried to sound nice and cheerful, only succeeded in sounding like Goldilocks saying *hello* when she walks in the door and smells porridge. "Señor Melendez, *una clienta para Usted.*"

The entryway was red tile, full of cool quiet and the smell of incense. Lots of incense, in thick blue veils. My blue eye smarted, filling with hot water. There was a sound of movement, and my hand leapt for the gun, fell away.

"Hola, bruja," he said at the end of the hall. "Come in. Been expecting you."

Melendez lowered himself down in a straight-backed leather armchair behind a massive oak desk cluttered with paper and tchotchkes. He called this room his study, and it was full of bookshelves holding leather-bound books—nothing Hutch would get excited over, these were just for decoration—and other, more useful tools of his trade. An empty fireplace, clean as a whistle, seemed just a set piece for the crossed rapiers hung over it. Both fine examples of Toledo steel, and worth more than the house itself *and* probably the neighbors' houses as well.

I surveyed the choices available. A padded footstool that would put me below him, literally, like I was a third grader. An overstuffed armchair that would swallow everything up to your neck. A penitent's chair made of iron, with a faded red horsehair cushion.

I elected to remain standing, and Melendez's broad brown face split in a yellow-toothed grin. He settled his ample ass deeper in his chair, his potbelly brushing the desk's edge. "Been a while."

"No murders traced to any of *your* followers lately." I folded my arms.

"You here about Ruth?" His dark eyes gleamed.

Well, there's either a very lucky guess, or he knows something. Guess which. "I'm here about Arthur Gregory. And the Cirque de Charnu."

"You here because Mama Zamba is calling in all her favors. She got an old feud against the devils, older than yours." He steepled his long, chubby brown fingers. In a blue chambray shirt and

jeans, a red kerchief tied around his straight black hair, he was in
that ageless space between twenty-nine and forty if you went by
his round, strangely unlined face. It was only the way he moved,
with a little betraying stiffness every once in a while, and the distance in his gaze that gave him away.

The *loa* can hold off age just like a Trader's bargain can. They
cannot grant immortality, but it gets awful close.

"If she keeps killing Cirque performers there's going to be
trouble. I don't have a lot of time to dance around." Impatience
boiled under my breastbone. I shelved it. "What do you know?"

"Oh, *bruja.*" He laughed. "You need a better question, you
gonna expect answers from me."

The urge to whip out a gun, squeeze off a shot for effect, and put
the barrel to his forehead and then *expect* answers from him leapt
up like a flame in the middle of my head. I took in a deep breath,
fixed him with my mismatched stare, and told myself firmly I was
not going to be shooting anyone unless it was necessary.

The trouble with that is, all of a sudden you can think it's necessary when it's not. Especially when you're deconstructing under
severe stress.

"Melendez." I tried to sound patient. "I've got a city that could
explode at any moment and a voodoo queen looking to cause a lot
of trouble. You fuck around with me and I just might decide to
look too hard at this sweet little deal you've got going for yourself.
Besides, with Zamba out of the picture soon you're looking at
being the reigning king of the scene around here. If, that is, she
doesn't show up and do you like she did the bitch of Greenlea. It
didn't seem like Lorelei had an easy death."

"Ah, Lorelei. She was Zamba's godmother. Seems like Zamba
cleaning up loose ends." He looked down at the desktop, ran one blunt
finger along a glossy strip of varnish peeking out from behind papers.

"Are you a loose end?" It was worth a shot.

"I belong to Chango." All jolliness dropped away, and his
broad moonface turned solemn. "The Twins, they have no hold on
me. My *patrón,* he whip their asses if they come near me. I in
strong with Chango. And you got some help too. Ogoun just waiting for you to come around."

My mouth was dry as desert sand. "I didn't think you had any truck with Ogoun."

He shrugged. "The spirits come when they will. You know. You called on them in the beginning of this. Papa Legba and Ogoun both watching you."

Well, training in dealing with possession has to take these sorts of things into account. I suppressed a shiver. The first time I'd brushed up against voodoo was during a ceremony devoted to Ogoun, Mikhail by my side. There was a skip, like a needle lifting from a record, and the next thing I knew I had a mouthful of fiery rum, Mikhail watching me very carefully, and the followers were drifting away toward the dinner table. He never would tell me what exactly I'd done when the drums lifted me out of myself. Broken glass had littered the floor of the peristyle, and there were curls of cigar smoke in the air. It had taken me a while to wash the smell of cigars away.

After that, Mikhail was very, very careful to teach me how to build an exorcist's hard etheric shell. I'd never had that problem again, thank God, but still. You never can tell when dealing with shit like this.

I fished the two Ziploc bags out of my coat. Straight razor and enamelware cup, both of them almost quivering with readiness. "What do these have to do with Zamba?"

He eyed my hands, then went pale under his brownness. *"Ay de mi."*

"Are we going to start talking, or are you gonna try yanking me around some more? Because I have to tell you, *señor,* my temper's getting a little thin." *Understatement of the year, isn't it?*

He was still staring at my hands. His eyes unfocused, brown irises sheened over as if with cataracts, a thin gray film spilling over his gaze. The air tightened, a breeze from nowhere riffling the papers on his desk, touching the leather-clad spines, and fingering the sheer curtains over the French doors looking onto the backyard's wide green expanse.

I braced myself.

When he spoke next, it was a different voice. His mouth moved, but the sound came from elsewhere, a mellow deep baritone crackling at the edges. *"Ay, mi sobrina. Bienvenidos a mi casa."*

The goose bumps rose again, hot this time instead of cold. My hair stirred, the silver chimes shifting, and my blue eye caught little dark shapes moving through the charged, heavy atmosphere that had suddenly settled inside the study. *"Buenos días, señor. Muchas gracias por su atencion."*

Hey, it never hurts to be polite.

Melendez's face worked itself like rubber, compressing and stretching. His mouth worked wetly. "You come here seeking knowledge, eh? What you give to Papa Chango?"

How about I don't rip you out of your follower there? How about I leave this place standing instead of burned down as a lesson in not fucking with me? I kept control of my temper, but just barely. It was getting harder and harder. "You wouldn't ask me if you didn't have something in mind already."

"*Es verdad.* Me and the Twins, we have a wager. They think their little *puta* is a match for the devils and for you. She pay them well, she always have."

I'll bet she does. There's all sorts of death lately she's been paying them with. "Payment isn't everything. There's more at stake here than just revenge. What does Arthur Gregory want?"

"I tell you what, *bruja. Mi hijo* here, he tell you all he know. In return, you owe me *una bala.* He lie, or he tell you nothing useful—and you put that *bala* through his *cabeza,* eh?"

Oh, for fuck's sake. "Why should I strike a bargain with you?"

The thing inhabiting Melendez's body laughed, a chortle that struck every exposed, shivering surface and blew my hair back. I smelled ozone, and rum. And cigar smoke, drifting across my sensitive nose. My eyes stung, smart and dumb alike.

"Because otherwise, *mi sobrina,* you ain't never gonna find that tick dug itself into the city's skin. She gonna bloat up with blood and strike the one she aimin' for, and you can't let that happen, can you? No. And this little *caballo* of mine know not just the *who* but the *why.* That what you wantin'. You just like every other *macizo;* you always sayin' *por que, por que?*"

It chuckled, moving Melendez's lips like ripples on the surface of a pond. "So what you say, *bruja grande de Santa Luz? Una bala, por la razon,* for the great *por que.*"

Jesus Christ. It always comes down to this, doesn't it. What part of myself am I willing to mortgage to get this case over and dealt with? "Deal." The word was ash in my mouth. Cigar ash. "But if you double-deal me, *señor,* this *caballo* is wormfood and you're on the outs within the borders of my city."

A good threat. I couldn't bar a *loa* from the city, of course— but I could make it hell on his followers. If I had to.

If it became *necessary.*

It laughed again. Chuckled long and hard, Melendez's hands jerking like brown paper puppets on strings. "We like you, *bruja. Mi hermano* Ogoun and me, we got a wager on you too. We be watching."

And just like that, it winked out. Melendez sagged, coughing, in his chair. A long jet of smoke spluttered through his lips, and his face hit the desktop with a solid thump.

It looked painful. He coughed, and more smoke billowed up. I swallowed a sarcastic little laugh. *If this turns into a case of spontaneous combustion, we're going to have a problem.*

Yeah, just add it to all my other problems. I stayed where I was as Melendez hacked, and the smoke gradually thinned.

When his bloodshot eyes swiveled up and he pushed himself upright, I sank my weight into my back foot, prepared to go any direction.

"Kismet." He coughed again, but without the smoke.

"Melendez." I sank down, coiling into myself like a spring. Just in case.

"I need a beer," he muttered. "Then I tell you *todo.*"

"Sounds good." I didn't relax. "Does Chango smoke every time he rides you?"

"*Chingada,* no." Amazingly enough, the round little man laughed. "Only when he mad, *bruja.* Only when he really fucking mad."

CHAPTER 23

I left his quiet little house a half hour later. I paused only once, standing on his threshold, to look back at the courtyard and the dry fountain. I was cold, and not even the white-yellow eye of the sun could warm me.

It was the damndest thing, but the Cirque's dogs didn't come up Melendez's driveway. Instead, they clustered up and down the street, each piece of knife-edged morning shadow full of writhing slender shapes and winking colorless-glowing eyes.

The Pontiac's door slammed and I stared at the steering wheel. Measured off a slice of it between my index fingers, bitten-down nails ragged, my apprentice-ring gleaming on my left third finger. Tendons stood out on the back of my scrawny hands, calloused from fighting and sparring, capable work-roughened hands.

Jesus.

When all else fails and you're looking at a huge clusterfuck, sometimes you just need a moment to sit and collect yourself before you start running the next lap toward the inevitable.

What came next?

The Cirque. Get out there and take a look at the newest body. Chances are you'll be able to triangulate her position from the traces, now that you know what she's doing and how they're linked. If you can get to her before she gets what she wants—

But there was another consideration. If Mama Zamba, *nee* Arthur Gregory, was out for vengeance against the Cirque, she had a right. Sloane had been working the case, which meant it fell to me to tie up loose ends and finish the job.

Helene took the brother in, and the fortuneteller—Moragh—had something to do with it. The Ringmaster too. That's who Zamba blames, at least. Reasonable as far as I can see.

But what about Ikaros? Why does she want to kill the hostage?

I reached over, grabbed Sloane's file from the passenger seat.

Saul should have been there with me. He would be looking at me right now, his head tilted slightly and his eyes soft and deep.

The pain hit me then, gulleywide sideways. I blinked back the tears rising hot and vicious. *Shut up,* I told myself. *Shut up and take it. You can take this.*

I hadn't really thought he would leave me. Well, I *had;* it was the song under every thought of him, the fear under every kiss. But I'd hoped.

That great human drug, hope. It makes fools of everyone, even tough-ass hunters. And I was so *tired.* When was the last time I'd slept?

"Goddammit," I said to the glaring-hot dash, the burning steering wheel, the flood of sunlight bleaching everything colorless-pale. "Do your *job,* Jill."

It was left to me. It was always left to me. That's what a hunter is—the last hope of the desperate, the last best line of defense against Hell's tide. No matter what shit was going on in my personal life, it was up to me to see that the entire fucking house of cards didn't fall.

My pager buzzed again. The goddamn thing just would not shut up. I fished it out with my free hand, glanced at it, and swore.

Perry, again. Which could only mean trouble.

I flipped the file open. Past the picture of Arthur Gregory's young, heartbreaking smile to the précis of the case.

Brother disappeared. Last known contact was outside the Carnaval de la Saleté. Suspects: Helene, hellbreed of the lesser type. Moragh, hellbreed of the higher type, refused to give information when questioned. Henri de Zamba, hellbreed of the higher type. Also refused to give information.

Holy shit. There it was—Arthur Gregory's gauntlet thrown down. *Zamba. I'll be damned.* It was there, staring me in the face. Another piece of the puzzle fell into place, clicking hard.

Maybe she wasn't trying to kill the hostage after all. Maybe she's been after the Ringmaster all this time, and it's just echoing through the bloodbond since the Trader would be his weak point. Jesus.

I slapped the file closed, dropped it on the passenger-side

floorboard, and twisted the key in the ignition. The Pontiac roared into life; I didn't bother buckling myself in.

Come on, Jill. Get this done, and you can rest.

It sounded good. The trouble is, as soon as this was done something else would come along.

I'll deal with that when it comes up. And if it does, that will mean I don't have to think.

There's something to be said for drowning your sorrows in work.

I parked on the bluff and locked my doors, then took the path down to the parking lot. The cars were hooded with dust, the paint already looking weary and sucked-dry. There were a lot of them, and the empty spots looked like knocked-out teeth. It was barely noon and the calliope was going full-bore, a souped-up version of "Let Me Call You Sweetheart" punctuating the air. The reek of cotton candy, animal shit, and fried fat painted the heavy motionless air. I checked the sky—over the mountains hung a dark smudge.

Rain, finally. Which would mean flash floods and misery, wet boots and cold hanging out on rooftops, steaming mornings and dripping against every surface. It would also mean old-fashioned hot chocolate, Saul's signature hash browns, and chili.

I pushed the thought away.

There were only two or three shufflers outside the ticket booth. The same Trader was on duty, her rhinestones sending back a vicious glitter, sweat-sheen greasing her pale skin as she kept as far as she could in the shade. I didn't pause, just strode straight past and jumped the turnstile. She gave a high piercing cry, but I paid no attention.

During the day, the Cirque did look shabby. Holes in signs, tawdry glitter, most of the booths deserted. The murmuring of Helletöng spilled under the surface, plucking at the visible world with flabby fingers. Dust rose in uneasy curls, and the calliope belched, missed a beat, caught itself, and went on.

Where is everyone?

I was cold, despite it being in the high nineties under the sun's assault. The alien scents of the Cirque swallowed me, teased at the inside of my skull. It was a few degrees cooler inside the Cirque's borders, but not enough to be a relief. Just enough to pull out some humidity and make every surface cloying and sweaty.

I heard a low wet chuckle and spun, steelshod heel grinding in dirt. My coat flared like a toreador's cape, the pockets weighted down.

Nothing but the shadow-dogs, crowding close. One slid a smoky paw out into the fall of sunlight and snatched it back, an angular curl of dust rising and dissipating on a breeze I didn't feel.

Something is very wrong here.

Another eerie cry went up, somewhere else in the Cirque. A thin, chill knife ran through my vitals.

They boiled out of the shadows, the dogs smoking with violet fumes, the hellbreed cringing and flinching, and the Traders hissing as they closed on me. The sun was suddenly my best ally, and my hand flashed for my whip just before the first one reached me.

CHAPTER 24

Adrenaline spiked through me, the taste of a new copper penny laid against my palate. The dogs clustered, hissing and smoking in the flat white glare of sunlight. They bled gushing gray smoke, their unskin bubbling. One crouched and sprang, hitting a Trader with a bony crunch. The Trader—long, skinny, walnut skin clustered with tufts of hair—screamed and went down, bleeding bright red tainted with black.

I'd already killed two 'breed and three Traders. The bodies lay twisted, hellbreed flesh stinking and simmering with thin black ichor running from its rents and breaks. The Trader bodies were jerking and twisting, contagion eating at the tissues, foulness simmering. My breath puffed a vapor-cloud as if it was subzero instead of scorching, and the silver in my hair rattled and buzzed.

The dogs pressed close, seeming not to notice the roasting on their surfaces. Blisters popped and oozed, and little black specks crawled over them.

It was a serious *what the fuck* moment, even for me.

The Cirque performers pulled back. Sharp glittering teeth, body paint, tawdry shimmers from rhinestones and glass paste. The skinny plague-dealer I'd seen at the entrance to the bigtop crouched in front of the dogs, his knees obscenely splayed under burlap breeches. His antique top hat was stove in, and his eyes glittered madly, dripping hellfire.

Daylight scored each flaw in their beauty, burned it deep, and put the twisting on display. The Traders writhed, caught between the desire to fling themselves at me and the snarling of the hounds.

Jesus, Mary, and Joseph. I tracked the front line of twisted faces, turning in a complete circle, one gun out, the whip jangling in the dust. *Do you suppose it's my cologne?*

The scar blazed with sudden acid fire, pulling on every nerve in my right arm, and every single humanoid form circling me, Trader or 'breed, fell face-first.

He picked his way through them, a mincing step and a tight-drawn mouth. The air peaked behind him in two turbulent whirls, and the breeze turned clotted, full of spoiled honey and dry sand. The whites of his eyes ran with trails and vein-traceries of indigo, his white-blond hair was standing up in soft spikes, and Perry looked *pissed.*

The shadow-dogs whined and cringed, the blisters on their hides smoking furiously.

I straightened, leveled the gun. "That's close enough." My ribs heaved with deep hard breaths.

"Oh, not nearly." His teeth glimmered, sharp and perfect white. Two more mincing steps, his polished wingtips picking delicately between tangled arms and legs. "Here is better." One more. "Or here."

The hammer clicked back as I put more pressure on the trigger. "Come on, hellspawn. Test my patience." *I fucking dare you.* It was an effort not to add the last four words.

"Now, now." But he stayed where he was. "It seems I did well, in insuring your life." A graceful sketch of a motion indicated the dogs. The 'breed and Traders whined, digging themselves into the dirt.

The last time I'd seen Perry in sunlight he'd looked almost trans-

parent, and extraordinarily unhappy. Right now he just looked furious, his eyebrows drawn together and dust swirling into two high
peaked points behind him. A ripple passed through all of them, and
I had the sudden, not-unwelcome thought that if I could just keep all
of them in the sunlight long enough, they might all implode like
vampires in bad B movies and save me a lot of trouble.

Sunlight is deadly to a lot of things, but it looked merely
uncomfortable to Perry. Just my luck. "Don't break your arm patting yourself on the back. What the fuck is going on here?"

He tilted his head to the side. A ripple ran under the surface of
his skin, a quick blemish gone as soon as the seeming reasserted
itself. "Oh, my dear. Didn't you receive my messages?"

"I've been a bit busy chasing down whoever has such a hard-
on for the Cirque performers since I last talked to you." But a
sinking sensation thudded into my stomach, and I was suddenly
not very happy about what he might say next.

There were any number of things that could make the Cirque
performers angry or stupid enough to attack me. Perry didn't let
me linger in suspense, though.

"You mean you haven't heard?" His face twisted up in a facsimile of dismay. Then he went and said the most horrible thing he
could have at that point. "My darling Kiss. The hostage was
attacked again, and lies near death."

Oh, shit. I braced myself. "I'll get to that in a minute." *And
here I thought they were pissed because I didn't pay for a ticket.*
"What about Moragh?"

"She is dead, eaten by the same monster. What more can concern you about her?" False interest brightened his blue eyes. The
rippling under his skin increased, like a pond rippling once a
stone's thrown in.

I gathered myself. *All right, Jill. Play this one very carefully.* "I
should take a look at whatever's left of her body, Pericles. And if
you're a really good little hellspawn I'll tell you who killed her."

I swear to God, he looked *disappointed.* Perry eyed me for a
long few moments, his fingers dangling at his sides, the dogs
whining and a low rumble of Helletöng rising like steam from the
'breed plastered to the dusty ground. The Traders twitched in

ways no human body should as his will passed over them, a tightening of corruption my blue eye could see all too well.

"Are there likely to be more deaths?" He cocked his head, buttery sunlight turning cold and cringing when it touched his pale hair and his linen-clad shoulders. The dogs growled, a rising note of unhappiness.

Four or five different things slid together in my head all at once. "Of course there are. Unless you get off your hellbreed ass and start helping me control the situation instead of trying to play it like a harmonica. It would be very upsetting to be second fiddle to the Ringmaster in my town, wouldn't it?" *Even temporarily.*

There. Not bad for a toss of the dice. I stared right at the bridge of his hellbreed nose, the naked scar on my arm running with soft wet fire, and wondered if I was going to have to kill them all. Or at least, take as many of them with me as possible.

That's the trick to staring down an unblinking hellbreed—just like scaring the shit out of a human being. Focus on the nose and your gaze grows piercing, a lot of their little glamours and fiddles don't work, and any move they make is generally telegraphed. Peripheral vision is a lot better at picking up that sort of twitchy almost-movement; that's what it's for.

Stare or not, though, even I might have some trouble with the entire Cirque *and* Perry on my ass.

The first consideration was that Perry needed a reason to be on my side—and *no* reason to let the Cirque run wild to gain some leverage on me. The second consideration was that if he was here, he wasn't watching the hostage.

The third was that I needed him if I was going to hold off the Cirque. I did not want to let them run riot through my city until someone else got a handle on them. Leon down south in Ridgefield or Anya over in the mountains had their own problems; this one was mine.

Last of all, I had to figure out what Perry knew and what side of the fence he was playing. As usual.

"You know what is causing this?" Did Perry sound, of all things, *tentative?*

Wonders never ceased.

"I haven't just been sitting on my fucking thumbs, Perry." I kept the gun steady, sharp hurtful gleams twinkling off the barrel. The sunlight was still so cold my shoulders were tight as bridge cables, and my head hurt. My eyes were dry and full of brambles. *Come on. Can we just have one time without a huge fucking production?*

No, of course we couldn't. These were *hellbreed,* for Christ's sake. Nothing was ever simple or easy. It was all a game, and you constantly had to stay a few jumps ahead.

Perry weighed me for a long moment. The dogs slunk back, smoking and bubbling. Their crystal eyes were tinted red now, veined through with cracks of magma. They vanished into the shadows, and the chill lessened a little. The smells of the Cirque didn't break, but the spoiled-honey-and-flies stink lessened.

The 'breed and Traders still writhed and jerked around us, as if a bomb had hit and we were the only unwounded. The scar sawed away at the nerves in my arm, Perry's attention moving slow and jelly-cold over me. I wished I'd thought to scoop up a fresh leather wristcuff to cover the goddamn thing.

"Then tell me, my dearest one." His tone was a numb-razor kindness. "Tell me who is responsible for this. I will kill him, and we will all be happy."

I almost laughed again, caught the sound before it could reach my throat.

Ha. Nice try. "No, Perry. I'm not telling you a goddamn thing. We're playing this my way." *Because if you got your claws into this, the next thing I knew I'd be yanked into going to the Monde again every month. And I'm sure you have something special planned for me. Not this time.* I lowered the gun, my arm creaking with the urge to shoot him in the head and start killing again.

It would be bad in the long term, but oh, the instant gratification was tempting.

Tension ticked tighter and tighter between us, a humming line. I kept staring at the bridge of his nose, breathing softly. My pulse was a steady river.

He finally hissed, a long steam-escaping sound of dissatisfaction. But my bluff held. "Very well. I warn you, though..."

Leather creaked as the gun slid back into its holster. I flipped the whip once, the flechettes jangling. "Save the threats, Pericles.

I need to see the fortuneteller's body—or whatever's left of it. And you need to be keeping both baby blues on that goddamn hostage. If he dies, you're the first hellbreed I'm killing."

As threats went, it wasn't a bad one. Especially considering I meant every word.

CHAPTER 25

The tent was hung with red velvet, cheap tin spangles, and a huge ugly stink. Black liquid was splashed on every surface, including the cracked slivers of a crystal ball on a small circular table draped with purple sateen. Fine gritty dust puffed every time the breeze plucked at the tent's edges, and the slice of hot daylight from the pulled-aside front flap didn't do much to dispel the gloom.

I had an unsettling notion that this hellbreed had snarled at me, on my first visit to the Cirque. But not enough of her was left to be sure.

I was still cold. Perry crowded behind me until I stepped away, not liking the faint touch of his breath on my hair. The ruby at my throat spat a single bloody spark, and silver in my hair shifted and buzzed, warning him off. "Why aren't you watching the hostage?"

"Oh, I like it much better here with you." His usual tone, bland and interested, with just the faintest sarcastic weight to the words.

"Go, Perry. Have them bring me a bottle of Barbancourt rum and some cornmeal."

"You came unprepared?" Mock-surprise, now. He skipped nimbly aside as I turned, avoiding both the sword of daylight through the flap and a bubbling streak of decaying hellbreed tissue. Fine white dust curled up, cringed away from the shine of his shoes.

"I didn't have time to stop at a *botanica*. You gonna stand here running your fucking mouth, or are you going to do what I tell you?"

"Where's your little kitty, my dear? Home lapping a bowl of cream?" His eyes glowed bright blue, the threading of indigo in his whites pulsing in time to some heartbeat too slow to be human.

"Saul isn't your concern, Perry." I was too tired to put much *fuck-you* into it. "Your concern right now is keeping that hostage breathing long enough for me to put an end to this."

"And afterward?"

Afterward you can go fuck yourself again, if it will reach. I folded my arms. "We'll deal with *after,* after. Hurry up."

"I think we should come to an agreement."

"You're about ten seconds away from me blowing another hole in your head. What you think doesn't matter."

His eyes glowed. A small flicker between his parted lips was his wet cherry-red tongue, gleaming in the dimness. "Not even if I'm the one keeping you alive? The performers here are restive, and the Ringmaster is recovering from a nasty bout of green smoke and cockroaches. Even Traders are so fragile."

Even you, he probably meant.

I am not a Trader. I'm a hunter. Don't forget that difference, Perry. "Five seconds." I stared at the air over his head. "And counting."

He sighed, spread his hands...and ducked out into the sunlight again, the shiver rippling through his linen suit as well as his skin as the sun, that great enemy of all darkness, touched him.

I hoped it hurt. I hoped every fucking second he spent out in the daylight hurt him.

A straight-backed wooden chair lay flung on the floor, soaked in rotting hellbreed ichor. There was something odd—a long hank of dead-black hair, tangled up in the muck. A few moments more of examination proved it to be a wig, with a kerchief tangled in it. The kerchief had once been red, and was now rotting as the acid ate at it. The wig's fake hair was stronger stuff, bubbling slightly as it was...digested.

"Ugh." I glanced up. *She was probably at the table when it started.*

Greasy antique playing cards scattered across the table. Five of spades, ace of spades, queen of spades, all spackled with steaming liquid rot and covered in teensy roach tracks. The crystal-ball shards vibrated slightly, and something lay tangled under the knife-sharp splinters. Even the base of twisted dull metal the crystal ball must have rested on was torn up, sharp jagged edges still quivering with distress.

The violence of this attack was far and away the worst. It looked like the hellbreed had literally exploded in chunks. Even with all the sacrifice Zamba had performed at her house—the killing of her closest followers—this was superlative.

Which meant Mama Zamba must've had some link to Moragh the fortuneteller. Something physical, the last piece of the puzzle.

Come on. Something has to be here. I was about to start tearing the tent apart when a round silvery glimmer caught my eye.

I crouched, the balls of my feet slipping slightly in greasy, bubbling gunk. Each piece of silver I wore quivered with blue light, blessing reacting with contamination.

"Bingo," I whispered. I shook a piece of fabric out of my pocket—a red bandanna, 51 colors like Gilberto's, left over from the last big case. I unknotted it, folded it over, and grabbed.

The pocket watch dangled, gunk dripping off it. Steam curled away from its steel curve. Not silver, and not gold, but still antique. "Blessed Maria." The words were numb on my lips, but the hellbreed ichor cringed, turning inert and dripping free. "Watch over us sinners, now and at the hour of our death."

Belief behind words neutralizes evil, one of the oldest tricks in the book.

I popped the case free. The watch had stopped at 11:59, and there was no way of knowing, but I would bet it was P.M. A plain face, with the Greek letter Omega right under the 12. The crystal wasn't cracked, and engraved on the outer edge of the front casing were three worn-down letters.

SRG. Samuel Gregory. I wondered what the "R" stood for.

There wasn't much about this case that I could feel good about. But I felt good about this, even with my coat hanging in hellbreed muck and my heart breaking inside my ribs.

"Gotcha," I said softly. "Gotcha, you bitch."

I closed the watch up and stowed it in my pocket. Stood, my

knees creaking, and surveyed the rest of the tent. A shadow fell across the flap and I whirled, hand to a gun.

It was the stuttering barker, Troy. His face twisted up, hard red flush high on his cheekbones. His mouth was a thin line, and his hair was mussed.

He held a bottle of Barbancourt rum. "H-h-h-here." The single syllable strangled itself on the way out of his mouth. "I-it w-was H-H-Helene's."

"Well, it's going to help catch her killer." I took the bottle, and he dug in his pocket. Came up with a much-wrinkled paper bag. I pointed. It seemed easier than making him talk. "Cornmeal?"

He contented himself with a nod and handed it over. "A-are y-you r-really g-g-g-going to—"

"I'm really going to fuck up Helene's killer, Troy." *Jesus. I'm reassuring a Trader.* "How's Ikaros?"

His thin shoulders came up, dropped. His eyes glittered with the flat shine of the dusted, and he seemed not to notice the stink filling the tent. The red suspenders were even more hopelessly frayed, and his white shirt looked wilted. "Th-th-they s-s-say you're n-not g-g-g-going to d-do an-ny-nything. Th-that—"

God, it was like pulling nails out of stubborn wood, listening to him talk. "I don't care what they say. I'm just interested in getting this over with. Get out of here."

His lip curled for a bare moment before turning into a thin bloodless line again, and he retreated out into the glare. I was left holding the rumpled bag of cornmeal and a half-full bottle of Barbancourt, standing in the middle of a rotting smear of hellbreed and staring at the shards of a crystal ball, clutching a pocket watch that ran with blue light under the surface of its steel casing.

I set the rum and the bag of cornmeal on one of the few unsullied spots on the table, yanked the cup out of my pocket. The watch fit inside, and when I drew the straight razor out and slid it into the cup the blue light didn't just lurk below the surface. It fizzed over, falling in a cascade of sparks. A shiver walked down my spine again.

"Oh yes." I tilted the cup, watching the blue light paint the fraying velvet of the walls, and the bottle of rum trembled against the tabletop. "I've got you now, Zamba."

*   *   *

So much of sorcery is pure will. You don't really have to do a damn thing except declare, *This is the way the world is.* People do it every day. The record plays just under the surface of their conscious minds, all those assumptions they make.

That's just the way it goes. Some things won't ever change.

It's also the principle that lets hellbreed, Sorrows, Middle Way adepts, and so many others slip through the cracks. People fear muggers or tax audits. They don't fear the things that crouch in the crevices, staring up with glowing eyes that don't obey human geometry.

Oh, sure, people subconsciously cringe away from a full-fledged 'breed or shiver when an *arkeus* passes close enough to touch. But they won't really *look*. They don't want to see.

And they will hurry away, if they can. Lock their car doors and forget.

Whatever weird confluence of genetics and opportunity makes a hunter, one thing is paramount: the ability to look steadily at the weirdness and the filth. The refusal to look away.

And add to that the stubbornness to refuse to accept that what you see has to stay the way you see it. I can't explain it any more clearly. It's the original sin, I suppose—the pride to stand toe to toe with God and say, *No, you did something wrong. You fucked up here, and it's my job to make it better. To fix it, as much as I can. Maybe you're too busy, maybe you have a great cosmic plan that accounts for all this suffering and hideousness—but I don't, I'm not you, and I'm going to fucking do something.*

It's just centimeters away from the pride that hellbreed think gives them the right to murder, rape, pillage, distort, and batten on the helpless.

But those centimeters count.

The straight razor rattled in the blue enamel cup. The pocket watch did too, blue sparks popping and fizzing as I held it in front of me, arms extended, knuckles and tendons standing up with the effort of keeping the wildly agitated metal still.

The rum burned in my mouth. I held it, my gag reflex quivering on the edge of kicking in, the alcohol fuming until my eyes watered and spilled over. The cornmeal, a fine thin line of it in a circle around me, shifted. Little grains of it rose, touched down again with slight whispering sounds.

They didn't scatter. They just lifted and plopped down again.

When physical material has already been sensitized to a load of etheric energy, it's easier to pump more force through it. My arms burned. My throat was on fire. Tears rolled down my cheeks.

I ignored it all. Fierce, relaxed concentration filled my skull. The cup leapt and rattled like a live thing, jerking so hard it would have dislocated my shoulder if hellbreed strength wasn't pouring through my right fist, scorching sliding down my wrist and pooling in my palm. My bones creaked. I dug my heels in, concentrating.

The pool of filth that used to be the fortuneteller bubbled. Her wig sent up curls of smoke. My blue eye narrowed, eyelid twitching madly as if I had some sort of tic. The strings under the surface of the visible snarled, ran together in a complex patterned knot.

Sometimes the best way to go about it is to unpick the knot, strand by strand. Then there's other times, when you just slice the goddamn thing in half and let the resulting reaction smack someone in the head.

Guess which one's my favorite.

In this space, half-sideways from myself, I could *see* the fine dusting over every surface, an etheric imprint like the scales on a butterfly's wings. Zamba had spent energy recklessly to reach this victim.

She must be getting close to the end, or desperate. The cup rattled, lunged forward.

The great hunter magics are largely sympathetic, as opposed to the controlling sorcery of, say, the Sorrows. Sympathetic magic is intensely personal; you have to know yourself before you can use it. One of the greatest dictums in hunter training: *know thyself.*

And of course, there are times when brute force instead of subtle knowledge is the best way to get things done.

I sucked in air through my rapidly filling nose, my lungs inflating. The rum was getting hotter and hotter in my mouth. The cornmeal shifted wildly, with a sound like static cling on a pair of really big metallic socks.

I gathered myself. The mental image solidified inside my head, seen with the unsight of my blue eye. Long blond dreadlocks, blue eyes, a narrow waist, a bony face with smallpox scars across the cheeks, a long blue and silver caftan kilted up to her knees. Mama Zamba was crouched, looking wildly around her, fat snakes of hair writhing. She could probably tell something was gathering, but not *what*.

I spat, a long trailing mist of rum that ignited in a puff of blue flame. The cup leapt again, dragging me a few inches, my heels stapling into the dusty ground. Cornmeal popped into flame too, sizzling. The smell was baking bread for just a moment, then shaded into burning starch.

Potential shifted, *might* became *is,* and the force left me in a huge painless gout. The tent flapped wildly, straining against its moorings, and the calliope music rose to a shriek.

Rum-fire and burning cornmeal winked out. The force yanking on the blue enamel cup snapped like a rubber band, and I sat down hard, skidding on my leather-clad ass as my teeth jolted together.

Jesus. Major sorcery always ends up with a pratfall. Reaction hit, like thunder after lightning. The strength went out of all my bones and I sagged, the scar singing one wet little satisfied note against my arm.

I heard my own breathing, harsh stentorian gasps. Blinked several times. Gray smoke billowed, wreathed the entire tent. The bubbling hellbreed ichor gave one or two last pops and settled, spent.

I swallowed, the reek of rum and burning baked goods sliming the back of my throat. "Checkmate," I said, softly, and wished I could lie down and sleep.

But there is no rest for the wicked, or for a hunter who has just bought a little breathing room. Zamba wouldn't be fucking with anyone at all until dark fell and the tide of magic turned. I pushed myself up on trembling hands and knees, wished Saul was there.

It was the wrong thought. A sob escaped halfway, I set my teeth and bit, choking it off. Pushed myself upright the rest of the way, every muscle screaming in protest.

Just a little longer, Jill. You've got a plan, stick to it.

It was good advice. But I was oh, so tired.

The iron voice of duty had no truck with my complaining. *Get moving. Finish the job.* I bent wearily, scooping the watch and the straight razor back into the cup.

Time for the next part of the plan.

CHAPTER 26

I found the Ringmaster by the simple expedient of collaring a passing Trader and putting a gun to the skinny, rhinestone-laden asshole's greasy head. I needn't have bothered—he just led me to the same broken-down Airstream trailer the hostage had been in before. There was a huge hole busted in the side of it, and a large black spot in the dirt where the Ringmaster had bled.

I went up the wrecked steps carefully as the Trader hissed behind me, set my foot over the threshold, and half-glanced over my shoulder. "Open your mouth again," I said softly, "and I will break every last one of your hell-trading teeth."

The hissing cut short as if someone had taken a kettle off the stove, and I edged into the darkness inside the ruined trailer.

Perry sat in a folding chair, leaning back, elbows on the arms and fingers steepled in front of his nose. The frowsty bed held a stick-thin blond figure, collapsed against pillows and breathing softly, with a gleam of silver at its throat.

The Ringmaster crouched easily at the end of the bed, his thin shoulders up and his top hat askew. Frayed red velvet strained at his shoulders and hung down, his jodhpurs stretched over his bony knees. He glanced back at me, his eyes burning orange in the dimness, and his lip lifted silently. I saw the flash of the boneridge that passed for his teeth, but he immediately turned back to the hostage and I let it go.

"Hello, darling." Perry's words slid against each other, Helletöng rumbling underneath them. "It has been an *interesting* morning."

"How's he doing?" My throat still burned from the rum. I

wondered if he could smell it on me. A colorless fume of sorcery still hung on me too, and no doubt he could smell that.

"Oh, I didn't know you *cared.*" Perry snorted slightly. "He suddenly quieted, not ten minutes ago. The magic pulling on him slackened, and he is sleeping."

"Pulling on him, huh?" *Now that's odd.* "What was the collar doing?"

"Sparking like all your curséd metal." The indigo threading through Perry's whites was black in the dimness, and the scar chuckled to itself like wet lips rubbing together. "It seemed to help, though."

I had to turn my back to him to check the hostage, and I was so tired I only felt the slightest ripple of unease up the muscles along my spine. My boots whispered through a drift of candy wrappers and paper trash. Something stuck under my heel, and Perry chuckled softly.

The sweat on me turned to ice. But I just lifted one of the hostage's eyelids and checked the pupil reaction: none. The dust-shine on the surface of the eyeball had turned thick and mucousy, dry and veined on the surface. His breath was regular and shallow, his ribs rising and dropping. There was no spare flesh on him, and he wore only a pair of stained jockey shorts. His skin was mottled like a night-growing fungus. Lines of spidery writing sank into the stretched, sunken skin, twitching sluggishly with his slow pulse.

The writing flinched away from my touch. My apprentice-ring sparked, and the collar took on a dim foxfire glow. The biggest pocket of my trench coat flapped slightly, as if a small animal nestled inside it.

Huh. Curiouser and curiouser.

I passed my palm down Ikaros's torso, the hellish scribbles fleeing my touch. The mottling also fled a little, but it still took two or three passes before Perry made a small spitting sound of annoyance.

"Do you *mind?*"

"Actually, I really don't. Sounds like you do, though." I kept looking. I wasn't quite sure what I was looking *for,* but the way the cup, razor, and watch trio was shaking in my pocket was an odd sign.

I glanced at the foot of the bed. The Ringmaster hissed softly, the boneridge's crevices grimed with something dark and dripping. Faint shadows crawled across his face, the traces of poisoning from blessed silver.

I stepped toward him. The hostage's breathing evened out, became deeper. The scar tingled, expectant.

"Jill." Perry's tone was a warning.

I'm in a trailer with two hellbreed I'm not killing and a Trader I'm trying to save. Jeez. "Just a second, Pericles." I eased forward another step, leather-clad shins whispering along the side of the foam mattress.

The rattling in my pocket decreased.

That isn't right. She's after the Ringmaster, isn't she? It's the only thing that makes sense. I looked back at the hostage, who stirred restlessly and curled up on his side, unconsciously making a lizardlike movement with his head to make the collar's spikes fold down on one side.

I wondered how long he'd been doing this, to be so easy with the thing.

The thought of what Ikaros might have paid for that might have made me shudder, if I hadn't been so tired.

"What did he Trade for?" The words fell into a sudden dangerous silence, filling the dark, trash-strewn interior. The jagged edge of sunlight falling over the door wasn't a beacon of hope—it was a sterile blanket. In the distance, the calliope rollicked on, and I suddenly wanted to find out where the music was coming from and fucking shoot the goddamn thing so I didn't have to listen to it.

"None of your business," the Ringmaster finally said, each sibilant laden with menace.

I turned my head, met his pumpkin-hellfire gaze. "You brought trouble to my town. There's people dead in the streets, and I've been attacked." *Besides, this is an old unfinished case, and I'm going to see it carried through.* "Any question I care to ask about, any dirty laundry I take an interest in, *is* my business. What did he Trade for?"

The Ringmaster did his best to stare me down. But Perry shifted slightly, the folding chair creaking, and the thin, crow-haired 'breed actually cowered, perched on the end of the bed like a vulture.

If this keeps up, Perry, I might just even get to like you. Or at least, hate you a very little bit less.

"Henri, this is excessively wearying." Perry sounded bored, but the Ringmaster flinched again. I took another half-step toward him, and the buzzing rattle in my pocket diminished again.

Another little piece of the puzzle fell into place. Not a big one, but one that stopped me and made me examine the hostage's face again in the dimness.

"For the same thing every hostage Trades for," the Ringmaster finally said. "For peace. Forgetting. An end to pain."

Why do I not believe that for a minute? "He had something he didn't want to remember?"

"Doesn't everyone? Even our kind has regrets." He shifted, and I saw his feet were bare, horny calloused toes gripping like fingers. The muscle under the skin flickered in ways no human meat would move. "Not many, true. But still."

Regrets from a hellbreed? Jesus. "Yeah, like you regret you didn't kill someone painfully enough? Whatever." For the hundredth time, I took a firmer hold on my temper. "What did he trade for?"

"I told you. He traded to forget. And he was valued here among us."

Valued, yeah. As a way to keep the hunters off your backs, or a way to allay suspicion? As a mascot? Don't break my heart. I let out a sigh, my cheeks puffing up and the sensation of Perry's eyes on my leather-clad back like ice against fevered skin. "I've got other business to transact. The attacks won't start again until dark, and I'll be back before sunset. Perry, you keep watch. And *you*." It was an effort not to jab a finger at the Ringmaster. "Clear out the bigtop. Before it's dark we're going to need the hostage in there and people watching the entrances and exits. The rest of your people need to be outside the city limits by the time dusk hits."

That got a reaction. The hellbreed stiffened, and the scar burned with sudden hurtful awareness. "You're throwing us out?" He showed his boneridge again, and a sudden certainty boiled up in me. If he mouthed off just one more goddamn time...

Calm down, Jill. Get some perspective. The exhaustion both helped and hindered. I was too tired to go on a homicidal rampage, but the chain on my temper was fraying.

Hard.

"No. I'm catching your killer and finishing this up. You give me any more flak and you're going to be auditioning a new Ringmaster instead of a new hostage. Get me?"

Hey, they're not the only ones who can threaten.

"I do not think—"

"Of course you don't." Perry's tone was smooth as silk. "It is not your strength. Our little hunter doesn't wish to lose whatever advantage she has. She will keep the identity of our killer secret until the last possible moment, to ensure we do not make alliance with him *and* to ensure this ends the way she wishes. With the Cirque firmly under control and myself, I suspect, neutralized."

It didn't sound bad when he said it, but I was kind of irritated that he twigged to it. More irritating was how surprised he sounded, as if he didn't think me capable of realizing my best chance of wrapping this up and making it so the 'breed didn't get any funny ideas was controlling the dispersal of information.

"The thing is," he continued meditatively, "she cannot be sure what I know. And here she is, with her back to me and her throat within reach of your claws. She must be very sure, this canny little wench, of at least one thing—that I want her alive for my own purposes."

The only thing I'm sure of right at this moment is that I'm not going to murder you just yet. And that I can't trust you as far as I could throw you with two broken arms. I said nothing, but the sudden drop in my pulse-rate was warning enough. If either of them moved on me now Zamba might just be a loose end to tie up at my leisure, instead of part of a ticking time bomb of an equation. "Don't flatter yourself, Perry. You're occasionally useful, but in the end you're just one thing."

His laugh was as cold and slow as the sudden chilling of the scar, a chunk of dry ice pressed against my skin, eating its way down. "And what is that?"

"Just another hellspawn." I swung toward the hole in the side of the trailer. "I'll be back by dusk. Nothing should pull on the hostage before then."

They rumbled at each other in töng, metal rubbing painfully against itself in some deserted trainyard. The Ringmaster's tone went up at the end, an inquisitive ear-flaying squeal, and Perry's deeper answering rumble swallowed it whole.

I stepped out into the curtain of golden light. The cold around me cracked reluctantly, threads of heat touching my leather-clad shoulders. The cup rattled a few times and was still, a weight in my largest pocket.

Calliope music surged and drifted. The shadows were alive, lean dogshapes twisting and leaping through them. The sun was higher, working through the shell of ice over me. It was going to be another scorcher of a day, and I wasn't going to get any more rest.

Come on, Jill. You can rest later. Right now, you've got to break a few traffic laws.

I lengthened my stride. Dust lifted on the morning breeze, and I caught a breath of cotton candy and sickness. The Cirque shimmered, even more frayed and tawdry in daylight, thick electrical cables strung between the tents. The avenues and alleys were deserted, but I could feel eyes on me.

I tried not to feel like I was retreating, and had to remind myself to keep my chin up as I headed for the entrance.

Galina met me at the door, in jeans and a gray T-shirt. "Jill, thank God. I remembered. I can't understand why I forgot—"

"Voodoo," I said shortly. *Memory is as easy as electronics to subvert. It's honest paper they have trouble with sometimes.* "Where's Gilberto?"

"Upstairs sleeping. I gave him a tranquilizer and set a healing on that arm of his. He seems okay enough." Her eyes were dark and troubled, and her marcel waves were slightly disarranged, pulled back under another red kerchief. "I was in the kitchen stirring up a batch of bone-ease and all of a sudden it hit me, like I'd known it all along. Listen—"

So Zamba's slipping and her loa *are no longer paying attention to certain things. Or it doesn't matter now that she's close to getting what she wants.* I made a restless movement. I was two steps ahead but I might not stay that way for long. "I need ammo, I need a place to work, and I need your help."

"Jill, *listen.* I think Mama Zamba is—"

"Is Arthur Gregory. He made a deal with the Twins, got a sex change or just dressed like a girl to throw everyone off the scent, and part of the deal was clouding his origins so nobody would guess or find him. It didn't work completely on you because you're a Sanctuary, and it didn't work on Sloane's files because of the defenses on Hutch's store and the standard defenses on every piece of hunter paper. I just spanked Zamba a good one this morning, and I'm working on no time and even less sleep. Can you get me some ammo and talk while I'm reloading? I'll need some other things, too."

The shop resounded around her, clear air thrumming like a bell for a moment, and I swayed on my feet. I could still smell cotton candy, and the reek of a hellbreed body boiling as it ate through cloth and false hair alike.

Galina folded her arms and examined me from top to toe. "Heavens. Where's Saul? You look terrible."

"Thanks. I think Saul left me." Said that way, it only managed to hurt like hell instead of cripple me.

"Left you?" A vertical crease showed up between her pretty eyebrows. "But—"

"Galina." I closed the door, the bell jangling discordantly. My arms ached, a low deep fierce pain. I'd probably pulled something trying to keep the cup still, and sorcery tells on the physical body even when you have the power to burn. Come to think of it, my ass hurt too. I would probably be bruised by midnight. "My love life can wait. If Zamba kills who she's aiming for, there's going to be heavy-duty problems and I'm too tired to deal with them. I've got a plan but I need your help. You can talk and help me at the same time."

"What do you need?" She was suddenly all practical attention, turning on her bare heel and setting off across the store toward the back counter.

"Rum. Hand mirrors. Florida water. Cigars. A little bit of luck, and everything you now remember about Samuel and Arthur Gregory." I took a step after her, and paused. "And ... you wouldn't happen to have any live chickens around, would you?"

"I don't deal in livestock; I send people to Zamba for that. Or used to, anyway."

Damn. But all of a sudden, a bright idea popped into my head. "Never mind, I can get 'em somewhere else. I'm going to need to use your phone, too. Oh, and cornmeal." I paused. "And I think I might need some heavy-duty firepower."

She didn't even blink. "Like?"

"Grenades. If this all goes south I'm going to need to kill a lot of 'breed *really* quickly."

CHAPTER 27

The sun was still a decent distance above the horizon when I goosed my Pontiac through the rows of parked cars under hoods and blankets of sparkling dust, bumped over a temporary speed bump, and got right up near the front gate. The same female Trader working the admissions booth didn't even glance up. There wasn't a single, shuffling soul in sight in the wide dusty strip in front of the booth, and a pall of white biscuit-flour dust hung over everything.

The heat was like oil, and I was glad. I'd washed my face at Galina's, but I was still grimed with dust as soon as I stepped out into the haze. The Trader in the booth stared as I opened the trunk and shrugged into the first bandolier. On went the belt, heavy with more ammo, and the second bandolier. The weight at shoulders and hips was enough to drive home just how fucking tired I was, and my eyes burned. I blinked away fine grit and picked up the black canvas bag, settled the strap diagonally across my body.

Jesus. I'm loaded up like a burro. I also got the flattish cage out of the backseat, thanking God I'd gotten a sedan and not the two-door coupe. If someone wanted to firebomb *this* car they had their work cut out for them, GM hadn't believed in fucking around with fiberglass in the '60s and this was one of the heaviest, widest mothers they ever built. Plus, the price had been right—it was a heap when I picked it up, but a month or two of heavy work and it was a solid, if not cherry, piece of American metal.

The chickens were okay, three balls of white feathers in a wire cage. Piper hadn't even asked me why I wanted them. "They're pecking and clucking, and I can't get rid of them until Monday," was what she said out loud. *Goddammit, take these fucking things away,* was the unspoken message.

And then she'd looked at me when I appeared in the door of her office, and said, "Jesus, Jill. You look awful."

It's about to get worse, I thought, and slammed the door. Stuffed my keys in their safe pocket, blew a kiss to my baby, and turned on one slick steelshod heel, stamped for the entrance.

"You can't leave that there!" the Trader called, her fingernails digging into the pasteboard counter. "Hey!"

My left hand had the cage, and my right actually cramped when I snatched it back from a gun butt. *Don't waste ammo on this bitch,* the cold clear voice of rationality said. *You're going to need it later.*

I didn't realize I was staring as her until she blundered backward, the spangles on her shirt sending up hard clear darts of light as she spilled right through the back of the little hutch where she crouched, deciding who could go in and get trapped by the Cirque. Must've been a helluva cushy job.

But not right now.

She vanished, and sunlight bounced through the empty booth. A flutter of small paper tickets puffed into the air, settled. I uncramped my fingers, shook them out, and took a deep breath.

Cool and calm, Jillybean. That's the way to do this.

I waited until I felt the little click inside my head, the one that meant I was rising away, disconnected, into the clear cold place where I could do what I had to without counting the cost. The space where murder was just semantics and the only thing that mattered was the task at hand. Anything else—pity, mercy, compassion—just fucked it up, just tangled the clarity of justice and made everything difficult.

It was a good thing Saul wasn't here. I couldn't do this with him around. Not with his quiet dark eyes watching me. And that was part of the problem, wasn't it? It wasn't him.

It was me.

But right now I hopped the stile, weighted down and maneuvering the wire cages with one hand. The ram's heads sparked, gathering the late hot sunlight and throwing it back viciously. I could swear I saw one of the blind snouts move, and the stile clicked once as I landed, a dry ominous sound.

Thou who, I thought. *Thou who has given me to fight evil, protect me, keep me from harm.*

Usually the Hunter's Prayer calms me. This time, it was no anodyne. It was a complement to the unsteady ball of rage under my ribs. *Because I want to be the one dishing out the harm tonight. Some divine help wouldn't hurt, if this plan's going to pull itself off.*

It was warm and still inside the Cirque. Balmy, even. The whole place was deserted. Maybe the girl in the booth had been an early-warning system, or maybe she didn't get the memo that everyone was supposed to be gone. Nothing moved except unsecured tent flaps, and the calliope was muted and limping along through a rendition of the "Cuckoo Waltz," wheezing and popping, straining like a locomotive going uphill.

Dusk was beginning to gather. The shadows had lengthened. I've seen a lot, and believe me when I say there is *nothing* creepier than a carnival at dusk. The midway games were all lit up, but nobody was in the booths. The dust tamped itself down where people's feet had shuffled. The ghost of cotton candy turned cloying and rotten, haunted the heavy stillness. The breeze mouthed the fringe over the goldfish bowl, whistled through the pegs of the Wheel of Fortune, made the Ring the Bell, Strongman!'s bell make a low hollow sound. I caught a glimpse of a carousel down one long avenue of tents, the horses rising and falling with a clatter. The mirrors ran with soft dead light even through the red glow of approaching sunset, and where the horses shifted into shadow a ripple ran as if their muscles moved. Carved manes tossed, and some of them trickled greasy, black-looking blood from sharptooth mouths.

A mouthful of fried-food scent, old grease gone rancid and

clotted, brushed by, and the chickens made soft broody sounds. A single white feather drifted down from the cage. THROW A RING, a hand-lettered sign barked at me, the white-painted words surrounded by leering faces, WIN A PRIZE. The rings chattered softly against the angled spikes, and I could almost see the pegs used to make the spikes impossible to hit.

I penetrated the tangled maze, heading for the bigtop's bulk. Its pennants flapped as the wind came up the river on its evening exhale, and I heard a distant mutter of thunder behind the calliope's mournful wrangling. The flat mineral tang of the water swept the fried food, animals, and spoiled candy away from me for a moment, and I was suddenly possessed of the intense urge to set the cages down, shuck all my weaponry, go back to the car, and drive. Somewhere, anywhere. Away from here and the job that had to be done. Away from the job that would kill me one of these days.

The carnival-breath closed around me again, walling away the clean scent of the river. All of a sudden I smelled popcorn and white vinegar, corn dogs and healthy human sweat. The calliope lunged forward into "Take Me Out to the Ballgame," and I remembered one of the few good times in my childhood, when my mother was between boyfriends. She had taken me to a Santa Luz Wheelwrights game, and we'd eaten hot dogs and cheered until we were hoarse.

Two weeks after that her new guy put her in the hospital and beat me to a pulp too. I was six.

Memory exploded, calliope music wrapping around me and tapping the inside of my skull, and I had another, deeper urge. To throw down the cage and the weapons, to retrace my steps and find that carousel, and to pick a horse. Any horse, it wouldn't matter. Though I would like one with tawny sides and dark eyes, and I was sure there would be one there waiting just for me. I could climb up on its back and ride, and one by one every memory I *didn't* want to keep would fall away like autumn leaves.

And if the horse shuddered and lurched then, if it grew fangs and the other horses clustered around with hellfire in their eyes and their teeth dripping, I would not care. I would willingly lie down, and it wouldn't be rough wooden planks that I felt. It would be the killing cold of a snowbank, and I would be back in the snow before Mikhail pulled me out.

Not tonight, little one, he'd said. But even then I'd known it was only a matter of time.

I shivered. The chickens made more soft noises. The tremor passed through me, and the calliope missed a single note.

If I went and got on that carousel, though, I would forget Saul. I would forget the low inquiring purr he used when he was sleepy and I moved against him in the warm nest of our bed. I would forget the way his hair curled, and the depth of his dark eyes. I would forget his hands warm on me, and the soothing when I sobbed and he would hold me, murmuring into my hair.

Even our volcanic fights, when we screamed at each other and the ghosts of my past would rise behind each edged word. Or the silence in Hutch's bookshop when I realized he was gone, most probably for good, because I didn't deserve him.

Remembering him would be a double-edged pleasure. But it was one I would hold to me in the dead watches of the night, when I was patrolling and my city was a collection of black and gray. Filth in its corners and the cries of innocents falling on deaf ears.

If I dropped what I was holding and went to the carousel, who would even try to fight for them? And who would remember Saul the way I did?

Trembling had me in its grip like a dog shaking a favorite chew toy. Sweat slicked my skin, ran down the channel of my spine. The chickens were squawking more loudly now, because their cage was jerking back and forth. I came back to myself with a rush, and found the shadows had lengthened. One lay over my boot-toes, and I looked up, confused.

The sun was sinking. How long had I been standing here?

Silver chimed as I shook my head, the charms clattering against each other. My apprentice-ring popped a spark, and the chickens took exception to that. I let out a harsh breath, my pulse hammering like I'd just run a hard mile. Feathers drifted to the ground, and I noticed the dust had swirled around me, streaks against my leather pants up to my thighs.

As if something had been rubbing against my legs.

The calliope surged again, but I couldn't identify the tune and it didn't pluck at me. It sounded dissatisfied. I took an experimental step forward, and the chickens calmed down. More thunder sounded, closer now. I checked the deepening bruise of the sky, found no clouds.

I understood more about the Cirque now. Much, much more than I ever wanted to.

My legs stopped trembling after another couple of steps. I swallowed a horrible bitter taste and almost choked on the regret and unsteady anger.

The bigtop wasn't far. I somehow made my weary legs go faster, and I walked toward it with my head held high.

CHAPTER 28

There was no guard at the door—just a red velvet rope I felt okay stepping over, since its arc almost dragged the strip of faded Astroturf leading into the maw. The plague-carrier's straight wooden chair was set to one side, flies buzzing around its encrusted surface. My coat whispered, and thunder growled again in the distance.

First impression: soaring space. The place was *huge*. At the far end was a collection of gleams and puffs of green vapor, and the back of my neck chilled when I realized it was the calliope, two stories high and belching lime-green steam. It wasn't any louder, certainly not loud enough to be heard all through the Cirque.

Next impression: empty seats, their wooden surfaces polished by God knew how many rear ends and backs, their arms carved. Some had straps lying open, others hungry metal hoops that clicked open and shut in time with the music, right where they could close over wrists and ankles. Some of the seats flipped up and down in tentative jerks.

Three knee-high wooden rings held vast circles of stained

sawdust. The two smaller, flanking circles held all sorts of weird metal cages and implements, some crusted with nameless fluids, others gleaming dully. The light came from nowhere, and rippled on the underside of the canvas like reflections from a pond's unquiet, scum-laced surface.

The biggest, central ring was mostly bare. Dark spatters and drips spoke in their own tongueless language—*that's high-impact splatter, and right there is arterial spray, and that's where someone was bludgeoned.* I forced myself to look away.

Set in the exact middle of the middle ring was a plain metal bedstead with a thin dun mattress that looked older than I felt. The hostage lay, curled into a fetal position, his narrow shadowed back to me. He was still wearing the same ratty boxers, and the collar glinted under his lank hair.

I stepped over the border of the ring, candystriped plywood faded and chipped this close up. As soon as I did, light glared, and I almost threw myself into a fighting crouch before I realized it was a spot from high up, and it highlighted the Ringmaster, standing at the other end of the circle. His face was a cadaver's leer, and he capered a little like a tired old horse, his red velvet coat glaring and the top hat sending back jets of dispirited aqueous light. His cane whirled once like a propeller, the green crystal globe humming as it clove thick air.

He danced again, his jodhpurs flapping and the boots landing hard on springy sawdust. Then he halted, jabbed the cane at me, and hissed.

I set the chickens down. They had gone deathly quiet, and the cage shook slightly. I didn't blame them a bit. The shadows in here leapt and swirled, but I didn't see any colorless crystal eyes or lean leaping forms. Even my blue eye was having trouble with the shifting shadows, the ether thick as pea soup.

But just because I didn't see them didn't mean they weren't there. And Perry had to be around here somewhere too.

The calliope quieted slightly, faint cheery music with an undertone of ripping flesh and splintered bone. I did my best to tune it out.

"Come on in and step right up, ladies and gentlemen! See the

hunter come into the ring! Yessir it's a sight for the ages, and tonight's show will be the one to end all shows! Hurry, hurry, find your seats—"

"Shut *up.*" My yell sliced right through his, and the scar woke to painful, agonized life, sending a hot bolt up my right arm. "And get out of the fucking ring."

"This is the seat of our power." All the bluster was gone. His eyes were sheets of orange fire, fat drops sizzling down his thin cheeks. He even wore stained white gloves, and the calliope agreed with him, singing along. It followed his breathing, a deep hitch whenever he sucked at the air to fuel that voice. "You heard the siren song, didn't you?"

Goddamn hellbreed. Tell me again why I'm helping you. "Henri." I sounded like a teacher addressing a recalcitrant third-grader, but it was just the exhaustion. "If you don't fucking get out of this ring I'm going to blow your head off."

The cane whirled again, once. His lips peeled back, and the faint lines running through the sharp boneridges that served him as teeth were no longer approximations of a human mouth.

No, they were all shark, and all pointed at me.

But I stood my ground, next to the chickens in their wire cage, fine white feathers now drifting upward on a random draft of air. Killing him and burning this entire horrorshow to the ground had a certain appeal.

But that would ruin the plan, Jill.

A wall of warm air flapped through the entrance, the canvas straining and ropes suddenly creaking. The shadows turned darker, and I knew instinctively that the sun had touched the horizon. *Not long now.*

"As you like." The Ringmaster capered back. "For now."

I picked up the cage and matched him step for step, forward as he retreated. By the time I reached the bed in the center, Henri de Zamba was a good twenty feet away toward another pair of flaps, a stage entrance. More spotlights buzzed into life, glaring circles of leprous white stabbing the seats. A shifting crowd murmur filled the tent. I half expected to see people shuffling in, their faces blank with the expectation of entertainment. This light would bleach them out, turn them into ghosts, and the calliope would murmur like it was murmuring now.

Another rattle of thunder sounded. I could barely hear it over the music.

I set the cage down. Dug in the black canvas bag. The white novenas in their glass sheaths went at the cardinal points, unlit. I circled around the bed and its deathly-still occupant, leaving a trickle of cornmeal. I made the circle as perfect as I could, etheric force bleeding out from the fingers of my right hand to guide it and keep it solid. The particles were unearthly yellow, like the sunlight even now bleeding away over the edge of the world.

The circle had to be big enough to contain the bed *and* another smaller circle traced at the foot. This one I tried not to hurry over, but the shadows in here were getting stronger. How long had I stood listening to the calliope and thinking about the carousel?

Just do it, Jill. Worry later.

The *veve* took shape, the spout of the plastic bottle of meal jittering a little as force ran smoothly through my hand. Alien curves unreeled, and the second smaller circle to one side grew almost without me noticing it. Cornmeal shifted and hissed over the sound of the calliope, and the lines twitched and tweaked until they were satisfied. The meal ran out, but the symbol completed itself out of nowhere.

A shiver walked down my spine again, salt crust from the cold sweat drying itched. *Great.*

The shadows were wine-dark now, well on their way to achieving solidity. Ikaros stirred and the Ringmaster hissed again.

Move it along, woman! The cigars almost fell out of my shaking hands, rolling in their sheaths. I tipped Florida water out, a sweet orange breath overriding the reek of animals and sawdust. When I looked next, the cigars had arranged themselves near each *veve,* short bristling hairs atop the circles.

The Ringmaster hissed again. I set the bottle of Barbancourt rum down, pulled the bag strap over my head, and reached down into its depths, bringing up a plastic bag of copper chloride.

"I do not recognize this sorcery." The Ringmaster paced closer to the edge of the containing circle. "I do not trust you."

"That makes us about even." I tipped all the copper chloride I could hold into my left hand. "You're the first one I'm going to kill if this doesn't work out. Just remember that."

The world held its breath. I pitched the bag and scooped up the rum, just in time. The long dusk exhale ended, and I felt the end of sunset all the way down to my bones.

I can always feel it. Sunset always wakes me up like five shots of espresso and a bullet whizzing past. I swear I can feel the deep breath Santa Luz takes at the moment of dawn or dusk, when the tide shifts and another day or night rises from the ashes of whatever preceded it.

The Ringmaster threw back his head and let out an eerie cry, the calliope pausing and thundering out every note it was capable of. The green vapor billowed, and faces appeared in it, long screaming gaunt ghostly faces. Their eyes burned orange, just like the Ringmaster's—

—and Ikaros, almost naked on his stained mattress, howled and went into seizure. His thin body bowed up into a hoop, and the collar bloomed with blue sparks as a point of violent green appeared up over the circle. It dilated, became a disc, and there was a pattering sound as roaches fell out of its glare and somehow avoided the circle I'd drawn. They landed in the sawdust and exploded in tiny gobbets of slime. The chickens made high-pitched, frantic sounds suddenly cut off in midsquawk. Their heads had been lopped cleanly off, blood briefly spraying in high-tension arcs.

Which was a good sign, if I was looking for one.

Time's up.

The cap on the rum spun off, I took a gulp, and threw the copper chloride over Ikaros. It flashed into sparks of blue flame, the cornmeal spat points of a deeper-blue static, and I sprayed the rum—

—just as the Ringmaster launched himself over the circle's barrier and hit me full-on, bones snapping as I flew into the seats and the hostage screamed a curlew cry.

What the fuck? But I knew. The Ringmaster must've thought *I* was the one fucking with the hostage. Goddamn hellbreed, they don't even trust themselves.

Let alone a hunter.

My hand slapped a gun butt, slipped away, and closed around a knifehilt. We hit, a crunch of thunderous pain, and something warm and wet flung itself out between my lips. One of my large knives stabbed forward, blue flame catching hold on the corruption in the air, and sank into his midsection with a *tchuk*. That took a little pep out of him, especially when I wrenched the blade back and forth, hellbreed strength pumping through my arm and stink exploding around me. Wooden splinters rammed into my back, skritching against leather.

I punched him twice in the face, the scar a white-hot coal burrowing into my arm. His hard crust broke, splitting where I'd poisoned him with silver before, and I lunged up out of the wreckage, getting solid footing and *pushing* with every ounce of strength I could dredge up.

My fist hit again, the scar squealing in satisfaction as I *pulled* on etheric energy, and the Ringmaster flew back. His top hat flew the other direction, out of sight. I scrambled up, my side afire with pain and the scar burning as it burrowed in toward the bone. Sick heat spilled through me, bones melding in an instant, and I retched, clear fluid and blood spattering through my mouth and nose before I whooped in a breath and flung myself forward. My abused lungs burned and warm claret trickled down my side, but I had no time to worry about that.

Because on the other side of the central ring, leaning forward as if pushing into a heavy wind, stood Mama Zamba. Her blond dreadlocks writhed behind her, her hands stretched out into claws, and she pushed against the shell of energy holding the cornmeal circle, her blue eyes gone wide and black above her pitted cheeks.

I've got you now, you bastard. My feet touched down and I vaulted, both guns coming out of the holsters. Her face tipped up and filled with sick green light, cockroaches spattering behind her and flooding forward, seeking a weakness in the circle, and her haunted eyes met mine.

CHAPTER 29

A tinkling childlike laugh. Sudden cold wetness and smell of salt and candy. And pain so immense it swallowed the world.

I'd hit something, and it had thrown me. *Hard.* A convulsion ran through me, muscles locking and nerves firing wildly in protest, a mutiny of the body.

I rolled onto my side, every inch of me protesting violently. Heaved and would have thrown up if my jaw hadn't locked. Silver crackled, the charms in my hair rustling, and my eyes were full of heat and something too sticky and red to be tears.

Thunder, again, not faraway but close and overwhelming. Ozone in the air. The calliope wheezing, limping brokenly through a descant. I pushed myself up and saw the Ringmaster's broken body trampled into sawdust. Black goop runneled his vanishing flesh. Arms and legs corkscrewed, twisting as death claimed the tissues.

I slid down the broken remains of several chairs. Gained my feet. Vomited a long string of blood. There were probably internal injuries. *Where the hell is Perry? I don't like it when I can't see him.*

It was enough that he was staying out of the way. I didn't want to deal with him *and* all this at the same time.

A barrier at ringside was just a three-bar fence, it took me two tries to hop it. And there, beyond the Ringmaster, Mama Zamba lay in the sawdust, writhing. Her dreadlocks were full of grit, and a spume of it jetted up as she convulsed, harsh ratcheting breaths blowing snot out through her nose. Bones crackled, and my smart eye saw the triple-lobed shimmering in the air over her.

The Twins were occupied with their follower. I gathered myself and bolted for the cornmeal circle. Another rattle of thunder shook the air inside the bigtop, a brief flash of acid white light made every detail stand out. Ikaros wasn't seizing anymore. He lay sprawled on the bed, chest rising and falling, the angular spiked hell-writing climbing over his flesh in fits and starts. His eyes were open, staring at the roof.

"Noooooooooooooooo!" Mama Zamba screamed, and her voice deepened, taking on a male timbre at the end. The bone-crackles took on a deeper, wetter sound, and my feet slipped in ichor-slimed sawdust. I was almost there, *almost there—*

Another bright-white flash, smell of ozone turned thick and cloying, and a huge warm hand cupped my back and flung me. I landed in a heap inside the cornmeal circle, looked up as I reached my knees.

Mama Zamba hung in the air, but she no longer looked even faintly female. Her face had *shifted,* cheekbones broadening and the smallpox scars deepening. Her eyes were now Arthur Gregory's eyes, glowing feverish gasflame-blue and horribly sane. The caftan flapped around her thickening legs, and he hit the edge of the cornmeal circle going full-speed.

Ka-POW! Lightning flashed. The resulting explosion knocked me back into the steel-framed bed, its footboard barking me a good one in the side, where my ribs were already tender from being broken once tonight. I collapsed, trying to get enough air in, my hands came up despite me and clutched at the bedframe. I had enough time to see the tendons standing out under my fishbelly-pale skin, blood sliming the back of my left hand and dulling the shine of my apprentice-ring, before the imperative to *get fucking moving!* boiled through me again and I hauled myself up.

Noise returned. I realized I'd been temporarily deafened as I landed hard on Ikaros, irrationally afraid the several pounds of ammo I was carrying would crush him. Squirmed, fell to the side, wrapped one hand around a bar in the headboard and braced myself, my right hand jabbing up.

The collar's spikes sank into my skin again. The pain was tiny compared to the rest of me. I found the release catch.

"Noooooooooooooo!" Arthur Gregory yelled again, and I snapped a glance up to see him flying toward the cornmeal circle again. I couldn't count on a lightning strike this time. Chango and the Twins had probably both interfered as much as they were able to.

The release catch was slimed with blood. I let out a hopeless sound, fingers scrabbling, caught in the spikes coming up from the collar. My apprentice-ring sparked under its mask of blood.

The catch miraculously parted. The collar opened like a flower, and I rolled off the bed, landing hard on my ass, my head hitting the frame. Silver chimed, a small noise lost in the sudden lunging scream of the calliope. Green vapor filled the air, full of the candy-sick corruption of Hell and a darker effluvia.

Ikaros screamed. So did Arthur Gregory.

I scrabbled away on hands and bootheels, muscle pulling loose of bone with hard popping sounds, flaring with pain like nails tearing my flesh. The cornmeal scattered as I plowed through the edge of the circle, and Arthur Gregory landed on the bed. Ikaros was already gone, though, rolling away on the opposite side.

The scar boiled, burrowing in toward bone. It never got any deeper, but I sometimes wondered what would happen if it did. Right now there wasn't time. I fumbled for a gun, for a knife to fling, anything. The calliope shrieked again, belching more green smoke, its brass pipes blooming with sick *ignus fatus* light, spinning off fat globes of bobbing will o' the wisps.

The hostage gained his feet in a spooky-quick lunge. He had a lot of pep for someone who had been writhing and twisting with seizures for a day or two. His eyes lit with the dusted glitter of a very pissed-off Trader. His jockey shorts flapped, scrawny-strong muscle popping out under his skin, where the mad angry runnels of hell-script fizzed, glyphs winking out of existence with tiny puffs of steam.

He drew himself up, and Arthur Gregory hopped off the bed. The caftan fluttered around his ankles, torn and stained all over now. The blond dreadlocks swayed.

Sudden silence filled the bigtop. My breathing was very loud, but so was theirs, twin gasps through constricted windpipes.

They faced each other, and my hand closed around a gun butt. I was moving through syrup.

Then Ikaros spoke. His face had squinched itself up, and he sounded very young.

"Arthur?" Tentatively. His broad farmboy paws knotted together. "Art?"

Arthur Gregory twitched.

Oh, holy shit. The last piece of the puzzle clicked into place. *That's why the attacks didn't kill him—they* were *attacks on the Ringmaster, not on the hostage! And—*

"Goddamn you," Arthur hissed. "God damn you to Hell."

Samuel Gregory spread his arms. "Already done. I've seen things you can't imagine." His face was no longer young. Instead, it was ancient and graven.

"You were here. The whole time." Arthur's hands dropped to his sides. He took two steps forward. The calliope simmered in its corner, a tremor rising up through the floor as if we were having an earthquake. "You were *here!*"

"I came here to forget it. Forget it *all*." Samuel's hands twisted together, fingers knotting. "Him. And her. *Mother.*" The single word was loaded with hatred, and I shivered.

"Even me?" Arthur drew himself up. His dreadlocks rasped against each other.

Samuel shrugged. "Even you. I'm...sorry."

He didn't sound sorry.

"I did everything for you," Arthur whispered. "Everything. All this. I sold my soul."

Samuel sounded unimpressed. "So did I. And you have to come here and *remind* me."

A hand closed over my shoulder. I flinched, but the fingers dug in. "Hush." Perry's hot breath touched my bloody cheek. "Be quiet, now. This is meant to be finished."

I pitched forward, but I was so tired. And his fingers bit down again, steel pins grinding my flesh. "I said *be still*." His whisper floated to my ear, a trickle of moisture that might have been blood or condensation from his breath sliding down toward my jawline. Frantic disgust roiled through me.

They stood staring at each other. The calliope regained its voice and whispered.

"God damn you." Arthur's throat had closed down on him. All that came out was a rasp. And too late I saw the knife in his broad, long-fingered hand. It glittered, starlike in the green pondlight. I let out a warning blurt, but Perry's other hand had clapped over my mouth. Dry skin against the slick of blood on me, and he drew me back.

Arthur Gregory lunged forward. Samuel collided with him, and the knife rammed itself home in his narrow chest. Samuel's arms were spread, strangler's hands limp and loose.

He had thrown himself on the blade. He folded down like a clockwork toy run out, and the corruption racing through his tissues distorted his face into an old man's before finally draining away, his body twitching and jerking as it turned into a bubbling smear.

My eyes rolled like a panicked horse's. I threw myself forward, but Perry dragged me back down again and I couldn't get leverage. His other arm was a bar of iron across my midriff. He crouched behind me, and the heat of him was like a boiler. The smell of charring leather rose.

"Quiet!" The rumble of Helletöng scoured my ear, already half-deaf and ringing from the vast and varied noises of the night.

Arthur Gregory went to his knees. The tripartite spinning of the Twins appeared briefly, a pale oval of light. They laughed, a cruel tinkling sound, and he stretched out his arms. Their faces blurred into each other before the slim androgynous figure silhouetted in the light turned its back and danced away.

Abandoning him.

The *loa* are fickle. Just as much as hellbreed are. And Arthur Gregory had used up all his credit with them.

His wail shattered the stillness. The calliope answered it, shaking the bigtop. Canvas rippled and fluttered, the ropes singing in distress.

Perry dragged me even further back, duckwalking. One of his knees dug briefly into my ribs and I made a small sound in the back of my throat, a red-hot bolt going up my cramping side and exploding in my neck. The scar blazed, agony unstringing my nerves. The collar still tangled in my fist, its spikes buried in my wrist. Hot blood smeared my right hand, and pretty much every other inch of me. My back was hot, and Perry hissed happily to himself as he rose, dragging me upright.

They flowed past us, bright eyes and twisted limbs, a tide of hellbreed. The plague-carrier I'd seen before was first among them, capering and jigging; he had found another red velvet coat somewhere. It was he who picked up the Ringmaster's cane, stealing it neatly from under another 'breed's questing fingers, and he twirled it neatly, cracking the other 'breed on the head and snarling. They pulled back a little, and he found the top hat too. It went onto his lank-haired noggin, and I was suddenly aware of hell-breed and Traders packing the entire bigtop, dancing in through the stage entrances, climbing through the stands, cheering and rumbling in töng.

Arthur Gregory was on his knees, sobbing. He bent over, his mouth distorted in a wet "o" of suffering. His eyes had turned dead-dark, and cold. Snot smeared on his upper lip. One of his dreadlocks came loose and fluttered to the churned, wet sawdust. Others followed, plopping free of his skull with odd little sounds.

The plague-carrier capered to Gregory's side, spinning the cane. The green crystal shivered and crackled, and when the carrier spread his stick-thin arms, the calliope tweeted. He jabbed the cane at it, green vapor cringing away from him, and the first few notes of "Be a Clown" rippled through the air.

The crowd cheered and hissed, arms raised, cheap glass and paste finery twinkling. Their eyes were bright and avid. None of the animals put in an appearance, but I swear I heard an elephant trumpet and the yowls of big cats. Yipping dogs. Perry's arm loosened. My boots touched the ground, finally. The shadows crawled and leapt with the Cirque's dogs, their eyes glowing and crackling.

"Ladies and gentlemen!" It was a ringmaster's voice, an impossible deep baritone coming from the plague-carrier's narrow little chest. *"Welcome to the Cirque Diabolique! We're all-new and renewed! We're pedal to the metal and shoulder to the wheel! And welcome our new hostage! What's your name, sonny?"*

The cane whirled again, and the crystal jabbed toward Arthur Gregory. Who screamed, his body buckling. He lifted his face to the bigtop's fabric roof swimming with sick green light and *howled.*

Their cries rose with his. Every single one of them, Trader and hellbreed, yowled like cats at the moon. The plague-carrier danced back, whirled, and blinked through space with the eerie speed of hellbreed. Perry's arm tightened again, but the thing just halted a bare four feet from us and gestured to the collar.

"Clip him and chain him." Strings of gummy yellow ick crawled over sharp teeth, and the 'breed exhaled foulness. "You have our thanks, hunter."

I opened my mouth, closed it again. Arthur howled again, the cords on his neck standing out. The plague-carrier danced back-ward, spinning the cane, and Perry shook me, recently broken bones twinging hard even though my body was doing its best to patch everything up.

"Do as he says, Jill." Perry's arms slithered away, I swayed on my feet. "He is theirs now."

It doesn't look like he knows it, I almost said. But the new Ringmaster halted next to Arthur, and put down one narrow hand. He smoothed the matted blond head, caressing, and made an odd clicking noise.

The dreadlocks finished falling, and new hair was growing in. Sickly yellow, and oddly feathery.

The collar jangled in my fist. I took an experimental step forward. My knee buckled, but I stayed upright. Perry made a low spitting sound, as if to chide me for swaying.

Arthur's blind eyes passed across me for a moment, and I opened my mouth again to protest. To say something, anything.

But the Ringmaster bent down and exhaled across Arthur's wide, now definitely male face. Which turned slack and grinning, vacant.

"It is ever so," Perry intoned behind me. "A life for a life."

"Life for a life," the assembled Cirque chorused. Even the cal-liope, weaving notes that sounded like words between the frantic strains of a song I didn't want to identify.

The new Ringmaster twitched, and pulled Arthur Gregory to his feet. "There," he said brightly. "Isn't that nice?" Foulness dripped down his chin. "Tell the nice lady your new name, my dear."

Arthur Gregory smiled under a mask of tears, snot, and black-ened sawdust. He mumbled something, his lips moving loosely.

"She didn't hear you." The plague-carrier glanced at me. His shoulders were tense, and I had a sudden insane vision of shooting *his* ass, too.

But I was so tired.

"Samuel," he said, louder, his mouth working oddly over the word. "I am Samuel. Now. I'm Sam." By the third time he repeated it, he sounded like he believed it.

The flat shine of the dusted lay over his irises, and I knew what he had bargained away. Who wouldn't want to get rid of the memories he must have been carrying? The guilt, and the shame, and the murder?

The new Ringmaster watched me avidly. I'm sure something of what I was feeling showed on my face. The biggest thing, though, was weary disgust. And relief that this was finally over.

"You have one more day," I croaked. "By dusk tomorrow I want you out of my city."

He swept a simulacrum of a bow, grinned his death's-head grin under the old top hat. The cane whirled, cleaving the air with a low sweet sound. "Of course."

I clipped the collar on Arthur Gregory and left him to his new demons.

CHAPTER 30

It was a relief to take the heavy weight of ammo off. I stowed the grenades carefully, tossed the black canvas bag into the trunk, and slammed it to find Perry leaning against my car, his pale hair and linen suit immaculate. The night was young, and as I stood there watching him, the first few shufflers arrived. A quick flicker of movement was a new Trader in the admissions booth—a round little dumpling of a male in a bowler hat and pencil moustache. His eyes glittered as a tall heavyset man in jeans and a stained *Friends Don't Let Friends Vote Democrat* T-shirt eased up to the booth and handed over a snub-nosed .38. The man's mouth worked wetly, his hair was uncombed, and he looked like a dreamer caught in a nightmare.

The Trader stamped his hand and motioned him past. The man stumbled through the turnstile, his hands plucking at the hem of his shirt. The big stain on the front, right over his belly, was very dark against his white fingers.

"Nothing ever really changes, you know." Perry's grin was wide and stainless, his bland blond mask firmly in place.

"You knew." I meant to sound accusing. I only managed "tired." I pulled the key out of the trunk's keyhole and clenched it in one nerveless fist. The scar had gone quiescent, humming slightly as etheric force pooled in it and spooled through my body, encouraging and compressing the natural processes of healing.

I was going to be hungry, to fuel the healing. In a little while.

Perry shrugged. "Not the specifics. But this is how the Cirque gains its new hostage." His face lengthened into mock-concern, and his eyes burned blue. "You didn't know?"

God, just go away. I'm tired. I lifted my chin slightly, drying blood crusting on my face. Thunder rumbled in the distance again, a sweet cool wind touching my hair. Silver jangled, and my scalp crawled. "I'm done here, Perry. Get off my car."

He didn't move. "Where is your cat? Have you lost your taste for bestiality at last? Though that was a lovely touch, with the chickens."

That wasn't me, Perry. That was a loa, *and it was payment.* "Leave Saul out of this." God, I was so heavy. It was an effort to focus on him, to force my weary body past another iron barrier of exhaustion. My eyes were crusty and hot, and adrenaline was fast losing its usefulness as a spur.

Too bad, Jill. Deal.

"He's been looking weary lately, my dear. And you look weary too." A pause, and then the silken trap. "I saved your life. You owe me."

So that's your game. I made a small beeping noise. "Nope, no deal. You helped out because you didn't want the Cirque loosening your grip on the city. I don't owe you a goddamn thing."

His grin widened, became sharklike. The essential inhumanity under his shell gaped and yawned. "You belong to me, hunter. It's only a matter of time."

It was a relief to find out he was lying. No matter how many times I feel that relief, it's always profound. "I'll tell you again: hold your breath until I call. Fuck off, Perry. I'm going home."

"You owe me," he insisted.

"I don't owe you jackshit." My fingers rested on a gun butt. If he attacked me now, I would probably lose—and lose badly. I was just too fucking tired.

But I would still inflict a lot of damage before I went down. And here outside the barriers of the Cirque he couldn't count on their help—*or* on them not running riot once I was out of the picture. It was the same basic situation, me playing them off against each other again.

It was necessary. But it still made me feel dirty, in the worst way. Like I might never get clean again.

The indigo threading through the whites of his blue-glowing eyes retreated a little. "Such a righteous soul you have, Kiss. I only ask an inch of it."

That's more than enough room to damn someone. "Not this time, Perry. Go home and suck eggs."

He bared his teeth, a swift snarl. I cleared leather and had both guns on him, back leg braced, arms straight. The scar woke, a blinding jolt of pain pouring salt on every recent injury. We faced each other, and the only sound was the shuffling of the doomed circling before they slid through the ramheaded turnstile into the Cirque's poisonous glow. With a *click, click, click.*

That and the calliope, singing softly. A well-satisfied, cheery little song threading just under the subliminal noise of my pulse. My coat flapped slightly, and the thunder drew closer. It smelled like rain.

Even the rain isn't enough to wash this off. I didn't blink. I barely even breathed. The world narrowed to Perry and me, facing each other over a chasm the width of a hair.

He bared his teeth again, another snarl. This one poured through the subaudible register, I could barely hear it even with the scar amping my senses into the superhuman. My pulse slowed, skin chilling under its mask of drying blood, sweat, spatters of rum and other fluids I didn't remember getting splashed with.

"Someday," he said, finally. "Some fine day, Kiss."

Maybe. But not tonight. "Not tonight, Perry. Get out of my sight."

He moved. I threw myself back and down, but he just went *over* me with the spooky stuttering speed of the damned. Hit the ground, and heard the fast light patter of his footsteps retreating toward the meatpacking district and the Monde Nuit. A chilling little laugh, fraying in the distance, and the calliope sighed.

I pushed myself wearily to my feet. Didn't look at the shuffling victims in front of the Cirque. *Not one more fucking thing tonight, please. Not one. Okay, God?*

There was no answer. There never is.

I got into my car, and got the hell out of there.

Epilogue

I sat in the car for a while. My garage is narrow, but well-equipped. I considered putting the seat back and sleeping right there. I itched all over and would feel crusty in the morning, as well as dirty inside and out. And I'm accustomed to the weight of my weaponry, but sleeping in my guns was a bad idea.

Still, the thought had merit. Especially when I thought of the empty house, and—

The door to the house opened. I blinked as a slice of warm electric light fell across the car. The figure in the door was tall, broad-shouldered, and his shorn hair was starred with silver. He stepped down into the garage and came to the driver's side, opened the door.

I shut my eyes. Tears rose.

Finally, he crouched down. His fingers touched my hair, brushed my cheek. He rubbed a little, dried blood crackling under sensitive fingertips.

"Jesus," Saul said quietly.

"I'm sorry." The words came out in a rush. "I shouldn't have said that. I shouldn't have—"

"Jill." Kindly, quietly, calmly. "Shut up."

I did.

His fingers circled my wrist, pulled gently. It was work getting out of the car, but he helped pull me upright. The door slammed, and he folded me in his arms. The sound of his pulse was a balm and blessing.

Are you staying? I couldn't make myself say it. *Don't leave me. Dear God, please, don't leave me.*

"I just want you to do one thing," he said into my filthy hair. I almost cringed.

Anything. Just stay with me. I stilled, waited.

"Just nod or shake your head. That's all. Now listen, Jill. Do you still need me? Do you want me around?"

"I—" How could he even ask me that? Didn't he *know?* Or was he saying that he felt *obligated?*

"Just nod or shake your head. I just want to know if you need me."

It took all I had to let my chin dip, come back up in the approximation of a nod.

"Do you still want me?" God help me, did Saul sound *tentative?*

It was too much. "Jesus Christ." The words exploded out of me. "Yes, Saul. *Yes.* Do you want me to beg? I will, if you—"

"Jill." He interrupted me, something he barely ever did. "I want you to shut up."

I shut up. For a few moments he just simply held me, and the clean male smell of him was enough to break down every last barrier. I tried to keep the sobs quiet, but they shook me too hard. The breeze off the desert rattled my garage door, and the last fading roll of thunder retreated.

He stroked my hair, held me, traced little patterns on my back. Cupped my nape, and purred his rumbling purr. When the sobs retreated a little, he tugged on me, and we made it to the door to the hall, moving in a weird double-stepping dance. He was so graceful, and I was too clumsy.

He lifted me up the step, got me into the hall, heeled the door closed. My coat flapped. My boots were heavy, the heels clicking against concrete. I probably needed to be hosed off.

I had to know. I dug in, brought him to a halt, but couldn't raise my eyes from his chest. "A-are you s-s-still—" I couldn't get the words out. I was shaking too hard.

"You're a fucking idiot," he informed me. "I'm staying, Jill. As long as you'll have me. I can't believe you think I'd leave you."

That did it. I broke down completely then, and as he half-carried me down the hall I cried. I couldn't tell if I was crying for myself or for Arthur Gregory, or for the whole goddamn world.

Tomorrow night I would have to get up and do this all over again. Make sure the Cirque left town and find out what new mischief was brewing under the night skies. It never ended, this job.

It never would. And now I owed a *loa* a bullet, I had an apprentice to train, and Perry was looking to be trouble again. How long could I keep up mortgaging bits of myself?

As long as you can, Jill. As long as God lets you.

But for right now, Saul held me. My legs failed me and I went down in a heap. He went down with me, and he held me just inside the door to the living room. The first spatters of rain rang hard on the warehouse roof. I cried without restraint, and he held me.

We all Trade for something.

And God help me, it was enough. He was enough.

I just hoped I would always be enough for him.

Acknowledgments

Thanks for this book go first and foremost to Mel Sanders, who listened to me talk about it for hours and hours. And next to Maddy, Nicky, and Gates—who listened to me talk about it for hours and hours. Next-to-last, but certainly not least, to Devi and Miriam, who also put up with me when I talked about it...for hours and hours.

And as usual, the biggest thanks to you, the Reader. Step right up, sit on down. And let me tell you a story.

I promise it won't take long.

Book 5

Heaven's Spite

For L.I.
Soon enough.

What like a bullet can undeceive!
—Herman Melville

CHAPTER 1

How fast does a man run, when Death is after him?

The Trader clambered up the rickety fire escape and I was right behind. If I'd had my whip I could have yanked his feet out from under him and had him down in a heartbeat. No use lamenting, had to work with what I had.

He was going too fast for me to just shoot him at the moment.

Didn't matter. I knew where he was headed. And though I hoped Saul would be quick enough to get her out of the way, it would be better if I killed him now.

Or got there first. And *then* killed him.

He went over the edge of the wall in one quick spiderlike scuttle and I flung myself up, the silver charms tied in my hair buzzing like a rattler's tail. The scar on my right wrist burned like a live coal pressed against my skin as I *pulled* etheric force through it. A sick tide of burning delight poured up my arm, I reached the top and was up and over so fast I collided with the Trader, my hellbreed-strong right fist jabbing forward to get him a good shot in the kidneys while my left hand tangled in his dark, dirty hair.

We rolled across the rooftop in a tangle of arms and legs, my leather trench coat snapping once and fluttering raggedly. It was singed and peppered with holes from the shotgun blast, where I'd lost my whip. I was covered in drying blood and very, *very* pissed off.

Just another night on the job.

Oh no you don't, fuckwad. One hand in his hair, the other one now full of knife hilt. The silver-loaded blade ran with crackling blue light as the blessing on it reacted to the breath of contamination wavering around the Trader's writhing. I caught an elbow in the face, my eye smarting and watering immediately, and slid the knife in up to the guard.

The Trader bucked. He was thin but strong. My fingers slipped, greasy with blood. I got a knee in, wrestled him down as he twisted—

—and he shot me four times.

They were just lead, not silverjacket slugs. Still, the violent shock of agony as four of them slammed through my torso was enough to throw me down for a few moments, stunned and gasping, the scar chuckling to itself as it flooded me with crackling etheric force. My body convulsed, stupid meat freaking out over a little thing like bullets. A curtain of red closed over my vision, and I heard retreating footsteps.

Get up, Jill. Get up now.

Another convulsion running through me, locking down every single muscle. I rolled onto my side as lung fluid and blood jetted from my mouth and nose. The contraction was so intense even my eyes watered, and I whooped in a deep breath. My hands scrabbled uselessly against dirty rooftop. My nails were bitten down to the quick; if they hadn't been I would've splintered them on tarpaper.

Get UP, you bitch!

My feet found the floor, the rest of me hauled itself upright, and I heard my voice from a dim, faraway place. I was cursing like a sailor who just found out shore leave was canceled. Etheric force crackled around me like heat lightning. I took stock of myself and took a single step.

So far so good.

Now go get him. Get him before he gets there.

I stumbled, almost fell flat on my face. Getting peppered with plain lead won't kill me, but if it hits a lot of vitals it's pretty damn uncomfortable. My flesh twitched, expelling bits and chunks of bullet, and I coughed again rackingly, got my passages clear. More stumbling steps, my right bootsole squeaking because it was blood-wet. The knife spun, blade reversed against my forearm, and I blinked. Took off again, because the Trader's matted black hair puffed up as he dropped over the side of the building.

Now I was mad.

Go get him, Jill. Get him quick and get him hard.

A waxing half moon hung overhead, Santa Luz shuddered underneath its glow, and I hurled myself forward again, going over the edge of the building with arms and legs pulled in just in case. The drop wasn't bad, and I had some luck—the stupid bastard decided to stand and fight rather than run off toward the civilian he'd marked for death.

He hit me hard, ramming us both into the brick wall of the building we'd just been tangling on top of. This rooftop was a chaos of girders and support structure for the water tank looming above us. I got my left arm free, flipped my wrist so the knife blade angled in, and stabbed.

Another piece of luck—his arm was up, and my aim was good. The knife sank in at a weird angle, the axillary region exposed and vulnerable and now full of silver-loaded steel. My knee came up so hard something in his groin popped like bubble gum, and I clocked him a good one with my hellbreed-strong right fist.

Stupid fuck. While he was running, or at least just trying to get *away*, he had a chance. But fighting a pitched battle with an angry helltainted hunter? Not a good idea.

He folded, keening, and I coughed up more blood. A hot sheen of it slicked my chin, splashed on my chest. I pitched forward, following him down. My knee hit, a jolt of silvery pain up my femur; I braced myself and yanked his head back. His scream turned into a harsh rasping as the neck extended, vocal cords suddenly stressed.

Another knife hilt slapped my palm and I jerked it free of the sheath. My right hand cramped, he made a whining noise as I bore down, my body weight pinning him. I'm tall for a female but still small when compared to most hellbreed, Traders, or what-have-you. The scar helps, gives me denser muscle and bone, but when it comes right down to it my only hope is leverage. I had some, but not enough.

Which meant I had to kill him quick.

The silver-loaded blade dragged across easily, parting helltainted flesh. A gush of hot, black-tinged blood sprayed out. Human blood looks black at night, but the darkness of hellbreed ichor tainting a Trader's vital fluids is in a class all its own.

Arterial spray goes amazingly far, especially when you have the rest of the body under tension and the head wrenched all the way back. The body slumped in my hands, a gurgle echoing against rooftop and girders, twitches racing through as corruption claimed the flesh. I used to think that if Traders could see one of them biting it and the St. Vitus's dance of contagion that eats up their tissues, they might think twice about making a bargain with hellbreed.

I don't think that anymore. Because really, what Trader thinks they're going to die? That's why they Trade—they think the rules don't apply to them. Every single one of them, you see, is *special*. A special little snowflake, entitled to kill, rape, terrify, and use whoever and whatever they want.

They think they can escape consequences. Sometimes they do.

But not while I'm around.

My legs didn't work too well. I scrabbled back from the body, a knife hilt in either fist. Fetched up against the brick wall, right next to the indent from earlier. Sobbing breaths as my own body struggled for oxygen, my eyes locked to the Trader's form as it disappeared into a slick of bubbling black grease starred with scorched, twisting bones.

Watch, milaya. My teacher's voice, quietly, inside my head. *You watch the death you make. Is only way.*

I watched until there was nothing recognizably human left. Even the bones dissolved, and by daybreak there would be only a lingering foulness to the air up here. I checked the angle of the building—any sunlight that came through the network of girders would take care of the rest. If the bones had remained I would've had to call up some banefire, to deny whatever hellbreed he'd Traded with the use of a nice fresh zombie corpse.

But no. He'd Traded hard, and he'd used his bargain recklessly, burning up whatever remained of his humanity. I coughed again, shuddered as the adrenaline dump poured through me with a taste like bitter copper. Training clamped down on the chemical soup, my pulse evening out and my ribs bringing down their heaving.

Just another day on the job. And we were three scant blocks from Molly Watling, his last planned victim. Who was probably scared out of her mind right now, even if Saul had shown up to get her out of the way.

It's not every day your ex-husband Trades with a hellbreed and shows up with a thirst for human flesh, hot blood, and terror. Trevor Watling had worked through his current wife, three strippers, and two ex-girlfriends, not to mention a mistress and another woman grabbed at a bus stop. His sole victim of opportunity, his practice run for the others.

Even killers start out small.

I blew out between my teeth. The reek was amazing, and I was covered in goop, guck, and blood. The night was young, and I had a line on the hellbreed Trevor Watling had Traded with. A hellbreed I was going to talk to, up close and personal, hopefully with some silverjacket lead, because that was my job.

Time to get back to work.

But I just stood there for a few more moments, staring blankly at the smear on the rooftop. I've given up wondering why some men think they own women enough to beat and kill them. It used to be like a natural disaster—just get out of the way and hope it doesn't get you. Then I thought about it until it threatened to drive me batshit, chewing over the incomprehensible over and over again.

Now it was enough just to stop what I could. But, Jesus, I'm so tired of it.

A vibrating buzz almost startled me. It was the pager in its padded pocket. I dug it out and glanced at it, and my entire body went cold.

What the fuck is he doing calling me?

I tested my legs. They were willing, capable little soldiers now that the crisis was over. My shirt was ruined, and my leather pants weren't far behind. Still, all my bits were covered, and my trench coat was ripped and tattered but still usable.

I got going.

My pager went off again, and when I slid it out of my pocket Concepción, the Filipina ER nurse, looked at me funny. But they're used to me at Mercy General, and Saul made soothing noises at the sobbing, red-haired almost-victim.

"Montaigne at the precinct will have details," I told the ER nurse, who nodded, making a notation on her clipboard. "She'll probably need sedation, I don't blame her."

The stolid motherly woman in neatly pressed scrubs nodded. "Rape kit?"

I shook my head. "No." *Thank God. I got there in time.*

Of course, if I hadn't, Molly Watling would be carted to the morgue, instead of driven to the ER or even forced to endure a rape exam. Small mercy, but I'd take it. Connie's expression said she'd take it, too; her relief was palpable.

"It's all right," Saul said soothingly. The silver tied in his hair with red thread gleamed under the fluorescents, and he didn't look washed out in the slightest. But then, Weres usually look good in any lighting. "You're safe now. Everything's okay."

The slim red-haired woman nodded. Fat tears trickled down her damp cheeks. She flinched whenever I looked at her.

"*Bueno.*" Connie patted the woman's arm. "Any injuries?"

I shook my head again. "Nope. Shock, though. Ex-husband."

Comprehension spread over Connie's face. No more needed to be said.

I rolled my shoulders back once, dispelling the aches settling in them. "So, sedation. Call Montaigne, get a trauma counselor over here, and Monty'll take care of the paperwork." County Health has counselors on standby, and so does the police department. *Especially* in cases like this. "I've got to get going."

Connie nodded and deftly subtracted Molly from Saul. The redhead didn't want to let go of his arm, and I completely understood. A big guy who looks like Native American romance-novel cheesecake, red warpaint on his high cheekbones? I'd be clinging too.

"Th-thank you." The almost-victim didn't even look at me. "F-for everything. I didn't th-think anyone would b-believe me."

Considering that her ex-husband had terrorized every woman before he'd killed them, and he'd been a real winner even *before* Trading, it made sense. If I'd been a little quicker on the uptake, I might've been able to save some of the other women as well.

But I couldn't think like that. I'd done what I could, right?

That never helps. Ever.

"He's not going to hurt you anymore." I sounded harsher than I needed to, and she actually jumped. "He's not going to hurt *anyone* anymore."

I expected her to flinch and cower again. God knows I'm hardly ever a comforting sight.

But she surprised me—lifting her chin, pushing her shoulders back. "I sh-should thank you t-too." She swallowed hard, forced herself to meet my eyes. It was probably uncomfortable—a lot of people have trouble with my mismatched gaze. One eye brown, one blue—it just seems to offend people on a deep nonverbal level when I stare them down.

And like every other hunter, I don't look away. It's disconcerting to civilians.

I nodded. "It's my job, Ms. Watling. I'm glad we got there in time." *Too late for those other women. But take what you can get, Jill.* I shifted my attention to Connie. "I need a phone."

"*Sí, señora.* Use the one at the desk." And just like that, I was dismissed. Connie bustled the woman away out of the curtained enclosure, and the regular sounds of a Tuesday night on the front lines swallowed the sharper refrain of a terrified, relieved woman dissolving into fresh sobs. The smell of Lysol and human pain stung my nose almost as much as the dissolving reek of a Trader's death.

Saul let out a sigh. He reached out, his hand cupping my shoulder. "Hello, kitten."

I leaned into the touch. The smile spreading over my face felt unnatural, until my heart made the funny jigging movement it usually did when he was around and a wave of relief caught up with me. "Hey, catkin. Good work."

"I knew he wouldn't get there before you." His own smile was a balm against my jagged nerves. He'd put on some weight, and the shadows under his eyes weren't so dark anymore. The grief wasn't hanging on him quite so heavily. "What's the next emergency?"

I shrugged, held up the pager. "Gilberto paged from home."

He absorbed this. "Not like him," he finally said. Which was as close as he would get to grudgingly admitting my apprentice was doing well.

"That's what I thought." I reached up with my left hand, squeezed his fingers where they rested against my shoulder. His skin was warm, but mine left a smudge of filth and blood on him.

He never seemed to mind, but I took my hand away and swallowed hard.

Saul examined me. "Well, let's see what he wants. And then, lunch?" Meaning the night was still young, and he'd like a slice of time alone with me.

It's kind of hard to roll around with your favorite Were when you've got a kid living with you, after all. I was about ready to start suggesting the car's backseat, but—how's this for irony—I hadn't had time yet. One thing after another, that's a hunter's life. "I don't see why not. I've got a line on the hellbreed Watling Traded with, too."

He nodded. The fringe on his jacket trembled, and he turned on one heel. "Sounds like a busy night."

"Aren't they all." I followed him out, past other curtained enclosures. Some were open, the machinery of saving lives standing by for the next high-adrenaline emergency. Some were closed, the curtains drawn to grant a sliver of privacy. Someone groaned from one, and a murmur of doctor's voices came from another. Mercy General's ER was always hopping.

The nurse at the desk just gave me a nod and pushed the phone over, then went back to questioning a blank-eyed man in Spanish through the sheet of bulletproof glass as she filled out a sheet of paperwork with neat precise scratches. The patient swayed and cradled his swollen, messily bandaged hand; he was pale under his coloring and smelled of burnt metal and cocaine. I kept half an eye on him while I punched 9 and my own number.

He picked up on the first ring. Slightly nasal boy's voice. *"Bruja?"*

"Gilberto. This better be good." I regretted it as soon as I said it. He wasn't the type to call me for nothing.

As usual, he didn't take it personally. A slight, wheezing laugh. "Package for you, *mi profesora*. Wrapped up with a pretty bow."

What? "A package?" My mouth went dry. "Gilberto—"

"Man who delivered it still here. *Uno rubio*, in a suit. Says he'll wait for you."

A blond, in a suit? The dryness poured down, invaded my throat. "Gilberto, listen to me very carefully—"

A slight sound as the phone was taken from my apprentice. I knew, from the very first breath, who was waiting for me at home.

"My darling Kiss." Perry's voice was smooth as silk, and full of nasty amusement. "He's quite a winning elf, your new house-boy. And *so* polite."

Think fast, Jill. My heart leapt nastily. The scar on my wrist turned hot and hard, swollen with corruption. As if he had just pressed his lips against my flesh again. "Pericles."

Saul went stiff next to me, his dark eyes flashing orange for a moment.

The hellbreed on the other end of the line laughed. "I have a gift for you, my darling. Come home and see it. I will be content with the boy until then."

He dropped the phone down into the cradle. The sound of the connection breaking was like the click of a bullet into the chamber.

I slammed my receiver down, pulling it at the last moment so I wouldn't break the rest of the phone. The man on the other side of the glass jumped, and the nurse twisted in her chair to look at me. I didn't bother to give a glance of apology, just looked at my Were.

Saul's eyes met mine, and I didn't have to explain a single thing. He turned so fast the fringe on his jacket flared, and he headed with long strides for the door that would take us out toward the exit. I was right behind him. The scar twitched under the flayed cuff of my trench coat. Saul's stride lengthened into a run.

So did mine.

CHAPTER 2

Sarvedo Street was dark and deserted this time of night. I didn't pull into the garage. I bailed out in front of my warehouse, barked a "Stay in the car!" at Saul, and hauled ass for the door. Steel-clad boot heels struck sparks from the concrete, the front door was open a crack, and I barreled through, rolling and coming up to sweep the front hall and wide-open space of the living room. The charms tied in my hair buzzed, a warning.

Gilberto was on the couch, dark eyes wide and thin sallow face almost bleached. His knees poked through the holes in his jeans and his red T-shirt glared against the couch's slipcover. He looked cheesy-sick, and I didn't blame him. Because on the other side of the coffee table, looking down at my apprentice like he was choosing bonbons out of a box, was a bland-faced, pale-haired hellbreed in a white linen suit.

My apprentice had Jack Karma's Bowie knife out, the silver loaded along the blade's flat running with blue light. He held the knife up, a tiny bar between him and the slender shape of the hellbreed, who was leaning forward, weight on his toes. Highly polished wingtips placed just so on the hardwood floor, his expensively cut platinum hair ruffled on a breeze that came from nowhere, Perry smiled a shark's smile. His chin jerked to the side and he almost moved before I was on him.

The shock grated through me, my aura fluorescing into the visible. Hard little sparks of blue crackled off sea-urchin spikes, an exorcist's aura hard and disciplined—and reacting to the soup of baneful intent in the air.

Gilberto let out a harsh yell, his voice breaking. Perry didn't speak, but that could have been because I had him on the floor, arm twisted up so far behind his back that whatever he had serving him for bones crackled, the gun pressed to the back of his shiny blond head. One of my boots was on his other wrist, flexing down until something else made a creaking, almost-snapping sound.

He gave a token heave or two and went still, the scar turning to soft velvet fire, sliding up my arm.

I would have preferred pain. Either way, the gun didn't waver. All of a sudden I understood why Mikhail had almost drawn on him the first time he'd shown up at the bar, sniffing around me. A million years ago, back when I was the apprentice and Mikhail was the hunter.

The longer I live, the more things just seem to repeat themselves.

Perry chuckled. "Kisssssss." Subvocal rumbling slid under the surface of the word, trailing away on a long hiss like a freight train's brakes failing on a long sharp hill. "*Darling.* So rough."

"Shut. Up." My knee dug into his back. I made sure I was braced, *watched* him. "Gil?"

A long, tense-ticking two seconds. My apprentice gulped. "*Sí, señora?*" No trace of sarcasm or machismo. That was either good... or very bad.

"Go out the front door. Saul's in the car. You two are going to have some lunch. I'll catch up with you." A nice even tone, but I did not relax. Perry didn't move, his body loose and unjointed against the floor. As if I was kneeling on a sack of loosely threaded bones in a bag of noisome fluid.

"*Sí, señora.*" He got up, slowly, like an old man. The Bowie knife boiled with blue light, and my finger tensed on the trigger.

It was time to make it very clear to a certain hellbreed that my apprentice was off-fucking-limits. If you give 'breed an inch, they *will* take twenty miles. Your only hope is to make it clear the first time.

And God help me, I liked making things violently clear to this particular 'breed. "Let's start at the beginning, Perry. *You do not threaten my apprentice.*"

He said nothing, just hissed. Which meant I wasn't getting through.

So I pistol-whipped him twice, bouncing his head off the floor. He hissed again and surged up, I shoved him back *down* and snapped a glance at Gilberto, who was stumbling in slow motion, a sleepwalker in a nightmare. But he was heading the right way, toward the front door. Saul would take care of him.

"Sweet nothings." The sibilants dragged out over the rumble of Helletöng. "Oh, my *darling.* I've missed you."

I stuck with the safest response possible. "You do not threaten my apprentice." And I was so close to blowing his head all over my living room floor. So, so close.

Not only because of the scar, rubbing against itself and moaning on my wrist. Not only because of Gilberto's cheese-sick cheeks or the fact that Perry was here, inside the house I slept in.

No. Because it would feel good. Too good. I hadn't seen Perry since the circus came to town, and that wasn't as long ago as I liked.

It would *never* be long enough.

"Of course not." Now he sounded irritated. "I came to bring you a gift. He was *entertainment.* Thoughtfully provided by—"

I hit him again. One more time, because it felt necessary. And another for luck. Once more because by then, I wanted to so bad I couldn't stop myself.

Hunters live on the ragged edge of adrenaline and violence. When all your problems are hellbreed, all your solutions start to look like murder. The trouble isn't that you're tempted to do it.

The trouble is that it feels so goddamn good.

Perry screamed, an inarticulate howl of rage and pain. I bore down as he tried to heave up, and the scar turned into barbwire instead of velvet, sawing against the nerves in my arm.

It was a physical effort to stop hitting him. I could have turned his head into hamburger, I had the firepower, but then I would have had to burn him and scatter the parts and ashes as far apart as possible. And what would the scar do if I killed him?

I just didn't know. But oh, God, I was getting so close to not caring.

It almost made me sweat. Threads of black ichor crawled through his hair. I settled the end of the gun barrel against his skull again and he went still.

Bingo, Jill. Even he isn't sure what you'll do.

It's nice when a hellbreed considers you unpredictable.

"Now." The sudden calm was a warning, just like the thunder of my pulse smoothing out, dropping into the steadiness of action. "Let me hear you say it, Pericles, so I know you *understand*."

"Dearest one." It must have been hard to talk with his face in the floor, but he managed. He even managed to sound cheerful, if you could call a tone like a razor slipping under cold flesh cheerful. "I was pulling your chain, Kiss. Such a nice chain it is, too. Attached to the wall of that conscience of yours."

I said nothing, but my hand tensed again. Such a little squeeze, and a .45 bullet would frag his head all to pieces. And then I'd find out what the scar would do without him behind it.

"I do not threaten your apprentice." A singsong, over a deep well of roaring Helletöng. The speech of the damned rattled the walls, made the floor groan.

"English, motherfucker." My throat had locked up, so it was a whisper. "You speak *English only* to me."

"Bigot." A soft, hurtful laugh. He had frozen under me, waiting. "Your maternal instincts are fetching, darling."

"Give me a reason, Perry." A certain amount of threatening theater is necessary to work this job. You stop the threats and the bitches start getting uppity.

But I meant it. I was begging him for a reason. To give me that opening. I could not just kill him out of hand.

That would make me just like him. Just like the things I hunted.

"Two gifts in one day? Woman, thy nature is greed." He laughed, the sound bubbling in a pool of black ichor. "Look on the table, Kiss."

I didn't. I looked down at the seeping mess of his head. The urge to slam him down a few more times trembled in my bones. My heel flexed down on his stretched-out wrist, and he made a squirming, uncomfortable movement.

Like a worm on a hook.

"Say it again." This time I sounded almost normal. A huge relief threatened to descend on me. If he mouthed off one more time, it was good enough provocation to shoot him. My conscience wouldn't raise a peep, that was the important thing.

"I do not threaten your apprentice." Level and bland. Like he'd gotten what he wanted.

Every muscle in my body tensed. I lunged aside, my heel grinding down sharply once more. I skipped back, and he rose in a black-spattered wave, shaking out his hands and turning to face me. His wrists crackled, and he made a queer sideways movement with his head, crunching noises inside his neck as he resettled himself inside his shell of normality.

Under the streaks and spatters of hellbreed gore, his face was...normal. No scrim of hurtful beauty, no sharp handsomeness. Even a hunter has to look closer than usual to see the *twisting* on him, the worm in the apple. I've given up wondering if the lack of beauty in his disguise makes him more scary, or less. It's one of those questions that will keep you from sleeping, and I need my sleep more than ever these days.

My gun was level, my aim settling right between his eyebrows. The scar turned back to velvet. My arm was straight, though. It did not waver. The silver in my hair rattled, and the chain at my throat holding the carved ruby warmed. So did my apprentice-ring, snug against my third left finger. The heat prickled and teased at my skin.

My peripheral vision snagged on a flicker of silver and white. A plain white paper box, tied with silver ribbon. A pretty, professionally made bow.

A present from a hellbreed is never a pleasant thing. And the more attractive the package, the less likely you're going to get something nice out of it.

My mouth was dry. "Take it away and go crawl back into your hole. I accept no gifts from you."

Not when he was looking to get me back into our bad old cycle. The scar and its attendant power for a slice of my time each month, that was the original deal—until he welshed and I got the scar's power for nothing.

Because I'd survived. And because I called his bluff. Yet another question that would keep me from sleeping—how deep had his tentacles been inside Inez Germaine's little operation? How much had he lost, gambling for the chance that he could make me damn myself? Once I did that, once I stepped into the abyss, I had a sneaking suspicion that he would own me.

He had been gambling for nothing less than my soul. And he was still looking to hook me.

The warehouse creaked around us, its usual nightly song as the wind came up off the river, whistling through the trainyards and the industrial section. Not all the noise was from the pressure of air outside, though. Some of the groaning and creaking was the strings under the physical world being plucked, both by my will and by flabby-corrupting hellbreed fingers. I met Perry's blue, blue stare and thought longingly of having him on the floor again and this time pulling the goddamn trigger.

"This gift you'll accept. It's more in the nature of recovered property." He stepped to the side, easily and slowly, I tracked him with the gun's snout. My left fingers dropped to my whip, and he grinned. White teeth flashed through the mask of thin viscous black dripping on his face. His suit would be ruined, a dark stain all the way down the front. His tie was steaming as polyester fibers reacted with hellbreed ichor. The rest of the fabric had to be natural—silk and cotton don't react the same way. They get eaten away, but they don't steam or smoke.

Just like a hellbreed to wear a polyester tie. A snorting sarcasm threatened to reach my lips. I killed it.

His gaze dropped to my left hand. "I'm not about to make trouble, my dear. I just want to see your face when you open my present. The boy's no challenge. You'll have your work cut out for you, making *him* into one of your kind."

That's none of your business, hellspawn. My blue eye was hot and dry, watching for a shiver of baneful intent. When I didn't respond, he chuckled softly as if I had.

The ribbon unfolded under his clever fingers. I tensed. It fell aside, and he opened the box with a quick flick, pulling his hand back and inhaling, shaking his long, elegant fingers as if they'd been singed.

"There." A sidelong glance at me. "Come and see, Kiss. And tell me what a good little hellspawn I am, bringing you what belongs to you. Scratch behind my ears, who's a good boy." A flicker between his lips—a wet, cherry-red tongue, scaled and supple. The flash of color was obscene against his bloodless pallor.

I ran through everything he could possibly mean with that statement, came up with nothing good. "Step back. Over there." I indicated a spot on the hardwood floor with my chin. Waited while he minced a bare foot, then two. "Further, Perry."

His mouth turned down, but he did mince back a few more steps. "Your mistrust wounds me. It really does. Here I've gone to all this *trouble*—"

"Shut up." I glanced down into the box, my whole body expecting him to jump me. The longer this went on, the more I expected something like that from him.

Hellbreed and Traders aren't known for impulse control.

Inside the box were glinting shapes that refused to make sense for a moment. I exhaled, hard, as if I'd been punched.

Mikhail's voice, from the secret space inside my head he always occupied. *Sekhmet is Eye of Ra, and this is Eye of Sekhmet. Been passed down,* milaya, *from hunter to hunter in Jack Karma's lineage. Before the first Karma we know little. But this is Talisman he had, for whatever reason. Is for my little snake when I am gone, no?*

And then I was there in that shitty little hotel room, Mikhail's life gurgling out through the hole in his throat and Melisande Belisa's tinkling laugh echoing as she fled. With this Talisman clutched in her spidery little fingers. It had probably bought her up quite a few ranks in the Sorrows' arcane and crowded hierarchy.

My shot went wide. Perry rammed into me, we slammed into

the wall across the living room. Drywall dust puffed out. His fingers closed around my right wrist, *squeezing*. Bones ground together and the scar sent a sick wave of hot delight up to my shoulder, his fingertips plucking as if my arm was a string instrument. He pressed against me, his other hand worming at my hip, looking for my whip handle. And there was something hard in his pants, too. Shoved right up against me as if I wasn't a hunter.

As if I was what I had been before Mikhail plucked me out of that snowbank.

A knife handle smacked into my left palm. I jerked it free and *cut*, the blade going in with little resistance. Silver in my hair and at my throat rattled and crackled, spitting blue sparks showering his marred, ichor-streaked face. He was grinning madly, and I didn't dare blink while I sheared through whatever served him as stomach muscle, finishing with a twist, and brought my knee up.

He recoiled, I heaved him away. The gun came down, but he knocked the barrel aside as I squeezed the trigger again. The bullet whined, dug a furrow out of the floor, and buried itself in the wall between living room and my bedroom. The scar shrieked with pain, napalm rubbed burning into skin.

My leg came up. I *kicked*, the blow unreeling, boot smashing solidly into his belly. A gush of black ichor pattered free. He folded over, arms wrapped over his stomach, and hissed, baring his teeth. The mask of bland normality slipped for a moment, and troubled air swirled in two points behind him, above his shoulders. The buzz of flies rattled everything in my living room, and the etheric protections laid in the walls tolled once like a bell.

It was a shame I couldn't consecrate the warehouse's grounds and keep him out of here permanently. I'd give up my monthly municipal check for that. But no—I'm a hunter, not a priest.

He fled, and I tracked him with the gun. My aim wasn't off—I plugged him twice in the back before he nipped smartly down the hall, footsteps too light to be human, hitting the ground oddly.

It was only after the front door banged closed and the sound of him running—northward, toward the meat-packing district and the Monde Nuit—faded too much even for my hellbreed-jacked hearing that I slumped against the hole in the wall. I tore my gaze away from the hall and stared at the box on the table.

Hard darts of silver glitter spiked up from the Talisman. My legs were unsteady. I made it, step by uncertain step, across what seemed like acres of floor, my boots gripping through a thin stinking scrim of hellbreed ichor. When I could look into the box fully, my smart eye watering and hot tears slicking that one cheek, I saw that it was, indeed, the Eye.

The ruby at my throat was a pale imitation of this barbaric red gem in its rough silver-claw setting. It glowed fierce crimson, darts of light shimmering into white glow at the edges. Its chain, large silver links that looked sharp enough to cut, was broken. Spilling out of the box, vibrating in place, the Talisman rattled as I drew closer.

I halted. But the necklace just vibrated more intensely on my coffee table, next to the stack of *Home Beautiful* and *Cook's Illustrated* Saul was always reading. A thin curl of smoke rose from the paper of the box.

Is it going to burn me? I was acutely aware of sweat touching the curve of my lower back, blood and hellbreed contamination all over my clothes, the scar humming a soft little chortle of corruption on my right wrist. And who was I kidding? *Both* my cheeks were wet, because my eyes were brimming with tears.

My throat clicked as I swallowed drily and blinked away the water, looking for traps. He'd had plenty of time to lay them, but I saw nothing except the burning etheric smear of an angry and awake Talisman. The smell of burning intensified.

The Talisman hummed, plucking at the strings under the world's surface. But not like a hellbreed. No, this was music. It was humming along with the song that naturally unmade things. The same music that triggered landslides and catastrophes, a great harmonic resonance instead of the crashing discordance of hellbreed corruption.

I don't even believe in Sekhmet, I'd told Mikhail.

And his response? *I don't either,* milaya. *But never hurts. Don't have to believe to do job. Just have to do.*

It took more courage than I thought I had left to take the final five steps to the table and reach down. I was prepared for sparks, or for a backlash of etheric energy to knock me away. Prepared for anything, actually, other than the thing that actually happened.

My fingers touched cool metal. The thready curls of smoke evaporated, leaving behind the smell of burning and the reek of rotting hellbreed. I found I was holding the Talisman, and the sharp edges of the chain brushed lovingly against my hand. They didn't cut, they just scratched a little.

Like fingernails against a lover's skin.

Oh, my God. The gem nestled in my palm and thrummed at me. When I lifted it to my throat, the broken links of the chain slid across my skin and melted together as if they'd never been ripped from a hunter's chest. The Talisman settled against my breastbone, its low humming note disappearing into the sound of wind touching the walls and the etheric protections settling back down.

And I knew, miserably, that I should have shot Perry when I had the chance. Because sooner or later I was going to have to go back to the Monde Nuit and ask him how he got his hellspawn hands on the gem my teacher's killer stole.

CHAPTER 3

Mickey's on Mayfair Hill is the kind of restaurant locals like to keep to themselves. Good food, a full bar down two steps in the back, pictures of film stars decking every wall, and a strict policy of toleration. It helps that Mayfair is the part of town where you can see same-sex couples walking hand in hand more often than not—the churches have rainbows on their signs, most of them stating unequivocally ALL ARE WELCOME!

The nightclubs are wildly popular, too. I'd call it a cliché, but that might get me in trouble.

It also helps that Mickey's is completely owned and mostly staffed by Weres. When you have claws and superstrength, tolerance takes on a whole new meaning.

Lean dark Theron met me at the door. The Werepanther's face was unusually solemn, and his shoulders came up a fraction as I swept the door closed. "Kid looks shaken up."

Not even a greeting. Weres are normally so polite, too.

"He should be." I glanced past him, saw Saul in our regular booth. Across from him, Gilberto slumped, staring at his beer bottle. The bottle's label was half picked off.

The kid wasn't old enough to drink, but that didn't matter in the barrio. It doesn't matter on the nightside, either. I turned a blind eye—God knows an apprentice is kept on a short enough leash otherwise.

Theron didn't move. The front of Mickey's is a narrow tiled foyer, a half wall holding back the tables to your left and the kitchen directly in front of you, with all its steam and heat. One of the cooks, a slim dark bird Were, was tossing a spatula, plucking it out of the air with graceful dexterity while he stared back at the freezer, tossing it again.

I finally looked up, met Theron's steady gaze. "What? Am I not allowed to come in?"

"I'd tell you to be gentle." Theron folded his arms. "But that's so not you."

I had washed my face, smearing my eyeliner and putting fresh on. But I hadn't bothered to change. I could spare the time to rinse my face, and I like to do it. The rest of me doesn't matter so much.

The Talisman hummed low on my breastbone, beneath the ruin of my black T-shirt. The shirt still covered all my bits, but I wished suddenly that I'd stopped to grab a new one. I used to wear shirts with witty sayings, but now I bought them—black, V-neck, three-quarter sleeve, slightly fitted—in job lots. Saul sometimes found nice ones at Goodwill, especially old concert shirts, but I bleed all over them so often I feel kind of bad about it. There's only so much he can do with a sewing machine and a T-shirt.

"Theron." I tried very hard for what could be considered a gentle tone. It sounded like I had something dry stuck in my throat, or like I'd been smoking a pack a day. "Why are you standing in my way?"

He leaned forward a little, on the balls of his feet. "You smell like burn—" Then his eyes dropped to my chest.

If I'd had any breasts to speak of after the workout I get all night, I might've been insulted. As it is, I'm scrawny in that department. Sometimes I wished I was a little more feminine, a little curvier, for Saul's sake. But no, a B cup is about all I get. The rest of me is packed tight with muscle and crisscrossed with scars.

Saul doesn't seem to mind. He traces some of the scars with his fingertips, gently. I usually let him.

Sometimes he even kisses them.

"Ah." Theron actually backed up, palms out as if he wanted to tell me to take it easy. "Sorry. My mistake."

I stalked past him. He actually skipped back out of my way as I hopped up the stairs to the tables. We were a regular dance team.

"Jill."

I didn't turn around. But I stopped, one hand light on the half wall. My nerves were twitching raw, and taking it out on a Were wasn't a good idea. He didn't deserve it.

"You smell like Mikhail," he said quietly. "I'll bring you a beer."

In other words, a peace offering. Not like he needed to. But goddamn Weres, they notice the damndest things. I did *not* raise a hand to the Talisman's lump under the ragged T-shirt.

Instead, I just braced myself and headed for the table, the flayed edges of my leather trench flapping a bit around my ankles.

Gilberto's color was better, but he would never be a prize. Sallow even on the best of days, with lank dark hair and a nose that belonged on an Aztec codex, acne scars pitting his cheeks, dead eyes. His long fingers played with the beer bottle, and as I approached he slid down further in the bench and took a long, throat-working draft.

I did not blame him at all.

I stopped and checked him, smart and dumb eye working together. Having an apprentice is like that—you add up everything you see, no matter how small. Constantly weighing. Not *judging*, because that implies they won't make it. *Weighing* in order to give them the best chance to make it.

After they show up on your doorstep and refuse to go home, that distinction is the least you can give them.

Gilberto's hands looked too big for his wrists, like a puppy's paws. He hadn't even finished growing yet, and you could tell it from the way he ate—hunched over the plate, as if someone or something would snatch it from him, shoveling the food down in great gulps.

That's the way kids in juvie eat, too. And prisoners.

He wasn't old enough to drink *or* vote. But those flat dark eyes belonged in a killer's face. Even in the ferment of the barrio, that kind of gaze makes people step back and reconsider, some without knowing quite why. He'd just graduated to being able to hold his own for thirty seconds in the sparring room against Saul. I watched, and weighed, while they went at it.

Gilberto did not give up. He kept getting up long past the moment when any rational person would have decided it wasn't worth it.

He had potential.

Right now he was still shaking a little. The fume of emotion on him was complex fear and shame, as well as defiance. Still just right. Of all the people I'd run across in my city, he was the only one who had even an inkling of what it takes to be a hunter. There had been a girl—Hope—not too long ago...but she hadn't lasted two weeks.

Sometimes they don't.

We're rare. It's probably a good thing. Without training we could end up worse than the things we hunt. Even with training, we're no picnic.

Saul glanced at me. His dark eyes widened a little, but he said nothing as I finished my once-over and strode up to the table.

I slid in next to my apprentice, bumping him with my hip as he scrambled to crowd up onto the wall. "Thought I'd find you here."

"*Bruja.*" Gilberto, getting the first shot in. He was actually sweating, and his pulse thudded along like he'd just run a marathon. "He was just there. One minute I'm sittin' on the couch, the next, *chingada*, there he is. He's *el Diablo*, right?"

Not quite. "Or so close it makes no difference. But he's just hellbreed, Gilberto. Relax, you did okay. Take a deep breath and get your pulse down; it's loud."

He gulped down a breath and concentrated. I waited as if we had all the time in the world. Saul studied me, a line between his dark eyebrows. The paint on his cheeks was still fresh, two bars of vivid red. I never asked why he did that. It just seemed fitting. And, well, I don't need to offer a comment on any Were's sartorial choices.

Not when I walk around in leather, silver, and increasingly

heavy eyeliner. The leather is so my skin doesn't get erased when I land on concrete. The silver is a mark of what I am, a bulwark against Hell's legions.

The eyeliner? Well...Saul isn't the only one who needs war paint.

Finally, Gilberto's pulse smoothed out. His eyelids fluttered, and I could almost *feel* him making that subconscious little *click*, shifting over into the place of calm. It was getting easier for him.

Saul was still watching me. I pulled the neck of my T-shirt down so he could see the barbaric, sharp-looking silver links. The top edge of the Talisman peeked out.

"Smells like a forest fire." His eyebrows came up slightly. "What is it?"

"The Eye of Sekhmet." It was hard work to keep my tone level. "What Belisa stole. When she..."

The unreality of it hit me sideways. I put my hands on the table, flat, and had to inhale deeply as well. The scar was dissatisfied, puckering against itself; I'd taken a spare leather cuff from the dish on the counter and buckled it on before I left. The relief from hellbreed-jacked sensory acuity was as intense as the new feeling now squirming around inside my uneasy belly.

That feeling was something suspiciously like fear.

"Oh." Saul absorbed this. Then, as usual, he gave me the right question. "How the hell did *he* get hold of it?"

I watched my left hand make a gun of thumb and index finger, cocked it, and shot at him. "Bang. Dead on, squire."

And then the next question: "What are you going to do?" His expression didn't change. Thoughtful, and worried.

I let out a sigh that was only half annoyance. It had taken me the whole trip down here to come up with what I *should* do instead of what I *wanted* to do. "I'm not going to do *anything*. Perry wants me down at the Monde. That's one place I'm not going. I have the Talisman, fine. It was mine in the first place. Belisa stole it. I'm not goddamn going to dance to his tune and come asking questions."

"Unless that's what he expects, you avoiding him."

Good point.

I snorted. Then shut my mouth, because Theron was back, setting two cold bottles of beer down for me, one dark microbrew for Saul, and a plate of cheese blintzes and hash browns, with a small dish of fresh strawberries on the side for my apprentice. That was worth a raised eyebrow, but Saul's twitch of a smile told me the Weres here were feeding Gilberto what they thought he *should* be eating, not anything he'd order.

Gilberto opened his eyes, stared at his plate, and shut his mouth before a word could escape.

He caught on quick.

Theron paused, dangling his tray in long, expressive fingers. "Other food'll be just a second. You want some water or something?"

Another peace offering. Was I really looking that temperamental tonight?

I shook my head, watching my fingers against the tabletop. Bitten-down nails, tendons standing out under fishbelly-white skin—I don't tan, I'm never up during the day—and a healing scrape across my left knuckles. The skin was repairing itself as I watched, the scar on my right wrist humming a dissatisfied little song. "No thanks." My lips felt a little numb, and the Eye was warm against my chest.

It was surreal. I never thought I'd be wearing Mikhail's greatest treasure. Not even while he was training me and saying, *Some day this will be yours.* I'd never thought that far ahead.

He'd seemed eternal to me. I guess your parents—or those you choose as your parents—always do. Until they're not.

Theron lingered a little longer, then left as one of the cooks swore. There was a hiss of something hitting the grill, and I looked up to find Saul watching me.

"*Chingada*," Gilberto mumbled. "No *frijoles*."

The laugh caught me by surprise. I bit it in half, swallowed it, and Saul's expression went from thoughtful to outright concerned.

"Do you think..." he began, but left the sentence hanging.

"I think I'm safer staying out of the Monde." Each word carefully held back from a sharp edge. "I think whatever Perry expects me to do, me ignoring this is not in his plan. Therefore, I am going to do what is *not* in his plan."

Saul nodded. Thought it over. "And the fact that he's fooling around with the Sorrows again?"

I took a long pull off one of my beer bottles. It hit the spot. There's nothing quite like a beer to bolster you in a situation like this. "That's why you're taking my apprentice to Galina's."

"Oh, man," aforesaid apprentice piped up. "*Again?* She just makes me take care of her plants."

"You have to be alive to be trained, Gil. And if the Sorrows grab you, you'll wish very hard you were dead." I kept my gaze steady, locked with Saul's.

My Were's dark eyes did not waver. "Where should I meet you after that?" Careful, tactful, and to the point.

In other words, *You're not leaving me behind, Jill. Don't even think about it.*

"I'm going to be visiting the son of a bitch who Traded with Watling." I set the bottle down with a click. Bacon was frying, and it smelled good. "I want that sewn up tonight."

But I didn't tell him where, even though I knew. I couldn't say what I suspected, but I did know I wanted Saul nowhere near where I was going tonight. Full 'breed nightclubs aren't healthy for Weres.

A short, sharp nod, his hair falling across his forehead. It had grown out, and he could tie charms to match mine in it now. A silver wheel gleamed near his left ear, knotted in with red thread. "So I'll just follow the screaming."

"Unless she decide to blow something up, man. Then you can follow the fire *and* screaming." Gilberto was looking down when I glanced at him, my mouth set in a straight line. He forked up a gigantic mouthful of hash browns, his arm curled around the plate. Shielding it.

I decided I wouldn't really take him to task, because it was true. "Gil, *poquito*, the adults are talking. *Cierra el pico.*"

He mumbled something impolite. I let it go. Picked up the bottle again and drained it. It went down easy, but it didn't quite get rid of the bitter taste in my mouth.

Saul tapped once on the tabletop, twice. Thinking. "I don't like this. It's not like one of his kind to give anything away."

"He needs something out of me, or he has a plan." I shrugged. Silver in my hair jangled a bit, restless. "Like every single other time he has a plan or wants something out of me. He'll have to deal with disappointment."

We looked at each other, Saul and I, and both of us knew it was pure bravado. I hadn't gone over the edge yet, even with Perry pushing and cajoling. I'd stood there and watched the abyss yawn right next to my toes, and the only thing that kept me from going down into damnation was...

...what?

Was sitting right across from me, playing with his beer bottle and looking worried, the way a Were almost never looked worried.

They don't usually date hunters. And I was helltainted to boot. We were an exception all over, Saul and me.

I slid out of the booth, pushed myself upright. "Get to Galina's. If all else fails I'll see you at home, at dawn." A judicious pause. "There's a mess there. Sorry about that."

"Jill—"

I shook my head. Silver clashed and chimed. A small sickle-shaped charm dangled in front of my eye for a moment, I tossed it back. "Got work to do, Saul. Depending on you to get my apprentice under cover. My instincts are tingling."

"I hear they have a cream for that. Jill—"

"The cream's for burning. Not for an unpleasant tingle. Give my apologies to Theron." I turned, sharply, and strode away. Made it outside without anything else happening, and let out a deep, dissatisfied breath. It was rude to leave before they fed me, but the night was wearing away and I wanted to get this wrapped up.

The Talisman's warm weight against my chest throbbed like a second heartbeat. Sooner or later Perry would come back, and I'd find out what he was dabbling in now.

But that didn't mean I couldn't question other hellbreed. And I knew exactly where to start.

With the hellspawn who was eyeing the number two position in Santa Luz's 'breed hierarchy. Who just happened to be the same spawn who had Traded with Trevor Watling.

What a coincidence.

CHAPTER 4

The Kat Klub was closed for good, Shen An Dua—the 'breed who ran it—dead in a stinking cellar room way back last year. But hellspawn are like pimps. There's always someone lower on the food chain willing to step up, if profit's to be had.

Down at First and Alohambra the granite bulk of the Piers Tower rises, one of the oldest skyscrapers in Santa Luz. Mikhail told me once that the property had been a mission long ago—before the town got big enough to attract hellbreed.

In other words, back when it was just the mission and a couple of chicken coops. And maybe a pig trough if the padres were lucky.

A gaudy sign shouting UNDER NEW MANAGEMENT had glared across the street for a couple weeks while the infighting went on. When the dust settled, I'd walked in and found that bastard Rutger supervising a small horde of contractors.

He'd gotten sassy. I shot him two or three times just to make him sit down and listen. Shen had been the *eminence grise* of Santa Luz, the only serious contender for Perry's position and a thorn in Perry's side. Rutger had big dreams, but that didn't mean I wasn't going to teach him who was boss. It was either that or have to kill him later and play roulette with whoever *his* replacement was.

So the Kat Klub was now the Folly. It kept the same hours—a cabaret changing to a nightclub at about midnight, rollicking along until dawn in defiance of the liquor laws. Which is no big deal; most nightside places wink at those kind of regulations. Cash changes hands, and the authorities wink, too. Of course, the cash mostly goes toward a hunter's salary. The municipal check every month, in fact.

I think that's called *irony*.

Instead of the stuffed cats and opium den vibe Shen An Dua had gone for, the Folly's décor was choke-a-baroque French bordello, with a side of lace and fringe.

It was just before midnight, so the cabaret was winding down. A female Trader in a painted-on latex outfit brought the cat-o'-ninetails up. Fluid spattered under the pulsing red lights. The cat's tails were wire, studded with barbs. Whatever she was whipping had six misshapen limbs and was the size of a tall man, stretched on an iron rack. It whimpered as the cat came down again with a sound like dissonant wind chimes.

The wires and barbs bit deep. The thing opened a hole at the top of its vague mass and howled. Hellbreed tittered. The Trader pivoted on her stiletto heels, brought the whip back and down again with an expert flick. There was a ripping sound as wet, pulsing flesh parted. A long vertical tear opened in the thing on the rack, and something white showed.

The collected 'breed and Traders stilled, expectantly.

A slender white hand rose. More wet sounds. A thin, curving arm. A knob of a shoulder. The Trader in black vinyl reached forward, the cat dangling in her other hand, and laced her fingers through the questing white hand like a girl grabbing a basket. She leaned back, hip jutting out, and pulled.

More wet tearing sounds, and a pale nakedness rose from the pile of steaming, lacerated flesh. High shallow breasts, wide dark eyes with the flat shine of the dusted, a cherry mouth, long wet strings of hair. Another Trader. Markings that could have been scars, tiger stripes on that dead-white, waxen flesh.

Polite applause. I had my back to the bar, a monstrous thing of mahogany and curlicued iron, silk scarves tied into the grillwork and fluttering upward in merry defiance of gravity. Sorcery and contamination crawled over the cloth, dripping onto the slowly corroding iron. The seaweed scarves flinched away from me, as every piece of silver I carried ran with blue light. Sparks didn't break free of the metal, but it was close.

The Talisman was still on my chest, like an alert little animal, frozen into immobility. I'd only seen Mikhail use it once or twice, when the situation was desperate. It was like the long, slim shape under its fall of amber silk in the sparring room—not to be touched until the need was dire.

But he'd *worn* the Eye everywhere.

Talismans are like that. You can't just leave them in a box.

They get irritable, and then you have an even bigger mess to clean up. I'd heard of a hunter in Kansas who had left a Talisman at home for too long and got three tornados in one day to show for it. At the same time he was working a string of disappearances and almost got his ass blown off by a Middle Way adept.

Embarrassing. I'm pretty sure he hasn't lived that one down yet. Still, considering the Talisman *he'd* been left with, I didn't blame him for thinking that maybe he shouldn't touch the damn thing any more than absolutely necessary.

The bartender was another Trader, tall and big-eyed, broad-shouldered—and with a messy line of vertical stitches closing his lips together. One of Rutger's little jokes.

Two vodkas, brief stings relished but gone by the time they hit the back of my throat, and I waited. Rutger was up in his office, probably watching the closed-circuit television. I could go up there and drag him out, but what would be the point?

No. I wanted this public, but I also wanted him to come to me. That would make the game mine, on my terms.

Admit it, Jill. You want to beat the shit out of someone. That's what you're aching to do, and if you do it in public you might not go over the edge. That edge that gets closer every time you do this.

Philosophizing in the middle of a hellbreed bar is a dangerous occupation. The risk of getting distracted is high. Still, I didn't jump when he appeared out of thin air with a sound like little voices tittering.

They like doing that.

"Ah, Kismet." Rutger's oily tenor, dripping with saccharine. "An honor to see you again. Enjoying the show?"

He was lean, and had a full head and a half on me. His skin was spilled ink. Not human-dark, or ethnic. No, his skin was literally *black*. It swallowed light with no sheen of human at all on its surface. A pointed chin, wide cheekbones, the slightly yellow cast of his too-sharp-to-be-human teeth, and a fluff of white thistle-down hair all competed to add creepiness. The final touch was his irises. A deep throbbing hurtful magenta, the pupils X-shaped. In the crux of the X lurked a leering, sterile point of red-purple light.

He liked velvet coats and ruffled-front shirts, breeches in odd gemlike colors, and high-heeled, shiny-buckled, pointy-toed shoes that should have looked absolutely ridiculous.

On this hellbreed, they looked very sharp. You could just imagine the edges of those shoes, heel or toe, slicing flesh. While he grinned with that V-shaped mouth, showing those shark-row teeth.

"No." I eyed his bodyguards—slabs of Trader muscle almost too dumb to be breathing. They looked like Frankenstein's monster crossed with a steroid burner's dream—even their muscles had lumps of muscle on top, like overyeasted bread.

And they were too far away, hanging back and staring at me with little piggy flat-shining eyes. I could have killed him twice before they got to me.

I bared my teeth, a bright sunny approximation of a smile. My left hand rested on the whip handle, and Rutger's eyes blinked— first one, then the other. Just like a lizard.

There was a crack of bone and a scream from the stage. It sounded like a peacock's cry, or a sexless being in fullthroated orgasm. Then it shaded up into agony before it was cut short on a gurgle.

Everyone else let out their breath. One Trader whistled, a keen piercing note that belonged more in a strip club than a murder cabaret.

Some people have no couth.

"Trevor Watling." The name fell into a well of silence. A single spark cracked from the carved ruby at my throat, and one of the bodyguards flinched. My smile widened just a trifle. It felt unnatural, a layer of paint over my skin.

Rutger shrugged. "Never heard of him."

I was kind of glad we were going to do this the hard way. He might have been, too, because he thought he was fast enough to jump me.

The corruption in them makes them easy to track. That's why hunters are human. We can track what we're akin to.

Quick as they are, a hunter's quicker. Especially with her reflexes amped up by a hellbreed scar. My boots hit the bar's shiny surface, and I pivoted slightly on one foot. My other lashed out, steel-shod heel cracking him square on the chin. The whip flashed, too, catching one of the bodyguards across his wide sweat-greased face. Rutger fell in slow motion, black ichor spraying in a wide perfect arc. I cleared leather, had the gun pointed at the next body-guard, my foot coming back, touching lightly.

The bartender, down at the other end of the curlicued mon-strosity, cowered. He didn't have a gun, but I couldn't bet on it staying that way. On the other hand, here I had the high ground.

And every eye was on me. The seaweed scarves dribbled, streaming away from me as the silver in my hair, at my throat and fingers and weapons, hissed and sparked. Each spark died quickly as it left my aura.

Up on the stage, there was a pool of waxen white striped with sluggish black, the slim body broken like a flower. The Trader in vinyl crouched, her hand on her cat-o'-nine, in a pool of garish spotlight that turned her eyes into blank holes. Some of the 'breed had half-risen from their seats, the waitstaff all stood, tense and ready. Some of them had hands inside their white jackets.

"Ah-ah-ah." Hard and bright, my voice rang out. Like a teacher admonishing a room full of third graders. "Now, now. Let's not be hasty. That's the penalty of lying a single time to a hunter in Santa Luz. Want to go for more?"

Rutger surged up from the floor. The gun settled on him. At my chest, the Talisman throbbed a little, a sore tooth. A thin curl of smoke rose from my T-shirt. I wasn't imagining it, but there were other things to worry about.

I'd broken the hellbreed's nose. Thin rivulets of black ichor threaded down, glittering against the odder darkness of his skin. His teeth champed. "*Bitch,*" he hissed.

Like I hadn't heard *that* one before. "I repeat. Trevor Watling."

"The Trade was legitimate," he hissed. Ichor bubbled down his chin.

He'd admitted it. Now we got to the fun part. "He stepped out-side the rules. You're liable."

A ratlike little gleam surfaced from the center of his pupils. I know that gleam.

The *how can I make this work for me* look. The one my mother had whenever one of her boyfriends got out the belt or the fist. The one in the eyes of the man who put me on a street corner to shiver.

The one in the eyes of every single john on that corner, in a car, in an alley or a cheap hotel room.

I *hate* that fucking look.

"Stay still." I didn't have to look at the second bodyguard to feel the way he was tensing up, getting ready. "Now, Rutger. Let's just say I don't want to have to train your replacement not to piddle on the floor." I stared at the bridge of his nose, knowing it would make my mismatched gaze piercing. And that the focus would warn me before he decided to move.

"You want something." It's hard for a hellbreed to look shocked. He managed it. A caricature of a human emotion, like every expression on a hellbreed's face. Except greed and sadistic pleasure, I guess.

I made a little beeping noise. Every nerve under my skin dilated, alert and quivering. "Wrong. *You* want something. You want to stay alive and continue your games in this tacky little nest. Now, I'm willing to think that your Trader didn't check in with you before committing his murderous little rampage. The only thing left for you to do is to prove your good faith. Give me a reason to decide your successor would be a bigger problem than you are."

Instinct alerted me. I dropped to one knee and fired in one smooth motion. Recoil jolted up my arm, almost too much for even a measure of superhuman strength. The bartender, a sawed-off shotgun in his stealthy little clawed hands, dropped like a stone. Half his head had evaporated.

Why I didn't switch to the bigger custom guns sooner was *so* beyond me.

Rutger had taken a half step forward. I trained the gun on him again. "See? You're just jumping at the chance to help, aren't you."

Another thin curl of smoke drifted up from my torn T-shirt. Rutger's pupils flared with diseased red-purple light, a bruise on the air. "What guarantee will you give?"

Please, you think I'm new at this game? "I don't give guarantees to hellspawn. You tell me about Perry's new houseguest, and I may decide to be charitable and overlook your Trader's stepping outside the bounds."

As soon as I said it, I knew I'd guessed right. Rutger stiffened, and the ratty gleam intensified. He telegraphed like a four-year-old reaching for candy. As soon as he twitched he knew he'd made a mistake, too, and I lowered the gun. The silver in my hair shifted, rattling. A blue spark popped from my apprentice-ring, and the hellbreed actually flinched. The scarves tied to the bar in front of me lay dead and dark now, bleeding clear fluid across the mirror-polished surface. A ripple ran through the assembled 'breed, and the Traders moved back in one clockwork motion.

"Oh, hit a nerve there, did I? Thank you." I sounded completely insincere. "Pleasant dreams, hellspawn."

When I hopped down from the bar, I expected him to jump me. Instead, he stepped mincingly aside. His shoes clicked like a woman's heels, but oddly. Hellbreed footsteps do not sound the same as human movement. They're too light, or too heavy, different musculature producing something that shivers the skin with its wrongness.

"He said you'd be here." A ripple ran through the assembled 'breed and Traders at the words. Rutger tried out a smile, light dancing oddly over his skin. The black bulged and rippled oddly, trying to contain whatever lived under the shell of human seeming. "And he said to tell you this: *he cannot hold back the tide forever.*"

The gun spoke again. I dropped, rolled, came up and the whip flashed out. The second bodyguard fell like a stalled ox between one step and the next, and Rutger let out a long rumble-roar of Helletöng, glasses chattering on the iron shelves behind the bar. The seaweed scarves, dripping with corruption, flattened and swayed. The ones that had cringed away from me shriveled, blackening afresh. The curse missed, flashing by like a freight train at midnight, and the whip spoke again. I didn't dive *away*, like he was obviously expecting. No, instead I pitched myself straight at the hellbreed and cracked him a good one with the gun butt after the flechettes finished tearing a chunk out of his chest. Blessed silver spat and crackled. Rutger howled, glass shattered from the sound, and while he was on the floor I kicked him twice, both good solid blows.

He curled like a worm on a hook, still screaming. The gun swept the massed ranks of hellbreed and they drew back, eyes shining, lips pulled up in snarls, and the scrim of beauty they wear faltering for a heart-stopping second.

"That makes it three times I've visited here and had to shoot an uppity 'breed or two. I wonder if maybe this place needs to be *cleansed.*" I had to raise my voice to be heard over Rutger's yelling. But you learn pretty quick to aim for a tone that slices through noise without seeming like you're yelling. I kicked Rutger again. "Shut *up.*"

"Pay." He bubbled and blurbled through ichor. "You'll pay for this, Kismet."

I swept the massed ranks of hellbreed one more time. They made no move. "You are *so* not in the position to be threatening, Rutger. Ta-ta, boys and girls. I'll be back."

When you've just put down the owner of a hellbreed nightclub, the right kind of exit is a sort of insouciant amble that is much faster than it looks. You don't want to give them time to think. But it is imperative not to look weak.

Or they will be on you in a moment.

"Kismet!" Helletöng rumbling under my name. *"I will kill you for this!"*

The Talisman on my chest gave a *thud* like a sledgehammer hitting the side of a refrigerator, and I turned on my heel. Retraced my steps, and the smoke coming up from my chest wasn't an illusion. It stung my eyes, and I had the sudden lunatic vision of my T-shirt burning off me in the middle of the Folly.

That never happened to Mikhail. What the hell?

The 'breed were all still as death. Bright eyes, painted lips, the shadows of what they really were rippling under their flesh.

I halted. Looked down at Rutger. Painted with hellbreed blood, down there on the floor, sniveling and whining. It wasn't a pretty sight.

Do not ever underestimate, milaya. Mikhail's voice inside my head. *Is fine way to get ass blown off sideways.*

"Come and try it." I didn't have to work to say it flatly. "Anytime, Rutger. That goes for every single Hell-trading one of you in this entire building. Whenever you're brave enough, *come and fucking try it.*"

To really finish it off right I should have kicked him one last time. But it was more of an insult to leave him there and saunter out the front door like I had all night, the smell of burning trailing in my wake.

And a very, very bad feeling starting in the middle of my chest.

CHAPTER 5

Beaky, skinny Hutch sat up and rubbed at his hazel eyes. He didn't quite squeal, but it was close. "What are you *doing?*"

I hadn't been in here for very long. Maybe twenty seconds, hearing him sleep and regretting that I was going to wake him up. I know what it's like to wake up with someone in the room, when you thought you were alone.

Hutch was lucky, though. It was just me.

"Same thing I do every time I wake you up in the middle of the night. Light." I flipped on the bedside lamp, almost forgetting how I looked. Hutch squeaked and fisted his eyes even harder.

His living quarters were up above the bookstore, and his bedroom was full of extra shelving. Clothes hung next to bits of high-priced computer corpses, ready for him to strip out and use at a moment's notice. He'd just come back from vacation two weeks ago, sunburnt and rested, and I'd met him at the airport with our local FBI liaison, Juan Rujillo. I'd finally gotten everything smoothed over from Hutch's last escapade—the one he wasn't covered for in court, because he hadn't been hacking at my request. No, he'd just been proving he was still bulletproof in cyberspace.

I guess I hadn't been keeping him busy enough. *That* was about to change.

"Jesus!" Hutch grabbed at the blankets. "Is it the cops? I haven't done anything, I *swear!*"

"You know, every time I hear you say that, it fills me with despair. Because I know you're lying or *about* to lie to me." I tried not to sound so grimly amused. "Wake up and get your glasses on, Hutchinson. I need you."

"Why don't you keep normal hours?" He turned even paler than usual the moment it escaped his mouth. I magnanimously refused to comment. Instead, I put my back to the wall near the door—or, if you want to be precise, to the overflowing bookcase right next to the door. "Never mind, forget I asked. What's up?"

"I want you to get on that goddamn computer and find something out for me." I did not tack on a *What did you think, I wanted to sing Christmas carols?* But it was close.

"What something am I finding?" He grabbed his glasses and put them on, blinked frowstily.

Something that will help me avert another fucking apocalypse. "I'll tell you once you're downstairs with some coffee."

"God." He groaned, levering himself up out of bed. "Why don't you pick on someone else?" His threadbare, penguin-covered boxers flapped; he picked them out of his ass crack and yawned. His narrow, sunken chest was sparse with wiry, reddish-dark hair, and you could see the scars up along the right side of his ribcage. Claw marks. You could see clearly where the hellbreed's three fingers had dug in, flexing.

There are reasons why Hutch doesn't ever want to get close to the nightside. He's wiser than most.

"Because I like you so much, sweets." I made a little kissy noise. Under the cuff, the scar was a wet, burning pucker. There was a hole in my T-shirt, and the red gleam of the Eye peered out through it. Above the Eye, the carved ruby—a pale imitation, to be sure—glowed as well. I did *not* reach up to play with it nervously, but my fingers itched.

He grabbed a Santa Luz Wheelwrights T-shirt from a pile of laundry on the floor, pulled it on over his head. "Don't *say* things like that. God. Go make me some coffee. Jesus H."

I slid out of the room and down the hall. The kitchen was as gleaming and shipshape as his room was messy and dusty. He had a state-of-the-art espresso and drip coffeemaker, complex enough to make a cappuccino by itself and pilot a rocket ship at the same time. I poked at it for a few moments, thought longingly of what a great sound it would make if I shot the damn thing, and figured out how to make the drip side work. After a search through every cabinet, I found the coffee canister in the fridge, exactly where

Saul would have put it. By the time Hutch shuffled down the hall, reeking of Right Guard and scrubbing under his T-shirt with one hand, there were six cups of coffee and more dribbling out.

"I made a whole pot," I said, and glanced at the window. Night pressed against the bulletproof glass. Each window up here was reinforced with silver-laced chicken wire.

"What am I looking for?" He looked marginally more awake, grabbed a Wheelwrights coffee mug, and yanked the coffeepot out. Thick dark liquid sploshed. "Jesus. You make coffee like my dad did."

If it's not strong, it's not coffee. I shrugged. "I need you to go digging all over. Find me any disaster, anywhere on the globe, in the past six months big enough to let a *talyn* or bigger hellbreed slip through. I want you to cross-reference it with everything you can find on Argoth."

He jerked. Coffee splashed. My hand arrived, caught the mug before it could fall more than a foot, and I straightened, subtracting the pot from him with my other hand. The liquid burned where it hit my hand; it soaked into the tattered sleeve of my coat. Hutch stepped back, barking his hip a good one on the counter. It was anyone's guess whether he was disturbed by Argoth's name or by me moving too quickly to be strictly normal.

"Holy *shit*. No way." He shook his head, his hair standing up in bedhead spikes. "Not that again. Really?"

"I don't know yet. Could be a red herring." I finished pouring, slid the pot back in, and offered him the dripping mug. "But I need everything you can get. If there's *any* breath of that bastard getting out of Hell and making trouble, I want to know where, what, and when. I also need you to brush up your Chaldean and look at the Sorrows calendar. See if there's anything shaking down there." A deep breath. I tried not to notice how he was going whiter than his usual pasty-boy at the thought. "There might be more."

"Sorrows and Argoth? Jesus Christ." He took the cup with shaking fingers. "They're connected?"

"I don't *know*, Hutch. I need you to do these things, and at noon today you pack everything you need for a siege and go to Galina's." *Because I am not about to lose my apprentice* or *my pet researcher.*

"Goddamn, Kismet. What kind of trouble are we talking about? No, wait. I don't wanna know. I'll get started right now. Anything else I should take to Galina's?"

"Just whatever you'll need to stay there for a while, and to keep up your research. Don't open up today." I cocked my head, listening. The entire neighborhood was quiet, and I'd made sure I was clean before even coming *near* the bookstore.

"Like customers are beating down my door anyway." He blew across the top of his coffee, snagged a pad of paper placed precisely under the yellow phone bolted to the wall at the end of the counter, and looked around for a pen. "Sorrows calendar. Argoth—hey, I thought you barred him from coming through. That time, what, two years ago or something? That case with the scurf."

"I did." *But it was close, Hutch. So close. You don't even want to know.* "But I can't be everywhere."

He gulped. If it was possible to go any paler, he probably would have. "Yeah. I, um, I got that. You okay? You look pretty pissed off. More than usual."

As well as covered in blood and blow-dried. I dredged up what could be called a smile. "Why, Hutch. I didn't know you *cared*."

He gave me the most evil look a weedy hacker boy I outweighed could possibly give. And to top it all off, my pager buzzed in its padded pocket.

When I dug it out and glanced at the number, I had to suppress the urge to roll my eyes. Never rains but it pours. "Can I use your phone?"

As if he was going to say no.

He backed up a couple more steps, as if I'd moved. "Go for it. As long as something doesn't crawl out of it when you're done. I'm gonna get to work."

"Nothing will crawl out of your phone, Hutch. Promise." I gave him a wide sunny smile, or as close to one as I could get. I even tried to make it unscary.

"That's what *you* say." He reached up, grabbed a box of energy bars from atop the sparkling-white fridge, and retreated with his coffee. I heard him stamp down the stairs, cursing, and picked up the phone.

It rang twice. I stared at the back of my left hand, the scrape across the knuckles healed up and looking weeks old instead of fresh. My fingers drummed on the countertop, bitten nails scratching the cheerful yellow tile. The Talisman was a warm weight against my chest, and a shiver went through me.

I can only hold the tide so long. Perry, standing in the warehouse and snarling at me. That case had almost ended up unleashing utter destruction on my city. The last time this Argoth came through into our world was in 1918, in Europe. The second Jack Karma—the one whose knife my apprentice had taken such a shine to—claimed the dubious honor of sending him back into Hell in Dresden, February 1945.

In the in-between time, Argoth had been a very busy boy. Some parts of the world were still reeling, between that and the great demonic outbreak in '29.

The phone picked up. "Sullivan," he barked.

"It's me. You rang?"

"Yeah. Me and the Badger, we got some live ones. Well, dead ones. But it looks like one of yours."

Jesus. "Where?"

"Cruzada. 153rd and Anita."

Out in the suburbs. "All right. I'm on my way. Hold the scene."

Like he needed me to tell him that. But he just made an affirmative noise and hung up.

There was little I could do until Hutch finished digging. The night was getting older by the second, and it already seemed too long. I drummed my fingertips for another few seconds, as if it would give me something useful.

Then I got going.

CHAPTER 6

The Cruzada district is a collection of suburban streets, most of the houses from the seventies and all of them needing to be taken on a street-by-street basis. Some are pretty nice, neat and clean, with hardworking neighbors who look out for each other. Some have crackhouses and shootings. The higher up and farther away from the river, the more likely there are to be bars on the windows and busted-down cars on the lawns.

Anita and 153rd was a buffer zone. Yellow grass slowly dying, bars on the windows that weren't for decoration, but plenty of the houses still had neat fences and all-weather children's toys scattered around. The air was heavy with the promise of spring, though the storms weren't threatening over the river yet and the desert cold had its winter bite. A scrim of snow still clung to the mountains and frost-rimed anywhere the sun didn't reach during the day.

It was three a.m. and dark even through the stain of orange citylight. The drunks would be making their way home, traffic fatalities occurring, the really bad domestic disturbances getting underway. In another couple hours the world would hold its breath for the long, dark shoal before dawn, the time when old people slip under the surface and drift away. But for right now, things would be hopping, one last frenzied burst of activity to take us through the night.

It wasn't hard to find the place. Two black-and-whites, their lights dappling blue and red, and a coroner's van lodged like splinters in the street in front of a trim fake-adobe. The adobe's door was open, a warm yellow block of electric light spilling out. Sullivan, his sparse, coppery hair catching fire under the reflected light, stood there talking to one of the blues. It was Jughead Vanner, the big blond unlucky one. He ran across weird nightside cases with distressing regularity. It was getting to be a joke with the crew of regular exorcists attached to the police department.

Some people are like that—unlucky. At least he knew who to call when things got weird. And he knew what kind of scene not to go barging into. He hadn't expressed any interest in the cases themselves yet, which was a good sign.

If he had, he probably would have ended up as an exorcist himself. Nobody can be unlucky *and* curious, and walk away untouched.

The gate in the chain-link fence was open, I pushed it further and it squawked. Sullivan and Vanner both glanced at me. The other black-and-whites were near the coroner's van; bullshitting since there was nothing for them to do, but they couldn't leave the scene until I cleared them.

"Hey, Kismet," Sullivan called. "Glad you could make it."

He looks like an overexposed photograph of a rumpled, thin man, despite the ruddy tinge to his hair. That washed-out exterior hides a mind so sharp it threatens to cut itself on a daily basis. Word was he'd almost ended up an accountant instead of a cop, and the finicky precision of his reasoning made me believe it. Of all the odd couples in Homicide, Sullivan and the Badger are probably the physically oddest.

He's lanky and almost transparent. She's round and solid-motherly, with a white streak in her iron-gray hair. She doesn't get her nickname from that, though. She gets it from being tenacious as hell. If she and Sullivan ever tangled, she would be the one holding him down and rubbing his face in the gravel.

At least, that's what the betting pool says. Odds are on the Badger any day of the week, and especially once a month.

She was in the hallway, arms crossed, her broad face solemn.

I took in the neatly clipped yellowing grass, touched with frost. People in the Cruzada have better things to spend their money on than astronomical water bills, especially in winter. No bikes or kid's toys, thank God. "I hurried right on over to get a hot date with you, Sullivan. What do we have?"

Vanner, as usual, flushed a bright scarlet and dropped his baby blues to my boots. He was the size of a small mountain, the beefy type that runs to fat early without hard exercise. "Neighbor called from the pay phone two blocks away at the Circle Mart. Said they heard screaming. Dispatch sent us out with backup. We got here, everything quiet. Except the front door was unlocked. We identi-fied ourselves, went in, and..."

The Badger stepped out, warm yellow electric light painting the stripe down the side of her head. "Hullo, Jill." A soft, unas-suming voice that had fooled a lot of perps into thinking she'd be easy to bowl over. "Pretty sure this is one of yours."

I nodded. My earrings swung, and silver shifted, chiming. Vanner flinched a little at the sound, covered it well. "How many?"

"Maybe four. It's...well." Her mouth turned tight, pulled against itself. "Come on in, take a look."

I stepped up onto the porch, sliding past Sullivan, who didn't move. Jughead pressed back against the wall like I had some sort of disease.

"You have the worst luck, Vanner." I tossed the words over my shoulder as the edges of my coat brushed his knee. "Seriously."

He mumbled something. His entire face was crimson now, flags of color spilling down his neck.

Sullivan snorted. "I think Jughead's got a crush on you. He keeps tripping over your kind of cases."

Nobody can taunt like a Homicide detective. It's like some sort of unwritten law. "Maybe that's because he's smart and perceptive. Ever think of that?"

"If he was, he wouldn't be working this job." Sullivan's fingers twitched.

"Exactly." I stepped into the hallway, my eyes roving. "And neither would you, right?"

"Bingo." The Badger let out a soft laugh, pushed her glasses up on the bridge of her nose. Dark circles scored under her eyes, and her shoulders were held stiffly, as if she expected a blow. "Now shut up, Sully. Leave the kid alone."

Sullivan muttered something uncomplimentary. The smile felt tight and unnatural on my face. Because as soon as I passed the threshold, the gassy, ripe smell of violent death filled my nose. It was enough to drive you back on your heels.

Huh. I stopped.

The entry hall was tiled in brick-red, and chilly. If there was any sort of heater or air-conditioning, it had been turned off. The smell should have just about knocked me over halfway up the path from the gate. Instead, it was like stepping through a curtain. One second, nothing but dust and the wind off the river. The next, the reek was so powerful my eyes threatened to water.

Badger was watching my face. She nodded, slightly.

Every nerve suddenly tingling-alert, I stopped dead. "Outside. Get those two off the front porch. Everyone pull back to at least the fence. Don't let anyone go just yet."

She nodded and padded away, shooing the boys in front of her.

For such a round little woman, she is amazingly light on her feet. I drew a gun, kept it low and to the side. Didn't ask her where the bodies were.

No use in asking what you're going to find out anyway.

Living room: faded brown couch, camp chairs, dinged-up yard-sale coffee table, big but old TV. Kitchen tiled in red, too, large window over the sink looking onto the backyard, clean, dry dishes in a rack. A large stockpot sat in the left-hand sink, full of water and a scrim of pinkish soap bubbles. Looked like someone had been cleaning up after spaghetti. The dining room held a table with six chairs, two places at the end stacked with bills. A white-board on the dining-room wall held five columns in black marker, each labeled neatly.

Joan. Elena. Alice. Kendall. LOVE!

Under each woman's name, chores and notes in different hand-writing and colors. Things like *Take out garbage* and *Electric bill*. In the LOVE column, two notes.

E, Kenny called. Said to call him back. And *A, picked up your dry cleaning, it's in your room. K.*

Two bathrooms, both clean and neat. One had a Post-it at eye level on the mirror over the antiquated sink—*Have u taken ur pill 2day?* And a smiley face. Three smallish bedrooms, one pin-neat and pink, the other two looking like bombs had hit them.

The master bedroom, at the end of the hall, was a soup of bruised etheric energy. I kept the gun ready as I tapped the door with my foot. Something was wrong with the hinges; the door opened only reluctantly and wanted to swing back closed. Either that, or the pulsating darkness inside the room wanted no witnesses.

Tiny crackles and sparkles of light preceded me, the sea-urchin spikes of my aura. I swept with the gun, my blue eye piercing and untangling a mess of threadlike tangles.

Oh, shit.

They lay on the king-sized bed, all four of them. Packed like sardines: one girl's head on the pillows, the next with her feet at the top of the bed, and so on. All utterly still, when viewed through my dumb eye. Through my blue eye, however, little crackles and twitches tingled through them. Nerve-death, some of it, bits of electricity still trying to connect over synaptic gaps. In most circumstances the body doesn't die all at once. Like living, death—even violent death—is most often a process.

But this cracking and twitching wasn't just nerve-death. It was flat out unnatural.

Sweet-sick corruption filled my nose. Vanner and his partner probably hadn't gone further than the door, and it was a damn good thing, too.

One of the bodies on the left, the one with its head pointing toward the foot of the bed, let out a gassy exhalation. The reek turned thick and clotted, like scabs pressing against the inside of my nostrils.

"*Sssssss...*" one of the bodies hissed, as trapped air escaped. The knotted foulness in the ether pressed *down*, obscenely, and the bodies jerked, writhing together. The scar tingled, and I reached over with my left hand, unsnapped the buckles, and tore the cuff off.

What was going to come next was not going to be pleasant.

If you've never seen a hellbreed reach through a rotting corpse, forcing the decaying meat and violated nerve endings to do its bidding, you're lucky. The body jerks in ways no human joints would, crackling like fat tossed in a fire as cellular reserves are depleted, and they make deep guttural sounds that are the closest frozen human vocal cords can get to Helletöng. It was a good thing Vanner's curiosity was nonexistent, because if he'd stepped over the threshold the way I was stepping now, I would have been looking at dead cops on this scene as well.

And I just hate that.

The four bodies wrenched into motion, squealing eerily with one voice. Every inch of silver on me sparked. I scanned the room one more time to make sure I wasn't missing anything. Then the one on the far right leapt off the bed with the jerky, disconnected speed of the damned, and I had no more time for caution.

If they got out into the front yard we were going to have serious problems.

CHAPTER 7

The last one had probably been an athlete, she was strong and quick, as the hellbreed's will cannibalized every scrap of flesh left on the skeleton's frame. My breath came hard and fast, blood slipping down my forehead as I tracked, bullets spattering the wall. Glass shattered, and the unearthly chorus of four corpses singing in hellspeak was reduced to just one guttural chanting.

She jagged for the hall leading to the front door, skin peeling back from wasted muscle and the eyes cloudy with low reddish hellfire. Two of the four had been in sweats and T-shirts with ragged, gaping, bloody holes in the front, one was naked, and this one was in a babydoll nightie of cream-colored material, also torn in the front. The ragged holes in their rib cages and flayed holes in their bellies, splintered white ribs showing and tissue flapping free, spatters of blood and other fluids, told me things I didn't want to know.

But first things first.

Since she was the last one up and moving around, I leapt on her halfway into the dining room. The impact knocked her down, bits of flesh splashing everywhere and the steady cadence of töng breaking for a thin half second before roaring back, like a radio coming in clear and strong through static.

The trick in putting down corpses hellbreed have taken control of is to either cause such massive damage the body can't move anymore, *or* break the etheric connection between 'breed and body. If you're dealing with more than one, you go for damage.

Which is always my favorite option, anyway. Call it a personality quirk.

Tangle of arms and legs. Splatter of stinking foulness, cold smoking fluid splashed in my face and I blew out through both nose and mouth, freeing the passages. I spend an awful lot of time wrestling around on the floor, getting leverage. Jujitsu is a *godsend*.

We rolled, and my right hand thrust into the stinking cavity in her chest.

Even if you suspect something so strongly, it's still a shock to have it confirmed. Her heart had been removed. Gristle scraped my slipping fingers, the body twisted and lurched with inhuman strength. It reminded me of fighting zombies, though zombies are a different proposition. For one thing, they're not impelled by a hellbreed's sheer power and desire to cause hurt. No, zombies are just like maddened animals.

Corpses with a hellbreed pulling their puppet strings, on the other hand, are cunning and ruthless.

The thing that used to be one of the girls on the whiteboard snarled as my fingers closed around something hard and egg-shaped. The tissue around it grabbed with slippery, grasping fingers, and my own voice rose, cutting through the babbling, grinding, tearing sound of Hell's language from a dead throat. I wasn't praying—no, I was cursing, yelling each filthy word I knew and combining them automatically. I dug in its chest, my legs wrapped around it, and my left hand punched the rotting face repeatedly.

The egg-shaped hardness almost squirted free, greased with noisome ick. But I yanked, and meat tore apart. The body spasmed, its hellfire dimming. Shattered wood flew as we struggled.

My fingers crunched down, the scar singing a piercing high note, burrowing hot as a dollop of melted lead into my wrist. The egg slipped free. I wrenched it all the way out of the gaping hole in the body's chest. Muscle and bone sagged aside, its frenetic activity snuffed out.

Harsh, ratcheting breathing filled my ears. It was my own. My pulse pounded. Cold sweat stood out all over me.

I shoved the body aside. Electric light from the fixture overhead was merciless, beating down like desert sun. The dining room was a mess—I'd had to fight while retreating down the hall, keeping them bottled up and away from the civilians out front. One of them could have gone out a window, if they'd gotten lucky. Or if I hadn't kept them bottled so hard. The last one *had* been looking to escape, probably to get out and cause a little havoc for their master, since I'd just come across a huge violation of the rules.

Whoever it was had to know I'd be along sooner or later to check this out. Thoughtful of them to leave a calling card. I lay on the floor, chest heaving to get enough breath in, and lifted the *bezoar*.

It glimmered nastily, a smooth, nacreous gleam from the packed-tight hairthreads it was made of. Pulsing with unnatural life, slippery with a weird clear fluid that dripped upward and vanished into smoke, the thing nestled in my palm.

This little seed, planted in a body, would make controlling easier. It was also something I could use to track the 'breed responsible. You don't see *bezoar* much; the act of destroying the body usually shreds them all to shit. Taking it out while the thing's still wiggling is key.

I swallowed hard, forced down nausea, and gained my feet in a convulsive rush.

The dining-room table was in splinters. One of the chairs was still whole, the others not so lucky. Cold, jelly-thickening blood splattered, already decaying and stinking, on all four walls and the French door.

My left hand was already digging in one of my pockets. Out came a square of white blessed silk, a little dingy from time spent stowed away.

Boy Scouts aren't the only ones who like to be prepared.

"Jesus." My own raw whisper took me by surprise, bounced back from the walls. The whiteboard was cracked, knocked down to the floor and rolled on. I probably had dry-erase marker smeared all over my coat. "Jesus Christ."

The silk went around the pulsing stone. The seeping liquid cringed from the blessing in the cloth. I had to use the breakfast bar between kitchen and dining room, laid the whole thing down and tied it up with quick gestures. Sorcery crackled on my fingertips, intent married to etheric force bleeding into the knots.

Most of the great hunter sorceries are sympathetic, echoes of a time when naked priestesses traced ley lines in dew-wet grass, using the earth's force as the basis for the simple magical theories of attraction and repulsion. And, not so incidentally, using that same force to push the night back from human settlements. To keep the dark at bay. Every hunter is an heir to that time and those sorceries.

"Thou Who," I found myself saying. Licked dry lips, continued. The Hunter's Prayer unreeled, with the ease of so many repetitions: "Thou Who hast given me to fight evil, protect me; keep me from harm." I skipped a bit, got to the important part. "O my Lord God, do not forsake me when I face Hell's legions. In Thy name and with Thy blessing, I go forth to cleanse the night."

A blue spark cracked. Two. The *bezoar* lay inert in a shield of white silk and blessing. A faint scratching sound came from the breakfast bar, and somewhere a hellbreed's rage mounted, but my hands were steady. I finished the last knot. "Amen."

Silence. The entire house was dead still. They were probably out there trying not to wonder what was going on. Sometimes I think it's worse to wait; other times I'm sure it's worse to see and know. After all, one of the more common responses to brushing up against the nightside is suicide.

A sharp pinch under my breastbone. I've lost good cops to the nightside. *My* cops, my eyes and ears, the people I protect. When you get down to it, there's not much difference between the work I do and their jobs. It's just a matter of degree.

Everything these days is just a matter of degree. It didn't used to be that way.

A tiny noise. I whirled, clearing leather, and saw Jughead Vanner in the doorway to the hall. His jaw dropped and his hands were up. He was so pale he was almost transparent, and sweat filmed his skin. His pupils were dilated, and he looked halfway to shock.

I lowered the gun, carefully. Tried to swallow my heart. "What the hell are you doing?"

He blinked. His mouth worked like a fish's. I holstered the gun, slid the wrapped, twitching *bezoar* into a pocket, and crossed the dining room in long swinging strides.

I grabbed his shoulders and *shoved* him all the way through the hall and across the living room. I'd gotten up a good head of steam, too, and when he hit the wall next to the barred window in the living room the impact jarred us both. "What. The *fuck*. Are you *doing*?"

"I...uh, I..." His mouth worked wetly. I shook him, shoved him back against the wall again. A thin thread of smoke teased my nostrils. The Talisman vibrated uneasily, tapping at my breastbone like impatient fingers.

"I said to *stay at the perimeter*! What about that did you not understand? God *damn* you, you could have been hurt!" I was yelling, full throat, and they could probably hear me all the way out by the fence. "When I say you *stay, you motherfucking stay*!"

I ran out of words and glared at him. My blue eye was dry and tingling, and I knew a crimson spark was dancing in the pupil's darkness. His Adam's apple bobbed as he swallowed convulsively. Dots of feverish red stood high up on his cheeks. I took a good look at him and swore, filthily. He shuddered at each word.

"Fucking stay right there, do *not move*," I spat, and checked the house one more time. Forensics was going to hate me for this. The bodies had been all neat in a row, but now the bedroom hall was an abattoir and bits were scattered everywhere.

Unfortunately, you do have to rip them up sometimes. I was lucky to extract the seed of corruption from one of them, something I could use to track the hellbreed responsible. The last body lay tangled on the floor in the dining room, amid the shattered wreckage of the table. Her face was turned to the light, the mouth wrenched open in a long silent scream, and that's the worst thing about corpses hellbreed have been playing with. They look like even death doesn't stop the agony.

This was turning out to be a long goddamn night.

CHAPTER 8

The Badger called in paramedics, and they treated Vanner for shock in an ambulance. "We kept hearing noises," she said quietly, watching them. "He just got more and more nervous, then headed in. I had a job to do keeping the rest of them here."

"You did fine." I hung up, handed her cell phone back. "Four bodies. I want a full workup on whatever's left of them. Find out which internal organs are missing. Find out who they are—"

"Already have, at least a bit. Student nurses from Saint Simeon. Pooling their rent, it looks like. Next of kin is going to be a bitch." She looked like she was sucking on something bitter.

Each one of them was probably a parent's pride and joy. The funerals were all going to have to be closed-casket. "Shit." I blew out a long breath between my teeth. "Tell Piper not to release the bodies until I give the okay."

It wasn't going to be pleasant for the families. But that was the way it was.

She nodded. Sullivan stood with the blues in a huddle near the gate. The sound of male bullshitting had a high sharp note it doesn't normally have, and the blues kept glancing at me. Short little nervous glances that skittered off the edge of my consciousness.

Vanner moaned, shapelessly. I looked at the house. A cloud of etheric bruising lingered, intensifying now that I'd unleashed sorcery inside its walls and ripped apart the bodies. One of the regular exorcists was going to have to come out and clean it. Probably Wallace, since Eva was on vacation and Benito was handling part of her caseload. Avery had enough to do keeping up with the police department. "Make sure Jughead gets one of the trauma counselors. And get Wallace out here for cleanup after Forensics is through."

She nodded, digging out one of the tiny pads of paper she was always carrying. A pen appeared, and she made notes. "Jughead, trauma. No release on bodies. Wallace out for cleanups. His number's still good?"

"The 3309? Hasn't changed for eight years." But the Badger's thoroughgoing little heart wouldn't let her take it for granted, and I knew as much. "Have I ever told you how much I love your eye for detail?"

"Don't let Sully hear you say that. He thinks my body's the only thing to love me for." A flash of a grin, but her eyes were dark and grieving. "I tell him the line starts on the left. He thinks I should make exceptions for him."

"Does your husband know Sullivan's desperately in love with you?" I played along. It sounds callous, but when you see lives cut short and bodies strewn in pieces, it's either gallows humor or screaming sobs.

I prefer the humor.

The Badger's smile did not ease. "Oh, no. Frank would kill him. Then I'd have to break in a whole new partner. And I just got this one housebroken—"

"Are you taking my name in vain again?" Sullivan called. He detached himself from the knot of blues and ambled over. He didn't look at my chest, where the Talisman was peeping out through its burnt hole. It was glowing, a fierce reddish gleam strong enough to read by if I was in a dark room.

I should calm down. I took a deep breath. It didn't work.

"Of course not." The Badger gave him a sweet smile. "Just talking about your bathroom habits. Anything else, Jill?"

"Phone records." I stared at the house, my eyebrows drawing together. "See if we can piece together their visitors, or an estimated time of death. I'll need to know what's missing from the bodies before I—" My mouth shut, jaw clenching for a moment before I focused again. *Or what's not missing.* "Have them rape-kitted, too."

"Jesus." Sullivan's lips turned down and he fished out a worn pack of Lucky Strikes.

The Badger was solemn. Jughead moaned again, but quietly. It was anyone's guess what had scared him more—seeing the decaying corpse up and moving around, or seeing me fighting it with inhuman speed.

I checked the sky, shuffled through everything I wanted to do, and got exactly nowhere. We were wearing toward dawn faster and faster, and all I could do was wait for Hutch to pull the references, wait for the autopsy to tell me what I should be suspecting.

Thrashing around without something more definite would only waste time and resources. Still... "I've got to get going. Buzz me when you've got something."

The Badger nodded, waving me away. Sullvan tipped me a salute. Jughead Vanner made a thin muttering noise, and the EMT in the back of the ambulance with him spoke up. "Blood pressure's fine. You're going to be okay, kiddo."

I wished I was that optimistic.

*   *   *

Mikhail's headstone is on the northern side of Beacon Hill's lush green, overlooking downtown and the mountains in the distance. The whole valley sprawls out, a vista as familiar as my own face in the mirror. I'd known, as soon as I saw the Talisman in the crushed paper box, that I would eventually end up here.

No use putting it off. And besides, better here than Perry's nightclub. If I went into the Monde like this, there was no telling what would happen.

I'd stopped at the edge of the barrio for a bottle of Stolichnaya—have I mentioned how loose the liquor laws are on the nightside?—and when I uncapped it the colorless fume could be an excuse for the prickling behind my eyes. I took a long hit and poured him a good healthy shot. It splashed on the granite stone. A faint whisper of traffic in the distance, the lamps along the periphery and at intervals failing to make any dent in the night. Darkness hugged the ground here, hung between the trees in rubbery sheets. The water they dump all over this place every day is a great psychic conductor. Grief and longing roiled under the surface of the neatly clipped grass.

I crouched easily, took another mouthful from the bottle. Swallowed, relished the brief sting. "Hi." A thin, breathy sound. "It's me." As if he wouldn't know.

Here was one place I still felt young. I knew his ashes were carefully scraped up from the pyre the Weres built him, safe in an alabaster jar in Galina's vault. But it was here at the gravestone that I felt his presence. I didn't think he'd be a stickler for tradition and only hang around his ashes. Or maybe it was just that I needed him here, out on a hillside with the whole city spread beneath us and the vast dark sky above. At Galina's, someone would be trying not to listen. And what could I do, wake her up in the middle of the night every time I wanted to talk to him?

I poured him another shot. The thin sound of the liquid hitting the stone vanished into the breeze, the river inhaling as dawn approached. I let out a long breath, my shoulders slumping a bit. A red gleam touched the puddle, hot and baleful even when reflected.

"So, yeah. I guess you've noticed the Eye. Perry dropped it off." It didn't sound like much when I said it out loud. But the night tensed around me. I glanced up. All quiet, trees standing watch over the soundly sleeping dead. "I've got a bad feeling about this, Misha."

I could almost hear him. *Bad feeling every day on this job, milaya. Is part of contract.*

Well, yeah, I knew that. Jeez. What would he *really* say to me?

It's one of the hardest things to get used to. No matter how well you know someone, when they die you will never know exactly what they'd say. Especially if you loved them.

Especially if you *still* love them, deep in that room in your heart where you keep the only things that truly matter. The baggage you take to your own personal desert island, the exile called life all of us are born into.

The Church holds it as a point of doctrine that hunters don't go to Heaven. Mikhail had been nominally Eastern Orthodox, with a few significant exceptions. *I go to Valhalla,* he had told me more than once. *Where the fight is the play, like movie.*

I'd only asked him once why someone from his part of the world would pick a Viking afterlife. *Because,* was his answer. *Now stop the asking stupid question,* milaya, *and do your kata.*

I found my free fingers were touching the Talisman's sharp-scratching edges. The gem thrummed, the carved ruby at my throat warming as well. The Eye purred like a kitten under my touch.

I put my hand down with an effort.

"I never got to ask you why you did it. Why you fell for that Sorrows bitch." I swallowed the rest of the question—*why you didn't stay with me. Why I wasn't enough.* Yet another thing I would never know.

The scar puckered and twitched, tasting the misery in the air. I hadn't bothered to cover it again. "I guess it doesn't matter." The words were ashes. "Not like any answer's gonna bring you back. But still."

A rustle of movement. I was up, the bottle hitting the ground and my right-hand gun free, before the shape resolved out of the darkness and I recognized him. I reholstered the gun and waited while he came up the hill. It was a courtesy to make noise while approaching.

When his deeper shadow finally detached itself from the rest of the night, I pitched the words to carry. "I thought you were going to wait for me at home."

Saul tilted his head slightly. Glitter of eyes, the silver in his hair glinting. "It smelled bad. And I knew you'd come up here." He avoided the headstone with respectful ease, striding around to the right, and stopped a couple feet away from me.

"Sorry." I could have been apologizing for both things. "I, uh. Well. It got messy in there. I busted Perry up a bit." I was suddenly aware of the rags of my T-shirt, rips in my leather pants, the reek of rotting corpse, the ick stiffening in my hair and the mess I'd left behind me just about everywhere tonight. Some days are like that. You just break everything as soon as you drag yourself up out of bed.

My trench coat fluttered. The wind was rising, and it was cold.

He bent and scooped up the bottle. It had landed on its bottom, fortunately. "What else did Perry say?"

"He hinted that a big-time 'breed was looking to come through." *Again,* I added silently. *Since I only narrowly slammed the door on him the last time.* It wasn't technically a lie, but the less Saul knew about that case the better. He worried enough as it was. "A 'breed with a big reason to hate any hunter of Jack Karma's lineage."

"Oh." He touched the bottle's open mouth to his lips, then handed it to me. A graceful gesture, like all Were movements. Polite, tactful, expressing everything. "Which is why you're going to invent some reason to ask me to stay at Galina's."

My face froze into a mask. *I didn't think I was that obvious.*

But who else knew me the way he did? "It crossed my mind," I admitted. Then, because it was dark and we were at my teacher's grave, because the Talisman throbbed like a sore tooth on my chest and I ached all over, especially with the heavy weight of the *bezoar* in my pocket, I told him the truth. "It would kill me to lose you, Saul."

He turned his head. Clean, beautiful profile presented as he looked down at the city. "I've done all right so far."

Damn touchy Weres. But at least he wasn't assuming I didn't need him around and clamming up. *That* was no good. "I'm not implying you can't take care of yourself. I just...Jesus, Saul. Please."

"Look." He pointed, a swift gesture taking in the lights huddled in the valley, cuddled against the blackness of the river's flow and the bulk of the looming mountains. The stars were hard, cold diamonds scattered over dirty velvet. "That's Santa Luz."

I know that. I lifted the bottle to my mouth, waited for him to make his point.

He waited a beat, as if he'd expected me to say something, then went on. "Every single innocent soul down in that valley is pulling on you from one direction. And I'm pulling from the other. How long is it going to be before we tear you in half?"

Is that what you think? That you're on different sides? The vodka burned my mouth. I swallowed. Dried blood crackled on my skin. "You're wrong. You both pull me in the same direction, Saul. The only thing pulling on the other side is...this. The things I'm trained to do. I commit murder every night. Several times, if everything's hopping and the 'breed are uppity." It was a night for uncomfortable truths. I would have expected us to be halfway to a screaming match by now. "Sometimes I wonder what makes me different from them." It was my turn to wait before giving him the answer. "Then I realize it's you."

"Jill—"

I wanted to get it all out. "I'm scared, Saul. I can't retire. This is the only thing I know how to do. The only thing I'm *capable* of. And if something happens to you, I am going to end up worse than the hellspawn. Because I won't care."

Silence, then, between us. I lifted the bottle, let a thin stream dip from it and plash on the headstone. None of us would get drunk—my helltainted metabolism ran too fast, and Weres burn through alcohol like it's sugar.

And Mikhail? He wasn't even here. It was just a stone I poured hooch on to make myself feel better.

Most of the time I was glad he was sleeping soundly. Because if he wasn't I would have to *make* him. Then there were the other times, when I almost didn't care.

I wanted him *back*.

Saul was very still, the charms in his hair glinting. "I wouldn't take the Long Road without you, Jill." Quietly, stubbornly. "Not even you could make me do that."

Sometimes talking to him felt like a cardiac arrest, like my heart was literally stopping. Or just hurting. What do you do when you love someone so much your body does that? You can't fight it, you can't shoot it, you can't do anything but let it happen. "I don't want to push my luck."

He stepped close. Paused. Stepped closer. His arm came over my shoulders, and the tension went out of me. I leaned into him, filth and dried blood making small crinkling sounds as my head dropped down. Silver chimed as charms hit each other, and I saw the red glow of the Talisman on my chest had muted to a glimmer. It faded as I leaned into him.

He let out a soft sigh. "It's not luck. I *chose* this, and so did you. We made a decision. Even if you let go, kitten, I'm still holding on."

A hot bubble rose up in my chest. It was a scream. I had to work to keep it locked down, swallowing several times. "Saul?" Again, the high, breathless voice. I sounded fifteen again. And scared.

"Shhh. Listen."

I did. Heard nothing but the breeze in the trees, whispering over the well-watered grass. Traffic in the distance. My heartbeat, a song in my ears. Silver clinking a little as Saul moved, lifting his chin.

"I'll go to Galina's." Quietly. His arm tightened around me.

Oh, thank God. "Thank—"

"Someone has to look after Gilberto. You've sent Hutch there too, I presume?"

I nodded. He could feel the movement against his shoulder. I reeked. He smelled of healthy cat Were, the dry-oily, slightly spicy tang of a brunet male. "Saul—"

"Don't thank me, Jill. I'm doing this for your peace of mind. I'll stay there for a day or so, but then I'm back on the job with you. It's a compromise."

Compromise, consensus, cooperation. It's how Weres work. It's also goddamn annoying. "You mean you're just staying there long enough for it to get dangerous."

"You see? A compromise." He even, damn him, sounded amused. "So Perry's hinting about a hellbreed coming through. What makes you believe him?"

"Besides the fact that he brought me a present?" I sounded as snide as Gilberto. "Nothing. He wants something, I'm going to hang back and make him work until I figure out *exactly* what's going on." The *bezoar* twitched in my pocket—another task to finish, before dawn if I could. "Then I'll start shooting. This may be the game that ends up with me killing him."

"Can't happen too soon," Saul murmured, and we were in wholehearted agreement on *that* score. "What are you doing tonight? Or this morning?"

The thing I wished I could say—*having some quality time with my favorite Were*—was tempting. It stuck in my throat like the lie it was, because I knew I was going to jump the gun and go hunting. "Tracking down a hellbreed who killed four student nurses over in Cruzada. When I'm done I'll come by Galina's. You can make me breakfast."

"And Hutch. And Gilberto. And Galina. We'll be a happy merry crowd." His arm squeezed gently, half a hug. "Come soon, huh? I know, I know. As soon as you can."

Another nod. "If I don't track this 'breed down by dawn I'll come by for breakfast. Promise."

"Good." He let go of me and stepped away. The wind touched where he used to be down the side of my body. A hunter doesn't care about external temperatures, but I felt abruptly cold.

But he cupped my chin in his hand. Warm skin, a Were's metabolism radiating heat. I leaned forward, he bent down, and our mouths met.

It should have been uncomfortable, kissing in front of Mikhail's gravestone. I had the oddest sense that Misha wouldn't mind. And then there was the hot, nasty feeling squirming under my breastbone for just a moment—*look, here's someone who wants me. Someone who hasn't run off with a Sorrow and ended up dead in a filthy hotel room.*

It wasn't fair. I didn't know why Mikhail had done...what he'd done. I just wanted him back. And the sex, I understood now, had just been another way to tie us together. High pressure and avail-

ability instead of...what I had here and now in front of me, his
fingers on my face and his purr thrumming through me, loosening my bones.

I didn't want to let him go, my dirty fingers twining in his
growing-out hair. But we both had to breathe more deeply after a
bit, so we stood, foreheads together, my eyes closed. His purr, a
Were's response to a mate's distress, settled into a subliminal
pressure. Minutes ticked by.

It was no use. I had work to do. Even if I knew I was going out
looking for a fight when I should be waiting for Hutch or Forensics to get back to me.

The vision of the last corpse's face, screaming silently and forever under the glare of the dining-room light fixture, printed itself
inside my eyelids. I didn't flinch, but I did make a small sound.
Immediately clamped my lips together.

I am about to do something stupid.

He let go of me, one finger at a time. Kissed my forehead, a
gentle pressure of lips. Then he was gone, boots just touching the
fresh, juicy grass. I listened as long as I could to the sound of his
footsteps, light and graceful-quick. They shifted as he blurred
into muscled, four-footed cougar form, still running faster than
anything normal could.

Super-acute hellbreed-jacked hearing was good for something.

I found I was still clutching the bottle of Stoli. It made a thin
musical sound as I upended it, washing Mikhail's headstone.
Alcohol fume wafted up, whisked away on a brisk breeze. The
river's inhale sped up as dawn approached. If I was going to
find—and serve bloody, screaming vengeance on—the 'breed
who had killed those girls, now was the time.

I won't lie. I wanted to kill something else tonight. And it
scared me even as I turned on my heel and vanished into the
darkness.

CHAPTER 9

The thinnest tendril of gray false dawn was touching the eastern horizon as I halted, the *bezoar* straining and writhing against blessed silk. I'd had to tighten the knots two or three times now. My apprentice-ring crackled with blue light, sparks under the surface of the metal occasionally breaking free with tiny snapping sounds, like itty-bitty razor teeth clicking together.

An iron gate stood ajar; the chain supposed to hold it broken and useless. They sometimes try to replace the padlock, but all it takes is dark falling for it to be burst into jagged metal shrapnel and the gate to drift open just a bit. Inviting.

The colorless, crumbling concrete wall is topped with razor wire. Behind it, the old Henderson Hill rises. The grass is long and always yellow now, clinging to life and sandy soil. Its buildings huddle together, spindly weeds forcing up through the cracks in the pavement squares and walkways. Several windows are broken, and no matter what time it is, it always seems a little darker the closer you get to the buildings. The wind makes odd sounds against every edge, even if no air is moving.

Sounds like faraway cries, or soft sobs. Or nasty, tittering laughter.

In 1927, construction on the new Henderson Hill was begun. It was almost finished when the great demonic outbreak of 1929 occurred.

That was too late for the inmates. They, like a lot of hunters we couldn't afford to lose, died in the first wave of attacks. They don't just call it Black Thursday because of the stock market, you know.

When some things come out of Hell, they come hungry. And the asylum, its physical structure impregnated with suffering from years of insanity and the torture that passed for treatment inside its walls, was a buffet.

The carnage here was blamed on a gas leak. Santa Luz's hunter at the time, Emerson Sloane, was still trying desperately to get a handle on things when he was ambushed and went on to whatever afterlife he'd chosen. The city went without a hunter until Mikhail showed up, fresh from postwar Europe and trained by one of the best—the second Jack Karma. Mikhail brought peace of a sort to the streets—or at least forced a lot of the stuff still running around to keep a low profile. It would take a long time and more hunters to truly tame the nightside.

We are so few. The Church—and other churches—tries to make sure we're funded and trained, and we have better firepower than ever, but even the best firepower is useless without someone capable of using it. I'd been at this for a while, and Gilberto was the only one out of plenty of candidates who even came close to measuring up.

Go figure. A murderous ex-gangbanger with a sarcasm habit and yours truly, the only help Santa Luz had against the nightside. Then there was Leon. I heard he'd been in the Army, in some South American country or something. And Anya Devi over the mountains, God alone knew where she came from.

No hunter likes to talk about what they were *before*.

I eased out of the shadows across the street from the gate. Psychic darkness swirled, coalesced between the posts. The *bezoar* twitched in my pocket, and my fingers made sure the knots were tight one more time.

The closer to dawn, the harder the fight. But any traces the 'breed who murdered those four girls had left would be fresh. That is, if they were smart enough to just leave, not stupid enough to stick around and wait for me.

Jill, you're lying. You need another fight the way a junkie needs another fix. That's why you're doing this.

I tried to tell myself one reason didn't cancel out the other. It didn't matter. I knew I was lying.

It's hard to look everywhere at once, especially when adrenaline is dumping into your bloodstream and nasty little flickering things are showing up in your peripheral vision. My blue eye turned hot and dry, untangling layer after layer of misery, agony, ill intent, cruelty—if ever a place deserved the name "haunted," the old Henderson Hill did. It was so bad up here, the psychic soup so thick, that even a lot of the nightside stayed away. I'd chased a not-quite-physical *arkeus* or two up into those chilly-thick halls. But the more physical 'breed and nightsiders give this place a wide berth.

The nastiness in Henderson Hill can hurt them, too. It doesn't care much *who* it hurts.

The gate let out a long moan as I approached. Nobody came down this part of Henderson Road, and there was a pocket of abandoned buildings washing up around the concrete walls. Before 1950, the entire complex had been loosely fenced; the public works department had put the walls up ostensibly to keep teenagers and hobos out. That was after the Carolyn Sparks incident, which you can find wildly varying descriptions of in the Noches County and Santa Luz Municipal library systems' microfiche. What you won't find is what really happened.

Trust me, you don't want to know. Suffice to say the boyfriend Miss Sparks thought loved her so much turned out to be a Middle Way adept just looking for someone to use as a gate. He'd talked her into coming out to the old spooky Hill on a dare.

There's no better gateway for some of the Abyssals than a gifted, untrained psychic, and the one who had come through... well, he ate Sparks's boyfriend and settled down inside the psychic's skin like a hand in a comfortable glove. It *almost* managed to raise another gate to bring a whole mess of its friends through. By *almost*, I mean it did for a split second, and released three more of them, before Mikhail could get out here to shut it down.

It took him a month to track all of them down. They went through civilians like a hot knife through butter. Misha never mentioned it directly. The notes he'd made in the file for the incident were gruesome enough.

The gate moaned even harder as I elbowed it. I knew better than to touch the metal with bare skin. Little sparks were visible all around me, the sea-urchin spikes of my aura crackling. There was enough ambient light for my hellbreed-jacked vision to have no trouble, but it was paired with a thick psychic darkness, a wet oppressive blanket almost blinding my smart eye's capability to look *between*, beneath, around.

The scar puckered wetly, chilled as if someone had licked the ridged tissue and blown on it. A shiver of sick delight spilled up the nerves of my right arm. Tasting the misery in the air, the scar pulsed as if it would swell.

I stepped over the threshold, Henderson Hill closing around me like a toothless, decaying mouth. The temperature dropped a good five degrees. A shiver passed through me, crown to soles, and my blue eye was suddenly alive with phantom images. Ghost faces, each one contorted in a rictus of terror or awful pleasure, swirled like smoke. Screams eddied soundlessly around me, moans and cries just at the edge of hearing. My skin was suddenly alive with little needling pinstrokes as insubstantial fingers brushed my shoulders, touched my hip, flinched away from the silver I carried.

It was getting bad up here. The spirits were almost visible, cheesecloth veils fluttering as the breeze veered. For an instant I smelled smoke, and the screams mounted, winding closer and closer. Etheric force crackled as I *pushed* outward, sweat springing up on my skin the way it never does unless I'm in a hard fight. Gravel scattered across the cracked driveway rattled like dry bones, pebbles lifting and dropping in place.

It's always that way—the first few seconds are the time when most trips to Henderson go wrong. The world rippled around me, and normality reasserted itself. The shades retreated to the edges of my vision, flickering in the corners. The sounds drew back, too. Having an exorcist's aura, hard and disciplined, is far from the worst ally when you're stepping on ground that's been unhallowed with a vengeance.

I let out a soft breath. Everything calmed down.

An untrained psychic might be drawn into the labyrinth of buildings and passages, deeper and deeper, until they ended up as a meal or one of the shades swirling around. Thank God most psychics, untrained or not, kept well away from this slice of real estate. Even normal people could get caught in the spider web of misery this place had become. Most of them had sense enough to stay clear.

The local exorcists called me instead of following if a victim headed for the Hill. There was a mute, scarred caretaker—the only person I'd ever seen here. He sat in the boiler room most of the time with a quart of rye, and I'd never figured out exactly *what* he was. Once, and only once, he'd appeared out of nowhere and walloped a writhing possession victim on the head with a shovel. The Possessor had been strong and wiry, using its victim's body recklessly, and the caretaker's appearance had given me a precious few seconds to get the vic down and mostly trussed up. The resultant quick and dirty exorcism had almost killed the victim, but I'd ripped the little bastard of a demon out and smashed it into screaming flinders.

The caretaker had merely shuffled off with his shovel. I felt bad about not thanking him, but with an unconscious human woman shivering and moaning in my arms, her blood pressure and pulse dropping fast, my options had been limited. And he'd never shown up again when I chased an *arkeus* or two around the halls. If I wanted to see him, I had to go around the corner of the building and penetrate the maze that used to be a quad for the inmates to shuffle around.

And I did not want to see that imitation of a garden again unless I absolutely had to.

I set off up the driveway. Pebbles shifted and clicked as I walked, the edges of my aura like a storm front setting off waves of disturbance. It was like walking under a blanket of something a little less heavy than water. Setting each foot carefully, every inch of me quivering with alertness.

"*Kissssssssssmet...*" A faint, faraway giggle. "*Kissssssmet, come closssser.*"

You bet I could. But not in a way they would like. I kept my mouth shut.

The main building loomed up the hill, all its windows dead eyes. The *bezoar* twitched, and I stopped. Slid my hand into my pocket and made sure the knots were tight one more time. Before carefully, gently, drawing it out.

A soundless buzz almost made me jump. It was my pager, silent in its padded pocket, vibrating insistently. *Not right now, dammit.* I promptly shut the sensation out and yanked the *bezoar* back as it tried to squirt free of my fingers.

A sick green light flashed in one of the upper windows. Third floor, fifth from the left. Odd that it was up there, instead of in the basement—hellbreed usually like dark holes. The darker, the better. But the Hill's basement is someplace not even a 'breed might want to be.

What the hell was a physical 'breed doing here? *Arkeus* don't murder so directly; they usually gain substantiality a little at a time by stealing it from Traders. It's a long process, and I usually kill them before they get halfway.

I leaned forward, each boot landing softly and rolling through, ready for any sudden movement.

None of the buildings were locked. There was no need, and in any case the locks went the same way the padlock on the front gate did. Boards were nailed up over random windows, as if the caretaker just came out and put a couple up for the hell of it every once in a while, a token show. It was like Band-Aids over leprosy.

As soon as the light flashed it was gone. My right hand curled around a gun butt as I stuffed the silk-wrapped lump back in my pocket. Seaweed-shifts of etheric interference blurred my smart eye, threatening to give me a headache.

That was the least of my problems. At least, if I couldn't get a lock through this static on the disturbance in the ether a hellbreed represented, they couldn't get a lock on *me*. Which meant I could come out of nowhere and knock them on their ass.

The steps were wide and oddly bleached. I went up them cautiously, eased across the wide porch, its columns cracked and dripping scabrous paint. A chorus of children's voices, screaming, roared between them. Echoes bounced, ruffling my hair and bowing the world in concentric ripples.

The scar turned hot and hard as it pumped etheric energy through me. *Now. Do it now.*

I uncoiled from the porch, one boot thudding home on the left-hand door. Cold air closed over me—outside on the grounds it's just cooler than normal. Inside, it's frigid, and my breath turned to steam. I hit the ground, rolled, and was upright again in time to see the short 'breed hanging in the air over me, lit by the weird, faint illumination filling the entire building. My pager was going crazy in my pocket again, but I didn't care, because I was in deep fucking shit.

It was the masked 'breed who does assassinations and dirty work all through Santa Luz. I say *masked* because he is, and "he" because it moves like a boy. The mask was a half veil, fluttering at the edges, and he wore loose-fitting black silk. He looked like a ninja in pajamas, complete with slippered tabi feet, except for the orange hellfire dripping from his black, black eyes. It crackled on his high cheekbones as it smeared, drops flying upward in merry defiance of gravity.

My arm jerked up, the gun spoke. Bullets spattered behind him as I tracked, rolling to the side. Henderson Hill rocked on its foundations, each silverjacketed round blowing a hole in the sweeping staircase's wall and puffing out dust. He was fast, even for a 'breed. I'd never gone up against him, because he confined himself to killing his fellow hellspawn and Traders.

I like to encourage that sort of behavior. As long as it makes *my* job easier.

He hit where I had been lying bare fractions of a second ago. My left hand jerked the whip free, it struck like a snake and missed, flechettes jangling. The sparks—sterile orange from him, cold blue from me—were photo flashes etching shadows on the rotting walls and ceiling. I skipped back, footsteps grinding in dirt and trash against the scarred ancient linoleum of what used to be the reception foyer.

On all fours, the assassin snarled behind his veil. His breath didn't paint the air with vapor. Mine swirled around my head like cigarette smoke.

Where plenty of them are tall packages of bad news, this 'breed is compact and skinny, almost childlike because of the weird proportion of the head to the limbs. White skin showed above the mask's sheen, pallid and waxy like a maggot's sides. Orange hellfire crawled and dripped, each droplet snapping out of existence as it rode the updraft of the hellspawn's fury.

I shook the whip, calculated the ammo I had left in the gun, squeezed off a shot. He lunged aside, but it clipped him low on the left. Black ichor sprayed. It wasn't a critical enough hit to put him down or slow him, but a few more like that and I'd send him back to Hell.

If I could stay alive long enough.

Still skipping back, the intake desk looming behind me under its drift of nameless, shapeless trash. Shadows spasmed and danced. Streaking with inhuman speed, he left a smear of fluorescent spangled hate behind him, each drop of hellbreed blood hissing as it hit turbulent air. I leapt, getting the high ground of the counter. It lurched under me like a living thing, rotting wood splintering, but I had my balance. The gun spoke again, its muzzle flash etching every line and angle for a brief instant as the whip cracked. My arm came down hard, leather singing as it stretched. My pager still buzzed, I ignored it.

Hit him now, hit him hard, *goddamn you Jill, hit him—*

The flechettes struck home, chiming, and the hellbreed howled. But he was so ungodly *fast*; he hit the desk and splinters smashed up in a wave. I was already airborne again, a tight-curled ball as my coat snapped once like wet laundry shaken before you put it on the line. Every muscle in my body straining against gravity, I *twisted* in midair and thumped down near the stairs, whirling and dropping to one knee, pointing the gun as the whip landed in a soft slithering coil...

...and the foyer was empty, from sagging walls to damaged ceiling. Thin curls of steam lifted from splattered hellbreed ichor, decaying rapidly. My ribs heaved; flickering with deep, harsh breaths that flashed into ice at the edges and fell in spatters of diamond frost. Dirty cheesecloth veils pressed close, tangling like wet weeds. The scar burned, throbbing, obscenely full.

Movement. The gun jerked, but it was just a twist of paper on a stray breath of air. The hellbreed's footsteps retreated, faltering. I'd hit him but good. I didn't have to chase him now—I knew who it was, and I could afford to go after him during the day when I'd have more of an edge.

I was beginning to think I'd need it.

I rose slowly. *Could be a trick. What's a 'breed doing here, though? Not an* arkeus, *either, a fully physical spawn.* Intuition tingled as Henderson Hill breathed around me. A whole cavalcade of little sounds—an old building creaking and ticking as dawn approached, rustles and half-heard cries as the spirits crowded around me, drawn by violence—

—and the thump-shuffle of halting footsteps.

I crouched easily, the whip dropped, and my hands reloading my right-hand gun with the speed of long habit. The *bezoar* twitched spastically in my pocket and my pager just would not stop vibrating. I was about to pull the damn thing out and shoot it.

My bitten-down fingernails scraped in dust and cold grime as I felt for the whip handle, grabbed it. Shook it a little, testing. I did not rise—if something jumped me, I was a smaller target and better off having my balance, even if every fiber of my body was screaming at me to move. To face whatever was coming at me standing up.

That's what training is for. To make sure you don't do something stupid. At least, to *help* you not do something stupid. The fine hairs on my neck and back and arms stood up, quivering like sea anemones, searching for danger.

A shadow moved in the hall to my left. I had a split second to decide whether it was real, unreal, or a threat either way. The gun pointed itself, my finger tightened on the trigger. I kept breathing, smooth swells as my body recovered from the tendon-popping strain of superhuman speed. My shoulders were bridge cables, the need to move drawing down tighter and tighter inside me.

Darkness swirled. My shot went wide, blowing out the doorjamb above his head, and a mild blue, cataract-clouded gaze met mine.

The caretaker pursed his scarred lips. The lower half of his face was a runnel of broken and battered tissue, parts of his cheeks and jaw suppurating under a shield of startlingly white gauze. No matter how many times I see it, I still feel the urge to flinch.

I lowered the gun. Tried not to look like I was gasping for breath. Stared at him.

The caretaker is scarecrow-thin, in a gray coverall with a name embroidered on the left breast pocket. The embroidery is just a mass of snarled stitches now, and the coverall washed so many times it's almost worn through at knees and elbows. Lines fan out from the corners of his eyes. His hair is indeterminate, somewhere between blond and dishwater. The only saving grace is those blue eyes, intelligent and mild even if they are filmed with gray. They looked at me, sad and wide, and I promptly mostly-dismissed him as a threat.

At least, he'd never been a threat before.

The masked 'breed was gone. Now I knew, or at least could

assume with a degree of certainty, who had killed those girls. But Jesus Christ, if he was killing *humans* . . .

. . . something was very wrong here.

The idea that maybe it was related to Perry's little present and dark hints was enough to break me out in a cold sweat.

I stayed crouched, every nerve alert and the scar humming as it sipped at the foulness in the air. The caretaker stopped, his hands hanging loose at his sides. A brief unease ran through me—not too long ago the circus had been in town and there had been a Trader with big paddlefish strangler's hands.

That case is over, Jill. Deal with what you got in front of you.

Nothing. The world was creeping closer to dawn, and I had a lead. I could track down the masked 'breed without too much trouble, and find out why he was killing humans. *After* I found out what he was doing here at Henderson Hill.

I straightened, slowly, my knees creaking. The caretaker was staring at me. As soon as I was fully upright, he nodded and pointed up the stairs.

Behind me.

I threw myself down and aside, both guns slapped out now and the whip discarded. It hit the ground with a soft slithering just as I felt like an idiot.

There was nothing there.

He shuffled forward, his ruined face coming into view. There was now amusement sparkling in those filmed-but-piercing eyes. His breath turned into a cloud, just like mine.

"Jesus," I said shakily. "Go ahead, laugh. I know you want to."

The sound of a living voice echoed oddly. The crowding spirits flinched away. I got to my feet, shaking dust and sand out of my hair. The caretaker shrugged, spreading those long fingers. An odd kind of clarity lingered around him, none of the ghosts playing tricks or pressing close to probe for openings. He didn't *look* like an exorcist. To my blue eye, he just looked . . . solid. And normal, but without the shifting fields of color that most often clung to living things.

Still, he breathed. And he was physical enough to hold a shovel. You learn to take what you can get on the nightside.

Again, he pointed at the stairs.

I holstered my guns, picked my whip up. "All right, all right. I'm going. I don't suppose you're coming with me."

But I was surprised again. He edged past me, carefully, his back to the bullet-scarred wall. I'd done a fair bit of damage; the desk still quivered with the dregs of violence. There was a hall in the east building, second floor, that was probably still reverberating from my *last* visit here.

I didn't like thinking about that. It was *freezing* in here, and even though temperature matters very little to a fully trained hunter this wasn't a physical cold. It was far worse. A soft rustling scraped through the foyer. The chairs tumbled along the far side, swept there and jumbled together, creaked sharply once. Like a shot, or a leather strap cracking down on unprotected flesh.

I stepped back. I didn't blame him for keeping his distance. He smiled very gently, his ruined mouth twisting against itself, and turned. He tested each step with a scarred work boot before committing his weight to it, and after he'd gone up four or five I moved to do the same.

The fifth floor had been a maximum-security ward. Some of the rooms were windowless, padding hanging in strangling, sticky scarves from the ceiling and walls. Others had bars and chicken wire holding glass that by some miracle hadn't broken, or else crystalline shards held in by wire. My pager kept going off, frantic in its padded pocket like a small bird's heartbeat. The *bezoar* twitched, too. My coat was beginning to feel like a live thing.

The caretaker kept to the middle of the hall, an exact distance away from either side. The heavy, reinforced doors occasionally twitched, each one ajar just a little.

Except for one most of the way down the hall. That one switched back and forth lazily, like a cat's tail as it contemplates a mouse. Nasty little titters hovered around us, the spike tips of my aura glittering sharp and the clarity around the caretaker moving with him, a double sphere of normalcy. A soft chill breeze full of medical antiseptic touched my face, shuffled through my dirty hair.

I couldn't wait to clean up. Soon enough.

I kept my right hand on a gun, and my left, deep in another

pocket, tightened the knots on the silk. I had a visual on the 'breed I was going to be questioning about this, but it would be silly to let the *bezoar* out of my grasp. Galina would have something to lock it down further, and as long as I had it there was nowhere the masked 'breed could go to escape me.

Not like he could escape me anywhere in Santa Luz anyway. When I get a real hard-on for a 'breed they don't stay hidden long. And it's not like he blends in.

The caretaker paused. Half-turned, and I saw his profile as he laid a finger against his mutilated lips. The bandaging on the bottom part of his face still startlingly white, even if crusted with seepage, and I wondered, just like I did every time, just what exactly he *was*. There was no sick-sweet perfume of hellish corruption hanging on him, and none of the other classifications of nightside or nonhuman seemed to fit him. The only place in this whole heap that wouldn't give someone the heebie-jeebies was his dark, dirty, *normal* boiler room, where he sat sucking on his bottle and staring at the walls.

I nodded and drew the gun. Kept it pointed at the floor, nice and easy. He set off again down the hall, and I found myself stepping only where he did. As if he was Mikhail and I was still an apprentice.

The Talisman sighed on my chest. No matter how much time goes by, missing someone never gets any better. You just learn to work around it.

The door's twitching motion sped up, imperceptibly. The hallway rippled like a funhouse mirror, the floor rumbling as if we were above a subway.

He stepped wide of the door, carefully turning himself. Moved sideways, crablike, to give me room. Pointed, with one long pale finger.

I edged around the door, trying to stay away from it and not get too close to the opposite wall. The door stopped twitching. Now it just quivered a little, jabbing out into the hall like an accusing finger.

Inside the room, the disturbance was so bad I had to shut my smart eye. For a moment the pictures didn't make sense, then they snapped together behind my eyes and bile rose in my throat. I backed up a half step, instinctively retreating, and a hand closed around my upper arm.

I almost punched him. Jumpy, jumpy.

The caretaker shook his head, and those sad eyes stopped me. He pointed again, and his ruined mouth opened. I waited for him to speak for the first time ever, but he just gave me the saddest look imaginable, closed his lips tightly, and pointed inside the room again.

This time I steeled myself, and looked with both smart and dumb eye. My pager quit buzzing, blessedly.

A misshapen hunk sat in the middle of the gouged linoleum, dripping with corruption. It was veiled with a fall of black cloth, but it was almost certainly a chunk of a hangman's tree. Various shapes squatted on its surface—a chalice of clotted scum, a claw from no creature that walked under the sun, other things whose intent was only to maim and harm. The altar wasn't finished, but the atmosphere here was already so poisoned they probably wouldn't need much. All it would take is the slightest push to gap the borders between *here* and *somewhere else* the smallest bit, and something could step through.

There were no vulnerable victims waiting in here, but the febrile boiling of agony, misery, hatred, and just plain nastiness here would be snack enough to feed something fresh out of Hell. There was no scoring on the walls, no drawn circle, and no parchment candles on wrought-iron pillars yet.

But there were four lumps of meat on the black material draped over the block. Small lumps, each about the size of a woman's fist.

I knew what they were. The rest of the organs missing from the student nurses would be at other evocation sites.

I cannot hold back the tide forever.

There's nothing that can tear down the walls between here and Hell like innocent flesh. I knew what the important part of the autopsy would say. I'd even bet my next municipal check that the four student nurses were all virgins, too.

My city was in deep trouble.

CHAPTER 10

couldn't get out of Henderson Hill fast enough. The caretaker shuffled away, his thin shoulders slumped under his coveralls, and I'd spent a few minutes of effort to coax whispering-blue banefire off my fingers. The last time I'd seen an altar like this, I'd been flinging yellow hellfire around, razing an entire airfield. It had taken a long time and concerted effort to call out the banefire instead.

Hellfire near an evocation altar is *such* a bad idea, there are barely words for it. The banefire struggled under the weight of contamination in the air, but finally I coaxed a wisp of blue up from my right-hand fingers. Once it had a good foothold, wreathing my hand in pale blue flames, singing in their hissing little whispers, I cast it at the altar. A blue streak roared foaming from my fingers and hit the nastiness squarely. It would burn clean and leave a thin layer of blessing in its wake, and if it spread to the surrounding rooms, so much the better.

I was seriously considering, like I did each time, burning down the entire goddamn place. But there was no way of doing it without hellfire, and like I said, bad *bad* idea.

Hellfire feeds on rage. It would be the psychic equivalent of a nuclear weapon, and it would leave even worse fallout.

I got out through the gate and stood for a moment, head down, listening to the chatters and whispers fading behind me. My skin crawled, not just from the dried blood, hellbreed ick, and other gunk coating me. The Talisman was quiescent, nestling under the rags of my shirt. Dawn was underway, the sky lightening to gray in the east and the first flush of color in a thin line along the horizon.

My pager went off again. I almost swore, checked the *bezoar* one more time, and dug the little electronic gadget out. Clicked back through the calls, once more wishing I could carry a cell phone. But no dice—pagers have a greater tolerance for sorcery, and with as much as I'm half-drowned, electrocuted, or other fun things, replacing a cell is a prohibitive expense. Especially since it's the police department that pays for it. Monty would have a cow if this one didn't last more than two weeks; I'd been having a bad run of it lately.

Montaigne was, in fact, calling me right now. Twice. I had a bad feeling about this.

I frowned. Galina, calling me. Several times. The pager quit vibrating, but immediately lit up again.

I juggled priorities for a moment. The autopsies wouldn't be done for hours, even with a rush on them. I had the *bezoar* and the capability of tracking that masked 'breed, plus I could figure out where he'd gone to ground without too much trouble. I needed to start digging to find out where the other evocation sites were, because bringing a high-class hellbreed through isn't something you undertake without a few planned backups.

I'd promised Saul breakfast. And if Galina was spamming my pager, something big was happening.

But first, I had to check in with Monty.

It never rains but it pours.

I cursed internally. Made a note to pick up my car from Galina's this morning, no matter what else was going on. And picked myself up into a weary run.

I must know where every working pay phone in the entire city is. When that infrastructure goes the way of the dodo, I'm either going to have to start carrying a cell and eat the cost of constantly replacing it, or I'm going to have to figure *something* out. Breaking and entering to use people's phones was the option I was most sneakingly in favor of, but one I suspected I'd never actually engage in. There are enough places open even in the dead time of early morning that I'd probably have no problem.

The closest phone was on Henderson after it jagged past Marivala Boulevard, in the corner of a stop-and-rob's cracked, dirty parking lot. The entire city had gone still, Santa Luz sinking into weariness before false dawn started coloring the eastern horizon and the nightside retreated glaring to its holes and burrows. I was hoping this wasn't going to be too complex, that Monty was just catching me up on forensics or something...but intuition as well as logic told me I was just trying to make myself feel better.

Oh, Jillybean, you are having one hell of a night, aren't you?

I had to stop and breathe before I plugged in my calling-card number, then dialed Montaigne.

"*What?*" he barked right after the second ring. He must've been sitting on the damn thing.

"It's me." I didn't have to work to sound tired. "What've you got?"

"Jesus Christ." Click of a lighter, a puffing inhale-exhale. He was smoking a cigarillo, dammit. In his office, despite the fact that all public buildings were supposed to be tobacco-free as of two months ago. And despite the doctor telling him to lay off.

I couldn't help myself. "Your wife's not going to like you smoking, Monty."

"Stay out of my marriage, Kismet." And boy, did he sound grim. I checked the sky again, decided it was about four in the morning, and winced inwardly. "Got a mass grave just outside the city limits. At least seven contenders, probably more. Weird work."

Crap. I thought about it for a second. "Bodies ripped up, some organs missing?"

"Oh yeah. They're crispy, too. Parks & Rec guy stumbled over it; Rosie and Paloma are out there. Rosie called in, said to get you on the wire and send her some fucking backup."

Jesus. I should've expected this. "Where?"

"Follow the Strip south and stop when you see the flashing lights. Do it as fast as you can, Channel Four's not there yet, but it's only a matter of time. Jesus." Another pause, and I heard him swallow. Probably coffee. At least, I hoped it was coffee. "Rosie says it's fragrant, too. Just a barrel of roses to start the day with."

"So you're in early, instead of late? When did that start?"

"I ain't got home yet, Kismet. Go take a look at this so I can fucking get there, okay?"

"Temper, temper." But he had a point, for something like this he was in his office playing central control until I got there and cleared the scene. "Cheer up, Montaigne. It could be a serial killer. A *normal* one."

His reply was unrepeatable, and he banged the phone down.

I set the receiver down with a grimace. Rubbed at my forehead, dried blood and gunk crackling off my skin. "Goddammit." It was just a whisper. Dawn was coming up fast.

I was going to have to catch a cab.

CHAPTER 11

The driver—a placid, tired, middle-aged Chicano I'd flagged down on Marivala—pulled over onto the shoulder, coming to a neat stop just behind a black-and-white with flashers lit up. They had two of the four lanes going south out of town blocked off, and it looked like Christmas had come early. His license said *Paloulian*, and I didn't ask how he'd ended up with a Greek surname. In return, he barely even looked at me. Relying on sheer outrageousness to slide under the notice of normal people has its benefits. Besides, any cabdriver on shift long enough to greet false dawn sees a *lot* of weird.

Paloulian threw his smoking Camel butt out the window as soon as I closed the back door. His tires chirped as he took off, and the IN SERVICE bar on top of his cab flicked out. He slewed left to get through the empty lanes and took the exit for the industrial park, probably meaning to turn around and head back north.

Thank God there was no traffic just yet, at least not going this direction. And people complain about *my* driving.

There were at least six black-and-whites, a couple of nondescripts with bubble lights going, and yellow tape fluttering. A Parks & Rec truck sat in the middle, a big white goose among the flock.

All the activity was past the ditch, in a stand of trashwood serving as a modesty screen. The Strip is pretty lonely right here, for all that a regular patrol goes through on the freeway to discourage drag racers. It doesn't work; pretty much twice a month in summer there's a bad bustup right where the freeway curves after coming out of downtown.

This part of the Strip was past where the races usually end.

The city limit's about a half mile back, the freeway arrowing for the desert and the steadily lightening horizon in a straight gray line. There are still exits for fast food, industrial parks, or tiny suburbs, but right here there was nothing but concrete, the divider between northbound and southbound, and a strip of greenery on either side surviving on periodic runoff from uphill, where blank fences stood scrawled with graffiti. *Greenery* is a deceptive term; it's mostly low slashwood and yellow weeds. Life clings to every breath of water out here, and clings *hard*.

I cocked my head. Dawn was coming fast, like a brass bell ringing along the eastern horizon. I'd be late for breakfast.

The question was, just how late?

I stalked for the carnival lights. The blue standing guard stiffened. It was "Crosseye" Garcia, so called to differentiate him from the twenty or so other Garcias on the force. Squat and balding, he didn't quite have a lazy eye, but it was close. If my own mismatched gaze makes people nervous, Crosseye's just makes them inclined to take him less seriously.

He doesn't quite have something to prove, but it's close.

"Hey, Garcia." I settled for a closed-mouth smile. "Where's Rosie?"

He jerked a thumb over his shoulder. "That way, with fuckin' Paloma. Take a barf bag. It's nice an' juicy."

"I heard they were crisped."

"Some. Go take a look, freakshow."

Considering Crosseye was only slightly less foulmouthed than "Fuckitall" Ramon, who never opened his mouth without an obscenity of breathtaking creativity slipping loose, I suppose I should've taken it as a compliment. I skirted the closest car and headed down the shoulder. "You've got such a winning personality. Goes with your smile."

His reply was unrepeatable. We were all in such a good mood this morning.

I hopped the ditch and headed into the slashwood. Murmuring, someone's voice raised in an exclamation of disgust. And something else.

A breath of smoky, corruption-laden perfume.

Pulse, respiration, my stride didn't change. But my right hand reached down, drew the gun free. Another high sharp note of disgust, and I heard Rosenfeld, sharp as a new brass tack, saying something about Forensics. Hunter's silence folded over me—the deep cloak of quiet that an apprentice learns early, because moving soundlessly is a survival skill.

There was a screen of brush along the top rim of a declivity. I edged along it to find the right angle. If there was a mass grave down there, I couldn't smell it. Which was bad.

I slid through the brush, following the drift of the corruption. This was a goddamn fire risk right next to the freeway. Maybe Parks & Rec had been out here on a preliminary sweep before they cleared it.

At the darkest time before dawn? Come on, Jill. Something's wrong here.

I kept the gun low as I stepped out of the brush.

I had a few seconds before they spotted me. Rosenfeld had lost more weight; she was just on the edge between looking good and stick-scary. She was on the far side of the site, her lantern jaw sticking out even more stubbornly than usual. Next to her, Ricky Paloma crouched easily, peering at something. Between us lay a shallow depression full of tangled shapes I didn't look too closely at yet. Blues ringed the scene, all of them recognizable. I spotted the one stranger before he saw me, and the silence over me deepened.

He wore a taupe-and-green Parks & Rec coverall. Weed-thin, a thatch of dark hair—but his shoes were wrong. They were wing-tips, not work boots. And the perfume of a hellbreed bargain clung to him.

Luck wasn't with me. He twitched, dark eyes rolling like glass marbles, maybe sensing a current of bloodlust in the predawn quiet. He saw me, but by then I was already moving. I cleared the fresh-scraped hole and twisted charred bodies in one leap, and I would have been on him like white on rice except for his immediate flinching backward leap. As it was, I jerked and my left boot smacked him in the head with a sound like a melon dropped on an icy sidewalk before he landed.

Rosenfeld yelled. Someone else cursed. The Trader went down in a heap, arms and legs bending oddly, and rolled. Dirt exploded up, and I got a stomach-loosening noseful of grave smell and the bad-pork stench of charred bodies before I hit again, just bare inches away from his scrambling.

"*Kismet!*" Rosenfeld yelled, but the cry was choked off midway as the Trader lunged up to kneeling, hands splayed on the ground and knees wide akimbo, his lip lifting and the yellowing stubs of his teeth cracking as he growled.

The gun roared. I had to not only get him down and cuff him for questioning, but I had to keep him away from the cops he had been standing around bullshitting with.

The defenseless mortal cops.

Lured them here, maybe. Or lured me. What the hell?

That's why the whip flashed forward, oddly quiet until it broke the shell of my silence; then silver-laced flechettes didn't jingle but cracked like silver lightning. They tore across his chest, and he howled.

I screamed, too, a short cry like a falcon's, and the gun was tracking him. He scrambled aside, but a single shot forced him into scrabbling to the right and back, *away* from my cops. He'd bargained for speed and probably strength, but I *anticipated,* and he jagged right into my next shot.

Which blew out his knee. The joint evaporated in a smear of red oatmeal flecked with white bone and the black lacing of hell-breed corruption. I was on him in a hot heartbeat, the whip doubled and slipping around his neck like it belonged there, my knee in his back and the other knee on his left arm. He tried to heave up, but when you lock the arm that high up they just have no goddamn leverage.

God bless jujitsu. Leverage is *good.*

"Mother*fucker!*" I yelled, cutting through the noise that was his howling and the screams of several grown men. I yanked back on the whip, twisting it, and choked him off. That brought down the volume somewhat. "Mother*fucking cock*sucking *son* of a *bitch*, what the *fuck* are you doing here? Huh? Having yourself some fun? *Huh? What the fuck are you doing here?*"

Rosie was making a lot of noise. I snapped a glance over my shoulder, just to make sure there wasn't anything nightside-ish to worry about. Nope, she was just getting the boys back, shoving

Paloma in front of her and yelling like a battlefield general. She was getting them into a firing line, and while I appreciated that, I was going to have to kick her ass for keeping herself and other cops in danger while I was working.

Just as soon as I took care of this fucker here. Which reminded me: I needed to ease up on the whip, or he was going to collect his eternal reward without telling me what he knew.

And we couldn't have that, now could we.

I untwisted the taut leather a little bit, listened to him wheeze. Snapped another glance back. Rosie had the blues spread out, some of them kneeling, their backs to the brush. *"Rosenfeld!"* I yelled. *"Get them back to the road, goddammit!"*

The Trader was shuddering. It took me a second or two to realize he was *laughing.* Cold fury boiled through me, I choked him a little, and the laughter cut off. Creaking leather loosened when I figured I'd shown him there was nothing funny about the situation.

I heard Rosie and the others moving. Thank God. "Now." I kept my balance. "Tell me what you're doing here, Trader, and I'll grant you a clean death."

Another weird, quacking laugh. Shaking his whole body like a seizure. If he felt his shattered knee, he didn't show it. "Hunter," he crooned, through a mouthful of dirt. I hoped I'd broken a few teeth. *"He* said you'd be here. This is a gift. *His* gift to you."

"Who?" No answer, so I choked up again a little until his body started juddering not with laughter but with panic. He was attached to his skin, this Trader. I let up a little. *"Who?"*

"Him." A retching, he spat dirt and snot and saliva. "The table's laid, the tide is turned. You're dead. You just don't know it."

Oh, please. Like I don't hear that or some variant every day. "The bodies. Who are they? Where are they from? It's not like I won't find out, so buy yourself some time. Make it easier on yourself."

He writhed under me, yellow grass smoking and flattening away as my aura hardened. He was strong, but he had no leverage. What the *hell* was he doing here?

A low creaking *sssssssssss* from behind me jerked my head around. The Trader started laughing again.

A thin line of blue hellfire crawled between the corpses, sharp little fingers poking and prodding. The bodies twisted and jerked, and the curse laid on them triggered with a *fwoosh* of flame. The Trader tried to heave me off, I shoved him back down and twisted the whip again to cut off that goddamn screeching laughter.

What the hell? But I knew. Someone was jerking me around. If I was called out here, something was happening somewhere *else*. Goddammit.

I braced myself, eased up a bit on the whip. "Tell me!" I yelled over the snap-crackle rush of unholy flame. The small clearing leapt with sterile light, shadows dancing like little imps. "Give me a motherfucking name, or I will start cutting!" *And hold bits of you in that goddamn fire over there for good measure.*

The Trader merely writhed. I realized something was wrong right before the secondary part of the curse laid on the bonfire of bodies snapped, a line of force snaking from the pit—

—straight for me. Or more precisely, for the Trader I was perched on top of.

Oh shi—

The world went white and turned over. I flew, weightless, and hit *hard*, snapping through brush and rolling to shed momentum. Thorns and other things tore at my coat, little grasping fingers. All the breath drove out of me in a huff, but no bones broke.

I struggled up to my feet, guns out, sweeping the clearing. The Trader was a twisting, jerking mass of flame and screaming. There was a sickening *crunch*; he fell like a dropped toy and lay in a burning heap. The bodies in the mass grave were writhing shadows, and the stench boiled out now that it was no longer laid under a shell of concealment. I scanned, trying to look everywhere at once, bracing for the attack. If a 'breed was going to hit me, they were going to do it now.

Nothing. The glare of hellfire stripped everything living of its substance, bleached the entire clearing and the bare branches on each trashwood bush. I waited, braced and ready, my pager going buzzwild again in my pocket. The *bezoar* had calmed down, just fluttering a little bit. It was like my coat was full of little animals, shivering away.

I exhaled sharply.

What the flying fuck?

This was a definite trap, but with no hellbreed lying in wait to kill me. So, the real problem was occurring elsewhere. And if Galina was trying this frantically to get hold of me...

First things first, Jill. Get that hellfire down, and check your cops for damage.

I got moving.

"I should kick your ass." I glared at Rosenfeld, but there was no heat to it. I was too relieved. The pile of bodies behind me smoked and let out a vile reek, the sky was brightening, and a plume of thin, greasy black smoke was rising in the windless hush. Curses and hellfire, what *next*?

"You looked like you could use some backup." Rosie glared back at me, her hands stuffed in the pockets of her leather jacket. She had wrinkled her nose exactly once at the smell. Beside her, Paloma held a snow-white handkerchief to his face. If it was an affectation, it was a useful one.

I could barely believe Rosie had agreed to Paloma. He was a mincing little martinet, and if he hadn't been so good at teasing order out of the chaos of long-cold homicide cases he would probably have been "promoted" into jockeying a desk somewhere Monty and his ilk decided he wouldn't do much harm. As it was, nobody wanted to partner up with the bastard, until Rosie had come back from her vacation ten pounds lighter and with those lines around her mouth, and stepped up to bat.

"Shoes," Paloma said from behind his handkerchief. His small, dark little eyes were avid. "He had the wrong shoes. The bodies were wrong, too. Naked and charred. It had your name all over it."

I nodded. Maybe he was trying to distract me from chewing Rosie a new one. If so, chivalry wasn't dead. But it was far more likely he was looking to get brownie points instead, so I magnanimously ignored him. "Jesus Christ, Rosie. The backup I need is not to worry about some of you catching a severe case of dead from tangling with a bastard Trader." I decided not to get bogged down in that. There was work to be done. "By the time you get Forensics out here the bodies will be cold; get them untangled. If we can identify *any* of them, I need to know yesterday." I'd already pulled out the Trader's wallet; I handed it over after glancing at the driver's license and memorizing the name and address. "Find out everything you can about this guy too, but *don't* go knocking on any doors. Just get me last-knowns. I'll check his truck before I leave; but I want you to go over it with a fine-tooth comb. I don't like the looks of this."

Rosie's jaw was set so hard it looked likely her teeth would shatter. She had to work to get them apart long enough to spit out two words. "What else?"

Jesus, Rosie. But I knew why she was angry. It had to do with a good cop's grave, and the fact that she still blamed herself. Or me. Or both of us.

If I'd just kept better tabs on Carper...but I hadn't. He'd brushed up against the nightside and paid the price, and I still hadn't found the dirty cop who'd pulled the trigger on me outside Galina's shop.

Goddammit, Jill, get back up on the horse. I scrubbed irritably at my forehead, dried blood and other gunk crackling as I worked it free. I'd pulled something in my leg, and it hurt enough that I shifted a little, easing it while the scar hummed wetly, pulling on etheric force. "Detail one of the black-and-whites to give me a ride. I've got to see what this was a distraction for."

I had a sick feeling beginning right under my breastbone. But *don't assume* is one of the first hunter laws for a reason. I didn't have enough information to guess at the pattern yet.

Paloma let out a whistling little laugh. "Hell of a distraction. Can't they just send you Christmas cards?"

My eyebrows shot up. If he cracked a few more like that I might actually get to like the prissy little bastard.

Rosie's face eased, bit by bit. "Careful, Ricky. That was suspiciously like a joke you just cracked there."

"Fuck you." He turned his nose up—quite a trick with the hankie still clapped against his face—and stepped gingerly away. I noticed, bemused, that he wore wingtips too. His were spitshine-polished, glossy black numbers. Even his socks matched his trousers.

He dug in the pocket of his natty gray suit for a cell phone, and I winced at the thought of whoever was on call for Forensics tonight coming out and getting a load of this. They were just going to love it.

Rosie and I faced each other. There was a lump in my throat and too much work pressing down on me. I settled for clapping her gingerly on the upper arm as I brushed past. My coat flapped a little, a whole new collection of rips and gouges letting air through. "Good work, Rosenfeld. You've got a hell of a battlefield yell."

"Thanks." The compliment apparently gave her no joy. "I suppose I'd better get the psychs out here too to eval everyone. That guy..." She glanced at the still-steaming pile of charred bones that had been the Trader.

Some of the cops were going to have nightmares after seeing me violate the laws of physics, not to mention the Trader's hellish snarl. The psych boys and girls were going to earn their cookies on this one.

"Yeah. Don't let anyone go home without a session with the counselors. I mean it. Even you, Rosie." *Because I would hate to lose any more cops to the nightside. I really would.*

You could never tell. A few people handled it just fine.

Others...not so much.

Her lip actually curled. "I don't need a fucking evaluation, Kismet. I've got pills for that."

And a patch of white in your hair you dye out every two weeks, not to mention some scars. You've seen the nightside and survived once. And she'd marched right down to my warehouse afterward to apologize for almost getting herself killed.

But sometimes it's the ones who have seen it before that crumble, too. You just can't ever tell. "Don't get cocky, Rosie. Get your eval and eat something, will you? You're losing your girlish figure."

"Don't you have some more property damage to commit, Kismet? Let me do my *job* here." All her walls up, a scowl to match one of Monty's best on her unpretty face, and she turned away. Paloma had jammed his phone shut and was issuing staccato orders; some of the blues were rolling their eyes. Rosie headed for the pile of charred flesh and stopped at its edge, looking down. Her shoulders were stiff, and her entire body closed in on itself like she wished she could disappear.

I let it go. My pager started buzzing again, and I told myself the prickling in my eyes was from the acrid smoke. The sun lifted above the rim of the earth, and I braced myself for a sleepless day.

CHAPTER 12

The Parks & Rec truck reeked of cigarette smoke and the fading perfume of hellbreed, but held nothing out of the ordinary. Vinyl seats, papers scattered everywhere, a plastic coffee cup half-full of ice-cold coffee and the rest filled up with used Camels filters. I glanced through the glove box, checked under the seats, gave the tires and undercarriage an exam.

Except for some fresh scratches on the bed, where something square and goddamn heavy had done a number on the paint job, there was nothing.

For the moment I was going to work on the assumption that the truck was stolen. I made sure there was nothing in there likely to make it blow up and cost me another couple cops, scanned it for any etheric disturbance, and decided to get out to Galina's. Cross-eye Garcia was tapped to give me a ride, and the entire way there he kept the scanner turned up to jet-takeoff level.

I guess I made him nervous. At least I kept the window down so he didn't have to smell me.

Golden light was beginning to stretch and lick between buildings by the time we got to the right neighborhood. He let me off a few streets away from Galina's, but before I got out I made sure he knew he wasn't going home until he had a session with the headshrinkers. He cursed me roundly for that, and I replied with a grin and a slam of his cruiser door.

"Fucking freakshow," he snarled before he gunned the engine and sped down the street, lights flashing.

I watched until he was out of sight, then disappeared into an alley, muscled up a fire escape, and cut across the rooftops. I circled Galina's house warily, twice. An exhausted dawn hush clung to concrete, brick, siding, and pavement. The etheric protections on Galina's shop reverberated uneasily, but they weren't tolling like bells.

I sometimes wondered how hunters in other cities functioned

without a Sanctuary around. Neutral supply of necessities to all the practitioners and quite a few of the nightsiders in a territory is the least of the services they provide. In Galina's case, she was the closest to a confessor I'd ever have.

The Church doesn't offer hunters Confession or Communion, because we traffic with Hell and commit the sin of murder every night. It was Galina who probably knew or guessed the most about me, with Mikhail dead. Saul didn't ask—he knew everything he needed to. Perry? Don't make me laugh—the more he thinks he knows, the less he actually does, and I want to keep it that way.

A chill finger touched my tired spine. *You're lying, Jill. He knows more than you think he does. You're only a hairsbreadth ahead each time he plays one of his games with you.*

A hairsbreadth was enough, wasn't it? I wasn't damned yet.

That was faint comfort indeed. And this was not a set of events guaranteed to make me feel better.

Ever since I'd gotten filled with plain lead right out in the middle of the street in front of the Sanctuary, I'd felt queasy coming in the front door. So this time, I dropped down soft as a cat from the neighboring rooftop, landing on hers. The greenhouse, its glass rapidly silvering as morning dew caught the dawn light, stood silent. Inside, green growing things breathed and dreamed.

The lock gave under my fingers and a tingle of sorcery. The color of the protections on the walls changed. I froze, and waited.

You do *not* drop in on a Sanctuary when she's upset. You let her know you're there, and you wait for her to let you in. Inside their thick walls, they have near-godlike powers.

I guess it makes up for being a tasty defenseless snack outside, kind of. But it would drive me utterly insane.

The protections calmed, flushing a dusky rose under a flood of mellow morning sunshine. I stepped inside, breathing in the smells of potting soil and fresh oxygen. My shoulders unhitched a little, before my pager buzzed again and cut off midway. Was that her calling again?

A long silver shape lay on a butcher-block table in the south quadrant of the greenhouse, placed for maximum exposure. It had been dead and black, a long time ago. Now the sunsword trembled eagerly against the table, its clawed crossguards chattering against the wood. The carved ruby at my throat woke up, warming, and the Talisman hummed a low, sustained note.

You can't have a sunsword without a key, after all. The Eye had been the original key, and with it gone, the ruby Mikhail had given me functioned quite handily as a secondary. Wearing both of them while I was worked up was bound to make the sunsword edgy.

The empty place in its clawed pommel held a glimmer of crimson light before I exhaled sharply, my will flexing. The sunsword went back to sleep, I drew in a nice deep breath, and the trapdoor in the floor was thrown open from below, slamming into the chair used to prop it so hard the chair leapt back like a bee-stung dog.

Galina clambered up through the hole. Her marcel waves were disarranged, there were dark circles under her green eyes, and she was in her sleeping gear: boxers and a ragged blue Popfuzz T-shirt. Behind her, Hutch peered up through the trapdoor, his hair sticking up like a bird's nest. He let out an undignified *eep!* and vanished.

"Jill." Galina was breathless. The mark of the Order at her throat—the quartered circle surrounded by a serpent, a solid chunk of silver—glimmered. The walls resounded to her distress, and the morning light was very kind to her. "Jill, be very careful. *Be very careful.*"

I almost rocked back on my heels. *Oh, Jesus.* "I got your pages. What's up?"

"I want you to be calm," she continued, running right over the top of me. "I just want you to be calm. Calm down."

"I'm perfectly calm." I was beginning to get a hell of a bad feeling, but I was nice and chilly. "What the fuck?"

A familiar dark head rose up through the trapdoor. But it wasn't Saul. It was Gilberto, and the instant he looked at me, his dead dark eyes flat and expressionless, I knew.

The world ground to a stop. I actually swayed.

"Oh, Jill." Galina backed up two steps when I looked at her, fetching up against another table, this one holding empty pots and small shovels, twine, bamboo rods for bracing weak plants. Everything jumped, once, like a group of trained dogs twitching in unison. "It was right out in the street. We couldn't—there was *nothing—*"

"Shut. Up." It isn't the sort of thing you say to a Sanctuary in her own home. But she stopped talking, high flags of color in her pale cheeks. My face felt strange, like it didn't belong to me. Lying against my bones like a mask. "Gilberto?"

He finished climbing up, brushed his lean brown hands together as if ridding them of dust. Coppery highlights came out in his lank dark hair as he stepped into a bar of sunshine. "You takin' me with you, *bruja*." Flat and unironic. "We gonna have to burn some fuckers for this, *es verdad*."

I didn't want to ask. My traitorous mouth opened. The most banal thing possible came out. "I'm late. Has Saul finished breakfast?"

Because there was still time for God to see He'd made a mistake, and take it back. I should have known better. God doesn't work that way.

He never has.

"Oh, Jill..." Galina's hand clapped over her mouth.

"They took him," Gilberto said. "They took *el gato hombre, mi profesora*. 'Breed and Traders. He put up a good fight. She"—he jerked his head at Galina, who grabbed the table as if it was driftwood and she was drowning—"knocked me 'cross the fuckin' room, ay? I was gonna go out."

Galina peeled her fingers away from her lips. "You would have gotten killed. Jill left you under *my* care. It was in the street; if he'd just been a little bit closer—"

Is he still alive? Not dead? "Galina." I didn't recognize my own voice. The trembling was in my arms, my legs. "Shut up. Please. Just for five seconds."

She did. If there had been a clock, it would have ticked heavily in the thick silence. The scar burned against my wrist, and the sunsword chattered once more against the table. It was hard work to get it to stay still, with the Eye on my chest and the ruby at my throat spitting sparks. *One, two.* Little crackles of blue electricity.

Three. Four. Five. Then I counted again, because I still couldn't put the words together. Finally, they came.

My throat was full of bitter ash. "Now." I had to work to speak above a whisper. "We're going to go downstairs. I need a new shirt and ammo. And grenades. And while you get those for me you are going to tell me *everything*."

"I go with you." Gilberto's face settled into sallow stubbornness. "You hear me, *bruja*? I go with you."

"Gilberto," I said very softly, "do not fuck with me right now. Tell me everything you remember while I get a clean shirt." I thought for a second. "And for God's sake don't get close to me." It hurt to say it. The sunsword chattered again, and my hands were making fists and uncurling, completely independent of me. "I'm not safe."

CHAPTER 13

The Pontiac leapt forward, clearing the slight hill and going airborne. Landed with a jolt. This was not my usual intuition-tingling run through the streets, threading through traffic like a spaceship flying low. No, this was pure *pedal to the metal, balls to the wall, get the hell out of my way, don't care if I do hit someone.* The engine thrummed, a subtle knocking I hadn't been able to suss out yet in its high-level harmonics.

For the first time while driving this fast, I didn't try to diagnose it. No, I just leaned forward, hands on the wheel, and willed the metal to go faster. Dawn was fully broken, morning everywhere bright as a hangover and full of knife-sharp shadows, the kind of solid black you only get very early on a clear morning in the winter desert.

Luckily every street I chose was pretty lonely at this hour, and the few black-and-whites that saw me knew my car. They don't interfere when I go screaming through the streets, no matter what time of day or night it is. Sometimes, if I've called in, they even cut traffic for me. Not often—they can't keep up.

Between the scene Rosenfeld and Paloma were still probably working and this, the betting pool was going to be a-chatter this morning. I hear they have a whole system for betting on when and where I'll show up, how long before someone sees me, how many bodies at the last scene I visited. Macabre? Maybe.

But they know that when I disappear, it's time to get nervous.

Gilberto had tried to insist on coming along. I'd ignored him, told Galina to keep him under wraps. I did not want my apprentice taken too. That would leave me with too many hellbreed to kill, and having to make a choice between my duty to him and the way my entire body burned at the thought of Saul in danger, in trouble, hurt...

I did not want to make that choice. I knew what I would choose, and it would damn me in the only place that mattered—my own conscience.

Tires screaming, I jagged around a lumbering streetsweeper, cut up 182nd the wrong way between the last block of Sarvedo and Tigalle, and floored the accelerator again. Now I was in the industrial section, bouncing over railroad tracks, approaching the Monde Nuit from the edges of the block of slaughterhouses that huddled near the railyards.

The drive from Galina's to the Monde can take as long as forty-five minutes in bad traffic. Twenty at normal speeds. I made it in ten and slewed into the parking lot, tires smoking, bailing out almost before the Pontiac had come to a stop. Running, each stride taking far too long. My coat snapped and fluttered like a flag in a stiff wind.

The Monde is a long low building, crouching in a shallow depression of brackish etheric contamination. There was usually muscle at the door, Trader beefbags the size of small outhouses, with utterly illegal submachine guns. The edges of the parking lot were unpaved, and dust rose in odd swirls as the corruption creeping out in concentric circles met the tired sunlight and flinched back.

I'd probably arrived just at shift change, because there were no bouncers looming outside. I hit the wide oak double doors so hard they both flew open, the hydraulic arms atop them popping hard as they exploded. Little bits of metal and plastic rained down, but I was already through. Sparks crackled, a roaring in my ears.

"Perry!" I yelled, the scar turned into a live coal pressed in the flesh of my arm. Jolts of pain sawed up my nerves. *"Goddamn you, Perry!"*

The place was deserted. No Traders finishing up the night's

games, no hellbreed at the bar, crouched on stools and hiding from the sun. The dance floor was empty, just like the stage. Dust danced in the golden shafts struggling in through keyhole skylights.

It was just like Perry to allow the sun, that great cleanser, a few fingers inside his hideout.

The only motion was at the bar, where Riverson set the bottle of vodka down with a click. His gray-filmed eyes, a little like the caretaker out at the Hill, fixed on me. But while the caretaker's gaze was mild and kind, Riverson's is just plain blind. Still, he sees a lot more than most with sight or Sight.

Behind him, bottles glowed on glass shelves. Some of them even held liquor instead of the various substances nightsiders used to give themselves a kick or two.

The vodka bottle shattered, liquid steaming as it hit dyed-russet concrete flooring. I had Riverson by the throat, dragging him over the bar. He was amazingly light, his strength only human. I don't know what he'd Traded to end up here, or how he survived night after night serving drinks to the scions of Hell.

I don't care, either. He's living on borrowed time just like the rest of them.

He flailed ineffectually. I batted one of his fists away and put the gun to his forehead. "Where?" I barked, and the word bounced back off the concrete, hurt my ears. "So help me, you helltrading blind man, I *will* kill you. *Where?*"

He choked, his face gone plummy and his filmed eyes rolling like a horse's. I realized he couldn't talk with me holding his throat like that and eased up a fraction, ready to clamp down again. I did not trust Riverson as far as I could throw him. Mikhail had come in here to pump the old man for information while I was still an apprentice. It was on one of those visits that Perry showed up at the end of the bar, dressed in pale linen and leering at me.

Misha had almost drawn down on him. Sometimes I thought it would have gone better if he had.

"—stop—" Riverson was still choking, and for a moment I struggled with the urge to close my fist and feel the little bones in his neck snap-crackle-pop. I could crush the larynx like a rotted fruit. It would take only a moment's worth of work, and it would be so worth it.

But it would not lead me to Saul.

I kept the gun to his forehead. Checked the interior of the Monde again. If Perry was upstairs in his white office, watching this on closed-circuit...but no. There was no betraying stain of a hellbreed's plucking at the fabric of reality in the whole building. Nothing but the syrupy well of etheric contamination, dark and swirling drowning-deep in some places. And Riverson's frail humanness, his pulse struggling as his face turned an even deeper plum-brick shade.

I eased up the rest of the way, though my entire body shook with the effort. "Talk fast, old man." Chill and sharp, I didn't sound like myself. I didn't sound like Mikhail, either. There was no edge of hurtful glee to my tone, either, which meant I didn't sound like Perry. Which was a blessing.

I might have shot someone, otherwise.

No, I sounded like a woman utterly prepared to kill whoever got in her way. Truth in advertising was making a comeback.

Riverson coughed, deep hacking sounds as his color eased. The colorless, nose-stinging fume of spilled vodka rose. "—*mercy*—" he managed to get out, and that was almost the last straw.

I pressed the gun to his forehead so hard I felt his skull under the thin skin, and the concrete under his head. "I am not in the business of mercy today, *old man*. Where is my Were?"

Shock softened his features. He coughed again, and even with the thick gray webbing covering his eyeballs he looked surprised and puzzled. "Huh?" Another deep racking sound, his entire body curling up like a worm on a fishhook. "What? The fuck?"

My temper almost snapped. The gun clicked, and he flinched.

"Did you miss the part where I am *not fucking around*?" The words hit a crescendo. "*Where is my Were, God damn you!*"

"I don't *know*!" Riverson yelled. "I was left here with a message! *Days* ago! *Jesus Christ Kismet don't shoot me, it's not my fault!*"

My fingers cramped with the need to squeeze the trigger. I lifted the gun, and it roared. The bullet smashed into a pile of electronic equipment on the stage. Sparks flew. Riverson screamed, the sound of a rabbit in a trap, and I pressed the smoking barrel to his forehead again. It sizzled. The scream ended on a whimper.

"Start talking." There was something in my throat. It made it hard to get the words out without a guttural growl.

The cold voice of calculation and percentage spoke up. *Don't kill him, Jill. Don't do it. Not yet.*

"It's not my fault! Perry left me here. He thought you'd be here before now, *way* before now. He's in trouble. Bad trouble."

"How exactly is that my problem?" But I had a sinking sensation in the middle of my belly, right next to the ball of unsteady rage.

"His problem *is* your problem, Kismet. They're bringing through another hellbreed. A bigger one. According to the higher-ups Perry hasn't been pulling his weight for years now. He's been fobbing them off with one excuse after another—"

I bounced his head off the concrete once. It felt good, but I didn't want to do it again. Might make it harder to question him if he got all dizzy and concussed. "Cry me a river and tell me another lie."

"No lie! *No lie!* Perry's in hiding! He needs your help! He even pulled in that Sorrows bitch—"

"Belisa." My breath hissed through the name. "Oh, I know. Where? Where is the son of a bitch? *And* that little whore too."

"I *don't know* where he is!" Screaming. Blood slicked the left side of his face, bright red. It stank of copper, only the faintest trace of black showing he'd Traded for something. "He's got some kind of hold on her, some collar, I don't know what! He left me here—bait, and with the message for you."

"What message?" I was regretting not killing him outright. Now I was going to have to let him live, at least until I found out everything he knew. *And* separated the fiction from the truth.

Something was nagging at me. *A gift. His gift to you.* I shelved it. More immediate things to worry about.

Riverson coughed, his throat rasping. "The back room. *That* room. He left you a present. *She's* in there."

For a moment the words refused to make sense. *Oh, my fucking God.* The world snapped into a different configuration behind my eyeballs. "Alive, or dead?"

"I don't know. Jesus Christ, Kismet—"

"There's an awful lot you don't know." Cold and considering.

"You're going to have to know something pretty soon, Riverson, to keep your head on your shoulders."

"I told you to stay away from him! I warned you not to come back! I did everything I could!" He didn't dare squirm. *"I did what Mikhail asked!"*

Another electric jolt through me. This was getting me nowhere. "You do not," I said, as quietly and evenly as I could, "speak my teacher's name, Riverson. The bitch is in the back room? *That* room?"

He almost nodded, caught himself when I jammed the gun against his skull again. "Y-yes. That room. Kismet, you should know something. That scar—the mark—"

"Did I ask you a question, Riverson?" I took the gun away but still held myself ready. He had only human strength, true.

But that could have just meant that he'd Traded for something else.

"You need to know." A whisper, like he was a kid scared of the dark. The blood slicking his face was too vivid, too bright. "If I don't tell you now, I'll never get a chance. *He* was always listening. Through my ears. Through my *head*."

He. One single syllable, carrying a weight of loathing and fear. No question who he was talking about, either. I dug for handcuffs, still keeping an eye on him. "Make it quick, then. I don't have time for this shit."

"Did you ever wonder why *he* made you the bargain?"

I almost shrugged, decided not to. It might disturb my balance. The cuffs jangled, their silver coating running with sluggish blue light. "He thinks he can get something." It was a moment's work to roll Riverson over, he offered no resistance. I had him cuffed in a few seconds, tested them. Good. "You can tell him he's wrong."

"You're wrong." The words were muffled against the floor. Head wounds are messy; he didn't look pretty. Still, it wouldn't kill him. It would be foolish to feel any sympathy.

"Do yourself a favor and don't piss me off right now, old man." I levered myself up, restrained the urge to kick him. It would serve no purpose. "And stay there."

Riverson actually laughed. The jagged edges of that sound rubbed every inch of me the wrong way. I took a deep breath. The first priority was finding Saul, but now I had to check that back room. I set off with long swinging strides.

If Melisande Belisa was back there, I would have a few words with her. And if it was a trap, I would spring it and find out what the fuck was happening. Either way, I won.

"He never let you do it with the lights on, did he?" Riverson yelled into the floor. His blood, slicking his face and dripping on the concrete, made the words bubble weirdly. "You never saw *his* mark, did you? Inside of the right thigh, high up, because Perry's not shy. A scar like a star."

I turned on my heel. My boot heels clicked. Three steps. Four. I reached Riverson again. Crouched, my hellbreed-strong right hand flashing out and curling in his graying hair. I dragged his face up, ignoring how the rest of his body torqued uncomfortably.

"What are you playing at?"

"Never with the lights on." His lips stretched, rubbery, around the words. "That's what he told me. Why no woman would ever see that scar. And he never wanted you to go down on—"

Cold went through me, and sick heat. The scar was a hot, hard knot on my wrist, tasting the corruption and misery filling this place. *Did he just say to me what I* think *he said to me?*

He *was* saying what I thought he was saying, I realized. He was intimating that my teacher had traded with Perry too.

My left hand flashed. The slap was a crack, and I dropped him. "Spread your filth elsewhere," I said softly, and Riverson sagged against the floor. A faint blubbery sound reached me.

The old man was crying. In messy gulps, like a child. My lip curled. If it was a mindfuck, it wasn't even worthy of the name. Mikhail and I had been closer than close, in bed and out of it...

...but here I was, with his Talisman again, heading back to see if his killer was waiting for me.

His *murderer*. The woman he had hidden from me. The Sorrows bitch who had killed him and stolen his treasure. He had lied to me about where he'd gone and what he'd done each time he went to hook up with her. In alleys, shitty hotel rooms, maybe even in his Mercedes. The same car I'd torched after the Weres built him a pyre to light him on his way to Valhalla.

And no, Mikhail never wanted me to go down on him. I'd been

too grateful for his tact, too starry-eyed with the thought that he wanted *me*, to ever do it. It isn't the sort of thing I like, especially given where I came from.

What he rescued me from when he pulled me from that snow-bank and told me *not tonight*.

He'd been a mass of scars. How could you tell one from another? Only a lover could. *I* could. But I'd never taken a look at that particular portion of his body. It just . . .

Oh, *shit*. Maybe it was a good mindfuck after all.

But I'd be damned if I would listen to it.

Doors in the Monde. One leads to a long corridor, rooms rented by the hour opening up on either side. Trades go down in here, meet-ings between the 'breed that carve up Santa Luz and occasionally test to see if I'm still on the job, various acts best hidden from daylight and even moonlight. Another leads behind the stage, to a long gallery where performers get ready before their "shows." There's one behind the bar that leads to the cellar, where the liquor and other liquids are stored.

The truly frightening one, behind a red velvet rope, opens up on narrow stairs that lead to Perry's white-carpeted, pristine apartment. I hadn't been up there in a good long while, and the last time—

Don't think about that, Jill. Focus on the job at hand.

I took the first door. Kicked it twice, the scar pumping etheric energy through me. The iron sounded like huge gong strikes, shock jolting all the way through me. Showy, but I wanted no surprises.

On the third kick, the door crumpled like paper. If Perry wanted to find me, he probably could through the etheric force I kept recklessly drawing through the scar. I'd keep using it freely, as long as I could. It gave me an edge.

And every time I pulled on it, I hope Perry felt it like a slap to the face. Especially now.

The corridor stretched off to the side. Any place hellbreed spend a lot of time in warps a little bit. The geometry starts look-ing weird, angles not fitting together right. It's enough to give you a headache if you're not a hunter. If you can't see below the *twist-*

ing and untangle the tricks of perception and illusion. My smart eye turned hot and dry, working overtime.

Nothing behind the door. But it smelled. Rot, both animal and vegetable, with the sharp copper tang of blood over it. The smell belched out over me with hot, sweaty meatbreath. My nose barely wrinkled. Of all the things about a hunter's job, the varied and disgusting stenches are not even close to the worst. You just learn to put your head down and go through.

It could be a metaphor for life, I guess.

The thought I'd been trying not to think came back with a vengeance. *His gift to you.* Who would leave an open mass grave for me? Especially one with curses that triggered into flame while someone was kidnapping my Were?

Who else? If it wasn't Perry, it was a hellbreed trying too hard.

I covered the hall with both guns. The room I was aiming for was at the very end. The door was ajar, too, a slice of ruddy light marrying with the low, ugly glow from the red bulbs marching down on either side of the hall.

"*Kismet!*" Riverson blubbered. "Don't! Get out of town! Go as far as you can! *He wants your soul!*"

Like I hadn't always known *that.* "Of course he does," I muttered. "That's nothing new." And I plunged forward into the hot close dimness.

The doors weren't staggered, and there was nothing waiting behind any of them. I went carefully, though impatience beat behind my heart, each thud of my pulse crying out for me to be doing something else. To start shooting and not stop until I'd untangled this whole mess and found my Were.

Moments ticked by. It was unbearably hot in here, but then it usually was. There's no air-conditioning in Hell.

The rooms were empty of living things. Some had beds, from narrow iron bedsteads to ornate four-posters complete with straps. A few had hard benches, or frames to strap bodies into. A few were completely empty, either tiled or carpeted on walls, floor, ceiling. All had drains in the middle of the floor and a slight slope downward from each wall, to make hosing off the night's effluvium easier.

The room at the end was normally a conference chamber, for

meetings. I nudged the door open further, guns ready and nerves at the breaking point. Crimson light washed the room—the chandelier had been taken out, replaced with a festoon of cords holding bare red bulbs like poisoned fruit. The long mirror-polished table was still there, but with one long zigzag crack down the middle. The chairs, even the iron throne that sat at the head of the table, were demolished. There wasn't anything left bigger than a pinkie-fingernail sliver.

It looked like a hell of a fight had gone down in here.

What the hell?

The wall at the end of the room, behind the ruin of the iron chair Perry settled in whenever there was a Big Meeting among the 'breed, dripped with slick metal worms. I blinked. After a moment I realized they were *chains*, and they moved slightly.

A wrongly musical clashing cut the static-laden silence. There, wrapped in orichalc-tainted chains, a slim female figure hung. Rags of deep blue silk twitched as she breathed, fitfully. Long blue-black hair, now tangled and rat-snarled. A hint of tilted cat-like to the eyes in her bruised mass of a face. Her skin was a little darker than the Sorrows usually preferred, but well within canons. Her eyes, if open, would be the limitless black of the adept who has practiced for more than four cycles of their calendar; black from lid to lid, no iris or white to break the unnatural gaze. She wore delicate golden eardrops, and the bruising of Chaldean my blue eye could see in her aura was disciplined, a parasitical symbiote.

The Elder Gods give to those who serve them well, almost as often as they consume them. The Elders are hungry, and ever since the shadowy Lords of the Trees locked them away from our world they've grown hungrier. The Sorrows can't hope to undo the great sorcery the *Imdarák* worked; a whole race burned up its life to seal the Elder Gods behind a wall.

But that wall could sometimes be breached. That was Sorrows' business.

Melisande looked like she'd been worked over pretty good. There was something clasped around her neck, too. A gleam of iron, but I couldn't see it through the writhing of the silvery chains.

Last time she'd played wounded on me, too. In conjunction with Perry. A shiver of loathing threatened to rise up my spine, was repressed, died away.

I examined everything from the door. What the hell had *happened* in here? Sorrows and hellbreed don't mix. At least, they don't *usually* mix. 'Breed wanted this world for their own as well, and they don't play nice or share.

I surprised myself by stepping into the room. Hellbreed taking my Were might not lead here, but Perry was bound to be my first suspect. And just look at the interesting things I was finding. The Talisman warmed against my skin, its chain vibrating slightly.

Of course it would react to the woman who had torn it from Mikhail's chest after she slit his throat. Or it could have been my response triggering the Eye's notice. The adrenaline dumping into my bloodstream, the rage rising, the little click inside my head threatening to occur yet again. That click is the sound of a bullet loaded into a clip. It is also the sound of lifting away, breaking free, of little things like mercy and compassion closed away so you can get what needs to be done, *done*. Without counting the cost, and without hesitating.

I don't know if I am a hunter because of the click...or in spite of it.

I kicked through shattered chairs, working my way up the side of the table. Every inch of silver on me warmed and ran with blue light. I swept the room with my left-hand gun, tested the walls with every nonphysical sense I possessed. No traps.

Nothing except the soft slither of the chains moving. The scar ran with soft wet fire, tasting the misery pressing down on every exposed surface. It pulsed, silently, and the chains shivered. Their slippery clashing intensified, and Melisande Belisa's breathing body sagged against their loosening. The thing around her neck shimmered faintly, but at this distance and with the interference of the orichalc chains I couldn't tell what was going on. Her eyelids fluttered. Her breathing changed, from shallow sipping to harsh rasps. Heaving against the chains, blood-crusted blue silk moving over her ribs.

It was not the throat-cut gurgle of Mikhail's body clasped in my arms, the life leaving him in great scarlet gouts. Red as the light, his blood, with no tinge of black. But then, I bled red, too. Without a single trace of corruption.

I wasn't going to start believing Riverson's lies. Not now.

Cold sweat stood out all over me. I lowered my right-hand gun. I didn't trust myself not to shoot her.

Goddammit, Jill, put her down. She's a Sorrow. Just like a goddamn rattlesnake. Kill it now before it bites.

But shooting her now would not help me get to the bottom of this. I breathed carefully, trying to calm down and think clearly. Also trying to get in enough oxygen through the nauseating, cloying reek.

I'd been held down by orichalc-tainted chains once. A bugfuck-crazy Sorrows Grand Mother wanted to use me to incubate one of their hungry, trapped Elder Gods. Melisande had baited me into the trap, and double-crossed Perry as well. If this was his idea of a gift, like a cat leaving a mouse at its human's door—

His gift to you.

But no. *No.* It was too easy, too simple. There was a hook in this bait. And if Perry had taken Saul, all bets were off.

I could not be *absolutely* certain Perry was responsible. But who else would do something like this?

Any hellbreed who hated me. Which meant any hellbreed in Santa Luz, or at least any 'breed crazy enough to think I would not tear the city apart to find them and administer vengeance.

I took another step. Agony raced up my right arm, cramping my fingers and sawing against the nerve strings. I exhaled, hard, against the sensation. It was for all the world like a red-hot key turning in the scar, digging in, tumblers clicking.

What the—

The chains *moved.* They slid away like fat snakes, and Melisande Belisa's body fell, a limp-jointed doll. Her skull cracked against laminated wood flooring laid over concrete. I felt a nasty burst of satisfaction, quickly smothered. I weighed the advisability of taking a closer look at that iron collar she was wearing. It looked like a heavy piece of work, and thin golden light glinted on it. I shifted my weight to step forward.

Outside, in the well of the Monde, I heard movement. A high, thin giggle. And Riverson's despairing scream.

CHAPTER 14

I just barely cleared the hall. Normally I'd want them to come at me one at a time, but Riverson was still screaming and I didn't want to be trapped with Belisa at my back, even if she was unconscious when I left her in the shattered conference room.

Four 'breed, dark-haired males. Just as many Traders, all of them frozen and snarling as I burst through the hole in the wall where the iron door used to be. One of the Traders—pale, shark's teeth, claws and joints altered strangely so he crouched like a spider—hunched over Riverson, tittering. My first shot took the titterer in the shoulder and he folded down shapelessly, a gout of black-laced crimson hanging in the air behind him as time slowed down and the mark turned into a live coal against my skin.

There's one certain way to get your ass handed to you while you're fighting hellbreed. That's to do it while distracted. Everything vanished but the fight in front of me, and it was a relief.

The Monde is familiar territory. I've fought there before, and I know its interior. I should have worked back along the wall to my left and gained the high ground of the stage. Instead I ended up in the middle of blank space, Traders circling and the 'breed hanging back, Riverson moaning like a child caught in a bad dream and twisting against the handcuffs.

I did not particularly care if he came down with a severe case of dead. I *did* care if he did so without giving me all the information he had, and I wasn't fool enough to think that he had. Yet.

When they recovered from the shock of finding me here instead of Perry, things were going to get ugly. So, I got ugly first.

Sometimes, the best defense is an attack. I put the one in front of me down with two shots, and the hole in the circling ring closed almost instantly. A half turn, another shot, but this one went wide because my instincts screamed and I threw myself aside, aiming to break for the stage. It was still my best shot, especially since all of them were focusing on me and not on the screaming blind bartender.

It just became a question of which ones were going to be in my way when I broke for it. But first I had to deal with the Trader leaping on me. The whip cracked, silver jangling.

No hunter carries a whip just because. We do it to give ourselves extra reach. It buys us those critical seconds of shock and pain, extends the circle of how far we can lay on the hurt. And this time it just might save my ass. If I could kill a few more of them.

The Trader dropped without a sound. Then they all jumped, and it became a melee.

When you're clearing a hellbreed hole, there's one good thing. You don't have to worry about where you're shooting, because every shot will get someone who deserves it. All I had to do here was avoid hitting Riverson, who technically *did* deserve it, but still.

The click inside my head sounded, and every edge and surface stood out in sharp clarity. The shining path of action and reaction unfurled inside my head, and I dropped into that state of fighter's grace where every bullet bends to your will and each one is a life taken. Hellbreed ichor splattered, I was somehow on my knees, bending back while firing, the whip curling. Then I was up again, a shutterclick of motion and I rolled sideways, gaining my feet in a convulsive leap as the body hit the concrete with a sound like a wet, rotting pumpkin tossed from an overpass. The stage was coming up fast, nobody between me and it, but any moment now one of the smarter ones might get the idea to head back toward Riverson and see if I twitched.

So I spun, heels skidding and striking sparks, and bolted straight for them again. They scattered, one of them keening in a high, unearthly wail. One more down, the blood exploding from his mouth and painting the floor in a splattering gout. I shot him again to make sure, calculations flashing through my brain. How much ammo was left in the gun, what the next move was, how far it was to Riverson, who was crawfishing wildly on the floor, trying to get out of the handcuffs. I could have used a silver-laced grenade, but the chances of fragging the person I had to question further were too high, and if I slowed down to get him behind the bar with me I might end up dead.

A copper-pale streak in the corner of my peripheral vision. *What the fu—*

The world turned over, hard. Down on the floor, trigger pulled, the 'breed on top of me snarling. It was the one with long greasy dreadlocks and a tubercular flush, cherry red lips widening and spraying me with hot acid spittle. Scrabbling, hand slapping a knife hilt and pulling it free, stabbing and twisting and had to *move* to get him *off* me, or I'd be swarmed and they would pull me limb from limb like a fly in the hands of a cruel little boy.

I shot him twice more, the silver smashing through his torso. This time I didn't have to switch to knives; the stupid bastard was lying on my guns. Crunching. Wet rasping sounds. A howl. A scream, cut short on a gurgle. I shoved the mass of decaying hell-breed off me and gained my knees—

—and stopped, staring in amazement.

Melisande Belisa, stark naked except for a heavy iron collar running with thin golden scratches, the bruising of Chaldean crawling over her skin and aura, twisted the last Trader's head in her delicate hands. The greenstick crack of a neck breaking echoed, and Riverson's screams died away. He hitched in a breath, but some instinct probably warned him to keep quiet and hope neither of us noticed him.

Those black eyes came up to mine, and under the mask of bruising on her face, the Sorrow smiled gently. Her teeth were small and white, one of the front ones jaggedly broken, and as I watched it fell out, hitting the concrete with a small definite sound. That gap-tooth grin was wide, friendly, and utterly chilling. A new sliver of white broke through the bloody pink cavern in her gums.

Just like a shark, I thought. *There's always another tooth waiting.*

Broken bodies lay strewn around. The last 'breed hit the door at a good clip, tumbling out into sunlight. I stared.

The Sorrow rose fluidly from her crouch. Took two tiny staggering steps. Then her black eyes rolled up into her head and she slumped, going to her knees and keeling over. The collar ran with weird gold wires of light. She ended up curled in the fetal position, and a rumble of sorcery died away, swirling back into her bruised, coppery skin. Shadows moved, like the dappled shade of leaves on a hot day, over her flesh.

Chaldean sorcery. How many of them had she put down?

Riverson was making a soft sucking sound like a child caught in a nightmare. For a few moments I just knelt there and stared.

Then the need to get moving started deep in my bones, an itch like chickenpox. I hauled myself up and dug in my pocket for another set of handcuffs.

Perry had redecorated, but not much. Plush white carpet, a mirrored bar gleaming along one side ranked with pristine clear bottles, either empty or full of shifting gray smoke that made screaming faces when I glanced at it. The bank of television screens was there, but only the closed-circuit ones were live, showing the interior of and entrances to the Monde. The others, usually filled with news feeds, were blank and dead like gouged-out eyes.

The bed, draped with white gauze and a snowy counterpane, was there too. Belisa's nakedness lay tossed over it, shadows crawling over her skin and retreating. The Chaldean sorcery would repair her inside and out, bringing her into perfect order soon enough. She hadn't taken nearly enough damage to put a Sorrow down.

I held the gauze down over his head wound, taped it. Didn't care if I caught his graying hair on the tape and he'd have to pull it off. Riverson shuddered. His filmy eyes blinked madly. His upper lip was slicked with snot.

At least he was still breathing.

"There." I took a deep breath. "Who were they, Riverson? Where do I start looking?" *And where is my Were?* I still couldn't rule out Perry taking him. Though I had to consider that maybe the masked 'breed could have something to do with it—but why would he, or whoever he was working for, distract me with a pile of bodies and take Saul? As an opening gambit? Why not just kill him, too?

That was an unhelpful thought. To say the least.

I glanced at the bed again, checking the Sorrow. She was out cold, or at least she looked like it.

I couldn't kill her just yet. I had to find out what she was up to.

I was beginning to wish I had access to some of those chains downstairs, though. Silver-plated handcuffs were not going to cut it for a Sorrow, though the collar looked vaguely familiar. The golden light turned out to be runes running under the surface of the metal, the queer, fluidly spiked writing of the Chaldean ceremonial alphabet.

Which was thought-provoking. The runes marched in orderly streams, like ants following formic trails.

He was shivering so hard his graying, blood-soaked hair quivered. "I. Thought. Thought we were. Dead."

"You almost were." *And you're close to it now, too.* I stepped back, my boots leaving dark prints on the carpet. There was a trail from the door to the bed, and I kept half an eye on the closed-circuit screens. "Start talking, blind man. You're a lucky bastard, you know that? Who were they? Who do they work for? What faction wants me dead this much?" *And where the hell is Perry?*

He swallowed several times, throat working. "I ..."

A slow singsong female purr came from the bed, the sibilants slightly slurred. "Oh, don't be shy." Melisande was awake. "Have you been telling secrets? You've been naughty, little man."

If you've ever heard a Sorrow pronounce the word *man*, you've heard the very meaning of contempt. There are two functions for males inside a Sorrows House—warrior drone or slave.

Neither has a very long life span.

Now I had to keep an eye on Belisa too, as well as the closed-circuit. Fortunately I'd settled myself against the bar at an angle where I could see everything and the door, too.

I would have bet it was right where Perry habitually stood. The thought filled me with unsteady loathing. That is, any sliver of me the red tide of rage wasn't flooding.

"Don't pay any attention to Chaldean whores, Riverson." The words fell flat in the motionless air. Here in Perry's bedroom, the corruption was thick and rank, and the scar plucked wetly against my forearm. The Talisman vibrated against my chest, a second heartbeat. "I'm all you need to worry about right now." *And boy howdy, should you be worrying.*

"I can tell you who has taken your pet, Judith." Soft and slip-sliding, she spoke as if she was in the incense-dark hush of a House. "I can tell you much more besides. I see my gift reached its destination intact. Do you like having it back?"

I was halfway to the bed without realizing it, the gun free in my hand and Riverson shrinking back against the glass and chrome of the bar. The effort of stopping made sweat spring up all over me, prickling as if each droplet was a fine hair.

That name. That goddamn name.

She'd cherry-picked it out of Mikhail's files, and it had won me the chance to slip free of the monthly visits to Perry. If Perry hadn't been so hot to use his newfound psychological leverage on me, I might have fallen neatly into his trap. Instead, I'd fallen into Belisa's.

And here she was again, mouthing the name of a dead girl. A girl with dark hair, wide, brown eyes and a bright, needy smile. A girl who had shivered on a street corner, whose ghost Mikhail had pulled out of a snowbank and *remade*.

The shadow of my right-hand gun twitched against pale carpeting. I forced the barrel down.

Careful, Jill. Be very careful. She's in cahoots with Perry. Don't do something that will damn you. There wasn't a good enough reason to kill her yet.

When she was on her feet and ready to fight back, when I knew what was going on and how she fit into it, when I had Saul back and this little situation all tied up neatly, *that* was when she could die.

But it would be so *satisfying* to blow her head off. And there she was, naked on the bed, one of her coppery haunches lifted as her body lay torqued. Her hair, tangled and sticky with dried blood and helbreed ichor, made small whispering sounds against the comforter. The bruises were fading, driven back by the leaf-dappled shadow of Chaldean. The collar was thick enough to clasp her neck and rest on her slim shoulders, and the Chaldean script on it made me uneasy.

"Funny." The word stuck in my throat. "Perry said it was from him. You two should get your stories straight."

She was wriggling over on her side to look at me. I lifted the gun again, and there was a small, definite *click*. She froze, and that was good. Because if she kept this up I really was going to empty a clip into her. And hope it worked.

And hope that killing someone when I knew I shouldn't didn't damn me enough for Perry to take out a mortgage on the parts of me he couldn't touch.

Still, one of her black eyes peeped over a fold in the coverlet. "Their little games. They always have to have their little games."

"Just like Sorrows." *Cut it short, goddammit. Something nasty is going on here, and you need to get to the bottom of it.*

"Our games are bigger, Judith."

Fury rose wine-dark inside me. The Talisman hummed. "Call me that one more time, Belisa, and I will ventilate your skull."

It didn't faze her. Then again, not much fazes them. "You haven't killed me yet. You're uncertain. I'll tell you a few things and you'll take the handcuffs *and* this damnable slave-collar off me. Then we will find your hellbreed friend, and after we bar passage to his superior we will spread his bowels upon the earth."

I wanted to shrug, but if I moved I knew I was going to squeeze the trigger. "I can do that without you."

"No, you can't. Not if they have your cat." She laughed, a sound like battered, wrongly musical wind chimes. "You don't even know what you're fighting."

"Argoth." The name made the heavy etheric bruising tighten, as if it expected a punch. Riverson shivered and moaned. It was a good guess.

She twitched, jerking. The collar ran with golden light, flaring. She laughed again, a pained rasp, and the glow settled.

Now that was interesting.

When she spoke it was a curiously atonal singsong, as if she'd memorized it. "Let's talk about something you're more interested in. Why do you think Perry has been so interested in your lineage, child? One of yours did his enemy a disservice. Now you must repay the debt." A slow blinking of the tar-black eye I could see. Like a snake's eye, actually, the lid never quite covering it. She moved, very slightly. "And how do you think the hunter of your lineage had the strength to shut away one of Hell's highest scions? He had help. He made a *bargain*."

I backed up, shot a glance at Riverson. He was so pale he was almost transparent, holding on to the minibar. The smoke in the bottles behind him flashed crystalline-blue for a moment, and I stilled. My blue eye deciphered no pulsing of ill intent.

"It's true," he said tonelessly. "Believe it or not, Kismet, it's true. Mikhail didn't tell you. I guess he didn't have time."

I couldn't help it. I glanced back at Belisa. Sourness filled my throat. There were a hell of a lot of things Mikhail hadn't told me. I suppose Riverson thought he was doing me a favor by reminding me.

The scar was flushed, obscenely full. I'd been pulling a lot of power through it, and it seemed to be getting steadily stronger, especially when I was worked up. I wondered, like I did so often, if Perry felt it. How many nights had he sat up here, possibly feeling it, while I killed things like him?

"Riverson," I whispered. "I told you not to say his name."

The gun jerked. The sound of the shot was a thunder crack.

Riverson howled, sliding off the stool. His knee was a mess of hamburger and blood, he hit the ground hard. I almost felt sorry for the old man.

Almost.

I was on him a second later, scooping him up. I carried him across the acres of white carpeting and dumped him on the bed, across Belisa. Her fingers worked like bloodless, active little maggots, twitching as she writhed against the handcuffs. I should have gagged her, but I didn't care enough to do it now.

And I didn't want to get any closer than I had to, collar or no. If I got much closer I wouldn't shoot her. I'd cut her fucking throat like she cut Mikhail's, and what I'd do afterward didn't bear mentioning.

And I would feel *good* about doing it, too. The abyss was howling my name, and this time it wasn't Perry pushing me to the edge.

Or was it?

Riverson kept screaming. I waited until he had to stop for breath. "Enjoy each other, kids. Hope the next set of 'breed finds you soon."

I knew Belisa would be out of the cuffs and on Riverson before anyone else could happen along. You can't trust a Sorrow around a man—they're carnivorous, like praying mantises.

It wasn't a nice thing to do. But I am not a nice person.

And to find Saul, I would get a whole lot nastier.

"*Kisssssmet!*" Riverson, howling. He'd got his breath back with a vengeance. "*Kissssmet I'm telling the truuuuuuuth!*"

"Yeah," I muttered as I turned on my heel. "Sure you are."

I got out of there.

CHAPTER 15

The *bezoar* tugged against white silk and a spider cage of silver filaments; Galina had the cage lying around and it worked like a charm. The knife, driven through the cage, held it against the passenger-side seat like a pinned butterfly. The silver in the blade sparked in waves, spume against a rocky shore.

Tires screaming, I jagged around a corner and up Fairview. Morning traffic was just getting started, and intuition tingled along my nerves. I cut the wheel sharply just as the *bezoar* leapt, the cage yanking against the knife, and I slapped it back down. The Pontiac was an automatic, so I didn't have to worry about shifting. It was a good thing, too. Because the *bezoar* went wild, tugging and straining against the silver threads, and I had to shove the knife more firmly into the upholstery again to keep it trapped. I cut the wheel once more, tires smoking, and slewed into a turn onto 139th, the direction the *bezoar* was pulling.

Tracking with a physical link is so easy, it's frightening.

Warehouses rose around me. The industrial district simmered under a flood of sunshine, day peeking wearily through the streets, trapping dust in the air. Soon the winter frost would break and we'd get a roil of spring storms and flash floods, settling into summer's crackheat glaze.

The *bezoar* rattled and sprang, to the left this time. Intuition warned me, a sharp prickle along my entire body, and I stood on the brakes. The car slewed, I realized I was swearing low and steadily under my breath, and I narrowly missed T-boning a semi. It hove out of the way, I smashed the pedal to the floor again and was off. The subtle knocking in the engine got fractionally louder.

I penetrated the tangle of warehouses and shipping yards, following the *bezoar*'s urging. It rattled around in the cage like an angry cancer. The nearer I got to its source, the more violently it moved, fighting against the blessing on the silk and the silver's sharp gleam.

My prey probably guessed I was tracking him. He'd be stupid not to.

I finally skidded to a stop outside a shambling warehouse on 154th and Chavez. Slid the knife free of the upholstery, the *bezoar* trying futilely to knock the cage into the footwell. Grabbed the little bastard, folding the cage down around it until it hummed like an angry bumblebee in my hand. It went into my pocket, where it felt like my pager trying to get my attention.

I knew this place. Years ago it had actually been a rave joint, hopping almost every night and raided sporadically by Santa Luz's brave boys and girls in blue. Then a couple Traders got involved with slipping roofies to kids they thought wouldn't be missed and then carting them out of town to a friendly slave ring.

It happens.

One of the rules of my town is "you don't play in the under-18 pool." I came down on those Traders as hard as I could, and chased the 'breed they'd Traded with, dispatching them all in a welter of blood and screaming. Then I'd eradicated every other 'breed within the city limits who was even tangentially involved.

Hellbreed function on profit and loss. I wanted to make it so expensive for them to trade in young bodies that they gave up.

I'm still working on it.

Weathered scraps of old crime-scene tape stapled to entrances and exits fluttered in the stiff morning breeze from the river. Bleached by the constant assault of sun and weather, they made little whispering sounds. The etheric bruising swirling ripe and rank over this place would have told me I'd found what I was looking for, if the *bezoar* hadn't already been going mad in my pocket.

I watched it for a few moments. The need to go find Saul and bring him out of whatever they were doing to him itched unbearably under my skin, but I had to go carefully. Running in half blind wouldn't save him. It would just get us both in more trouble.

I was now assuming whoever took him was tied to the evocation site I'd found. If Perry wasn't involved—which I was by no means sure of—this was my next best guess. If Perry *was* involved, and had the masked 'breed running around doing dirty work while he pulled on other strings, this was going to get nastier before it got better.

The congestion tightened. Whoever was in there could feel me approaching. Sorcery will make a hunter's apprentice a full-blown psychic before long—if they survive. It also has the benefit of helping a hunter pop up just where the filthy bastard isn't looking.

Jill. You're too distracted. You can't go in there like this.

I told the voice of reason to take a hike. If something that could lead me to Saul was in there, that's where I was going, dammit. It made little sense for anyone to mess with my Were. They had to know that taking him would only make me determined to knock down anything in my way to—

Maybe they do. Maybe they're distracting you, just like they distracted you with a pile of bodies to take him. Maybe, just maybe, you should be looking somewhere else, for something else. Like Argoth.

Hutch still needed time to sort through a mound of data. He was going as fast as he could, but I was asking him to find needles in haystacks, and do it at a distance instead of at his home with access to every text the hunters in my line had accumulated.

I breathed out softly through my nose, suddenly aware I was making an odd sound. A sort of whistling moan as I breathed. How long had I been doing that? And the shaking running through me, what was that? I was too well trained not to know that it meant I was dangerously close to running on emotion instead of calculation.

The world narrowed. I shut my eyes, my smart blue eye piercing the meat of my eyelid to show me the still-contracting bruising over the warehouse in front of me. Night after night of kids dancing and hungry Traders preying made for a messy psychic "house," and banefire wouldn't have done much good at this point. Charged atmospheres can go either way, holy or unholy.

Guess which one is more common.

I am doing this case all wrong. I should have been focusing on the bigger priority—finding out if they were, indeed, trying to bring Argoth through. And if so, the location of every evocation site—so I could get there to disrupt them in time. Any hellbreed higher-class than a *talyn* is seriously bad news, and if what Hutch had said about Argoth last time was any indication, he was *definitely* above that classification.

It was an interesting question: how did Perry's dark hints, Riverson's ravings, or Belisa's silken lies go together? Which of them to believe? Or believe none of them? If there was a deeper game being played here, I needed to get to the bottom of it.

If it was Saul's life balanced against the lives of everyone in my city in a hellbreed game . . .

Something inside my chest cracked a little. I was making that whistling moan again.

I swallowed it, hard. A bitter tang coated the back of my throat. *Whatever you're going to do, Jill, get cracking. Do it now.*

I set my shoulders. Drew my right-hand gun, thought about it, and kept my left hand free. I struck out for the north side of the warehouse. There was a fire escape back there that should do a little better than the front door—more cover, and kicking down the front door and yelling hadn't done a thing at the Monde. It's always been my favorite way to go.

But maybe it was time to change it up a bit.

Catwalks zigged back and forth inside the warehouse's cavernous sprawl. Thin fingers of daylight touched down through the holes in the roof or gaps between the boards on the windows. The day's heat had begun to creep into corners, gathering strength.

It smelled of dust, rat fur, metal, and the sick-sweet tang of hellbreed. A faint copper note of blood. But no healthy brunet spice of Were. Instead, the wet reek of danger and brooding, nasty sorcery, incense and perfect-tallow burning.

Those in the trade call it perfect-tallow, at least. The candles stink and make an ungodly psychic mess. That's because they're made from people.

Well, their bodies, anyway. How many candles would the charred bodies out by the freeway have made?

I eased along a catwalk, silence drawn over me like a cloak. Each step torturingly slow, weight spread out, toes and the ball of the foot testing before weight shifted in increments. I couldn't be sure if my heavier muscle and bone would break the rickety grating or wring a betraying groan out of the struts. My eyes roved. The shadows were too thick, sorcery lurking in their depths. The entire place breathed, dust moving oddly and the light behaving like it shouldn't, bouncing off odd corners and falling into deep black wells without a gleam or a sigh.

Another tangle of metal stretched over what had been the dance floor, a wide expanse of cracked concrete. The kids had brought in plywood, scraps of scavenged linoleum, cardboard, to make a patchwork. The cardboard and linoleum were slowly rotting, the plywood had been stolen for God knew what. It was surprising that more of the metal hadn't been scrapped, but I'd lay odds that all the copper wiring left over had been sold to the recycling plant. I wondered if any of the DJs had been back to collect their stereo equipment since the moment I'd dropped down from the ceiling and started killing Traders.

If they hadn't been back, some foolhardy asshole had probably stumbled across it. People are too inquisitive for their own goddamn good.

Especially hunters. It's one of the things that makes us, well, *us*.

A low unhealthy blot of rectangular blackness sat in the middle of the dance floor. It pulsed like an obscene heart, and I checked the moon cycle inside my head again. Dark moon was best for this, and we had a week of waxing and another two of waning before the walls between here and Hell were even close to gapping without some serious help.

So this was a secondary site? But it was further along than the one at Henderson Hill. The altar crouched like a live beast, dozing in the middle of all that empty space. My blue eye caught flashes of ill intent, nasty little tingles of sorcery and bad feeling.

The *bezoar* stilled in my pocket, tiny tremors like a frightened rabbit quivering through heavy leather. I paused, silent as cancer or a snake under a rock, weight braced and the gun low but ready.

The *bezoar* quit trembling and tugged, very faintly.

Straight down.

The catwalk screeched as I pushed off, airborne and turning. I was over the railing and dropping like a stone. Gunfire crackled, bullets spattering as the 'breed hissed up at me, leaping from a gantry below, bone claws extended and the mask fluttering at its edges.

A moment of sheer savage glee, white-hot, went through me. *You again? Oh, good. Here, have some of this aggression I've been saving up.*

Falling. Firing into him as I *twisted*, his claws tangling in my coat and shredding the leather even further. He was aiming for the *bezoar*, I realized as my foot flicked out. There was no weight behind the kick since we were both in midair, but it did jolt home and we tumbled free of each other, leather ripping. I was screaming, a rising cry of female effort tearing through the gloom with a bright razor edge.

Impact. We hit the altar squarely. No give; it was like hitting concrete. Nothing broke for once, because I spilled over to the side and rolled free, bleeding momentum. It was a good thing, too, because he was leaping for me. The gun jerked up instinctively. Fire burst from the muzzle, I hit him square in the chest and rolled, whip jerking loose. Knee up, boot grinding in anonymous dust and dirt, a shard of broken glass eating itself into smaller pieces under the steelshod heel. Striking true, the jangling end of the whip sparking with fierce blue light. He tumbled aside, soundless, black ichor spattering.

I scrambled up. Time to press my advantage. Shot him twice more, tracking him, every bullet now striking home because the world had turned into a clear crystal dish with my path mapped out in a ribbon of light.

When you fight every night, reflex takes on a whole new meaning. Sometimes, and only sometimes, you hit a fight where *everything* comes together. Your entire body dilates and compresses at the same time, and suddenly everything is easy. I've heard it called a peak experience. There's nothing peak about it—you find that out the next evening, when you've pulled a muscle or two and you roll out of bed groaning to do it all again.

But while it lasts, it's better than chocolate.

I knew where he was going to move next, and fired before he could get there. The third shot took him in the ball of the shoulder joint and he was down, flopping like a landed fish. White chips of something like bone showed in the mess of his shoulder, black silk shredding. I was on him in a heartbeat, dropping the whip and driving the knife into hellbreed flesh with a solid *tchuk!* like a solid axe sinking into dry wood. My right-hand gun slid into its holster, because I *knew* this was going to be a knife fight from here on out.

Something was wrong. It nagged at the clarity of action, but I shoved it aside because I had to concentrate *now*.

He roared and threw me off. I careened, weightless, hanging in the air a moment before hitting a tangle of metal struts with a crunch. Hot agony speared my left arm and I thrashed, falling with a thud and narrowly missing cracking my head against a sharp-sheared edge. The snap of my left humerus breaking was a red scream, but I was on my feet again in a moment, hurling myself forward to meet the hellbreed with another shattering jolt. It tore the mask halfway free, and I caught a glimpse of copper skin and an alien, gaping vertical slit of a maw before my second-biggest knife dragged through hellbreed flesh like it was water, spilling noisome reek in a heavy gush.

No wonder he doesn't talk. A fleeting thought; that orifice didn't look like it could shape a single word.

But something was definitely wrong. He didn't try to rip my spleen out the hard way, and something about his skin nagged at me. His bony arms closed around me with a crackle like lightning. He pitched aside, inhuman muscles coiling and releasing, and a heaving, grinding sound filled the world, ending with a jarring clang.

We rolled, fetching up against steel bars with a stunning jolt. But I had my largest knife out, too. Silver sizzled, parting tainted flesh. I *twisted* it, wrist straining and arm bent oddly, the broken edges of my left humerus grinding together so hard black sparkles danced over my vision. Great heaving, sobbing breaths as my ribs flickered. The hellbreed's body jerked, corruption spilling through its tissues. The gaping, vertical maw of the mouth under the mask champed, yellow foam painting its thin lipless edges.

Shit. I hadn't meant to kill him so completely—I'd thought he was more durable. Now who was I going to question?

Wait a second, Jill. This guy's all wrong.

I struggled free of the swiftly decomposing remnants of the body, black silk sizzling a little as the ichor worked at it. The mask was a twisted rag, and his eyes were now collapsing holes. But something was wrong, very wrong, and when I raised my head, the silver still buzzing in my hair, I finally realized why he hadn't eviscerated me.

He'd been too busy knocking me into the trap.

What had seemed a random jumble of metal had fallen from the ceiling, fresh weld spots glowing with the peculiar white gleam of orichalc. Part of it fitted over the empty altar, caging it securely, and the entire thing quivered around me like it wanted to take flight. The metal had driven deep into the concrete, like fingers sinking into butter.

The body on the floor really started to stink. I froze, examining the tangle of metal now webbing us both.

An orichalc-tainted cage? What the—

A faint movement, silk against inhuman skin. I cleared leather in an instant, and the guns didn't dip as the clarity of battle left me and I began to suspect I was in deep fucking shit.

The 'breed melded out of the gloom, at the far end of the dance floor. The *bezoar* twitched in my pocket again, demonic little fingers tugging at my coat. Same compact build, same flutter of black silk, and maggot-white skin. The mask moved slightly as whatever was under it gapped its wide mouth, breathing softly.

He was *white*, not copper-skinned.

Oh, fucking hell.

I took two steps forward. It brought me closer to the crazy-crack jumble of steel, and the metal moved. Runes crawled over it, visible only to my blue eye—weird, angular writing, curved only in specific spots. It glowed a sickly gold, moving like a spider's scuttle when the web is touched.

Chaldean. Just like Belisa's new necklace.

Think, Jill. Think fast. I drew back. Saw my whip handle on the other side of the bars, just barely in reach, the rest of the leather and silver jangles stretching out across the floor in a ribbon of stars. I leapt for it, because the 'breed at the other end of the dance floor twitched. If I could reach the whip I could—

POW!

My fingertips scraped concrete before I was flung away. I hit the cage on the other side, and the Chaldean struck again like a snake, tossing me down to the floor. The screaming I heard from far away was me. My voice cracked, raging in a high unlovely torrent of obscenities.

The 'breed hissed as he twitched my whip out of the way with the tip of one slippered foot. I realized the other masked 'breed hadn't been wearing those goddamn tabi footies, either. He'd been a double.

I cursed myself for running on emotion instead of brains right before the cold concrete darkness reached up to swallow me.

CHAPTER 16

I came back to consciousness slowly and piecemeal. Lying on my side, cheek against a rotting piece of cardboard, my entire body felt pulled apart and put back together wrong. I lay completely still, my breathing not changing as I surfaced. Hard things dug into my ribs, stomach, arms—my left arm twinged faintly, but the scar was humming with deep etheric force. Like a flash flood rumbling through an empty canyon, moments before the wall of water crashes into you.

So. I had my guns, my knives, the grenades. My arm was healed up and the scar was awake and angry. The *bezoar* was still vibrating in my pocket. I'd been taken in by that masked bastard and was now in an orichalc-tainted cage crawling with Chaldean.

Belisa. Did she know I'd leave her at the Monde? Jesus.

That's the thing with Sorrows. They are masters of the mind-fuck; they make even hellbreed look simple. What was that collar on her for? I didn't know nearly enough.

And speak of the devil: "I know you're awake." A soft whisper, still as if she was in the incense hush of a House.

I kept my eyes mostly closed. The world was a soft blur. It still smelled like the same warehouse, and I kicked myself for not realizing the tang of incense was a Sorrows blend instead of the heavy noxious reek 'breed use for their rituals. Sorrows use perfect-tallow too, it's one of the few overlaps between their different sorceries.

I could have kicked myself six ways from Sunday. Running on emotion will fuck you up big time and leave you trapped.

Slight huff of breath, a sigh like a teacher with a difficult student. "Jill. I *know* you're awake."

I couldn't pin down the location of the voice. It could be a speaker system or a very slight sorcery to misdirect. Either was a good idea, especially since I still had my guns. They might have me trapped, but I was carrying a lot of ammo. I could probably figure out something with the grenades, too, to bust myself out of this predicament.

At least she wasn't calling me a dead girl's name anymore. Small mercies.

I lay there for a few more moments. My right wrist was under me, the scar twitching in my flesh. The stench of rotting hellbreed coated the back of my throat.

No sign of Saul here. My innards whirled violently for a moment. I suppressed a retch.

Another small sigh. "Come now, child. This is not especially mature of you."

It could be a recording, filtered through different speakers so I couldn't get a lock on it. And why was she talking to me like I was one of her cursed initiates? The other Sorrows bitch—Inez—had done that, too. They probably had a file a mile thick on me. Did every female hunter have trouble with the goddamn termite queens, or just me?

That's a dangerous thought, Jill. Prioritize. You're lying here on the floor. That won't help you find Saul or stop this evocation. It doesn't matter who they're bringing through, it's your job to get to the bottom of this and stop it posthaste.

There was more, of course. Riverson had done his job well, planting a seed of doubt. I still couldn't bring myself to believe Mikhail'd had a hellbreed mark. The very thought tried to send a shudder of loathing through me. I clamped down on everything—heartbeat, respiration, blood pressure, all my training narrowing to a single point.

"I offered to tell you where your cat was," Belisa breathed, and it sounded like she was standing right over me. A faint touch of air against my cheek, spiced with incense, like a single paintbrush hair drawn along my dirty skin. I was beginning to think I'd never be clean again.

It was a trick. It *had* to be.

The pressure intensified, became metallic. As if a scalpel was gently touching me, just before a whisper of more pressure is applied and the skin splits along the razor edge. It drew itself up my cheek, over the hill of my cheekbone, and dipped down into the valley of my eyesocket.

I lunged up and away, the sensation fading like cobwebs and Melisande Belisa's genuinely amused laughter ringing all through the warehouse. I did not draw a gun, but ended up kneeling as far away from all the sides of the cage as I could. This put me at the edge of the lake of black hellbreed scrim, my boot toe touching it.

A bright idea crawled through my head. I froze, my eyes moving over every surface. Both my hands were fists, and a chill slid over me. Like I'd just been doused in cold water, or like a fever had just broken. Sweat greased my skin, and a thin tendril of it kissed the scar's pucker. The too-intense wash of hellbreed-amped senses was beginning to seem almost normal, just like every time I had the cuff off for a while.

The warehouse was dark. How long had I been out? The altar, under a mass of twisted, jagged metal, throbbed a single dissatisfied pulse. It wasn't empty now, no sir. Chalice, claw, and candles, not to mention lumps of human organs, scattered across its surface. I wondered briefly, pointlessly, how many of those organs had been in the charred bodies near the freeway, or if there was another mass grave waiting somewhere for me to find it.

The thought of being unconscious so close to the altar—not to mention while someone laid the altar, though they could have done it with sorcery, I supposed—was enough to give me the willies. If, that is, I didn't already have so many other problems that one looked like a cakewalk. Tiny sounds—chittering, nasty, whispering laughter—filled each corner. It was meant to be disorienting, but my blue eye wasn't fooled. It's disconcerting to *hear* things running for you while your eyes swear you're alone and in no danger. Even more disconcerting to feel the brushes against you, ripples of Chaldean glyphs sliding through the cage's physical structure pushing air around.

"The blind man wasn't lying," she whispered. "Mikhail did have a scar. Star-shaped, inside of the right thigh. It was full of their corruption. He was worried he would die before he could find someone to take his place *and* the corruption itself. That's how it works, my dear. Haven't you wondered why your *zilffari'ak* watches over you so assiduously? Yours is a soul he has no intention of losing. The others, well. He could wait, and watch, for *you*."

Gee, I'm honored. Of all the things that have ever happened to me, having a Sorrow whisper sweet nothings about a hellbreed's motivations has to be one of the weirdest. And that's really saying something.

The urge to swallow hard rose. I repressed it. *Give nothing away, Jill.* Instead I turned in a full circle, examining the cage.

"Don't tell her." The second whining nasal voice was a surprise. "Let her anticipate the worst."

"Shut the fuck up, Rutger." My voice surprised me, echoed oddly against the cage. It quivered as if it wanted to clamp down on me, a gigantic veined hand with leprous-white spots. "The adults are talking."

Silence crackled. I drew my left-hand gun, holstered my right, and shook my fingers out. Took stock of myself from head to foot. *This might end up hurting a bit.*

"Oh, hunter." Rutger giggled, a high mincing noise. "You and your master are both going to burn. He'll be demoted to licking boots, and you'll be dragged to Hell screaming."

"Been there. Done that. Wiped off with the T-shirt." I stretched my fingers, tendons flickering in the back of my hand as I wiggled them. *First step is getting out of here. But that one's going to be a lulu.*

"Imbecile." Belisa, very softly. "If *he* finds out you're disloyal he'll make you uncomfortable. You'd better pray your plan works." A slight scuffle, changing direction in midsound. She had to be using sorcery to disguise where she was. Rutger, however, was not. And he had just moved—away from her, it sounded like.

I stored up their words for later. Interesting. Did the stupid hellbreed not realize she was a Sorrow? You'd think he would be staying as far away from her as he could.

And where was that masked bastard? The *bezoar* was quiet in my pocket. I could still track him with it, and next time I wouldn't be so easily taken in.

At least, I hoped.

"Shut up, witch-whore. Just because I'm not the one holding your leash doesn't mean you can yap." Rutger was moving again, restless tapping sounds. He was still wearing those sharp-edged heels. I had a vivid mental image of him kicking a body on the floor, shut it away with a physical effort.

My hand relaxed. The scar chuckled to itself, a wet lipless unsound against the flesh of my arm. Silver shifted and sparked. The Talisman pulsed once on my chest, and I considered using it for only a half second.

No. the situation wasn't that dire yet. I could still recover this. I *could*.

My fingers tingled.

"You're simply lucky I have *this* leeway to act and no more. If you weren't so useful, or if this damnable thing wasn't on me, I would..." Belisa, softly, each word coming from a different quadrant of the warehouse.

"You would what? What, exactly, would you do?" Rutger's sneer was palpable. "Pray to one of your spent, ancient masters?"

A long breath of silence, while I was doing some praying of my own. I prayed for them to be so involved with each other they wouldn't notice what I was up to. It was hard work, the fierce relaxed concentration of sorcery when my entire body was jittering from adrenaline overload and the thought of Saul trapped somewhere, maybe in a cage as well, beating inside my brain.

The tingling in my fingers crested.

Banefire whispered. Tiny blue sparks wreathed my hand, popping free of the skin, coalescing on my fingertips. You'd think they wouldn't have left me alive, with my ammo and my guns. They were either monumentally stupid, or they had something nasty and inescapable in mind.

Since Belisa wasn't stupid, guess what my money was on. There was a third option—that they couldn't get inside the cage. They were saving me for something.

Like an evocation, perhaps? Something about the situation was off, and if I had some time to think I could tease it out. That wasn't a luxury I possessed right now.

Stop reacting and start thinking, Jill. Slow and easy, now.

"I do not need to pray to deal with an upstart *zilfjari'ak*. Even if I am currently unable to do as I like." Belisa's dulcet tone turned to a hiss. I had to admit, I liked it better that way.

"Yes, well, one of *us* put that little necklace on you. It suits you." Rutger tittered.

A susurrus of silk against unholy skin. My ears perked up. High, behind me, to my left. So the masked bastard was still here, too.

The banefire slid against itself, almost dying under the weight of corruption in the air. *Please, no. God, cut me a break on this one, please?*

Even hunters aren't immune to pleading with an uncaring god. The thing is, while we reflexively do so, we know there really isn't any point.

God's busy. It's up to us.

I kept my right hand low and close to my side, in the folds of my tattered, torn coat. The scar twinged sharply. I exhaled, a slow, soft breath. Concentration came in fits and starts, and the banefire sang a sad little dirge in a chorus of dead children's voices.

More sounds—scuffles, a wet ripping. Good news for me.

Another soft sliding of silk. How could I have been taken in by a stupid double? Because I was running blind. All someone had to do was take Saul, threaten to hurt him, and I—

The banefire blazed up. My hand jerked away from my coat, and the shadows were suddenly cutting sharp, like a photo flash, every surface the bright blue-white light fell on bleached and curling with steam. Someone yelled, a long low rumble of Helletöng, and metal screeched and tore.

I threw myself backward and cast the banefire straight at the altar in one motion. It would hit the stored-up corruption there and consume it, and then once it had a good hold it would go for the bars.

I could only hope the resultant explosion wouldn't kill *me*, too. But better to die here than at the mercy of whatever Belisa—or whoever was holding her leash—had planned.

CHAPTER 17

The altar went up in a gout of brilliant blue, screaming faces in the twisting flames. Grasping fingers of fire caressed the cage.

Metal screamed, deafening, as if it were a living thing being tortured. The concussion knocked me back, and I had time enough for a split-second, hopeful thought—maybe the Chaldean sorcery on the bars would be spent now?

If it hadn't, I was looking at being the ball in a giant game of tennis between razor-studded rackets.

Impact. Red-black pain jolted through me. I lost consciousness briefly, stars whirling through my skull, and I wondered if I'd been too smart for my own good.

It wouldn't be the first time.

Shutterclicks of red and bright blazing blue. The banefire had a good purchase now, and was roaring. Regular orange flame was twisting, too, a clean and normal light under the black belch of smoke. The iron was curling like paper. So that was what it did to Chaldean sorcery impregnating orichalc-tainted steel. I should have Hutch write that down—

Get up, milaya. Mikhail's voice. *Get up now. Or I will hit you again.*

When he said that, he always meant it. It made me move when nothing else could.

I scrambled, my body not obeying me quite right. My left arm felt like it had broken again and I was swimming through molasses. I knew the pain would be right behind me, and I just had to move fast enough for it to stay *behind* me and not catch up.

Moving, though, would be the problem. Great chunks of burning stuff fell from the ceiling, orange and blue flame mixing in long banners. My feet went out from under me, slipping on a wash of something bubbling and foul, and it was a good thing, too. If I hadn't slipped, going heavily to my knees and almost biting a chunk out of my tongue, Rutger would have collided with me. As it was, every inch of silver on me fluoresced with blue sparks, bane-fire howled, and the edge of one of his sharp little shoes clocked me on the back of the head. I rolled, tucking everything in.

The pain caught up with me. Every joint, muscle, and bone in my body screamed, the scar a dumb lump of burning meat on my right wrist, and I fumbled for a gun.

The inside of the warehouse was alive with leaping blue flame. Banefire squealed and cried, the children's voices rising in a glass-ine chorus. And other sounds, ones I couldn't quite make out because my ears were full of something warm, trickles of fluid sliding down my neck. Even that touch of moisture couldn't cool the heat. The Eye on my chest throbbed, and it took effort I couldn't afford to quiet the thing.

Howls. Cries. Gunfire. Someone yelling my name—a human voice, young, breaking in the upper registers.

What the hell?

I floundered on the floor. *Get up. Jill, get UP.* I made it to hands and knees, coughed. An amazing jet of bright-red blood splashed on the floor. No trace or taint of black in it.

Every time I bled red it was a relief. Except there was so *much* of it.

Why was the entire warehouse burning? The banefire should have just busted the cage. It must have reacted with the Chaldean. I really needed to get Hutch on that to figure it out.

I should have been healing. The scar should have been pump-ing etheric energy through me. Instead, my arms almost failed, slipping on the blood and the bubbling mix of foulness coating the floor. Smoke roiled, coating the inside of my throat. A hellbreed screamed, the cry rising up to earshattering volume before it was cut short on a gurgle.

I hoped it was Rutger. But who would kill him? Belisa? *Why?*

Worry about getting up first, Jill.

Good advice. Except something dark appeared in the corner of my peripheral vision, and I threw myself back and rolled, hands going for my guns and the barrels coming up, but slow, too slow.

Something was badly wrong inside my torso, darkness beating at the edges of my vision. Even my smart eye was clouding up.

The masked 'breed hung in the air over me, banefire bleaching each edge, fold, and crease of his ninja pajamas. I knew, with a sudden sickening thump, that I wasn't going to get the guns up fast enough. I knew he would come down and there would be a wet final crunch, and if I survived it I would have to go for my knives, but there was nothing in the world that would save me now. The scar was dead, not even a trickle of etheric power working up the nerve channels of my arm. He was descending from the apex of his leap, and the slow motion was not my speed working overtime but from the dragging slowness of a nightmare. One I wouldn't ever wake up from.

CRUNCH. A pale blur hit him from the side. They tumbled, and another flash of black filled up the world. The snap-crackle of flame turned into a roar, and if the fire didn't get me I was probably going to bleed to death.

The scar had finally failed me. Had Perry planned this all along? None of it made any sense. Nothing did.

That's what you always think before a case starts to jell. The thought rolled under a breaker of agony as my entire body seized up. The dumb meat thought it could get away from the pain by flopping around uselessly. I'd been relying on the scar too much. Just like any Trader, using up the bargain and spending what made me human.

Oh, Mikhail, they're lying about you. They have to be.

"*Chingada!*" someone yelled, and more gunfire spattered. Growls and yowls, almost swallowed in the fire.

"Found her!" A familiar voice, very close. Hands on me. I struck out weakly. "Holy *shi*—"

"We're trying to help!" Another voice, female, with a snarl running under the words. It was a clean sound, not the twisted groan of a hellbreed.

Weres? Here? What?

Lifted. Body bumping. Broken bones ground together. I cried out.

"Bad shape!" Theron yelled. "Move move *move!*"

What the hell is he doing here? But I couldn't get a breath in.

Something was pressing on my chest. A heavy weight, hard to dislodge enough to get a breath in.

I fell back into darkness. My last thought, crystal-clear and oddly calm, danced for what seemed a very long time before unknowing swallowed it.

If the Weres came down here they're in danger. I'm going to just kill Theron.

CHAPTER 18

Clear!" A hellbreed's voice, töng rubbing and squealing below its surface. "Move *back!*"

"You'd better not—"

"Get *back,* Theron! Let him!" That voice. Female, with a snap of command under its softness, so familiar. Why?

White light slammed through me. The scar lit up, finally. I might have wished it hadn't, because it sent a grinding jolt up my arm as if it was going to rip the appendage off, and I convulsed again, blood spraying slick and hot past my lips.

"Oh, you're not going yet." The hellbreed chuckled, like he was having a grand old time. I knew who it was now, and I couldn't fight. My body simply wasn't obeying any command I was giving it. The most I could manage was thrashing.

Fever-warm, inhuman fingers clamped down on my forehead. The scar keened, zapped me again. A flare of sterile light filled my head, chasing out the sound of fire and screaming.

Oh God—

Another zap. This one found every bruise, every break, every torn muscle, and filled it with acid. Broken bones twitching and melding, all the pain of healing compressed into bare seconds. Silver crackled, and Perry hissed.

"Just a little more, my darling," he whispered. "Just a very little more. Then you can rest."

I didn't believe it. Thrashed more, or tried to. Weak limbs twitching, I heard someone shapelessly moaning and knew it was me. I was saying something, over and over, the only prayer I had left.

"Saul... *Saul*..."

"Jesus," Theron said quietly. What was *he* doing here?

Then, the biggest surprise of all. I recognized the woman's voice. *What is Anya doing here? She's supposed to be over the mountains in her own territory.* "She's going to be okay, kid."

What the hell?

"*Chingada.*" Gilberto's tenor, breaking at the end of the word. "What's he doing?"

"I'm repairing my investment." Perry clicked his tongue thoughtfully. "It's unpleasant work. Perhaps you should look away."

"You just better hope she keep breathing, *cabron.*" Gil sounded steady enough.

"Have no fear, little boy. Our dear Kismet has not seen the last of this weary earth just yet. She has *ever* so much more to accomplish." A soft chuckle, like a razor blade against numb skin.

A silver nail ran through me from crown to soles. The world lifted up and shook me off like a flea from a dog's back. I clung desperately, fingers and toes slipping. Rammed back into my racked, convulsing body, skin stretching, an obscene, dying scream filling my smoke-burned throat.

"This is what you get," Perry murmured. "Banefire. What next? Too impulsive by half, Kiss."

"Saul," I whispered. But the machine trained into my head clicked into life. I wasn't dead yet, and the scar settled down, humming nastily to itself while it repaired bone and stitched together muscle tissue. I coughed, retching. Blood steamed and spattered. There was a roaring, and sirens in the distance. It was a welcome sound.

It meant the cavalry was on its way. But if they got here and hellbreed were hanging around, not to mention Belisa, then I was looking at possible casualties. And where was that masked bastard? Had he survived? Why had Belisa jumped him? Or had it been her?

I jerked into full consciousness, slapping Perry's hands away. He made a small spitting sound of annoyance, and tried to grab my head again.

The gun smacked into his ribs. My fingers were slick and wet, but steady enough. "Back. Off." I coughed, spat more blood. It dribbled down my cheek, because I was flat on my back. Lying on pavement, the entire scene drenched with unholy light. The bane-fire had burnt itself mostly out, and now the entire warehouse was a mass of regular old orange and yellow flame. A pillar of black smoke rose, garishly underlit, and it was looking like it would involve the structures on either side too unless the fire department could do something soon. It was morning, gray light just touching the tops of the mountains. I'd lost a whole day in there, somehow.

Shit. Monty's going to have a heart attack over this one.

"A thank-you would be nice." Perry's pale hair was mussed, soot grimed into it. Under the mask of smoke and dirt, he was grinning. His eyes twinkled. "Since I did just drag you out of the dragon's maw."

Another coughing fit rasped at my throat, I pushed it down and back. The gun was steady, jammed up into his ribs, plenty of play in the trigger but that could change in a heartbeat. "Back *off.*"

He moved away, gingerly. The pale linen suit was spattered with blood, hellbreed ichor, other fluids. Tarnished with smoke, and crisped in a few places. No wonder he looked like he'd had a good time. His wingtips were still glossy, though, and you could see the suit had been ironed and starched at a not-too-distant point in the past.

"Eh, *profesora.*" Gil, from behind me and to my right. "Thought you was a goner."

I did too, kid. "Gilberto?" The word slurred. My mouth wasn't working correctly. The scar crawled against the flesh of my wrist. Perry's smile turning to a wolflike leer as the fire sent shadows dancing.

"Right here. *Los gatos hombres aquí.*"

Well, thanks. I figured that out. "I told you. To stay at Galina's."

Slight snort. "I ain't too good at listening, *chica.*"

"I got that." I found out my body would move. Shaky, like a newborn colt. My arms and legs creaked as I moved. The scar chuckled and hummed, behaving just like it normally did. A velvet tide of pleasure slid up my arm—Perry, trying to make me react.

I kept the gun trained on him as I hauled myself up. "Anya? Anya Devi?" Coughed again, spat a mouthful of something bright red.

"Here." Very quietly, also to my right. If I knew her, she had her guns trained on Perry too.

"And...Theron?" I had to know who *else* was here.

"We're here, Jill." A growl ran under the edge of Theron's voice. He sounded like one pissed-off Were. Galina had probably told him what was happening. Or at least about Saul, because I didn't have a clue what was happening otherwise. And if she did, she would have told me.

"Not just one beast, but dozens." Perry shrugged. "We should move from here, dear one."

"Shut. Up." *Until I figure out what the fuck you're doing here.* "Anya, what the fuck?"

"Your house, Jill." She sounded calm, and utterly certain. "Then we'll ask all the questions we need to. Perry will meet us there. With the Sorrow."

My heart gave the sort of leap usually reserved for teenage girls in horror movies, right when the bad guy bursts out of the shadows. I couldn't take my eyes off Perry, but if Belisa was around...

Perry heard the hike in my pulse, and his grin widened. "Don't worry." His tone was a parody of soothing, coming out of that lean, grinning face. "I don't intend on leaving her behind again to get into mischief. She served my purpose—proof of my good faith. Just like that pretty bauble you're wearing."

For a bare second I contemplated unleashing the Talisman. It would make a smoking crater out of whatever remained of the warehouse. I wasn't sure it would kill Perry, but it could make him very uncomfortable.

The fact that I was even considering it meant I wasn't thinking straight. I made a harsh, almost physical effort to prioritize, clear my head, and figure out what to do next.

Perry leaned forward, all his weight on the balls of his feet. The wingtips gleamed, incongruously clean. "After we're done, Jill, you can have the Sorrow. We can get a room. Just she and thee, and some pretty shiny blades. Won't that be nice?"

It was a relief to find out I could still tell when he was laying a trap. The guns lowered, and the scar settled down, a live coal pressed into my wrist.

I never thought I'd be glad to feel that. The strength pouring up my arm was an unhealthy glow, like a cocaine rush. It would give out soon, and the fog of fatigue would set in until I could get some other fuel in me.

I needed to be somewhere safer than the open street when that happened. This was getting me no closer to my objectives. Either Saul was dead and vengeance needed to be planned, or he was alive and needing a rescue I couldn't accomplish if I was dragging. Not to mention the fact that someone planning on bringing a big-time hellbreed through might or might not be related to the whole mess.

I'd already fucked up by running on emotion.

Perry and I studied each other. The sirens drew closer.

I thought of saying something. Like, *If you've taken him, Perry, you will die.* But it would serve no purpose. He had to already know that.

Just like he knew I wasn't going to shoot him now.

On to the next problem, Jill. "Belisa," I croaked. "Where?"

"Oh, I've put the chain on *that* little cat. She won't be selling you to my enemies again. At least, not just yet." He tipped his head back a little. My eyes didn't want to focus past him, but I saw her. She crouched, in tattered blue silk, rocking back and forth. Her black eyes were empty, and her long fall of dark hair was mussed and full of soot. My right hand jerked, the gun almost locking on her, before I forced it down.

Perry turned smartly on his heel, reached down, and picked up a length of chain from the pavement. He twitched it, and Belisa pitched forward a little, the chain jingling where it met the collar's metal gleam.

The collar positively crawled with the same golden tracery of Chaldean runes as the cage had. No glaring white spots of orichalc, though. She rose awkwardly, and I noticed that her feet were bare and horribly battered. She left dark bloody prints on the pavement as she stumbled forward.

"Little snake." Perry's half-fond tone was utterly chilling. "Did you enjoy your half freedom? Now we'll see who you betray. I expected you to do something like this, seeking to cheat me of my prize."

Oh, God. Bile crawled up into my throat.

I backed up. It was probably a bad idea. The way my legs were shaking I ran the real risk of going down in a heap. I almost ran into Theron, who closed a hand around my shoulder. I realized several other Weres were moving to surround me. Amalia—a lioness of the Norte Luz pride—had two vertical stripes of black painted down each perfect golden cheek. Some of the bird Weres had feathers in their hair; others wore variations of the paint Saul sometimes used. Red, black, white—they were dressed for battle.

And there, a mop of dark hair and a pair of bright blue eyes. Anya, in a long leather duster. Her guns were out, pointed steadily at Perry. The silver in her hair—beads instead of charms, and threaded onto small braids in the dark hanging mass—ran with blue light.

It's always a good thing to see another hunter. But if she was here, shit was about to get more complicated than it already was.

Theron's lean dark face was set. "Let's go."

"Oh, but I'm having so much *fun.*" Perry twitched the chain again. The links made a tinkling, icy sound under the roar of the inferno. Belisa swayed toward him, pliant and terribly empty-eyed. "Would you like to hold her leash, Kiss? It's an experience."

Gorge rose hot and fast again. *Oh, God, what have I done?* I reeled back into the Weres. Theron was leaning forward, a snarl thrumming under his skin. Anya was still covering Perry, her strong-jawed face set as if she smelled something even more horrific than usual. Gilberto, carrying a snub-nosed .38, probably loaned from the Weres, came into view. His sallow face was alight; he looked about ready to lunge for Perry. The gun was lifting, and the savage joy in his eyes warned me.

I pitched forward, grabbed his arm, sank my fingers in. The scar gave a flare of pain, as if someone had tried to yank out the knot of corruption by its roots.

"No." I held Gilberto's gaze for a long second. He resisted, but even with every bone and muscle in my body weakened I was more than a match for his skinny human strength. "No, Gil. *No.*"

"You better not, boy." Anya's drawl, soft and clear, chill with certainty. "You fire at him, I'll be the one to knock some sense into you. Right after she finishes."

Perry giggled, a high sharp note of glee. Gil swore, and the shaking in me must have infected him, too. The sirens were almost here, and dawn was coming fast.

I let the Weres draw me away, Theron's hands gentle and the collective rumbling from them shaking me down to my bones.

I only looked back once, but the firelit street was empty. Perry and Belisa were gone.

But I could still hear him laughing.

Saul had cleaned up a little before he'd been snatched, but my warehouse still stank of hellbreed. I went straight for the bathroom and into the shower. I couldn't stand the filth one more second. Plus, the warm water would give me another short-term burst of energy.

And I could also load up on more ammo.

It took me more time than I liked to clean up. I kept having to stop, staring at my hands, willing the shaking to go away. Stupid, stupid, *stupid*. But assuming Perry had taken Saul was reasonable, especially with the way—

Who was I kidding? Assuming is *never* reasonable. I'd lost precious time and wasted resources going off half-cocked. I'd gotten caught, trapped. My Weres and my apprentice had put themselves in danger to rescue me, and *that* was a fine kettle of fish they should never have had reason to open.

Weres don't fight hellbreed. They get hurt too badly. There is no corruption in the Weres that will allow them to outthink, track, or eradicate a 'breed. Traders are dangerous, too, but a Were has a chance against something that's basically human.

Against 'breed? No. Yet plenty of them had shown up to save my bacon. Or because one of their own was taken. Either way, they'd put themselves in danger. That wasn't their job.

It was mine. I was sucking at my *job*.

I looked up at the mirror, my bathroom wavering around me for a split second as if it was underwater. The scar twinged sharply, and the sound of cold iron chain links crashed inside my head.

Christ. Buckle up, Jill.

"*Profesora*?" Gil, in the door. He had an armful of black leather.

"I should kick your ass." I pulled the hem of the fresh T-shirt down. "You were supposed to stay at Galina's."

"An' you were gonna bring back *su marido*." He shut his mouth as soon as I half-turned and looked at him. The fall of black leather in his arms was a fresh custom-made leather trench; I'd found a new supplier who didn't balk at sewing in the ammo loops and extra pockets to my exacting specifications. I buy them in bulk, and my last supplier had been hauled in on tax evasion charges.

For once, it was completely mundane and not anything to do with me. I'd almost forgotten what that felt like.

I couldn't go off half-cocked on my apprentice for telling the truth. "Gil."

He shrugged, offered me the coat. "*Es muerto*?"

"He's not dead." I took the coat, held it up and shook it a little. Slid into it, then started slipping the contents of my old pockets into the new ones.

"How you know?"

I don't. I just refuse to believe it. "Nobody wants that much trouble from me."

"*El Diablo rubio*, he might. He don't like Saul."

"Of course he doesn't. 'Breed don't like Weres. The feeling's mutual." I looked up. A chilly silver charm touched my cheek before I tucked the curl it weighted down behind my ear. "Wait a second. Is Perry here?"

"*Sí*. With the *chica* on a leash." Gil was pale under his sallowness. There were bruised-looking circles under his dark, flat eyes. "Sparring room. *La otra cazadora* is drinking some licorice shit. Says she shoulda known you'd end up like this."

"Great." I scooped up the caged *bezoar*. It quivered unhappily. If you've never taken a shower while keeping an eye on a twitching corruption-seed in a silver cage, count yourself lucky. Down it went into a padded pocket. "The Weres?"

"Some out watching the neighborhood. Others looking round your kitchen. I told 'em not to take *el gato*'s copper-bottoms." A faint smile touched the corners of his thin lips.

I found my eyeliner. Considered just leaving it, but I needed every inch of protection I could get if I was going to face down Perry again. My hands were not steady, and neither was the rest of me. The fatigue fog was creeping up quick. "Yeah, well, if they take any of his enameled cast iron either there'll be hell to pay."

The sheer unreality of it rose and walloped me sideways. I took a deep breath, grabbed the counter, and willed my body to buck up. Etheric energy trickled through the scar, coiling up my arm like ivy.

Take it one problem at a time. I focused on the most immediate thing, opened my eyes, and put on my Teacher Face. "A few of the Weres will take you back to Galina's."

His pointed chin lifted, stubborn. "I done good."

My temper almost snapped. I took a firm grip on it, and on myself. *Don't, Jill. He's just a kid. He's your apprentice, dammit.* "You disobeyed a direct order and put yourself in danger."

"Weres said I done good." Lank hair shaken back, hands curling into fists. I was not handling this right. My entire body felt heavy and pale because replacing a few pints of blood takes a lot out of you, even if you've got a hellbreed mark and the benefit of sorcerous training.

Had the mark not been working because of the banefire? I'd never been completely encircled by banefire before, not while I had the scar. Another thing to set Hutch working on. Sure. I could just throw that on his plate and see what he came up with.

Wonder of wonders, my pager was still working. I know because it went off then, buzzing on the counter like a small poisonous rattler.

I swayed. Closed my eyes, eyeliner in one hand, the other making a fist to match Gilberto's. Calmed my runaway pulse, breathed in deep. Shuffled priorities inside my head, and told the ball of unsteady rage inside my chest to sit back and let me *work*, goddammit. My pager cycled through the buzz and cut itself off. The Talisman grumbled against my chest.

Where is he? Are they hurting him? Whoever they are. If he's harmed I will...

I couldn't afford to get worked up now. I shoved the anger down into a box, slapped a lid on it, and pushed it away. As a coping mechanism, it sucked. As a short-term solution so I could *think*, it was all right. For now.

I breathed deeply, dispelling the rage. Now was the time to be cold, to use a hunter's chill calculation.

"*Profesora.*" Gil, very close. Was he about to touch me? I hoped not.

I was so not safe right now. My bitten-down fingernails scraped against the butt of a gun, and I opened my eyes. The world rushed back in, a sharp torrent of color and hard edges. I stepped away along the bathroom counter, the edge of my coat brushing the dark wood cabinets underneath. I hadn't stepped back into my boots, so my calluses rasped against the hardwood.

Gil's hand dropped back down to his side. "*Lo siento.*"

"Get my boots." The words were a harsh croak. I turned back to the mirror, leaned in, and brought the eyeliner up. I was going to lay it on thick for this. "And for the love of God don't get so close to me. I am not safe." *Not for a human, anyway. And you're still all too fragile, Gil.*

"You ain't gonna hurt me." He sounded supremely confident. "You're gonna kick the shit out of whoever took *el gato*." But, thank God, he was moving away into my bedroom to find a pair of boots.

"Damn right I am." Still, I had an uneasy feeling.

Now I had to face Anya. And there's nothing like a fellow hunter for seeing right through any lies you tell yourself.

Gilberto had understated the case a bit. The warehouse was *full* of Weres. As soon as I stepped out of my bedroom, I had to put up with being touched no matter how unsteady I felt.

It was to reassure them, I knew. Bird Weres breathed in my face, the cat Weres brushed my shoulder or got way inside my personal space and smelled me, and there was even a hollow-eyed spider Were who walked right up and delicately laid her fingertips on my cheeks, staring at me for a few moments. She looked familiar, but her mate—smaller and slimmer than her, even—hustled her away. After trickling his fingers over the sleeve of my coat.

I suffered it. It's the way they say they're happy I'm still here, and it's also how they show they care. Gilberto was bundled off with a group of four Weres, bound for Galina's. He didn't like it, but I wasn't in a mood to argue.

I found Anya Devi perched on the breakfast bar, her steel-toed boots dangling and a modified 9 mm in her left hand. A bottle of venomous green liquor sat obediently at her right side, and I caught the whiff of licorice.

Anya believes in absinthe the way other people believe in immunization, football, or sex. It's a panacea. It was the way Mikhail had felt about vodka.

Me? I'm a firm believer in Jack Daniels. But I'll take whatever's handy.

She lifted the bottle as soon as she saw me. Her apprentice-ring, a silver claddagh, threw a hard sharp dart of light back at the overhead fixtures. Anya is built a little smaller than me, but she makes up for it with pure dangerous brains. She didn't come back from Hell at the end of her apprenticeship with anything extra, unless you count the utter crazed determination in those baby blues. She and the Weres ran herd in Sierra Cancion over the mountains, keeping the scurf population down and the hellbreed and Traders guessing.

Long nose, straight eyebrows, the faint shadow of a scar on her right cheek, a claw mark slipping down from the outside corner of her eye like a tear. The usual *bindi* above and between her eyes, this time a miniature ruby. I hear it's a subdermal piercing, but I don't ask. I'm not one to throw sartorial stones. The usual silver hoops in her ears, small ones so they don't get ripped free in the middle of a fight. A dangling carnelian rosary, its cross resting against her navel. She'd put on a little more weight, all muscle by the looks of it, and her navy-blue T-shirt was ripped and dotted with blood. Some of her leather was scorched, too.

We regarded each other for a few moments. The Weres drew away, tactfully. One of them had his head in my fridge, muttering, and there was the smell of something sweet in the oven fighting with the reek of 'breed ichor.

She tipped her chin up a fraction, finally. "Kismet."

I copied the motion. "Devi."

Another few beats of silence, the kind of quiet that rises between two old gunfighters. Then a grin spread over her face and she hopped down, landing light and lithe as a cat. "Good to see you. We've got problems."

I'll say. "I'd ask what you're doing here, but something tells me I'm going to find out." *And it's not going to be pretty or simple.*

"Oh, yeah. And I'd ask you what that hellbreed is doing with a Sorrow chained up in your sparring room, and what the hell 'breed are doing kidnapping Weres. But something tells me I'm going to find out." Her mouth firmed a little. "It's *him*, isn't it. Perry."

I nodded. My neck creaked. Her eyes dropped to my chest. If I could feel the Talisman humming sleepily along under my T-shirt, she could probably sense the etheric disturbance it created.

I hooked a finger carefully under the sharp edges of the chain, and drew the Eye out. The light changed, taking on a redder cast, and the Weres all went very still for a few seconds. "Perry brought me this. The Sorrow is Belisa. Someone's looking to bring a high-level hellspawn through, maybe with Belisa's help as she double-crosses Perry, maybe not. There were bodies controlled by a 'breed assassin, an evocation altar, and a mass grave that lit up like a goddamn bonfire when I got there. And my Were is some-where out there at the mercy of hellbreed." I paused, running back over it. "Not sure they're connected." My pager lit up again. I dug it out and checked. The Badger, again. She was next on my list. "And my fucking pager keeps going off."

One corner of Anya's mouth lifted slightly. "Well. This should be interesting. Whoever they're trying to bring through, they started trying over in my territory. I've been chasing evocation altars for a week or so now. Hutch called me, and when I got here that blond 'breed was at Galina's. He said you were in deep shit; my Weres put the word out and we went out to find you. That new apprentice of yours is a piece of work."

"That's why I took him in." I absorbed this. Whatever was in the oven smelled really good, but the scrim of rotting 'breed over it wasn't going to win it any prizes. "They started in your terri-tory? What are they using to fuel it?"

"Mostly hearts. Two nuns, a nineteen-year-old boy, a clutch of schoolgirls, and one old lady with a bunch of cats Balthazar just *had* had to find homes for. Apprentices." One shoulder lifted, dropped. I had a little over half a head and several pounds on her, but if we ever tangled I wasn't sure either of us would come away whole. Balthazar was her apprentice—he'd come out to keep a lid on things while I went on my honeymoon with Saul.

"You have any idea who they're trying to bring through?" *Please don't say Argoth.* But I wasn't holding out any real hope.

"Just some whispers about some asshole called Julius, maybe. Whoever *he* is, I'm told he likes virgins." She snorted. "Is he going to get a surprise, this day and age."

Wait. "Julius? You're sure?"

Her smile widened, and it wasn't nice at all. It was, in fact, the kind of smile where you wanted to take a step back and look for a wall to protect your kidneys. "I couldn't swear to it. I've just heard the name. Why?"

I don't think Anya knows she can grin like that. It makes me wonder what my own face looks like sometime. "That just means I can stop Hutch from going on a wild goose chase and possibly aim him at something more productive. He'll enjoy that."

Perry's hints about Argoth, dropped to Rutger, weren't a good enough basis to worry about it. Anya's information was. She was a hunter. It meant her word was as good as honest silver.

Of course, she wasn't sure, or she would have said so. And there was the little matter of the Trader and the pile of charred bodies. *A gift for you.* But still.

"I don't think Hutch really *enjoys* much. Have you found any evocation sites here?" She took a hit from the absinthe bottle, rolling it in her mouth like it was fine wine.

I winced. I've never liked licorice. "Two. I think the one at the warehouse was a primary." *But I'm not sure.* "You getting graves with charred bodies?"

"Yeah, they're burning them after they take the sweetmeats out. There was a site in that warehouse?" Now she looked grave.

"Yeah. And an orichalc-tainted cage." I headed for the phone. "Give me a couple minutes, okay? Then we'll powwow."

She waved her fingers over her shoulder as she turned away. The bullwhip, neatly coiled at her side, swung just like her coat.

"And eat. You need it. I think we should take a peek at what that 'breed's doing to that Sorrow. Since they seem to be involved up to the hip on this."

God damn. It was good to have another hunter around.

CHAPTER 19

J ill?" The Badger, sounding a little less than calm. Which meant severe trouble. "Thank God."

"What? More bodies?" *Not like I have time for them. Jesus.*

"No. Vanner. He's gone. Disappeared from the hospital. The trauma counselor says he's still in shock. She's afraid he'll..." The Badger's voice didn't break, but it was close.

"Tell all the black-and-whites to look for him. I'll do my best too." *Goddammit. Shit, shit, shit.* "How did he check himself out?"

"That's the weird thing. He didn't. He's just gone." Then Badger dropped the other shoe. "His uniform's still there, though. Wherever he is, he's in his hospital johnny."

"Oh, *Christ*." I tried not to sound aggravated. "Okay. Keep a surveillance on the scene he stumbled across, he might go back there. Put out an APB on him, and roust Montaigne." *Sorry, Monty.* "Tell him to get whoever he can working Vanner's trail. See if we can pull him in."

"Sully's raising Montaigne now. Anything else?"

I struggled to *think*. There was one more thing. "Call Wallace again. Give him the situation. See if he and Benito can scare up anything."

"Okay." She sounded a lot more reasonable now. Of course, nobody could ever call the Badger unreasonable. But I could hear the relief now that she had a list of things to do.

"When he shows up, have Wallace or Benito or Avery take custody. Do *not* put him in a holding cell. Got it?"

"Oh." I could hear the wheels turning as she took this in. "All right."

"Good. Have the next of kin been contacted on those bodies yet?"

She actually sounded surprised. "Not yet. Figured it was better to hold off until I heard from you again."

Meaning, she was hoping I'd call and tell her it was all right to release them. Even the Badge cavils at telling a civilian family they can't collect their violated dead. I hated to have to ask them to do it. "And Rosie and Paloma, do they have anything on the other site?"

"I checked with Rosie not a half hour ago. Not yet. Stanton's having a hissy fit over the number of bodies. Going to have to start putting them in nooks and crannies." She moved the phone a little. I could just see her at her cluttered desk.

"Stanton's always having a hissy. One more thing. Warehouse fire, 154th and Chavez. Start the paperwork for a paranormal incident, if you find any bodies buzz me again."

"Jesus *Christ*." For a moment there she sounded like Monty. "You're a busy little girl, Kismet."

"The moment the nightside slows down, I will too. Thanks, Badge. Keep me updated, and I'll keep an eye out for Vanner."

"All right." She hung up, and I stood there for a second staring at the phone. The Weres were quiet, but someone was stirring something briskly in the kitchen. The tapping of a metal whisk inside a glass mixing bowl sounded so familiar, as if Saul was standing there after a long night's work, making breakfast. Probably burritos, because nothing goes down after a night of killing hellbreed like eggs, ham, potatoes, chipotle Tabasco, cilantro, and a nice cold beer.

I shook the thought away. *Focus, Jill.* Picked up the phone, dialed again. "Galina? It's Jill. Put Hutch on."

She didn't waste time asking me what was going on. "Oh, thank goodness...*Hutch! It's Jill!*"

I heard him bitching all the way up to the phone. "Worried *sick* about you," he ended up mumbling, as Galina handed the phone over. "Jesus Christ. What?"

I could just see him standing there with pen and a pad of paper, bracing himself. Thank God he had enough sense to stay where I put him. Not like my disobedient apprentice.

"The hellbreed someone may be trying to bring through is probably named Julius." I spelled it for him. "Cross-reference it with Perry, see what you come up with. Do you have anything on the Sorrows calendar yet?"

"Nothing, we're in the Dead Time. Something interesting, though; there was a Sorrows House burned in Louisiana a week ago. Completely torched. Resident hunter out there—it's Benny Cross, by the way, he says hi—says hellfire was involved."

Louisiana. Okay. "Did he mention the spectrum?"

"I knew you'd ask. Green, shading up into blue." Hutch's tone dropped to a whisper. "Bad news."

Yeah, anything above orange on the spectrum was *incredibly* bad news. The saving grace was that the higher on the spectrum, the less likely a 'breed was to be wholly physical, which meant sorcery and banefire could be used to disrupt them.

On the other hand, I'd seen Perry produce blue hellfire. And he was all-too-disturbingly physical. This put a whole new wrinkle in the equation.

"Did Benny say anything else?"

"Just that the Sorrows are mad as hell. He's watching them go after hellbreed. Not getting in the middle of that unless they drag a civilian in, he says."

Reasonable of him. If 'breed and Sorrows were looking to off each other, it made his job easier. Mostly. "Yeah. Okay, next thing. Would banefire break the link between a Trader and a 'breed? Like, a complete encirclement of banefire, cut it off completely?"

Silence crackled over the phone line. I shoved down the impatient need to say something more while he worked it around in his head. There was a sizzle of something hitting a hot pan, and I smelled eggs. Missing Saul rose like a stone in my throat. Was he in pain? Was someone maybe torturing him?

I told that line of thought to take a hike. It just laughed at me and kept on going. That's the problem with seeing so much of the nightside. Your imagination just works too damn well, because it has a *lot* of food to keep it going.

"It's possible," Hutch finally said. "Very possible. Banefire creates a psychic barrier as well as a physical one. What's going on, Jill?"

"Do you really want to know, Hutchinson?" I sounded more savage than usual, had to stop myself. "Look, dig up anything you can out of the theory books, okay? Check Malvern and the Breisler." I considered telling him to go through the hunter records in Galina's vault for the hell of it, but what would I tell him to look for? Evidence that Mikhail or Jack Karma had an agreement with a hellbreed?

I didn't want to believe it. But the poisonous seed of doubt was planted. God damn Perry.

Too late. He's as damned as he's going to get. You need to make sure you don't follow him.

"Breakfast in ten minutes," the Were in my kitchen said quietly, and murmurs went around. I felt their attention, though they were tactfully not listening. It felt like more had arrived, too. The fridge was going to be picked bare, and they would restock my groceries before they left.

"When you put it that way..." Hutch gave a long-suffering sigh. "Should I still keep digging for that Argoth asshole?"

Thank God for you, Hutch. I rested the phone on my shoulder, so I could check my guns. They were where they always were. I forced my hands away. "Yes. I'm not ruling that out *just* yet. Better safe than sorry."

Scratching of pencil against paper. "Okay. Look up Julius, keep working Argoth angle, cross-check with Perry, check for banefire breaking connections between 'breed and Traders. Is there anything else on this Julius character, anything at all?"

"He likes virgins." I snorted. "Does that make you feel safer, or not?"

"I went to *college*," he informed me huffily, and hung up. I laid the phone down gently, restraining the urge to slam it into the cradle and crack the plastic. The Talisman trembled on my chest, like a live thing.

It was a live thing. Now I couldn't even remember Mikhail wearing it without thinking of Perry. Or Belisa.

Sunlight strengthened in the skylights. I stood there, staring at the phone for a moment and breathing deeply. Keeping the lid on that box of rage bouncing around at the bottom of my chest.

"All done up?" Anya, at my shoulder. She was so damn *quiet*, even for a hunter. I almost twitched. "Let's get this over with, so we can eat. I'm starving."

She was always starving. No wonder she got along with Weres so well.

It was an uncharitable thought. My entire body hurt, vicious little nips of pain all over. Even my hair hurt, the charms weighing it down. "Yeah." But I stared at the phone for another couple of seconds, willing it to ring and tell me something useful.

Something like, *It's me, kitten, I'm free and coming home.*

A hand on my shoulder. This time I did twitch, but did not draw a gun. I found Anya examining me. She didn't look perplexed or concerned. There was a faint vertical crease between her eyebrows, and I saw the beginnings of crow's-feet radiating from the outside corners of those blue eyes.

There is a disconcerting directness to a hunter's gaze when they're completely focusing on you. It's a hunter's job never to look away—we bear witness, and we watch what others can't bear to.

Mikhail taught me that. He'd been old for a hunter when I met him, but still lethal. And here was Anya—I remembered her as an apprentice, the first time Larssen brought her over to help Mikhail and me with a Black Mist infestation let loose by a circle of cannibalistic Traders. She had been quiet and watchful even then, the kind of girl who would vanish at a crowded party until you struck up a conversation and realized just how pretty and smart she really was. "Hides her light under a bushel," was Larssen's succinct sum-up.

She was getting older, too. While I looked just the same. I only *felt* old.

"Maybe breakfast first?" She actually looked hopeful.

"No." My throat was dry. "Let's get this over with."

The etheric protections on my warehouse walls were awake, tendrils of blue light sliding through the physical structure. My blue eye, and the unphysical gauze layer of Sight over the natural world, could see it clearly enough. Anya immediately moved a few steps to my left, and I knew without looking that she'd drawn one of her guns.

The sparring space was large and open, hardwood-floored, skylights everywhere filling up with gold. I could have wished for some more sunlight, but wishing never did anyone any good.

Mirrors and a ballet barre marched down one side of the room. Weapons were hung on the other three walls; at the far end, pride of place went to a long shape under a fall of amber silk. The spear quivered gently, sensing a current of bloodlust in the air. Between the lance and the Talisman humming sleepily on my chest, I could probably handle Perry if I had to.

It was a comforting thought. For a certain value of comforting, I guess. The fact that I would rather not lay a hand on the spear unless I *had* to was incidental. Wasn't it?

In the middle of the open space, Melisande Belisa knelt, her battered feet still bleeding a little on the hardwood. Her silks were torn, and she reeked of smoke. The iron collar clasped her delicate neck, laid against her shoulders like a yoke, and thin threads of blood slid down from where it rubbed against her skin. The Chaldean marks on it ran with diseased gold. Her black eyes were completely blank.

The chain crawled with those same golden runes. They unraveled halfway up its length. *Now that's interesting.* I hadn't asked Hutch about collars for a Sorrow. I was going to have to do that.

He was really earning every single moment's worth of effort I'd spent on getting him back home without federal charges.

Perry crouched in front of the Sorrow. He was immaculate again, and I wondered where he'd cleaned up. The pit of my stomach turned over hard, thinking of him in any of my bathrooms. Or, maybe worse, not having to—just stepping out of the grime and smoke tarnish and somehow becoming his usual self.

They were both moving slightly. Perry would lean forward a little, shifting his weight, and Belisa would lean back just as infinitesimally. Then he would relax, rocking back, and she would go back to her slump-shouldered kneeling.

He was making a slight crooning sound, too, like a child trying to entice a reluctant dog.

A nasty, sociopathic little child.

My gorge rose. I swallowed bitterness. "Pericles." It had all the snap of command I was used to putting into it. "Answers."

He was silent for fractionally longer than was polite. At least it stopped that goddamn crooning. "Hello, darling." Soft, reasonable, bland. "Do you like her? She's so wonderfully *decorative.*

And so predictable, too. Always treacherous. You appreciate that in a woman after a while. Constancy of its own sort."

I kept my hand away from my guns with an effort. "Tell me about Julius, Perry."

He was still for a whole long-ticking fifteen seconds. Utterly, eerily still—not the stillness of a hunter, which contains little bits of motion in its own way. No, this was as if he'd turned into an inanimate object. The scar was full of soft fire, little brushes against it like the wet rasp of a cherry-red, scaled tongue.

When he did move, it was to slowly straighten, his legs stretching out. He made a queer little twitch with his head. Something inside his neck crackled a little. "There are other things I'd rather tell you about." He didn't turn to face us, and Anya drifted another few steps, stepping soundlessly.

It was a comfort to have another hunter in the room.

"Start with Julius, Perry. Save the rest of it."

"Oh, but you'll want to hear this. It seems my lackey was rather a naughty boy. He gave you a gift I had no intention of giving just yet, but I can't begrudge it to you. Tell me, how does it feel to know your teacher bore the same cross you do?"

A gift for you. For a moment I thought he'd meant the bodies near the freeway, and bile rose in my throat. Then the meaning hit home.

My jaw set so hard my teeth ached. Basic healing sorcery means they don't shatter or fall out very easily. Still, there was something creaking in my mouth. The creaking slid down my neck, and the scar was soft velvet. Wet pleasure slid up the nerve channels, touching my shoulder like a lover's hand.

It was just like being in the room off his white bedroom, the one with the tiles and the iron rack and him fiddling with the scar, trying to make me react. Trying to make me jump the way he wanted me to.

Anya glanced at me. The silver in her hair slid soundlessly. Her eyebrows were up, her lips slightly parted as if she wanted to say something. Her leather duster whispered slightly as she moved again, covering Perry from another angle that would mean she could shoot clear of Belisa.

I wanted to tell her not to bother. The sooner that snake's head was chopped off, the better.

Then why didn't you do it, Jill?

Because doing it for the wrong reason would damn me. Even more thoroughly than a hunter could be said to be damned in the first place. Even if nobody else knew the difference, *I* would, and that was all that mattered. Knowing that difference and doing it anyway would make me no better than the things I hunted.

And then Perry's little smile would turn into a sawtooth grin, and I would pay for every single insult I'd ever offered him.

That would keep him busy for a long, long while. And he'd make sure I was awake for all of it.

Oh, I knew. I'd known since the beginning. I'd realized it the moment he'd made the offer, that cherry-red tongue flickering out to touch his bloodless lips. Perry and I were playing this game for different reasons. I wanted the power to keep cleansing the night.

He wanted something else. Something that would end with me even worse than a Trader.

"I know Riverson told you." Silken, even, each word just so. "I regret I wasn't there to see your face. Such an interesting shade of white. Almost as pale as you are now."

"Julius." I managed the one word, found I could use others. "Your immediate superior?"

"I? I *have* no superior, my darling. And certainly no equal, in this world or in Hell." Now he turned on one elegant heel, and though his suit was perfectly clean and his hair neatly arranged, his face was still streaked with smoke. It glared at me, that mask of banality, the even regular features unassuming except for the shadow of twisting under them, like a knife under a blanket. His eyes burned blue, a sterile inferno as far away from Anya's clear steady gaze as it was possible to get.

"Hellspawn," the other hunter said, softly but with an edge of incredible disdain. "Answer the question."

"Little human hunter." He didn't look away from me. "You're interfering with business not your own."

"Ooooh, scary." Her tone said very clearly that she wasn't impressed. "Kismet?"

It took two tries to make my throat work. Fortunately the words came out just right—bored, with an edge of menace. "Julius, Perry. Your immediate superior, coming through to ask you a few questions. Belisa playing both sides against the middle again. You should have learned not to mess with Sorrows last time."

The snarl drifting over his bland face was a balm. It disturbed the mask of humanity for a critical half second. Now I was in control of myself, and I slid the gun free of the holster.

Anya exhaled softly. But her pulse was even and steady, marching along. Mikhail was always on me about my pulse. My heart cracked, but no expression reached my face. "One more time, Pericles. Julius. Rutger planning on moving you aside, since Shen didn't manage?"

He considered me. Lifted one hand, tapped a finger to his smoke-grimed lips. "Don't you ever wonder why your teacher sought out his death at the hands of a Sorrows whore?"

"That's none of your business." I raised the gun. "The next time you sass me, Pericles, it's going to be a bullet. Start talking about Julius."

"It started with Jack Karma. The first one, dear, not the pale copy. I'd been looking for a hunter lineage with certain...peculiar qualities, and I finally found one. The Karma children have always had such charming personalities. A fault line right down the middle, hair-thin but so vulnerable."

I'll admit it. I lost my temper. Two steps forward, Anya drifting with me, and my finger tightened on the trigger. "Julius, Perry! Start fucking talking."

He actually smirked, the bastard. "Language, Kiss. Such indelicate—"

I took another step forward, but Anya was quicker. The knife blurred, parting the air with a low sweet sound, and sank into his throat. He folded down, making a very undignified choking sound, and I stood and stared like a civilian.

Anya glanced at me. "You didn't know? How could you *not* know?" She now had both guns out, and pointed at Perry while he keeled over onto the floor with a far-too-heavy thump.

The world shifted underneath me. Just a few inches, but that was enough.

Riverson I didn't have to believe. But Anya was hunter, and hunters don't lie. Not to each other.

We *can't*.

I actually swayed, half-turning and staring at her. My mouth dropped open, but no sound came out. The .45 almost slid free of my fingers; they spasmed shut at the last moment.

I found my voice, a harsh croak that didn't sound like me at all. "What?"

"I thought you just didn't talk about it." Her coat whispered as she stepped aside again, to make sure her angle of fire was still clear. "Jesus, Kismet. How could you not know?"

"I . . ."

Perry gurgled. He reached up, fingers closing around the knife hilt. Worked it back and forth. An obscene squishing sound came from the unholy flesh while black ichor welled up sluggishly. She'd pegged him right in the larynx, missing the arteries neatly. A double-bladed dagger with a plain black hilt, just the thing for shutting up sassy-ass hellbreed.

He choked, writhing, working the blade back and forth in the wound. The squishing sounds got worse.

"Mikhail had a bargain with this piece of garbage, too. I don't know about either Karma, though. You seriously didn't . . ." Something occurred to her then. She considered me, blue eyes gone cold. "Huh."

"Breakfast!" a Were yelled from the other room. A ripple of appreciative sound went through the rest of the warehouse, a counterpoint to Perry's gagging. The knife slid free on a gush of black ichor with a weird, opalescent sheen.

Perry was still grinning. His mouth worked, but he didn't speak. The hole in his throat, his shell breached by the blessed silver loading the blade, would be slow to heal. But he still looked like a cat full of canary.

My stomach curled up against itself. "Mikhail." I sounded like I'd been punched.

"We've got other problems." Her chin jutted forward a little, indicating the hellbreed on the floor. Melisande Belisa still crouched. The pool of ichor almost touched her knees. "Like what the fuck he's doing with a Sorrow."

"He . . ." I swallowed hard, again. My stomach closed up even tighter, as if it would throw the mouthful of spit right back out. The Talisman rumbled unhappily on my chest, almost like Saul's purr. Except Saul would comfort me, and this unsteady deep thrum wasn't comforting at all. It was like the whine of a jet engine before something goes terribly wrong and the plane rediscovers gravity in a big way. "Met her before. A while ago." A horrible supposition rose inside me like bad gas in a mine shaft.

"I'll just bet." The corner of Anya's mouth lifted slightly. "Kismet…"

Perry knew Belisa from that case, the one with the bugfuck-crazy Sorrows Grand Mother and her job to shove a Chaldean Elder God into my resisting body. But what if, just *what if*, he'd known her before?

How had Mikhail met Belisa? I'd often wondered. Usually in the long, dark watches of the night, while I patrolled the city looking for trouble. I used to come back to it like peeling at a scab, until time had given me other things to think about.

Pieces of the puzzle slid together inside my head. I inhaled sharply, and Anya actually yelled as I leapt.

I was on Perry in a heartbeat, pistol-whipping him. His head bounced. Bone cracked, black fluid spraying, and even though he had a hole torn in his throat the hellbreed was making a queer chuffing noise that I realized was *laughter*.

He was *laughing* at me.

The world turned red. I was not flailing wildly. No, the instinct and expertise of years of murderous combat every night was filling me in an ice-burning torrent, and I hit to kill.

Chaos, the world turning over. Bright stars flashed across the red sheet my vision had become.

Someone had just punched me.

I hit the floor and wrestled with them. Whoever it was, they were unholy quick and strong, and they didn't move like a 'breed. No claws, and someone was yelling my name. Someone I should recognize.

But first I had to kill *him*. They had my left hand locked, arm twisted bruising-hard, someone supple and dangerous as a python in my grasp. Suddenly more hands were clamping down on me, hard but not with the hurtful prick of hellbreed claws. I heard someone screaming obscenities in a ragged, cracked, unlovely voice, and realized it was me.

I also realized I was under a pile of Weres, and they were having trouble holding me down. Anya had dragged me off of Perry. I'd been trying to kill him by pistol-whipping him. Or with my bare hands.

Oh, shit. I'd lost it.

He'd finally found a way to make me react. Only it hadn't been Perry, it had been her.

If she said it, it had to be true.

Oh, God. A wrecked scream rose up inside me, was throttled, died with a whining, hurt sound.

I struggled, but not with the hands holding me down. With *myself.* The scar was a brand, pressed into scorching flesh, laughing in a low, nasty whisper nobody else could hear. The abyss howled, and I pulled myself back from it with an effort that bowed me up into a hoop, every muscle locking down and my throat on fire, trying to scramble back from the howling madness opening up inside my head, inside my chest, inside everything that made me myself.

I made it. Just barely. Closer than I'd ever been.

I went limp. They sagged down on me, and I hoped I hadn't hurt someone. "Anya?" I whispered. "OhGod. God, oh God."

"God*dam*mit." I heard the click of silver-plated handcuffs. "Is she all right?"

"We can't sedate a hunter." It sounded like Amalia. "She'll burn right through—"

The very suggestion of sedation made me heave up from the floor again, struggling madly. They bore down, a tangle of arms and legs and more-than-human weight.

"Jill! Goddammit, Jill, calm down!" Anya, the snap of command under her sweet high-pitched voice. "*Calm down or I will make you, hunter!*"

She probably used that tone on her apprentices. It worked. I lay still as death. My eyes squeezed shut so hard tracers fired geometric shapes and whorls in the darkness behind my lids. The glow of the living beings on top of me poured in through the dumb meat of my left eyelid, my smart eye piercing the veils. Even when I tried to shut it out, I could not look away.

"Kismet." Still with the crisp bite of authority. "Are you reasonable?"

No, I am not reasonable. This is not reasonable. I made some sort of noise, whether affirmation or denial I couldn't tell, but it was apparently good enough.

One by one the Weres flowed away. They were all lionesses, their tawny hair falling in beautiful ripples and their eyes lambent. One of them was Amalia, and she leaned down, offering her hand. Muscle stood out under the bare, burnished skin of her upper arms. Her mouth was drawn tight, though, and her entire face was set and paler than a Were had any right to be.

I reached up as if drowning. Her warm fingers threaded through mine, and she hauled me to my feet. As soon as I had my balance she was away, stepping with the peculiar soft-footed glide of a cat Were, and a longing to see Saul shook me right down to my bootsoles.

Anya had Perry handcuffed on the floor. He was a mess. The urge to cross the intervening space and start kicking him with my own steel-toed boots rose, was repressed. Did not die away. The Talisman made a thin keening sound, and a curl of smoke rose to my nose. My aura crackled restlessly. Every piece of silver on me was warm and running with blue light.

"Jill." Anya, very carefully. "Are you reasonable?"

I cleared my throat. Swallowed twice. Stared at the hamburger mess of Perry's face. The grin was still there, white teeth flashing through meat and a chortling gurgle far back in his throat.

He had finally, after all this time, made me react.

"Jill." Anya, again.

Hunters do not lie to each other. We can't. It's too dangerous. Not only that, but each hunter has descended into Hell at the end of their apprenticeship, trusting their teacher to hold the line and bring them out alive. If you ask an apprentice what the line's made of, you'll get varying theoretical answers. If you ask a hunter, you'll only get one. It's why we don't even shade the truth.

It's so simple, really. You can't lie to someone else who has been loved like that. Loved so hard it pulls you out of Hell itself.

Mikhail. Bitter acid filled my mouth. "No." The word stung my throat. "I am very fucking far from reasonable, Anya Devi." Was that water on my cheeks? I was crying?

Why? God, why *cry* at a time like this? It had to be blood. I was bleeding salt and water from the knowledge.

"It's true." Was there a rock caught in her throat, too? Did she have to pull every word out of that raw bleeding place inside that makes us what we are? "I swear it's true. I thought you knew."

Idiots, Mikhail said. *They think we do this for them. There is only one reason for to do what we do,* milaya. *It is for to quiet screaming in our own heads.*

Hearing him in my head used to be a double-edged comfort. Now it tore at everything I'd ever believed about him.

"Is there anything else?" My hands were fists. I had no idea where my gun had gone, and that was bad. A hunter doesn't lose track of something like that. I licked my scorch-dry lips. "Is there any fucking thing else someone *forgot* to tell me?"

"He must have had his rea—" She shut up as I looked at her. My blue eye was burning, and I knew there would be a pinprick of red in the depths of my pupil.

And I honestly do not know what I would have done if the loud, clanging chime of my doorbell hadn't rung. It cut the tension like a knife, and every Were in the building tensed. Intuition hit me with a sick thump, right in the solar plexus.

I turned on my heel and ran for the door.

CHAPTER 20

The envelope, heavy cream-colored linen paper, stank of hell-breed. The sweet candy sickness mixed with rotting ichor, cinnamon rolls, and breakfast smells, as well as the spice and healthy fur tang of Weres. There were no obvious traps or tingles of sorcery on it.

Someone had spent some effort to get it delivered right to my door. Whoever it was had evaded the watch the Weres had set, and they all looked grave about that. It didn't stop them from queuing up for breakfast, though. I sank down on the couch—an old orange Naugahyde monster Saul had slipcovered. It was about the first thing he'd done when he moved in. Other than throwing out all my kitchen gear and starting afresh. It was a good thing I had municipal funding; he'd about wiped me out when it came to pots and pans.

Stop stalling, Jill.

Anya stood at the end of the coffee table, watching me. Like she expected me to go bugshit again at any moment. She had her absinthe bottle out and took a swig as she stared at me.

I tore the envelope open. Two photographs and an 8½-by-11 sheet of the same expensive linen paper. The writing was copperplate script, the ink rusty and watery, scratched on with what I'd bet was an iron nib.

The first picture. Black-and-white, glossy, high quality. I stared at it for a few moments, my pulse pounding in my ears. Handed it to Anya.

It was Saul, whole and unharmed, lying on the floor of an iron cage. Taken between bars, it focused on his profile. His eyes were open, but he had curled up, one arm under his head. Grace in every line of his long, lean body, his boots and fringed jacket gone but the rest of his clothing there. He looked a little disarranged, and the paint on his cheeks was drying and flaking off. The cage was square, and as far as I could tell there was no Chaldean scoring on the bars.

They would have other ways of keeping a Were quiescent. He was obviously not dead.

Anything could happen, though.

The second picture was taken with a telephoto lens. A slight figure, hunching his shoulders as he went through Galina's front door. A nose that could have come from an Aztec codex, pitted cheeks, and his lank hair.

Gilberto.

I handed that photograph over, too. It quivered a little bit in my fingers.

The note was short and to the point.

Via Dolorosa, at dawn tomorrow. Come to the middle of the bridge and wait.

It was signed with a twisted little sketch—a glyph that looked like a crying mouth behind clawed fingers. That was the closest the little bastards could get to writing Helletöng down. It was a name-mark, and a huge break. I could get it to Hutch and find out who was working to bring this Julius, or whoever, through. That was just one short step to serving justice on him, her, or it.

Justice? No. *Vengeance.* Screaming, bone-breaking, blood-spattering vengeance.

Via Dolorosa had to be Wailer Memorial Bridge, lifting up from downtown and flying over the river, leading to the highway that ran under the bluffs. There wasn't much room for anything but freight yards and a sad shantytown or two. Every morning you could see some of the homeless trudging across the bridge toward the better pickings of the city's beating heart.

I handed the letter to Anya. It fluttered like a bird in my unsteady fingers. And I wondered just where Rutger and that god-damn 'breed in black pajamas were. I hadn't seen their bodies, so they were possibly still alive.

And "possibly" will bite you on the ass at every opportunity, when you're dealing with hellbreed.

"It's a trap," she said immediately. "Probably set by that son of a bitch in there or one of his vassals. There's no cover on that bridge. Bet you anything it's being watched now, too."

"Yes." I nodded. Silver chimed. I took my hand away from a gun butt when she gave me a meaningful stare. "Exactly."

"You're not going to do it." Flat and final.

I couldn't lie, so I just stared at the paper. *Her* hands were steady. There was a scrape on her right knuckles, thin threads of healing sorcery sunk into the skin and binding everything together. If I didn't have the scar, I'd be a mass of healing sorcery by this point too. I probably wouldn't have tried banefire in that cage, either.

There were so many things I couldn't have survived or done without the mark of Perry's lips on my wrist. I'd never caught the smell of sicksweet corruption on Mikhail...but then, after Perry had given me the mark and my enhanced senses, had Mikhail's mark vanished?

No, because Belisa had seen it. Or was that another lie? Did the scar remain even if the bargain was cleared?

I shuddered at the thought.

Anya dropped the letter on the coffee table. It fell as if it was heavier than it had any right to be. Leather creaked as she folded her arms, the cape of her duster moving as her shoulders came up. "Jill. You're *not* going to do it. Not without me."

I searched for a reasonable answer. Finally found one. "You have to shut down those other evocation sites. The Weres can't do it; it takes a hunter. There might be other mass graves lying around, too."

"How are we going to—" She caught on. "No. No *way*. Jill, for Christ's sake. You go in there like this, he'll eat you alive."

She had a point. "He hasn't yet." I clasped my hands, my apprentice-ring glinting sharply. I remembered Mikhail fitting it on my third left finger, a small strange smile on his aquiline face. *There, little snake. Honest silver, on vein to heart. You are apprentice. Now it begins.* And his eyes, bluer and paler than Anya's, cool and considering. Weighing me. "What else didn't Mikhail tell me?"

She spread her hands. "I don't know."

The smell of food was drowning out everything else, and I didn't know whether to be happy or revolted about that. It was just masking the hellbreed stink now. Just putting a pretty face on it.

I sank back into the couch. Stared at the ceiling. The skylights were full of thin hot winter gold now. I'd lost a lot of time knocked out in that warehouse, behind bars running with Chaldean runes. It was small comfort that Rutger or Belisa hadn't pulled off whatever they were attempting. The more fools they, leaving me in there with my weapons...

...but could I take anything about the whole episode for granted? I couldn't.

Whatever was going on, Perry was playing for keeps. There might be others working at cross-purposes; God knows hellbreed don't cooperate. It had all the makings of a clusterfuck in progress, and not much in the way of stopping it unless I put on my big-girl panties and started getting some shit *done*.

When I brought my chin back down, I found Anya watching me. There was also a plate of breakfast—eggs, pancakes, hash browns, and cut-up cantaloupe that Saul had been planning on using for a fruit salad as soon as he could get by the farmer's market—held at eye level by a somber Theron. He wore a Trixies T-shirt, jeans, and the expression of an unhappy but determined Were.

My heart wrung down on itself.

"Gilberto." My lips were numb. "They might grab him outside Galina's."

"We've already sent more Weres." Theron's mouth was set in a thin line.

"Hellbreed—" I began.

"Shut up." He shoved the plate in my face again. "And eat. No, we don't go up against hellbreed. We can buy him some time to get to Sanctuary, maybe. Make it harder for them to steal him away. But *you* need to eat."

I grabbed the plate, because otherwise he would have pushed it right up my nose. "Theron, goddammit—"

"You're about to do that Lone Ranger shit, Jill. It never ends well." He gave me a level, dark glare, then turned on his heel and stalked away.

Jesus. Taken down a peg by a *Were*. And not a word about Saul. Of course, it would be tactless to say anything about it, wouldn't it? They were the soul of tact.

And if he was dead, they wouldn't speak his name. They have some funny ideas about that. Ancestor-worshipping people usually do.

I set the plate down on the coffee table. A young bird Were, brown feathers tied fluttering in his sleek dark bowl cut, handed another plate to Anya, holding a fork against the side with his thumb. They were going to have to break out the paper plates and picnic cutlery in a bit; I didn't have nearly enough china for the crowd in here.

"He's right. You get stupid now, we'll lose a hunter. And quite possibly more Weres." Anya crouched, setting down her absinthe bottle. She started shoveling in the food as if it was oatmeal, neatly and ferociously. She hunched a little, too, the way you do in juvie or prison.

Just like Gil. It had taken me forever to learn to eat like a civilian. I'd done it for Saul, mostly. He was big on manners.

I stood up. Anya tensed, her fork in midair. "What the hell do you think—"

"I am going to take those two somewhere else." Brittle calm enveloped me. "You round up the Weres and get out of here. I want you to kill every evocation site you can find and liaise with Montaigne in case there are more bodies. I'll question Perry and leave any information I get with Hutch."

She shook her head, vigorously. "Bad idea. *Bad* idea."

"They'll come for me, here or wherever I am, before dawn tomorrow. Meeting on the bridge is just a ploy. There's another game being played here, and I want to find out what it is before it gets any deeper *or* another hellbreed comes through to wipe my city off the map." My fingers ran lightly over weapons—guns, knives, my bullwhip, my full pockets, everything stowed away. "They won't give me a whole day to get my feet under me and make plans. I don't want the Weres catching any *more* flak. And Perry will answer every one of my questions." *Every single one. God help us both. But especially me.*

She didn't think much of that idea, either. "You can't trust him not to—"

"Anya. I've been playing Perry for years now. Since before Mikhail...left." *Died, Jill. Call it what it is. That Sorrows bitch that cut his throat is in there, and you haven't killed her yet. Do you know what you're doing?* I told that little worried voice to take a hike. Checked my ammo again, the equivalent of a nervous tic for a hunter. "I haven't done too badly."

Meaning: *I'm not damned yet.*

"If you didn't even know that he—" She shut up when I stepped away, leaving the plate on the coffee table. Saul had thrown away the ruins of the box and its silver bow, too, probably with fistfuls of salt. He knew what precautions to take, now.

Too bad it hadn't saved him.

Had they meant to kidnap him here? Should I have asked him to go straight to Galina's? Were they tracking him even as he left the cemetery?

I brought myself back to the present with a jerk. My aura wasn't crackling anymore, and that was good. The Talisman was a sleeping weight on my chest, heavy and warm. Like a consoling hand. "No matter what I knew, or know, or should have known, Mikhail's dead and my city's in danger. My best bet is getting that fucking hellbreed to a place where I can deal with him. With you and the Weres getting those evocation sites shut down, I have a chance of getting Saul out of this alive and my city another few days of rolling along. Do it, Anya."

"Jill? *Jill!* You're not going to—"

I walked away.

CHAPTER 21

I figured the Monde Nuit was the last place anyone would expect me to go at this point. Shafts of sunlight pierced the gloom, because the lights downstairs were all turned off now. The entire place looked like a stage set, dusty and disused, every angle subtly off and placed that way for show.

Perry was trussed up like a Christmas goose, double pairs of silver-plated handcuffs doing their duty at wrists and ankles, the larger sizes around his elbows and knees. Anya had gagged him, too. His eyes were closed; the gaping hole in his throat was closed but not completely healed. He mercifully didn't even try to squawk. He was heavy deadweight, and I checked the cuffs every time I set him down.

Belisa obeyed every time the chain was twitched, stumbling around as if she was blind. She'd follow verbal directions, too, and I wondered if she was playing dumb or if the chain had something to do with it. With just the collar on she'd been pretty peppy, and obviously she couldn't take it off.

Another mystery to solve.

Still, I heaved a sigh of relief when I got them both up the stairs and into the office. The chain pulsed obscenely in my hand, Chaldean runes flinching away from my fingers. The metal was warm; it almost felt alive.

The white bed was torn to shreds, the bar a ruin of glass and mirror shards. Riverson was nowhere in sight. But the closed-circuit cameras were still working. I put Belisa in a corner facing the wall, like the bad little girl she was. It was work to haul Perry's unresisting weight along the floor, but getting him up the stairs had been the hard part. The scar was burning, the feeling working deeper and deeper, as if it would hit bone soon. It never had yet—but still.

The small room leading off his office/bedroom was glaring white tile on all four walls and the floor. An iron rack stood off-center, closer to the far wall than the door. The ceiling was a blank pane of fluorescents, their harsh glare bouncing off the table set to the right along the wall.

A rosewood case, its gold latches unbuckled, sat in the precise middle of the table. As if waiting for me. My skin turned cold and tight, except for the hard little pinprick bumps of gooseflesh.

Perry didn't struggle as I got him fastened into the iron rack. His eyes were still closed, lips moving slightly around the leather strap of the gag. Spread-eagled, slumping from his arms, the front of his shirt blackened and his suit spattered. I made sure he was fastened in securely, testing each strap twice. His fingers moved like little white spider legs, and he didn't help or hinder. I popped the gag, and his mouth gave it up without complaint. It was slick and wet, but I stuffed it in a pocket anyway.

When I stepped back, his eyes opened slowly. For a moment he looked half blind, indigo threading through the whites like veins and sending questing tendrils into his glowing irises. His lips still moved, writhing obscenely, and a faint rumble of Helletöng rattled away from him in concentric rings.

I waved an admonishing finger. "Now, now. None of that."

The töng bled away, like a freight train vanishing in the distance. He stared at me, and the indigo retreated from his irises. Finally, he licked his lips, and his voice was a hoarse ruin of itself. "We were always going to come to this, Kiss. *Always.*"

Careful, Jill. Make this his mistake, not yours. "Let's start with Saul, Perry. Who has him?"

"Perhaps I did take your cat." He grinned through a mask of rotting ichor. "Perhaps not. What are you going to do now?"

It wasn't time to play the biggest card I had, yet. Instead, I reached up and touched the Talisman. It arched up under my fingers, cool metal that somehow conveyed the impression of faraway flame, a heat not quite felt against my skin. "Who has him now?"

The strap across his forehead was as tight as it would go. He tried to move his head, couldn't, and rolled his eyes, still grinning. "Now why would I tell you that? With him out of the way, you're so much more amenable. So much more *pliant*."

That's what you think. I turned away. Headed for the table. The rosewood was slick and satiny as I opened the case.

The flechettes lay arranged neatly against dark-blue velvet, each one a razor gleam. There were tiny ones that fit over the fingertips, curved and straight ones as long as my hand, other assorted shapes and sizes. The largest was as long as my forearm, its cutting edge curved slightly and a blood-groove scoring down its fluid length.

"Ohhhhhhh..." Perry sighed. "How much will you hurt me, Kiss? You see what a *good* little hellspawn I am. I take things from your hand I would take from no other."

Don't tempt me. But it was too late for that. I took my time, running my fingers over the flechette handles, considering each and every one.

I'd used them all. Before Perry had welshed on his end of the deal by playing with Sorrows, I'd been in here every month. More often than not he had me strap him into the frame and start cutting. Sometimes it was a beating, and he grinned each time I broke his pale, hard hellbreed shell. Once he lounged in his bed, narrow pale hairless chest exposed, and toyed with a dish of strawberries while he asked me questions. What my favorite color was. What I wanted to be when I grew up. What I thought of politics.

All a game, to get me to respond. Gathering up little bits of psychology, storing it up for the day I stepped over that hairline crack and into his world.

The day I was damned. The day he owned me.

It might end up being today, if you let it. Careful, Jill.

I picked up the largest flechette. The metal handle, scored for traction like a gun butt, was ice-cold. The scar chilled, too, a warning.

My face settled against itself. My pulse dropped, as if I was waiting on a rooftop for a target to show. I wasn't as calm as I could be. For one thing, the skin of my right cheek was twitching as if a seamstress was plucking at it with a needle.

For another, the Talisman was rumbling too. Louder than the Helletöng, the subsonics striking the tiled walls and reverberating. The Eye's song swallowed the unmusical nastiness of Helletöng, turning each limping broken hiss and groaning curse on its head, blending it into an even greater theme.

Something about that helped, though I don't know why. I let out a sharp breath and was suddenly, mostly, back in control of myself.

Except for another worried little thought. Why would Perry give it back to me?

When I turned, I found Perry considering me. The indigo had bled out of his eyes, and they were bright, glowing blue around the too-dark pupil. The border between pupil and iris shifted, each an amorphous blob of darkness with a red spark buried in its depths.

He'd never done *that* before.

The tip of his tongue crept out, wet cherry-red, and touched the corner of his mouth. "You look lovely."

I felt the smile pull up my mouth, baring my teeth. An animal's grimace as I crossed the room. "Why, Perry. Thank you." The tip of the flechette caressed his cheek. I considered it, drew it up his smoke-tarnished skin to the corner of his left eye. "How would you like to be blind?"

Not a twitch of uneasiness, but he was so very still. "You can't."

"I can put silver in the holes once I've dug your baby blues out." I cocked my head. "Wouldn't that be interesting."

His expression—interested, avid—didn't change. "Then I could no longer see your beauty, Kiss. I would miss that."

The tip dug in a little. There was nothing human under that shell, but I was fairly sure if I twisted my wrist and scooped, the eye would pop out. I knew the blade was sharp enough to cut him, whatever metal it was. No silver, because it didn't fire with blue sparks when it got near him.

"Last chance, Pericles." The calm descended on me. "Saul. Who has him?"

He grinned. Like a skull.

And then he told me. I didn't even have to cut him once.

CHAPTER 22

gunned the engine. Beside me in the passenger seat, buckled in like an unresisting doll, Melisande Belisa swayed. I wanted to keep an eye on her. And leaving her with Perry seemed...wrong.

For all I knew, Perry was still strapped in that rack. God alone knew how he got unstrapped at the end of our long-ago monthly sessions, but then he'd had flunkies. There was nobody in the building to come get him out.

I hoped he'd stay there for a while. Long enough for me to get this done and figure out a way to deal with him.

The tires squealed as the car spun, a roostertail of golden dust rising. The car leapt forward obediently. The day was well underway, noon past and the sun sinking from its apex. The chain hanging from Belisa's collar clanked as I hit the corner coming out of the Monde's parking lot and stepped on the gas. There wouldn't be many people on the street, but—

My pager buzzed. I dug it out, one hand on the wheel and the pedal to the floor. Intuition tingled along my nerves. I hit the brakes and narrowly avoided a pickup truck running a stop sign on Soledad Street. The driver was obviously drunk, careening away in a flash with ranchero music blaring.

One look at the number on my pager convinced me to pull over. There was a phone booth at Soledad and 168th. I cut the wheel hard and Belisa slumped in the seat. The chain jingled musically, a queerly wrong clashing, and I wondered where Riverson had got himself to. If, that is, Belisa had left him alive.

One more of those questions I had no time to answer. I pulled over, hit the parking brake, and took the keys with me.

Galina's phone rang twice before Hutch picked up. "Jill?"

"It's me. Is Gilberto there?"

"I thought he was with you. Anya Devi came through, she's looking for you. But there's something else. Listen, Jill—"

I cursed. Considered putting my fist through the plastic shell of the booth. Stared at the car. Belisa was deathly still, slumped against the window, and the Chaldean running through the chain flickered gold.

Yes, I parked where I could keep an eye on her. Just because she hadn't been any trouble so far was no indication.

"Shut up." Hutch actually snapped at me. I shut my mouth. "Listen, Jill. This Julius, the hellbreed? Likes virgins, looks like a manlier version of Buster Keaton, according to the description—"

"Cute," I muttered. "What about him?"

"He's already out. He surfaced two and a half weeks ago. In Louisiana."

There was a glimmer inside my car, a foxfire glow fighting with the sunlight. It was the golden glyphs, brightening. Was she struggling against the chain?

I should kill her. It would be so easy. Just a moment's worth of work and I could be done with the whole thing.

Then what Hutch had said hit home. "Oh, shit," I whispered.

"Yeah. I called Benny Cross again, on a hunch. He's madder than a wet hen, there's a full-scale war between the Sorrows and Julius's henchmen spilling over onto civilians. Julius is nowhere to be found. Benny says to be fucking careful."

"Hutch." I struggled to breathe. "What kind of chain binds a Sorrow? What does it look like?"

He was silent for a full five seconds. "Meteorite iron, I guess. It has to be bloodworked and runed; they use them for the *Pas'zhuruk*, where they eat their own. Expensive, it'd cost you an arm and a leg to get one, assuming you could pry it out of a House. Regular pin and lock on the collar, and once the collar's on the Sorrow's a slave, but has some agency. Add a chain of the same stuff and they're catatonic."

Pas'zhuruk. "Isn't that where they sacrifice a Grand Mother to one of the Elders?"

"Yeah. Um, listen. Gilberto's not here. Thought he was with you."

Fuck. "Any Weres showed up yet?"

"No, none of them either. What the fuck is—no, scratch that. I don't want to know. What do you want me to do?"

Wise man. "Call my house, see if you can raise Anya. Or get her pager. If all else fails, she'll check in with you." I shuffled priorities. Evocation altars meant they were planning on bringing *someone* through. It was too expensive a ploy to waste just to keep me chasing my tail...or maybe not. Still, I couldn't take that chance. "Tell her to evacuate my house pronto, and that Gil's been snatched, unless he shows up with the Weres. Tell her not to send any more Weres to Galina's or after me, that I have a line on Saul, and that Julius is out and making trouble. Tell her to find and burn those evocation sites as fast as she can. I don't have locations."

He was scratching furiously on a pad of paper again. "Anything else?"

"Call the Badger. Have her check every John Doe homicide in the last three weeks for anything funky. And *do not step foot outside*. I don't want to rescue you, too."

"Oh, for fuck's—come on, Jill. I don't go outside when you tell me to stay in. I just *don't.*"

"Good. Make sure Galina stays undercover too. And keep digging—cross-reference for any other hellbreed with a link to Perry that would need or just like virgin flesh to break out of Hell."

"You got it. Anything—"

"No. Stay inside." *And pray for me.* I didn't add that. He didn't need the stress. I did hang up, and leaned inside the pay phone for a moment, watching my car.

Belisa was helpless. It was the best shot I'd get. And she killed Mikhail.

I turned my right wrist over, looked at the scar. It was just the same—the print of Perry's lips, now flushed because of the etheric energy humming through it.

Mikhail.

"I don't care." My voice took me by surprise. "He must have had his reasons. He *had* to have his reasons."

Had Belisa killed him before he could find the way to tell me?

It doesn't fucking matter. Perry's out of the way for the moment. You've got a line on Saul. Go get him, then you can get to the bottom of the rest of this. And when it's over, you're going to seriously consider killing Perry. I don't care if the scar is useful, this is Too Far.

The nasty little idea that this was just what Perry would want me to think so he could damn me—or so he could help me damn myself—just wouldn't go away. So I ignored it.

Big mistake.

CHAPTER 23

It was just as Perry said—a nice three-story in Greenlea, never my favorite part of Santa Luz.

Greenlea is just north of downtown, in the shopping district. If you're really looking, you can sometimes catch a glimpse of the granite Jesus on top of Sisters of Mercy, glowering at the financial district. But Greenlea's organic froufrou boutiques and pretty little restaurants don't like seeing it. Sometimes I think it's an act of will that keeps that particular landmark obscured from certain places in the city, especially around downtown.

The last time I'd been down here, I'd been tracking down a voodoo queen's rage before it could unleash a hellbreed's idea of a circus on my town. *That* would have been unpleasant, and Perry had been up to his eyebrows in it as well.

Crackerbox houses, postage-stamp yards, yuppies and the upwardly mobile jealously watching for any sign of weakness in their neighbors. The bitch who used to live out here—Lorelei—had made quite a living for herself from their petty squabbles, for a *very* long time.

Her bakery and coffee shop was now a place claiming to sell vegan Thai and Indian food. I shuddered at the mere notion, and Saul had looked puzzled when he saw the sign.

You can't explain vegan ethnic to a carnivore. You just *can't*.

The entire neighborhood—centered around one street with two high-end bookstores, vegan eateries, a coffee shop, and a couple of kitschy-klatch places selling overpriced junk—was quiet. There's a few antique stores down at one end, and a fancy bakery and two pricey bars at the other. This particular house was at Seventh and

Mariposa, a high wooden fence around its tiny yard and every window glazed with venetian blinds. Everyone was at work, looking to afford the property taxes, and the main shopping drag was two blocks over. The street was quiet, but it wouldn't stay that way when quitting time arrived and the hipsters came home.

I parked two blocks away behind a closed-down whole-foods warehouse just to be sure, then pushed Belisa into the backseat and laid her down, making sure the pin holding the collar closed was secure. The chain rattled. She sighed. Her flayed feet were healing. Long tangled dark hair, and if she closed her eyes you could see where she would be pretty. The exotic sort of woman a man would look twice at on the street.

But those black eyes were holes into another place. She didn't close them. I had to watch for a few seconds to make sure she was blinking.

My right hand moved. The gun was out of its holster in a hot heartbeat, barrel pressed against her forehead. It would be so *easy*, and the mess in the backseat wouldn't be the worst thing I've ever cleaned up.

No, Jill. Don't do it.

She blinked again. Utterly helpless. Revulsion twisted my stomach.

Not this way. If you kill her, make it clean. Don't be like what you hunt.

You don't live long as a hunter if you're not willing to just get the fucking job done, with whatever means are to hand. But there is a line you cannot cross, and the only guide for where that line is rests inside your skull. You could call it conscience, I guess. It's not your teacher or your lover, it's not even God. Because you can fool all of them, some of the time. When it counts.

The only person you take accounting with as a hunter is *yourself*. And I knew as surely as I was breathing, if I pulled the trigger on Melisande Belisa right now, I would be damning myself. It would be easy for Perry to own me after that step.

I breathed out a soft curse. I was wet with sweat, the way I never am unless I've been fighting hard. The clammy-cold film reeked of adrenaline and a bitter copper tang.

Fear.

It was a struggle to put the gun away. My arm actually physically resisted, muscles locking. I tipped my head back and swore, and finally got the .45 back in its dark little home.

I closed Belisa in the car and left her there. It would get hot with the thin winter sun beating down, but I found I didn't care.

I shimmied up over the board fence from the house next door and dropped down cat-soft. Drew my right-hand gun again, surveyed the backyard. The grass hadn't been cut, and the entire house was a brackish bruise of etheric contamination.

Oh yeah. We've got hellbreed. Hang on, Saul. I'm coming.

No cover. It was bare as a bone except for metallic trash cans clustered near the high wooden gate to the front. Coming over that way might have caused a racket.

Three concrete steps up to the back door. My blue eye caught no betraying quiver of ill intent, nothing to suggest there were hellbreed here beyond the thick etheric bruising. No hint of Saul.

But then, they would want to keep him well hidden. In a basement, probably, since the picture had shown him on concrete.

Hold on, baby. I'm on my way.

A thin high horsetail cloud scudded in front of the sun, the light darkening a bit. It was a bad omen, but it was still daylight.

The doorknob was ice-cold. I exhaled softly between my teeth, sorcery tingling in my fingers. The scar tensed, sensing something it was akin to. I wondered if Perry had managed to get out of the iron rack yet, banished the thought. Sorcery requires fierce, relaxed concentration, and if I kept thinking about Perry and what he'd told me I was going to be anything but relaxed.

The deadbolt eased free with a *snick*. I winced, waited. No sound. It was child's play to undo the other lock, and I twisted the knob a little at a time. It eased free.

I shoved it open, stepping to the side in case they opened fire, then stepped back and dove through, rolling to come up in a crouch. It was a hall that had been turned into a utility room, a washer and dryer standing to attention and a little bamboo-mat thing to clean your shoes.

Dead silence, sunlight falling through windows. The gun tracked, every inch of me alert and quivering, ready for all hell to break loose.

Nothing. Not a peep. A tang of hellbreed corruption, sick-sweet, and a fading ghost of dark spice and clean fur, familiar to me as my own breath.

Saul.

Nothing. No betraying creaks or little whispers, no sense of breathing habitation houses get when someone's around. I braced my back against the wall, drawing my other gun. My stomach turned over hard as I gapped my mouth, tasting the air. There was another smell under the perfume of supernatural. It was the gassy note of mortal death.

No.

The kitchen was as empty as a dry well, all the cabinets closed and the sinks clear. Whoever lived here was a big believer in minimalism. Either that or they spent so much money affording the house they couldn't buy more than a cheap round table and two scavenged chairs.

There was the door that probably led to the cellar, open just a crack. Nothing but darkness beyond. I ghosted up to it through two bars of wintry sun, toed it until it swung wide and disclosed wooden stairs going down into absolute darkness. There was a light switch, difficult to flip with my elbow but I managed it. The little sound it made was loud in the thick silence.

I was suspecting there weren't any hellbreed in the house. If there weren't...

The stairs were solid, at least. I hate going down cellar stairs, they're often open and something reaching through to grab you isn't just for horror movies. So I went down fast, easier to keep my balance *and* gave me an edge if anything was waiting to trip me up.

But there was nothing. I reached the bottom, slid along the wall, and ended up in a defensible corner.

The cellar was empty. The concrete floor was cracked and uneven in places, but I could see the marks where something very heavy had been scraped around.

There were other marks, too. A smear of something that was red paint, a different color from the faint bloodstains. And something else. A shapeless lump of material. Suede, its fringes lying dead and discarded.

Hot bile whipped the back of my throat. It was a good thing I *hadn't* eaten. I would have spread every bite of it over the concrete floor.

A faint whispering sound. My head jerked up, tracking it. A rushing, like water. My blue eye pierced the etheric bruising for a second; I saw the geometric shapes of a hellbreed curse sparking and flowing in an intricate pattern.

The Talisman sang, a high piercing note. I immediately bolted for the steps, and that was probably what saved me. Because I smelled smoke, and the house overhead exploded with a dry *wump* that sucked a draft of cool air past me. I made the kitchen just in time to dive for the utility room as a wall of orange flame with blue wires at its edges burst through from the living room. The curse had triggered up on the top floor and moved down, probably to catch me like a rat in a rain barrel.

Another trap. I'd walked right into it, and I had a sneaking suspicion the owners of this place would be among the dead near the freeway.

And the hellbreed had moved Saul.

I dove out the back door a bare fraction of a second before the wall of hell-fueled fire coughed free. Rolled, came up and swept the yard with both guns. Nothing but the pale glare of fire in sunlight, sweeping up the brick like great, grasping, throb-veined hands, the flames oily and edged with blue. The heat was monstrous, crisping the grass as I skipped back. The board fence was smoldering.

Holy shit. I ran up against the boards, not quite believing what I was seeing. Survival took over, the guns were stowed, and I was on top of the fence in a heartbeat, balanced like a tightrope walker.

Something exploded. The concussion blew me off the fence. I flew, weightless, hit another fence hard, wood splintering in great jagged pieces. Glass shattered—the shock wave blew out windows in neighboring houses. I hit something else with a snapping *crunch* and found myself in the ruins of a kid's swing set. The cheap metal had twisted and bent instead of breaking, or I'd have been wearing some of it *through* me.

It was broad fucking daylight. Next would come sirens and attention. I swore internally, struggled to my feet, and vanished.

CHAPTER 24

The sun was sinking fast when my pager buzzed. I picked a sliver of glass out of my hair and sighed. Belisa sighed too, in the backseat.

I didn't like that.

Of the four locations Perry had given me, three had evidence of Saul's presence...and traps. I was now certain—the kind of cold certainty that settles on me halfway through a case—that the people who had lived in each place were all resting in the morgue.

The fourth locale, a dun-painted McMansion on the edge of the suburbs, had the carpet yanked up in the empty master bedroom, marks on the floor where a huge heavy object had been placed, probably brought in through the French doors. There were *also* five little guard-breed—little yappy things that looked like Lhasa Apsos with burning-red eyes. One of them had sunk vicious, needle-sharp teeth into my calf before I could break its neck. I would have worried about the sound of gunfire, except the mansion's neighbors were far enough away that it didn't matter.

Goddamn little dogs. Of course, if they were as large as German shepherds they'd be much more dangerous. They were just a demonic *annoyance*, especially if you had other 'breed or Traders to worry about.

But there hadn't been anything bigger. I was chasing my own tail, goddammit.

I dug the pager out. They had to be moving Saul every few hours. I should have known they would, especially if Perry had any notion of where he was likely to be held. Now I was wishing I *had* cut him, and cut him deep.

That wouldn't have led you to Saul. Of course, this isn't doing a whole hell of a lot, either.

I found a Circle K and pulled into the lot. Glanced back at Belisa, made sure the collar was still snugly on. Here I was ferrying around a woman I should have killed on sight. God had a sick, sick sense of humor.

But I knew that. I'd known it since I was five years old.

"No sense," I whispered to the pager's glow. "This makes no fucking sense. As usual."

But I was not quite being honest with myself. I had a bad bad feeling, down deep in my gut.

I dialed, it rang twice and she picked up. "Jill."

"Hey, Badge. What do you have for me?"

She got right down to business. "You wanted to know about funky John Does in the last three weeks?"

"Yeah?" I tried not to feel like a bloodhound straining at the leash.

"Rosie and I have been digging all day. The short answer is, there's none. But there's something else."

"Like what?" Her sense of the weird was almost as finely tuned as Carper's had been. I shut my eyes at the thought of Carp, sleeping under a counterpane of green.

"Like disappearances up twenty percent. Rosie crunched some numbers. Adult disappearances are holding steady. It's the kid ones that are accounting for the bump."

"Huh." If it was summer, the numbers might make sense. Kids get into trouble when school's out, here as well as everywhere else.

But a spike of twenty percent? That was something. In winter too. "When did it start?"

"Let's see...two weeks ago, missing persons reports did a sudden jump. Among kids too young to be runaways. We took a look at unsolved numbers in the last two weeks compared to unsolved over the last three years, and allowed for a certain percentage of retrievals—"

"Badge, you're a wonder." The sun slid below the horizon, and Santa Luz took its regular nightly breath before the plunge.

"Don't I know it. And they're up twenty percent, even accounting for variables in weather and unemployment. Does that help?"

Kind of. It tells me we are looking at a new high-level hellbreed in town, a hungry one. What were those evocation altars for? Just to keep me chasing my tail? To bring through someone else?

A sudden, blinding thought occurred to me. The victims I'd taken the *bezoar* from had to have been virgins, but it might have been a fluke or a crime of opportunity. In Anya's territory, the virgin flesh might have been just to create extra punch in doing an evocation while the moon was wrong. Nothing pierces the walls of Hell like innocent flesh—and if they were attempting an evocation out of phase to bring someone *else* through, they'd need all the help they could get.

The pattern showed itself for a blinding moment. The scar buzzed on my wrist, etheric energy jolting up my arm. The *bezoar*, securely caged, twitched madly in my pocket as if someone was yanking at my coat. I looked up, and every sorcerous sense I had informed me shit was about to get ugly.

I didn't need intuition to tell me that. All I had to do was look at the creeping dusklit shadows clustering up to my car. Those shadows had eyes like flat russet coins, and teeth that sparked with phosphorescence. They hunched and lunged through the shadows with the peculiar, crippled speed of the damned.

"Jill?" Badger said cautiously. "You still there?"

"Gotta go. Keep digging, give my best to Rosie. And thanks." I hung up, drew my guns. One of the low twisted things leapt up on the trunk of the Pontiac, and the car's springs groaned as it growled. Its muzzle twisted up, showing ancient, yellowed teeth. Its front paws were shaped like hands except for the two or three extra fingers, enlarged knuckles, and tarnished ivory claws. It dented the metal, and irrationally, all I could think of was the paint job.

"Son of a *bitch*," I yelled, and launched myself forward. They melded out of the gathering dark, four of them, and spread out. *Oh, this is gonna be fun.*

At least I was sure I'd been poking around in the right way. They wouldn't send *rongeurdos*—bonedogs—after me if I hadn't been wandering around closer and closer to the truth.

The first one coiled down on its haunches, sprang with a deadly scraping of claws on concrete. I faded to the side, hit it twice at the top of its leap. It fell with a thump, steaming and scrabbling as blessed silver punched a hole in its shell and fragmented, filling it with poison.

The worst thing about the bonedogs is that they hunt in packs.

The best thing? They die and *stay* down when you breach them with silver shot. And they never run by day.

Of course, that didn't do me any good now.

As soon as I put that one down, another was leaping for me. I heard the little *ding* as the Circle K's door opened, and I hoped nobody was coming out to take a look at the ruckus. You'd think even in the suburbs they would know to stay indoors when they hear gunshots.

My own leap was reflex, like a cat jumping back from a striking snake. I landed hard, already pitching to my right to draw them away from the convenience store's entrance and whoever was stupid enough to be walking in or out. My boot flashed out, and the crunching shock of it meeting a *rongeurdo*'s face jolted all the way up to my hip, but I was already turning and shooting the other one with both guns. *Pushing* off, arms pulled close and angular momentum conserved enough to give me a spin. When I faced the other two my left hand held my whip instead of a gun, and I felt much more sanguine about the situation. The whip jingled as I shook it, assuring myself of free play. "All right, you sonsabitches." My voice, a bright thread over the deep twisting Helletöng-accented growls. "Come get some."

The Talisman thumped on my chest, its song of destruction hiking up a notch.

One hung back as the other slunk forward, head down and lips lifted over a slavering snarl. Yellow foam spattered, writhing into cracks in the pavement in long oily ropes.

I was bracing myself for the one in front to leap when the one behind flung its head up and howled.

The howl was answered. Eastward, another cry lifted into the night. Then, to the south, another one.

Oh, fuck. Kill them quick, Jill.

I swung forward. Hip leading for the whip work, the force uncoiling through me and flinging out through my hand, gun speaking at the same moment as the bonedog jerked aside to avoid jingling razor-sharp silver. The second, his duty done, leapt too, but I'd gotten the first right through his broad canine skull. He dropped like a stone and I had the last one to worry about.

The last one was the smartest. He looked at me, those eyes

widening and turning bright crimson instead of a low punky russet glow. The sky was indigo now. In winter, night falls quick and hard in the desert.

The thing scrabbled backward, turned tail, and ran.

I leapt for my car. Fast as I am, I can't follow a bonedog on foot. With a V8 under me, though, I can track it as far as possible.

If the *bezoar* was reacting, I could track it even farther. That masked son of a bitch might have survived, but he wouldn't survive what I was about to do to him. I could find out who he was really working for as a bonus.

But I thought I knew. And the knowledge chilled me all the way down to the bone.

You've gone too fucking far this time, you son of a bitch.

I piled into the car. She roused with a purr, and her tires smoked as I spun the wheel. I let off the brake and peeled out. There was an *oof* from the backseat, but I couldn't do more than glance in the rearview and get a jumble of shadowy impressions, a flash of pale-copper flesh and the chain jingling. A merry, Christmas-like sound, but if you knew the real story behind Santa Claus you'd probably never want to hear sleigh bells again.

Hellbreed aren't the only things that like tender little children. And don't even get me started on the Tooth Fairy.

The bonedog was just visible down the street, nipping smartly around to the right. I gunned the engine and the Pontiac leapt for it, happy to be going fast again. The knocking in the upper registers of the engine's roar was even *more* pronounced, I was really going to have to nail that down—

I checked the rearview again. Shadows ran like ink on wet paper. Little spots of red in the distance, loping along two by two.

More bonedogs.

The accelerator was already jammed against the floor.

Now it was a race.

CHAPTER 25

A long, looping trail of rubber came to an abrupt stop. Something had blown in the engine. It didn't matter—I bailed out, not caring that Belisa had rolled forward and was now half on the floor in the back.

She could stay there. I'd settle her hash after I settled Perry's, when this was done.

The gates were shaking like epileptic hands. They banged together, and Henderson Hill rose behind them.

But something was wrong. It should have been a starlit sky, the waxing moon already risen like a yellow-silver coin. Instead, the vault of heaven was black, the stars blotted out and an unnatural dark covering my city like an old, veined hand.

Oh, this isn't going to be fun.

I timed it just right, plunged between the gates. The Hill closed around me, I didn't have time to slow down and see if it was going to try to make things tricky. Besides, something *else* was wrong— the bath of ice-cold prickles was much weaker than it should have been. I should have been hopping one step ahead of Henderson Hill's voices, sparking off the thick sludge of etheric bruising.

Instead, the ghosts rushed at me in rotting cheesecloth veils. Their mouths were open in distorted screams. They poured through and past as if I was an empty door, splashing against the threshold where the bonedogs pulled up short, snarling.

The *bezoar* went nuts inside my pocket, straining against the silver cage and the leather. Buzzing like an angry bumblebee. A really big one.

One of the bonedogs put a paw over the threshold and snatched it back with a Helletöng-laden squeal, like metal rubbing against itself in an empty, echoing stadium. The Hill's ghosts trembled on the edge of visibility, twisting together in boneless contortions to make a weird flowing screen.

A long black smear was the remains of the bonedog I'd chased in here. It bubbled, the eyes rolling free like weird crystalline fruits, the nerve roots decaying strings of quartz.

Now that's weird. Back here again, just like a bad dream. And why does it feel so strange, Jill? Oh, this is great. Just fucking great.

I didn't stop to ask myself why the Hill's ghosts would be holding the bonedogs back. I just dug in my pocket for the *bezoar* while lengthening my stride, and bolted for the lowering bulk of Henderson Hill.

The sky was still featurelessly black. I kicked in a boarded-up door, the *bezoar* rattling and straining when I shoved it back in my pocket. I found myself staring at a hall with a slight upward slope. This was the building on the north side of the quad, a huge brooding monstrosity. It vibrated with agony and fear, but something was muting the force of the Hill's terrible cold unlife.

The doors marching down the hall jerked and shuddered. Normally they'd be opening and closing hungrily, and the entire hall would stretch to infinity, a trick of light and shade. There was a long smear on the floor, some dark weeping fluid, and I hopped over it. *Making a lot of noise. They have to know I'm coming.*

That's okay, an iron voice inside me replied. *Get Saul, kick their asses, and close up whatever door they're opening to Hell. One two three, easy as can be.*

I should have checked the entire Hill for a secondary evocation site. Either that or they'd come back, since this was too good a snack to resist for whoever they were bringing through. But goddammit, physical 'breed didn't come up here!

Unless the reward—or the threat by their master on the other side of the walls separating worlds—was greater than the cost.

Up the hall, avoiding the heavy doors as they sluggishly swung wide to catch at the unwary, the *bezoar* straining against the leather of my coat and sending up a thin keening sound. I smelled smoke, the Talisman rumbling against my chest, and when I reached the top of the slope and the circular hall around the huge operating theater opened up, I was prepared for the crosscurrent, a psychic torrent raging around the still, horrible eye of where a great many of the old Hill's worst excesses had gone down.

I was so braced for it, as a matter of fact, that I almost fell over when it didn't show up. I actually stopped for a moment, braced in the threshold.

The hall should have been alive with screaming faces, weird noises, and a strong current of not-quite air pushing against every surface. Instead, it was a dingy, institutional hallway, curving out of sight on either end. My breath still puffed out in a freezing cloud, and my hair still stirred on a not-quite breeze.

But the roaring weirdness was gone.

Shit, shit shit—I hooked around the corner, running for the secondary door to the operating theater.

The one they used to wheel the bodies out through.

There were windows, long narrow strips of chicken-wire-laced glass up too high for anyone to peer through them. Maybe they were psychological. They ran with diseased blue light, the corners dripping fat little blobs of it to sizzle against the chipped layers of yellow paint. The scar sent a jolt of agonizing pain up my arm, but my hand didn't waver, freighted with the gun. My boot soles pounded on the water-damaged linoleum. Each step seemed to take a lifetime, but I knew I was moving much faster than an ordinary human—or even an ordinary hunter.

I skidded, turning, and hit the secondary door with megaton force. The Talisman's thrumming went up a full octave, and my aura began to sparkle with little sea-urchin specks of light. The door exploded, steel flying as shrapnel—

—and I was through, rolling, coming up with both guns and taking in the lay of the land.

The operating theater was concave, with two or three concrete terraces that used to hold audiences back in the days of electroshock and experimentation. The space at the bottom of the bowl was wide enough for two iron cages, one of them twisted and battered a bit, and an altar. The fluorescent glare of the lights blinked and buzzed, and the entire place was just *full* of robed, cowled hellbreed.

I shot the first one and didn't have time to check the cages. Because between them, right where the central operating table would have sat, was an evocation altar—a pulsing blot of blackness and corruption. And atop it was a pale spinning oval of light.

It was an egg, and if they kept feeding it etheric force it would crack, and when it did the walls between here and elsewhere would gap just a little, and *something* would slip through.

Something old and hungry that Jack Karma had sent back to Hell during a firestorm in Dresden, decades ago.

The 'breed exploded into motion. I'd already put down two of them, one with a head shot and another with a glancing blow. Now all I had to do was stay one step ahead of them, and not shoot whoever was in the cages.

One of the hellbreed screamed, Helletöng like metal and glass buildings rubbing each other during an earthquake, and the curse hit me squarely. Right in the gut. The world turned over, I flew up toward the ceiling, but that was okay—twisting in midair, shaking the remains of the 'breed's curse like so much water from a duck's back, still firing. The fragments of hellbreed nastiness flew free, flapping their leathery wings, so many pieces of shadow careening through space. Momentum bled, etheric force crystallizing around me, and I hit the ceiling a glancing blow. Old warped glass fixtures shattered.

Falling, then. I was going to hit hard, braced myself, still firing. By the time I crunched into one of the concrete terraces with a terrible snapping sound, I had my whip free. It slithered, hit the floor, and my ribs ran with agonizing pain. The scar burned, burrowing into my flesh like acid, and the 'breed leapt for me, hanging in the air with his robe and cowl fluttering, arms up, claws extended, and his legs drawn up like a spider flicked into a candle flame.

Split-second reflex was all I had. The whip's end was airborne, my side giving a hot flare of spiked agony as muscles pulled against broken ribs. I caught him as he was already heading down from the apex of his leap, the other 'breed hanging back for some reason, and that was bad news.

He was slight and dark, with a handsome bladed face the flechettes tore across with a smart crackling jingle. Skipping aside, reaching the next terraced step up and my legs bending and tensing, flung up with a leap that was half instinct and half desperation. If they were avoiding me, waiting for this guy to finish me off, he was probably a Big Cheese. I had never seen him before, which meant he wasn't local.

Which, ten to one, told me I was looking at Perry's boss, the one trying to bring Argoth through. He did look kind of like a handsomer Buster Keaton, right down to the pouting lips.

And since Perry could produce hellfire in the blue spectrum, his boss was likely to be more badass than one tired hunter could handle.

For a brief moment I thought of unleashing the Talisman. But with the spinning egg over the evocation altar hungrily grabbing at all the power it could find, that was a monumentally bad idea.

Dammit.

Julius howled, and the windows shattered, blown outward. I gained my footing on the uppermost tier of concrete, a few busted wooden seats to my left and clear running room to my right. Shook the whip free as my ribs fused together with heavy red pain, the scar like hot lead whittling deeper and deeper as I aimed. *One shot, God, come on, one shot, give me a good shot here—*

I pointed and squeezed, praying.

I hit him. I knew I hit him, too—his sleek head snapped back and black ichor flew.

But then his chin came down, the hurt sealing itself over and the hard carapace of a hellbreed flowing like so much molten sugar, and he hissed at me, baring his pearly, shark-sharp teeth.

I heard a high nasty giggle from one of the watching 'breed, and braced myself. This was going to hurt, and I was down to four shots left in the extended clip.

Goddammit.

The lights—and who the hell changed the bulbs in here, anyway?—flickered. Glass rained down, and the bits of curse flapped in lethargic circles. The scar gave an agonizing wet crunch of pain, and I hissed in a breath, broken ribs twitching with pain. Every hellbreed in the operating room crouched except Julius, whose blue eyes widened—

—before more glass shattered. Perry resolved out of thin air and knocked him on his ass. The screen of bland normality over Perry had dropped, and for a heartbeat or two I saw *underneath*— the thing that inhabited his shell snarled and crouched before leaping down toward the altar, on a trajectory that would take him right to where Julius was landing.

Go figure. I was actually not unhappy to see him. Despite the fact that he was playing me and his boss off against each other for some reason.

My fingers moved mechanically, tucking the whip and reloading. I was almost able to aim again before one of the other 'breed decided to take care of what the boss couldn't, and as I threw myself away toward the wooden chair, I saw the mask fluttering over the lower half of his wax-white face and knew who I was facing.

Oh yeah. This just keeps getting better.

CHAPTER 26

Rule number two of fighting 'breed: *keep moving.* Even if your ribs are broken and your entire body feels like it's been passed through a meat grinder, don't slow down. Slowing down means dying.

What little I could see of the masked 'breed's face was a ruin of scar tissue. Guess Belisa hadn't put him down for good, but it wasn't for lack of trying. I bounced like a jackrabbit, whip uncurling, knew he'd dodge, and swung back, my leg flashing out to kick a lean dark cowled 'breed in the face. The shock jolted all the way through me, but it did knock the son of a bitch away and into a snarling mass of 'breed vying to take Perry's guts out the hard way. Including Julius, but Perry seemed to be doing all right and I had all I could handle in front of me.

I landed on the twisted cage to the right and snapped a glance down. It took a moment for it to register, because I immediately had to hop aside, my whip flying out again and my gun speaking with a sharp crackling roar. The recoil grated in my shoulder. The scar writhed on my wrist like a live thing. I landed on the other cage, and the roaring of the thrashing hellbreed kicked up a notch. They hit the altar squarely, and the pale egg of etheric force began to spin.

That's not good. So not good. But I couldn't worry about that, because the masked 'breed was stalking me again, and this time I was sure he wasn't a copy. He was just too goddamn fast, and he had his little tabi booties on, the bastard.

And to top it all off, the cages were empty.

What the hell? But I had no time, because Perry was thrown back like a meteorite, a streak of black ichor and the incandescence of pure unholy rage trailing him. He hit the concrete so hard he dented it, and the *crack* was loud enough to drown out everything else.

Julius snarled and leapt on him, I shot the masked 'breed twice, and began to think of how I could get out of here while Perry was still ass-deep in angry 'breed. If Saul and Gilberto weren't here— but there was that pale egg of light needing to be dealt with, and the evocation altar too. Good luck calling up banefire while dealing with the Great Masked Ninja in Pajamas.

There was only one thing to do.

This is going to hurt.

Tensing, stupid body bracing itself for a hit it knew was coming, I leapt from the top of the cage, my boots skidding on the slick iron. Falling, right for the pale egg. The silver I carried, not to mention my hard thick exorcist-trained aura, would disrupt it. I'd be thrown like popcorn, again. I'd been doing a lot of that lately.

I might also lose an arm or a leg. Or more. Details, details. But I'd slam the door closed on the toes of the 'breed trying to come through, and that was worth the risk.

It's always worth the risk.

I hung in the air for a long crystalline second. The body was still flinching, like that was going to change the outcome. The rest of me kept firing, the masked 'breed having realized what I was going to do and spitting a stream of curses like rancid lasers at me. They were too slow. I was going to make it.

But the world paused, the way it will do when something truly significant happens. There, in the door I'd kicked in, a pair of familiar figures: one male, one female. The female had a vacant smile, her black eyes wide and hungry as collapsed neutron stars. The collar around her slim neck had rubbed through her skin, biting into her shoulders as well, and blood slid down her tattered blue silk. The Chaldean wasn't healing her fast enough.

Lilith Saintcrow

The other was the caretaker, his filmed eyes wide and the clarity around him brighter than the fluorescents. He reached up, slowly, and his clever thin fingers touched the locking pin holding the chain to the collar. Hellbreed hung in the air, their motion arrested, and I saw—No, I thought I saw...

No, I *saw*. I saw the light shining through the caretaker's façade of mute blind scarring, his hair turning a feathery gold—and the things behind him, reaching up in spires of snowy white, what were they? Wings, but not of any terrestrial bird. Glowing, in a way that seemed oddly tip-of-the-tongue familiar.

My blue eye *burned*, a twinge of acid fire spearing back into my brain. I could not look away from the light, dear God, the *light* pouring through him like dawn breaking, a dawn that was not tired or old...

What the hell?

The pin holding the chain to the collar clicked free. The chain slithered, clashing all the way down, but the collar stayed put. Melisande Belisa inhaled sharply, and hurtful intelligence came back into her black eyes. She looked across the confused jumble of 'breed doing their best to kill each other, and I swear to God I saw an awful sanity in her gaze.

The caretaker's lips were moving. He whispered in her ear, his eyes unfilmed for a long terrible moment, piercing blue casting shadows against her face. The shadows of Chaldean moving over her aura flinched back from that blue glow.

The chain finished hitting the floor with a slither, and she was already moving. Time made a snapping sound, like a huge rubber band breaking, and the noise of an almighty huge fight broke over me like a wave. My hair blew back on a breeze from nowhere, my coat flapped, and something out of the ordinary had indeed happened.

Because instead of falling into the oval of light and cutting off the door between here and Hell, I landed with bonecracking force in *front* of the altar, a short howl escaping my abused lips. And the masked 'breed was on me in a heartbeat. I shot him twice, but he was too close.

Now it was time for knife work.

*　　*　　*

He tried to grab my head and slam it into the altar's base. I wriggled away, and he'd taken so much damage he was moving slowly, at least for him. I jerked my leg up, the bony part of my knee sinking into what passed for his groin and meeting something weirdly squishy. That was only a distraction, though, because my largest knife had sunk in to the hilt, only the crossguard stopping it from vanishing into his belly. I wrenched it back and forth, the reek of hellbreed guts spilling free assaulting me. Hot noisome fluids bathed my hand.

The noise was incredible. Now I knew what happened when a Sorrow went up against a 'breed. It wasn't pretty. But between her and Perry, Julius might have a lot of trouble, and if I could just get *up*—

The assassin slumped atop me, corruption racing through his tissues. His fingers flexed, and I half-swallowed a scream. His claws grated between my ribs, and I was losing yet more blood. The scarring on his coppery face cracked apart, fine noxious dust bleeding out.

That meant he was dying. Thank God. I'd worry about the next 'breed to step up and start committing assassinations when I survived this.

If I survived this.

Get up, Jill.

But there was a problem with that. My body would not obey me. I blinked warm wetness out of my eyes, every muscle tensing and the scar a cicatrice of fierce heat on my wrist. There was a horrible *draining* sensation, worse than any blood loss I'd ever felt. A warm lassitude spread up my ankles.

I stared up at the pale egg. It was spinning now, filaments of it reaching out and snagging the flying bits of curse as they got too close. Each little bat-flapping thing went into the hungry maw. That was where most of the nasty psychic force of the Hill had gone, too. A nice snack for whoever was waiting under Hell's dry screaming skies, probably impatiently tapping a clawed and twisted foot.

He would have to step through to claim that snack, though.

And he can't do that if you get up and stop him. So DO it!

Swearing at myself didn't work. But my body twitched.

Something hit the floor next to me—a hellbreed claw, ripped free of its owner's body and smoking with corruption. It twisted and flexed, wet, rancid dust pouring out of it in veined streams.

Will and life roared back into me. There was an odd ringing in my ears. My body suddenly obeyed, jerking up off the floor. A split second later, something huge barreled for me and I leapt aside instinctively, knife in one hand and my whip flashing out. It hit the bleeding mass of Julius squarely, and his resultant roar was a wall of warm air pushing me back. My boots slipped in greasy crud—bits of hellbreed rained down, plopping obscenely and still twitching as they hit.

A blue blur streaked by. Belisa, her battered feet slapping the stone and her mouth a rictus of effort, leapt with fluid effortless authority onto Julius. She clawed at him, screaming in the heavy consonant-laden mess of Chaldean, the bruising of the parasite on her aura turned as dark and sonorous as mountain thunder. Perry, just as battered and wearing a mad death's-head grin, was right behind her. They descended on the hapless 'breed, and I snapped a glance up.

The room that had been full of Hell's citizens was now an abattoir. Rotting bits of 'breed were *everywhere*. My breath came in short, hard sobs; the scar went back to chuckling as it tasted the death and misery riding the air. It sent a jolt up my arm, and the terrible draining sensation swirled away.

Julius howled. Both of them were ripping at him, like a pair of wolves at a carcass. His head smashed against the altar, right where mine had been a few seconds ago. Bile burned the back of my throat, I retched silently and pointlessly. Belisa made a guttural noise, the chanting in Chaldean hitting a vicious peak and the collar flashing with deep gold, and she finally grabbed Julius's head in her strong slender hands.

I was expecting a quick movement and the green-stick crack of a breaking neck. But no. Her flexible thumbs dug and gripped, and she popped his eyes like two overripe grapes. The 'breed's spine arced up into a hoop, his heels drumming the concrete, and corruption raced through his tissues.

If I'd eaten lately, it would have come up in a tasteless rush. As it was, I retched again and stumbled back, slipping and sliding. The floor was awash.

Perry was suddenly there, resolving out of thin air with a sound like nasty laughter trailing him. "Enjoying the show, my dear?" His ribs heaved, but he didn't sound at all out of breath. "What a pleasant little interlude. I've waited to do that for *so long.*"

"P-P-P—" My lips refused to shape his name. I wasn't looking at him. I was looking *past* him, at the spinning egg. A hairline crack had appeared in its center, a thin line of darkness.

Melisande Belisa threw back her head and howled. It was an animal's cry, except for the all-too-human rage tinting it.

The hairline crack widened. My right hand swept down, sheathed my largest knife, and was heading for my gun when Perry grabbed my wrist and squeezed, grinding the small bones together. "Oh, no you don't. She's expendable, my darling. I still have plans for—"

My left fist, braced with the whip handle, got him in the belly. It was a good solid punch, and that did make him lose all his air. My other fist crashed into his face and his head snapped back. I kicked him, too, and the Talisman made a rustling, roaring sound.

I hadn't used it, had I? No, if I'd used it this whole place would be a crater and the door to Hell would be busted wide open. And yet...

Perry went down. He slid back along the floor, fetching up against concrete with another stunning sound.

And the pale, spinning oval over the altar...

Cracked.

CHAPTER 27

Belisa howled, a guttural, abused scream. A hairline crack, darker than the pit of a black hole, zigzagged through the spinning egg of light. It widened, just a little, and something white showed.

The Sorrow rose. She cast a glance back over her shoulder, her face slack and terribly graven. Bruises crawled over her skin, the shadows of Chaldean sorcery doing what they could to ameliorate the damage. But she was in bad shape, bleeding all over, her tangled hair smoking at each knot.

Each inch of silver on me ran with blue flame. My head was full of screaming noise.

"*Kill*," Perry hissed, from where I'd kicked him. "*Kill it now!*"

I lifted my gun slowly. It was a terrible dream, fighting through syrup, my muscles full of lead.

Belisa's chin dipped wearily. She pitched forward just as the egg stopped spinning.

The thing that slid its malformed hand through the barrier between this world and Hell twitched. I heard myself screaming, sanity shuddering aside from the sight. They do not dress when they are at home, and when they come through and take on a semblance of flesh it's enough to drive any ordinary person mad. Wet salt trickles slid down from my eyes, slid from my nose and ears.

They were not tears.

There was a rushing, the physical fabric of our world terribly assaulted, ripping and stretching. My screams, terrible enough to make the Hill shudder all the way down to its misery-soaked foundations. Perry, hissing in squealgroan Helletöng, and under it all, so quiet and so final, Mikhail's voice from across a gulf of years. Long nights spent turning over everything about his death, remembering him, all folding aside and compressing into what he would say if he was here. Or maybe just the only defense my psyche had against the *thing* struggling to birth itself completely.

Now, Mikhail said. *Kill now,* milaya. *Do not hesitate.*

My teacher's killer was in the way.

The scar crunched on my wrist. I squeezed the trigger. *Both* triggers, and I saw the booming trail of shock waves as the bullets cut air. Belisa's fingers had turned to claws, Chaldean spiking the soup of noise, and she tore at the not-quite-substantial flesh of the thing. Blue light crawled over her as if she wore silver, the same blue that the caretaker's eyes had flashed. The shadows of the Chaldean parasite flinched aside, for some incomprehensible reason.

I was still screaming as the bullets tore through her and the egg as well. The collar made a zinging, popping noise, the golden runes shutterclicks of racing, diseased light. Her body shook and juddered as she forced the thing behind the rip in the world *back*, and the physical fabric of the place humans call home snapped shut with a sound like a heavy iron door slamming. The bristling, misshapen appendage thumped down to the floor.

Belisa's fingers, human again, plucked weakly at the collar. She was a servant of the gods who were here long before demons, the inimical forces the shadowy Lords of the Trees trapped in another place long ago. It was a Pyrrhic victory; the *Imdarák* didn't survive, either. And the Sorrows are always looking to bring their masters back. The 'breed? Well, they're always looking to bring more of their kind. It's like two different conventions fighting over the same hotel.

If anyone could have slammed a door between here and Hell shut, it was a Sorrow.

But *why*? And the caretaker, what was he—

My knees folded. I hit the ground. Henderson Hill whispered around me like the end of a bell's tolling, reverberations dying in glue-thick air.

Oh, no.

Belisa folded over. I'd emptied a clip. Sorrows can heal amazingly fast, but she was probably exhausted after all the fun and games.

Her knees hit the concrete in front of the altar. Blood flowered, spattered on the floor. She shook her head, tangled hair swaying. The golden runes on the collar snuffed out, one by one.

"Ahhhhh." It was a long satisfied sigh, escaping Perry's bleeding lips. "Oh, yes. *Yesssssssss.*"

The scar drew up on my wrist and began to ache. This wasn't the usual burning as I yanked etheric energy through it. I tore my eyes from Belisa's slumped form and turned my right wrist up.

The print of Perry's lips was not a scar, now. It was *black*, as if the flesh itself was rotting, and it pulsed obscenely. As I watched the edges frayed, little blue vein-maps crawling under the surface of my flesh.

And I knew why. I could have shot around her.

But I'd chosen not to.

Melisande Belisa's body hit the floor too, next to the swiftly rotting hellbreed appendage. The last rune on the collar winked out. There was a terrible mortal stench—even a Sorrow's sphincter relaxes when death takes them. The blood spread out from her body in little tendrils. Soon it would make a pool. A lake.

The tendrils made a screaming face for a moment, traced on the cracked and blackened floor, before a wash of bright-red blood poured over and obscured it. I sagged, my mouth open and the gun falling out of my right hand.

"At last." Perry, on his feet now. He danced a little capering jig, and I saw one of his shoes had been lost somewhere. His sock was pale cream, and absolutely filthy. "A hunter of my very own. My darling one, my Kiss, we are going to—"

I don't know why he forgot I had another gun in my left hand. I raised it, and the shot took him right in the chest.

The scar shrieked with agony. But each time he'd fiddled with it over the years, each time he'd used it to fuck with my nervous system, he was training me to disregard it. My right hand curled up into a seizure-lock, but the left was fine. I got him twice more in the chest before he snarled and was on me, knocking the gun away. His free hand closed around my throat, and my back hit the floor. He snarled into my face, his breath an exhalation of spoiled honey, and I heard the buzz of dead metallic flies in a chlorine-painted bottle, bashing at the sides as they tried to escape.

I fought for leverage, but he was too quick and I was exhausted. And damned besides. The knowledge beat inside my head like a drum, robbing me of the clarity of a hunter's reactions. All I had left was...

...what?

Saul. It was like breaking water and taking a breath. "You. *You* have him. All the time, *it was you.*"

He'd played both me *and* Julius. The rest of the pattern came clear now. He hadn't been trying to bring a higher-up hellbreed through; he'd been stringing along the other 'breed trying to bring Argoth out. And Perry had set out to kill his immediate superior with my help as well—or with Belisa's. The whisper of Argoth was to keep me chasing my tail while he worked me into a corner—with the Talisman to knock me off balance and the revelation of Mikhail's bargain to keep me there. It was all a game, every set of obstacles balanced against the others and working at cross-purposes.

The prize wasn't any power or position game among 'breed. He wasn't playing to get any higher in the hierarchy.

No. *I* was the prize. And I'd fallen right into his trap.

He'd won. At last.

"Oh, darling. Not personally, of course." He leaned in and sniffed, taking a good lungful. It couldn't be pleasant—reek of hellbreed death, blood and human death, corruption and whatever foulness was spread all over me. "This has been so entertaining. And there's more to come." He grinned, a terrible grimace. "Via Dolorosa, my darling. At dawn. Don't disobey—or that black rot will start to spread. You won't like it."

I heaved up, but he shoved me back down. The extra strength from the scar had deserted me now. I was only weakly human, hunter or no, and my body started reminding me I'd been abusing it far past the norm, even for me.

Perry leaned forward. His tongue snaked between his blood-less lips, wet and cherry-red. A drop of clear liquid hung trembling at the tip. Little bits of blue hellfire danced and dazzled in whatever that liquid was, and I was suddenly very certain I didn't want it touching my skin.

The drop slid back up his tongue, hellfire crackling in the spaces between the scales. The rough tongue tip touched my cheek, flicking along the skin. It caressed my jawbone, slid down to touch the pulse beating a frantic tattoo in my throat. Rasping, dryly.

It reeled back up between his lips with a snap. The Hill shuddered again, and I exhaled. My right hand was still cramped up, my fingers an absurd claw.

But my left curled around a knife hilt. I braced myself slowly, tensing muscle by recalcitrant muscle.

"Come see me at dawn, my darling." He breathed in my face again, a hot dry draft from a desert of powdered bones. "I've waited for this *so* long. Best savored, don't you agree?"

I exploded into motion, slashing. But he was already gone, glass shattering and his footsteps a rapid light beat. The Hill shuddered, settling in itself, and little sparkles began as my aura pushed against the psychic soup spilling into the nerve center of the hill like wine into a glass. The force that had been gathered, held to open a gap and feed a fresh hungry 'breed, was exploding out from confinement.

I had to get out of here.

I rolled to one side. Pushed myself up. A single drop of blood fell from my nose. It hit the concrete, flowered into a star.

I looked at the black traceries defiling the clean red. Melisande Belisa's body still slumped, the bruising of Chaldean settling in to do its work of erasing her from the world. They were dead the moment they took vows. Most of them had no choice, they were born into the Houses—a Mother impregnated by a soldier drone, bred like cattle.

Had I been aiming at her?

Why do you ask, Jill? You know you were.

Scrambled to my feet. My right hand relaxed slightly, fingers shaking out. I felt a plucking at the scar, but nothing else. No etheric energy swelled through it to mend my body, nothing. It might as well have been a rotting lump of flesh.

That's exactly what it is, Jill. The truth of what I'd done hit home. I'd solved two problems at once, but it hadn't been clean vengeance. I'd killed her because the entire time she'd been in the car, she'd been wearing on my nerves. It didn't matter that she was Perry's servant in all this.

I had killed her while she was helping to seal the rip in the world. And I'd done it not because she was a threat, but because I couldn't stand to have Mikhail's killer breathing one more moment.

I had damned myself.

The Talisman was a warm weight on my chest. It hadn't turned on me yet. How long would it last?

Just long enough, I promised myself.

My left hand could still make a base for the banefire. I concentrated, *hard*, as the flaming blue wisps fought me in a way they never had before. But they came, moaning and crying, and they *burned*. Bubbling, blistering the skin.

That sacred fire burned me.

I cast the banefire. It hit the altar and roared up in a sheet of cleansing flame. I could have stayed and let it take me too.

But I had things to do.

CHAPTER 28

The sky had cleared, bright diamond points of stars glaring through the bowl of night.

The warehouse was echoingly empty. The Weres had cleaned up and restocked the fridge. The food probably wouldn't go bad— they'd gather here afterward for Saul, if I succeeded.

Not if, Jill. When. You're just damned, not out. But then I would move, and the leather cuff on my right wrist would rub against the blackened scar. A jolt of sick pain would go through me, and I would almost flinch.

I walked from room to room, stashing ammo, touching things. I'd never noticed how bare and drafty the entire place had looked before Saul moved in. The weapons and the clothes were mine. Everything else . . . well.

The sheets were still tangled from the last time we'd rolled out of bed to catch Trevor Watling. Saul had slipcovered the old orange Naugahyde couch in pale linen, stocked the kitchen with cooking gadgets, arranged little things on shelves and even hung an ailing wandering Jew up in the living room, in a fantastically knotted macramé holder complete with orange beads and the faint smell of reefer—a thrift-store find he'd been so proud of. The laundry room was arranged the way he liked it, the detergent within easy reach and the eight different kinds of fabric softener sheets ranked neatly on top of the dryer.

Everywhere I looked, there was something he'd touched. I opened the kitchen cabinets, ran my knuckles over the fridge's cool white glow. The dishwasher had finished running, and it was full. The drying rack was full of the last load of pots and pans from breakfast, not arranged the way he would have, but still.

I filled up on ammo. Loaded a couple more clips. Considering writing a note. Decided it was a cliché. Anya would piece it together, one way or another.

Before I left, I stood for a long time in our bedroom door,

looking at the peaks and valleys of the sheets and thin blankets. He ran warm, and I never needed much in the way of covers. We slept during the day, the bed set out in the middle of the floor so I could see anything creeping up on me.

The low hurt sound I was making shocked me back into myself. There were still other things to do. I'd just meant to come here to get some ammo, and...

The Eye twitched on my chest, a tiny dissatisfied movement. I wiped my cheeks and touched it with a tentative, tear-wet finger. No crackle of electricity. It wasn't going to get rid of me just yet.

But under the cuff, the blue veining was spreading from the blackened lip print. Up my arm, in tiny increments.

"God," I whispered. "You bastard."

I wasn't sure who I was talking to. Mikhail? Perry? God Himself?

I didn't have nearly enough time with him.

But I couldn't bitch about it. There was nobody else to blame. I'd damned myself.

The clock next to the bed showed the time in pitiless little red numbers. My car was dead, and I had to get to Via Dolorosa. I ached all over, healing sorcery crackling through me in little blue threads. It didn't burn like banefire, but it was probably only a matter of time.

Only human strength and healing.

It would have to be enough.

I made sure I had enough ammo. Stalked into the weapons room, stared at the long slim shape under its fall of amber silk. I couldn't take the spear—it was just asking for trouble. The sunsword might help, but one look at me and Galina would know there was something wrong. Plus, why drag more trouble to her door? She and Hutch were safe, and that was where I wanted them.

After all, I'd sucked at protecting Gil and Saul. Now every innocent in my city was going to be at risk. Perry had to have more of a plan, and without me to keep him in check...

Goddammit. There isn't any way out. There hasn't ever been.

I couldn't even blame God. *I'd* done it.

I came back to myself with a jolt. The clock read five minutes later. I'd just checked out, like a CD skip.

Can't afford to do that. Something left to do, Jill. Then you know what's going to happen.

I turned on one steel-shod heel. My coat flared out. I realized I was running my fingers over gun butts, checking each knife hilt, my hands roaming over my body like I was in a music video or something. I dropped them with an effort just as my pager went off.

I fished it out, gingerly. It was Badger again.

She could wait. Dawn was coming soon.

The cab let me off at the end of the Wailer Bridge, made a neat three-point, and drove away maybe a little faster than was necessary. The driver wasn't Paloulian—it was a big, thick good ol' boy in a flannel shirt and greasy jeans, with a ponytail under his bald spot and the radio tuned to AM talk.

It just goes to show you can get a cab to anywhere, even Hell. If you know how.

The eastern horizon was paling, scudding clouds over the mountains breaking up in cottony streamers. A faint glow of pink showed where the sun would crown and push itself up.

A long, long night was ending.

The bridge is a concrete monstrosity with high gothic pillars, built during the big public works binge of the thirties to try and keep Santa Luz from bleeding to death. Every once in a while someone would make noise about renovation, and about whose job it was anyway to pay for said renovation, and on and on. Then there would be a big public outcry about the homeless who lived under the bridge's glower on the river's banks, especially the ones you could see trudging over every morning, heading for downtown. They shuffled like the hopeless, and sometimes one of them would go over the side and into the water's uncaring embrace.

They were mine just like everyone else in Santa Luz. There were predators even here, and I'd chased cases over on this side of the river before.

Today, though, the Wailer stood empty. There wasn't even a stream of traffic for the industrial park and docks on the other side. I kept thinking that someday they were going to zone in some residential and spread up into the canyons like Los Angeles. But no, why do that and worry about landslides during spring downpours when you had the rest of the desert stretching away from the river's artery to fill up? There were a couple retreat mansions up there, mostly people with more money than sense, but nothing else.

Four lanes. A yellow line down the middle. The city really needed some dividers out here, but they were engaged with a running fight with county over who was going to pay for *that*. It's the oldest story of bureaucracy—who's going to foot the bill?

Except I knew who was going to be paying on this bridge today. It was yours truly.

I went slowly, looking for traps. Nothing on this side of the bridge, but it made an odd sound—humming a little, as if it was cables instead of concrete. The water underneath, and the rebar inside, would make it an excellent psychic conductor.

I stopped halfway, scanning with every sense I owned. Having the scar gone was like being blind; I hadn't realized how much I depended on hyperacute senses and jacked-up healing. I was back to being an ordinary hunter—about as far away from a normal person as possible, but still. I was used to so much more.

Nothing. Even my blue eye was oddly clouded.

The wind came off the river, ruffling my hair. I wondered what would happen when the silver started to burn my skin.

You've got a while, Jill. Use it.

This could have been just another ploy. But I didn't think it was. The glyph on the letter, tucked safely in one of my pockets, had to be Perry's name in their language. Or another lie—maybe Julius's. Perry had neatly double-crossed Julius as well. That's the thing about 'breed—they can't even trust each other.

What, after all, do you think Hell is?

The image of Belisa's body, slumped in front of the altar under a pall of bruise-dark Chaldean, rose up in front of me in vivid detail. I could have counted each of her tangled dark hairs and named every bruise and cut. Memory is a curse.

I'd known as soon as I fired that I'd done something wrong.

What the—

I whirled. Footsteps. Lots of them, and the sky was darker than it had any right to be. Dawn wasn't far off—but the closer to dawn, the harder the fight. And if what I was hearing wasn't just a trick of sound bouncing off the waters, I was in even deeper shit.

They massed at either end of the bridge. Hellbreed and Traders, a crowd of them. Bright eyes, painted lips, curve of hips and glimmer of dewy skin, the beauty of the damned on display. On the city side of the river, shapes appeared. I had to blink a couple times before they resolved into a coherent picture behind my eyes.

Crosses. They were carrying two twelve-foot crosses. A slight figure on one, a heavier male figure with silver in his hair in the other. My blue eye turned hot and dry, and I did not let out the breath I was holding until I could focus ... and saw the glow of living creatures around both of them.

Gilberto slumped against whatever was holding him to the rough wood. Saul's head was down, his hair hanging. I saw lashings, instead of nails. They were only *tied* to the things.

The mockery made my stomach turn over hard. I swallowed hard, and almost wished I hadn't.

The Talisman made a low angry noise against my chest. A curl of smoke drifted up, tickled my nose. I eased my right-hand gun out. My hand might cramp up again if Perry wanted to play a little game, but I still had my left. Which closed around the bullwhip's handle, and I set my feet against the bridge's surface.

If a semi comes along, it's going to ruin this lovely picture. All of them coming out to see the hunter get hers. They're going to enjoy this.

"Behold!" someone screamed from above. I snapped a glance up—hellbreed, crawling on the bridge. Like maggots in a wound, seething. Except maggots actually did something useful by cleaning up dead flesh. "*The sacrifice!*"

Oh, honey, if you're talking about me, you'd best be warned. I'm not a good sacrifice. I tend to stick in the craw when you try to eat me. I bit back a murderous, contemptuous little laugh. The world narrowed down, became basic.

The only thing that mattered was getting Gilberto and Saul off those crosses. Saul might still be able to run, Gilberto was a chancier proposition, but either of them would stand a better chance if I could somehow get them free.

Where are you, you son of a bitch?

The scar crunched with sick pain, all the way down my cramping fingers. I blew out between my teeth.

There was Perry in a pale linen suit, capering in front of the mob of hellbreed on the city side. His legs moving in ways no biped's should, he cracked his heels together and danced. The throng of 'breed and Traders were humming, a weird subsonic note with the squealing groan of Helletöng underneath it, rubbing against the fabric of the physical until it frayed.

They were about to bring the crosses onto the bridge. Some of them were dancing too, little jig steps. Behind Perry, to his left, Rutger minced. I could even hear the tip-tapping of his ridiculous shoes against the road.

So, Rutger had been playing according to Perry's dictates all along. Color me unsurprised.

"Thou Who has given me to fight evil," I whispered, my lips barely shaping the words, "keep me from harm."

It was useless, just like everything else.

Now, Jill. Do some good.

I launched myself toward death. Without the scar's eerie stuttering speed, but still—I was hunter enough to move pretty damn fast. My heels struck sparks as my stride lengthened, and a cry went up from the hellbreed on the mountain side of the bridge. The entire structure reverberated, and the Talisman warmed against my skin. Like a lover's hand, fingers trailing down between my breasts.

I needed my breath for running, but I heard a cry of rising effort anyway. It was too high to be male, and it echoed oddly. The crowd broke, streaming past Perry and leaping for me. The crosses dipped crazily, and I suddenly understood they were going to throw my Were and apprentice over the side just to be assholes.

Well, it wasn't surprising. It even had a kind of mad hellish poetry to it, just what you'd expect from Perry.

The scar was dead, but I pulled on it anyway. A thin trickle of etheric force slid through it, a wire of nasty heat up my arm. Perry stopped in mid-caper, his eyes blazing infernos. The thing that wore his human shell rippled through pale skin, and his grin was a shark's.

Gunfire. But I hadn't shot anyone yet. I was still just out of optimal range, and—

There was a commotion behind the screen of 'breed and Traders. Then the screaming started, and I was within range. I leapt as I reached the first of them, my own gun speaking. Howls and screams lifted—that's one thing about facing a crowd of Hell's citizens.

You don't have to watch where you shoot as much. And with the only two people who mattered to me up on the crosses, I didn't have to worry about hitting them.

My right hand seized up, the scar fighting for control. I could *feel* it, thin little tendrils of corruption yanking on muscles and nerves. But nightly murder will make shooting more than a habit. It will burn it so deep into your hands you don't have to think—if you're breathing you're fighting, and the scar wasn't deep enough yet to reach that yet.

It was a losing fight. But then, it always was. The tide of Hell is so broad, so deep, we can't hope to do more than hold it a little while.

I cannot hold back the tide forever. Another misdirection, a good one because it held the seed of truth. Perry hadn't wanted Argoth to come through and come gunning for me. He just wanted me to damn myself, and he'd worked it so I could. It had taken him years, but he'd done it.

The entire bridge shuddered, and I heard something familiar. *Very* familiar. When Anya fights, she cusses almost as much as I do. I saw her, breaking through the hellbreed like an avenging angel, firing with both hands and moving inhumanly fast. Hunter-fast, as fast as I was moving now.

Behind her, there was a roil of struggling figures. Weres, more than I'd ever seen in one place before. They were swarming the Traders and trying like hell to stay out of the way of the 'breed. The 'breed were concentrating on Anya, but she was giving them so much trouble it was going to take a while.

And up on the top of one of the crosses, Saul raised his silver-starred head.

CHAPTER 29

C runch.

The whip snapped and Rutger danced back. Perry snarled. The scar boiling with agony on my wrist, I was too slow because I had to fight it. Its tendrils were all the way up to my elbow now, twisting and yanking.

I was screaming. My only battle cry now.

"Saul! Saul! Saul!" His name, over and over again, while the Weres clustered the Traders holding the crosses. Lionesses leapt, and if you haven't seen the Norte or Sud Luz pack lionesses work together to take down a kill, you've missed one of the most amazing sights on earth.

The huge splintered things jerked and danced crazily; Gilberto's head flopping and Saul moving, looking around. I couldn't watch, I had my hands full; Rutger skipped toe-tapping aside and Perry leapt for me. I faded to my left, firing, how I was going to reload with a cramping hand and the whip keeping them back was an open question. Perry darted in, took a shot in the shoulder, and snarled. My wrist bloomed with hot acid pain, and he wasn't bleeding the way he should have been.

That was worrying. If I'd had time to worry, that is.

I was still screaming Saul's name when Anya appeared, her arms up, the sunsword's silver length rising forever from her hands. Shock jolted through me.

She can't use that without a—

The Eye dilated on my chest, singing a long high sustained note of power.

This is why two hunters can take on an army of hellbreed. Because it never occurs to 'breed to give, or to help each other. Each one of them is out for himself, plain and simple, in any melee. None of them ever thinks to *share.*

You can't use a sunsword without a key. But I *reached,* an unphysical movement from the Eye on my chest toward the blade's hilt, a hand held out in thin air. A red glimmer showed in the empty space trapped in the sunsword's hilt, whirling as it strengthened.

I might have been damned, but I was still hunter enough to help her. She'd expected me to understand and use the Eye as the key, both of us working in tandem to hold back the tide.

Anya caught hold, strong slim mental fingers in mine. The silver in her hair crackled with blue sparks, and the sun was almost up over the horizon. If we could last long enough for it to break free, we might have a chance.

Flame blossomed against the sunsword's razor-silver edge. The Eye twitched on my chest, and the fire deepened golden-orange. A thin wire of white ran through the blade's center, the red gleam in the hilt suddenly a small star, and the fire coughed as it exploded free.

Dawn was early today. The light drenched the bridge, and the leaping sinuous forms of the bonedogs howled and cowered. Rutger screamed, falling in slow motion, as the sword descended.

The scar fought, clawing at the meat of my arm, for control. I shot Perry again, but I was too slow, the world dragging me down and my body refusing to put up with one more damn thing. He collided with me, a huge snapping crunch that turned the world over, I flew. Hit the concrete bridge railing, more things breaking inside me, and a warm gout of blood exploded between my lips.

The crosses swayed, but the Traders had broken and were fleeing. The 'breed hanging in the bridge's spires slid away like oil, hissing at the terrible light spreading from the sunsword. Anya screamed, a hawk's cry, and stabbed down. The blade slid through Rutger's chest as if through soft butter, sinking into the concrete below just as effortlessly. Pavement scorched, and the 'breed's dying scream was lost in the inferno roar as the sunsword burned, cleansing the corruption.

Don't let go, Jill. Whatever happened to me, I had to keep the sunsword going. The Eye was a warm weight on my chest, humming along happily as something burned.

Don't you dare let go.

I tried to get up. My chest was broken, a fragile eggshell in pieces. The warmth between my lips was blood, I coughed up more. Perry bore down on me, his face avid with terrible glee, each footstep making the bridge sway like tall grass in a high wind.

The crosses were down now, Weres crowding them. They were cutting the leather straps free, and as I rolled my head painfully to get a better look, charms digging through my hair and into my skull, I saw two of them lift Saul tenderly between them. Perry's footsteps drew closer, each one like the heartbeat of some huge monstrous thing.

Relief burst inside me. I turned my head back. Looked up at him.

The sunsword's light etched lines on his face, eating at the shell of seeming he wore. I coughed again, fresh blood welling up. The scar jolted with sick heat, etheric force like a mass of red-hot wires sliding up the nerve channels and fusing flesh and bone back together. Healing me, probably so he could do more damage. And the corruption from the scar was spreading up to my shoulder.

I cried out, scrabbling weakly, a small sound lost in the chaos.

He loomed over me, his lips shaping words I didn't want to hear. Just two of them, really.

You're mine.

Helpless, I just lay and watched. *Get up, Jill. Get up and kick his ass.*

But Saul was safe, and the Weres had Gilberto too. There was nothing left to do but hold the sunsword's fire steady, the Eye burning as my blood touched it—

"Goddamn motherfucking sonofabitch, get the fuck away from her!"

Anya. The sunsword's light turned fierce white, the glare of full noon as the sun lifted its first limb over the rim of the mountains, and the world was lost in that brilliance. The light filled my eyes, my mouth, my nose, all the way down to my toes. I held the sunsword in sight as long as I could, realizing the hopeless broken cawing sounds I was hearing as quiet fell on the bridge were my own screams, my voice ruined.

The shadow that was Perry flinched aside from the assault of light. He was really such a small thing, that shadow.

I blacked out briefly, surfaced still holding the line to the sunsword. Nothing mattered but that line, etheric force thundering through it, and the cleansing light. If I was lucky, it would burn me to ash too, and—

"Let it go, Jill!" Anya yelled. "Let it *go*, or you'll melt the bridge! *Let go, hunter!*"

Again, that snap of command.

So I did, my mental fingers loosening. The white-hot glare receded, bit by bit, and the Eye hummed softly. The sense of pressure building inside the Talisman had bled off significantly. Like the spear hanging in my weapons room, it needed to be drained every once in a while, or it would get dangerous.

Even more dangerous than it usually was, that is. I had to tell Gilberto about it. So many things I had to do.

I lay there. There was a crackle, and a warm bath of sensation. It was healing sorcery, and if Anya was doing that, it meant the fight was over. I shut my eyes and let her work.

If I wasn't dead, I had to be able to walk for what I had to do next. But for the moment I just lay there on the bridge, listening as the Weres spoke softly and the sounds of hellbreed and Traders fleeing retreated in the distance.

CHAPTER 30

Galina freed the stethescope's earbuds with a practiced motion. "He'll be fine," she said quietly. Her eyes glowed green, and the sunlight pouring through the window made her skin luminous. "A little bit of shock. They starved him. No sign of beatings or other abuse."

My fists refused to unclench. For once, I didn't try to hide it. "You promise? You *swear?*"

"Of course." She gave me an odd look, her necklace flashing against her white throat. "Are you all right?"

In other words: *What the fuck, Jill? You never doubted me before.*

"I just want to be sure," I mumbled. Stared at Saul's sleeping face. He was gaunt, and the yellow tint to his copper skin was new. His fingers were too thin, bony knobs.

Their metabolisms run a lot faster than regular humans'. It's one reason why Weres are all about the munchies.

I wanted to lie down on the bed next to him. Put my arms around him and whisper, *It's all okay, you're safe now.* But the scar was still burning. The corruption had been driven back, healing sorcery pushing it away as thin blue threads settled in and bound bone back together, repaired blood vessels and muscles, swirled through me and made every inch of silver on me glow softly. My right hand cramped, fingers squeezing down as if I held Perry's throat between them.

"Gilberto?" I whispered.

Galina sighed. But she was smiling wistfully. "Young. He'll bounce back. I gather he gave them quite a time. Doesn't know when to quit, that boy."

Sanctuaries are gentle souls. It's really terrible that so few people pass their entrance exams. The world could do with a few more.

"No, he doesn't." *It's part of being a hunter.*

Theron knocked at the door. The smell smoked off him in waves, an unhappy cat Were sending out a musk of aggression and combat readiness. "Kid's awake. Asking for you."

I nodded. "The altars?"

"We found four of them. Devi spiked them all. We had just enough time to get to the bridge. You okay?"

"Fine," I lied. It left my lips easily, a preparation for the other lies I was going to have to tell today. "Galina, can you give me a minute?"

"Sure. I should mix up some boneset for Gil anyway." She gave me another curious look, her eyes darkening before they cleared, and I had to work to keep my face set. "Are you sure you're all right, Jill?"

"Peachy. Just, you know. Tired." I exhaled sharply. "I'm getting too old for this shit."

"Pshaw. Mikhail said that all the time." She grinned, slipped past me, and I saw her brush against Theron's arm as she left. He looked down, a private smile curling his lips, and my heart swelled up, lodged in my throat. They'd been dancing around each other for a while.

What else did Mikhail say to you, Galina? I didn't ask. What could she tell me? A big fat nothing, that's what.

Nothing that could save me.

She went down the hall to her spare bedroom. I heard Hutch ask her a question, her soft reply. It was like listening through cotton wool, I didn't have the scar jacking me up into redline sensitivity.

I never thought I'd miss that.

"Jill?" Theron sounded uneasy. I dragged my attention away from Saul's gaunt, yellow face.

"Tell him I love him." I didn't sound like myself. Who was the woman using my voice? It was a thin, colorless murmur. "Do you hear me, Theron? When he wakes up, you tell him that."

"You're going to tell him yourself." A crease appeared between his eyebrows. I hoped my face wasn't betraying me. "Right?"

"Yes." Another lie. Really racking them up. What did it matter? "Of course. But I want you to tell him as soon as he opens his eyes, Theron. It has to be the first thing he hears. Promise me."

He examined me, top to toe, for a long moment. I was covered in gunk, I hadn't even washed my face yet. Normally I like at least my cheeks and forehead clean, if nothing else. But this time I'd left the grime. I already felt filthy all the way down inside where soap couldn't reach. No washcloth was going to help.

"Theron." I tried not to sound like I was pleading. Failed miserably. "Please."

He nodded once, his dark sleek head dipping. "I promise. It will be the first thing he hears."

"Good." I did not look at the bed again. Closed the sight of Saul's face against the crisp, white pillowcase away, deep in my chest where the pain was already beginning. Took the first step away.

The steps got easier. I brushed past Theron, who took a deep breath. I was hoping the smell of the Eye, its forest-fire burning, would cover up everything else. He didn't move, just stood stock still as the ribbon-flayed edge of my coat brushed his leg.

"Jill?"

I paused, between one step and the next. If he asked me…"Huh?"

"Don't do anything stupid." He stared at the bed, that line still between his eyebrows, his profile clean and classic. They're all so *beautiful*, the human flaws burnished away.

It's enough to make you sick.

I found something closer to my regular tone. "I'm a *hunter*, Theron. It's part of the job description. See you."

I didn't precisely hurry out of there and down the stairs, but I didn't take my time either.

Past the kitchen, where Weres congregated, speaking softly. I made it up the ladder, quietly but not *too* quietly, as if I just wanted a moment alone or to check on the sunsword. I reached the greenhouse, climbing up through the trapdoor, and found my escape path blocked.

I should have known Anya would be waiting for me.

She held a cup of coffee, the venomous-green absinthe bottle set on the table where the sunsword glittered. It drank in the morning light, no glimmer of red in the empty space its hilt curled around. Its clawed finials twitched a little, like the paw of a dreaming cat. That was all.

Anya studied me. Half her face was bruised, the swelling visibly retreating under the fine thin blue lines of healing sorcery. I looked back at her.

Silver glittered in her hair and at her throat, her apprentice-ring sending a hard dart of light into a corner as she lifted her coffee cup. It paused on the way to her lips. She lowered it, set it on the table.

Silence stretched between us. Her clear blue gaze, no quarter asked or given.

I'd thought I could lie even to a fellow hunter now. I was wrong.

I reached down with my left hand, slowly. Pushed my right sleeve up, heavy leather dried stiff with blood and other things. Unsnapped the buckle. Dropped the cuff on the floor, and turned my wrist so she could see.

The air left her all in a rush, as if she'd taken a good hard sucker punch. "Jesus," she finally whispered, the sibilants lasting a long time. "Jill—"

"This stays between us." I was now back to sounding like

myself, clear and brassy. All hail Jill Kismet, the great pretender. "I'm going to take care of it."

She didn't disbelieve me, not precisely. "How the hell are you going to do that?"

I shrugged.

She read it on my face, and another sharp exhale left her. "And if…"

I suppose I should have been grateful that she couldn't bring herself to ask the question. So I answered it anyway. "If it doesn't work, Anya, you will have to hunt me down. No pity, no mercy, no *nothing*. Kill me before I'm a danger to my city. Kill Perry too. Burn him, scatter the ashes as far as you can. Clear?"

She grabbed the absinthe bottle. Tipped it up, took a good long healthy draft, her throat working. "Shit."

"Promise me, Anya Devi. Give me your word." Now I just sounded weary. My cheek twitched, a muscle in it committing rebellion. The scar cringed under the assault of sunlight, I kept it out. The pain was a balm.

She lowered the bottle. Wiped the back of her mouth with one hand. "You have my word." Quietly.

I dropped my right hand. With my left, I pulled the Talisman up. Freed the sharp links from my hair, gently. It was hard to do one-handed, but I managed. I took six steps, laid the Eye on the table. The sunsword quivered. "For Gilberto. Will you…"

"You don't even have to ask. I'll train him."

Then she offered me the bottle.

Tears rose hot and prickling. I pushed them down. Took a swallow, the licorice tang turning my stomach over and my cracked lips stinging. When I handed it back to her, she didn't wipe the mouth of the bottle. Instead, her gaze holding mine, she lifted it to her lips too.

I bit the inside of my cheek. Hard, so hard I tasted blood. The thought that it would be tinged with black made my stomach revolve again. There were so many things I wanted to say. Things like *thank you*, or even *I love you*.

Because I do. We are lonely creatures, we hunters. We have to love each other. We are the only ones who understand, the only ones who will.

Except I wasn't a hunter anymore, was I.

"I need a car," I croaked. "It won't be coming back."

"Shit." It was a pale attempt at a joke, and neither of us smiled. She dug in her pocket and fished out two keys on a keychain that also held a cast-silver wishbone. "Here's my spares. Take them."

I nodded. Tweezed them delicately out of her fingers, but she was quick—she caught my wrist. Warm human skin against mine, and she tugged a little. We stood under the flood of clean yellow light.

She licked her lips. "Mikhail was a good hunter." As if daring me to disagree.

It was hard to get anything out, around the lump in my throat. "One of the best."

"So are you." Her mouth set. "You do what you have to, Jill. I'll take care of everything here."

My face crumpled. I squeezed my left hand into a fist around the keys, sharp edges digging into my palm. The scar burbled unhappily, and the thin creeping tendrils of corruption slid another few millimeters up my arm.

Just like gangrene.

She let go of me, a centimeter at a time. I stepped away, set my shoulders. The protections on Galina's walls shimmered.

"I'm parked west of here, around the corner." Anya's hand fell back to her side. She held the absinthe bottle like a lifeline. "*Vaya con Dios*, Kismet."

"*Y tú también*, Devi." I half-turned and headed for the door. By the time Galina realized I was leaving, I'd already be out.

My cheeks were hot and slick with saltwater. By the time I hit the door, I was running.

CHAPTER 31

The closest freeway on-ramp took me north and slightly west, toward the fierce heart of the desert. Anya's car was a newer Ford Escort, fire-engine red and with no pickup at all. A cheap plastic glow-in-the-dark rosary hung from the mirror, and she had four bobblehead hula girls stuck to the dash, one of them with cropped punk hair. They bobbed and swayed, their gentle vacuous smiles faintly creepy.

The thing barely went seventy. Still, it was wheels. I drove all afternoon, the windows down and sheer golden sunlight parting in shimmering veils. Past the city signs, out to where the road met the horizon. That's the thing about America—you get to some places and there's so much space. It's amazing and faintly nauseating that people pack themselves into cities, living on top of each other like rats in a warren.

If it was summer the tar on the road would have been sticky. As it was, it was one of those rare winter days that's almost balmy, a cloudless pale sky and the sun like a white coin. It's the kind of weather snowbirds come down for, to bake all the aches out of their bones.

When the shadows started lengthening I checked the map, found a handy access road, and slowed down in time to catch it. The car bounced and juddered over washboard ruts, and it was a good thing Anya wasn't expecting her car back. The suspension probably wouldn't survive this.

I saw an outcropping I recognized, guesstimated the distance, and turned the wheel hard. There was no ditch, so the car immediately bounced and wallowed in sandy soil. I worked the accelerator—the brake will make you fishtail worse than anything in sand or snow. At least Anya understood about keeping her car in reasonably good condition. Leon Budge, out Ridgefield way, seemed to keep his truck going with spit and baling wire.

The rocks in the distance were a little farther away than I'd thought, and the sun was touching the horizon by the time I skidded to a stop, a roostertail of dust hanging in the evening air. This far out there was no breath of the river, just the smell of heat and the peculiar flat-iron tang of bone-dry air in winter. The desert smells of minerals, like dried blood without the rust.

My right arm hung limp. I made sure the windows were rolled up, got out of the car, and stretched.

I thought I'd remembered this place correctly, and of course I was right. The outcropping was marked on survey maps, at the edge of a lunar landscape dotted with other rocks, some bigger than houses, others bigger than skyscrapers. Other than that, it seems empty. There's life everywhere in the desert if you know where to look, but in late afternoon it appears barren as an alien planet.

I stepped onto fine sand, into the mouth of a pile of black stone. The semicircle of stacked black rock was glossy, a type that didn't belong in this area. Heaven alone knew what had dropped it here. Inside, the sand was fine and thick, blown in by a wind that some-how avoided sending trash or tumbleweeds along. It was sterile and clean, and I picked the edge farthest inside.

Thirst stung my throat. I hadn't brought a drop of water, and my stupid stomach growled loudly, thinking it was time to get some chow since the bad part was past.

The flesh is always so weak, no matter how hard you train it. I didn't have the heart to explain to my stupid body that the worst was coming.

Outside, the wind moaned against sharp glassy edges. I slid out my left-hand gun and settled down cross-legged, my back to the stone's cup but not touching it, leaving me a good three or four feet of room. Etheric force hummed sleepily through this rock, and the air was a few degrees cooler than outside. I checked the ammo, a trick to do one-handed, and settled the gun in my lap.

I waited.

The sun sank by degrees. I had to pee. It was an urge just like hunger, and I ignored it. Drew the hunter's cloak of silence over me. Peeled my right sleeve up a little, looked at the inside of my wrist.

The mark was hard and cancerous now, the skin swollen and hot. The thin unhealthy threads of corruption spreading were now hard and black as well, a shiny crackglaze on my skin. My entire arm felt numb up to the ball of my shoulder, occasional pins and needles jabbing and tingling.

Night falls quick out in the desert. I breathed deep, brought my pulse down. As soon as the sun touched the horizon, I concentrated on my left hand.

Not long now. Not long at all.

The banefire hurt. It *burned*. Blisters rose on my left hand, and silver shifted uneasily in my hair, rattling. The silver chain of my ruby necklace, the apprentice-ring on my third left finger, all warmed dangerously. But the twisting blue flames came, bubbling and boiling. I flicked my fingers, and the banefire leapt. It obeyed, snaking in a ragged circle from one curve of rock to the other. I was tucked safely inside here, and as soon as the circle of banefire closed there was a not-quite-physical *snap*.

My right arm cramped, curling up as if the triceps had been cut. The ball of my right fist struck my shoulder, and I made a small hurt sound.

"This won't do any good." Perry melded out of the shadows.

He was immaculate. White linen suit, wine-red tie, but snake-skin boots instead of the usual polished wingtips. His hair was longer, and messy. Instead of his usual blandness, his face had morphed into sharp, severe handsomeness. The bladed curves of his cheekbones could have gotten him a modeling contract, even if the photographer could have caught a glimpse of what lay below.

He took a mincing step forward, but the rock creaked and groaned. Banefire leapt and he froze, staring at me.

Thank you, God. My left-hand fingers found a knife hilt. I drew the blade free. Shifted a little bit, careful to keep the gun in my lap. "How long have you been working on this, Perry?"

"Longer than you can imagine." He was utterly still, but his mouth twitched into a wide, mad, hungry grin. "One must be careful, don't you find? When one has a plan, one must be very exquisitely careful. Everything must be just so."

"You never intended to let Julius live, but he distracted every-one nicely. If Argoth would have come through, you would have bargained with me to send him back." My chin dipped, I nodded wearily. "If he didn't you were sure I'd damn myself with Belisa. Or, if not, I'd trade myself for Saul's safety. Any way you sliced it, you won."

"I traded some rather large favors to acquire the collar and chain. Then it was only a matter of finding the Sorrow to go into it. Simpler than I thought, too. She never managed to go very far from you, darling. You fascinated her."

Not anymore. I tried forcing my right arm to uncurl. It didn't want to. I struggled, sweating, and the banefire hissed. It cast weird leaping shadows all over the rock, turned Perry's face into a caricature of handsomeness. He moved slightly, shifting his weight, and the banefire leapt again.

Mikhail had brought me out to these rocks once. It's good to know where places of power are, even if they're a day's drive from your territory. You just never know. The humming force inside the stones fueled the banefire nicely, and as long as I concentrated...

He watched as I uncurled my arm, inch by inch. His lips parted slightly, avid, and the red flash of his scaled tongue flicked once, twice. "A deal's a deal."

I set the knifeblade against the meat of my right hand, drew it across with a butterfly kiss. It stung, and flesh parted. Red welled up.

I stared at it in the shifting light. The tracery of black at its edges mocked me.

I drove the knife into the sand next to me. Picked up the gun. Hefted it, and looked at him.

If his grin got any wider, the top of his head would flip open.

I pointed the gun at him and smiled. The expression sat oddly on my face. He hissed, Helletöng rumbling in the back of his throat.

I almost understood the words, too. A shiver raced down my spine.

"You can't escape me." The rock groaned as his voice lashed at it, little glassy bits flaking away. They plopped down on the sand with odd ringing sounds. "The fire won't last forever, my darling. Then I'll step over your line in the sand, and you'll find out what it means to be mine."

"Think again." I bent my left arm. Fitted the gun's barrel inside my mouth. My eyes were dry, my body tensing against the inevitable.

Comprehension hit. Perry snarled and lunged at the banefire. It roared up, a sheet of blue flame. Twisting faces writhed in its smokeless glow, their mouths open as they whisper-screamed.

I glanced down at the slice on my palm. Still bleeding. It was hard to tell if the black traceries were still there. For a moment, I wondered.

Then I brought myself back to the thing I had to do. Stupid

body, getting all worked up. What the will demands, the body will do—but it also tries to wriggle, sometimes.

Not this time.

"Kiss!" he howled. *"You're mine! MINE! You cannot escape me!"*

I saw Saul's face, yellow and exhausted, against the white pillow. I smelled him, the musk and fur of a healthy cat Were. I saw Galina's wide green eyes and marcel waves, Hutch's shy smile, Gilberto's fierce, glittering dark gaze. I saw them all, saw my city perched on the river's edge, its skyscrapers throwing back dusk's last light with a vengeance before the dark things crawled out of their holes. I saw Anya perched on Galina's roof with her green bottle, staring down at the street and wondering if I had the strength to do this. Wondering if she would have to hunt me down, if I failed here.

And I heard Mikhail. *There, little snake. Honest silver, on vein to heart. You are apprentice. Now it begins.*

I love you, I thought. *I love you all.*

"You cannot escape!" Perry screamed, throwing himself at the banefire again. It sizzled and roared, and the rocks around me begin to ring like a crystal wineglass stroked just right. If this kept up they might shatter.

Wouldn't *that* be a sight.

"Do you hear me, hunter? You cannot escape me!"

Watch me, I thought, and squeezed both eyes shut. The banefire roared as he tried again to get through, actually thrusting a hand through its wall, snatching it back with a shattering howl as the skin blackened and curled. It was now or never.

I pulled the trig—

Book 6

Angel Town

To all the survivors

An army that continues to fight on regardless of the outcome must be considered a well-trained army, whether it is well led or not.
—John Mosier, *The Blitzkrieg Myth*

Decensus ad Infernos

*I*n the shifting wood of suicides that borders the cold rivers of
Hell, what is one tree more or less?

They are a mosaic, those trees. Every shade of the rainbow,
and hues humans cannot see. Every color except one, but that has
changed.

There is one white tree, a slender birchlike shape. Instead of a
screaming face hidden in the bark, there is a sleeping woman
carved with swift strokes. Eyes closed, mouth relaxed, she is a
peaceful pale pillar amid the cold shifting.

For Hell is frozen, a chill that burns. The trees shake their
leaves, roaring filling their branches.

Under the spinning-nausea sky holding dry stars of alien
geometry, something new may happen, might happen, will
happen...

...is happening now.

Pinpricks of light settle into the white tree's naked branches.
She has not been here long enough to grow the dark tumescent
leaves every other tree shakes now. The screaming of their distress mounts, for these trees are conscious. Their bloodshot eyes
are always open, their distended mouths always moving.

The pinpricks move like fireflies on a summer evening, each
one a semaphore gracefully unconnected to the whole. They
crown the tree with light, weaving tiny trails of phosphorescence
in the gasping-cold fluid that passes for air. They tangle the
streamers, and the storm is very close.

Hell has noticed this intrusion. And Hell is not pleased.

The trails of light form a complex net. The other trees thrash.

Takemetakemetakeme, *they scream, a rising chorus of the damned. Their roots hold fast, sunk deep in metallic ash. The river rises, white streaks of foam clutching its oilsheen surface. Leaves splatter, torn free, and their stinking blood makes great splotches on the dry ground. A cloud of buzzing black rises from each splotch, feeding greedily on the glistening fluid.*

The net is almost complete. Almost. Hell's skies are whipped with fury, the storm breaking over the first edge of the wood as screaming thunder. Maggot-white lightning scorches. The pale net over the white tree draws close, like a woman pulling her hair back.

Long dark curling hair, spangled with silver.

The storm descends, ripping trees apart. The souls of the damned explode with screams that would turn the world to bleeding ice, if the world heard. The ashes of their destruction will sink into the carpet of the woods, each separate particle growing another tree.

For there is always more agony in Hell.

The net collapses, silvery filaments winding themselves in. It shrinks to a point of brilliance, and the shadows this light casts are cleansed. They etch themselves on the ash, and under the wrack of the storm is a sound like a soft sigh.

The light winks out.

A few tiny, crystalline-white feathers fall, but they snuff themselves out before they reach the heaving ground.

The white tree no longer stands. It is gone.

And Hell itself shakes.

I: Anastasis

Buzzing. In my head. All around me. Creeping in. A rattling roar, filling my skull. Crawling into my teeth, sticky little insect feet all over my face, feelers probing at my lips. They move, hot and pinprick-tiny, and that sound is enough to drag me screaming out of...

...where?

Dark. It was dark, and there was no air. Sand filled my mouth, but the little things crawling on me weren't sand. They were *alive*, and they were droning loud enough to drown out everything but the sounds I was making. Terrifying sounds. Suffocating, it was in my mouth and my nose too, lungs starved, heart a suddenly pounding drum.

Scrabbling through sand, dirt everywhere, the buzzing turning into a roar as they lifted off me. The insects didn't sting, just made that horrible sound and flew in disturbed little circles.

I exploded out of the shallow grave, my screams barely piercing the rumbling roar. Little bits of flying things buzzed angrily, flashing lights struck me like hammers and I fell, scrabbling, the wasps still crawling and buzzing and trying to probe through my mouth and nose and ears and eyes and hands and feet and belly.

They were still eating, because flesh had rotted.

I had rotted.

I scrubbed at myself as the train lumbered past. That was the light and the roaring. My back hit something solid and I jolted to a stop. The wasps crawled over me, and when I forced air out through my nose it blew slimy chunks of snot-laced sand away.

I collapsed against the low retaining wall, breath sobbing in and out. My head rang like a gong, I bent over and vomited up a mass of dark, writhing liquid.

The stench was awesome, titanic, a living thing. It crawled on the breeze, pressed against me, and I vomited again. This time it was long strands of gooey white, splatting. Coming from nowhere and passing through me, landing in twisting runnels.

Just like cotton candy! a gleeful, hateful voice crowed inside my head. The eggwhite was all over me, loathsome slime turning the sand into rasping dampness.

I squeezed my knees together, bent over, and whooped in a deep breath. The wasps crawled, and other bits of insect life clung to me. Maggots. Other things. Of course—out in the desert, the bugs get to you. Especially in a shallow grave, when there's been trauma to the tissues.

I grabbed my head. The sound was immense, filling me to the brim, the roaring swallowing my scream. Gobbets of rotting flesh fell away, the wasps angrily swarming, and the train rumbled away into the distance.

Leaving me alone. In the night.

In the *dark*.

I tore at the rotting flesh cloaking me. It peeled away in noisome strips, and under it I was whole, slick with slime. I retched again, a huge tearing coming all the way up from my toes, and produced an amazing gout of that slippery eggwhite stuff again.

Ectoplasm? But—The thought floated away as the pain came down on me, laid me open. Skull cracked wide, bones twisting, everything in me creaking and re-forming. My knees refused to give, my short-bitten nails dug through the cloak of rotting and found my own skin underneath.

I scrambled along the retaining wall. The grave yawned, leering, crawling with disturbed insect life. I fell on sand, grubbed up handfuls of it, and scrubbed at myself. I didn't care if it stripped skin off and left me bleeding, didn't care if it went down to bone, I just wanted the rot *away*.

Under the mess of decaying flesh was a torn T-shirt, rags of what had been leather pants. At least I had some clothes. I was barefoot.

I collapsed to my knees on the sand, looked up.

A full moon hung grinning in the sky, bloated cheese-yellow. The hard, clear points of stars glittered, and steam slid free of my skin.

Whole skin. Clear, unblemished, scraped in places. But not rotting.

The pain retreated abruptly. My questing fingers found filthy hair, stiff with sand and God knew what else. The wasps were sluggish—it gets cold out here at night. Everything else was burrowing to escape the chill.

It's cold in Hell, too. So cold. That thought threatened to tip me over into howling madness, so it vanished. Swept under the rug. Hey presto.

My skull was still there. Hard curves of bone, tender at the back. I let out a sob. Held my hands out, flipped them palm-up. They shook like palsied things.

Branches. Like branches.

But the image fled as soon as it arrived, mercifully. My forearms were pale under the screen of filth. On my right wrist, just above the softest part, something glittered. Hard, like a diamond. It caught the moonlight and sent back a dart of brilliance, straight through my aching skull. The sight filled me with unsteady loathing, and I shut my eyes.

Start with the obvious first. Who am I?

The train's rumble receded.

Who am I?

I tilted my head back and screamed, a lonely curlew cry. Because I didn't know.

CHAPTER 1

I shivered, pushed the door open. My feet left bloody prints on faded blue-speckled linoleum.

The diner was deserted. Long white lunch counter with chrome napkin holders, pies under glass domes, and the smell of industrial coffee fought with the reek around me. The night wind had scrubbed the worst of the stink away, but I still felt it like a cloud breathing from my skin.

Why I was worried about that when I was dripping with sandy, crusted filth, bare- and bloody-footed, and wild-haired in the rags of leather pants and a T-shirt was beyond me. Still...it bothered me. Something about my hair bothered me, too. I felt completely naked, even though all my bits were mostly covered. I was too scrawny for there to be much to look at anyway. Pared down to scarecrow bone, muscle wasted away, my elbows bigger than my biceps, my knees knobs.

The diner sat alone off the highway, its windows glowing gold with warm electric light. Two ancient, spaceship-shaped gas pumps stood outside in a glare of buzzing fluorescents. No car was visible for miles in any direction. In the distance, the glow of a city rose, staining the night. I'd been heading for that glow for a slow, stumbling eternity, reeling drunkenly on the blacktop because the shoulder was full of pebbles and other things. Broken glass. Cigarette butts. Nameless, random trash.

I was just another piece of refuse, blowing along.

The booths marched away, all covered in blue vinyl. The tables were spotless, their chrome edges sharp-bright. The window booths even had sprays of artificial violets in tiny mass-produced white ceramic vases, the kinds with pebbled sides and wide mouths.

For a moment I had a memory, but it slipped away like a catfish in muddy water. I stood there on an industrial-grade rubber mat that used to say WELCOME in bright white paint. The *E* and the *OM* were scuffed into invisibility by God alone knew how many feet.

The place probably did a land-office business during the day. Maybe.

"Justaminnit!" someone yelled from the kitchen. There was a sizzle, and the heavy sound of a commercial freezer slamming shut. "Be right with ya!"

Yeah, great. I don't even have any money. There was a phone in a booth outside the front door, but who the hell would I call?

I didn't even know my own name.

"Well, good eveni—gooood gravy *Marie*!" The man hove into sight, two hundred fifty pounds if he was an ounce, most of it straining to escape his white T-shirt and the stained apron slung loincloth-style below his considerable belly. Despite that, he looked hard, and the lightness of his step told me he could do some damage if he wanted to.

If he had to.

But he simply stopped and stared at me. "God*damn*, girl, what happened to you?"

How the hell did I know? I'd just clawed my way out of a god-damn grave. I opened my mouth, shut it.

The door opened behind me. Instinct spiked under my skin; I jerked to the side. My bare, bleeding feet slapped down, braced for action. I ducked, my hand blurring up in a fist.

But broad, warm fingers closed around my filthy, naked upper arm.

He set me on my feet. Taller than me, stoop-shouldered and wiry, his dishwater hair laying close to the skull, and a shadow of acid-melt scarring over the lower half of his face. I stared, a sound like rushing water filling my head, and his ruined lips twitched. You could see where the scars had been really bad, but they were...were they?

Yes, they were retreating. I knew it because I'd seen him before. The black curtain over whatever had happened to me didn't part, but I *knew* him.

"You," I whispered.

"I'm about to call the Authority." Apron Man crossed his beefy forearms. "What the *fuck* is—"

The scarred man looked up. His eyes were bright blue, and that was wrong, too. Something shifted under the skin of his face, and his mouth opened slightly. No sound came out on the slight, soft exhale, but the fat man shut up.

"Well, why'n' tcha *say* so?" he mumbled. "Nobody ever *tells* me nothin'. Coffee, comin' up."

Blue Eyes looked down at me. Then, as if it was the most natural thing in the world, he raised his other hand, indicating the booths. Like he was asking me where I wanted to sit.

Those eyes. They'd been filmed before, gray cataracts hooding them. And the scarring had been much, much worse, in runnels and pleats like the flesh had been reshaped with acid. He'd worn gray coveralls, and the name tag had been a snarl of faded thread.

"I know you." My voice cracked halfway through. "How do I know you?"

He shrugged a little, and indicated the booths again.

Great.

Well, there wasn't anything else I was doing. I picked a booth along the wall, since the windows made my nape prickle and I needed to see the front door.

Why? Why do I need to see it?

I just did, that was all.

He let me choose my side, slid in across from me. Fine threads of gold glittered in his hair under the lights. There were fluorescents in here, too, but over the door and the window booths were incandescent bulbs. It made the light softer, actually—fluorescents are hell on everyone.

Sand fell off me. The scrim of eggwhite goop in my mouth tasted of ashes. My skin prickled with insect grime. Bloody footprints tracked in from the front door, and now that I was sitting I felt just how filthy and exhausted I was. Every part of me had been pulled apart and put back together by someone who had no fucking idea what they were doing.

I stared at Blue Eyes. He regarded me mildly, his ruined mouth curving up in what could have been a small smile. Strings of dirty hair fell in my face, and it seemed wrong. I tried again to think of what my hair *should* look like. Got exactly nowhere.

We sat like that for a while, until Apron Man brought two heavy, steaming china cups and plunked them down. He gave me an incurious glance and walked away, his heavy shoes blurring two of my footprints.

What the hell?

Blue Eyes cupped his hands around his mug. Looked at me.

I figured I could ask, at least. "Who am I?"

Blue Eyes shrugged. It was a very expressive shrug. Now that I was sitting down, the shaking started. It began in my feet and worked its way through my bones one at a time, until I was shivering like a junkie. The neon OPEN sign in the window buzzed, and Apron Man began to sing as something sizzled on the grill. An old Johnny Cash tune, "Long Black Veil."

How could I know that, and not know my own name?

My stomach cramped. "You know me," I hazarded. "But you can't talk?"

Another small shrug, this one different than the last.

"You *won't* talk."

This earned me a nod.

Well, great. "How am I...Jesus. You...I..." I looked down at myself. The trembling threatened to rob me of words. "I know you somehow."

Another nod. Then he made a slow, deliberate movement, reaching under the table like he was digging in a pocket. Faint alarm ran through me, tasting like copper through the ashy sludge in my mouth.

He laid the gun on the tabletop, its barrel carefully pointed away from either of us. I stared, my mouth hanging open as he picked up his coffee mug, deliberately, and drank.

It was a .45, custom-built. A nice piece of hardware, dull black, a real cannon. I knew what it would feel like if I picked it up. I knew the heft and the pull, knew exactly how much pressure to apply on the trigger. I could *feel* that the butt was reinforced as well for pistol-whipping.

"My gun." I sounded like all the air had been punched out of me. "That's mine. I have a gun." *Or I had one. And you're returning it.*

Blue Eyes nodded. He set down his mug with a decisive little click, then edged the butt a little closer to me with one fingertip. A faint breeze touched my face. His mouth opened as if he would say something profound, but then he shut it tightly and shook his head. *Sorry, Charlie. No can speak.*

"You're going to have to help me here. Give me a verb, or something." The shaking started tapering off. Sand slid off my clothes, pattered on the bench and the floor. The thought of a shower filled me with sudden longing. Maybe some food, too. A bed to sleep in, because I was so, so tired.

Dead tired.

Nausea cramped under my breastbone again. Blue Eyes was fiddling around under the table once more. This time he came up with something very small. A tiny metallic sound as he laid it on the table, his palm covering it.

A gun, and something else. I looked up.

His face changed. With the cataracts over his eyes peeled away, those eyes spoke for him. Right now, they burned with pure agonizing sadness. The expression drew his mouth down, and I found out the scarring *was* retreating. It shrank on his face a little, the skin smoothing out. I blinked.

His hand lifted.

It was a ring. A simple circle of silver, and my heart leapt like a landed fish inside my chest. Scruffed up and obviously worn, I knew that if I picked it up I would see the etching on the inside. Tiny scratches of Cyrillic, the only thing I would ever know how to read in that alphabet, because someone had shown me a long time ago.

Do svidaniya, it said. "Go with God."

The other meaning: "goodbye."

Bile whipped the back of my throat. I picked up my mug with dream-slow fingers. It was too hot, but I took a searing gulp of the acrid coffee anyway. It tasted like it had been on a burner for a while, but it was better than the eggwhite crap.

Ectoplasm. It was ectoplasm. Something's happened.

Hot water filled my eyes. A tear rolled down my cheek, and Blue Eyes nodded. He pointed at my right hand, and I knew without asking what he meant. I set my mug down and turned my hand over, looking at the thing embedded in my right wrist. Just in the softest part, above the pulse's frantic tattoo.

It was fever-hot, a glittering, colorless, diamond-shaped gem set in my skin. Its edges frayed, like it had been surgically implanted and then pulled around a bit. It spasmed and settled like a shivering little animal. That tiny twitching tremble communicated itself up the bones of my arm, settling in my shoulder with a high hard hum.

Fear whipped through me, and a bald edge of anger like smoking insulation.

"What the fuck is *this*?" I whispered.

His lips moved slightly, and the flesh on his face crawled. Like there were bugs underneath. I pressed back into the booth, my torn heels sending up a shriek as I shoved them into the floor, my right hand darting for the gun with scary, instinctive speed. Fingers curling, my arm tensing, the barrel trained unerringly at his head.

Familiar. Done this before, too.

He pointed again at my right wrist. His lips moved slightly. The words slid into my head, interlocking puzzle pieces of meaning.

When you're ready.

One moment he was there, solid and real. The next, there was a *pop* of collapsing air, and the booth was empty. Another breeze feathered against my face, touching the crusted strings of my hair. I flinched, the gun lowering as I scanned the entire place.

Empty. Except for Apron Boy, who came shuffling out from the kitchen. Quick as a wink, I had the gun under the table. My left hand scooped up the ring, and the feel of cool metal sent a zing through me, like tinfoil against metal fillings.

Apron Boy held a steaming plate, which he plopped down in front of me along with silverware wrapped in a paper napkin. "Nice guy," he said. "Paid for your breakfast, at least. You eat right on up, honey." He looked expectantly at me, expecting some kind of conversational volley back.

I cleared my throat. "Yeah. Thanks."

That seemed to satisfy him. He hove away, moving side to side like a walrus shouldering up onto a rocky beach, but lightly, his feet planted with care. The plate held ham, scrambled eggs, hash browns.

It looked good.

Eat while you can, Jill.

A klieg light went on inside my head. "Jill," I whispered. "I'm Jill."

I tucked the gun safely away. The ring fitted securely on my third left finger. Was I married?

A pair of dark eyes, silver-scarred hair, and fluid grace. He half-turned, reaching for something beside the stove, and the clean economy of motion made my heart skip a beat.

As soon as the image came, it vanished. I shook my head. More sand slipped free in a hissing rush, but none of it fell into the food. I was suddenly hungry. Not just hungry.

Famished

A gun. A ring. And whatever that thing was on my wrist. And vanishing blue-eyed mutes. Whoever I was, I was certainly *interesting.*

Well, as long as the food was here, I'd take it. I'd worry about what to do afterward.

I hunkered down, stripped the napkin off the stamped-metal knife and fork and spoon, and started shoveling it in.

CHAPTER 2

By the time I quit, Apron Man had refilled my coffee twice and brought out two more plates. I couldn't get full, felt like a pig. At first the food just vanished into the huge hole in my gut, but after the second plate I slowed down a bit. I was in the middle of the third before I began to feel halfway satisfied—biscuits and gravy, sausage patties, a mountain of wheat toast dripping with butter, a smaller plate of huevos rancheros with a side of rice. It was enough to put a grown man in the hospital, but it looked good to me. I did my best, but the yawning emptiness in me suddenly filled halfway through the eggs. The plates looked like something feral had been at them, but Apron Boy didn't say a word, just took them as soon as I pushed them away, then came back with the coffee pot and a slice of coconut cream pie.

I didn't even know if I liked coconut cream pie. I sat there and looked at the piped decorative cream and the little shaved bits of toasted nutflesh and felt sick. Then I wondered if chocolate cream would've been worse. Or cherry. Or...

How could I know about pie and not know who I was?

The gun's heavy weight rested against my side. *Jill. You're Jill, and you're armed. Focus on that, the rest will take care of itself.*

"Sure be glad to close up early tonight." Apron Man shuffled back with another cup of coffee. He wedged himself into the other side of the booth with a sigh. "Get off my old dogs. I'm going into town, give you a lift."

Another one of those silences, and I figured out he was waiting for me to say something. "Really? That's...nice." My voice was a papery husk. "Town?"

He shrugged. "Santa Luz. The bad old lady herself. You'd have to walk a fair ways. Told your friend I'd give you a lift, since he was goin' elsewhere."

Was he, now. I'll just bet. I picked up the clean fork, cut off the tip of the pie slice. "Nice of you." Awkward, like the words were sharp edges and I had to hold them just right.

"Yeah, well. Got to do what we can to he'p each other. You got somewhere in town you're goin'?"

I don't even know my name. Just how to hold this gun. And that if I wanted to, I could be across this table with this cheapass fork stuck in your carotid in a hot half second. It played out in vivid Technicolor inside my head—spurting blood, the greenstick crack of a neck breaking, the things I could do. "No. Just the city limits will do."

He gave me a dubious look, but his attention was snagged by the pie. "Is it gone off? I wouldn't think so, ol' Onorious brought it in this morning."

Onorious? "It's good." It was a lie, I hadn't tasted it yet. But the rest of the food was good. I slid the plate over into the middle of the table. "Want to share?"

His face lit up. "Boy howdy!" And wouldn't you know it, he had a spoon. He must've been waiting for me to ask.

I put my forkful in my mouth, studied his wide walrus face. He looked...kind. But something bothered me. I barely tasted the pie, but it was okay. I could get to like coconut cream. "What are you doing out here?"

He shrugged, chewing vigorously. Swallowed in a rush, took a gulp of coffee. "Landed here a while ago. Get a fair amount of business. People drive, they get hungry. And here I am. Gas pumps still work, but mostly it's the phone and the cookin'. People come in for the phone, and it smells so good they want to have a bite."

I nodded. My right hand came up, I offered it across the table. The gleam on the underside of my wrist sent a small rainbow winging across the Formica. "Jill."

He grinned even wider. It was a nice smile, broad white teeth with not a trace of food clinging to them. The corners of his eyes crinkled up, and for a moment something golden moved in the depths of his eyes.

You could see where he had been handsome, once.

His hairy paw closed over my filthy, smaller hand. "Martin. Martin D. Pores, atcher service. Honor to meetcha. Now, what do you say we finish up this here piece of pie and get movin'? Dawn's a-going to break afore you step over that limit, miss."

Dawn? But I was past questioning by then, really. A great wave of exhaustion crashed over me. My stomach was full, I had a gun and the ring, and that was all that was important right now. "I'm tired." I sounded like a cranky child.

He considered me for a long few seconds, and if I'd been less tired I might've been concerned about the things moving deep in his gaze. "I'll bet you are. You want to visit the ladies' while I get this all closed up?"

The car was a 1975 Mercury wagon, faded fake-wood paneling and handling like a whale. The engine had a slight knock to it, one

I caught myself trying to suss out. For all that, it was comfortable. There's just something about a piece of American heavy metal when you can stretch your filthy battered feet out and watch the miles slip away like silk under the wheels. The ribbon of white paint running alongside the freeway reeled us along just like a big silent fish on a hook.

Martin kept it five under the speed limit, and he drove like an old granny. It didn't matter. There was nobody else on the road at this hour. The stars were hard clear points of light, each one a diamond, and the moon was low.

"You like music, Miss Jill?"

I thought about it. Did I? Didn't everyone? I decided on a good answer. "Yes."

"Well, that's good. Music's a good thing." He twisted the shiny silver knob and caught what must have been an oldies station, because Johnny Cash was singing about shooting a man in Reno just to watch him die.

I shivered. It couldn't have smelled good with me in the car, so I'd rolled my window down. Fresh, cold air poured over me, the roaring of the slipstream almost making words. I propped my filthy hair against the back of the seat and sighed.

Martin kept both his beefy paws on the wheel. He hummed along as Cash turned into the Mamas and the Papas, singing about nobody getting fat but Mama Cass. My eyelids were suddenly heavy.

Stay alert, Jill.

But there was no way. I'd had a hell of a day. Night. Whatever.

The hum of the engine and the song of the wheels were both soothing. With a full stomach and the heater finally blowing warm air into the car, I fell asleep to Martin's tuneless humming.

Just like a newborn baby.

CHAPTER 3

I drove the knife into the sand next to me. Picked up the gun. Hefted it, and looked at him.

If his grin got any wider, the top of his head would flip open.

I pointed the gun at him, and smiled. The expression sat oddly on my face. He hissed, Helletöng rumbling in the back of his throat.

I almost understood the words, too. A shiver raced down my spine.

"You can't escape me." The rock groaned as his voice lashed at it, little glassy bits flaking away. They plopped down on the sand with odd ringing sounds. "The fire won't last forever, my darling. Then I'll step over your line in the sand, and you'll find out what it means to be mine."

"Think again." I bent my left arm. Fitted the gun's barrel inside my mouth. My eyes were dry, my body tensing against the inevitable.

Comprehension hit. Perry snarled and lunged at the banefire. It roared up, a sheet of blue flame. Twisting faces writhed in its smokeless glow, their mouths open as they whisper-screamed.

I glanced down at the slice on my palm. Still bleeding. It was hard to tell if the black traceries were still there. For a moment, I wondered.

Then I brought myself back to the thing I had to do. Stupid body, getting all worked up. What the will demands, the body will do—but it also tries to wriggle, sometimes.

Not this time.

"Kiss!" he howled. "You're mine! MINE! You cannot escape me!"

I saw Saul's face, yellow and exhausted, against the white pillow. I smelled him, the musk and fur of a healthy cat Were. I saw Galina's wide green eyes and marcel waves, Hutch's shy smile, Gilberto's fierce glittering-dark gaze. I saw them all, saw my city

hunched on the river's edge, its skyscrapers throwing back dusk's
last light with a vengeance before the dark things crawled out of
their holes. I saw Anya perched on Galina's roof with her green
bottle, staring down at the street and wondering if I had the
strength to do this. Wondering if she would have to hunt me down,
if I failed here.

And I heard Mikhail. There, little snake. Honest silver, on vein
to heart. You are apprentice. Now it begins.

I love you, *I thought.* I love you all.

"You cannot escape!" Perry screamed, throwing himself at
the banefire again. It sizzled and roared, and the rocks around me
begin to ring like a crystal wineglass stroked just right. If this kept
up they might shatter.

Wouldn't that be a sight.

"Do you hear me, hunter? You cannot escape me!"

Watch me, *I thought, and squeezed both eyes shut. The bane-*
fire roared as he tried again to get through, actually thrusting a
hand through its wall, snatching it back with a shattering howl as
the skin blackened and curled. It was now or never.

I squeezed the trig—

—up from the concrete with a southpaw punch, bone shattering
as my fist hit. My foot flicked out, heel striking sharply in the second man's midriff, and I was beginning to wake up. The alley
tilted crazily, both sides leaning toward each other like old drinking buddies, and the rotting refuse in choke-deep drifts along its
sides smelled about as horrible as I did. Faint grayish light seeped
in through the crack of sky showing above. The sky was weeping
a little, a diseased eye.

There were two more of them, one with a chain that rattled
musically as he shook it. Cold fear and exhilaration spilled
through me like wine.

Gutter trash, Jill. Not worth your time.

But my body wasn't listening. It knew better than I did, and I
was suddenly across the distance separating me from Chain Boy,
my knee coming up and sinking into his groin with a short meaty
sound. He folded down, and I had the gun in my right hand,

pointed at the last man. He fetched up like a dog at the end of his tether.

A chain's only good if you can use it. It's also only good for a very short distance, shorter than you'd think.

For a moment I wondered how I knew that.

The fourth man was actually a boy. A weedy little boy with greasy lank hair and a lean, sallow face, a leather jacket that creaked like the cow was still mooing and hadn't missed it yet, and pegged jeans that looked dipped in motor oil. The switchblade made a small clatter as it hit the concrete, dropping from his nerveless hand. My finger tightened on the trigger.

He's just a kid. Come on.

But that kid would've followed his buddies in raping and possibly killing me if I was what they'd thought I was.

Wait. What am I? It said something that even sleeping like the dead, I kept hold of a gun.

I didn't see the Mercury. Martin D. Pores, nice guy and granny driver, had left me in an alley. Nice of him. Why was I surprised? Of course he would, it was the way things were going.

Pay attention! A sharp phantom slap, my head snapping aside, and my right foot flicked out again, catching sneaky Guy #2 in the knee. *Crack* like well-seasoned firewood when the axe split it, and he folded down with a rabbit-scream.

Must've hurt.

The boy in the motorcycle jacket just stood there and shivered. I don't know what he saw on my face, but it gave him some trouble. Maybe it was the mismatched eyes, one blue, one brown, that I'd found staring at me in the diner's restroom mirror. Maybe it was the gunk smeared all over me.

Maybe it was even the gun.

"Go home," I rasped. My voice didn't want to work quite right. "Go to school. Get a job and stop hanging out in alleys."

His head bobbed, lank hair falling forward in strings. He reminded me of someone, but I couldn't say just *who*. Someone with a flat, dark stare, someone I knew because . . .

. . . it was gone. Just for a second, I had it. Then it retreated, maddeningly.

He turned tail and ran, his sneakers whispering over concrete and kicking aside random bits of trash.

I spun, slowly, in a complete circle, marking every fallen body. The gun swept like a searchlight, tracking by itself to cover possible hiding places before I even thought of it. An easy instinctive movement, just like breathing. Whoever I was, I'd spent a lot of time doing this.

Training, milaya. A gruff, harsh voice, the words freighted with a foreign accent and cut off short and sharp. *It gets into bones. Run all the way deep.*

Who was that? My right hand jerked a little, as if the gem set on the inside of my wrist was twitching, pulling me.

He'd trained me well. The guys were down and moaning, except for the first one—the one I'd punched, his cheekbone shattered and bits of white tooth flecking the wet hole of his twisted-open mouth. He lay utterly still, with his head at an odd angle.

Oh, Christ, did I kill someone?

The sudden certainty that it wasn't the first time poured down my back, ice cubes trickling. Nobody who handled a gun like this could be innocent.

I backed up two steps, bare feet on cold concrete. At least I wasn't bleeding anymore. Maybe I was toughening up.

You clawed your way up out of a grave. I'd say that's pretty damn tough. The question is, what do you do now?

I had a full belly. But I needed shelter, and some more clothes wouldn't be amiss.

A quick search of the two moaning men produced rolls of cash as thick as my forearm. Plus little plastic baggies full of illegal smokable stuff, switchblades, and two guns—a .38 and a 9mm. I tossed them down the alley so the boys didn't get any ideas, and considered the guy I'd punched. After a second or two of thought, I found another roll of cash as well as more baggies on him. He was still breathing, the air bubbling through the bloody mess of his mouth. I'd broken his cheekbone and quite a few of his teeth. My hand didn't hurt at all, and how had I blinked across space to take out Chain Boy?

The gem on my right wrist glittered, colorless, a hard dart of light as dawn strengthened and spilled more illumination through the crack serving as the alley's ceiling.

You don't know your own strength, girl.

"I guess not," I muttered. "Jesus."

I got the hell out of there.

CHAPTER 4

The crackling plastic bags on the tiny room's colorless bed gave up a black V-neck T-shirt and a pair of jeans that were a little too big, but I hadn't been able to try them on. It was bad enough waiting in the shadows for the gigantic Walmart a mile away to open. By 9 a.m. when the doors whooshed wide, I was a bundle of exposed, dirty, and vulnerable nerves.

I shouldn't have worried. Those employees don't bat an eye. I guess no matter what I looked like, they'd seen worse. After getting an eyeful of the crowd waiting to scramble on in and get their cheap shit even cheaper, I won't exactly say I was heartened—but I was feeling a little more anonymous.

I remembered my shoe size, at least, but the sneakers felt weird, too light and flexible. The holster for the .45—I'd stuck it in the waistband of my ruined leather pants while shopping, just like a good American—didn't *quite* do it, but a little duct tape fixed that right up. The .45 ammunition had been reasonably cheap, and as soon as I put it in my basket I'd felt soothed.

Whoever I was, I didn't like being unarmed. Or short of ammo. I was hoping the modifications on the gun hadn't made it unable to fire a basic clip, but there it was.

I found a place on the edge of the barrio. Some clear instinct warned me not to go any further into that tangle of streets, so I just picked a likely-looking hotel and paid for two nights. Cash up front, no ID requested or given. It was the kind of place usually rented by the hour, and after about 2 p.m. it started doing a brisk trade. Footsteps, soft cries, some screams, doors opening and closing. I didn't listen too close. It was bad enough that my hearing was jacked up into the red, and I could smell every single person who had ever used this tiny room.

Sirens. Jackhammers. Traffic.

At least the shower worked. It was tepid, but there was decent water pressure. The drain almost clogged, sand and gunk sliding off me in sheets. I didn't bother with the towels. Who knew what vermin they were carrying? Instead I wrung my hair out and air-dried. The wheezing air conditioner didn't help very much against an egg-on-the-sidewalk sort of day, a glare of heavy sunlight golden against the barred window. It was like being in prison, only with a door that locked on your side.

Which meant it wasn't very much like prison at all.

Once I was dressed and the gun was checked, cleaned with a just-bought kit, and set on the flimsy bolted-down nightstand, I lay down on top of the cheap chintz bed-spread and let out a long sigh. The ruined, filthy clothes were in a plastic bag; I'd dump them elsewhere. Something told me it was best to leave no traces.

My hair was already drying, raveling up into dark curls. I was pale, and the face in the mirror was nothing special except for the mismatched eyes. Long, thin nose, mouth pulled tight and thin, bruise-colored shadows under said eyes almost reaching down to the prominent cheekbones. I looked half starved. I was hungry again.

Who the hell am I?

Evidence: one silver ring with Cyrillic script inside, one gun, one weird gemlike thing implanted in my right wrist. Speed and strength enough to take on four men without breaking a sweat. Of course, there was the little matter of Martin Pores and his vanishing Mercury, but if I had just dug my way up out of a shallow grave maybe I'd hallucinated that bit and just wandered around dreaming of diner food.

I couldn't rule that out.

The only other thing was the tattoo. A black tribal-looking scorpion, high up on the inside of my right thigh. It itched and tingled, but maybe that was only because I'd scrubbed at it, thinking it was dirt.

My hands were capable and callused. My battered feet were healed, too. No sign of the bloody mess they'd been after walking miles of highway. Even if I'd just been wandering around in a hallucination, I'd been shoeless and bleeding. But now you couldn't tell.

For some reason, I turned my head and looked at the window. My hair felt weird. Like there should have been something in it. Lots of little somethings digging into the back of my head. Tiny gleams, little hard things.

For just a moment I had it, but it slipped away again. Frustration rose hard and hot in my throat, I swallowed it.

I knew my first name. I knew I didn't have a problem killing someone, but I preferred not to.

At least, not when they're human. When they're something else...

Something else?

"Maybe I'm insane." My own voice caught me off guard, hit the flimsy walls and bounced back to me. "That's an option, too. Consider all the alternatives, Kismet."

Kismet?

Another light turned on inside my head. Jill Kismet.

That's who I am. But who is she?

I waited, but nothing else came up. It was daylight. Sleepytime, because daylight was...safe.

I tested that thought. It felt right. "Daylight's for sleeping," I whispered. "Night is when I work."

Well, that was comforting to know. Or not.

I closed my eyes, told the gnawing in my belly to go away, and waited for dusk.

It was as good a plan as any.

CHAPTER 5

I reached down with my left hand, slowly. Pushed my right sleeve up, heavy leather dried stiff with blood and other things. Unsnapped the buckle. Dropped the cuff on the floor, and turned my wrist so she could see.

The air left her all in a rush, as if she'd taken a good, hard sucker punch. "Jesus," she finally whispered, the sibilants lasting a long time. "Jill—"

"This stays between us." I was now back to sounding like myself, clear and brassy. All hail Jill Kismet, the great pretender. *"I'm going to take care of it."*

She didn't disbelieve me, not precisely. *"How the hell are you going to do that?"*

I shrugged.

She read it on my face, and another sharp exhale left her. *"And if…"*

I suppose I should have been grateful that she couldn't bring herself to ask the question. So I answered it anyway. *"If it doesn't work, Anya, you will have to hunt me down. No pity, no mercy, no nothing. Kill me before I'm a danger to my city. Kill Perry, too. Burn him, scatter the ashes as far as you can. Clear?"*

She grabbed the absinthe bottle. Tipped it up, took a good, long, healthy draft, her throat working. *"Shit."*

"Promise me, Anya Devi. Give me your word." Now I just sounded weary. My cheek twitched, a muscle in it committing rebellion. The scar cringed under the assault of sunlight, I kept it out. The pain was a balm.

She lowered the bottle. Wiped the back of her mouth with one hand. *"You have my word."* Quietly.

I dropped my right hand. With my left, I pulled the Talisman up. Freed the sharp links from my hair, gently. It was hard to do one-handed, but I managed. I took six steps, laid the Eye on the table. The sunsword quivered. *"For Gilberto. Will you…"*

"You don't even have to ask. I'll train him."

Then she offered me the bottle.

Tears rose hot and prickling. I pushed them down. Took a swallow, the licorice tang turning my stomach over and my cracked lips stinging. When I handed it back to her, she didn't wipe the mouth of the bottle. Instead, her gaze holding mine, she lifted it to her lips, too.

I bit the inside of my cheek. Hard, so hard I tasted blood. The thought that it would be tinged with black made my stomach revolve again. There were so many things I wanted to say. Things like Thank you, *or even,* I love you.

Because I do. We are lonely creatures, we hunters. We have to love each other. We are the only ones who understand, the only ones who will ever understand.

Except I wasn't a hunter anymore, was I?

"I need a car," I croaked. "It won't be coming back."

When I woke, the dream faded. For a second I had everything, it trembled inside my head...then it was gone. And I needed to go, too. Dusk was rising, and something told me the hotel might not be...safe. The need to get out and move itched under my skin.

I found out something else, too: I liked heights. I especially liked gliding along rooftops like a ghost, peering into the streets below. Looking for something I couldn't define while dusk rose from every corner, cloaking the city in peculiar static heat, the rising wind bringing me an oddly familiar tang of river as everything exhaled.

Preparing for the plunge into darkness.

Everything about it was familiar. Even the shapes of the city streets, the arterial bloodflow of traffic, the quiet neighborhoods and the back alleys, the parts that lit up only when the light failed. And yet, everything was unfamiliar—the sneakers were too light, and I felt oddly naked. Like I should have more, a heavy weight on my shoulders and something flapping at my ankles, something on my face and those little weights tied into my hair. Not to mention the fact that my left hand kept dropping to my side like it expected to find another gun. Or something else.

The city revolved inside my head. I knew the street names, sometimes only after I dropped down to their level and looked around a bit. The town clung to the banks of the river, a big granite Jesus on top of a hospital downtown spread his arms in a menacing blessing, nightclubs pounded and weird things skittered in the shadows. Every building greeted me with a secret smile, little bits of the geography whirling like snowflakes until they settled against the rest of my mental map.

It was next to the granite Jesus, looking out over all those tiny dots of light, that something else stirred inside my aching head. I crouched in Christ's spreadeagle shadow, watching the very last dregs of light swirl out of the sky, and sniffed the wind. Even in summer, nights out in the desert can get chilly. No trace of moisture in the air, but a thin faint thread of something candyspiced and wicked tickled my nose.

What the hell's that? Half-rising from the crouch, keeping to cover, I almost swayed because I didn't have a counterweight hanging behind me to keep me steady. A cloak of stillness folded over me, my pulse dropping, my entire body chilling. Gooseflesh rose hard like little rubbery fists under my skin, I ignored it.

Follow that. It's not supposed to be here.

I was moving before I knew it, bolting across the rooftop, the world around me blurring. Hit the edge going full speed, a moment of weightlessness, and smacked the pavement stories below with a crack like a shotgun and a breathless feeling of *holy shit did I just do that?*

I would've been laughing with crazy joy, if not for the gun unholstering itself and the sudden fierce buzzing in my right arm, like a band of metallic flies was breaking for the surface of an infection. Right at my wrist, too. It pulled me along on a reel of silk, I flashed through a deserted alley and straight up a brick wall, barely touching the rough surface, my left hand catching at the top and heaving me over with little effort.

It was like flying. And I might've liked some time to enjoy it before I collided with a long tall thin thing out of a nightmare, its flesh glowing waxen-pale as it snarled, flying backward with its legs and arms drawn in, spiderlike. Its eyes glowed with a powdery sheen, and the thing it had been crouching over was a rag of bloody bone and meat that had once been a human being.

Trader. Put him down quick, Jill. But not so quick you can't question him.

Well, at least now I had a goal.

He smashed through two struts, snapping them like matchsticks, and the strength flooding my veins was definitely bolting up my right arm from the . . . thing, the gem, whatever it was. I was on him in a hot heartbeat, punching him twice and something cracking in his torso; we skidded and a lick of hot pain went up my arm. Skin erased by concrete, the smell of blood, and the Trader's chin jutted forward. His teeth were sharklike points, steaming saliva dripping and foaming, and we hit a retaining wall with a sound like a good hard break on a pool table. Something snapped in my side just like the struts, the pain was a spur. His teeth buried themselves in my shoulder, grating on bone, I screamed. Not with the pain.

No. I screamed in pure frustration. I knew what to do, but I didn't have the tools to do it. I didn't have my knives, or my coat, or—

The gun bucked in my hand, its roar oddly muffled. A hole opened in his back, the exit wound blossoming obscenely. The Trader howled through his mouthful of my flesh, blood squirting and whatever venom he had on those sharp triangular teeth burning as it sizzled, spattering my neck.

He didn't quit.

I shot him again, twisting, and the thought—*thank God for judo, Jillybean, get him good*—seemed completely normal. Another hole opened in his back. Why was he *still* moving? Squeezed the trigger again, and his torso was mangled now. Another hole opened in his back, this one spattering and spraying wider than the first two. A mist of copper droplets hung in the air.

I got lucky.

The flat, shine-dusted eyes glazed. He twitched, teeth grinding in the ruin of my shoulder, and I let out a sound that probably would've haunted a nightmare or two if there was anyone around to hear. It took working the gun barrel into his mouth and cracking the jaw to get the teeth to loosen up as his body twitched and jerked. I jammed it further back—he was still twitching—and squeezed the trigger again, the roar way too close for comfort.

The back of its head evaporated.

Corruption raced through its tissues, little veins of dust spilling from a crackglaze like fine porcelain glued back together and unceremoniously busted again.

Would've been easier with my knives. Where are my fucking knives? It didn't matter. I scrambled out of his slackening embrace, my sneakers squishing and sliding in a tide of brackish fluid. It was blood. But the edges of the red fluid held a taint of black, hungrily threading through and turning it to dust as the body twitched and jerked, heels drumming in a weird dance against the rooftop, the mangled head spilling brainmeal as the neck twisted. My ribs flickered; heaving breaths shaking me like wet laundry. I hit one of the listing iron struts reaching up like fingers—it was bent crazily where he'd gone right through it.

Yes, I could see now it was a he. He'd been naked, and his genitals were altered, too. Barbed and spiked, like...I don't even know what like.

They always go for body mods. Part of the personality of someone who'll trade their soul away. I know that. It was a relief to find something I did know for sure. Even if this was weird as fuck.

I was making a whistling sound. Hyperventilating. Something inside me clamped down, made my pulse and respiration calmer, my eyes locked on the twitching, disintegrating body.

You must watch death you make, a man whispered from my soupy, darkened memory. *Is only way,* milaya.

Mikhail. I remembered his name, now, with a lurching mental effort. Sweat stood out, cold and slick, all over me. The gun was steady, pointed at the swiftly rotting corpse as if it might take a mind to get up for round two.

You never know. You just never know.

My shoulder burned, but I ignored it. The gun didn't waver. So this was what I did. I leapt off multistory buildings like I was stepping off a patio. I found weird smells. I got into fights on rooftops.

I killed things that shouldn't exist.

The gem on my wrist glowed softly.

When you're ready.

Is that what he'd meant, my blue-eyed breakfast-buying hallucination? Was I having another hallucination now?

That's the trouble with waking up in your own grave. A whole lot of weird shit suddenly seems pretty reasonable.

Maybe that wasn't your grave. Maybe your name isn't Jill. Maybe Mikhail is something else. Can't assume. That's what he said, all the time. "Do not ever assume. Is quickest way to get ass blown sideways."

I stared at the bubbling mass until it was clear it wasn't going to get up and come after me again. The night air was full of traffic sounds, faraway sirens, whispered secrets. My shoulder had stopped bleeding. When I looked down, craning my neck, the bubbling pink froth squeezing out of the flesh as it knit itself back together sizzled a little, eating at the T-shirt. Bile whipped the back of my throat, I forced it down by swallowing. Bad idea, because then it hit my stomach and revolved. I was kind of glad I hadn't eaten anything, because I heaved once before I got myself back together and used the spar behind me to muscle my way back to standing. My knees definitely felt gooshy.

The next step was examining the victim and looking for evidence. Like a cop.

Not a cop. A hunter. You do what the cops can't.

My own voice, hard and clear, addressing a class of bright-faced boys and girls in blue dress uniforms.

I will be blunt, rookies. You'll all be required to memorize the number for my answering service, which will page me. Pray you never have to use that number. Three or four of you will have to. A few of you won't have time to, but you can rest assured that when you come up against the nightside and get slaughtered, I'll find your killer and serve justice on him, her, or it. And I will also lay your soul to rest if killing you is just the beginning.

"Holy fuck," I whispered. The city whispered and chuckled.

I shuffled like an old woman, back to the victim. There was a pile of clothing—workman's boots, overalls, a red plaid shirt, a billfold in one of the pockets. A nice wad of fifties and hundreds that I took without compunction, ID showing a sullen, lean face— it was dark up here, but I had no trouble picking out the features of the thing I'd just killed. Back when it had been human, its name had been Eric Allen Dodge, and he lived in the Cruzada district. Staring at the address gave me a map of the city, different routes I could take to get out to his house if I needed to give it a looksee. There was one more thing, and I held it while I crouched to look at the rag of meat and bone he'd been hunched over when I hit him.

The victim was female. There was enough of her left to tell, mostly because the breasts were chopped free and laid to one side and her plumbing was oddly untouched.

He must've been saving that for last. My gorge rose again. What did it say about me that I could guess?

Not enough blood on the roof, so he'd killed her elsewhere and brought the body here. Her heart, a fist-sized lump of flesh, was set neatly aside with her tatas. There were other bits, something that was probably her liver, long strings of guts. Her face had been savaged. About all I could tell was that she'd probably been dish-water blonde or light brunette; her shoulder-length hair was matted with clotted blood and filth. White slivers of teeth poked through the hamburger of what was left of her features.

Her left hand. A gleam of gold—wedding ring, on the third finger. Just where silver rested on my own left hand.

"*Do svidanye*," I murmured, and looked at the only other thing that'd been in Dodge's wallet.

It was a plain, thick, dove-gray business card. MONDE NUIT, it said, and an address out near the meatpacking district. I knew exactly where the meatpacking district was, and the location seemed... familiar.

More than familiar.

Wasn't this just my lucky night.

CHAPTER 6

The place looked foul. The atmosphere over it had thickened like a bruise, my left eye smarting and watering as it untangled layer after layer of rotting cheesecloth. *Etheric bruising,* my helpful unmemory piped up. *That means it's a haunt. You know what a haunt is, right? A place where wild animals go to feed. There's 'breed in there, and Traders. You need silver.*

Silver. My right hand flashed up, touched my hair. That's what should be there. Silver charms. Tied in with red thread. It was traditional.

Doesn't help me now, though.

I loitered at the edge of the parking lot, sunk in shadows. There was brush here, and I crouched easily, sometimes moving to keep muscles from stiffening, sometimes utterly still and watching. The place looked familiar—a long, low building, parking lot shading to gravel at the edges, a couple of gorillas at the door and a line waiting to go in. Faint thumping bass reached me as I studied the shapes of the people in line. They moved... oddly. Scary quicksilver grace or twitching almost-stasis, and even at this distance I could see the twisting under the surface of their normal shapes. The twisting threatened to give me a headache until I figured out I could simply make a note of it and it would stop bothering me. I just had to acknowledge it.

Someone in there knows who I am.

But these were things like the thing I'd killed on the roof. *Wrong.* And very, very bad. I had no silver. Just the business card and—

A long black limousine took a right into the parking lot, crunching on gravel before bumping inelegantly up onto cracked pavement. The line twittered and whispered with excitement. The car glowed, wet light from the tangle of red neon over the building's front sliding over its sleek flanks. My focus narrowed and I leaned forward, coming up out of the crouch as if compelled. My body obeyed smoothly, but my right wrist twinged. I glanced down, but the gem set in the skin was the same, a colorless sparkle. The wind touched my hair, playing with the curls, cool with the flat metal tang of river water, the desert's sand-baked exhale picking up the water and vanishing.

The limo banked easily, like a small plane, and one of the bouncers stepped forward to open the door. I took another two steps, gravel oddly soundless underfoot. My right hand touched the gun butt, fingers running over it like they expected to read Braille.

A pale head. He rose out of the car on the other side, and a rippling sigh of excitement went through the line. I moved forward, impelled, cutting through a line of dusty parked cars. The limousine scorched, dirt-free, the only thing in the lot that didn't look tired or filthy. My hand curled around the gun, but I didn't draw it yet. The ring on my left hand ran with blue light, a seashine gleam.

They became aware of me in stages, as if I was a storm moving through from the mountains. First the eerie-graceful part of the line, with their seashell hips and liner-drenched eyes, stilled. Their heads came up, and sculpted nostrils flared. Cherry-glazed lips parted, and a collective exhale lifted from them along with a bath of nose-tingling corruption.

They were beautiful, but under that beauty lay the *twisting.*

The jerky, oddly-shaped ones were next. They hissed, lips lifting and sharp-filed teeth showing, some of them crouching. One of them, a broad wide manshape dressed in a caricature of a construction worker's plaid shirt and Carhartts, his work boots stained with something dark and fetid, actually growled. The sound rose in a rumble like boulders grinding together, and some sure instinct made me pause, staring at him. Yellow eyes, unholy foxfire in the irises and the pupils flaring and constricting like a cobra's head. He tensed as his knees slowly bent.

He's getting ready to spring.

Movement. The pale head of hair was approaching. They cringed and fell back from him, but I didn't look. I stared at the Trader, my fingers slowly tightening on the gun. If he jumped me I had some running room and cover in the parking lot. Maybe I could tangle them up and—

There was a blur of motion, cream-colored linen streaking. A pale clawed hand flashed out, and the construction worker fell sideways, arterial spray blooming high and red. The drops hung in a perfect arc, and I saw each one was tinged with that tracery of black, hungrily gobbling at the fluid as it splashed.

Holy shit. I stared.

He stepped out of the way, polished wingtips gleaming just like the car, and my gaze snapped to him. The gun left its holster with a whisper, and my arm was straight and braced.

Pallid hair in a layered razor cut. Blue eyes, and the face wasn't beautiful. He looked normal—average lips, average cheekbones, an average all-American nose. The suit was linen, sharply-creased and expensive, and the eyes were bright blue. He regarded me with pleasant, cheerful interest, and I blinked before my left eye gave a twinge and I caught a glimpse of the *twisting* rippling under his flawless skin. A wine-red tie, he lifted his right hand and touched the half-Windsor knot, as if it had been knocked a millimeter out of place. Taller than me, his shoulders braced and his hips narrow, my mouth suddenly filling with copper adrenaline and my pulse dropping into a low steady rhythm.

Because this was a face I knew.

His left hand twitched. The fingers drew up like claws, and his paleness was a shade or two darker there. Something had happened to that hand, something my brain shied away from even as it threatened to plunge through the fog and *remember*. A spark popped from my ring's silver surface, photoflash blue.

"I know you." My lips were numb, but I simply sounded wondering. "From..." Words failed me, balked and twisted away. "From somewhere. I *know* you."

He studied me for another long moment. His smile widened.

He actually *grinned*. Pearly teeth, very sharp but very normal as well. It was a television newscaster's beaming, wide and practiced. Those blue eyes lit up, and another ripple went through the crowd.

"Of course you know me." Even his voice was reassuringly normal. Bland as the rest of him. "Our darling little Kismet, returned. How lovely." He stepped forward off the curb, but the bruisers looming behind him—one with a submachine gun, the other just a pile of over-yeasted muscle—didn't move. I almost twitched, but *he* made a soothing noise. A low exhale, his tongue clicking as if I was an animal to be gentled. "You look beautiful."

CHAPTER 7

I twitched outright this time, nervously, the gun tracking him. He paid no attention, heel-and-toeing it across the concrete as if we were on a dance floor. He only stopped when I took a restless step sideways, and that brought him up short. But he leaned forward, balanced on his toes, his entire body focusing on me.

"My lovely," he whispered. "My own. Of *course* I know you. What have they done to you?"

They? Whoever it was left me in the desert. In a grave. I rotted, but I came back.

No. That wasn't quite right. I hadn't come back. I'd been *sent*.

"They sent me back. To...I don't know." It was work to whisper. My throat was suddenly dry. Queasy heat boiled through my stomach, and I was suddenly aware the entire crowd of them was too still to be human.

If they jump you now, a clear cold voice warned me, *you're not going to have an easy time of it. You're not even really armed. Just this gun with useless ammunition. You need silver. And lots of it.*

Well, it was a fine time to remember that. And what did this have to do with the thing on the rooftop and the flayed, opened-up body, its organs set neatly aside?

I backed up, even more nervously. One step, two. He kept leaning forward.

"Don't." His unwounded hand came forward. The body of the Trader behind him slumped, twitching and jerking as corruption raced through its tissues. "Don't leave, dear one. Come inside. You look hungry."

What a coincidence. I was suddenly *starving*, and empty blowtorch-hole in my guts. I examined his face. Whatever lived underneath that skin rippled.

It didn't look good, and the business card in the wallet of a murderous *thing* was not an endorsement. But...he was familiar. Whoever he was, I *knew* him.

That doesn't mean he's any good.

Did I have any other option?

My gun lowered slightly. The night exhaled around me, dangerous sharp edges and the neon glaring, the hunger suddenly all through me. My right wrist twitched, a fish-hook under the skin yanking restlessly.

"That's it," he crooned. "Come inside. There's a bed, and sharp shiny things to make you feel safer. You want knives, don't you."

A guilty start almost made it to the surface. I stared at him.

His smile widened just a notch. "And a gun or two. And a long, long black coat. And shining chiming things to tie in your lovely hair." His tongue flicked out and touched his bloodless lower lip. In the uncertain ruddy light it was a startling wet cherry-red, rasping against the skin. That quick little flicker made me nervous again, and I sidled another step. That brought him forward in a rush, fluidly, his bones moving in ways a human's shouldn't.

Even that was familiar. Half-disgust boiled under my breastbone. The other half was something I couldn't name. "Perry." I found his name. But nothing else. It was like thinking through mud. "You're Perry."

His irises glowed, sterile, cold blue. Thin threads of indigo slid through the whites of his eyes, a vein-map. His pupils dilated a little. "At your service. In every conceivable way, Kiss. That's what I call you. A pretty name for a pretty girl. Come. There's food. And drink. And a place to rest." His head cocked slightly. "And answers. You would like answers, wouldn't you? Your perennial plaint: *Tell me why.*" A short, beckoning motion, his long, expressive fingers flicking. "You'll be under my protection, darling one. Nothing to fear. Just come, and let me soothe you."

It sounded good. Better than good. For a moment something else trembled under the surface of my memory, but it retreated again. Maddening, the feeling that I should know. That I should *understand*, instead of pushing myself blindly forward from place to place. The ring was warm, a forgiving touch against my flesh.

The gun twitched. My finger eased off the trigger. It lowered slightly. "First tell me something."

"Oh, anything." He eased toward me again, supple and weightless as if he was simply painted on the air. "Anything you like."

I searched through every question I had. There were too many of them crowding me. His pupils swelled, and the roaring sound filtered into my head again. The wasps, eating and buzzing, little tiny insect feet prodding as they crawled over me again. A galvanic shudder racked me. The gun dropped even further.

"Who am I?" I whispered. "What the hell *are* you?"

The laugh was another rumble, as if a freight train was passing me by again. It came from him, a subvocal roar, plucking at the strings under the surface of the world, and his fingers closed around my arm. Everything in me cringed away from that touch, but his fingers were warm and exquisitely gentle.

"You are my Kiss." Very gently, experimentally, he pulled on my arm. The ring sparked again, but it was unimportant. I followed, numb, the wasp-roar filling my skull like the cotton wool of illness. "And I, my darling? I am Legion. I am unconquerable fire." His grin was absolutely cheerful, and oddly terrifying, but all the soothing in the world was in that voice. "But don't worry. I am also your humble host this momentous evening. You've arrived just in time."

He led me past the bouncers, the submachine gun dangling as

they watched, slack faced. The crowd muttered, hissing, but he paid them no notice. The doors were open, a red velvet curtain hanging in tattered folds, and he drew me through it and into the pounding music. I could barely gasp in a breath before the noise folded over my head like wings, and his grip on my arm never faltered.

I had a confused impression of swirling bodies on a dance floor lit with migraine stabs of brittle light, a monstrosity of a bar with two slim male shapes handing out what could have been drinks in twisted sparkling glasses, the press of the crowd alternately fever-ish and cold. The whirling crowd snarled, pressing back against each other as stipples of light flashed around me. Those little spar-kles weren't from the disco ball—and who the hell has a disco ball nowadays? It was a slowly spinning planet, ponderous, a great silver fruit that pulsed with malevolence.

No, those little sparkles were half-unseen spikes surrounding me, their tips fluorescing up into the visible. An aura.

An exorcist's aura. Be careful, Jill.

I wished that voice had spoken up before. I'd killed a thing on the rooftop, a thing like these *things*. Now here I was in the middle of them, nowhere near as terrified as I should be.

This was *normal*. And what did that say about me?

It had something to do with him. With his hand on my arm and the thrumming growl coming through him, the noise that carried us both through the press of the crowd.

There was an iron door behind a frayed red velvet rope, and as soon as he pulled me through and the door shut with a clang I found myself on a staircase, going up.

So far so good. I'd been here before, several times. The gun dangled in my nerveless hand. He drew me up the stairs, and under the bass-throb attack of the music played at jet-takeoff lev-els I swear I heard him humming. A happy little tune, wandering along like a drunken sailor past alleys full of cold, dark eyes.

Another door crouched at the top, and he pushed it open. White light flooded the stairwell, and I blinked.

The room was white, too. An expanse of white carpet, a mir-rored bar to one side, a huge swan bed swathed in bleached mosquito netting, a bank of television screens flickering at odd intervals. Some of them were dark, some fuzzed with static; others showed the club's interior and exterior, flicking rapidly through surveillance angles. Still more held news feeds, footage of explosions and disasters shuddered soundlessly. Once the door slid shut it was eerily quiet, a faint thumping through the floor all that remained of the noise below, a dozing animal's heartbeat.

He led me across the room, pushed me down on the bed. I sat without demur, my feet placed side by side like good little soldiers. He finally let go of my arm, stepped back, and brushed at stray strands of my hair that had come loose.

I didn't flinch. I just waited for clues, my eyes fixed on the blue gleam running under the ring's surface.

"There." The smile was still wide, but he looked pained. "That is…perfect. Just *perfect*. I've often thought that if I could have you sit just there, just so, all the problems would fade into insignificance."

"Problems?" I cradled the gun in my lap. The buzzing wouldn't go away. Rattling, chrome wasps in a bottle.

The thought that some of the carnivorous insects might have been left inside, maybe in my sinus cavities, nibbling at my brain, sent a rippling jolt through me. The bed made a soft shushing sound, silk sliding and netting twitching. The bottles racked above the mirrored bar were all clear glass. Some held gray smoke, shifting in screaming-face shapes. Others held jewel-glowing liquids, and the harsh white light stroked them.

"I have no problems, darling. Now that you're in my sight. Apple of my eye, flesh of my flesh." He stalked to the bar, his wingtips crushing the pristine carpet. "And you must be hungry. One moment."

My breathing had turned shallow. The horrific buzzing rattled my skull, I hunched my shoulders and went still. The air was curiously flat in here. The bed smelled faintly of fabric softener, but that was it. There was nothing else. It was the equivalent of a blank page.

There's something you're not seeing. Look deeper. Look again.

If I could get the meat inside my head to stop sounding like an overworked lawnmower on crack, I would. The sound crested, filling my bones, shaking me like a terrier with a toy in its sharp white needle-teeth. My ribs heaved, lungs burning, as if I was chasing something across rooftops.

The business card was crumpled, but I lifted it anyway. It still said the same thing.

Think. A card in a wallet. Doesn't mean much. Or it could mean everything. Which one are you betting on?

"*Et voilà*," he murmured. A flicker of motion jerked my head up, and I stared.

In the middle of the arctic expanse of carpet, a table had bloomed. Covered by a fall of snowy linen, a bloody half-closed rose in a vase like fluted ice, two places set with exquisitely simple porcelain. Forks and knives and spoons of heavy, pale golden metal. A bleached, brassy candle-holder like a twisted tree held thin white tapers. Their flames were colorless, standing straight up.

"Now." He indicated the chair with its back to the bed, a high-backed, spine-shouldered piece of pallid metal with a cushion of faded-red velvet. "I have no violinist, and no apples. But I think we shall do very well. Come, sit."

The buzzing receded like a sand-gurgling wave. I crushed the business card in my fist, suddenly very sure I didn't want the twisting under his skin to see it.

"I." My throat closed up. I cleared it, a harsh sound rustling the mosquito netting. "I, ah, have questions."

"Of course you do." He set down two water-clear champagne flutes. "And I'm in a position to give you answers. Plenty of them, too."

"Then start." My voice didn't belong to me. There was some other woman using it, her mouth twisted half up into a pained, professional smile and her hand ready on the gun in my lap. She peered out through my eyes, taking note of everything in the room and chalking it all up on mental lists—how easy it would be to get her hands on it, how much damage it would do, what her chances were. Percentages and likelihoods, all whirring inside our shared brain like clockwork gears. "Who buried me in the desert?"

"Well." A dusty bottle appeared out of nowhere. Its cork popped deftly free with a wrenching, violated sound, and the fizzing, pale-amber fluid poured in a couth stream into the flutes. "Hardly dinner conversation, Kiss. But I suppose you have a right to know." He set the bottle down with a click and picked up both glasses, cocking his head as he stared at me. His tongue flicked again, a blot of cherry-red, shocking against the paleness. "When I saw you last, you were dead."

"When was that?" She shifted slightly, the woman suddenly using my body, and cursed us both for putting us right in the most vulnerable location in the whole damn room.

"Oh, about two months ago." His teeth flashed, lips parting. "What would you like for dinner, my dear?"

I shifted again, uneasily. I was *starving*, but that other woman was warning me not to take a single sip or bite of anything he'd give me.

Where had she been when Martin Pores was feeding me?

"Knives." I swallowed hard. "You said knives. And...a coat."

"Don't be uncivilized. Sit over here." Faintly annoyed now, a shadow between those feathered eyebrows. The rippling under his skin had quieted, but the indigo threading through the whites of his eyes warned me.

My legs tensed. They carried me upright, and the gun dropped to my side. His teeth looked a lot sharper now.

So did the rest of him. A shadow of bladed handsomeness passed over his face, his eyes burning.

One step, two, my sneakers making little dry sounds against the carpet. Everything up here was new, freshly unwrapped. Like the whole stage had just been waiting for me to step onto it, under a brilliant skull-white spotlight.

"Right here." He indicated the chair. "That's a good girl. We'll have a nice, happy dinner. The first of many."

Does that mean I've never eaten here before? I think that's a fair guess. And I'll bet I had my reasons. The time for me to make any move was narrowing, ticking away in microseconds. The gun twitched, my pulse thudding along even and sonorous like a deep underground river, my right wrist suddenly burning. The buzzing had moved out into my fingertips, and it fought to bring the gun up, squeeze off a shot and let—

Footsteps. High and hard. The door burst open, and I whirled, gun trained on the new arrival.

CHAPTER 8

Perry was suddenly *there*, slim pale fingers tensing and crackling at the man's throat. Man, or boy, he was so slight I couldn't tell. His ears came up to high points and his teeth were only bluntly human, but dapples of shadow-bruising ran over his skin, and his hair writhed in fat brown dreadlocks like it had a mind of its own.

He choked, and Perry hissed. The sound was freight trains rubbing together at midnight in a cold deserted yard, overstressed metal squealing in pain.

Helletöng, I realized. The language of the damned.

Which gave me all sorts of interesting ideas about the position I was in. The hiss-roar died away, and the Trader's face turned an unpleasant purplish.

"I thought I said I wasn't to be disturbed." Perry cocked his head, each word quiet and level. "This had better be—"

"—*caught*—" The Trader choked again, and Perry eased up.

"What?" More töng, plucking at the strings below the surface of the world. I could glimpse the spreading stain, corruption welling up and torquing reality one way or another, my blue eye suddenly hot and dry. "Speak *up*," Perry snarled.

He probably could, if you weren't holding him a foot off the floor and cutting off his air. But I kept that thought to myself. It would probably be unhelpful in this situation.

It was looking like I was going to need all the help I could get. Lights were turning on inside my head, flickering in rapid fire, and the things they showed weren't very nice at all.

"Caught one," the Trader wheezed as the fingers in his throat loosened slightly. "We caught one. Watching us."

"Indeed." Perry went still for a few seconds. A hot, dry draft reeking of spoiled honey brushed the room. Even immobile, you could see his molecules trying to escape, jittering away. Under his suit coat his back shifted, something straining inside the shape he wore. Horror crawled up into my throat, my brain shivering away from the suggestion underneath. Like a twisted alien body under a blanket, so horribly *wrong* a chill walks up your spine with ice-glass feet.

I've seen that before, though. I survived seeing it. I know I did.

Perry glanced to the side, his profile severe and handsome, a classical statue's long nose and relaxed mouth. His eyes scorched, and he made a sudden swift movement. A greenstick *crack* echoed, the Trader's feet flailed, and the hellbreed dropped him like a dirty rag.

Bile whipped the back of my throat. My face stayed frozen, numb. *Keep your pulse down.* Training clamped down on my hindbrain; I could actually *feel* the pressure sinking in, hormonal balance mercilessly controlled, heartbeat and respiration struggling to escape those iron fingers.

Mikhail was always on me to keep my pulse down. I stared at the body as it slumped to the side, twitching and juddering, dusky corruption racing through its tissues. The naked, hairless chest, the ribs flared oddly to support different musculature, legs in a pair of fluttering black pants caked with something filthy and iron-smelling at the bottom. The stink of death-loosened sphincters ballooned out, exploding across the sterile unsmell, and I shivered.

Then I stilled, hoping that hadn't been a mistake.

"There's no need to fear." Was he trying to sound *soothing*? Perry rolled his shoulders back in their sockets, cartilage crunching. "This will only take a moment, darling mine. You can even watch."

He stood there, staring to the side, the indigo threads in the whites of his eyes swelling and retreating obscenely. As if expecting a reply.

I searched for something to say. Finally, I cleared my throat again. "Is that what's called killing the messenger?"

He actually *laughed*, and the horrible thing wasn't how loud it was. No, it was the sheer gleeful hatred, his lips smacking like I'd just told the world's funniest joke. The laugh cut off in midstream as more swelling crackles slid around under his pale, perfect skin.

"You could say that." He stepped daintily aside as the corpse's legs jerked. "But it's also a lesson. They shouldn't interrupt me, not while I'm with *you*." A sidelong glance, sipping at my face. "Come along. This should be...*instructive*."

What else could I do? I followed.

Down on the ground floor, twenty seconds spent passing from one iron door to another along the edge of the vast belly of the Monde. The damned paid no attention, writhing against each other while the disco ball spun slightly faster and the music took on a screaming, spiked edge. I glanced out over their sea of chains and leather and slim legs, sweet curves and the bloom of powdery rot on each of them, and something else lit up inside my head.

Hunter, Jill. You're a hunter. And these are what you kill.

Which opened up huge new vistas of contemplation I had no luxury to indulge in, because this second door gave onto a hall lit by low bloody neon tangles, crawling like worms against the wood-paneled walls, and my fingers tightened on the gun again. More doors marched down the hallway on either side, and again recognition rose to choke me. Little half-remembered scenes played out inside my skull, the woman who shared my body unlocking mental doors and throwing them open—just like Perry, his hair and clothes now dyed scarlet, chose a door on the left and flung it wide.

"Well, well, well," he chanted, mincing into the room beyond. "What have we here? Oh, look. A stray cat."

A cold spear went through me. *Cat?*

The last time I'd been here, these doors had all been standing open, torn-out teeth in a dead smile. Behind the one at the far end of the hall had been a table shattered to matchsticks, an iron throne demolished, and something hanging in silvery chains. Something horribly battered, and as I'd walked in the chains had rasped against each other, fat, dry-sliding tongues.

I stared down the hall. If I walked to the end, would I find a room where the table was put back together as if it had never been broken, mirror-polished and solid? And the throne at the end... would its metal spikes be repaired? Or would a new one have been brought in?

A low, terrible growl cut across the hallway. It was a cleaner sound than 'töng, and it turned another key inside the broken lock my head had become.

—pair of dark eyes, tawny sides moving, the sun picking out gold along a cat's sleek lines, and he nuzzled my throat, kissing while I shook. The crisis tore through me again, and the kiss turned to a bite, pressure applied with infinite care, the skin bruising as he sucked. The neck's erogenous in the extreme for a cat Were, and Saul—

Saul? I jolted back into myself. My lips shaped the word, but I said nothing.

He was *important.* My pulse sped a fraction, control clamped down, and I began to get a very bad feeling about all this.

"Hold it down. She'll want to see this." A low, delighted laugh, and the wasp-buzz was a dark curtain inside my head, bulging over some horrible, unknowable shape. "Oh, this couldn't have been better if we'd *planned* it. Kiss?" Calling me, like a dog. "Kiss, my darling, come inside."

I hated him calling me that. Another key, another broken lock, muscles hardening as I *twisted* it. The effort was both physical and mental, the gem on my wrist scorching, threads of silvery pain sliding up the nerve channels all the way to my elbow.

This time, the buzzing was a curtain of shining metallic insect bodies, and the gem on my wrist vibrated as the curtain pulled aside. Dawn rose inside my head, but it was the sterile white light of a nuclear sunrise, everything inside me turning over and shattering as consciousness flooded me.

Jill. Jill Kismet. Hunter.

The memories slammed through me all at once, my entire body locking down, muscles spasming and ruthlessly controlled. Fighting in the dark, night after night spent cleansing the city streets of things like the dancing mob in the belly of this building—and Perry, pulling the strings, our bargain sealed by a scarred lip-print on my right wrist.

I hated everything about him. Everything. But that wasn't important right now. Training jacked my hormone balance, adrenaline a bright copper flood across my tongue, the bloody neon light flashing as my eyelashes fluttered. The ring was a scorch on my left hand, silver reacting to the etheric contamination filling this bruised, hollow place. I dropped back into myself with a thud, and heard Perry laugh again. A low, very satisfied chuckle, a razor against numb flesh. There was a wet sound, and the growl cut short as if a door had slammed in the middle of it.

I knew that sound. It was a Were. Probably a cat Were, too. He'd just been punched in the gut.

If there was a Were here at the Monde, he was looking at a whole lot of hurt. And if it was who I thought it was...

...I couldn't let that happen.

CHAPTER 9

Immobility shattered. My eyes flicked open. I drew in a deep breath spiced with hellbreed corruption, the copper stink of blood, and a sudden colorless fume of rage.

I *moved*.

The door slammed open, hitting a wide-load Trader— chunky-thick, plaid shirt, bare feet misshapen and horned with calluses—with a sound like an axe sinking into good, dry cordwood. I twisted in midair, gun roaring, and the second Trader— slim, dark, head exploding in a mess of bone and brain—folded down. A head shot, and a good one, but how I was going to deal with Perry was a whole 'nother ball of wax. I landed, whirling as Perry made a sound like a frozen mountainside calving, chunks of overstressed icy stone groaning and tearing free.

The room was small, a brass drain hole glinting in the middle of the shallow-sloped concrete floor. Soaked in the neon glow, my foot flicked out, catching the third Trader—blonde, female, modded out with claws and blood-glowing compound eyes—just under the chin with a jolt and a sound of bone breaking, like glass hammers shattering in a burlap bag. *Should really have boots for this sort of work.* The thought was there and gone in a flash, because I dropped, instinct taking over as a pale smear bulleted past me. It was Perry, snarling, his hands outstretched, and if I hadn't shed momentum and hit the ground he would've crashed right into me. As it was, he hit the wall with a *crack* that might've been funny if he hadn't still been making that huge rock-crushing noise.

The man they'd been holding up slumped, his body heading shapelessly for the floor. I grabbed him and flung us both backward toward the door as Perry slid down the wall. Spiderweb cracks radiated out from the crater he'd put in the dark-smeared wood paneling, and a pair of chains hanging on the opposite wall jangled musically, little spots of white gleaming on their thin surfaces.

Orichalc-tainted titanium chains. I had no time to think about what they would do to whatever they would chain down in here.

Time to go to work, Jillybean.

The glass tangles lighting the room swayed, shadows dipping crazily. My sneakers slipped, and I felt, of all things, a brief burst of silver-sharp irritation. *Would never happen in boots, why couldn't they bury me with my boots on?* The gem on my right wrist turned scorching, a tide of wine-red strength flooding up the bones and veins, jolting in my shoulder and roaring through the rest of me.

I was hoping it wasn't Perry's force I was drawing off. Whose else could it be? It didn't matter. Deal with the devil and dance another day.

Nice to know some things hadn't changed.

Neon tubing smashed with a tinkle as I ran right into the wall across the hall, the man's bulk surprisingly heavy. I had one hand wrapped in his skein of dark hair, the other tangled in the shredded remains of his T-shirt, and he was bleeding. The blood was red, no trace of black at its fringes, and I hauled him up. My back burned, glass slivers digging in, and warmth trickled down from broken skin.

His head tipped back, a lean dark face horribly bruised and swelling, and a heatless shock of recognition went through me.

Wait. Not Saul. "Theron!" I yelled, and pitched aside. We went down in a heap, rolling, and another part of my aching head lit up under klieg-light memory. *Theron. Werepanther. Works at Mickey's out on Mayfair. Good backup.* "Get *up*! Let's *move*!"

Which brought up a problem: I had no weapons except the

gun, not even any silver-coated ammo, and another consideration surfaced, one I had no time to indulge because a massive sound rose from the room we'd just vacated.

Perry was not going to be happy. Just guess how I knew *that*.

What would've happened if I'd eaten something? A chill walked down my bloody back, but Theron was up. He shook his head, stared up at me like he didn't quite credit what he was seeing.

"Move!" I yelled, and shoved him toward the end of the hall that gave out into the Monde's interior. No exit the other way, and legions of the damned between us and the outside.

Fun times, Jill! Never a boring moment! Get your ass moving!

Theron took off, a graceful unerring lope much faster than I thought he'd be able to move. I skip-shuffled back just as the Trader I'd hit with the door was propelled out into the hall, wide shoulders slumped and his face a mask of black-tinged blood from his mashed nose. Somehow it had splattered *everywhere*, and a fresh gout stained his flapping Hawaiian shirt as he saw me and snarled, hunching like a demonic football player. His modified feet twisted so the toes splayed and great horny toenail-claws dug into the flooring.

Don't worry about him. Worry about Perry, who's due out any sec—

The doorway evaporated. A wash of crackling-blue hellfire burst out, unholy flames blooming with a hiss I could hear even over the pounding throb of music through the walls. The glare swallowed the crouching Trader whole, and he went up like a fatty candle.

I drove backward, legs pumping, hoping I wouldn't tangle with the Were as we both flung ourselves for the door that would lead out into the Monde. Trigger-finger cramping, lungs burning, had to remember to breathe, steps jolting up through my hips and shoulders as my sneaker-clad feet stamped hard, I threw myself back just as Perry rounded the corner, wreathed in pale-blue livid hellfire and his bland face suddenly sharply starving-handsome again.

I didn't hit the door because Theron had, busting it clear off its hinges with a short bark of effort, a cat's coughing cry. So I sailed back, crashing into a knot of dance-writhing Traders, scrabbling to get *up get up get UP* just as the flames belled out again, little tiny fingers sinking into the wall on either side of the hole. Perry was suddenly *there*, filling up the space.

And he looked *pissed*.

CHAPTER 10

I was up again in a hot second, my heel grinding into something soft and my elbow whapping a female Trader a good one in the face. The music was still going, and I hoped like hell Theron had already made it past the bar. He'd have only the Traders at the door to worry about then, and he could be out in the night in a moment, vanished with a Were's speed and agility.

What was he doing here in the first place? What's going on?

That wasn't my problem right now. My problem was the hell-breed who stepped mincingly out of the blurring, grasping fingers of blue flame and twitched his shoulders, the air peaking in high points of disturbance behind and above him. His eyes were the same color as the hellfire, indigo spreading around the edges of the burning irises and threading down over his cheeks in a vein-map tattoo. Everything turned over inside me. I remembered something else—*yellow flame dripping from my hand as I pulled on the mark on my right wrist, etheric force jolting up my shoulder, sick fury and rage twining together to fuel the fire as I burned the whole hellish mess to the ground—*

I gained my balance with a huge lunging effort, raising the gun. *Keep moving.* More skip-shuffling back, covering ground as fast as physics would let me, the noise was massive and confusion just starting to spread out in ripples.

Two shots popped off, both of them good solid hits. Perry's head snapped back, a gush of thin black ichor hanging in the air as time slowed down and details stood out sharp and clear. Still moving back, flicker of motion in the corner of my eye, I threw myself aside as a stick-thin male Trader in a black T-shirt and jeans leapt for me.

A dark blur hit the Trader from the side, a coughing roar cutting the sonic wall of music. Spatters of leprous light flicked as the ball overhead swung, and the mood of the crowd tipped crazily.

Theron had the Trader down, blurring through panther form into humanoid, claws tearing. The shape-between isn't anyplace Weres linger, but even there they are beautiful, and he'd just saved my bacon.

Except I'd been planning for that hit, and now I was scrambling to recover as Perry's head tipped back down, the ichor closing over the hurt and sealing it away. Without silver, bullets would barely slow him down.

Great.

Perry twitched his shoulders again, grinned murderously, and launched himself for me with the eerie stuttering speed of hellbreed. The crowd exploded away, the grace of confusion vanishing as awareness of the fight raced through them like ink dropped in water.

"*Jill!*" Theron yelled, and I had at least the satisfaction of him knowing who I was. If we got out of here, I could ask *him* some questions, too.

Like how I'd ended up dead. Who had buried me. And what the bloody blue *fuck* was going on.

"*Get out!*" I screamed. "*Theron! Get the fuck ou—*"

Perry *arrived*, blinking through space, and my right wrist sent a spike of clear, hot pain all the way up my arm, detonating in my shoulder, tearing across my ribs, and jerking down my legs in one swift lunge. I spun, hip twitching out to provide momentum, my foot coming up as the gem in my flesh let out a high, crystal-stroked sound. My sneaker crashed into Perry's jaw, force transferred and the jolt snapping something low in my right leg; red pain bolting up to my hip. Knees pulled in, the world turning over as I pushed off, deflecting him by critical degrees, and at least I was light without weapons or anything else hanging on me.

I *flew*.

Landed hard, breath driven out of me in a howl as my abused

right leg gave way, and Theron was suddenly *there*. Skidding to a stop, fingers tented on the floor, bruised face a mask of effort as he snarled. I almost overbalanced, but he uncoiled with sweet grace, legs driving him up as his hand closed around my left arm and Perry tumbled through the crowd, knocking over Traders and other 'breed like ninepins. He hit them hard, too, the crunching of bones breaking and screams of the wounded drowned out the feedback squealing of the music.

Theron left the ground in a leap of such effortless natural authority I half-expected it to be easy for me too. I pushed gracelessly with both legs, trying to help, ignoring the bones grinding together in my right shin, a red firework of agony.

His grip popped my shoulder out of its socket with a high, hard burst of pain, my head snapping aside and tendons screaming, the rest of me a boneless flag flopping in the wind. We tore through the moth-eaten red velvet curtain and burst out into the cool darkness outside just as the music juddered to a halt behind us and Perry's cheated howl shattered several chickenwire-laced, painted-black windows.

The parking lot reeled drunkenly as Theron yanked me again. A submachine gun opened up in a burst of deafening chatter, glass shattering and metal pop-pinging as bullets dug a sewing-machine trail behind us. My stretched shoulder gave another flare of deep-purple pain, a symphony of damage playing colors behind my eyelids as I tried to return fire.

This ammo won't do any good. Been lucky so far, but luck won't hold. Goddammit.

We hit yet again, Theron compressing like a spring, and plunged into the scrub brush at the edges of the lot. He cursed, the whisper-screaming of obscenities over a deep rumbling groan. Nobody knows where a feline Were's purr comes from, but this was a warning growl, shaking my bones and sending a deep pulse of heat through torn muscle and abused flesh.

Behind us, screams and cries lifted into the chill night air.

Now they were hunting us.

Being carried along by a cat Were is an exotic experience, even if you can understand what's happening to you. Being dragged by a cursing, slowly healing, very angry Werepanther was a new one even for me.

Or at least, it felt new. I hoped it was.

He skidded aside, and the dark of an alley swallowed us. I hung, almost limp, in his grasp. My entire body twitched, the meat senselessly protesting a brush with its own mortality. Stupid body, getting all worked up because I could have died.

I guess even if you've done it once, it's not something you want to do again.

"Jesus," he kept saying. "It's you. It's *you.*" Like he couldn't believe it. Like he was relieved.

I seconded that emotion. Except I was tired, and hungry, and nothing about tonight was going in a way that could remotely be considered well.

But I knew who I was. I knew who he was, I knew what we both were, and I knew enough about Perry to guess we should keep running.

I just couldn't figure out how I'd ended up dead.

Theron propped me against the alley wall, long sensitive fingers feeling for my shoulder. "This is gonna hurt," he announced, and I nodded.

"Do i—" I began, but he popped the balltop of the humerus back into the socket before I could finish. I swallowed a half-scream, my teeth driving hard into my lower lip and bursts of color exploding behind my closed eyelids again.

"Sorry." He sounded genuinely sorry, too. His breath touched my cheek, I found out my head was lolling. "Jesus Christ, Jill. It's *you.*"

"So they tell me." I tilted my head, straining my ears. *They're going to be after us.* Everything on me hurt savagely, muscles twitch-screaming and bruises rising for the surface of my skin. My right wrist burned, a live coal pressed into the flesh—but the heat was strangely soothing. It didn't feel normal. *Yeah. Normal. We've missed* that *train by a mile.* "We can't stay here."

"Where have you been?" He still had my arm, as if I might disappear if he let go. "You tell me that. Where have you *been*? Saul..."

I perked up at the sound of that name. "Saul? Is he all right?"

His eyes flashed gold-green for a moment, rods and cones

reacting differently than a human's at night. Then a brief sheen of orange—when Weres and 'breed get excited, the eyes get all glowy. The knowledge slid into place like I'd always known. Maybe I had.

It didn't disturb me. Weres were safe.

I was sure of that much, at least.

"He's..." He stared at me for a long moment, his jaw working and the bruises crawling up his face livid even in the gloom. "You...don't remember?"

"I woke up last night in my own grave, Theron. I'm not sure what I remember. Or who." My knees felt suspiciously weak, I leaned back into the wall. Whatever was dumped in the trash piles here reeked to high heaven, but at least it might cover up *our* smell. Neither of us were too fresh right now. I reeked of gunfire, rotting Trader blood, and effort, Theron of musky, unhappy cat Were and fresh blood. We both carried the sweet whiff of hell-breed corruption.

It was a heady mix, but not a particularly nice one. My shoulder throbbed, but I took stock and discovered I could fight. If I had to. And he was moving okay for a Were who'd been taken in by hellbreed.

Lucky. We were both goddamn lucky. I holstered the gun. It was next to useless against 'breed without silvercoated ammo.

But I'd find a way to make it work.

I searched for a way to explain where I'd been. I didn't even know how to explain it to *myself.* "I remember some things. Others, not so much, and some things I only remember too late." *Like hating Perry. He seemed so familiar.* I was too tired to even shudder. "Glad I found you."

"Me too. They were about to...look, you don't know *anything?* Where have you been?"

My pulse dropped, breathing evening out. It wasn't relaxation— my jacked-up hearing caught the pitter-patter of hellbreed feet, too light or too heavy to be human, too fast or way too slow. Probably some Traders, too, and drawing close. "Dead, Theron. Weren't you listening? We've got to get out of here, they're looking for us."

"You even *smell* different," he muttered, but he grabbed my arm again. "I can run. You just hold on."

"I can run—" I began to protest, but he simply yanked at me while he turned, a graceful, complex movement ending up with my arms around his throat. He straightened, and my legs came up instinctively around his middle. Just like an uncle taking a kid piggyback riding, and I was breathing in his hair.

"We're running for the barrio," he said over his shoulder. "Relatively safe there, even with the war."

"War?" I took a deep breath. Cat Were, musk and wildness—familiar, but it wasn't him I was thinking of.

Saul. Where are you, catkin?

The last thing I remembered was Galina's face when she told me he'd been taken. By hellbreed. But there was a maddening blank spot after that, bruise-colored, aching, and blank as a dead TV monitor. I had no time to settle down and *think* and try to figure out what to do about it.

"War on Weres, Jill. You've been out a while. Things are...complex." He tilted his head and tensed.

The skittering footsteps drew closer. The night pulled itself taut, a drumskin over vibrating hatred. "I can fight." But I held on.

He burst into motion, bolting for the blind end of the alley. Up the wall in a breathless rush, and the city yawed underneath. Fur scraped my arms, he dropped halfway into catform, and I hugged him as tight as I could, my right wrist coming alive with sweet piercing pain. I hoped I wasn't throttling him—and I hoped he could run fast enough.

Because a choked cry rent the darkness behind us, and I knew they'd found our trail.

CHAPTER 11

We almost made it. The edge of the barrio was temptingly close, but there were just too many of them. They were between us and safety, and we crouched on a rooftop in the lee of a billboard for car insurance. Traffic crawled along Lluvia Avenue below, rubies one way and diamonds the other, civilians with no idea a running battle was going on above their heads.

I slid from Theron's back as he gasped, his sides heaving. Hauling my ass around probably hadn't done him any good.

"Catch your breath," I told him, and slid the gun free. Even if the ammo was no good, it would at least slow the Traders down, and if I could bleed them out badly enough the corruption of their bargains would finish them off.

Hellbreed were a different proposition. But I'd think of something. "Run for the barrio. I'll draw them off."

"You...and your...Lone Ranger...shit." He didn't look good—cheesy-pale, those bruises, and if my eyes weren't fooling me, thinner than when we'd started this whole barrel of fun. His metabolism was at scorch level to heal him and provide the speed he'd just used to cart me halfway across the city. "Never...ends...well."

Now that sounds familiar, too. I cast an eye out over the rooftop. "Quit talking. It's wasting breath, and I need you ready to run when I make a diversion."

He gulped, his sides heaving, and shuddered. His breathing evened out, and he closed his eyes. "You have...*no* weapons. How...are—"

"I've got *a* weapon, I'll think of something." I checked the gun, my fingers moving with ease. The ammo clipped to my new belt, worse than useless, was still comforting. "More than one way to skin a hellbreed, Theron."

"What do you remember?" He was perking up. This was a good hiding place. I almost didn't want to leave it, but sooner or later they *would* find us. When they did, it would be ugly. He needed food, and rest, and the cold machine of calculation inside my head piped up with the thought that maybe he could tell someone who would care that I was walking around...alive? Kind of alive? Undead? Not-dead-anymore?

Did I have any friends?

"I sort of remember Galina telling me hellbreed took Saul. Not much after that. Or before, for that matter." I sounded flip and casual, unconcerned. *Don't let him know you're worried, too.* Scanned the rooftop, crouched in a well of shadow, my ears perked for any faint hint of the things I'd spent the years since Mikhail's death hunting.I remembered now, murderous nights and adrenaline-soaked cases, the world skating close to the edge of apocalypse with distressing regularity, and the Traders and 'breed working, busy as beavers, to send it careening over that edge.

I couldn't kill them all. For one thing, more would replace the ones I put down, just like pimps and dealers moving into suddenly vacated territory. Always more where those come from, and hungry, too.

But I managed to kill enough to keep them slinking in the shadows, instead of swaggering. No wonder they'd all snarled at me.

And Perry, what had he been planning to do with me?

Don't worry about that right now. Keep your attention on the roof.

To give the Were credit, he didn't look very surprised. "Saul's ... alive. Last I saw."

Relief exploded inside my chest, so hard I almost sagged. "Oh. Okay. Good." But something bothered me. "Last you saw?"

"He's in the barrio."

Well, that wasn't bad. Weres ran herd on the barrio's seethe, since a girl with my skin tone could catch too much flak there. "And?"

"It's complex, hunter. Listen—"

"Hold that thought." I tensed, prickling silence closing over me. *The first thing any apprentice learns*, I heard Mikhail murmur, way back in the soup my head was threatening to become. *To be quiet little snake under rock.*

Apprentice. Gilberto. Lank hair, acne-pitted skin, dead eyes. *My* apprentice. The chain of memory pulled taut, the curtain in my head rippling, but I had no time to follow that chain into the cold deep and see what it dredged up.

Because there, at the edge of the rooftop, a shadow slunk. Lifted its wax-bald head, sweat gleaming over its naked hairless chest.

It crouched. The snuffling sounds carried clearly, and Theron had become a statue next to me, the way a cat will pause with a paw in the air when something catches its attention.

Are there more? My eyes moved, silently, the blue one hot and dry as it looked *beneath* the visible. The strings under the surface of the world resonated, each quivering individually as the tension in its neighbors communicated itself. *Can't see them. Doesn't mean they're not there.*

The Trader hunched, and sniffed again. It was on all fours, its haunches higher than its head and encased in a ripped pair of faded jeans. Its face was damn near buried in the floor of the roof, and those snuffling sounds were wetly suggestive.

I couldn't even tell if it had originally been male or female, and at this distance only a suggestion of the body modifications it had Traded for could be picked out, even with my vision on overdrive and my left eye suddenly feeding way more information than I needed directly into my brain.

"Theron," I whispered, barely mouthing the words. "When I move, run for the barrio. Don't argue."

He said nothing. My right wrist hummed, a subaudible warning.

The thing snaked its head, muscle rippling oddly up its bare back. A flat shine reflected from its eyeballs, like a drift of pollen on stagnant water under a strong light. *Dusted. Trader, not 'breed.*

Hellbreed eyes actually *glow.* If you can call that diseased shine a form of "light." There aren't proper words for it.

Thank God.

I was barely aware of moving, streaking across the rooftop, sneakered feet slapping. The Trader's malformed head flung up, and I saw the dustshine runneling over eyeballs dried and useless as raisins. The nose was a ruined cavity, double sinus-dishes like sinkholes, the mouth wet and open to take in more air. That mouth was slit on either side, cheeks gashed so it could open even wider. A spiked collar strapped around its skinny throat, leather and brassy metal both glowing with unholy foxfire.

That's so it doesn't swallow the prey, like a cormorant. I had enough time to think that before I hit with a crunch, tumbling it off the roof. It shrieked, a high panicked cry, and I shot it four times while we were still in midair. *Bleed it out, rip its throat out if you can, brace yourself, Jilly-bean, this is gonna hurt.*

I hoped Theron was running.

* * *

Hit *hard*, spilling to the side in a tangling roll to shed momentum, bones snapping, and the Trader's cry cut off midway. *Made enough noise.* My right leg crunched with agony, my tender shoulder gave a high, sustained soprano note of overstress, my head hit concrete with a stunning crack, and I *yanked* on all the etheric force I could reach.

It jolted up my arm, hot and pure, a completely different sensation from the hot twisted flood of Perry's mark. Add that to the list of things I didn't have any goddamn time to figure out—I jackrabbited to my feet, the shattered edges of my right femur grating together, and the pain was a spur as the gem on my wrist lit up like a Christmas ornament and etheric force tied the bone back together. The sea-urchin spines of my aura, hardened by countless exorcisms, lit up, too. The points of light swirled around me in a perfect sphere, and brakes squealed. Tires shredded as the 'breed closed in, traffic snarling around me.

I'd landed right in the middle of the goddamn road. An ungodly screech, and the first hellbreed jagged toward me from the right, leaving the ground in a leap that violated physics and sanity all at once. It was a female, long golden hair in dreadlock snarls and her too-white teeth bared as they lengthened, her eyes full of low red hellfire dripping, riding the updraft of her rage and crackling out of existence. She wore fluttering orange silk, a loose shirt and pajama pants. Her claws were bony scythes.

Think fast, Jill. I threw myself aside, a nail of red pain in my thigh, my feet thudding onto the hood of a big red SUV oddly slewed in the road. A teenage boy in the driver's seat gawped at me, and I leapt again, straining, the gem on my wrist feeding a burst of controlled fire through me. Blue light flashed—another spark from the ring—and I was still gawdawful *fast*, almost hellbreed-fast, especially when I wasn't weighed down by weapons and a long black coat.

Though I'd like my coat now. And some ammo. And for my birthday I'd really like a pony. Ignored the thought, my foot flicked out, and I kicked the dreadlocked 'breed in the face. The impact jolted up to my hip, taking a break in my still-healing femur, and I screamed as she did, two cries of female effort.

No, three. I couldn't worry about the third one. I dropped back down onto the SUV's roof, and the 'breed twisted. For one eternal moment she hung in the air over me, time slowing down and I braced myself because her claws were still out and this was going to hurt when she landed. I had nothing but the gun and it was rising but the ammo wouldn't help.

The third voice was a stream of obscenities cutting across the 'breed's desperate howl and my own. Gunfire crackled and the dreadlocked 'breed tumbled aside, half her head evaporating in a mess of black ichor and zombie oatmeal.

What the fuck? That wasn't me!

The newcomer uncoiled over me with a bound that was pure poetry, long leather duster flapping once like wet laundry shaken with an authoritative *crack!* Silver sparked and popped in her hair, beads tied to tiny braids in the straight shoulder-length mass, and her blue eyes were alight with hard joy. The ruby above and between her eyebrows was a point of living flame, and she turned in midair, firing at another hellbreed streaking out of the shadows.

Holy shit, I know her!

But I could not for the life of me come up with her name. An angry swarm of buzzing scraped the inside of my temples as I strained, frozen for a few critical moments.

The Trader who landed on the hood of a small black sports car, legs swelling with muscle and his entire body lengthening as he exploded out of the crouch and for her back probably didn't know her name either. He'd never learn it, either, because I shot him four times in midflight, the recoil jolting up my arm controlled almost as an afterthought. The hollow points tore up his head and chest bad enough to put him down on the road with a thud.

Hopefully the bleeding out would do the rest, but if it didn't I'd figure something else out.

Horns screeched. A rending crash, a blue minivan rear-ending another SUV down the line. Someone was screaming from the sidewalk, I hoped it wasn't collateral damage. *Fucking civilians, we're doing this out in the middle of the road, what the fuck?*

The woman landed, her right-hand gun blurring into its holster and her fingers jerking at something attached to her belt. "*Status!*" she yelled, and wonder of wonders, I understood exactly what she meant.

She was asking if I could fight. I could, I'd be more than happy to, it would make me ecstatic, I just needed some goddamn ammo that would put these fuckers *down*.

"No ammo!" I rolled off the SUV's roof and landed with a jolt on the road. My legs burned, bone messily healing, crackling as etheric force jerked at them to set the breaks correctly. It was the gem on my wrist doing it, and I didn't care. Traffic was at a complete standstill. "Civilians all over! Werepanther up on the rooftop, hope he's headed for the barrio! Fucking hellbreed chasing us! *Perry!*"

"Figures." She half-turned, eyes roving. Every piece of silver on her ran with blue sparks under the surface, and the ring on my third left finger responded with crackling of its own. "What you packing?"

".45. One. Nothing else. Regular ammo." Frustration turned the words into hard little bullets, but I sounded tight-mouth amused.

There was another impact. We both turned, guns coming up, and the thing in her right hand was a bullwhip, sharpsilver spines jingling at its end. She twitched it a little, assuring free play, and my fingers suddenly itched. I wanted one, too, in the worst way.

Theron rose from a crouch. "Devi." He tipped his head. "Look who's back."

Her name lit up inside my head, another klieg light of memory and meaning. *Devi. Anya Devi.* I let out a sigh of relief. If she was here, things had just gotten exponentially better.

So why did my heart suddenly pound in my wrists and throat for a moment, before training clamped down again? Why did I feel suddenly guilty?

Her face twisted a little, smoothed out. "Barrio?"

He shrugged, eyes lambent. "Was trying."

"Galina's." She glanced at me like I would protest, but I didn't have a damn thing to say. I scanned the perimeter, kept my fool mouth shut.

Theron looked relieved and stubborn all at once. "Can't make it. Too many of them, wait for daylight."

I lowered my gun, did another half turn. Traffic was hell-to-breakfast higgledy-piggledy, and people were actually starting to get out of their cars to get a closer gander at the trouble. Idiot lookie-lous.

But then, they didn't know hellbreed were on the loose. We kept it a secret, we hunters.

Monty's going to have kittens over this. Was I in the middle of a case? Were the cops betting on when I'd show up again, was Vice running the pool on sightings of me, nervous because I'd been out of action for a little bit?

We had to vanish soon, or the crowd would get hurt. As it was, the cops were going to have trouble with this one.

The woman sighed. "Goddamn stubborn Weres. Jill? You with me?"

Do you even need to ask, Devi? But I probably would've asked me, too. "Yeah."

"Are you safe?"

I looked over my shoulder, shaking aside my tangled hair. The scar down her right cheek was flushed, and she didn't look happy. Her gaze was disconcertingly direct, and for a moment I thought I could see all the way into the back of her brain. I didn't look away. "Safe?" I sounded honestly puzzled. I was a *hunter.* What was she really asking?

"Never mind. Here." Her left hand flicked, tossing something; I plucked it out of the air.

It was an extended clip, and I caught a glint of silver from the top bullet peeking out. Silverjacket rounds, just the thing to pierce a 'breed's tough shell and poison them, weaken them enough so you could tear them to itty-bitty pieces and make the night a fractionally safer place.

For the umpteenth time that long, long night, relief swamped me. The waves of feeling under my skin were like caffeine jolts, or like some drug that hadn't been invented yet.

Thank you, God. My fingers flew, drawing the old clip out, clearing the chamber, racking the new clip, chambering a round. The relief turned into a calm steadiness.

Now we can do some shit. Oh yeah.

She drew her left-hand gun again. A howl rose on the exhaust-laden wind, and sirens began baying in the distance. The ruby at her forehead gave a sharp glitter, and I saw old yellow-green bruising on the side of her neck. "Stay low. You hear me, Kismet? No heroics. Stay low, follow Theron, and I'll do the rest. And Jill?"

"Yeah?" My throat was full. The buzz inside my head crested, threatening to shake me. Her territory was over the mountains, why was she here?

I said goodbye to her once. And she promised to do...something. What? What was it?

"If you become a liability, I'll put you down myself." She was braced for action, I realized. As if I was the enemy.

Or as if I was a question mark.

That was new, and unwelcome. We were hunters, she and I. It's a bond deeper than blood, and there are no lies told or implied, no quarter asked or given. Why would she even *say* that?

My right wrist ached, and I had a sudden, very bad feeling about all this. But the first wave of hellbreed had massed and moved out into the streetlamp glow, civilians were screaming, and Theron arrived right next to me, his hand curling around my left arm again. Devi let out a short sharp breath, and every inch of silver on her ran with blue light.

"Time to go," Theron said, and the race was on.

II: Kyrie Eleison

CHAPTER 12

Ramshackle frame houses slumped in a jam-packed neighborhood deep in the barrio's seethe. The street here was maybe paved once, but patches of dirt rose up through the ancient concrete-like mange. Chain-link fences enclosed haphazard, yellow-grassed, postage-stamp yards, and patches of sidewalk here and there were linked together with dusty boardwalks that looked ancient as the *Mayflower*. Everything looked deserted, but I would have bet my roll of stolen cash *and* my gun that there were eyes on us.

I leaned against Theron, my stomach empty and a hot weight of bile rising in my throat. "Fuuuuck," I whispered, drawing the single syllable out, and Anya Devi laughed, a sarcastic bark. Her coat was flayed by hellbreed claws, her hair was scorched, and her eyes were alight. Dried blood crusted her hair and her cheek, and thin blue lines of healing sorcery sank into her skin, pulsing through her aura.

I'd wanted to help apply the sorcery, since God knew I had enough etheric force humming through my right hand. But she'd shied away. Just like I'd twitched away from Perry.

I didn't know if I liked that.

She was braced against a graffiti-scarred storefront, leaning forward, elbows on her bent knees while her sides heaved. Her breathing evened out, and she shook her head, silver chiming. "They want you *bad*, sweetheart. That's a good sign." She checked the street. "We're clear. Theron?"

He ran his free hand back through wildly mussed dark hair.

The bruises were getting better, but the circles under his eyes were so dark they looked painted on. His shirt flapped low on his right side, crusted with blood, but he was moving all right. "I could use a burrito. And a good stiff drink wouldn't go amiss either."

"In a few minutes. Jill?"

I wiggled my left toes. I'd somehow lost a sneaker, and my sock was torn up and filthy. I wasn't bleeding very badly. Everything on me ached, but the wounds just closed up on their own each time the gem sent another hard, high burst of singing rattles through me. It felt like a jet plane just before takeoff. "Food sounds good." *Booze sounds better. And a chance to sit down and think about some shit wouldn't be bad either.*

"Good fucking deal." Devi hauled herself up. "Wait a second, though."

Her hand came down and gripped my right wrist. I almost flinched, the motion controlling itself as she turned my hand palm up, the gun pointed off to the side. Theron had my other arm, and I was effectively trapped.

But I suffered it. For a bare half second I wanted to twitch away, but my control reasserted itself. She was a *hunter.*

I could trust her.

She studied the gem in the streetlamp glow, blue eyes unblinking. "Huh. Where'd you get that?"

"It was on me when I woke up." I weighed it as she glanced up at me, decided to drop the other shoe. "In...in a grave."

"Yeah?"

"Shallow. Out in the desert. Just off a railroad line. I caught a ride into town last night." I shuddered. *There was a diner, and a blue-eyed man who gave me my gun back. And Martin Pores, nice guy who pulled a vanishing act.* "Almost got mugged. Then I went to Walmart."

Theron made a small sound. We both looked at him. His mouth was twitching. Another snorting half laugh escaped him, and one corner of Anya's mouth twisted up.

She sobered almost immediately. She eyed the trickle of hot blood easing down from my scalp. Head wounds are messy; this one had been caused by a bit of shrapnel, and it was still weeping a little. I'd probably have lost most of the pints I was carrying if not for the healing.

Superhuman healing. As if I was still hellbreed-tainted. But the gem didn't *feel* like Perry's mark on me—the scarred lip-print, a hard little nugget of corruption working in toward the bone.

This was something different. And I didn't like the idea that she might be checking me for...what?

Which just brought up the question of what the hell had happened, what had ended up with me in a shallow grave and a hole in my memory the size of the breathing city itself.

Her free hand came up, and she smeared a little of the blood on my forehead. Rubbed it between her fingers, considering, and actually sniffed it. Examined her fingers in the warm electric glow from the bodega's porch light. Racks of novenas in the window behind her rippled, and I blinked, swaying.

"Devi?" Theron, carefully.

"She's clear. I don't know how or why, but she's clean." Anya blew out between her lips, her *bindi* winking at me. This close, I could see that it was, indeed, a subdermal piercing. You'd think the prospect of getting hit in the face would've made her refrain, but I *so* wasn't one to throw sartorial stones. "I suppose if you knew what'd happened to you, Kismet, you'd let me in on it?"

"I have some memories," I repeated. My eyebrows drew together as the hornet buzz returned, threading under the surface of my brain. "Fragments. I remember...I was on my way to the Monde to question Perry. Because...Saul. They had Saul." And now I had a question of my own. "What are you checking me for, Devi?"

"Great." She said it like a curse, and let go of my wrist, wiping her bloody fingers on her leather pants.

I seriously wanted a pair myself. My jeans were torn and flapping. Some of the pints I'd lost were a result of roadrash—you get to going faster than the average human, and you can erase a met- ric *fuckton* of skin.

"Devi?" Very carefully, each word calm and neutral. "What are you checking me for?"

She shook her head, silver beads chiming. "Later. All right, Theron. You're right. Let's go. But then I'm taking her to Galina's."

He nodded. "Come on, Jill. Someone wants to see you."

I took hold of my fraying temper. If Devi wanted to clue me in later, fine. I could trust her that far. "Great." I didn't have to work to sound sarcastic. "Is it someone else who wants to kill me?"

"Oh, no." He paused. "At least, I'm almost sure he doesn't." He seemed to find this hilarious, and snickered at his own joke as he drew me away from the bodega and out into the street. Anya drifted behind us, rearguarding. Dust rose on the faint night breeze, Santa Luz taking a deep breath in the long dark shoal before dawn.

"Wonderful." I let out a short, choppy, frustrated sigh. "But I would like to know what the fuck *happened* to me." *Boy, would I ever. And I want weapons. And some more silver.*

And while I'm dreaming, I'd like a pony, too.

"Later, Jill." My fellow hunter didn't sound happy. "When we get to Sanctuary, I'll tell you everything I know. We've pieced together some of it. But the only person who knows everything is you." She paused. "*Was* you."

Fantastic. That's just great. This is getting better and better.

Still, things were looking up.

CHAPTER 13

The house looked like a ruin, its porch sagging and groaning under our weight. But when Theron opened the unlocked door, a heavenly smell of bacon and eggs came drifting out, and the entry hall was brightly lit and tile-floored. Stairs went up to the second level, a wrought-iron banister rising in a sweet curve, and it was obvious someone had spent serious time making the inside as beautiful as the outside was decrepit.

I stood there, my sock foot smearing blood and dirt on the tiles, and blinked. Down the hall was even more bright light, and someone was humming tunelessly as a hiss of something cooking in a pan reached us. Devi crowded in behind me, sweeping the door shut and locking it. "Jesus." She blew out between her teeth, and you could hear her eyes roll as if she was a teenager. "I mean, *really*."

"Who would try to break in or steal from us *here*?" Theron swept his hair back. He was perking up big time. "Hello the house! Break out the *cervezas* and bring me a burrito! Look what I've got!"

The arch off to our left was suddenly full of motion. Two women, their long, tawny hair hanging loose except for twin braids holding it back from their faces, appeared. *Weres*, I realized, seeing their fluid economy of motion, their wide, high-cheekboned faces. Their arms were bare and rippling with clean muscle, both of them in flannel button-downs with the sleeves ripped off. Barefoot and dark-eyed, they were both utterly beautiful.

Something hot rose in my throat. I blinked.

"Jesus fucking Christ," the one on the right said, staring at me. "It's ... is it? It *is*!"

I realized I knew her face just as Theron laughed again.

"Amalia." I studied her. And the other female. *Lioness, both of them. From the Norte Luz pride.* The sensation of puzzle pieces sliding together, dropping with a click, was beginning to be disconcertingly constant. "Rahel."

They stared. Their jaws dropped, but Amalia pulled herself together first. "He's upstairs." The hall was suddenly crowded as she pushed past Theron, stepping close to me and brushing his hand away. "It's ... brace yourself." A glance at the Werepanther. "Have you told her?"

He spread his hands helplessly. "Look at us. There hasn't been *time*. I was over by the Monde, just poking around—"

"Ah, yes," Anya Devi piped up. "*This* was the story I wanted to hear. Come on, I need food. And absinthe. Please tell me you have some."

Amalia's grip on my arm was just short of bruising. "He hasn't told you *anything*?" She pulled me up the staircase, each hardwood step sanded and glowing mellow gold. The good smell of healthy Were and cooking mixed together, and I began to feel like

I might have survived the last few hours. "You look awful, by the way."

"Thanks." The word was turned into sandpaper by the rock in my throat. "There wasn't time to say anything. We've been on the run. Look—"

"He's fading. But you'll fix that *right* up." She virtually hauled me upstairs, and the balustrade turned out to run all the way along the open hall. Bedroom doors opened up off to the right, and at the end of the hall an antique iron mission cross hung on the bathroom door. I knew it was the bathroom because the door was half open, and I saw a slice of white tile and scrubbed-gleaming chrome, the edge of a claw-footed tub. "I'll bring you something to eat. Maybe you can persuade him to eat too, he needs it. He's going to be so..." She stopped dead, took a deep breath. "Listen to me babbling on. How are you? Are you all right?"

It was too much concern all at once. "Fine," I mumbled. My fingers dropped to the gun butt, smoothed the warm, comforting metal. A very nasty supposition was rising in my head, like bad gas in a mine shaft. *Fading? I don't like the sound of that.* "Um. Amalia—"

She didn't listen, just set off again. Paused for half a second by the second door on the right. "Brace yourself. Really. It's...my God. Come on." She twisted the balky old glass-crystal knob—everything in the house looked like it had been restored from one hell of an estate sale. "Saul?" Her voice dropped, became soft, questioning. "Saul, I've brought someone to see you."

My heart leapt into my throat. It hit the rock that had been sitting there for a good half hour, mixed with the bile coating my windpipe, and twisted so hard I almost choked.

Saul? The room was dark. Amalia drew me in, and the sudden gloom confused me. My one sneaker squeaked on the hardwood floor, and an overstressed tremor went through me, my skeleton deciding it could shiver itself to pieces now that the fun and games was over.

The room was very plain. White cotton drapes over a small window, a white iron bed, a long human shape on it. He was curled up, sparks of silver in his dark hair, and my skin tightened all over me.

Was I afraid? Yes. Or no, I wasn't afraid.

I was outright *terrified*.

"Saul?" It was a harsh croak. I tore my arm out of Amalia's grasp, and she let me. There was a cherrywood washstand by the door, my hip bumped it as I took two unsteady steps.

The shape on the bed didn't stir. A rattling sound rose from it—a long, shallow, tortured breath. The silver in his hair was charms, ones I knew.

Because I'd given him every one of them. Tied most of them in with red thread, too, while sunlight fell over us and a cat Were's purr made the air sleepy and golden. Sometimes he would drum his long coppery fingers on my bare knee, and I would laugh.

I was halfway to the bed before I stopped, remembering how filthy I was.

That never mattered to him. I inhaled sharply.

It smelled *sick* in here. Dry and terrible, a rasping against my sensitive nose. Like a hole an animal had crawled into to die. It was clean, certainly, every corner scrubbed and the bedcovers and drapes bleached and starched. Still, the reek of illness brushed the walls with shrunken centipede fingers.

Oh, God. "What's wrong with him?" I whispered. It was a useless question. I could guess.

"Matesickness." Amalia's own whisper made the air move uneasily around me, little bits of fur and feathers brushing my drying sweat. "The closer you can get to him, the better. Lie down next to him. He needs to know you're alive." She backed up, reaching for the doorknob. "We thought you were dead. Weres don't survive without their mates. You know that."

"I was—" I began, but she swept the door closed, leaving me alone in the dark. I swallowed, hard. *I* was *dead*. The sudden certainty shook me all the way down to my filthy, aching toes.

I was *dead, and Perry had something to do with it. Maybe even a lot to do with it. And now...Saul.* My pulse picked up, a thin high hard beat in my wrists and throat and ankles, behind my knees, my chest a hollow cave.

The shape on the bed stirred. Just a little. I saw a gleam of dark eyes under silver-starred hair. Only it wasn't just the silver. There were pale streaks, gray or white, and that was new.

I took a single step. "Saul?" High and breathy, like a little girl.

He twitched. The rattling in-breath intensified. The gem on my wrist gave out a thin sound, like crystal stroked by a wet fingertip.

When you're ready.

I was beginning to think I wasn't ready for anything about this. But it was too late. I'd already clawed my way up out of my own grave, hadn't I?

You can't do that and not accept the consequences.

CHAPTER 14

My knees hit the side of the bed. I stared down at him. His back was to me, and even in the dimness I could see he was skeletal. The sharp boniness of a hip under his boxers, ribs standing out in stark relief, shoulder blades like fragile wings. His head was too big for his neck, and he tipped it back. The silver moved in his hair, chiming sweetly, and a gout of something hot boiled up inside me. There was nothing in my stomach to throw up, but the shaking all through me demanded I *do* something. Kill whatever was hurting him, hold it down and put a bullet or twenty through its head—

"Jill?" A faint whisper. He inhaled, another long rasping rattle.

As if he could smell me, as filthy as I was. Shame boiled through me. God, couldn't I *ever* be clean?

No. You've never been clean, and he always was. Always.

The wetness on my cheeks was either tears or blood. "God," I whispered back. "*God.*"

That managed to make him move. Slowly, painfully, hitching one hip up, rolling. My hands were fists. One of his scarecrow hands lifted, dropped back down on the white lace coverlet. He tried again, reaching up, and I grabbed that hand with both of mine.

He jerked in surprise. For a mad moment I was sure I'd hurt him, tried to ease up, but his fingers bore down with surprising hysterical strength. He pulled, and I went down onto the bed, trying not to land on him.

His stick-thin arms closed around me. The shudders came in waves, I wasn't sure if he was shaking, or me, or both of us, because he was saying my name. Over and over again, in that dry cricket-whisper that hurt my own throat, and I sobbed without restraint. He was *kissing* me, I realized, his thin lips landing on my bloody forehead, his leg snaking up and over me, body curled around mine as if he could hold us both down while a storm passed overhead.

Only the storm was inside my buzzing, aching head. Memory exploded, shrapnel tearing through my brain.

"I just want you to do one thing," he said into my filthy hair. I almost cringed.

Anything. Just stay with me. *I stilled, waited.*

"Just nod or shake your head. That's all. Now listen, Jill. Do you still need me? Do you want me around?"

"I—" How could he even ask me that? Didn't he know? Or was he saying that he felt obligated?

"Just nod or shake your head. I just want to know if you need me."

It took all I had to let my chin dip, come back up in the approximation of a nod.

"Do you still want me?" God help me, did Saul sound tentative?

It was too much. "Jesus Christ." *The words exploded out of me.* "Yes, Saul. Yes. Do you want me to beg? I will, if you—"

"Jill." He interrupted me, something he barely ever did. "I want you to shut up."

I shut up. For a few moments he just simply held me, and the clean male smell of him was enough to break down every last barrier. I tried to keep the sobs quiet, but they shook me too hard. The breeze off the desert rattled my garage door, and the last fading roll of thunder retreated.

He stroked my hair, held me, traced little patterns on my back. Cupped my nape, and purred his rumbling purr. When the sobs retreated a little, he tugged on me, and we made it to the door to the hall, moving in a weird double-stepping dance. He was so graceful, and I was too clumsy.

He lifted me up the step, got me into the hall, heeled the door closed. My coat flapped. My boots were heavy, clicking against concrete. I probably needed to be hosed off.

I had to know. I dug in, brought him to a halt, but couldn't raise my eyes from his chest. "A-are you s-s-still—" I couldn't get the words out. I was shaking too hard.

"You're a fucking idiot," he informed me. "I'm staying, Jill. As long as you'll have me. I can't believe you think I'd leave you."

I cried for a long time, there in the dark. He held me, stick arms strong for a Were who was wasting away, and he kept repeating my name.

How could I possibly have forgotten *him*? Even if I forgot myself, I would remember him. If I was blind I would know him. I hadn't even known what I was missing, but it had been him.

I should have been looking for him as soon as I clawed up into the night and screamed.

I was. I didn't know it, but I was. And I couldn't even tell if that was a lie I was telling myself or the bare honest truth, because the sobs were coming so hard and fast they shook both of us.

We curled around each other like morning glory vines, and for that short while everything else faded away. He didn't say anything else, and neither did I.

There was no need.

It was the first good sleep I'd had since I'd come up out of the grave, and it wasn't nearly long enough.

The gun was up, pressure on the trigger and my arm straight and braced. I blinked, and Anya Devi, her blue eyes narrowed, held both hands up, one of them freighted with a glowing-green glass bottle. "Easy there, killer." She even sounded amused, the tiny silver hoops in her ears glinting. Her coat brushed her ankles, and I realized she was tense and ready. I wouldn't put it past her to dodge a bullet.

But she wasn't my enemy.

I lowered the gun, pushed myself up on one elbow.

The room was empty. Westering sunlight poured past the sheer white drapes, and crusty, dried crap crackled on my skin. I hadn't even washed my face. I felt cotton-stuffed, the way you do if you've ever fallen asleep after a long wracking bout of sobbing. Like I'd been cleaned out and Novocained. My mouth tasted fucking awful, too. My foot had swollen inside the one sneaker I still had on, and I wanted a hot shower, a gallon of coffee, and some weapons.

Not necessarily in that order.

Devi answered my first question before I could ask. "He's downstairs, eating. Has a lot of body mass to put back on." She offered me the venom-green bottle as I sat up, sheepishly lowering the gun the rest of the way. I sniffed cautiously and smelled licorice and alcohol.

Absinthe. Devi believes in the stuff the way other people believe in football, God, or sex. Mikhail'd felt that way about vodka. Me, I can take it or leave it—I save all my love for the tools to get the job done.

No. I don't. I save most of it for him. The rock in my throat eased, miraculously. "Sorry." Liquid sloshed in the bottle, I made a face. "What the fuck?"

"Good for you, cures everything. Go on, take a hit." One corner of her mouth quirked slightly. "Or do you remember hating it?"

I lifted it to my mouth. Took a swallow. It burned all the way down, and it was unspeakably foul. "Gah." My face squinched up, it coated the back of my throat and went off in my stomach like a bomb. But I took another long swallow. That was as brave as I could get.

It was booze, after all. And a belt was just the thing to bolster me.

She accepted the bottle back, took a long hit, her throat working. Then she lowered herself cautiously into a high-backed mission-style chair by the bed, the one thing I'd missed last night. Leather creaked as she sank down with a sigh.

"So." She studied the bottle. "You bleed clean. That's not a 'breed mark on your arm anymore. Couple months ago you disappeared. Found my car torched out in the desert, plus one very large crater that reeked of angry hell-breed out where those goddamn stones are. Or where they *were*, I should say, because whatever it was shattered them and fucked up the ley lines but good. We're in the middle of a war here, and all of a sudden you show up at the Monde, bust Theron out just in time, and..." Her straight eyebrows went up, the scar down her right cheek—the claw had dug in right at the outside of her eye, like a tear—crinkling a little as her mouth twisted. The *bindi* gleamed, a sharp dart of light. I studied it while I waited for her to finish the thought.

While she decided what to do with me, was more like it. I had no illusion that anything else was going on. She was up on everything happening in my town, and I was... what?

Confused, still not thinking straight, and still exhausted.

"I bled clean before," I managed, through the pinhole my throat had become. "Even though I had the mark."

She said nothing. Examining me like a gunfighter, the silver in her hair glowing, her gaze disconcertingly direct, like every hunter's. Crow's-feet touched the outer edges of her eyes, and the lines as her mouth pulled tight against itself would only keep carving themselves deeper from now on.

It is our job to keep gazing, unflinching, on the worst Hell has to throw at us. It is our job to never look away.

When she said nothing else, the silence stretched uncomfortably. I stood it as long as I could. I itched all over, and the need to find more weapons itched as well, right under my skin where nothing but metal and ammo would scratch. "I barely even remembered my own name. I killed a Trader on a rooftop. He had a card for the Monde. I went there. Perry seemed... glad to see me."

She let out a short, plosive breath and settled into immobility. The quality of a hunter's concentration can spook civilians; something about our trained stillness just makes them uncomfortable. "Right into the lion's den. Well, at least *that* hasn't changed."

I searched for words to boil the whole complex tangle down to its essentials. "He was...I heard Theron. I thought it was Saul. Everything came back. At least, everything up until a certain point. So I got him the hell out of there."

"Good. He shouldn't have been there." She let out a sigh, her shoulders sagging for a moment. "So here's the million-dollar question, Kismet." She took another hit off the bottle, venom-green liquid sloshing. "You still a hunter?"

Why the hell would you ask me that? "It's not like I have a choice of career options."

As soon as I said it, I knew it wasn't strictly true. You could lay it down and walk away at any moment. Nobody would say a word, or judge you.

Idiots, Mikhail used to snarl sometimes. *They think we do this for them. Is only one reason to do,* milaya, *and that is for to quiet screaming in our own heads.*

I found out I'd laid the gun in my lap, and I was twisting the ring around my finger. *Do svidanye.*

Honest silver, on vein to heart. Now it begins. Bile crept up into my mouth. It took a few hard swallows before I could speak, the silvery insectile curtain inside my head shifting a little as... something... peeked out.

"Mikhail," I whispered. "I found out... something. About him."

She nodded. "You did. Here's another million-dollar question, Kismet. Do you want the last two and a half months back? Or d'you want to head out onto the Rez with that Were of yours? There's no..." She paused, swallowed hard. Her eyes had darkened. "There's no obligation, Jill. You did what you had to do."

"What did I do?" I was honestly puzzled, and the hornet buzz inside my head threatened to rise again, swallowing thought whole and triggering reaction. I shoved it away, my shoulders tensing as if I'd been hit. "That's the one thing I can't remember. I woke up in my own *grave*, Devi. I'm as confused as it's possible to get. I'm digging myself up, then this guy drops me off in an alley, and all I can think of is getting some ammo. But I didn't remember the silver, or...*Jesus* fuck-me *Christ.* Of *course* I want my goddamn memory back. What are you thinking?"

"I have... an idea." The admission, pulled out of her. "But have you considered that you might not want your memory? That there might be things you'd prefer to forget? This isn't the type of job that gives you happy dreams. Saul loves you, you've got a chance to—"

I slid off the bed. I had to get that goddamn sneaker off before it turned my foot gangrenous. "There's a war on? Against Weres?" *And you expect me to sneak off into the sunset. Great. Well, now I know what you really think of me, right? Great.*

She let out a longer sigh, one she probably practiced on her apprentices. "They're driven into the barrio. Galina's doing what she can, but—you remember Galina, right?"

"Of course." I limped for the door. "I remember almost everything, up to the moment I pulled up in front of the Monde. I was working on a case, which I'm guessing is wrapped up now. Can you find me some clean clothes? And more weapons?"

"I can, but Jill—"

"I've got to pee." And with that, I made an inglorious retreat out into the hall. I wasn't lying—I really did have to piss like a racehorse.

But I was afraid that if I stayed in there any longer I'd lose my temper. Or, even worse, I would look down at the space on the bed next to me, the pillow still dented from Saul's beautiful, wasted head, and entertain ideas of riding off into the sunset after all.

CHAPTER 15

I was taller than Anya, and broader in the hips. But the leather pants fit me just fine, and the black Angelcake Devilshake T-shirt too. I knew that wasn't mine—I'd started buying my tees plain and in job lots, because they ended up shot and blood-drenched, not to mention sliced, diced, and dipped in unspeakable foulness so much. Just like the rest of me.

Even the sports bra and unmentionables fit just fine. There was a pair of scarred leather boots that looked damn familiar, and hugged my feet as if they'd been broken in but good.

But it was the weapons that did it.

Another modified .45, this one shiny instead of dull black. Holsters for both the old gun and the new. A complicated array of leather straps that came alive in my hands, buckling itself on like an octopus hugging me, holding weapons. Knives with silver loaded along the flats, from the big main-gauche to a slim stiletto almost lost in its sheath. Cartridges of silverjacket ammo, and the crackling-new bullwhip with wicked-sharp sweetsilver jingles at its tip, secured in its own little loop.

The coat was a little too long, a black leather trench instead of a duster like Devi's, and it smelled like comfort. Copious pockets and more loops sewn in for the pile of ammo Devi had brought up in two paper grocery bags. The more I slipped into the loops, the better I felt.

"Thou who," I whispered, and shut my mouth. The prayer had no place here, but it kept going under the surface of my conscious thought. When I repeated it, the wasp-noise retreated, left me alone.

Thou who hast given me to fight evil, protect me; keep me from harm.

Except it was useless. I'd ended up dead. There were Weres hiding in the barrio. And Anya was still here, instead of back over the mountains in her own territory, keeping the scurf down and the Traders under wraps.

The bathroom was white tile, clean as a whistle, and my dirty clothing had been whisked away by a tight-lipped Amalia. The shower was ancient, the kind with the curtain attached to a hoop bolted to the wall, and the mirror showed a gaunt woman with mismatched, exhaustion-ringed eyes and a habit of not meeting her own gaze. I was milk-pale, but the shaking in my hands went down with every weapon I strapped on.

Oh, yes. This was what I'd been missing.

The knock startled me, and I thought it was Anya. But when I swept the door open, it was him.

He was still too thin, leaning against the wall. The plaid flannel shirt and jeans hung scarecrow on him, and his hair fell in his dark eyes, scarred with small silver charms. His cheekbones stood out sharply, his proud nose a blade of bone and skin, and his mouth turned down at both corners.

My jaw dropped. I stared.

Weres are beautiful. There is no corruption in them, nothing like a hellbreed or Trader. Hunters can track 'breed; humans have an advantage in hunting what we're akin to. But in Weres, everything is burnished. It's humanity, yes... but with so much of the crap burned away.

He was holding something up, his expressive fingers just knobs of bone and skin. "I thought..." His voice was a rasp, he coughed and the words came a little easier. "Thought you'd want this."

It was a stick of kohl eyeliner. I grabbed for it. "My God. Thank you. I didn't even know I was missing—"

"Are you all right?" The words cut across mine, and all of a sudden the leather on my back didn't feel very much like armor anymore. "What *happened* to you? I couldn't find you anywhere, Jill. Not even the wind carried a hint. You were *gone.*"

Everyone keeps asking where I was. You'd think I'd know. "I woke up in my own grave." The words were beginning to sound routine.

Not really.

He stared at me. Not disbelievingly. Apparently the idea that I could wake up in my own grave wasn't very outlandish to him.

Of course not. He knew me better than anyone.

I searched for something else to say. "I'm here now." I clutched the eyeliner like it was going to try to escape. "The last thing I remember is screeching up to the Monde, because they'd taken you. Right outside Galina's. Perry..." *Perry, I knew him.* I shook the thought away, damp strings of hair touching my cheeks. "Devi says she's got a way for me to remember how the case ended up."

He stepped forward, stopped. Braced one shoulder against the wall. I thought of the bone underneath pressing out through wasted muscle and skin, how much that had to hurt. "Are you sure you want to?"

The only thing I'm sure of right now is that every bit of firepower I strap on makes me feel better. Oh, and that I'm going to put a bullet or twelve in the head of anything that hurts you. A good grocery list to start out with, right? "She says she can do it. She's got an idea, I guess, and as soon as she tells me I can get started—"

"No." A shake of his beautiful, wasted head. One of the charms—a silver wheel, tied in with faded red thread—moved against his temple. "Are you sure you want to remember?"

"I...yeah. Of course." I backed up a step, shifted my weight as if I was going to turn. The fragile stick in my fist creaked a little, and I eased up on it. "I've got to. There was Perry, and Belisa was mixed up in it. The Eye, too—Gilberto's probably got that. Gil's at Galina's, I'm betting."

He thought this over, watching me, those dark eyes soft. Almost wounded.

"Yeah," Saul finally said, heavily. "Locked up tight, poor kid. Just let me get some more food, and we'll get going."

That might not be such a good idea—I opened my mouth to protest, but he beat me to it.

"Don't even start with me." His head dropped forward wearily, and he glared at my chin through his lackluster, silver-scarred hair. "If you're going, I'm going. I'm not losing you again."

"You didn't—" I began, but I couldn't finish. The words lodged in my throat, because I was suddenly sure that I had been lost, and in a big way.

Utterly lost.

"Here's what I know." He reached up, brown fingers gripping the doorjamb. "You told Theron to make sure the first thing I heard when I woke up was *She loves you.* And Devi, God damn her, always finding a reason not to be in the room when I showed up. Until I cornered her and she told me you'd been . . . that you'd bargained yourself away. For *me.*"

I blinked. *Was that what happened? Who did I . . .* My brain shivered inside its bone casing. I shuddered.

"And I couldn't find you," he continued. His free hand flicked, and flashes of silver chimed as they hit the floor. My gaze didn't drop down to check, riveted to his face. "I couldn't find you anywhere. Even *inside.* You were gone. I went half mad looking for you. Then I came back to the barrio to die." He waved aside my instinctive protest, knobs and spindles of bone moving under his skin. "And now, here you are. Inside and out."

"Saul—" The thing in my throat wouldn't let anything else get past. Just his name.

He shook his head, so hard I was afraid he'd snap his wasted, scrawny neck. His fingers tensed against the jamb. Wood groaned. "No. Everywhere you go now, I'm going with you. *Everywhere.*" He turned on his heel, sharply, and stamped away. The hall almost rocked around him, one gaunt Were with the burned-candle smell of anger trailing behind him in eddies and swirls.

Even their anger is clean. It doesn't twist into hatred. You won't ever find a Were Trading.

But you might find a hunter Trading, a deep voice whispered inside me. *You just might. Especially for what she loves.*

What she can't do without.

I found out I was trembling. A wave of shudders went through me, but I bent over anyway. I found the charms and tweezed them up delicately. Three of them—a tiny silver shoe like the one from the Monopoly game, a Celtic cross, an exquisitely carved spider.

It was there, on my knees, clutching the eyeliner and the small bits of silver, that it hit me.

The blue-eyed mute who had paid for my breakfast and given me my gun. He had seemed familiar. Too familiar.

And now I knew who he was. The knowledge opened up another door in my head, but only halfway.

Halfway was enough.

"Shit," I muttered, there on the floor. "Oh, God. God." My arms came up, and I hugged myself, rocking back and forth.

God didn't answer.

He never does.

CHAPTER 16

I stamped down the stairs and found everyone in the kitchen. Everyone, that is, meaning a crowd starting with an unhappy-looking pair of lionesses, Theron nursing a beer, Anya Devi chowing down at a table littered with plates, and Saul right next to her, doing his level best to destroy a mountain of beans and rice. A huge pan of what looked like beef enchiladas verdes heaped with cheese sat to one side, and between pulls off a Corona bottle he was doing very well at taking the whole load of food down without chewing much.

The house muttered and sighed, because there were other Weres now too. A bird Were bent over the stove, something sizzling, as another lean tawny cat Were—*Ruby*; I found her name with a lurching mental effort—set down a pair of grocery bags and stared openly at me. Several other cat Weres were crammed in the living room, and the only reason why more weren't in the kitchen/dining room was because it literally wouldn't hold any more. The first story was full to bursting, and I was lucky to be able to squeeze through the hall downstairs.

As it was, I stepped into the kitchen and let out a long breath. I had enough eyeliner smeared on to make me feel like a raccoon, and the long leather trench whispered reassuringly as I came to a halt, boots placed precisely and the three charms knotted into my hair with dental floss I'd found in the bathroom cabinet.

Hey, whatever works.

Everyone except the bird Were, feathers fluttering in the updraft in his dark shoulder-length hair, looked at me. I squared my shoulders and tried not to feel like a carnival sideshow.

Except it was too late for that. I was armed and dangerous now, and for the first time since I scrabbled up out of the sand with filth covering me I felt...

...human. Or, like I knew who I was. Or like I belonged in my skin. Even if the thought of a carnival sent another rippling shudder through me, ruthlessly quelled. I remembered *that* case, thank you very much.

Devi swallowed a forkful of paella and blinked at me. "Nice to see you up and around. Get some food, we've got to get out of here."

I shrugged, rolling my shoulders under the heavy leather. The T-shirt was vintage, and the lettering on it was going to give someone a perfect target to aim at, but I couldn't cavil. It would probably get shot off me or blood-drenched in no time at all. "I'm good. We're headed to Galina's?"

Saul stopped shoveling long enough to glare at me. "Jill." A rumble filled his thin, wasted chest. "Sit. Eat."

I dropped down into the only free chair at the table, and the bird Were was suddenly there, banging down a huge plate of steak, eggs, and crispy hash browns. Fragrant steam wafted up, and there was a fork buried in the potatoes. He took a load of dishes away, table space magically appearing. His long nose twitched once, the feathers in his hair fluttered, and he hurried back into the kitchen, dismissing my faint thank-you with a nod.

Anya grinned, the corners of her eyes crinkling. The beads in her hair chimed sweetly. "Now I *have* seen everything." She took another huge forkful of paella and washed it down with a gulp of absinthe.

I shuddered at the thought, and stared at the plate.

Perry was trying to feed me, too. Everyone trying to shove something down my gullet.

Which brought me back to my blue-eyed mute and the diner. I still wasn't sure if that was a hallucination. But he and Martin Pores had been the first to feed me.

It probably meant something, but what? No clue. I'd wait until we got to Galina's and sort everything out. Sounded like a reasonable plan, right?

Steam rose from the browned potatoes, the fluffy eggs, the strips of medium-rare steak. Anya shoved a glass bottle of ketchup over with one hand, then grabbed her absinthe and took another long healthy drag.

The sorcery will burn it out of her. Not like Leon and his constant beer-swilling, to dull the something-extra he came back from Hell with—

My head snapped aside as if I'd been slapped. The heavy butcher-block table rattled, my fingers curling around its edge and sinking in, the gem giving a subsonic thrill all through me. Plates and cups waltzed, chattering together, and Anya was on her feet, the chair shoved back with a squeaking groan that might have been funny if she hadn't had both hands on her guns.

"Easy there." Saul barely looked up from his methodical shoveling-in. "Both of you settle *down*. Trying to *eat* here."

Ruby, in the kitchen, peered out with wide dark eyes. She'd gone down into a half crouch, but the bird Were simply racked dishes in the open dishwasher, hooked it shut with a foot, and twisted it on. "Pizza next!" he sang out in a light tenor. "Extra cheese. Rube, unpack those for me, will you? Then you're on drying duty."

I picked up the fork, awkwardly. A thin lattice of golden-fried potato hung from it, still steaming. My other hand still clutched the table. "I, ah." My throat was full of sand. "Just thought of something. That's all."

A long silence, broken only by the methodical chink of Saul's spoon against his bowl. The rice and beans were vanishing at an amazing rate, and the enchiladas were going down just as smoothly. You could almost *see* the food being converted into muscle, filling him back out again. His shoulders weren't hunched, but I thought of the way kids eat in juvie—protecting the plate, arm curled around it, and the blank look as they took it down as quickly as possible.

They eat that way in prison, too. You *ate that way, before and after Mikhail found you in that snowbank. You only stopped when Saul started coaxing you to use some manners.*

Another soundless explosion touched off inside my skull. "Mikhail. Something about him. And Belisa, that Sorrows bitch." I searched Devi's face. "And... Perry."

Her *bindi* flashed, a dart of bloody light. She lowered herself down gingerly. "Yeah." Just the single word, no more. And she, I noticed, almost hunched over her plate as well, before straightening a little self-consciously, taking another hit of absinthe, and going back to making the food disappear.

I took a bite. The hash browns crunched, salted and heavenly. I swallowed carefully. It scorched on the way down, and the bird Were came back out with another bottle of beer, so cold it smoked with vapor, and a king-sized mug of what proved to be thick black coffee.

From there it was easy. But I kept thinking of diner food, possible hallucinations, ol' Blue Eyes, the Sorrow who killed my teacher, the gaps in my memory...

...and Perry's snow-white table with its blood-clot rose in the crystal vase.

The burst of frantic loathing that went through me turned the food to ashes, but I kept chewing and swallowing. I needed the fuel.

The city drowned under sharp honey sunlight, dust rising on an oven-hot, unsteady breeze. A rattling, mottled-green Chevy pickup was our only transportation, Theron and Saul both hopping lithely into the bed and Anya twisting the key with a little more force than absolutely necessary. The engine roused, protesting, and I caught a shadow of movement from inside the house. Weres, peering out through the windows like frightened children.

War against Weres. I should ask about that.

Anya pumped the gas pedal, and the engine caught. "Only

wheels we've got right now. Mine got torched, yours wouldn't run—"

"Sorry," I mumbled, staring out the window. Even with the leather and the pounds of weaponry I wasn't hot, my temperature regulating itself with only a faint passing ghost of sweat touching my skin before I remembered I didn't have to. The deep rumble of the engine was soothing, and I caught myself thinking I could probably tune this beast up. Wouldn't take more than a couple afternoons, you can get Chevy parts easy enough. And they respond well to both threats and blandishments.

Not like that Pontiac. She was a lady, but damn she was hard to please. Something had happened to her engine, though. It was in the middle of that blank spot in my head. I'd been working that case pretty hard, and half mad with agony over Saul...

"No worries. Jesus." She dropped it into gear, and for a moment I considered grabbing for the dash. It wasn't a completely unwarranted thought, because she floored it, and we jounced down the street in a rumbling roar. I thought of glancing back to check the Weres, too, but they could probably hold on. Even if Devi did wrench the wheel and send us careening down an indifferently paved cross street.

This was familiar, too, only I was used to being behind the wheel as we bounced through negligible traffic. We certainly didn't stand out in this rig.

Not in the barrio.

Anya reached for the radio knob, drew her hand back. "So," she called over the wind rushing in through the windows, "we're pretty safe as long as we're in the barrio. Outside, though..."

I actually twitched with surprise. How could we not be safe? "It's daylight!" I yelled back.

"Of course it is." She fished a pair of Jackie O sunglasses out of her coat, slid them on, twisted the wheel, and we slewed and bumped up onto slightly better pavement. "But that isn't stopping *them*, Jill. Just relax. Coming back from the dead was the trick of the week, but I've got one better."

"Nice to know you have a plan." I grabbed at the door as she swerved wildly around another turn.

She must not have heard me right. "We're heading for Sanctuary," she called over the windroar, and reached for the radio. Snapped the knob all the way over, and the wail of a country song filled the cab.

Great.

CHAPTER 17

The bells over the door jingled, and we piled in through a sheet of cascading redgold, energy flushing deep purple as it sealed us inside. With the Weres crowding behind we couldn't slow down, and I was halfway across the small occult shop before skidding to a stop, guns flicking out.

The ride here had been spine-tingling but uneventful—if by *uneventful* you mean "almost got into six different traffic accidents, lost a cop in the industrial district, and bailed out of the truck with the tires still smoking." Now I knew how other people felt when *I* drove.

It occurred to me to ask why the cops didn't recognize her ride, but with the radio going supersonic and her lips moving as she cursed steadily, it didn't seem like a good time.

Shelves of books and candles stood against the walls like good little soldiers, and there was a large rack holding crystals and stones in small bins. Another wooden rack held amulet-making materials—leather, bits of bone, beads, feathers, and less-nice things. Glass cases slumbered under falls of dusty golden sunlight, and the air quivered a little as the walls ran with purple light. My smart eye watered, trying to pierce the curtains of etheric force.

But that wasn't what was bothering me right now. Anya let out a short sharp yell, and the Weres behind me suddenly let loose with twin growls, shelves of books and candles and other assorted trivia—including the glass cases and the racks—vibrating as the Sanctuary's walls resounded like the curves of a gigantic bell.

Galina spread her arms, green eyes alight and her dark marcel waves slightly disarranged. She was in full robes, smoky gray silk glowing with pigeonthroat sheen, the medallion of the Order—a quartered circle inside a snake's supple curve, cast in some light silvery metal—running with white radiance against her chest.

But that wasn't why I had my guns out. You'd have to be crazy to draw on a Sanc inside her own walls. They settle, drive in their roots deep, and are near godlike inside their hallowed homes. Outside, they're a tasty, almost-defenseless snack. But hunters, Weres, and even most 'breed or Traders will smack you down *hard* if you attack your local Sanc. Neutral supply of necessities is the least they provide.

No, I had both guns out and braced because of the hell-breed near the sleek black cash register, his eyes glowing sterile blue and his pale hair ruffling as he saw me—and grinned.

"*Jill!*" Galina yelled, and the walls tolled their deep bell note of restrained power again. Each hair on my body stood straight up, my skin shrinking with reaction, and I found myself suddenly hoping she wasn't going to lose her temper.

It can get awful uncomfortable inside when a Sanc loses their temper.

"Darling." Perry's lip lifted, his pearly teeth bluntly human but too, too white. The silent snarl turned into a bright, bland, sunny smile, the kind a real-estate broker will use right before moving in for the kill. "*So* good of you to come."

Galina's open palm, flung out toward him, twitched. "Don't make me, Perry." Flat and loaded with terrible power, the single sentence turned the air inside the shop to frost. "Jill. Jesus Christ. *Pax*, hunter. Put the guns down."

My breath turned to a white cloud. Every muscle in my body protested. Anya Devi drifted away to the right, and I was suddenly certain she was getting a better angle on Perry. An angle that would leave Galina out of the line of fire.

My stomach cramped, my arms aching and tingling. If I needed to know how Anya felt about me, it was all in that subtle movement. We were hunters. If I was going to throw down, even inside a Sanc's hallowed walls, she was ready to back me.

"Stay where you are, Anya." Galina was having none of this. "Jill, put your guns *down*."

Perry took a single step forward. Galina's hand twitched and he halted, a ripple running under his pale skin. Like tiny mice, begging to escape. The pale linen of his suit was dotted with black ichor, hems and cuffs sending up little threads of steam, but he looked pristine under it.

Like he could just step out from under the spatter stains and they would fall to the ground with tiny little *plash*ing sounds.

Splashback. He's been killing other hellbreed. Because we got away? Maybe. I took in the spatter patterns as I lowered the guns, slowly. So slowly, my arms straining, every muscle locking and fighting me.

I walked right into the Monde with nothing but plain lead in my gun. Jesus. My skin chilled again reflexively, and I tasted copper. *What would have happened if I'd eaten something there?*

There was no deciding which was worse: being helpless and mostly unconscious of the danger, or looking back and seeing how badly things *could* have gone.

Perry's grin widened, the further down the barrels went. He shook his head slightly, white-blond hair sliding back from his face like raw silk. He changed hairstyles like some women change shoes, but very subtly. You had to look to see what he'd done each time.

And I did not like that I knew that, or how closely it meant I watched him.

"You left too soon, Kiss." The sheer good humor, as if we were at a party and he was dropping banal gossip. A hot draft of desert wind, laden with the scent of spoiled honey, brushed every surface. "Always in such a hurry."

Buzzing pressed itself inside my skull, tiny insect feet prickling over my hands and face. I even felt them *inside*, chitinous bodies and dragging stingers pressing behind my cheekbones, running lightly over the surface of my brain as the buzz became a roar. They were crawling and eating, and my fingers almost shook with the urge to rip at the skin of my face and peel them off—

"Back *off*, Perry!" Galina's walls shivered again, the bell-gong sound rattling through my bones. "If I toss you out, you're never coming back in. Settle *down*."

"I just want to talk to her." He sounded so *reasonable*. I blinked furiously, my left cheek twitching as if a seamstress had her needle in and was plucking at the flesh. "Just a little tête-à-tête with my darling one, surely it can do no harm?"

"Galina." Devi, her tone slicing through his. "Get him the fuck out of here, or I won't be responsible for what happens."

All those threats. Blandishments. Pulling on me like dogs with a bone, except I was armed and ready the way a bone never is. The machine inside my head started calculating whether or not I could aim and squeeze both triggers before Galina twitched and made all of us mighty uncomfortable.

The machine returned a number I didn't like, no matter how many times I ran it.

"Everyone just simmer down." The air hardened, pressing against all of us, Galina's temper fraying. "I can separate you all like toddlers at the lunch table if I have to. Perry, you're done here. Leave."

"I don't have what I came for." Soft, deadly, the sliding sound of another step. "Kiss. My dearest. I have all the answers you could ever want, and I *ache* to give them to you. All you have to do—"

I fought to keep the guns down. Because sooner or later I was going to chance it, no matter what the numbers in my head said.

It wasn't surprising someone interrupted him. What was surprising was that it was Saul.

Weres don't take on 'breed. Traders, yes, because Traders are still at bottom human. But there's no corruption in Weres that can track and anticipate a 'breed.

The thrumming growl under his words said very clearly that Saul didn't care. "Step any closer, hellspawn, and *I will kill you.*"

The world narrowed to a pinhole of light, darkness crawling around the edges. Galina's shop trembled like oil on disturbed water, afternoon sunlight suddenly brittle and chill through the windows. Air-conditioning soughed, the humming in the walls oddly distorted, shimmers of energy cycling up. Galina's arms tensed, and her green eyes flamed. Red-gold Sanctuary sorcery smoked in the walls.

"Little puss." Amused, disdainful, Perry's chin lifted. His face had changed, cheekbones turning to blades and severe handsomeness rising from under the blandness. Helletöng grumbled, its flabby fingers picking at the strings under the surface of the visible. "I will deal with you in my own time. Go back to lapping milk and clawing at walls. Kiss…" The sibilant turned into a hiss. "When you're ready, *come and find me.*"

When you're ready. Silver spat and crackled with blue sparks, bleeding free of the metal. My aura rippled, the gem vibrating against my wrist. The rattling hum rippled and crawled over my shoulders, sliding under my clothes. Leather rustled, my hair ruffling on a breeze that came from nowhere, Galina's shop trembling around us both. The wooden floor groaned sharply, once.

Perry *winked out.* A *pop* of collapsing air, a draft of rotting, spoiled honey, an obscenely warm breeze caressing my face. My guns jerked up, but there was nothing for them to track, and the Sanctuary shielding made a low overstressed noise, rocks shredding under contradictory gravitational pulls. Galina chanted something, low and furious, and my fingers cramped.

I was sweating, great clear drops of water standing out on my skin. And shaking too, like a horse run too hard.

"What. The fuck." Anya sounded puzzled. "Lina?"

The world righted itself. "Well, that was unexpected." The Sanctuary blew out a frustrated sigh. "Jill?"

I thudded back into myself. My arms were straight, and even though I shook, the guns were absolutely steady. They were up.

Maybe I would have been fast enough, after all.

Training. Goes bone deep. "Jesus," I whispered.

Galina skidded to a stop right next to me. I almost twitched. Hunters don't like it when someone gets too close. But I lowered the guns, and my fingers eased off the triggers.

And Galina, wonder of wonders, threw her arms around me. She hugged me, her walls suddenly tolling a greeting instead of a threat. She was rounded at hip and breast the way I was not, and her hair smelled of incense and green growing things. The murder under my skin retreated from that softness.

CHAPTER 18

The Sanctuary gave up trying to shake me and hugged me again, and she was actually *crying*. Her soft, unlined face blotched up, and the defenses in her walls made another low, unhappy sound. She looked for all the world like a grade-school girl crying in the bathroom.

Galina was old, though. Old enough to remember the hunters before me.

Old enough to know things I didn't.

"—*worried* about you!" she finished up into my leather-clad shoulder. The rest of her smelled like fabric softener, smoky sorcery, apples, and an acrid tang of worry and tension. "What the hell happened? It's been *months*! One second we had Saul back, everything was wrapped up, and then—"

"Give her a second, Galina." Theron folded his arms, leaning against a glass case. Mummified alligators, a scatter of tarot-card packets, and wristlets with brass bells crouched inside the case along with statuettes and chunks of semiprecious stones. "Our Kismet's come back from the dead, it looks like. Saved my ass over at the Monde."

"And you should *not* have been there, Were," Devi piped up, with a meaningful eyeroll. "First things first, though. What the fuck was that asshole doing here? And Galina, while you're explaining that to me, I need one of your vaults. Altar and circle." The other hunter drew in a deep breath. "Jill's going *between*."

I blinked again. That was her plan?

Well, great. That's just peachy. Someone stop the world, please, I want to get off.

I slid each gun back into its dark home, quietly, my breath coming hard and high and my arms weak as noodles. *Jesus. Jesus Christ. Perry.*

You could've heard a pin drop. Galina held me at arm's length, peering up at me. Dark hair fell in my face, the silver spider weighing down a curl, and I just stood there and suffered it.

There really wasn't any other choice. And I needed a few seconds to get myself together, so to speak. Something was rising under the hole torn in my memory, and I didn't like the look of it.

Saul took two steps forward. He was still gaunt, but the sheer amount of food he'd managed to pour down his throat was showing. The dark circles under his burning eyes had gone down a little, too.

Or maybe I was just hoping they had.

Had he really been ready to throw himself at Perry? The thought of *that* particular dance number, even within Galina's hallowed walls, was enough to turn everything inside me cold and loose.

"*Between?*" He sounded mildly enquiring, but a rumble poured under the surface of the word. "That's it? That's your wonderful idea?"

"Oh, Lord." Theron sighed. "This is not going to end well." He leaned against the case like we hadn't just seen a 'breed wink out of existence. Of course, Galina *had* told Perry to leave. But still… I had never seen a 'breed do that before.

I'd never *heard* of a 'breed doing that before, either.

Come on, Jill. With the holes in your head, can you be sure?

Still, he'd done things before that made him different from the usual scion of Hell. The only thing I was getting any surer of was that Perry was a separate fish indeed. I had a cold, sinking suspicion deep down in my gut, and I wasn't liking it. As much as Mikhail taught me not to assume, this was looking very very bad.

Anya shrugged and slid past Galina, her leather duster creaking slightly. She was pale. "It's the only thing I can think of, Were. The bigger question is, though—"

"You'd better think again."

God, give me patience. But there was no answer. I was on my own, as usual.

I tipped my head back. "Stop it." I sounded very small. "I'm doing what she says."

"I've got a better way to bring a memory back. But nobody

asked me." Anger glittered and smoked under Saul's tone, and that growl spread out, rattling the windows facing the street. The Chevy sat in a glare of afternoon sun, its pale patches leprous. The telephone poles up and down Jimenez wavered slightly in the heat. The air-conditioning kicked on, soughing cold air through vents, and the walls of the shop resounded again, but gently, all its power held in check. "And that hellspawn son of a bitch is here, *inside* Sanctuary, and gets close enough to touch her, and none of you *do* anything? What the fuck is going on?"

"Ease up, Saul." Theron, oddly conciliatory. Of course, he was a Were.

But Saul didn't sound like a Were. Saul sounded downright furious.

"I *lost my mate*." Saul was suddenly next to me, his fingers curling around my shoulder. "And the only thing you can think of is throwing her *between*? She *doesn't remember*."

"You..." Galina's hands dropped to her sides. She cocked her head, her marcelled waves falling just-so, and glanced from my face up over my shoulder, then at Theron. "What *happened*, Jill?"

I get the feeling I should be asking you *that.* "I *don't know*. Not much, anyway." I kept my hands away from the guns with an effort that threatened to make me sweat even under the AC. The shudder that went through me made my own leather coat creak, weapons shifting. "Devi says I can remember how I wrapped up that case. I'm down with that. So let's just get it over with." I made a lunging mental effort, trying to prioritize. "No. Wait. Wait just a second. Where's Gilberto, and goddammit, what was Perry doing here?"

"Gil's upstairs." Galina's soft mouth turned down at the corners. "With Hutch. I wanted them both safe and out of the way."

Well, hooray for that. One thing to be happy about, I guess.

"And Perry?" Anya had turned away, studying the fall of sunlight through the windows. Tension sang in the set of her slim shoulders. "I am very, very interested in why *he's* here, Sanctuary."

The Sanc actually shot her a quelling glance. It would've been magnificently effective, maybe, if Devi had been looking. "He was waiting." Galina's gaze darted to me, and for a moment, I could have sworn she looked almost frightened. "For Jill."

* * *

I plunged my hands into the stream of cold water. The upstairs bathroom was familiar, sun falling in through the skylight and caressing every surface. She'd chosen a nice soothing blue up here, with little Art Deco accents. Maybe she realized she looked like a silent film star, so she might as well have a stage set.

They were fighting down in the kitchen. Saul's voice, raised, rattling the walls. Galina's unhappy but patient. Anya Devi throwing in a spiked comment every now and again, just often enough to keep it at a boil. She wasn't going to win any smoothing-the-waters awards.

It wasn't like her. Devi knew Weres better than anyone—they helped her hunt the scurf infestation in Sierra Cancion, keeping it as contained as possible. Weres are scurf's natural enemies, and Anya was close to a Were herself, what with the munchies and her disciplined ferocity.

Still, the situation here was enough to tax anyone's temper. And hunters aren't known for interpersonal patience.

The bathroom door quivered, and when I glanced up, a scrawny-tall cholo stood there eyeing me. Lank dark hair fell in his acne-pitted face, without a hairnet for once, and his dark eyes were even more flat and lifeless than they had been. He'd put on some more muscle and shot up a couple inches, and the way he braced himself, leaning lightly against the doorjamb, told me someone had been training him.

Anya. You asked her to. Or she just did what another hunter would have done, stepped in to finish what you started.

There was a gleam on his chest, a razor-linked chain holding a barbaric, bloody gem. It rested uneasily against his faded flannel button-down. If he'd been shirtless, his narrow face with its high bladed nose might've been a little less pizza and a little more Aztec.

My apprentice's hands twitched a little. Jeans and engineer boots, his fingernails were clean, and I was assessing him from top to toe before he even opened his mouth.

Weighing. Measuring. As if I was still his mentor. Small wonder—he'd chosen me, not Devi, and I winced when I thought of what this must be doing to him.

"Eh, *profesora*." He grinned. A shark's wide humorless smile, curving his thin lips, and in that moment you could see a flash of who he might have been. "Had enough vacation, gonna go back to work?"

I almost snorted. *Was I just worrying about this kid?* But there was a hair-fine tremor under his façade. Gilberto Rosario Perez-Ayala had a shark's smile, true. Even in the barrio's seethe that grin would make seasoned gangbang cholos step back and reconsider.

But on the inside, he was a hunter's apprentice. With the dangerous but exactly right mix of need, aggression, loyalty, a goddamn bundle of twitchy neuroses, and a need to prove himself big enough to get him into serious trouble if he wasn't trained hard—and trained right.

Which was my job, and I'd failed by dying on him.

"Gilberto." I dipped my chin at the bloody, sullen gem on his chest. "That needs to be drained. And soon."

I didn't ask how the Eye of Sekhmet had ended up on *him*. The last time I'd seen my teacher's greatest prize, its razor-edged chain had been hugging my own neck.

Because Perry had left it in my warehouse. A present. *In the nature of recovered property.*

That snagged a deduction out of the soup of memory. "Belisa." I stared at the Eye, and it responded, its humming almost breaking into the audible as etheric force tensed like a fist. "He got it from Belisa, somehow."

Gilberto shrugged. His long spider fingers worked at the chain, but it wasn't any good, he couldn't get any purchase. It was kind of funny, seeing such a male reaction to jewelry.

He finally gave up and lifted the gem carefully from his chest, gingerly sliding his fingers under and working the chain around his ears and the rest of his head. "Makes me nervous." Sunlight gilded highlights into his hair, but it was merciless to his pitted cheeks. "Devi, she say to hold it for you. She thought you weren't comin' back. *Estupida.* But I took it anyway. You hold what you got to, *profesora.* Learned that somewhere else."

You hold what you got to. He wasn't old enough to know how true that really was. "Yeah." The water slid over my hands. I scrubbed them against each other as if they had blood on them. Which, given my job, was a good possibility. The sink was chill white porcelain, and it felt good to just let the water carry everything away.

Jill, you're hiding. What the hell?

He offered it, the sharp links dangling from his fist. There was a healing scrape across the back of his left hand, looked like mat-burn. How was Devi finding time to spar with him, if there was a war on Weres and all sorts of other shit going on?

The Eye's gleam sharpened, and the stream of water over my hands warmed. I shut off the faucet and flicked my fingers. "Keep it. It's safer with you." *Because if I take that, I'm going hunting for Perry. And that is probably what he wants, so it's a Very Bad Idea.*

Gilberto shrugged, his shoulders hunching. "You went off to dance with *la Muerta, profesora*. Months you been gone, and things going to hell." He acknowledged the pun with a curled lip, and the Eye hummed slightly in his grip. The chain trembled a little, its links scraping.

Like lovers' fingernails. I knew what that felt like.

Gil watched my face. "What you gonna do? We drowning. Losing turf every day, and *la otra cazadora* ain't got time to see the half of it. Weres getting squeezed onto Mayfair and the barrio, and I'm not thinking Mayfair gonna hold out much longer."

I shuddered. Mickey's was out on Mayfair, the only Were-run restaurant I knew of. Plenty of nightsiders caught a meal or a cuppa joe there, and it was relatively neutral ground.

Neutral, that is, as long as the hellbreed hadn't declared open war on Weres and were making it dangerous during the *day*. This was all sorts of wrong, and it pointed to something big.

Trust Gil to put it in terms of a gang war, too. It actually wasn't a half-bad metaphor.

The Eye quivered, dangling from his fingers. Every inch of skin on me prickled, as if I were standing on a flat plain right in a thunderstorm's path, the tallest thing around.

"*Profesora?*" The trembling in him was more pronounced. "What we do now?"

Like this wasn't a disaster in progress I didn't have a clue about how to start solving. It was like five shots of espresso and a bullet whizzing past, like dusk falling, a jolt that peeled back layers of confusion and woke me out of a stupor.

My apprentice was counting on me. Every soul in this city was counting on me to figure out what the 'breed were up to, and fast.

Why else had I been sent back? I'd said that. *They sent me.*

Sent, brought, what the hell, didn't matter. I tipped my head back, rolled my aching shoulders in their sockets. Leather creaked, and the gem on my wrist sent a little zing through me, a needle-sharp nerve-thrill.

Vacation's over, Jill. Get back to work.

Everything clicked into place. My chin came down and my eyes opened. I tapped two damp fingers on a gun butt, thinking, and Gil's face eased visibly.

"*Profesora?*" No longer tentative, but he was waiting for direction. The Eye made a low, dissatisfied sound.

"Put that thing back on, Gil. You're my apprentice; it's yours. I've got to go downstairs and break up that fight." I took a deep breath. "If I'm going to go *between*, it's better sooner than later. Anya'll hold the Eye while I do; it'll even drain it and solve two problems at once."

It was a great plan. It might even have worked.

The kitchen wasn't quite in an uproar. Still, Theron had wisely taken himself off somewhere, probably to the greenhouse.

Weres don't like conflict.

Galina stood near the butcher-block island, her hands up, glancing from one end of the room to the other like a tennis spectator. Saul, near the door to the hall with his arms folded and legs spread, actually *scowled* at my fellow hunter. "You're not. And that's *final.*"

"I am not even going to—" Anya halted, glancing at me as I appeared in the doorway. A curious look spread over her face, and she dug in a right-hand pocket, still frowning at me. She fished out, of all things, a pager, and glanced at it.

That's right. I was dead, so she took over the messaging service. Either that or it was transferred to hers. I wonder if Monty moans at her about replacement costs, too.

"Montaigne," she said, flatly, and I almost started. "*Shit*." She stalked for the phone by the end of the counter, and Galina's shoulders relaxed slightly.

"Hey." Saul's arms loosened. The circles under his eyes were fading, and I wondered how long it would be before Galina started feeding him, too. He was still too damn thin. "You okay?"

"Peachy." I did what I should have done in the first place— reached out, touched his bony shoulder. Fever heat bled through his T-shirt, and I reeled him in. He came willingly enough, and when I closed my arms around him he let out a shuddering sigh. He's taller than me, but his head came down to rest on my shoulder, his entire body sagging, and I held him. Slid my fingers through his hair, and I was still stronger than even a strictly human hunter. Because he leaned into me, and I held him with no trouble, just a little awkwardness.

"You don't even smell the same," he murmured. "But it's you. It *is*."

Was he trying to convince himself? My heart squeezed down on itself, hard. What could I say? *It is me, don't worry*? That was ridiculous, and a lie, too.

I wasn't sure just who I was, right now. And even though I didn't want him to worry, there wasn't a hell of a lot else he could do.

And really, it was time to worry. It was time to worry a *lot*.

"It's me," Devi said into the phone. A long pause, and the tinny scratch of another voice over a phone line brushed at the tense silence. If I concentrated, I could hear it more clearly.

I didn't. I stroked the rough silk of Saul's hair. "It's okay," I whispered, and the sheets of energy cloaking Galina's walls lightened.

Go figure. For once, I was being soothing. Should've known it wouldn't last.

"Really." Devi tapped her fingers on the counter, once. Frustration or impatience or habit, I couldn't tell. "Okay. Tell Eva to keep them away from that place, have her hold Sullivan and Creary there so we can question them. Do *not* let them go any closer to that—yeah, okay, I know you know. And relax. I've got good news for once."

Another short pause, then a jagged little laugh. "Very good news, Monty. Keep your hat on and have faith. We're on our way."

Faith? That's not anything I'd ever say, Devi. Sullivan and Creary—that would be Sull and the Badger, homicide detectives. Eva was one of the regular exorcists working Santa Luz's night-side, handling standard cases and calling me in for anything out of the ordinary.

Devi smacked the phone down like it had personally offended her. "Galina? I need an ammo refill. And some grenades."

"Got it." Galina sounded relieved to be given something to *do*. The herbs in the bay window breathed out spice, basking in a flood of sunlight that was no longer pale and brittle with winter. She took off at a dead run, her slippers whisking the wooden floor as the house settled with an audible thump. Her robes swished lightly.

Anya's attention turning to me was a physical weight. "Jill?"

Saul stiffened, but I kept stroking his hair. "That was Monty."

"It was. Saddle up, change of plans."

"Good deal." I tried not to feel relieved, failed miserably. "What's boiling over now?"

"Missing rookie cop. Vanner. Something about him being at a crime site and going shocky-weird?" Anya's tone was light, but the inside of my head clicked and shifted.

I let Saul draw away. "Vanner. I remember him." *Called him Jughead. Was always running across weird scenes.* "Where did they find him?"

"Eva brought him in a week after you disappeared. He was up at New Hill—"

I blinked. *Goddammit.* "What was wrong with him?"

"Catatonic. I gave him a looksee, but there was nothing we could do. They kept him in one of the barred rooms at the Hill; two days ago he vanished."

Jesus. A chill walked down my spine. Vanishing from a barred room at New Hill is a Houdini act and a half. The last I'd seen of Vanner, he'd been in shock, in the back of an ambulance, after seeing me fight hellbreed-controlled corpses. "Vanished. Out of a barred room. Okay."

Anya nodded, the beads in her hair clicking as braids fell

forward. "Well, Creary found him. She called in Eva, and as soon as that Faberge-painting bitch showed up, the rookie made a bee-line for guess where."

"Where?" But a sick feeling began under my breast-bone, a spot of heat like acid reflux.

I had the idea that I already knew where Jughead Vanner was going. It made a sick kind of sense, like cases start to do once they heat up.

Anya's mouth drew down at both corners. "Where else? Henderson Hill. The *old* one."

I couldn't even feel good about guessing right. Of course. Of *course* it had to be the one place a regular exorcist—and many nightsiders—wouldn't go. A psychic whirlpool of agony, fear, and degradation, especially since the great demonic outbreak of 1929, when the inmates had ceased being prey for sadistic jailors and turned into a buffet for Hell's escaped scions.

Ever since '29 hunters have been not just mostly out-numbered. We'd been outright fighting a losing battle, for all that we give it everything we have—and everything we can beg, bor-row, steal, multiply, murder, liberate, or otherwise get our hands on.

It is not enough.

And what the hell was Vanner doing heading for that place?

Anya watched me, very carefully. Like I should know some-thing else.

I kept my hands away from the gun butts with an effort. My face was a mask. I *did* know something else about that place. Or, more precisely, there was someone I suspected I'd find at Hender-son Hill. Someone I wanted to talk to.

If he would talk. If I could *make* him talk.

So I ignored the tiny chills walking all over me. "Let's go."

"Not without me." Saul's hands actually turned into fists, his shoulders squared as if he expected round however-many-they-were-at-now.

I reached, once again, for diplomacy. It was a goddamn mira-cle. "It'd be nice if I could go with Devi to watch my back, and you stay here and fuel up. I can pretty much tell you're not going to go for that."

I was right. Again. When I didn't want to be.

"What part of *everywhere* do you not understand?" The question was mild enough, but his hands curled into fists again, and weariness swamped me.

The old me would have argued, or at least given it the old college try. He was safest here in Sanctuary...but he'd been taken from the street right outside. I remembered *that*. I remembered Galina telling me to calm down when I found out, up in the greenhouse. I remembered burning rubber out to the Monde, and something there waiting for me. Something huge, a thing I bumped up against the edges of, my brain shying away like a skittish horse. The black cloth bulging over that memory was wearing thin, little bits peeking out through its moth-eaten, merciful darkness.

Right now he's safer right where you can see him, Jill. So you can make sure nothing happens to him. Or you can kill whatever touches him.

With this amount of ammo and my knives securely strapped in, not to mention the creaking-new bullwhip, it sounded doable. More than doable.

It sounded good.

And if it saved me from descending into the chaos of *between* to look directly at whatever had happened to turn my memory into Swiss cheese and kill me, then bring me back...well. Maybe I was a coward for feeling relieved, but it was getting to where I didn't care as much as I should.

"Fine." I didn't recognize my own voice. "Get ready, then. You'd better go armed."

CHAPTER 19

Out of the four of them, Eva took it best when we showed up. Sullivan went even paler than usual, only his receding coppery hair under his bleached-out Stetson showing any color. His thin hands twisted together, and he drew himself up and back into the inadequate shade provided by a warehouse's side as if I might not notice him if he hid well enough.

Montaigne, in an ill-fitting sports jacket despite the heat, stared. His bulldog jaw dropped, and he hadn't shaved in a while. Cigar smoke drifted across his scent, and the tang of whiskey. There were bags big enough to carry a week's worth of luggage under his eyes.

The Badger was actually in a tank top and jeans, the white streak at her temple glowing and her round, pale face sweating. She is, like some heavy people, astonishingly light on her feet, and many a perp has been surprised when he thinks the rotund little lady cop's the easiest one to escape or overwhelm. She acquired her nickname even before her streak began, working a downtown beat and quietly, in her own unassuming way, taking absolutely no shit from anyone. Right now she stared, and I had the uncomfortable idea that coming back from the dead is not guaranteed to keep you any friends.

Eva, slim and dark, hopped down from the hood of Avery's Jeep and strode toward us. She gave Devi a brief nod, looked curiously at Saul, and swept her long hair back over her shoulder.

Devi contented herself with nodding back, for once, and moved over into the shade. Sullivan let out a sound that might've been an undignified *eep*, quickly turned into a cough.

"Nice to see you." Eva blinked under the assault of sunshine, wiping her fingers on her jeans. "Christ."

Thanks. I was dead. I didn't glance back at the truck, where Saul leaned against the hood. The silver in his hair was bright starring, and he munched slowly on an energy bar while his eyes took in the street in controlled arcs. "Vanner. He was catatonic the whole time?"

"About as long as you've been AWOL, sweets. Ave and the boys will be happy you've shown up."

"You still dating Avery?"

She shrugged, and a small smile lifted the corners of her cheerleader-pretty mouth. And she apparently got the message, because she glanced away up the hill. "Sometimes I let him think so."

Even in the sun, you could feel a suggestion of a chill draft. She was right at the edge of the Hill's etheric shadow, and the only surprise about that was how far the stagnant bruising in the fabric of reality had spread.

Should really do something about that. But what was there to do? Banefire might burn the whole place to the ground and leave a blessing in its wake...but that amount of bane might turn into just-plain-fire at the edges, and with the slumped warehouses and converted offices hunching around here, we could be looking at a huge burnout.

Before, the scar would have provided me with hellfire. But hellfire around this sort of stagnation and misery would just drive the scar in deeper.

And with all the Hill's accumulating force to fuel it, it would spread even further. No, hellfire was *so* not a good idea.

"Good deal. So, yeah. How did Vanner present?"

All the amusement fell away. "Catatonic. Both me and Devi scanned him, he was...inert. In every possible way. I checked him weekly over at New Henderson Hill." She glanced up the street and actually shivered, her tiny gold-ball earrings winking before disappearing behind her hair and her safari jacket rippling. "Now?" Her shoulders hunched. "I think something's riding him."

"Possessor?" It was a risk, but they didn't usually go for men. Well, it was about 60–40 in favor of females. But Possessors favored morbidly religious middle-class shutins, not reasonably irreligious rookie cops locked up in asylums.

Still, anything's possible, and he'd gone shocky after brushing up against the nightside. And even before that, Vanner had shown up at a fair number of odd homicide or burglary scenes, crimes with a nightside connection.

We'd even joked about it. Or at least, Badge and Sully had.

Eva shrugged. "I don't know how he would've caught one, and there's no marks. He disappeared from New Hill two days ago, hasn't slept or eaten that I can tell. Slippery little fuck, whatever it is, but altogether too active to be a Possessor. Plus, it doesn't *smell* right."

Out of the four regular exorcists, Ave comes closest to being a hunter candidate through sheer adrenaline-junkie insanity. It's Eva who comes closest through cool calculation and the tendency to be three or four steps ahead of everyone else.

They make a good pair. I was actually hoping A very wouldn't let her slip through his fingers the way he usually lets women go.

"So. Smart, mobile, smells different than a Possessor..." I tapped at a gun butt. "All right. You can take the cops and head out as soon as Devi's done. And *be nice.*"

She spread her hands, a plain silver band on her left index finger flashing. "Bitch is the one with the problem, Jill. Not me. Can I just register how happy I am to see you?"

Likewise. If you only knew. "Duly noted. Hey, how have cases been lately?"

"Hopping. We're all working for the cops now, not just Ave, and on shift so we can get some sleep. It's never been this bad." And there it was, printed all over her dusky, weary face. The transparent, slightly squeamish relief you see when you show up to handle the weird so people can go back to Happy Meals and vodka tonics. Or what passes for normal to an exorcist. They're good souls, fighting the good fight, and some of them could almost be hunters.

But not quite.

"No worries. We're on it." I restrained the urge to clap her on the shoulder. Eva most definitely did *not* like to be touched. I wondered how Avery managed it.

"Yeah, well, it's been getting progressively worse the longer *she's* been here. I mean, she handles it, Jill. But she's not you."

Oh, for Chrissake. "She's a hunter, Eva. Come on. I want to talk to the cops and then send you guys home. Monty's not sleeping again, is he."

"Murder rate's spiked. The media's blaming it on the heat, but..." Another shrug, her hands spreading. "Not just murder but all sorts of fun. Rape, arson, assault, and enough weird to make it feel like thirteen o'clock all day. We've gotten to the point where even triage isn't helping."

"Well, fuck. Come on." It looked like whatever case had shot me in the head and left me out in the desert wasn't over. I half-turned, glanced at the deserted street. Something was troubling my city. Of course the legions of Hell flood in when a hunter goes missing. We're barely enough to stem the tide as it is.

But this was exceptional. And when the exceptional shows up, a hunter gets nervous.

Saul had gone still, looking the same direction I was, the empty wrapper closed in his fist. I headed for the knot of cops, my trench flapping a little and Eva drifting reluctantly in my wake.

"It's about goddamn time," Montaigne greeted me. He coughed, and it had a deep rasp to it I didn't like. "Where have you *been*?"

"Dead, Monty. You want to keep asking questions like that, or you want to tell me what you've got?"

"Hi, Jill." Badge folded her ample arms over her equally ample bosom. She blinked, as if dazed. "You look like shit."

"Thanks." I glanced at Sullivan, who visibly flinched. It wasn't like him. Of course, he would probably have been an accountant if he wasn't a cop; he had a feel for the nitpicky detail and he liked things neat. That was his trouble—he liked everything all *explained*. "Vanner?"

"He's . . ." It was Badge's turn to glance around uncomfortably. Neither of the guys gave her a hand. "He's changed, Jill. He's scrambling around on all fours, but it's definitely him. Fast, too. Guerrero here says we're not supposed to get any closer to the old Hill."

"Yeah, that's a good idea. You know the drill." Everything clicked into place. This situation, at least, I knew how to handle. "Relax, boys and girls. Kismet's on the job."

"Thank fucking God." Monty muttered. "I suppose you need another pager, too."

"It wouldn't hurt. But I'll be with Devi, just buzz her for the time being."

He hunched his wide shoulders. "Fine. Jesus H. Menace to property."

Well, that was good. If Monty was bitching about property, he was relatively okay.

"I haven't blown anything up yet today, Montaigne. Give it a rest." *But you should've seen me the other night. I busted up the Monde but good.* Another chill walked up my back. The gem rang softly, like a crystal wineglass stroked by a delicate, damp fingertip.

Devi was staring down the street as well. She'd gone completely still. "Jill?"

"Let's roll. Go home, everyone. Good work."

"I suppose I can't tell you to be gentle," Badger called after us. She probably *had* to say it. She is, after all, a mother.

The county put up a concrete wall around the old Hill after the Carolyn Sparks episode. Which was a reasonable response, given that that had involved a Major Abyssal, an untrained psychic, and a string of murders that made even a seasoned hunter blanch. I've seen the file—even with only black-and-white photos it's enough to give you nightmares.

Someone even occasionally tries to put a fresh padlock on the front gate. Come nightfall, however, the padlock is always busted wide open, shrapnel scattered in a wide arc, and the iron gates stand open just a little.

Inviting.

The gravel drive inside the gate was moving. Little bits of it popped up and turned over with an insectile clicking, as if the whole expanse thought it was popcorn while it's still just bursting sporadically. Before the big explosion.

I cocked my head and stared, one hand loosely on a knife hilt. It was, I suppose, a hunter's equivalent of a nervous tic. "Jesus," I breathed.

Anya laughed, a jagged, brittle sound. The gravel settled down, little gray stones twitching in the sunlight. "Thank God dusk is a ways off."

"Look." Saul pointed. Scuff marks on the scattered ground, and smears of something on the gate itself. My eyes narrowed, and I didn't need to get any closer to tell that the stains were fresh, and crimson.

Anya and I both drew our right-hand guns, a weirdly synchronized motion. We could've been on the stage.

"Take point." Anya indicated the gates. "I'll follow in three. Were?"

"I'm a tracker." Saul crouched fluidly, the fringe on his suede jacket fluttering. It almost hurt me to see how it hung on him; he was so thin. "I'll be fine. This is just like spot-jumping scurfholes on the Rez."

I blew out a short breath. "Okay. Give me three, Anya, then come in. Give *her* three, Saul, then you come in. If something's going to go wrong, it'll go in the first few seconds. Christ, I've never seen it so bad here."

"You sure about that?" But Devi, tight-lipped, just shook her bead-weighted hair with a heavy chiming when I glanced over. "We're burning daylight. Do it."

Still, I took another few precious seconds to study the gates. Wrought iron, quivering just slightly, and the gravel moving uneasily behind them. It shouldn't have been this bad.

Something happened here. Something fed the Hill. Shit. Inhale, exhale, watching the gates with their seaweed drifting, just a little bit too quickly to be the wind moving them, just a little too slow to be anything else.

Some hunters say it's not the big weird that wallops you the hardest. It's the just-slightly-off, the subtly wrong. Because it echoes inside your head and builds until you want to scream. I've lost civilians to both. Some people crack just seeing a body-modded Trader. Some go screamingly, eye-clawingly, gratefully insane when faced with something that breaks all their base-level assumptions about how the world works.

Still others take the whole enchilada, seem okay, then walk home and ventilate themselves.

You just can't ever tell. You can only visit the grave afterward and feel the horrific tightness in your chest that means you didn't do a good enough job protecting them.

Personally I think both the big and the little weird are hideous, and depending on when they hit, they can take the legs right out from under a normal person. Even a hunter gets a chill now and again. We're trained, and we're ready, but nobody is ever *really* ready for the weird all the time.

At least a hunter has an explanation, and a job to do.

The gates clanged wide, my boots hitting them squarely, and I landed on popping, pinging gravel. Little chunks of stone rose, whirling, and my aura fluoresced into the visible, hard little sea-urchin spikes tipped with points of light. That shell flexed, a sphere of normalcy asserting itself, and a tide of whisper-screams rose around me. My hair lifted on a not-quite breeze, and my left eye turned dry and itchy, untangling tricks of perception and snarled etheric strings. The lines quivered, and I could almost-See the passage of *something else* through here recently. More spots and spatters of blood. Someone was moving fast.

Well, at least we had a trail. And for a hunter, blood's as good as neon arrows.

The buffeting increased, but I had my feet planted, and the gem gave another high clear hard ringing all through my bones. I *pushed*, bearing down as if I was ripping a Possessor out of a hapless victim inch by inch.

Most often, they code and you have to jump-start their hearts and get them to a hospital. It's a tremendous psychic shock—all your mental cupboards torn open, furniture hacked apart, windows smashed, the Possessor digging in with its little claws, woven into mental architecture over weeks or months of dedicated pawing and fingering.

Pushing, pressure mounting behind my eyes, hearing the snap of a leather coat as Devi landed, the Hill rousing itself like a sleepy beast. An almost-physical click as the compression vanished, it was work not to stagger. My left hand was a fist, cramping, I shook my fingers out.

Saul was beside me, stamping his right leg twice. It was like striking a drum, and the driveway shuddered before it settled. His eyes were lambent even under the assault of sunshine, and as he straightened it was suddenly easier to breathe.

Anya's *bindi* flashed, the beads in her hair rattling, and it was a relief to see the same speckled sea-urchin shape to her aura. She opened her eyes cautiously, and took a step forward. The gravel was still in a perfect circle around her booted feet, just as Saul and I carried an area of eerie stillness with us. Outside those calm patches, the gravel popped up, flinging itself about knee-high.

We waited.

The Hill calmed slightly. It was rumbling and unhappy, quivering on the edge of sentience. Before, it would have been cold and tricky during the day, active and dangerous at night.

Now, even under the sun, it felt *treacherous*. And the cold was not physical. It lay under the daylight with its own heavy weight, a prickling like tiny feet wandering all over me, probing delicately into every cavity, tickling every inch.

I shuddered, threw the thought aside, and a buzzing rose momentarily inside my skull.

Oh, you tricky bastard. No, thank you. Another *flex*, sweat popping out along the curve of my lower back. Even with a hunter's regulation of body temperature, a few things will make you damp up.

Sorcerous effort. Combat. Sex.

Terror.

The black hole inside my head yawned, and for one vertiginous second I was skating its edge as the walls between me and however I had ended up in a shallow grave crumbled.

Oh, Jill, you are fucked for sure. A soft, merry voice, my own, inside the dark reaches of my skull. *Fucked six ways from Sunday and hung upside down, too. This was where it happened.*

Where *what* happened, though? I returned to myself with a jolt. Saul's hand over my shoulder, claws needle-poking through the tough leather, just felt, not breaking the borrowed skin. His mouth was close to my ear, warm breath on my skin, and for a bare moment a tide of hot feeling rushed through me, too complex to unravel before my sightless eyes blinked and started relaying information to my busy little brain again.

"Kismet?" Devi, thinly controlled.

"Steady." The gun was pointed down and to the side, thank God. "Steady as a rock, babe."

"Doubt it." But she set off, soundless over the gravel, with a sliding, rolling, hipwise step. "Follow the yellow brick road, children."

"Ding-dong, the bitch is dead," I muttered. Only, if the bitch was dead, that bitch was me. Under the dirt with my socks rolled up.

Great. Now was a bad time to be thinking those sorts of things.

Anya laughed again, but softly, lighting with a feral intensity that turned her into a very pretty woman indeed, blue eyes firing and her mouth turning up. *Hides her light under a bushel*, her teacher had remarked to Mikhail, back when we were apprentices. The sort of girl who would wallflower at a party until you actually spoke to her and realized what a sharp mind was behind that pleasant face.

She led along the trail and I swept next, Saul behind and slightly to my left. It was like moving after Mikhail, stepping only where he did, breathing only as he did. You can't get closer to another human being than when they're trusting you to do your job and watch their back. Anticipating, guessing, responding to every breath of chill intent against the skin, taking over the angles like clockwork so each is covered, gaze moving in smooth arcs, the little hitch in Anya's breathing when the gravel began to pop like shrimp in a sauté pan. It evened out immediately, and I thought our hearts were probably matching beat for beat, too.

She was heading for the main steps, and I wondered if the air inside was still reverberating from my last visit here—or at least the last visit I remembered. If the front desk was still smashed, if there was still violence in the air—and if there was a room upstairs where I'd taken apart a hellbreed-built altar, bile burning my throat and the banefire whispering and aching to escape my control.

And the scar on your arm aching as it tried to burrow in toward the bone, Jill. Don't forget that. Another soft, sliding, nasty little voice. *The little scar Perry gave you. The mark of Cain.*

Cain shot his brother, though. I just shot my pimp. And oh, Christ, I did not want to go back to that night, to the hole in Val's forehead and the ticking of the clock on the wall. The ticking that would turn into a buzz as tiny feet crawled over my rotting flesh.

"Stop." My voice cut the thick, cloying silence. "Devi. The windows."

She glanced up. "What?"

Someone—probably the caretaker who lived in the boiler room, with his filmed gaze, scarred face, and his quart of rye— sometimes haphazardly nailed boards over the windows. They were Band-Aids on gunshot wounds, mostly, with the look of just being put up for appearances.

But now those boards were gone. The five floors of Henderson Hill's public front—offices on the two lower levels, progressively tighter security on the next three, but no heavy equipment, that was saved for other buildings—stared at us with compound centipede eyes. Some windows were starred with breakage, but the chicken wire mostly held everything up. Scarred, but not broken. On some hungry, avid little windows the cracks looked decorative.

Like war paint, or the crackglaze in the makeup of an aging hooker.

"The windows. Some were covered, before."

She was halfway through a one-syllable obscenity when chaos broke loose.

CHAPTER 20

Henderson Hill's front door shattered and the gravel rose in popping, excited bursts. I caught a flash of motion—something pale and human-shaped, flung aside as the attacker streaked down the stone stairs, straight for us, its claws making deadly little snicking noises.

The thing was long, and low, and bullet-lethal. Anya hopped aside, whip already in her hand and flicking forward neatly, and I'd already squeezed the trigger twice as Saul faded behind me. It moved like a hellbreed, stuttering through space, and was between us in an instant, snarling and hunching, blood steaming on it. The sunlight drew lashes of scorch-smoke from its hide, but it merely bared broken, shark-sharp yellowglass teeth and snapped, ignoring the assault of that clean light. Its eyes were coins of diseased green flame, and as soon as they locked on me the thing let out a shattering squealgrowl and doubled on itself, flexible spine cracking as its back scythe-claws dug in.

This was not a *rongeurdo*, a bonedog made by hellbreed that never ran by day. No, this was one of the creatures of Hell itself, and it was—

"*Hellhound!*" Anya yelled, the word disappearing into a string of gutter Latin as she chanted, hunter sorcery rising in thin blue lines as every inch of silver on her flamed.

Well, shit, I could've told you that. A flash of annoyance like bright sour sugar against my tongue, but the hound was in the air, body stretched out in a lean unlovely curve.

Hit me, sound like worlds colliding, blood exploding from my mouth, something snapping in my side as we tumbled. I shot it twice more and had my knee up before we hit the ground, flung gravel pelting both of us. The hound snarled again, a low rumble of Helletöng boiling from its narrow ungainly snout, and the impact knocked me free.

Up on my feet, ribs howling, boot soles sending up a spray of gravel as the gem poured a hot tide of strength up my arm. Leather flapping—those curved claws are *hell* even on tough cowhide—I skipped to the side, gun coming up and my left hand shaking my whip free with a quick sine-wave movement from my shoulder.

It was a relief to have a clear-cut problem in front of me, even if I coughed and nails of agony cramped through my left side. Creaking pops as the ribs snapped out and messily fused together, etheric force jolting through my bone structure like an earthquake through a skyscraper, and when the hound leapt again, steaming and smoking and howling in töng, Anya's chanting reached a fevered pitch behind me. If I could keep it busy enough, she could slow it down, then we could tear the goddamn thing apart.

What was in the door? But Saul was already gone, scrambling past us up the stairs and plunging into the Hill's maw. I had to forget about it, trust that he would take care of himself and—

CRACK. It hit me again, and this time we simply blinked through space and smashed into the stone steps. The gem rang, a piercing overstressed note, and my scream was cut short.

If I'd been paying fucking *attention*, I would've used the whip instead of letting it smack me that time. More bones snapping, my head hit sandstone with stunning force and I actually pistol-whipped the thing instead of shooting it, my left fist coming up too, freighted with leather whip handle, and clocking it on the other side of its head. 'Breed mostly have a hard outer shell you can breach with silver, but hellhounds are elastic over hard bones, the skull a titanium curve under a gooshy, slippery-thick layer of congealed darkness birthing yet more scorchsteam as the sun lashed it. It reeked of corruption, and the gem hissed angrily on my wrist.

Anya's chant spiraled up into a scream. My left arm was up, and the thing's jaws closed, teeth driving in. It had its back legs braced and snaked its misshapen head, hot bloody foam spattering as it shook me like a piece of wet laundry. Lines of blue sorcery bit, driving deep, and Anya yanked back. If the thing hadn't been loosening up to take another bite of me, I would have gone with it as she whipped it back away from me, a hawkscream of effort escaping her as she pivoted, hip popping out and boots scraping through hop-bouncing gravel.

The thing howled like a freight train with failed brakes on a steep grade. Warm trickles sliding down my neck because the noise was *wrong*—it reverberated through the ice bath of the Hill's charged atmosphere and tore at sanity itself, an amplified squeal of psychic feedback.

"*Inside!*" Devi yelled, and I was already scrambling to my feet, letting out a scream of my own as broken bones ground and my left arm *burned*, if its bite was septic we were looking at fun times.

Never a dull moment around you, Jill. Get UP!

She didn't grab me to haul me up, but she didn't bound past me, either. She covered as I made it, awkwardly, up the stone steps, struggling into the building.

It was good tactical thinking. One-third of our force was inside here, we had a civilian we needed to track and lock down, and inside a building the number of approaches a hellhound could use were reduced.

Blood spattered the scarred, ancient black-and-white linoleum squares. I scrabbled through on all fours, rolled while sweeping, and was on one knee with the gun braced as Anya plunged through behind me.

I was right. I could see the damage from my last visit. The monstrous wooden reception desk had a hole blown in it, a jumble of wooden chairs and trash at one end of the room vibrated uneasily, and Saul was on the stairs holding down a writhing, spitting mass of paleness that had once been Jughead Vanner. The hellhound had tossed Jughead aside to deal with us, the bigger threat.

Might have saved his life. Goddamn.

One booted foot off to the side, his coppery fingers clamped on Vanner's nape, my Were glanced at me and his dark eyes widened slightly.

"Status!" Anya yelled.

I coughed, spat. Etheric force tingled all through me, and my left arm cramped up as the gem fought whatever toxin had been smeared on the thing's teeth. Or in its blood-foaming saliva. Or whatever.

The world trembled and came back, the Hill shivering all over. "*Jill!*" Anya didn't sound happy.

Buckle up, Kismet. Just buckle up. "Fine!" I barked, and shook the whip slightly. I had to swing my shoulder back and forth to do it, my arm had seized up. "Ready to tango. Saul?"

"He's strong." Quiet, clinical. "You're bleeding."

Well, no shit. That's how these things always end up. "I'll live, it's closing up. Devi?"

"What do you wanna bet that hound isn't coming back?" She moved back and to her left, finding a good angle, both guns covering the door. Outside our little spheres of normalcy, the air was thicker. Almost opaque, like dust-fogged glass. Paper trash twisted and ruffled at random, half-seen shapes flickering and my blue eye burning as it tried to focus *through*.

"I don't take losing bets." I levered myself up, coughed rackingly again. *Move it, Jill.* "Saul, what's wrong with him? Is he bit?" A hellhound bite could do any number of things to a person. *Bad* things.

"Don't know." Saul's back tensed as Vanner writhed, bare toenails scratching the linoleum. The stairs groaned sharply, once. "Steady, friend."

It was hard work to lever myself up and turn my back on the door, even though I knew Anya was watching. My ribs ached, and my left arm flopped a little, huge jagged waves of pins-and-needles cramping up from my fingers, exploding in my shoulder, sliding down to grip at my ribs, grinding in my knees each time my boots hit the floor. Half-heard voices rose in a whispering tide, little unseen fingers tickling the edges of my vision. The bright spangles tipping each spike of my aura winked uneasily, little stars. "It's *bad* in here. Jesus."

"Something happened." Devi, carefully neutral. "My guess is that fucking blue-eyed 'breed was in it up to his neck." She paused. "And Belisa."

Yeah, I noticed my apprentice had the Eye. Subtle, Devi. "So it would seem." I approached cautiously, each step tested before I committed my weight. Thin traceries of steam rose from my flayed sleeve. "I'm cuffing Vanner."

"You sure it's him? Maybe it's his cousin."

"I'll revise my assumption when I get to him." The banter was supposed to soothe our nerves. I don't know how well it was doing for her, but for me, not so good. My arm came back to life in a scalding rush, and the flechettes on the whip's end jingled merrily as I stowed it. My fingers were finally obeying me again.

She magnanimously didn't mention that I'd pulled a rookie mistake and gotten myself hit. Nice of her.

Saul had our victim's right arm twisted up behind his back so far it looked ready to separate the ball joint; along with the knee in his back and the lock at his nape it looked reasonably secure. Which was wrong. Because even a weakened Were should have no trouble at all holding down a human, especially one that presumably had been lolling catatonic in a chair for months and shagging ass all over the city for the past couple days.

Oh yeah. This just keeps getting better.

CHAPTER 21

It *was* Jughead Vanner, and something was seriously wrong with him. There was so much blood I couldn't tell if he'd been bitten. The reinforced silver-coated cuffs went at his wrists and elbows, and I flipped him over while Saul straightened, glancing mildly around like he was interested in the scenery.

"Jesus," I muttered, and the memory of the last time I'd seen Vanner hit me right in the gut. It was that house. The one with the dead girls a hellbreed had harvested organs from, the girls that got

up and started moving while I was there. Vanner had come in—
maybe to help, maybe to gawk, even though he knew the rules.

They all did. When I say *stay*, they stay like good little boys
and girls.

Back then Vanner had been a big lumbering rookie, blue-eyed
corn-fed All-American steak with a habit of blushing and stam-
mering whenever I spoke to him. Now he was wasted down to
pasty skin, bruised crescents of shocky flesh under his rolling
eyes and the remains of a filthy, bloodsoaked hospital johnny covering a skinny torso that had once been an advertisement for
weightlifting. He'd found a pair of canvas pants, too, and God
alone knew what color they were originally. Now they were
stained, smeared with sixteen different flavors of street grease
and claret, and he'd lost control of some very basic functions most
of us get a handle on before we're three.

Wonderful.

I grabbed Vanner's unshaven chin. The hair on his cheeks was
more stubborn than the mop on his head, once leonine blond and
high and tight, but now just a few soft strands over a naked white
domed scalp. His jaw worked loosely, spittle drooling down his
chin, and he shrieked.

The Hill shrieked back.

Mottled rashing burns spread down Vanner's throat, a distinctive bright-red wattling. Like radiation. The other skin was dead
white, and it rippled as his back bowed and he shrieked again.

Ohshit. "Vanner?" I snapped. "*Vanner!*" I found his first name
with a lurching mental effort. "*Christopher!*"

He moaned, far gone, eyes rolling up, their whites yellowed as
old teeth. His bare heels drummed into the linoleum as I wrestled
him back down. "Something in him all right. Can't tell what it—"

"Jill!" Devi moved forward, light even steps. "Incoming!"

Poor Vanner. He'd run so hard, and so long, and he had reached
the end of it. There was a boom and a snarling of Helletöng as the
hellhound hit Henderson Hill's front door, and the skin over the
parasite-thing breeding in a Santa Luz cop, one of *my* cops, peeled
back and burst.

The unhuman shape came up out of him in a looping stream

that resolved itself into a narrow canine head, sharp needle teeth made of basalt and slick eggwhite ectoplasm clinging along it. Bones crackled, forelimbs lengthening and hindlegs shortening, muscle roiling and shifting as it assumed its shape. The 'plasm splattered, and the bits of it that hit the Hill's turbulence hung in midair, spinning little milky spheres. I was chanting myself now, bastard Latin strung together in an ancient prayer pagans had stolen and Christians had stolen back, and thin blue lines of sorcery snapped into being. My apprentice-ring sparked, the three charms in my hair did too, and I went over backward. The whip doubled and looped, caught just over the thing's head, locked up as its teeth champed an inch from my nose. It had mad, wide blue eyes burning with unholy fire, and it was slick-wet with the noisome fluid of its birth. Short blond hair bristled all over its hyena-shaped body, and for a single sickening moment my blue eye saw Vanner himself in the thing, his hands turned to needle-fine but lethal razor claws and his entire body a lean compact weight. Like a nightmare the thing scrabbled at my chest, and another massive sound was the hellhound and Anya screaming at each other, gunfire popping and Saul's enraged roar.

This is not good not good not good—my fingers, slick with ectoplasmic goo, didn't slip. I tightened up, shoving the thing back, and it choked, spraying me with more foulness. *God*dam*mit, get up and help them! That's a hellhound! Saul's over there! Fucking kill this thing, get up and kill the other thing, and let's get this* done*!*

The gem shrieked, a crystalline, overstressed note, glass tearing apart instead of breaking. Red pain jolted up my arm, exploding in my shoulder, and for a long moment it was Perry with his lips on my skin again, the scar melting with sick delight, him fiddling with my nerves and trying to make me respond. To jump in any direction, as long as he could just get a reaction, *any* reaction, from me.

It's not the scar it's something else the scar's gone ohGod the scar's gone where—

The hole in my memory gaped, yawning... and I fell in with the hot breath of the beast on my face. The Hill screamed like a woman in labor, and time... stopped.

*   *   *

The Sorrow rose. She cast a glance back over her shoulder, her face slack and terribly graven. Bruises crawled over her skin, the shadows of Chaldean sorcery doing what they could to ameliorate the damage. But she was in bad shape, bleeding all over, her tangled hair smoking at each knot.

Each inch of silver on me ran with blue flame. My head was full of screaming noise.

"Kill," Perry hissed, from where I'd kicked him. "Kill it now!"

I lifted my gun, slowly. It was a terrible dream, fighting through syrup, my muscles full of lead.

Belisa's chin dipped wearily. She pitched forward just as the egg stopped spinning.

The thing that slid its malformed hand through the barrier between this world and Hell twitched. I heard myself screaming, sanity shuddering aside from the sight. They do not dress when they are at home, and when they come through and take on a semblance of flesh it's enough to drive any ordinary person mad. Wet salt trickles slid down from my eyes, slid from my nose and ears.

They were not tears.

There was a rushing, the physical fabric of our world terribly assaulted, ripping and stretching. My screams, terrible enough to make the Hill shudder all the way down to its misery-soaked foundations. Perry, hissing in squeal-groan Helletöng, and under it all, so quiet and so final, Mikhail's voice from across a gulf of years. Long nights spent turning over everything about his death, remembering him, all folding aside and compressing into what he would say if he was here. Or maybe just the only defense my psyche had against the thing struggling to birth itself completely.

Now, *Mikhail said.* Kill now, milaya. Do not hesitate.

My teacher's killer was in the way.

The scar crunched on my wrist. I squeezed the trigger. Both triggers, and I saw the booming trail of shockwaves as the bullets cut air. Belisa's fingers had turned to claws, Chaldean spiking the soup of noise, and she tore at the not-quite-substantial flesh of the thing. Blue light crawled over her as if she wore silver, the same blue that the caretaker's eyes had flashed. The shadows of the

Chaldean parasite flinched aside, for some incomprehensible reason.

I was still screaming as the bullets tore through her and the egg as well. The collar made a zinging, popping noise, the golden runes sliding over the collar shutterclicks of racing, diseased light. Her body shook and juddered as she forced the thing behind the rip in the world back, and the physical fabric of the place humans call home snapped shut with a sound like a heavy iron door slamming. The bristling, misshapen appendage thumped down to the floor.

Belisa's fingers, human again, plucked weakly at the collar. She was a servant of the gods who were here long before demons, the inimical forces the shadowy Lords of the Trees trapped in another place long ago. It was a Pyrrhic victory; the Imdarák *didn't survive their victory, either. And the Sorrows are always looking to bring their masters back. The 'breed? Well, they're always looking to bring more of their kind. It's like two different conventions fighting over the same hotel.*

If anyone could have slammed a door between here and Hell shut, it was a Sorrow.

But why? *And the caretaker, what was he—*

My knees folded. I hit the ground. Henderson Hill whispered around me like the end of a bell's tolling, reverberations dying in glue-thick air.

Oh, no.

Belisa folded over. I'd emptied a clip. Sorrows can heal amazingly fast, but she was probably exhausted after all the fun and games.

Her knees hit the concrete in front of the altar. Blood flowered, spattered on the floor. She shook her head, tangled hair swaying. The golden runes on the collar snuffed out, one by one.

"Ahhhhh." It was a long satisfied sigh, escaping Perry's bleeding lips. "Oh, yes. Yessssssssss."

The scar drew up on my wrist and began to ache. This wasn't the usual burning as I yanked etheric energy through it. I tore my eyes from Belisa's slumped form and turned my right wrist up.

The print of Perry's lips was not a scar now. It was black, as if

the flesh itself was rotting, and it pulsed obscenely. As I watched
the edges frayed, little blue vein-maps crawling under the surface
of my flesh.
*   And I knew why. I could have shot around her.*
*   But I'd chosen not to.*

The dog-thing that used to be Vanner hung motionless over me.
Further away, seen through vibrating, glassy air, Anya Devi
extended in a leap, her long dark hair a silver-scarred banner. One
of the bullets was just exiting the gun in her left hand, the explosion behind it clearly visible. Saul crouched on the grimy black-
and-white squares, the fringe on his jacket unsettled, standing
straight up. They were utterly, eerily still.

The hellhound itself was leaping for Anya. It was wounded,
sprays of black ichor hanging behind it like fine lacework scarves.

"We have a little time," he said.

Henderson Hill's caretaker crouched easily next to me, stroking the sleek head of the canine thing on top of me. Same faded
coveralls, with the snarl of embroidery hiding his name. His eyes
were bright clean blue, no longer filmed. And the shadow of scarring on his face was clearing up nicely. Alone of all the things at
the Hill, he'd always just looked solid.

Normal.

Well, this sort of shot the idea of *normal* in the head, didn't it?
He wasn't any species of nightsider I'd ever come across. He was
something else. I'd been wanting to talk to him, and I'd thought I
might find him here. Or even just a clue to where he was likely to
be hiding once he dropped a quarter in me, pulled my arm, and set
me spinning.

He'd brought Belisa to the operating room and turned her loose
on the hellbreed in there. He'd also bought me breakfast right after
I clawed my way out of my own grave. He'd given me my gun and
my ring.

Which made him a question mark, at best.

I blinked. *What the fuck?* My fingers cramped on the whip, I
kept the tension up. Everything stayed still, the movie of life
paused and nobody thinking to warn me about it. So I wet my lips

and wished I hadn't, something foul was spread on my face. "What. The fuck."

He grinned, a boyish expression, while he scratched behind the dog-thing's ears with his expressive, callused hand. The shadow of sorrow in those blue eyes didn't lighten. "Do you know how liberating it is to actually *speak*? Don't worry," he added in a rush. "I mean you no harm."

Oh, I'm not so sure about that. "Get this thing off me." A harsh croak, something stuck in my throat.

"Can't. I can only break the laws of the physical so far. Little Judy, listen to me."

I went stiff. Resisting. My jaw creaked when I finally loosened it enough. "Don't. Call me. That." *That's a dead girl's name, and I've had enough of people saying it to me.*

"Very well. Kismet, then. You named yourself for Fate, didn't you. As a holy avenger. Much the way your predecessor Jack Karma did. You're rather amazingly alike; all of you choose those like yourselves. It's..." He shrugged slightly. His tan workman's boots made a small sound as he shifted, their rubber soles grinding on dust and dirt. "It hurts to see, sometimes."

"What the fuck *are* you?" I breathed. Because the gem was making a low, satisfied note, and the flood of etheric energy up my arm had turned warm and caramel-soft.

Well, that answered *that* question, didn't it.

"Call me Mike. I'd shake your hand, but you're busy. Kismet, Hyperion must be stopped."

Hyperion?

My brain did another one of those sideways jags. *Perry. That's what other hellbreed call him. Galina calls him Pericles, because he's old. Mikhail just called him "that motherfucker at the Monde."* My breath jagged in, with a ratcheting sound. "No kidding."

"You don't understand. *Everything* has been according to his plan. Everything. Except your final act—the little break in the pattern. Do you remember what you did?"

My head ached, fiercely. The buzzing came back, rising inside me on a black tide. "No." I struggled, achieved exactly nothing. I was nailed in place. I could breathe, and my heart was a live wire jumping and sizzling inside my chest. I could even tighten up on the creaking leather of the whip.

But I couldn't move.

"You sacrificed yourself, Kismet. For the sake of many." He was grave now, a blush of color high up on his cheekbones. Before, he'd been horrifically scarred, the gray film over his eyes somehow making him gentler. This man looked like the caretaker's handsome older brother, his hair lifting and curling, taking on a richer gold. "That makes...certain things...possible."

Now it was a laugh, tearing free of my resisting chest. "What things? What the hell?"

He leaned down even further. Those eyes were pitiless, terrible. They were not burning with a hellbreed's fire. No, they were simply sad. A sadness like a knife to the heart, numb grief when the night rises and the bottle is empty and the voice of every failure and weakness starts to rumble in the bottom of your brain like a bad earthquake.

Cops get that look after a while, sometimes in stages, sometimes all at once. Other hunters, too. Sometimes, looking in the mirror while I smeared eyeliner on, I've caught glimpses of it.

It's the look of seeing too much. Of being unable to turn away.

"Go to Hyperion. Do what is necessary to convince him you're intrigued. Pretend your friends have thrown you out, whatever you like. But *go*. I am asking you to play Judas to a hellbreed, so that when he laughs in the moment of his triumph you can strike him down. You can be our avenging hand."

Which brought up the very first question I needed to ask, the first of many I wanted fully answered. "And who the hell is *we*, white man?"

I didn't think he'd get the joke, but he smiled. It was a terrible smile as well, that sadness staining through the expression, and a sick feeling began right under my breast-bone. A low, nasty buzz mounted in my ears, little sticky feet probing and tickling all over my face, down my throat, down my aching, immobile body.

"You know who we are." His shoulders set.

"I don't know a single—" I began, but my heart was skipping triple time, and his hands were coming forward. He was going to *touch* me, and everything in me cringed away from the notion. "No. Don't. *Don't.*"

"I'm sorry," he whispered. "I would bear this for you, if I could."

I strained, black spots dancing at the edges of my vision, sweat rising in huge pearly drops, terror like wine filling my veins. I made a helpless sound, and I hated it immediately. It was the gasp of a very bright, very needy dark-haired girl huddled in her bedroom or shivering on a street corner, a girl under someone's fists. A girl begging and pleading. *Please. Please don't. Oh please don't.*

"I have been with thee from the beginning," he said very softly, and his fingers clamped on my head. White light exploded inside my skull, and it *hurt.*

It was like dying all over again. Or mercifully—or maybe just practically—I can't now say what it felt like. I can't remember.

And I don't ever want to.

CHAPTER 22

Hip popped up, heel stamping down, massive lung-tearing effort and the doglike thing spun to the side as I wrenched its head and flung it. Shove at the head and the body will follow; it's a basic law of anatomy. My whip reeled free, flechettes spilling out with a jingle, and I was up in a hot heartbeat, whip end snaking out and me right behind it. Throwing myself across space to crash into the hellhound at the apex of its leap, whip looping and turned taut, straining. Gunfire popped, bullets splattering behind us, and I wasn't quite sure why I'd done this.

Then I remembered. Saul.

We hit the shipwrecked desk, and my right hand was full of knife hilt. The blade slid in, twisted, the silver laid along its flat flaring with sudden blue radiance, and the warmth on my chin was blood as the thing snarled in my face. It couldn't get any purchase; the whip was now wrapped around it and pulled tight, my legs clamped around it too and the tearing in my side was ribs broken, *again, dammit, can I just go five seconds without another bone snapping please God thank you—*

I bent back as the head snaked forward, teeth snapping near my throat, rank hot breath touching my chin and Henderson Hill shuddering again on its foundations. The knife punctured its gluey hide, cut deep, drag on the blade as unholy muscle gripped it, silver hissing and sparking as it grated hard against ribs. Tearing it free, rolling, splinters shredding against my coat's surface, the cubbyholes behind the desk exhaling dust as a current of bloodlust foamed up their surface, and I cut the thing's throat in one sweep.

Arterial gush sprayed, thin black-brackish and stinking. I blinked it away, knee coming up, and realized I'd almost taken the hound's head off. The neck broke with a glassy snap as I heaved it aside, dusty corruption racing through its tissues; it slumped off the desk and fell.

The voices in the air around me sighed, a hundred little sharp-toothed children all exhaling in wonder. For a moment the Hill pressed down, the psychic ferment shoving against my aura like it wanted to get *in*.

I pushed air out past my lips, *hard*, blowing through a thin scrim of hellbreed ichor. The shit was all *over* me, dammit. But there was that second thing to worry about too, and I was already rolling, dropping off the desk with a jolt, legs and ribs protesting as etheric force hummed through me and I shook the whip, the knife spun and held with the flat of the blade back along my arm. Anya could shoot the fuckers all she wanted, but my forte was knife-work, and it was looking like I could take a hell of a lot more damage than she could.

You know what we are, he whispered inside my head.

Mike. What kind of a name was that for what I suspected he *might* be?

Anya was covering the door. Saul stood, brushing his shoulders gingerly, as if he'd been showered with dust.

"Where?" One clipped syllable, but I said it too loud and the foyer rippled. The spangles of Anya's aura, their spines popping out and shifting uneasily, roiled as she sighed and slowly lowered her guns. Her coat creaked a little as she did, and the tension humming through her made lines of force swirl in the thickened, dusty air.

"It ran off." She spared me one swift, very blue, very annoyed glance. "You want to tell me what the *hell* just happened here, Kismet?"

"Something was *in* Vanner. It busted free, I slapped it pretty hard and took out the hellhound, and Vanner . . . Jesus Christ, what *was* that? I haven't seen anything like that before."

"I have. Dogsbody." Tight and unamused. "Why the fuck did it run off?"

Gooseflesh rippled under my skin before training clamped down on my hindbrain. I shivered. *No fucking way. "That* was a dogsbody?" *Should've taken my head clean off. Jesus Christ.* "It can't be. Nobody's bleeding." I shut my mouth, realized how absurd it sounded. "Well, except for me. But that's normal."

"Take a look. That rag laying on the stairs is just skin. That rookie's a day-running dog full of hellhound venom now, and we'd better get going if we're gonna track him."

"No need." My mouth was numb. The knife slid into a sheath, I slid my right-hand gun free just in case. Everything inside me was shaking and shivering. An internal earthquake, bits popping and shattering inside my skull, puzzle pieces dropping into place.

Still too much I don't know.

"No need," I repeated. The Hall quivered, and a cold draft blew between us, rustling paper trash with a sound like drowned fingers slipping free of their skin. "I know where he's going."

We made it back to Galina's just as afternoon shadows began lengthening. The heat was a hammerblow, the worst of the day, and Anya was white-knuckled on the steering wheel. The way some of the shadows were twisting oddly, I didn't blame her. And with Saul riding terribly exposed back in the truck bed, it was a nerve-wracking slalom for me, too. Especially since I could swear we were followed, or at least *watched.* I just couldn't tell who was doing the watching.

Anya slammed the absinthe bottle down on the butcher-block table. Venomous green liquid sloshed inside it. "All right. I've had it. Talk."

Galina still kept the Jack Daniels in the cabinet above her ancient Frigidaire. I had to go up on tiptoe to get it, and I left a smear on the fridge's chilly white enamel. The hellhound's ichor was drying to a gummy black paste on me, and I was filthy with the ancient dust of Henderson Hill.

Low golden light fell over the herbs in Galina's kitchen window, and the Sanctuary was in the door watching both of us, her hands tightly laced together. Her tone was soft, conciliatory. "He's downstairs pacing. Theron is watching him. Gil's trying to escape through the sunroom, and Hutch won't come out of the vault."

"Vault's a good place for him." I worked the top free, considered the bottle, and took a long pull. It burned going down, and I could pretend it was the alcohol heat making my eyesight waver. The gem purred on my wrist. "Nervous type, our Hutch. Has anyone told him I'm alive?"

"Jill—" Galina, trying to forestall the explosion.

It didn't work. Anya Devi had waited long enough. "Kismet, start *fucking talking*. I've been keeping this town on the map since you disappeared, and now this? *This?* You just vanished and reappeared across a whole fuckload of empty space. Not even hellbreed are that fast. And why didn't that dogsbody tear you up, huh? What did you *do* out there?"

The world stopped, and I had a visitation from a hallucination. I grimaced at the fridge. My hair hung in long strings, matted with hellbreed ick, and I didn't have nearly enough silver to tie into it. "Do you believe in God?"

"What?" My fellow hunter sounded about ready to have a heart attack.

I didn't blame her. "It's a simple fucking question, Devi. Do you?" I took another hit off the bottle, to stop myself from saying more.

"No." Sharply, now. Liquid sloshing inside a bottle. "I believe in booze, and in ammo, and in being prepared. But God? No. *Fuck* no."

"Neither do I." It gave me no comfort to admit it. "I pray like everyone else, when my ass is going to be blown sideways. But I don't believe. Hellbreed I believe in, and they predate anything we might think of as *God*, right? By a long shot."

"I like history." Anya drummed her fingers on the tabletop. "Really I do. And philosophy's a great discipline too. Foundation of the humanities. But for fuck's sweet everloving sake, Jill, not *now*."

I held out my right hand. It shook, slightly, the tremor running through my bones making the flesh quiver. I didn't have a lot of flesh on me to shiver, still scrawny as hell. My stomach twisted on itself, and I was guessing my metabolism was burning as hot as a Were's for a while to speed the healing. My ribs were tender, and my shirt was a blood-soaked rag.

Also, I needed to calm down. Unfortunately, that didn't look like it had any goddamn chance of happening.

I stared at the Frigidaire and the smears I'd left on it. I fouled everything I touched, didn't I. I had from the beginning, from the moment I ruined my mother's rootless life by being conceived. Then there were her fist-happy boyfriends, and the street boys, and Val. So many shapes of men.

And Mikhail? If I'd been better, faster, stronger, maybe he could have told me about the bargain he'd made with Perry. He wouldn't have hidden it from me, which meant maybe Perry wouldn't have been able to jerk me from one end to the other and play me so neatly—and finally, finally trap me.

"I remember what I did now," I whispered. "I damned myself. Didn't I."

"Galina." Scrape of a chair as Anya stood up. "Give us the room, huh? And keep the boys downstairs."

"But—" Galina must have swallowed any objection, because the next sound I heard was her bare footsteps shushing away.

They sounded, for the first time, like an old woman's shuffle instead of a girl's light step.

Devi approached, softly but definitely making noise. "Something on your mind, Jill? You bleed clean, and I don't know what that thing on your wrist is, but it isn't hellbreed. I bet you went out into the desert and played one last game with Perry, and got free the only way you could." Reasonable, even, spacing out the chain of logic. "That far, at least, I can get on my own. But what the fuck else, Jill? What else happened?"

I blinked, a trickle of warm salty water easing down my filthy cheek. The booze wasn't doing any good. It might as well have been milk.

I am asking you to play Judas to a hellbreed. Either it was a hallucination who'd bought me breakfast and slipped Belisa's leash, or it was real. If it was real, I was just given my marching orders, wasn't I?

But orders from who, and why? And if it *wasn't* real, was it because I wanted to go back to the Monde? Or because I was looking for a way out, any way out of what was going to happen next, so I could ease my conscience and go riding off into the sunset with Saul? Leaving Anya to pick up the pieces. If she could.

She'd certainly try. She was *hunter.*

What did that make me?

"Belisa's dead." I weighed both words, found them wanting. The rest stuck in my throat, but I had to force them loose somehow. "I shot her because I wanted to. It wasn't a clean kill, Devi."

"Yeah, well." She paused. I sensed her nearness. "I don't blame you. But that's not the point, is it."

Thank God she understood. But of course she did.

She was a *hunter.* We commit the sin of murder every night, we who police the nightside. When you're trained to do that, when mayhem is an everyday occurrence, you have to have something to keep you from going over the edge. From making you worse than the things you hunt.

There's a lot of words for it, but I've only ever found one.

"No. It's not." I capped the bottle again. "Perry's planning something big. The caretaker out at Henderson Hill is in on it somehow. I've got to dig further." The half-formed idea that had been trying to wriggle its way out from under a bunch of soupy terror finally came out into the light, and I let out a long sigh.

Thank God. One card in my hand, at least.

Devi folded her arms, leather creaking. "Okay. What do you need me to do?"

Because this was my city, right? I was the resident hunter. Even if I'd clawed my way up out of a grave and couldn't remember my own fucking name, I was *responsible.* There was no getting away from it. If I did drive off with Saul, sooner or later I wouldn't be able to live with myself.

And we all knew where *that* ended, didn't we. With me between the rock and the hard place, where I had all the freedom in the world—but I could only make one choice, because of who I was. How I'd been made.

Oh yes, God exists, even though I don't believe in Him. He absolutely exists. And He is a sadistic fuck.

I gave myself a mental shake. *Focus, Jill.* "Tell Galina to keep Saul here. Keep him in the vaults if you have to. He's going to go nuts, but if you let him outside alone, he's going to die." *Perry will kill him. Just to show me he can.*

He wasn't even safe with me, no matter how much I wanted him right where I could see him. How craven of me was it to let him come along to the Hill, even?

Self-loathing turned to spurs right under my skin. It was difficult to think through the noise in my head, but I managed.

Anya didn't hesitate. "Done."

Well, that was the easy part. "Call Montaigne and have him list Vanner as a line-of-duty casualty. Full honors and a memorial service. We don't have a body and we never will." The rag of skin left behind at the Hill wasn't anything we could bury, and was eaten by banefire now anyway. A thought occurred to me, I went up on tiptoes again to put the JD away. If I kept looking at it I was going to finish the whole damn bottle, and with a metabolism running this hot it wouldn't do any good. "Get hold of Badger. Have her pull every car Vanner's owned in the last four years off the DMV and list them for you. Keep my pager, I'll use that number and Galina's to check in." *If I'm still alive to check in. If I pull this off.*

"Okay."

I wasn't imagining it. She actually sounded relieved I'd started firing on all cylinders again. *Stop it*, I wanted to say. *You're a full-blown hunter too. What the fuck do you need me for?*

Well, I was Santa Luz's hunter. I was also the only damn person who could possibly worm Perry's big plan out of him.

Lucky, lucky me.

"Get Hutch on the computer." I couldn't believe I was saying it, staring at the fresh smudges and smears I'd left on Galina's cherished icebox. It looked like a thirties-era rendition of a spaceship, all rounded and solid, the Frigidaire logo polished but still showing little signs of age. Rusting and flaking, its chrome giving up the battle. Evan a Sanc can't completely stop time. "Have him beg, borrow, hack or tap everything he can about Perry. Especially about what Perry was doing in the twenties. Tell him not to worry about anything, I'll authorize whatever he wants to do retroactively. You understand? Give Hutch the T1 line and carte blanche. Get *everything* on Perry, but don't let Hutch leave Sanctuary either, even if there's books he needs at the shop. Have him find them in some other library, twist whatever arms you have to."

"Jesus." It was the first time I ever heard her sound shocked. "All right. What else?"

"Saul. Tell him..."

She waited.

"Tell him I'm coming back. Tell him even dying won't stop me, and he's not allowed to let himself waste, because I'm going to need him."

She said nothing. Maybe she knew it was a lie. But when I finally turned on my heel and looked at her, I found out her cheeks were wet too. Her hands were fists. The scar down her cheek flushed, and for a moment she was so beautifully ugly my heart threatened to crack.

"And you be careful. I'll keep Perry as busy as I can, but this is likely to be nasty."

She found her voice. "What about Gilberto?"

My conscience squirmed. I clamped down on it as hard as I could. "Gil's coming with me. We're going to visit someone." *If he wants to. If he decides to.*

But he was my apprentice. I already knew what he'd say.

CHAPTER 23

Melendez still lived on the north edge of the Riverhurst section, where the lawns were green and wide under the bloody dye of dusk. Sprinklers were going full tap among the fake adobes and the few Cape Cods, the expensive mock Tudors and other ersatz-glitz refugees. If you wanted truly antique houses you would go over to Greenlea where the yuppies elbowed each other over twenties mock-Victorians and organic boutiques. Or toward the edge of the suburbs, where there was a belt of poverty-stricken structures from the forties and fifties hanging on from before the blight of tofu housing development started.

Gilberto yanked the hand brake. I didn't ask where he'd gotten the small black Volkswagen from; in return, he didn't ask me what we were doing. He kept it below the speed limit, obeyed all traffic laws, and generally piloted the thing like an old granny. He even whistled tunelessly below his breath. Like he was having a good time.

Since Mama Zamba had disappeared, Melendez was no longer jester of the local voodoo court. He didn't have Zamba's appetite for gore and grotesque, but he did have a stranglehold on power—and he was in very good odor with his patron Chango. Anyone who parlays with a non-human intelligence is suspect in a hunter's book, but I was living in a glass house at this point. Not only that, but Melendez had been... helpful, once or twice. In a limited sort of way, when he could see his own advantage.

Or when I had him by the balls.

The noise in my head had cleared a little, and I was feeling more like myself. Gilberto ghosted behind me, stepping only where I did, his pulse slow and even. I glanced back, and the half-grin fell off his face, almost shattering on the sidewalk.

This is serious business, I'd told him, *and there needs to be no goddamn funny stuff. No face, no insults, no nothing. You keep your manners on, your mouth shut, and you don't draw unless I do.*

Sí, señora bruja, he'd said, and it looked like he meant it.

Melendez's faux-adobe hacienda sat behind its round concrete driveway. A brick bank in the middle of the heat-shimmering concrete held heavy-blooming rosebushes, a monkey puzzle tree, and a bank of silvery-green rue. Lemon balm tried its best to choke everything else in the bed, but aggressive pruning held it back. The fountain in the middle of the driveway was bone-dry, the concrete cherub who was usually shooting water out of his tiny little peeper looking sadly dejected. My smart eye watered, but I detected nothing other than the usual febrile etheric congestion.

Afternoons Melendez was usually ministering to the faithful at his storefront out on Parraroyos, nonprofit under the tax law but donations encouraged, drumming and chicken dinners pretty much every night. Today, though, I was pretty sure he'd be here. That's one thing about being psychic—sometimes you're home when someone wants you.

Gilberto hung back as we approached the wide iron gate, until I motioned him forward. I very pointedly did not ease a gun free of the holster. Busting in shooting and yelling wasn't going to be necessary, no matter how much I liked the idea.

"Be cool, Gil."

"I am very fuckin' cool, *profesora*. Don' worry 'bout me none."

I shouldn't be bringing you here. I swallowed hard and crossed the driveway, checking the sun. Not much daylight left.

Everything around me rippled, chills spreading down my spine. The gem sang, vibrating on my wrist. I kept going, stepped through the gate, the courtyard closing around me. Another fountain here, seashell shaped, also dry. Was he having trouble paying his water bill? Not likely.

I didn't even get to ring the bell. As soon as I stepped up to the door, there was a sound of locks chucking open. The door creaked as it swung inward, and a rotund little Hispanic male eyed me. He wore a bowling shirt festooned with pineapples, a pair of jeans, and there was a hint of a smile around his wide mouth.

"Señor Melendez." I kept my hands where he could see them.

He studied me for a long, tense-ticking fifteen seconds. His gaze traveled up over my shoulder, and I knew Gilberto was staring back. Melendez waved one pudgy hand, as if shooing away an insect. He examined me from top to toe, taking his time.

I suffered it.

"*Ay de mi*," the little butterball finally breathed. "*Ay, mamacita*, you took *El Camino Negro*. And you come back."

No shit. "I've got a few questions."

He nodded thoughtfully. "Bet you do. I just bet you do." He seemed content to just leave it at that, sucking at his upper lip, and didn't move. The heat was a thick blanket, I tasted sand and rot, and buzzing rose inside my head. A ghost of sweat touched my back, training clamped down and I kept my hands loose with an effort.

"Melendez." I didn't raise my voice. "Your cooperation is *not* optional."

"And what about *mi patrón*, eh?" He grinned, his teeth shocking white. The spirits paid for good dental care, at least.

"His isn't optional, either." I stepped forward, Gilberto following silent behind me. Melendez retreated, and the cool and quiet of the voodoo king's house enfolded us.

The kitchen was stainless steel and sharp edges, a bluetiled floor and every surface painfully scrubbed. The light was warm and electric, even though there was a wide window looking out onto the blue shimmering jewel of the pool in the backyard. A faint tang of cigar smoke hung in the air-conditioned breeze, and the tall silver fridge stopped humming. Uncomfortable silence rose, and when I pointed Gilberto dropped onto a tall stool at the breakfast bar. His shoulders hunched before I gave him a meaningful look; he straightened and buttoned his lip.

Nice to know I still had the quelling glance.

Melendez opened the fridge. Glass clinked, and he came out with a couple brown bottles of expensive microbrew. He cracked the beers with practiced twists, and handed me one. "You got to know," he said finally. "You owe Chango a bullet, *bruja*. Don't think he forgot."

"I haven't forgotten either. This is about something else." I took a long pull off the bottle. "Time's a factor, Melendez. So spit it out."

He took a pull off his beer, made a face. "I ain't got much to spit. It ain't pretty out there, *bruja*. Faustina on Seventy-third, she dead. Mark Hope, he dead too. That cocksucker on Martell Avenue with his fancy cigarettes, gone. Luisa de la Rocha, Manuelita Rojo, that Dama Miercoles bitch, they gone too."

"Wait. Hang on." I stared at him. *That's every big mover in the voodoo community, for Christ's sake. "All* of them? You're telling me they're dead?"

"Well, they ain't in fucking Baja, fuck." He took another pull. "*Es Los Otros, los diablos*. No warning. *La Familia*, they gave no warning. Just, one second everything fine. Then bam! Dead, dead, *muerto*, and the spirits screaming about the treaty broken."

Gilberto shifted uneasily on his stool, his hands cupping his sharp elbows, and under his sallowness his pitted cheeks were pale. He stared at me, and I was abruptly reminded of just how young he was. Had I ever been that wide-eyed?

"No warning? When was this?"

"Couple months ago." Melendez's eyes glittered sleepily, hooded. The cigar smell drifted across the room, and a thin thread of smoke curled up from the open mouth of the beer bottle.

This just keeps getting better. "So the hellbreed all of a sudden started killing voodoo practitioners. The movers and shakers. Why are you still alive?"

A sneer twisted his plump face. "I in *strong* with Chango, *bruja.* You know dat. He tell me long as I stay inside he protect me. Now here you come. What you want, eh?"

It took several long throat-working swallows to get the beer down. I didn't taste a single bit of it, which was a shame. Nothing like getting an unexpected gift to make a cold beer go down nice and easy.

"I want to talk to Chango." Might as well get it all out in the open. "About several things, but we can start with Perry."

"*El Diablo Rubio?*" Melendez paled and set the bottle down with a click. Beads of condensation on its surface glittered. The pool sent dappled reflections through the window, making a pattern-play on the roof. "Aaaaaah."

The lights flickered. The reek of cigar smoke thickened, and my hand dropped casually to a gun butt. Gilberto hunched on the stool, his eyes wide, and as much as I wanted to give him a reassuring glance, I didn't. I watched Melendez, who seemed to swell inside his chinos and blinding-white shirt.

"*El Diablo Rubio,*" I echoed softly. "*Sí. Buenas tardes, Señor Chango.*"

A long, low, grating laugh, too big to come from Melendez's chest. Smoke rose from his cuffs, eddying in swirls that opened like crying mouths. Little fingers of vapor threaded across the tiles, reaching for me. "*Buenas tardes, hija.*" It wasn't the little man's voice—it was richer, deeper, and crackling with authority. "Still owe me *una bala*, bitch."

"I haven't welshed yet," I reminded him. My bitten fingernails tapped the gun butt. "Perry, señor. I'm looking to hand *los diablos* a world of hurt, and I haven't forgotten the help you gave me last time."

The spirit riding Melendez's body rolled his shoulders back in their sockets, his rib cage oddly torqued. Tendons popped, creaking. The smoke billowed, knee-deep now, but swirling uneasily away from me and Gilberto.

It eyed me, a spark of red inside each of Melendez's dilated pupils, before his eyes rolled back in his head. Still, the spark remained, burning against the whites, a tiny blood-gem.

My right wrist ached, force humming up my arm and shaking my shoulder. I waited.

"*Una bala*," he said finally. "In *el rubio diablo's cabeza*. You kill him for us."

Well, isn't that handy. It was my turn to shrug. "That's the plan. What can you tell me about *El Rubio*'s little game?"

The bloody pinpricks rolled, fastened on Gilberto. "Why you bring him here? Little man in a big man's house. He got too much brag in him, *bruja*."

"Don't you look at him." Snap of command, I straightened, and my fingers had curled around the gun butt. "You're dealing with me, *padre, no me chingues*."

And God help me, but it reminded me of the first time I'd seen Perry down at the end of the bar in the Monde. Mikhail had said very much the same thing, and at the time I hadn't wondered why they seemed to know each other, since Perry had been new in town. The old hellbreed who used to run Santa Luz had just died a bloody, screaming death, but I hadn't seen it. I'd been locked up at Galina's during *that* whole set of events, still an apprentice, prowling and trying to escape through the greenhouse too.

Nothing ever changes, Jill. Ever.

The spirit twitched. Melendez's whole body jerked, knees bending. His boat shoes scuffed against the tiles, a sad, squeaking sound. "We lost too many, *bruja hija*. Not weak, but you on you own. I look after *mi hijo* here much as I can, and him *only*, when dat *rubio cabron* come callin'."

"Understood." And it was probably for the best, too. "What's Perry planning, señor? Tell me everything, leaving nothing out."

That was the most important question, and I didn't know how long the *loa* would ride his horse. The smoke thickened, curdling.

Melendez's body let out a long slow hiss. "*La Lanza*. Yes. He aims to use *la Lanza*, and open the door all the way."

My skin chilled, gooseflesh threatening to rise. "Open the door?"

"Between here and *there, mi hija*. Between you and them. Like they did before, *mi hija*. This time they have *la Lanza*, and it will prop door open like broomstick."

Oh, my God. There was only one thing that could possibly mean. I went cold all over, and glittering little insects with sharp tiny feet prickled me everywhere. "*Y la Lanza? Qué es eso?*"

"*La Lanza*." Another long hiss of escaping air, another frothing billow of cigar smoke. "*El rubio*, he hide it under the eyes of *los santos*, and he lie to keep you away from it and from *los padres, sus amigos* no more. *Es la Lanza del Destino*, and *los diablos* can't touch it. Only *las marionetas de carne*, the ones they bargain with."

Oh, Jesus. Jesus Christ. I hadn't realized I was gripping the counter with my right hand. Indigo tiles groaned as the gem made a low melodic sound, and I had to work my fingers free with an effort. I'd left splintered marks. "Tell me where, *señor de los parraroyos. Where* are they going to throw the party?"

But Melendez swayed. "Owe me a bullet, bitch," the spirit rumbled through his mouth, and the entire kitchen rattled. "Go serve it to *el rubio*. And if you die before you do it, I find you, and I make you *pay*."

Oh, no worries about that. "Don't threaten me." I couldn't kill a *loa*, but I could make things very uncomfortable for his followers.

If I survived this.

"*La puerta no debe abrirse, bruja*. Stop him. They send you back for this."

Really. Thanks. I would never have guessed. My mouth was so dry I had trouble forming the words. "*Gracias*, señor."

Melendez sagged against the fridge. He held the beer bottle like it was an artifact from another civilization, and I was momentarily grateful Chango hadn't been in a glass-chewing mood. You

don't get hurt doing something like that—the spirits take care of
their own—but it can be uncomfortable. Afterward.

His eyelids fluttered. Normal human eyes now, dark, their
pupils humanly round but flaring and constricting wildly. His
knees buckled, I caught him before he hit the ground, the empty
beer bottle flung away. Gilberto was off the stool, his hand flashing out and closing around the neck, neatest trick of the week, and
the Eye on his chest sent a dart of bloody light splashing against
the window.

Melendez lay in my arms like wet washing, curiously boneless
before consciousness flooded him again and he stiffened.

"Easy." I braced him, he was so *light*. A breakable doll in a
breakable world. "Easy there, señor. Everything's copacetic."

You're in shock, Jill. But I just held him until sanity flooded his
dark gaze again, conscious of the smell of his aftershave—something heavy and orange-musky, expensive Florida water. I got
him on his feet by the simple expedient of pushing myself up,
strength humming in my bones even if my knees were suspiciously mooshy. I got him propped against the counter, and I think
it was the first time I'd ever seen Melendez actually, honestly
terrified.

"Gil." I glanced through the thinning smoke. It smelled like a
bar in here. "Get us a few more beers, huh?"

"*Sí.*" My apprentice was still pale, and the Eye gleamed against
his narrow chest. His flannel shirt flapped as he straightened and
headed for the fridge.

"*Madre de Dios,*" Melendez breathed.

"No shit." I made sure he was steady enough to stand. My
brain thrashed like a rat in a cage, I took a deep breath and forced
stillness. *I need a plan, and a good one. Don't have one. So I guess
we just wing it. As usual.* "We need to talk, Melendez. I'm leaving
Gil here for a while."

CHAPTER 24

Night fell hard on Santa Luz, sinking her teeth in and shaking a little. Neon greased the dry streets, and the whole city was restless.

I walked into the Monde like I owned the place, steel-shod heels clicking and my coat swinging heavily. I hadn't stopped to clean up, so I was covered in hellhound filth, but I had borrowed a handful's worth more of charms from Anya. I tied them into my hair while sitting in the parking lot, in Gilberto's little Volkswagen.

As armor, they sucked, even though they ran with blue light the deeper I penetrated the etheric bruising laying over the nightclub. But I had my gear, and my coat, and my aura flaming with bright spikes. I had the eyeliner, now smeared and messy enough to make me look bruised under the scrim of decay. I had all the ammo I could carry.

I even had a couple grenades; they'd been packed in the trunk. Gilberto was a sneaky little boy, but right now, I wasn't going to scold him. No, I was just going to hope he was sneaky enough to stay one hop ahead of everyone.

Just like me.

The damned pressed close. All hellbreed tonight, and all beautiful. Every single one of them aware of me as I forced my way to the bar. And it was time for another shock, because in addition to the two Traders dispensing libations there was a familiar, lined face and a pair of filmed, sightless eyes. Riverson's hair was a shock of white, and he moved with jerky, mechanical quickness. Every motion looked painful.

Serves you right, motherfucker. Still, he'd tried to warn me. Too late and too little, but he'd tried.

Unless that was part of Perry's royal mindfuck, too.

Riverson went dead still as I approached, one of his hands holding a bottle of Stoli, the other cupped around a delicate fluted glass. I didn't quite turn my back on the mass of 'breed writhing on the dance floor. The damage from my earlier visit had been repaired, and the disco ball was sending little screaming jets of light all over. Whenever the lights paused, you could see they were shaped like skulls. Laughing little skulls.

Well, that's an interior decorating trend that's never going to hit the big time. At least, I hope it won't. It's so fucking tacky. I reached over, quick as a snake, and grabbed the Stoli bottle. Took a healthy slug, saluted Riverson. "Well, hello, you helltrading sonofabitch," I yelled over the noise. "How's tricks?"

His mouth worked wetly for a moment. One of his teeth had been broken, a jagged stub that must have hurt like hell. His fingers tightened on the glass. "You shouldn't be here!" he finally yelled back. "God *damn* it, Kismet, you shouldn't *be* here!"

I took another belt. As a bracer, it didn't do much. The thought of Gilberto out in the dark, deep in Riverhurst with a voodoo king who made most Traders look sweet and innocent, was better.

Still, Melendez was at least as frightened of me as he was of Perry. He'd keep Gil safe tonight and put his part of the plan in motion. More than that I couldn't ask for—and if he didn't take care of my apprentice I would come back and do more than break a few dishes.

I was *through* with fucking around.

Riverson stiffened. The glass shattered in his hand, and all expression left his face as blood welled between his clutching fingers.

I felt him arrive like a storm front, a flash of paleness and his fingers were over mine. Perry took the vodka bottle, raised it to his lips, and grinned at me, the blandness dropping for a moment. High cheekbones, bladed nose, sterile beauty shining briefly before the screen of average came back up. His bright blue gaze fastened on me, indigo threads staining his whites with an inky vein-map, and the music took on fresh frenetic urgency.

The disco ball sped up, and the assorted hellbreed leapt and gamboled. They drifted away from the bar to pack the dance floor, faces blank and beautiful, the twisting of rot underneath candygloss corruption flickering through them like wind through high wheat.

The woman, Mikhail had reminded me so often, *has advantage in bargain like this.*

And God, I was hoping it was true.

"You shouldn't be here." Perry's lips shaped the words, they sliced through the jet roar with no difficulty at all. "Not yet."

Come on, Jill. This is just like working a sharkjohn. The kind that will pay double if you perform according to his little script. The cold calculation wasn't a hunter's totting up of percentages and averages—no, this was an older feeling.

It was the mental scrabble that lights a ratlike gleam in a quarry's eyes. The *how can I make this work for me* gleam, the one my mother used to get when her boyfriends got too drunk or too loud and she started thinking about how to make their attention fasten on something else, anything else.

Even me.

My right hand flicked forward. I grabbed the bottle, slid it out of his hand, and took another hit. The glass was too warm, body-warm, and the thought that his lips had touched it sent a bolt of hot nausea through me.

I tipped the bottle further. Liquid chugged and churned. I kept swallowing, and Perry's gaze dropped. Not high enough to be watching my mouth, not low enough to be watching my chest.

He was staring at my throat as it worked, the liquor sliding down and exploding in my stomach, a brief heat lightning. The tip of Perry's cherry-red tongue poked out, for just a bare second, gleaming wet and rough-scaled.

The last of the vodka vanished down my throat. I slammed the bottle down, a gun crack that managed to cut through the music. My apprentice-ring spat a single spark, bright blue and quickly snuffed.

"*Do svidanye*," I yelled, and I grinned with all the sunny good humor I could muster. "Hello and good night!"

Perry cocked his blond head. The light ran over him, the tiny skulldapples screaming as they touched the pressed linen of his suit. He was even wearing bleached suede wingtips, for God's sake.

You're carrying this much too far. Maybe the vodka was affecting me after all. But no, I just felt cold all the way through. Making myself ice, the real me curling up inside my head and a stranger taking over.

The stranger was hard and cruel, and she had no trouble surviving. She'd shot Val in the head, and she was the one Mikhail had rescued from a snowbank that night. It was probably *her* who made me refuse to die. Certainly she'd been the one who had pulled the trigger in that circle of banefire, breaking my skull and brain open for the hornets to devour.

I might be weak, but that bitch never gave up. And I was going to need all of her to pull this off.

Okay, Jill. It's time to start the game.

Still grinning like a goddamn fool, I reached out.

And I grabbed Perry's hand.

CHAPTER 25

The room upstairs was no longer so white. Maybe I was just seeing it through a screen of vodka heat, or my own hopelessness. The carpet was softer, dove gray, and the bed was still crisp but cream instead of a bleached cloud. The mirrors all looked dimmer, not hurtfully clear and bright, but the television screens still held their familiar news feeds, static crawling from one to another in blinking, random loops and whorls.

I let go of Perry's feverish, marble-hard fingers and took perverse pleasure in stamping smeared tracks across the carpet. Vaulted the mirrored bar, my dirty hand leaving a streak on its surface, and examined the bottles. "Not much of a choice here, you know. I've always wanted to ask what's in these." *Talking too much, Jill. Bring the focus back to him.* I looked over my shoulder.

Perry shut the door, and his fingers flicked. There was the *chuk* of a lock engaging, and he stood for a moment with his pale head down. The hand I hadn't touched was in his pocket, and for a moment he almost looked human.

Almost. Except for the little ripples passing through him, as something else twitched under the surface.

I selected one bottle, full of shimmering sapphire liquid. It looked oily. I touched its slim neck, pulled it forward a little. A little more. It teetered on the edge of the glass shelf for a long heart-stopping moment, plummeted.

The crash went right through the room. Perry didn't move. Blue liquid spread out slowly, gelatinous. Steam lifted from its surface.

I selected another bottle. This one held shifting gray smoke, a screaming face in its depths becoming a picture of dismay as I tugged, sliding it exquisitely slowly across the shelf. Again, the teetering, the will-she-won't-she.

Oh, she will. She always will, but on her own terms.

It was so easy to break. I flicked a dirty, chewed-down finger-nail, the bottle plummeted, and the smoke oozed up with a small sound, like a cricket's breathless chirrup in the distance.

"Stop," Perry said mildly.

But he didn't move, so I did it again. This time I selected a tall thin bottle full of a milky white liquid that spun strangely when I scooped it up and hurled it across the room.

Before it hit the wall he was suddenly *there*, but I'd anticipated and was on the bar again, boots grinding as I landed cat-footed, and he skidded to a stop.

I didn't go for the whip.

He was on the other end of the counter, his wingtips placed just so on the glass surface, solemn-faced as he hardly ever was. That was wrong—I wanted him smiling, but still. I'd rattled him.

Good for me.

We examined each other, standing on the bar like a couple of cheesy B-movie gunfighters. The indigo was gone from his eyes. They were very blue, shadows moving in poisonous depths. "Dangerous," he said, again very quietly. "For you. Here."

Well, let's see if we can't get you interested. "I'm for sale, Pericles. Bid high."

His gaze had fastened on my throat again. "What is this, Kiss? A misguided attempt at sacrifice?" He cocked his head, his cheek twitching just slightly before it settled. "What do you remember of the last time you tried?"

All of it. The hornets buzzed and prickled, pinprick mouths chewing at my flesh. Eating my brain, scouring my skull. "Enough."

"Really." His fingers flicked, and a silver chain dropped from them, running with blue sparks. His face was set in a grimace, like he was smelling something hideous. It was in his shadowed hand, the one he'd tried to reach through the banefire circle with.

I wondered how long it had taken for the fingers to uncurl and uncramp, if it had hurt when the skin started to grow back.

The chain held a rose-carved ruby as long as my thumb. I'd used it as a key for the sunsword after Mikhail was dead and the Eye of Sekhmet stolen by his killer. The stone was cracked now, but still alive with clear crimson light. It sizzled, still vibrating with the shock of its wearer's death.

My death. I tasted vodka fumes and bitterness, the sharp metal tang of fear. If you're not afraid when dealing with hellbreed, you're not paying attention. Inattention is just *asking* to get fucked up six ways from Sunday, and all the way to breakfast too.

"For you," he said lightly. "A memento, worn next to my heart. The only thing I allowed myself to keep."

You buried me. Well, isn't that sentimental of you. For a moment we stood, sizing each other up.

"I remember enough," I repeated. "Come on, Perry. I'm sure there's other buyers. I'm a useful tool."

"How do I know you'll stay bought?" Whimsical, now. "Oh, darling Kiss. Don't play this game with me. You'll lose."

That's yesterday's news. I already lost. But we've already established I don't know when to fucking well quit. "You don't know *what* game I'm playing, Perry." It was time for a bit of truth turned sideways. That was a hell-breed specialty—just enough honesty to bait the lure. You can't deal with them, night after night, and not know it. Know it—and know how to do it yourself. "I spend my nights killing hellbreed, but there's always more and more of you. And all of them, all those oblivious fucking people I kill you to protect, they fall all over themselves making deals with you night and day. The world threatens to end and I yank it back, I break every bone in my body, I even put a bullet through my own head and you know what? Even then I'm not allowed to rest. I'm *tired*."

He dangled the necklace, ignoring the silver biting at his hand. Sparks popped. "As are we all. The point?"

Shit. "You're not interested. Fine." I hopped off the counter.

Or at least, that's what I had planned. He hit me in midair and we slammed into the wall near the door with a rattling crunch. The gem hummed on my wrist, sleepy under the weight of honeyed etheric corruption.

Perry inhaled, his nose buried in my throat, his hands clamped around my wrists. He only had an inch or so on me, if I dropped my knee and brought the other one up I could nail him pretty hard, or I could kick and take out *his* knee and wrench myself sideways, breaking free, my hand slapping on a gun butt.

But I didn't. I just hung there, silver pressed against my right hand dangerously warm, responding to hellbreed contamination. The ruby dangled, scorch-bright, and my breath came in shallow rasps. Heat rolled off him, a terrible cold fire, and even if the thing inhabiting his skin wasn't human it felt like he had a pretty respectable hardon. Shoved right up against me.

Oh, we've been here before. At least he's interested, right? Good sign, wouldn't you say?

I told that rabbit-jumping part of me to shut the fuck up and struggled to control my pulse. My heart settled into a high, hard thumping, ready for fight or flight, adrenaline touching the back of my tongue with a copper finger.

"I didn't say I had no interest," Perry breathed against my throat, obscenely warm and wet. Condensation gathered on my skin, and every inch of flesh on me crawled. "I didn't say that at *all*. Please, continue."

Sure instinct ignited in my head. *Now* I could bite back. I gave him a love tap to the knee and shoved him, and he stumbled away. I punched him, too, a good hard crack that snapped his face aside, and I finished with a ringing open-handed slap on the other cheek. Just like I hadn't taken the next step to turn this into more of a fight, now he did not. He simply stepped back another foot or so, making a quick sideways motion to resettle his jaw. Then he dropped his chin and looked at me.

The dirt on me had smeared on his linen, too, but the grin was back. It was wider than ever, his patented old I-could-buy-this-if-I-cared-to expression, its sheer amoral good will capable of sending a shudder up even a hunter's spine.

I met it with my own fey careless grimace, defiance and terror
gasfumes just looking for a spark. My pulse settled down, dropping into the high-spaced gallop of impending action, and I knew
he could hear it. The music thudded away underneath us, but neither of us paid any attention. I straightened, shook my right hand
out once, fingers loose and easy. The gem had gone quiescent, but
etheric force hummed through my bones.

"Don't fuck with me," I said tonelessly. "I'm *this* close to walking out, Perry, and you'll never see me again. I'll retire to fucking
Bermuda while you're still here thumbing your ass and playing
little hopscotch games with whatever hunter comes along to
replace me."

He took this in. Swung the ruby in a tight, tense little circle. It
sparked, once, a bloody point of light. "What am I buying, my
lovely? I seem to remember being cheated once before."

"*You* welshed. Not me." It was out before I could stop myself,
but his grin widened. He spun the ruby, the chain making little
groaning noises as it whirred, faster and faster. "Don't you ever
want to find out what would happen if I was willing? Or are you
one of those stupid bastards who just likes the chase?"

A little moue now, the flush on his cheek where I'd hit him
dying down and leaving him pale and perfect again. "It *has* been a
long chase. And full of such tender moments. I find your homicidal little displays charming, darling, and you know how much
I...*love*...you." The snarl drifting over his face sent a ripple
through the entire room. Behind him, television screens fuzzed
with static.

Oh, good Christ, if this is love, I don't want to see hate. "It's not
love." I folded my arms and raised my chin. The air tightened, and
I knew this dance. If he jumped me again we were going to have a
hell of a tango. It wouldn't stop until one or both of us were bleeding, and once I started beating on him, I wasn't sure I would stop.

Or vice versa.

So I pulled out my last card and threw it on the table. "You're
the only one who understands, Pericles." Soft, as if the admission
was pulled out by force. "A fucking hell-breed, and you're the
only one. You *know* me."

And like all good lies, it was true. I hadn't gone on mortgaging bits of myself for the glory of it. Sometimes I hadn't even for the speed and strength a hellbreed scar could give me.

No, sometimes—*plenty* of times—I'd done this just to see if I could. To walk right up to the edge, to prove I was different from him, to make him respond. To get out the razor and make the mark, and laugh at the sting.

There was no way he could play with me so effectively, otherwise.

Idiots, Mikhail sneered in my memory. *They think we do this for them. Is only one reason to do*, milaya. *It is for to quiet screaming in our own head.*

Every time I walked away from Perry breathing, it was like walking away from a car wreck, leaving an old life behind and striking out for parts unknown. Like being pulled out of a snowbank by a pair of hard callused hands and told *Not tonight, little one.*

Maybe it took shooting myself in the head before I could admit I *liked* having the power to play with him, too.

God help me. But there was no help for this. I was on my own. Like always.

Perry stared. The tip of his wet, red tongue slid out again, touched the corner of his bloodless lips. His eyes glowed, twin blue infernos casting shadows down his cheeks, and the air behind him ruffled into two points of disturbance high over his shoulders. The reek of spoiled honey trembled around us both. A buzz of chrome flies in chlorinated bottles mounted, matching the wasps' singing as their little mouths and feet prickled all over me. The cracked ruby swung, its circles shrinking as his slim hard fingers curled.

He's not going to bite. "Fine." I took two steps toward the door, sliding along the wall. "See you."

"You actually surprised me." His fingers flicked, the necklace vanishing into his palm. Now the dark threads were in his eyes, spreading from his irises, eating the whites. "I thought you would love life too much, like all those other insects." His fist tightened, a narrow artist's hand clutching at a coin for a magic trick. Shadows slid over the skin like clouds reflected in a glass of milk, and blue sparks struggled between his clenched fingers. "But not you, my Kiss. No. You were already dead, so pulling that trigger was no trouble at all." Quietly now, the softest and most seductive of all his voices. "You've been dead a long time."

There was no way I could argue. I was dead long before Mikhail plucked me from that snowbank. I'd been born dead, and fighting it didn't make much difference. The whole thing was pointless, except for Saul.

Oh, God. I couldn't think about him right now. At least he was safe.

Perry took a soft, gliding step closer, infinitely slow. "They suspect you, don't they. Your fellow hunter, your Sanctuary, the beasts you call your friends. You can feel the suspicion breathing on your back, and it *twists* in you, doesn't it. Knife in the wound." Another step.

It wasn't true. It *wasn't.*

But I was shaking. Because Anya had checked to see if I was bleeding clean. Theron hadn't been suspicious at all, Weres weren't like that. If I'd still been tainted somehow, if I hadn't had the strength to pull the trigger, it would have fallen to Anya to hunt me. To keep me from doing any more goddamn harm.

It wasn't true.

So why was I trembling? In great waves, weapons shifting and leather creaking a little as they slid through me. The closer he got, the more I shook.

It was because I knew that tone, the soft reasonableness. He was about to slide the knife in, and I had to stand there and let him do it.

"Or maybe it's that you suspect yourself," Perry murmured. "You always have, Kiss. You push yourself so hard, because down at the very bottom, *you* understand *me.* We're twins, my darling, and I waited so, so long for you." A soft sigh, and he was so close now the exhalation touched my hair, too warm and too damp. "We are the ones crying outside their circle of light. We are the ones they cast away. We are the sufferers, and on our backs they build golden cities." His fingers were on my shoulders, very gently, and he eased me forward.

It's not true, I reminded myself. *Perry never suffered a day in his hellborn life. Never.*

"Do you remember your visits to me?" he whispered into my hair.

Another shudder went through my bones, this one violent, and his heavy, marble-hard arms closed around me, cold water dragging at a swimmer's boots.

Of course I remembered.

Most often, he would have me strap him into the iron rack in the other room, and the rosewood case with the blades was always on the little gurney. He would order me to start cutting, and he wouldn't make a sound as the bright metal parted his flesh and made hellbreed ichor run in thin black stinking streams.

"Do you remember what I said, each time you stopped?"

More, he would whisper, or let out with a breath like a sob. *More*. The shaking had me all over now. Great, clear drops of sweat cut through the filth on me, one of them tracing down my cheek like a tear, another fingering the shallow channel of my spine.

"If I atoned enough, my darling Kiss, do you think I would one day bleed as red as your oblivious ones? I've tried. You've *seen* me try."

Oh, God. The water was closing over my head. He sounded so reasonable, and I was exhausted. There was no way this was going to work.

"You're hellbreed," I whispered, but it was the last gasp of a drowning woman.

"Even a hellbreed can dream." So softly, into my hair, a spot of condensation on my scalp. When he stepped backward I didn't resist, I came with him. He walked me across the room, and he loosened the coat from my shoulders. It fell away like a heavy skin, and he unbuckled the weapons-harness and let that fall, too. The ammo belt lay on the floor like a snake, and the bed was cloud-soft. I sank into it like I was falling through heavy water, and the mattress didn't creak as it accepted his weight next to mine.

You can do this. It's Judas to a hellbreed, you can do this.

But I was horribly naked, and on a bed with him. The worst part was that it felt...familiar.

Not safe. And not comfortable, even though the bed was soft

and I was filthy and hungry and so tired. And most definitely not like lying next to Saul—

I stiffened, shut that thought away.

The hellbreed made a small, soothing noise. He held me, arms like flexible stone, his chin atop my head. "Rest," he said, very softly. "Just rest, Kiss. You're so very tired. Sleep."

The music coming through the floor was a heartbeat, and we floated in the bed. He even stroked my dirty hair, so gently, despite the silver that hissed and crackled at his nearness.

"Or if you can't sleep," he murmured, "simply close your eyes, and I will do the rest."

And I did. We lay there, hunter and hellbreed, and he made soothing little noises while I sobbed.

CHAPTER 26

There was a shower in the white-tiled room I'd often cut Perry up in, and my skin crawled at using it. But the water was hot, the towels were fluffy, and I kept an eye on my coat and my weapons the whole time. I probably didn't have to, because the hellbreed was playing house with a vengeance, humming to himself while he brought the towels in, arranging them just so. He brought me a stack of black silk T-shirts—medium, V-neck, three-quarter sleeve, just what I liked to wear in cotton. And leather pants, too, and I had to shudder when they crawled up my hips. They fit like they'd been made for me, and wasn't that thought-provoking?

He even watched me get dressed, but that wasn't a huge deal. Dating a Were will give you a whole new definition of nakedness, and I've been tied down naked to an altar and almost-sacrificed. Skin doesn't bother me.

But the way he licked his lips with that rough cherry-red tongue was disconcerting. And even more disconcerting was shrugging into my coat and finding it clean. It also reeked of candyspiced wickedness, just like the whole Monde. My hands roamed, finding

the pockets full of ammo, everything as it should be, my whip at
my side and my guns heavy at my hips and everything right with
the world.

When I turned around again, blinking under the sallow glare
of fluorescents, Perry was holding something. A flat case, rosewood, balanced on his palms. "For you."

Another present? My stomach turned over, hard. The case was
just the right size for one of those shiny knives, the kind that
weren't silver because they didn't react to him. Light and razor
sharp, with hatching on the handles for a better grip.

They were so *cold.*

I froze. The iron rack was set off to one side against the wall,
but if he sauntered over to it and ordered me to strap him in...

He actually rolled his eyes. Back in the linen, immaculate, but
even his tie was raw pale silk now. Those shoes of bleached suede
were creamy against the white tile. "It's not going to *bite* you, darling. That's past."

Oh, is it? It would be idiotic to relax now. So I just stood and
looked at him until he made a small amused sound and passed one
hard, narrow hand over the top of the box. There was a click, and
the lid opened like a flower.

There, on rich red velvet, were the charms. Honest silver, each
one running with blue light in the choked atmosphere, and a spool
of red silk thread to tie them with. Nine of them, twisted shapes,
fluid and somehow-wrong, creatures that walked under no earthly
sun, clawed and furred and winged, vibrating against the velvet.

The silence from downstairs was deafening. Was it the middle
of the day? My internal clock was all wonky, and I hadn't slept. Or
had I? I'd drifted in and out, rocked in Perry's arms. The familiar-
ity bothered me.

Well, I had so much else bothering me at this point, it was
pretty academic, wasn't it?

"A hellbreed giving me silver." I addressed the air over his
head. "Now I *have* seen everything."

"Not quite." Did the bland smile falter slightly? It came back as
soon as it slipped. "Do you like them?"

On the one hand, all the silver I could get my hands on was a good idea. On the other, I wouldn't put it past Perry to make them start crawling over my scalp, digging in with their sharp little pin-prick feet.

"They're gorgeous." And they were, in the twisted way the damned are beautiful. I swallowed. "Thank you."

Did he actually look *pleased*? "Well." A slight cough. "I thought, perhaps..."

I braced myself, hands loose and ready.

"*Will* you relax?" he snapped, before taking back that honey-and-butter tone he liked so much. "My dearest one, you are here of your own will. As my *guest*, and my own darling, lovely, oh-so-unbending Kiss. Furthermore, you are a very particular piece of a very particular plan, and I will be *very* vexed should you come to any harm."

"You wanted to kill me the other night." I probably shouldn't have reminded him.

The snarl drifted its way across his face like a thunderstorm coming down from the mountains. "I don't like it when you con-sort with beasts."

I've heard that before. I watched, fascinated, while his skin rippled a little. As if tiny little insects were running underneath the poreless, elastic stoniness.

It drained away, the indigo threads vanishing from his whites. "After all, jealousy is a besetting sin, isn't it. Such a lovely sin, either soft or hard, such an *instructive* tool." Quiet, reflective, he tilted the case. "If you don't like them..."

"I do." I even sounded like I did. "Perry—"

I don't know what I was going to say. But he interrupted me.

"Good." He offered the case. "I would tie them in your lovely hair, my dearest, but, well. *Silver.* Soon that will cease to matter."

I avoided touching him, but I took the flat length of wood. It was surprisingly heavy. His hands dropped to his sides, and I studied the charms. Bile rose briefly in my throat, *Why would sil-ver not matter? Because you're going to do what no hellbreed ever has, and if you pull it off, well, you're right, it won't matter.* "And why is that?"

"It's a surprise." He pressed his hands together, a parody of praying—but then he bowed slightly, and his lips pursed in that bland face. Like he wanted to say more, like he held a secret too delightful to contain.

Cold sweat broke out all over me. The box tipped, I righted it, and he backed up two silent steps.

"Tie your shinies on, my darling, and come downstairs. We have guests, and it doesn't do to keep guests waiting."

"Soul of politeness," I muttered, and the hellbreed *laughed*. A deep, rich chuckle, like he was having a fantastic time. He headed for the door, while I stood there like an idiot. The blue glow running under the surface of the silver submerged, thin threads of it remaining like healing sorcery, reacting to etheric contamination.

Halfway there, he stopped. He did not *quite* glance over his shoulder, but he did turn his head, and the three-quarters profile was chillingly beautiful, some trick of fluorescent light and passing shade.

"You recall Belisa, of course." Level and dead serious. "Always treacherous. Which is a woman's own sort of constancy, isn't it? And it earned her a bullet to the head. After she'd been so *useful*, too."

The sweat turned to ice. I opened my mouth, but nothing came out, and the hum of the fluorescents dug at my skull.

Perry's profile turned to a grinning satyr's mask. His shoulders moved briefly as he settled himself further inside his human shell. "And cover up that *thing* on your wrist, darling. It's distracting."

He swept the door shut, still grinning, and I found out I was shaking again. The charms rolled on the velvet and chimed together, sweetly musical. The red thread fell and hit like a blood clot on the white, white floor.

III: Libera Me

CHAPTER 27

The worst part wasn't going down the stairs with the charms tied in my hair. It wasn't even opening the door and stepping out into the vast daytime cavern of the Monde, tiny golden shafts of sunlight struggling through the dust and thickening. It also wasn't the sight of Riverson flung backward over the bar, his mouth slack in an upside-down scream and his hand still dripping blood. His filmed eyes were closed forever, and the terror frozen on his dead face was enough to give any reasonable person nightmares.

I barely glanced, storing it away for later, because the worst thing was the ripple that went through the assembled hellbreed packed into the Monde's throat. They filled the dance floor, brushing against the bar and its bloody cargo. The Traders at the door were grotesque slabs of muscle with submachine guns and slack mouths. There were no other Traders; it was strictly a 'breed affair.

Hellbreed lips parted, the female mouths candyglossed and the males' merely sculpted, and they smiled at me like a collection of dotty old aunts beaming at a favored family baby.

"There she is." Perry stood on the stage, his hands in his pockets. It spoiled the lines of his suit, but he didn't look like he cared. Since he was grinning ear to ear. "Our lovely one, our own Kiss."

Oh, great. Every inch of silver on me ran with blue light, and the gem on my wrist muttered softly, buzzing in my bones. The hellbreed smiles didn't cease, and under their hard, flexible skins little ripples churned. Their eyes burned, glowing with excitement.

I swept the door closed. The sound of it catching shut was loud in the sudden murmuring stillness. The crowd was utterly still. *Here during the day. Perry must have called a meeting. Why? So he can impress me?*

Only one of them didn't look happy. He was a tall stocky 'breed with glare-yellow eyes, his skin dappled with inky stains. Frayed designer jeans, sharp bony claws, and the handsome face of a pimp who can afford to slide the knife in once a wrinkle or two shows up on a working girl's face. He stared at me, his lip lifting, but before he could open his mouth there was a low, rumbling growl.

The dogsbody lumbered out of the darkness behind the bar, slinking along. It had matured, and its close blond pelt was wiry and glossy. Its eyes were crystalline, flicking over the assembled 'breed as it placed its paws just so. There was something wrong with those eyes, but I couldn't think of just what.

The gun drew itself free, my finger on the trigger and my pulse dropping into the steady rhythm of impending action. It would be just *like* Perry to have a dog attack me in full view of his little throng.

But there was a whisper next to me, and Perry's fevered fingers on my wrist. "Hush, darling one. Wait."

I could still feel the thing's throat against my whip as I choked it, my coat was still flapping from its claws, and he wanted me to *wait*?

The dogsbody padded forward, its claws snicking softly on the floor. Perry's hand tightened. It was too close, if it bunched its hindquarters and sprang...

It was terrible, the way you could still see the shadow of human hands under its paws, and a weird roll to its humpbacked gait showed you it had been bipedal once. Its head dropped, snaking at the end of its adapted neck, and it slowed. It was close enough to spring, and I didn't want to die here in the Monde. It would mean breaking Perry's arm, or worse, but—

The dogsbody gave a sigh, settling down on its haunches. It

lowered its front end, and it crawled belly-down on the floor, whining, until it reached my feet. Its tongue was black, too, and it lapped at my boots, still stained with hellhound ichor. The slimy trails it left behind glistened, and revulsion jolted up my legs to engulf the rest of me.

A huge retch filled my stomach, crawled up my throat. I swallowed so hard the effort left me blinking. A sigh went through the hellbreed, and a mutter of Helletöng like faraway thunder in the middle of a flint-cold night.

"See?" Perry, slowly releasing me, one finger at a time. "We're *all* at your feet, my darling." More loudly now, playing to the audience. "Do any of you worms doubt me? She's hunter, she's human, and she's *mine*, here of her own will. With her to wield it—"

"It's a long way from owning one of the monkeys to coaxing it to wield *that*," the piebald hellbreed piped up. "And she stinks of the Other Side. What are you playing at, Hyperion?"

Perry turned, and there was a general drawing away. The 'breed were packed in here like sardines in a can, but they managed to find the space to leave the piebald standing alone.

Dominance, I realized. *This kid's looking to take a bite out of Perry. Interesting.*

What was even more interesting was that he was a 'breed I hadn't seen before. I knew all the players—or at least, I had a couple months ago.

"Oh, the *Other Side*." Sarcasm dripped from Perry's words, and the floor groaned sharply. "When have they ever taken an interest? Fear of them restrains us, is that it? I am no longer content to be restrained."

"Your lord father—" Piebald hesitated, because the Monde had gone still, and hot air breathed along every surface.

Father? Oh, my God, you mean someone actually gave birth to that? Hellbreed reproduction is not my area of expertise—I just kill the motherfuckers—but I supposed it was possible. And the thought made my stomach turn over again, harder this time.

"Oh, yes, my dear Halis. Let's mention *him*. Really, you're a bad guest." Perry's smile was wide and utterly chilling. He bore down on the piebald, hands still in his pockets, his shoulders square. The dogsbody had finished licking my boots and whined, deep in its throat. The sound was a glassy squeal, diamond claws on a mirror.

The Other Side. Wield it. Betcha ten bucks he means la Lanza, *according to Melendez, and I have to find out where he's keeping it.* I couldn't look everywhere at once, and I didn't want to. I watched Perry's linen-clad back, and when the dogsbody hunched itself up to crouch against my leg I almost retched again.

The piebald 'breed seemed to shrink, hunching his shoulders as sallowness rose on his pale parts. Even his hair was patchwork. "Don't be hasty." He swallowed, visibly. "I know where it is, I'm the one who can get it for you—"

"Oh, but I think we'll do quite well without you." Perry's sheer goodwill was terrifying. I still had the gun in my hand, loosely pointed at the floor. "*I* know where the Lance was, too, and even now I know where it *is*. Because it happens to be in my keeping, along with my darling Kiss."

Stop him. Judas to a hellbreed. The caretaker's eyes, bright blue now, and the dogsbody's teeth at my throat. He'd been stroking the thing's head, scratching behind its ears. Its eyes had been blue, Jughead Vanner's eyes with hellfire dripping through them, but now they were colorless crystals.

Just like the gem in my wrist.

"Really, Halis. Did you think to challenge me? Here? *Now?*" Perry made a little clicking sound, tongue against teeth, and stepped mincingly past the piebald 'breed. "Kiss?"

It took two tries before my voice would work, because I knew what was coming. "What?" At least the word came out right, bored and flat.

But whatever it was Perry wanted, Halis decided it was better off unsaid. He was deadly silent about it too, blinking through space with the stuttering speed of a hellbreed who means business. I was already tracking him with my right-hand gun, whip loosened and chiming as it flicked forward, one hip cocked and ready to swing back.

CHAPTER 28

I didn't even see the dogsbody move. One moment it was right next to me. The next, it hit the flying 'breed with a boneshatter crunch, and several 'breed shrank back as ichor splattered. The dogsbody's jaw crackled, and it made a sound like a hyena late at night.

I ignored a cramp of nausea, backed up a few more steps to get some room in case the piebald threw off the dog-thing and came for me.

I shouldn't have worried. Because a dogsbody, like a hellhound or a *rongeurdo*, knows its work. The crunching of teeth settled into wet chewing slurps as it settled down to its feast, crouching, only the gleam of one colorless gemlike eye as it watched me. One flat ear was pricked, too, standing alert.

Like a good dog with a bone, waiting for his master's call.

Oh, Jesus. The world paled, came back in a rush of color. I actually staggered back, regained my footing, and gave myself a sharp mental slap. Looking weak in the middle of a crowd of 'breed is not a good way to go.

"How nice," Perry murmured. "Our Kiss has a pet. Well, would anyone *else* like to dispute our little plan? No? Good. Then you are all excused to work my will."

They didn't move. Some of them stared at me, avid, mouths slightly open and eyes burning. Another ripple ran through them, titters and half-heard whispers.

"Oh, yes. That reminds me." Perry half-turned, looked at the stage. "I want that Were's head. If the other beasts will not give him up, move into the barrio." His grin turned wide and white, his tongue flickering once. "Kill them too."

"It'll be difficult." This from a tall female, so skinny the alien bones rubbed against the inside of her parchment skin. "That's their ground, they know it better than we—"

"Nevertheless." Perry waved a hand. "Children, children, you are Hell's scions. I trust you'll find a way."

I found my voice. "Perry—"

"You may leave us now," he said quietly, and Helletöng filled the spaces between the words with misshapen drowning things bubbling in a cold vault. The hellbreed moved for the exits in a wave of seashell hips and painted eyes, chitterings and moanings and sighs behind them.

"Perry." *I am still a hunter. And this is my town.* "Leave the Weres alone."

"If they would hand over the one that shared your bed, my dearest, I would. But no, they're intransigent."

I almost choked. "What do you—"

"I had him once before, and I would have kept him after you were mine. Now I don't need him, so I won't keep him, but I want him for just a few moments, Kiss. Can't you guess why?"

"So you can take lessons on how to be a decent human being?" I probably shouldn't have said it. Judas to a hell-breed, sure, but he wasn't going to touch my Weres.

Especially Saul.

The hellbreed were slipping away, and I still had my gun out.

But Perry had simply hopped up on the stage. 'Töng grumbled and swirled through the sun-pierced dimness, and all the hell-breed were scurrying to their cars under the assault of the cleansing light of day. "Too late now."

Salvage this, Jill. Assert some control. "Perry. Go after the Weres, and the deal's off."

"You should have said that earlier." He spread his arms, a paleness against the dark cavern of the stage. "All they have to do is hand over your kitten, my dove. Wouldn't it be nice to see him again? They move him from place to place, but sooner or later they'll see reason."

"Fine." I turned, and the dogsbody lifted its snuffling head from its snack. The piebald 'breed was rotting quickly, and my gorge rose again. The smell was something else, and to have your nose buried in it... "You send 'breed into the barrio, Perry, and you'll never see them ag—"

"Do you honestly think you can threaten me now?" He had my

arm, suddenly, fingers biting in, and the dogsbody growled. "And you'd better leash that thing, before you lose it. There is a *limit* to what I allow you, Kismet."

I hit him hard, a good solid crack to the face. His chin snapped back and the gun was level, pointed into his chest. The whip jingled a little, and the dogsbody growled again.

"Shut up," I said, and the thing that used to be Jughead Vanner did.

The silence was immense. The hellbreed had drained away, and the dripping from Riverson's outflung hand had stopped. *Why kill Riverson? This isn't like you, Perry.*

None of this made sense. Had I just made a huge mistake, or was I doing what I was supposed to? Had I thrown away any advantage over Perry by letting him think I was here willingly? Did any of this fucking *matter*?

Of course it matters. Melendez's loa wants the debt repaid, but I can't do that until I know where and when Perry's planning his party.

"Sweet nothings," Perry hissed. He wiped at his mouth with the back of one narrow hand. "Oh, I've *missed* you."

"You won't miss me if you declare open season on Weres. I'll be right up close, once I finish with the hellbreed you send into the barrio." The shaking had me again, but the gun was solid. *Fuck this, fuck everything. I'll kill them, then I'll take Saul and—*

And what? Ride off into the sunset while Chango got a hard-on for me and Anya braced herself for the next wave of hellbreed to come in? Because there were always more.

Or even, here's a thought, what if Perry had a little plan for Anya too? Or if something fatal happened to her? Hunters were tough, but also as mortal as everyone else.

And what would happen to my city, all the oblivious who liked signing deals with hellbreed and the others who had no idea they even existed? What *then*?

Stop, little snake, Mikhail whispered inside my memory. *Anger is no good. It makes things distort, yes? It makes you stupid.*

Hearing him used to be a comfort. Now it had teeth. I'd signed myself up for the scar because Misha had said it was a good idea.

He hadn't told me he needed someone to take his place in the deal with Perry. Would he ever have told me? Couldn't he find the fucking words?

I would have done it anyway, for him. If he just would have *asked*. Add that to the list of my sins.

I swallowed. *Be clear and cold for this, Jill. You have to be.* "Besides, what does it matter? I left him, Perry. I'm here."

"Here, yes. Now." His mouth was flushed, a bruised scarlet line. "But I want you *more* than here, Kismet. I will take everything you love, everything that has ever loved you, and I will break it until there is only me. *Only* me."

Oh, for fuck's sake. Great. He's gone insane. "Well, that's a great Christmas list, Perry. Too bad it's summer. Why don't you tell me about the Lance instead?"

It wasn't very elegant, but at least it got his attention. He was still for a full ten seconds, Helletöng groaning and rumbling under the surface of the visible, and I knew I had his complete attention.

"Oh, that." He waved a hand. "It's not important. Yet."

"If you're wanting me to do something with it, it is." The gun was level, but he seemed to take no notice of it. My fingers tightened on the whip's handle.

"Oh, Kiss. Never bored while you're near me." The grin was back, and wider than ever. "You may go now, my lovely. Tell your friends I am coming for them. And tell whoever sank that stinking thing in your arm that they are welcome to try and stop me." He spread his arms. "It is *my* time, now."

I backed up a step. Two. My heart beat thinly in my chest, echoing in my wrists and temples. "You seriously want me to leave?"

"Take your dog. That's a nice trick, too, I'll ask how you did it sometime. Later, when I'm not so busy." He watched me as I took another step. "Yes, I want you to go. It's Wednesday now. Come back tomorrow, we'll dance and dine. The world will end, and you will help me end it."

Fuck it all. I can't do it. "I should kill you now." My finger tightened on the trigger. I knew exactly how much pull would send a bullet through him.

But one bullet wouldn't do it. I'd have to start shooting, then I'd have to hack him in pieces, and call the banefire. And hope to hell it put him down.

Don't. You can't kill him yet, there's something even worse waiting in the wings. Play along, Jill. "I should," I repeated. "I should ventilate you right fucking now."

His grin turned savage, and the shadow of handsomeness was back, burning away the screen of blandness. "Likewise, I'm sure. But my primrose path, my darling, you can't afford to. You don't know nearly enough about what I want, or how I'm going to get it. So run along and ask some questions, and meet me tomorrow. About dusk, I should think."

This is not going well at all. "Perry—"

A thin tremor passed through him. A draft of spoiled honey brushed along the tense air between us. "For the love of your pale little God, my darling, go. I find myself growing murderous." Perry headed for the second door, the one leading to the red-neon hall. He left a scar behind him, viscous darkness peaking and eddying. The Monde grumbled, settling lower into itself, like an animal in a dark cave.

You've only got one more, Jill. Make it good. "Why Riverson? Perry, why Riverson?"

He snarled, a deep throbbing noise. "Go. Away."

"Why Riverson?" I yelled. "God *damn* you, answer me!"

"Because he robbed me of you!" Perry screamed, and the whole place shook. Dust pattered from the ceiling. His head dropped forward and his shoulders heaved, linen stretching and rippling as it fought to contain him.

For a second I was sure he was going to turn around and leap on me, and that would have made it all right to kill him according to the abacus inside my head. The *conscience.* The thing that kept poking me no matter which way I turned, the stranger who had made me a hunter in the first place. And then I would go tell Melendez that Chango should be satisfied, collect Gil, and go find Henderson Hill's caretaker, with his blue eyes and his vanishing scars.

And I would get some answers. All the answers he would give me willingly, and any others I felt like beating out of him.

"He robbed me of you," Perry said again, but very softly, like a killing frost creeping down from the desert. "There is my first warning, Kiss. All your friends. *All*. Even those who are not quite your friends. Everyone you have cast your eye upon, they are marked for death. You will have only me." His tone dropped, confidential and musing. "And I will have everything."

He stood there for another moment, while everything around him shook, spiderlines of reaction etching themselves on the Monde's floor—concrete covered in hardwood, the dance floor something else entirely, glimmering black.

I waited, hoping. And I was right. Perry had to throw one more bone in the pot to make it boil.

It was a good one, too. "And when you see my brother Michael, ask *him* about your resurrection. Ask *him* about the game you're so blindly stumbling through."

Call me Mike. The hornets buzzed, speaking to me with their pinprick feet, a tattoo of warning.

I got out of there. The dogsbody padded after me, and the sunlight didn't smoke on its wiry blond hide.

"Oh, thank *God*," Galina breathed. "He's gone mad, Jill. I can barely—"

"Shut it." It was rude, but I was beyond caring. "Where's Devi?"

Sound of movement. "Here," Anya Devi said, carefully. "Jill?"

"Perry's got something big planned for tomorrow night." I braced my hand against the phone booth's scratched, clear plastic. Sarvedo Street was deserted even this far up, and the sunlight was too thin. I kept seeing odd shadows, my blue eye hot and dry.

"Hutch is running on coffee and nerves. He says he's found an old etching or something, prior to any knowns. Saul's tearing up whatever room Galina locks him in—"

"Devi." My throat was dry. "Tell Hutch to drop everything. Instead, get him on the horn and call every hunter we know of. *Everyone*, do you hear me? Every single one of us. This thing Perry's planning has something to do with a portal to Hell, possibly *huge*, and have him crosscheck with a 'breed called Halis, spelling unknown. And something else. *La Lanza de Destino*, Spear of Destino. Lance of Destiny. Whatever."

"There's so many—" she began. She was about to say there were plenty of things masquerading as Spears of Destiny, and some of them were even Talismans. Every long piece of wood around in the Middle Ages with some etheric force in it was a goddamn "Spear of Destiny," it was a needle in a historical haystack.

"I know there's a million of them knocking around, but have him dig. And there's..." I almost choked. How could I even begin to explain? "Never mind. Get everyone we can for tomorrow before dusk."

She swore, but under her breath. "What else?"

Of course, you knew there had to be more. "The hellbreed are moving to take the barrio. Get everyone under cover. The Weres on Mayfair, too."

She cursed again. "Of course. Perry's been trying to get his hands on Saul for months, and now that you're back... Jill, what *is* it with you and that hellbreed? Mikhail had a deal with him and you took it over, sure, but he never played for Mikhail this way—"

"I don't know." The words stung my chapped lips as they slid free, and I didn't sound truthful even to myself. *Oh, you know all right. It's because deep down, you're the same thing. Twins. You proved it yourself, didn't you?* "Did the Badger come up with anything?"

"Vanner's cars? Let's see. A red Dodge pickup, two motorcycles—he was a Honda dude, fucking poser—a blue Buick four-door, a—"

"Blue Buick. Four-door. License plate?"

She reeled off a string of numbers and letters.

It matched up. One more question, then, to keep me warm. "When did he get rid of it?"

"A couple months before you disappeared. You need the date and the buyer?"

"No." I shut my eyes briefly, leaning against the phone booth's shell. My memory was cruel now, showing connections in a pitiless white glare, like the sun beating down or the wide white carpet in Perry's bedroom. "Jesus," I whispered. That tied up *that* loose end. Vanner hadn't been nervous around me all the time because he had a habit of walking in on the weird.

He'd been nervous because he'd tried to kill me once, during the case that lost me one of my cops and almost, *almost* turned my city into a wasteland. Only the 'breed pulling the strings hadn't warned him to use silverjacket ammo on a helltainted hunter. And doubly nervous afterward because he hadn't killed me, and he was in deep to that same hellbreed. I hadn't smelled any corruption on him, but it wasn't out of the question. Most likely he'd been full human and angling for a Trade...

...and that was a question mark, too, wasn't it? Perry's enemies were likely dead by now, if his treatment of Halis was any indication. Shen An Dua—the 'breed who I would've pointed the finger at—was dead, and so were Rutger and that pajama-masked psycho who'd been trying to kill me last time. There was nobody left to send a poisonous hellhound after one crooked cop.

Except Perry. Who would have wanted me down but not out, since my agreement with him kept him at the top of the hellbreed food chain in Santa Luz. He very well might not have warned a stupid human slave to use silver-jacket. And Perry could *always* use a pair of eyes on the police force, couldn't he.

Or maybe Vanner had just been a crooked cop, tried to kill me, found out he couldn't, and went looking for something on the nightside that would keep him safe in the event that I kept digging and found out who'd been driving that blue Buick. Especially since Harvill, the DA who had been the prime node of corruption on that case, had ended up dead, too. Just how Vanner connected to Harvill I didn't know, but someone could probably tell me if I cared to find out. Now that I knew where to look.

I glanced out into the street, where the dogsbody padded back and forth, sunlight drenching its blond hide, its colorless jewel-eyes glittering. I tasted bile, and the gem on my wrist twinged sharply.

Why was a hellhound chasing him? Unless Perry wanted him back. Or maybe...

Devi's tone crackled with thinly controlled impatience. "Jill? Throw me a bone here. Give me something, anything, come on."

I'm having hallucinations about Henderson Hill's blue-eyed caretaker. Only they're not hallucinations, because he bought me

breakfast and gave me a gun. "If I could, I would. Just get everyone you can, Devi, and watch your ass. Put Saul on the line."

"I'm not your fucking secretary." But she laid the phone down,
and I heard Galina's murmured questions, Devi's sharp reply.
"She wants to talk to him. If it'll stop him doing this crazy shit,
I'm all for it." Bootheels coming down hard as Devi stamped
away. "*Hutch!* Get your skinny ass up here!"

I waited, breathing deep. Fed another eight quarters into the
phone. Devi had probably tucked a phone card into my coat, but it
didn't matter. The coins dropped in, pieces of silver to pay the
ferryman.

Cells are expensive and finicky, and the more advanced they
get the more sorcery messes them up; once pay phones were a
thing of the past I was going to have to figure something else out.
Right now, breaking and entering to use someone's phone sounded
like the most satisfying option. As well as the most educational
and entertaining.

Always assuming I survived long enough.

Static burst over the phone line. Then a listening silence. I
could hear him breathing, deep even swells, a sound of effort temporarily checked.

"Saul?" I always sounded breathy and silly over the phone
with him. "Saul, please. You've got to calm down."

"Where. Are. You?" The words vibrated over the lines and
carried all the fury in the world into my ear, and gooseflesh spilled
down my back.

"Galina's going to keep you there, Saul. I can't afford to lose
you."

"I *told* you—" he began, and it wasn't like every other fight
we'd ever had. Usually I was the one losing my shit while he tried
to stay rational. This time it was him losing his shit, and if he lost
it enough, it wasn't going to be easy to slow him down.

I had to get it all out at once, before he got his head up. "Saul.
Perry will kill you. If he does, I'm damned and he will have no
trouble getting me to do anything he wants. You are the only goddamn thing that matters to me, all right? The *only* thing. *I don't
even care about my fucking city, Saul.*" I let that sink in, and

wonder of wonders, he was quiet. I swallowed, expecting the world to rock out from underneath me from the blasphemy.

What did that say about me? Santa Luz could get wiped off the map, and as long as Saul was alive I'd count it chump change. That was *wrong*, because I was a hunter...but that was the way it was. And if it stopped him long enough for me to get a word of sanity in edgewise, I didn't care. "Just stay put and when I'm done with this, you can yell at me all you want. But I need you to rest, I need you to eat, and I need you to be strong so that when this is done you can load me in a car and get me the hell out of this god-forsaken town. *Please.*"

Silence. The rage crackling over the line didn't abate.

"Please." It was a little girl's whisper. "Saul, *please.* I came back from Hell for you."

And here I was, racking up the lies. I didn't remember where I'd come back from. I had a suspicion that I didn't want to, and another sneaking suspicion that it hadn't been Poughkeepsie.

Hell was as good a guess as any.

Besides, I know Hell exists. The evidence is all around, every day, rubbed in your face. And the descent into hell-breed territory is the final step that makes a hunter—no, wait. The final step is the *return*, with your teacher holding the line and the souls of the damned screaming in your ears.

Heaven? Never been there. Unless being in Saul's arms on a sunny afternoon counts. Which it probably does, if I'm lucky.

If I deserved it. If I pulled this off and saved the weary world for him one more time.

A clatter. Footsteps stamping away. A low, rumbling growl dying out.

"Jill?" Galina, softly. "He's calmer. Theron and I are taking turns cooking; now he might even eat. I won't let him out. Are you all right? Is Gilberto okay?"

She was such a gentle soul. My stomach turned over hard. The dogsbody lifted its head, crystalline eyes fixed on the middle distance down Sarvedo Street.

"Gil was fine when I gave him his marching orders. Galina, *keep Saul there.* I don't care what you have to do, just keep him safe."

"I already promised." Solemn now. "What's going on? It's Perry, isn't it. What's he doing?"

Taking me apart one piece at a time. And repeating the worst part of modern history, thank you very much. "Something big. Look, I need you to do something for me."

"Of course."

The dogsbody slunk closer, still staring down the street. Under the golden wires of its hair, sharply defined muscles moved under black skin. "Start making silverjacket bullets. Get the Sanctuary ready for all the hunters who can reach Santa Luz in the next twenty-four hours. And Galina?"

"What?"

"Do you pray?"

She sounded surprised. "Well, the Order's quite catholic, in the old sense—"

"Good. Start praying. Maybe it will help."

CHAPTER 29

The warehouse was full of ghosts.

It stood on the wrong side of the tracks, and from the outside it was just another dusty, decaying bit of urban infrastructure. Inside, though, it was space and light and the stamp of Saul's presence everywhere. It looked just the same as it had the last time I'd been here.

When I'd been preparing to go die.

I'd left the bed tangled and some cupboards open; the huge orange Naugahyde couch with the pretty slipcover Saul had made was dirty; I'd been covered in filth, as usual. Thin blue lines of etheric protection hummed in the walls, fading until I stepped inside, gathering strength from my presence. Dust lay thick over everything, and even though Gilberto or Anya had been out to lock up and keep everything tidy, it still smelled like an abandoned house. Places start to rot very quickly, etherically and physically, once they're uninhabited. It smelled sour and stale, and that would just about drive Saul nuts. He'd start scrubbing everything he could reach.

My eyes blurred, hot water brimming. I blinked it away. The dogsbody padded behind me, whining softly to itself, and ignoring it wasn't making it vanish.

Not that I thought it would, but I didn't have the heart to shoot the damn thing.

Yet.

I strode through the empty rooms of our life together and stepped into the wide, wood-floored sparring room. Mirrored tiles along one side, a ballet barre firmly bolted to them; weapons hanging on the other three. There was one empty spot—a fall of amber silk crushed on the floor, and I don't know why I was surprised. Of course someone had taken the hunk of pre-Atlantean meteorite iron, with its dragon heads and scythelike blades.

I had a moment's worth of unease, wondering...but no, the weapon Mikhail had handed down to me couldn't possibly be called *la Lanza de Destino*. For one thing, it was too old, and it wasn't wooden. Anya would have taken it to store in Galina's vaults.

No windows, but skylights drenching everything with late-afternoon honey, dust motes dancing as the gem gave a hard piercing note, like a crystal wineglass right before it shatters.

My guns leapt free, trained on a column of sunlight. Dust coalesced, a single spark flared white, and he was suddenly *there*.

I didn't shoot him. But it was close.

Call-Me-Mike the caretaker regarded me mildly, his blue eyes glowing. The sun picked out fine threads of gold in his no-longer-dishwater hair, and instead of the jump-suit he wore jeans and a plain white T-shirt. All he needed was a duck's-ass pompadour and a pack of Lucky Strikes rolled up in his sleeve.

The dogsbody whined and slumped next to me, shivering.

"What the fuck *are* you?" I'll admit it, I yelled. The words cracked, bounced back from the mirrors, set the dust swirling in tiny tornados.

Mike shrugged, a loose easy movement. "It's not important."

"It is to me." I didn't lower the guns. The idea that I could just start shooting every nonhuman or non-Were involved in this whole scenario was wonderfully comforting. I wondered if I had enough ammo. "Perry says hello, *brother Michael*. He's planning something for tomorrow night to send the world down the drain. But you know that, don't you. What was the point of sending me there?"

Mike shrugged, spreading his hands. The light made him insubstantial, just another ghost here with all the dust and the memories. "It was...necessary."

You son of a bitch. "Was shooting myself in the head necessary too? You're the *Other Side*, Perry says. We're bleeding and dying down here, where the fuck are *you*? Why are you just showing up now?" My ribs heaved. I didn't realize I was shouting until the echoes came back, the entire warehouse creaking like a tree in a high breeze. The triggers eased down a millimeter, another. Squeezing off a few rounds would just about start this conversation off right.

Sorrow, then, darkening those blue, blue eyes. Not sterile like Perry's, a warm summer color. But so terribly sad. "It's not that simple. I'm bending the rules enough as it is. So much depends on you, and of course..." Another slight movement, hands spread. "Of course I wish I could do more. It...it's painful, to see such suffering."

Well, isn't that big of you. "Wind me up and set me loose, right? Just throw me at the enemy. I've been fighting this war for years, and it never gets any better. I've been down in the streets trying to hold back the tide. There's no goddamn hope at all. And you've been sitting up at Henderson Hill the entire *fucking* time, doing *fucking* nothing, just waiting for...for what? For Perry? Is that it? You're in cahoots?"

"I wouldn't say that. He's part of the Pattern, as you are. As I am. But...there are disturbing signs. He's..." Another helpless shrug. "Even if I had the words, you wouldn't understand. I can't even offer you a dispensation. If you do this—stop Hyperion, save your fellows, and recover the Lance—you will not be rewarded. There is no glory, no recompense."

A harsh cawing laugh shook its way free of my chest. *Well, shit, that's par for the course.* "So why should I bother, huh? Because you brought me back? Is that it?"

"It's part of the Pattern, but I can't explain that either. *Kismet*. Did you really expect to name yourself that and not be called upon?"

It was like talking to Mikhail in one of his vodka-soaked philosophical moods. Baffling, opaque, and frustratingly-familiar enough to drive me to the heavy bag. I searched for something that would wring an answer out of him. I'm used to dealing with hellbreed, where you question them, then you hurt them, then you question them some more.

Something told me that would be a bad idea with this guy, whatever he was. "Perry called you his brother. You're related?"

Another gentle, rueful smile. "Is a mirror related to the image it holds?"

Oh, for fuck's sake. Disgusted, I lowered the guns. I was shaking again, and all I wanted was to lie down and sleep. Next to Saul, if possible. Let the world end, it had been lurching along before I came along to be a hunter just fine.

Focus, Jill! I blinked. A puzzle piece snapped down inside my head. "He needs me for something. *La Lanza de Destino*, Melendez called it; the only trouble is, there's several of *those* floating around. I at least know it's not the chunk of meteorite Mikhail left me. The important thing is, Perry can't use it. What does he want it used *on*?"

Mike nodded, the patient teacher beaming at a recalcitrant but gifted student. "*Very* good. But your task is simply to strike him down when he has achieved the first half of his purpose. It's very important, Kismet."

"So he wants me to do something for him, and you want me to murder him but you won't tell me exactly why." The guns lowered slightly. "I'd do it for free, you know. That bastard has gone too far." *And so have you.*

The caretaker crouched, suddenly, a fluid movement. I twitched, stopped myself at the last moment.

The dogsbody whined and leaned forward. It glanced up at me, colorless eyes suddenly pleading, and the sickness revolving behind my breastbone rose another notch. "Jesus Christ," I whispered, suddenly very sure. "The hellhound was chasing him to shut him up. Perry was just cleaning up a loose end."

"This one has paid for what he's done." Michael held out a hand, just touching the edge of the sunlight. Stroking it, the finely drawn border where light met air. "And it's fitting that he should protect you now, isn't it?"

God, there's not much difference between you and a hellbreed, is there. Maybe I should start killing you both. "This isn't getting us anywhere. What the fuck are you, and why are you here?"

"I came to give you comfort, Kismet." He cocked his head, glancing up at me. The dogsbody didn't move, but its shaking slid up my leg. The gem groaned, etheric force thrumming up my arm. "And to explain, as far as I am able, what Hyperion wishes to do."

"It's about fucking time." I lowered the guns, nice and slow. "I'm waiting."

So he told me, in plain words. And I listened. By the end of it his voice was a brass bell, stroked softly in a forgotten chapel, and I was cold all over. The dogsbody whined even louder, crouching next to me and shivering. The sunlight dimmed, and by the time he finished I was on my knees too, hugging myself, staring at him.

"Saul," I whispered.

The caretaker was glowing now, his skin burnished and his eyes burning feverishly. My own blue eye ached, piercing the veil of the visible—his outline rippled, eddies and currents passing through the snarled fabric of reality. "Do it for him. Do it for love. Please, Kismet. You are the only one who can."

"I . . ." *But Saul. I promised him.* "I promised."

"If you will not do this, we are lost." He shrugged. "The Pattern will right itself in some other way, I suppose. But there will be terrible suffering, not just among those you love. I can only ask, Kismet, Jill, whatever you want to name yourself. You are free to refuse."

Oh, fuck. "You know I can't." Hopeless, pale little words. "You have to know I can't. That's not a way out, you know I was *made* this way. So I can't turn you down. *God* made me this way, and don't you dare fucking tell me He didn't."

"Do you believe in such a cruelty?" Michael sighed. "You're so willing to hurt yourself." The rippling through him was more pronounced now, bits of him wavering as if under clear, heavy water. Sunlight dimmed further, a cloud drifting between us and heaven's eye. "Goodbye, beloved."

Metal clattered somewhere, but my eyes were full of light. Just like that, he was gone. The dogsbody shuddered, pressing against me, and unhealthy heat boiled from its hide. I swallowed several times, and the world spun. When I came back to myself I was hunched over, my forehead against cool hardwood and awful knowledge beating inside my brain.

I was probably going insane. Coming back from the dead will do that to you, I guess. Or maybe this was a different version of Hell, one I'd been extra-special nominated to.

One that felt just like my life.

Get up, little snake. Mikhail, in my memory. Why hadn't he ever told me about his bargain with Perry? Could he just not find the words? Did he not care enough to . . . but no.

No.

Mikhail was my teacher. He'd held the line when I made my first trip to the hellbreeds' home, the one that turned me into a full-fledged hunter and gave me my smart eye. He'd loved me the way only a hunter can love another hunter, right down to the bones and back.

He must have had a reason.

I had my marching orders. Ol' Blue Eyes had been a busy, busy boy. He was just so helpful, feeding me and giving me weapons, showing up to push me in another direction, poking and prodding.

I made my legs straighten by the simple expedient of cursing at them, levered myself up from the floor.

"They want a sacrificial lamb." My voice sounded odd. The dogsbody stopped whining and made an inquisitive *rrowr* sound that might have been funny if it hadn't been so pathetic. "Boy, are they going to get a surprise."

CHAPTER 30

Dawn found me in a cemetery.

The northern side of Beacon Hill's lush greenness looked out over the valley, the mountains rising in the distance and the river a bright colorless ribbon as the sky lightened. I sat on the wet grass, sprinklers going overtime in the dark to compensate for the desiccation that would hit later in the day. The water had stopped, thank God, but everything squelched underneath me.

I put my chin on my knees.

The dogsbody slunk closer. It settled down with a sigh, its unhealthy heat steaming in the predawn chill. Around sunrise Santa Luz always smells like metallic sand as the city inhales, filling its lungs from the wasted desert all around, mixing it with exhaust and the effluvia of thousands of people going about their lives.

The gravestone shimmered, polished white rock. I'd dug up Mikhail's ashes a while ago and had Galina put them in one of her vaults. Still, it was here that I felt his presence most strongly, and it was here I sometimes came to talk to him. Galina's perfectly polite, but I don't like having conversations with my dead teacher where other people can hear.

Call me secretive.

I held myself absolutely still. The sky slowly turned gray, stars winking out and a few birds warming up for their morning chorus. What a waste it was to water the ground here. In the first place, water's a great psychic conductor, and the grief soaking this place echoed in every molecule. And in the second, why not spend some of that water on the living? They needed it more.

The only need of the dead is to sleep unmolested.

You're kind of sucking at that, aren't you, Jill. I squeezed my eyes shut, opened them. The gravestone was just the same.

Mikhail Illich Tolstoi. Nothing else, not even the years of his tenure on earth. Why bother, when I would remember it and it was in the files? It wouldn't matter to anyone else. Except maybe Gilberto, when he finished his training.

I wouldn't be around to see that, would I.

I stirred a little, shifting to relieve muscles threatening to cramp. The dogsbody was still, its weird eyes closed and its breath softly chuffing in and out. Just like a hound, really.

I'd never had a pet.

Are you crazy? This thing's dangerous. Plus, it's basically hellbreed, even if Call-Me-Mike did...whatever he did to it. A shiver went through me.

I was stalling.

"Misha." The word rode a breathy scree of air. "Mish, Misha-Mik, if you're there, I could use a friendly ear."

Well, strictly speaking, listening was all he *could* do, right? He was fucking dead. Passed on. Joined the choir eternal. Had I met him, wherever I'd been after I pulled the trigger and broke my skull open like a pumpkin dropped off an overpass?

If I rubbed under my hair, I only felt the bumps and ridges anyone's head acquires after a few hard knocks. No shrapnel. Just a tenderness in places, like old bruising. A faint twinge.

"Why?" I whispered, staring at his grave. "Why didn't you tell me you had a deal with Perry and you needed me to take your place? Why didn't you tell me about Belisa? Why didn't you take me with you? Why did you pull me out of that snowbank in the first place? Why *me*? And Jesus Christ, Misha, why could I come back if you couldn't? Or is it just that you didn't want to?"

I go to Valhalla, he'd told me more than once, *where fight is like play. Like movie.*

I guess that was his idea of a good time.

"Why, Misha? I would've done anything you asked. Hell, I would've given Perry a lot more to buy you free. I would..." I ran up against the wall of what I *would* have done, what I'd've given if he'd just asked me.

Why hadn't he?

A while ago, I'd visited Melendez and Chango had deigned to speak to me. It had been a different case—the circus had come to town, and someone was looking for vengeance. Voodoo and hellbreed don't mix, and I'd been looking to get the whole thing tied up and safely stowed before open warfare broke out and the Cirque was given free rein in my town.

You meatpuppets, Chango had snorted with magnificent disdain. *You always got to know why.*

"It would sure fucking help," I muttered, and wiped at my cheeks with callused palms. Why the fuck was I crying? Another *why* question.

Shit.

"Was it worth it?" That was a new question. I sounded ridiculously young, and I stared at the white blur of the headstone. "Melisande. *Belisa*. Did you love her? Or were you just looking to get free? Was *she* worth it? You had *me*, Misha. Was I not enough?"

Of course I wasn't enough, never had been. I'd been born without some essential thing everyone else seemed to have. There was an emptiness in me, way down deep, and even if it had been the reason everyone who should have loved me couldn't, it was what kept me alive long enough to escape. Long enough to survive and meet Mikhail. And even then, I hadn't been enough.

The only person who shouldn't have loved me was Saul. And go figure, he did.

At least he's safe. But if you end up dead again, Jill, what's that going to do? He'll starve. He'll get matesick, he'll go down. Weres don't go to Hell, and you know that's where you're bound. If there was a heaven you'd've seen it by now. Hot water flooded my eyes, trickled down my cheeks. My nose was full. I'd given up wiping my cheeks.

"It's not fair." Lo and hallelujah, I was five years old again. "It's just not *fair*, God damn you."

The eastern sky was rosy. The birds burst into song, a great swell of twittering music. It stopped, started again. The hush returned, this time threaded with liquid birdsong. It was funny how noise could be a component of early-morning silence.

I was on my feet before I knew it, steel-shod heels sinking into wet grass and mud. "I should leave it here to rot. All of it. Everything. Including you, Misha. You lied to me."

By omission, yes. But still a lie. Hunters aren't supposed to lie to each other. When you've been loved so hard that the love turns into a rope that pulls you free of Hell's cold shifting borders, you can see it in another hunter's eyes. It's raw and bloody and it aches, but you can't lie to someone who's been loved like that.

Mikhail *had* loved me. He'd pulled me out of Hell. What if his lie had been a mercy, instead of deceit? Why would he have done that?

Fuck. We're back to the whys.

I held up one finger. "You loved me." Another. "So you lied to save me. You couldn't hold Perry off much longer. But you thought *I* could."

A third finger. "Mike. The caretaker. Judas to a hell-breed. He can't interfere much more than he already has."

A fourth. "A Lance. And Perry planning a repeat of '29."

1929, the Black Year. The year when the hellbreed had opened up multiple doors, and escaped en masse from Hell's embrace.

Unwilling, I glanced up.

The eastern horizon was a furnace. Caught in the valley, Santa Luz turned over, sighed, and began waking up. The skyscrapers glittered, and for a moment the whole city was open inside my head, the streets that made its arteries and the buildings its bones. The people moving through it, the city's dream made flesh, but so vulnerable. They had no idea what abyss was yawning under their feet, and every night, even since before Mikhail's death, I'd been fighting to keep them safe. There was no reward, no prize; few of them even knew my name.

So why did *I* do it? Why hadn't I taken Mikhail's other offer— therapy, education, a way off the streets, my past wiped clear and a fresh chance at life as a civilian? I'd never even considered it.

Because I'd wanted so badly to be worthy of what he'd done when he pulled me out of that snowdrift. Funny, that year it had snowed; I couldn't remember a single white winter in the time since.

My thumb popped out. "My city."

My city.

Now I looked at my callused palm and fingers, the lines running across flesh, the bones of my knuckles. My hand curled into a fist, and the gem muttered sleepily against my wrist. When you got right down to it, was it any different from the scar of Perry's lips on me?

Do it for Saul. Do it for love.

"I can't." There it was. "There isn't enough left in me. *You* made sure of that. All of you fighting for a piece of me, pushing me around like a rat in a maze. Jesus."

What did that make me? If I couldn't do this for love, what did it make me?

Who the fuck cares? I'm going to do it anyway. None of it matters. Except Saul.

Even if he was going to go down after I threw myself into this losing game, at least he'd be going down in a world where he had a *chance.* Where the hellbreed were checked. Not permanently, that would take a goddamn miracle. But I could keep the world spinning a little longer, and make it a little safer.

It didn't matter if I was doing it for them, or for myself. At least, I wasn't going to let it matter.

"I love you," I told Mikhail's headstone. For a moment I had a crazed hallucination of my right fist punching, the shock grinding the white stone to powder. I could do it, I was suddenly sure of that. Before, it had been hellbreed-jacked strength. Now the power came from somewhere else, and I didn't have a clue what I would do if it deserted me. "Mikhail," I whispered. "I hate you, too."

I didn't recognize my own voice. Irrational, sudden fear drilled through me. I hunched my shoulders and waited. One breath. Two.

Nothing happened.

I looked up again at my city. The sun's limb lifted sleepily from the horizon, swords of gold piercing the sky, and I felt dawn in my bones like the ocean must feel its tides.

Another idea hit me. I actually rocked back on my heels, my brain jolting inside its heavy bonecase. The dogsbody lifted itself up, the imprint of its scorch on wet grass steaming, and shook itself. The flat ears pricked forward, and it stared adoringly up at me. It actually *did* look like a hound, and even my blue eye could find no trace of Jughead Vanner left in its long lean body.

"Shit," I breathed. "Shit shit *shit*. Come on."

The absurdity of talking to myself on Beacon Hill was enough to make me grin as I spun on my heel and left Mikhail's glowing headstone behind. The dogsbody loped next to me as my stride lengthened, my coat flapping, and I broke into a run as the day came up like thunder.

CHAPTER 31

H UTCHINSON'S BOOKS, USED & RARE, glowed in faded gold leaf on the wide dusty front window. I remembered how proud he'd been when we'd changed the name over from Chatham's, and how soon the gold leaf had started to look dry and dusty, like it had never been anything else.

He'd left the desktop, and while it booted up I grabbed a couple references from the *other* part of the store—the climate-controlled bit where he kept a hunter's library. That library earned him some nice tax breaks and justified me saving his bacon when he was caught hacking something he shouldn't be. Weedy little Hutch thought he was ten feet tall and bulletproof in cyberspace, and it didn't help that he was usually right.

I stacked the D'Aventine and Miguel de la Foya on the desk, sweeping aside a clutter of paper and setting a cup of moldering coffee higher up on the file cabinet behind his antique cubbyholed desk. The place was beginning to smell of sharpish rot and neglect, the dust and paper covering the peppery tang of a refugee emergency. I hadn't given him much time to pack.

I was grateful I'd sent him off, however.

Everyone you love. Every one you cast your eye upon.

Was Perry really that jealous? Or was it just a way to distract me? To keep me running until—

The monitor blinked. I flipped open the D'Aventine, checking the binder that had been right next to it—a laboriously cross-checked index, and an old one. Hutch had bitched endlessly about the old dot-matrix even after he'd gone through two new laser printers by now, the same way old ladies complain about beaus who jilted them in youth. I'd learned to just make another pot of coffee when he started in on that.

I wrote down page numbers and checked the de la Foya and the *Scribus Aeternum*, tapping a pencil while I scanned. I checked Kelley's *Habits of the Damned* and Carré's *The Outbreak of 1929: Its Causes and Effects*. Also, Hartmann's *Catholic Myths* and Artur Fountaine's *La guerre d'Inferne*.

I knew what I was looking for. Confirmation and explication instead of a needle in a haystack. Still, I came up empty. Nothing about a particular Spear of Destiny that would fit the bill, and nothing about Perry even in Carré, who was generally held to be the authority on '29. Even if he was a terrible writer, he was pretty much always dead-on.

The constellation of intangibles that made the Outbreak possible—astronomical and astrological energies aligned to weaken the walls between the Visible and the other worlds, the Infernals collecting Talismans used to power the Portals in different locations, the carefully nurtured scurf infestations and overheated economy—were monstrous enough. Some Infernals have admitted there was a Leader who forced an alliance long enough for the portals to be achieved synchronously on different continents; there are even whispers of a full-blown hellmouth that stood for hours, admitting a flood of Infernals to our helpless world—

He goes on for *pages*, refusing to speculate further but giving tantalizing hints, reporting rumors and in the next breath reminding the reader to rely only on the things that can be verified. The trouble is, 'breed don't like appearing in the historical record. Carré had been a researcher much like Hutch; he'd disappeared in 1942. The hunter he'd been attached to—Simon Saint-Just—had also gone missing.

It had not been a good time to be a hunter in Europe. Hell, things had been bad all over, and it wasn't until the mid-sixties that we got some sort of handle on things.

A hellmouth. A full-blown hellmouth, instead of the barriers between here and the hellbreed home gapping for just an instant to let a single monster through. Perry certainly didn't dream small, and if it had happened once before, it could be done again.

A Leader who forced an alliance... What had Perry said to me, more than once?

I cannot hold back the tide forever. I'd stopped one of his bosses from coming through twice now. Or more precisely, Belisa had stopped him last time, before I'd shot her.

And damned myself.

Each time, the big bad boss had been struggling to step through a fractional gap, sliding into the fleshly world. That was bad enough. A full-blown hellmouth—a passageway to Hell held open for God knows how long—was going to be exponentially worse.

How's he going to power it? Ten to one says this Lanza del Destino. Major Talismans of a certain type can power a hellmouth for a while, but I can't think of a Spear that applies. I sighed, rolled my head back on my sore, aching neck. The dogsbody dozed near the front door, seeming content just to lay there.

Was I going to have to feed it soon? Did they stock hellbreed dog chow at the supermarket? I wondered briefly if that was tax-deductible and closed Carré with a snap. Hutch was going to have a fit if I didn't reshelve everything.

Well, if he has one, it'll mean I'm around to see it. That'd be nice. I considered the screensaver for a moment—pictures of cats with weird captions, shuffling by in random order. It vanished as soon as I tapped the space key.

"Okay," I said to the dusty silence. The air conditioner kicked on, cool air soughing through the store and Hutch's silent, dark apartment upstairs. "Let's hope digital is better than analog for this, huh?"

It took me two hours of hunt-and-pecking and cross-referencing, broken only by a trip upstairs to make some coffee. Hutch's fridge was unhappy in the extreme, so I left it closed after grabbing the canister of espresso-ground. I considered taking the garbage out, but one peek under the sink convinced me it was best left to itself. I was trying to stop a catastrophe here, not playing Molly Maid.

Halfway through that pot of java, I leaned toward the computer screen. I'd finally signed into Hutch's remote worktop, seeing what he'd pulled up recently. It was eerie that I could see what he'd last been looking at and when—he'd been up late last night, not going to bed until near dawn. I would've been on Beacon Hill by then.

All excited about a woodcut, Devi had said. There were plenty of files in the image folder, I started going through them methodically. They bloomed over the expensive flatscreen monitor, and most of them were Perry.

Bingo.

Here Perry was caught by a telephoto lens, a black-and-white of him getting out of a car on a city street. The back of the photo, part of the same image file, held Mikhail's spiky backward-leaning script: *1969, Buenos Aires.* Another, this one in glaring color, clipped from a newspaper archive, all about new management at the Monde Nuit, decades later.

I stared at the date.

It was right after Mikhail had pulled me out of the snow. I shook my head, silver chiming in my hair. *Huh.*

Another black-and-white, Perry leaning against a bar and smiling, white fedora pushed back on his head, his shark smile showing up in the mirror between gleaming bottles. *Berlin, 1934.* Back when the first Jack Karma was working Germany. That was pretty much the first mention of him I'd ever been able to dig up.

I found the woodcut just as another scalding cup of coffee was going down. Mid-sixteenth century, originally from Bremen, now part of a museum collection. Thick black inked lines; the carver had been a genius. It was small as such things went, but exquisitely detailed—two cavorting figures under a full moon, facing a tall thin man in a long dark coat, his broadsword slanting up and flames running along its edge. He was unquestionably a hunter, and a long thin casket lay on the ground behind him. The title was *Der Schutz der ersten Spear,* and an electric bolt shot through me.

The two attackers leered. One of them was unquestionably the late and unlamented piebald Halis, floppy hair and all, claws and teeth bared.

The other was Perry, a spot of white in the woodcut's florid lines, a slim orchid.

"Oh, you son of a bitch," I whispered. "I've got you now."

Only I didn't. It took most of the afternoon before I had him, and when I did I was sweating, my teeth were chattering, and Hutch had run out of coffee.

CHAPTER 32

I dialed Galina, but she didn't pick up. Which was odd.

I paged Anya from Hutch's shop too, but there was no answer. Of course, she was probably in the barrio, trying to get the Weres to safety. I dialed my own answering service, but it just rang endlessly. I even tried ringing Monty, but after getting his voice mail for the fifth time I just hung up.

From not remembering a single damn thing, I'd gone to being able to pull phone numbers out like I was shuffling through a card file. It was a goddamn pity nobody was listening, and the sun was past its apogee. The shadows were lengthening, and the dogsbody was nervous. At least, he *looked* nervous, pacing back and forth in front of the shop door, muscles rippling under blond hair. Whining while I dialed and dialed, getting no response.

"Galina should be picking up," I muttered. "What the fuck?"

He couldn't give me any reply, black-skinned ears fuzzed with blond fur laid flat against his ungainly head. Just that grumble, deep in his throat, spiraling up to an inquisitive at the end. I was still sweating, every nerve in me jumping and frayed raw.

"*Fuck!*" I finally snarled, and slammed the phone down. Just then, someone tapped on the glass, and the dogsbody growled, deep and low.

I stalked between bookcases, my hand on a gun, peered at the dusty window.

He tapped again. I almost fell over myself unlocking the door, grabbed his collar, and dragged him in. "What the hell are you—"

Gilberto's sides heaved. His face was painted with bright blood, and he was shaking. For all that, his dark eyes were alight, no longer flat and dead, and he looked completely, fully alive.

"*Mala suerte,*" he gasped. "*Mala* fuckin' *suerte, chingada.* Melendez, he prolly dead."

I locked the door and dragged him further into the shop. The air-conditioning soughed on again, and I smelled burned coffee and the flat copper tang of human fear and blood over the dust and paper.

I propped him against a bookcase in the Classics section and took a deep breath. "Why aren't you at Galina's, then? That's where you were supposed to—"

"Been there." He closed his eyes, gulping down air. "*Chingada, mi profesora,* the whole place burning."

"Burning? A *Sanctuary*?" I stared at him like he'd gone mad.

"Barrio too. City's rollin' like Saturday night. *Estamos corriendo en la chingada, mi profesora,* we are fucked for sure. Was *el Rubio* at Melendez's. Old man tole me run, tole me you'd be here. Almost din't make it out." He was gaining his breath rapidly, eyelids fluttering. "Ran for Lina's, but it was on fire. Crawling with 'breed. Hopped away. Had to steal a horse."

Considering what he was telling me, I didn't even want to take him to task for minor auto theft. "Galina's shop was burning? The whole thing?"

"Blue flames, *profesora.* Screamin'." He'd regained his breath by now. "Whole goddamn thing. Looked bad."

Saul. Everything inside me turned over hard. *Oh, God. Saul.*

But Galina had the vaults. It would be simple for her to just get everyone downstairs and rebuild. Blue flames, though. And whoever heard of someone burning down a Sanctuary? It would take the equivalent of a sorcerous nuke to do it. Not worth the trouble when they could just rebuild like a tree growing in fast-forward...

"The fire. Blue. Hellfire, Gil?"

"Looked like. Listen, I ain't sure I'm clear—"

Meaning he wasn't sure if hellbreed had followed him. "It's nice of you to be worried. Don't be." The machine inside my head clicked on, calculating, assessing, weighing. "It'll take more than that to keep Galina down." *He wants her incommunicado.* It was the only explanation. And without Galina to hold messages and ammo, Anya and I were looking at some difficulty. "Go upstairs. Bathroom's second door on the left, grab the first-aid kit and wash the blood off. Then come down here, be ready to roll."

"*Sí.*" He took off down the hall with enviable speed. Guess the

young bounce back quick. And it was probably a relief to have someone giving him orders so he could just put his head down and *do*.

I remembered that feeling from my own apprentice days.

I peered out the front window, surveying the street. The shadows were clustering, the sky hot blue and cloudless. All the same,
static electricity prickled under my skin.

"Fuck," I said, stupidly, under my breath. Like it was a secret.
"*Der ersten Spear.*" The Prime Spear. The first spear-shaped Talisman. "Perry, you son of a bitch."

*Well, Jill, what did you expect? He's been planning this for
decades.*

Another thought hit me, so suddenly I actually jerked and a
half-amazed laugh burst out of me. "Of course. It's Black Thursday, all over again."

The dogsbody made a short barking sound, like it was echoing
my laughter. Outside, the shadows sizzled, and several of them
lengthened. I didn't like the way they were creeping toward the
store, the world behind them warping into a colorless fuming
wasteland. The blue of the sky was lensed with smoke now, and I
snapped my fingers at the dogsbody. Its ears perked again.

"Come on, you. Guess we're not letting Gil come back down
after all."

"Where we goin'?" Gil yelled, clutching the bandage to his upper
arm. His torn sleeve flapped in the wind roaring through the broken windows, I slewed the wheel to the right and shot us through a
red light with half a foot to spare, ignoring the blare of a horn
from a semi and nudging us over into the left lane. Oncoming
traffic was a bitch, but the tingle of intuition running along my
nerves told me left was the way to play this part of our run.

I've never been in an accident. Basic precognition is good for
something. Besides, the rush of traffic might slow down pursuit.

It was nice to be behind the wheel again. Sort of.

"Sacred Grace!" I yelled back. The blue Nissan didn't have
much pickup, but it was maneuverable, and that counts for a lot.
Still, it was making a knocking noise I didn't much like, and if I sent
it over another few railroad tracks at high speed the tires weren't
going to be happy. "Where'd you get *this* car from, anyway?"

"My cousin!" Thin blue lines of healing sorcery crawled under the bandage on his arm, knitting flesh together. He was armed, too, and grinning so widely I could see his fillings. "Discount *por la familia*! Got it cheap!"

"Next time tell him to sell you American, for Christ's sake!" I twisted the wheel again, we skidded around a corner, I feathered the brake and stamped the accelerator and we were off again. Gunfire erupted behind us, perilously close to our tires. *They probably don't know I'm driving. Perry needs me to make his little plan work. Or was he lying about that, too?*

"Why we goin to church, eh?" Gilberto had a 9mm out, sunlight sparking viciously off its edges. "Father Gui owe you money?"

He owes me a lot more than that. "He's got something Perry wants!" I yelled. "Now shut up and put that thing away!"

He whooped as we smoked into a turn at the north end of Salvador Avenue, near Jordan's headshop. I hoped to hell she was under cover. Gil's pulse was jackhammering, but I didn't have the breath or time to get on him to calm it. The dogsbody was flattened in the backseat, and if it was making any noise I couldn't tell. A thundering *pop* and the car slewed wildly, of *course* we'd lost a tire, it was the way these things went. I hit another corner, floored it, ignored the grinding, wished it was a stick instead of automatic for the fiftieth time, and realized I was cursing steadily, a song of obscenities as familiar as breath. Tendons stood out on the backs of my hands as I fought the steering, forcing the car to do what I wanted as it bucked and shuddered.

We cleared the curb with a bump and soared, hit the steps and the car teetered for a long moment. "No no no *no no*—," I chanted, willing it to stay upright, and we thudded back down, listing terribly. I'd bought us a few seconds. *"Inside!"* I barked. "Move your ass!"

Gil was already bailing. The dogsbody wriggled out through the back window and I covered them, skipping backward up the stairs as the shadows down the street warped. Bullets chipped and plowed up the steps behind me, Gil hit the doors like a bomb and the dogsbody leapt, its claws scratching on stone. I flung myself back and Gil kicked the door again, neatest trick of the week, slamming it shut. The lock was broken, deadbolt wrenched free, I bounced up and swept the church's interior with both guns.

Sacred space, won't hold them for long though. Not when they're this motivated. "Gui!" I yelled, a harsh cawing in the sudden gloom. "Guillermo! Rosas? Ignacio?"

"Dios," Gilberto breathed, and crossed himself. My eyes finished adjusting, and I let out a short frustrated sound. The dogsbody shivered, hunching next to me, steam drifting from its blondness.

The priests had taken refuge here, instead of the chapel attached to the school. This late in the day, maybe they'd sent the kids home. I *hoped* they had. Their rooms—they still called them cells, a sort of monastic joke—in the parsonage building would be empty too. Here was safest.

Only it hadn't turned out to be safe after all. Not when the forces of Hell were this goddamn enthusiastic.

Old thin Ignacio was in the middle of a jumble of broken pews, his body contorted into an enthusiastic back-bend. The new redheaded one, Father Blake, had died near the confessional, and the arterial spray had even reached the racks of candles lit for sinners and prayers. Every inch of stained glass was covered with a thick layer of soot, and the pews—all terribly jumbled and splintered—were scorched.

Fat jolly Rosas, who had never liked me, was on the steps to the altar. He'd been flung over the crucifix, his guts spread in a tangle of gray loops and whorls. The crucifix itself had been torn down and mutilated, and in its place was nailed...

Bile burned my throat.

Gilberto was whispering. *"Aunque pase por el valle de sombra de muerte, no temeré mal alguno. Porque Tú estás conmigo."* He took two steps to the side, leaned over, and heaved.

"La primera Lanza was here all the time." I sounded like I'd been punched. "For *years."*

A long time ago, there had been a case involving a fire-strike spear. Guillermo had lied to me then, but he'd been protecting an even bigger secret. *I can't let you break your oath,* Rosas had told him, and relations between me and the boys of Sacred Grace had been decidedly chilly ever since. I never played basketball with sleek dark Guillermo anymore, and we kept the exorcisms strictly business.

The altar had been torn to bits, something wrenched from its depths. Of course, hide one of the most powerful Talismans on earth in plain sight. That had probably been Rosas's idea. My boots slipped in the blood and foulness on the steps. The stench of a battlefield was overpowering. No matter how many times you smell death, it never gets usual. It never becomes routine.

Rosas's face was twisted in horror. He'd died in a bad way. *Not so jolly now, fat man.* From the way he'd been flung, he'd probably been trying to protect Gui, buy him enough time to reach the altar and the artifact inside.

The very thing Perry was after.

It has been in my keeping all this time.

The case had also involved a wendigo and the Sorrows. Now I remembered that *Perry* had shown up during the hunt with the firestrike—the only weapon capable of killing the goddamn thing the Sorrows had been using to hunt me. I'd only had Perry's word that he'd gotten the firestrike from Sacred Grace. He'd told Saul as much, and since Saul had told *me* I'd taken it as truth.

Perry could not have stepped on this consecrated ground, could he? No. But he *had* been up to his eyebrows in that case, with Melisande Belisa, and neatly misdirected me. *Never assume* is the rule when it came to hellbreed, and it had been only a small mistake on my part. A tiny link in the chain, but enough.

Not to mention Perry had planted distrust between me and Father Gui. Which must have warmed his cold, dead hellbreed heart all the way through. If I hadn't assumed the firestrike was what the priests were hiding, I would have come back and torn the whole place apart until I found everything—and the Spear they had been hiding all along would have ended up in Galina's vaults, where Perry couldn't lay his hands on it *ever*, world without end, amen.

It was all so simple, now. Somehow Perry had gotten wind of the Spear, hidden out here in the middle of nowhere. The other thing he needed was a hunter to wield it. I'd assumed the firestrike had been what Sacred Grace had been hiding, and relations between me and the priests had been decidedly frosty ever since. It was a pity, because Gui probably would have eventually told me, vow of secrecy or not.

We were, after all, friends. Or we had been. Had he wanted to tell me, any of those times he tried to talk to me and I ignored him, keeping the conversation to the exorcism at hand? Had the secret been burning in him all this time?

It didn't matter now. With the Spear right where Perry could keep an eye on it, all he had to do was wait for me to damn myself. He'd waited *years*.

And all that time I'd been oblivious.

Never assume, milaya. *Is shortest way to get ass blown sideways.*

"FUCK!" I screamed, and the word hit the walls, richocheting back to sting me. Gilberto crossed himself again, reflexively.

Little creaks and cracklings ran through the church walls. The building groaned, etheric contamination spreading as the murder and hatred boiled. *Wait. Wait just a second. Hellbreed can't touch it, and the ground's sanctified. So he sent Traders to open up the way and contaminate. What do you want to bet some of them are still here?* "Gil. Behind me."

He moved immediately, thank God. "You see something, *bruja?"*

"Listen." I kept both guns loosely pointed down. "They're still in the building, or at least, *some* of them are. Nine o'clock, there's a door. Move toward it, nice and easy."

The dogsbody growled and looked up, a quick inquiring movement. "Hey," I said, and its ear flicked at me. "Go with Gil. Protect him."

The hound shook its narrow head, then padded toward my apprentice. *Well, there's that, at least.* "Gil. Get out of here, go—"

Now we hit the stubbornness, at the worst possible time. "Ain't leavin you, *profesora."*

I would have kicked his ass for it, but the choir loft exploded and the church was suddenly full of hellbreed, its walls shuddering at the violation. A century of blessing and sacred belief rose to push the intruders out, but it was damaged now. The Traders had broken it with murder and suffering, and theft.

The blessing, crackling fine lines of blue, beat ineffectually at the damned as they swarmed. They hissed, jaws distending, their beauty sliding aside, and every single one of them was 'breed instead of Trader. Fast, brutal, and harder to kill. There were at least a dozen of them. They didn't look like they cared very much that Perry supposedly wanted me alive.

This is not going to end well.

CHAPTER 33

Father Gui's body hit the altar with a meaty thump. I followed, blood slicking my lips and the knife sinking in past a hard hell-breed shell, twisting through the suction of unholy muscle. We slid down the wall, the gem singing in my wrist as it pumped etheric force through me, every muscle cramping and my breath a harsh ratcheting as I swore, again, obscenities interweaving with a chanted prayer in bastard Latin. The 'breed exhaled foulness in my face, but he was already dying, thin cracks of dusty corruption racing through his skin as the silver's poison spread.

Gilberto screamed, a high breaking note of rage, and fired again. The dogsbody made another one of those wrenching guttural noises, and my boots jolted down. I heaved the rotting body away, it fell on Gui's wracked and lifeless frame with a wet splorch.

Sorry, padre. Wish we could shoot some hoops instead. The dogsbody hunched, snarling, and I crashed into the 'breed crouching in front of my whey-faced apprentice. He was giving a good account of himself, but it was only a matter of time. The 'breed went down in a heap; I cut its throat with one swift motion and the dogsbody was on it too, jaws crunching with sickening finality. The 'breed exploded in a shower of brackish fluid, dust spilling from its veins, and I rose from the tangle, spinning the knife. "Come on!" I yelled, the knife sliding back into its sheath, and we were out the door before more of our pursuers decided to chance the inside of the church. The murder would echo here for a long time, eating further at the blessing in the walls until someone could get out here to clean it up.

I might even be the one cleaning, if I survived this.

"Need transport!" Gil yelled.

Well, at least he was thinking. "Don't *worry*!" We pounded down the hall, smell of chalk and incense, vestments hung on one side and the wine cabinet locked behind gilt-edged froufrou, my coat snapping and the silver in my hair buzzing and spitting blue sparks. It was dark in here, the lights flickering and buzzing. The sharp-edged charms Perry had given me were heavy, twitching as if alive. "Gonna have to steal a car!"

"Aw, *chica*." Gilberto coughed rackingly. He was keeping up so far, but soon his strength would start to flag. There was only so much healing sorcery could do, and both I and the dogsbody were moving with eerie speed. "You a real role model."

"Bite me, kiddo." Our footsteps sounded like one runner, until I left the ground in a leap that blew the outside door clean off its hinges. I rode it down, guns out, and swept as a howl went up.

The sun was low in the west, not setting yet but damn close, and clouds were boiling over what had been a blue vault. Greenyellow stormlight filled the alley; there was a basketball hoop bolted above the one-car garage at the dead end. The garage door was open, and I didn't have time to remember playing horse with Father Gui as an apprentice, both of us talking smack and the priest's three-pointers marvels of accuracy. He crossed himself after each one. Misha would be drinking a beer and watching, occasionally catcalling a point of advice that was of no earthly use whatsoever as Father Rosas sat next to him in a sagging lawn chair and glowered disapprovingly.

No, no time to think about it and feel the rage or the grief, because there was a car backed into the garage, pointed out at the alley. It was the church's only vehicle, the ancient Cadillac Ignacio had picked up for a song and I'd rebuilt and cherried out, long ago in the dim time after Mikhail's death. No time to remember working on it, Ignacio handing me tools and Gui asking me soft questions about what this or that part of the engine did. "*Get in!*" I yelled; there were lean shapes at the alley's mouth.

The key was in the ignition, and it reeked of Ignacio's cigars. Gil was coughing, gone cheesy-pale in a way I didn't like at all, and the dogsbody growled as the tools hung on pegboards chattered, the entire garage rocking like a ship in a storm as the church tolled its distress.

The shapes at the end of the alley were hellhounds, their eyes full of venomous, greenish glow. I twisted the key and was rewarded with a throbbing purr. The old girl still remembered me. "*This* is a car!" I barked. "This is the kind of car you steal, Gil! Good old American heavy metal!"

He slumped in the seat, but his quick brown fingers were busy reloading. "They don' look happy, *bruja*." Another cough, but I'd snapped the parking brake and dropped it into gear. I floored it and the Caddy leapt forward like it had never intended to stay still.

"*Fuck* them!" I yelled, and we hit the massed bodies at the end of the alley with a crunch. The Caddy snarled, the dogsbody let out a yowl, and we were through as the sky muttered with thunder.

"Where we goin'?" Gilberto grabbed for his window, rolling it up, and I had a mad desire to flick on the air-conditioning.

Shit if I know, kid. But it hit me like lightning, Melendez's mouth shaping a spirit's words, and understanding broke through me like water through a bombed dam. It could have been intuition, or the gem in my wrist suddenly singing in a language I understood, or just the most insane option at this point. But as soon as it occurred to me, I knew it was right.

The speedometer's needle popped up past sixty and I stood on the brake, twisting into a bootlegger's turn, fishtailing as hellhounds boiled out of the shadows, their hides leprous with steam in the scabbed light. They closed around us like a wave, running, their obsidian-chip teeth champing between gobbets of poisonous foam, and Gilberto let out a short miserable cry as he realized they were *herding* us.

"Gonna play some baseball, Gil. It's the World Series, and I'm on call." My breath came in heaving gasps, and my cheeks were wet. The world was doing funny things seen through my left eye, jumping and twitching as the strings under the fleshly curtain were plucked and torn. "Listen carefully, and *don't argue.*"

IV: Dies Irae

CHAPTER 34

There was nobody on the streets. I wasn't surprised—even numbskull civilians will stay inside when the sky looks like a ripening bruise and the air is full of scorching that feels like an ice bath. Now that we were going the way they wanted, the 'breed hung back, letting the hounds nip and harry us through the streets. I made a few attempts to shake them, just because I don't like being chased. Mother Mary on a pogo stick, how I *hate* to be pursued.

But there was nothing left to do, and Gilberto did *not* look good. He clutched at the gun like it was a Grail, and his lips moved a little as if he was praying.

It was a good idea, but I had no time.

"You hear me?" I finished, as we hit International Way and the four lanes ribboned around us, every light turning green as we sped through, tires smoking and the hell-hounds pouring around us in a steaming wave. "No heroics, Gil. You get the *fuck* out of here and strike for Ridgefield. Leon'll take you in."

Gil's chin set stubbornly.

"Gilberto. You're a liability, not a help. You go, or I swear to God I'll beat the shit out of you myself." It was a good threat. I even sounded like I meant it.

"You goin' in there to die." Flatly, as if he was talking about the nice weather we were having lately. "*Mi hermano*, he look like this, like you. Right before he got shot."

I almost winced. His brother was not a safe subject, the past reaching out its tentacles to strangle us all. "They can't kill me, kid." I sounded weary even to myself. "Perry needs me for this." *A Trader can steal a Talisman, but not wield it. Not for very long, anyway—but if he's using it to power the hellmouth... Still, I'm the Judas for the Other Side. I have to make it a little longer, right?*

It was *so* not a comforting thought.

Gilberto's chin set itself, stubbornly. "So I go in. Watch your back."

"No."

"*Profesora*—"

"No, Gil. You have your orders, goddammit."

"*Profesora*—"

"*No*." I said it a lot more sharply than I meant to, and hit the brakes, slewing us sideways as International dove down to follow the river. The stadium was here, hulking like a giant animal over a bone, one of the places in the city where you can't see the huge granite Jesus on top of Mercy General. Sometimes I'm pretty sure it's an act of will that keeps that particular landmark from being visible in some pockets of urban real estate. "I'm counting on you, Gilberto. Don't let me down."

He mumbled something. I smashed the accelerator again, spun us into another turn, stood on the brake. "I can't *hear* you, apprentice." Snap of command.

"*Sí,*" he said, scowling. "*Sí, profesora.*" Just like a good soldier.

Just like me, when Mikhail would tell me what was what. Would I ever reach the point where I'd trade Gil for my own mark, sell him to Perry to buy a little more time? Or bargain him into it out of love, believing that he could do what I couldn't and stop *el rubio Diablo* from spinning the wheel and landing a double zero?

I don't want to find out. It ends here. "Good fucking deal." We rocked to a stop, tire smoke rising in sharp-toothed shapes around us. The hellhounds flowed in a leaping circle, stormlight running wetly over their smoking hides as thunder rumbled again. "Gil..."

He stared out the window, sallow, pitted jaw working.

"You're my apprentice," I said, finally. "And you're a good one. You won't understand for a long, long time. But I love you, and I'm sorry. It's not your fault."

I hit the latch and was outside in a hot second, leaning down to glance through the back window. "Stay with Gil," I said, sharply, and the dogsbody settled into the backseat, whining. Every hair on my body tried to stand straight up, I heard hellhound claws skritching and scratching, and the splatter of foam from their panting mouths. The circle tightened, pressing closer, and I glanced up at the sky.

The clouds lowered, sickly greenish-black. Lightning crawled through their billows, occasionally lancing with a *crack* like a belt hitting naked flesh. I slammed the door, Gilberto already shimmying over into the driver's side. The Cadillac purred, a plastic rosary swinging from the rearview—maybe it was Father Gui's, maybe Rosa's—and Gilberto stared through the window, his dark eyes suddenly wet.

I told him what I wish Misha had told me, I realized, and swallowed hard. The hellhounds didn't draw any closer.

I stepped back once, twice. The engine revved, the tires chirped...

...and the hellhounds flowed aside at the last moment, leaving a clear path for Gilberto as the wine-red Caddy shot up Martin Luther, its engine singing in mingled pain and relief.

The Santa Luz Stadium and Convention Center was a squat, graceless concrete dome, pathways cut up and down its sides like ribbons of frosting on a particularly nasty soot-gray cake. Normally, a gigantic American flag fluttered atop it, waving like a stripper's pasty, but the three squat glass towers of the nearby convention center leered at an empty flagpole now, reflecting bright white flashes as the storm closed over Santa Luz. No rain, everything hot with that queer icy heat, the edges of my coat flirting as the wind teased them. My right hand touched a gun, and I felt very exposed standing here.

Almost naked.

I swallowed again, waited as the Cadillac's roar was lost even to my jacked-up hearing. *"Do svidanye,"* I whispered. My left hand had already closed around the whip's handle.

If they wanted me to go in there, they were going to have to work for it.

Unfortunately, the hellhounds took me up on the challenge. They moved in, heads down and snaking, a whole massed tide of them, and I gave ground. The whip flicked, breaking tough skin and loosing spatters of stinking ichor, but I didn't draw the gun.

I had no bullets to waste, now.

They herded me past the ticket booths—all their glass shattered, glinting back little fractures of lightning—and the crowd-control turnstiles, the aluminum tubes twisted back in weird contorted flower-shapes. Someone had certainly been smoothing the path for me.

The primrose path, Jillybean. All the way down to Hell.

When the dogs got too close I flicked the whip at them, and one or two screamed in high, childlike voices. Thunder was a constant roar now, and I *felt* the sun touch the horizon, beginning its slow nightly drowning. The city shivered, concrete groaning, and the wind from the river howled through empty parking lots, tearing at the edges of the dome.

Darkness rose from the corners of the earth, and the hellhounds herded me into a long, low corridor. I heard a mutter, the bulk of the storm shut away. They'd stopped steaming under the lash of daylight, but the press of their bodies made the air quiver with unhealthy heat.

The corridor curved, and for a long time it seemed like I'd be in it forever, the hounds pressing forward to nip at and drive me along, my whip flicking with a jingle of blessed silver every few moments to hold them back. I skip-shuffled along, my back to one wall or the other, and ghastly fluorescent tubes fizzed and blinked overhead. Chipped paint on the concrete turned sickly as the hounds brushed against it, and the little dapples of my sea-urchin aura showed up, punctuating the etheric bruising with tiny crackles.

The corridor terminated in a set of double doors, pulsing as the air behind them pressed close with a crowd-murmur. The hounds stopped, some of them crouching on their haunches, tongues lolling and yellow foam dripping, wriggling into cracks in the floor with subtle hisses.

He must really be excited. I bit back a bitter little laugh. *All this trouble, Perry, when you knew I'd show up anyway.*

One of the hounds hiss-growled very softly, its lip curling back from glassine teeth. I jingled the whip and the beast cowered back into the mass.

Gonna see what's behind Door Number One, Jillian? Oh yeah, you bet. Right now. I eased along the wall, keeping an eye on the hellhounds. *Right fucking now. He's been setting this up for decades.*

Be a shame to keep him waiting.

I pushed against the crossbar. The door opened, sterile white light flooded through, and the sound of a crowd belched into the hall on a tide of dry candy corruption. The hounds pressed further back, and for a moment I considered taking them on until I ran out of ammo.

But that would be a waste. I had better things to use my bullets on.

I braced the door wide and stepped out into the glare.

CHAPTER 35

Whatever game we were going to be playing, it wasn't baseball.

The playing field was venomous green, usually Astroturf but now transmuted into short fleshy spikes that twisted and rippled obscenely as the crowd-roar passed over them. The glare was amazing, a nuclear flash prolonged until it was a scream of whiteness, a world-killing light. I blinked, my eyes watering, and forced myself to scan.

The field was bare and green, an indecent hump in the middle with a low block of darkness placed precisely on its crest. The sound was immense, swelling through feedback and screaming, the roar lifting my hair and blowing it back as etheric bruising tightened and my aura sparked, every inch of silver on me running with blue light.

It halted, a sudden silence filling the vast dome, and that quiet stole all the breath out of my lungs, the way a sudden jolt at the end of a rope will. Training clamped down, my lungs shocked back into working and my pulse dropping as my right-hand gun cleared leather. A rush of warm air slid past me and toward the closing doors; they latched shut with the clicks of bullets loaded in a clip.

Perry laughed. He spread his arms and grinned with sheer mad good humor. "*Darling!* One appreciates punctuality in a woman, almost as much as one appreciates beauty. Then again, my dearest one, you are *so* worth waiting for."

He wore black. A thin V-neck sweater and narrow pleated trousers, a sword of darkness against all the glare. His hair was pale tarnished silk, and his eyes glowed hellhound-blue. The change from his usual white linen was a shock, too, and my busy little brain started worrying at it. What did it *mean*?

Just let it go, Jill. You'll find out soon enough.

Super-acute senses are sometimes a curse. My eyes stung, but I caught movement up in the stadium seats, behind the screen of glare. *How many? Sounds like a lot, but echoes, hard to tell. Jesus.* I kept the gun trained on Perry, shook the whip slightly to assure myself of free play. "Actually, *Hyperion*, I'm early."

"We can argue later, my dove. And Brother Michael?"

"He sends his love." An answering grin pulled my lips back from my teeth. "You're being an asshole, Perry."

"Oh, you wound me. I have kept faith with you in every possible way. I allow you so much more than I would ever allow another." He backed up a step, two, his wingtips touching the fat blades of not-grass with slight squelching sounds. "For example, it was necessary to allow you to betray me. Or whatever you thought you were doing, darling. I don't expect you to be anything other than what you are."

"Which is what, Perry? What do you think I am?"

"My unwilling ally, darling. My enfleshment, my entrapment, and my lovely, lovely doom. In the old sense, of course. *Doom* as in 'inescapable.'" He actually lifted a hand and blew me a kiss. A susurrus went through the invisible crowd, a breaker of whispered titters. "Come here, dearest. Come see what your suitor has created, all for you."

I shot myself in the head to get away from you, Perry. Don't pretend you've got my interests at heart. But sick knowledge impelled me forward.

I had to *see.*

The altar was long and low, made of black volcanic glass instead of a chunk of a hangman's tree. I took it in with short, sipping little glances, between scanning the rest of the stadium. It seats an ungodly number of people for Wheelwrights games and other foolishness, a real sink of taxpayer dollars from the seventies when everything was whiskey-a-go-go out here in the desert. Santa Luz fought like hell to get the stadium pried out of the grip of the Noches County seat, and the success was Pyrrhic when everything went over budget and repairs started coming due.

And now it was full of hellbreed and Traders, bright-eyed and staring, whispering at each other. Popcorn passed from hand to hand, and I smelled hot dogs and hellbreed. The place wasn't quite packed yet, but it was filling up.

This is not good.

My pulse settled down. The sudden calm would be ominous, because it meant I was ready for action. But Perry just smiled, and the scuffle of finding seats intensified.

It was the altar's surface that made my throat seize up and my stomach sink. Twisted runes—the closest you can get to Helletöng in written form—were scored deep into the volcanic glass, their sharp edges full of diseased blue hellfire. There was a chalice of heavy golden metal, full of clotted scum. Not gold, because pure elemental metal—copper, silver, gold—is always a bane to them. Silver works best, and the silver in my hair was sparking continuously now. My apprentice-ring was dangerously warm.

There were other things on the altar. Deformed claws, lumps of meat. Organs from their victims, a loop of hanging-rope, a knife of sharp alien geometry... and the Lance.

La Primera Lanza del Destino, wrenched from its hiding spot at Sacred Grace, lay on the unholy altar, curls of steam rising around it as it shivered uneasily.

A long, fluted cylinder of dark, stained wood, or a metal veined and carved to look like wood. It vibrated also, etheric force barely held in check, and its long, leaf-shaped blades looked too delicate to do any harm, both of them trembling like high school kids on a first date.

The world spun out from under me. I knew what it was, now. Hutch's books had shown me everything once I knew where to look.

The granddaddy of all Talismans, the one all other Spears are copied from, the Spear of Undoing. No wonder the Church had kept it so secret. It was older than the pagans, far older than the savior they prayed to, and it probably hadn't been anywhere near his martyrdom . . . but still. It was a Major Talisman, and you don't leave those lying around. Especially when they have a nasty habit of being able to *unmake* things.

"It's not going to work." My voice was a thin tremor from the dry cave of my mouth. "There's no way it's going to work."

"Oh, you're such a *pessimist*." Perry sighed. "We have everything we need, my dearest. You and I will deal with my master, the hellmouth will remain open, and when the smoke has cleared, we shall be the undisputed rulers of a world remade in our own image."

Whose image? Not mine, you bastard. "Your master?"

"Father, master, whatever." He shrugged. "You didn't think I was *common*, did you, Kiss? I've taken an interest in your line for a very long time. And in Dresden, lo these many years ago, your predecessor Jack Karma and I had a meeting of minds. I gave him something he wanted, he gave me something I needed. And beautiful music was made."

This much, at least, I knew about. "Argoth. Your *father*?"

"One of many, darling. I told you, I am Legion. But *he* is very, very angry. You've barred him twice now. Ever since dear Jack sent him back, he's been aching and frothing to return and play games in this most fascinating of worlds. And to reclaim me, of course." He tilted his head, grinning at me. The silence was full of whispers, nasty mouthings, wet silk against sweating legs. "He thinks I'm going to help him."

"Aren't you?" I edged closer to the altar, but Perry resolved out of thin air next to me. The air tore itself apart with malevolent children's laughter. His fingers closed around my upper arm, slim steel bands, and I went very still, my left hand still on my whip handle.

"Now, now. Close enough for the moment. Don't be hasty." His fingers flicked, claws sliding free of pale narrow hardness, and leather tore. Perry grabbed my wrist, locking it.

He drew in a deep breath, his ribs crackling as they expanded. *"My children!"* he roared, and I almost flinched. His fingers bit down, and he shoved me back from the altar. *"Now is the hour of our glory!"*

"Glory!" A sea's foaming roil. The crowd went wild, arms lifted, claws and fists shaken. They howled and screamed and yapped, Trader and damned, all of them twisting under their screens of human flesh.

I stumbled back, using Perry's shove to get some space. Ran through the next few minutes in my head. There was just too much that could go wrong—

"Open the door!" Perry yelled, and the exotic thought that I was going to witness the creation of a hellmouth got me moving.

"The door, the door!" the crowd screamed back, and surged forward against the metal rails keeping them off the ten-foot drop to the stadium's floor. *"Open the door!"*

Thou Who, I thought, as my weight dropped back into my left leg, muscles tensing in preparation. *Thou Who hast given me to fight evil, protect me, keep me from harm.*

It was now or never. I exploded into a leap, aiming for the altar. If I could get my hands on the Lance—

Except it was too late. The gem on my wrist screamed, a high thin note like glass shivering into breaking, and Perry grabbed my ankle. He twisted, his fingers sinking into my boot with a sickening crunch, and hurled me across the field.

CHAPTER 36

Tucking, rolling, the not-grass splorching underneath me and sending up a rank, juicy reek. I fetched up against the goalpost at the north end of the field, and the gigantic hollow sound it made would have been funny if the red rage of pain hadn't swallowed me whole. I was on my feet in an instant, whip shaken free and the not-grass suddenly sticky underfoot, gripping my bootsoles like an angry insect-eating carpet. The gem wailed, my ribs popping out with crunching wet noises, and I whooped in a breath as I jagged to the side, heel grinding down and my entire body a scream of agony. The whip struck across Perry's chest, silver biting, flaying his sweater and the white marble-hard shell underneath.

"Lovely!" he screamed. *"Just like old times, Kiss! Kiss me again!"*

Backing up, a glance shot at the altar where the 'breed made a circle, pushing the Traders in front of them. Slack-mouthed, their eyes bright with the shine of the dusted, the Traders pressed forward, and the deep thrumming all through the stadium wasn't just the blood in my ears.

That's where he's going to get the initial charge to break open the hellmouth. Traders. A whole lot of them.

And with that much ritual death, plus a Talisman to fuel it, he could keep a gap in the walls of the world open for a while.

It made a mad sort of sense, really. Innocent flesh breaks the walls between here and Hell better than anything else, but in a pinch other death will do. And if it's the death of the damned, it's the next best thing to innocent. Because none of the damned ever really thinks they're going to be the one.

Death is for other people, like payment and guilt. The damned believe they're *special.*

I suppose we all believe that, way down deep.

The gun spoke twice, holes blown in Perry's sweater. Black ichor flew, splattering, but not enough of it. Perry grinned, a death's-head smile, and leapt for me. I faded back, still firing, and the fact that I still didn't know nearly enough about exactly *what* he was rose up to bite me.

He produced hellfire in the blue spectrum, when anything above orange is seriously bad news. He wasn't an *arkeus* or a *talyn*, because he had always been all-too-disturbingly physical. And right now he was acting like the bullets were bee stings—a little irritating, certainly, but not putting him down the way a load of silver should.

He flashed through space with the stuttering, eerie speed of hellbreed, but I was one step ahead of him, leaping up and to the side as muscles pulled against flash-healing bones in my side and my ankle gave an almost-unheeded flare of sick burning pain. The squelching underfoot heaved, whatever had taken the place of Astroturf trying to throw me, and if I could just get my hands on the Lance and a few more seconds' lead time I could disrupt the altar and maybe take down enough of them to—

Perry hit me with another sickening sound, and I flew up into the bleachers, twisting and firing as blood burst from my lips. Red blood, no trace of black corruption. The gem screamed, pumping etheric force through me on a wave of bright white, and the cry was echoed by the crowd at the altar. Traders were being pulled down, hellbreed hands narrow and hard and clawed and hairy quelling their struggles as the mood inside the stadium tipped over into glee and terror.

The Traders had Traded, and now the bill was due.

He hopped up the bleachers towards me, black wingtips leaving wet black prints, the crowd had pulled away from this section and I suspected that was why he'd thrown me up here. He was *playing* with me, cat with mouse, and the knowledge filled me with welcome fury.

Do not get angry, Mikhail had always warned me. *Makes you stupid.*

I couldn't help it.

The Traders began screaming, and the stadium was an echo chamber, collecting the cries in massive sheaves and throwing them back down to earth. *Didn't count on being the sacrifice, did you? Serves you right.* I was up on my feet again, steel-shod heels chiming soundlessly as I found my balance in a wide aisle, Perry hopping up the steps in a mockery of dancing, his joints moving in sickeningly wrong jerks.

The stadium howled, concrete vibrating in distress, and Perry flung out a hand. Blue hellfire splashed up the seats to my right. I was already moving, flinging myself through a wall of super-heated air, leather crisping and smoking, landing braced on two seats and pushing off, *twisting* in midair as my coat gave a snap like wet laundry, and my feet skidded across the not-grass, throwing up huge chunks of rotting foulness. Traders were dying in droves, the deep rumbling of Helletöng swallowing their screams whole, and a pale oval of brightness was spinning over the altar.

Jesus Christ! It was going too quickly—of course, he'd had a lot of time to prepare. The altar was heaped with harvested organs, and the Traders were falling at the hands of the hellbreed they'd Traded with, corruption-reek filling up the vast bowl space. The bodies fell, twitching, dust eating through them and spiraling up on hot drafts, spinning eddies of it coalescing and sprouting curse-wings. The baby curses flapped, squawking in 'töng, and glaring white light stabbed through me as Perry hit me again, driving me down into the not-grass. I choked, spitting to clear my mouth, my abused ribs giving another howl, and the knife was in my hand as we rolled to a stop, the blade dragging against his shell and biting in, silver sparking and hissing.

He jerked back as if stung, grabbed my wrist, and twisted, the knifeblade running with blue light, ichor sizzling on the metal. I punched him twice with my free hand, fist braced with my whip handle, black ichor flying. I spat again, tasting foul oil-soaked dirt, knee coming up as my heel stamped down, but he was too heavy and getting heavier, the physical world rippling around him as etheric force ran through us both. The gem was a wild high melody over the subsonic fright-train grumble of 'töng, and I was suddenly in the desert again, clawing my way up out of sand with the hornets buzzing and eating all over me, screaming and chok-ing as ectoplasm and grit filled my mouth.

"Beautiful!" Perry yelled in my ear, even though I punched him again. His head snapped back, more ichor flew, and he was grinning through a thin black mask of it as his chin came back down.

I screamed, struggling, and the world skipped like someone had jostled the CD player it was spinning in. It came back, but only at a quarter of its usual speed, the curse-birds gaining strength and mass and slowly beating their wings and the screams of dying Traders running like colored oil on a wet plate.

Perry held my wrists. He was impossibly heavy, as if gravity had decided he was an exception to every rule. Ichor dripped down his face, and he blinked at me, first one mad blue eye, then the other. "Judith," he crooned, under the soupy feedback of the titanic noise raging in slow motion around us. "My darling. My *flesh.*"

Don't. Call. Me. That. Rage ignited, I heaved up under him, breaking my right hand free with another screaming twist. The knife flicked, biting his abdomen again. We rolled, the fetid green juice of the crushed not-grass sliding and slipping over us both like birth fluid.

The world snapped forward, catching up with itself, and I heard a familiar battlefield yell.

Thank fucking God. Relief then, hot and acid against my throat.

The hunters had arrived.

CHAPTER 37

The tranced Traders were still dying, but now the hellbreed were dying too. I saw Benny Cross from Louisiana, his ferret face alight as he opened fire with both guns; Sloane from gray rain-drenched Seattle, the charms in his hair chiming as he swung two silver-plated *escrima* sticks, Leon from Ridgefield, his battered tan duster scorched and spotted with blood while Rosita, his modified rifle, roared. Thierry Parvus from Saskatchewan, dropping out of the sky like God's avenging while the copper charms on his boots' fringes rattled and spat, Emoke Kolada and Dmitri Roslan, John Blake and John Carver and John Gray and Jack Quint and Jack Hell, Louis Darmor and MaryAnn Bright, too many to list. Some of them I only knew from word of mouth, others I knew because I'd worked with them; a few had come to Santa Luz to help out once or twice and I'd returned the favor. Many of them I didn't know at all, but they were all hunters, elemental metal jingling and long coats swinging as they waded into the fray, their auras cracking with sea-urchin spikes like my own.

Their cries were a bright counterpoint over the rumble of 'töng, and I could have wept. Because we do something the 'breed don't ever do: we work together. It means every hunter is worth more than their weight when it comes to holding back Hell's tide; even when there's a mass of them, every one of Hell's scions only thinks of his own advantage. The hunters moved in tightly disciplined bands, cutting through the crowds, and I saw Anya Devi, her beads running with blue light and Benny Cross at her back, heading straight for the altar.

If even one of us could reach the altar, we could nip Perry's little plan right in the ass.

Oh, God, oh God thank you—

Perry snarled, my fingers in his hair, and I slammed his skull against the yielding ground. It felt wonderful, so I did it again, realized it wasn't going to do any good just as he got his wits about him and heaved up, tossing me away. I landed catfooted, had my balance in a split second, and leapt after him.

He was heading for the altar. He was too impossibly fast, streaking through trembling, overloaded reality. Anya was bogged down in a knot of struggling 'breed and Traders, her guns literally blazing and her scream of frustration a rising hawk-cry of effort.

Don't worry, I'm on it, just keep going—

Another roar filled the stadium, and I didn't have time to blink or even really register the fact that Weres had begun pouring into the stadium through flung-wide doors, leaping gracefully and flickering between animal and human form, clustering dazed Traders and bringing them down, trying like hell to avoid the 'breed. Lionesses, tawny-armed and honey-haired, working together to take down their prey, other cat Weres simply, magnificently fought; the bird Weres flickered through their feathered changeforms and raked with long talons. If they could keep the Traders away from the ritual death meted out near the altar, just maybe...

But we were doomed, because Perry was faster than all of us.

He cleared a thrashing knot of 'breed in a single leap, and hurled himself at the pale oval spinning atop the altar's black crouch. The curse-birds swarmed down, ripping past him in black bullet-shreds, and the oval became a dome of pitiless white light.

He couldn't touch a Major Talisman. But he didn't have to. All he had to do was get it close enough to the hungry orifice.

His foot flicked out, and he kicked the Lance directly into the incipient hellmouth.

The world exploded.

I was down and rolling as the shockwave passed over me, the fabric of reality bunching and twisting as it was torn rudely open. Bodies went flying, ichor splattering, and the noise was so big I moved in a bubble of silence as soon as it started, hot fluid trickles slipping down from my ears, kissing my neck. The pain was silver nails driven through my skull, a warm gush of blood loosing itself from my nose, but I was already committed to the leap. A collapsing hellbreed, his mouth a soundless scream of agony, folded as my boot kissed the top of his head, propelling me forward, my whip hand flicking forward and the gun in my other hand now.

Too late. The door was open.

Hellbreath streamed free, a wave of heat so fierce it was cold, and it was a good thing I was temporarily deaf. Surviving Traders fell, hands clapped to their ears, screaming silently. I had no time to think about how the Weres were handling this, I was too busy, bracing myself for the hit as a tide of half-seen shapes burst free of the hole in the world.

This wasn't a regular portal, a hair-thin millisecond gap in the world for something to slip through. This was a full-fledged hell-mouth, the dome of white light an obscene abscess swelling, pushing against the altar's surface, hellbreed crawling out of the yawning light as Hell shoved them free.

I strained through air gone thick as lead, committed to my leap, as the mouth pulsed once, drooling hellbreed and the shadowy forms of *arkeus* like pus. Perry lifted his arms, braced against the flood of his kith and kin, and leaned forward. His mouth stretched, and the long grinding of Helletöng was a single word, rubbing through the deaf-noise and spearing every cell of my body.

The hole clotted, and for one second as I hung above him I

thought perhaps it had closed of its own accord. But no, it was just heaving around something almost too big for it, and I must have known on some level. Because the gun was back on its holster before I hit the ground, my whip jolting free, and I dove for the altar as the hellmouth pursed its thin lips and vomited.

The gem on my wrist gave a hard, painful jerk. My whip uncoiled, silver jangling silently. My right-hand gun spoke, burning flooding my arm and the gem shrieking. If I hadn't been swimming in so much pain already, the sudden cramp might have brought me to my knees.

I opened my mouth to scream if I had to, but there was no *time*. The world burst out into hypercolor, even more vivid than the superacute senses the gem gave me. At the same time, everything slowed down, my hip popping forward because always, in whip and stave work, it's the hip that leads. Temporary deafness fraying at the edges as the whip stretched, blurring-fast, and the thing vomited through the hellmouth leaned back, its foot crushing against the wooden Lance as it shuddered on the altar's top. Ash rose as the Lance twisted, bits of it grinding away finer and finer as the hellmouth chewed at its stored-up power.

The *thing* that had come through was an amorphous bipedal shape, silhouetted against the glow—hellbreed are like Elder Gods, they do not dress when they are at home, but when they come over into the physical they need *some* kind of shape. There's a moment just as they're coming through where you can glimpse their alienness, and it can drive you howlingly, gratefully insane.

But I was already halfway there, fury rising inside me. A chilling, glassy sound broke out of my mouth, burning my throat. Even through the deafness I heard it, like murder in a cold room at midnight, and we struck—the whip and I—at the same time, with physical and etheric force.

And we got his attention.

The world went white. Landing, *hard*, throwing up a sheet of juicy foul green and clods of oily black not-dirt, knocking over hellbreed like ninepins, the jolt snapping bones with sweet pain, blood bursting free in scarlet banners. The gem screamed on my wrist, and a shock ran through me from crown to feet as it tried to patch me up and get me fighting again. Everything tilted sideways, and something damp kissed my cheek.

Rain. It was rain. The roof was crumbling, concrete chunks falling with silent, eerie grace, smoke thinning as water fell from the sky and lightning flashed again and again.

They had come.

They shone, sliding down through the gaps in the dissolving roof like cosmic firemen, clarity glittering on their armor and their wings. No guns for them—they had swords and slender spears, bows and knives, chains and flails. They moved among the hellbreed, winnowing, and Hell's scions were screaming in terror but still standing to fight.

They had no choice.

The clarity around the newcomers shone through the hellbreeds' twisting, stripping off their masks and the rotten applebloom of damned beauty.

He landed next to me, his hair a furnace of gold and his blue eyes alight, and leaned down. The gem gave a heatless, massive twinge all through my broken bones. His hand closed around mine and he pulled as if I weighed less than nothing, hauling me to my feet.

"This is the help we can give!" Michael the Caretaker said. The words cut through the deafness, laid right in the center of my brain. I was so far gone I didn't even feel a weary satisfaction at seeing the wings behind him, glorious white and feathered like a vulture's, spread wide, glowing like the sun. *"Human hands must end this!"*

Oh, I'll end it, I thought, and another cold, adrenaline-fueled little laugh burst out of me as Michael swung aside, his sword coming up with a sweet singing, cleaving the cringing air.

Perry fell back, snarling, and he had a sword of his own. Its blade was tarry black, drinking in the light, but I promptly shelved him as a problem and looked to find the badass who had just stepped through from Hell.

I'd settle Perry's hash later. Still, if the caretaker wanted to save me the trouble, that was fine with me. I had other fish to kill.

CHAPTER 38

The hole in the world glowed white-hot, and more hellbreed were draining through. The big one—Argoth, a nightmare made flesh now—crouched as he finished settling into form, a sheet of glaucous film tearing from the inside as he used his claws. He stood, naked, and my boots were thudding onto the squishy field, jolting agony through me like wine, laughing at the idea that I could be stopped by the blood I was losing or a little thing like the broken bones grating together, desperately trying to heal as the gem sang a descant of impossible, strained beauty.

I left the ground, sound coming back in stuttering bursts as my eardrums healed with spikes of wet red pain. Roaring, screaming, weeping, the cracks of thunder and wet sizzling sounds, hunters screaming their battle cries and Weres making a lot of noise, gunfire spattering—

Impact. Or not. I missed him.

He *twisted* aside, his mad blue eyes wide with delight, and the first shock was that he looked like Perry. Or maybe Perry was just a pale copy of this creature, a marvel of twisted pale beauty, his mouth a cruelly luscious crimson slash, his ears coming up to high points poking through the frayed mat of spun-platinum hair. Force transferred and I was thrown, the whip handle biting my hands as it was ripped free and the gem resonating to the chaos around me. Landed again, all the breath and sense knocked out of me. My body decided now was a fine time to just take a little vacation. Just lay there and breathe for a second, except I couldn't get any air in.

Get UP! But nothing would obey me, my hands flayed and the broken bones healing but too slowly, everything inside me straining and even my will—that trainable, teachable thing that drives the body, that *makes* it obey—wasn't working. What the mind requires, the body will do; but the body has its limits. Sorcerous gem or not, I suspected I'd reached mine.

Well, maybe not *suspected*. More like, *found out*.

A shadow fell over me. My eyes rolled. It was Argoth, standing with the Lance shaking unhappily in his pale, beautifully shaped hand. It wept and strained to get away, ash rising on a hot updraft, and he snarled.

He shouldn't have been able to touch it, but it was probably drained from holding the hellmouth open. Tracers of ash ribboned back as the hungry mouth yawed, wind screaming as it sucked, shrinking—but not fast enough. It was gorged with incredible power, and it would close itself—but Argoth was *here*.

Perry could do all sorts of crap he wasn't supposed to; why should I have expected his father, original, whatever, to be different?

I noticed, with a variety of shocked, swimming amusement, that his long, amber-burnished fingernails were buffed. *Well, if you're going to step out of Hell, you might as well make sure you've got a manicure, right?* It was the merry voice of doom, caroling inside my weary skull, but the only thing I felt was exhaustion and a great drowsy sense of having let them down.

Wake up! Move! It was my own voice, shrilling at me. Usually when I'm hurt bad there's someone else inside my skull, pushing me.

But I had nobody left.

He lifted the wooden Lance, glare of lightning playing along the slick, ash-weeping blade, and a wide, beautiful-ugly, triumphant smile twisted his face. *Now* he looked like a hellbreed, the shadow of the thing freshly released from Hell's cold, screaming confinement rippling under his skin.

I braced myself to die again.

Then his head jerked back, black ichor spattering. And again. Bullet holes bloomed on his chest, and my head lolled drunkenly enough to see Gilberto, widelegged in the shooting stance I'd taught him, making his triangle and aiming nicely, squeeze the trigger again. His eyes were bright and lively, he was covered in black stinking 'breed rot, the bandage on his arm was torn and flapping, and the Eye of Sekhmet glowed on his chest, sending up a curl of smoke that wreathed his sallow, young-old face.

He was *laughing*. Even as Argoth let out a banshee wail that dwarfed all other sound and spun the spear, the bullet holes closing over and sealing the hurt away. Silver wasn't going to put this bitch down.

The wall of sound hit Gil, and he tumbled over backward. But the dogsbody was already in the air, its blond hide streaked with spatters of smoking black, and it hit the baddest hellbreed I'd ever seen with a crunch I felt all the way down on the ground.

Now get up, Mikhail said inside my head, and I could swear...

No. I don't need to swear. I *saw*.

One of the winged things was near me, a familiar hitching limp as he eased his sore knee, that clarity blooming over him in a waterfall of light. Not the sterile white nuclear light from the hellmouth, but the white of a clean sheet of paper, a freshly bleached sheet, sunshine on sugar sand, joy and sunrise. He leaned down, his hair a mop of pure silver, and grabbed my arm. It was the same hand, hard and callused from daily practice and nightly hunting. The same long nose and narrow mouth, the same pale blue eyes with dark lashes, the same cleft in his chin and the same vulnerable notch where his collarbones met the breastbone. He didn't look tired, but there was still the faint shadow of knowledge in his eyes. His wings were iron-gray, like his hair used to be, and there was the scar along his jawline, now a thread of gold against his skin. And another scar on his throat, a thick, golden torq.

His mouth opened, but nothing came out. My teacher's voice whispered directly inside my head, even as his lips soundlessly shaped the words.

Now get up, milaya, *and kick bastard back to Hell where he belong.*

He gave me a little push, as if we were in the sparring room and I had to do it again, but faster and better this time. I stumbled, glancing down to find my footing, new strength pouring through me and the gem resonating on my wrist.

When I looked up, he was gone. The dogsbody landed in a heap next to me, scrabbling weakly for a moment before going limp, twisted on itself. Its eyes fell shut, and it gave a little sigh.

Argoth grinned, licking his red, red lips. His tongue was purplish, shocking against the rest of his beauty, flickering between sharp white teeth. The world was tearing itself to pieces around us, but we stared at each other for a few heartbeats, and he lifted the warping, trembling Lance slightly.

I let out a long breath, my ribs finally healing fully with snapping crackles. The hellmouth pulsed behind him, casting knife-sharp twisting shadows, and the flood of Hell's icy heat lifted my blood-soaked hair. I lifted my filthy hands, and the sharp pin-pricks of Perry's charms dug into my skull as they moved rest-lessly. The hornet buzz filled my head.

That's so strange. Now I remember being dead.

Then he was on me, the Lance moving so fast it blurred, still wicked sharp even through the shredding of ash rising from every surface, screaming its bloodlust and defiance. But I'd thrown myself forward, already inside the arc of his attack, and grabbed.

My right hand closed on the Lance's haft, and its chill jolted up my arms. Argoth had raw power, and a hellbreed's ability to twist things into obeying him. But I was a hunter, and I was human, and I had an edge when it came to forcing a Major Talisman to do what *I* wanted it to.

Or so I hoped.

Because after all, we made the Talismans. They're *ours*. They do not come from Hell.

My left hand clamped down over his, my fingers biting with preternatural strength, and we were face-to-face for a long, shat-tering moment while I drove him back. There was a warm wind behind me, and it smelled of peppery adrenaline and vodka, leather and musk and the warm smell of Mikhail's skin as he lay beside me in our shared bed. I *pushed*, and the wind behind me wasn't just Mikhail. It was my fellow hunters, Anya and Gilberto, and Monty and my cops; it was my city exhaling as dawn rose and shuddering as dusk fell, while I prowled its rooftops and alleys; it was the hornets buzzing and the spear singing a glassy bloodlust cry, the gem burning on my wrist and every inch of silver on me suddenly running with the same clarity that folded around the winged things.

And finally, it was Saul, his eyes dark with pleasure as he sighed into my hair. Saul cooking pancakes and yawning, his sleepy smile a reward all its own. Saul holding me while I wept, my own arms around him as we both shook, the promise of pain shared and halved in the darkness.

You will not survive, Michael had told me. *You will have to sacrifice yourself again to destroy Hyperion.*

All I felt, finally, was relief that Saul was safe with Galina.

I drove forward, legs pumping, and Argoth's face corkscrewed in on itself as he realized what I was about to do. He tried to let go of the spear, but I had his right hand locked too. The gem sang on my wrist, a rising tide of light inside my bones.

I pushed against him, close as a lover, his hot rank breath in my face and his teeth champing, spattering me with yellow foam.

Not so pretty now, are we.

I threw us both into the hellmouth. The silver I was carrying and my hunter's aura would disrupt it. The shock would shred my physical structure, but that was a small price to pay.

Wasn't it?

Mercifully, everything went black.

CHAPTER 39

C onfusion.

"Hold her head up." A familiar voice, but so tired, almost slurring the words. "Jesus."

Stutter-flashes of light. Rumbling as the storm retreated, cold rain lashing down. I was wet all over, and freezing. Every part of me burned with savage pain. Someone's arm under my head, sharp little charms biting into my skull. Heaving breaths; someone was moaning.

I'll bet there's a lot of wounded. Then, muzzy amazement. *Wait.*

"I'm not dead?" I actually said it out loud, my lips rubbery, sounding like a dumbfounded drunkard.

A short growl-cough of a laugh, one I recognized. "No. Not yet."

My eyes flew open. I tried to move, too, my entire body tensing, but Saul's arm tightened under my head. He was haggard and damp with rain, and the blood on his face made every part of me cold with fear.

"Relax," he said, gently but firmly. "Just settle down for a second, okay?"

"Galina—" I began.

"She's okay. Mad as hell, but okay. We're going to have to have a talk, Jillian."

I stared at him. There was crusted stuff in my eyes. I blinked. Lightning spattered through the clouds. The stadium's roof was a gigantic gaping hole. The whole place was peppered with huge chunks of concrete, as if the gods of urban architecture had decided to throw up over everything.

Monty is just going to have a fit. It was a good thought, a sane thought. It meant I was alive. Saul's mouth was drawn tight, and he looked fine. Bloody, but fine.

"You are never doing that to me again," he informed me. "I swear, Jill. If you even try I'll..." He ran out of words, his irises flaring with orange as the cougar came close to the surface. It retreated, and the rumble in his chest was a growl.

My lips were cracked. My mouth tasted foul. But I managed to get the words out, only slurring them a little. "Nothing. Could be worse. Than losing. You."

A flash of pain crossed his face, and it tore at my heart. I never wanted to hurt him. But he simply leaned forward, his other arm slipping around me as well, and pulled me close. We clung to each other, one bone-thin Were and a very tired hunter, and if there were tears on my cheeks nobody saw and I didn't care.

He was alive. So was I.

It had to be enough.

We didn't get to stay like that, though. "Jill?" Anya Devi, softly.

Saul's arms loosened. I found I could move. "Jesus," I moaned, and someone laughed.

"Always did know how to throw a party, darlin'." Leon's Texas drawl was thick as cream. He must've been tired. "Nice friends you got. Where you find them?"

"Oh, shut up." Anya sighed. "Jill. Please."

I got my legs working again. Saul helped. He hauled me up carefully, I still weighed more than I should. Denser muscle, denser bone, the gem sparking on my wrist, humming a low note of satisfaction. My skin crawled. I was covered in guck and goop and I stank to high heaven.

Everything stank. The not-grass was dying, lashed by cold water. The altar was crushed under a huge shipwreck-shape of concrete, a charred stick jetting up from its crest. After a second I realized it was a flagpole, and the char-tattered rags hanging from it were anonymous. The hellbreed and Traders were either dead or fled, but there were bodies *everywhere*. Mounds of corpses, and grim-faced Weres picking through them, looking for survivors.

Or looking for their kin, or for hunters.

"Did we..." I steadied myself against Saul's shoulder. *Did we lose anyone?* I couldn't say it.

"Some. Maybe." Anya was wet clear through, leaning on Theron. The Werepanther looked somber, but Devi just looked tired. "We'll deal with that in a bit. There's...something you should see."

Oh, Christ, what now? But I squared myself, wearily, and found I could stand. Not very steadily, but I could at least hold myself upright. I could even fight, if I had to.

Except what was left to kill?

I had a sneaking suspicion I was about to find out.

The Lance lay near the altar, twisted like the flagpole, quivering a subaudible hum of distress and frustrated anger. It was weak, very weak. All the force it had accumulated was now spent, and all it could do was shake like a whipped dog.

Dog. "Gilberto?" I whispered. "And the...the dog?"

"Gil's fine." Anya pointed. "See?"

My apprentice was bandaging Benny Cross's leg. Half of Gil's hair was singed off, Benny was covered in all kinds of crap, and the dogsbody slumped next to Gilberto, hanging its narrow head. It glanced at me, ears pricking, but it looked as tired as Anya. As tired as I felt.

Thank you. I didn't even know who I was thanking. "Good deal," I rasped. "Okay. What's next? Point me at it. I'll kill it."

"Good." Devi shook herself away from Theron with a quick glance of thanks. "Because it's Perry. Sort of. And if you don't ventilate that fucker, I just might."

CHAPTER 40

At the northern edge of the battlefield, a few of the winged things had gathered. The rain avoided them.

They didn't turn as Anya and I approached, Saul and Theron hanging back with perfect Were tact. A few other hunters—Dmitri Roslan, Jack Quint, a short, hard-faced woman I realized was Belle de Sud herself, with her long brown fingers flicking uneasily at her whip handle, four or five others—stood in a loose semicircle, watching. Dmitri flicked me a salute, his usual grin absent; I returned it without thinking.

I couldn't help it. I stared at the wings. They were all white, some with flecks of brown. And *huge*, managing to look perfectly natural instead of a violation of biology. The clarity had faded to a slow gleam around them, no longer hurtfully bright. They faced something chained to the goalpost, glints of gold shifting as the blackened, charred thing moved slightly. A ripple of tension went through the winged, as if they expected him to break the thin golden bonds and start making trouble again.

Bitterness filled my mouth. Anya tapped at a gun butt, her face set.

The tallest of them half-turned as I halted next to him. It was Michael the Caretaker, and there was no shadow of scarring left on his face. His wings drooped a little, as if he was tired, too. His eyes were the same, though, bright and mild, that shadow of pain sending an answering twinge through me.

"You understand," he said, quiet.

I don't understand this at all. "Yes," I heard myself say, dully, a good pupil aiming to please. "Sacrifice."

Michael nodded. "You were willing, again, even when there

was no hope. That creates a...new thing, you could say, in the Pattern." He looked back at the charred form, and his shoulders dropped again. "His father is dead. He is utterly flesh now, as he wished to be." A world of sadness in the words. "The choice is yours, to spare or to kill."

I didn't want to think about that yet. "Where's Mikhail?" My hands were fists. "I *saw* him. He was here. Where is he?"

Michael shrugged. One wing flicked, delicately, sending a clean breeze over my filthy cheeks. "Only the ones present are here."

"Well, no shit." Sarcasm gave me fresh strength. The gem muttered, etheric force trickling back through me. I needed food, and rest, and maybe a couple pints of something eye-wateringly alcoholic before I'd be anything close to my mettle, but right at the moment I didn't care. I was shaking.

But not with the weakness. No.

With *rage*.

He turned, this time facing me fully. "Love cannot be forced. Love is only given, freely." A faint smile, but he didn't look happy. Instead, it was that sorrow again. "Love is only *proved*, though it asks no proof in return. This is important, but it is not our task here. We are to witness your choice." Again a wing dipped, indicating the blackened body, and I was forgetting I'd ever seen him without the snowy feathered expanses.

My fists ached. "What were you doing down there in the Hill's boiler room all this time, huh? Just waiting for this?"

"Witnessing." He nodded slightly, as if the question was expected, weighed his answer, and added more. "Serving the Pattern."

"Your Pattern fucking *blows*." It wasn't up to my usual standards. I sounded more like Gilberto than myself. "It's *insane*. It hurts good people. It's not fair."

"It is," he said gravely, "all we have."

He made a sudden movement, and another ripple went through the winged things. But he'd just unlimbered his sword from somewhere. It was a heavy broadsword piece of work, too tall for me, with wicked finials on the guard and a ruby the size of a fist at the end of the pommel. It looked razor sharp, and its bright blade smoked with dappled light.

It looked a little like the sunsword. Well, the sunsword was a toothpick compared to this, but still, you could see an echo.

He presented me with the hilt. Anya breathed an obscenity.

"It is your choice," Michael repeated.

It was hard work to shake my right hand out. Even harder to touch the damn thing. Warm strength poured down my arm from the cool metal, and Michael nodded approvingly.

I probably looked ridiculous, stepping across the sludge-dying not-grass, gingerly and awkwardly holding a broadsword almost as long as I was tall away from me. The winged stepped back in unison, but the hunters moved forward, almost as if prearranged.

Is this part of his fucking Pattern too? The bitterness was all through me.

He'd been burned, terribly. Weeping cracks coated his charred flesh, but his eyes were still the same sterile blue. The dome of his skull without any hair to cover it was subtly wrong, and he seemed smaller. Of course, anyone's going to look small covered in fourth-degree burns and chained to a goalpost, right?

Even a hellbreed.

His lips cracked. Thick colorless fluid wept from them. "Kissssssss." Sighing, like a lover.

"Hyperion. *Perry.*" I swallowed hard. My palms might have been sweating, or it might have been the rain or the filth making the hilt slippery. The sword hummed, a thunderbolt contained. His own black blade lay in pieces around him, and Perry raised his burned-bared head and stared at me. "Or should I say, Argoth."

A shrug. More blackened skin broke, a brittle sugarglaze. How he was still alive? "Only a part of him. A fragment. Insurance, originally. A doppelgänger, meant to be a placeholder here, in case the masters needed hands in this world."

It was my turn to nod slightly. "But you wanted more. Slipped the leash, made a deal with Jack Karma, and got the original locked away in Hell. Then you started planning how to get all of the original's power, all the other pieces of him." I coughed, tasted smoke. Thunder roiled in the distance, and the rain intensified. "But for that, you needed a hunter. Because you didn't just want all of your father. You wanted to be *real*. Anything above an *arkeus* isn't usually physical, it can be disrupted and once it is, goodbye and good night. The bargain with Karma and his line kept you here and gave you a simulacrum of flesh, and you could afford to settle down and wait for a hunter who could take on your poppa *and* keep you bolted to the physical world at the same time." *You followed Mikhail all the way from Europe. That's almost why he drew on you in the Monde that first time I saw you. Did he think he was free of you? Not likely. So what was he thinking?*

Would I ever know?

His tongue flickered, startling cherry-red. He studied me for a long time, and I let him. The sword quivered heavily, but my arm wasn't tired. It was building in me, the knowledge of what I had to do.

"I am flesh now," he finally hissed. "*Flesh*, my darling one. You made it possible. You killed the *original*, as you so quaintly call him. I am his heir, and we are linked. I am your other half. We're the same coin, my love."

Negation rose inside me. But I nodded again, slowly. He was at least partly right. I'd been mortgaging bits of myself to Perry for years, telling myself it didn't make me a Trader. It gave me the strength to police the nightside more effectively, and his mark on me had been the punishment I deserved.

For everything.

No. I couldn't afford to lie here. He was right. There was only a thread-thin edge between Perry and me. A coin's edge. He had waited for me for a very long time. Waited for the hunter who was, at bottom, *like* him.

We are the ones crying in the dark, and on our backs they build golden cities.

God help me, I understood.

"So what is it to be?" More of his brittle skin cracking as he shifted. The thin golden chains sent up threads of steam, whisked away by the cold wet breeze. "Cut me loose, and take your place as my keeper? Think of what you can do, with me your willing slave. Think of the battles you can win." Another wriggling motion.

He might eventually squirm free, I realized. But it didn't seem important.

"Or strike me down with that avenging sword—overcompensating a bit, aren't we? And damn yourself with murdering the helpless, whose only crime was to wait for you and love you?" Those white teeth were now grimed with thin pinkish fluid, darker lines accumulating between them. He writhed again. "I waited so, so long for you, my dove. Theirs is not the only Pattern."

There. That's what he's after. "No," I dimly heard myself say, through the roaring in my ears. "I suppose it isn't."

"We can make a new one," he whispered. "Just you and me. A *fair* one. You can mete out justice, and I will make it total. Just let me loose."

I stepped closer, boots squishing in the muck. "I suppose it isn't the only pattern." Louder now, clear and strong. "It's not even the one that *matters*."

Perry gazed up at me. "Let me free." So soft, all the promise in the world. "You will never be lonely, Kiss. Not so long as I am able to comfort you."

Oh, God. The problem wasn't that he said it.

The problem was that it was *true*. There was only a hairsbreadth of difference between Perry...and me. Or at least, the part of me that made sure I survived. The stranger who lived inside me, strong and ruthless where I was weak. And with him dead, I would be—down in the secret place where the animal of survival crouches, the part of me that was coldly determined to do what *had* to be done—*alone*.

Utterly alone.

The sword rose, thrumming, its blade suddenly pouring with white radiance. Perry bared his teeth, more skin crackling, and the golden chain burst with a tinkle. My right wrist flamed with cramping pain, but I brought the blade down with a scream. It cut, the goalpost singing before it groaned and tipped, smashing into the wet ground with a *plorch*.

Lifted and flung, my right arm on fire, torn out by the roots, every nerve screaming...and I landed, hard, my fingers forced open and the sword clattering away. Rustling filled the broken bowl of the stadium, and they took wing, spiraling up with a grace and authority that forced a dry barking sob from my aching, parched throat.

The last one bent over me, blue eyes dark with sorrow. But he was smiling, and he laid one warm finger to my lips. Warmth broke over me in a wave, white light filling my head for one long glorious moment.

Well done, he whispered. Or maybe it wasn't him. Maybe I just thought he did. Maybe I needed someone to say it.

In any case, there was a pop of collapsing air, and he vanished.

I lay there in the rain, fresh cold sludge working up through my hair and the tatters of my coat, with my right arm flung up as if to protect me.

My whole, naked, unmarked right arm.

CHAPTER 41

We had Galina to thank. Pissing off a Sanctuary by attempting to burn down her house from the outside is not a good idea, and she'd done something Sancs only keep for emergencies—somehow opening a space down in her vaults for hunters to step through from other Sanctuaries. They'd been flooding into Santa Luz ever since I'd made that frantic phone call to Anya Devi, and with them working from the top and other hunters working from the bottom, as well as Galina's control over the wrecked physical structure of her house, they'd broken through before dusk.

It didn't take a genius to figure out something big was going down, either. With the sky going dark and hellbreed and Traders popping up everywhere and making for the stadium, you only had to have half a brain in your head to figure out where the big event was going down.

Montaigne was moaning about property damage. Anya filled out the reams of paperwork for a Major Paranormal Incident so we could get government funding. Flash floods had claimed a couple lives, whole sections of the barrio were burned down, the morgue was groaning at the seams from the citywide spree of murder, arson, and other hellbreed fun. Most of the other hunters had only stayed to help deal with the cleanup in the stadium— banefire and yellow tape, just to be sure, and the Lance reduced to cold, metallic ash scraped into an alabaster jar—and headed back to their cities.

We're not much on goodbyes. So mostly they just slid out of town after exchanging a few words with me or Devi.

A few stayed. We'd lost four hunters and six Weres. One of the Weres was Rahel, and, oddly enough, that was the thing I cried over, hunched next to Saul's bed with my face in my knees, snot slicking my upper lip as I shook and sobbed as quietly as possible. I bit the smooth, unmarked skin on my right wrist where a scar in the shape of a pair of lips had been pressed, where the gem had shivered free of my flesh. I was still stronger and faster than even the average hunter, but there was no mark on me.

It's not even the only pattern that matters.

A bunch of 'breed had escaped through the hellmouth. Things were going to be hopping all over—but at least we'd staved off the *big* catastrophe. Argoth was no more, and there hadn't been any other prepared hellmouths.

Just the one. Just Perry's lunge toward fleshly incarnation. With me as his linchpin and Argoth's power behind him, what would he have been able to do?

What wouldn't he have done?

Galina's house and shop were fully rebuilt in a matter of eighteen hours, growing up from the ground like a mushroom. You can't keep a Sanc down for long; even if Perry had succeeded in locking her temporarily inside her vault and making her mad. She stalked around muttering for a while, checking every inch of her house and making tiny adjustments while the walls shivered with redgold sheets of cascading energy.

We all stayed out of her way, except for Theron.

The dogsbody had vanished. One moment it was there at the stadium, the next...gone. I didn't mention it to Devi.

Gilberto was in the barrio with some other hunter apprentices and Leon Budge, helping the Weres rebuild. Mickey's on Mayfair had gone down in a three-alarm fire—more hellbreed work—but they would rebuild.

Saul slept through most of it, but every time he woke up I was at his bedside. Devi handled the rest. It was one more thing to thank her for. Every time I tried, though, she just rolled her eyes and waved an absinthe bottle at me, threatening to make me drink until I shut up.

I shut up.

When Saul woke, he ate. I carried tray after tray of food up the stairs, watched him fill out bit by bit, listened to his breathing.

I did not think about Perry. Or about wings. I didn't sleep much, either. Maybe I was afraid of dreaming.

Hello? I asked the silence inside my chest. *Who am I? Tell me who I am now.*

There was no answer.

Anya tapped on the door one long, drowsy-sunny afternoon. Saul was sleeping deeply on his side, his hair streaked with tawny lights. I held a finger to my lips and tiptoed to the door. Left it open a crack so I could hear him.

"You can take the truck," Devi said bluntly, her *bindi* glimmering. She pushed a bead-weighted strand of hair behind her ear. "Get out, get away, get your head cleared out. There's nothing you can do here."

I slumped against the wall, one hand on a knife hilt. She was tense, I realized, and I left my fingers fall away. "I'm a liability." Flatly, daring her to disagree.

"You need a *vacation,*" she corrected. "You've done enough for a while, and if you keep pushing you're going to kill yourself. Or Saul. Or both, and I don't want to deal with that."

I moved, restless. Looked at the floor. Our boots were placed just so, both of us braced and ready for action.

"Mikhail," I said finally. "He was there."

Her chin dipped a fraction, the scar down her right cheek flushing. "Maybe he was. *I'm* not going to fucking disagree. I'm not even going to speculate who or what those bird-things were. Nobody is."

At least, not out loud. Well, thank God for that. But I shivered. "One thing."

"Okay." She didn't even ask *what*. Just agreed.

My heart twisted, I pushed down the pressure in my throat. "The Monde." My throat was so dry. It was work to get the sounds out. "Burn it. Banefire. Please."

"Of course. Jill." Her hand on my arm, brutally short fingernails digging in. Her duster made a sound, but my arms were bare; I wore only a T-shirt and a pair of spare leather pants. "Perry's dead. Absolutely *dead*. He's not coming back."

You promise? Because I wouldn't put it past him. But she was a hunter, and I looked up. We held each other's gaze for a long time, possibly an eternity. And I found out, gratefully, that *I* couldn't lie to a fellow hunter.

"I'm afraid either way, Devi," I whispered.

She nodded. There was nothing else to say, so she didn't bother. She just let me fold forward until my head was on her shoulder, and the silent sobbing that shook me was like an earthquake. She stroked my hair, touching the sharp-spined charms he'd given me, and they didn't bite either of us.

Misericordia

We left near dusk, stealing out like a pair of thieves. At least, we would have sneaked out if Galina hadn't packed everything for us and Theron hadn't cooked a gluttonous farewell meal, during which Anya stalked in reeking of smoke and nodded at me.

The Monde was gutted. I didn't even have to go check.

She stayed only long enough for a silent beer before vanishing again. Gilberto sucked down a couple beers, too, ate a whole pan of tamales, and informed me he was going to be working in the barrio with the Weres, not to mention training with Devi, until I came back.

"We still need to discuss you not following orders," I muttered.

He actually *winked* at me, and left with a couple bird Weres who didn't look at me. They were probably kin of the deceased, but they said nothing.

Weres don't talk about their dead.

I turned the key and the Chevy roared into life. Theron waved, then ducked back inside Galina's store, the bell tinkling and gleaming as the door closed. I dropped the car into gear, popped the brake, and pulled out slowly even though the street was deserted. Turned left at the bottom of the slight hill, and began threading our way toward the freeway.

When we reached Miguel and 147th, Saul let out a sigh.

"We'll stop over the state line for a snack." I kept my eyes on the road. "And, you know, if you get tired..."

"I'm *fine*, kitten." Slightly irritated.

"Here." I dug in my pocket. The new coat was stiff, and I was hoping I could go for at least a week without it getting ripped or blown off me. We were supposed to be embarking on a vacation, but there were a lot of new hellbreed around.

Trouble might find us.

I fished out an unopened pack of Charvils. "Congrats. Galina says you can smoke again."

"Thank *God*," he said with feeling, grabbing for it, and I surprised myself by laughing. It was a harsh, cracked sound, but it felt good.

The rearview mirror was alive with reflected sunset, but a shadow flickered in its depths. I stood on the brake and we skidded to a stop, Saul's right hand slapped down on the dash.

"Jill?" Quiet, but with a thread of a growl underneath.

I hit the seat belt catch and hopped out, the gun held low and ready. Scanned the rooftops, every hair quivering, my nape crawling with gooseflesh. Readiness settled over me, and it felt so good I could have cried.

A long lean shape flickered out of the alley to my right, and I sighed. Eased my finger off the trigger. "Christ."

Saul's door opened. "Is that what I think it is?"

The dogsbody's fur gleamed golden. It was rail-thin, and it cringed as it trot-walked up to me, ears back and flat, stubby tail tucked as far as it could go. When it got within twenty feet, its front end came down, and it finished by literally crawling on its belly. The ugly thing heaved to a stop right in front of my boots, and I shut my eyes, listening to its quick wheezing breaths.

Sweat stood out all over me. I lifted the gun, just a little.

The dog whined. Softly. Saul was still and quiet, watching.

I could just bend down, put the barrel against the thing's domed head, and pull the trigger. Easy, so very easy.

The dogsbody whined again, and shuddered. Its head was on my boots.

No, Jill. It was my conscience, speaking loud and clear. *You don't get a chance to practice mercy every day.*

My cheeks were wet. I forced my eyes open. The sun was dying, and the usual wind from the river cut across the buildings, laden with desert sand and exhaust. The dog sighed, its eyes closed.

I slid the gun back into its holster. Cleared my throat. Still, I sounded choked. "Put the gate down, will you?"

Saul said nothing. His footsteps were soft, and the screech of the tailgate covered up whatever he might have muttered. I moved my toes and the dog looked up, its eyes wide and dark now. Not blue, and not pale, colorless crystalline. Relief tasted like thin copper; my mouth was full of it. I swiped at my nose with the back of my hand.

"Get in," I said harshly.

The dog hauled itself up. It shambled to the end of the truck and made a graceless clumsy scrabble, its nails clicking on the bed as Saul slammed the gate. It settled down with a sigh, right next to the spare tire, and closed its weary eyes again.

I got back in and slammed my own door. Saul was a moment behind me. The engine idled; someone had done some tune-up on it. Probably one of the Weres, Devi wasn't a big car person and Leon held his own truck together with spit and baling wire.

The click of a lighter sounded very loud in the cab's hush. Saul inhaled and blew out a cloud of cherry-scented smoke.

"I'm sorry," I managed through the rock in my throat. "I can't—"

"I always wanted a hound." Saul grabbed his seat belt. I mechanically followed suit.

"I..." Everything I wanted to say balled up inside me, and he glanced over. A half smile curled up one corner of his mouth, and the pressure inside my chest eased. How the hell did he do that? Would I ever figure it out? "I thought cats don't like dogs." I dropped it into gear again, eased us forward toward Fifth Street and the freeway onramps.

"That's not a dog. It's a *hound*. Completely different." Saul snorted, took another drag. "Hope it eats Purina."

"Yeah." I braked for the red light on Fifth, we rolled to a stop. Traffic was light here, for once, and if we were lucky we'd be out of town in twenty minutes. "Saul?"

"Hmm?" He settled further, stretching his legs out.

"I love you."

I'm surprised he heard me, because I couldn't say it very loud. But his reply was clear and distinct.

"I love you, too, kitten."

By the time we crossed the state line he'd scooted over to the middle seat belt, I had my arm around him, and we drove on into the desert night.

finis

Acknowledgments

Thanks are due first of all to Maddy and Nicky, my twin reasons for enduring. After that, my endless gratitude goes to Miriam Kriss and Devi Pillai, for believing in Jill—and in me—even when I did neither. Thanks are also due to the long-suffering Jennifer Flax, and to the usual suspects: Mel Sanders, my bestie; Christa Hickey, who teaches me how to be brave; and Sixten Zeiss, for love and coffee.

Last but not least, dear Reader, I shall continue to thank you in the way we both like best: by telling more stories. Come in, sit down. I hope you like this one...

Glossary

Arkeus: A roaming corruptor escaped from Hell.

Banefire: A cleansing, sorcerous flame.

Black Mist: A roaming psychic contagion; a symbiotic parasite inhabiting the host's nervous system and bloodstream.

Chutsharak: A Chaldean obscenity, loosely translated as "Oh, *fuck*."

Demon: A term loosely used to designate any nonhuman predator with sorcerous ability or a connection to Hell.

Exorcism: Tearing loose a psychic parasite from its host.

Hellbreed: A blanket term for a wide array of demons, half demons, or other species escaped or sent from Hell.

Hellfire: The spectrum of sorcerous flame employed by hellbreed for a variety of uses.

Hunter: A trained human who keeps the balance between the nightside and regular humans; extrahuman law enforcement.

Imdarák: Shadowy former race who drove the Elder Gods from the physical plane; also called the Lords of the Trees.

Martindale Squad: The FBI division responsible for tracking nightside crime across state lines and at the federal level; mostly staffed with hunters and Weres.

Middle Way: Worshippers of Chaos, Middle Way adepts are usually sociopathic and sorcerous loners. Occasionally covens of Middle Way adepts will come together to control a territory or for a specific purpose.

OtherSight: Second sight, the ability to see sorcerous energy. Can also mean precognition.

Possessor: An insubstantial, low-class demon specializing in occupying and controlling humans; the prime reason for exorcists.

Scurf: Also called *nosferatim*, a semipsychic viral infection responsible for legends of blood-hungry corpses, vampires, or nosferatu. Also, someone infected by the scurf virus.

Sorrow: A worshipper of the Chaldean Elder Gods.

Sorrows House: A House inhabited by Sorrows, with a vault for invocation or evocation of Elder Gods.

Sorrows Mother: A high-ranking female of a Sorrows House.

Talyn: A hellbreed, higher in rank than an *arkeus* or a Possessor, usually insubstantial due to the nature of the physical world.

Trader: A human who makes a "deal" with a hellbreed, usually for worldly gain or power.

Utt'huruk: A bird-headed demon.

Were: Blanket term for several species who shapeshift into animal (for example, cougar, wolf, or spider) or half-animal (wererat or *khentauri*) form.

A Note on Kismet

Hopefully, after six books, I have once again earned a little lee-way to bore you, dear Reader, with a closing word.

Jill Kismet started out as a "what-if?" character. I was tired of paranormal heroes and heroines who had adversarial relation-ships with law enforcement. If there were things that went bump in the night, I reasoned, the cops (and other first responders) would be more than glad to have a specialist on hand to deal with them. I asked myself what that specialist might look like, what kind of person would be attracted to that type of job. How they would deal with the stress of the paranormal, what sort of enemies they might face.

However, when Jill strolled onto the page in *Hunter's Prayer* (which I actually wrote first) and began speaking, something much deeper than a "what if?" happened. *It's not the type of work you can put on a business card*, she said, and I immediately felt a galvanic thrill along every nerve ending I owned. The more I wrote, the more it seemed Jill had just been waiting for me to sit still long enough to hear her. (I didn't even know why she'd cho-sen the name "Kismet" until *Flesh Circus*.)

It is very unfair of me to compare characters, though such comparisons are all but inevitable. I'm often asked about Jill and Dante Valentine: if they're sisters, if they came from the same place. They most emphatically do *not*. Danny Valentine is a bro-ken character. Jill is not broken—bent a little, maybe, but still whole. I think that is the critical difference between them, though they both have smart mouths and a love of weaponry, as well as a streak of sheer adrenaline-junkie grade-A crazy.

Hey, write what you know, right?

Writing Kismet took me through some pretty dark times. I won't deny that sometimes, writing a gruesome scene—the clinic in *Hunter's Prayer*, the scurf-hole in *Redemption Alley*, the Cirque itself, at Carper's graveside, the scrabble out of her own grave—I found solace in the fact that no matter how bad I had it, my character had it worse. I also can't deny that many of the issues I wrestle with found an expression in her. As I noted in my goodbye essay on the Valentine series, any story about the possible future—or even about an alternate present—ends up saying far more about the writer than anything else. The filter the story passes through shapes it, for good or for ill.

Oddly, the character who affected me the most over the Kismet series isn't Jill. It's Perry.

If I did not feel physically filthy, if I didn't crave a hot shower and scrubbing every time he wandered onto the page, I went back and dug deeper and did it again. As much as I loathe him, I ended up pitying him as well. That's the tragedy of hellbreed—they carry their punishment with them. As Milton remarked, *"The mind is its own place, and in itself / Can make a Heaven of Hell, a Hell of Heaven."*

Human beings are very good at doing this as well.

Other characters came from different places. Saul was, in my original plans, only on board for one book. He was supposed to be a cautionary tale about how people with itchy trigger fingers and vigilante complexes are hard to have relationships with. Nobody was more surprised than me when the two of them made it work. I am asked many questions about Saul, and I have always wanted to note that if Saul's and Jill's genders were reversed, the vast majority of those questions would never see the light of day. They would simply match a number of assumptions and be let go.

Gilberto surprised me too. I had no idea why he was so important in *Redemption Alley*, but he literally would not go away. It was only later that I understood why. Monty and the various Santa Luz cops—fighting the good fight, being Jill's backup, extending to her the rough take-no-prisoners compassion they give to each other—are homages to the silent heroes who, every day, respond first and do their best to keep other people safe. More than that, however, they are people Jill cares about. If there is a grace that saves her from becoming what Perry wants her to be, it lies in that caring.

Galina represents another type of courage—those who quietly and patiently guard and build. And dear, sweet Hutch, bulletproof in cyberspace and a weenie everywhere else, is probably the most gallant of the bunch.

Still, I had no Grand Statement I wanted to make with Jill. I had no agenda, unless it was to tell a good story in as unflinching a manner as possible. Jill's job is not to look away; in that, hunters have a great deal in common with writers. I firmly believe that if a writer is honest, if the writer doesn't punk out or look away, that their story will have the ring of truth, and it will reach the readers it needs to. I have done the best I could.

I am sad to say goodbye to Jill. But it's time. Other stories are knocking at the door. All that remains is to thank you, dear Reader. Without you, this would be pretty useless, right? So, thank you very much for reading. I hope you've enjoyed it. And I cannot wait to tell you more stories.

But there will always be a part of me in Santa Luz, watching the moon rise over the bad old lady herself, while rooftops lie in shadow and neon smears the street. There will always be a jingle of silver flechettes and the creak of leather, and the sense that someone is watching even the darkest corners of the city. Someone is out there to right the wrongs, someone is going toe-to-toe and looking to settle the score. In some part of me, Jill Kismet will always be on the job.

I wouldn't have it any other way.

extras

meet the author

Daron Gldow

Lilith Saintcrow was born in New Mexico, bounced around the world as an Air Force brat, and fell in love with writing when she was ten years old. She currently lives in Vancouver, WA. Find out more about the author at www.lilithsaintcrow.com.

introducing

**If you enjoyed
JILL KISMET,
look out for**

THE IRON WYRM AFFAIR

Bannon and Clare: Book 1

by Lilith Saintcrow

*Emma Bannon, forensic sorceress in the service of the Empire,
has a mission: to protect Archibald Clare, a failed, unregistered
mentath. His skills of deduction are legendary, and her own
sorcery is not inconsiderable. It doesn't help much that they barely
tolerate each other, or that Bannon's Shield, Mikal, might just
be a traitor himself. Or that the conspiracy killing registered
mentaths and sorcerers alike will just as likely kill them as
seduce them into treachery toward their Queen.*

*In an alternate London where illogical magic has turned the
Industrial Revolution on its head, Bannon and Clare now face
hostility, treason, cannon fire, black sorcery, and the
problem of reliably finding hansom cabs.*

The game is afoot.

When the young dark-haired woman stepped into his parlour, Archibald Clare was only mildly intrigued. Her companion was of more immediate interest, a tall man in a close-fitting velvet jacket, moving with a grace that bespoke some experience with physical mayhem. The way he carried himself, lightly and easily, with a clean economy of movement—not to mention the way his eyes roved in controlled arcs—all but shouted danger. He was hatless, too, and wore curious boots.

The chain of deduction led Clare in an extraordinary direction, and he cast another glance at the woman to verify it.

Yes. Of no more than middle height, and slight, she was in very dark green. Fine cloth, a trifle antiquated, though the sleeves were close as fashion now dictated, and her bonnet perched just so on brown curls, its brim small enough that it would not interfere with her side vision. However, her skirts were divided, her boots serviceable instead of decorative—though of just as fine a quality as the man's—and her jewellery was eccentric, to say the least. Emerald drops worth a fortune at her ears, and the necklace was an amber cabochon large enough to be a baleful eye. Two rings on gloved hands, one with a dull unprecious black stone and the other a star sapphire a royal family might have envied.

extras

The man had a lean face to match the rest of him, strange yellow eyes, and tidy dark hair still dewed with crystal droplets from the light rain falling over Londinium tonight. The moisture, however, did not cling to her. One more piece of evidence, and Clare did not much like where it led.

He set the viola and its bow down, nudging aside a stack of paper with careful precision, and waited for the opening gambit. As he had suspected, *she* spoke.

"Good evening, sir. You are Dr Archibald Clare. Distinguished author of *The Art and Science of Observation*." She paused. Aristocratic nose, firm mouth, very decided for such a childlike face. "Bachelor. And very-recently-unregistered mentath."

"Sorceress." Clare steepled his fingers under his very long, very sensitive nose. Her toilette favoured musk, of course, for a brunette. Still, the scent was not common, and it held an edge of something acrid that should have been troublesome instead of strangely pleasing. "And a Shield. I would invite you to sit, but I hardly think you will."

A slight smile; her chin lifted. She did not give her name, as if she expected him to suspect it. Her curls, if they were not natural, were very close. There was a slight bit of untidiness to them—some recent exertion, perhaps? "Since there is no seat available, *sir*, I am to take that as one of your deductions?"

Even the hassock had a pile of papers and books stacked terrifyingly high. He had been researching, of course. The intersections between musical scale and the behaviour of certain tiny animals. It was the intervals, perhaps. Each note held its own space. He was seeking to determine which set of spaces would make the insects (and later, other things) possibly—

Clare waved one pale, long-fingered hand. Emotion was threatening, prickling at his throat. With a certain rational annoyance he labelled it as *fear*, and dismissed it. There was

1379

very little chance she meant him harm. The man was a larger question, but if *she* meant him no harm, the man certainly did not. "If you like. Speak quickly, I am occupied."

She cast one eloquent glance over the room. If not for the efforts of the landlady, Mrs Ginn, dirty dishes would have been stacked on every horizontal surface. As it was, his quarters were cluttered with a full set of alembics and burners, glass jars of various substances, shallow dishes for knocking his pipe clean. The tabac smoke blunted the damned sensitivity in his nose just enough, and he wished for his pipe. The acridity in her scent was becoming more marked, and very definitely not unpleasant.

The room's disorder even threatened the grate, the mantel above it groaning under a weight of books and handwritten journals stacked every which way.

The sorceress, finishing her unhurried investigation, next examined him from tip to toe. He was in his dressing gown, and his pipe had long since grown cold. His feet were in the rubbed-bare slippers, and if it had not been past the hour of reasonable entertaining he might have been vaguely uncomfortable at the idea of a lady seeing him in such disrepair. Red-eyed, his hair mussed, and unshaven, he was in no condition to receive company.

He was, in fact, the picture of a mentath about to implode from boredom. If she knew some of the circumstances behind his recent ill luck, she would guess he was closer to imploding and fusing his faculties into unworkable porridge than was advisable, comfortable... or even sane.

Yet if she knew the circumstances behind his ill luck, would she look so calm? He did not know nearly enough yet. Frustration tickled behind his eyes, the sensation of pounding and seething inside the cup of his skull easing a fraction as he considered the possibilities of her arrival.

Her gloved hand rose, and she held up a card. It was dun-coloured, and before she tossed it—a passionless, accurate flick of her fingers that snapped it through intervening space neat as you please, as if she dealt faro—he had already deduced and verified its provenance.

He plucked it out of the air. "I am called to the service of the Crown. You are to hold my leash. It is, of course, urgent. Does it have to do with an art professor?" For it had been some time since he had crossed wits with Dr Vance, and *that* would distract him most handily. The man was a deuced wonderful adversary.

His sally was only worth a raised eyebrow. She must have practised that look in the mirror; her features were strangely childlike, and the effect of the very adult expression was...odd. "No. It *is* urgent, and Mikal will stand guard while you...dress. I shall be in the hansom outside. You have ten minutes, sir."

With that, she turned on her heel. Her skirts made a low, sweet sound, and the man was already holding the door. She glanced up, those wide dark eyes flashing once, and a ghost of a smile touched her soft mouth.

Interesting. Clare added that to the chain of deduction. He only hoped this problem would last more than a night and provide him further relief. If the young Queen or one of the ministers had sent a summons card, it promised to be very diverting indeed.

It was a delight to have something unknown, but within guessing reach. He sniffed the card. A faint trace of musk, but no violet-water. Not the Queen personally, then. He had not thought it likely—why would Her Majesty trouble herself with *him*? It was a faint joy to find he was correct.

His faculties were, evidently, not porridge *yet*.

The ink was correct as well, just the faintest bitter astringent note as he inhaled deeply. The crest on the front was absolutely genuine, and the handwriting on the back was firm and masculine, not to mention familiar. *Why, it's Cedric.*

In other words, the Chancellor of the Exchequer, Lord Grayson. The Prime Minister was new and inexperienced, since the Queen had banished her lady mother's creatures from her Cabinet, and Grayson had survived with, no doubt, some measure of cunning or because someone thought him incompetent enough to do no harm. Having been at Yton with the man, Clare was inclined to lean towards the former.

And dear old Cedric had exerted his influence so Clare was merely unregistered and not facing imprisonment, a mercy that had teeth. Even more interesting.

Miss Emma Bannon is our representative. Please use haste, and discretion.

Emma Bannon. Clare had never heard the name before, but then a sorceress would not wish her name bruited about overmuch. Just as a mentath, registered or no, would not. So he made a special note of it, adding everything about the woman to the mental drawer that bore her name. She would not take a carved nameplate. No, Miss Bannon's plate would be yellowed parchment, with dragonsblood ink tracing out the letters of her name in a clear, feminine hand.

The man's drawer was featureless blank metal, burnished to a high gloss. He waited by the open door. Cleared his throat, a low rumble. Meant to hurry Clare along, no doubt.

Clare opened one eye, just a sliver. "There are nine and a quarter minutes left. Do *not* make unnecessary noise, sir."

The man—a sorceress's Shield, meant to guard against physical danger while the sorceress dealt with more arcane perils—remained silent, but his mouth firmed. He did not look amused.

Mikal. His colour was too dark and his features too aquiline to be properly Britannic. Perhaps Tinkerfolk? Or even from the Indus?

For the moment, he decided, the man's drawer could remain metal. He did not know enough about him. It would have to do. One thing was certain: if the sorceress had left one of her Shields with him, she was standing guard against some more than mundane threat outside. Which meant the problem he was about to address was most likely fiendishly complex, extraordinarily important, and worth more than a day or two of his busy brain's feverish working.

Thank God. The relief was palpable.

Clare shot to his feet and began packing.

Chapter One

A Pleasant Evening Ride

Emma Bannon, Sorceress Prime and servant to Britannia's current incarnation, mentally ran through every foul word that would never cross the lips of a lady. She timed them to the clockhorse's steady jogtrot, and her awareness dilated. The simmering cauldron of the streets was just as it always was; there was no breath of ill intent.

Of course, there had not been earlier, either, when she had been a quarter-hour too late to save the *other* unregistered mentath. It was only one of the many things about this situation seemingly designed to try her often considerable patience.

Mikal would be taking the rooftop road, running while she sat at ease in a hired carriage. It was the knowledge that while he did so he could forget some things that eased her conscience, though not completely.

Still, he was a Shield. He would not consent to share a carriage with her unless he was certain of her safety. And there was not room enough to manoeuvre in a two-person conveyance, should he require it.

She was heartily sick of hired carts. Her own carriages were *far* more comfortable, but this matter required discretion. Having it shouted to the heavens that she was alert to the pattern under these occurrences might not precisely frighten her opponents, but it would become more difficult to attack them from an unexpected quarter. Which was, she had to admit, her preferred method.

Even a Prime can benefit from guile, Llew had often remarked. And of course, she would think of him. She seemed constitutionally incapable of leaving well enough alone, and *that* irritated her as well.

Beside her, Clare dozed. He was a very thin man, with a long, mournful face; his gloves were darned but his waistcoat was of fine cloth, though it had seen better days. His eyes were blue, and they glittered feverishly under half-closed lids. An unregistered mentath would find it difficult to secure proper employment, and by the looks of his quarters, Clare had been suffering from boredom for several weeks, desperately seeking a series of experiments to exercise his active brain.

Mentath was like sorcerous talent. If not trained, and *used*, it turned on its bearer.

At least he had found time to shave, and he had brought two bags. One, no doubt, held linens. God alone knew what was in the second. Perhaps she should apply deduction to the problem, as if she did not have several others crowding her attention at the moment.

Chief among said problems were the murderers, who had so far eluded her efforts. Queen Victrix was young, and just recently freed from the confines of her domineering mother's sway. Her new Consort, Alberich, was a moderating influence—but he did not have enough power at Court just yet to be an effective shield for Britannia's incarnation.

The ruling spirit was old, and wise, but Her vessels...well, they were not indestructible.

And that, Emma told herself sternly, *is as far as we shall go with such a train of thought.* She found herself rubbing the sardonyx on her left middle finger, polishing it with her opposite thumb. Even through her thin gloves, the stone prickled hotly. Her posture did not change, but her awareness contracted. She felt for the source of the disturbance, flashing through and discarding a number of fine invisible threads.

Blast and bother. Other words, less polite, rose as well. Her pulse and respiration did not change, but she tasted a faint tang of adrenaline before sorcerous training clamped tight on such functions to free her from some of flesh's more...distracting... reactions.

"I say, whatever is the matter?" Archibald Clare's blue eyes were wide open now, and he looked interested. Almost, dare she think it, intrigued. It did nothing for his long, almost ugly features. His cloth was serviceable, though hardly elegant—one could infer that a mentath had other priorities than fashion, even if he had an eye for quality and the means to purchase such. But at least he was cleaner than he had been, and had arrived in the hansom in nine and a half minutes precisely. Now they were on Sarpesson Street, threading through amusement-seekers and those whom a little rain would not deter from their nightly appointments.

The disturbance peaked, and a not-quite-seen starburst of gunpowder igniting flashed through the ordered lattices of her consciousness.

The clockhorse screamed as his reins were jerked, and the hansom yawed alarmingly. Archibald Clare's hand dashed for the door handle, but Emma was already moving. Her arms closed around the tall, fragile man, and she shouted a Word that exploded the cab away from them both. Shards and splinters, driven outwards, peppered the street surface. The glass of the cab's tiny windows broke with a high, sweet tinkle, grinding into crystalline dust.

extras

Shouts. Screams. Pounding footsteps. Emma struggled upright, shaking her skirts with numb hands. The horse had gone avast, rearing and plunging, throwing tiny metal slivers and dribs of oil as well as stray crackling sparks of sorcery, but the traces were tangled and it stood little chance of running loose. The driver was gone, and she snapped a quick glance at the over-hanging rooftops before the unhealthy canine shapes resolved out of thinning rain, slinking low as gaslamp gleam painted their slick, heaving sides.

Sootdogs. Oh, how unpleasant. The one that had leapt on the hansom's roof had most likely taken the driver, and Emma cursed aloud now as it landed with a thump, its shining hide running with vapour.

"*Most* unusual!" Archibald Clare yelled. He had gained his feet as well, and his eyes were alight now. The mournfulness had vanished. He had also produced a queerly barrelled pistol, which would be of *no* use against the dog-shaped sorcerous things now gathering. "*Quite* diverting!"

The star sapphire on her right third finger warmed. A globe-shield shimmered into being, and to the roil of smoulder-ing wood, gunpowder and fear was added another scent: the smoke-gloss of sorcery. One of the sootdogs leapt, crashing into the shield, and the shock sent Emma to her knees, holding grimly. Both her hands were outstretched now, and her tongue occupied in chanting.

Sarpesson Street was neither deserted nor crowded at this late hour. The people gathering to watch the outcome of a han-som crash pushed against those onlookers alert enough to note that something entirely different was occurring, and the resul-tant chaos was merely noise to be shunted aside as her concen-tration narrowed.

Where is Mikal?

She had no time to wonder further. The sootdogs hunched and wove closer, snarling. Their packed-cinder sides heaved and black tongues lolled between obsidian-chip teeth; they could strip a large adult male to bone in under a minute. There were the onlookers to think of as well, and Clare behind and to her right, laughing as he sighted down the odd little pistol's chunky nose. Only he was not pointing it at the dogs, thank God. He was aiming for the rooftop.

You idiot. The chant filled her mouth. She could spare no words to tell him not to fire, that Mikal was—

The lead dog crashed against the shield. Emma's body jerked as the impact tore through her, but she held steady, the sapphire now a ringing blue flame. Her voice rose, a clear contralto, and she assayed the difficult rill of notes that would split her focus and make another Major Work possible.

That was part of what made a Prime—the ability to concentrate completely on multiple channellings of ætheric force. One's capacity could not be infinite, just like the charge of force carried and renewed every Tideturn.

But one did not need infinite capacity. *One needs only slightly more capacity than the problem at hand calls for,* as her third-form Sophological Studies professor had often intoned.

Mikal arrived.

His dark green coat fluttered as he landed in the midst of the dogs, a Shield's fury glimmering to Sight, bright spatters and spangles invisible to normal vision. The sorcery-made things cringed, snapping; his blades tore through their insubstantial hides. The charmsilver laid along the knives' flats, as well as the will to strike, would be of far more use than Mr Clare's pistol.

Which spoke, behind her, the ball tearing through the shield from a direction the protection wasn't meant to hold. The fabric of the shield collapsed, and Emma had just enough time to deflect the backlash, tearing a hole in the brick-faced fabric of the street and exploding the clockhorse into gobbets of metal and rags of flesh, before one of the dogs turned with stomach-churning speed and launched itself at her—and the man she had been charged to protect.

She shrieked another Word through the chant's descant, her hand snapping out again, fingers contorted in a gesture definitely *not* acceptable in polite company. The ray of ætheric force smashed through brick dust, destroying even more of the road's surface, and crunched into the sootdog.

Emma bolted to her feet, snapping her hand back, and the line of force followed as the dog crumpled, whining and shattering into fragments. She could not hold the forcewhip for very long, but if more of the dogs came—

The last one died under Mikal's flashing knives. He muttered something in his native tongue, whirled on his heel, and stalked toward his Prime. That normally meant the battle was finished.

Yet Emma's mind was not eased. She half turned, chant dying on her lips and her gaze roving, searching. Heard the mutter of the crowd, dangerously frightened. Sorcerous force pulsed and bled from her fingers, a fountain of crimson sparks popping against the rainy air. For a moment the mood of the crowd threatened to distract her, but she closed it away and concentrated, seeking the source of the disturbance.

Sorcerous traces glowed, faint and fading, as the man who had fired the initial shot—most likely to mark them for the dogs—fled. He had some sort of defence laid on him, meant to keep him from a sorcerer's notice.

Perhaps from a sorcerer, but not from a Prime. Not from me, oh no. The dead see all. Her Discipline was of the Black, and it was moments like these when she would be glad of its practicality—if she could spare the attention.

Time spun outwards, dilating, as she followed him over rooftops and down into a stinking alley, refuse piled high on each side, running with the taste of fear and blood in his mouth. Something had injured him.

Mikal? But then why did he not kill the man—

The world jolted underneath her, a stunning blow to her shoulder, a great spiked roil of pain through her chest. Mikal screamed, but she was breathless. Sorcerous force spilled free, uncontained, and other screams rose.

She could possibly injure someone.

Emma came back to herself, clutching at her shoulder. Hot blood welled between her fingers, and the green silk would be ruined. Not to mention her gloves.

At least they had shot her, and not the mentath.

Oh, damn. The pain crested again, became a giant animal with its teeth in her flesh.

Mikal caught her. His mouth moved soundlessly, and Emma sought with desperate fury to contain the force thundering through her. Backlash could cause yet more damage, to the street and to onlookers, if she let it loose.

A Prime's uncontrolled force was nothing to be trifled with.

It was the traditional function of a Shield to handle such overflow, but if he had only wounded the fellow on the roof she could not trust that he was not part of—

"Let it GO!" Mikal roared, and the ætheric bonds between them flamed into painful life. She fought it, seeking to contain what she could, and her skull exploded with pain.

She knew no more.